The
Darkness
That
Slept

Keegan and Tristen Kozinski
Kozinskibooks.com

Cover Illustration: Keegan Kozinski
Edited by: Tracy Wolf

Contact: keeganandtristenbooks@gmail.com

If you notice any quality issues with this manuscript, please contact us.

Live Long
Laugh Longer

Also by Keegan & Tristen Kozinski
THE CITY OF LOCKED DOORS

Free short stories @ Apple books, Kobo, Barnes&Noble
NEMESIS
DEATH'S BACKDOOR
A COMPANY OF TRAITORS

Table of Contents

1

Antiark

6617A.O.M.
Approximately 30th day of the New Order incursion.

~The North, older than all other corners of the world and isolated by the Rhawn mountains, is a land of mysteries and legends, where the laws governing other lands submit more easily than they govern. It is a remnant of the Before Age, and the domain of a being older than mortal existence: *Winsyria.* In this, the Third Age, his power is diminished, his influence restricted to The North. Nevertheless, he remains the caretaker of his people, feared and loathed by the ascended gods since a time older than reminiscence; and until all creation fails, he will continue to rule The North.~

Deep within The North, protected by the Rhawn Mountains, a circle of ancient trees swayed in the ceaseless wind burdened, yet uncompromising, beneath the undisturbed ice of millennia. Stately firs pierced the tenebrous sky while dominant spruces stretched protective limbs over the shorter rowans and shaded the mingled willows. A wall of stout cypress, eucalyptus, and baobabs concealed the trunks of these primordial sentries, their grandeur undiminished by their inferior height. A magnificent sequoia reigned over all of these from the center of a white lake, its graceful limbs also stretched out protectively over its attendants. The implacable northern wind caressed the sequoia's fragile, golden leaves as snowflakes kissed its alabaster skin.

Men did not venture here often for the Rhawn are perilous to ascend and worse to descend, and this sanctuary was secreted deep within their peeks.

A howl reached down the sheer pass leading up to the glade, and the sanctuary stirred in welcome, its drowsy soul rousing from a century of isolation. A White Wolf of Winsyria materialized from the eternal blizzard and strolled into the circle of trees. The unearthly canine settled beside the pond and started to drink, its eyes alive with an unnatural intelligence.

The Wolf remained unperturbed when a second figure materialized from the storm; a man advancing with a hesitant step, his features defined by the tundra-cold eyes, the pale northern hair, and the scars dealt to his skin by his harsh motherland.

The deranger scanned the lake, probing through the dense fog veiling its surface. Although the mist stretched out to embrace him, one could still see the bow of rare black rowan hanging across his shoulder beside a quiver of three dozen arrows fletched with the feathers of black swans.

A ripple stroked the abnormally serene water, alerting the deranger that his presence was noted. Chagrined, though no sign of it broke the impassivity of his features, the deranger drew his cowl back.

He smiled at his foolishness, a rare moment of unveiled humor for him, recollecting that his skill would not conceal him from the man he sought. The deranger—a Ranger-Warden of Winsyria—thus named by the Northern people due to his habitual insanity of braving The North's harshest maelstroms, walked to the lake's bank and knelt beside the Wolf. Closing hazel eyes, he slipped into a half trance, allowing his mind to relinquish the constraints of his body. With the air of beginning a ritual, he unsheathed his glass sword and plunged it into the water, returning the blade to the forge of its birth. The true North welcomed him; mists and half-formed shadows granted him wordless visions of beauty and solitude that transcended both distance and time.

To an outsider, The North was a sinister land encircled by baleful mountains; but to those within those mountains, the land was a haven.

Submerged in the ancient majesty of his homeland, the deranger lost track of time, drifting until the mists receded from the lake's crystalline waters and unveiled another man kneeling, immersed to his breast. The deranger exhaled a long breath, relinquishing his trance, and unsheathed the glass sword from the water, its spine shimmering with captured light; the impurities cleansed.

The Rhawn Mountains murmured, their voices like grinding stone. The deranger glanced up, not for fear of the Rhawn or *Winsyria's* storms— they were facets of a home he cherished—but for what they portended.

The immersed man stood, tied back the locks of bronze hair and strode to the shore, water streaming down his naked torso over an intricate tapestry of indigo tattoos. "Hello, Maern." The High-Warden spoke with a soft, graceful cadence despite his size, and at his words, the storm calmed.

Maern stood, sheathing the glass sword but hesitating to speak. "The New Order has entered The North, circumventing Adriat under cover of night, battle, and enchantments. Some four thousand of them." Maern fell into step, and the White Wolf followed.

"Yes, and they bring demons in their company." The High-Warden slowed, aligning his stride with his companion's.

"The war that Lord Dellak predicted has arrived."

"None of us ever doubted his words; we've had time to prepare for this."

Maern nodded, beginning to struggle through the fresh snow. In contrast, the High-Warden moved easily, leaving no history of his passage as they ventured deeper into the Rhawn Mountains. Unperturbed by the arduous trek, Maern continued, "Lord Antiark solicits your aid."

"I know, but I cannot aid him. This is a war whose entirety we do not yet fully comprehend. There are other evils out there with their eyes fixed on us while other, fouler things, stir. Messages of portentous events rise on dark wings, and the *Hounds of Karrassain* walk this land again. In the West, Cardolyn Tyier broods upon his throne, eyes cast heavenwards."

At the mention of *Karrassain*, a prison for gods and their ilk, Maern's step faltered.

The High-Warden continued undeterred, "For the first time in decades, Tiberius Whyte leaves Apelium to converse with the last Avenar Prince while Morrehiegann laughs in his dark tower, gloating over our plight and inner conflicts. Rumors speak in susurrations; the harbinger of something terrible that has long slumbered. A Dread Lord walks the Mortal Kingdoms again, and with this messiah's arrival, the curse inflicted upon the Avenar Princes is reawakened."

The High-Warden arrived at a simple abode—carven from the mountain as if grown—and opened its door, beckoning both man and Wolf to enter. Maern hurried inward and the High-Warden followed, bending under the high door frame. The Wolf entered last, at ease in the deteriorating weather.

Motioning Maern to a chair before the hearth, the High-Warden donned a shirt from the mattress in a corner. The Wolf claimed the hearthstones with a satisfied huff, sniffing and rubbing the dense, scented furs that blanketed the floor. Within the hearth, the house's kelbrok slumbered heavily, steam rising from the nostrils on its beak with every exhale. Its large scales flared periodically, exposing the vibrant blue skin beneath and expelling drafts of heat. It lay coiled around a darkened, half-eaten cedar log.

Allowing the heat to sooth him, Maern brooded, uneasy with his lack of knowledge. The North always balanced on war's precipice with the Light and Dark Pantheons ruling the exterior world, forever ravenous to enter but denied the necessary conduit. Gods needed devotees to manifest their will upon the world, mortals to pray and seek their miracles in true belief, and none such existed in The North. In this slow process of rumination, realization struck. "The gods will fall on us like crows upon the dead."

"Yes, the gods will come: *Telacra* shall ride the backs of her New Order, and *Malbreyth* will invade as the first drop of human blood falls. *Jaidar* will enter through the flames and agony as the slightest threads of chaos sunder our unity; and where *Jaidar* goes, *Enecki* soon follows."

Maern watched shadows cast by the kelbrok's light flicker across the hearth's interior, contorting into myriad shapes and guises. First, there was a solitary Wolf running in place and then its brethren joined it, their heads lifted in the ancient lament they had sung since the first dawn.

The High-Warden continued, "Still, it is not the gods I fear; everything is stirring, both the evils in their prisons and the guardians in their holds, some of which have been asleep so long they will not recognize the world. I fear what will be demanded of them."

He took the vacant seat, offering Maern dark bread and cold mutton while a tea kettle whistled from a hook over the kelbrok. The High-Warden took a pair of mugs from pegs driven into the walls and poured tea into each. Maern accepted a mug, beginning to murmur his gratitude but fell silent as something flickered through the High-Warden's eyes. "*Winsyria* recedes; his power is no longer used as it was. Many consider it a weakening, but it is not; a bargain has been struck, and I cannot see its laws. All paths hence are shadowed; I do not know which road is best. I think we are all pawns for now, and until I discover more, we shall remain thus. The question is: Who's controlling the game?"

At these last words, a shiver ran through Maern's blood. He leaned back, setting aside his repast and clasping the tea mug for warmth. His mind wandered the roads of queries and doubts, guessing at players he could not conceive.

Hours passed before Maern surfaced from his thoughts. The kelbrok had waken and was gradually swallowing the cedar log whole. Night had fallen, calling the Wolf away to its eternal song, and the High-Warden stood at the hearth, bronze eyes veiled with internal shadows.

Maern stood, reaching for his glass sword. He felt a summons from The North, a silent reminder that his labors were incomplete. The derangers patrolled the trackless North, searching for whatever managed to slip past

Adriat. They gave little heed to the affairs of kingdoms and empires, of armies or warlords. They guarded the land while lesser men guard their children.

"You will be needed in Antiark."

"I know. I can hear their pleas, the dead accusing and the living bitter; I cannot help either. I have my own tasks waiting. When it is done, I will lend my strength to Antiark." The High-Warden knelt to offer the kelbrok a new log, which it sniffed then declined. "I suspect this war shall reach its wretched fingers into our heartland up to the walls of Antiark. I believe those who call The North home shall trade tranquility for power and tainted gold."

"You speak of the Weshac."

"Yes. Their latest pretense of a king is dead. Even if he were not, the laws governing their race are fragile. The New Order will find an easy alliance with the outcasts."

The High-Warden walked to a corner and retrieved the twin pale swords reclining there. The magnificent weapons belonged to him from a time lost to memory, and throughout that time, they had rarely seen the light. They were Talwars, as long from pommel to tip as the average man stands. Though they were heavier than a normal man could wield, the High-Warden held them easily. A full two inches in width at the spine and six inches of blade at the base, the weapons curved, expanding to a near foot before tapering to a point.

"Will you serve, High-Warden?" This question revealed Maern's purpose: a task given to him by Lord Antiark. The query itself was merely decorum, a petition of the High-Warden in days of war: *In peace, none shall command greater authority than the High-Warden, though he shall not reign. In times of war, none shall supersede the Lord of Antiark, though the Lord of Antiark has no command over the High-Warden unless the High-Warden submits to his commands.* This passage declares the High-Warden subordinate to none, unless he submits to Lord Antiark during times of war.

The High-Warden of Winsyria served a single purpose: a guard against the supernatural forces the Mortal Kingdoms harbored. The Lord of Antiark was the sentinel against the mortal tyrants who thrive on the profits of war; only the *Winter Court* exceeded his authority within The North.

"No, Maern, I will not serve."

Maern expected nothing else after listening to the High-Warden. "What are the tasks you mentioned?" he queried, intending to convey Lord Antiark's offer of assistance, yet no answer came. The High-Warden, at last, looked up, his eyes raw with fury; a fury inflamed by every black boot treading the soil of his home.

"Though already beset, The North is better served by the prevention of any other foe seeking spoils. These are tasks neither the derangers nor Lord Antiark should interfere with. You still have time though, so rest, and resume your obligations in the morning. Cherish this peace, for it will be hard to find in the days ahead." The High-Warden gestured to a mattress in another corner.

"High-Warden, if I may, how are you doing? The North can't be taking this gently."

"My state is irrelevant, I have a *Burden* to fulfill, and you rest to take. Leave the door open when you go."

The deranger accepted. His fatigue, masked while he conversed with the High-Warden, returned in full. Wrapping himself in the woolen blankets, he watched through heavy lids as the High-Warden brushed one callused hand across an ornate pommel. Maern closed his eyes, accepting this gift of tranquility and trusting the High-Warden of Winsyria to accomplish the necessary tasks.

Pulling the intricate scabbards encasing the Talwars across his shoulders, the High-Warden released a breath. The Talwars knew the hour of their first song neared, the scent of that forthcoming moment draped the air.

He commenced his final preparations, first mounding wood beside the kelbrok, then retrieving the remaining meat and bread for Maern. Finally glancing to ensure nothing was displaced, he exited into the storm, knowing he would never return.

He could feel The North's wrath. It desired to unleash itself on the intruders, to ravage them until nothing remained. Interlaced with that rage, however, he felt its elemental instinctive fear and almost wept for it. The North knew the gods would come seeking to crush and shackle it to their Pantheon, nothing more than a broken wolfhound kept for amusement and display.

Feeling their rage reverberating through the earth, he looked toward the Rhawn Mountains, intimidating with their razor peaks and lethal ice storms. The earth trembled, and the heavens thundered with their rage, threatening to split; and they would split, they would shatter if ever he relinquished his hold. The North was gathering its strength. Whether he wished it or not, this land would destroy itself before yielding to the Pantheon. Turning south, he began his journey to Antiark.

Throughout the eternal memory of immortals, the Rhawn had preserved The North as an impenetrable barrier guarding the land. As he stepped onto their black roots, snaking along and beneath the snow, the winds died and the ever-shrouding mist engulfed him. Laying callused hands on the primordial rock, the High-Warden greeted the Rhawn Mountains. They slept now, dreamless and wrathful in their protective vigil. Still, they answered him, rising from their memories at the touch of an old friend. He soothed their troubled thoughts with a murmured promise.

He journeyed southward toward the numberless peaks in an ethereal twilight. He was never alone; the Rhawn Mountains always accompanied him, and The North surrounded him, as real and present as a friend. He heard the wind just beyond his reach, saw the trees thrashing in shared fury while their leaves of gold, burgundy, and emerald fluttered. He opened himself to the natural land and let it fill him, sharing itself and taking from him what he gave freely.

The High-Warden completed the journey of weeks in hours, with the Rhawn opening crevices for him and the mist bending distance to hasten his pace until he attained one of the many summits where The North opened, like a tapestry, in all its beauty.

Twelve cities rose across the country of men within The North, beginning with Adriat in Winter's Gate and concluding with Antiark in Winsyria's Cradle. Adriat was the City of War, and the only entrance into The North men dared take because only fools travel The Northern Ocean.

The High-Warden looked to the four horizons, soliciting knowledge of current events, and the wind answered his summons. He saw longships with wolf prows searching for a river flowing inland. He saw a serpent of men slithering across the earth racing toward Antiark, pursued by Lord Adriat's legions.

Yet they were just men, and in the heavens above loomed their goddess, a presence vast as the world: *Telacra,* Lady of Darkness and Treachery. She brooded over The North and her disciples, waiting for her moment to join them, to manifest a fragment of her being in the physical world, to claim The North. He would not allow that to transpire, for her or any of her kin to despoil his land.

Telacra was the first, but others waited behind: her brother, *Malbreyth,* Lord of War and Storms, and her father, *Jaidar,* god of Chaos. A fourth god sat upon the Dark Pantheon, but his presence had yet to mass in the sky.

The High-Warden of Winsyria issued a final farewell to what he relinquished before commencing his descent of the mountain toward Antiark and the world of men.

When the first men fled through Winter's Gate into the northlands from the oppressive gods and Elder Races, *Winsyria* gave them asylum. He called the *Annuir'Hyme* to rise and molded its water into the glass city of Antiark. He parted the clouds, allowing starlight to illuminate his refuge. The stars, however, did more than cast light: they danced. Whether they were solitary lights or vast constellations, the stars wove across the heavens, shifting and swirling in an eternal, slow ballet. It was here under the stars and in a glass city straddling the *Annuir'Hyme* that the race of northern men was born twelve thousand years ago.

Even in The North where hard men tower over their softer cousins in the Summer-lands and know many wonders, the High-Warden elicited stares. He entered through the gates by the long crystalline bridge leading to Antiark from the mainland. The glass portcullis chimed in the wind as he traversed it, and the trickle of people arriving or departing slowed to watch him. A dozen guards in white oudakc—thick, ankle-length outside coats—reclined around the entrance speaking of inconsequential matters and jesting while their piercing eyes measured all who entered. Deceptively indolent wolfhounds lay on the crystalline ground at their feet, chewing bones and lolling contentedly.

The guards noted his approach from the periphery of their vision, hands resting on long-hilted swords. He bowed in passing, making no attempt to introduce himself or conceal the weapons across his shoulders. They did not—could not—question him. Something in his mien conferred his power, his *Burden*, and his sacrifice, placing him above inquiry. Thus, though never having seen him, the guards knew and welcomed him. He felt the city stir as well, recognizing and greeting him with pleasure but also disquiet; Antiark feared for her people.

Slipping from the press of men and women going about their morning activities, he soothed her fears, asking her to trust him as he approached one of the rivers that comprised the city's thoroughfares. A flotilla of small coracles populated the river, propelled by the currents to ferry passengers across the city without an oarsman.

He reached the riverbank and a coracle slipped free from the current, running aground near him on the glass shore despite the absence of a dock. He boarded and grasped its stern, propelling the coracle into the gentle currents.

A short while later the coracle slid aground, rasping across the ice as he stepped from the glass vessel onto the shore of Antiark's final bastion. The

Citadel was a dour structure, its towers and walls a stark contrast to the northern tundra with their black, sharply hewn stone. The immense iron portcullis stood shut, its vicious jaws lodged in the ice as a reminder of when The North belonged to a more bestial era when mortal men bowed to wolves. Amalgamated tragedy, joy, and anguish hung in the air like curtains for windows that never open: an echo of the Citadel's past lords. Derangers patrolled its parapets and lingered at the solitary gate, their faces unseen within the fabric of their coats, watching The North with eyes that saw beyond Antiark's walls.

The High-Warden approached the gate, his arrival going unnoted until the portcullis lifted of its own accord, drawing the derangers' attention. One fell into step. "May we be of service, High-Warden?"

"No, you cannot. My words are for Lord Antiark alone." He paused before continuing, reminding himself of courtesies. "I would like to speak with Lord Antiark in as short a time as can be arranged without inconveniencing him." The deranger nodded as they ascended the wide stairs and entered the main domicile.

Where the outside stonework was sterile and forbidding, the inside was beautiful. Its stonework was perfect: without scars, dents, or mortar grooves. Patterns of colored glass blanketed the walls, preserving the memories of past lords and safeguarding their rare joys from the currents of time.

They crossed the antechamber, the High-Warden's strides hushed on the intricate floor. A thousand strands of silver and cobalt glass flared with soft light at his steps. They formed a pattern too intricate to map, each strand twining the names of past Lords and High-Wardens. His name also rested somewhere in the pattern, surrounded by the names of other men both greater and lesser than himself. Across from the hall leading into the main complex, a pair of rowan doors opened of their own accord, welcoming him.

The High-Warden bowed to the deranger. "Please, inform Lord Antiark of my arrival." He watched the deranger leave before entering. The doors closed behind him, barring anyone who did not bear the *Burden*.

He entered a vast room seething with heat, the walls to either side of him masked by towering mahogany bookshelves and a dozen hearths with enormous kelbroks, some of the females warming clutches of eggs. He doffed his boots in an alcove at the entrance and then continued onto the blanket of white furs, more out of respect than necessity. Dirt rarely clung to him. The heat dimmed with his passage, yielding to the essence of winter slumbering in his heart as he wove through furnished chairs and mismatched tables.

The oldest books waited on the far wall, their covers gray, torn, or nonexistent while the script on their spines endured. Some recalled the Before

Age, others transmitted visions of *Lord Arthramain Roy'al* and his wars of conquest. The last, those nearest to the shadow-bound ceiling, were loath to surrender their secrets and often obscured them with barren pages and spilled ink. They spoke of forgotten memories, of The North itself and the elemental force known as the *Oracle*.

He halted at the far wall, his eyes scaling the shelves until they found the pewter carving of a serpentine dragon twisting along the sixth ledge. The High-Warden extended his right hand and traced the beast's curved tail, rising and falling with the sinuous stone, feeling the ancestral carving of scales and horns. The dragon's crest caught his forefinger, opening a minute gash so a drop of his violet blood could slip down the dragon's face and into its open maw. He withdrew, his offering complete.

The dragon's head turned toward him, its maw closing to taste the blood's purity. A shiver ran the length of its form, expanding to cascade through the books, and with its passage, it all became glass: a reflective mirror that nevertheless held its original shape.

The High-Warden stepped into the mirror and entered a library of water that surged up, around, through and over another set of glass books. Even the floor underfoot was comprised of water that pulsed a subtle emerald with every step he took. A gentle ecstasy enfolded him as *Winsyria's* quintessence awoke. The whole of this land touched him, transmitting the joy of spring's first awakenings scarred by the portent of rising war.

He waited, knowing the time for the books would come later, and soon a glass figure emerged from the coursing walls, light glinting off its countless facets. This fraction of *Winsyria* stepped forward and spoke voicelessly, his arctic words entering the High-Warden's mind, *"Much time has passed since we last spoke."*

"Yes, by the standards of mortal men," the High-Warden said, bowing to his lord. "Soon my reckonings will transcend that if they have not already. I do not know whether this pains me yet."

"It will not pain you now or for decades to come, but it will as all the choices, losses, and broken promises of centuries weigh upon you unrelenting. You shall learn to hate both it and humanity when the ceaseless passing centuries convert to millennia then eons, and as, piece by piece, you are denied all the gifts of mortality. You are eternal, and in living among mortals, you will truly learn all it entails."

"I know. Just as I know my years of solitude have ended."

"Yes, and it will bring new pain. I wish such torments need not fall upon the shoulders of any, and I wish I could change your fate, High-Warden. But know this; if a burden must fall, let it fall to one who can bear it."

"I accepted the *Burdening*; I will carry it until another is selected."

"I ask for nothing more, and it is still more than I would ask of you."

The High-Warden nodded, as a vibration shook the still water. "I can no longer sense you in the earth, my lord, no longer hear you in the wind or taste you in the water, and sometimes the cold now bites my skin; where have you gone?"

"Nowhere, but I am forbidden from aiding in this war. There was an old debt, and I have been called to answer."

"For how long will this pact hold you?"

"Until this war is done." The crystalline figure looked heavenwards. *"My time is up, High-Warden. We will not speak again until the war reaches its conclusion."* Winsyria's form scattered and merged with the water, restarting the current.

The High-Warden immersed a hand into the circling waters, feeling only the pressure of a stream, and extracted a book.

He took the slender book in hand, the glass cover undulating beneath his fingers and shaping itself to his hand. Careful of its fragility, he opened the first page, watching the scripture write itself. The words spoke of the ritual he needed, a means to awaken and summon the eldest Rhawn.

A sound broke across the room, sending contrary ripples eddying along the walls. The High-Warden noted the footfalls of Lord Antiark and the accompanying flash of emerald light but continued to read the progressing script, reassuring himself of the essential knowledge. A bare foot touched the water, giving less retort than a mouse might have.

"Greetings, Lord Antiark." He shut the book, his words unleashing a ripple through the water and glass.

The quiet footfalls ceased as Lord Antiark reached him. "I hope you are faring well, High-Warden; it seems like you haven't aged a day." Lord Antiark inclined his head, the frosted locks of his pale hair drawn back from a wide, unassuming brow. He wore a deep blue indakc—a tight, knee-length indoor coat intended for daywear—lined with white fur but had abstained from formal garb. "I remember you coming to speak with my grandfather all those years ago when he accepted his *Burden*. I remember being frightened of you because of your tattoos and size." Lord Antiark smiled, brushing off his own words.

The High-Warden nodded, recalling the child this man had been those decades before. He remembered the boy for his laughter, made all the stronger because of his heritage. The Lord Antiarks were not blessed with joyous lives; they are the caretakers of a land wild in its aggression and must balance all of mortality's pain coupled with the agonies of immortality. His laughter was one of the reasons the High-Warden had not traveled to Antiark on the eve of his *Burdening*: he already knew the man.

"You have grown," the High-Warden said dryly.

Lord Antiark chuckled. "How can you recognize me?"

The High-Warden ignored the question. "The war brings me to Antiark, though not to aid in her defense."

The smile fled Lord Antiark's face. "I expected as much, but I had hoped."

The High-Warden raised a hand to forestall further words. "This invasion opens a breach in the *Barrier* that segregates this land from the gods and their ilk. This cavity broadens every day the New Order remains in The North. Their gods are waiting for the slightest opportunity. They cannot enter, not yet; the *Barrier* still denies them entrance."

"I know of the *Barrier*, but how can it defy the power of four gods with *Winsyria* gone?"

"The *Barrier* is not a solid wall; it is a layered defense with each layer bound to a specific divinity. If they desire to enter, the gods must fight alone."

Lord Antiark nodded, a slight furrowing of his brow the only sign of his rage at the invasion. "What are your intentions?"

The High-Warden responded with dry humor, "Intend? I intend to seal every cavity before the gods use them. If that is unsuccessful, I intend to rip the eyes out of any god who dares enter and hold them until the breach closes. And if all else fails, I intend to bleed as much as The North requires." The High-Warden replaced the book, the water coiling up his arm. With a gentle motion, he coaxed it back into the river.

"What do you require of us?" Lord Antiark turned to depart.

"Of Antiark itself? Nothing." The High-Warden followed the man, passing through the glass doorway and into the library.

"If you require nothing of Antiark, why come at all? The forefathers tell me you examined everything in the library years ago?"

"Immortality dominates my blood in many ways, but three centuries are long enough for any man to forget, and I cannot afford to err."

"What do you need?"

"I require nothing of you; I need a wizard."

Lord Antiark frowned. "Are we so weak that we need to plead for aid from outsiders?"

"The North is not lacking; I am. What I am in body, if not in soul, is averse to an essential rite. I need to enact a summons, and wizards are my sole recourse."

"Are you certain? Your past with them is fractious. Moreover, Falain Durensev has grown influential in the council's deliberations."

The High-Warden answered with a measured voice, "I need the aid of a wizard, not Falain Durensev; I trust one will remember they live in The North."

"One of them will."

The High-Warden looked at Lord Antiark for a while. "You are like your ancestors in many ways but different also."

"How so?"

Stepping away with a gesture of farewell, the High-Warden gave Lord Antiark the hint of a smile. "There is more hope and laughter. Two qualities your grandfather lacked for all his strength of character."

"Wait, High-Warden."

"Yes?"

Lord Antiark gently touched his forearm. "As one of the few of those in this land that can truly understand what it means to be connected to The North, I want to ask how you are doing. Not the land, for I feel its violation everywhere, but you."

A long silence ensued, then, "I am enraged, Lord Antiark. It is not something I habitually enjoy being."

2

Slade Lammerock

6616 A.O.M.

Slade Lammerock slithered through Tellor's congested streets. He swayed continuously, sometimes dodging around protruding elbows or heaped goods, other times sneaking into people's pockets, snooping through their personal affairs and then returning the baubles with none the wiser. He also entertained himself by tossing kisses at strange women or batting his eyelashes at young, handsome fellows he "accidentally" collided with. Often the poor men froze mid-step, watching as their tormentor vanished then reappeared with a final blown kiss.

Despite his antics, no one paid Slade any real attention. They were more concerned with surviving the sunny, near painfully humid day and enjoying its city-wide festivities. He, on the other hand, merely ambled about until his affairs came calling.

This happened soon enough, arriving as a screech that pierced the messy clamor and drew his attention skyward to a circling hawk, just as it tucked wings and dove toward him.

It landed at his feet with surprising grace, thick, granite feathers scraping closed as it hopped forward and pecked at Slade's boots. "Ah, feeling a tad impatient, are we?" The young man grinned, crouching down and offering one of his gloved fingers as a perch. "Come now, tell me your sorrows."

The stone-bird gave him a flat unamused stare. "Very well then, keep your secrets. Instead, how about I"—the bird pecked at his hand—"oh alright, I'll let you convey your message."

The avian's beak opened, reciting in the voice of a man whose misspent youth afflicted him with a rasping cough. "Our uninvited guest just arrived at Trader's Gate; it is the fifth-Vigil. At the current rate of admissions, she will enter shortly. How shall we proceed?" Finished, the hawk gave another cry, this one laced with the distinct tone of a question.

"Return message: see, I told you she'd pick this way." Slade glanced down his street to where the towering portcullis known as Trader's Gate loomed. "Gloating aside, I'm already here, so I'll handle things." He then hurled his hand upwards and the hawk, voicing a final screech, departed.

Directing his steps toward the gate, Slade scanned the admissions line and spotted a tall, auburn haired woman who stood with arms crossed, tapping a foot as the gate-guards checked her papers. Weight shifting forward, she made an obviously curt inquiry; whereupon the guard stiffened.

A slim, articulate eyebrow lifted upward and Slade produced a reed flute. With a light skip and the beginnings of a dance, he added yet another song to the already prevalent wash of drums and lutes.

The guard looked up, eyes sweeping the crowd until they alighted upon Slade. Still performing, the young man beckoned, inviting him to join the festivities. The guard simply resumed his job, waving the woman through with all difficulties apparently resolved.

At the sudden switch, her eyes narrowed; nevertheless, she snatched her papers and marched into the massive port city of Tellor, setting foot upon its umber cobblestones with hardly a glance.

Continuing his tune, Slade let the crowd drag him along behind her: his uninvited guest.

Over time the woman's confidence faded, ground to dust by an hour spent wandering through unfamiliar streets. With each intersection, she dawdled longer, weighing her options or glancing back the way she had come.

Any native could easily diagnose the problem as her needing directions and so he strolled to the nearest shop: a little tent watched over by a creature best described as a feathered monkey. As for the monkey's contractor, an obscenely fat man who bravely grew a beard despite the appalling results.

Slade leaned against the counter and lightly tapped its overlord's arm, pulling the man's attention around then wagging eyebrows to prod him into broaching a conversation.

"What can I do for you, good sir?"

"That pretty lady looks lost; perhaps you might assist her?"

The man scowled at him. "You seem perfectly capable."

"I've never visited this side of town before, so we share the same affliction." Slade smiled cheerfully, and after a brief indecision, the vendor grumbled and then lumbered off to aid the woman.

Taking advantage of the stall's defenseless state, Slade pulled a stalk of grain from his satchel and fed it to the shop's adari—a mysterious, monkey-esque creature defined by its narrowed, glowing eyes and enveloping robes—bribing it to ensure no scream sounded when he pilfered a package of candied apple slices. He then walked right past the woman who, still oblivious to Slade, gave the shop's vendor a grateful nod and began searching her pockets, unwittingly buying Slade's snack.

With her and Slade's positions reversed, she resumed her journey, continuing until the sun relinquished its earlier position and began marching to its next guard-post, where it would wait for another hour. As the shadows retreated, she glanced skyward, marked the Vigil shift and then examined the surrounding food stalls, eventually settling for one that supplied tediously flavored lunches for a nominal expense.

Slade chose an establishment whose green and gold banner proclaimed it served eastern cuisine. Hopping onto one of the six barstools, Slade reached for the small, bronze counter bell etched with strange runes: a tool meant for scaring off malignant spirits. Helping in the defense were several iron bottles with identical runes swinging from the awning and humming softly as they threatened imprisonment to any mischievous spirits wandering past. Most cultures considered these methods pure superstition, but all agreed that touching another's charm was a call for misfortune.

Slade had spent the last three months attempting to ring the bell. Heartbeats before his fingers brushed against its chill surface, the shop's yellow feathered adari hissed through its concealing cowl and a tall, skeletal woman stretched over the counter to slap his hand with a spatula.

"Master Lammerock, shall I prepare the usual?" Despite her assault, the woman continued eyeing the skillets sizzling before her, each adorned by three to four cakes of varying sizes. The woman's hands blurred as she swapped between skillets, sliding a spatula under each light brown patty and flipping them skyward before focusing on the next skillet, allowing the airborne cakes to land wherever they wanted. Somehow each cake landed on the appropriate skillet, their upturned faces an appetizing golden brown. With all the cakes flipped, she leaned over the griddles and moved the bell outside of Slade's reach.

"Of course, as if I would forego our little game?" Teeth flashing, he placed his customary bet atop the counter.

With scarce a hiccup, the vendor dug into a drawer, produced a sheaf of thick wax paper and chose a finished cake, setting it at the paper's center where it was promptly wrapped. After preparing a second cake, she disappeared behind the counter, bending to investigate an oven's contents. She reappeared a second later holding two pies with mysterious contents. Sprinkling them with an unknown spice, she wrapped the pies and, setting them atop the cakes, relinquished the mysterious collection into Slade's custody. If she failed to surprise his taste buds, their permanent wager ensured she bought his next meal.

"Terribly grateful."

Overhead, the adari dipped a quill and wrote a careful note in the massive, steel bound ledger that served as both seat and occupation, all the while eyeing Slade with the indiscriminatory suspicion of its species.

Slade, meanwhile, checked on his uninvited guest, discovering that a truculent customer was delaying her line's progress. Exploiting this delay, he crossed the street to procure two skins of mulberry juice. These in hand, Slade returned to the skeletal woman's stall, claimed a seat by the bar and set one aside. He flashed the owner a grin and picked up a small vial conveniently laid to his right. Thus armed, he mixed its contents with the second skin of juice. Whoever imbibed the drugged liquid would feel a minimal euphoria while their natural suspicion diminished.

Once he was finished, Slade dropped the vial into his satchel and withdrew six unmarked packages that he placed on the bar. Without glancing away from her griddles, the woman quickly concealed them behind her counter.

His chores addressed for the present, Slade collected the uncontaminated juice but left the drugged one lying atop the bar. His ducklings would ensure their uninvited guest received his contribution and whatever minor effects it could wreak.

In the meantime, he decided to wait atop the second of Tellor's three towering walls because it overlooked those sectors allocated to unofficial performances. Upon arriving though, Slade first scoured the base for suitable entertainment, ducking under banners hung to commemorate Cardolyn Tyer's birth and dodging between the sweat smeared people hunkering in the wall's shade.

A cacophony of cheers arose, breaking his stride and drawing his attention to a crowd of spectators exchanging coins. A second roar burgeoned and again money changed hands, only to switch ownership a third time when another roar sounded. A quick glance confirmed Slade's disappointing suspicion; the bets belonged to the legal variety and thus were merely frowned upon.

Nevertheless, Slade grinned and raced toward the battlements, jumping onto a lift just as its metal gears started clanking, pulling both him and a squad of guards upward. Atop the wall, the prevailing scent of the ocean became far more noticeable. Another benefit was that he could enjoy the spectacle without impediment while also watching for his uninvited guest, correcting her movements if necessary.

Below him seven entertainers—four men and three women—stood within a cleared area, listening to the crowd's adulation interspersed with the occasional obscenity, bowing before one and cheerfully ignoring the other.

At a signal from the performers, the audience's merriment receded to a constrained din.

In unison the women tumbled from the scene, bestowing the figurative stage onto their compatriots. The men juggled glinting swords, flaming torches, and twisted hatchets. They performed blade dances, various gymnastics, and balanced knives in doubtful places. One time they abandoned the script to belch fire at another performer, setting the poor man aflame and causing untold merriment.

Mid-performance, Slade noticed his uninvited guest approaching with lunch in hand. He began whistling a haphazard tune that, by all rights, the spectators should have drowned out. But a male performer looked up, listening intently as his head bobbed along with the melody. At its conclusion, the man gave Slade an affirmative nod, sighted the woman immediately, and joined the closing act of the performance.

The women entered then, stepping onto the stage with calm dignity as showers of coins greeted their arrival. Ignoring the coins, they began an elaborate series of vaults, cartwheels, and handstands designed to tease the audience with a hint of what awaited them.

At the end of this intro one woman slid into a graceful split, extending her hands upward—palms facing the sun—to create a podium for another who ran forward and flipped onto it, hands first. Except perfect balance eluded them, and every heartbeat threatened collapse. With each dangerous tilt, the audience groaned; with each last second correction, the audience lost its ability to exhale. Slowly, however, the two women worked their way to absolute equilibrium. The instant they did, a third woman scaled the tower to erect her own handstand, balancing on the feet of her predecessor. This time neither a twitch nor a tremor shook the display. Long, breathless seconds ticked by as the audience waited for the first quiver, the first hint of imminent collapse. This intimation was never given. The uppermost woman vaulted off, landing in a crouch and quickly rising to catch the second performer when she dismounted, forming another tower. Hands locked, the women allowed their display to fall backward, collapsing into an arch that the third woman hurdled with a double flip. It was one performance among several and each successive routine strained belief once again. Their more implausible feats included dancing across wires, contorting themselves into astonishing postures, and escaping impossible situations.

Despite knowing the demonstration by heart, Slade applauded and whooped right alongside the audience, attention ever fixed on his uninvited guest.

At the show's conclusion, the spectators dispersed, some wandering lost, some hunting food, most seeking amusement elsewhere. His uninvited guest paused for directions, then joined the first group. Slade elected to finish his meal, watching as three performers donned various disguises to trail the woman.

Tossing his greasy wrapper into a specially prepared fire, Slade hopped from the parapets. If he hurried, he could arrive fashionably late.

Hearing a set of footsteps, he turned and found a Theanne guard patrolling in his direction. *Actually, that reminds me. I need an extra pair of hands on the docks.* Bouncing to his feet, Slade gave the guard a wave. "Hello there, I wonder if I might steal a moment of your time?"

The man started slightly, then glanced from Slade down both sections of wall. At last he performed a curt bow. "My lord, do you have a license to be up here?"

Despite being strangers, pins hooked into their respective collars revealed their station, their family, their occupation, and any award either might have won. A gold pin adorned Slade's collar, its surface bearing his father's crest. The soldier, conversely, possessed two silver pins, one denoting his middle-class rank and a second revealing both his military service and rank.

"Of course I do. Now about that stolen moment, I have a proposition for—" The guard extended an expectant hand, prompting Slade to begin patting his various pockets. "Oh my, it appears I've misplaced it."

"Then I must request that you accompany me."

It appears I'll have to ask someone else. Slade heaved an exaggerated sigh. "If you insist." The guard made a sharp about-face and led Slade to the nearest lift, where he politely but inflexibly assisted him on his way.

Walking the umber cobblestones once again, Slade merged with the flow of traffic and let it take him wherever it wished. He had to make a random appearance and what better way to achieve that then by not knowing his own destination.

Eventually he was deposited alongside an alleyway so murky the other members of its species would have cast sideways glances at it. A few steps down its cobwebbed mouth, Slade began slipping in between the numerous strings that bisected its length. Curiously, several tiny bells hung from each yellow cord making it near impossible to traverse the alley without causing a disturbance. In Slade's case, he practiced touching the bells without they themselves noticing it.

At the alley's rear sat an iron-grate. Grabbing its slimy green bars, he lifted it and then stepped onto the ladder underneath, sliding out from the thick, humid heat of the surface into a gloomy, cloying damp, and the prickling sense of everything around him holding still and watching: a sensation reserved for Tellor's sewers.

After a brief listen, Slade disappeared down the right-hand path, fingers trailing along the damp wall. His current schedule forbade disoriented wanderings, and his clothing decried the thought of falling into the scummy river moping along beside him.

Soon he caught the sounds of life, beginning with a quiet, many-throated groan and a muted cry of triumph. Next he heard the intermittent songs; tasteless ballads sung with no regard for either skill or beauty. Upon drawing nearer, he also distinguished the occasional word or familiar voice. Lastly Slade heard the prayers: a combination of muttered entreaties, damnations, and bargains all offered to the same god. *Kis'Maat*, God of Luck and Fate: patron of the streets.

He found and triggered the secret latch easily, air whistling past as the stone wall retracted several inches before sliding sideways.

He waved at the startled faces of those concealed within, twenty-five assorted men and women scattered across various dice games. "Don't let me disturb you, pray continue." Hesitantly the rattling resumed as players returned to their illegal games.

Slade beckoned the gamekeeper over, facing away from the crowd and pulling the man in close. "My friend, you've only been here a week, but I have already caught you cheating me. This is a tad disappointing, and obviously I'll have to deduct a substantial portion from your wages; more importantly, we desperately need to work on your technique. See if we can work out the kinks." The man gave a confused nod. "Fantastic, now for the interesting bit." He reached into his satchel, producing three sets of identical dice. "These are loaded dice, be careful not to raise suspicions when you use them. I want you to lose for the next month, allow rumors of our ... misfortune to spread, let these tales entice a large crowd and then lose big. Afterwards, you can start winning again; do it subtly though, I don't want to scare off potential customers."

The gamekeeper bowed once, then departed, leaving a smirking Slade behind him. If all transpired according to plan, this gambling den would lose a significant amount of money but gain several loyal patrons.

Half-an-hour later, Slade—once again walking the salt-laced air of Tellor's streets—passed under an elaborate archway, all gussied up in banners of silver and blue, and entered the Great-Market at Tellor's heart. It stood among the few things that rejected the Empire's strict order, overflowing its designated borders to crash against the third wall and flow well beyond the second.

A cacophony of scents, colors, sounds, and people dominated the scene, teasing him with the possibilities contained therein; all it needed was a single step. Slade, however, needed to reach his destination before the next Vigil shift, at least if he still wanted to be fashionably late. So, he rallied his determination and dove headfirst into the writhing torrent of shouting vendors, jostling shoulders, and ubiquitous confusion.

Slade avoided any possible siren calls by focusing on the cobblestones, using all but a piece of his attention which he saved for the sharks infesting this particular sea: pickpockets.

They attacked his purse three times. Twice the prospective criminal was an orphan searching for their next meal. In both cases, Slade patted the ruffians' heads and directed them to easier, more lucrative targets. The final pickpocket was a handsome youth dressed in a Thearch's attire, an excellent suitor for the most fastidious wallet. Slade, the eternal gentleman, decided to help the young lord by relieving him of all excess valuables that might encumber him.

Despite these travails, Slade almost succeeded in crossing the Great-Market. Almost, however, was the same as utter failure. As he neared the far edge, his absentminded gaze wandered across a quaint shop tucked into a back corner. An old man flitted about it, his capable hands straightening and polishing already resplendent merchandise.

Just like that, Slade's attention fell prey to the murmuring of hats, the seductive whispers of scarves, and the expectant silence that belonged to sashes alone.

Amongst this multitude of apparel, one specific item fascinated his gaze and forced his slow, deliberate tread out of its predetermined path. This mutiny notwithstanding, Slade sauntered to the old man's stall with all manner of disinterest. Opposite him the proprietor now lounged on a stool, its legs creaking as he leaned back against his counter. Neither fooled the other.

The old vender's adari leaned forward suspiciously while he merely watched Slade from under lowered brows. "Does anything strike your fancy, my lord?"

Slade suppressed a smile; since he'd concealed his Thearch pin before entering the Great-Market, the old man was clearly trying to charm the money from his purse. "I am simply inspecting your ... wares." He incorporated a slight pause, suggesting he mistrusted the quality of said wares, before offering an opportunity. "I'd hoped to find something suitable for a masquerade, but it seems I'm destined for disappointment." Slade shrugged, feigning a departure.

"Please, my lord, rest for a spell." The vendor leapt forward and ushered him to the newly vacated seat. "Allow me to present a few choice products, I'm sure they will both satisfy your impeccable taste and fulfill any requirements."

Slade, heaving a sigh directed more at himself and his overly generous nature than the old man, accepted the offered seat.

"My wares are of the best quality, my lord, I assure you. Take this specimen for instance." The hat he proffered was a firm, wide brimmed example burnished to a glistening black. Also, it was the very object of Slade's fascination.

"This article, my lord, was crafted with the finest materials; resources so rare that master craftsmen strain to procure them. The results, however, are incontestable. This purchase will satisfy your every need from durability to comfort." Causing Slade's eyebrows to rise slightly, he presented it for inspection.

"I assume the material is waterproof?" Slade asked, running his fingers over the silky brim and then donning the article, already suspecting its perfect fit.

"Entirely so, my lord."

"Very well, I shall offer you two bronze-crowns."

"For the young lord, my first customer of the day, I can part with it for three silver-sails."

Slade gave a low whistle and returned the hat, drumming his fingers upon the counter. "One silver-sail."

"Two silver-sails and three bronze-crowns."

'That's the same price you sly old fox. Though I may look too slim to be an Imperial citizen, I am very much a native here.' "Three bronze-crowns," Slade replied, changing his own denominations to return the favor.

"Oh, how you attempt to ruin me." Bantering tone notwithstanding, the man's jaw adopted a stubborn edge. "This fine article cost four bronze-crowns to make; why I could sell it for two silver-sails if I were allotted a more hospitable market space."

A large reduction in price; either the man was desperate, or he tired of the game. Slade shook his head, rejecting the price, then caught the man's hand as he moved to reshelve the hat. "I may have an ulterior proposition; one I think you will enjoy." The vendor stilled, his ears perking up. "You, good sir, will give me this hat, that most outrageously sized peacock feather, and the crimson band hanging from that nail."

"And in return for my generosity?"

"I offer you this most magnanimous gift." Slade delved into his satchel and withdrew an embellished envelope with a flourish, giving the old man a wink.

A quick skim of the contents had the vendor's wide-eyed gaze lifting to Slade. "This is a writ from Governor Warsein, allowing me to sell my wares anywhere I wish." His awestruck gaze returned to the prize he held, the document wrinkling under his forceful grip. "I could sell my wares at the center of the Great-Market. *Enecki* bless me, I could sell at the very feet of the Imperial Emperor's statue."

"Now that is a bold location. I wish I'd thought of it myself. Do we have a bargain?"

The man, entranced by the Governor's Writ and oblivious to his surroundings, nodded.

Slade hopped from the stool, leaned over the counter and collected his various purchases, afterwards spending a mere heartbeat to construct his masterpiece. The crimson band found itself wrapped around the hat's bowl and the dark, ostentatious peacock feather was thrust in between the two. *'There, absolutely marvelous.'* True, the acquisition left him short one writ, but he could always produce another before the appointed hour.

Whistling a lively melody, he finished trekking across the Great-Market and turned down a side street, following it into the convoluted alleyways of Tellor: a place where even a compass could lose its way. At the center of this warren, beyond the twisting corridors, past the innumerable dead-ends, through the countless stalkers, footpads, and other individuals of similar occupation, a meeting waited for him. First he had one last errand; a smuggler friend who needed help unloading cargo and sneaking it past any Theanne guards patrolling the wharf.

Almost as if summoned by the thought, three pale-skinned, ruggedly dressed men stepped from the shadows, flanking him on all sides.

"Why hello, gentlemen. You new in town?" At his tone, the three footpads exchanged glances, the one in front hastily making complex finger signs toward his companions. *Ah, friends from Carr'Selain.'* "Believe it or not, this is a fortuitous encounter for me. Any of you curious to hear a proposition?"

With this and his detour in the Great-Market, Slade doubted he could still arrive fashionably late; that said, he could arrive exceptionally late and be extremely fashionable.

Slade entered through the back door, but only after his long delicate fingers danced across multiple locks of increasing difficulty. His choice lacked any serious motivation, amounting to a casual disdain for the front door because of its traditionalism and how crawling through windows was undignified. *Of course, considering my chosen profession, the back door seems equally traditional.* Closing it soundlessly behind himself, he allowed shadow to swallow the room, but neither the furniture gratuitously scattered across the carpet nor the prevailing obscurity hindered him. With a relaxed posture that belied the numerous traps crowding his path, Slade crossed to an oaken door.

There he paused, waiting to see if somebody had detected him. But long, tedious seconds elapsed and … nothing. A grin split his face, eyebrows tipping inward as he started tapping out a simple beat on the door. This quickly progressed to a more complicated stanza and then the crowning display of his impromptu concert, an in-the-moment inspiration that required both hands and a breakneck tempo, the sort to outclass a three-armed man.

The faint chatter hitherto seeping through the door fell away, silence stretching until footsteps thumped across the room and the door cracked open. Warm, spectacled eyes peered out. They belonged to a towering man with blonde hair that was shaved along the sides and grown long enough to pull into a ponytail. "Who's there?"

"Ah, my dear, sweet, foolish subjects, I dread to consider what sorry tales your lives would have told without my patronage. I tremble to think what horrors you would have endured sans my guidance. I almost gibber from the thought of what terrors you might experience if someone kidnapped my patient, nurturing self." Bent near double by unspeakable despair, Slade's head shook from side to side.

"It's him alright," the door-guard called over his shoulder, stepping aside.

"You forgot to ask me what the password is."

"We have a password?"

"Of course we do, Haram, all shady dealings require a password."

"Um, alright... What is the password then?"

"Utterly useless ukuleles."

"Um, that's correct; you can come in now."

Slade threw his hands into the air. "No, it's not; that was a decoy password; the true password is psychopathic paraphernalia. If you can't remember it, what's the point in having a password?"

Haram braced his arm against the door. "I actually remembered the password; but I wasn't sure you did, so I pretended to fall for the decoy."

"That is complete hogwash."

"Yes, just like your passwords."

"Excellent." Trotting past the huge man, Slade assumed his customary position at center stage and spun a slow circle, favoring his crew with a broad grin. "Have you, my servants, slaves, and devoted sycophants, enjoyed my absence?"

A quick tally accounted for all twelve members, including the acrobats from earlier. Among the numerous, allegedly solitary crews Slade managed, this was his oldest and most skilled. That said, neither their ability nor their history bought his secrets, subjecting them to the same blissful ignorance as the others. Except for Haram.

"*Jinsorren* grant me patience. Slade, could you occasionally start a conversation with the proper use of our names and a culturally accepted greeting? You know, as etiquette demands?" His bald-headed questioner dropped into one of the many fresh-faced couches and pulled her feet up onto the cushions, leaving her shoes behind so they wouldn't smear char over the designs. Even now, after multiple cleanings into their resumed and unpaid tenancy, charcoal still darkened the room's stone and colored its air with the scent of ash, ensuring his ducklings remembered to be more careful in the future.

As for the room's current adornments, Slade had decided to provide them for his personal comfort after the flames doomed the house to inhospitality. Unfortunately, his crew had promptly claimed the chairs as their own, heartlessly disregarding his threats of unending torture.

"Why ever should I concern myself with something as defunct as etiquette?" Slade raised both eyebrows, extending his arms in either direction. "Especially since you ladies don the most delightful pouts when I disregard it? And we mustn't forget our male companions who offer boundless merriment while pushing their besotted minds to untangle the convoluted greetings my tongue weaves in the place of convention." Noticing slight discontent creeping through his male followers, Slade patted the nearest one on the shoulder. "Well, alright. Your pouts can be adorable too. It might even be true as I've never seen any of you pout before. I'm starting to think the mere act of pouting would demean your manhood beyond recovery."

Off to the side, Haram shook a sleeping crewmember, slipped a pillow under their head and then raised a hand. "Might I suggest we shelve this topic for a later date, perhaps when you don't arrive quite so … on time. We need to discuss our uninvited guest and develop a plan for how to proceed."

Slade huffed, blowing a strand of hair from his eyes. "Oh, very well; but be quick, time is neither so cheap nor so copious that someone besides me can waste it without fruit."

The man nodded, adjusting his square, gold-rimmed glasses before addressing the room. "As you may have guessed, the Thieves' Guild has infiltrated Tellor once again—"

The reactive groan was so universal that the room itself might have joined in. "Didn't we just finish evicting a shipment of their goons?"

"Are they actually Carr'Selain's people or more assassins he's hired to go after Slade?"

"We don't have time for this either way, not with the mansion job coming up."

"And that's dangerous enough as is."

"How many incursions have there been this month? Four?"

'Oh no, far more than that. But for you personally, yes.' Slade raised his hands, calming the storm of chatter. "This time is significantly more interesting than past visits. Carr'Selain has seen fit to send a bright eyed, bushy tailed representative in lieu of assassins or more thugs. Rumor is that he wants a meeting, though we're not supposed to know its him."

"What? Where did you hear that?"

"A mostly reliable source: myself."

Whispered conversation erupted around the room, continuing until Haram gestured for silence. "Our uninvited guest is a woman in her middling twenties; she has dark auburn hair, almost red, and blue eyes." The man leveled a stern expression on his companions, pinning each to their seats. "She is armed; more importantly we suspect she is a Rat. Be careful when approaching or following her."

The guild's field agents fell into two categories: Rats and Mice. The former steal objects of value from anywhere and anyone—occasionally sequestering people if need be—and handle any violence; whereas the latter uses subterfuge to appropriate information. Information about everything and everyone.

"With the important details covered," Slade said, taking the room's attention back for himself. "All that remains is for me to speculate on what impression we should cultivate for our dear guest." He twisted to the side and lifted his right hand toward the ceiling, making a fist. At the same time, he expanded his chest and lengthened his waist, spine arching ever so slightly to convey a sense of dignity. "Shall we go for impressive and influential, or perhaps the lucky fool?" His posture shifted, becoming the type of stance one expects from a man who hasn't suffered a rainy day in his entire life and is foolish enough to believe this good fortune arises from his own skill rather than the universe's design. "On the other hand, we might do a bit of both, an influential upstart perhaps." Again his posture changed, becoming the epitome of a young, conceited man who climbed above his station. "Better yet, we could nurture an idea so profound, so far beyond understanding it boggles her mind." Slade rubbed his hands together and cackled with the malignity of a truly evil mastermind.

"I'm not sure it matters. We think she's an experienced combatant, but from what I've observed, she lacks skill in subterfuge." These faint words came from a young woman who kneeled to Slade's right. She bent over a square coffee table, inspecting a gigantic map that exceeded the edges and draped onto the floor.

Slade swiveled in place, facing the young woman with the sort of grin that welcomed the uncertain and invited easy conversation. "Why do you say that?"

Nevertheless, her countenance flooded with color, and her nose quickly buried itself in the map. From that refuge, she mumbled a reluctant explanation, "Our guest walks straight ahead, neither glancing over her shoulder to search for possible tails nor weaving her way amongst the crowds."

Slade allowed himself a small, inner sigh. If Emily glanced up once throughout the entire meeting, *Kis'Maat's* benign eye was upon him today. Perhaps he should purchase a new map for her; her current specimen resembled a fisherman's net.

"An adequate deduction. Well done." This, of course, caused her face to reignite but a little encouragement never hurt, and Slade intended to use every possible weapon in his war against shyness. Refocusing on his crew, he waited to see if someone wanted to offer an opinion.

None presented either hand or thought, electing to wallow in shameless expectancy.

Slade grinned, clapping his hands together. "You realize that I adore you all? With this business of allowing me to make the final decisions, I get the distinct impression of being in charge. Why, it's almost as if I actually lead this crew of rogues and scoundrels, like I am the true mastermind behind our exploits." For effect, Slade danced a little jig and hummed a brief snatch of tune, laughing silently as they stared at him with the usual blend of expressions: horror, amusement, shock, and long-suffering patience.

"Slade, you command with an iron grip and abuse us mercilessly; of course you're in charge." A woman yawned and stretched back with luxurious pleasure. "Now concerning your accusation that we leave all the decisions in your lap; in our defense, something must alleviate the enormous pressure resting on our young shoulders. Furthermore, it's always amusing to grant you free reign and enjoy the ensuing havoc."

"Besides, it's obvious that you wish to parade your latest acquisition." The dark-haired Samara added, giving the apparel an admiring glance. "Such a marvelous acquisition deserves a proper maiden voyage."

"I am sooo glad you noticed." Slade winked and gave a tip of the hat. "With how you study me, notice my feelings and my clothes, one might suspect you for a spy." Of course she was a spy. He always made sure to have at least one. It paid to keep one's enemies close, preferably in a position of supposed power. "Well, you indolent worms, there's work that needs doing. Let's go yank wool over the eyes of an inexperienced damsel in distress." This time grins answered Slade's own, except for one man who looked confused.

"So which charade will you employ?" Haram asked, but Slade only tapped the side of his nose.

One by one or in pairs, they left the house and ran to their assigned positions. Before long Slade stood alone, waiting for the moment to make his grand entrance. A little deliberation never hurt anybody though, particularly when the deliberation created drama, and Slade loved drama.

3

The Tragnashi

6617 A.O.M.

Dunes of burnished sand rolled over the trackless desert, surpassing tempest waves in their mountainous heights. A vindictive sun reigned over them from one of the day's earliest Vigils, long ago having incinerated all but the hardiest life to red dust. In the near distance, immense towers jutted like a forest of pine trees from a plunging chasm that extended southward beyond the sight of any human eye, and in length from one edge of the Avarus Desert to the other. These towers reached wearily skyward, ravaged by time and sun until the stone stooped from exhaustion and misery, echoes of a ruined glory.

A Raven, small for its kind and possessing the emerald eyes of a human, soared southward in defiance of the sun's oppression, attention fixed upon the withered city. It banked and dove, passing the immense towers and countless bridges until they eclipsed the sun overhead, many casting shadows over three hundred men long. Diving beneath a filthy clothesline, the Raven circled a ponderous tower and dove again, navigating the worn structures and arching bridges to the chasm's walls where it continued descending. It pulled up just shy of the chasm's foundation, where smooth stone gave way to the jagged, tusk-like rocks, tenacious vines, and emaciated bracken that provided a frail shelter to the few species hardy enough to survive.

At this foundation ran the chasm's architect. Here, where water exceeds measurable value, the *Annuir'Hyme* is worshiped beyond any man, god, or sun. The Raven ascended through the bridges again, searching for the city's heart. It found the Coliseum near the chasm's middle, within reach of the sun yet not close enough to endanger lives. The Coliseum was a compound of a dozen arenas interconnected through bridges, interred passageways, and walls. These stadiums differed from one another in their environments, some containing swamps, others infernos, small jungles or any number of seasonal attractions, but all shared the pillars: towering structures supporting ornate balconies for the Kalvonders to enjoy the spectacles of blood. Stands on the octagonal walls provided seating and shade for inferior men.

The Coliseum was the largest of the arena complexes scattered across Sahdaen, and the nearest to the old Remanas Palace. It was here the Kalvonders poured their most extravagant displays of power to terrify, quell, and satiate the Avaran populace.

The arenas hosted a series of gladiatorial entertainments on the culmination of every four Turnings, or forty-eight days, called the Angorat'Wass where Tragnashi combat one another and a variety of monsters. The Tragnashi are literally soul-less: individuals owned to the very fabric of their existence by Kalvonders.

The Raven descended, continuing to circle the Coliseum as it sought a particular man. It found him on a pillar overlooking the swampland arena, alone but for his attendant and ordered rows of vacant seats. It dove, circled once and alighted on the balcony's railing. Ancient burgundy fabric draped the railing and floor, displaying an immense gold summoning pentacle from Isaracc: a collapsed empire of wizards. It would have been vibrant despite the years, but Avarans and Kalvonders had long since defaced it with paints and filth. A wizard from that empire—long dead of course—dangled from a pillar to the right, mummified in sumptuous violet cloth, golden runes, and chemicals.

Valeriius, the sole Kalvonder currently occupying the balcony, glanced at the Raven. The balcony's other occupant was a slave woman with waist-length hair braided into a dozen interlocking chains and adorned with bone jewelry to designate her station. She looked up at the Raven's descent, revealing severe lacerations marring her features and rough black hued skin. She was Aparthii, an itinerant people living outside the Avaran Holds.

The slave averted her eyes before Valeriius noticed her lifted brow, but not so low as to miss his glanced command. She hastened to remove the preserving lid and present a glass tureen to her master. Within, nestled cubes of frozen blood varying every color of the spectrum. Valeriius selected a violet piece and resumed his bored demeanor.

Valeriius was neither tall nor short, neither handsome nor ugly, and neither muscular nor overweight. His unbound hair was medium length and his stance ambivalent. He walked with a quiescent stroll and spoke with banal lethargy. In summary: forgettable and unassuming. His only notable aspect was a cane of pure amethyst wrapped in carved vines of ebony and rowan. If one looked close enough, its core shimmered with slowly pulsing light.

Behind Valeriius the balcony's cloth door flapped inward to admit a quartet of his guards. Their faces were concealed behind nondescript veils, marking them as eunuchs. The veils were a façade, serving instead to conceal the pale skin and large eyes of eastern sell-swords. Avarans abhorred foreigners, but eastern sell-swords far surpassed any warrior caste inhabiting the Avarus Desert, so Valeriius made an exception. Even the best Avarans barely constituted warriors, too addicted to the Kalvonders' abundant and varied intoxicants to become adept warriors. It was a disgruntling result but sufferable in view of the control and wealth it provided.

Cautious to maintain the appropriate distance, the sell-swords knelt before Valeriius, pressing their brows to the floor. After an appropriate span, their commander raised his brow and Valeriius nodded once, suffering him to straighten. "Valeriius Kalvonder, Krell Kalvonder desires an audience." The sell-sword resumed his abasement.

Valeriius deliberated. Krell desired either to exact tribute or discuss the possibility of an alliance. Either way, his response was the same: a waved hand indicating the sell-sword should admit Krell. His guest, however, did not wait for the summons. She stormed into view with all the grace of a schismatic boulder, a slave racing to drape the adjacent chair with a lush emerald cloth. It gleamed with the luster of an Artisan Weave but the woven and stenciled images—a few carrion birds and a string of tall, spear-shaped flowers—spoke of common work with fat lines and simplistic designs. She collapsed into the seat, exuding just enough arrogance to compound her dominance but not enough to merit retaliation.

Krell immediately began patting her multiple chins and forehead with a silk handkerchief before adjusting her apparel with bulbous hands and smoothing the seat-cloth to best display its artistry. Her retinue trailed her, the half-dozen guards first, followed by her numerous remaining slaves and contracted attendants: specialists courted through offers of wealth and power. All but the guards lowered themselves to the floor.

To skilled Kalvonders, attendants provided further opportunity for manipulation and deceit with their number, specializations, attire, and wealth all blending into a mirage that would entrap the incautious.

The first of her three attendants was a guardian of the Mercenary's Guild, armored in a gambeson with an iron shield slung across his back and shoulder-length hair pulled tight across his skull by ivory pins. The next was her gamekeeper, dressed in a white over-tunic with the minor embellishments of his class. He wore his hair just above the shoulders, betraying his lack of proficiency, and woven into three separate tails. The final man was her assassin. He dressed in black, his lowered face concealed behind a conforming mask, and his hair styled into an elaborate knot of braids. The man displayed a single skulled dagger on his hip, marking him as a minor assassin at best.

Krell's gamekeeper conferred that she enjoyed the many violent southern sports, but his lack of gaudy embellishments signified she lacked the wealth to hire a true master of the art. The guardian and assassin in her retinue suggested ties to the guilds. The evidence of their true allegiance indicated she was deeply indebted to their masters.

Valeriius had no attendants, blatantly declaring his lack of wealth and prestige. When another Kalvonder saw him surrounded only by slaves and guards, they would view him as weak, inexperienced, and easily manipulated. The contempt they derived from these opinions blinded them, impairing their already fumbling intellects.

Valeriius waited as the obese woman shifted in her seat, the heavy flesh of her body sagging like warm gelatin. Upon realizing the futility of her endeavor, she slumped forward with a snap of her fingers. One of her servants, a male child slave who bore more scars than he did locks of his waist-length hair, scurried forward bearing a chilled wineskin. She snatched the wine and raised it to her lips for a long gulp. The slave ran back to hide in the mass of her retainers.

Krell lowered the wineskin with a belch, plastered a counterfeit smile across her swollen, overpainted features and spoke, "It is a pleasure to finally make your acquaintance, Valeriius!" She made a lilting gesture to exemplify the intensity of her emotions and gulped more wine.

"The pleasure is mutual."

The inebriated woman tittered and gulped her wine. When she lowered the wineskin, she replaced it with a larger no less sickening smile. "I have been watching you for some time now."

Throughout the last Turning, Valeriius had been steadily feeding Krell a feast of rumors and lies regarding information he possessed that, if brought to light, could destroy her. She had devoured his banquet of lies like a prize-winning pig until, through gradual submersion, she drowned in them.

Trailing another gulp, Krell resumed her discourse, "What with Greole Kalvonder's death, wisdom dictates we ally ourselves." Greole had been her sole ally; thus Valeriius ordained his destruction. The death of her ally left Krell as the sole distributor of a rare, hyper-addictive toxin. This solitude made her vulnerable while the resource made her a target. She needed an ally. Krell, however, was an unimportant member of the Kalvonder hierarchy; necessity demanded she find an inferior ally or, at least, an equal she did not fear. Of the Kalvonders in Sahdaen, only Valeriius matched these requirements. With little more than a score of warriors and a small fortune, Valeriius lacked the military threat Krell brought to their conference; her meager intelligence, however, more than settled this imbalance.

Every law of politics and self-preservation dictated Valeriius should leap at the opportunity to make an alliance with Krell. Her military power was insignificant compared to most Kalvonders, but it still allegedly far surpassed his own and would fortify his position substantially.

"We both know why you seek an alliance with me, Krell." He waved a hand delicately toward her. "You need time, time only I can provide with any modicum of fidelity." While he spoke, she gulped more red wine. The liquor, though, did little to obscure the pale fright dominating her features. "So, let us dispense with these time-consuming political games." Valeriius reclined, nodding for Krell to present her offer.

She blinked, mouth hanging agog as her befuddled mind tried to rouse itself from intoxication. Finally she smiled in a confused manner and spoke, "Very well, how …"—she struggled for words complementing on the surface but insulting at the core—"concise. Let's see, huh?" Her brows crinkled and she shook her head. "Ahh, yes, yes … it should begin with a promise of both offensive and defensive military support, yes? A large portion of the Anatay drug also, not equal but certainly profitable." Krell collapsed back into her seat and drank the rest of her new wine flask before reaching for another.

"I will match your brevity. I desire all you offer, but you will also nominate me as the sole heir to your estates in the event of your death." Valeriius inclined his head, ceding her the opportunity to ponder his convoluted overture. In the higher echelons of Kalvonder hierarchy, Valeriius' offered alliance was a statement of superiority and a gamble on who could murder their ally first.

Krell examined his features with a calculating light in her beady, drunken eyes, and he matched her gaze. Ultimately, she looked away, and Valeriius resumed surveying the arena.

Krell coughed, her decision made. "The Inheritance Article would be mutual." She glared, challenging him to refute her.

Valeriius gave the woman a tentative smile. "Of course."

Her manner becoming subdued, she foraged through the voluminous folds of her dress to withdraw a svelte quill. It was an object of wrought gold and vibrant mahogany, marked at its base with the single rune unique to its species. Valeriius extended his left hand, and Krell surrendered the precious object.

Valeriius explored the quill, his deft fingers stroking its length without missing any detail. It was a Blood-Quill, doubtlessly inherited through countless generations of her family for a single, primordial function.

He returned the Blood-Quill, and she raised it to her lips, kissing the rune at its base. Withdrawing the Quill, she lifted her right hand and pricked her thumb on the tip. A grimace flashed across her features as she reversed the Blood-Quill and pressed her thumb into the rune at its base, bathing the sigil in blood. Krell gestured for another slave to bring a page of vellum. Placing it across her knees, she wrote the laws of their alliance in her blood.

When she finished, Krell offered Valeriius the Blood-Quill, her features paler now despite the drunken blush. Accepting it, he did as she had done; first slicing his palm, then writing the oath and his name in blood.

With their alliance forged and bound in blood, Valeriius waited for his vow to take hold. The Blood-Oath's ethereal constraints gripped him, fettering his actions and forcing him, despite his formidable will, to abide by the oath he swore. Valeriius ignored the sensation and watched the vellum's lettering gracefully warp from recognizable script to archaic words of power. The letters, older than any script in all the Avarus Desert, eclipsed his knowledge to decipher. They were the *Arthramainian* script, the words of kings.

Rising to his feet with smooth grace, Valeriius gestured for Krell to accompany him and for their guards to stay back. Wrapping Krell's arm in his own, Valeriius advanced to the balustrade and allowed his attention to wander the arena. At his side, Krell settled her bulbous form upon the railing with a repulsive sigh. Meanwhile, their movement surreptitious, Valeriius' sell-swords rose and positioned themselves behind Krell's guards.

He regarded her, knowing it was irrelevant if she caught him; a woman like her would see only a man intoxicated by her beauty. Valeriius, however, sought a reaction rather than beauty; specifically, her reaction to the sudden gurgles of her dying guards as his sell-swords struck. Her attendants shrieked, their wails of fear theatrically distraught, while her slaves recoiled in shocked silence.

He watched the horror dawn across Krell's features, watched as terror consumed her visage, and watched as her jaw worked in a desperate, futile attempt at speech, then thrust her over the edge and into the swamp below. She flailed in the quagmire and screamed as he took a seat on the balustrade just beyond her reach.

She managed to rise above the black water and, gasping for air, waded toward the shore, oblivious to the leeches on her until their numbing poison wore off. Throwing back her head, she screamed, scratching at her arms and face with such wild desperation she tore her skin. The massive woman floundered nearer to the shore and stumbled into the leeches' nest. Krell resurfaced after a moment, her bloated skin almost invisible beneath the leeches. Valeriius simply watched, taking care to exhibit no excitement, pleasure or disgust as the leeches devoured her.

The leeches would inject their embryo into her bloodstream, using her flesh to protect their young until they matured. At that point, the colony would seek new hunting grounds. Nothing would disrupt this life cycle because everything feared the leech colonies.

Valeriius continued to observe Krell's struggles. At first her flailing grew stronger, but her movements quickly attenuated, becoming little more than uncommon spasms. The death wouldn't serve his prestige among other Kalvonders, or entertain the gossip mongers long, but expedience suited his intentions better than spectacle.

With nothing left to witness, Valeriius returned to his seat, beckoning for Krell's scarred slave to hasten forward and hurl himself into a posture of abject submission. "You are to go to the mansion of the late Krell Kalvonder and present this document to her entire household. After they accept its authenticity, you will inform them of their mistress' demise, and that they are now my property." The slave dared to look up, and Valeriius, noting his bloodshot eyes, ground the slave's head back into the floor with a boot. "Furthermore, all household members will cease the consumption of intoxicating drugs. Let those who cannot survive the deprivation die; I will not suffer addicts. Understood?" The slave cowered.

Valeriius allowed his new slave time to memorize the commands before continuing, "You will transfer my new holdings discretely through the sewers. Make certain there are no witnesses. When you've collected everything of value, burn her estates." Valeriius paused, a thought occurring to him. Two other Kalvonder mansions abutted Krell's residence. Neither possessed much wealth or power, but if handled correctly, Valeriius could acquire a profit from them. "Ensure the fire expands to the residences of Trayvo and Hraven Kalvonder." Valeriius dismissed the slave and addressed the sell-swords. "Send a message to the others. Tell them to infiltrate Trayvo and Hraven's mansions while they remain occupied with the Angorat'Wass. They are to pillage everything within easy reach." His sell-swords bowed in the manner of the Autumn-lands and departed.

There were hundreds of Kalvonders in Sahdaen, but only a few were noteworthy, and it was these Valeriius now sought. Xexeross and Trerrock surveyed the morning's festivities from the edge of their balcony, heads tilted toward one another in discourse. Trerrock, a masked brooding figure, vied with Xexeross' towering, passionate aura. Together they formed two-thirds of Sahdaen's ruling Triad; and though neither was the crowning jewel, they were both powerful enough to threaten annihilation on each other and the third member.

Almost every Kalvonder across the Avarus Desert built their power on a mixture of lies, coercion, and alliances. The lower they ranked in the pyramid, the more they relied on these assets to survive. Trerrock, Xexeross, and Ureign—the ruling Triad—alone were exempt from that need. Their individual wealth, power, and military strength were the equivalent of a small kingdom.

Trerrock, an immortal by all reports, had been visiting galas and Angorat'Wasses for over a century, appearing at each one masked and bearing a naked crimson blade at his side. He built his fortune and amassed his power over the generations, quietly ascending to his current prominence.

Xexeross had been a warlord prior to declaring himself a Kalvonder, and prestige did nothing to temper his predilections. Even now, after a decade on the Triad, Xexeross still relentlessly consumed the lesser Kalvonders and oppressed the greater.

The final member of the Triad was a mystery to all. Ureign had appeared one night in the doorway of a lavish gala, thunder heralding his arrival and lightning marking his entrance. They had challenged his presence, declaring him unfit to join their company, and in rejoinder, he butchered them all. Then awash in the blood of his rivals, Ureign declared himself lord of the Triad and set about constructing an unassailable bastion of fear, opulence, and prestige. Now three decades later, rumors would have all believe that Ureign's army numbered upward of a thousand soldiers. Valeriius knew it approximated thrice that, plus assorted specialists.

The thunderous beating of a drum attracted Valeriius' attention to the four sobbing children huddled together on a dais. Over the centuries, the Kalvonders had found that simply sending Tragnashi to brawl with one another grew tedious. Thus they inserted beasts into the arena, and later on objectives. These children were one such objective. If the victorious contender managed to collect the heads from any of these children, he would receive a prize, which could be almost anything he desired and even, for exceptional performances, exclusion from the subsequent Angorat'Wass.

Across the arena, the spectators began to cheer.

Dieharamon waited in silence, suppressing his fear, his hate, and all the silent screams commanding him to oppose this evil, pleading he defy this madness he was on the brink of re-entering. His emotions were frighteningly easy to suppress after sixteen years of fighting and killing in the Angorat'Wass.

The individual memories had faded, amalgamating into a shapeless river that would inevitably spit out a nightmare whenever he thought better of himself.

He waited just outside the sunlight reaching in from the arena, peering outward, waiting for the moment they sent him in to start killing again. Although he looked, Dieharamon did not truly see the arena. Its high curving walls were branded in his memory, a permanent scar that would forever haunt his fractured sleep. He could see the forest of pillars rising from the noxious swamps even with his eyes closed. Something always lurked in those waters, stalking its prey with a swish of black scales. It was the same for every arena.

Dieharamon looked at his new gloves, their once black leather now scuffed and faded, the seams stretched and buckles rusted. He clenched his hands against a spike of fear; these were his second pair this month alone. Valeriius would not be pleased.

He always wore gloves, both the obligation and the articles imposed upon him by Valeriius. In recent years, the gloves had begun deteriorating without any visible explanation but never at this rate. He groaned, knowing it was futile to conceal the ruined gloves. Valeriius would replace them, but he would also exact payment.

He retreated deeper into the tunnel, distancing himself from the cheering crowd outside, and leaned against the wall, pulling his waist-length braid over his shoulder.

The braid marked him as a Tragnashi, while the countless bone shards and intricately woven knots signified a gladiator. As for the length, a gladiator's hair was never cut because they never survived long enough for length to cause difficulty.

Hearing a roar, he returned to the tunnel's entrance and assessed the arena beyond with a callus eye, scanning the four sobbing children crouched at its epicenter. A hundred gladiators stalked them, waiting only for the last thunderous drumbeat to commence their small war.

The gladiators, all of them Tragnashi, ranged from mere children to young men who would have already fathered a litter of children. Looking at the circle, Dieharamon noted an irregularity: a woman.

Female Tragnashi were no less common than male; their suffering just differed. The Kalvonders used female Tragnashi to breed because any child born of a Tragnashi is a Tragnashi. Thus they increased their fortune until the woman could bear no more children and then sent her to the Angorat'Wass. Few women ever survived their fertile years, killed by disease or the labor of unremitting childbirth.

The drum's thunder ceased, and the Angorat'Wass began. The youngest gladiators were drugged to corrupt their minds, twisting their delicate sensibilities into a combination of feral instinct and raw blood-lust. The older gladiators would be drowning in enhancing drugs and anesthetics. Dieharamon had taken his share of those drugs when they first consigned him to the arena. As he matured, Valeriius had reduced his dosages until, having removed them entirely, he declared to all of Sahdaen that his gladiator fought without augmentations.

The arena exploded with a deafening roar as the gladiators charged. The woman slit her throat instantly, knowing what awaited her in the arena. Dieharamon had seen it before, gladiators waiting until the match neared conclusion to take turns raping the woman before killing her and one another.

The younger gladiators lasted only minutes despite their chemical savagery. Their reach was too short and their strength too insignificant to compete with their larger, more experienced foes. Some called these opening minutes a baptism: an act of consecration to prepare the field for all the matches of the Angorat'Wass that would follow. Truthfully, these commencing moments amounted to little more than undecipherable carnage. The actual competition would begin after this initial massacre resolved with the surviving participants forming alliances to hunt and destroy the truly dangerous among them: the survivors of past conflicts. These alliances never lasted though. The moment a back was turned in arrogance or idiocy, betrayal took another life.

Initially the conflict centered around the four prize children with the embattled gladiators struggling for dominance, and the opportunity to safely claim one of them. As the conflict progressed, the circle of gladiators scattered across the arena. It was then that the Kalmarads unleashed their hoarded monstrosities. The swamps erupted—heralding the arena's newest arrivals— as its native monsters burst from their prisons to assail the gladiators. Meanwhile, caught in the center of this horror, the four children still huddled together on their raised dais, safe from the beasts.

The last two gladiators were a youth of thirteen summers and a man of sixteen. One carried a net and trident, while the other held a shield and a broken sickle blade.

The younger gladiator charged, hurling his net only to have the elder gladiator raise his shield and bat it aside with derisive ease. However, in doing so, he blinded himself, allowing the younger gladiator to thrust the trident into his groin. The elder gladiator screamed, lurching back and clutching the trident's haft. The younger gladiator drove his opponent back, forcing him toward a small cavity in the island upon which they fought. This cavity lurked in nocuous stillness while the rest of the swamp broiled in frenzied feeding.

Screaming his triumph, the younger gladiator gave one final shove and thrust his opponent into the cavity. The elder gladiator had managed a single terrified cry before he submerged into the thrashing water. Heedless of his abandoned trident, the younger gladiator fled toward the dais, all his remaining strength focused on escaping whatever horror brooded in that cavity.

Meanwhile, one of the drugged children leapt onto the back of a feasting crustacean. The beast spun in a blur of orange claws and snapped at the child straddling its ridged shell.

Just barely evading the abomination's claws, the child retaliated with a jagged rock, smashing the stone repeatedly into the crustacean's head.

Dieharamon could see what the child fought to obtain: a simple bone knife clutched in the fist of a half-devoured gladiator.

A terrified scream pierced the throng's clamor, drawing Dieharamon's attention back to the elder gladiator. Horror welled within him as he registered what the Kalmarads had buried in that small cavity: a Vultaki.

A Vultaki is comparable to a centipede with a shell of thick, overlapping plates and a hundred twisted, gray limbs. Two antennae sprouted from its head, which when the Vultaki rested was covered by a helmet-like carapace. This Vultaki, however, had its carapace withdrawn, revealing the wide circular maw.

It was small for its species, barely four feet long when they are known to grow upwards of a dozen. It enwrapped the elder gladiator's torso and drove its legs into his flesh, pumping him full of venom and eggs. With a last spasm, the Vultaki fell away, her body inert and drained of color as it slid back into the cavity.

The elder gladiator soon followed it, his body contorting as the Vultaki queen's eggs hatched. The larvae within him would spend months devouring him from the inside, using his body as protection until they grew large enough to survive on their own. When insufficient meat remained to feed them, they would devour one another until only one remained. The surviving Vultaki, always a queen, would emerge several years later already impregnated with a brood of larvae.

The Vultaki eats only two things throughout its lifetime; first is the host and second are its eggs. They are ambush predators that wait motionless for decades in dark waters sustained by their eggs. The Vultaki queen uses the nutrients of her eggs to produce more eggs and grow larger in a self-sustaining cycle. Once she reaches a dozen feet long, a Vultaki queen can endure the insemination of its young and survive indefinitely.

The younger gladiator attained the safety of the massive dais where, his victory assured, he lifted his voice in a wordless cry of triumph. At his pronouncement, the countless spectators roared back in salute. They loved champions as they loved bloodshed. Dieharamon ignored the victorious champion, focusing on the small child and the crustacean instead.

Armed with only the jagged stone, the child continued pounding the engorged monstrosity until it finally died. Hurling his makeshift weapon aside, the child dove into the fetid water, scrambling to claim the bone knife. Upon the dais, the younger gladiator still screamed his victory, ignoring the absence of a horn validating his triumph. He did not fear a quartet of unarmed children.

Wrenching the bone knife from the dead gladiator's hand, the child turned back to the object of his fear. The gladiator remained oblivious to his peril up to the moment the child stabbed him just under his left shoulder blade, rupturing his spleen.

The horns and drums sounded, declaring the murderous child the victor. A thunderous voice bellowed over the crowd, suppressing their jubilation, "Victor, against all the odds, unarmed and unprepared, you have managed to achieve dominance. Now all you must do is take the blood of your fellows and receive your reward!" The child stepped back, casting aside the dagger as he closed his eyes and covered his ears. One of the four, however, did not hesitate. He rushed forward to grasp the discarded knife and drove it into the victor's throat with a cry. The kill was brief and accompanied by riotous laughter from the spectators; they loathed a weak victor.

Dieharamon rolled his shoulders and stretched in preparation for his fight. He sought the weapons scattered across the arena. The weapons and cadavers from past fights were left to bake in the sun until one of the resident monsters devoured them.

His attention was drawn back when the voice boomed, "We have our true victor!" The spectators applauded the child with raucous cries and stomping feet. When they subsided, the speaker resumed, "Your prize waits at the entrance to the Coliseum, victor." The child looked up, a spark of hope rising on his soiled features only to die with the speaker's parting words, "We are eager to watch you compete in the next Angorat'Wass." The spectators exploded into a roar, and the youth knelt beside those he had killed. He begged with words lost in the crowd for them not to be dead. It took a ruddy-faced guard to remove the child, clearing the road for more bloodshed.

The arena's summons called Dieharamon forward, and taking a last calming breath, he answered. The spectators called his name, demanding he fulfil his function and provide some small value to society. He hated them, or maybe he just hated everything. It was hard to say with Valeriius' influence manipulating his emotions, honing his fear into shuddering desperation, and his hate into murderous intent.

He lunged to the right, his eyes locking upon a youth scrambling to extract a javelin embedded in a gladiator. Dieharamon reached him in two strides, and all the youth's veteran scars did not matter. He died like anyone else when Dieharamon snapped his neck.

Dieharamon tossed the cadaver aside and crouched to collect the javelin. He scanned the arena for approaching foes and immediately noticed the dozen or so gladiators warily approaching him, each one armed with a weapon procured from the dead.

Their leader was easy to discern; even lingering behind the formation, he dwarfed his fellows. Dieharamon measured the distance, reared back and flung the javelin. It smashed into the man's solar plexus and drove through, lodging into the ground behind him and arching his body back in a grotesque parody of stance. The alliance members shared one glance at his corpse and then devolved.

Satisfied he was in no immediate peril, Dieharamon searched for, and found, another weapon—a pair of twin pewter hatchets currently dismembering a screaming foe while their obese master cackled.

Dieharamon assessed his quarry for an instant and then hurtled forward, his long legs propelling him over the grisly sand in great strides and over the waterways in bounds. The obese gladiator heard his approach and spun, moving with incongruous dexterity to brace himself. When he saw Dieharamon's reckless charge, a leer split his face and he stepped forward, slashing with one hatchet. Like so many others, the obese gladiator saw only Dieharamon's size and failed to compensate for his mobility.

He discovered this error a moment later when his hatchet met air and threw him off balance. Slipping in after the hatchet, Dieharamon hammered the gladiator's midsection. He twisted out from under the toppling gladiator, lifted his hands and brought them crashing down onto his opponent's exposed neck, snapping the vertebrae.

As he bent low and ripped the pewter hatchets from his opponent, a shadow fell over him. Without thinking he plunged desperately into the swamp. It was a gamble he would fare better against whatever the morass concealed. The cold gnawed at his skin as tendrils of plants grasped at his arms, and the swamp's jutting bed scraped at his underside. He dragged himself further in, feeling the swamp hiss as his assailant hacked at the water.

Something ominous gave way beneath his hand, but before he could react, a scaled body encircled his chest and constricted, forcing the air from his lungs in a surge of bubbles. Clawing at the throttling coils, he set his feet and lunged for the surface. The dark water parted lethargically, loath to release its captive any more than the serpent wanted to release its prey.

He broke the surface with a strangled gasp, the water churning about his waist as he struggled to escape the serpent's coils. He pressed outward, but the serpent tightened its grip and bit his shoulder. He arched back with a scream, and the serpent dragged him back under.

He fought to disentangle himself from the serpent's grip, all the while struggling against its sedative. His movements growing sluggish, Dieharamon wriggled until his right arm slipped in the serpent's grasp, almost shirking its embrace entirely. But the coils readjusted and increased the pressure to his chest. During the split second it took the serpent to retighten its grip, he dragged his other arm free, reached up, caught the serpent's head and crushed it.

The serpent's coils slipped away, swishing as they sank. His lungs screaming, Dieharamon lunged for the surface and exploded onto the beach with a coarse gasp. No longer concerned with which bank he climbed, Dieharamon clambered to his knees and retched, which provided all the opportunity another gladiator needed to press a spear to his chest.

The gladiator grinned and stepped forward, thrusting his spear to drive Dieharamon back into the water. He felt the water lapping eagerly at his heels and glanced back, searching for the nearest landmass. All he saw was another ominous ripple arching through the water toward him.

The gladiator's triumphant sneer evolved into full laughter. "Let's see you survive that!"

His opponent tried to thrust again, but Dieharamon lurched aside, caught the spear and propelled the gladiator into the water.

Squealing, the gladiator recoiled, desperate to escape the water. Dieharamon struck in that instant of vulnerability and crushed his opponent's throat with a fist. The man gurgled once before slumping into the water.

Dieharamon trudged over, collected the hatchets, and then observed his surroundings. The conflict approached its conclusion with less than a dozen exhausted gladiators vying against one another in scattered duels.

A strange tranquility enveloped the arena as he crouched there assessing the battle. Curious, Dieharamon glanced up toward the stands where the four thousand awed spectators watched him. The silence broke with a roar after a long hesitation of disbelief. It took Dieharamon a while to realize why they screamed; no one survived the beasts of the arena, and yet he was alive.

Dieharamon glanced to Valeriius.

As always, the man sat alone at the base of a pillar. Something predatory and calculating always hung about Valeriius, haunting Dieharamon whenever they spoke and festering in the recesses of his mind whenever they were separated.

He inspected Dieharamon with a tilted head, his ever-present cane lazily held in one hand while his other rested atop the balustrade's beryl curtains. Valeriius nodded once, as vast a compliment as a Kalvonder ever bestowed upon their Tragnashi. In return Dieharamon bowed and touched a fist to his forehead, acknowledging that Valeriius owned his soul.

Dieharamon turned back to the conflict and the half-dozen survivors now approaching him. These survivors had also noted the silence, and in that silence, they had discovered him. Desperation drove them into one last alliance.

In a voice too soft for any man to hear, Dieharamon whispered, *"Arawn*, take mercy on my soul." Though he hated the gods and feared magic, death was something he understood so intimately he could no longer fear it. He hurled himself forward as his prayer echoed back to him beneath the pounding of his blood as if something had heard it. Thus, heedless of the perils his words would bring, Dieharamon screamed out, "Fore-gods burn you, *Ashshand!*" At his furious cry, a primordial cold filled him, and he cringed. Though his words went unheard by men, *Ashshand* stirred at his curse.

The first gladiator, wielding a shield and spear, ignored his companions' warnings and engaged Dieharamon without a thought for the gravity of his error. Dieharamon ducked beneath the swipe, a burning sensation welling up within his breast, setting his blood alight and sharpening his vision. The gladiator lunged forward but struck air as Dieharamon pivoted around the spear, caught his shield, and dragged it down with one hatchet while the other smashed into his skull.

Separating from the corpse and spinning right, Dieharamon swept a hatchet low to parry a thrusting spiked mace. The attacking gladiator stumbled forward, and Dieharamon severed his spine with a blow before continuing past.

He spun, the right hatchet digging into the throat of a third foe encroaching on his left side. Continuing his revolution, Dieharamon threw the left hatchet end-over-end into the forehead of a fourth gladiator lingering at the back. A fragile clay dagger bit into his already-injured shoulder and shattered. Grimacing, he twisted, grabbed the man's arm, braced it against his ax haft and broke it.

The gladiator careened back into his last ally, clutching his arm as blood welled up between fingers. Dieharamon advanced, smashing his last hatchet into the injured man's chest, and pursued the final gladiator. His quarry turned on a heel and fled, hopelessly seeking to escape but tripped with a wailing cry. The gladiator managed a single whimper before Dieharamon stomped on his throat.

The audience waited in a disbelieving hush, most struggling to accept what they just witnessed, and then erupted. Avarans loved victors and victories, the bloodier the victory, the better. In response, Dieharamon bowed in slow succession to the arena's four corners.

When he rose from the last obeisance, Dieharamon faced south where the chief Kalmarads stood on the brink of their column. The Triad reclined behind them.

With a wide smile upon his features, the Kalmarad opened his arms, paying the Kalvonders at his back no more heed than he would a common Avaran. The fool probably wouldn't survive the night. To insult any Kalvonder was an egregious error in judgment. To insult a member of the Triad was suicide.

The Kalmarad lifted his arms, palms facing heavenward in a call for silence. "Once more, brave gladiator, you are our champion! Another chapter is added to your heroic saga!" A roar from the crowd echoed his words but fell silent when he raised a hand again. "And so you, our greatest gladiator and champion; you, a legend and inspiration, shall be the first gladiator to hear of the ultimate Angorat'Wass!" The audience waited breathless for the grand revelation. "On the first day of this subsequent Turning, when the sun first breaks through the heavens a new Angorat'Wass will be held. Every gladiator in Sahdaen will compete with their brother and sister gladiators as allies!"

An image of the next Angorat'Wass rose in his mind, depicting hundreds of gladiators striving against one another in a roiling mass of bodies crushed so tightly together they could barely move. Dieharamon glanced at Valeriius and wondered why he would orchestrate the death of every gladiator in Sahdaen.

4

Tasha

Tasha kicked one of the offending walls, but failed to alleviate how the tiny room kept crowding inward. She voiced a low snarl, batting at the rising cloud of ash before stomping to the open doorway and conducting a cursory inspection. Nothing.

Swallowing a scream, Tasha discarded the fresh air and buttery sunlight for the smoky interior. Once there, she resumed pacing and considered what came after this moment, defined, as it was, by someone's acute absence. If her contact arrived, Tasha would complete her assigned task. If his absence continued though, matters became far less certain. Stubbornness demanded she loiter in Tellor and search for another method to contact her absent host; while other less truculent emotions suggested she leave tomorrow and save money otherwise spent on lodgings.

She discarded her first option almost immediately. It was ill-advised to go rummaging through a foreign city in search of its criminal king, especially when that king hated the Thieves' Guild as much as it hated him. Besides, she had no idea how Carr'Selain contacted him in the first place. No, it was best to return her new impressively expensive clothes and leave the city tomorrow. Well, except for the boots. *Enecki* knew she needed a pair without holes.

The gray damp of that morning had seen Tasha sitting at her vanity long before she actually needed to, applying cheap makeup with deft strokes, grumbling at the necessity, and then spending the better part of an hour wrangling her hair into some semblance of a style. Still, when she finished, Tasha had glanced into a small, cracked mirror and found herself smiling at the reflection.

She later departed Tellor via a back gate and reentered legally, suffering through admittance to cultivate the appearance she'd just arrived. Following some difficulties with her papers, Tasha had wandered around until she stumbled across the meeting point, all the while subtly checking for tails.

Unfortunately, the foreign city combined with the sheer number of revelers basically ensured a belated arrival.

Tasha had rushed through the door with an apology already balanced on the tip of her tongue, but panic immediately locked her steps. The room was deserted. With thoughts rapidly skewing toward the gravest of possible ramifications, she had conducted a cursory inspection and discovered to surging relief that she'd simply arrived first.

Now half-an-hour later, she still waited for her contact. "*Jaidar*, bless you." She growled, kicking a stone down the path she had paced in the dusty floor.

"Are you expecting someone, my Dear? Perhaps a dashing rogue who will dash around and around until finally sweeping your feet out from underneath you?" Tasha whirled at the unexpected voice, habit more than conscious effort drawing her knives; whereupon the intruder—a young man, fresh faced and innocent except for a whiff of mischief—dropped his teasing smile to throw both hands skyward. "Modern culture is entirely rife with barbarians. Sheath your weapons lest you hurt someone, me in particular."

Not quite relaxing, Tasha scanned him for a concealed weapon, found none, and then quickly examined his two collar pins: one silver and one bronze. The silver pin was embossed with a ship and proclaimed his status as a merchant, while the bronze denoted his heritage as a farmer through its emblazoned pitchfork. Finally she scanned the youth's face, noting its handsomely angular but decidedly non-western features before settling on his wide-brimmed hat. "Who are you?" His innocuous appearance notwithstanding, Tasha shuffled backward, shifting little by little until her back faced a corner and she had a clear path to the nearest window.

"Who me?"

"Yes, you," Tasha snapped, sheathing her knives. *'It looks like he's just a friendly idiot; he's no threat… Not unless my contact decides now is the perfect time to appear and jump to conclusions. I need to get rid of this idiot before we both end up with slit throats.'* "On second thought, I don't care. Go make yourself scarce."

The young man clapped his hands. "Ooh, a secret meeting undoubtedly filled with all manner of dastardly conspiracies. Are we planning a rebellion, a birthday party, an elopement?"

"What? No!"

"So, we arranged this top-secret meeting without intending to conspire?"

"Yes, wait, no. I mean, there is no secret meeting. Now will you please leave; I'm waiting for somebody who gets antsy around strangers."

"If he gets antsy around strangers, conspiracy feels like a bad line of work. That's all about meeting new people and making friends. Speaking of making friends, I don't believe we've introduced ourselves yet."

"I'm not going to give you my name."

"Really? It seems like the height of impropriety to start an acquaintance without first introducing oneself."

She ground her teeth, fighting against the sudden urge to strangle the boy. "My name is Tasha Bloomhale, may *Enecki* illuminate your life and defend you against *Jaidar*." She steepled her fingers and gave a harsh, cursory bow.

"Slade Lammerock, now and forever at the service of one so beautiful." Forgoing the steepled fingers, he swept the hat from his head and bowed so low his ponytail touched the ground. From there he twisted, staring up with a lopsided grin.

"Whatever." Tasha rolled her eyes, then stopped as his name registered. "You? You're Slade Lammerock? No. No, you can't be. I don't know how you learned that name, but who are you and what happened to my contact?" Her thrumming nerves, only just relaxing, tightened all over again. "Did you kill him?"

"Hardly. The whole contact business is a needlessly complex and archaic tradition; I discontinued the practice ages ago."

"Just how stupid do you think I am?"

"Believe it or not, I think you're moderately clever."

"Shut up. You are not Slade Lammerock."

"Slade Lammerock is who I am, as I am who Slade Lammerock is." He rose from his exaggerated obeisance. "I understand your doubts, however misguided, and indeed I suffer identical worries. Imagine the hypocrisy if I wasn't myself? Luckily I am myself, which means I need only to convince you. A simple matter, albeit one that introduces another, far more complex difficulty. Where shall I dispose this newly baseless doubt that was formally directed at me and my supposed identity? That it needs redistribution is beyond question; homeless doubt without proper target or reason will only fester and expand; but who to bestow it upon? Obviously, no one who actually deserves it, and we can't exactly distribute it equally because spreading your doubt willy-nilly would burden you with that terrible affliction known as wholesale distrust. What's worse, *I* might once again fall prey to this—"

"Stop," Tasha shouted, finally breaking the landslide of words. "A clever tongue won't sell your story; the mere fact you're trying only makes it harder. A thief-lord does not persuade; he forces his rivals to believe through deceit or brutal action."

"Be careful, my Dear," he purred, losing his veneer of innocence in a way that sent a chill down her spine. "Idle words and a careless tongue make for a dangerous pastime. I now know this was an arranged encounter, one whose participants are a beautiful, mysterious woman"—Slade gestured toward her—"and a thief-lord renowned for coercing others to his whim." He splayed a hand across his chest. "This whole affair stinks of a shoddy adventure novel or perhaps a cheap romance."

"No, I am not here to meet with a thief-lord." Tasha massaged her brow, biting back on her temper. "That … that was my tongue running away with itself."

"First, you accuse me of propagating mistruths, then, without bothering to wait a suitable grace period, you dive head-first into hypocrisy. Oh, the depths society has fallen!" He reeled backward, throwing an arm across his brow. "Oh, to barely miss a time when trust rampaged through our hearts, a time when honesty was law rather than the exception or pleasant surprise, a time when all men had integrity and utter derision for those who failed to uphold these commandments."

"Will you stop and—" But Slade's rhetoric plowed on.

"Why must I, the epitome of these ideals, suffer as the common man suffers? I, who in my little toe, possess more scruples and honesty than a hundred, nay a thousand, men whether they be kings or paupers."

*'What in **Enecki's** blessed name is going on with this man?'* Insane or not, she needed him gone. "Would you listen to me for one sec–"

"They should be damned, damned and burned at the stake. Roasted to a turn and served at the Imperial Emperor's feast." His hand exploded outward, pointing a quivering finger at Tasha as malevolence sparked in his gaze. "I know the perfect candidate to start with."

"Be silent you little pest." She strode forward, grabbed his dark waistcoat and shook him. "Don't you understand, you're meddling in something that could get us both killed."

"Well, since you asked so nicely," he said, shifting abruptly to reasoned calm. "Now confess, how did you know I lied about being this fantastic Slade Lammerock person? How do you know me better than I know myself? Because despite your ignorance concerning my actual identity, you're certain of whom I'm not, which far exceeds what the average person knows about themselves, let alone others. If you don't know who you are, how can you know who you're not?"

Instinct warned this was a trap, but she didn't have time to argue with him. "If I explain it, will you leave?"

"You have my totally dishonest promise that I shall."

She did not like that answer, not at all. *If this boy is a random passerby, why the façade and how does he know Slade Lammerock's name? The man's existence is supposed to be a secret. What's going on? Are the reports wrong? Is he simply well-informed or is this lunatic a subordinate or …'*—Tasha swore silently—*'or is he some sort of rival?'*

"Eyewitnesses describe Lammerock as a man in his late forties with graying hair and blue eyes; you're not even twenty yet." Tasha's gaze flicked to his countenance. A clever disguise could alter faces, hair, and weight. Eyes, on the other hand, remained consistent. What she found caused her thoughts to stumble; one eye was a dark sparkling jade while its sibling shone like sun-lit emeralds.

"True enough," her opponent said, filling the pause. "Unless one listens to rumor. I'm sure you've heard the tales of my escapades? Of glorious subterfuge, malevolent puppetry, and masterful disguises? Of course, since my identity is still under review, this is all hypothetical, but … a thought has just occurred to me. What if I—once again in the hypothetical sense—hired an imposter to confuse and mislead your so-called witnesses? Everyone knows they're spies."

"That's impossible." Tasha grimaced. "Our spies are the best; they never make mistakes." Obviously the youth was either a subordinate or rival to Slade Lammerock.

Smirking, the youth raised a hand to one side of his mouth, leaned forward, and whispered as if conveying a secret. "Mine are better."

Tasha snorted. "No, they're not. No one is. Besides, I doubt friendless Slade Lammerock, a man habituated to assassination attempts and contending with one of the most dangerous enemies in the Empire, would stroll into a meeting blindly. Now if he sent a proxy to spring any possible traps, well … that's a viable strategy. It would also explain why there aren't any traps or fail-safes in the building. There's no need." Just a little needle to provoke him, test his reaction.

"Rumor, that most dastardly of creatures, once again provides me with a counter argument. Supposedly my hypothetical self is one of the most devious tacticians alive; what if I erected my various fail-safes after you arrived? I believe this would also explain my unfortunate tardiness."

"That's unlikely." She batted a hand through the air. "There's only so much you could arrange if I'm already here and none of it in secret."

"What if we moved really, really quietly?"

Tasha gritted her teeth. "Fine. Since those arguments seem beyond your comprehension, I shall resort to easier ones."

He flicked a hand. "Crude insults, how boorish."

"Let's begin with your clothing, shall we."

"Please do. I'm practically breathless with anticipation for what I presume are thoroughly considered arguments filled with disgustingly logical conjectures."

Suppressing a growl, Tasha pressed on. "The hat is bad enough, but then you paired it with that atrocious feather; together they practically scream pay attention to me."

Slade removed the article, twisting it every-which-way as he examined it. "Contrary to popular opinion, looking ostentatious does not mean one is ostentatious; besides, I like this hat. It makes me look … dashing."

"All the young ladies will blow kisses and throw flowers at your feet when you tread Dancer's Walk. Neither gallantry nor a dashing appearance will save you from the noose."

"Agree to disagree; I simply must find myself a city where a rich young lady rules and win my pardon, if not her hand through pure gallantry." The youth waggled his eyebrows, suggesting he had found such a place and seduced its incumbent queen long since.

Her mounting tension finally snapped and she strode forward, pressing a knife to his throat. "Enough games. Take me to Slade Lammerock. Take me to the man so proficient, so skilled he can waltz through Cardolyn Tyier's palace clear as day and skip out twirling the Imperial Emperor's crown around one finger."

"That's a marvelous fire-side tale, though not much given to historical accuracy." Slade's head lolled to one side, unmindful of the weapon pressed to his throat. "If recounted accurately, the whole affair takes place under a full moon with neither I nor Slade Lammerock—since you haven't decided which of us is which yet—involving ourselves; the genius who conceived that diabolical plot was a little kooky for my taste." Slade heaved a sigh, looking up mournfully. "The poor fool failed. He tripped at an inopportune moment, dropped the crown, and convinced the guards to assault him with all due tenacity."

"You act like you were there." Tasha's temper was a flash storm. Already the rains receded, leaving her in a flush of embarrassment made all the sharper by her still drawn knife.

"I may have been the one who stretched the tripwire across the courtyard. Anyway, Imperial courts sentenced the poor guy to a lifetime in our northern-most cells for his idiocy. But never you fear; in appreciation of his efforts, I lent him an escape artist who negotiated a three-day sentence."

"Idiocy? You're the one who sabotaged his escape!"

"A technicality," he said flapping a hand. "Oh, by the way, I stole a gold bracelet inlaid with enough jewels to buy a small town, not the Imperial Emperor's crown. Its former owner endured tremendous difficulty to recover her prized ornament and conceal certain indiscretions involved with it, eventually discovering the bauble with a rather slimy merchant." The youth's amusement began leaking into his voice. "I hear he was quite the character, standing no taller than a man's chest and having aged well into his nineties. In fact, while attempting to appear younger, he dyed his hair a nice shiny black." Doffing his hat, Slade smoothed back his own similarly colored hair.

"I don't believe it," Tasha whispered, her sudden belief surprising her as much as it failed to astonish him. "You're telling the truth."

"Yes. I try not to lie; I find it makes it harder to trust me."

She turned away and began to pace, unconsciously embracing soliloquy. "You're so young, too young; the guild master must know and yet he doesn't." Her shoulders stiffened, squaring a little as she faced him once again. "It doesn't matter. For what it's worth, I'm sorry; but my orders were clear." Sheathing the knife, Tasha clapped once.

Two men dropped from the rafters, landing beside Slade to seize and twist his arms behind his back. It was easy and uncomplicated, and Tasha felt her stomach muscles easing for the first time in days. Perhaps, just maybe she could pull this off. But unnervingly, Slade grinned at her.

"Your hand is quite marvelous." His mouth contorted into a momentary grimace as one thug twisted his elbow painfully, the other going so far as to lay a knife across his throat.

"What do you mean?" Tasha lounged against a nearby wall, feigning indifference at his treatment. *I can't order them to let up, not while he's grinning at me like a cat that just broke something.*

"I presume you are familiar with the rules of cards?" Tasha shrugged. "Well, considering how hands of cards go, you have an excellent set. I'd equate it to a flush." Her thugs shifted in place, sharing a glance before inspecting their captive. Ultimately, they tightened their grips, until Slade twisted about sharply. "I know goons think with their muscles, but that's no reason to break my arms." He switched his glare to the other thug, the motion tracing a shallow cut across his throat.

"They'll kill you for so much as winking."

"Oh?" he asked, his entire countenance brightening. "Like this?" And then he winked.

Her thugs reacted according to procedure. One assumed full control over the rebellious captive while his cohort moved in front and slammed a fist into Slade's stomach. Ignoring the resulting gasp, the man caught Slade's head and smashed it against his knee.

A heartbeat later Slade was upright again, wearing the same annoying grin. "I suggest you perform an immediate, yet still courageous, retreat. This is my domain, and I have protected it well. An army of my specially trained, grotesquely bloodthirsty gnats will soon leave you feeling very … sleepy."

The first thug produced a set of iron knuckles. "Does the word surrender mean anything to you? How about stubbornness or obstinacy?"

"I admit those are some of my more endearing traits." Slade spat blood on the thug's boots. "As for surrender, well I'm considering it with ever-increasing affection, especially when confronted by a woman of such dazzling beauty as she who leads you."

Before her over-eager thug punched Slade again, Tasha strode forward and pulled his fist down. "Enough, we have to move before his crew discovers we've taken him."

"My Dear, a bat could have foreseen your duplicity. Instead of focusing on your flimsy schemes and scrambling escape; let's address something more interesting: the second reason behind my imminent surrender." He grinned, then indicated Tasha with a nod. "Despite her beauty, it is you, my friends, who offer the greatest inducement. I can barely control my terror and subsequent balling when faced with such gentlemen as yourselves. Indeed, a simple glance in your general direction has blinded an entire—" A thug's iron-shod fist shattered Slade's dialogue.

But when he prepared to strike again, Tasha cuffed the back of his head. "Once was enough. Our orders made it clear: do no irreparable damage. Carr'Selain has uses for him."

"Ah, the benefit of being useful; I am untouchable."

Discarding any compassion, she grabbed the youth's chin and forced his head in various directions. "Are you experiencing blurry vision or nausea? Is there any chance you suffered a concussion?" *Not that it would matter. I doubt any blow could addle him further.*

"With your delicate sun-kissed skin brushing against me and my eyes sinking ever-deeper into your oceanic gaze, I stand at the pinnacle of health." One thug rolled his eyes, a fitting counterpart to his companion's soft whistle. "For you I would trudge, nay walk—nay again. I would run barefoot from one extremity of the endlessly endless southern desert to the other. Furthermore, I'd do it blindfolded if you waited at the end of my endlessly endless trek with your lovely countenance, tender caress and—"

"Enough. You answered my question. Now I suggest you keep a guarded tongue; my patience is shallow to begin with, and you've already drawn deeply. Next time I'll let these men beat you senseless." Tasha's grip tightened, an unconscious reaction to the creeping certainty that something was about to go very wrong.

Sure enough, a dangerous glint sparked in Slade's mismatched eyes. "In fact let me demonstrate my perfect health." He stomped on his captors' feet, contorted his body to evade the knife and wriggled free. He straightened instantly, coughed once, and adjusted his tangled clothing. Each deed took a mere second, yet Tasha's goons crumpled as he finished, a dart buried under their ears.

"Like I said," Slade began, sweeping imaginary dust from his person, "you–"

Tasha slid forward, her knife attacks short, abrupt, and accurate. She sliced at his throat, stabbed at his chest, slashed at his stomach, targeting any weakness that presented itself; but Slade thwarted each one gracefully, sometimes slapping the knife aside, sometimes dodging the bare minimum required.

Tasha dropped low, attempting to sweep his legs out from under him. Slade sprang over the attack, landed and fell into a roll, putting distance between them. "Now, my Dear, let's return to civility, violence is most unseemly." Slade dodged to the right, a knife burying in the wall at his left. "I guess not." He glided right again, slapping aside Tasha's latest attack and grabbing her wrist. Using her arm like a lever, he slammed her into a nearby wall and locked the arm behind her back.

Except Tasha wasn't dazed. Down came her foot, stomping on his toes; back flew her head, smashing his already tender nose.

With scarcely a breath between actions, she twisted in place and, discarding the pain it caused her shoulder, slammed an elbow into his face. Breaking from his loosened grip, she pivoted, smashing a knee in his gut before rolling around his body and wrapping an arm across his throat. A sharp pain, akin to a gnat's bite, sprouted at the back of her neck, but she ignored it and hammered Slade into a wall.

As she drew back, intent on repeating the maneuver, Slade hooked a foot around her ankle. She fell hard, dragging Slade with her; he however, rolled elegantly to his feet.

Lurching upward, she stumbled once then darted forward only to collapse, a bizarre weakness creeping through her body.

"Like I said, you have a good hand, but I have the jester, which trumps all. Don't worry about the weakness, the drug's effects will subside in a few minutes." He removed a handkerchief from his pocket and proceeded to soak up the blood streaming from his nose. "This looks like an appropriate time to scream for help. However, if that notion disturbs your fragile sensibilities, I'm sure we can reach an agreement. Let's say your soul for your life?"

Tasha snarled something intelligible, ignoring the weakness and forcing her body into a kneeling position, simultaneously reaching for her closest weapon. Anger, pride, and sheer stubbornness buckled under a rising tide of fear, as location by location her hands failed to produce a weapon.

"My Dear, are you searching for something?" He gasped softly. "Pray don't say you've lost something?"

At the tone of his voice, Tasha looked over slowly to find one of her knives balanced on the tip of his finger. As for the rest of her weaponry, it all sat neatly arranged in his emerald sash, including the poisoned hairpins.

They observed each other in silence, Tasha reassessing her enemy for the second time while Slade completed his no-doubt unflattering estimation of her.

"What happens now?" she asked, feeling sick to her stomach. He had to be furious, there was no other possible reaction. Which meant that if she was lucky, his practicality would overrule his temper and he would send her back as a message of his dominance, someone ransomed after light abuse left them short a finger or toe.

Those rules, however, applied to polite society: the politics of guilds and nobles. Tasha had forfeited that protection when she accepted the completely random, entirely unearned mission to meet with and kidnap Slade Lammerock. It had been a stupid move. A desperate move.

The underworld gossip mongers had discovered him five years earlier. Ever since, the Thieves' Guild had sought to either eliminate or conscript him. Both proved impossible because they never caught more than glimpses or extravagant rumors, generating a stalemate that persisted until they discovered his center of power in Tellor. They hurried to escalate the war and immediately started losing it, their every attempt to infiltrate, oust, or assassinate failing. Most of their operatives never made it inside Tellor, their assassins chased shadows, and their spies returned fruitless, with amnesia, or not at all.

Thinking about the missing ones, Tasha wondered if he would accept the relatively cheap price of her arm or demand a leg.

At last Slade spoke, "What were your masters thinking? Besides the obvious, I mean. What did they hope to gain by capturing me? Killing seems altogether neater."

She blinked, stumbling over absent sneers, gloating words, and promises of unending torture. "Umm, … I don't know; we're not encouraged to ask questions. I guess it limits our backstabbing opportunities."

"Hmm," he began to pace, thinking aloud, "what is Carr'Selain planning? He might try conscripting me, but the kidnapping portion of this debacle makes it a tad bold for such uncertain rewards. The guild can't even guarantee my obedience, setting aside torture, which tends to backfire rather excitingly."

Her nausea didn't leave, but at the realization that she wasn't slated for immediate removal and butchery, Tasha's mind picked itself up out of its despondency and set about getting her the *Jaidar* blessed Abyss out of there. "What do you mean bold? We're not averse to kidnapping people, nobility or otherwise." *'Keep him talking. Buy time.'*

"Yes, you kidnap the rich and powerful but never without assurances or political backing. Shadows and secrecy become your masters a little too well for anything else. More importantly, they avoid any escapade without guaranteed success." Slade gave an absent-minded wave of his hand. "Kidnapping me is bold because your masters have no political backing, no certain victory, no assurances of safety, and no secrecy. Whereas I have all the above."

"They are not my masters; nor as you insinuate, am I their slave," Tasha snapped, attempting to gain her feet with less than sterling success.

"No matter which guild one serves, they all assert their control and steer your thoughts toward a single overriding purpose: How best may I serve? In the end, guild allegiance is a handsome word for slavery, an honorable term for a dirty truth. And if a perspicacious individual attempts flight, he or she courts death." He stopped and faced her. "I could suggest that you flee while you're already outside; flee before the Thieves' Guild recognizes your potential. I won't though, you'd just ignore me."

"Wait, how did you know my affiliations?" He had spoken so confidently and given the information so blithely, she hadn't thought to question it before. "Our letter didn't mention any particular guild. I could have been a diplomat from the Merchants' Guild or an acolyte in the Assassins' Guild?"

"I didn't send the Merchants' Guild a gold sealed letter detailing my current whereabouts. Those people are far too paranoid; they wouldn't trust a card sent by an old acquaintance let alone one sealed with gold and penned by a complete stranger. Why they might die from sheer terror thinking it was a bomb." Slade gave her a pointed stare. "Very smart of them actually; paranoia is underrated." He then strode for the door and glanced skyward, determining the time.

"Do you have a pressing date with someone?" Tasha asked, a spark of hope tickling her stomach. *'If he has business elsewhere, that could mean he doesn't have time for me.* **Enecki** *bless me, I could keep all my toes.'* Feeling the bizarre numbness recede somewhat, she finally rose with the help of some awkward flailing.

"Yes, but it's one I'd rather avoid. Assassins can be such demanding guests."

"What are you talking about? Carr'Selain closed the bounty before I left."

"Don't worry these aren't yours. They're a delightful family of freelancers that stop by every couple months. We've become quite chummy over the years; I only wish they didn't overstay their welcome so often. There's no need for concern though, I'll protect you from their … attentions."

"I don't need your protection. Why would you even offer it?"

Slade grinned. Then took three rapid steps, fell to his knees and snatched one of her hands, dragging it to his heart. "Because through your glory, beauty, and charm you have secured my everlasting affection. I now live for your happiness. You own my body, mind, and soul. Your wish is my desire, your desire is my wish, your hate my hate, your love my love. As for your problems, well they're still your problems. Aside from that, secrets alone come between us, but I will happily divulge mine if you reciprocate."

Eyes bulging, Tasha froze like a woman in a painting, standing stock still until suppressed laughter erupted from all around. She whirled, searching for its source and finding nothing.

"Ah-hem. If it please you, great lady, I still await your answer." She pivoted and there, still kneeling, was Slade Lammerock, still holding her hand and still grinning at the not-so-amusing situation.

"Get away from me!" Tasha wrenched her hand to no effect and then reared back, throwing her entire body into the following punch. Even as it flew though, her mind screamed at her. *'Oh gods, what have I done.* **Enecki** *help me, I've just signed my own death warrant.'*

Just as she poised to leap over Slade's prone form and bolt outside, the young man propped himself up on one elbow to rub his jaw. "I'll take that as a no."

The complete lack of rancor stalled her. *'What in the Abyss is going on here. One minute he's bordering on insanity, the next he's acting as even tempered as a rock. I don't understand.'* Tasha could almost feel her nerves beginning to fray. "Enough games. What are you going to do with me?"

"With you?" Slade's head lolled back thoughtfully. "Well, I can't think of anything to benefit me. I guess I could arrange something dastardly for your entertainment."

"There's no need to exert yourself on my account," Tasha said hastily, to which Slade shrugged again. "Sooo, does that mean I can leave?" It was such an idiotic question, she almost felt like laughing. She didn't even know why she asked it.

"You may depart whenever the inclination strikes you."

"What?"

"I said you can leave, my Dear. Please stay within city boundaries until the festival ends." Flipping onto his feet, Slade strode to where her thugs lay in a crumpled heap.

Seeing this halfway to the door, Tasha cursed herself but paused. "What will you do with them?"

"I also suggest you murder your conscience forthwith. This is a dangerous game to play if scruples control your actions. That aside, they'll come around with nasty headaches and empty purses."

Tasha hesitated then extended her hand. "Seeing as you're in a generous mood, could I have my knives back?"

"Hmm, no."

"*Jaidar* bless you, why not?" She stepped forward, hands curling into fists at her side. "Is that your plan? Let me leave unarmed and hope some footpad knocks me off?"

"Do you really think I need such indirect methods?"

"Return my weapons then. Aside from my death, what can you possibly achieve by withholding them?"

"Securing my continued pristine health maybe?" He pointed to the thin cut drawn across his neck. "With weapons comes the incentive to use them."

"But—"

"Oh pish-posh." He flapped his hand at her. "We deviate from the subject at hand or the subject at hand several moments earlier." She opened her mouth to protest again. Slade, however, spoke first, "I have figured out why the Thieves' Guild really sent you."

Tasha rubbed her brow hard enough for a little blotch to appear. "I'm sorry but I don't really care at the present."

"The answer is simple: your masters recognize how hopeless such childish attacks are." Slade began to pace again, this time glancing at her repeatedly as if delivering a lecture. "Why initialize an attack destined to fail? And if they foretold its fate, why send a Rat to ensure their plot bore fruit." He spoke swiftly and articulately, snaring Tasha despite herself. "This mixture of conclusions and questions lead me to believe they planned something deeper. What if triumph was never the objective? What if they sought failure rather than success? This suggests they needed to gauge my worth, my skill as a thief-lord without endangering me." Slade spoke with increasing speed, warming to his subject like a burgeoning fire. "What if they intended this whole escapade as a test? But why leave you unaware … unless you're a part of the scheme and they didn't want to risk the truth on a terrible actor. What better way to seduce me into unwitting failure than by facing me against a young woman? If I succeeded, the tests would establish both my physical talents and my resistance to manipulation. There's probably a third one too, such things always come in threes: a future test perhaps." Slade whirled toward her, grinning with a sudden revelation. "They must test my nerve, my boldness to see if I'm willing to reach for prizes beyond most men."

"Are you suggesting the guild's testing your capability for something?"

"Yes, my Dear, that is exactly what I'm suggesting. If I'm not mistaken, they wish to conduct a joint heist."

"That's insane, Carr'Selain hates your guts." Except his confidence was so powerful that Tasha felt an annoying thread of belief worm into her mind despite all the contradictory reasons.

Again he began to pace, stopping after a few short steps and beginning to rub his hands together. "My Dear, they want my help stealing something impossible. Why do they want me specifically? Well, they're enthralled by the marvelous delusion that I completed a similar caper before."

"And what might that … oh no, you can't be serious?"

Slade grinned at her triumphantly. "They want to steal something from the Imperial Emperor Cardolyn Tyier himself. Probably *Akravast*, his divinely forged sword. Not only that, they wish to sack his coffers and raid his libraries, or at least, I do."

5

Running With Devils

As you lie there you stare up and you see that the sky is a maw as wide as your horizons, and within it there is a multitude of other maws, all hollow and gnashing. They consume neither flesh nor blood but pain, and the demons feed them ours lest they and the Abyss be devoured instead.

Translated excerpt from *Memoirs of a Condemned Demon* by an Isaracci wizard.

The fourth day of the New Order's incursion.

Brimares felt her armor prickle long before she heard his approach, but permitted herself no reaction other than to continue stirring coals with a rejected branding iron. The New Order's encampment flailed around her, the sea of long tents groaning from the hammering wind and appearing more white than black beneath their crusted ice despite the night's shroud. As she crouched on the embers, huddled against the firepit's raised embankment, a second gasp of relief swelled from the encampment, verbalized as a hiss of melting frost and visualized in a rise of steam to the already prevalent haze. This second iteration of heat-prayers warmed her skin, diminishing the bone-aching, lung-burning, murderously-intent cold by a sliver.

Kell'MachChain strolled past her, dropping from the embankment and onto the dying flames with a menacing caress across her cheek, his advent provoking the exhausted coals into renewed life. She crushed the urge to flinch at his touch and locked him with a dead-eyed stare as he settled across from her, illuminated from below by the embers and shadowed from above by the night.

He watched her, smiling his small, insidious grin, saying nothing, and she watched him back, the air distorting around both of them from the heat of their bodies. He reminded her of the Abyss, of air that burned and fires that twisted, of hungry machines that tore flesh, and seas of ash. Someone else might have cowered from him, but fear bred malice in Kell'MachChain, stimulated his appetite for cruelty, and that might get her killed.

She relinquished the branding iron to the coals, its handle mangled and enflamed by her tension. The motion pulled a lock of her blood-red hair to dangle over her eyes, but she let it hang, hackles rising from the palpable violence burgeoning in Kell'MachChain. Her own violence reared in kind, as tangible within her as the Chaos in her veins. She strangled it and watched his lips quirk upwards.

"No, no, please go ahead. Don't let me stop you." He chuckled, his left hand gliding through a languid, munificent gesture for her hair. She complied, hooking the lock of hair behind an ear, more to appease him than actual need; it hadn't obscured her vision of him anymore than the dark did. That damning grin widened further, and with it, a hideous, putrid yellow flame erupted upon his palm and in his eyes. They were demon eyes, burning maelstroms roiling with all the colors of violence: her eyes.

Kell'MachChain laughed aloud, a sound of contempt that sent the flame swirling giddily around his fingers.

Then his elegant brow lowered, his lips curled, and his hand lazily flicked the Chaos-Fire at her. She recoiled from the motion, the flames splintering into a storm of molten hornets that stabbed her features, retreated and stabbed again, igniting her flesh. She snatched at them, gouging her own features with the serrated edges of her gauntlets but catching the flames and extinguishing them. Kell'MachChain laughed again, harder, and the coals erupted into another crimson flare.

Brimares shook the blood and skin from her gauntlets and then scraped the rest off in the coals, provoking a flare of her own. Where her blood struck the ice or snow it hissed and burned through, sizzling against the hard earth below. She ignored it, the searing pain in her features already fading as her face knit itself back together.

As it did so, and the blood drained from her eyes, Brimares glimpsed something in her periphery. She lunged forward, an arm slashing behind her to smash against iron. A clawed hand snapped on her face, dragging her back as a black knife slid across her throat, opening her skin just enough to bleed.

Kell'MachChain chuckled softly. "You have a pretty face, and I'd wager you had all the boys drooling over you. I doubt any of them would fancy you now, your condition and all. Still, there are benefits." He waited, expecting some sound, some reaction. "You're a quiet one. I wonder, would you scream if I dug out an eye?" The dagger's tip rose to kiss her pupil, spinning ever so slowly as Kell'MachChain began humming.

He liked that particular weapon; it was something he had collected from the Abyss. "You know, this is my third time out of the Abyss; well, fourth if you count my life prior to glorious damnation, but well, I don't count that. It's just not the same thing. Anyway, when the Abyss first spat me out, I didn't know what to do with myself; I had all of this power, all of this fire burning within and no one to burn. Can you imagine it? Thankfully, that encumbrance failed to last; I soon found more than enough to play with. How are you enjoying your first vacation from hell? I admit The North is not the most pleasant location, but it's an improvement." Kell'MachChain waited. Brimares denied him her voice.

He sighed and shoved her into the coals, prompting them into renewed brilliance. "Your no fun. At least not yet. I didn't spend a hundred years being tortured to not learn anything. I'll get you to scream one way or another."

Brimares straightened, the flames licking her armored feet and turning the metal electric blue, incapable of harming her without the effects of foreign magic.

She faced Kell'MachChain, waiting for him to decide whether to continue tormenting her or release her as incompetent entertainment. Tonight he chose the latter, his expression of contempt and cruelty evolving into curiosity. "Have you changed yet; shown your other face?"

She turned from him without comment and climbed the firepit's embankment into the shrieking wind, lashing sleet, and floundering army. Soldiers in black chainmail and gambeson-clad mercenaries struggled from the haze around her, deconstructing tents, packing sleds, harnessing beasts of burden, or struggling into armor. Officers waved shuttered lamps, their brilliance scarcely visible as orbs of yellow light amidst the blinding storm, to direct and guide their squads, keeping the men anchored in the camp. Ropes also bound the mercenaries into pairs or groups, and the black-armored soldiers, elites trained by the New Order, carried spells upon their collars that functioned as compasses, directing them to their commanding officer and the New Order's generals.

Totems reared throughout all of it, anywhere between ten and six feet high, wrought by an amalgamation of wood and iron sung into shape and fused with Shards of Divinity. Their black surface gleamed with silver scripture from *Telacra*, arranged and outlined as if in pages, detailing events from her history and her spoken will. They marked whatever land they touched as *Telacra's*, sanctifying it to her and her followers, strengthening them and permitting them to access her in prayer—even in The North, where no god could transgress.

Brimares continued trudging deeper into the encampment, navigating extinguished firepits, the frozen bodies of sentries, and ducking aside whenever one of the enormous, armored bears or boars lumbered past, led by their handlers. The New Order's commanders watched her as she passed, their dark eyes vibrant with their goddess' benediction and their collars blazing with the third lodestone spell. She could feel the dark energies of their goddess whenever she neared them, an aura of poisons and treachery, of the night and secrecy cast by the Shard of Divinity each harbored within.

A horn sounded, calling the vanguard to assemble and mount and causing the spells on the New Order's collars to flash. Brimares disregarded it; she and her kin did not serve in the vanguard.

She slowed, recognizing the futility of discovering another campfire in the disappearing camp. The main force would depart soon, their dead left to rot just as the dead had been abandoned when the New Order bypassed Winter's Gate three days prior.

She remembered ascending the hill's peak and witnessing the true North for the first time. She remembered the baleful winds as they tore the warmth from her blood. She remembered the shocked cries of men collapsing under the weight of snow, their faces turning blue then black. Most of all she remembered Adriat crouched in the pass like a cornered wolverine, its walls black and hewn from the Rhawn Mountains.

Winter's Gate represented the sole eastern means of entering The North, leaving a suicidal assault on Adriat their only recourse. Thus the New Order erected their encampment: digging trenches, constructing siege engines, and spitting volleys of arrows at the high walls before settling in to wait for night, and in so doing lured Adriat's soldiers to the front wall. Then at midnight, Kheldar Ferain summoned the demons and the New Order's elite to muster. The priests joined their prayercraft and wove a shroud of liquid night to hide them from Adriat's sentries.

Brimares remembered the liquid night rising about her, clawing through empty air and blinding her to what lay beyond it. She remembered Kheldar Ferain's cold dispassion as he ordered their allies to assault Adriat's unbreakable parapets.

Thousands died before they attained the walls and hundreds more as they scaled them. Meanwhile, the New Order elite slipped past Adriat under cover of this distraction, navigating the miserable outcropping of broken stone that separated Adriat from the *Annuir'Hyme*. It was little wider than a man's shoulders, treacherous under the best circumstances, and fully in Adriat's daunting shadow but, under the battle's shroud, delivered them inside.

Once beyond Winter's Gate, they reunited with the mercenaries smuggled into The North over the last decade, becoming the first army to breach Winter's Gate since the Mad Kings.

As the cold descended for the first time, they learned the true depth of their hubris. Enchanted armor and weapons cracked, leather split, and beasts of burden died in seconds. The storms arrived seconds later, smashing their ranks with howling winds and slashing their skin with shards of ice. The sleet fell in vast oppressive sheets, obscuring their vision by its sheer amount and causing soldiers to buckle beneath its weight. Finally the Wolves began their howling, a piercing song to ravage courage and sow despair. She caught a glimpse of those Wolves, beasts larger than the New Order's destriers. They stood in a line behind them, condemning the host to The North's nonexistent mercy.

A sudden stillness and silence roused Brimares from her recollections. She stilled entirely, rigid at the absence of wind and the encompassing silence. Soldiers froze all around her, vainly trying to pierce the mist. Then the warning screams began.

Instinctively her armor clicked, its ridges smoothing out and merging into a seamless suit. She dove, rolling through the snow into a twelve-man tent and curled up as tight as she could. Vaguely she heard soldiers scrambling in, one shoving himself up against her.

The temperature plummeted.

First there was only the howling wind, then came the ice in a barrage of needle-thin icicles. She heard the cries of men as they were struck, and the dull clang as ice drove through their armor once, twice, a hundred times until their voices stopped. She felt the icicles shatter on her armor over and over, their leeching cold creeping over her. The assault attenuated to its former vehemence moments later, repulsed by the clerics and the dark paladins.

Brimares stood cautiously. Her helmet clicked open, merging into the back and shoulder pieces of her armor. She heard ice crunch and spun around, her armor flaring in open threat. The two elite soldiers, their black armor dented beneath a coat of sleet, halted.

She relaxed, her flared armor subsiding. They released groans and looked at the seven mercenaries lying in expanding pools of blood. Four of the prostrate soldiers were still alive, but only two of those had any chance of surviving. Brimares shuddered—the smell of blood taunting her nostrils and tongue—then crossed to the survivors and began killing them.

The two elite soldiers aided her in this and then looted their comrades before departing in a flurry of barked commands. Brimares left on their heels, entering a scene of devastation.

It was as if she viewed Death's playground. Everywhere she looked, she could almost see Him prancing about in infantile glee, pointing this way and that to boast. She heard the screams of the dying, the agonized whinnies of horses, and the bleating of dying oxen. She heard the pleading wails of the injured as they were looted, and their screams as they were murdered.

She resumed her earlier wandering journey, tromping through the encampment until she reached the median of empty ground that separated the mercenaries from the New Order. A palisade of stagnant black energy awaited her on the median's inside edge, conjured with razor-edged stakes twice the height of a man and offering a single visible entrance where five sergeants crouched. They stood at her approach, scanning up and down her length with clinical demeanor.

One of them advanced, clamping her jaw with his right hand while his left hand fingered the silver knife on his belt. She endured the sharp sting of a foreign essence crawling through her and waited. The sergeant completed his inspection and stepped to the side, nodding her through. As she did so, a warmth prickled against her chest.

Once beyond the palisade, the haze cleared slightly and the storm's wrath diminished, blunted by stronger prayers, but Brimares lengthened her stride, diverging from the primary road to slip between two unattended trains of the enormous sleds. The horses harnessed to them shied away, but she passed between them until one did not: a black stallion with bright eyes. She slowed then approached it, one hand extended with her gauntlet retracted. It regarded her with a proud stare and tossed its head, warning her off. She felt a flicker of real sorrow. A creature like this should not have been a beast of burden, it deserved so much more. The horse continued to regard her, fully aware of the bloodline it carried. She stepped forward again, almost close enough to touch, and here, where no one else could hear her, she whispered to the stallion, words from before her crime condemned her to the Abyss. It listened, then lipped her fingers and permitted her touch. She stroked it gratefully, then crouched and raked the thick curls of her hair back. She performed a final survey of her vicinity before reaching down her collar to grasp a delicate chain and remove the necklace, grimacing when her armor sheared through it.

A ring gleamed silver and white amid a pool of sleek ivory links. It was a dainty thing, unadorned with jewelry or enchantments but radiated purpose. It should sear her flesh, devour the chaos in her blood—for silver abhors demons—but it left her skin unblemished. The ring was made of strings, more strings than she could count; with the smallest threads, too small to define, woven together to create thicker strands which, in turn, accreted into thicker strands. It remained warm, cautioning her against something.

Brimares closed her eyes and leaned back against the sled. Bittersweet memories rose in her thoughts. Of all she had been preceding her damnation, only the ring endured, its grip somehow defying the Abyss and clinging to her despite three centuries of torment. Now it served as a reminder of who she had been before. And what she had done.

"That is an extraordinary ring you possess." Brimares surged to her feet, her fragment of peace evaporating. The speaker lounged opposite her, his eyes black and colder than any void she had ever known, and his clothing a thick unnatural white, from the leather of his boots to his exquisite coat. He extended a hand, palm up in silent inquiry. "One wonders how a she-demon came to possess such a rare artifact." Brimares stepped away from him, clasping the ring behind her back. The stallion lipped her hair in passing.

The man lowered his hand, displaying no hint of malice. "Do you have a name? I know you are one of the Perdition demons the sorcerer summoned. My humble opinion is you are neither Cellar'Veer nor Kell'MachChain, being they are, or were, men. Nor are you a creature of lesser damnation, thus you are the third greater demon and, therefore, mine."

Her eyes locked onto the man's eyes despite the bitter chill filling her core from the contact. The man smiled, his eyes flashing something Brimares could not define.

"Yes, you were summoned at my behest and council. Kale Saragion opposed the act. He preferred a more experienced denizen, a rival to fetter Kell'MachChain. It is fortunate the demon in question had just acquired a new master and was unavailable for service. I managed to convince him any woman who gains herself three centuries in the Abyss is worthy of summoning. Now, may I inspect your ring?"

Her trepidation increased; what manner of individual altered the Abyss' tides and actively manipulated the availability of its demons? She remembered him; one did not forget those present at their first summoning.

Brimares stepped back, slow and definite, her hackles rising and her armor flaring.

"Do you comprehend what it is you hold so covetously in your hand?" He advanced, and Brimares stumbled back, almost falling. He stopped. "It does not matter; what does, is from whom you received it and that you never reveal it again. I would offer to keep it for you, but you would not accept it.

Brimares hastened her retreat, feeling the open air behind her where the sled train ended. The man strolled after her with a lifted eyebrow. "At least allow me to present myself to your erudite judgement. I am Salem of the

East, counselor to the Sorcerer Kale Saragion. Please, tell me your birth name, child."

Mere feet from the black-armored soldiers assembling into the vanguard, Brimares halted. This man, Salem, declared himself the servant of the sorcerer. She knew this as a lie. No servant reclines in his master's throne and mocks the master in the midst of a summoning.

She faced him, bracing herself to suffer whatever the man desired. Whoever this man was, he could not be worse than the Abyss.

He stopped before her, close enough to touch if that was his whim. "Not all of those who rule this army are ignorant, and Kell'MachChain, in particular, would recognize that ring. The New Order has been gentle with you thus far, in part because the lesser of them fear the Chaos in your veins, and in part because they have nothing to obtain from you, which will change the moment they recognize that ring. They will try and take it from you, not realizing it is impossible; that ring will never leave your possession unless you give it willingly."

Brimares resisted every urge to run, though her whole body screamed for flight.

Salem grinned abruptly and changed track. "Who did you kill to earn three centuries in the Abyss and more? Which petty king or wizard? Unless ... it was not something you did, but something you did not do?"

Before he could press further, the earth shook beneath them. Brimares glanced over her shoulder and beyond the sleds for what she knew was coming. Cellar'Veer advanced parallel to them, dwarfing mounted men and sleds, each stride reverberating through the earth. Of all the demons, Cellar'Veer alone wore his bestial face, the one tainted by Chaos and twisted into a violent mockery of animals. This choice was probably one of the reasons no one came within a dozen feet of Cellar'Veer: who in their right mind approaches an eighteen-foot tall bear with the flesh of crimson iron and blood of molten fire.

Brimares recoiled from him, fear raising her hackles and baring her teeth in a snarl, knowing Cellar'Veer would attempt to take the ring from her if he ever discovered it. She could not trust Salem, so she took the split ivory links in both hands and roused the Chaos within her. It ignited at her summons and spilled a storm of fire and searing pain into her veins, but she had not survived the Abyss by being weak. She collared the Chaos as she would an unbroken stallion, and compelled it to fulfill her desire, causing the necklace to fuse.

Cellar'Veer lifted his head in unison to her use of the Chaos and shifted his trajectory toward her direction. She donned the necklace and stuffed the ring into her armor just moments before he arrived.

His shadow, contorting and writhing, passed over and dwarfed her, its human head hurled back in unheard agony. She ignored her own shadow, which was a transient thing in constant shift—sometimes human and sometimes bestial—and faced him, quelling the urge to snarl and bark. Cellar'Veer grunted, shoving the two sleds separating them aside as if they were toys, and lowered himself to four paws before her, speaking in a voice of molten iron rasping against itself. "Why are you wasting Chaos?"

Brimares retreated, bumping into the opposite sled train and refusing him response. Chaos was a demon's lifeblood and their very finite power. All of them, from Kell'MachChain to their most insignificant pack member, would die if they used too much of their Chaos.

He snarled, demanding a response; but again, she refused, her lips parting to issue a growl, her fists opening into claws and her armor flaring open in a surge of fire as her Chaos mounted. She could not contend against Kell'MachChain; he was too old, too full of Chaos; but she could defy Cellar'Veer, a creature of instinct and brute strength.

Cellar'Veer barked, his double jaws snapping open and shut in a heartbeat to unleash a wave of putrid breath. Brimares answered his threat with a challenge, baring her extending incisors and further enflaming the Chaos. While Brimares was ignorant as to how deep the Chaos ran in her blood, she knew the extent of Cellar'Veer's corruption perfectly. He used the Chaos to make himself invulnerable, to heal his injuries and augment his physical strength to extremes. Small mountains had collapsed on Cellar'Veer and done him no harm, wizardry and magecraft had met equal failure. Cellar'Veer never stayed long in the Abyss.

He growled once more and relented, hackles lowering. "Don't squander your power." He then addressed Salem, "Kheldar Ferain wants to speak with you and the demons before we march."

"By all means, let's not keep him waiting." Cellar'Veer snarled at the blatant condescension and reared back onto his hind legs. "Oh, calm yourself, I am not challenging you for pack dominance." Salem dismissed the beast with a wave of his gloved hand. "Return to Ferain and tell him I will speak with him at my pleasure."

Salem turned back to Brimares as Cellar'Veer departed. "Though it may vex you to admit it, Cellar'Veer is correct; you should not waste the Chaos in your blood on trivialities. Its every use shortens your lifespan, bringing the hour of your return to Perdition closer. The High-Warden will not fall to cheap parlor gimmicks or timid manipulations of Chaos. You will need everything in your blood to destroy him, and perhaps supplementary energies. This High-Warden is old, four hundred years old, with three centuries of dominion over this land. Even Kell'MachChain does not comprehend the entirety of what you are to confront."

Salem strolled past, entering the press of soldiers and beckoning her to follow. Brimares trailed after him, entering the currents with far less grace. When she reached Salem, he spoke, "I would show you something later, a piece of past events, the last war to strike The North. Until then, you will accompany me."

They arrived at the swath of magic-charred earth that functioned as the encampment's epicenter. Salem strode between the encircling totems and across its naked, frozen earth without ill effect, but she staggered, muscles seizing and armor fastening tight upon her limbs, turning cold and inert. Her blood chilled as well and her Chaos dimmed, stripping her of its warmth and fire. She buckled, vomiting as *Telacra's* black influence suffused her; surrounded by her effigies, this earth worshiped the dark goddess, and Brimares served a different god. Salem paused in his languorous advance to glance back with an expectant gaze. She wiped bile from her mouth and staggered after him toward a table ringed in men: the New Order's commanders.

There were seven in total, more than half of a complete circle. The first was tall, his eyes ancient and dark with the Shard of his goddess. He faced them with violence in every sinew, his black robes billowing in the ceaseless wind and a loose chain of merged wood and iron hanging across his chest. A series of three lockets hung from its links, two carved of dark wood and one of gray, but all three radiated divinity. They were prayer-oaths, promises sworn to a god to fulfill some immense task or quest. All members of the New Order wore similar chains, though the lockets varied in number, hue, and purpose with one exception: they all shared an oath to destroy Cardolyn Tyier and his Paladin Order.

Another man, armored in full plate, grasped the bishop's shoulder. His every motion exuding hubris and acerbic contempt, he yanked Bishop Viral back to his seat. Then with a flick of his blond hair and a lewd grin, he looked at her. His delicate, almost feminine, features glowed with a vibrant energy in sharp contrast to his vapid eyes. He was one of the dark paladins: *Telacra's* highest servants. But unlike his kin, he wore no oath to her or any god. A single amulet of black iron hung from his chain.

A second dark paladin sat across from the bishop, holding a cracked mug in one hand and tossing a pair of seven-sided die in the other. He was older than the Blond Knight, his dexterous features framed in thinning black hair. He was clean-shaven and wore no armor or weapons except for the butcher's knife driven into the table before him, burdened with gray-white amulets. He watched all of them as a contemptuous god watched mortals. He was Sorran, one of the twin brothers who ruled a cult of Death-Addicts.

Indifferent to those gathered here, his brother, Eredar, idled atop a rock, sharpening a knife. Even in full plate, he was smaller than his brother and most of his companions. He wore a coronet on his fleshy brow, a declaration of allegiance more than supremacy; the obsidian skull carved onto the coronet marked him as a Death-Worshipper: a particularly nasty breed of religious extremists ensconced deep within the East. He looked up at her approach, surveyed her with round, childlike eyes, and resumed his labors. In that glance, she had seen enough to hate him though.

A fifth man lurched in a surge of feverish energy, his wild eyes unceasing as they dashed to her and past. He perspired despite the cold, his left hand clasping and releasing the hilt of a sword in blind zealotry. He was Patriarch Kadrin, one of the highest members of the New Order's religious hierarchy.

Salem arrived at the table and inclined his head in greeting. Across from him, Kheldar Ferain—chief among the four dark paladins—stood, the black plate of his armor glistening from the falling snow. He towered over them all with vicious eyes and an expression like storm clouds. The chain across his chest bore three black amulets, two of which were open, seething with *Telacra's* energy: oaths fulfilled.

A small Raven cawed and flew from Kheldar Ferain's shoulder, circling the assembled lords, to perch on Salem's arm. It pecked at his hand when he reached up to caress the feathers of her breast, and gracefully stepped onto his finger.

Kell'MachChain, followed by the other demons, strode into their midst and greeted the dark paladins with a derisive bow. "At last, all of the lords of this host are gathered. I wonder, does The North weep in terror for what it must face, or has it found enough courage to resist us in the wake of your goddess' inevitable defeat?"

"You can be an idiot whenever you so choose," Kheldar Ferain growled, "but you will leave your taunts for when you play with the other hell-spawn. Even if *Telacra* is defeated, as impossible as that is, it will not affect the outcome: The North's time of heathenism is over."

"I will play my games wherever I please. It would be wiser to command only those you are certain you can control. I am not of the New Order, and there is nothing on this Mortal Kingdom you can use to harm me."

Kell'MachChain advanced a step closer, the plates of his armor clicking with anticipation.

"If you're lacking entertainment, Kell'MachChain, go torment some of the mercenaries. Just don't kill them."

Salem snorted. "Well, I am certain that will increase morale among the recruits."

"And who are you?" Kell'MachChain turned the force of his gaze upon Salem.

"I am Salem, a humble wanderer of the East and assistant to Kale Saragion, Dark Consort to *Telacra*—your master."

"Yes, I remember your name. He said it on a couple of occasions, and I don't mean the sorcerer." Kell'MachChain smiled wolfishly.

"Yes, yes, you are terrifying; imagine I am weeping oceans of tears and begging profusely for you to forgive my every trespass, etc. etc."

On his shoulder, the Raven cawed once in raucous laughter. Brimares shifted, her skin prickling with nervous energy. The violence on the air was both palpable and suffocating.

"Enough!" Kheldar Ferain barked. "We are here on a united purpose: war. Your every lust, every sadistic passion, every whim shall be sated when we sack Antiark. Until then, direct your violence at the Northerners. All of you serve the Dark Consort by one means or another, and he named me commander."

"And what is your command, Ferain?" Sorran leaned forward, setting his bone-dry mug on the table, and tearing his knife free, stabbed the table again. "As I recall, there are thirty thousand Northerners hunting us."

Brimares flinched, the Chaos within her growing hungry as the mug's stench of blood teased her nostrils and tongue.

"If this is to be the moment we challenge the Dark Consort's decision, I ask why we are using demons?" Patriarch Kadrin smashed his fist on the table, snarling his words with such vigor saliva flew from his mouth. "Are we so weak that we cannot destroy our enemies alone? Must we ally ourselves with the Abyss?"

"Kadrin, unless you are willing to challenge the High-Warden of Winsyria alone in their stead, you will accept the presence of the demons until I deem them unnecessary." He directed his attention to the company as a whole. "As for the hunters, we are two days ahead; they will not catch us."

The Blond Knight laughed. "I for one do not mind the presence of the demons; they are sure to have a variety of uses. I am certain every one of them has a unique skill we might exploit. Dark Lord, what were the restrictions placed upon the demons by the Dark Consort?" Though he spoke to Kheldar Ferain, his eyes never wavered from Brimares.

"They are to follow my commands so long as those commands do not interfere with their primary objective. They are not to cause the New Order harm by their action or inaction, nor may they ever assume command."

"But which of us are they to obey?" Bishop Viral leaned over the table, striving to weave his own net of dominion.

Brimares felt the Shard of Divinity stir within Viral, lending preternatural strength to his voice. She saw the wood pale beneath his hands, his shoulders swell outward and his fingertips darken with stolen color.

"They are to follow the commands of only the Dark Consort, myself, and their pack alpha." Kheldar Ferain glanced at him, breaking Viral's subtle onslaught as he would porcelain. "Their energy is for their purpose, and they are not to be interfered with. Understood?"

The lords sneered and grumbled but accepted his edict.

Amidst those susurrations, the scratch of the oilstone ceased. Eredar stalked toward the table, his supple features twisted with fury. "Why do we flee when there is killing to be done? Stray dogs harry at our heels, leaving the sheep all around us unguarded. Why have we not turned our eyes to the other northern cities? They are unguarded!"

"That would delay us too much, giving Adriat the time it needs to catch up," Kheldar said. "And I will not send a sortie; not a man would survive this cursed land."

Kadrin surged to his feet. "Do you actually believe those tales? That putrid mysticism bred to ensure loyalty? *Winsyria* does not exist; this land is dead."

Kheldar Ferain turned on him. "I doubt *Winsyria* is only mysticism. And even if he is, the High-Warden is not, nor is the power he wields. Something guards this land, and I will not ignore it. The Mad Kings ignored it, and they suffered for—"

"You promised us blood, you promised us war, and you promised us we could take all the lives we desired, and we have yet to take any." Sorran's eyes flashed in open threat. "Are we to assume the Dark Consort does not keep his promises? Should we keep to our oaths if he does not?"

"You will drown in death when we sack Antiark, Sorran; until then, keep yourselves in check," Kheldar said.

The table fell silent as all watched the two brothers match Kheldar Ferain's stare. Salem poured himself a glass of wine from the vessel on the table, humming merry notes.

"And what happens, Ferain, if we don't keep ourselves in check? Are you going to destroy us? Last time I looked, there was a lot of dying going on around here, and you know what that does to us." Eredar smirked, his hand resting on the dagger's hilt.

Kadrin hissed, "You would challenge Ferain? The Dark Consort gave him command; to challenge him is to challenge the New Order itself. He is the agent of *Telacra*, of your goddess! Bow, bow and beseech absolution!" He struck the table with an open hand, spittle flying between his yellowing teeth.

The Blond Knight faced Kheldar Ferain with a sadistic curl to his feminine lips. "They don't exactly worship *Telacra*. I believe they give oaths to *Morgan* on the last day of the Turning."

Bishop Viral shifted his weight, eyes flicking back and forth between the two. He loathed the demons, and thus Kheldar Ferain for forcing them upon him, but he feared Kheldar Ferain and the Dark Consort above all others. Viral gathered himself up, clenching his gauntleted fingers with a rasp. "To contest the sorcerer, our Dark Consort, is to beg for death. I will not challenge the path he dictates, nor will I be destroyed for standing idle when others challenge him."

Brimares hovered far behind the cluster of men now, hoping she was beyond the fallout's radius. She doubted it though, but suspected retreating further would attract their attention. The other lesser demons just cowered, and Kell'MachChain gloried in the midst of it all.

Around them, the army continued to gather into squads and battalions. The vanguard had formed, five hundred armored knights in full plate atop massive destriers that would plow a road through the shoulder-high snow for the sleds and infantry.

The wind struck in absolute silence, throwing the lesser demons to the earth and causing the greater demons to lurch. A crack rent the air, and the table was shattered. Brimares heard someone scream, the voice twisted by anger or pain. She collapsed, fighting to breathe as pain lanced up her limbs and the cold dug into her. She ignited the Chaos in her blood, hurling tides of searing pain and heat throughout her body. A thunderous voice spoke, breaking through The North's assault with barked commands in a tongue she could not understand and the retching scent of sulfur.

"DOL'VARYURAN KAR SEMINATAR DASS BIIRENAEDONAEDARAEDAEN TELACRA!"

A primal shock crashed through Brimares, deafening and blinding her as the goddess was invoked. She screamed, clutching at her bleeding ears in a futile attempt to protect them from the divine words ricocheting through her skull with the force of a blacksmith's hammer.

The thunderous words eventually tapered off, allowing her to see, hear, and feel again. Kheldar Ferain stood amid the table's wreckage, his stark features outlined with the power of his goddess. After him, the brothers were the first to stand, followed by the Blond Knight, Patriarch Kadrin, Bishop Viral, and Kell'MachChain. The lesser demons followed suit. Of them all, Salem alone seemed unfazed by the assault. He stood to the side, drinking his wine and caressing the Raven on his shoulder as she raked her beak through her wings.

Brushing snow off his cuirass, Sorran turned a venomous eye on Kadrin. "Patriarch Kadrin, do you still believe the tales are only mysticism and lies?"

"Flash freezes are a common enough occurrence in The North; do not attribute them to omnipotent deities of lost eras and legends." He glanced northward with a twitch of his ashen face.

Still crouched, Brimares watched Kadrin, uncertain if his perspiration derived from fear or anger.

Kheldar Ferain strode from the wreckage, smashing the cracked remains of a chair in passing. His gauntleted hand swept out in a volatile gesture of abusive command, the splayed fingers entrapping the attention of his valets and squires. "Bring us our horses; we ride with the vanguard today. Detain us any longer, and you'll wish you were quarry slaves." He faced the brothers and spat, "You have one day and fifteen knights to exact retribution and satiate yourselves but do so only on the unguarded villages. You will both suffer five lashes for every man lost, ten for every destrier, and twenty for every hour you're late. Now go!"

Sorran withdrew a pair of figurines from a pouch on his belt and hurled them to the earth with a terse incantation. Hellish fumes exploded upward when they landed, engulfing Sorran and his brother in a sulfurous veil.

A moment passed, and the noxious fumes ebbed, exposing the brothers as they swung into the saddles of two monstrous stallions. Sorran tossed Kheldar Ferain a grin and, driving silver spurs into his beast's flank, cantered off with his brother in tow.

Kheldar Ferain watched them depart with disgust before addressing Salem, "Send that damned bird of yours to watch them; let's hope it will be of some use if they lose control."

The Raven looked at him and cawed, batting it wings and clutching Salem's coat. Salem grasped the protesting Raven and hurled her into flight.

While everyone else watched the Raven depart, Brimares observed Salem, wondering what power made him a lord of the army. Of all the New

Order, he alone endured the cold without ill-effect despite wearing rich fabrics better suited to the courts of kings. Salem met her puzzled gaze with a smile, ensnaring her eyes in the obscurity of his own. He waved a hand and swung into the saddle of a white mare. Beside him, Kheldar Ferain hauled his armored bulk into the saddle of an armored destrier outfitted with a great-bow and quiver. Viral followed their lead, mounting a docile mare that shied away from the unruly stallion struggling to unseat Kadrin.

A roan stallion thrashed outside the group, its feet planted and digging furrows in the mud as two burly squires fought to drag it forward. The Blond Knight grinned and strode toward it, causing the roan to thrash in the squires' hold, throwing one of them to the ground but still failing to escape. The Blond Knight grasped the reins with a savage hand and swung into the saddle with all the ease of an expert equestrian. He drove his golden spurs into the roan's flank, causing it to rear as he wrenched it about in what would have been a vision of majestic beauty if you ignored the scars of previous encouragements. The roan dropped back to the ground with a fragile whinny and shuffled toward the other lords.

Kheldar Ferain glared at his commanders. "Kadrin, you ride at the column's head; Viral you take the center. I don't want any surprises, so keep watch. The rest of us will ride with the vanguard. Salem, do whatever you want but don't stray. If those derangers attack, you will be called on to fight. Move out!" Kheldar Ferain pulled his stallion about and spurred it toward the front lines. "Darkness reign!" The other New Order lords echoed his battle cry with varying degrees of enthusiasm and followed into the storm. With their departure, and the deconstruction of their sanctified grounds, it reasserted its wrath; the wind, sleet, and haze doubled, plunging everything around them into obscurity.

Kell'MachChain snorted, beckoned his demons to follow, and sprinted after the dark paladins, keeping pace with the horses. Cellar'Veer strolled after Kheldar Ferain, showing no interest in keeping pace but, through sheer size alone, managing to outdistance the infantry. Brimares waited to distance herself from everyone else before following at a half-run and positioning herself near the sled train at the center of the army's column. The totems, shifted in the last moments of decamping, erected regularly atop the cargo sleds caused her discomfort, but the commanders were also less likely to find her here.

Even as she thought that Salem cantered up alongside her, appearing from the storm between two files of soldiers. "Do you want to know about the commanders of this glorious host, why they joined the New Order? Do you want to know which ones to fear?" The wind shrieked incessantly, and soldiers slogged to either side, battling just to stay upright beneath the land's assault, but Salem suffered no difficulty in making himself audible. "Were I you, I would not worry on the accounts of Kadrin and Viral. The former is a fanatic so devoted to the cause he will take not a step without prior consent from a superior. Viral has power, else he would not be present, but he is also a coward and loath to use his power for fear he might need it. Kheldar Ferain is a soldier; he will not ruin his resources unless necessary. If you adhere to his rule, you will have no reason to fear him.

"The brothers Sorran and Eredar, however, you should fear. They joined the New Order because the New Order will bring war to the whole of this Mortal Kingdom, and war is death. They don't care for whom they fight so long as they can kill. Eredar is a slave to his passions, but Sorran is psychopathic and in full control of both his passions and his brother. That said, Eredar is not an idiot; he is as conniving as his brother. He just doesn't bother with restraint. I find them interesting to study and entertaining to watch. They are like wolfhounds hunting the same sheep as the wolf, made unpredictable and savage by their fear of it. Amusingly, they do not comprehend the wolf is neither alone nor the alpha. That is why it is entertaining to watch them harass Ferain, wagering subconsciously that they will have the strength to defy the New Order's vengeance.

"Now the last of their number, the Knight with the blond hair, his blood runs in the same veins, only he wears a different face. The brothers, they joined to kill men; he joined to watch men die. He's one of the men who would start a fire just to watch the forest burn; one of those men who start wars just to watch nations collapse."

Suddenly Salem tapped his heels into his mount, surging it into her path. Brimares lunged back, trying to evade him only to slip and skid to a halt beneath his horse. Salem leaned down, his grin vanishing. "Tell me, Brimares, which of them do you fear more? The two who desire only to slaughter men and feast on them, or the one who wants to watch men die?" Straightening, Salem tapped his heels into the horse's flank and rode toward the vanguard, a stain of white amid the black.

Brimares thrust herself from the snow, melting ice streaming through her armor, soaking her to the bone. Once out of the snow, her body's heat returned, evaporating the water and allowing the fire within her to recover. Demons had two weaknesses: silver and ice. Silver purged them of Chaos, while the cold robbed them of life because they had known nothing but fire for years. She forced herself to follow in the vanguard's wake, slogging through the slush they left.

Her steps slowed further as she watched the New Order's ranks pass. All those who might command or pursue her had their attention diverted, so she stared toward the south and the Summer-lands. Could she escape? It would be easy to avoid the pursuing army and slip past Adriat along the same road she entered. She could outrun any man because demons did not suffer from exhaustion and were stronger than any mortal man. As for her task, the command to eliminate the High-Warden of Winsyria, no time limit had been given. Once beyond the Rhawn Mountains, she could hide from Kell'MachChain and the Abyss.

It was a foolish idea and a broken hope; she could not outrun Kell'MachChain or Cellar'Veer. If they caught her scent, she would be dragged back to the New Order and returned to the Abyss.

So she resumed her trek, marching north to find and kill the High-Warden of Winsyria.

6

The City Of Bridges

Valeriius watched Dieharamon stare at the Kalmarad before throwing a shrewd look his way, his features locked in the cold façade he donned for the arena. Valeriius was not surprised by this reaction; despite his appearance and station in life, Dieharamon was not stupid.

Valeriius turned his attention to the Triad. Trerrock's face was masked, but Xexeross wore a twisted visage of fury. Ureign leered from the comforts of his overflowing debauchery; he was wealthy enough to sustain his impending loss and cared nothing for the lives it would cost.

Valeriius leaned down and whispered into a guard's ear, "The Kalmarad is not to leave his pillar alive. Frame a prominent Kalvonder." He tapped the guard's left shoulder with his cane, warning him to accomplish the task without delay. The guard nodded, rose and scampered through the exit.

One of his remaining sell-swords hurried to part the door curtain as two others slipped into the room beyond, intent on verifying its safety. Valeriius followed without delaying for their return.

Dieharamon sat in silence, his wounds bound but throbbing. His eyes were closed tight as he fought to ignore the dry sobs slinking out from the farthest corner. Except for the crying child, Dieharamon was alone in the subterranean chamber. He sat on a weathered, blood-stained reed mat—one of several running the length of the room—waiting for the guards to retract the cloth door and allow his departure. He ached to leave the cold chamber with its haunting memories of past victories, ached to lose himself in the Sahdaen Hold.

The Avaran cities were named Holds because they were the only places Avarans could survive in the Avarus Desert. They inhabited the massive chasms dug by the *Annuir'Hyme's* branches. The river provided the water needed to survive, and the walls afforded protection from the sun. Sahdaen was the largest, and oldest, southern Hold and the epicenter of Avaran culture. No other Hold boasted as many Kalvonders, or as many of the cloth and silk Artisan Families.

The Holds were built on massive, interconnected stone bridges fashioned by men and strengthened with magecraft and Archient magic. With over six thousand bridges, some referred to Sahdaen as the City of Bridges.

The collision of beads and the swish of cloth drew his attention to the doorway. The scent of lavender slipped through the door curtain, preceding a man with a shaven head charred from, and covered with, ceremonial ashes. Heavy violet robes swallowed his small frame, cheap but abundantly decorated with sun lizards, which were sacred to Ashshand.

All men, mage or Kalvonder, heeded *Ashshand's* prelates for they mirrored their deity's cruelty. The Great-Immortal was powerful, and his strength made his Clergy powerful, powerful enough to dissuade the greatest Kalvonders from challenging them. An uneasy peace existed between the two factions: the Kalvonders left the prelates alone, and the prelates obeyed the Kalvonders' reign.

The prelate glanced at Dieharamon, sniffed, and turned his unnerving gaze to the cowering child. The Clergy of *Ashshand* were fanatics sworn into the Great-Immortal's service and bound to the cleansing of the Avarus Desert. Their oaths required the collection and binding of souls to *Ashshand,* and the eradication of all nonbelievers.

With the languid stride of the mighty, the prelate approached the child, who squeezed further into the corner and cowered with widening eyes and frantic breath.

"Child, do you fear the Flame-Lord *Ashshand?*" His voice rang off the walls. Small and frightened, the boy nodded before hiding his face again. "That is as it should be." The prelate laid both hands upon the child's head, and the boy recoiled at the abrupt contact. "Those who do not fear mighty *Ashshand* are heathens and monsters. Only those who fear *Ashshand* can hope for salvation. Through respect born of rightful terror can your stay in this holy land be sanctified."

His face falling behind a cold mask, the prelate resumed in a gentler voice: a lying voice, "Child, look at me." The boy complied as if unable to refuse, and the prelate continued in the same voice, "Where there is love, there must also be fear. Where there is love, there is pain. Where there is love, there must be trust. Where there is trust, trials will follow. Where there are trials, there is yet more pain. These are not our tenants, nor are they the tenants of the Avaran people. They are truths few dare to acknowledge."

The prelate's left hand disappeared into his robes to withdraw an amethyst pendant bound in charred iron wrought to resemble flames.

Amethyst stones served to strengthen, to hold, to bind, to summon, and a hundred other spells that drew energy from the human soul. In the Avarus Desert though, their most common use was the imprisonment of souls—namely, Tragnashi. The darker and richer the amethyst, the more souls it held. The elder amethysts, those holding souls from across centuries, were rumored to have upward of ten thousand. They could be recognized by the constant shine of their exterior skin. There were rumors of mythical amethysts holding yet more souls. Andeor'Vallen supposedly had one such amethyst in the pommel of the golden Stone Blade. This, however, was fact; it possessed upward of a hundred thousand souls and glowed with inner brilliance.

The prelate held the pendant before the child's eyes; it attracted them like a magnet as it spun slowly on its chain. Dieharamon had no need to avert his gaze from the amulet for he had no soul to give. With the child hypnotized, the prelate lifted his hand. An orange flame rose from the center of his palm.

The fire danced across the prelate's hand, a bridge for the reaping of a soul. Sweat beaded the prelate's brow, dripping down his long plump face and leaving trails in his oiled skin. The flame flared brighter, spinning once and turning a bright amethyst. The boy's soul fled his body, flowing from his eyes—white and ethereal—and into the amulet, causing it to flare with white brilliance before fading. The prelate returned the amulet to his robes.

The child slumped to the floor, whimpering as his hair faded to gray. The child's body followed, becoming thin and sickly as the glow that surrounded him, unseen but perceived, was extinguished. He was now Tragnashi: soul-less. He would experience hunger and thirst, heat and cold, pain and pleasure because these are of the flesh not the soul; but he would feel only the emotions his master determined.

The prelate shoved the child aside with his foot and spoke, "Welcome into *Ashshand's* care. If you survive, you will be accepted into the Clergy. Consider these your initiation trials." Without further words, the prelate began his departure but paused to inspect Dieharamon. Dieharamon growled. The prelate flinched and hastened his departure; he was not the first man unnerved by Dieharamon's un-Tragnashi-like behavior.

Dieharamon waited for the footsteps to fade, until he was certain they were alone, before moving to where the child sprawled on the floor. He touched the boy's chest and felt the aching chill it now harbored. He lifted his right hand from the child and laid it upon the hollow of his own frigid sternum.

'I pray your life turns for the better because for now it is damned.' It was not a prayer to the gods he hated; it was a broken plea to anyone who would listen. Like all Tragnashi prayers, Dieharamon felt his wither and die.

The child awoke with a cough, and Dieharamon pulled him up as gently as he could. The coughing gave way to wheezing and then to a simple, heavy silence. A shudder went through the child, and tears gathered at the corners of his eyes. Suddenly the child folded himself into Dieharamon, crying not for sorrow but for the void where his soul should have been.

Shocked, Dieharamon did nothing at first. Then he embraced the child. He should have kicked him away and told him to shut up as other Tragnashi would have. Instead, he cradled the child, aching with shared pain and wishing he could do more than just suffer in tandem. At a loss for how to provide more comfort, he brushed a hand across the boy's forehead, discovering the *brand* seared there. The Kalmarads would never trust the day's entertainment to the foolish whims of children. They must have *branded* him when the initial victor failed to slaughter his companions, inciting a murderous rage.

A sharp, barked command broke the partial silence of the chamber, "Shut the brat up." The newly arrived speaker was a tall youth, just beginning to gain the weight of manhood. New scars covered his arrogant features and frame. *Brands* lined his arms, a history of scars detailing back the years of preparation inflicted upon him for the Angorat'Wass.

Dieharamon softly squeezed the child tighter, offering what little protection he could, and glowered at the gladiator, but the gladiator ignored the warning. He was intoxicated with the aftereffects of accepting a *branding*. All magic left the body tingling: a result of mortals tampering with the immortal. Like the addiction to drugs, the consequences were perilous.

The gladiator advanced with a snarl, threatening him through movement and posture. Dieharamon ignored him and returned his attention to the child. Two things were obvious to him: first, was this gladiator had no fear of him; second, he was oblivious to who Dieharamon was. No living Tragnashi or sane warrior across Sahdaen would challenge him on equal terms. Dieharamon had killed all he could stomach for today though.

This act of dismissal enraged the gladiator further, sending him lunging forward with a wordless cry. He never landed a strike. Dieharamon surged to his feet, one hand sweeping out to parry his foe's grasping hands and the other snapping forward into his stomach.

The gladiator fell with a groan, clutching his midsection as Dieharamon returned his attention to the child. He found the boy staring up at him in terror, the dry tears gone from his eyes. Dieharamon shrugged. "I'm not your enemy and hurting you is the last thing I want to do, even though it may be inevitable." When the child continued to stare at him, Dieharamon sighed and sat on the mat beside him, the boy barely sitting as high as his elbows. "Stars, I hope I'm not the one to kill you." He looked down and tried to muster a smile. "It wouldn't be a fair fight."

The child met his eyes, the doubt and fear fading. "I don't want to fight. I don't want to die."

Dieharamon looked away, unable to stand his gaze. "You don't have a choice."

The child leaned forward and buried his face in Dieharamon's chest, wrapping himself into another embrace. Dieharamon let him, his eyes wandering to the opulent statue opposite them. A statue of *Arawn*, or *Morgan* as the Winter-lands knew him, God of the Dead; the second of the only two deities Avarans worshiped. The first is *Ashshand*, the Southern Great-Immortal. The statue depicted the feared god seated upon a throne with an open book on his lap, with the various carrion birds—his servants in the mortal world—gathered about his feet. Though *Arawn* appeared to be reading the book, the pages were blank to represent how the Avarans saw the *Book of Souls*.

Two additional victors eventually entered the holding room from the various passages. The elder of the two nodded once to Dieharamon and hastened to the farthest mat from him. Dieharamon ignored this; he had long since grown accustomed to the unease his presence caused in older gladiators. Unlike their younger rivals, the older gladiators knew victory and the hope of survival it brought. They had proven themselves strong in the arena, sometimes over the course of months; the price of victory, however, was that champions must collide. For gladiators, that meant facing Dieharamon, and he never lost. Thus they respected and hated him for he was their executioner.

Dieharamon heard the guards approach and stood long before they stepped through the cloth door. The boy followed suit, clinging to his arm like a drowning man; but Dieharamon gestured for the boy to hide as best he could, for there were few laws in the arena and thousands of drunks with lost bets. The Kalvonders permitted it because Tragnashi rarely died from the encounters and they could charge the perpetrators for damage, more often than not condemning them and their entire family to slavery.

The ominous tromp of boots on the stone floor ceased, then the door flap burst open and a guard swaggered in, stumbling with a wineskin in one hand and a clinking purse in the other. He sniggered and slumped against the door frame. "You can leave now." He hiccupped and stumbled out.

The other gladiators rushed to squeeze through the small exit, avoiding Dieharamon with lowered eyes. Dieharamon began to follow, but the patter of bare feet arrested his attention. He halted, not looking back. "You don't want to go where I am going. Valeriius Kalvonder is not a kind man."

"Dava."

Dieharamon froze, hoping the child had not given his name. "W—What?"

"My name is Dava."

Dieharamon's heart sank. Names were dangerous and, for someone like Dieharamon, only led to two things: exploitation or friendship, and both only resulted in pain.

In the moments following Dava's words, names paraded across Dieharamon mind, names belonging to people that once befriended him, all of them dead, more than one by his hand.

He closed his eyes, hoping to anyone who would listen that this time would be different. The hope was a lie to himself, one he didn't believe. The result never changed. "Alright."

Dava looked up, surprise evident.

Dieharamon forced himself to meet the boy's gaze. "Take care, Dava. A name is not something to give away freely."

In the security of his mind, Dieharamon pleaded to the child, *'Please, do not place your trust in anyone, and most of all not me.'* It did not matter that Dava had bound himself to Dieharamon, he still begged. His silent entreaties became a litany as he stepped into the subterranean world of Sahdaen with Dava clinging to his side.

There are three sectors to every Avaran Hold: the bridges, the caverns, and the river. The bridges comprise most of the Hold and house the main populace. The caverns, immense conduits carven into the chasm walls, enshrine and protect the fodder, meat, and insect farms. Beyond these designations, the Holds are separated into lower and higher precincts. Lower Sahdaen harbors the powerful and Upper Sahdaen the rest. Kalvonders abide almost exclusively on the ground level along the *Annuir'Hyme*.

After traversing the gladiator borough, scarcely more than hollowed out crevices connecting rooms and butchering stations, Dieharamon scaled an excavated ladder to a primary tunnel and the suffocating masses crowding it.

He shoved into the torrent, dragging Dava up behind him, then around to his front. He pressed forward, doing his best to ignore the crushed bodies and filth, and protect Dava from the press.

A prickle along his skin caused Dieharamon to pause. Then with a racking shiver of preternatural cold, he drove sideways, hefting Dava until they attained the wall, then dropping and ensconcing him with his body. Dava shifted with a muffled complaint, pushing until Dieharamon loosened his hold.

The prickling on Dieharamon's skin worsened and expanded as an ursine man with large eyes appeared in the distance, his brow inked with a wolf's head: an eastern sigil for exiles. He wore full plate armor, real iron the likes of which Dieharamon had never seen, and carried a long morning star across his back. Over his armor, he wore a thin gray coat of fine but mundane fabric lined with silver sigils: a mage.

The Easterner pierced the crowd contemptuously, probably on some Kalvonder or Clergy errand; no one else could even afford the equipment he wore. The armor alone would have fed an Avaran family for years, had there actually been food to buy.

Dieharamon pressed himself and Dava harder against the wall and quailed. He had no fear of mages, their power resided in the elements. But the world's other magics did frighten him, and a chill wrought by the Easterner's advance bespoke more than magecraft: wizardry.

A jackal-headed *daemon* trailed the Easterner's heels, leashed to his belt by a chain of amethyst links infused with soulcraft. It snapped a hissing lipless jaw at the nearest Avarans and scrabbled at the ground with barbed claws attached to long human fingers. Its sapphire skin glinted with a swirl of magic that rolled up from its limbs to the yellow crest running down its back.

The Easterner marched past Dieharamon without a glance; the *daemon* almost did likewise, its steps delicate, almost feminine, but as it passed Dieharamon, it acknowledged him with a flick of cobalt eyes and a low rumble.

Dieharamon sighed relief as the crowds swallowed them and rested his head against the passage's cool stone, trying to calm his thundering heart. He shivered with a premonition that he would meet the Easterner again.

Exhaling, Dieharamon forced himself to relax. "Come on, let's go."

A blistering wind swept down the suffocating passage as he neared the exit, pummeling him with more scents than he could count. The floor inclined, revealing the exit with another surge of oppressive heat. He pushed through the Avarans rushing to enter the stadium for the next match.

He squinted heavenwards as they stepped outside into the splintered sunlight. Through the massive network of bridges, he saw the sun at its third-Vigil. Contained and amplified by the chasm's walls, the heat had attained a suffocating pitch. He quickly looked down again, rejecting the taunting openness. He had once tormented himself with dreams of escape, of avenging himself on Valeriius when he grew stronger. The years passed and he began to dream of being saved, of some western merchant buying him out of pity or, in his more fantastical imaginings, a knight crashing through Valeriius' door. He didn't hope for anything anymore.

Releasing his grip on Dava, Dieharamon moved from the entranceway and slumped against one of the columns supporting the bridge overhead. A larger pillar sprouted a short distance off the bridge, its immense girth ringed in ropes and protrusions. J'sasur, six-limbed behemoths that resembled toads from the Winter-lands, scaled its sides, hauling cloth lifts burdened with leather sacks and clays urns, or ferrying Kalvonders on much finer lengths of fabric.

Back near the entrance, Dava shifted nervously, attention flicking between Dieharamon and the crowd.

"Well, come on. We're not going anywhere yet, let the crowds die first," Dieharamon called, sliding to the ground with a scrape of sand, spiked braid pulled down his front so as not to prick himself. Dava crossed to and crouched before him, barefoot on the hot stone, waiting. Dieharamon's heart sank a little further.

"Dava, ..."—the boy looked at him—"do you have anywhere to go?"

"No, they'll kill me if I return, have to pay back what they got."

Dieharamon nodded dully; he'd figured as much. "You weren't part of a guild? Just the street clan?" If Dava owed a guild anything, they would collect their due in excess from him and anyone near him long before the next Angorat'Wass occurred.

"No, just the clan. Guilds wouldn't buy me."

"Family sold you to pay off a debt?" This question once caused him pain, now it engendered nothing.

Dava just shrugged. "Yes, a reprieve for our room."

Dieharamon pointed at the nearby cathedral, a tower-like shard of black stone suspended from the bridges by crooked onyx shafts. "I could take you to the Clergy?" Dava shook his head. "There's nowhere else. You can't sleep on the bridges down here, and if you go up top, they'll kill you." His gut clenched even as he talked. He'd heard rumors of what happened in cathedrals and seen enough on Valeriius' habitual visits to believe them. But the Clergy had food and a scrap of interest in Dava's survival. Maybe enough to spare him the worse they were capable of.

Dava shook his head, clenching his small fists. "I won't go to the Clergy. Not again."

"Okay, but you need someplace to go, and you can't follow me to Valeriius."

Dava traced the pavement with a foot. "Why not? You won't hurt me."

"Because Valeriius is a Kalvonder, Dava. If you're lucky, he'll kill you and incriminate another Kalvonder." When Dava gave no answer, Dieharamon tapped his shoulder. "Do you know why Kalvonders slaughter children in the arena? Because it's horrifying, and Valeriius is no different; on occasions, he is worse. You don't want to be under someone like that–" He broke with a cough, the wind spitting hot sand into his face, further irritating his parched throat. He turned from the wind, raising a hand to his mouth against another onslaught of coughs. He fumbled a small flask from under his shirt, pulled the cap out with his teeth and drank a quick swallow, just enough to ease his throat. Dieharamon recapped the flask, ignoring the familiar awful taste. Even with the *Annuir'Hyme* running at their feet, the Kalvonders deemed water too precious for the lesser Avarans. Therefore, they allowed Avarans to drink only the bitterest wines. Of course, there was never enough to keep the whole of Sahdaen satisfied; thus the Kalvonders created and controlled another need for survival.

Dieharamon began to return the flask but saw Dava staring. He offered the flask to Dava, who ripped it out of his hands without question. Dava raised it to his lips and gulped, wine spilling down his cheeks. Dieharamon yanked the flask back before Dava managed another gulp. "Don't drink all of it!" He recapped the flask and replaced it beneath his shirt on the belt that kept it bound to his midsection. Dava flushed in shame but still greedily licked at the wine on his chin.

In watching him, however, Dieharamon felt an idea stir, something that didn't fill him with nausea. "I guess you could pedal drugs for the Entertainers' Guild. They'll feed, house, and pay you, and make sure you are still capable of competing at the end of the Turning. If not that, they always need children for other tasks. You won't get paid for those, but you will be fed and housed."

"What are these other tasks? Do you know any of them?"

Dieharamon nodded slowly, preparing himself for a trek through Sahdaen's pleasure houses. "The Entertainers' Guild is still a guild, Dava, though they paint themselves prettier and wear fancier clothing. If you go to them, you will be bound to them, indebted for the rest of your life or until the Clergy enforces its claim. But you don't have much life left so what harm is there? They could have you do anything from carrying the instruments of the musicians to watching over the dancers in case they're attacked. That work for you?"

Dava gave a weak nod. They both knew he needed to find shelter because being a Tragnashi in the Angorat'Wass was no protection against those who wandered the streets at night. Without protection, Dava would never survive the nights.

Dieharamon stood. "No point in delay." He jerked his head for Dava to follow and stepped to the ledge. On the exterior of the pillar, a stone ladder connected them with the other bridges. He grabbed the ladder, swung onto it and descended. Though the Entertainers' Guild hawked its wares to anyone who could pay, they built guild houses in Lower-Sahdaen where the actual wealth of the city resided.

Two descents later, Dieharamon stepped off the ladder into an alleyway with Dava swinging after him. Stone structures lined either side of the street, butting up against each other with leather-paned windows and adorning streams of cheap cloth. Hired thugs watched from balconies overhead, the richest outfitted with reed or clay armor. More cloth stretched over the roads, shielding them from the heat and whatever debris higher levels discarded.

To prevent the crowd separating them, Dieharamon grasped Dava by the shoulders before plunging into the roaring flood of people. Music from hundreds of un-housed musicians cascaded over them, competing and striving for an audience. Dancers swayed through the crowds, their sheer dresses tossing in the wind and discordant against the drab robes most Avaran wore. Prostitutes loitered outside doors, leaning barefoot against the frames, dressed in britches, and shredded shirts, their hair cleaned and glistening with scented oils. The drug masters hawked from the entrance of alleyways with banners enumerating their merchandise, and their faces and hair dyed. Old wizard corpses decorated one out of every twenty structures, most of which featured some defaced or scarred sigil or spells over the windows and doors.

Dieharamon pressed forward, glaring at any entertainer that dared draw near and resisting the urge to spit or hack whenever the wind blasted him with the hundred conflicting aromas of drugs and wine. After half-an-hour searching, and several robbery attempts, he discovered an Entertainers' Guild house.

He pulled Dava from the crowd and toward the entrance, the aperture laden with faded sanguine curtains in a dozen shades and a purple carpet that disappeared inside. At his approach, an Avaran woman wearing sheer clothing and the painted blue teardrops on her cheeks of a dancer emerged. She smiled and curtseyed, revealing the unnatural white teeth of a Vabor addict. "What will be your pleasure, Tragnashi?" She straightened with a sway of hips and an unfaltering smile.

"I have a boy to sell, and I hear your masters are always eager to buy, but I won't have him whoring or drug pedaling."

The dancer gave a coy laugh and sashayed forward to turn Dava's face for a better view. "You know you'll get less if you don't sell him to the whore and drug masters? Children always sell toxins faster and are popular in the whorehouse; that's why they don't last long." Dieharamon nodded; his jaw set. The dancer shrugged. "Oh well, it's not me who's losing money. There are plenty of other tasks that need doing. Is the child yours or did you find him in Upper-Sahdaen? Not that it matters overmuch."

"He found me, and we fashioned an arrangement. I get to sell him so long as it's not to whore or peddle drugs."

The dancer tittered and flapped a hand at him. "Oh, just sell him to whore anyway! It's not like he can run away. Besides, what's a deal broken with a child? Come on; I'm sure there would be a hefty payment and your pick of a night's entertainment for the boy; he is *very* pretty. With a little makeup and the right cloth, he would look divine!"

Dieharamon shook his head. "No, I cannot break contracts if I wish to live a full life." He had no contract that protected Dava, but with luck, his word would be enough to dissuade the dancer from continuing to badger him.

The dancer gave a theatrical sigh and strolled back to the door. "Come on, I will see whether we can procure you an audience with the house-keeper. I can't promise you anything though."

They followed her along the carpet and into the obscured guild house. A corridor of doorways opened before them, each curtained with cheap brown cloth, most of it ratty. The corridor ended at a reed door set in a narrow embrasure. The dancer retrieved a key from around her neck and opened it with a waft of perfume from beyond. "They're waiting for you inside. If the house-keeper has acceded to your request, they will permit you past; if he has not, they will return you to me."

Dieharamon grimaced, not asking how they knew to expect him. So much of control resided in convincing others you wielded more power than you truly did. Lies, mystery, and ostensibly impossible events were all devices the Guilds, the Clergy, and the Kalvonders used to expand the tapestry of façades, cruelties, and truths they wove. He nodded acknowledgement and entered with Dava in tow.

Everything within was carpeted in burgundy, barring only the ceiling. Cushions abounded through the room, some long enough to lay upon and others abutting low tables with mild intoxicants, puzzle boxes, and dice. Avarans of all stations populated the room, waiting their turn with the Entertainers' Guild's prize laborers. Serving boys scuttled around, bearing complimentary wine, and for the richest patrons, a slice of fruit. Bruisers stalked the perimeter and lounged in doorways, armed with bone bludgeons and knives.

Dieharamon and Dava crossed to the room's center, where a shriveled Avaran man sat upon a dais with black quills, inking a silk scroll. Squinting bleary eyes, the occupant noted Dieharamon's approach, uttered a low sound of revulsion, and ceased writing long enough to indicate a door behind him. Dieharamon obeyed.

The door swung inward at his touch, teasing with a brush of faint enchantments from within. Two men and a woman greeted him with upraised glances. One man reclined on a circular bed, bare-chested to reveal a sculpted musculature and as much of his rich skin tone as possible. His braided hair was beautiful, designed to give further allure to a beautiful face. The second man stood near the room's center, his wrinkled visage painted and his hair gray despite coloring. He lacked the beauty of his companion with a harsh protrusive jaw and a face too accustomed to contempt and scowls to have ever possessed beauty. The woman lounged on a bench with a rough, if brightly hued, gold seat-cloth, strumming a harp in idle amusement. She wore a mask over her lower face that highlighted vivid eyes and the intricate pattern painted around them. She wore glistening pin-prick jewels on her provocative robes, and a pair of silk gloves lay beside her.

A shattered pentacle occupied an alcove to Dieharamon's right, the stone tiles scoured with chisel marks and the Isaracc script painted over, though it seemed in need of another coat since the words were beginning to bleed through again.

"So I hear a man has a boy for us to buy, then I hear the boy won't be sold into whoring or for selling drugs. But I say fine; we always have a need for a child with quick feet. Then I hear the boy's a Tragnashi, and not only that, but his vendor is also a Tragnashi and not just any Tragnashi, but Dieharamon Tragnashi: the hero of the Angorat'Wass! And I ask myself: What's that bastard doing in my guild house?"

The man on the bed stretched and purred, regarding Dieharamon with blatant avarice. "He's here to sell us a boy, Baetar; what else do you expect? And oh, that boy is so pretty, such a shame I can't have him! Why, with a face like that, I would make sure he survived infancy! Ooh, imagine what he'll be like as a man grown; the ladies will be killing one another to have a go!"

"I don't care about your whores! I want to know why Dieharamon Tragnashi is selling me one of his own!"

Dieharamon avoided their eyes, skin crawling. They wouldn't kill him because he served Valeriius, but they might kill Dava, and there would be nothing he could do. "This is an easy way to make money without angering any of my fellows. The boy needs someplace to stay for a Turning; he can work for his food and lodging."

The house-keeper scowled. "And why does he need lodging for only a Turning? Is he poisoned, taken with the plague?"

Dieharamon hastily shook his head. "No, he's in the next Angorat'Wass. So he has a Turning to wait and nowhere to live."

On the bed, the man dipped his pinky into a glass bowl of yellow paste and reapplied it to a strip of raw flesh and crumbling paste on his right hand, shuddering. "Oh, that is such a tragic waste! Please let's help him, Baetar."

The house-keeper turned his scowl on the reclining man before returning it to Dieharamon. "He's dead in a Turning, and you expect us to not only house and feed him but to pay for him also? And we can't whore him out?"

Dieharamon grit his teeth, and straightened his back and shoulders to loom over the much smaller man as best he could. "Yes, I do. But I don't expect full price. I know you can make a lot more off this child in a week than he will cost. I know how much money a serving boy can lift off a drunk or addict." He knew because he'd done it for Valeriius to other Kalvonders.

The lilting music ceased, segueing into the woman's voice, "And he has no prior connections to one of the other guilds or a Kalvonder to worry us? Nothing in his past or future that might inconvenience us? To whom is his soul bound?"

"There is nothing, no prior involvement with the guilds or a Kalvonder, only a minor gang that wants him dead. He is soul bound to the Clergy, but they have abandoned him to prove himself in the next Angorat'Wass. If he survives, they will claim him; but until then he will be all yours."

The woman lifted a long finger to touch her lips. "I see no difficulty in acquiring the boy, Baetar. I think a glass bead for every day of service is a suitable payment. As for the boy, he will be maintained to repay his service." She resumed playing the harp, humming in accord.

The house-keeper paced between the harp on the left side of the room and the sofa on the right, muttering to himself all the while. He stopped pacing and spat, "All right, we will take the boy for twelve glass beads and not a shard more! That is the only offer you're going to get."

Dieharamon nodded and released his grip on Dava. The house-keeper scrounged through a pouch on his belt for a handful of glass beads. Dieharamon extended his hand towards the house-keeper, who counted out the money. With every bead that fell into his hand, Dieharamon fought the urge to cringe. He knew this was the best for Dava, and his best chance at survival until the Angorat'Wass. Still, it sickened Dieharamon.

When the house-keeper had counted the last bead, Dieharamon closed his fist and stepped back. "I would like to speak with the boy in private, then he is all yours." The house-keeper waved him off and resumed his aggressive pacing. Dieharamon led Dava to the pentacle's alcove for the scrap of privacy it afforded, shuddering as he crossed the arcane lines and trying to ignore how the script seemed to sharpen.

He knelt. "Dava, are you sure?"

Dava nodded. "Yes, I've lifted lots of purses before. I'll be fine; this is better than Upper-Sahdaen." He shuddered.

"Alright. Here, take the glass beads; they're not mine." He stepped back as Dava gaped at them. "It's probably best to keep those hidden."

Dieharamon began to depart, but Dava caught his arm. "Will I see you again?"

"I don't know. I doubt it, but I don't know. I pray it will not be twelve days from now in the arena." He gently broke Dava's grip and then left the guild house, refusing to look back as he directed his steps to the chasm's southern wall.

7

Touring Tellor

For the second time that day, Tasha stood motionless, struggling with some insanity Slade had spoken. Steal *Akravast*? That idea stepped well beyond insane. The Imperial Emperor's divine sword was not some trivial artifact spelled to breathe fire or pierce metal like butter, legends said it broke continents apart. For Slade Lammerock, the Thieves' Guild, or anyone else to contemplate stealing it was … insane. Merely touching the weapon, incinerated mortals. Yet, nothing less would induce Carr'Selain to offer a ceasefire let alone seek an alliance.

Tasha exhaled and, unable to stand still any longer, began to pace. "Alright, let me get this straight. You're basing your whole ridiculous theory on the assumption that Carr'Selain orchestrated this … farce, just to measure your skills before opening negotiations. A conjecture that you fabricated through unfounded deductions and leaps in logic.

"Yep, sure did. If it helps, consider this: two random goons and one Rat barely suffice to kidnap sheep; yet you're supposed to abduct a thief lord from his center of power."

It was a good point. The inadequate manpower certainly implied that something else brewed under the surface. Unfortunately, Tasha's only theory was that someone wanted her gone, but she doubted anyone hated her enough to orchestrate her demise. *'But what the hell do I know. I didn't think the higher-ups would recognize my corpse let alone my name, yet look at me now: ill-equipped, ill-qualified, and one lunatic's whim away from death.'* "Fine, we'll run with your mad-cap idea as our working theory." Tasha flexed her fingers, trying to siphon off the energy buzzing through her. "If nothing else, they said you were smart, and I might as well trust them."

"Excellent, though I feel obligated to warn you about some potential gerrymandering in the reports. It's likely your master downplayed my intelligence to reduce my perceived threat and prevent fear from infecting the masses. I—being an honest, morally upright person—reject such tactics,

91

relaying the full truth and fearlessly embracing both my awesome intellect and their lack of such." Clasping his hands together, Slade glanced skyward. "Unfortunately, my crippling humility prevents me from gloating about either one as it properly deserves."

She gave a short bark of laughter. "On first impression, I doubt you and humility have even stood in the same room before."

Slade huffed, crossing his arms and stamping a foot in mock outrage. "I'm modest to a fault. Why my middle name is Self-effacing and my second to last is Humble."

"Gods above, even your name's dishonest."

"Hardly. My fourth name is 'Unreservedly' and my fifth is 'Guileless', so obviously you can trust me."

"You have a very long and very strange name."

"Longer and stranger than you know. Pity the guild reports didn't make note because it looks incredible when inscribed on paper: very distinguished."

Tasha rolled her eyes. "Yes, because that's just as important as uncovering your location and your appearance and how you …"—her brow wrinkled, recalling a beautiful, flowing line scribbled in the margins—"have a tendency to invent random anecdotes?"

Slade flapped a hand. "Don't believe such vile slander. Obviously those reports mislead you with despicable frequency. Why just last week I was regaling my minions with an interesting, totally unfabricated, tale when the unabashed skeptics declared my holy truth false. Fortunately, a second witness granted me absolution: a man of unquestionable honesty, a man who has never spoken a lie, a man of such titanic moral fiber that upon being accosted by footpads, he—rather than speak falsehoods—gave exceedingly detailed instruction on the gold beneath his ex-wife's house."

The corners of Tasha's mouth curved into a bitter smile. *At least the reports got something right.* "Look, I have no interest in hearing about the drunk who thought he witnessed something you made-up–"

"The fact he's Tellor's most prominent drunk is irrelevant." Slade peered down his nose at her, rising to his full and—as Tasha suddenly realized—slightly unimpressive height. "Just because he enjoyed a few drinks doesn't make him untrustworthy. If anything, you can be doubly certain of what he saw. Regardless, my friend was stumbling down the street, pondering his two favorite subjects when a squirrel dropped into his path and hurled all thoughts of booze and honesty from his mind. At first, my friend feared the rodent planned to assault him, who'd think any different when an animal, dressed in the raiment of an utter scallywag, leaps from concealment and starts gesticulating with a rusty cutlass." Slade mimed the squirrel's antics, flailing about with an imaginary blade. "But the devilishly handsome rodent planned a far more lucrative scheme. After securing the premises, the squirrel rose onto its haunches and, gods strike me dead if either I or my witness lie, gave a sharp, piercing whistle. An instant later, two more critters sprang from hiding. The first was a bedraggled, auburn-furred cat who wore the most scandalous outfit imaginable: an article that made her gender abundantly clear. Alongside her stood a distressingly adorable chipmunk, who discarded propriety altogether by strutting around in nothing but her fur; this I might add was the color of purest silver." Slade grinned at Tasha, evincing such pure enjoyment that her own mouth quirked upward.

"Anyway, the squirrel began pointing and chattering at the other two, so engrossed in his rhetoric he straight up ignored my friend. Faced by this impassioned speech, the cat rolled its eyes skyward and served the orator her best disdain. But the squirrel continued undeterred, probably because his second audience member listened with unmatched rapture." Slade continued miming the events of his story, adopting both the pose of an orator and its accompanying gestures. "Upon finishing his stirring harangue, our squirrel discarded verbosity and started barking orders at a terrific rate, sending the cat dashing across the street to where Tellor's largest confectionery operated. Meanwhile, his second cohort rushed in another direction, tasked with running interference. Throughout all of this, my friend stood in drunken stupefaction, dabbing at his brow and muttering various exclamations as those three devils executed a spectacular heist. At the height of excitement, the squirrel fought twenty guardsmen, the cat seduced the store owner, and the chipmunk secured the confectionary, pouring bag after bag into a massive wheelbarrow."

"And how did these … creatures escape?" Tasha asked.

"The sea, of course. They hopped atop the wheelbarrow and careened down to the wharf, causing an ungodly racket before barreling across the docks and flying free, ultimately landing in the water. Afterwards, they sailed into the sunset jeering their defeated enemies." Slade finished his performance by retreating into the 'distance', waving a fist and stage-shouting unintelligible insults. Upon reaching the back wall, he bounded forward. "Anyway, considering the despicable penchant your masters have for lying and withholding information, one almost suspects they don't have your best interest at heart."

Tasha's slight smile vanished. "Oh, and I suppose you tell your peons every nuisance, every potential threat, every path that could fork one way or the other?"

"I tell my toadies nothing. I designate orders, outline a timetable, and occasionally teach my minions how to do their assignment. Heck, my peons consider themselves lucky if they know what job they're supposed to do."

"That's barbaric! How do they react to the unexpected if they don't even know what job they're doing?"

"Because, my Dear, I warn them against every possible situation."

"No one is that smart, certainly not a sixteen-year-old–"

"Eighteen," Slade corrected, crossing his arms.

"Fine, eighteen-year-old boy. No one can predict their enemy's every move, let alone account for sheer bloody chance."

"Yet, here I stand, nary a scratch marring my body. I am as unmarked as when I first drew breath."

She snorted, staring pointedly at the scab forming across his neck. "Take due note of my utter disbelief."

"I would denude instantly, thus proving my words, but I'm afraid of agitating your delicate sensibilities. If you insist though, I will gladly remove any apparel you deem"—he wagged his eyebrows—"excessive."

"And there went the last of my patience. Good-bye, Slade Lammerock. Contact me if something arises; I'm sure you know how." Nothing else remained at this point. Either she believed Slade's wild conspiracy theory, or she discarded it as pure fabrication. Whichever path she selected, Tasha's next task remained unchanged. Hopefully, Carr'Selain would believe her report, provided Tasha's handlers didn't burn it for being drug addled ramblings.

Wordlessly, Slade bowed and motioned toward the open door.

Tasha didn't move, however, rooted in place by the man's glittering eyes.

Finally the pressure grew intolerable, and she muttered a curse, stalking across the room with shoulders hunched against the forthcoming rebuke. Except none came and with every step pressure built in her skull, making it ever harder to repress simply bolting for the door.

Through it all, Slade waited calmly, innocently. She knew he planned something though. She knew it. She knew it right until she marched past and stepped through the open doorway into sunlight.

Relief swamped Tasha, a near gut punch that promptly reversed itself when Slade fell into step and snaked an arm through hers. "In the recent excitement, I quite lost myself and more importantly my manners. You're visiting a strange city with foreign roads, foreign powers, and foreign nuances. Let me assign a guide who'll navigate these turbulent, unfamiliar waters for you." He grinned at her. "I nominate myself."

"No, thank you; I am already acquainted with your city. A guide would be redundant." Tasha twisted away, trying to free her arm without success.

"I insist. In fact, I demand this boon. Today, this singular day when the Empire embraces excess, is the worst possible day to wander around lost. This time last year, Tellor recovered twelve lost children, endured hundreds of robberies, dozens of drunken brawls, and several explosions. All this on top of the usual reprobates who cheat, murder, gang-press, and tickle with despicable frequency nowadays. It's embarrassing really, a blight on Tellor's honor, how brazen these criminal activities have become. Someone should address this insufferable state of affairs; perhaps we could contact the chief criminal in this sector?"

She looked straight ahead, ignoring the inane question and the vibrant, slightly unnerving eyes staring at her. "I doubt it," she snapped finally. "Involving bureaucracy only solves excessive haste, and that's when a lawful government manages affairs. Calling upon an organization of dishonest, morally bankrupt individuals might do less and a good sight worse." She made one last, sudden effort to free herself, but failed and settled for making Slade's life awkward by tucking the arm into her side. Surprisingly, he allowed this. "Fine, we'll tour the block, then go our separate ways. I've other affairs to manage. Loafing isn't one of them."

"Pish posh, I'll serve as both your personal assistant and guide. We can manage your affairs as we tour. Take this right please." He nudged her down an alley without breaking dialogue. "Speaking of tours, have you seen Cardolyn Tyier's statue yet? You know it took nearly sixty years to build and required specialty equipment every step of the way?"

"Of course." Without looking, Tasha pointed to where the sky lay sandwiched between two flanking roofs. Piercing that cerulean void as a mountain might, was the colossal, sandstone depiction of Cardolyn Tyier complete with glorious, beautiful *Akravast* sheathed at his hip and an enormous war-hammer slanted across his shoulder. "It's rather difficult to miss, I saw it two days out. Impressive but not worth an up-close inspection."

"In that case, let's settle for wandering around Tellor; possibly sneak down the back-alleys and get mugged or visit the docks to sword fight with the giant wharf-cranes before fleeing an army of Theanne guards. Nothing too exciting." He paused midway down the alley, a zinc coated pipe to his left receiving a light rap. "The roofs will have less traffic. After you, my Dear."

Reluctantly, eyeing him warily the entire while, Tasha stepped on the bolted wheel connecting two pipe sections, grabbed a second wheel overhead, and propelled herself up the makeshift ladder. Only a series of metal bands kept it from swaying underneath her, limiting movement to a dull rattle and a gentle grinding against brick.

Slade, meanwhile, resumed his former dialogue, sounding directly beneath her despite—as far as she could guess—not having stepped onto the pipe yet. "As your newly and duly appointed assistant, we need to discuss today's surprises, plan your future, and write a truly fantastic report. The last one we can do while strolling along the face of Tellor's third wall; you dictate and I'll scribble."

"Wait, shouldn't we walk atop the wall?"

"Nonsense, such activities belong to the unimaginative. Though if you're skittish, we can practice by hanging from a balcony."

"How am I supposed to write my report let alone find lodgings while hanging from a balcony?" Tasha grunted, silently cursing Tellor's muggy heat as she hauled herself over a junction between multiple pipes and onto a stone ledge halfway up the building. From there she mounted one of its four jumbo water-drums, grabbed the gutters feeding them, and dragged herself onto the expectedly flat roof.

"Well, the balcony could attach to an inn or maybe the room where all your tawdry romances happen. If all else fails, I can always provide suitable accommodations." Almost before she had time to look back, Slade was climbing onto the roof alongside her.

'Gods, I didn't even feel him on the pipe.' "Thanks, but no thanks; your help would make some of my tasks inconvenient."

Slade reclaimed her arm and patted her hand. "Think of it like this: so long as I escort you, the task won't befall one of my decidedly untrustworthy goons. Your intimidating beauty already besieges their fragile minds. *Enecki* help us if they discover you're intelligent as well. They'd capture and lock you in a tower so fast that the dust wouldn't even stir let alone realize it needed to." Tugging her along the roof's edge, he led to an old board laid between buildings.

"Well that makes my situation all sorts of rosy and pink, doesn't it? Instead of a lackwit minion, the devil himself escorts me."

"I only moonlight as the devil, my Dear. I'm hardly a true professional, though my regulars do say I have the requisite charisma and a certain … devilish charm." Performing a playfully chivalrous bow, he handed Tasha onto the creaking board and then followed her across, paying no mind to how it bowed several inches into the plummet below. "My goons, conversely, have pursued different qualities, disdaining traits like my physical allure and bottomless intellect."

'Alright, enough of that. Time to deflate him a little.' "Slade, you treat your companions with such rampant disrespect, one would almost think you're intimidated by them. Are we worried by the possibility of a coup perhaps?"

"Their coup would be an interesting diversion, if only because of the unintended comedy. Even if it were successful, I would still ridicule them ceaselessly and continue ridiculing them until they accomplished something heroically stupid; whereupon I would redouble my efforts. I alone can complete said acts with any degree of certainty."

Jumping a gap squeezed between their building and a much taller one, Slade latched onto a wall pipe—the swirls of cleansing runes suggesting that it fed into the kitchen—and climbed past three windows onto a large, communal terrace. Leaving a swearing Tasha to surmount the encircling balustrade by herself, he approached a cute little stand that supplied nearby buildings with small necessities and homemade trinkets.

Muttering a cursory greeting to the skinny woman presiding over it, Slade began sifting through the shop's jewelry, causing the vermillion adari to shift forward watchfully.

Tasha, upon seeing what Slade did, stopped dead. *'You've got to be bloody joking. He's dragged my ass up here just so I can watch him shop? Jaidar bless it, I have better things to do.'* But she didn't stomp away. She wasn't sure he'd let her. Instead, Tasha just leaned back against the shop to simmer and hopefully extract something useful. "I think arrogance might be leading you to an over-exerted sense of competence. Which is probably making for a dangerous habit wherein you boast to your followers while simultaneously deriding them. If that's true, I really can't understand their loyalty; neither fear nor money sway it."

Slade cast her a sideways glance. "And what do you know about their loyalty?"

Tasha met his gaze with a sly, suggestive smile. *'Can you trust your men?'* Then she nodded at the arranged jewelry. "You should buy your lady something nice, she deserves a reward for enduring your … unique personality. How about the necklace in the corner, a little debutante-ish but tasteful."

"Spitefully life has deprived me of a lady friend, undoubtedly because she and Death separated recently." Slade tossed her a quick grin. "Rumor is that their careers caused problems." His hand darted forward, snatching an earring from the miscellaneous pile and dangling it before the vendor, making its silver chain glint while the obsidian shard swung lazily. "Demotal singolar tiheas Kelly'afa?"

The woman stared at Slade in surprise before joyfully responding, uttering a torrent of bizarre syllables that sounded more like a single word than an entire sentence. Tasha quickly gave up dissecting it and, unable to sit still any longer, levered herself off the shop's counter. Behind her, the discourse continued for several exchanges, both making excited gestures with Slade indicating Tasha on occasion. Ultimately, he barked a final sentence and pounded the table's surface, making its adornments jingle. The stall owner considered his words, gave a decisive nod and reached out for payment. Slade captured her hand with a vigorous shake.

Freeing herself, the woman reached out a second time. "Kekkay sinc'tulo shah."

Heaving a melodramatic sigh, Slade fished inside his waistcoat and flipped two coins at the woman. "A pleasure doing business with you, madam." After collecting both his earring and a silver-chain necklace with an amethyst teardrop, he departed.

'*Finally,*' Tasha thought, correcting course and letting her strides quicken until she drew abreast with him. "One mismatched earring won't exactly thrill your lady-friend, even less when she discovers how egregiously the vendor gypped you. Ironic that a thief lord can't price jewelry."

"We've already discussed my amorous deficiency, remember. This is to reward myself for becoming the fourth most-favorite and influential person in my life. It's quite the honor."

'*Wait. Someone else has more influence over Slade than he does himself?*' "Alright, I'll bite. Who are the others?"

"Well, in first place, there's Nocturnal me and in second, we have Morning-post-breakfast me, who's been enjoying a meteoric rise of late: he used to be sixth. To celebrate, we all chipped in and bought him a new hat, but the ungrateful sod promptly regifted it to Afternoon me. This hurt his polls a little, almost enough for Evening me to sneak ahead and claim second place."

Tasha rubbed her eyes. "Of course."

Slade slipped the ornament into his ear. "Now be honest, haven't I become unspeakably dashing for a few bronze-sails?"

Tasha snorted. "Dashing isn't the word that comes to mind. And if you paid with bronze-sails, both she and I hallucinated."

Rather than answering, Slade began a singsong rhyme. "Unique to millions am I, but no different to the passing eye; forged for deception, a criminal's mind housed my conception. We are both fools without aid, one by name the other by trade. Cut past my skin and discover who committed a sin."

"You gave her counterfeit coins, fool's gold? Somehow I did not expect that from you."

"We're both crooks, albeit of lesser and greater caliber; propriety demands we cheat each other or, at least, attempt to." Slade tossed the necklace upward, grinning as reflected light sparkled. "Besides, she bought something of mine with those exact coins last month."

'Okay, that's … actually kind of funny. Seems he has some inkling of justice after all. Sure it's strained through muddy water, but still…' She ducked under a clothesline and then navigated several clustered tables. "That doesn't change the earing being a complete waste of money, but I will grudgingly admit the necklace is beautiful."

"Good. I thought my perceptive eye noticed your perceptive eye noticing this perceptive bauble." As she waded through that, Tasha missed both the warning grin and her chance to escape. In a blink, he had ducked behind her and clasped the necklace around her throat. With a gasp, she tried yanking it off, but Slade stopped her. "The cards foretell a grim future; Fate, it seems, has dealt you a harrowing road, my Dear. Whether misfortune comes at my hands or those of your masters I cannot say. Either way, please accept this gift as an apology for what the future holds."

"No." Tasha's stomach twisted. Not from his appalling sincerity, but from her inability to hear the deception. "You cannot buy my … whatever it is your trying to buy with this." She jerked at the necklace.

"Who said anything about buying?"

"You don't ply strangers with expensive gifts unless you want something in return."

"Oh, come now, it's a gift between friends. Besides, what could you possibly know that I do not? What could you possibly supply that I don't already have?"

Tasha's retort died on her tongue, murdered by this rather embarrassing truth. "Dammit, why can't you just leave me alone. I don't want you near me, I don't want a tour of your damned city, and I certainly don't want this accursed necklace."

"Hmm, I could almost express that same sentiment to Carr'Selain." This brought her to a grinding halt. "Regardless, I'm afraid I must insist upon the necklace. It has a tracing spell that will free manpower for … more lucrative ventures. I had hoped you'd accept it as a gift, without realizing the true selfishness behind my generosity."

She barked a short laugh. "You expect me to believe that you need manpower? This is your gods-damned city. I'd be surprised if I tipped a rock and didn't send three of your minions skittering for cover." Again Tasha jerked the necklace. "So what's this actually about? A death charm? A punishment device? Some sort of safeguard in case I become a nuisance?"

Slade recaptured Tasha's arm and, nudging past her slight resistance, led her over the top of a decorative arch and the crowds of chattering pedestrians beneath. "No mortal exists beyond my control. Threats, subterfuge, or the clink of coins can purchase anybody's loyalty. If these fail, I'll adopt the more artful techniques of subtle manipulation and carefully arranged pieces. Soon enough everyone dances to my strings."

"I'm not a puppet."

"Not mine, no. In celebration of that fact, let's make a deal. You wear the necklace from now until tomorrow morning, and I'll return these." A flip of his wrist caused her three poisoned hairpins to materialize between his fingers, no thought given to how easily their needle like points could pierce his black leather, elbow length gloves.

"Done." She snatched them from his grip. "Give me a long knife too. Save me the trouble of stealing one later."

He grinned at her. "I already did. But enough of such boring subjects. Prepare yourself for a story beset by the deepest woes, a legend stuffed with the most monumental triumphs, a chronicle blessed by the grandest of characters: me."

Tasha stopped in the middle of verifying he had indeed returned a knife. "Oh, for the love of *Enecki* and Order itself; you're killing me here."

"Seeing as you're practically dying from anticipation, I'll begin immediately. As you might guess, my lady minions are so infatuated with me they can't think in crooked sentences let alone straight ones."

"Oh are they now?"

"Indubitably." And Slade smiled, but not with his typical mischief or arrogance. Instead, it was light and eager, almost like he was inviting her out to play. "What's worse, the men suffer from an identical infatuation with the women. So every fortnight—I set strict rules on fraternizing—everyone may campaign for the affection of their romantic interest. The men employ sweet but rather simple tactics, wherein they demonstrate or proclaim their undying love. The women, conversely, run to and leap straight off the edge of desperation, employing every imaginable art or chicanery to win my affection. Most are unmentionable near innocent ears like yours." Tasha snorted. "Anyway, how am I supposed to react when faced with such an enterprising predicament? What can a man do when all his goons would qualify for lovelorn sap of the year?"

"Clean house perhaps? I hear murder is an excellent way to solve difficulties."

"Believe me, I tried that most inelegant of solutions, except their love was so strong they rose from a butchered heap and rejoined my service."

'Note to self: matching Slade's absurdity does not work.'

"So after much deliberation, many long journeys to consult equally baffled wise men and the occasional talking llama, I formulated a suitable scheme. The answer is simplicity itself: I need somebody who won't fall hopelessly in love with me or one of my crew. Additionally, this person must possess all the wit and charm I demand from my associates."

"Might I suggest a celibate misogynist, perhaps one with an academic vocation?"

"Tragically, whenever I find someone who can resist a woman's temptation, he commonly suffers from an agonizing compulsion to safeguard my honor and will brutally thrash people over imagined slights. These events happen with such alarming frequency, I almost suspect my honor has shed its existence as an abstract concept, wandered off to enjoy its own life and is now manipulating my companions into resolving its personal vendettas."

"I see." Whether from relief at possessing weapons again or grudging acceptance of Slade's inevitable detours, she found sitting captive and just listening ... easier. She still practically vibrated from suppressed energy, but she wasn't ripping her hair out.

"And so my difficulties stand revealed to a gawking, jeering audience." Slade moaned, hiding behind his hands.

"Is there anything else?"

"Ah yes, there's certainly more." Grabbing a rope, he swung across to a lower building, landed atop the balustrade and sent a flock of seagulls winging away with indignant squawks. "You see, if I found a woman who could resist the allure of romance, she'd inevitably work as a high-priestess for the most godless religious order ever invented: one dedicated to abstinence." Slade shivered. "Her ethics, convictions, and other peculiarities would define our relationship through endless conflict: her fighting tooth, nail, hammer, and tongs to make me an upstanding citizen, while I cajoled, tempted, and mocked her into becoming an unrivaled hedonist."

Slade shook his head in quiet disappointment, then raised a finger. "Now don't believe all my difficulties revolve around those few psychoses. My potential companion can pick from a wealth of afflictions. They could be too smart for proper manipulation or psychopathic, and if neither an acute intellect nor a lack of empathy plagues them, then scruples intercede or they're insane enough to think they know better than I do."

'He's thought about this before, that or he has an unparalleled ability to spew drivel. I wonder if there's more history here and less story than I thought.'

Swinging after him, she dropped onto the balustrade and jumped off. "One solution could be to find a companion from a different race, culture, and class. The problem of your honor is still present; but considering your typical associates, I'm sure you're only a crude joke away from finding someone who doesn't give a rat's ass about honor."

"That still leaves the question of where I might find such a sublime candidate?"

"I haven't the slightest idea."

"Precisely, and now we've discovered the heart of my troubles." Slade, despite his gloomy predicament, pronounced this cheerfully.

"Maybe if I knew why you needed a companion, I could offer better advice."

"I'm departing Tellor in search of adventure, something minions don't complement very well. Hence a companion."

"Why? Your life here is easy and enriching."

Slade contemplated the question, idly hopping onto and balancing his way across some unfinished scaffolding. "I'm bored. The streets that once radiated potential now stand actualized. All my trivial schemes and their sparse complications now leave me dissatisfied. Worse yet, the unease I inspire in my opponents no longer amuses me. I've lost all interest in writing epics; instead, I'm urged to enact them."

"Do you have the slightest idea of what adventuring requires?" *'We've only just bloody found him. The last thing I need is for him to go charging off into the wild.'*

Reaching the edge of the roof and finding their next building partially demolished by laborers replacing old clay and thatch with brick and shingles, Tasha joined her captor on the scaffolding just as he transitioned to its ladder. A quick slide returned them both to the dark umber of Tellor's cobblestones.

"I've already ordered the necessary preparations. Something you'll undoubtedly argue, using my supposed inexperience as your main weapon. But, if you allow me a measure of competence, then a companion is my final necessity. Without one, I fear the solitude will oblige me to converse with the only available partner: myself. While our conversation would be undoubtedly scintillating, think of the reactions when people saw me conversing with, to all appearance, the wind?"

"I doubt their opinion would change; people already think you're mad. But even assuming you've prepared correctly, are you trained to defend yourself? If not, bandits or wild boars or roving Weshac will kill and deposit you before *Morgan's* glass throne in short order. There aren't enough knights errant to–" Slade blurred in Tasha's periphery, two fingers jabbing the back of her knee.

Instantly the world cavorted about Tasha, its dance reaching an abrupt end when her nose scraped across cobblestones and she began struggling to roll over despite a needle pricked leg. Then Slade stole the sky by leaning over her. "Take care upon Tellor's streets, my Dear; blood, treachery, and innocent death were used to water the mortar."

"Gods dammit, Slade, why? Are you bipolar or just a royal bastard?"

"From the very moment I introduced myself, you've rejected my every claim, practically steeping yourself in disbelief." He crossed his arms behind his back, not looming or glowering merely commenting. "As such, I thought to dispense with the pleasantries and convince you prematurely."

"Forgive me a little doubt; you're not exactly what I expected."

"Shame on me if I were." He slid a relaxed, open hand toward her and she—somewhat hesitantly—accepted, letting the sun haloed man drag her back to her feet.

"What did you mean by that treachery nonsense anyway?"

"Just a chapter from the hush-hush book of world history. Two centuries ago, this land belonged to a group of nomadic tribes collectively known as the Leor'Hana: a fierce people dedicated to the horse, the bow, and honoring the land."

Tasha suppressed the urge to drop her head back and whine. "I didn't ask for a history lesson."

"Ah, but this isn't just a history lesson. It's an illicit history lesson. Here there be secrets."

"… You have my attention."

"I thought so." Slade crossed the street, leading Tasha around a steel wagon loaded with granite blocks larger than a man squared. "Now first secret, despite their itinerant nature the Leor'Hana built a fortress deep within their lands, a sanctuary serving as capital, reservoir, and yearly gathering point. A city we now call Tellor."

"But Cardolyn Tyier built Tellor."

Slade merely shook his head. "Most everything in the Empire is built atop the bones of our predecessors and Tellor is no exception. The foundations have been here for centuries, we simply demolished the huts. Anyway, our Imperial Emperor needed materials for his expanding empire and Tellor had an abundance: metals, mines, and even lumber. The Leor'Hana, however, refused all terms, caring only to preserve a land that once housed their ancestors and would soon house their children.

"Skirmishes sparked at our every encounter, soon escalating to raids obscured by flimsy fictions. Then, on the cusp of outright war, a message reached the Leor'Hana's chief-of-chiefs, informing him about a delegation that was coming to resolve the situation. Two weeks later, the Imperial Emperor himself rode into Tellor."

"Wait, in person?"

"In person," Slade confirmed. "The Leor'Hana, obeying a custom older than memory, showered Cardolyn and his twenty paladins with gifts of ivory, furs, and all things they found precious. The poor, who had nothing else to offer, gave Cardolyn Tyier baskets filled with something the Leor'Hana called Tears of the Sun. We call it gold." Tasha swore under her breath. "The Leor'Hana chief-of-chiefs strode down his temple's steps, welcoming the Imperial Emperor with open arms, asking about his journey, and calling him brother. Cardolyn Tyier responded in kind, praising the city and even marveling at its crown jewel: the one and only temple dedicated to *Iothar*."

Tasha frowned. "*Iothar?*"

"Great-Immortal of the West."

"Tellor has no such building."

"That's because Cardolyn Tyier killed its god and subverted it. He tore down its murals, made bonfires of its paintings and broke anything—statues, writings, alters, braziers, floors—anything that might serve for remembrance. He replaced it all with attire better suited to the worship of *Enecki*."

"You're lying; to house *Enecki* in a heathen's temple would be ... would be ..."

"Sacrilege?"

"Yes!" Tasha snapped, hairs on the back of her neck prickling at such casual indifference.

"Why? What's sacrilegious about setting up shop in the carcass of a murdered religion?" His innocent first question had almost provoked an explosive response, but then he continued and Tasha's retort died on her tongue. "Thus I present our second secret. Want to hear another?" He leaned forward, smiling broadly. "*Iothar's* not as dead as Cardolyn thinks." With that he winked and left her standing in the middle of the street.

Gradually a realization crept to the fore of her thoughts. *'He left me. I could just leave. I should just leave.'* She twisted, looking back the way she'd come. *'I'm uninformed, ill-prepared, and bloody lost as to what my actual purpose here is. I don't even know why they chose me, except as an expendable piece.'* Tasha found her jaw clenching, a companion to her small, vicious smile. *'This really is an appalling hand of cards they delt me. Well, **Jaidar** bless them too.'*

Swiveling, she stomped after Slade. "Alright, so we have a cult lurking somewhere in the Empire. What happened next?"

"Techa'noka, the chief-of-chiefs, invited our Imperial Emperor to a feast utterly unlike our humble affairs," Slade's voice dropped to a low, soothing cadence. "The Leor'Hana celebrate for weeks or entire months, and during this time everyone enjoys the prepared delights. The paladins ate, drank, or slept as the fancy took them, reclining on couches stuffed with sweet-smelling herbs while naked slaves plied them with delicacies." Slade paused, then leaned in close. "This ease was a ruse. While Techa'noka's men lost themselves in revelry, Cardolyn Tyier prepared, scouting, swaying slaves, and convincing the less honorable chiefs. Come the height of revelry, he drugged the wells and poisoned the wine, granting a painless death to Techa'noka and his loyal chiefs. The remaining Leor'Hana infuriated beyond measure, charged the paladin delegation. But the paladins drew flaming swords and cast aside their festival robes, revealing armor that shone gold with the blessings of *Enecki*. Lastly the Imperial Emperor himself rose, weaponless, towering above all and marching forward with hands of fire, reshaping the world into cinder and ruin.

"The battle ended long before a crimson sunrise peaked over the horizon and illuminated a city that coursed with blood. Those waking on that terrible morning bore witness as the still cooling heat from Cardolyn Tyier's fists dried the blood to brown, then black and finally mere specks on the wind. However, the land would not suffer this cleansing, this forgetting, and the very stone turned underfoot, darkening to umber red. Ever since, no cobble can be laid but which flakes and becomes a reminder of our treachery." Slade stomped the umber cobblestones with his boot. "But our story and secrets don't end there. Before departing, Cardolyn Tyier had extracted a promise from each of his twenty knights: any who accompanied him would pay their debt ten years hence, not a moment sooner or later. Of the twenty, fear or guilt compelled all but one to break that vow. Failure, however, greeted them all equally. Come the ten year anniversary they reunited, some in chains, some in rags. That evening, nineteen succumbed to their preferred death or cold execution. As for the remaining paladin, he drank wine mixed with a drop of Cardolyn Tyier's blood. He alone would bear the weight of their treachery, carrying it throughout the long centuries of his life."

"Do you have any proof, or is this just another one of your fables?"

"All twenty paladins kept a diary by order of Cardolyn Tyier. After their deaths, the Imperial Emperor placed one in each of the Empire's largest cities. Four, by strange happenstance, found homes in Tellor. This, my Dear, concludes your final secret."

In the following silence, Slade slowed his normally energetic stride and let Tasha absorb, unobtrusively guiding her across the city. Ultimately, she shook away her distant gaze and looked to him. "Where are you taking me now?"

"I think it's time for a snack, don't you? Ever tasted southern cuisine?"

"No, foreign cooking doesn't really inter–"

"Of course you haven't; it is exceptionally pricey, and you commoners are destitute beyond comprehension."

"Thank you for enlightening me as to my finances; I hadn't realized their decrepitude."

"Fear not, my Dear, this is one experience I prohibit you to forego. In light of my recent announcement, I shall assume the cost. Prepare to eat whether you're hungry or not." Slade rounded a corner, dragging her into view of a restaurant.

"Death by Southern Food? Are they serious?" Tasha dug her heels in, self-preservation warning against entering any shop whose sign depicted one man gorging himself while his companion writhed on the floor, apparently set aflame by—and to the hilarity of—his laughing meal.

"Of course not, the sign is comedic. Humor opens tight purses, and what merriment cannot free, the cooking does."

"What does the owner do with the bodies after he's finished opening their purses?"

"It doesn't matter. This food is worth dying for." Disregarding her protests, Slade weaved through the crowd toward a raised patio decorated with the usual panoply of southern iconography, blatant stereotypes, and grossly incorrect misapprehensions. Once under its violet canopy, Slade rose onto his tiptoes, voiced a triumphant cry and bounded off through the clustered diners, snatching an unoccupied table just before someone else. Tasha advanced slower, navigating the crooked chairs and ever-shifting limbs to accept the seat he held for her.

A moment later, Slade was rattling off bizarre foods to a passing waitress who—almost without breaking stride—steepled fingers, bowed and then rushed off, annotating everything.

"You know something, I am beginning to understand why you don't have a sweetheart." Tasha started ticking off fingers one by one, absently flexing and releasing her leg muscles so her knee wouldn't start bouncing and rattle the table. "Murderous food, spying jewelry, enchanting stories, and let's not forget your charming personality."

"Being charming is uneventful and boring, best to make a spot of trouble. As for the story, you can't really blame me for the contents of history."

"Maybe not, but while we're on the subject, why did you want to tell me about the Leor'Hana?"

Slade's eyebrows arched the barest centimeter. "What makes you think I wanted to?"

"Because my mercenaries beat your ass and you flirted with me. A logical question wouldn't land me face first in the ground."

Slade smiled, looking—strangely enough—almost triumphant. "I was curious. I'd pressed you temperamentally, physically, and wanted to do so ideologically."

"All that because you were … curious?"

"Obviously. A better question would be why?"

"Alright, why are you so curious?"

Slade merely grinned, tapping the side of his nose. "Enough opening labyrinths and teaching curiosity to the cat. Our lunch is here."

"So soon?" Even as Tasha twisted, their server swayed past and swept a circuit around the table, her broad tray slanted so the various platters slid free. Then, before the last plate stopped rattling, she whipped the breadbasket from atop her head and rushed off again, now thumbing through the tallow-colored letters Slade had snuck into her apron pocket.

Politely ignoring the latter half of this, Tasha courageously reached for a piece of breaded meat drizzled with purple sauce. Slade, however, snatched the dish away. "I'll serve, my Dear." He grabbed a pair of foreign utensils and loaded her plate with select morsels, showing no preference between the simpler foods like the numerous stuffed breads or the more extravagant southern concoctions. Judging from appearances alone, many of the extravagant varieties were the offspring of a dye shop and a gruel factory. Other dishes resembled a sort of salad comprised of various diced roots mixed with crumbled meats and equally bizarre seasonings. Thankfully, the deserts looked fairly tame.

"What's that yellow dish?"

"Opaca, I don't know the ingredients, but it tastes wonderful."

"So this yellow slop might swim in drugs or something."

"Nonsense, drugs aren't allowed in the Paladin Empire, and smuggling is well-nigh impossible. Only the most daring, handsome, and skilled smugglers attempt it. Not that I'd know anything about that, of course. I only import the most excruciatingly legal merchandise."

"I see. So what have you 'imported' recently?" Selecting the most innocuous loaf, she tore off a piece and chose a spread at random. Before she even lifted the small wooden bowl, Slade plucked it from her fingers and replaced it with a lime colored sauce.

"Oh, nothing much, a few minor stimulants, the occasional enhancer, and a frightening amount of painkillers. The army and hospitals buy them at exorbitant prices."

Tasha frowned then shrugged it aside. "Well, considering how profitable it is, perhaps I should invest in contraband." *'Contraband yes, drugs absolutely not.'* Giving the lime colored sauce a tentative whiff, Tasha spread a thin layer over her bread. Once again Slade interposed, sighing as he spooned on the appropriate amount.

"I advise against it; sleep would become a distant friend. Paranoia, paperwork, and a multitude of forgotten details would forever plague you, becoming your one true nemesis. Trust me, the high-life is not for you."

"Yet here I stand, a Rat in the Thieves' Guild. Not the tamest occupation." Tasha eyed the piece of bread. Mustering herself, she took a nibble and doubled over hacking, spewing food across the table.

Unperturbed, Slade brushed the debris from his waistcoat. "Admittedly southern cuisine is colorful, but that's no reason to bombard it across your host." Still coughing, Tasha's face grew increasingly florid. "Oh, enough dramatics, my Dear." Slade poured a glass of pomegranate juice and slipped around the table to help her drink it.

"Whoever built this place chose an apt name." She gasped. "I bet they have a graveyard hidden out back for deceased customers."

"They certainly do, a cheery place filled with sunshine, bright grass, and many daisies. But don't fear the cooking, it won't kill you and might well resurrect you. I hear it is the primary reason we have undead stalking the land."

"If their cooking is necromantic, that's reason enough to leave southern fare alone." Tasha tried nudging her plate away, but Slade pushed it right back.

"Nonsense, who doesn't wish to cheat death; such a story will regale your grandchildren without end."

"If I wanted stories, I'd have plenty after meeting you. Besides, I doubt their parents would approve of me filling their impressionable minds with such fancies."

"Ah, but envision how much they'd learn from stalking my footsteps."

"An eccentric thief lord is not a good role model." Tentatively she chose another morsel from her plate. This time the flavors eased onto her tongue, and Tasha found herself actually enjoying the taste.

Come the end of the meal, where they scraped excess food into the trash bin and stacked plates, knives, spoons, and forks in their respective baskets, Tasha had grown as enamored of southern food as Slade.

Unperturbed by the people swirling around him, and likewise ignored, a man stood utterly still in the middle of the street, staring fixedly as the couple rose from their table and came walking toward him. However, even as the city ignored him, one person stared back with unwavering, mis-matched green eyes.

Much later—well after the sun surrendered the night's canvas to his wife—Tasha paced her cramped room, ducking the low hanging crossbars, yanking her shirt off sticky skin, dodging the support beam that speared up through her floor, and slouching where the ceiling slanted.

As usual she couldn't sleep. As usual she couldn't blunt all her nagging questions, vying doubts, and prophesized failures. As usual in the absence of distractions—of tasks—she couldn't even sit without restless energy buzzing through her, compelling movement. As usual she couldn't sleep.

'Is Slade's insane theory about Carr'Selain accurate? And if so, what am I supposed to do now? What am I supposed—hell what can I even accomplish? And why was I, of all people, chosen? If Slade's right, then me being sent because I'm expendable doesn't make sense and—'

Muffled wagon wheels snared Tasha's attention, their dull creek and clatter entrapping her for a split second as they passed beneath her window. She couldn't say how, but in that moment Tellor's oppressive humidity shifted, weighing heavier even as the sweaty, clinging atmosphere stepped back. Most bizarrely and quite possibly imagined, a whisper of sharp, chilly mountain air.

Tasha escaped her split-second reverie and dashed to the small flung open window, where she leaned out to see a luxurious carriage roll by, unadorned apart from simple carpentry and surrounded by paladin knights. As for the occupants themselves, naught but mystery and shadowed curtains which Tasha stared into unblinkingly.

Then these twitched aside and an older, powerfully built man peered out, iron grey eyes looking directly at her window. *'Enecki bless me. What is the Imperial Emperor's Will doing in Tellor?'*

8

The Northern Wizard Council

The High-Warden stepped out into The North and the last of the Citadel's heat fled his body. He felt no longing for its return. The North ran too deep in his blood for the cold to affect him. Nodding to the guards, he descended the Citadel's wide stairs and crossed the bailey. A gentle flurry of snow began as he emerged from the Citadel's outer wall onto the glass shore beyond. A new coracle waited there, gliding on the soft currents. He boarded, and it gently slid out onto the river, turning against the current without struggle or pitch. He moved to the prow and watched Antiark slip past, her crystalline structures dusted with snow and elegantly joined, framed by slim roads and occasionally connected to other islands by arching bridges. Thousands inhabited those streets and rivers, but their presence never rose above a murmur, even in laughter. The populace thrummed with a gentle rhythm, peaceful and content within Lord Antiark's presence despite the war. None of them could sense *Telacra* in the sky, creeping over The North like an eclipse, nearing her moment.

His coracle rounded a garden island and came into view of his destination: The Northern Tower of Wizardry. Five Towers of Wizardry existed across the world attended by monolithic, levitating crystal shards. Only three of the Towers boasted all six shards, one for each of wizardry's three facets—*Vydur, Kysuir,* and *Asiiu* or, in basic terms, *Destruction, Manipulation,* and *Restoration*—and three for mages, warlocks, and sorcerers. The third wizard shards were more commemorate now as *Asiiu* had been lost since the fall of Arthramain Roy'al.

The coracle stilled as it crossed into the static water of the Tower's stone dock, a belt of water and shallow protrusions that encircled the island. He retrieved a glass oar resting in hooks on the coracle's side and traversed the remaining distance to dock on the tiled bank.

Suspended hundreds of feet off the ground by a single perilous stairway, the Tower loomed at the island's center, surrounded by statues on pedestals of obsidian and gold depicting men and creatures as they cowered, cavorted, allured, or reclined in various semblances, humming with *Kysuir* energy. Blithe emerald and sapphire streams riddled the courtyard, bathing the statues' feet and swirling about them like strings of silk.

The statues turned with his advent, trailing his progress through their midst with concealed trepidation. He disregarded them and moments later they resumed their initial stillness, heeding an unheard command to permit him entrance.

He paused at the stair, remembering his last visit to the Tower before beginning his ascent. The first stair swirled at his step, changing colors and assuming imagery from some notable event the Tower's past. The second stair changed as well, regaling him with a different event. Necessity had blinded him to the artistry during his previous visit, now he permitted himself to appreciate it.

The Tower's history unfolded as he climbed and eventually manifested into a familiar step: his own. Images formed, beginning the story it would tell for as long as the Tower stood.

A powerful eastern wizard came to The North, consumed with avarice and violence, seeking the eradication of the warlocks that had found asylum here. The North rejected his desires, refusing to dissolve its protection of the warlocks. Decades passed and the wizard began studying The North's secrets, enticed by the power of a *Burdening*. He endeavored to court *Winsyria*, wooing him as he would a fair maiden with beneficent acts and ostentatious promises. His acts increased his eminence within the northern Tower, achieving him a seat on a lesser council but earned him nothing of *Winsyria's* favor.

The years continued and impatience spliced with rapacious lust began festering in his mind. Neither the lords nor the High-Warden died; they endured, abiding their *Burdens*. His desire drove him to the Abyss, where power is always brokered. Such was his lust that he refused to believe *Winsyria* chose his High-Wardens with care. Therefore, in blind avarice, he called forth devils and abused their power until he created a monstrosity strong enough to destroy his preeminent rival, the previous High-Warden. He succeeded. However, in the hour of his triumph, another man accepted the Burden. Enraged, the wizard unleashed his creation upon the new High-Warden, betraying his hand only to have his horror destroyed and his deceit revealed. The Abyss had concealed his duplicity from *Winsyria*, and his lies had deceived his brethren, but now, with the demise of his monstrosity, both his lies and the Abyss' involvement were revealed.

The new High-Warden journeyed to the northern Tower of Wizardry where the murderous wizard resided. A massive statue, lifeless beyond the will of its creator and crowned with a lion's head, challenged him. It stood taller by half than the High-Warden and twice the size of normal men. Iron swords would have splintered upon its hide and fire might have scarred it, yet, with nothing more than his hands, the High-Warden shattered it.

The wizards had watched from their tower, and The Northland had waited, ready should the High-Warden call for vengeance. Within the Tower, fearful of The North, the wizards scrambled to discover the traitor. The wizard surrendered himself to their judgement, speaking poisoned words to his fellows and the High-Warden, giving a face to all the shadows, nightmares, and nameless horrors that crawl from the Abyss unnoticed by men or gods. He spoke of venom in his blood and how it twisted his thoughts and corrupted his actions.

The High-Warden did not believe the man, but he allowed for the possibility of truth, choosing to suffer the guilty rather than condemn the innocent.

The High-Warden resumed his ascent, his mind rampant with a conflux of disruptive emotions varying from anger to wonder at the beauty a man millennia dead had woven.

He reached the Tower's door—unassuming despite the power strata imbued into it throughout millennia—a few minutes later. The door opened almost immediately, revealing an apprentice robed in orange. The youth hurried out, scampering to escape the doorway.

The High-Warden inclined his head in greeting and entered.

The fifth-year apprentice closed the door and strolled past the High-Warden into the brightly lit antechamber, his hands folding into the sleeves of his robes. His countenance displayed the subtle agelessness wizards acquire through years of practicing their craft.

Wizardry was available to any with the intelligence and willpower to master it; however, when a family practiced it across generations, the magic attached to their bloodline, granting affinity.

The initiates in the Tower wore first white, to mirror their lack of knowledge, followed by green and finally blue as they concluded their initiation. If an initiate passed his trials, he became an apprentice and donned crimson succeeded by orange and lavender before ultimately graduating.

The curving halls, resounded with cries and movements of men and women in white, green, and blue as they rushed to and from their classes with youthful exuberance. For the most part, they ignored the occasional warlock pair threading through the crowd in somber black.

Power radiated off almost everyone in the halls, fluctuating wildly across every surface. The uncontrolled energy caused no harm as it was unmolded, but everyone felt its irritating effects and constantly scratched. The masters and lavender apprentices alone held their power fully in check, their tightly knit energy acting like a boulder in the river of untamed power.

The High-Warden felt the awed eyes of initiates and apprentices examining him from every direction. Most watched him because of his size, but a few—Northerners—recognized him and sought to wrestle secrets from his appearance. The rest were simply drawn to him without knowing why.

The orange-robed apprentice scampered to keep pace. "I will take you to the council. They are eager to hear your petition." His words held a query because secrets always sold well. The High-Warden disregarded the unspoken query, directing his strides toward one of the many stairways.

There were many ways of traversing the Tower, some ordinary, some perilous, and some hidden. Of these, the stairs are the most common and safest. The High-Warden waved the apprentice away, confident in his ability to ascend the Tower. When the apprentice refused to depart, he spoke his dismissal aloud, "Leave me." The apprentice departed with a lowered head, nursing a perceived insult.

The High-Warden shook his head and began his ascent, slipping around a cluster of lesser initiates as they conversed animatedly. The number of initiates gradually attenuated as he climbed the stairs, fading away until there were only dark robed apprentices and instructors. It was not long before he only saw warlocks, apprentices in lavender, and full-fledged wizards.

He passed through an arching doorway into a vacant chamber of red masonry with white veins. Twelve stone guardians posed in the room's corners, their feet attended by diminutive clay figurines. These statues were the works of the current council members, one for each of the twelve, built in the hours preceding their inauguration to replace the old. Of the twelve, one foul obsidian carving reeked of his rival.

Demons also waited in the chamber, greater than the stone animates and greater than their masters. They were bound to this chamber and had been since its construction. They were invisible to most eyes, even the High-Warden couldn't see past their human faces to the beasts slumbering beneath the skin.

Two tall demons inspected him, their faces a fiery red and beautiful despite the frailties and scars of their past lives. They hissed at his ingress but pointed toward a door at the far right, one of five closed entrances. The other four were portals, means to transcend distance without physical exertion and arrive at similar doors in other Towers. One of them had ceased to work long ago, its magic falling dormant in the hour of *Lord Arthramain Roy'al's* death. It had once offered passage to the central Tower of Wizardry, but that Tower had long since fallen into a state of half death.

The High-Warden acknowledged the demons and approached the door, careful to touch nothing. The demons shied away and threatened him with meaningless snarls; both sides knew their threats bordered on the immaterial.

They were mortal souls damned to the Abyss by a paladin knight. The burning Chaos of the Abyss warped them, usurping their mortality and their blood, changing them over time into demons. The longer they endure in the Abyss, the greater the perversion became and, in turn, the greater they became upon reentering the Mortal Kingdoms. *Jaidar* permitted wizards to extract and bind these tortured souls to their service, alleviating their agonies for a short time.

The door opened easily at a touch, the elegant mahogany handles darkening beneath his skin. Magic, wild and unformed, billowed out as it opened, contradicting the obdurate spells at its core.

He ducked into a white room, the stone an empty canvas awaiting the master's brush to give it life and purpose. Ethereal scents tickled his nostrils; pine and maple slid through his senses in lulling harmonies, mingling with the scents of autumn and rain. Then it changed, giving way to wheat and fertile soil. Other aromas flittered across his senses, never lasting for more than a dozen heartbeats, yet never diminishing entirely.

He advanced to the room's center, his eyes exploring it without haste. The walls quivered with his strides, bending to his presence and will. They faded like the earliest memories, giving way to tundra and distant black mountains. Winter swirled around them, its scent growing to dominance, the wind capturing snow and ice to curtain the chamber's confines.

Twelve Arch-Wizards watched his arrival without comment. Not one of them were alike; some dressed peculiarly in the feathers of rare birds or adornments ranging from masks of copper links to leather shirts framed with bleached bone. Some sat or reclined in near nudity: their skin painted a myriad of different shades or etched with sigils that stored knowledge or enhanced their art. Beside almost every one of the twelve, either at their shoulder or at their feet, was a demon. Most wore their human faces, bodies encased in symbiotic, charred red armor, but a rare few wore their demon guises and sprawled about as metal beasts, their eyes and mouths aflame, belching evanescent fumes.

The council observed him with maintained dispassion; they feared to anger him but were loath to concede any power. Individually they were powerful, a wealth of spells to reap cataclysmic destruction upon anything within their reach, and together their strength bordered on the divine.

After taut seconds of scrutiny, the High-Warden's eyes fell upon his aggressor from those centuries before.

Falain Durensev sat with an aspect vacillating between hate and blatant vengeful lust; one of the few dressed in the wealth of kings and the only one in pure crimson. The High-Warden's rage surged at Falain's choice of apparel, scarce believing any man possessed such arrogance. Crimson, while not outright forbidden, belonged solely to *Lord Arthramain Roy'al* and his Crimson Empire. To wear crimson is the highest of conceit unless blood is shared, for he had claimed it with these words: *'Mine is an empire built upon, with, and through crimson blood. Though it can be said thus of all empires, none in their construction or fall have cost more lives than I have in the building of my Crimson Empire, and for this I weep.'* Now, he understood Lord Antiark's reservations about the council.

The rivals locked eyes, and the High-Warden nodded in greeting, receiving a contemptuous sneer in return. Leaning back in his sumptuous throne, Falain Durensev veered his gaze to the avian-like demon perched on his shoulder.

The High-Warden switched his gaze to the man seated before him. His salt-pepper hair was thinning on his brow and chin, showing the marks of spells gone amiss—scars many of the wizards here shared. He wore no adornments, sigils, or cloth to amplify his power and instead dressed for comfort with loose western clothes and oiled boots. A few pins decorated his high collar, but nothing else. There was a carving knife on his belt, an unfinished figurine on the armrest of his chair and wood shavings in his lap.

He stood, head bowed in greeting as the room shifted from winter to an autumn forest and the scent of maple and hot cider. "My greetings, High-Warden, how can we be of service to The North?"

The High-Warden inclined his head in acknowledgement, respecting the man as an equal. Before he could respond, Falain interceded, his voice steeped in contempt and loathing, "That is not the proper query, Caddon." The derision in his words was for the wizard and the High-Warden both, though he addressed his colleagues. The chamber became fiery and dark to compliment the scents of brimstone and ash. "We should be asking whether this man deserves our assistance." A triumphant inflection colored his last words as he favored the High-Warden with a wide grin, disregarding Caddon's evident exasperation. "Well, do you merit our aid, Northman?"

The High-Warden considered his response; words of praise and bargains, words that unveiled the fury and disgust within him, and words that did neither. Ignoring the silence demanding his answer, the High-Warden spoke only when he felt certain of his words; he needed their aid, "I will not bandy words, Arch-Wizard Durensev; I serve a higher purpose than your pride. Either the council will accede to my request or I will search for another wizard more amenable to my plea." The wizard council might deny his request, but they could not forbid other wizards from doing so.

Falain Durensev's features turned red, his eyes burning with spited wrath. To his right, Caddon Fayre laughed. "High-Warden, it appears you know our rules better than one of our own council. Again, how can we, or if need be, I, be of service to The North?"

He faced Caddon Fayre, the sole council member unattended by a demonic entity, and spoke before Falain could interrupt again, "I require a wizard with enough skill and power to execute a deep summoning."

Falain lunged forward, maintaining his seat with a vice-grip on the armrest. "See?" Spittle flew from his mouth as he shrieked and gesticulated at the High-Warden, as if by this gesture he could prove his claims irrefutable. "See? He demands we summon entities just lesser than gods, that we endanger ourselves in matters of no consequence to us. I—"

"Quiet," Caddon barked as the scenery changed again, and in that instant, the High-Warden saw the signs of a protracted struggle for dominance. "High-Warden, please continue."

"I ask that you trust me when I say the only person imperiled by these actions is myself."

The wizards preserved their silence, each wondering at the depths of their Northern involvement. They measured a favor of the High-Warden against the animosity of the East. They knew nothing of him except for indistinct rumors, and only a little more of The North. They all knew of, though they might not comprehend, the *Burden*.

The hush collapsed to Falain rising tall upon his throne, eyes dominated in furor and the power he held. "You are all fools to consider this!" The demon on his shoulder vaulted forward, warping mid-flight, the iron feathers giving way to human limbs coated in serrated crimson plating. It landed on all fours to growl and slink behind the High-Warden, its mouth spread wide and hissing.

He paid the creature no heed.

When his words met with silence, Falain Durensev, never one to surrender for lack of interest, renewed his rhetoric, "This man asks us, feigning humility, for our assistance. Yet, not once has he done aught for us. Instead, he has done harm. Not only has he forsaken the gods, rightful rulers of men, but he has allowed and sanctioned the practice of black magic in The

North. Is it not his *Burden* to guard The North from evil?" Falain spun to face his colleagues. "The warlocks endanger themselves and others through their practice of magic unbound by the laws set in place for our safety! I have heard the Lord of Antiark is one of these heathens who practice feral magic. How can we, who are greater than kings, hope to influence others to abandon their own petty rivalries and ambitions when we harbor such malice?" Wild in his hatred, Falain frothed like a feral beast, spitting out words with a guttural hate.

When Falain drew a breath to persist, Caddon interposed, "Falain, we are not and should never be greater than kings. We have our art; that should be enough."

Falain turned on Caddon. "What do you know?" He swiped his hand through the air between them. "You, with your wisdom of the past, know nothing except for what lies hidden in books. You are lost to the wisdom of the future, bound by the laws that have ever governed us. It is time we change those laws." Falain drew his rampant words to a halt, forcing control over his passion. "I say, let us assume sovereignty, let us command rulers such as that fool Lord Antiark. Let us command kings who have fire in their hearts but lack the foresight to tread paths of glory. Let us counsel men such as Cardolyn Tyier, so they never act blindly; let us fight tyranny where it entrenches itself: in the thrones of kings!"

The High-Warden stepped forward, drawn by the proposed tyranny this man lauded beneath a façade of magnanimous intentions. "Tyranny does not favor only thrones, Arch-Wizard Durensev. It sprouts from the blind masses striving for false ideals spoken to them by men with beautiful, treacherous words." In the echoes following his remonstration, the High-Warden's eyes burned cold.

"How loquacious, almost eloquent, of you, High-Warden." Falain waved a hand in dismissal, sniggering. "But how can one such as you know aught of theology? We speak of kings and avarice, of ambition and betrayal. You, in all the inherent idiocy of your arrogant people, know nothing of what you presume yourself to be above, but which you exude with every breath."

"Enough!" Caddon Fayre stood, and for all his graying hairs and small stature, the man towered over the other council members. Even Falain realized he had transgressed and cringed, though his conceit and ire remained prominent on his features. Resuming his seat, Falain suffered Caddon Fayre's unequivocal command.

Caddon continued, "I will end this now. High-Warden, this council is above nations and cannot involve itself in this matter. The council refuses to aid you. Still, our laws forbid us to restrict the actions of any wizard lest they be involved in matters of Darkness. Thus I offer myself and whatever aid I can to you." He stepped off his throne.

A statuesque woman with pale hair and a youthful face spoke, "You are the head of this council, Caddon. You cannot take a perilous road alone. These are uncertain days; we cannot be left without our leaders. What if the New Order decides to make themselves our enemies?"

Caddon laughed, lifting his hand as a white squirrel scampered out from his sleeve. "No need to fear. If I am needed, look to Andrea." Caddon crouched and placed the squirrel on the floor. It cowered there for a moment, shocked at the separation, then fled back to Caddon's leg with a squeak. The man smiled and scooped the protesting animal in his hands, caressing its small head.

The High-Warden watched an indigo light pass between man and animal. The small creature glowed indigo for an instant before the light faded to a thread and gently touched the squirrel's mind. After bidding his wordless farewell, Caddon set the squirrel down and it scampered towards the woman, who knelt from her chair to catch it mid-leap. The squirrel scaled the woman's arm to conceal itself in her hair. "Very well, love, I will care for him and the Tower, so long as this is a brief sojourn." They shared a glance, a lifetime of emotions and memories imparted over a span of seconds.

"Dear, I walk in the company of one whose glory shames the achievements of our forefathers. Few are the perils that will not flee before us by leagues; nor will I be gone long, it is only a summoning." Caddon turned his focus to Falain, who appeared pleased with the decision. "Falain Durensev, listen to my words with care. Long ago you committed a transgression, a crime for which you have not suffered—"

"It was not a crime …" Falain lost his words in wronged fury and then found them again as he surged off his throne, "I erred, and for this I have suffered more than aught you could do!" Despite his protests, Falain's eyes resembled those of a fox cornered by the hunt.

"That is of no matter, Falain. You were allowed your life on the hinge of this man's doubt. Before you seek to challenge his goodwill again, examine your own past."

Feverish in rage and contempt, Falain Durensev stormed back to his throne. Breathing heavily, he threw himself into the seat; lips parted in a snarl.

The High-Warden turned from the council with a bow of gratitude. Followed by Caddon Fayre, he departed, the chamber's small door swinging outward. At his egress, the walls changed once more. Everything vanished, replaced by ruins and overturned thrones. The wind lamented, and in the shadows cast by decrepit walls, some foul creature with a tormented body slunk across the ground. It lasted for the space of a heartbeat then fled, leaving him questions and a troubled warning.

Caddon tilted his head back and, with his eyes wide and glazed, chanted low words, amassing arcane power. His words took shape, becoming a verse of summoning.

His demon arrived without excitement, slipping beneath one of the chamber's doors in a cloud of ash, forming into the shadow of a man and then immersing itself in his shadow. Caddon smiled. "Did you enjoy your vacation?"

The shadow flowed across the floor as the demon shifted before responding in a dead voice, "It served well enough, Arch-Wizard." The demon stilled, conjuring an uninviting air, dissuading further conversation. Caddon shrugged and left the antechamber. The High-Warden trailed after him, waiting patiently for him to voice his questions.

Caddon began as they arrived at the Tower's central stair, "Now that you have my support, what is the task?"

"The North is at war, and with war comes all manner of crows and scavengers. Foremost among these vast flocks are the gods."

Caddon caught his breath. "The gods?"

"Yes. The North has long survived as a land forsaking all touched by that accursed Pantheon and its twelve deities of Shadow, Light, and Darkness: the twelve gods of men. Inevitably war will debilitate The North, and this weakness will cause fractures in the *Barrier*, fractures through which the gods can enter. Once they enter, none of us will boast strength enough to break their hold, even with all Northern might to aid us."

Caddon Fayre's breathing quickened, his mind latching onto what the High-Warden described, and his intention of defying the gods. "And how do you intend this denial, High-Warden?"

"There are more entities of the Before Age than *Winsyria*; I intend to bargain with them to ensure select gods do not enter." The High-Warden resumed descending.

Caddon lengthened his strides to keep pace, trying to accept the High-Warden's words. "Which gods?"

"*Malbreyth*: God of War, *Telacra*: Goddess of Shadows, Darkness, and Betrayal, and of course their father, *Jaidar*."

Caddon nodded, though the thought of defying the gods broke all logic. Nevertheless, he knew the gods would assault The North if the opportunity arose, and if *Jaidar* was denied, *Enecki* would gain no foothold, thus neither would the lesser gods of the Pantheon. Of the remaining gods, only *Morgan* freely accessed The North, for no Mortal Kingdom could deny him by any power. "How do you intend to accomplish this? To defy the gods is not an act often done, even in our colored past."

"I will pay the price necessary to call Northern entities and convince them to use their combined strength to shield The North. These entities have enough strength to defy the gods, no matter their wrath."

"Then what need do you have of me?"

"I need your help to summon the Rhawn Mountains. Their spirits are tied to their mountains and cannot leave unless called with a formal summons using wizardry. Thus I need a wizard to conduct the summons."

"Why not just travel to the mountains themselves?"

"Because I need more than one spirit and the greatest of the Rhawn must all be present if they are to bring their strength fully to bear on *Telacra*."

Caddon considered the High-Warden's words. If he spoke true, Caddon needed to complete a summoning from before the era of men or gods. This summoning would be something primordial and require more than just vast power. The great works of elder days could not be done anywhere, only in locations of deep magic; locations that endured in The North, revered by all its inhabitants. "Where will we complete this summons?"

The High-Warden slowed his strides, allowing Caddon to slacken his running pace. "It is below Antiark. All cities have their catacombs and secrets; their crypts of forgotten stone obscuring resonances from the Before-Age."

Stepping free of the Tower, he inhaled the wind with its thousands of flavors and tasted the joyous life exploding out of the snowflakes. The Northern sun's frail light broke through the brooding heavens in a flash of golden light—a harbinger of **Enecki's** arrival—and shattered his moment of peace.

He shifted aside, allowing Caddon, who muttered an incantation against the cold, to exit the Tower and begin their descent.

Stepping from the final stair into the forest of stone, he came to a sudden halt, one boot upon the earth, one still on the stair. Behind him, Caddon halted. With a low growl, the High-Warden finished his descent, his gaze flicking heavenwards. A brittle flutter of wings answered his attention as a sickly bird fell from the sky; its wing beats infrequent and scarce strong enough to keep it aloft. He caught the falling bird, a foul taint oozing off its feathers. Internally the North's rage multiplied, straining against his restrictions and increasing the strain upon his mind.

Crooning, he brushed a thumb over the falcon's breast, clearing away a coat of putrid, black dust. The falcon revived at his touch, its eyes blinking open as its chest rose with a shallow breath. With a gentle hand, he turned the falcon over and ran his fingers through its feathers, scraping away the corruption as one would wash the dirt off a plate. Slowly, color returned to the falcon's feathers, their tarnished state ameliorating until a sheen of gloss coated its wings. "There, it's better now." He lifted it to eye level. "Now, tell me what's wrong."

The falcon made no sound but nuzzled its head in the palm of his hand. The High-Warden cocked his head, the wind rustling around them, a low susurration that demanded his attention. His face hardening, the High-Warden said, "Show me." His eyes misted over, changing to mirror the falcon's. The wind's susurrations increased, though no breeze touched them or any of the surrounding trees.

A deep snarl, starting low and growing stronger, emanated from the High-Warden, startling Caddon. "What's wrong?" Caddon watched the High-Warden's eyes revert to normal, barring the sudden, icy rage overflowing within them.

The High-Warden cast the falcon into the skies, the temperature plummeting. "Something has occurred, Arch-Wizard; it is best you remain here while I deal with it. I promised the council there was no danger to you; that is a promise I cannot keep if you accompany me."

The High-Warden strode forward, power coalescing about him like winds in a hurricane, thickening the air and focusing the attention of all those with the eyes to see.

"High-Warden, I would accompany you." He gave no sign of slowing, so Caddon broke into a jog. "I am not of The North, but this land has housed me for a hundred and ten years; it is more a home to me than the West. Let me help."

The High-Warden glanced at him, no softening in his eyes of winter. He spoke and his words rumbled with the age of mountains, seared with the cold of winter's heart, "I cannot promise your safety or usefulness, nor will I risk your loss or suffer the retribution that derives from it."

Caddon moved to stand before him, stalling his advance with a hand. "The North will not suffer for this. I promise."

The High-Warden considered him and then stepped past. "Follow me."

9

A Harbinger Of Crows

Dieharamon leaned on the crumbling stone balustrade, watching the *Annuir'Hyme* rush past. He could feel the river's power through the stone. He saw it in the incandescent, unblemished water. He heard it in the ancient thunder of its currents and tasted it in the exquisite spray.

Buckets on ropes trundled up past him, dripping water onto the intricately painted tiles underfoot and soaking in the red dust that blanketed them. Teams of Avaran slaves hauled ropes attached to the pulleys from scaffolding throughout the Hold, ferrying the priceless water to the chasm walls and the farms burrowed there: drug farms, meat farms, insect farms and even a few fruit or vegetable gardens, all owned by one Kalvonder or another. Almost no Avarans even knew how to grow food anymore or raise cattle; the Kalvonders had ensured it.

Avaran warriors patrolled on either side of him, masked to indicate loyalty devoted solely to Sahdaen. It was a shallow truth: Kalvonders had heavy purses and represented most of the people that mattered in Sahdaen, meaning they represented most of Sahdaen.

More Avarans labored bare backed just below Dieharamon, hacking at the wall of Quosh reeds growing along the *Annuir'Hyme* with stone sickles. The hard brown reeds rattled at every thwack, filling the air with red dust from their seeds. It was brutal work, and the best most Avarans could hope to achieve, offering both proximity to the water and security from the sun.

The Kalvonders' residences lined the precipice behind him, some built close enough to exchange wineskins and others partitioned by a vast distance of unworked stone.

A shudder coursed through the balustrade, reminding Dieharamon how truly old this part of Sahdaen was. Everything was cracked; the tiles, the walls, the statues, and the mansions; magecraft could deter structural entropy for only so long. These were the ancestral abodes of the oldest Kalvonder families, bound in blood to their descendants. Most were empty, their sand-dusted window frames barren of glass or shutters. Every door was an ivory masterpiece of elaborately carved images, equal parts chronicle and avowal of supremacy. Despite their power and cunning, Kalvonder families died through conflict, betrayal, debt or, on the rare occasion, just age. In the wake of this, their mansions are closed, and their possessions locked within until an heir surfaces to reopen them, or another is appointed. Not that any bloodline with that authority had appeared since the Dragon Lords fell. Not even the Wizard Kings of Isaracc had succeeded, and they had tried repeatedly over a millennium.

Except, Valeriius was one such resurfaced heir. His ancestors had been eradicated centuries prior in the fall of Isaracc. Only one child survived the empire's sundering, Valeriius' antecedent. Generations passed and his family gradually accrued affluence until Valeriius reopened his ancestral doors. Or so the story went. In truth, it was the wild fantasy of drug-addled Avarans fused to the measured speculation of Kalvonders trying vainly to breach the smoke and mirrors Valeriius never stopped fashioning.

Dieharamon pushed off the balustrade and headed southward, his thoughts lingering on Dava. Overhead the sun ascended to its seventh-Vigil, marking the late hour; he had dallied too long, first with Dava and now with the *Annuir'Hyme*. Valeriius tolerated Dieharamon's quirks and wanderings, but his patience was finite. Dieharamon was more than a gladiator; he was a bruiser, an intimidator, a trophy, a servant, a protector, and assassin; in fact, he was anything Valeriius thought him capable of. The only task he never set for Dieharamon was breeding.

He passed beneath a statue of *Ashshand*—depicted here as a serpent— and shifted to put as much distance between himself and the effigy as possible. The Avarans worshiped *Ashshand* from fear. The fear did not originate in the Clergy, but they propagated it gleefully, expanding their authority ever further across the Avarus Desert, dragging the Avarans ever deeper into their control.

The statues of *Ashshand* grew more abundant and lavish the further south he trod, rendering the rare statues of *Arawn* all the more insignificant.

He hastened his stride, eager to escape the watchful eyes of *Ashshand* and *Arawn*. Looking ahead he saw Valeriius' mansion climbing sedately up the chasm's walls, its towers peeked in luscious mahogany. He hesitated just outside the mansion, one foot on the wide sandstone stair.

One of the sentries shoved off his column with a swaggering sneer and strolled down the stairs, grinding a clay pipe between his blackened teeth and slapping the red dust from his cheap robe. He stopped three steps up from Dieharamon, chewed pensively and exhaled a cloud of green vapors with a contented huff. "Did you enjoy your ramble? I hope you did because Valeriius sent the whole lot of us out searching for you a couple hours back."

The guard smiled, snickering to his friends with a flash of malevolence, and struck him. Dieharamon teetered off the steps, one hand snapping out to catch the attending banister. The guard inhaled again, a deep, unnatural intake, and belched more smoke in his face. "Do you know what it's like trying to find a man in this Hold? Now here you are, just walking up like you don't know the hour and are a freeman." The guard sauntered down a couple stairs, until he stood level with Dieharamon, and struck him again.

Dieharamon felt his ire surge, a habit cultivated by Valeriius, but repressed it. The guard leaned closer until their noses almost touched, his breath bombarding Dieharamon with the scent and flavor of a dozen separate drugs. The guard grinned and attempted, unsuccessfully, to shove him. "I think you owe me."

Dieharamon thrust back, easily tossing the guard onto his backside. "No, I don't."

The guard scrambled to his feet, hissing in affronted rage. "You'll do as I say if you want to live! I won't be whipped for you, not without getting something back!"

The guard lunged forward, but Dieharamon shoved him back with a hand. "I will not kill for you, I will not die for you, and I will not bleed for you. Now control yourself before Valeriius sends me to kill you." He stepped past the guard, grappling with his own mounting rage. The other guards let him pass and rushed to intercept their companion when he scrambled to his feet with a torrent of profanity. They knew their companion's life was forfeit if his drug use reached Valeriius, so their actions were to avert their own summary executions.

Dieharamon hesitated at the ivory doors, inspecting the hundreds of faces inscribed thereupon with a hand half extended toward the latch. The images centered on a pair of men, both monolithic and godlike as they effused power in rolling tides of devastation. They strove against one another, one unarmed while the other held a steel maul and celestial sword. A sea of faces and warring bodies surrounded them, the insignificant conflict of lesser men whose girth gave it spurious importance. The scene depicted a pivotal moment in Cardolyn Tyier's war of conquest. It recreated the commencement of the Border War, where the Southern forces finally managed to halt the Imperial Emperor's advance.

The battle occurred along the Inland Sea's southern shore. The vastly superior Avaran host waited on the beach in horrified witness as Cardolyn Tyier's fleet sailed implacably through a sea the god emperor had set aflame, their sails billowing in a divine wind, and the air drowning beneath the weight of their drums. It was to be the last battle in Cardolyn Tyier's war of conquest. The Imperial Emperor had already devoured all lands south of the Rhawn Mountains, up until the Inland Sea, and west of the *Annuir'Hyme*, shattering the remnants of Isaracc in the process.

With their puppet kingdom shattered, the Kalvonders abandoned their northern territories to Cardolyn Tyier. In preparation for his inevitable advance, they summoned their hoards to gather upon the Inland Sea and hurled their vanguard across the waters to contest Cardolyn Tyier's onslaught. In response, the Imperial Emperor had set the sea ablaze, incinerating every Southern Trireme in seconds. To this day, the Inland Sea continues to regurgitate charred carrion and cracked debris for anglers to discover.

Cardolyn Tyier resumed his march of conquest immediately, leaving hewn forests and salted earth in his wake. The Kalvonders contested Cardolyn Tyier's landing, hurling their unnumbered thousands against his disembarking legions. The flames devouring the Inland Sea became red with blood. The elements commanded by the Southern mages clashed with the amalgamated power of the wizards, paladins, and clerics serving Cardolyn Tyier.

Siege engines anchored on the decks of massive dreadnaughts hurled crates of burning pitch into the Southern ranks. The light of both the stars and the moon failed, obscured behind a curtain of arrows and wizard fire while the Imperial Army methodically pressed up the beach, leaving a carpet of dead in their wake.

Eventually the Avarans broke before the Imperial Army's advance. They fled, scattering their implements of war, crushing their earthen ramparts, and trampling on the wounded. The perfect Imperial ranks expanded in their wake, driving azure pennants into the stained sand.

For a Turning, the Imperial Army lingered on the coast, excavating trenches and erecting fortifications. The wind never slowed in its drive southward, propelling an endless stream of galleons and dreadnoughts laden with soldiers and supplies. The Imperial Army burgeoned over those twelve days, amassing two hundred thousand infantry and twenty thousand cavalry.

Scrambling to reform their forces, the Kalvonders watched Cardolyn Tyier amass his legions and supplies. They knew they could not defeat the Imperial Emperor. Thus, far from any Hold, the Kalvonders gathered centuries of hoarded power and twisted the little soulcraft they knew into a new guise. They birthed a monstrosity, binding it to them as they bound their Tragnashi. Then the Kalvonders sent their monster to the Inland Sea to challenge Cardolyn Tyier.

They began their counterattack with the new Turning, hurling their renewed hoards against Cardolyn Tyier's legions. Under the fall of night and the monstrosity's command, the Southern host swarmed the entrenched Imperial Army.

They warred throughout the long hours of the night, but with the Inland Sea at their back, the Imperial Army had no retreat. Through sheer numbers, the Kalvonders' host began to prevail, swallowing the barricades and trenches, drowning their foes in a sea of lives cast forward without a thought for the cost in blood. Simultaneously, the Kalvonders' monstrosity ravaged the Imperial ranks.

When dawn came, the Imperial Army verged on collapse, exhausted from the night of war, horrified by the wanton disregard for life. The dead overflowed the trenches, broke the barricades, and suffocated the living. The roiling sea of Avarans never faltered, never ended and never ceased crashing into the Imperial Army. However, with the rising dawn, Cardolyn Tyier, the Imperial Emperor and god-spawn, answered the Kalvonders' challenge.

He descended from the heavens, ablaze like a falling star, and struck the earth, rupturing it for miles. The Avarans fled, leaving their monstrosity to combat Cardolyn Tyier. The creature hurled itself against the god-spawn, every blow sundering the world further. Cardolyn Tyier smote his foe, destroying the amethyst body but failing to kill the wretched soul. This was the commencement of the Border War.

The Kalvonders have warred with the Imperial Army for the last hundred years, futilely attempting to drive their foe back across the sea. To this day, no one knows why the Imperial Emperor stayed his advance.

Dieharamon did not know why the door depicted the scene of Cardolyn Tyier and the monster's battle, or what the image concealed; Valeriius' residence far predated the conflict depicted here. Still, he always took a moment to inspect the door, to remind himself the Kalvonders were far from impregnable. The Kalvonders maintained the battle was a victory and reinforced this assertion at every opportunity. It was all a façade, however; every Kalvonder and Avaran knew Cardolyn Tyier would destroy them all whenever he decided to finish his conquest.

The ivory portal screeched, opening inward just enough for him to slip into the musty darkness. A shuffling Avaran closed the door behind him, throwing the antechamber into almost complete obscurity. Dieharamon blinked at the entrenched shadows, watching the vague shape of a decrepit Avaran exit through a side doorway. As his eyes adjusted to the unlit hall, he began to distinguish its contents.

He glimpsed slaves in dark attire scurrying through the antechamber with muted steps and furtive murmurs while bone-clad guards surveyed all that transpired from the doorways and columns without disturbing the eerie silence, their gazes deceptively lax. He also saw a few beleaguered retainers navigating the antechamber as well, creeping in their finery and heavy robes, cautious to maintain Valeriius' ordained serenity.

Striding through the ranks of statuesque columns, his steps echoed through the hall, contrasting the terrified silence everyone else fought to maintain.

Instinct slowed and quieted his step as he neared the hall's daunting centerpiece: an onyx statue standing twice the height of a man on two legs, twisting at the waist to peer over stooped shoulders. It was dog-like with an elongated cranium and jaw, but the skin was rough and plated.

The crushing weight of an ancient consciousness settled on Dieharamon, compelling him to avert his eyes and lengthen his stride. The statue, or rather the Archient, stalked his movements, blinking once with every step. The Archient's intellect was wild and immortal, sizzling as it jumped from thought to thought in bursts of momentum. The air was laden with the flavor of its power, teasing his senses and making him twitch with nervous energy.

The Archient settled onto its forepaws with a low rumble, calling Dieharamon to halt and turn. It stepped from the dais, nostrils flaring as a second pair of lids clicked shut, changing the color of its liquid eyes from orange to indigo.

Immortal and endowed with pure magic for blood, the Archients were the alpha predators of the Avarus Desert. For the most part, they kept to themselves and wandered the vast southern wastelands, feeding on the equally violent fauna. However, they would occasionally ally themselves with men and trade their power for a mortal lifetime of pampering and worship. This particular Archient, *Eunarhe*, had allied itself with Valeriius.

Dieharamon had no idea what Valeriius had offered *Eunarhe*. What he did know was that it was one of only three Archients in Sahdaen, two of which were recorded while *Eunarhe* was not. One had allied itself with Kyar, a Kalvonder of middling influence, and the other served Trerrock, one of the Triad.

Dieharamon lifted his hands mollifyingly. *Eunarhe* growled again, pressing its flaring nostrils up against his throat and sneezing. It reared with a snarl, sending Dieharamon staggering back, his throat burning from *Eunarhe's* touch. The Archient gazed upon him, and every servant, slave, attendant, and guard across the antechamber froze. *Eunarhe* shook its head and turned away with a snort. Dieharamon watched in bewilderment as *Eunarhe* returned to its dais. He brushed a hand over his throat, feeling the burnt skin.

Eunarhe always noted Dieharamon's passage but never to this extent. More than once, Dieharamon had seen *Eunarhe* crush an intruder or newcomer into a slop that was later fed to the Takk Hounds. Without fail, they were revealed to be assassins or men bound to another Kalvonder. Dieharamon must have done something to warrant *Eunarhe's* attention, but he could think of nothing.

He slowly continued inward, releasing a sigh as the Archient continued to ignore him, and slipped away through a small arch with a sheet of leather for a door. He let the flap close behind him and began his descent, first counting the steps and then the doorways. The walls were smooth beneath his hand, carved out of the stone rather than built with weak mortar and human hands.

He turned right at the third doorway and pushed through a thin barrier of string beads. The clatter of beads caused those on the other side to glance over, the single oil lantern's negligible light painting ghastly shadows on the walls.

The walls held centuries of scratched words from those condemned to an existence as Tragnashi. The words were etched in a dozen different tongues heralding from the West, East, and South. Some were prayers, others: hopes, vows of redemption or hate, and a rare few were recitations, tales of the past or the present. Dieharamon had always known which was which. The vows were always written in blood; the recitations were written in the corners with a constrained hand. Hopes were the fewest he found and always hidden away in alcoves or behind the furniture for fear of discovery. The prayers outnumbered all others combined, covering the cracked walls with rank upon rank of uneven calligraphy. Once, Dieharamon had written his share of prayers, vows, and hopes. That was long past now, and every word obliterated by his own hand.

He pushed inward through the beads; his shoulders hunched beneath the low ceiling. The four of them watched him, their hair bound in the braid of Tragnashi. They kneeled or sat on the floor around a short, cracked table held together by fraying ropes of leather and tattered clothing too moth-eaten for any other use. His boots rasped on the floor as he inched by, pressed against the right wall for lack of space.

Twelve sleeping alcoves occupied the walls, six to a side and each just large enough for a man to curl up inside. Most of them were empty, but some had a trinket or memory stashed within. Dieharamon passed these without a glance and took a seat in the last alcove.

Staring at his hands, he exhaled and rubbed them together. The other four kept silent, waiting for him to speak. At last he looked up, rubbing his neck. "As you can see, I am still alive." Their tension dissipated and they all settled back. Suppressing a grimace, Dieharamon undid the collar of his shirt against a sudden flush of heat. "Well, who's dead?"

The four at the table set aside their dice and bones. The one nearest to Dieharamon twisted in his seat to face him and made a shallow gesture of greeting before leaning back against the table. "Vowran's dead."

Dieharamon tugged at his collar again. "Nine months is still more than any of you expected. Who, or what, killed him?"

The Avaran shrugged and spat. "He had the Fire Pit today; one of the geysers torched him. Damned bastard refused to die, so Ysar ran him through after he finished with everybody else. About time he died too; I lost a lot betting for him to die over these last months. Speaking of which, how did you know he was going to make it over seven months, but not the full year?"

Dieharamon scratched his neck, the flush of heat spreading. "He was an eastern lordling; they're always trained for war. Moreover, he had something to fight for. If he survived a year in the arena, his Kalvonder would send him back in exchange for his younger brother—the one that sold him." The Avaran nodded, and Dieharamon shrugged. "It was simple enough; with his strength, training and lack of prior drugging to destroy his intellect, no gladiator rivaled him. And he wouldn't survive the year because his Kalvonder profited more from his defeat than his success."

An Avaran with a face of scars and missing teeth leaned across the table. "What did you get today, Dieharamon? Anyone notable?"

"No, the Kalvonders won't let their prized gladiators fight me anymore; and I was given the swamp."

Taor, the scarred Avaran, leaned back with a snort. "Well, someone clearly wants you dead. Twelve swamps running, *Ashshand* must really hate you."

Dieharamon shrugged again, suppressing the urge to flinch when Taor spoke the Great-Immortal's name. "I'll survive."

The Avaran who spoke first chuckled, showing off stained and filed teeth, "That you do, Dieharamon, that you do. I reckon you could have killed Vowran and saved me a lot of work in the process! I would have shared the money if you killed him when I asked you to!" The Avaran, Fatar, dug into a bowl of undercooked beetles with a grin and tossed one into his mouth.

Taor pulled the bowl out of his reach. "If you have any more there won't be enough to last us through the Turning." He refocused on Dieharamon. "As we mentioned, Ysar survived along with Kass and Jaur. Hyr and Qurr didn't; killed each other in the forest. Rather, Hyr killed him, then died of blood loss leaving some coward as the victor." Taor sighed. "Ah, I liked Hyr. I wish he could have lasted a little longer than four months."

Dieharamon pressed his head against the ceiling of his alcove, watching the shadows dance on the opposite wall. "How long is it now that Ysar, Kass, and Jaur have survived? Also, is there anybody else, anybody new?"

Fatar laughed, interrupting Taor, "Ysar's a year old now and officially the second oldest after you. Though he won't be living much longer, rumor is he's looking real ugly now. He's missing a little too much and has a few too many things broken." Fatar spat again and giggled.

Taor glared at Fatar. "Kass is at five months now and good for at least another month so long as he doesn't get paired against Jaur or Ysar. Jaur's only three months, but no one's touched that monster yet. I don't like him; he loves killing a little too much. But I guess that is what to expect from a man groomed since birth for the arena. Everybody's saying he was bred to kill you, and after what I've seen, I don't doubt it. Jaur always hunts the largest competitors first; takes out their legs then lets the beasts finish them off. As for newcomers, there are two that survived their third Angorat'Wass, though one's pretty scarred up. A handful of others have survived four. The two who survived their third bout are Oreh, the scarred one, and Prii."

Dieharamon nodded, he had seen Jaur fight; he always watched those who survived. He tapped his fist against the alcove, working his jaw and trying to find the words.

One of the other Avarans leaned forward, scrutinizing him through the flamboyant shadows. "What's wrong?"

"They are organizing a special Angorat'Wass in which every gladiator across Sahdaen will compete. It is to occur at the end of this Turning. So if anybody owes you, collect it now while they're still alive." The other four Tragnashi fell silent, even Fatar.

Fatar's shock slowly became a smirk. "That's it! Your times up, bastard! You're not surviving this!" He threw his head back with a howl of laughter, stomping his feet into the floor with such force the table shook.

Dieharamon's temper surged. "Don't you think I know that?" This only augmented Fatar's merriment. Dieharamon averted his eyes, trying to ignore Fatar's glee, trying to control his rising anger. He pulled at the collar of his shirt again, trying to release some of the feverish heat afflicting his skin. The motion caused his gloves to further deteriorate.

Fatar leaned forward onto his knees, still grinning. "Is the little man angry? Are you scared of dying? Of facing your divine judgement for the hundreds of us you've killed? I can tell you it won't be pretty, not with how you hate the gods!"

Taor leaned across the table and slapped the back of Fatar's head. "Someone really needs to kill you. Ask yourself, what happens when Dieharamon dies? Guess what the answer is: it means one of us is going into the arena next. Moreover, none of us is going to survive as long as he did, which means we're going to start dying off. I don't know about you, but I don't want to die."

Fatar reclined onto the table. "Don't worry, Taor, I'm in the arena next when Dieharamon's dead, and I won't be dying easily. After this Turning, no other Kalvonder will have anybody that knows anything about fighting, and no one's as good at killing as I am. Not even Dieharamon; he's too soft."

Dieharamon began pacing, rolling his shoulders to burn away the energy prickling along his limbs. He ignored Fatar's comment, knowing that cruelty did not increase his chances of survival. Strength, skill, and brutality augmented his survivability, the last because it assured quick kills and inspired fear. Fatar continued laughing, but Taor, noting his restless energy, focused on Dieharamon. Taor hefted the oil lantern to cast the light further in Dieharamon's direction. "You all right?"

"Yes, yes, I'm fine, Taor. Go back to your game."

Taor ignored him and slipped around the table, lifting the lamp higher. Dieharamon winced and tugged at his collar again, fighting the urge to pace. It felt like there was a flame blossoming in the cavity of his chest. The fire burned him, but it was a burn closer to pleasure than pain. Taor lifted a hand and ran it across his forehead. "You're sweating, Dieharamon, and you have a high fever. Your eyes are dilated and losing their color." Taor gave an aggrieved sigh. "You didn't take your medicine this morning."

"I hate that stuff."

Taor shook his head in reprimand. "So you keep telling us, but you just can't stop taking them; your body is addicted. If you stop taking them, you will die. Besides, you know what follows when you deprive an addict." Taor pushed Dieharamon towards the back of the room. "And I am not going to die because you refused to accept logic and the inevitable result of your stubbornness. Go take your medicine; they are still in the cabinet unless you burned them."

Dieharamon began to refuse Taor's command, but a wave of nausea stole his words. He doubled over, hacking as Taor caught him. "See, it's already started. Can you honestly say you are strong enough to survive the denial? Can you honestly say you won't hurt us when we have to stop you taking more than you can handle?"

Dieharamon could not. He had seen too many men lost in their addictions. He had seen lone men with wild eyes and not a weapon to their name assault whole caravans. He had seen entire streets burn in a fit of rage when a supplier refused someone incapable of paying. Dieharamon slowly pulled himself up and sagged in defeat.

Taor hurried to a waist-high cabinet recessed into the left wall. Pulling aside the covering fabric, he retrieved a clay vial the length of his hand. Taor returned and offered it to him. "Here."

He accepted it, braced himself against the harsh flavor, and took a quick gulp before thrusting the vial back at Taor. The volatile drug rolled down his throat, silencing the burning within. He spat out what remained of the vile flavor and slumped into his alcove, ice spreading through his insides until he ached with it. He curled up and scrunched into the alcove, shivering as they all stared at him. Taor tossed a threadbare blanket over him, but it did nothing to alleviate the ice.

A burst of pain woke Dieharamon, sending him lurching upright against the ceiling of his alcove. Gasping through the fog of sleep, he tumbled onto the floor in a heap. The boot landed again, smashing into his side and flipping him over before pressing down.

"Wake up," a masculine voice barked as the boot shoved him against the wall and relented.

Coughing, Dieharamon scrambled to a sitting position against the wall and looked at his antagonist. The Avaran glowered at him, arms crossed as the corners of his supercilious lips curled. He wore rich boots pulled over extravagant trousers. A loose silk shirt climbed high about his throat, marking him as a favored servant. Over these, he wore a long orange coat open at the front and snug on the shoulders from extra padding. Flames were inked into the coat alongside runes and salamanders, warning all others of what this man was. Still half asleep from his medicine, Dieharamon crawled to his feet and bowed at the waist, low enough to erase any perceived slight but not so low as he would to a Kalvonder. "What is the will of Valeriius Kalvonder, mage-born?"

The fire mage moved as if to strike Dieharamon but hesitated, glancing at the door in annoyance. Dieharamon followed his gaze but saw nothing through the bead curtains. "It is the will of Valeriius Kalvonder that you join him in his chambers, Dieharamon Tragnashi." The fire mage bent and hauled Dieharamon to his feet, almost throwing him forward in the process.

Straightening, he glanced questioningly at Taor where he hugged the room's far wall, as far from the fire mage as he could get. Taor shrugged and continued watching the fire mage as he strode past and thrust the table aside. Dieharamon hastily followed him, his eyes focused on the ground.

Outside the room, the corridors echoed with the quiet tread of servants and guards rushing about their obligations. The servants walked or slipped past Dieharamon innocuously, but the guards shoved him aside at every opportunity. As one though, they avoided the fire mage.

They ascended through the passages, the temperature increasing with every floor. The lights diminished in both number and vibrancy, restricted to the increasingly rare doors and passageways. In contrast, the statues of *Arawn*, each one carrying his chained book and lantern, grew more prevalent. If Valeriius worshiped any god, it was the God of Death.

Gradually the other occupants of the passageways attenuated, first the servants then the guards. All the while, Dieharamon walked ahead of the fire mage in silence. The fire mage's nervous twitch and glances did little to improve his state of mind; fire mages hated being surrounded by large amounts of stone.

At the passage's end, his steps slowed as he neared the pool of light around Valeriius' simple door, and for once, the fire mage did not strike him. He glanced back, wondering why, and discovered his escort had not entered the circle of light.

"What are you waiting for?" the fire mage asked slowly, enunciating each word with weighted precision. If Dieharamon arrived late, the fire mage would suffer.

Dieharamon returned his attention to the door. He inched closer, advancing uneasily between the flanking statues on either side of the door and crouching beneath their upraised hands. They made no movement to deter him, causing his heart to sink further. Taking a last calming breath, Dieharamon knocked twice.

Soundlessly the door swung inward of its own volition, revealing the tasteful chamber beyond. Candles hung from the ceiling, throwing their gentle light across towering shelves laden with books, silk scrolls, clay tablets, and glass spheres. An opulent ruby chandelier hung over a large mahogany desk bearing further scrolls and books. Behind the desk, standing beside his chair was Valeriius Kalvonder.

The Kalvonder was scrutinizing one of the glass spheres from the shelves, but when the door opened, Valeriius glanced up with a serpentine flick of his eyes. His cool gaze scanned Dieharamon briefly before motioning him to a mat on the desk's other side. Dieharamon obeyed, keeping his eyes averted. Valeriius resumed his inspection of the glass sphere, lifting it higher for better light.

When Valeriius continued ignoring him, Dieharamon glanced over the manuscripts splayed across the desk. He could read the Merchant's tongue and Avaran Shi-Ta—low tongue—but possessed only a rudimentary knowledge of the Isaracc alphabet. Not that he ever hoped to possess more than a rudimentary understanding of Isaracci; that language was an intentional cipher designed by the Empire's founders to disguise their spell casting. The only race even capable of fully understanding it was Avarans. Still, he could recognize most of the tongues written on the manuscripts. In his brief glance, he noted a dozen languages from across the Mortal Kingdoms, a few recognizable only due to their rarity. He saw the thin, sprawling hieroglyphics of Isaracc, the rough, ordered letterings of the Paladin Empire, the runes of the Lynn, the beautiful arching calligraphy of the Ie'Dara, and the flowing streams of Blessed Remanas.

At last Valeriius set down the sphere, a reservoir of knowledge called an *Acculm*, and focused his attention on a large book lying open across his desk. "Dieharamon, do you know aught of the Descendant Empires?"

Dieharamon nodded once then, at a slight nod from Valeriius Kalvonder, elaborated with only a trivial stutter, "The three Descendant Empires are nations that believed themselves the true inheritors of *Lord Arthramain Roy'al's* kingdom. The first was Rhiatan, a democracy that rose to prominence a little after the fall of Blessed Remanas. The second Descendant Empire was Alarach, a republic born in the alliance that destroyed Andaur. The third Descendant Empire is the Paladin Empire of Cardolyn Tyier which ascended to dominance by breaking its predecessor: Isaracc."

Valeriius tapped a word on the open manuscript. "As you are originally from the Paladin Empire, do you know anything of the Rhiatan script?" Dieharamon shook his head. "This manuscript is written in the Rhiatan tongue. It was written in the first years after the Crimson Empire's fall and speaks of something that will soon become profoundly important to Kalvonders and Avarans alike." Closing the book, Valeriius spun it to face Dieharamon, motioning for him to read the title. Perspiring, Dieharamon leaned over the table. He could not read the beautiful script; the golden lettering defied his knowledge.

Valeriius waited while Dieharamon struggled before speaking. "It is a history of the Muntalabac House, a main perpetrator in the Succession War. It is mostly a list of names and the associated atrocities." The torches and candles scattered across the room flared and dimmed. Valeriius regarded Dieharamon and smiled, something coiling in his eyes.

Knowing it could lead to painful repercussion, Dieharamon nevertheless queried, "Why are the Muntalabacs important?"

Valeriius ignored Dieharamon's question. "This book is significant because it is a window into their lives and their acts; their hubris and their violence, their power and their fetters." Valeriius spoke slowly, each word articulated and controlled. His gestures resembled his speech: slow and methodical.

Dieharamon felt a shiver run the length of his spine. "But what does a man thousands of years dead have to do with the Avarans?"

Valeriius smiled. "Time heals all wounds, corrupts all memories and reveals all things, Dieharamon." Valeriius stroked his fingers over the manuscript's cover and it undulated, shrinking to the size of a hand, the cover changing to new leather, and its title warping into a different tongue.

Valeriius pushed the book aside, his long fingers tapping the opulent cover. At this signal, there came the sound of pattering feet as the Aparthii slave woman rose from a mat behind the desk to collect the book. "Return that to the proper library this time."

She touched her brow to the desk and fled; the book held close to her breast.

Valeriius sat in his backless chair, resting his elbows on the cushioned armrests and clasping his hands. His seat cloth, a gentle mauve in color, gleamed with the luster of a true Artisan Weaver, but carried a single design, this too radiantly fine: a slim, sinuous dragon in gold along the top edge. "Time has certainly taken its due toll on the Muntalabacs and Avenar. The former is already forgotten, their atrocities and their labors attributed to other, lesser men. The Avenar have fared little better; they are seen as little more than philanthropic bureaucrats with illusions of divinity."

Dieharamon rubbed his forehead as an ache began pounding in his skull. Desperately he sought for why Valeriius was interested in a lost noble house. He did not seek their power when he had just declared it forgotten.

"But …"—he hesitated—"why do they matter?"

Again Valeriius smiled. "Because less than a fortnight's journey from us is a delegation, emissaries even, bearing tidings of war. In their midst, is a man called Sinnitar Muntalabac." Every candle flame in the room cowered in upon itself. "This delegation is preceded by a murder of twisted and blighted crows that owe no allegiance to *Arawn*. They are the harbinger of Sinnitar Muntalabac's coming. He sends them because we of the South have not forgotten; we remember and we are prepared to welcome the return of our

Masters. And so must you. Conveniently, he will arrive just in time for your performance in the next Angorat'Wass."

10

A Dreamer's Hall

The thirty-first day of the New Order's incursion.

The coracle carrying the High-Warden and Caddon slowed as it crossed from the city currents into the sheltered lake. The water beneath them balked at progressing but continued when the High-Warden urged it forward. Secluded from the city by mist, a forested island with a bank of white sand occupied the lake. It was one of many gardens intended for meandering or reflection scattered throughout Antiark. Except a shapeless evil now beset it, causing the trees to stoop beneath the weight of corruption and tumors of rot to swell across the sand.

The High-Warden inhaled, tasting the stagnant air, and grimaced. There was more to the corruption than a sickness in the trees; the air festered on his tongue, and the wind blowing from the island felt like tar on his skin.

This poison derived from something ancient, an evil imprisoned since before this Age began. The High-Warden knew little more than that. *Winsyria* had clouded The North's memory of it and confided only its existence to him. This evil was meant to be forgotten. However, in the final moments of its imprisonment, some pieces escaped, scattering to the far corners but unable to cross the Rhawn Mountains. It was the High-Wardens' obligation to eradicate those pieces, but they were elusive, little more than memories or rampant emotions sustained by what they destroyed. Most had been purged over the last millennia, but one appeared to have survived. At least, he hoped so; the possibility existed that current events had debilitated the bindings, allowing the original monster to escape. If this proved true, the High-Warden feared for The North. Creatures were bound during the Age of Gods for a reason.

The coracle ran ashore, scraping the sand and conflicting starkly with the ravenous black veins of corruption extending toward the water. The *Annuir'Hyme* churned in wild rage, cleansing the corruption wherever it touched. The High-Warden vaulted ashore, crouching to dig his fingers into the sand. The corruption flared white at his touch and turned to ash, receding toward the forest.

Caddon followed, stumbling as he stepped onto the beach. His face contorted in sudden pain and he buckled forward, shocked by the corruption. The High-Warden caught his arm, steadying him. "Stay close; it will dull the pain."

A groan emanated from the woods, every tree distorting to the left. The sapphire leaves and bark that should have been white rippled like water as the forest reversed direction, arching to the right, its leaves changing color, through black to rust. The High-Warden advanced to the trees, trying to soothe their pain and shield them. His fingers twitched as they touched an unseen barrier taunting him with the agonized screams of animals. He shattered the barrier, sending the corruption raving into the forest, and drew a pair of curved knives from his belt. Caddon took the proffered weapon, his face pinched from the corruption's residual effects. "What is this for?"

"Mercy." The High-Warden entered the forest, vanishing before Caddon could follow. Bracing himself, Caddon pursued.

The air was thick with a hate that burned their eyes and scoured their throats. The shadows did not resist the light; they forbid it with clawed hands reaching across the boughs of trees and over the earth. Undeterred, the High-Warden slipped further into the forest, brushing a hand against each tree he passed, lessening its suffering. With each touch, he left a white handprint on the bark and withdrew a hand covered with ashes.

An agonized shriek pierced the pall of silence and a stag burst from the underbrush. It crashed, stumbling over roots and through briars toward them, its eyes swollen and veined black. Massive tumors protruded along its spine and around the joints of its legs, some of them ruptured and spilling vile ichors. This creature—driven to madness—rammed into a tree, causing a tumor to explode and spray sizzling bile.

The High-Warden stepped forward, grasped the full-grown stag by the antlers and drove the knife into the tortured animal's heart, ending its misery. He shot a glance over to where Caddon stared in shock. "Kill any that you can."

The earth shifted around the hart's body, black tendrils reaching up hungering fingers to consume the rotting cadaver. Those fingers dug into the animal's skin, darkening the blood running from its many injuries, and dragged it into the earth.

"What is this?" Caddon peered around, endeavoring to pierce the darkness of shifting trees and roots. The bark and leaves flashed black before turning emerald, drawing strength from the High-Warden's presence.

"Evil is a term I hesitate to use, but this, this is an old evil. It has been imprisoned in The North for millennia, bound by *Winsyria*'s power. With the Great-Immortal's absence, it has resurfaced."

"What is it?" Caddon shifted, his senses screaming a warning.

A shadow flitted across the trees, swirling into an emblem: that of a sword thrusting down. A silhouette taller than any man Caddon had seen, excluding the High-Warden, materialized from the forest and reached for the sword.

"Tell your demon no fire; we dare not invite *Jaidar* here to add further malice." The High-Warden, following Caddon's gaze to the shadows, paused and grasped him by the shoulder, breaking the shadow's hold. He pressed onward, pulling Caddon gently along behind him. "If you see something in the shadows, don't look. Do not challenge it, for it will destroy you from within. Stay close."

Caddon risked a glance back at the shadow, but it was gone.

They continued through the forest killing anything tainted by the corruption. Caddon struggled to stay afoot as they traversed deeper into the forest, the land growing ever more corrupted. The earth soon turned gray, strangled by the countless black tendrils superimposing everything. They watched peaceful animals tear each other asunder, and wolves impale themselves onto broken tree limbs with such insane energy their skulls split. They stepped over uprooted trees that bled sap and through underbrush suffocating beneath the corruption's weight.

Everywhere the High-Warden tread, the corruption abated. The shadows lifted and the black tendrils withdrew. The land would sigh in relief and shake itself as if waking from a nightmare only to crumble beneath the corruption again after the High-Warden passed.

After more mercy killings than Caddon cared to remember, they attained the forest's heart. Here, the forest endured, resisting the corruption destroying everything else, except for the central tree. The Ancient reigned immense with old grandeur and simultaneously black with disease. Its branches were leafless, and its scant bark was cracked from incessant bleeding.

The High-Warden entered the clearing, his strides cleansing the mossy bank. Caddon followed, his eyes exploring the vast, tortured Ancient. Taking his borrowed knife by the blade, he lifted the collar of his tunic and withdrew an amulet. It sparked to life in his hands, the power invested in its core stirring at his summons. He felt the *Vydur* stored within, felt rampaging fury, the ceaseless, revolving implosions of its nature striving to break free of its prison. He siphoned just a thread of the power within. There was no danger in using *Vydur* because, unlike the demons, *Vydur* was untainted by *Jaidar's* Chaos.

The *Vydur* within flared at his summons, inundating his body with the searing cold of wizardry and erupting into the knife. The undiluted, unshaped destruction of *Vydur* turned the now tainted blade into an icy, liquid glass dripping through Caddon's clenched fist. He cast the purified remnants aside, hoping he would not have need of the knife later, and shackled the *Vydur* back in the amulet. This accomplished, Caddon reverted his attention to his companion.

The High-Warden looked at the Ancient from the bank of its surrounding lake. The water churned, thrashing against the pervading oily corruption. Like the hands of the damned reaching for deliverance, the pure waters lapped up the bank toward the High-Warden. He answered them, striding into the lake, with ripples of sapphire light, and incinerating the corruption.

The corruption retaliated, surging past him from the forest to coalesce upon the lake and the dying Ancient.

He advanced deeper into the water, each step hurling undulations of sapphire light to cleanse and fortify the lake.

Waist deep in water, he reached the Ancient, the black tendrils writhing across its surface parting with a hiss. He pressed his hand against the bark, causing the Ancient to shudder. The hissing amplified as the black tendrils grudgingly parted, splitting and cracking like the shell of a chrysalis to reveal something crouched amid the Ancient's ruin. The thing in the shadows shifted, advancing upon him without daring the light. Mandibles clacking, the swollen aberration descended toward him, suspended on black webs.

"I am the High-Warden of Winsyria. You are of the Old Darkness, a last cry of rage it uttered before incarceration."

The arachnid clicked, rubbing its forelegs together and hissing in mixed glee and hunger. "No, I am not. I am the venom that will corrupt and destroy The North; that will feast upon her until she is nothing but a tormented husk. I am a promise of reckless hate and reasonless violence, an oath of ancient vengeance and broken laws." The arachnid inched closer, tenebrous strands of corruptive webbing intertwining beneath the bulbous mass of its thorax. The arachnid spoke again, viscous saliva bursting from its maw, "I will consume you, trespasser, and your death will nourish my ascension."

It struck, lurching half off its ledge to slash at him, but he twisted aside, his unblemished knife blurring. The arachnid staggered back, vile blood splattering the water and sizzling. The blade flashed again, severing webs and dismounting the arachnid from its perch. The creature fell shrieking into the lake.

A heartbeat later, filth billowed up to the surface, and its carcass emerged already disintegrating into white ash. The High-Warden flipped the arachnid over, unveiling its glistening gray underbelly, transparent like glass and vacant. He growled and submerged the carcass before returning to the shore.

Sheathing his unblemished knife, the High-Warden exited the lake. "Arch-Wizard, how much fire do you have?"

Caddon blinked. "I can conjure all you require, why?"

The High-Warden ignored the query, directing his gaze to the dozen derangers emerging from the forest in a semi-circle, their white cloaks motionless in the renewed wind and their glass blades driven into the earth. They bowed as one, answering the need without necessity for summons.

A deranger unsheathed his blade from the earth and stepped forward. "What needs to be done, High-Warden?"

"What I destroyed was but a vessel. I need to cut down the Ancient and burn out this evil; the forest will take care of itself after the corruption's heat is expunged."

The faces of the twelve men hardened. Their hands tightened and their backs straightened. They stood like a wall, hardening themselves to the task of removing an Ancient.

The twelve stepped forward, lifting their blades and clasping the hilts to their chests as a new form took shape in the tree. The twelve derangers encircled the High-Warden and offered him their blades. The water churned behind him, indicating a second arachnid gestated on the Ancient. The vile chrysalis split with a grotesque retort, and the arachnid climbed out, reborn and oozing The North's corrupted life essence.

The High-Warden reached for the extended hilt of a sword. Accepting it, he paused at a noise from above and lifted his eyes to the forest's copse. A murder of crows perched there in eerie stillness while a solitary Raven sat perched atop the Ancient, untouched by the rapacious corruption.

The High-Warden directed his sword at the Raven. "Kill that." The derangers, their attention now also on the murder of crows gathering around the lake, followed his eyes. The swordless deranger grabbed the longbow bound to his quiver, drew it—the string attaching itself mid-draw—knocked an arrow and released it in a fluid motion. The arrow hummed its death hymn and passed harmlessly by the fleeing Raven as it cawed in mockery.

The deranger prepared another arrow, but the High-Warden gestured for him to halt. "You won't kill it now." The Raven banked, circling the gathered men, taunting them. He watched it, the glass sword's tip touching the earth. From the trees, the crows joined it, cawing and mocking, hopping on their perches, sending blackened leaves falling into the wind and the lake. The cacophony rose to a strident pitch, causing the arachnid to scream in rage and thrash frantically on its perch, breaking the Ancient's smaller branches.

The circling Raven slowed and halted inches from the High-Warden's face. It cawed once, and the murder fell silent, but the arachnid continued thrashing, breaking the Ancient further. The last branch supporting the arachnid groaned, fractures opening along its length. The Raven returned toward the lake and dove, angling to run its left-wing tip through the water, leaving a stain in its wake. The water pulsed and changed to seething blood. Content with what it achieved, the Raven disappeared into the heavens followed by the murder.

Awash in the departing murder's chaotic shadows, the High-Warden watched the seething blood scale the bank. He took another sword and joined the twin blades, pressing one atop the other as they merged. One by one, he joined twelve blades, the singular growing heavier with every union until all were joined and glowing with a cerulean light. The blood-lake surged, straining for the High-Warden and hissing as it scorched the earth.

Drawing their cowls, the derangers knelt in a circle around the lake, their hands pressed on the tortured earth— arresting the corruption's spread.

The High-Warden returned to the blood-lake, which besieged him with churning waves once again. He advanced undaunted by its assault.

The forest whimpered and leaned inward, branches snapping. The arachnid skittered on a larger limb, snapping and rising on its hind limbs, towering over the High-Warden by half-a-dozen feet. Its girth bulged, turning scarlet as it leeched malevolent energy from the contaminated water. The High-Warden paused, the glass sword held before him—a small light in the deepening shadows. He directed its tip to the arachnid and tightened his grip on the hilt. The forest quieted, sighing as a weight was lifted; the trees leaned back, roots burrowing in the earth anew. The arachnid hissed and retreated. "This land has survived greater evils than you with lesser guardians than I. You will fail; you have already failed."

The arachnid dashed forward, slashing at the High-Warden with an enraged scream, but the branch supporting it cracked beneath its weight. The arachnid plummeted to the bloody water with a cry. But instead of submerging it as before, the bloody water churned and welled up like a pedestal beneath the arachnid as it righted itself. The High-Warden glided forward and slashed, severing the water pedestal at its base and upending the arachnid. The bloody lake welled up again, catching the arachnid again. The High-Warden drew back, raising the glass sword high overhead and drove it into the lake. The cerulean light in the blade flared, searing the blood and healing the tainted water. The arachnid howled and scampered back to the Ancient. The High-Warden stalked after it, driving the arachnid to the shore, where its tumid body shriveled and the livid red and black of its hide tarnished.

The tone of its voice changed, insect-like clicks usurped by a rabid feral cry as it lunged for the ring of derangers. But its movements were ponderous and disjointed, so they repelled it easily. The arachnid righted itself on quivering limbs and shuffled to face the High-Warden. It gathered itself and lunged forward in a final, desperate assault.

The High-Warden advanced, the glass sword flashing to sever the arachnid in twain and cast it thrashing into the water. Black ichors boiled out from its body in a teeming morass of disintegrating flesh. The shadows fled into the trees with a final shriek.

The High-Warden sighed, his heart lightening as the malice abated. He returned to the Ancient, calling stillness to remove any lingering misery. Behind him the forest shook off the last shadows and corruption amid a cacophony of animal sounds as the land cleansed itself.

Caddon watched from the bank, feeling as if he was the bystander in a fable. He had seen shadows without light or casters, water turning into blood, and a hero striving against a villain.

The High-Warden brushed a gentle hand across the Ancient's trunk, mourning the impending death he felt. He closed his eyes and touched his brow to it in mourning. He felt its suffering and its rage at the corruption it had contained, and gently enveloped its spirit into his own. He communed gently, pulling it from its rage. "Rest now; it is done. Your burden is upheld." He felt it calm, releasing its anger like a moth shedding its cocoon. "All these years, you imprisoned it, safeguarding your children." He withdrew from their link, offering wordless gratitude. "Your essence will return to the father and reunite with the land, where you will feed a decade's new growth. I can do no more for you." The last of the Ancient escaped the cairn of its body. The spirit slipped through him, rejoining the earth.

He opened his eyes, seeing only something foul and twisted where the Ancient once reigned. He withdrew a step and took a single pearly flower from its lowest branch. He slipped the many-layered bloom gently onto the water, where it lingered before floating to the bank.

The High-Warden concentrated his will into the length of his sword. The corrupted tree lashed outward with its remaining strength, its branches belaboring him and putrid resin exploding from the bark. He struck, sundering the branches like dried bracken until only the trunk remained, a thin scar running down its stump. He drew back, swinging the sword up and then down.

The tree split in an implosion of water and taint a dozen feet high. It left a bitter testament to its presence: an eviscerated base, sinking to the lake's bottom. Reversing his grip, the High-Warden lifted the blade and drove it through the base as it sunk, destroying the last of it. The water surged again, lurching up the bank with the force of the corruption's demise. The tide of water ceased at the derangers, crashing up and receding.

The High-Warden searched for the bloom and, finding it, touched his hand to the crystalline water, calling ripples to bring the bloom back to him. The lake swirled, ferrying it toward him. The bloom arrived seconds later, joyous in youth and eager to grow. Its fragile roots, already inches long, entwined his welcoming hand. Humming a low song, he lifted the bloom from the water and stepped closer to the Ancient's foundation, beckoning Caddon forward.

Caddon hesitated on the bank, leery of entering what had just been blood. He shook his head to dispel the haunting images and advanced into the lake. The water froze beneath his step, and he hesitated again, uncertain of the ice, before testing it. When it did not break, he proceeded. The High-Warden watched him approach, his hand outstretched.

Reaching the dead Ancient, he grasped the High-Warden's forearm and braced himself against slipping, though his gaze inevitably found the Ancient's ruins in the water. He exhaled at the sadness of it and called the *Vydur* in the amulet again, filling his hands with purifying flame. The water withdrew around him, exposing the split stump. Caddon cast the flames upon it, searing away the last of the Ancient and the last threads of corruption. He persisted until only charred earth remained, the glass sword melting upon the charred ruins.

Gently, the High-Warden took the bloom and set it upon the lake. "You will be birthed in the remnants of your predecessor; draw upon his memories and the strength of the forest to grow. Take up the mantle when you are strong enough to guard this sanctuary until you are called to join the father." The High-Warden slipped the bloom over the crystalline water until he touched the glass pool entrenched in the lake floor. Releasing the bloom's roots, he rose and watched them swim through the liquid glass. It would be decades before the new Ancient could reign, until then the forest would need constant vigilance.

The derangers were already slipping back into the forest. Some would leave Antiark on other tasks, and some would linger to watch the forest.

The High-Warden exited the lake, his clothes dry and his mind returning to the more pressing task of defying the gods. "We must hurry; *Telacra* is ready to begin her assault."

Caddon sprinted after the High-Warden. "What do you intend to do about her?"

"What men call the *Barrier* is not a wall of wizardry or sorcery, Arch-Wizard; it is a law etched into the soul of this land and its inhabitants, man and beast. But now that *Winsyria* has retreated from the world, the law's divine weight has diminished. I can bolster the dwindling power with my own strength, but it is an imperfect treatment, a suppression of the symptoms rather than a cure. This vulnerability provides her with an opportunity, and the longer this conflict lasts, the less strength I will have for the stronger gods of the Dark Pantheon: **Malbreyth** and *Jaidar*. I need help, someone to fortify the *Barrier* against her while I contest the other gods."

"What do you mean? What entity can be more powerful than the gods, they are ascended?"

"The Mortal Kingdoms have seen three Ages: this one ruled by mortals and its predecessor by gods. Can you imagine the masters of the first Age all died with it?"

Caddon hesitated, conserving his impulsive words before their utterance, but the High-Warden waved for him to continue. "I must ask if that Age ended, would it not have done so for a reason, and would it not be better to leave it dead?"

"Of course it died for a reason: their time was up, and the Mortal Kingdoms required new lords." Ahead of them, glistening off the ice and through the trees, the sunlight penetrated the forest's shadows, calling them onward. "There will come a time when our Age ends, Arch-Wizard, and a new power rises to claim it. It will be a race we know, an infant race still far from maturity. Our current Age will end in a vast war to encompass the whole of the Mortal Kingdoms. The few who survive will vanish to become a memory or a fable worshiped for a few short years."

At the forest's edge, he waited for Caddon to cover the distance separating them before saying, "Begin harnessing your energy, Arch-Wizard."

Caddon nodded, his hand pressing against a tree to steady himself from their frantic pace. Black fumes issued from his shadow, preceding his demon as it stepped out.

The High-Warden watched as Caddon Fayre began the amassing of his power, watched as an inner flame ignited. In time Caddon's breast glowed incandescent with golden power. The gentle warmth of *Kysuir*, the facet of manipulation, rolled along the High-Warden's skin, causing his clothing to ripple.

Caddon exhaled, glancing up, his eyes aflame with golden energy. "Are you ready, Arch-Wizard?"

When he spoke, Caddon's voice emanated deeper than customary, distorted by the energy he contained, "Yes."

The High-Warden stepped from the forest onto the bank, entering the light and unadulterated wrath of The North. The river raged and the winds shrieked, demanding retribution on the invading goddess. Caddon doubled over as he exited the forest, gasping as the warmth fled his skin.

The High-Warden reached back and grasped him, preventing him from collapsing under the strain of the cold. He helped the beleaguered Caddon to the river, where a new coracle bobbed. He laid Caddon at the prow, the man's skin like ice beneath his palms, and shoved off.

The High-Warden brushed past the demon, leaving the coracle's journey in the river's control. "No fire." The demon hissed but acquiesced, leaving the High-Warden to ameliorate whatever ailed its master. The High-Warden inspected the *Sithe* clutching and screaming at Caddon in abject terror.

The *Sithe*, a lesser northern spirit, was no more than a vague shape in the wind, catching the falling snow to give itself density. There was no strength in its thrashings; but its fear removed all warmth, changing whatever it sought comfort from to a frozen husk. Frost was already beginning to crust Caddon's clothing.

The High-Warden touched the *Sithe*. "Shh, shh, calm yourself; he is not your enemy." He continued murmuring soothing words as his eyes rose to the sky where thousands of *Sithes* fled on the wind, more than he had ever seen. They were easily frightened creatures that became blind to all else when frightened.

Through inching measures, the *Sithe* calmed and released its hold, lolled by the memory of *Winsyria* in his voice and the pacifying music of his words. Still whispering, the High-Warden took the *Sithe* and, leaning over the rim, slipped it into the water, where it sank, already possessed by a deep slumber.

He kept speaking, his words extending beyond the reach of his voice. It would be better for the *Sithes* to sleep until this ended. The winds carried his words across Antiark to the terrified *Sithes*. Slowly, their seething fear abated, and the wind carried them to the river. None of them resisted, they were not malign creatures, merely wild and intemperate. The North was an old land and copious with wild spirits and entities. It is the task of the High-Warden and the derangers to shepherd these creatures, guarding them while ensuring they caused no harm. As the *Sithes* calmed, the crushing cold abated, relinquishing The North to its customary frigid atmosphere.

The wizard looked up, improved in part if not in whole, and gave him a shivering grin. "I didn't expect it to be this cold."

"It is always colder in times of war. And trust me, Arch-Wizard; The North has yet to declare war. The land is only turning bitter because it feels threatened; consider it the growling of a dog before it bites. Wise men will hope the dog isn't rabid. Now you can use the fire." This last piece, the High-Warden directed toward Caddon's demon. The demon materialized in the shape of a man and pressed its hands onto Caddon's brow, channeling warmth. The High-Warden watched in silence, observing its human face. Demons have two faces, a human, the one they wore prior to their damning, and a bestial form that mirrors their tortured soul. From the human aspect, only the power they held could be learned, but from the bestial, which was the physical representation of their mortal soul, much could be ascertained. Greater demons, those who had endured the Abyss for centuries, learned how to manipulate their bestowed faces, to change the visages they could assume.

Caddon's demon met the High-Warden's gaze with disparate human eyes. It spoke with a strangely human voice, "You know they've set my kin upon you?"

"If you speak of the New Order, yes, I know."

"I know who they sent after you; the rivers of Chaos yearn for their return. Three are greater demons; one is nothing more than a beast, every vestige of human soul eradicated by the Abyss. Despite his near invulnerability, Cellar'Veer is not the one to fear; that's an old friend of mine: Kell'MachChain. He is old, ancient even, harkening back to a time The North should remember well. How much do you know of the Mad Kings?"

"I know enough; I know what drove them mad; I know of their bargain, and I know of their origin. I know of the Dread Lords and Taelan Muntalabac."

"The Dread Lord is dead and only the remembrance of his malice endures; though that memory is powerful and stretches it shadows far, even beyond death."

"I have no fear of Kell'MachChain or any that share the infestation of his blood. It is my Burden to destroy his ilk; the dark paladins erred to believe any could destroy me."

"That may be true but ask yourself this: Who told them you could be killed with demon fire? Also, beware of Kell'MachChain; he derives from more sinister origins than most of us reclining in the Abyss and is of the few who truly merits *Jaidar's* ministrations. In times long past, Kell'MachChain was scarce a man; he was a lieutenant of the Dread Lord Taelan Muntalabac. As a mortal, he was a warlock addicted to the power he could unleash and the lives he could ruin; he approximated himself to a god. He saw the Dread Lord as a means to acquire further power and joined him. He watched as the Mad Kings were incarnated into vessels of horror and insanity. He joined them when they sold their mortal inheritance of redemption for power. Except, what Taelan Muntalabac gave Kell'MachChain proved inadequate. Thus Kell'MachChain began his machinations to usurp the Dread Lord. The idiot. Taelan Muntalabac danced him on his puppet strings until they fell limp. Then he severed them. Taelan Muntalabac damned him to an eternity in the Abyss; or rather, he anchored his soul to it like one's soul is bound to the body. None of the malice he leeched from Taelan Muntalabac will have diminished in all the years he has burned. I wonder: how will the High-Warden of Winsyria measure against the disciple of a Dread Lord."

The demon subsided into silence, retreating from his master's side to conceal itself in Caddon's shadow. Perturbed, the High-Warden moved to the prow, his eyes reaching southward for the invading New Order. He did not fear Kell'MachChain; he did, however, fear a Dread Lord, because even dead Dread Lords tended to cause havoc. His eyes open but unseeing, the High-Warden searched The North for the demons, but the New Order's veil obscured them.

He refocused on his surroundings as the coracle ran ashore and vaulted over the side. Caddon hurried to follow, his eyes still incandescent with his wizardry and his color much improved. Despite their haste, they failed to reach the Citadel's doors before the assault began.

Telacra, Goddess of Darkness and Treachery, hurled her amassed power against the law denying her admittance. The High-Warden stumbled beneath the sudden force crashing down on the *Barrier*. Bracing his lowered form with his hand and a knee, he stared upward with glazed eyes. He saw the dark clouds of *Telacra's* assault pulsing across every horizon as they besieged The North, and pushed back. He fused his being into the *Barrier*, reinforcing it and shirking the immense weight of the goddess' being unto himself. All the while, The North raged harder, almost insane in its wroth and pain, railing against his grip.

The High-Warden stood, tremulous beneath the unseen weight, and proceeded, addressing Caddon in a strained voice, "We must hurry; *Telacra* has begun her siege. She is unaccustomed to open conflict where lies and shadows are of little aid, but desperation and the terror of her father's hunger is an untapped well of strength; *Malbreyth* also harries her, knowing her failure will only strengthen him."

As before, when he entered the Citadel's courtyard every eye sought him, their minds igniting with his presence. Across the compound, the White Wolves of Winsyria howled against the burgeoning dark; a challenge to the goddess and a welcome to the High-Warden. A scattered group of derangers stood beside the Wolves; their own eyes locked on Caddon's demon as they entered. It shrank at their stares, hissing soft threats and scouring the derangers' rowan bows. Already it could feel the poisonous cold of those weapons, crueler than the weather withering its skin. At an unspoken command from Caddon, the demon changed itself into a man of dark hair and scarred complexion and stepped from Caddon's shadow. The Wolves evinced no concern toward the creature and, after a brief glance at them, the derangers mirrored their demeanor.

Striding through the doors, the High-Warden, gestured for the circle of derangers to depart. "Leave us; this is not for the eyes of men." Their eyes briefly fastened on Caddon Fayre and the demon, warning both with their glances, then they left. Most departed the Citadel entirely, but a few slipped deeper into the bastion, closing all doors in their wake.

The Wolves took the places within the entrance hall vacated by the derangers. The floor began spinning as the door closed, churning beneath the transparent surface in a whirlpool of swirling names until one spiraled upward with his name. It radiated silver light, growing brighter as he called into himself all the power of the Burdening. Despite the long sleep, a sleep that had yet to be broken since the last invasion, the power surged into him, vengeful and cold, protective and loving.

Inhaling the power coursing like a river that was aflame and frozen in the same breath, he intoned words that weighed heavily on the demon and Caddon. The White Wolves observed in silence, their own eyes burning bright silver in reflection of the High-Warden's. Beneath him, the floor continued to twist onto itself, the names fading away.

When the High-Warden spoke, his voice remained unchanged despite all the power he now held, "You have no need to comprehend, Arch-Wizard, only to follow. I now am all that stands between the gods and The North, and the time runs short." The High-Warden sank through the floor, causing the smooth stone to ripple. Caddon listened for the tremors that surely should have been released at such an act of power that warped stone. Yet, he heard and felt nothing.

Caddon surrendered his futile search and followed the High-Warden. His feet slid into the stone, submerging into a liquid denser than water.

Underneath the gateway, the High-Warden stood at the heart of a stone maze formed of graves without depth or mass, without names or dates. The spirits within called out to him in tongues lost to men. They spoke words of dragons and entities dead long before the gods ascended: words discordant with the tremors from the *Dreamer* slumbering here.

It was not only immortals that were interred here, but men also rested in the catacombs of Antiark. The High-Wardens of old shifted, consciousness returning a semblance of life to them, and formed themselves bodies of spirit, each glowing with evanescent light. He bowed to them, honoring their services in life and death. Should an intruder trespass here, he would never leave. These souls kept vigil in death over what they had guarded in life.

A dozen pools glimmered in the rock around him, of which he stood in the shallowest, a pond of luminescent water that provided the only discernible light. Behind him a quiet shift in the water revealed his companion's arrival. Caddon's gasp confirmed it.

"Arch Wizard, allow your mind to open. Allow the ritual to take you but do not hold it. Let it fill you for the length of the summoning and let it disperse at the end."

Caddon allowed his mind to expand and memories suffused him, drowning out his mortality with ephemeral knowledge. This change would recede when he relinquished the borrowed knowledge; though some of it would endure in his spirit, an unmeasured deepening of the soul.

While the awareness of the ritual yielded to Caddon, the High-Warden strode forward and the wizard followed detachedly. The passage ran only a few paces before it opened into a cavern large enough to contain Antiark's Citadel. A shallow stone bridge extended over a depthless black lake. Despite its nature, the water was transparent, allowing everyone to see the skeletal dragon curled on the floor, crowned and merciless despite its slumber.

The *Dreamer* shifted uneasily in its ceaseless dream, sensing the consciousness now entering its eternal tomb. The *Dreamer* was ancient, older than the gods and mortals. This was its prison: age. It had lived too long, too many memories dominated it, too many for a mortal creature. Those memories gave it power, but that power drove it insane. The *Dreamers* had burned the world in their joint madness, ending the Before-Age and beginning the Age of Gods. The world recovered over eons, but some scars remained. Now, the *Dreamers* slept. If they awoke, their memories would destroy them and all that surrounded them. They dream their memories, forgetting them over the eons but never forgetting the knowledge and the power.

The High-Warden continued, repelling the will and thoughts of the *Dreamer*, and came to a halt at the precipice. The wizard hesitated; he knew what lay sleeping and feared to waken it. "Arch-Wizard, we must finish this."

Caddon assumed his place, knowing it without the need of query. As the summons mounted, his vivid eyes rolled back, and he spoke—the harsh words scarring his tongue and throat. The Rhawn heard him, and he heard the land's need throbbing in their hearts. Slowly they awakened, stirring from millennia of slumber. They journeyed through the mountains and rivers of The North, soared on the wind and dove through the stonework of men until they reached the High-Warden deep in the bowels of Antiark.

The High-Warden watched them shape their ethereal images and bowed. The last entity materialized at the forefront and stepped onto the bridge. His form solidified as he touched, for the first time in millennia, the stone of mortals. His words were somnolent, yet somehow thunderous in anger at *Telacra*. "High-Warden." In these simple words, an existence of meaning was imparted, an eternity of emotions no man could ever experience or comprehend. "You would ask something of us."

"Yes," the High-Warden said, accepting the knowledge that he laid his Burden upon their shoulders. The Rhawn spirit knew what was to be asked but waited all the same; for there is as much power in the asking as there is in the giving. "The gods have initiated their assault: an assault I cannot defeat alone."

"It is not in our power to defy the gods; the conflict would destroy us to no purpose."

"I ask only that you lend power to the Law of Forbiddance and deny *Telacra* entrance."

"There is a price, High-Warden, a price dictated by the power you would claim. Will you accept it?"

"Yes."

The entities nodded as one. "All things have a price, High-Warden. Often, it is a price we cannot comprehend, a price exceeding what is gained. As in all things, this burden you would have us bear has such a price. This price is twofold, an unwarranted death and a damned life. Are you willing to pay this price still?"

"Yes."

"The Pact is wrought: temporary power for a death and a life. The first concerns the weapons of destruction crafted for you. None other could wield them, and yet they still wait to be drawn. This will change, as it always must, and upon their drawing, it will be against a man who is neither a foe nor a danger to The North: a man who was and is an ally. When your blades are drawn against him, he must die." They fell silent, their ethereal faces expressionless, and one by one departed.

Another weight settled on his shoulders as he turned from the departing spirits. He knelt and lifted the unconscious wizard, collapsed at the completion of the summoning. He felt the Rhawn assume their burden and smite *Telacra* from The North, liberating him of her weight. His shoulders roused slightly, and a tired sigh of relief slid from his lips, but his thought inevitably returned to the heavens and the scornful laughter echoing through them.

High overhead, *Malbreyth*, God of War, began to manifest in The Northern sky, and with him The North's rage mounted.

11

A Meeting Of Paladins

Leaning back against a property wall, Slade sat immersed within the past, carefully graphing and projecting how its innumerable tentacles would stretch out to rearrange life. Whenever possible he manipulated these, ensuring they worked towards his ends rather than personal whim. Occasionally, however, the future resisted.

Slade found himself grinning.

Tasha Bloomhale was promising to be an intractable piece, her past throwing up a giant, distrustful wall that would rebuff most techniques. This left a solitary alternative—namely, subjecting Tasha to and subsequently rescuing her from certain death, except certain death tended to end in tragedy.

His conundrum still unresolved, Slade surfaced and reached to the side, giving the garden door a light push before levering himself off the wall and stepping through onto a limestone walkway. He followed its meandering, decidedly non-Imperial lead across a stone garden that was home to numerous statues, raised flower beds, the odd birdhouse, one sandstone mansion, and a set of steps. This last obstacle he surmounted with a series of jumps, each hop avoiding tiles of ill-repute to land atop those he deemed lucky. It was a childish game, but it carried him to the summit and hopefully garnered some ever-useful luck.

Cracking the front door, Slade snuck into the unlit entrance hall and paused as a stranger's voice issued from the library, goosebumps rising along his arms. It was a man, his tones warm and soothing with a magnetic cadence and an articulation that favored neither the strenuous dictation of nobility nor the poorly attached syllables of common folk.

Cain—Slade's stepfather—responded, their discourse flowing with the ease of long acquaintance, covering a tedious subject that probably resulted from the presence of a demure, predominantly silent young woman.

Slade eased a step further from the library and the stranger inside it. There were tiny silver bells tinkling in a recess of his mind: the one labeled dangerous. Intent on evading any involvement, he crept toward the staircase and managed half before a door opened above him. Preceded by the patter of quiet feet, an old woman descended the stairs, her bright eyes piercing the late-night easily.

Wisp-like he slid sideways, hiding in one of the decorative recesses and letting the woman shuffle past with her basket of fresh linen. For the guests, no doubt. A step below him, however, she gasped and started tipping forward.

Just before she fell, Slade steadied her shoulder. "Be careful; we can't have you hurting yourself and spell ruin for the entire household."

"Oh! Master Lammerock, you're back."

"Yes, but if possible, I'd–"

"Master Cain is entertaining guests in the library. He requested your presence as soon as you return."

"I guessed as much. Do we know who they are?"

Before the woman—Freida—could answer, one of the library doors swung open with a flood of light and Cain Lammerock's imposing silhouette entered the gap. "Slade, stop dawdling. We have guests, and they are anxious to meet you. It appears they've heard some ... interesting tales concerning your social life." A thread of humor snuck into his usually inflectionless voice, but it quickly changed to subtle warning. "Entertain your best manners tonight, these are important people. Tiberius Whyte has–"

"The Will of the Emperor?" Slade asked, vaulting the stair rail.

"Yes; he's an old friend. Respect him accordingly."

"Father, when have I ever disrespected one of your acquaintances?" Slade adopted a smile so innocent it reeked of benign intent. "If I did, may your knights lock me in the stockade for my heinous transgression, may the ground swallow my contemptible self for indulging such disrespect, may the sky boil with crimson flames for my dishonoring you so grievously, may the seas and oceans turn to dust if I embraced such utter depravity. If I ever–"

A hand gloved in scars clamped on his shoulder. "They have waited long enough, Slade, come along." Few possessed the will to deny Cain's requests, especially when pinned under his storm-cloud gaze. Some of the more timid souls even feared violence, which was preposterous; Cain never lost control.

Deterred by neither handicap, Slade wriggled free and dove around his stepfather into the library. He swept its creamy bookcases with a glance, located each occupant and then—maintaining a watch over the first occupant—disregarded both warnings to be polite. Crossing the room, he plunged to his knees before a fifteen-year-old girl, captured her hands in the middle of steepling, and clasped them to his chest. "Sweet fiancée, we meet at last. Oh, joyful day." He surged upward, kissing her cheek lightly before subsiding again. "Your beauty outshines the stars themselves, nay the entire night sky, nay again the glory of a thousand sunsets. To think my incompetent spies declared you *merely* pretty. Oh, truly *Kis'Maat's* benign eye is upon me. *Me* of all people! That we're bound to an arranged and irrevocable marriage is a gift beyond belief, beyond what my criminal self deserves! Once again I worship the gods because my divine and unquestioning faith has been rekindled by their unbound generosity." During this heartfelt confession, Slade watched her lovely, pale countenance turn increasingly pink and frantic, her eyes widen and a million responses rush through her head only to scatter at his proximity.

Then intruded the warm, soothing voice from earlier, its owner extending across the couch to disengage Slade's hands. "I'm afraid your spies are even worse than you assume. Neither I nor my ward agreed to any marital arrangement. You appear to have stumbled into a case of mistaken identity."

By the time Tiberius Whyte finished speaking, Slade had realized why the man's voice caused the ringing bells. It conveyed nothing. The perfectly balanced inflections stripped away all color, all accent, leaving behind an amorphous diction that could pass anywhere without remark. That was a mystery for later. For now…

"Oh, what a calamity! To watch the gods turn away and smile at another, to feel *Sammahale's* terrible wrath scorch the lush ground under my feet, making perfect soil for seeds of despair. My one pride and joy ripped from my clutching fingers, and my glorious future torn to bitter shreds." Slade flailed with broad, exaggerated gestures that perfectly detailed his torment. "Oh gods above, better to endure the end of all life than suffer this doom, surely that pain would prove infinitely sweeter than this heartbreak. But the most harrowing part to this grindstone of my soul, is that I can't even propose matrimony because I'm already betrothed. Oh, calamities of calamities, may *Jaidar* reap my soul and drag it to the heart of the Abyss; I have nothing left to live for." Collapsing slowly to the ground, Slade cupped his distraught face and rolled despondently.

A breathless anticipatory silence ensued, ending when the girl, Feylin, dared a low exhale, mistakenly believing her ordeal concluded. At this signal, Slade surged with sudden hope. Before she realized it, he had taken her hands for prisoners and was showering them with kisses. "At a single word from your luscious lips, I will murder my fiancée so we can fulfill our grand romance. Furthermore, I shall—"

Cain grabbed Slade's collar, lifting him from the ground and depositing him in a cushioned chair. "I apologize for my errant son; he has no sense of propriety, etiquette, or decorum. That, or he chooses to ignore them."

Tiberius dismissed this with a wave. "Feylin and I are more amused than insulted." The girl's instant horrified reaction disproved this assertion. "Besides, Lady Senna, in her infinite wisdom, forewarned us of his ... peculiarities. As such, we came expecting this possibility." By natural progression, their eyes alighted upon the woman who slept across the arms of a large, pudgy chair. Even with her countenance laboring beneath an unhealthy pallor, Senna Lammerock's beauty snared the gaze, an ensorcellment of articulate eyebrows and luminous eyes, of strawberry blonde hair that bounced and haloed an elegant jaw, of an upturned nose that tended to wrinkle when she laughed, of full lips made distinctive by the ever-present quirk of mischief, of grace turned ephemeral by languid starvation.

Refocusing upon the conversation, Tiberius leaned toward Feylin and nudged her with an elbow. "Who would have guessed you would bewitch your first suitor tonight, and such a level-headed man also?" She only blushed and sank deeper into her couch.

Externally, Slade listened with polite interest. Internally, he listened to everything else: his mother's quiet breathing, Cain's slow tread across carpeted floors, the sound of metal clinking as Tiberius toyed with knicknacks, the partially finished decanter of wine splashing into a glass. Something important was afoot but not tonight. While both men expressed atypical restlessness, the wine was social and Senna dozed, plus Feylin seemed an odd addition to such potentially grim affairs.

Cain moved beside his wife, leaning over to brush aside Senna's hair. "Please forgive my lapse as host, I must carry my wife to bed. Her day has been exhausting and she needs rest."

"There's no need to apologize, Cain. I was about to suggest it myself."

Cain nodded once, kneeling and gently lifting Senna in his arms before carrying her from the room. As they stepped through the double doors, she shifted in her sleep, asking a mumbled question only he could hear.

"Yes, Slade has returned and with not a single feather askew. Go back to sleep." The woman smiled and cuddled deeper into his embrace, slipping to the edge of sleep once again and murmuring to him. Cain nodded and began humming, lulling her over the final threshold.

The door clicked shut, an innocent sound to signal Slade's release. He exploded to his feet and darted to claim Tiberius' hand, pumping the man's arm excessively. "Many fair greetings honored guests. Seeing as my father is acting like his usual taciturn self, I'll take it upon myself to ensure a light, fluffy atmosphere in which to conduct our undoubtedly shady dealings. To this end, I shall employ any number of devious, twisted, or obscene methods, including poking merciless fun at you—our guests—and deriding our mutual acquaintances. If that fails, I'll resort to sadistic humor because everybody loves sadistic humor. But"—Slade raised a finger—"if you're too illustrious to be everybody, then I can regale you with jokes appropriate for the most innocent ears. I can also inundate you with polite conversation and gossip about the most intriguing subjects. If all else fails, I'll adopt the very soul of boredom." Slade stepped back, exuding the most cheerful expectancy.

Tiberius regarded his newly liberated hand absently, flexing without hurry. "No, I do not think adopting the very soul of boredom will be necessary. I can now see how your mother thought you equal parts wonderful and peculiar."

"Only the ordinary are limited to a single designating characteristic, and ordinary—as I've decided to start saying—is for the poor dreary people who infest our cities with such dreadful profusion, hence, the term ordinary. I, conversely, aspire to a different, far more enviable appellation. Unfathomably Intricate has a nice ring to it, no?"

"Sounds exhausting, though I am curious how you intend to cultivate that particular appellation. People rarely pick their own."

Slade flapped a hand. "Simplicity itself. All I require are two basic steps: first, remove any alternatives; second, introduce my preferred name while convincing my victims they conceived it themselves. Now, you might ask, how I intend to implant these seeds of insidious suggestion? Once again the answer is simplicity itself; I shall manipulate my persona until I am both mysterious and incomprehensible. The first via a little voodoo, a couple shrunken heads, and a cloud of smoke, perhaps a strange aroma as well. As for the second, I need only prove that I am, indeed, incomprehensible, and I shall achieve this by revealing all the defects of my character." Slade grinned, his expression adopting a sinister air. "Mortals, arrogant creatures that they are, find the deficiencies of others incomprehensible. Their own, conversely, are perfectly understandable and almost laudable."

Tiberius held Slade's mis-matched eyes without contest, and dropped them just as unconcernedly, stretching sideways to hook the long-necked decanter from his side table and top off his wine. In moving, he revealed the five pins sewn along his shirt's collar. Most people wore two. "I have heard a great deal about you, Slade Lammerock, even squirreled away in Apelium. Your father saw fit to write numerous letters describing your character, antics, and general development." Slade mimed a gasp, earning a nod from Tiberius. "Yes, I was quite surprised myself. Alongside this frankly unnerving talkativeness, he grew dangerously close to bragging at times." Slade's eyebrows rose even higher, and Tiberius resettled into his seat with an amusement that rested less in the curve of his mouth and more the wrinkles of his eyes. "I should probably have taken those letters to heart and learned not to have expectations concerning you. Tell me, what prompts a young, handsome man to bare his defects for the dubious reward of a self-selected title?"

"The world has a multiplicity of reasons; they're simply winnowed by the value we place on our shortcomings." Slade—without quite losing site of Tiberius—crossed the library's spiral patterned carpets to the curved, single pane window that occupied the back wall. "In my case, I don't value them very highly at all, so my potential reasons are limitless." Slade pulled one of three golden cords. "That said, revealing one's shortcomings can be equally courageous and foolish. So only the foolishly brave or the brave fools initiate transactions like this … and me of course."

Feylin glanced up—a question climbing to the tip of her tongue—and Slade whirled with a broad, tooth-baring grin. She hastily looked back down, flushing to the tips of her ears.

Slade frowned; it became infinitely harder to play with an audience who refused to participate. Luckily, participation was non-negotiable. "Never fear, Miss Feylin, I am prepared to answer all questions, even the unasked ones. You see, I consider all brave men fools because charging headlong into danger is extremely unwise. Furthermore, I deem the foolish brave because it takes depthless courage, titanic perseverance, and monumental resolve to sail through life's rivers in, effectively, a sinking ship."

As Feylin cringed, Tiberius offered the barest hint of a crooked smile. "It would be an adventure to discuss philosophy with you, Slade Lammerock, if only to watch as you delight in calling white black and black green. What twisted, convoluted roads would be tread, what iconoclastic views brought to light."

"And now I have a question for you, my Lord Tiberius." Approaching the armchair to the paladin's right, Slade stepped over the armrest onto the dented cushion and dropped into a cross-legged sit, bracing his chin atop one hand. "What does the final pin on your collar signify?" The first of the five displayed a hand brandishing a war-hammer: the symbol for paladin knights. The second bore the symbol of Tiberius' fife: two doves and a sword. The next displayed a scroll thrust through a crown: the symbol for the Will of the Imperial Emperor. And the fourth displayed a chess king, denoting his status as a military general. The final pin, iron and smaller than the other four, bore two eye-like engravings.

With an unconscious mien to the motion, Tiberius brushed a thumb across the final broach. "It was a gift from the Lynn. During the closing years of the Fae war, the Empire marched on their home in Drak'marr. However, as the first battles and skirmishes began bloodying the grass, an … ancestor of mine worked to convince the Imperial Emperor that a lengthy conflict was undesirable. Notoriously Cardolyn Tyier requires more convincing than most, especially after proclaiming that he would defeat the Lynn … personally if necessary. But, raising more than a few eyebrows, this man secured the emperor's permission to ride north, whereupon he braved the mountains alone. Drak'marr isn't so untraversable as the *Rhawn*, but its mountains are … crueler, less tolerant of intrusion, and there are no derangers to safeguard those who lose their way. My ancestor did not lose his way, he found the front door and waited for months. Eventually, the Lynn capitulated and offered their hospitality. During the successive negotiations, he disdained all contact with Cardolyn Tyier and effectively assumed Imperial authority, for which the penalty is death. Instead, Cardolyn Tyier named him the Emperor's Will and made the post hereditary." Tiberius let his hand drop. "The Lynn, conversely, gave him a lighter title: Iron-Eyes, for the iron in his gaze and the iron in his soul. Hence this rather unimpressive heirloom."

Slade leaned back in his chair and nodded absently, rotating two fingers around each other. Unlike the legends of old where gods strode the land and heroes like Rowan Silverwood slew necromancer kings, the story lacked a certain grandeur. Nevertheless, the telling sent a quiet thrill through his veins. What's more, there was the delicious aroma of important details being left out.

Tiberius, for his part, observed Slade with his head tilted minutely, finger idly tracing the rim of his wine glass. "If you're inclined, perhaps we can exchange one answer for another." Slade's attention snapped back to Tiberius, followed by a light nod. "Do you know what Cain plans for your immediate future?" The question rung as innocuous, but the man sat too casually within Slade's reach. Most everyone, from Thearcs to Theonaughts, and paladin knights—even Cain Lammerock on occasion—had a tendency to eye Slade like a silent, invisible timer that was counting down overhead. The fact Tiberius seemed indifferent merited a touch of caution.

"I cannot say I do. We have a mutual, unstated agreement wherein neither snoops through the other's schemes."

Behind Slade, the library door glided open to admit Cain, who immediately stepped to one side, preventing it from closing. "You may place the food on a table and then retire."

"As you wish, Master Lammerock." Frieda entered with an embossed tray and several platters of cold food.

"Once again, I apologize for my absence, but I am certain my son entertained you. I can only hope he kept these entertainments within the bounds of propriety."

"Father!" Slade gasped, clapping a hand to his chest. "I've adopted my best behavior tonight, the type of comportment only found in outdated etiquette novels." He indicated Frieda. "Besides, I ordered dinner. What possible mischief could I have gotten into?"

"Cain, relax. Your son proved to be an acceptable host, albeit one averse to simply discussing the weather." Tiberius beckoned Frieda over and then cleared his end table, passing the decanter to Feylin, pocketing the pens and setting a small half-carved turtle on the middle couch seat, where it scarcely got comfortable before Frieda recovered the animal and gave it to Slade. The turtle secured, she placed her tray, curtseyed, and departed.

Tiberius was already sifting through the arranged meats, fruits, and cheeses to prepare a couple plates. The first he filled with exotic items like sushi or mango. The second received more commonplace fare like yellow cheese and ham. When both were well stocked, he laid the second plate atop his lap and handed the first to Feylin, who murmured a quiet, "thank you." Employing a slow, graceful technique out of style by nearly a century, they began eating.

Snagging a few orange slices while moving past, Slade deposited the turtle atop a shelf where it helped steady a few drunken Herbology books. Afterwards he resumed his seat, snagging the entire bowl of cherries. "My Lord Tiberius, if I may ask, what brings you to our sunny, beach side slice of the Empire?"

Tiberius' heavy, blockish, and extremely western brows lowered, finally denting his equanimity. "If only it were to enjoy your beach and sun, but no. I've come on two separate purposes. The first is Imperial business that coincided with my plans, so I agreed to address it. We'll discuss that later. My second and primary purpose, however, is curing Senna." The man's grizzled head fell back against the couch and he breathed a sigh. "If possible, I would have departed the moment I received your letter two years ago. It's just that … it wasn't time to leave yet."

"I didn't expect you to come. I was just appraising you of the situation." Of all Cain's acquaintances across the Empire, every foreign dignitary and correspondent, Tiberius was probably the only one to receive a letter.

"I know. Even so, staying was the hardest choice I've made in decades." Tiberius rubbed his face then straightened. "The past is done and I'm finally here, thank the gods. From your description, I'm afraid her affliction is worse than a common illness."

Tiberius' abilities ranged across multiple fields, most notably the broken remnants of magical healing. All knowledge concerning the practice had died centuries ago, forgotten by everyone except the western dragons and those who were ancient long before the loss. Neither shared knowledge. Thus, Tiberius spent his life chasing rumors, striking bargains, and collecting tattered threads.

"The surgeons and apothecaries believe that her disease originated within the Avarus Desert. It vaguely resembles other Southern afflictions and might have mutated while crossing the Inland Sea, elsewise it wouldn't survive our moderate climate." Finally Cain sat down, even relaxing enough to undo the top button of his uniform. "I am uncertain though, the Empire's Ward Spires should expel foreign illnesses."

"The surgeons are wrong." This was not delivered harshly or arrogantly but with a note of fatigue. "I've searched Apelium's library extensively, focusing on primarily Western, Southern, and Islander pathogens. At best her symptoms showed a passing correlation." Tiberius gave a slight bitter smile. "If it's not in my library, it probably doesn't exist. There are only two larger collections."

"If not the South, where does it originate?" Slade asked, nudging Cain with the cherries until he caved and indulged his slight addiction. "I spent months scouring Tellor's libraries and bookstores for any tidbit, and while they can't compare to Apelium, I investigated everything from poison to magical backlash and still found nothing."

"I fear this sickness stems from the East." The room stilled.

"Are you certain?" Tiberius' silence was answer enough and Cain rose, eyes flicking to Slade. "We should discuss this alone." When Slade moved to follow, he pointed back at the vacated chair. "Stay here. Politely keep our guest company."

Slade subsided with a frown, abruptly finding himself staring at the wrong side of a door. No matter, he would fix that.

Once the conversation started in earnest, Slade stood, shushed Feylin's scandalized expression and then skulked to the offending doors. Crouching down, he pressed an ear against the keyhole only to discover that both paladins spoke in a mysterious, foreign tongue.

Huffing, Slade slunk back to his erstwhile companion as she studied her lap with the fervor of someone wishing they'd mastered invisibility. Stopping in front of her, he coughed politely. "Miss Feylin, while doing nothing untoward in that corner, I noticed your appalling lack of entertainment. As your host, I feel obliged to resolve this issue. May I sit?"

This spurred a stolen glance at his face followed by an immediate dose of slight, rather obvious panic and finally—after much mental scrambling—a shrug.

"Your generosity is unequaled by anything except your beauty." He sat down at an angle. "Now, if you're willing, I'd love to be regaled with a few exciting tales from your youth; I am fearfully anxious to learn about the woman I almost married."

Feylin scooted sideways, scrunching herself into the corner. "I doubt my stories would entertain you."

"You needn't worry about me, I'm already entertained; I'm getting us acquainted so you can be entertained as well. So ..." He performed a leading gesture.

Feylin shook her head, flushing a little. "A stranger who peeked into my life would see an endless line of books. This is my first adventure and it's largely been a carriage ride."

"Well, that's a shame; I'd only wish a boring adventure on my worst enemy. That said, if you think your tale is too indescribably boring for conversation, you could always invent something." Feylin blinked, making direct, prolonged eye-contact for the first time, and Slade grinned. "Go on, delight us with the story of how you were taken hostage by a one eyed giant." She just stared at him though, too awkward and too unsure of how to respond. "No good, I see. Well, we need to find a subject soon or I'll start gossiping about myself and that would be the height of presumption. Hmm, let's consider… We certainly can't discuss the books I've read and criticizing those in powers would be difficult on account of your innocence and youth; it takes a well-seasoned mind to enjoy the devastating insults I heap upon our overlords."

Feylin eyes snapped up, her chin thrust out and a surgical chill entered her voice, "My youth is no more an obstruction than yours, Slade Lammerock. In fact, it's clear that adolescence unhinges your faculties more than mine. Whatever the chosen topic, I'm sure I can–" She halted, a blush flaming her cheeks.

Slade's grin had only broadened though. "You're right of course; youth has no effect on intelligence or seasoning unless you happen to be a sprig of oregano, in which case age should have sapped all your mind's flavor by now."

Silent, Feylin stared fixedly at her lap.

"Is that all I get? One thoroughly deserved scolding after I risked life, limb, and stylish waistcoat to rescue you from tedium? Why any moment now our respective guardians could storm through the door in a hurricane of splinters, grab my shirt collar, the seat of my pants, and hurl me into the nearest dung-heap. All in perfect, synchronized unison." Slade raised his eyebrows in a silent invitation that went declined. "This, of course, would lead any rational mind to wonder why I risk such terrible retribution for your little, blue-eyed self?" He leaned back, hands cupped behind his head. "Since you're a vocal, forthright lady, I shall embrace the same candor. I'm a spy. Lord Tiberius, hired me to stalk your every step in utter silence and complete obscurity, supervising your actions and ensuring your continued prosperity."

Feylin frowned at her lap, cast him a confused glance, looked back to her lap, waited a second and then, "If you're supposed to be a spy tasked with stalking me in complete obscurity, why share the information?"

"Ah ha!" Slade gesticulated skyward sharply, making her jump. "Because that story is a ruse masking my true intentions, which are deeper and far more sinister than you can imagine."

"Oh, … I see." Hesitantly, she crept out from her corner. "Sooo what are your true intentions?"

Looking around surreptitiously, Slade leaned over and whispered, "I'm here to sequester a certain beautiful, light-haired damsel and elope with her into the sunrise, where we shall live in blissful adoration until she grows old and ugly; whereupon I shall escape with the next beautiful maiden to cross my path."

Feylin had to have expected it. Even so, she couldn't quite muster a response and so they sat there, Slade starring expectantly while she peeked in short, anxious bursts. Then his eyebrows began to prance atop his forehead, surprising both a giggle and a response from her. "I don't know, living in the sunrise might get a little bright sometimes."

"I'm flexible. How does an underwater palace sound? I've also got a castle somewhere; we just need to find it. In a stroke of pure brilliance, I built the glorious structure atop a cloud, which, as you well know, is an ungovernable species. They're forever chasing wind nymphs, rising and falling without a thought given to their tenants and bursting into tears at the most inopportune times. Have you ever wondered why clouds cry all the time?" Mutely, Feylin shook her head. "Well, it's because they're hopeless romantics.

Not only do these fluffy creatures insist on breaking each other's hearts once or twice a day, they're also addicted to watching human love affairs. Since men profess their undying love whenever a toad burps and women give their hearts away the moment they've finished gluing the pieces together, it's no wonder clouds perfected weeping. I will say this for them: their poetry is heavenly." He winked at her. "So, where's it to be, Lady Feylin, cloud castle, underwater palace, or sunrise villa?"

"I don't know."

"You should consider Doth'Ammorian. I haven't visited for an age, but it's lovely during late summer and early autumn." Flanked by Cain, Tiberius spoke from just inside the library, his powerful shoulders relaxed and his hand resting lightly upon the doorhandle, yet his steady, gray eyes weighed upon Slade—still bearing all the equanimity in the world—but now with the unmistakable message that Slade needed to behave himself. "Your mother forgot to mention persistence when detailing your character, Slade. Perhaps, considering your other traits, I might have guessed."

"My obstinate streak only appears sporadically because I rarely struggle with anything."

"Although I admire your dedication; please allow Feylin time to consider before pressing her further."

Slade rose, offering Feylin his open hand; whereupon she slowly, warily gave over the very tips of her fingers, earning a brilliant smile.

"It seems we've been discovered, sweet lady. I must flee." He bowed, placing a chaste kiss upon her fingers. Blushing, the instant Slade released his light grip, Feylin burrowed her hand within the safety of her lap.

Tiberius watched this in silence, eyebrows raised slightly, then reclaimed his former seat. "Slade, one of your mother's stories caught my interest earlier. Apparently, you have the endearing habit of befriending Tellor's homeless and unfortunate, frequently bringing them home for dinner as a precursor to adopting them like stray puppies. Rumor says you typically indoctrinate these poor souls into a heretical cult or a criminal syndicate with aspirations of world domination?"

"I'm pretty sure my mother started those. There are a few others, some with significantly more accuracy and others with significantly less. All embellished."

"Such is an unavoidable truth; every rumor monger alive believes he alone knows what happened or what makes an exciting story. The idle hands of a clever tongue will make the simplest tale into a legend."

"To be honest, I'm a little guilty of that myself. But I doubt this was your intended discussion."

"Slade, I would like a favor from you. Two actually." Articulated by another equally powerful man, the request might have struck as peculiar. From Tiberius, spoken in his calm and unhurried voice, it seemed perfectly normal.

"Ask away, Lord Tiberius, and disregard my vaunted ethics, they have a loose association with morality. There's no depravity too depraved, no atrocity too atrocious, no barbarity too barbarous for a friend of my father."

"Well, that's a relief to hear;" the paladin lord said dryly. "I must confess, that possibility had concerned me. As for my first request, Feylin has never visited Tellor. Help her explore the city and, if possible, explain how to navigate unfamiliar territory." Tiberius leaned forward briefly, pinning Slade to his chair. "Do this without proposing marriage every other street."

"It'll be my pleasure to escort your delightful ward."

"Now for the second favor. By any chance, have you heard the rumor that someone plans to steal *Akravast*?"

Cain's head whipped around. "Tiberius, if that's a joke, it's in appalling taste."

"It may be a joke, but it's not one of my design. I usually have better taste."

Slade shrugged. "I've heard it mentioned a few times, even spread the rumor myself. People pay attention when they learn some fool plans on stealing the Imperial Emperor's birthday present."

"The Imperial Emperor believes there is an actual threat, and thus he's offering fifteen hundred gold crowns to whoever apprehends these criminals."

On the surface, Slade's eyebrows rose in faint surprise. Underneath the surface, he pinched himself to stifle gasping laughter. *'Oh what glorious, sublime irony! The moment I get involved, the past rushes forward and complicates things in a beautifully spectacular way.'* Slade almost shook his head. *'I'd regret starting those rumors in the first place if it weren't so amusing.'* "So, our omnipotent Emperor fears that a monster's hiding under his bed, planning to steal his toys. How does that concern me? You can't possibly think I have any intention of running around and stealing divine swords."

"It concerns you less than your friends and their contacts in Tellor's underworld. I already have men poking around, but no one likes talking to soldiers and we're having trouble even finding the underworld. At best we catch glimpses of illicit activities: an illegal gambling ring, the odd smuggling operation, a bit of spilled drugs. Within hours, however, everything vanishes, leaving behind a tapestry of dead ends. You're the first person to admit Tellor has an underworld. Everyone else is oblivious or pretending to be. It's rather disconcerting."

"What exactly would you have my friends do?"

"If they're comfortable with it, ask around. Elsewise, I only need one or two names, people with guaranteed knowledge that I can speak to personally: a foot in the door, that's all."

"How would speaking with them personally result differently from dispatching a common soldier? You represent the same difficulties only multiplied."

"One of the benefits to old age is that I've had a great deal of practice talking to people. They will speak with me."

Looking into the man's steady gray eyes, Slade knew the words for true, which made the whole affair significantly more dangerous. Closing his own eyes, Slade leaned back and started stroking his eyebrows, envisioning every potential outcome. "Alright, I'll see if they're willing, but there will be no contact between you and them. No names exchanged. I'd rather they avoid any potential backlash. As for me, I'll keep my ears open while escorting Miss Feylin, though I fear the endless drudgery of my presence will bore her unto tears."

Only Tiberius heard Feylin's snort of disbelief, but he kept a studiously controlled face. "Thank you. Keep your eyes open as well."

"Unfortunately, my eyes will be wholly devoted to observing your beautiful ward." Slade swiveled toward Feylin and propped his chin upon both hands, breathing a dreamy sigh.

"Slade, one last moment of gravity please. These are dangerous waters. Whoever intends on stealing *Akravast* is either powerful or insane, stupid's not an option. Be careful who you discuss this affair with. If you tell the wrong friend and they idly tell someone else, it starts a chain reaction that might culminate with you or one of your friends murdered. Can you defend yourself?"

"I taught him swordplay when he was younger, but he's fallen out of practice since then." Cain stroked his mustache thoughtfully. "That said, Slade is proficient at knife fighting and martial arts."

Slade gasped loudly, fanning himself with one hand while draping the other across his brow. "Oh, such a compliment. Quick, Father, fetch my smelling salts; I do believe I feel faint."

Cain shook his head, wearing the barest hint of a smile.

12

A Dread Lord's Council

The thirtieth day of the New Order's incursion.

A boot smashing into Brimares' back woke her from the fiery haze she had wrapped around herself. She sprawled forward into the sleet, plowing through a sheet of thawing ice and snow before lurching to her feet.

A horse snorted, bringing her around with bared teeth and a flare of heat as the sled train and soldiers continued past, shambling with the night's lateness. The Blond Knight pulled up beside her with a mercurial grin, slathered in melting ice and partially obscured by the raging storm. "At last the fair maiden answers the hero's advances." His eyes glimmered through the haze, devoid of concern, expecting no resistance, and by all rights, she should have offered none. But the Chaos seethed within her, and unlike Kell'MachChain, the Blond Knight did not require her actually suffering to torment her.

She exploded to her feet and vaulted over his head, spraying sleet as she twisted mid-air and gouged fingers into his pauldrons. His armor shredded like paper under her serrated gauntlets but caught on their flared ridges nonetheless, giving her the leverage to tear him from his saddle.

They both landed on the horse's opposite flank, he on his back and she in a crouch with her fingers still entrenched in his armor. He cursed, surging up from the snow and thrashing in her grip but succeeding only in further shredding his armor. She lunged backward, dragging the Blond Knight up over her shoulder and hurling him into a nearby birch. The tree splintered with a brittle crack, showering its environs with frozen beetles, wood chips, termites, and leaves. She settled low, the Chaos stirring within her, excited by the violence. It never truly slept, merely subsided enough that she could ignore it, but it required very little to waken.

The Blond Knight lay supine for a minute and then slowly stood, visible only as an indistinct silhouette through the blizzard, and flicked his pale hair. The marching mercenaries began parting around them, scrambling over the waist-high snow as best they could to circumvent the demon and paladin.

Brimares retreated, quelling her Chaos' roaring violence, and collided with one of the sleds from the train. The mercenaries perched atop it, huddling against the totem in their sopping cloaks, rebuffed her with a flurry of catcalls, laughter, wagers, and kicks, gleeful at the prospect of someone else suffering—as if this meant anything to her besides an inconvenience.

The Blond Knight approached, radiating belligerence despite his sheathed blade. He spat a wad of blood onto the crusted snow and stroked his sword's pommel, one hand resting comfortably at his side, conflicting with his vengeful tilt. "I like a little fight, there's no joy in the easy conquests, but you deserve what's coming, and I will hear you beg. I'll make sure everyone hears."

His words projected across the storm, charged with the divinity he harbored and booming. She began circling him, assessing, calculating. This gave him brief pause, then he resumed advancing, steel blade whistling from its sheath as tendrils of black fire grew in his unburdened hand.

She spared the black sword a glance and disregarded it to watch the Blond Knight's fire; the blade would cause her little harm, but the fire—fueled by a goddess' divinity—would. And she needed every drop of Chaos if she intended to kill the High-Warden, and survive.

"You're intriguing. One moment passive, the next lusting after blood. I wonder, will you eat your kin after they die? Or have you somehow remained untainted by every hell they cast you into?" Brimares continued to circle, now facing the sleds instead of away from them. Mercenaries trudged behind her, a dozen ranks deep and bent almost double. The Blond Knight lengthened his stride, lips parting in an elated grin, knowing she could not kill him without repercussions.

She spun around and bolted, helmet forming as the flared edges of her armor snapped close. He roared and lunged into pursuit. Her first step hurled her to within feet of the mercenaries, the second launched her over them in a spinning vault. She landed on the other side and crashed through the ice and snow to the frozen earth, submerging to her chest outside of the column. The snow hissed and melted against her armor, gushing down her sides as the storm swallowed her again, but she lurched and crawled free of the slush. The Blond Knight screamed from within the column, augmented voice cracking through the wind to demand her return. She slammed a foot onto the solid ice and erupted into a sprint down the army.

Her sprint delivered her to the front ranks and Kheldar Ferain's dubious protection, where she slowed and slipped into the marching lines.

Several of the soldiers glanced at her or shied away from her arrival, but she ignored them. Kheldar Ferain might not care what happened to her, but according to Salem, he wouldn't allow their march to falter because his soldiers could not contain their lust. Especially not with day so close to breaking.

The little that remained of the night gradually cracked overhead, splintered by the lances of an azure dawn glowing through the haze. With it the temperature dipped lower, their prayers of warmth diminishing as *Telacra's* prime hours concluded. Moments later a sergeant rode across the front ranks bellowing commands she could scarcely hear, "We camp at that hill; sentries start watch immediately; the rest of you erect the fortifications and dig the trenches. Fires are a priority, and no one is to go beyond the palisades once they are finished." The soldiers around her twisted in place, wearily tapping on the shoulder plates of their neighbors to relay the message. She mimicked them, still wary of the Blond Knight's pursuit, but peered past the sergeant from the corner of her eye, endeavoring to glimpse their campsite through the storm and find someplace to hide, preferably near the outer fires.

A skeletal crest jutted up in the near distance, outlined with jagged edges and a series of slim, haughty peaks. What had once been a delicate forest of crape myrtles speckled the tor's roots with mutilated trunks and a graveyard of curving branches. The sky above it, however, blushed with thousands of red myrtle blooms gliding on a contradictorily gentle wind, shockingly vibrant and flowing north like a river into the sapphire dawn.

"You, she-demon!" She jerked at the hostile cry and faced the sergeant. "Kheldar Ferain summons you to the command post." Brimares nodded, but the sergeant had already ridden away calling out further orders. She glanced about for the Blond Knight and started toward the distant summit, watching every solider she passed.

A sense of foreboding wreathed the solitary hill, thickening as she neared and making her skin crawl despite the fires igniting across it. Mercifully the storm diminished as she neared, blunted by the totems being raised along the tor's natural moat: a thin branch of the *Annuir'Hyme* that had collided with the hill's easternmost tip and forked.

Brimares faltered a few feet later, arrested by the sight of three stone longboats moored in the river's shallows, inert despite the aggressive water. The wolf-prows of raiders crowned each of them, and bloody hand and paw-prints marked their sides. Their owners—hunched, thick-furred figures with extended snouts—strewed the bank, conversing in barks and yips, tending fires, fishing, sharpening weapons in packs, or just prowling impatiently, sometimes on two legs and something on all fours. Weshac.

The scattered Weshac stirred at her approach, many rising from their occupations to observe her. Two answered her arrival, leaving the company of their brethren to detain her while a third sprinted down the riverbank. Brimares halted and let them stalk around her, ghosting over the snow she wallowed in and inhaling to taste her scent. They performed two circuits, sniffing constantly and prodding her with a granite spear once before settling between her and the *Annuir'Hyme*.

Brimares cautiously moved to circumvent them, but their spears fell with a whoosh, cracking against her pauldrons and thrusting her back with accompanying snarls. They briefly held their spears ready, then lifted them as all signs of aggression evaporated. Brimares settled back to wait, the Chaos simmering higher within her, eager for the violence these half-feral creatures offered. She'd encountered their kind before, even seen them die in the months leading to her damnation. They had frightened her once, when she was a girl listening to tales of the cities they'd burnt.

A voice extended from behind the Weshac, speaking in a tongue she did not recognize. The two sentries retreated with a subservient huff, yielding to the speaker. He was also a Weshac, but unlike his fellows, he was dressed in basic human winter apparel with only vestigial fur coating the back of his hands and head to betray his true nature. Unlike the men she accompanied, he wore a long, dense coat with a hood and the flaps rolled slightly up his calves. It bore no insignia or coloring.

This new Weshac motioned the sentries back. "I must apologize; they are newly arrived and have yet to adapt to the warmer climates and civilization; they will be politer in a couple of weeks." He squinted at her with vertical pupils. "You're not human."

Brimares snorted and watched the white tattoos swirl across his black fur and skin. A quick glance told her the two sentries also shared the flowing tattoos; if anything, theirs were starker. She had heard of the Weshacs' living tattoos. The white tattoos on their black skin designated these Weshac as renegades.

The articulate Weshac surveyed her again. "You are one of the hell-spawn summoned to assassinate the High-Warden." She nodded. "We were told to expect you; come, Kheldar Ferain is atop the hill." The Weshac turned and strode to the river. She followed, glancing to either side as Weshac gathered to watch her pass. Some barked at her in their animal tongue, the exact meaning lost but the tones of challenge and fear.

The Weshac conducted her to the *Annuir'Hyme* where a flotilla of pulley-drawn rafts waited, many in transit between the two banks with Weshac and soldiers aboard. The mercenaries were regulated to the land surrounding the tor and currently occupied in raising external embankments to function as walls.

The Weshac paused at the river's edge, one boot submerged and the other planted on a protruding rock. "That will take you across the *Annuir'Hyme;* but beware, all the river needs is one incautious moment to destroy you." His hand extended, indicating first a raft of weathered, seamless stone then the shrouded currents. "Cling to the railing and hold close to the deck."

She mounted the raft and it instantly lurched forward, throwing her against the railing. Cursing internally, Brimares lowered herself to the deck, wishing she knew how to swim. Not that it would have mattered. The river would have destroyed her if she so much as touched a finger to it.

Crossing the river required a few minutes, though it felt far longer and ended with the raft scraping into a ramshackle dock where two huge Weshac heaved on the ropes. Six New Order soldiers huddled around a brazier nearby and regarded her shivering form with distrust. She lurched off, returning their glares as another spray of ice and water struck them. They cursed and spat, motioning her up the icy beach.

The only life inhabiting the hill was the vanguard. These black armored soldiers scurried through the camp assiduously erecting fortifications, cooking, tending to the horses, standing sentry, and lighting every fire the hill could sustain. Not one of them spared her a glance or tried to impede her progress.

Brimares continued her ascent until she found the New Order's lords convened atop the hill within their circle of totems, the peak around them splintered and disrupted by sharp stone protrusions. There were twelve men present in all, the five New Order lords and Salem standing opposite five Weshac. A New Order lieutenant thrashed upon the ground before a fire, flailing with enough force to fracture his bones.

She crept closer, noticing her kin standing at the periphery and avoiding them entirely. The lesser demons observed nervously, whispering amongst themselves, while Kell'MachChain mocked their temerity with a grin.

Patriarch Kadrin sidled toward Kheldar Ferain, licking his lips. "What is this spell, Commander? Witchcraft, sorcery?"

"No, this is Sinnitar Muntalabac come to tell us something." Kheldar Ferain jerked his head, motioning Kadrin to retreat. The patriarch happily accepted, scampering behind the pacing Bishop Viral.

Salem chuckled. "That is only true in a sense, Kheldar; this is a Dread Lord come to smash your illusions of power, to uproot your courage, and to eviscerate your pride. You will need a new lieutenant when he is done."

The fire died, releasing the pre-dawn obscurity to swallow them all. The shadows dissolved a second later when green light swelled into life across the hill, emerging from Kheldar Ferain's hand to unveil the lieutenant where he knelt before the ashes. His eyes and mouth bled darkness beneath the tenebrous red light of an inverted pentacle seared into his brow. That darkness oozed over his skin, dripping slowly to the earth like tar. Where it landed, the snow bubbled and spat, hissing steam as it gave way to graying earth below. The drops began to coalesce, circling through and around the lords and demons. More darkness emerged from the ashes, amalgamating to assume a human shape.

The lieutenant moaned, his skin now black and drawn taut across warped bones. All the youth and vigor that had characterized his body were gone, siphoned away by whatever malice possessed him. The lieutenant's back arched, his head crashing to the earth as a last scream split the air, marking the moment of his life's theft. Amidst the ashes, the specter of a man attained completion. He dwarfed everyone present, his eyes scathing with crimson light. The ashes sparked back to life around his feet, shining a venomous yellow.

Brimares dared a look from the specter's eyes to the embers. She saw an inverted pentacle with the silhouette of a man at its center and lines of fire that ate the earth and poisoned the air.

In unison to the specter's completion, the demons and the dark paladins retreated; the greater among them cowering while the lesser shriveled in terror. Only Salem, unfazed by the apparition, and Kell'MachChain, standing erect with eyes fixed on the specter, did not cower.

In the lowest voice Brimares had heard him use, Kell'MachChain murmured to himself, "But you're all dead."

The specter ignored Kell'MachChain and faced Kheldar Ferain, surveying the dark paladin in absolute conceit. "Dark Lord, I bring you counsel, knowledge, and a warning. You are an idiot; that sorcerer is an idiot." Contempt suffused his words, and Kheldar Ferain growled, a hand rising to the haft of his ax. The specter snorted. "Don't, it would be better for the New Order if you do not add insane and dead to your collection of faults. I come as an ally."

"What do you want, Sinnitar?" Kheldar Ferain did not move his hand, but Brimares could see him withering to cowardice beneath the specter's presence. Kell'MachChain began to shake his head in long, unnoticed movements. The Weshac cowered; their weapons discarded if not outright broken.

Sinnitar shifted on the embers to survey the mound's peak. "I see you have advanced in the world, Kheldar. I remember you when you were no more than a sniveling rat of a whore's son, killing the weak to terrify the strong. I remember watching you punish that lout who challenged your rule of the streets; it was with a rock you picked up off the street, if you don't recall. Tell me, what does it feel like to wield power after the crime and poverty of the streets? Does anything noble exist now after Fate has had its fun? But you do have power now, which is more than I expected of the wretch you were. Is it true power though? Or do you still have to rape the smaller boys to keep the larger ones in line?"

"I don't like you, whatever you are. Best state your business and make reverence before I decide to start killing." Sorran's knife flashed in the illumination when he stepped to the fore. Behind him, Eredar followed in his shadow, a satisfied glint in both of their eyes. The prayer-oaths clattered on their chests, one of the gray lockets for both brothers hanging open and radiating *Alkarred's* presence. She heard rumors of what those particular oaths were: they had vowed to kill men personally in the plague god's name.

The specter addressed them. "I see the sorcerer has commenced searching the East for our lost monsters. I commend him; we left many prizes through the centuries. Yes, we created your kind, or rather Taelan did, but it was our power that gave birth to what you are. There used to be hundreds of you, the Mad Kings' assassins. Now you are nothing more than dogs we twisted into something we fancied. Even now, I could unmake you and do so with such pain a demon would scream. You're not even full-bloods. Run, go back to your master. Wretches, are you all that endures of our work?"

Sorran and Eredar both stilled, rage contorting their features.

"But there are others worthier of note and appraisal in your midst. Come forward, Kell'MachChain; tell me, are you enjoying your gift? How is damnation? How deep have you gone into the Abyss? I believe Taelan bound you for eternity. I should put you back there; I promise to listen as you scream."

"I don't fear you; my power is vast and Chaos runs in my blood. I do not fear you."

"Everyone fears us. Tell me, Kheldar, where is the Mad King? You boast so many other trinkets from Taelan?"

"What do you want, Sinnitar?" Kheldar Ferain stepped forward, the veins in his neck distended on rage and fear.

Brimares could feel that same terror pounding in her blood and in her skull. It was not a natural fear, a sickness infested it, feeding her panic, giving rise to every vile emotion within her.

"What do I want? I am here to give you advice, knowledge, and assistance. *Telacra* will not be here much longer. You will be alone in The North, bereft of your precious goddess. The High-Warden has stirred at last, and the lock is set; all he must do is turn the key. Before the next dusk sets, *Telacra* will be banished from The North. Complete your prayers tonight, for they shall be the last she answers until this war ends. Fill your Shards and cast every spell you can. *Telacra* will be generous for she tastes only victory, ignorant of her rising defeat.

As for the demons, ignore that sorcerer's commands. Don't send them after the High-Warden. Keep them close, use their power to burn Antiark's walls. To hurl them against the High-Warden would waste them. He was bred for the single purpose of killing their ilk. Use silver arrows from afar when he comes to defend Antiark; end him thus and you might survive."

"I do not believe any man is prepared for three greater demons and their attending thralls, Sinnitar."

"I could. I can kill all of you, the whole army with a sword, with a stick, with a rock, with a pebble, with my hands, with a word if I was blindfolded and chained. You are not true powers in this world, Kheldar. The New Order is weak, mewling infants ripped from the bleeding womb of their dying mother. The Old Order had power, but that power was lost in the breaking. All you have are soldiers and a few clerics. You have no comprehension of power. The High-Warden will destroy your demons, then hunt you and your entire army. Your power will prove insignificant."

"You are eloquent as ever, Sinnitar. Have you heard from your brother of late? Or better still, speak to us of events in the West. My heart palpitates at the thought of hearing about your successes. I am certain they are many." Salem made a gesture of invitation to accompany his welcoming smile.

"I see that sorcerer sent you after all, Salem. It does not matter; you don't matter. The events in the West are no longer of my concern; I have the Iron. The sorcerer now sends me South, idiot that he is. I will join you when matters there are concluded. Now for the warnings, Tiberius Whyte is moving. He has spoken to a man called Cain: Cain Lammerock. Cardolyn Tyier will not be blind to your movements; he may send a legion of knights. I suggest you hurry; Antiark must fall."

A raucous cry interrupted Sinnitar, and Salem's small Raven descended from the night. She circled Sinnitar, cawing with laughter, before reclaiming her perch on Salem's shoulder.

In her wake, the Blond Knight rode into the light and dismounted before Sinnitar. The Blond Knight observed the specter, demonstrating no fear. In return the object of his attention stared at him in unconcealed contempt. The Blond Knight spoke, "I expected more from a Dread Lord than parlor tricks. Are you not supposed to make the night weep from terror? Where is your power? Why do I not fear you?"

"You are blind and you do fear us, only the realization eludes you, concealing itself behind your arrogance. You consider yourself an agent of malice, you consider yourself, though the term is cliché, a villain. You lust for power, and to have your every desire satiated until you die of the feast. Do you believe that since others fear you, terror passes you by; that it has no hold on your heart? You have killed maybe a dozen men. Yet, Kheldar Ferain killed over a hundred during a smaller span, and Kell'MachChain a thousand. And yet, they do not compare to that she-demon holding her distance. On a caprice, she ended more than all of you combined. You are nothing." Sinnitar extended a hand toward the Blond Knight, who smirked and ignored the gesture. Sinnitar laughed. "You have some truly sweet nightmares. Take this as a gift." Sinnitar's hand withdrew from the Blond Knight's face, leaving behind a slack face and bleeding eyes. "Go; enjoy my present; our hospitality is generous." Sinnitar faced Kheldar Ferain again, behind him the Blond Knight collapsed, dead but for the beat of his heart.

"Tell me, how do you intend to sack Antiark? The walls are high and the city grows as it needs and repairs every breach before it begins. The streets will move, and the rivers will drown your soldiers. The earth will clutch at your boots, and the wind will scream in your ears as it tears the flesh from your fragile bones. Your soldiers will be underfed and weak from sleepless nights. You will have two days to carry those walls and the citadel, two days to dispatch the High-Warden, Lord Antiark, and every soul in the city. There can be nothing left, not a stone, not a trickle of water lest the city rebuild itself."

"Our force is superior, and if the Weshac were to join, it would be vast. Two assaults, one from the east, the other from the west. We would not bother with blowing down the walls, and instead use *Telacra's* power to assault the Citadel and the Tower for neither are of Antiark. But the Weshac are not cooperating; they dislike the notion of assaulting Antiark."

Salem laughed. "Would you not hesitate? If it were the seat of *Telacra's* power in this Mortal Kingdom, would you attack it rashly? Antiark is an old and powerful city with many secrets. Every soul in there will fight, and moreover, there is a reason why the Weshac never raid a Northern city: there's no way out. The city will close itself around you and become your tomb, so even in victory you find defeat."

"Well, that is a matter I can resolve." Sinnitar turned to the cowering Weshac. They heard his words and shrieked. "Oh good, they still remember… Look at me!" In unison, they faced him. "That is better, is it not?" The Weshac nodded, each rising at the thrall of his words. His left hand reached toward them, fingers extended, dark energy coalescing about the knuckles. Trickles of wispy, frail light began slipping from the Weshacs' eyes, streaking through the air to touch his fingertips. Then the Weshacs gave a united howl, the light hardening and gushing free into Sinnitar, where it was consumed. He reverted his focus to Kheldar Ferain, the light still streaming into his hand. "They should be more compliant now."

Their transformation finished in moments, leaving the five Weshac as statues waiting for something, for anything really. They were empty vessels in need of filling and until something was given to them, they would remain thus until starvation or dehydration killed them. "I should be going; there is little else I can do for you here. Give Lord Antiark my fondest regards; tell him the Dread Lord sends his greetings. Enjoy my gifts while they last; you are about to be entirely on your own, except for me."

"What ... Do ... You … Want?" Kheldar Ferain drew and thrust his ax toward Sinnitar, blind in rage and unanswered or reasoned fear. "You can't be here just to advise us. What damned machinations are you attempting?"

"You are a fool, Kheldar. I want nothing from you. I wish to see Antiark burn, because it is a bastion of courage and light in a world quickly submitting to our shadow; and I do not refer to the New Order. The reign of Light is ending, and the New Order will burn with it. Know this, I have bought your soul, and when you die, your death will belong to me. On another note, there is a paladin tracking you." Sinnitar vanished, abandoning them to the bitter odor of fear.

In his absence, Brimares found his words echoing through her mind, proclaiming her doomed to die by the High-Warden, and her hands clenched to fists. Then there was the paladin, a member of the organization that condemned humans to the Abyss. A member of the order that condemned *her* to the last three hundred years of torture. Her Chaos simmered higher.

13

The Paladin

The thirty-fifth day of the New Order's incursion.

A bitter wind blew from the mountains, bearing a storm of Northern ice and snow. Yet, this was not The North; a full day's walk separated Lionel from Winter's Gate.

Heedless of the vermin skittering all around, he turned his attention to the derelict cathedral as the old wood creaked. The Shard of Divinity near his heart pulsed, warning him to purge the evil here before it successfully took root.

This was just one of many things that had stirred in the New Order's wake, a menagerie of small horrors emboldened by the devastation they sowed. This malice took the shape of a witch and siren that had assaulted the village a day ago, slaughtering and feasting on the inhabitants before besieging the cathedral.

Lionel had felt the cathedral's fall and mourned the deaths of its caretakers: his brothers in faith. The morning brought a divine summons: a command to avenge their deaths and render aid to any survivors.

Now, he stood on the cathedral's stairs, surrounded by signs of truncated lives: the children's toys, the cookware, the wagons, the footprints, the withered flowerbeds, the animal stalls, the pavilions, and the market. The only living things here were the pestilence-ridden vermin and insects, both too occupied with their new kingdom to bother him.

The cathedral's shattered doors groaned on rusted hinges as he ascended, taunting him with a chilling exhale. He unsheathed his long sword—a blade of true enchantment whose spells and prayers had been fused with it throughout its crafting, instead of simply being temporarily enchanted in the hours before battle—and pushed inside. The darkness bathed him like thin, fouled oil, suffocating his senses and sapping his strength. Lionel woke his Shard of Divinity, calling up a thread of latent power to illuminate his blessed sword. The scent of nutmeg filled his nostrils and tongue, its bitter aftertaste warning him that it neared depletion.

The light routed the entrenched shadows just far enough to reveal blood splashed across the threshold. He knelt and dipped a finger into it, watching it sizzle and turn black on his gauntlets. He counted the seconds as it simmered away, then took another globule and dropped it on his tongue, grimacing at the acrid taste. It was stronger than it should have been but still human; the witch was young and probably weak.

Lionel sat back on his haunches, listening. Every young witch was bound to a familiar, a lesser entity, through which she would augment her abilities. It was an old pact, created before the dawn of this Age, dictating the witch feed her blood to the familiar who in turn granted her power. This contract was finite, however. A familiar cannot grow stronger; therefore the witch always surpassed it. At that moment, the witch will discard her familiar in favor of rituals or stronger entities to augment her power.

Lionel listened but heard nothing until the cathedral's fractured wooden doors closed behind him. He raised his light and risked a glance back, but the shadows resisted it, taunting him and thickening. He moved to the door's frame and retrieved one of the engraved torches, igniting it into golden life with his shard. The shadows scattered, hissing almost inaudibly as nutmeg filled his nostrils again.

Abandoning the entrance, Lionel prowled deeper into the cathedral, trudging through splintered pews and toppled statues that reeked of urine and feces. The cracked images of saints gazed blindly from the walls, their eyes gouged from the stonework. Glass crunched under his step, drawing his eyes first down then up to the shattered remnants of a stained-glass ceiling.

He crossed the chamber, pausing at the podium where a copy of the *Amarthayiss* occupied the pedestal, a sliver of Order and Light amid the devastation. Lionel exhaled in relief and placed a hand upon the sacred tome: it was not the original *Amarthayiss*, book of *Enecki*, for to brush against such a divine artifact would have incinerated him. This was a lesser facsimile created to further the word of *Enecki*. It retained some of the original's power, however, and was a treasure Lionel could not leave behind. So he nestled it in his satchel and buckled the flap shut with a murmured invocation.

With the book secured, Lionel proceeded into the living quarters through a charred doorway. The room was a swamp of eviscerated books and bedding intermingled with corpses. Thumb bones littered the floor, split down the middle and sucked clean of marrow in testament to the witch's growing appetite.

He knelt beside one man lying separate from the others, his slacken face pressed into a pool of oddly fresh blood. Lionel cleared out a space so he could lay his torch down without igniting the scattered papers, and resumed his inspection. Much like the blood the corpse appeared fresh, but its skin stung cold to the touch. With an ominous premonition, Lionel overturned the corpse and cursed wordlessly, bile rising in his throat. On the man's brow was the mark of Chaos: two circles, one within the other, both chained and pierced by thirteen lances.

The mark explained much, especially why a young witch and a syren would assault a temple of *Enecki*. If the witch had bound herself to *Jaidar* instead of a familiar, she would have both the power and the desire to defile one of *Enecki's* temples. Still, it made no sense. If bound to *Jaidar*, the witch would have no need of a familiar and no need to drink blood or devour marrow. There was more astir than the cathedral's desecration. As if to validate this conclusion, his torch flickered and died.

Lionel left the torch where it lay and vacated the library, moving toward an archway on the opposite wall. As he neared, a cold breath slithered up the waiting stair to greet him. He flinched at its touch and ignited his sword with light, routing the suddenly heavier darkness. It receded from his light, causing the room to warm as it fled downstairs. Lionel pursued.

The stairway led to the scriptorium, where economical chairs sat at desks laden with books, ink vials, and loose paper. A progression of increasingly ink-stained brothers occupied those chairs in various postures, some slumped upon their desks and others slouched back with open mouths.

Lionel hesitated, noting the mark painted in blood on the floor: thirteen crimson spears expanding from the room's center, perforating two circles of runes and chains to touch the walls. It was a mark of ownership, *Jaidar's* mark. The witch and syren had done more than defile one of *Enecki's* temples; they had fully invoked a god, and *Jaidar* answered.

Even the various consorts only used partial rituals, invoking a mere fraction of their god's consciousness. But if answered, a full invocation concentrated a god's intellect into a single moment of time and space when it normally encompassed centuries. Such actions always resulted in consequences.

Usually, the ensuing devastation occurred immediately, but *Jaidar's* effect on the Mortal Kingdoms had always been erratic, sometimes resulting in a fallout that occurred centuries prior to or after the original invocation.

The more Lionel learned, the more obvious it became that both the witch and syren desired something concealed here. But what?

Careful to avoid the pentacle, Lionel traversed the desks, checking each scribe's brow for *Jaidar's* mark and finding it without fail.

Another arch waited across the room; its door wedged open with a loose stone. He paused at it, catching the murmurs of a chant below. He tried to decipher the words but only recognized a fragment of their meaning. Grasping the chain around his throat and whispering a swift prayer, Lionel stepped through the archway onto the cobweb-draped stair.

His cloak swept the steps as he descended, pulling back in the dense cobwebs to reveal a brigandine and full suit of armor. He paused at the final step, his presence concealed by the extended wall, and listened. Quiet footsteps and labored breathing reached him, almost muffled by the sound of boiling water and the scent of new death. There was a rasp of iron on stone, the clink of weapons against armor, and the senseless mutterings of a mind newly lost.

He crouched and stole a glance around the corner. There were five of them: all tall, muscular men collected for those attributes, which signified a female witch. They were armed with only the most basic implements: a pair of axes and three haphazard bludgeons. A second, longer glance revealed the spells inscribed on their skin were few and thin, the ink barely visible against their gaunt flesh. The presence of a second door proved of greater interest, however. Cathedrals—even the largest—are comprised of a kitchen, a library, a main hall, and the dormitories, yet there was another door nestled in the kitchen's back corner. The door stood ajar, flanked by two stone monks, which marked the syren as male. The witch's chanting faltered from beyond the doorway and resumed.

Lionel crept a few steps back up the stair, contemplating his options. He disliked the thought of a frontal assault against five opponents, their poor equipment notwithstanding. Besides, any conflict would attract at least the syren and possibly the witch. He dared not challenge both of them simultaneously with his Shard so depleted, and either one was dangerous on their own. The syren, in particular, concerned him, for they were an old and malignant race with centuries of cultivated hate. They only ventured from their caves as adults and only to acquire something of immense value.

He had precious few options, and stealth was not one of them. He sighed, recognizing there was no time to deliberate, and ignited his Shard, molding its power to deafen himself against the syren's *song*. Then speaking in the sacred tongue of *Enecki*, Lionel touched the blade of his sword, turning the iron a bright cherry and then bathing it in golden fire. As he spoke, however, the witch's servants fell silent, recognizing the invocation of an ascended god.

Still amassing power, Lionel stepped into the open and flung his hand upward, a fierce, golden light blooming in his palm.

The witch's servants recoiled, shrieking their hatred and agony as every shadow fled. One, his skin boiling from contact with the divine light, wrenched a helm over his eyes and charged, flailing with a bludgeon.

Lionel decapitated him with a backhand swipe and advanced, hurling fire at another with his free hand. The remaining three staggered upright, yanking their helms down with wordless snarls, and charged.

Lionel backpedaled, manifesting his Shard's power into physical shape. It formed slowly in dense golden teardrops and cascaded along the edges of his armor to his palm. He snapped his arm out, simultaneously hurling and molding the amassed divine energy. It struck the back doorway and expanded into a golden barricade, imprisoning its occupants while he dealt with their adherents. Then the thralls reached him.

He dove aside at the last instant, forcing them to change course. The smaller thralls managed the shift, twisting in step to spring after him, but the largest careened into a wall. Lionel parried a lumbering swipe and plunged forward, hammering his vastly superior weight into his unarmored assailant before flowing around to parry and turn the second thrall's assault.

It was a simple maneuver, one of the beginning stances for the *Daaru* blade-form, but it was devastating against an untrained foe. In that single maneuver, Lionel stole all his opponent's strength, momentum, and balance, then with a flick of his wrist, expended it with crushing finality, caving in his opponent's chest. A quick thrust executed the other thrall, leaving only one.

He spun toward the larger thrall, slashing upward and across to sever his reaching arms. The thrall ploughed onward, crashing into Lionel and driving him back. Lionel staggered, righted himself and shoved back, hurling the thrall to the ground, where it thrashed, golden flames roaring up its arms from his earlier cut. It tried to rise several times but ultimately crumbled away to ash.

Lionel stepped away from the corpse, panting, and turned his attention to the doorway. His barrier bulged outward, riddled with veins of dark energy. A shriek tore through the barrier, strangling every other sound as it climbed toward a crescendo, "Where is it?"

His barrier shattered, hurling golden shards across the room. Lionel cursed and lunged for the stairs, concealing himself from his new foes. There was a breath of silence, then the low furious hiss of a syren; he could hear again. Muttering another curse, Lionel crept further up the stairs and began a new verse, restoring the tattered threads of his earlier prayer.

Shrieking, the syren surged forward and around the corner, the heavy coils of its lower body piling against the walls. Lionel slashed, his blade flaring golden, and drove the monster back. Rearing up, the syren struck, its jade talons scouring his left bracer and the wall. Lionel stumbled up the stair, slashing haphazardly only to have his blade sheer into the wall and catch. The syren reared higher, filling the passage from floor to ceiling with its sinuous bulk, and inhaled.

There was a hush of culmination, and then the syren's jaw opened in that fatal scream of its race. The walls rippled and his skin turned cold, but his prayer held, protecting him against the syren's *song*. Lionel clambered to his feet, fighting through the concussive sonic battery. He lurched downward, wrenching his blade free of the wall, and thrust it at his foe.

The syren slapped his weak thrust aside and retreated, unnerved by the failure of its *song*. Lionel lunged after it, hacking and slashing, desperate to prevent it from singing again.

A second cry tore through the room, "Where is it?" And a twisted, burning, canine creature stepped from the doorway with a girl mounted atop it: the witch. "You took it! It was promised to me, all the power, all the secrets, everything! And you took it! It is mine; mine, you hear me. I will have it, and you will be dead! Give me it, give me the book!"

Lionel flared his Shard, summoning everything he could bear to hold. The syren reared back and surged forward, the *song* again rising to its lips. Lionel answered with golden flames, hurling them from his left hand as he charged his foe. Fire engulfed the syren, stealing its voice and breaking its momentum. He danced past with two swift strikes, one to the syren's flank and the second impaling the reeling syren from behind. It spasmed and then fell with a thud, leaving him alone with the witch and her demon.

Lionel leapt back, twisting toward the creature as it charged, its maw wide with wanton bloodlust and innate odium. He sidestepped, slashing as it past and lacerating its eye. They parted, Lionel whirling toward them as the demon raked furrows in the floor and settled. He screamed a challenge and smashed his left fist into his chest, unleashing a rain of golden threads along his armor. They struck the floor and flared out into a four-walled diamond around him.

The demon threw itself against the barrier, howling and spitting molten saliva. The barrier retaliated, blasting the demon off with a crackle of energy. It staggered and straightened but relented. The witch, however, thrust her forefinger at Lionel, words oozing from her tongue in the beginnings of a curse.

Lionel drove his sword into the floor and knelt, his voice rising in an old prayer from the *Amarthayiss* an instant before the curse struck. He gasped, almost buckling beneath the impact, but clutched his sword tighter and ignited his Shard.

The opposing powers ravaged one another with the blind hatred of anathemas, consuming both each other and the energies fueling them in seconds. Ultimately, the curse withered first and died, leaving Lionel to sag forward as the psalm faded from his tongue. The cathedral's floor hummed beneath him, almost vibrating with divine power, reacting to his presence as a scion of *Enecki*.

He stood, exhaling an unsteady breath, and leveled his sword on the witch. He could tell her power was exhausted from her shuddering gasps and the way her skin cracked liked baked clay, but that didn't make her less dangerous.

She straightened, her anemic features scoured with new lines, and extended a trembling hand. Thin energy coalesced down her arm, gathering in her palm until, with a whimpered gasp, her efforts failed and she crumpled, motionless except for the rise and fall of her shoulders.

The demon discarded its mistress with a shake of its matted shoulders and charged, flames bleeding from the cracks and fissures of its body. It collided with the barrier a second time, shattering it amid an eruption of ichor and fire, and continued forward. Lionel flowed around it, gouging out its eye with a slash, but the demon twisted with inhuman dexterity and hammered his side with an immense forepaw, shearing his armor and bruising him. Still reeling, Lionel struck again, impaling the demon's surviving eye. It shrieked, more in fury than agony, and flung him across the room.

Lionel slammed into the far wall with the rasp of iron on stone and staggered to his feet, vision blurry from the impact. Across from him, the demon shook its ridged head, shedding a rain of molten ichor. There could be no retreat between them, no relent or mercy for they were opposites: Order and Chaos.

The demon screamed its battle cry and lunged, flames igniting in its ruined eyes. Lionel attempted another slashing sidestep, but it compensated and collided with him, knocking the blade from his hand and crushing him against the wall.

Lionel gasped and then clawed at its head, digging his thumbs into its eye sockets. The demon shrieked and clamped on his shoulder, wrenching him back and forth across the wall, frenzied by his blood. Twisting, Lionel managed to liberate a dagger from his belt, and drove it into the demon's throat, causing its flesh to blister and froth. The demon released him with an agonized howl and reared back, stumbling and crashing through its death throes.

Lionel forced his aching body to stand and trudged forward, one arm clutching his side while the other collected his sword. The demon writhed and snapped at him, helpless as he raised his sword and stabbed down, silencing it. Then he faced the witch, steeling his heart against the lie of her age and the innocence of her face. She turned at his approach, tears welling at her eyes. Lionel hesitated; witches were fearless, their power consumed that emotion.

She spoke, her voice a quavering sob, "P–...p...please."

Lionel growled and lifted his sword overhead but vacillated on the brink of execution. Those amber, hauntingly human eyes stared up at him, pleading.

His sword drifted lower; no one knew all of magic's laws, the dark magics in particular. Still weeping, the girl crawled toward him through an array of disjointed murmurs. "H–...help me." The tip of Lionel's sword brushed the ground, ringing a single metallic note. "It hurts ... her voice in my head ... laughing, hurting always hurting."

He knelt, aching to comfort her. "It's alright; I'm here." Doffing his gauntlets, he pulled her head into his chest and awakened his Shard. The girl sobbed unrestrainedly, attempting words but succeeding only in whimpering. "It's alright; you're safe now. I'm going to help you, stop her from hurting you." Never ceasing his low, comforting murmurs, Lionel molded his Shard's light, fashioning an ember in the fingers of his hand. The energy pranced across his palm and slid into the girl's body. She moaned, deep and agonized, her arms wrapping around his neck. Hot tears fell against his cheek, burning with the remnants of whatever taint possessed her.

His ember pulsed, searching the recesses of her thoughts and soul for enduring malice. The ember throbbed, probing deeper, and died. Lionel shoved the witch back but failed to prevent her hands from closing around his throat. Her weeping warped into a low cackle as she squeezed harder, crooked nails perforating his skin. Lionel ignored her attempts to strangle him, grasped her skull as she cackled and wrenched, snapping her neck. She jerked and sagged, slipping from his arms to sprawl across the floor. Witches died like any other woman; the difficulty was in keeping them dead.

Lionel slumped forward onto his hands, holding his breath and listening for anything that broke the pervasive quiet. Seconds passed and he heard only his heartbeat, allowing him a gentle sigh.

He stood and collected his sword, cleaning it with a stained cloth until every trace of blood had vanished. Then he tossed the cloth onto the witch's body with the words of a prayer, raised the blade overhead and decapitated her. There was no blood, for witches bound to a familiar do not bleed. This, more than anything else, kept him from losing his supper.

After that, he hurried to collect the kitchen's spare kindling and mound it around her corpse, ignoring the syren and thralls for their deaths were final. When he no longer saw the corpse, he lit the flame and stepped back, swallowing as the awful stench rose. The flames climbed, slow to catch the wood but eager for the witch.

Lionel moved to the center of the room and knelt, drawing a silver knife from his boot as he began a psalm of cleansing. His words were not loud, but they were enough. He slid the knife through the witch's lips and pried her jaw open, exposing blackened teeth. First, he excised her tongue at the base and tossed it onto the flames. Then he laid the blade flat on each eye, watching the skin blister and pus. The magic-devouring silver would sear her lids shut, blinding her and barring the last exits for when her itinerant soul returned. Lastly, he cut every adornment—regardless of its nature—from her hair and skin, depriving her of vessels for her power.

A witch's soul always returns to her body; this is a law they cannot break; but, if the body is destroyed, their souls are released to find another mortal vessel. Thus the body is burned, except for the head from which the tongue is removed and the eyes seared, ensuring she can neither cast spells nor escape.

Sickened to his heart, Lionel tied the witch's head to his belt by its matted hair, collected his weapons and started toward the mysterious room, summoning a light that bobbed between his fingers. He expected some new peril to arise at every step, but no monster swelled up from the shadows to crush him, no ancient trap sprang with the hiss and crunch of gears, and no spells denied him passage. In fact only the cobwebs deterred him. They hung across the doorway and from the walls in vast sheets with strands thicker than his thumb and more than one ensnared rodent. He touched one tentatively and felt a spark of power. They were not natural spider webs.

Past the doorway, he encountered a chamber blanketed in dead warding runes and frowned; these were not runes to bar intruders but to imprison something.

A short flight of stairs ran down the wall to a cracked floor and a raised dais. An empty book-pedestal occupied the dais, its wrought iron frame twisted and broken.

Lionel shuddered, unable to disavow the sensation he was entering the crypt of some long-exiled abomination, and descended, one hand running along the wall to explore the runes and spells carved there. The air thickened as he advanced, growing cold. A strange dread stirred in his heart as his hand brushed across magic after magic: the chill of wizardry, the many incenses and flavors of prayercraft, the burn of magecraft, and the phantom agony of demon fire. There were other magics, some he knew and many he did not, but they all shared a purpose: incarceration.

He reached the floor, flinching at the dulled remains of more spells, and raised his light for a better view. Fissures riddled the floor, divulging bloated roots while apertures split the walls from floor to ceiling, their edges bleeding magic. But he saw nothing to explain why this room existed, nor anything that so much as hinted at its creators.

Lionel mounted the dais and brushed a hand across the wreckage of the gaunt podium, hoping for an echo of its divine power or a memory of what had been stolen. He did not search for the item itself, knowing the witch and syren had found it missing.

He dismounted the dais and approached the far wall to touch the defiled wardings. They flickered at his touch, sensing and drawing strength from an adherent of *Enecki*. This gave him hope; stone had always boasted a better memory than iron.

Scraping away the grime of centuries, Lionel began a coaxing prayer to reawaken the dormant power. It answered warily, seeping from the wall to immerse his hands. Fractured memories blurred in his mind, often fragmented or repeating, images of black wings, an evanescent woman, and the stolen book. He probed deeper, meticulously weaving together the images to create a cohesive recollection.

The scent of smoke disrupted him as he delved, jarring him with a sudden, violent cough. He stumbled back, raising a forearm to cover his mouth and nostrils. The fire should not have expanded so quickly; it should have taken an hour to progress beyond the witch's corpse. Lurching toward the stair, he dashed upward. In his haste, he failed to notice the small Raven following him out.

14

The Palace Of Dragons

Dieharamon followed in Valeriius' shadow, his shoulders hunched beneath the young night's chill and the splendor of the Remanas Palace. A cold wind swept through the chasm, tugging their procession's finery and shearing through his thin, accentuating dress suit. He shuddered and directed a mistrustful glance at the carrion birds perched all around them in droves, an endless choir of red-eyes monsters. Mostly they favored the thin, crumbling bridges over the palace, structures erected in recent decades without the blessing of the old craftsmen and magic. Originally the space had been vacant, letting the sun shine unopposed upon the seat of the Dragon Lords' authority, now it creaked with bland, decrepit walkways.

The Ramanas Palace, former seat of the Dragon Lords, towered before them, spearing the heavens with twelve spires and spanning miles in width. Its walls of gold, jade, and ivory glittered in the fractured moonlight, simultaneously radiant against the dark and staggering in their beauty. Rank upon rank of bridges extended from it, bedecked in all the riches they could sustain and lined with dragon-masked guards in white, all to intimidate the approaching emissaries. The Kalvonders would greet them with spectacles of excess, awe them with a heritage that eclipsed millennia. Only then, robed in the trappings of their lavish grandeur, would they hear the New Order speak.

The wealthiest Kalvonders had arrived first, congregating throughout the early hours of the day to enjoy the palace's normally forbidden grounds. The guild lords and clergymen arrived next with the former appearing in solitude and the latter in a starkly controlled horde. Now, with night freshly risen, the lesser Kalvonders were permitted to enter.

As always, Valeriius chose to come last, forever maintaining the illusion of impotence. He approached the palace guarded by a mere half-dozen poorly equipped warriors and a handful of slaves. For retainers he employed the most generic pair imaginable: a guardian and assassin, neither dressed lavishly nor exhibited trophies to boast their skill. Either display would have earned him contempt, together they labeled him immaterial, little better than an Avaran.

Tonight he wore a brocaded tunic of gold and jade, crowned with a shallow hood of silver drawn over his brow. A pair of coattails draped just past his knees, accenting the movement of his darkly clothed legs and guiding any inspecting eyes to his conspicuously amethyst-laden boots; a subliminal threat few Kalvonders had to stoop to.

It was also unusual for Kalvonders to flaunt their gladiators, but Dieharamon was the cornerstone of Valeriius' wealth, a legend in his own right, and one of the most valuable possessions in all of Sahdaen. So Valeriius paraded him, taunting the other Kalvonders with something they could never have. It also served to remind all who saw him that the grand Angorat'Wass neared upon the following morrow, when Dieharamon would enter an arena specially crafted for this moment to fight and die with thousands of others. No one expected him to survive, but all expected a legendary display. He would murder hundreds.

They passed between the entrance's soaring marble doors, leaving the ranks of dragon-masked soldiers behind—for their blood was too impure to tarnish the sanctified palace stonework.

Inside they entered a courtyard that glowed with the full glory of day, illumined by a hundred thousand torches affixed to every wall, pillar, and brazier that would sustain them. Valeriius advanced in the blazing light unperturbed, but Dieharamon quailed, one arm raised against the painful brilliance. A moment later, his vision adjusted, revealing a forest of statues carved from ivory, stone, onyx, and jade. They surrounded the palace in a ring of a hundred ranks, depicting *Arawn*, *Ashshand*, nameless warriors, and most of all, the twelve Dragon Lords.

The Dragon Lords had appeared in the South on wings of fire and light as the Crimson Empire of *Lord Arthramain Roy'al* crumbled into ruin. They were his servants, assigned with a sacred geas to protect this corner of his empire. Thus, as the world burned with his dying Age, the Dragon Lords claimed the South and preserved it from the nightmare.

They ruled for twelve hundred years, for no mortal being or creature could contest them, and only twice during those centuries did war come to Blessed Remanas. The first war was an attempted reunification of the Crimson Empire by the would-be emperor of Rhiatan, but his endeavor failed in a storm of dragon-fire.

The second war occurred at the end of their reign, born of a long-nurtured avarice. One of the twelve lost sight of his purpose. He succumbed to the lure of power, to the lust of solitary dominance without rivals or fetters. And so, he reacquainted the land with misery.

The ensuing civil war destroyed Blessed Remanas and spawned a new horror upon the world, for the traitor could not defeat his kin with the weapons he possessed. Compelled by desperation, he sacrificed himself to a darker magic and arose upon a tide of blood, black sorcery, and rubble, reborn as Morrehiegann.

When the war ended, ten Dragon Lords lay upon the last battlefield, their sacred bodies carrion for the crows. In their deaths, however, they achieved victory, routing Morrehiegann to Paranoia where Andeor'Vallen, last of the twelve, pursued him.

The two fought a war of vengeance and hate, and such was their power that the earth was splintered and mountains pulverized. In the heavens, the last two lieutenants of *Lord Arthramain Roy'al* fought as dragons themselves, a mass of flames and sinuous scaled limbs. Fueled by rage, Andeor'Vallen proved the stronger, and as the sun set, he cast his sworn brother to the earth. Grief-stricken and scarred in both body and spirit, Andeor'Vallen returned south where he locked himself away in the Remanas Palace, and never ventured out again. However, lying amid the ruin of his shattered body, Morrehiegann's eyes opened.

Though his body perished in the battle, his spirit endured through dark magic and a terrible contract. It fled the dying mortal vessel to a dark sanctuary crafted of forbidden power where, his evolution complete, Morrehiegann spawned a new era of night over Paranoia. Later, his dominion would be broken at the beginning of a conflict that persists to this day.

Valeriius perused the forest of statues with an air of barely contained boredom, every look weighted with contempt and every murmured phrase thick with disgust. His peers accompanied him in this perusal, though they saw it more as an opportunity to converse with one another or the servants of superior Kalvonders.

They ignored him for the most part, disdaining his inconsequence and the brutish inelegance of his displayed emotions. Nevertheless, Dieharamon felt more than one gaze stalking Valeriius. With the Anatay drug in his sole possession and Krell Kalvonder's resources at his disposal, Valeriius represented the beginning of a new power play in Sahdaen. One that could upset the Kalvonder hierarchy.

One Kalvonder rose from his seat on an Andeor'Vallen statue, brushed off his loose robes and strolled toward Valeriius. Two men and a woman trailed in his shadow, their intermingled glances of boredom and suspicion unfeigned. The first man wore a lavish shield across his back, accentuating the already dominant physique. The second man slunk after the first, his visage tattooed with an auburn arachnid and faintly charred: an alchemist. The woman sashayed behind her master, the lower half of her face masked with gold muslin while the upper half gleamed beneath vivid paints. The Kalvonder himself walked with a lanky stride, his shoulders slouched from habit and his skin pasty from hours underground in the food mines. Slim rings of gold, silver, and ruby glittered on his beige robes, interwoven in the resplendent Artisan Weave, and upon the haft of the iron-linked whip dangling from his side. He also wore mint green gloves of Artisan Weave, the silk so fine and thin you could see the skin beneath with the sigils of proprietorship inked across the back of his hand: he owned one of the blood lines that wove Artisan Silk.

His visitor reached them with a wide, black-toothed grin and a gesture to encompass their surroundings. "Is it not glorious? The splendor of this Hold shames all others, and I have seen my share." As he completed the gesture, he glanced at Dieharamon and his eyes flashed greedily, not only with avarice to possess but also at Dieharamon's inevitable fate in the arena.

"Yes, it is impressive and also an egregious waste."

The nameless Kalvonder snorted, a thumb burnishing his whip. "How can any of this magnificence be a waste? Are we not about to host a dominant Eastern faction? Do we not walk paths of gold, swim in rivers of jade, and dress ourselves in ivory sheets? You cannot squander what you are drowning in."

Valeriius indicated their surroundings with a lithe hand, mocking his companion's earlier motion. "The New Order does not come to us in search of beguilement or wealth, Lyrrh Kalvonder. You will gain no purchase on them through this display. They serve gods, you fool, and what are we to them?"

An incensed snort burst from Lyrrh's nostrils. "Remember who you declare a fool, Valeriius! You may now wield a shred of power, but it is nothing, nothing, compared to mine!"

"I have no need of your support or esteem, Lyrrh Kalvonder, and your enmity could serve me well. All of Sahdaen separates our residences, and your reach is short; so I will deem you a fool when you present yourself as one. Now, what is the purpose of this tedious dialogue?"

The man made a visible effort to restrain his emotions. "I merely wondered if you knew the origin of this so-called New Order. My operatives tell me it is a religious cult devoted to *Telacra* but little else. I hoped a scholar such as yourself might enlighten me further, but now I see you are a mislaid infant struggling to tread water in the seas of his forefathers. I will take my leave—"

Smooth as the striking adder, Valeriius' cane struck Lyrrh's side, forestalling his departure. "It is no trouble, though their history does lack interesting events. They find their origin in the Guild Wars some five centuries past, during Cardolyn Tyier's ascension, may the blood boil in his veins. After his ascension, the Imperial Emperor rewrote most of the Paladin Order's guiding tenants. However, some older paladins defied his amendments and fled east to find a new deity, where they became what they are today: the New Order."

Valeriius smiled, the expression as much a veiled threat as profound contempt, and lowered his cane. "Now, go and tell your allies about me; rage and insult them until they abandon you. However, before they discard you, make certain they know I will not parlay on their terms. If they wish an alliance or a blind eye from me, let them come crawling across the floor begging with their lies and their tribute." Valeriius strode off, heedless of the other Kalvonder's spluttering diatribe.

Even after the crowd swallowed Lyrrh, Valeriius moved with concentrated purpose, surveying the amassed Kalvonders as he would a heifer at auction. But as they toured the crowd, proceeding to make not one but several circuits, Dieharamon realized Valeriius was not searching for someone but making his presence known, grinding his recent ascension into the minds of every prospective rival, demanding their attention. Yet, by the very act of doing so, he marked himself as infantile.

Gradually Valeriius conducted them to a low wall of worked masonry attired in luxuriant flower vines and bobbing soul-lights. Its effervescent blooms of red and blue swayed in the breeze, offering an image of quiescent beauty to contrast the excess splendor surrounding them. A simple iron door offered ingress into the garden beyond.

Valeriius paused on this threshold. "Leave your weapons at the gate; there will be no violence or its implements in these gardens. We must obey the laws set by *Lord Arthramain Roy'al.*"

Dieharamon hurried to divest himself of his various knives and hatchets and lay them beside the door. When he finished, Valeriius motioned for his two retainers to wait outside, and entered.

Dieharamon followed, feeling as if a veil was being drawn across the world, quieting the tumult outside and painting over the harsh southern stone with gentle verdure. The garden seemed half-asleep, its grounds wandered by unbroken marble paths and its trees draped with pale white lights. Fountains whispered amidst the foliage, their rims wreathed in delicate purple vines and their waters glimmering with an innate glow. It was all alien to him, and utterly beautiful.

A woman emerged from deeper in the garden, her silver and emerald robes mingling effortlessly in the flora and her hair cut short in palace custom. "What do you seek of these gardens, Valeriius Kalvonder?"

"I am in search of Thanen Kalvonder, keeper. Is he here, or must I seek elsewhere?"

"Thanen Kalvonder has indeed sought sanctuary here. If you do not intend to agitate him, I will guide you."

"Please do."

"Follow me, then."

The palace-keeper conducted them further into the garden, the star-crowned heavens gradually becoming hidden behind a veil of scented trees. The ethereal white lights grew more numerous in unison, heightening the already prevalent sense of unreality and painting the world over with twilight. For the most part, they encountered no one else, only keepers tending the garden or travelling to some other task.

Eventually they reached a willow tree set on the bank of a stone pool beside an ivory bench. The palace-keeper advanced to the willow and parted its branches. "Valeriius Kalvonder, if it pleases you."

Thanen acknowledged them with a flick of his eyes, then gently took the farthest edge of his barely off-white seat-cloth and folded it into a slim strip running parallel to his leg. The Artisan weave gleamed, and the breathtaking images woven upon it in black lines changed with every fold, recounting a simple story that concluded with the final turn.

Valeriius retrieved his mauve seat-cloth from within his robes and unrolled it over the span Thanen cleared, then he smoothed it, leaned his cane against the bench and sat. "Thanen."

"What do you want?" Thanen asked, his features expressionless and his eyes veiled behind long lashes.

"What all those who seek you desire: access to your secrets."

"And why should I barter with you, Valeriius? Despite the power you've acquired, you remain insignificant, and eastern sell-swords will not change that."

"The sell-swords are not my only secret, Thanen." He snapped a willow branch and presented it to his companion. "And I happen to know some of yours."

"It's adorable you think that matters in the least. Secrets are just leverage, and I hold leverage over some of us that are truly frightening, anyone of whom would eagerly erase you at my behest."

Valeriius dropped the unaccepted willow branch. "I do not seek conflict, Thanen. I mention my knowledge only to acquire your full attention and to ensure my safety after."

"The one you have found, the other is still in suspension; I have no intention of suffering Krell's fate."

"Krell was an irritation and a hindrance; you know she amounted to nothing more than a drunkard and a brute. She was inferior, unfitting of the name Kalvonder and ill-suited to any alliance. To bind myself to her would be like tying myself to an anchor."

"I do not argue your accusations, Valeriius. I simply state I will not ally myself with a mad viper."

"I do not expect an alliance in writing and blood, words will suffice."

"And what would I gain from our alliance?"

"I intend to ascend on the turbulence caused by the New Order, which would reward you with influence you might otherwise never achieve. Especially if I am the viper you believe."

Thanen laughed. "Very well, I will set you a task, Valeriius. If you succeed, I will bind myself to you; if you fail, you will condemn yourself to me. I will give you one secret to start this wager, and you will kill one man for me, agreed?"

Valeriius considered. "Agreed. I will kill Lyrrh Kalvonder."

Thanen gave him a dangerous reappraisal. "Yes, that is a good choice. I will consider your offer. Now, whose secret do you want?"

A rustle interrupted them as the palace-keeper parted the willow branches. "My apologies, Valeriius and Thanen Kalvonder, but the New Order is soon to arrive." Thanen nodded and she retreated.

Valeriius waited until she disappeared before resuming, "That ulcer on Lyrrh Kalvonder's throat, it's not a typical malady, is it?"

"Be cautious, Valeriius, our kind abhor intelligent rivals; in particular, those they once perceived as inferior. And yes, Lyrrh, the fool, is addicted to demon blood. Or rather, he is addicted to diluted Chaos.

"The supplier could not manage Lyrrh's need and died for his failure. As a result, Lyrrh is growing desperate. His supply thins by the day and he knows he cannot survive the withdrawal. Now we have emissaries to greet."

Vast and comprised of a dozen tiers, the palace's greeting chamber surrounded Valeriius in gilded splendor. The floor ascended level by level as it progressed outward from the room's center, each tier hundreds of feet wide and laden with tables, slaves, guards, statues, thrones, guild lords, and Kalvonders. Curtained alcoves lined the walls between the tapestries and paintings. Three long atriums, likewise curtained, stretched from wall to wall overlooking the audience chamber from various heights. Thin staircases scaled the walls to the atriums, serving as the only access routes. Light suffused the entire chamber in gold, refusing to allow even the most infantile shadow.

Valeriius observed proceedings from the lowest atrium's railing, his delicate hands resting on the balustrade. The atrium's secluded interior waited behind him, illuminated by faintly glowing amethysts set in the curtain walls and their jade columns. The sable carpeting underfoot was edged in gold, and thick enough to mask the floor. Weathered tables peeked out from curtained alcoves to either side of Valeriius, their burnished mahogany cracked from the southern heat.

Alone except for Dieharamon, he watched his fellow Kalvonders mill below him because they, and not the emissaries, held the power. The New order would never truly threaten the Avarus Desert, no army besides that of *Lord Arthramain Roy'al* ever had.

Therefore he scanned their faces for apprehension, listened to their flowing dialogues for stutter or flaw and hunted their postures for quiver or stiffness, forever seeking a vulnerability to exploit.

Of the Kalvonders present, only Ureign and Trerrock displayed no disgruntlement at the delay. They observed the proceedings with indifference, preparing for a long contest of wills with the eastern delegation. Their greatest hindrance was a lack of knowledge, for the Kalvonders as a whole knew only rumors of the New Order; thankfully, the New Order shared this ignorance.

Valeriius, however, had monitored the New Order from the moment they unveiled themselves, noting every change in their motives and nature. The New Order had once protected the weak, now it sowed malice.

The New Order had concealed itself in the East for five-hundred years, growing stronger and spreading their influence. Now they were ready to begin their war on Cardolyn Tyier. But the Paladin Empire had its allies, so the New Order needed allies. Thus they came south.

The Avarans shared their hatred of Cardolyn Tyier, which made them agreeable to a potential alliance. The Avarans also feared everything they did not know, which made them easy to manipulate. Lastly, the Kalvonders were corrupt and abusive, which eliminated any need for the New Order to conceal their intent. What they failed to realize, however, was the Kalvonders were not Avarans and every fraction the New Order's equals.

Tidings had also reached Valeriius of an assault on Winter's Gate, no doubt an attempt to undermine the rather tenuous alliance binding The North and the West. If successful, the invasion might unbalance the scales in the New Order's favor, and they needed every advantage against Cardolyn Tyier.

Valeriius dug into his rich apparel and withdrew a small pewter statue of *Arawn*. It depicted the unaligned god as a hooded figure seated in his customary throne bent forward with age. He set it on the railing to greet the New Order upon their arrival.

The doors swung open, groaning on strained hinges and revealing the New Order's delegation. First to enter was a tall man in black robes, his mercurial eyes relentlessly hunting those with true power. Age visibly weighed on him, causing him to shuffle with the assistance of a staff, but that physical debility belied his power for he stood high in his goddesses' favor.

Valeriius rejected the man as a fool, and instead sought the one called Sinnitar Muntalabac.

The tall man continued his advance, beckoning as he went. A thunder of boots answered his gesture, preceding ranks of New Order's soldiers in black chainmail and robed priests.

The actual emissaries followed soon after, robed in the dark vestments of their order and the white scarves of diplomats. They advanced quietly, harmlessly, but their presence brooded with power and their eyes gleamed the unnatural ebony of those sworn to *Telacra*.

They assembled before the Kalvonders and bowed, evincing an illusion of humility they never fully sold. The gift bearers flooded in behind them, bearing a dazzling fortune in gold, silver, and art.

Valeriius had no desire for the wealth they poured across the tiles in wanton abundance, his attention owed allegiance only to the man entering in their wake. He crossed the threshold with a stride of autocratic oppression, heralded by a cloud of tactile dread and an imperious gaze.

This man Valeriius recognized as Sinnitar Muntalabac; no other within the chamber possessed such a presence of unrestrained malice. No other presence squeezed the mind for the simple sin of being regarded.

The Dread Lord was a huge man, towering over all others by a full head and shoulders. His skin was a silken black, offset by the crimson beads tattooed over his exposed flesh in convoluted patterns and corrupt sigils. His eyes were a broad venomous yellow, his clothing heavy, dark, and taut across a daunting musculature. Bestiality loomed in his shadow, a broiling, pervasive spirit-presence that caused fragile men to cower at his approach and stronger men to flinch. Despite all of this, Sinnitar Muntalabac traversed the hall unseen, his every step one of effortless grace.

An unmistakable blade occupied his back, its onyx sheath decorated with silver runes and gold vines. The blade was slim to the point of frailty and half its bearer's height from pommel to tip; yet only a fool would have believed it frail. The handle was a masterpiece of silver stone worked into the semblance of a dragon in flight. Its coiled tail formed the handle and its spread wings the cross-guard. Common knowledge said the dragon's neck and head extended out onto the blade, the maw open and eschewing flames.

A Stone Blade of the Dragon Lords had returned to the Avarus Desert.

Every tale spoken by men or inscribed in books hinted at their creation; *Lord Arthramain Roy'al* had made them, and in the hours of their birth granted them sentience. They lived, for all their hearts were flowing stone, brimming with thoughts, memories, and emotions. Nonetheless, they were still tools of destruction, and in the hands of their wielders, horrific to behold, capable of shattering mountains and reweaving the *Annuir'Hyme*.

With the fall of the Dragon Lords, despair befell eleven of the twelve swords. They slipped into a terrible madness and lost all they had once been. Their natures inverted with no diminishment of power, and all that had once aimed to preserve the world turned toward its destruction. Only the sword of Andeor'Vallen withstood the madness because he alone survived Morrehiegann's betrayal.

No one knew the exact shape their madness took, for none could wield a Stone Blade and remain sane. Their call is sweet and tantalizing, beckoning all species alike for they need a wielder to work their influence. They whisper of acts done by heroes and the wealth of kingdoms. They offer the might of gods and the fulfillment of every desire, and corrupt those desires to their uttermost end regardless of their nature.

Now Sinnitar Muntalabac carried the Stone Blade as its master.

———————

Sinnitar Muntalabac smiled at the Kalvonder overhead and bowed, wondering if he should grant him a glimpse of the truth. The man had already pierced his Veil, seeing him when he should have been nothing more than an errant shadow; how much more could he bear to witness?

Stolen Wings susurrated in his mind, calling him to feast, to strip off his pretense of humanity and drive all who looked upon him mad. The Dread

Lord smiled and soothed the voracious monstrosity. *'Soon, but not yet. We must destroy them first.'* The weapon hummed in response, prying ever-deeper into his consciousness and resuming its incessant whispers of dominance. All it knew was the hunger for devastation and the need to be its progenitor. Through Sinnitar Muntalabac, it had found the route to achieve that.

A flare of violet light and a brush of movement drew his attention to where one of the Avaran Tragnashi hurried to his master with a tray of sweetmeats. There upon his disfigured brow was an old *Arthramainian* rune, still livid from its recent infliction. *'So this is the famed soulcraft Avarans are so proud of, and so deeply ignorant of.'*

The Dread Lord raised a fist and spoke, his glove blackening. "All things obey the word of the *Roy'als*."

Invisible to all except himself, a burning rune materialized between him and the slave: his family's *brand*, an inverted pentacle. Even if they heard him speak, none could have translated his words, but their meaning echoed across the hall: *Muntalabac*.

The Tragnashi collapsed without a word, the sigil *branded* on his heart and the void of his soul. When he woke, he would know only Sinnitar's desire, speak only his words and serve only his purpose. He belonged to them now, body, mind, and soul.

Sinnitar distanced himself from the emissaries, laying a hand flat across the breast of a slave and befouling her soul. It was easy, for there was nothing in Sahdaen to constrain him, and every act or thought of malice, every drop of suffering, fed him, and his appetite knew no satiation.

Sinnitar proceeded through the slaves, *branding* each and consuming their souls until his body seethed with dark energy. Then he spoke in a voice black as pitch, his words almost singsong, *"At my summons, darkness comes to me with greed and hunger burning and a perversion most malign. It flies on dread wings laden with terror to the minds of all who my presence enfolds. Into each of them it plants a seed of fear in mind and body, where it will grow until it is too vast to be burned and too deep to uproot."* The Dread Lord thrust his united hands forward, sowing a crop of spectral embryos birthed from tortured souls and blood magic. *"Now, rise."*

Plague-like, the seeds took root in the Kalvonders and Avarans alike, latching onto their minds and drinking of all the small fears they refused to confront. These seeds, though small in their youth, would soon propagate and infest others, ensnaring all of Sahdaen in paranoia.

However, four men resisted the curse.

The first was a corpulent Kalvonder at the forefront of his kin, a man who silently observed the proceedings with eyes corrupted by a joyous insanity. The second man stood to the left of the first, his face masked by an intricate design of crimson bronze. The third was the Kalvonder atop the bridge, and the fourth a Tragnashi behind him.

The first, Ureign Kalvonder, withstood because fear could never truly find purchase in the insane mind, it just becomes another facet of the insanity. The curse had invaded the second man, Trerrock, only to be consumed by whatever his mask concealed. The third had simply resisted the curse, and the unnamed Tragnashi harbored an undefined power that had protected him.

Sinnitar began his ascent toward the atrium, letting a sliver of his presence worm free.

Valeriius perceived the Dread Lord's approach in the light dying at his back, and in the leeching cold taking sway over him, squeezing until all voices of kindness, mercy, compassion, and love died; usurped by hatred, obsession, avarice, lust, cruelty, and fear.

He greeted the man with a regal nod and then deliberately resumed his vigil. Despite this display of apathy, every ounce of his intellect was focused on the Dread Lord, rendering all else a haze of color and sound.

The man assumed a place beside him, his presence like a leaden coat.

"Few," Valeriius began in a voice of polite interest, "would dare wear the inverted pentacle. Fewer still among those who know its significance."

"The world has not forgotten all of its wisdom, then. But I wonder, do you know its history, Kalvonder? Or are you just parroting your mother's fables?"

"Mother, father, book, and song." Valeriius made a dismissive gesture. "I am called Valeriius, you are Sinnitar Muntalabac."

"And do you know what that *name* means, Valeriius Kalvonder?"

"I know your bloodline died out a few centuries ago, which makes me wonder how you're standing here now? But I am more interested in what you want from me?"

"I am aware that you avoided my hex. Doing so without betraying your nature piqued my interest, made me wonder what else you could offer me in return for power."

"I do not need you to fulfill my ambitions, and any contract with you would erase my individuality, rendering profit defunct."

The Dread Lord's voice thickened around Valeriius, dulling his eyes, clouding his ears, and tangling his mind with wayward thoughts. "You don't seem to comprehend what I can offer, though I do not blame you; you are banal, an utterly prosaic specimen of humanity. Your attempts at grandeur are a tawdry affection, like a whore dousing herself in perfume to pretend class. I am not ordinary, and through me, you can attain a shred of true Grace."

Valeriius tightened his thoughts, sharpening them to knives against the Dread Lord's obfuscation. "I look to the horizons and see nothing I do not desire and cannot achieve. I intend to rule over kings, and I do not need your intercession."

The pressure relented. "It is foolish to focus on such a shortsighted desire as power for an ultimate goal. Power is a medium."

"Power is the ultimate currency." Valeriius stepped back from the railing, collecting the statue of *Arawn* as he did so.

"You will find it a frail shield when the night falls on Sahdaen. Those who reject me always end in tragedy."

"I do not doubt your power; I know a confrontation between us would result in my destruction. Yet, at this point our scales are matched. You have only begun your preparations, mine near fruition. You will need more than a vague threat and an offer of slavery to sway my allegiance." He departed the atrium without another word.

The Dread Lord let him go; he had not sought out the Kalvonder to dominate him, only to assess him. Though the former conclusion would have been welcome. Ultimately, the Kalvonder's resistance, whether he found success or failure, mattered little. Each would result in Sahdaen's despair, and that served the Dread Lord's intent.

15

Geas Of Dread

Alien and undeniable, the summons throbbed in Dieharamon's blood, calling him ever downward through a world cast of shadows and mist, a prisoner in his own body. A pageantry of spectral figures and half-heard sentences surrounded him as he delved through the Dragon Lords' palace, but they passed through, by, and around him obliviously, offering no more resistance than the walls.

The mist-laden world around him thrummed with the call's power, echoing with the reverberation of a voice he could not hear, and swirled with light. It was at once lovely and appalling, unknowable and primal, celestial and very much mortal. Yet in this brilliant, insubstantial world, Dieharamon saw an eroding darkness in the veins of light, a poison swallowing all of it bit by bit.

Gradually two pillars of white stone appeared from the shadows and mist ahead of him, painfully sharp against the flux but offering an island of constancy amidst the chaos. They beckoned him voicelessly, and as he passed through their archway, admitted by a door of nebulous insubstantial shadows, the shadow world faded, giving way to the mortal existence and releasing the summons.

Dieharamon found himself in an octagonal room of polished black granite segmented by more of the white pillars. An empty circlet levitated in the room's center, its blush-hued chiseled stone reminding him of a crown. Unlit teardrop lanterns hung just out of reach, swishing with mournful creeks and glinting in the vague light.

He searched for what had summoned him yet saw only a pair of iron doors set in the wall and a mound of rumpled silk lying discarded in the corner. He shivered; the air felt laden with memories and the promise that if he delved far enough, he could retrieve them. Thus when he spoke, he did so in a rasping whisper, terrified of what might answer, "Why am I here?"

201

At first nothing responded. Then within his thoughts, the softest of tugs pulled on his mind, coaxing his eyes to the abandoned silk. His eyes passed over and around the cloth, searching for anything to merit his attention, but as previously, he saw nothing. A shiver prickled up his spine, feeding his fear. He hated, above all else, what he could not comprehend. Again something tugged his mind toward the silk. It lay almost flat with barely any creases; but something minute could be hidden underneath it.

Dieharamon shook his head and retreated, fumbling for the door. He had no desire to see anything hidden in this chamber by the Dragon Lords; such things should remain hidden, such things should not be touched, most of all by those with no right to hold them. But as he was retreating, he inexplicably fell.

His eyes remained locked on the black silk throughout the fall, and to some extent, he barely realized he was falling until he landed. Some small, detached part of his intellect wondered how he had fallen in this barren room, but the majority of his consciousness was awash in fear.

Then as incomprehensible as the fall itself, his dull impact sent a gust of air across the chamber to lift the cloth. The wispy fabric fluttered for an instant, revealing a black orb upon the floor.

That one glance was sufficient. A need to see the orb awoke within him, urging him to his feet and across the chamber. He knew his mind was being tampered with, but that knowledge was as useless to him as the memory of water to a man in the desert.

Crouching helplessly, Dieharamon snatched the cloth away. Immediate awe bridled within him, eliciting a whimper and driving him back. The damage was done, and no act by god or man could avert what was to follow.

Dropping to his hands and knees, Dieharamon stared at the orb. It was modest, no larger than his hand, and perfectly formed without dent or mar. The substance of its body resembled glass, yet with an opaque interior that spiraled ever inward, defying all attempts to see beyond its obscurity. A tiny golden flame materialized at its epicenter, and a soft voice spoke into Dieharamon's mind, sliding in between the recesses of his thoughts and the callused scar of his memories. *"Take me to the pedestal."* There was no resisting the orb's command, so Dieharamon acceded without defiance.

The orb spoke again as he set it on the suspended circlet, *"We do not have time, Dieharamon. Soon the Last Guardian will return to confine my vision again, and there is much you need to know about forthcoming events."*

He stumbled back from the orb, entreating with broken words, "But can't he be delayed?" It was a blind plea, spoken through a haze of panic.

"No! And it would only bring you an ill fate if he was delayed!" The delicate voice sheared through Dieharamon's clouded mind, forcing clarity into his scattered thoughts.

In the absence of restraint, however, his anger found purchase and retaliated, driving him to his feet. "And who are you to command me?" He spun to leave, forgetting in his haste and wrath that the orb could just recall him.

"No! You cannot!"

Dieharamon screamed as his limbs locked, and hurled his will against the foreign mind. "Why not?" Desperation suffused the artifact's voice, and that terrified him.

"The SoulReaver will take you if you do not heed us."

Dieharamon stilled, some primeval part of him quailing in response to the uttered name. "What is a SoulReaver, and why—"

"There is no time! I must show you."

Dieharamon's vision began to fade, but he railed against the orb's pull. "No! What you are, what is the SoulReaver?"

"I am an Accumulary, and I will show you your sole chance of survival in the war to come..."

He found himself in a demure room decorated by spare paintings, gold-tipped furnishings, and bountiful firelight. Three tapestries occupied most of the wall space, two smaller pieces on the northern and southern walls and a larger on the western. The northern tapestry was scarcely recognizable through its etiolated colors but seemed to depict a woman with black hair. The southern tapestry had survived the years with better grace, remaining distinguishable as a white, unsheathed sword on a crimson field. A crown hung on the wide cross-guard, echoing the three rings glistening on its blade. Both images unnerved Dieharamon for they were ancient and carried weight beyond their fabric.

The final tapestry portrayed five men, one at the forefront, two a step behind him and then a final two at the edge, small and tucked into the background as if an afterthought. He recognized only the central man, and no one could have mistaken him. *Lord Arthramain Roy'al* loomed over his companions, a naked white blade in his hand and a gold crown on his harsh brow.

Of the other two discernible figures, one was sinewy and gaunt with haggard features and the other larger with significantly more tenebrous aspect. The first stood hunched on the left, his arms crossed and twin blades adorning his figure, one at his hip and the other on his shoulder. This man boasted hard, silver eyes, and hair to match.

Of the three, only the third man smiled. His smile, however, in the midst of a small goatee, was something Dieharamon fervently desired never to encounter. Beyond that he dressed in a black, side-buttoned coat, and wore his hair in a thick braid down to his knees, accenting a high brow.

Besides the tapestries, the spacious chamber housed a pair of chairs and a large hickory table that projected a conjured map of a forest and mountains. Unsettled by the magic, Dieharamon directed his attention to the two living men at the table instead. The first glowed with energy and strength, his light-brown eyes confident with purpose, intelligence, and a spark of laughter. The rough-hewn locks of his hair were a golden-blond and draped warmly over his brow as he leaned along the table rim with splayed hands, staring at the map.

The second man's posture and demeanor were quieter than his companion's, but when his steel gray eyes flicked from the table to his companion, they defied the illusionary frailty cast by his graying hair and lined face. "Are you certain you want to send Dayada?"

The first man raked his hair back in frustration. "We don't have a choice, Tiberius. You and I can't go, and there's no one else to send."

"Yes, but is it worth risking Dayada? He's not ready for a Dread Lord."

The first man thrust off the table and started pacing only to cease when his eyes found the door. His shoulders slumped. "It is in his blood. He'll have to face them eventually, Tiberius. We can't change that. Besides, you said this was important."

"It does not matter how important the man is; I would not risk Dayada on a hopeless endeavor. You of all people, Tarram, should be wary of the Muntalabacs."

"Yes," he replied softly, "I am an Avenar, and I am exhausted. We're almost out of blood to give, Tiberius. It's just me, Dayada, and his sister." He leaned forward, rubbing his eyes. "I can feel them growing stronger, somewhere out there I can't find, and they're spreading: East, South, and West. Gods, I can even feel traces of them in The North."

"You are not alone, Tarram. They are as near to extinction as you."

"They are not; they are where they wish to be, Tiberius, and have been for two millennia. We have fought, hunted, and resisted them for all these centuries and have achieved nothing but our own diminishment." Tarram fell back into his chair. "I do not know what to do."

"I wish I could help you more, but something has changed and I cannot see what. A coin has been flipped and a gambit made, ushering us towards an ending we are blind to. We must either fall beneath their shadow or rise above it as we always have. We must persevere and hope *Lord Arthramain Roy'al* did not err."

Tarram Avenar exhaled a soft breath and pulled himself upright. "What do you need from me?"

A strange sensation welled within Dieharamon that caused him to shiver, a sense of purpose and something else long denied to him: hope. There was strength in the Avenar's voice, strength awful to behold against the weight it held.

"... I fear you are right, Tarram. The time has come when we can longer protect Dayada. We can only pray he will not be consumed as Rhettaris was."

Something in Tiberius' words seemed to spark a revelation in Tarram. He responded slowly, cautious of the words he spoke and their significance, "You believe Dayada has a pivotal role in our story, that he will see the two Dread Kings rise?"

"Yes, and I fear what will come of it. *Jaidar* stands in *Etherea* amassing his power, while Morrehiegann marshals more dark energy in Paranoia than I have seen since Vanner Muntalabac tortured this earth. The New Order is emerging from their centuries of concealment, and soon enough I believe Cardolyn Tyier shall find himself and his empire embroiled in a convergence."

Dieharamon sought the *Accumulary* with his mind. "Why show me this? Who are they? Who is Dayada? What has this to do with me?"

"You must find the one of whom they spoke. You must find Dayada Avenar and hope he can protect you from the SoulReaver."

"What does the SoulReaver want with me, and why should I trust you?"

"You must trust me because you have no other chance. If you do not find Dayada Avenar, the SoulReaver will–" The *Accumulary* ceased mid-thought. *"He's here."*

"Who is?"

"The SoulReaver Muntalabac." The *Accumulary* winked out.

"Wait! No! Come back!" Dieharamon grasped the orb and energy surged through him, setting his blood alight and driving him to the floor. That's when he felt it, an irresistible presence taking hold of him, drawing his eyes along the granite floor to a pair of iron-soled boots and the silver-wreathed wood of a black sheath.

His breath faltered, and for the length of that unspent breath, he could not force his eyes above the scabbard. Then his gaze scaled up the dark apparel of the man standing before him until it found the Dread Lord's eyes.

The shadow world rose around him again, and in it he saw the man standing as a gaping, ravenous maw, his ethereal form bloated with a thousand agonized faces. The world drowned in his shadow, every light snuffed and all existence balanced on the precipice of annihilation.

"Who are you?"

"I am Sinnitar Muntalabac."

Dread filled Dieharamon. He knew the meaning of that name, knew it instinctively even without the knowledge given to him by Valeriius and the *Accumulary.* Yet it took standing in the Dread Lord's presence for him to truly understand it. There would be no end to the night. He retreated, fighting the urge to prostrate himself in a gibbering mess.

The Dread Lord followed him. "And who are you?" Again the voice almost brought Dieharamon to his knees, but names had power, and few knew this truth better than the Avarans. So he said nothing.

Impatience flared in the Dread Lord's eyes, becoming a snarl. "What is your name?"

Dieharamon just kept retreating, teeth clamped shut on the name that screamed for release. The Dread Lord's snarl turned into a grin. He spoke and his voice caused the chamber to cower. "Down."

Dieharamon slammed to his hands and knees in a bow, forehead grinding into the floor. He tried to rise with a strangled growl, but nothing obeyed him, not even his own lungs. For that aching moment, Sinnitar Muntalabac ruled him in his entirety.

Slowly, agonizingly, Dieharamon twisted his head to glower at the man. The unnatural dread remained, but his fear was gone, usurped by a desperate rage and the power igniting at his core.

The Dread Lord ignored him and strode past, his gaze fixed on the *Accumulary.* He reached out, grasped it and the *Accumulary* exploded into renewed life, engulfing the chamber in a storm of wrathful power and blinding radiance.

That storm washed over Dieharamon in an instant, banishing his thoughts and casting his will into ruins. Yet the Dread Lord stood before it unaffected, a scar amidst the brilliance as he lifted the orb and spoke, "You will serve me." His words sheared through the maelstrom, silencing it with the first syllable and strangling it into submission.

In that instant, Dieharamon knew Sinnitar Muntalabac should never be allowed to master the *Accumulary.*

He fumbled through the wreckage of his will, trying to discover some reservoir of strength to combat Sinnitar. But only the power answered him, rising on his desperation and marking the first time he ever voluntarily summoned it. Strength surged along his limbs, setting him aflame with that undefined, inexplicable power. He did not know where it came from, but his fear of the Dread Lord eclipsed his fear of magic and that was enough.

Even knowing he could not contest him, Dieharamon stood and howled his challenge. The Dread Lord replied with a smirk, his hand ablaze in the *Accumulary's* golden fire. Dieharamon threw himself forward, tackling the Dread Lord about the waist and staggering him a miniscule slide back. Sinnitar twisted with the impact, grabbed Dieharamon by the shoulder and threw him into the wall.

Dieharamon rolled to his knees with a snarl, pain grinding down his spine, and lunged back to his feet and forward. The Dread Lord kicked him back into the wall, expelling the breath from his lungs along with a burst of blood.

He slumped back to his hands and knees, gasping as the Dread Lord crossed to him. He struggled to rise, but Sinnitar grabbed his forehead and slammed it into the wall, shattering his grip on the power. The strength fled, leaving him powerless and fighting just to maintain conscious through the agony.

Sinnitar dropped him with a snort and returned his attention to the *Accumulary's* burning depths. "You are nothing, Tragnashi." An inexorable force wormed into Dieharamon's breast, crushing him into the wall. "You of all men were born to follow and be broken." The pressure lessened momentarily and then returned in full. "How it must burn to know you possess such power and, yet, be incapable of harnessing it." He dropped low, inspecting Dieharamon with a musing expression. "Such power shouldn't be wasted."

He uttered a word then, a horrible word in a tongue that defied comprehension. A word that cracked through Dieharamon's mind and threw his body into a vicious, contorting arch.

Dieharamon screamed, not in pain but in horror for some instinctual part of him understood he was being marked; that his existence was being claimed. He felt a wrangling, sinuous taint latching on his mind, filling his mouth with bile and his nostrils with blood. He felt himself submerging in darkness, drowning in it as he resisted the Dread Lord's subjugation.

Sinnitar Muntalabac stepped back, directing his left hand toward Dieharamon as rasping words slithered from his lips, "Within this palace resides an ancient artifact: the *Pathfinder Shard*. You will find this artifact and bring it to me upon the morrow of the new day."

Dieharamon whimpered, his eyes shut tight against the foreign malice within him as he pleaded for salvation without words or hope. Its thin blackness tightened on his heart and spirit, consuming both until there was only fear.

"By a means formed of Insidious Dread, let these commands cross the bridge crafted of Insidious Dread. By the venom of Insidious Dread, let these commands take hold over a host unwilling like venom with no cure, venom born of Insidious Dread. Let the Insidious Dread that birthed it, enforce it; so that these commands dominate the will, mind, body, and soul of the unwilling host, and thus reach their completion, furthering the Insidious Dread that birthed and enforced them!"

With those words, Dieharamon felt the commands take hold, dragging his body up through the pain of torn muscles and fractured bones. Some part of him tried to fight that terrible command, tried to reclaim his own body, but he could no more defy those commands than he could swim in the *Annuir'Hyme.*

Sinnitar Muntalabac did not speak again, whether in the verse of his dread power or in the simple prose of men. He merely turned from Dieharamon and strode from the chamber.

With his first step, he shrouded himself in the screams and misery of a thousand tortured souls. With his second, he discarded the *Accumulary* and it crashed to the floor, resounding with the screams of failing empires and dying kings.

For a single damning moment as the Dread Lord left, Dieharamon managed to resist the monstrous tendril enveloping his spirit. For a single moment of courage found in some false sense of heroism, Dieharamon's human spirit resisted the Dread Lord's touch. Then his world changed, and all that existed was fear and the Dread Lord's will.

Without heed to his aching body, Dieharamon rose. He felt no pain or hindrance. There was no warmth in his body either; the golden flames that had burned within were extinguished. Dieharamon knew he was on the brink of accomplishing something horrific. Nevertheless, he could not resist the force driving him toward the door. All he knew was the desire to serve Sinnitar Muntalabac.

A thought, however, intruded on his mind as he stepped through the iron door. Singing with a passion and power long harbored in secret, it spoke a command equal in strength to the Dread Lord's will, *"Find Dayada Avenar."* And with these words, healing suffused Dieharamon, knitting his torn flesh, easing his aching muscles, and ameliorating his fractured bones. At the name's utterance, however, something ancient and murderous awoke within him. This fury was without reason or control; and in that chaos, Dieharamon found a spark of denial.

16

Matching Dresses

A deep, clear boom rattled through the sandstone foyer and Slade leaned out over the second-floor railing. "Frieda," he called down, "welcome our guest before they catch pneumonia." Walking just underneath her precariously balanced employer, the woman glanced up, curtseyed and then set aside her basket of laundry.

As she moved to the front door, Slade abandoned his dubious position for a quick trot across the balcony toward a staircase with a curving descent along the left wall. "Well? Who has the gall to disturb our solitude? Do they bring cookies?"

Frieda dispelled the images circling the enchanted mirror. "A young woman I don't recognize is pacing the front porch. She has blue eyes and long, poorly styled auburn hair flecked with red."

"Oh, good. Our guest is a guest of mine." Leaping the final three steps, he promptly claimed center stage, lowered his brows and struck a commanding pose, exaggerating everything to the point of absurdity.

Frieda, sniffing with the extraordinary hauteur that only an aged servant could muster, opened the door and allowed a gust of searing wind to invade the foyer. "Please come in, my lady." She gave a little curtsy then side-stepped, one hand motioning inward.

"Thank the gods, you finally answered. Don't butlers sleep on the doorstep, or something?" Too busy escaping the weather for proper introductions, their guest darted inside first, then steepled her fingers and gave a belated bow. "Tasha Bloomhale, may *Enecki's* light forever shine upon you."

"I am only a servant, my lady, not the butler. He suffered heatstroke yesterday, so Master Lammerock gave him the day off."

"Master Lammerock?" Tasha's gaze snapped up. *The reports said nothing about Slade being a Thearch, let alone one of sufficient rank to merit this*

209

grandiose mansion.' Upon reading her directions, she thought he simply worked here as camouflage.

"My lady, can I prepare you a glass of iced water or some chilled mulberry juice perhaps?"

'So far everything else has proved wrong, why should his bloody station differ?' Tasha sighed inwardly then nodded to the old woman. "Some juice would be wonderful, thanks. Oh, and when you have a moment, please find Slade." Frieda pointed behind Tasha, who—with some chagrin—realized he stood five steps behind her. "Ah, there you are."

Slade, his absurd pose forgotten when Tasha failed to notice him, hastily resumed the posture. "Here I am indeed, most observant lady." He gave her a meaningful glance before turning to Frieda and dropping his sonorous tone. "I imagine she'll also welcome a damp cloth and most certainly one of my mother's old dresses: the white one, I think."

"As you wish, Master Lammerock. Can I provide anything else, my lady?" When Tasha shook her head, Frieda dropped a final curtsey and departed at a brisk trot, pausing to collect her discarded basket.

Closing the distance between them with his usual grin, Slade first caught then kissed her hand, lips barely touching the skin. "Your presence is a summer breeze, my Dear. A divine blessing that makes me well-nigh inconsolable with joy."

"Whatever reason you have for calling me today, I expect it to be a damn good one." Tasha yanked her hand free and thrust both it and its sibling into the security of her pockets. "Consider your answer carefully."

"Due to my recent neglect, I thought to assure you of my continuing affections lest your heart grow disconsolate or embittered. As for this inconvenient heat, I'm terribly sorry, but I feared you might catch pneumonia, so I contacted a wizard and had him rustle up a little sunshine. Apparently, he sneezed at an inopportune moment and botched the whole affair." Slade shook his head, tut-tutting. "On the flip side, I hear the Avarus Desert is enjoying its week of snow."

"Slade, the only reason you've 'neglected' me is because it served your purpose, and the only reason you've returned now is because it also serves your purpose." He shrugged, neither denying nor admitting to her accusation. "And I don't a need a dress."

He recoiled. "No! You cannot mean that. I exist in a state of permanent, gibbering terror at the thought of your refusal. I dread the mere suggestion of you disdaining this spectacular vestment I've so munificently offered. I balance on the precipice of insanity simply considering the awful notion." All of a sudden he switched gears, becoming calm and reasonable.

"You see my inborn apprehension believes your fragile disposition may well prove your undoing when confronted by such ostentatious heat. Sunstroke, that great indifferent enemy, will undoubtedly kill you, preventing the unfettered pleasure to come from the consummation of our inevitable marital massacre."

"I would pay a silver-crown to anybody who can repeat a quarter of that."

"Well, since you're offeri–" Tasha all but leapt forward, clapping a hand over his mouth.

"While you adore your own voice, I find its constant drone bothersome. Please remain silent or at least comparatively so." Tasha felt Slade's grin press into the palm of her hand. "Why do you want to give me a dress anyway?" Letting her hand drop, she executed a hasty retreat; *Enecki* knew standing close to him was dangerous.

"While wearing trousers, you adopt an unsettling masculinity that your warlike temperament fails to dispel with awesome gusto."

Tasha gasped, cupping both cheeks and widened her eyes to their limit. "You don't say?"

"The dress is part of an elaborate scheme to change your appearance from rancid barbarian to refined damsel."

"My clothing is none of your affair."

Slade wagged at finger at her. "Tasha, you're a representative of the Thieves' Guild and scallywags in general. How dare you besmirch my infamous name with your tawdry outfits."

"Slade, for someone who might steal *Akravast*—undoubtedly causing the Empire's greatest upheaval in centuries—you're oddly worried about your reputation."

He clapped one hand to his chest and thrust it's sibling toward the horizon with splayed fingers. "My worshipers look to me for guidance, speaking their desperate prayers in the hope that I'll resolve their difficulties. How might they react upon learning I'm represented by a woman dressed as a man? Why they would desert me in droves, searching elsewhere for the guidance they believe I'm unfit to deliver. I shudder to contemplate what depraved scoundrel might undertake this onus with unclean intentions. Gasp! What if it's the Thieves' Guild?"

"Seeing as I'm not your representative, you have nothing to worry about."

"They think you are."

"I never agreed to that."

"Too late, I just nominated you. You really shouldn't submit a resume without intending to accept the job."

"I didn't submit a resume!"

"Of course not. I submitted it for you. Be sure to dress accordingly for work."

Tasha hurled her hands skyward. "The dress probably won't even fit!"

"Let's say I've discovered your measurements through tireless, delightful examination."

"Enough! End of discussion. I don't need a dress, certainly not one your mother wore." Her protests flowed to either side of Slade without so much as brushing his shoulder.

Frieda returned then, carrying a silver tray with a decanter, three glasses, and an icebox dressed in heavy condensation. At that point, Tasha stopped listening to Slade entirely. But the young man continued listing arguments until the old woman walked up behind him; whereupon he reached back and deftly stole her tray.

"If the benefits I describe leave you unsatisfied, I can easily devise more." Smiling pleasantly, he brought the tray around and proffered it to her. "Glass of juice, my Dear?"

"Yes please." She snatched a glass at random, lifting it halfway to her mouth before realizing it's depressing emptiness. Somewhat chagrined, she held it out and Slade, lifting the decanter far beyond the necessary height, poured a long, glistening stream of mulberry juice into her glass before spinning the tray so the icebox faced her. Ignoring the ice, she finished the juice in a single draught.

"Frieda, please fetch my mother's dress," Slade said, taking Tasha's glass and scooping it through the ice box. "Our fate as sun-charred meat mustn't wait any longer than absolutely necessary."

"As Master Slade wishes. Can I provide anything else?" Frieda asked, reaching for the sequestered tray.

"Ah, yes. Please inform Miss Feylin that we're ready to depart whenever she is." Slade lifted the tray overhead, eliciting a piqued huff from the servant. While society considered a noble carrying a tray unseemly, it downright disapproved of an elderly servant hopping around to reclaim said tray. "Also, please give Miss Feylin the dress we received from the tailor earlier. And Frieda, don't disclose that it arrived today."

The old woman pursed her lips. "I understand, Master Slade."

As she bustled off, Slade shook his head. "Forgive her sour temperament, Frieda's a renowned sore loser. One time she punished me with cold baths for a week just because she lost a game of chess." A grin stole across his face. "Truth be told, I find it all rather amusing; besides, I did cheat."

"Slade, you find everything amusing. Why the tussle though?"

"Frieda belongs to the elder breed of servants. A fierce, tenacious species who take offense when their masters do anything considered low work." Slade abandoned the tray atop a decorative table and vanished through a side door, quickly reappearing with a large, cushioned chair that he set beside Tasha. "This insult is, of course, preposterous." He tapped the chair.

"I'm fine."

"My Dear, you just walked halfway across the city to unwittingly join an adventure that will require yet more walking. Sit while you can."

She glared at him in part truculence and part narrow-eyed suspicion, then—unwilling to reveal anything he might use against her—forced herself to sit and hold still. This entailed pressing bootheels against chair legs and squeezing golden knobs on the ends of armrests, hoping Slade wouldn't notice either.

An unexpected boon to this effort came when her restless gaze passed over the ceiling. Whether from rebellious architects or a product of Lammerock wealth, the tiles overhead deviated from the usual monochrome design. In fact, Slade's house stepped beyond simple deviation into outright creativity by covering their ceiling with pillowed clouds and blue oblivion. The true affront to Imperial sensibilities arose from the little faces concealed within each cloud. Some of these laughed or whispered jokes, while others pulled faces and mocked the occupants below.

Slade followed her gaze with a smile. "My mother hates cloudy days, so my father painted eternally sunny skies on the first floor and starry nights on the second. She suggested we paint the floors and walls too, but he worried our guests might lose their sense of direction."

After a moment, Tasha's amusement faded and she caught his vibrant green, still unnerving, eyes. "Slade, we need to discuss a delicate matter; I received an envoy with Carr'Selain's personal signature. "It–" She hesitated, glanced around the tall, pale room and leaned closer. "It confirms than an official delegation should arrive next week, only I got a second message from the delegation itself. Apparently, they decided today better suited their schedule."

"I received the same messages or, more accurately, intercepted the same messages. It's not all sunshine, roses, and theory vindication, however. Some of those delegates owe allegiance to Syndros Nomarr."

"That doesn't make any sense. Why is Carr'Selain sending assassins to kill you if he's planning on negotiating? There's no reason unless … unless he's unaware or someone else hired them?"

"I have no doubt Carr'Selain is fully aware of their presence. I suspect he's simply choosing not to interfere with Syndros Nomarr; quite wisely I must say."

Tasha cursed, knuckling her forehead. "Perfect, just perfect. First, they lie about my objective here, then they hide the bloody assassins coming with the delegation. What am I supposed to do in this situation?"

"Nothing, these shadowy characters aren't your problem; Carr'Selain made that clear by not informing you. That said, if you got doped up on your own morality and leapt upon their swords for my sake, I'd jeer along with everybody else. I doubt we'll need such heroics though."

This casual deferral of obligation left Tasha starring. "Why aren't you infuriated that Carr'Selain's leading assassins straight to your door, and this while he's preparing negotiations?"

"They are lions without claws or teeth, suited only to the parade. Plus I sent a sternly worded letter that will assuredly change their intentions."

"Alright then, if you're not bothered, I see no reason to concern myself on your behalf."

"That's the spirit."

"How can you say that? This is practically a betrayal!"

"My Dear, while I sympathize with your position, this isn't the place for such clandestine subjects."

Her next words caught, burning atop her tongue. "Alright fine. New subject. Who's this girl that's supposed to accompany us. Can we get rid of her?"

"That's a difficult proposition. Besides, you have no idea who she is. This mysterious personage could be a distant, long-lost grandmother or, better still, a formerly betrayed and now forgotten sister."

"Unlikely. I memorized my entire family tree by age ten."

"Public tree or secret tree?"

"Both."

"In that case, she's probably not your long-lost grandmother. Disappointing. Anyway, Miss Feylin, our guest, is ward to the renowned paladin Tiberius Whyte. A name you're no doubt acquainted with."

First one moment, then a second passed. "What in the names of all twelve gods are you doing rubbing shoulders with the ward of Tiberius-*Jaidar* blessed-Whyte?"

"Just lucky, I guess. He's a family friend."

"Your family is friends with Tiberius Whyte and yet you're"—she floundered for a moment—"stealing?"

Slade grinned. "I'm a complicated person."

Tasha slumped back, shock briefly overcoming her thrumming nerves. "Well, this does explains why leaving her behind is a difficult proposition. Tiberius would skin you alive if we left his ward wandering around some random marketplace. What are they doing in Tellor anyway? Tiberius Whyte hasn't left Apelium in years." She paused, eyes growing wide. "*Enecki* bless me. The Will of the Emperor is sleeping under your roof isn't he? How doesn't the city know about this? Did you break the rumor wheel and poison the women spinning it?"

The way Tasha swore by *Enecki* fascinated Slade. Most people swore by the gods best favoring their chosen profession, *Enecki* for nobles, *Kis'Maat* for criminals, and *Malbreyth* for soldiers. *Jaidar* was the exception. Everyone swore by *Jaidar*.

"The city's well aware but pretends otherwise for the sake of propriety." Slade smirked at her. "If Tiberius snuck in disguised as a goat herder, Tellor would know within the hour."

"And now we're burdened with equal notoriety." Tasha sighed, running a hand down over her eyes.

"Not quite. Few people know Tiberius Whyte has a ward. We'll be the picture of unremarkable, especially since I ordered a pair of matching dresses to help you pass as siblings. Miss Feylin is, of course, oblivious to the deception."

Her shoulders slumped. "Very well. It's a potential disaster, but I can't see much choice."

"Great. Now, let's reopen negotiations on that dress of yours."

"You mean *your* dress. No matter what insane logic you invent, I won't wear it."

"Contrary to your vile supposition, the logic I intend to combat and inevitably overcome your truculence with is contemptibly sane." He began to pace. "Yes, our current weather is occasionally enjoyable, but more commonly it's an oppressive warlord with particular animosity for the darkly clothed." Slade gestured at Tasha, indicating her sturdy, high-collared coat, brown leggings and silver sash, all respectably Imperial fashion and absolute misery. "The dress—which I myself sewed from the silk of countless murderous spiders—is white, cool, and equipped with several pouches designed to smuggle useful contraband."

"First, you're wearing black. Second, nobody would believe we're sisters, so what's the catch? Also, you said the dress belonged to your mother."

"Well, I modified the dress, and *Sammahale* has difficulty seeing the color black so I'm good. As for the last detail"—Slade heaved a dramatic sigh—"I'm afraid you've outsmarted me once again, my Dear. I really suggest sailing along with the current; learn to let the minor details go." He began kneading Tasha's shoulders with an absentminded air. "Unfortunately, the catch is confidential information. Your position is far too prestigious, and I cannot possibly trust you with any secrets until after you've secured a demotion. Let's say jobless vagabond. In the meantime, know you can trust me even when you distrust me. I know what is best, and I shall do my best to see the best done; for today that means anonymity."

Tasha shook herself free, rose, and started pacing. "If you refuse to elaborate on the dress, at least explain why you called me over here."

"The Imperial Emperor is apparently both omnipresent and omnipotent; he knows you intend to steal *Akravast*. All things told, his response is quite moderate." Slade grinned at her, forearms resting atop the chair. "He declared the scheme equitable to treason. Any person foolish enough to attempt it will be caught and executed with all the cruel imagination his torturers possess. Then again, he could settle for less creative deaths, such as boiling oil or a well-polished hatchet. Oooh, I can just see it, the ax descending through the morning sun, glittering even as it performs the decapitation." Hands clasped in pious anticipation, Slade spun a circle and Tasha, halfway through swallowing back sudden nausea, abruptly clapped a hand to her forehead.

"Of course! This explains why Carr'Selain is reaching out to you. He needs a proxy because Cardolyn Tyier's eye is fixed on the Thieves' Guild: the only people who would even consider stealing *Akravast*."

"And me apparently, except now the Imperial Emperor is deliciously aware of Carr'Selain's intentions." Slade slid into the vacated chair. "The game has changed, becoming infinitely more perilous. My playful fantasies aside, can you even imagine what sentence they would assign us, this Empire that takes fingers from pickpockets? Likely not a long, enjoyable prison retreat. What can the guild possibly offer me to risk near certain execution? What convinced Carr'Selain that I would even consider it or, better yet, what deceived him about the quality of truth found in my legends?"

Tash broke eye-contact. *Why the hell is he asking me? He probably knows more about Carr'Selain and his plans than I do.* He kept staring at her though, and so she sighed. "For the past three nights, I've asked myself the same question. Why would the King-of-Thieves approach you—a dangerous unknown—when there are others with far more experience? Last night, I think I stumbled across the answer."

"Please, my Dear, regale me with your epiphany."

Tasha met Slade's mismatched eyes, his faintly smug expression amplifying her doubts. *What if I'm wrong? What if I make a fool of myself? Actually, considering how I botched that kidnap attempt, voicing a stupid idea isn't all that terrible.*' Then she noticed his ever-present laughter and realized he was hiding something. But what and why? Tasha could only think of one way to find out. *'Like blind trust, doubt has its place and both should be ignored by rote.*' Bracing herself for his derision, she pressed on. "I believe it's because the rumors aren't rumors; you've stolen from Cardolyn Tyier before. I don't know when, how, or why, but you've snuck into the Imperial palace and took something so important that none besides the highest authorities heard of it. Tongues, however, inevitably slipped and the rumor wheel began spinning and nothing, no force, no clever manipulation of lies, could stop its turning. Still, it was only rumor … unless someone sold the secret to Carr'Selain." Tasha paused, laying a hand atop her chest and feeling its oddly quick tempo. "I know you refuted this story earlier, claiming something about it being someone else and that you only wanted a golden bracelet or maybe a necklace or whatever. It's not important. What's important is that the whole debacle was a distraction for your true target: half-a-million gold crowns that simply vanished from Imperial coffers. Considering no one got hanged, I doubt it was embezzlement. But I think the scheme goes deeper because most people know about the missing gold, indicating that isn't the secret they're keeping. What if this enormous sum was just another shroud, a glimmering curtain to disguise your true mark. Seeing as I've no idea what you took, it worked. Although, I'm almost certain the object was bound by the Law of Right."

"Now, Tasha," Slade said, wagging a finger at her, "your theory is not only preposterous in the extreme, never mind its accuracy, but the wild imagination thus displayed is a doorway leading to unimaginable peril. You cannot let random fancies murder your logic. It's bad form, and it gives criminals a reputation for being unreliable and prone to exaggeration, if not outright insane. It's all downhill from there."

"I think people care more about our occupation than our mental state."

"Ah-ha, that's where you're wrong. Popular fiction has romanticized our profession. Thievery is now a popularity contest judged by the common people; the rogues with charming tongues and beautiful faces will survive while our constables hunt down the true ruffians of society."

"Oh? And I suppose you rank quite highly?"

"On the contrary, the people don't know I exist and have no perception of me. Though I'm faintly tickled by the notion that if aware, they'd perceive me as an artist. An artist, and if you like, predictable."

"Predictable? How so?"

Slade grinned. "Because I play each and every possible character, and scripts never change, only the words. When I adopt a villainous character, you will know my scheme instantly. First, capture the damsel; second, world domination." He rose, stepped onto the chair and immediately hunched over, rubbing his hands together vigorously while cackling. "Have no fear, however. For the damsel—played by the ever-fabulous Slade Lammerock—is a plucky creature who will escape and warn the outrageously handsome hero—also played by the charming Slade Lammerock—of the villain's plans." He smoothed back his hair and struck a heroic pose. "These two protagonists will embark upon a quest to save the world from domination." Hopping down, he stumbled across the room with one hand raised against a stinging wind. "At the conclusion of which, their adoring admirers will elect the devastatingly gorgeous hero as king of the world, and he will take the damsel as his queen." Slade clasped an invisible bride to his chest, giving the sequestered beauty a lasting kiss. "The story isn't finished yet because at the apex of celebrations the people realize the world was never saved from domination. They'd simply given it to a different overlord. Such was the protagonists' devilish scheme from the onset, a plan they concocted with their childhood friend: the villain." Reeking of self-satisfaction, Slade reseated himself as if inhabiting a throne. A second later, white flower petals began fluttering down around him, some catching on his dark, silky hair while others settled atop his shoulders with an almost artistic flare.

Slade plucked one from his lap, then both he and Tasha looked up to where his mother stood on the balcony overhead, one arm cradling a bundle of flowers while its sibling collected the petals and sprinkled them over the edge. "Every performer deserves flowers, though I do wonder where you learned such impressive skills." Smiling, Senna began her descent, bare feet poking out from underneath her light satin gown with every step and torso swaying gently on occasion, necessitating a light touch to the bannister. "I hear so little of my son's whereabouts he might as well be lost in some barren wasteland. I've even grown so desperate that I tried hiring the Thieves' Guild to spy on him; strangely enough, all my letters get mislaid." She gave Slade a pointed glance before looking back up the stairs. "Come on, sweetheart, they're waiting for you."

Previously hesitating just out of sight, Feylin crept into view, holding a square of folded cloth to her chest. Twice now she had joined Slade on excursions, each time accompanied by the mediating force of either Cain or Tiberius, though yesterday had seen a brief exception. Today, she accompanied him entirely without their protection.

'So,' Tasha mused, staring up at the girl. *This is the ward of Tiberius Whyte.'* She looked small and clean. Small—even here in wealth and society that should have comfortably inhabited her accustomed domain—and clean, but not the clean of freshly laundered clothes. The clean of a shirt just set out upon the shop counter, the clean of a silk shirt stored in a box and kept at the back of a pristine warehouse. Aside from that the girl was pretty, with perfect posture and anxious fiddling and large, round eyes of an uninspired blue, eyes that struck Tasha being a poor color for that particular face. *'At least she's quiet and not some giggling, high-pitched annoyance.'*

"Mother, what are you doing up and about?" Slade asked, moving to embrace her and placing a quick kiss on either cheek. "I thought Tiberius prescribed a morning of supreme indolence?"

"Neither your father nor Tiberius will return until later, so unless someone snitches, I've all morning to rebel." A mischievous smile akin to Slade's own grin slid into place. "Besides, I know when industry or indolence is required." She laughed. "Now if your father was the one pampering me, I would pretend such dreadful infirmity as to need his undivided attention for days on end."

"Mother, Tiberius is a powerful, experienced healer. If he prescribes rest, please follow his suggestion."

As Slade fussed over his mother, Tasha found herself watching him with a slight frown. His voice sounded oddly deep without its ever-present levity, just as his body looked strange and wooden without his usual exaggerated gestures.

"Slade, who's the mother here? Who spent the last eighteen years raising trouble disguised as a boy; caring for him, comforting him, and giving advice he ultimately ignored?" Senna cupped his cheek. "I'll have both you and your father know that I survived perfectly well by myself; at least, until you appeared riding on a tornado's back." She kissed his brow. "I've always enjoyed a good storm though."

"A thousand times you've told that story, always forgetting how my arrival improved your life dramatically." Slade's grin met his mother's smile. "For instance, please recall the meat that occasionally snuck onto our table. Unless I misremember, the event arose in direct correlation to my efforts."

"My dear boy, we both know you stole all that meat. I still wonder how they never caught you." Her gaze misted over as memories briefly swallowed the present, then her smile broadened and she faced Tasha. "Here, sweetheart, Frieda said Slade was pilfering this for you." Exchanging items with Feylin, she stepped around her son, and offered Tasha a folded dress.

Unwilling to disdain the gift, Tasha took the gown by its shoulders. "It's beautiful," she admitted grudgingly, the feather-light material falling like shimmering water to hang below her knees.

Feylin, conversely, watched through narrowed eyes, her gaze swapping between Tasha's new dress and her own. However, before she gathered the courage to speak, Slade snatched the dress from Tasha and held it to his chest like one does when checking their reflection.

"Of course, it is. Particularly when the appropriate light caresses it. The color changes to silver, see?" He began swishing from side to side, demonstrating the effect.

Senna shook her head. "Whatever his failings, Slade can select a beautiful gown."

"But Slade told me this was one of your old dresses," Tasha said.

"True, and the finest I owned until a few years ago." She smiled. "Slade bought it when a certain gentleman asked me to dinner, but I refused since I had nothing respectable to wear. Upon hearing this, my little boy pestered the man's name from me and instantly disappeared." If possible, the story embarrassed Slade, who became very engrossed with his swishing. "Slade reappeared late next morning with that dress in hand. When I asked about his adventures, he concocted some grand tale bursting with unimaginable peril, daring escapes, and another hundred improbable events. Eventually I learned how Slade visited Cain and coerced money from him. Imagine that; a scrawny, twelve-year-old boy bullying one of the Empire's most formidable paladin lords." Senna shook her head in disbelief. "Anyway, when Cain asked what Slade wanted the money for, he grinned at him and said, 'I'm going to buy my mother a dress. Come pick her up at eight.' Stunned, Cain let Slade escape with the entire purse." Senna chuckled. "When I learned the amount Slade … um … borrowed, I almost fainted. It was a fortune, at least by my standards, and more than enough to buy a dress. I never learned how Slade spent the rest, he claimed to have built a secret castle somewhere." Smiling at Tasha, Senna shrugged. "He'll denounce anything of the sort, but at heart, Slade's a romantic."

As predicted, he greeted this assertion with a derisive snort. "Since you are both intelligent, sophisticated women, I'm sure you realize that dresses bore me unto death. Let's hurry along, before we hurl our chaotically arranged schedule into complete order." Slade passed Tasha the dress, tapping his foot with exaggerated impatience. "At this rate, I shall die of boredom and bleed all over the floor, and I cannot possibly advocate such dalliances. The governor has issued an invitation, welcoming all resident nobility to his mansion for an evening's entertainment. Just imagine the reactions if I entered dressed in blood. Why, everyone would lose their appetites." Slade dug into his satchel, producing an envelope. "Our attendance is specifically requested, no doubt as a shadow invitation to any guest we may or may not have." He nodded toward Feylin.

Senna opened the letter, quickly skimming its contents. "Governor Warsein waited longer than I expected. We finished all our preparations yesterday and I'm actually quite excited. Your father—the sweet man—is even pretending to have a smidgen of interest because I haven't been to a party in years. It's probably killing him not to complain about the inevitable politicking. But that's all for later, in the meantime, let's not disrupt Slade's carefully ordered chaos." The woman shooed Tasha toward the stairs. "Quickly now, off to the changing room. It's the first door on your left."

Tasha wanted to refuse, but something about Senna made the idea of being rude inconceivable. So, reluctantly, she climbed the stairs.

Waiting until the door closed above them, Senna confronted Slade with a raised eyebrow. "That girl is a bit old for you?"

"It's not what you think, Mother." Slade grinned, holding his hands up palms out. "She's only the friend of a friend of no friend of mine. We are acquaintances, nothing more, at least for my part; as for her, I fear she regards me with an unholy passion."

"She dislikes you that much, does she?" Senna teased, making Feylin stifle a burst of laughter. "Oh, glory from above, I forgot to introduce you two—"

"Don't worry, Mother, we met with all due formality three days ago, introduced as we were by our respective guardians." A small smile tugged at his lips.

In response, Senna's expression contorted into one of confusion then pain with a thin coating of desperation. "But … she arrived … yesterday, and … and you were sleeping? You were sleeping, right?" Thin palms pressed up against eyes as she tried sorting through the jumble, and from behind her shoulder Feylin glanced, wide-eyed, at Slade.

Slade, however, shook his head, pressing a finger to his lips for a single heartbeat.

"Mother, perhaps you should go lay down. Maybe drink some of those medicines the apothecary gave us, they're supposed to help." And they did, insomuch as suppressing the symptoms counted as helping: reducing the fever chills, sedating her enough that she could sleep through the headaches, and keeping her a little … displaced.

Senna hastily lowered her hands. "No, no. I'm fine. I remember now, I was just having a momentary lapse. Silly me, of course you arrived three days ago." She smiled broadly. "So you two met? How did that go?"

"It was a … unique experience." Feylin blushed, glancing at her shoes. "But I suggest you ask Tiberius; Slade tends to embellish."

"Embellish, ha; I clearly remember rescuing you from a fearsome dragon of epic proportions and delightfully repugnant character. Tell me, what kind of embellishments does that story need?"

Senna rounded on Slade. "Again with the marriage proposals, Slade; eventually, one of these girls will think your sincere and accept the offer. What happens then?"

"That possibility is why I restrict myself to pretty girls. If one accepts my proposal, either through spite or ignorance, my tormenter will at least possess an exquisite countenance paired with the ability to occasionally surprise me." Slade grinned, swooping forward and kissing his mother's cheek before swiveling to grab Feylin's hand. "Come, Miss Whyte, let's migrate to the depressing gloom outside."

Stepping from the cool relief of Slade's home into the blinding flare and oppressive warmth beyond, Feylin gasped then tried back peddling only to feel Slade brush against her as he closed the door and followed her out. Twisting to negotiate re–entrance, she stopped, eyes widening with outright horror at his dark, layered clothing. "Gods above, how can you stand this heat?"

"By standing still and imagining my unimaginable allure to all the young ladies passing by." He then pulled his great, feathered hat—its brim now adorned by a line of silver runes—from his satchel and plopped it atop his head. "Plus a hat to protect my fine skinned self from *Sammahale's* glare." Slade grinned at her, his teeth flashing in the shade. "But what about the ivory skin you leave unprotected? As your chaperone, I must remedy this situation immediately. Tell me are there any styles of hat you prefer?"

"Oh, no, you mustn't." Feylin—for once knowing what exactly to say—hastily retreated, both hands raised in case her self-appointed chaperone went digging through his mysterious satchel yet again. Something he did at the slightest provocation, producing one useful or improbable item after the next. Not even Tiberius could guess how it worked. *'Then again,'* she thought, *'neither could his crew and if anybody should know, it'd be them.'*

She'd met the various members yesterday when Slade offered to introduce everyone and Cain—their actual chaperone—immediately opted out, leaving her without bulwark against the most playful, charming, and generally irresponsible group she had ever encountered.

Feylin, pressing back against the cool, sandstone blocks of his home, found herself eyeing Slade as he rattled off the various hats that might suit her, describing each with those talkative hands of his. *'Now that I think about it, he seems oddly … not exactly secretive, but reserved when it comes to personal details. No one at the party'*—because what else did you call a cacophony of practical jokes, drinking, acrobatics, and illegal gambling—*'knew anything about him beyond their personal horror stories.'* By the end of festivities, Feylin had uncovered little and started suspecting that Slade proposing on their first meeting was actually his version of being polite and mellow. Whereupon she got distracted by him and his satchel distributing books among his crew, one or two occasionally landing atop empty chairs to wait for absent members. Each seemed incongruous, possessing titles like *The Secret of Agriculture, The Art of Fine Baking,* or *One Hundred and One Crochet Stitches;* all together they far exceeded the supposed limit of his satchel. Seeing one heavily armed man receive his copy of *Divine Flower Arrangements* with obvious delight, Feylin had assumed the whole affair was an inside joke, which somehow left her all the more curious about the satchel. And now, for the umpteenth time, she puzzled over it.

'You realize, the simplest solution is just asking him for an explanation, yes? People make inquiries all the time. Give a war cry like Tiberius said to do when you were younger, psyche yourself up, and ask the question.' Feylin took a breath. *'Wait, do a silent war cry. You don't want him thinking you're peculiar. Whew, that was close. Alright, on three. One, two, three. Yaaaah!'* And with that rather unintimidating cry, she blurted out, "Slade, how is your satchel enchanted?"

He took the abrupt subject change in stride. "I wondered when you would ask. There is a terrible power suffusing this satchel, Miss Feylin; are you sure you want to know?"

She winced at the honorific. "Yes, though you can or … umm if you don't mind, please…" She took a breath. *'You got this, Feylin. You're already prying into his secrets and digging up his personal life, what's a minor request? Go on, psyche yourself up again. Yahhha!'* "Please don't call me Miss, just Feylin is fine." Rather belatedly, she made an attempt at nonchalance, but suspected her blush and shifting feet spoiled the effect.

"Well, my newly christened, Feylin, allow me to elaborate." He leaned forward, adopting the air of one who wished to convey a secret, voice dropping low and tenebrous. "My satchel is a gateway to Oblivion: a realm devoid of either time or essence. If you dropped something, a bird perhaps, into this satchel it would fall and fall, never reaching the bottom of an endless chasm. Unable to fly since there's no wind. Unable to land since there's no ground. Unable to live since there's no life. Unable to exist since there's no existence. Unable to die since there's no death." Slade raised a hand, forestalling her objections. "The nature of Oblivion is … nothing. If you peeked into the realm of Oblivion, you would see nothing. Not the absence of all things, not even an all-encompassing black because black is color and color is something. You wouldn't recall what you saw, because there was nothing to see." Feylin shivered, large, heavily lashed eyes entranced by the dark words and enthralling voice. "It takes an exceptionally powerful wizard to bend Oblivion to his will; those who fail die, slowly corrupted from within. Dark tendrils creep from pupils long since consigned to nightmares, infecting bright, colorful irises before escaping and spreading to the rest of the body. Beautiful, ivory skin becomes swollen and red. Blood seeps from ears, eyes, and nails. A man's strong body will twist in unimagined ways. A beautiful woman will shrivel under a single moon cycle." Slade paused, letting the anticipation build. "But not always, some possess the unwavering willpower needed to dominate this nothingness, and their future overflows with unlimited potential." Silence reigned briefly, lasting until he grinned. "Except, this glory is death in disguise. No man eludes Oblivion forever."

"Why not pursue a different livelihood?"

Turning, Feylin looked up into the penetrating, unrelenting, saturated blue eyes of Slade's companion. She was taller than Slade, almost as tall as Cain even, only without the strictly controlled demeanor and adherence to proper conduct that ensured he felt mostly safe if unapproachable. The woman, conversely, felt raw or perhaps like a spring wound until every wire screamed and one unfortunately snapped twig might result in practiced violence. A distinct impression that Senna's beautiful dress, the woman's lovely wooden hairpins, and her long, beautifully sun-catching auburn hair failed to alleviate. Leaving Feylin with the impression of a woman who could, in fact, intimidate with a battle cry.

"If they possessed enough willpower to tame Oblivion, they should use that same resolve to ignore its lure." The woman's eyes swept Feylin, then switched to Slade, lowering into a slight 'only sort of contemplating murder' glare.

"The dress makes you even more stunning than I imagined. However did my besotted mind develop such an intriguing design."

"Slade, enough. I'm no beauty."

"There are endless types of beauty, my Dear; if we lack one, we often possess another."

"Agree to disagree."

"Agree to disagree on our agreeing to disagree, I simply haven't convinced you yet."

"Being pretty has only one use: attention. Not really something I'm looking for."

"You're right, of course. Beauty is a crushing burden, which is why the gods only give it to those titanic few who can bare the weight. You, my Dear, must have a truly awesome soul."

The woman rolled her eyes, which, of all things, was what made her less intimidating. "Answer my question please."

Slade harrumphed. "My Dear, if you persist with this crotchety demeanor, I shall be forced to call off our engagement, no matter your tear-sodden pleas to the contrary."

"Would you really? For me?"

Feylin couldn't help herself, she laughed and Slade grinned. "For you, my Dear, I would do anything." He leaned forward, once again drawing an atmosphere of sweet darkness about himself. "Tasha," he spoke the name softly, seductively. "You know how delicious the temptation of power is, the almost physical ecstasy of money and the satiated lust that arises from uncontested will. Alone they make powerful enemies. Together, they form an unstoppable force that topples nations. And all the while Oblivion taints the soul, slowly eroding your restraint and distancing you from morality. You ask why practitioners cannot walk away. I ask, how can they resist?" Slade shook his head, closing his eyes at such bleakness. Opening one, he peeked at his audience. "Your expressions of dumbstruck wonder are beyond any compliment."

Feylin blinked and shook her head as if clearing the cobwebs. "You should have been a storyteller."

"I think wisdom advises he continue with his present occupation," Tasha said, the barest touch of amusement coloring her brusque tone. "Otherwise stories of the incredibly handsome, unbelievably intelligent adventurer Slade Lammerock would flood the Empire and the tower princess would come back into fashion."

"Tasha, I do believe our relationship is improving; the idea that such a compliment might pass your lips was beyond my wildest dreams." He sidled closer, holding a hand to his mouth. "Between us, I came quite close to believing the rumors concerning your gorgeous self."

"And what might those rumors be?"

"Oh, nothing much, a bit of idle gossip concerning your studiously amoral compass, a few errant tales regarding your sociopathic tendencies, and a certain preference for the fairer sex."

Tasha threw her hand skyward. "Praised be *Enecki*, Slade has finally insulted me."

Slade pressed both hands to his chest, one drumming against the other to suggest an elevated heart rate. "I do believe I see matrimony on the horizon, its tidal wave of pale silk accompanied by the sound of church bells. Feylin, you simply must be our bridesmaid. We'll invite the whole city. *Telacra* can be the maid of honor and *Morgan* shall be best man."

Smiling, Tasha shook her head and turned to Feylin, steepling her fingers for a slight obeisance. "I don't believe we've met. My name is–"

"Miss Feylin Whyte, may I present Tasha Bloomhale," Slade interposed. "She's the Imperial Emperor's most proficient spy, here on a mission so steeped in secrecy that I only discovered it a year ago. Its secrecy is so secretive, the Imperial Emperor himself doesn't know about her mission." He leaned in, one hand pressed to the side of his mouth. "Personally, I think she's the Emperor's Shadow." With that he swept in the opposite direction, rising slightly to lay an arm across Tasha's shoulders. "Allow me to introduce Miss Feylin, a divinity whom I cursed with mortality and thus made hopelessly enamored of me." Slade leaned close once again. "I believe her love is a disgraceful subterfuge designed to recover her immortality." Straightening, he grasped a hand from either woman and shook efficiently. "Now we've concluded introductions, we can begin the adventure, and let me assure you that the enjoyment derived from this escapade will be terrible indeed." He beamed then clapped his hands. "The hour grows late, the day hot, and our clothes damp; let's not tarry."

"Where are we going?" Tasha eased a toe into the sunlight, little by little abandoning the shade. As for her question, Slade merely tapped the side of his nose—eyes glittering from an unspoken joke—and skipped down the steps.

Feylin trotted after him, realized this was an untenable speed and modified her pace; whereupon Slade slid an arm through hers, attempting the same with Tasha when she descended. Tasha, however, rebuffed the advance.

Slade grinned. Their route was long and riddled with opportunities for sequestering.

17

Playing With Cards

"Prepare yourselves, my charming companions, for we've braved sun and sea breeze to arrive at last." Slade swept his arm across the horizon, indicating what resembled the colorful offspring between a tent village and a marketplace. The sprawling mess occupied Tellor's eastern face, squashed into the corner where the first wall met the city's outer edge and the land gave way to an enormous sea-cliff. An identical cliff curtailed Tellor's western side and together they formed the base for one of the city's most distinctive features: three long, blade like promontories—broad across the surface, slim along the edge—that jutted over Tellor's two ports and the land bridge separating the Inland Sea from the ocean. "Come on, let's socialize."

They descended a short stair onto grass strewn with ancient flakes of rusted bronze and set out across the park, weaving their way through scattered metal trees that—according to Slade—had fallen into hibernation centuries ago. As they approached the house-sized, polychromatic tents, the residents gradually lost their ambiguity and Tasha's steps slowed. *Gods above, most of them couldn't fit under a door without stooping.*

Feylin, conversely, hastened, dashing several steps before spinning back toward Slade, her eyes sparkling as much as the night sky. "We're visiting the Ie'Calla, right? You've taken us to one of their villages."

"Yes indeed, I–"

"Oh, I've never seen one before. I've only read books and asked Tiberius things." She swiveled to rush ahead again, but Slade caught her arm, which left her undeterred. "He says that they're nomadic but can't see across long distances, and that the Imperial Emperor lets them govern themselves and that they're impossible to steal from."

"All true." Slade smiled. "Legends claim that *Kis'Maat* himself couldn't pick an Ie'Calla's pocket."

"Come on, come on. Let's go."

Watching the young woman tug against Slade's grip with feet that practically churned up the ground, Tasha felt a smile creep into place. *'Pampered and blessed and sheltered far beyond what is healthy, but at least she gets honestly excited and for more than dresses and lace.'*

Just ahead of them a child glanced up, squinted, and then gave a squeal of delight, forsaking her duties as miscellaneous collector and charging in their direction.

"How old is she?" Tasha asked, giving a small return wave as the girl skipped circles around them.

"In our years, I'd say she was a little over six." Producing a scrap of cloth, Slade knelt and, bowing his head, offered it up to the girl who stood an inch or two taller than Feylin.

Giggling, she accepted the gift, examining it with luminous, large pupiled eyes then gasping as it changed color.

Drawn by her earlier cry, other Ie'Calla now ambled forward with a tide of children preceding them. Alongside the children came a towering adult, who approached Tasha and bowed over her languidly. His skin had a pale green pigment that warmed to yellow around the cheekbones, and—while alien—didn't leave her skin crawling, neither did his absent ears or the two simple slits that served him as a nose. "Please," he said, pressing a bracelet into her palm, the dusky wood engraved with frogs and crisscrossed by colorful string, "accept this gift and our sorrow for your past." The Ie'Calla said nothing more, merely inclined his head and stepped away, leaving her locked in place.

Then she snatched Slade's arm, stomach muscles clenched tight. "What is he talking about? What did he mean?"

"It seems rather straightforward, my Dear; he's feeling sympathetic towards you."

"I don't want his sympathy. I want to know how and what he's learned, also why he picked me for this." Tasha brandished the bracelet, pausing mid-gesture as her eyes narrowed abruptly. "Unless this is another one of your games?"

"A good thought but incorrect. As for why he chose you, presumably because you've encountered a few rough patches in your history."

'Of course you'd say its incorrect, not like you'd admit to it … except, he might actually admit it. Jaidar bless it, why can't he just lie like a normal person.' Tasha released his arm and stepped back. "I'm no more unfortunate than any street orphaned brat. Why me?" From the corner of her vision, she vaguely noticed Feylin's head cock at this, but couldn't be bothered at the moment. It wasn't true anyway. Slade, however, swallowed it easily.

"Ah, that explains it. The Ie'Calla hold that no child should grow up an orphan, whatever their race, their heritage, or crimes their ancestors might have committed." Taking her wrist, he slid the bracelet into place. "It's common for Ie'Calla to adopt children and stray animals, often times picking them up right off the street. They just know, somehow. I wouldn't worry about it." Patting her hand, he turned to greet the general mass of older Ie'Calla arriving, many carrying exquisitely woven rugs or beautiful ceramics for hawking. "You two run along and mingle now but be careful. Touching their Eleeky is incredibly disrespectful."

Feylin stopped mid-dash. "What?"

"Their hair."

"Why?" Tasha asked, eyeing the mass of thick leathery cords hanging from each Ie'Calla head.

"Eleeky are a living part of Ie'Calla anatomy, possessing their own blood and muscles. More importantly, they're incredibly sensitive. But that's enough of lecturing. Go on, shoo." Offering a grin and a wave, Slade marched off into the crowd.

He spent a couple of minutes wandering among the Ie'Calla, exchanging coins for slips of paper, scraps of cloth, pieces of clay, and even a couple wooden tablets, basically anything an Ie'Calla might have at hand for writing. These transactions came to an abrupt halt when a towering woman accosted him with a yellow shirt. "Ooh, what a beautiful garment," Slade cooed, grinning as his words spawned a pleased blush. In human years, she was barely sixteen. "How much does it cost?"

"Shanna'shen sells it for one bronze-crown."

'Well, that altogether seems like a fair price so either she's new to this or it's shabby merchandise.' Taking Shanna'shen's hands, Slade adopted his most beseeching eyes. "My funds are woefully inadequate. Perhaps a lovely lady like yourself would consider reducing her price so I might have at least one beautiful thing?"

The girl giggled. "Perhaps, Shanna'shen can sell shirt for two bronze-scepters." Slade winked at her and waggled his eyebrows, and she burst into outright laughter. "One bronze-scepter and no less, they'll scold Shanna'shen otherwise." Standing on tiptoes, Slade kissed his fingers and pressed them against her cheek. A moment later she was skipping across the park, intent on spending her profits in Tellor's Great-Market.

Stuffing the shirt into his satchel, he pivoted and collided with a pillar dressed in bright orange robes. "Slade Lammerock, the silver-tongued bane, why must you beguile our young with your clever words and charming smile?" Rather than sounding bitter, he spoke with the same leisurely tones as all Ie'Calla.

"You wound me, Delain'Delar. I'm selflessly teaching your children to beware wily snakes like myself, plus she made an excellent profit."

Bright purple eyes crinkled with mirth. "A less perceptive human would have only seen our masterful reputation not the countless errors torturing the embroidery. They would have paid accordingly. However, those same humans would have paid nothing at all upon knowing what you know. It was a generous act, Slade Lammerock, and we're humbled by this. Allow me to refund your acquisition or at least compensate some of the cost."

"Ah, but, Delain'Delar, what if I intended to buy such a wonderful disaster?"

After thinking for a moment, the Ie'Calla gave a crooked grin. "So, who will you insult with this gift? A rival?"

"My secrets are mine alone; just as your secrets belong to you."

"Ah, but no one keeps secrets from you, Slade Lammerock. Every man's secrets lie in your safekeeping." The Ie'Calla withdrew a bundle of scrolls. "Speaking of safekeeping, I took the liberty of inscribing these with all our noticings, harder to misplace this way."

"Wonderful," Slade said, opening a scroll and peeking at the bright, carefully written notes, "but … not in alphabetical order, I see."

Delain'Delar shrugged. "I tried. Also, I made certain to note all the especially curious happenings." He leaned closer, setting a massive hand atop Slade's shoulder and speaking in a low, slightly less relaxed tone. "More strangers snuck in with the last caravan. Friends of yours, I think; they asked many questions and we gave many wrong answers, but we also gave a few correct ones to those who paid. All their portraits come free of charge. Be careful."

"Most generous of you." Slade tossed him a purse. "Do you have my other purchase?"

The Ie'Calla nodded, digging through an inside pocket and producing a small redwood box. "Be cautious. Though the interior is padded, the contents are fragile and will lose potency if exposed. May the dream they weave possess limitless color. Fare thee well, Slade Lammerock."

"May *Enecki* guard you and your children," Slade murmured to the departing figure before looking around. A little to his right, he saw Tasha fending off three Ie'Calla women—each armed with a garishly colored dress—and leapt to her rescue. "Beautiful ladies, please allow my companion her rest; she's newly arrived and long poor."

Predatory gazes latched onto Slade and wares got extended, but he shushed them elsewhere.

"Why did they listen to you? I've been trying to escape for the past ten minutes."

"After many years and titanic effort, I convinced even the most dubious that I was stubborner. Here take this." Slade passed his newly acquired shirt to Tasha.

"What's this for? I don't need any gifts."

"It's not a gift." Hopping atop a barrel, he peered over the exceptionally tall Ie'Calla. "It's a refugee fleeing from a young, lovely mistress who tortured it horribly."

"Since I didn't pay for it, I'm pretty sure that still constitutes as a gift."

"And you would be correct were anyone besides myself involved; I operate beyond the cruel oppression of such plebian guidelines. If it helps, think of the shirt as a gross insult. Ah, there she is."

"A gift can't be an insult, Slade." Tasha called before sighing and following him as he swept off to rescue Feylin. A gaggle of children had surrounded the young woman, oohing and ahhing over her blond, nearly white hair. One particularly resourceful boy even snuck up with a pair of scissors.

Luckily, Slade managed to prevent the intended butchery, swiping the scissors from surprised fingers and then releasing paper sailboats that flew off through the tents with giggling children in pursuit. "Feylin, I suggest tying up your hair; Ie'Calla children like stealing the brightly colored specimens. That aside, I think we've mingled enough, making now the perfect time to enjoy the main event. Come along."

Feylin, her countenance flushed by excitement, scurried in pursuit, bombarding him with questions. "How do they hear? How long do they live? Which type of magic do they prefer? Are they mages or wizards?"

"Their Eleeky sense vibrations in the air, serving in place of ears and alerting the Ie'Calla to each movement made within a crowd, also granting them unparalleled linguistical abilities. As for their magical inclinations, wizardry; though in general they practice a rare type of divination. It presents multiple possibilities rather than the single most popular candidate."

Listening as Slade lectured, Feylin and Tasha stumbled through the maze of tents, ducking under guylines and occasionally shifting the all-encompassing clutter to one side. Ie'Calla suffered from a condition wherein they found it near impossible to clean up after themselves. Clothes collected atop misplaced chairs or lay scattered across the ground, sharing the space with all manner of pots and boxes and drawers that held an equally varied clientele. Everything migrated constantly too, since pets ran wild and the Ie'Calla worked whenever the impulse struck, simply grabbing whatever or whoever's tools lay within reach. These habits meant stray bits of yarn, pottery shards, and wood dust covered every conceivable surface, damning the tent village to further chaos. Yet, the Ie'Calla never lost anything.

Slade, turning a corner, spun and walked the next stretch backwards, flawlessly navigating the dangerous terrain with arms thrown wide. "May I present this afternoon's entertainment, the marvelous, the incomparable, the reality defining, secret banishing, ineffably stylish Fate-House of Josarra'Josi."

Behind him rose the Ie'Calla's gaudiest tent. It had green, pink, and orange stripes running across the entire surface except for where pale squares made space for embroidered pictures; all in all, a perfectly horrendous design.

"Long name for a place with no sign," Tasha said, jumping some drawers and then catching Feylin when she rushed the same leap. Rather than recovering her balance, however, Feylin used Tasha to redirect her momentum and sent herself hopping forward.

"A Fate-House? Is that where they tell fortunes? Real fortunes?"

"Yes, real fortunes. Well, most of the time."

"How do people even find the place?" Tasha asked, examining the surrounding clutter. "There's no writing or anything."

Slade shrugged. "I'm ninety-five percent certain there is a sign; it's just squirreled away in storage somewhere."

"Can we talk about this later, please?" Feylin asked, practically bouncing up and down, then abruptly reaching for the tent's flap.

Slade's hand clapped over hers, snatching it to the side. "Thresholds are sacred to the Ie'Calla because they lack any permanent home. No stranger can touch or cross them without explicit permission." He met her widened eyes without hint of sparkle or jest. "These are an amicable people unless you violate their laws, whereupon they drown you in the nearest rain barrel, offering their sincerest condolences to your family and friends."

"How are we supposed to get in then?"

"Ah, well there's usually a bell or wooden drum or … something to make noise." Slade scanned the area. "Huh, those also appear to be in storage."

"Where do you find the time to learn all this?" Tasha shook her head. "I expect this breadth of knowledge from a wizened old scholar, not a young man with plenty of affairs that need his attention."

"Sleep is an old friend and we have a regular rendezvous, but he's deathly afraid of the dark so I am invariably left waiting. Generally, I pass the time reading, but I've also dabbled—unsuccessfully—in darning socks and even took up dark magic again." Slade heaved a sigh. "I've tried taking him to a psychiatrist. It was the least I could do since my practicing dark magic is what started this whole predicament—word from the wise, never practice dark magic with your friends—but the poor fellow won't even answer the door. The moment I show up, he starts screaming and chucking lamps or lit torches and demanding that I leave. Understandable considering my condition, but still a mite discourteous."

"Your condition?" Feylin asked, starting slightly when this produced an immediate pained groan from Tasha.

Without hesitation, however, Slade leapt atop a pile of firewood. "I am the Great Goddess *Telacra*, lady queen of darkness and mistress of terror, treachery, and torture usurped by my treacherous siblings and cast down to the mortal plane!"

Feylin stared, a little horrified, and Tasha crossed her arms, poised between laughing and hurling the nearest wooden figurine at him for his blasphemy. Luckily, the tent's inhabitant spoke up from inside, "Does Josi hear rightly? Is Slade Lammerock come visiting alongside her guests? Does he again bring friends for Josi to impress or is he come to let her seek out his missing future?" The tent flap pulled aside, revealing an Ie'Calla woman who was only a full head and shoulders above Slade, her Eleeky trailing across the ground and her eyes bright with pleasure.

Slade swept a bow. "Indeed tis I, your ever-adoring enigma, come with pretty ladies for you to impress."

"Come in, come in; enter Josi's abode freely and without reprisal." The woman retreated inside, letting the tent flap swish close and expelled a gust of cooling wind.

Both women gasped in the sudden chill, glancing from the entrance to Slade, who nodded. "We may now enter without losing our breath."

Renouncing further questions, they pushed the tent flap aside and dove into the glittering void of the night sky. Beautifully detailed constellations were embroidered into the walls of the tent, all original and all enchanted to exude a faint glow.

As they stood there, uncertain where to move, a series of small warm lamps materialized and slowly illuminated the particulars of day-to-day life: several large trunks, an old sleeping mat, the disordered residents of a writing desk, and a blackened cast iron stove that lurked in the back alongside its wood basket. Lastly, a table and three chairs held court at the tent's center.

"Come, come. Make yourselves at home and partake of Josi's repast." She waved them forward repeatedly then bent over a trunk, kicking its sides and soundly battering the latch before leaping away as the lid burst open. She then dove in headfirst.

Obeying their host, Feylin trotted over and started inspecting the table's contents. She quickly identified the pitchers as containing peach juice, iced water, and cool mint tea. The trays meanwhile held an assortment of finger food, largely granola, exotic berries, and nuts. Best of all, a loaf of steaming bread presided over the congregation, flanked on all sides by crocks of jelly and butter.

Tasha frowned at the spread. "It's like she expected us," she whispered to Slade as he passed by with a random chair.

"She expected you, me not so much. I'm very unexpected."

"Be serious, please. I don't like this."

"That's because you loathe the unexpected."

"What?"

"My Dear, you detest surprises with the unconditional hatred of mortal enemies; they're the result of something you didn't foresee and thus can't control. It's a reasonable sentiment but unnecessary, nothing untoward is happening." Slade squeezed her shoulder reassuringly, then passed over the chair. "Here, take this." Unthinking, she obeyed, whereupon he pranced off grinning.

Rolling her eyes, Tasha lugged the chair over and sat down, only then realizing that he had swiped her pillow. Interrupting Tasha's forthcoming complaint, Josi cried triumphantly and dived further into her trunk. She briefly reappeared holding an old bag and a small treasure chest, both of which she callously discarded before vanishing again. When she next appeared, Josi held four cups of scattered heritage, material, and design. Upon turning about though, her expression fell. "Why-oh-why are Josi's beautiful guests not eating?"

"That dreadful scoundrel Heat has stolen their appetite, but I'm sure they'll recover presently." Slade, ignoring Josi's motherly clucks over the girls, began loading his plate with various snacks. "In the meantime, please read our fortunes in The Cards of *Kis'Maat* or at least sit and rest your feet awhile." He patted the chair next to him.

Josi gave each girl a last worried glance, then hesitantly sat beside Slade. "Since handsome Slade asks, how can Josi refuse?" She cleared a broad space, produced a deck of cards and began to hum a soft, deep throated tune that lingered beautifully. Called by the music, a mysterious resonance filled the tent accompanied by a slight physical weight.

Josi lifted her arm, hand hovering above the cards as sea green power blossomed within her palm. Slowly, gracefully the cards exuded their own glow, consuming her magic until they shone with a steady, opaque light. Next the deck started shuffling itself. Cards leapt from the pile, soaring around the room in complex circular patterns that ended with them returning to their deck.

Twisting about, both Feylin and Tasha strained to see the undersides. The cards, however, were blank.

Josi's hand snapped out, seizing a card and slapping it down, making both women jump. It depicted a monk, his eyes bound with a ragged cloth and a quarterstaff cradled in one arm. "The Warrior Priest: a protector of the weak, righter of wrongs; one who discards physical sight for the spiritual kind. He trudges the weary, endless roads of immortals and, like all such entities, can impart much wisdom; wisdom you will need." The card shifted, morphing into a different one altogether. Gone was the blind monk; in his place, stood a tall, gaunt man who wore tattered chainmail and carried two swords slung across his back. Most disturbing of all, he had two bloody iron stakes rammed through his eyes. "Be forewarned, madness twists his thoughts. Alignment: Prince of the Wandering House."

Josi seized a second card mid-flight, slapping it alongside the first. "Fate also stalks among you. It's the whirlpool that never ceases and the boulder that crushes anything mortal or physical to dust. *Kis'Maat's* strings glisten and stick like spiderwebs, warping your lives to a larger design." Fate's card exhibited a huge twenty-sided die that blurred, spinning within the confines of its painting. "Alignment: Jester of the Divine House."

The Ie'Calla woman plucked a third card from the air. "*Amarrion*: time, immortality, the present, the past, and the future made one. Master of the ceaseless. Your life will be fraught with the schemes of immortals. Alignment: Priest of the Divine House." A card decorated by an hourglass whose sands actively fell.

A fourth card joined the other three. "The Bloody Crown: royalty or the war of kings and maybe the blood of the *Roy'als*. War is coming, a war of succession, a war of subjugation, a war of desperation; war is coming. Alignment: the Wandering House, unranked." Josi slapped two cards down simultaneously and pushed them together, creating one picture; a man whose face was covered by a mask, one half of which cried while the other laughed. "The Masked Man: he who wears a solitary face that is many faces. He will both guide and manipulate your every move. Alignment: none." Her hands blurred, simultaneously catching a new card and sweeping the table clean. The cards she swept aside flew into the air, rejoining the endless procession.

"*Jaidar:* all is upturned. Primary alignment: King of the Cursed House. Secondary alignment: Prince of the Divine House." This last card displayed a burning pentacle whose flames ate the card from within, singeing its edges black.

Josi caught another card. "The Wheel That Never Ends: the seasons, day and night, a man who dies then lives, dies then lives, dies then lives, forever doomed to this pattern. Death follows in his wake, maybe yours, maybe another's. Alignment: the Dark House, unranked." The last card displayed an iron wheel, spiked and bound in chains.

Josi swept the table clean again, snatching a series of cards from the air and placing them in a neat line, tapping each in turn. "The Cloaked Man: he is an assassin, spy, and betrayer, or perhaps, a shadowy friend with an obscure purpose. Alignment: unknown." A man, dressed in cavorting shadows, stared up from the card, his face hidden behind the darkness.

"Resurgence and Cataclysm." A man walking across a frozen sea without a horizon. "Something or someone returning from lost roads and bringing with them the end of days."

The third card displayed a pair of hands gripping each other over a war-torn battlefield. "Alliance: one will bargain with demons or against them, attempting to avoid an inevitable war." Josi placed two more cards on top of the table. One bore a disk whose surface exhibited a battle between Light and Dark, the balance of power fluctuating constantly. The other depicted a tree, warped and poisoned by sickly green tendrils that crept from the black-hafted, crook-bladed spear leaned against its trunk. "The Poisoned Tree: what cannot fall sick is claimed by disease, a poison without cure and a plague without beginning or end." This card also changed, becoming a physically twisted, near-broken man who grinned with a savage glee. This image lasted a moment before changing into a broad-shouldered warrior who dressed in black armor carrying the crook-bladed spear from earlier. Blood, poison, and disease dripped from his hand while his step corroded the ground underfoot. On his brow rested a dark iron crown. "The Lord of Plague: an old darkness set free, his prison broken, ready to savage the earth again. Alignment: Lord of the Dark House." Josi shifted her finger to the other card. "Good and Evil, Chaos and Order, Death and Life: opposite sides of the same coin; the powers of Light and Dark prepare to continue their endless war. Alignment: Divine House, unranked." The card had changed and now displayed two armored men, one in gold the other in black.

Josi cleared the table of cards and then, with great deliberation, arranged five new cards before her. Flipping the first, she spoke, "The Prison of Gods: the *Hounds* are hunting, and their master takes a side. Alignment:

Wandering House, unranked." This card depicted six massive black dogs circling a wrought iron key. Josi flipped over the next card, displaying a tall copper haired man standing atop an ice-bound mountain; a halo of golden light surrounded him. "The Mortal Servant: a man who serves the divine." She flipped the same card twice in quick succession; her first revolution displaying a man who stood outside a city with its gates locked against him. When Josi flipped the card again, she revealed a knight carrying an overlarge shield. "His duty is changed: cast out, banished, exiled; he shall be your protector against forces like the one he formerly served. Alignment: the Wandering House, unranked." The next card she flipped illustrated an indistinct character atop a mountain ridge, hurling bolts of lightning. "The Raven Witch: she who cursed the gods and plans to do so again. Alignment: Queen of the Wandering house." Josi passed her hand over the card, and the scene changed, switching to a golden-haired man who held his hand aloft to catch the lightning cast from above. "Her nemesis is the Sun Mage: his light shall guide and protect you. Alignment: the Divine House, unranked." The Ie'Calla woman flipped over the fourth card to show its face; a well-dressed, handsome man standing over the corpse of another man. Except the second man was no man at all, rather some half-dragon thing horribly warped and deformed. This card changed as well. Now it showed two knights fighting over a young boy; the first dressed in red and the second in white. "The Hunter and the Protector: you are hunted by powers beyond your abilities but standing with you is the Guardian." The fifth and last card, when overturned, was blank. "The future grows unclear, and the gods summon the Prophet, the Oracle, and the Augur."

The humming drifted off and the cards faded into blank canvas, lethargically shuffling themselves one last time. Josi stared at the neatly piled deck, the quiet creeping by until she covered her face with trembling hands. "Josi weeps for her friends. Gods, Great-Immortals, deep evils, and death bringers all contest their future while unknown companions wander scattered and distracted. The cards have spoken, and Josi has born witness."

Silence and two sets of wide blue eyes—one vibrant, one dull and flecked with glittering silver—met her words, Tasha staring forcefully with white knuckled hands gripping her armrest while Feylin seemed a touch distant, as if struggling to shirk an enchantment.

"Well, I don't know about any of you"—Slade shrugged—"but I intend to sequester a second helping." Grabbing the bread, he cut a slice for each of them. When they didn't leap on the food, he delivered a withering glare. "I'd hate to finish this delightful meal all by my lonesome."

Tasha shook herself and took a deep, steadying breath. "Yes, I believe my appetite has returned." She then reached for some mint tea and gave the still absorbed Feylin a rough bump with her shoulder. "Snap out of it, I highly doubt it's as serious as we think. Most of that stuff is so vague it could be said about anyone."

"Not me," Slade chirped, dolloping jelly on Feylin's bread.

"That's because you're the one tasked with creating the disarray and chaos."

"Tasked? No, I do that for my own pleasure."

"Why am I not surprised?"

Looking between them, her eyes no longer distant, Feylin took a tentative bite, then another with more gusto. Together they picked the table clean, stacked their plates at the center, chatted and gradually relaxed, finally departing.

"What do you think it all means?" Feylin broached as they meandered through the colorful tents and bronze trees of the Ie'Calla home. "How much is true as opposed to false?" She'd taken a breath before asking, determined to hold his gaze directly. Except, the moment he looked across, she blushed and found her shoes again.

"I do not know. Mysterious villains hunting you and Tasha seems plausible. Rumor has it that she grew up street-side, which is an easy place to find perilous enemies, and you're an obvious target because of Tiberius."

I guess that makes sense, but what about him… Go on, you know you can ask. You've pestered him enough that he probably expects it. Just like before. One, two, three and … "Does someone hunt you, Slade Lammerock?" It still came out a touch abruptly, but the asking itself seemed easier than before.

"We all have enemies, Feylin, I think it's best that mine remain personal."

'Oh, … okay. I apologize for prying." *See? I pushed too far and now he thinks I'm nosy. But why wouldn't he tell me? Ahhh, now I'm even more curious.'

"There, there. No need to look so depressed. I'm sure you'll liberate a few of my actually decent secrets eventually."

"And what makes knowing someone's enemies a poor secret?" Tasha asked. "It can reveal so much about their character."

"A useful secret and a decent secret aren't necessarily the same thing. For instance, it's remarkably useful to unearth your governor's embezzling habit, but that hardly qualifies as exciting. In my case, knowing who abhors me is likely to make you slap your forehead and say 'ohhh, that makes sense'; whereas knowing why they're my enemies is far more interesting."

'What does that mean?'

"And before you ask, no I won't reveal what I've done to deserve such moderate and really quite reasonable loathing."

Tasha dropped back a pace, skirting around the group and beginning to walk alongside Feylin, peering down with blue, unrelenting eyes and bringing a light, probably undeserved sweat to Feylin's hands. Then she struck out with a playful nudge. "He probably flirted with governor Warsein's daughter and broke her heart."

"Not exactly," Slade said as Feylin giggled. "I only flirted with her to disguise my forbidden love with her brother Amonn. We intended to elope later that week, but our romance was doomed to heartbreak because, under all his pretty words and sweet nothings, Amonn's a cad and a scoundrel. Anyway, after realizing my folly, I returned to his sister, but she was furious and chucked me out on my tail." Slade shook his head. "We're not enemies though. She has since forgiven me, and Amonn's devolved into an … irritation."

"The governor then." Feylin suggested, blushing promptly after.

Slade grinned. "Maybe, maybe not; I've still no intention of telling you. How about I spill somebody else's secret instead?" The two women shared a glance then nodded. "Tellor's foundries are heating up."

"Aw shit." Tasha ran a hand through her hair.

"What? What does that mean?"

"It means Cardolyn Tyier's preparing his next war."

"How do Tellor's foundries mean we're going to war?"

Slade pointed at a massive smoke cloud. "Over a hundred years ago, Tellor was equipped with a thousand foundries that proceeded to supply half the Empire with everything from armaments to raw steel. Some records say the sky all but disappeared behind ash clouds. Other records describe the scene like a hellscape. Then came his next war and the Imperial Emperor added the second largest foundry in the Empire, doubling production and creating a dark, ashen winter that blanketed half the West. Even the *Annuir'Hyme* ran gray from all the ash. Our forests still haven't recovered."

"But why? Why start another war? It doesn't make sense."

Slade shrugged. "He needs no other justification than he is god-spawn, the greatest power currently living, the dragon that has everyone else holding their breath and praying he sleeps just a little longer."

"But why?" Feylin asked for the third time, almost whispering.

"He's waging his father's war on the mortal plane and he's winning. It doesn't matter that it's a senseless fight, the Empire's people don't care. Five hundred years ago he saved them from brutality, starvation, and slavery at the hands of a dying Alarach Empire. He made new mortar from the blood and rubble of our predecessor, and he built an empire destined to withstand the poisoning of time. Cardolyn Tyier has given us everything we now possess: our unity, our prosperity, our power, and even our direction. After five hundred years of safety and comfort, the people worship him more than they do his father. They'd fight any war he asked."

A hawk's cry sounded directly above them, and Slade veered to a statue he then climbed. Tasha stopped directly beneath him with rolled eyes, but Feylin hung back as a rosy heat spread across her cheeks, almost certain she could hear snickers and horrified gasps from nearby.

As for the statue, she would have sworn the poor thing looked disgruntled.

From his position atop its head, Slade waved down and then reached skyward, offering a perch. After the bird accepted, he shifted it to his shoulder and listened as it spoke a flood of gibberish, nodding periodically.

'Looks like we might be here for a while.' Hesitantly, with eyes peeled for any fingers pointing their way, Feylin sidled closer and perched on the statue's base. She spent a moment trying to decipher the gibberish above, then sighed and propped her chin between her hands. "Sometimes I wish messages didn't come encrypted."

"I don't," Tasha said, relaxing beside her and crossing arms in such a way that Feylin—with a quick pitter patter to her heart—noticed the pale scars slicing back and forth across the skin.

"Oh? Why?" *'I wonder what she does? Caravan Guard? Ring fighter? Mercenary?'*

"I prefer privacy over hearing secrets. Besides, any message carried by a bird is either important or bad news, and neither concerns us. If you're curious about someone's private affairs, snoop the polite way: hire a Mouse from Carr'Selain." A tad aggressively, Tasha began picking pieces of lint from her sleeve.

"A what from who?"

"A Mouse is someone who steals information and Carr'Selain's the leader of the Thieves' Guild."

"Oh, … I see." Lifting a bit of reed from the ground, Feylin began sketching in the dust. "I'm still curious."

Beside her, Tasha's picking worsened to fidgeting and the woman quickly resumed her feet. "Don't let your imagination runaway with you; important doesn't mean interesting."

Feylin conceded this with another sigh, sketching more random lines. As time progressed, a dragon formed, causing her to frown and quickly push a boot through the drawing.

"Why'd you do that? It was coming along nicely."

"No, not really. The proportions were incorrect." The other woman looked about to argue, then shrugged and turned away, leaving Feylin to stare groundward for a moment. "Hey, Tasha?"

"Yes?"

"Are you one of those, um … people he's adopted? Slade I mean."

"Do I look like I need help from a skinny teenager?"

"No."

"Exactly."

"So, you're not a member of his crew?'

"Gods no. Why do you ask?"

"Tiberius asked Slade to investigate something for him and I was hoping you knew a little about it; Tiberius won't tell me anything. He thinks it's safer."

"Probably is. Slade hasn't mentioned anything though, or he did and I discounted it."

"Oh…"

"I'll give your ear a tug if anything falls into my lap, but the best person to ask would be Slade."

"I don't think he'll tell my anything, not with Tiberius making it clear that I'm to be uninvolved."

"Slade plays the game however he wants to; if he feels like telling you, he will. If he doesn't, he won't."

Before Feylin could ask her next question, the man himself landed between them with a plume of dust. "I'm sorry but a pressing matter requires my immediate attention. Tasha, please escort our delightful companion to my house; I'll return later."

"What did the message say? Is everything alright?" Feylin asked, rising to her feet.

"Everything is perfectly fine. It's simply that a few deadly assassins have come to brutally murder me." Slade flashed a grin. "Should be quite the shindig."

"Oh, okay." Feylin stepped back a pace, unsure how to respond and feeling a twinge of hurt. *'Quit that,'* she told herself, *'he likes his secrets—his very interesting secrets—and there's no reason for him to tell you anything. You're not friends yet, merely acquaintances.'*

Tasha, of course, proved less compliant, stomping right through his polite dismissal to loom over him. "Slade, what really happened?"

This produced an exaggerated gasp of outrage, the voicer of said gasp rearing back with a hand pressed to his chest. "You would accuse me of lying? Shame on you and all your ancestors with a double serving for your descendants."

Tasha frowned, glanced at Feylin then stepped in close. "Tell me."

Considering her, he leaned in close enough to nibble an ear. From the faint whispers Feylin heard, he clearly did very little nibbling. It became clearer still when Tasha broke away, stamped the ground and swore.

Slade grinned, darting forward to plant a kiss on her cheek. "Aw, so you do care for me." Tasha growled something unintelligible and kicked at him ineffectually, sending him dancing off into the crowd.

"So what's going on?"

"From what little Slade told me, something that's none of our business."

"Assassins really aren't after him, are they?"

"Don't be ridiculous. If assassins hunted him, we would all be scurrying home."

"Can't we help in some way?"

"Like I said before, this affair is none of our business. The best plan is to return to Slade's house and hope for answers later."

Frowning, she followed Tasha down the road, smelling a series of partial truths but unsure how to pursue. *'Based on Slade's reaction, I don't think anything dangerous happened. I mean, he's not exactly a soldier, so him charging headlong into danger seems unlikely. Right? But then why did Tasha react that way? He obviously told her something and … I don't think it surprised her. Whatever just happened, is she involved?'* Feylin stumbled. *'Wait, does this have something to do with Akravast?'*

Tasha, meanwhile, silently thanked *Enecki* that Feylin was neither stubborn nor spoiled. Ten years earlier, Tasha's heels would have dug furrows through stone until she heard the full story.

18

Passages Of Stone

Compelled by the Dread Lord's dominion, Dieharamon tread through the palace within the embrace of a cloying shroud that tugged at his sanity and spoke to the vilest corners of his mind. This time, however, Dieharamon did not seek to command his mounting fury: he fed it, and along with it, the inferno seething at his core, hoping they would liberate him.

Despite the Dread Lord's urgency, he progressed slowly, impeded by a morass of latent power—so thick it became a physical burden—and coughing fits provoked by the centuries of accumulated dust. Nondescript black doors looked on from either side of the ancient, mostly forgotten passageways, offering no solace and denying the world entrance.

As he ventured deeper into the palace, the labyrinth grew darker and the magic denser until his skin vibrated with it. His blood flashed from chillingly cold to boiling hot ceaselessly, his clothing fluttered despite the lack of wind, and his braid writhed on his back. Even the stone had grown pliant over the years and now yielded beneath his steps.

Abruptly Dieharamon felt a change in the air, a fluctuation in the bruising weight of magic that eased the stress on his body and relieved his vacillating temperature. Nevertheless, he stilled, searching for what had provoked the change.

He knew little of magic, but the Dread Lord's geas rooted one of his eyes in the spirit world, granting him a flawed vision of what that entailed, revealing both a golden rune of concealment etched onto the wall and the slim entrance of a veiled path beside it. He recoiled at the prospect of entering it, but Sinnitar's geas was undeniable. So he obeyed and fire answered his first step. It swelled around him from the walls and floor in a tide, consuming his world in a dusty golden haze. He lurched back, screaming and flailing at his clothing only to strike an unseen barrier. Horror welled within him, and in that instant, he realized something strange: he felt no pain. Dieharamon stilled, staring at his undamaged skin and clothing in disbelief.

The Dread Lord's power thrashed inside him, clawing at the void of his soul and drinking of his life force to sustain itself. The flames pursued it, slipping beneath Dieharamon's flesh and burrowing to his core, incinerating the Dread Lord's hold as it went.

Dieharamon collapsed, trembling with a sensation of release: of physical, tangible relief in his body and thoughts as the Dread Lord's corruption was routed.

His spirit vision faded, but phantom images of the palace's spell work remained, seared into his mind, along with a glimmer of the prevalent magic. In that brilliance he saw something discordant: a dozen man-like silhouettes crouched in malevolent famine, staring at him from beyond the unseen barrier, waiting. He quailed under their glares, assaulted by the same primal terror the Dread Lord engendered; he could not fight them, and even if he could bypass the barrier, he could not traverse them for his fear, which left only the passage downward.

Thus he descended, relying on luck and the phantom images to survive whatever spell work he encountered and deliver an escape route. It proved a futile endeavor. The passage simply ran on without variance, offering only locked doors and shallow alcoves. His lingering vision faded during the descent, diminishing with the elapse of time until it expired completely. He froze with its absence, the dim corridor illuminated only by the traces of magic visible to everyone. He stood at the edge of a sunken room fashioned entirely from jade with twelve walls and doors, three for each cardinal direction, aligned with the primal lands, and a thirteenth wall for the entrance he occupied. No radiance or power glimmered within, nothing to forewarn his advance, but even so his skin crawled and his mind ached; he did not trust what lay beyond, not when magic flow through the corridor all around him thick as wind.

Still, he possessed no other route and could only step into the chamber. Sound barraged him the instant he stepped foot onto the jade floor, a cacophony that could not be described as words or music, only as something alien, but he knew it for magic all the same. He cursed and clamped his hands to his ears, but magical things paid little heed to the blood and sinew of men. Logic gradually emerged from the cacophony, allowing him to parse meaning from the deluge: it derived from the doors, some of it a demand for his approach, and the rest a warning.

He staggered back toward the entrance, frantic for the relief it harbored as a foul sensation twisted in his gut. He slowed, mind dragging helplessly inward toward the expanding morass of sound, caught on tethers he could not see. The Dread Lord's geas yawned awake and consumed him again, snaring his thoughts and slithering through his veins like knives to take root in muscle and bone. He screamed futilely, but his body pivoted in place and retraced its steps across the jade room to the southern wall.

His gripped the second door and heaved, shaking it in its casing but achieving no effect. The geas coiled inside him and gouged deeper, burrowing until it discovered the blazing fount at his core and latched on. Dieharamon shrieked, his blood afire with raped power and his body contorting back. The geas threw him into the door, shattering it with a kick and eschewing dust. He stumbled inside, hacking and shuddering as an ethereal summons boomed out.

Spectral flames ignited as he entered, illuminating a throng of scattered relics in assorted displays or locked receptacles. The magical cacophony instantly doubled, almost deafening him with their awful, alien noise. He advanced, glancing from artifact to artifact in search of the *Pathfinder Shard*.

Ultimately, he found it in a secluded nook, swathed in the cobwebs of long-dead arachnids. It resembled an Avaran Arshendi: a twin-bladed knife that ran the length of a man's forearm, with a hilt wrought from ivory and gold, its onyx blade charred with a rune: *Pathfinder*.

The hilt pulsed at his touch, extracting its name from his unwilling lips, *"Pathfinder."* The chamber shuddered and stilled, the walls freezing mid-undulation. He ignored the chamber's unnatural movement for in uttering its name, the *Pathfinder Shard* had unveiled its purpose. It existed to fashion paths through any barrier, distance, or intervening power. It created a colossal bridge through which any number of thousands could travel without trace. For this power, it demanded a soul, a life, and a memory: the elements necessary to its construction.

Dieharamon retreated, not for fear of the artifact but to observe its entirety. The *Pathfinder Shard* brooded beneath a looming pall of death, a shroud of unsatiated violence that called him to wield it. His abhorrence of the Kalvonders answered, demanding he claim the *Pathfinder Shard* and free himself of Valeriius.

The clatter of feet ruptured his thoughts, pulling him around with a muttered profanity. He cast about for anything he could use to defend himself and found nothing.

The guardians slipped through the arching doorway with feral grace, the light glinting off jade skin, like the antechamber outside. They had waited centuries for something to disturb the palace's treasures, for anything to transgress on their sacred domain. They had lived centuries on the brink of starvation, for their bindings allowed them only to feed on those who transgressed. Yet, they were but precursors. A deeper summons slithered against the periphery of his senses.

Dieharamon retreated, desperately groping for a weapon. The geas burgeoned within him, gouging its talons deeper into the fount of power at his core and pulling his gaze to a bronze sword. He recoiled with a mental protest, loathing magic even in his possessed state, but the geas dragged his hand forward and grasped it.

The bronze sword erupted in Dieharamon's mind, simultaneously unveiling its history and seeking dominion.

The blade originated from the Age of Gods and had been revered as a divinity by a tribe of the Aparthiis' predecessors. They had made daily sacrifices of lamb marrow and virgin blood until a passing nomad stole and interred the blade out of fear for its insatiable hunger.

It slumbered for millennia until a Dragon Lord unearthed it while excavating a well. The sword attempted to subjugate the Dragon Lord but failed, leading to its eventual incarceration in the palace vaults. The bronze blade and its entire ilk were named *Harvester*: a species of artifact that leeched strength and sentience by consuming life.

Suffused with the *Harvester's* power and sick to his core with the geas' perversion, Dieharamon confronted the encroaching animates. They prowled along the corners of his periphery, Takk hound-like with their apish shoulders and crocodilian jaws. He retreated, answering their dull hisses in kind and striving to avoid encirclement.

Internally, the *Harvester's* consciousness coursed through him, ravenous and primal until it struck the geas. The Dread Lord's geas retaliated, unwilling to relinquish its host.

Dieharamon ignored the battle; even if he could have affected the outcome, the guardians demanded all his attention. They surged at him, baying louder as their rage mounted. The *Harvester's* blade flashed scarlet as he swept at the Takk hounds, momentarily repelling them. They renewed their assault without hesitation, tearing at his flesh and clothing in a frenzy. Yet, ensorcelled by the power flooding his veins and the Dread Lord's will, Dieharamon felt nothing.

As the first Takk hounds fell, Dieharamon seized the moment of reprieve and leapt back, toppling stands and upending chests into their path, desperate for a solution to his predicament. They pursued, vaulting over his impediments only to stumble as they landed, caught off guard as the room distorted violently. It warped in both hue and shape, turning various shades of vermillion and curving in on itself like the interior of a sphere, foreshadowing the approach of greater denizens.

A Takk hound struck in that instant, propelling him into and up the wall with a note of unearthly music, and lacerating his front with its secondary limbs. Dieharamon screamed and tore the beast open from stomach to jaw with the *Harvester*.

It was then that the Dread Lord's curse reared anew, having suppressed the *Harvester*, and thrust him into a wild ploy. He pivoted and dove from the enraged Takk hounds, doing his best to ignore how the air hissed like a frightened cat and groaned with the caress of a mounting storm: a *rift* was forming.

He came up with a vertical slash, shearing through one Takk hound and facing the *Pathfinder Shard*. There was a moment of dawning horror as the *Harvester's* lingering sentience realized his intent. He brought the bronze sword crashing onto the *Pathfinder Shard's* left edge, sacrificing the *Harvester's* soul to make a portal.

In the same moment, a thunderous crack split the air behind Dieharamon, marking the *rift's* completion. It split the air from floor to ceiling, a jagged emerald gash that pulsed with the contractions of a mother giving birth. The first entity arrived immediately, materializing just as the *Harvester* exploded, toppling Dieharamon and bludgeoning it back into the *rift*.

Screaming but uninjured by the discharge, the entity latched clawed hands onto the *rift's* edges and dragged itself forward, furious at the hubris from such an inferior creature. A second *rift* formed beside the first, eschewing another bear-like *daemon* into the Mortal Kingdoms.

The second *daemon* charged Dieharamon without pause, scattering the Takk hounds with a bellowing shake of its antler-crowned head. The first *daemon*, a many-limbed violet-plumed monstrosity, launched forward with a piercing cry.

Dieharamon discarded the *Harvester's* ruins, grasped the *Pathfinder Shard* and planted it at the base of its pedestal. The stone undulated and spat, smearing Dieharamon and the first *daemon* in liquid basalt and marble. He maintained his grip, clutching the *Pathfinder Shard* even as a pool of shadows expanded beneath him.

The *daemons* lunged forward with enraged cries, but the shadows embraced Dieharamon, submerging him in their depths.

As they closed, three powers grasped Dieharamon: the first was the *Pathfinder Shard*, intent on completing its journey; the second, Sinnitar Muntalabac, desirous of claiming his prize; and the third, Andeor'Vallen, his presence dwarfing the others.

Besieged by both a Dread Lord and a Dragon Lord, the *Pathfinder Shard* faltered and light glimmered through the portal's enfolding dark. Sinnitar Muntalabac reasserted his grip, but even he could not defy a Dragon Lord in his domain, not yet at least.

But in the last instant, a fourth irrefutable will claimed him, erasing all other claims as easily as monks discard a ruined sheet of paper, and eased Dieharamon into the *Lake of Dreams*.

19

In Pursuit Of The New Order

Lionel watched the temple burn from the tree line, his destrier stamping the ground in mingled displeasure and satisfaction. He could not save the temple from its corruption, but he could preserve the land upon which it stood and start its healing.

The wind brushed him, scraping the last flecks of blood and soot from his armor and inviting him to come North. Few others would have recognized it as an invitation, but Lionel knew The North and wind seldom tamed fires.

He sighed, lamenting the long ride ahead of him, but the New Order had already gained a day, and he could not risk lagging further.

Murmuring a final prayer of farewell to *Enecki*, Lionel mounted Arrad, his broad and long sword sheathed on the destrier's flanks. He opened a dilapidated saddlebag and retrieved a golden idol about twice the length of his hand. It hummed at his touch, faint due to the late night, only hours shy of morning, but Lionel chanted regardless, enacting a fundamental rite of devotion.

It glowed gently, infusing his Shard with a trickle of power, like drops in an empty glass. He would need higher rituals and the dawn to restore his Shard fully, but for now, he returned the idol to his saddlebags and turned his gaze to the distant Rhawn, afflicted by a vague sense of foreboding he could not place.

The sensation passed, but its impression lingered, disturbing Lionel's thoughts as he began preparing the witch for travel. First, he doused her hair and eyes in valerian to ensure sleep, then plugged her mouth and ears with ingots of myrrh and frankincense before ultimately sewing her mouth shut with black thread.

When he finished, Lionel restored everything to its proper place and urged his destrier north, the path illuminated by the bountiful stars. "Let's go, Arrad, there is nothing else for us here."

Hours later

Lionel smelled the rotting cadavers and heard the gorging crows long before Winter's Gate ever crested on the horizon. He glimpsed them soon after, a flock so dense he could barely see the sky, reigning over a battlefield that resembled a black scar on the ice. Beyond the dead stood the Watchers; two statues carved from the Rhawn Mountains as if wrought by the hands of gods. They flanked the *Annuir'Hyme*, their lofty crowns veiled by clouds, wreathed in thunder and scraped almost featureless by the eons. Miles separated them, but even at that distance you could see they reflected one another.

Lionel pulled Arrad to a halt, his emotions a jumble of trepidation, relief, and elation ensnared by memories from ten years of self-imposed exile. He had washed upon the banks of the *Annuir'Hyme* two decades past, bereft of all knowledge, a boy with the mind of an infant. A childless couple found and adopted him, raising Lionel as a Northerner for the next eleven years until *they* came.

Lionel dispelled his memories and spurred Arrad forward, struggling to calm an increasingly unsettled mind. It was not the witch that unsettled him, but the unnatural garnet-hued skies that gradually consumed his vision and the earth so gorged on death it supported a thin glacier of blood. Even the *Annuir'Hyme* ran scarlet near the bank, its banks littered with the metal and coins of all who had fallen into it.

Nauseous, Lionel directed Arrad's steps toward to *Annuir'Hyme*, one hand placed firmly on the witch's head lest death fuel her energy somehow. He dismounted a little short of the bank and traversed the remaining distance with open hands, heels ringing on the littered gold, silver, and buckles. The river greeted him with a roar, lashing up the banks and spitting a gush of handle-less blades and strapless armor. Lionel hesitated at the discharge then pressed forward, unsteady on the slick metal.

The river receded gradually, mounting into a wall and exposing a bed of anhydrous sand in invitation. He obeyed, shivering as its rage enveloped him. The *Annuir'Hyme* still tasted the massacre, still felt the taint in its water, the violation inflicted upon the land by the avarice of men, and it rarely forgave a transgression.

Lionel raised the witch's head, teeth clenched as he fought to speak through the *Annuir'Hyme's* presence. "I ask you to cleanse this evil, for there is no *Lithian Wood* near and I cannot carry it with me."

The water stilled, and the witch's head slowly spun toward him, eyes thrashing beneath her charred lids. She reached for him, seeking to divert his mind. He shrugged her off, but desperation gave her strength and her mind found purchase. He retaliated, igniting his Shard and sparking a conflagration on her skull. She recoiled, her assault shattering as a terror he did not understand assailed her. Then the river engulfed them, tearing her from his grip and submerging him in its freezing tumult.

He tumbled downstream, his armor smashing against the stones and scoring the sand. One of his flailing hands caught a protruding rock, and the other scrabbled at the floor. They held for an instant, then he glimpsed an indistinct man amidst the raging currents and his grip broke.

The river wrenched him upward, stripping him of what little power remained in his Shard and evicting him onto the bank, cleansed of all malice. He lay there gasping, exhausted, and bruised, unable even to rise until Arrad nuzzled him, declaring it was time to stop moping. Lionel pushed Arrad's head aside with a groan, but still obeyed his destrier's urgings. Satisfied, Arrad knelt with an air of long-suffering resignation, ready for him to mount.

Lionel bristled. "I know I should be more careful, but I signed where you got drafted; I need some wild tales to prove I'm doing anything." Despite his protests, he crawled into the saddle and prodded Arrad toward Winter's Gate.

The stars began winking out overhead, shrouded by storm clouds and the encroaching night. He bound his cloak tighter and kicked Arrad into a gallop, fearing what the storm portended. *Winsyria* never took well to intrusions. The last tyrant asinine enough to assault The North lost everything in days and afflicted the world with the worst winters it had experienced in centuries.

Crows erupted as Lionel approached the battlefield, screeching a cacophony of rabid caws that stalled Arrad short of the corpses. Lionel ducked over the destrier's head, shielding him until the carrion birds finally resettled further in the slaughter to resume their desecrations.

All carrion birds were caretakers of dead souls; they ferried them from the battlefields, prisons, and utmost extremities of the world to find their place in *Morgan's* realms, safeguarding them against the thefts of mortals. However, these were not *Morgan's* birds; they ravaged the dead with a visceral, macabre glee and no thought for the souls still imprisoned within.

He spurred Arrad forward, circumventing one cadaver mound populated by a choir of rooks, his skin prickling beneath their predatory scrutiny. One, an impossibly large abomination, expanded four wings and screeched a challenge.

Lionel spat a curse but Arrad did not hesitate; driven by instinct and training, he bolted for Winter's Gate, scattering the amassed birds in search of the Watcher's shadow, which none yet populated.

Even as they started, however, a crow larger than a hunting dog dove into the Watcher's shadow ahead of Lionel. It stabbed its beak into the eye of a frozen corpse and wrenched it free with such force the body jerked.

"Blood and Iron!" Lionel cursed again, his sword singing free of its sheath and erupting into light, fueled by its own prayercraft rather than his Shard.

The crow's left eye flared crimson with a mess of red veins, seething unmistakably into the shape of an inverted pentacle. Lionel smashed his heels into Arrad's side, urging him toward the monstrous bird and hacking at it. The crow vaulted into flight, easily evading him with a cackle. In that instant, Lionel glimpsed a struggling, ethereal figure caught between its wings, then the crow flew into the southern horizon.

Lionel lowered his sword, shivering within. He knew the taste of fear, but this was different, quieter. It burrowed deeper than fear but, unlike terror, it didn't erase his thoughts. Instead, it whispered of misery, despair, and venomous, lingering nightmares.

The East, somewhere in the holding of House Madasz:

Thyme
The man stood alone but for the dead, his form decrepit from centuries. He and his victims shared this moment, tranquil in the absence of wroth and desire. Their wordless communion proceeded, witnessed only by the night and the carrion birds. However, like everything else, neither dared approach him.

A surreptitious wind swept the plateau, murmuring like an old, favored sycophant. The banners, once held in righteous fury, now flecked the cadavers of their bearers. The few still upright creaked and billowed in bloodstained testament.

He had been a tall man once, and well suited to legends. His unseeing, visceral eyes surveyed the dead from beneath a high brow and matted locks of ivory hair stained almost black with filth. Even his armor seemed to droop, its former resplendence long faded, and its minute, interlocking plates rusted over. Two swords hung at his side: their blades obsidian and silver, and their handles black rowan. His coat, once crimson as blood, had degraded to gray rags.

A Raven settled on the ground near him, disrupting the monstrous carrion birds gorging on his victims. He glanced at her, and the Raven returned his stare, unfazed by his inhuman eyes and the silver haze that obscured any hint of iris or pupil.

"Hello, Seren." His lax hand tensed, preparing to snag her neck and twist until her head burst. The Raven hopped back, cawing in open mockery. His hand fell, but he still watched her.

To the north, beyond the Rhawn's callus peaks, he felt something primordial touch the daylight, and an old desire stirred. Without hesitation, he strode northward, the Raven taking flight behind him. For an instant, he tasted something sweet, something refusing to desert him regardless of his having long ago surrendered it. He crushed it.

The carrion birds followed, drowning all other sound beneath the thunder of their wings and abandoning the unfinished dead, for they never hungered in his company. Still, only the Raven flew close, making him question her presence, and what her master desired. Not that either question truly interested him.

The leagues passed beneath his untiring steps, night turning to day and rolling hills to forests that shifted at his traversal. The briars and vines retreated from his touch, the moss cringed under his step, and the trees groaned from his path. He paused, freckled in broken sunlight, and sniffed. The air smelled like the *Annuir'Hyme*—not *it* specifically, but something that shared its nature: a *Lithian Wood*.

He resumed, his tread lightening as the *Lithian Wood's* flutes murmured their soporific melodies. Those who obeyed their song slept in the canopy, bound to trees in the hundreds, a wealth of malevolence for those strong enough to claim it. He ignored them, indifferent to dead witches: Light or Dark.

The trees thinned as he advanced, opening into a clearing where the Raven preened on a rock alone because the other carrion birds dared not enter a *Lithian Wood*.

The ground here whimpered, its moss torn away and the earth lacerated by wagon tracks. He halted, listening for something beyond the *Lithian Wood's* haunting melody. When nothing spoke, he knelt to explore the tracks with a hand, divining their direction and proprietors as a grin slowly formed; an Army of Purgeance traversed this wood.

The caravan crawled behind the slaves and mercenaries clearing a path through the underbrush, its supply wagons, slave train, and merchants reduced to a perilously thin guard detail because of it. Worse still, the *Lithian Wood* continued to deny all of them sleep, further eroding their safety.

The whole venture teetered on fate's whim, and the blindest traveler could recognize the forest's ire. Frightened stories vaulted from ear to ear, spreading dissent, sowing doubt and promoting chaos, all accented by a single, recurring question: Was it wise to continue? With over two hundred men and women—an amalgamation of soldiers, slaves, and travelers—the complaints became a low, incessant thunder.

The caravan master, an eastern lordling of negligible standing, disregarded the complaints, recognizing them as hollow, and continued his perusal of the caravan. His gambeson and shield caused him no grievance as he was a large man and acclimated to warfare since birth. Like his father, he had joined the Army of Purgeance for the power it offered. In fact, much of his family's current wealth derived from the Army of Purgeance and generations of spurious oaths to their precepts. It was a tradition he intended to perpetuate.

He reached the final wagon and reined in as the three mounted guards bowed. He ignored them and parted its flaps to inspect the cargo: scores of eastern-style spears, their four-edged tips glinting in the partial sunlight, and all accounted for.

Satisfied, the caravan master relinquished the flap and returned to the caravan's head, where he addressed the troop's mercenary commander, "How much farther to this damn forest?"

The other man laughed around wad of tobacco. "Why? Does the fact we're surrounded by dead witches unsettle you? Knowing some of them hung here in your grandfather's time."

"I don't care about the witch heads; I just want this trip done." The caravan master sheathed his pipe and beckoned to a slave, who rushed forward with a wineskin. He snatched the wine and struck the young Avaran's face, throwing him to the ground. "Be quicker."

"Yes, of course, master." The slave scrambled to a less offensive distance.

The caravan master removed the stopper and drank, only to spit out the wine with a profanity. "It's hot, you bastard son of a cur!" He flung the wineskin at the slave. "You think I want hot wine in this heat! Bring me another!"

The slave fled, clutching the discarded skin to his chest.

A scout emerged from the forest at a sprint and dropped to his knee. "Sir, there is an old man approaching from the east, he–"

"Why should I care if some idiotic grandfather is traveling this cursed wood?"

"The man is armed and shadowed by a murder of crows."

"Some wild enchanter or other devilry then. Where are your companions?"

"Observing his progress…," the scout trailed off, his attention riveted on a broken man approaching the laborers with two bloodied swords.

"Is that him?"

"Yes, sir."

"Fetch the guards."

The scout sprinted down the caravan, screaming his summons.

The mercenary captain drew his long sword with a snort. "I'll handle him." He spurred his stallion to within half-a-dozen paces of the old man. "Halt or we wil–" The mercenary's head tumbled off his shoulders with a dull thud, and the old man continued, unperturbed.

"Archers, kill him!" Heedless of his command, the mercenaries charged, the first of them dying before their weapons ever cleared their sheaths. And still, the old man continued, his form shrouded in a blur of black and silver blades.

Arrows sang into flight and then dove, most tasting blood but none striking the old man.

Seething, the caravan master ripped a horn from his belt and sounded it, calling every guard to battle as another arrow volley launched overhead.

Cavalry thundered past an instant later, lowering their spears as a scattered contingent of foot soldiers followed.

The caravan master started to grin, confident in his swarming force, only for it to falter when the old man refused to die.

He vaulted up onto and danced across the backs of the stallions, his blades flicking across the riders' throats with impunity.

The caravan master cursed again, wrenched his sword free of its sheath, and kicked a slave forward. "What are you waiting for?" He kicked another slave in the back. "Kill him!"

Thyme wove through their ranks, slaughtering at will and absently noting the caravan master's charge. The mercenaries parted for the advance, but he pursued them, owing no mercy to any who served the Army of Purgeance for gold.

A man lunged a spear at him, frantically swinging the haft back and forth and screaming. Thyme killed him with a thrust.

The caravan master galloped past, swinging his sword like a bludgeon. Thyme evaded the hacking blade, slaughtering one man as his other blade flashed across the stallion's throat. The beast collapsed, throwing its rider to crash against the ground, roll to his feet and charge. Thyme spun, slitting another man's throat and severing the caravan master's hand at the wrist.

The man buckled, clutching the stump of his arm and shrieking as Thyme extended the tip of his obsidian blade to kiss his throat. "Yield."

"Never you—"

Thyme decapitated him with a sweep of the silver blade. They would all submit.

The howling slaves crashed upon him, their momentum inexorable even if they had seen their master die. He slaughtered them with indiscriminate apathy, but they continued all the same, powerless against centuries of bondage. The surviving guards fled in their wake, blindly seeking salvation in the forest that would only destroy them when night fell. Thyme let them go.

Finally, shattered by fear and exhaustion, one man yielded. He dropped to his knees, screaming words of reverence and servitude as if speaking to a lost god, and Thyme stilled. His blind eyes focused on the praying Avaran, causing the other slaves to freeze as well.

Terrified, the Avaran prostrated himself further, pressing his brow into the soil and weeping. Thyme stepped past, raising his blade to the silent masses. "Yield."

They knelt as one, weapons discarded, brows grinding into the dirt and voices rising in ancient prayers of veneration.

Satisfied, Thyme sheathed his blades, blood spilling from the scabbards, and continued north, abandoning over a hundred dead to the carrion birds.

20
Dark Dreams

Dieharamon awoke in torpid ease upon the boughs of a rowan tree, distantly aware that he basked in the dreams of a foreign mind. The bark shone a rich sable in the dancing light while the leaves shimmered with the eternally setting sky's luminescence and boasted all the colors of autumn. Beneath him, the tree's roots writhed across the surface of an ocean, swimming towards one of the infinite horizons where clouds, shaped like long-forgotten creatures, danced with slow grace. A wayward water droplet splattered his chin and flowed up off his cheek, swaying in rhythm to the distant music that presided over this realm, as did everything else within it.

From his perch, Dieharamon watched the world unfurl around him, weaving itself without haste or languor into images and then stories. It was a collage of everything the Dreamer had once treasured and desired, an old and oft-visited sanctuary from the waking world's cruelties, and a hope to see something beyond the Avarus Desert's smoldering wastes.

The ocean's surface frolicked with memories in the silhouettes of men, only instead of flesh and cloth, they wore flashing colors. They pulsed red for passion, saffron for joy, emerald for contentment, and lavender with a hint of rose for something unspeakably precious. Lines of cobalt flowed to and fro across the surface, connecting memories and seamlessly forming and undoing an eternal tapestry.

Dieharamon inhaled deeply, savoring the permeating scents of jasmine and spearmint, lavender and pine, before springing from the rowan tree's bough with a laugh. He settled barefoot on the warm ocean, and laughed again, devoid of fear, doubt, and anxiety.

He was content, and that was the closest thing to joy he had experienced in years.

A distant cry drew Dieharamon's focus northward where golden light flashed on sapphire scales. The Elthari soared past, its two glorious, feathered wings flaring open as its long neck and serpentine body twined serenely. It swooped low and around Dieharamon, reveling in the sheer joy of flight. Its massive eyes, alight with bliss, met his for an instance and then it ascended anew, round face raised to the light.

The Elthari were one of the oldest mortal species and a cousin to dragons. More magic flowed in their veins than any other creature's, potent but beyond their ability to harness. It concentrated in their scales and the blue ivory of their claws, the first curing and the second granting immense physical strength. For these gifts, humans hunted the Elthari unto the brink of extinction. The passive giants had fled to the world's furthest extremities, and millennia had passed since any mortal saw one. Its presence marked this as an ancient dream.

Thunder peeled in the east, and the Dream Realm stilled, subsiding into a nocuous silence. A chill caressed Dieharamon, corrupting his breath into fog as strips of black ice lanced across the ocean's surface. He spun, his tranquility shattered.

A black storm yawned upon the horizon, effacing the dream as it expanded and plunging what remained into obscurity. All light and sound died, leaving Dieharamon alone in a gray twilight, surrounded by the silhouettes of trees and memories. From the storm, towering above him like a castle wall with ice spreading from its footsteps, skin wrought of night and a single crimson eye in its right socket, a dog emerged.

Dieharamon retreated, hands splayed before him and his mind rebelling at what he saw. The *Hound* raised its immense head and howled, drowning the world in the screech of chains and the barring of unseen doors. The storm worsened at its cry, devouring what little warmth and vibrancy survived in the dream and crushing Dieharamon beneath its immeasurable weight. He buckled, blind except for the crimson eye approaching him through the obscurity.

Yet in that instant, a familiar, awful presence enfolded him, Sinnitar dragging him into a new dream just as he had sought to extricate him from the palace. He hung between the two dreams for an eternal second, the entirety of both inundating his mind, and then the second embraced him.

The new Dream welcomed him with a burning city and a bed of smoking ash. The heat followed, strangling his breath and oppressing his body.

He staggered upright, gaping at the shattered structures, streams of blood, and half-charred skeletons. A searing gust of air buffeted him, besieging his nostrils with the stench of blood, charred flesh, and soot, and his body with chunks of bone. Finally, above all else, he felt the Dreamer's odium.

An ash mound to his right quivered and exploded into carrion birds. He cursed as they swarmed him and ducked beneath his arm, batting at them with his free hand. Yet amidst the deluge of their wings, he glimpsed someone, a woman with shorn hair and pale skin. Then she vanished, and every bird crumbled to ashes on the wind.

Dieharamon stood hesitantly, afflicted by the sense he knew this place beneath the fire and the blood. A child shuffled past, barefoot on the embers, her auburn skin charred. He stumbled, horror and shock first stripping him of balance, then sending him sprinting down to Sahdaen's main road.

He blasted through a clothesline and skidded to halt, the street before him swallowed by Avarans marching past, their foreheads *branded* with Sinnitar Muntalabac's inverted pentacle. The Dread Lord rode at their front, his essence manifested in the nightmare around them, for all of this—every rape and murder, every burning scream and tortured child—was him in his unveiled truth.

The Dread Lord pulled his mount from the procession, and extended a gauntleted fist toward Dieharamon, finger crooking to command his approach. "This is my vision for Sahdaen; I imagine you find it pleasing." The hand fell, clamping on Dieharamon's head as he arrived. "But you don't have to share it. You have power, and I can help you realize its potential."

Dieharamon cowered, every inch of him revolting at the offer and yet unable to voice his refusal.

"That's not an appropriate ans—"

Thunder boomed, echoing with the refrains of a metallic growl, and the *Hound* stepped into the dream, crushing a stone cart underfoot.

Sinnitar's mount, a nightmarish creature fashioned of thorn and sinew, reared in challenge, releasing Dieharamon from the Dread Lord's grip. Sinnitar drove it back to the ground and launched a maelstrom of black fire against the *Hound*, engulfing it only for the flames to be shirked with a roll of its head.

Liberated of the Dread Lord's grasp, Dieharamon scrambled across the ground, desperate to find shelter. A familiar touch answered, beckoning him from this dream and deeper into the *Lake*. Mentally spent, he acceded and the dream faded to a final lingering image of the Dread Lord and the *Hound*.

Dieharamon traversed a dozen Dream Realms, every threshold opening with a gasp and closing with a murmur of song. He never lingered for more than a second, but it sufficed for the entirety of each new Dream Realm to inundate and overwhelm his consciousness.

He fell until his mind verged on collapse, finding no relief even in the fathomless ether between worlds, his consciousness constantly besieged by a thousand fragmented images. Gasping, coughing, and exhausted, he finally tumbled into one last Realm.

Time slipped from Dieharamon as he lay huddled on the grass. The onslaught of Dreams had passed, but their phantoms endured; a multitude of worlds thronging in his mind, crowded with voices that roared, screamed, wept, and laughed, overwrought with emotions he could not contain.

Gradually the voices and the images faded, causing his ragged gasps to ameliorate and for consciousness to ease back into him. He half opened his eyes to a haze of light. When it caused him no pain, he opened them fully to bask in whatever Dream offered him asylum.

He lay on a path of moss-adorned stonework, staring at an emerald blanket of spring grass dotted with nasturtiums, snapdragons, and hyacinths. Trees stretched overhead, lush with fruit and bestowing their shade in huge swathes over the blooming flowers. Petals of all colors scattered the ground, often sweeping up on the gentle breezes that caressed the enclosed garden.

The Dreamer sat across from him, surveying his garden from a bench of carved stone. He was a tall man with proud shoulders and a strange, preternatural grace. In the distance, as if behind a wall, voices laughed—a woman's and a child's—the remnants of a lost dream the Dreamer refused to abandon.

Dieharamon hesitantly stood, feeling small though he towered over the seated Dreamer, and bowed. "Who ... who are you? And ... how did I get here?" He stumbled in his address, strangled by awe and the sensation that he should not be standing here. He wasn't worth it.

The Dreamer responded slowly, "I was ... many contradictions, now I am one." He lapsed into silence, and Dieharamon let him be despite the questions badgering for release. Eventually the Dreamer spoke, "I pulled you into the *Lake of Dreams* as a safeguard from the Dread Lord, but he pursued, interrupting my hold so you fell into a Dream Realm neither of us chose. The *Hound of Karrasain* found you there, attracted by the mark seared into your being. After that, guided by your connection, the Dread Lord summoned you into a vision he designed, allowing me to gleam your location and, ultimately, bring you here."

"But who are you?"

"Confiding my nature would only muddle your head, and you need clear vision for the war to come."

"How do you know me? And what war? Cardolyn Tyier's? Someone else's? The Muntalabac's?"

The Dream Realm blackened at the last word, echoing with the tolls of ancient conflict and shrieking via the wind. All else slumped beneath a pall of resentment and fear, burdened with a history Dieharamon had only glimpsed when he stepped into the Dread Lord's manifestation. He shrunk on himself, feeling tiny and misplaced, a lost tool.

The Dreamer sighed gently. "Few things elude my notice, Dieharamon, much less someone who will have as much impact on the Mortal Kingdoms as you."

"Impact? How? I am Tragnashi. I am powerless. Nor would I ever want to—"

The Dreamer swept a hand and storm clouds billowed into existence, frothing with lightning, rain, and thunder but silent. "War obscures all horizons, and neither I nor the gods can pierce its veil. Yet, sometimes, cracks appear, and I glimpse what lies beyond. I saw you and, among other things, the *Oracle* reborn."

"What war?" Dieharamon whispered desperately, exhausted by the Dreamer's riddles and terrified of any war that involved gods and *Oracles*.

His plea earned only silence, and when the Dreamer finally spoke, his voice had changed, gaining weight and implacability, "Someone is playing with you, with the gods, and the Great-Immortals; all while three ancient powers and a long-slumbering evil have resurfaced: war *is* inevitable."

"Only three? Just tonight alone, I have been manipulated by a Dread Lord, an ancient artifact, dragged here by you, and attacked by a dog the size of a house. And we can't forget somebody already owns my soul; so, I think there's more than one person playing with me!" Dieharamon controlled himself with an effort. "Who is he and what does he want?"

"I don't know, but he's focused on you."

"How do you know I'm important and not just a bystander?"

"Your Age does not have a word for it, but in my time it was called a *Knowing,* and they do not lie. Your fate, however, remains ambiguous, and as such, is susceptible to change." The word he spoke did not resemble any language Dieharamon had heard or knew, but it impressed its meaning upon him nonetheless: Knowing.

Still wary, Dieharamon sat beside the Dreamer, trying to calculate the repercussions of all he had heard. "How can I choose my fate when my soul is not my own?"

"You will reclaim your soul, that is inevitable; but it is how you reclaim it that will dictate your fate."

Dieharamon flinched, haunted by the image of wolves over a grave. "How do I choose the right path?"

"You must decide that for yourself."

"What if I chose to walk in evil? How is that the right path?"

"That is not my choice. You *must* relearn autonomy, Dieharamon, otherwise your fate will destroy you."

Dieharamon slumped back with a half-hearted snort. "You won't tell me anything."

The man shook his head with the ghost of a long-forgotten smile. "No, but I can give you a little guidance. Find Dayada Avenar. Pay no heed to how he acts or what you know of him; when the time comes, you must trust him. He is the second hinge upon which your fate hangs, and the only man who can shield you from the Dread Lord."

Dieharamon froze. *I'm not alone? There's someone out there than can help me. Save me.'* He nodded, schooling his thoughts before they spiraled from his control. *'Maybe ... maybe he'll even free me.'*

The Dreamer stood, and for the shortest breath, gold flashed upon his brow. "The gods cannot contain me entirely, no matter the strength they expend. The boundaries of their prison are too close to the *Lake of Dreams*, which does not obey them. Here, I tread as I will, and no power they possess can hinder me. If you claim your soul through flame or bargain, return to the *Lake of Dreams,* and I will do my best to aid you. If your soul is given, however, do not return to these waters." As he spoke, a fiery glory kindled around him, fading only as he fell silent and extended a gentle hand to Dieharamon's brow. "You must now rest, but your sleep will be dreamless. When you awake, the Dread Lord's hold will be untethered, but you will not wake where you entered; and if you encounter the Dread Lord again, he can restore the *brand*."

Sleep enfolded Dieharamon, easing him into its warmth. As he submerged, however, he heard the Dreamer's voice from a distance, "And yet, before you return, I believe there is one last dream you should see."

"Whose?"

"Yours."

21

Memory

The void of unformed dreams withdrew from Dieharamon's consciousness, exposing a vista of rolling hills, browning flora and cracked dirt. He reclined atop a knoll, shielded from the looming sun by an oak tree as finches flew westward overhead.

Raising a hand to screen his eyes, Dieharamon vacated the oak's shade. The Dreamer had said this was his dream, yet he had no recollection of it, and the view, despite its brilliance, inspired only grief.

"Why did you send me here?" he asked, but of course, the Dreamer gave no response. Shaking his head, Dieharamon trudged west, prompted by a faceless yearning.

A stream flowed around the knoll, its continuity broken by protruding stones and the occasional small amphibian. A distant, almost forgotten, memory told him the stream derived from a much larger river, but he pushed that knowledge away and vaulted the stream.

A boy and a girl ran down along the stream, spraying one another and laughing without noticing him, causing the ache in his chest to worsen. He followed, the water splashing his ankles. The boy remained oblivious, but the girl glanced back, her giggles faltering. Halting, he waved, but the girl gave no response. She had an innocent face, full of joy and framed by the golden locks common among westerners. She was also blind, her eyes misted over and unfocused as they stared through him.

Dieharamon tentatively stepped forward, extending a hand. Before he could touch her, the boy, her brother by appearances, called her to hasten and they resumed their trek. Dieharamon dropped his hand, feeling to his very core that he should recognize the girl but failing utterly.

Making no attempt to conceal his pursuit, he trailed them along the stream, wondering every step how the girl kept her footing on the slick stones. Her brother never bothered to glance back or to aid her. He simply urged her to keep up, that they were almost there.

The river concluded at a plate of untarnished white stone, converging with other streams into a shallow pool. The boy dashed forward, shrieking his glee; but Dieharamon faltered on the stone's edge, affixed by the stare of a split effigy. Seven of them encircled the pool, each shattered, burnt, or in some other way destroyed, their wood long-ago faded to lifeless gray and their markings either gouged out or scarred. Dresses littered their feet, varying across every hue, style, and echelons of wealth, from noblewomen's to rough homespun; offerings, Dieharamon thought, though he knew not why.

The girl settled on the pool's rim, immersing her legs without thought for the mud on her worn dress. Her brother splashed, and she retaliated with a laughing kick. He submerged, evading her splash, and then resurfaced explosively, showering her.

As they frolicked, a small Raven perched on one of the effigies. The brother, sighting it, shushed his sister to silence, waving though she could not see. Still giggling, though striving mightily to control it, she obeyed. "What is it?"

The brother inched toward her, whispering, "There's a Raven!"

"So? What's wrong with a Raven? I think they're pretty birds!"

"Oh, yes! Pretty black birds with a cruel intelligence! Birds of darkness they're called and with good reason! I've never heard of a Raven bringing good tidings. Except to *Lord Arthramain Roy'al;* but that barely counts because they were bound to him, and it was only ever that one. Still, Old Man Farl calls them servants of evil, messengers for the dead god. You can't trust birds like that."

"I still think they're pretty. Besides, they ferry souls for *Morgan*. You would end up wandering lost if it weren't for them." She extended her arm toward the bird and whistled, but the Raven ignored her, preferring to groom its feathers.

"You can't see anything; how do you know it's pretty?"

The sister opened a bag hanging from her shoulder. "I just know; besides, when have you ever seen an ugly bird?" She extracted a half-loaf of bread, tore off a hunk, and offered it to the Raven, who surveyed her before deigning to accept.

She giggled and alternated between feeding and stroking the Raven. Her brother, rolling his eyes, waded over to her. "If you get cursed, don't blame me and don't spread it around!"

The sister cooed, "It won't curse me; it's a nice bird."

Her brother tentatively started stroking it as well. "I wonder what it's doing this far west?"

"I thought Ravens lived everywhere?"

"Not really; they prefer the East or the northern borders. They don't like the South for some reason, probably the heat, and avoid the deep West because it's *Enecki's* land and they serve *Morgan*."

Sighing at the foolishness of girls, the boy submerged and dove for her feet. She yanked them out, laughing as he tried to tickle her and turning her body to shield the Raven when he resurfaced with a splash. "Don't, you'll scare it away!"

He gave her a sullen look and dove back into the water, swimming dejectedly until a thought bloomed in his eyes. Launching forward, he vaulted up beside her with a conspiratorial glance. "Wanna see something cool? A secret?"

"What kind of secret? Not like that weird bone you gave me the other day?"

He scooted forward. "A big secret! But you have to promise not to tell anyone, or I won't show you."

"Oh." Her shoulders slumped. "You shouldn't tell me you have a secret if you have to show it to me."

He snorted dismissively. "I told you about this place, and you couldn't see it! This is a secret or, at least, would be if some people didn't go telling Father."

"This is different; I can touch it, feel it. I can drink the water, smell the flowers, the grass, and the dirt; hear the fish and the frogs!"

"You will be able to feel this also. I promise! Only, this is a real secret, you cannot tell Father, Mother, or anyone."

"Alright, I promise not to tell anyone. What's your secret?"

He stared at her long and hard. "Alright, give me your hand." She complied, and he cupped it, features scrunching with effort. Gradually his breathing assumed a shallow rhythm, and hers altered to match. Slowly, gently, golden flames burgeoned across their skin.

She gasped. "What is this?"

"It's fire. My fire."

"But it didn't burn me?"

"It never burns me; and I didn't want it to burn you, so why would it?"

"You mean you can make it hurt people? Have you?"

"No! I haven't hurt anybody. I swear! It's just there's the feeling I can, and it scares me. But other than that, it's awesome, isn't it?" He leaned back with an exhausted sigh and let the flames die.

"Yes, it is. And don't worry, I won't tell anyone."

"That's good because I don't think it's a gift from *Enecki*." He glared at the Raven. "And make sure that thing doesn't bring bad luck; Father says we've had enough as is it, even without the drought."

She bit her lip. "I don't think our bad luck's run out yet. Mother and Father are scared and talking about southerners crossing the Inland Sea."

The brother's face tightened, but he spoke with confidence, "Don't worry. If anything happens the guards will handle it." The boy finally glanced Dieharamon's way, his eyes aflame with golden fire, and Dieharamon buckled.

This was no dream. It was a memory.

His sister began to speak again, but the world faded and then changed. Images swirled in on a tide of sound and gaiety. Dieharamon stumbled and spun, caught in a whirl of people on a street lined by wooden houses, lanterns, and decorations. He pulled free of the festivities, staggering to collapse on the steps of a dilapidated porch.

He had a sister.

The sky groaned overhead, a roll of thunder to protest the dormant storm in its bloated womb. Mangled but vaguely comprehensible voices reached Dieharamon. They carried unspoken inflections of hope, always accompanied by one word spoken in relief: rain.

His sister and younger self rushed through the crowd and up the stairs of an adjacent porch, slowing as they attained the awning's uncertain protection. His younger self opened the door for his sister and nudged her inward, cautious of the Raven still perched on her shoulder. Dieharamon followed, phasing through the closing door.

An inadequate candle shed light from a central table, illuminating shuttered windows, dirt floors, and warped walls. Spider webs cluttered the ceiling corners, and rats scuttled through the shadows in search of absent food.

A hollow-cheeked woman emerged from the back room, a smile warming her haggard appearance. "How was the river?"

Dieharamon's younger self claimed a seat at the table. "It was fun until I noticed the storm."

His sister snorted, feeling her way to the hearth, and the raven jumped from her shoulder to alight on the mantle. "You didn't notice anything."

"Of course I did, even though there wasn't a wisp of cloud in the sky!"

His sister crawled from the hearth with a cat in her arms. "You always smell a storm first, and you can't smell anything." Clutching the feline to her chest, she joined them at the table.

Dieharamon stepped forward, their words and presence fading from his mind as he extended a tremulous hand toward the strange, almost remembered, pins adorning his mother's collar. At the last moment, however, he instead tried cupping her cheek. His hand phased through and he dropped it, afflicted by a bone-deep ache. Wordlessly, he retreated to the hearth to wait.

The thunder roared with increasing violence as the night progressed, always followed by cracks of dry lightning and a blistering wind. His mother, unfazed by the quivering walls, alternated between stirring a pot on the rekindled hearth and disappearing into the back room with his younger self. It continued thus until the door opened with a rush of humid air to admit a man in a soldier's azure uniform.

Dieharamon's sister glanced up from her thin soup and smiled. "Hello, Father. Looks like the rain's finally come."

"Yes, I just hope it doesn't flood the fields." He shared a tired smile and doffed his overcoat. "Where are your mother and brother? The back?"

"Yes, trying to catch rats for tomorrow. I think they caught one, but they're trying for more in case their luck holds." She frowned. "I hope they don't try much longer; luck doesn't like being pressed."

"I'm sure it doesn't, but still, I'm glad it's decided to show a kinder face; so let's pray it holds, eh?"

She shook her head, absently, fiddling with her spoon. "I don't trust luck, Father, and I don't think we should pray for more."

He kissed her. "Don't worry, if anything happens, I'll be here to take care of it."

"I thought I heard your voice." Dieharamon's mother emerged from the back room, eliciting a smile from her husband and presenting a pair of dead rats. "Look what we caught, and Dieharamon's got another cornered." She shared a quick kiss and proceeded into the kitchen area, followed by Dieharamon's younger self with another rat. The cat trailed them, pompous with conceit for avoiding work.

His father nudged his sister. "See, nothing to worry about, our luck's still smiling."

Dieharamon's younger self crawled into a seat beside them. "What do you mean, see?"

"Oh nothing, your sister was just—" A wail interrupted his father, sending him rushing to open the shutters. He cursed and slammed them shut. "There's a fire at the gate, and the whole wall's going up." He yanked his discarded coat off the floor. "Take the children to the church."

Dieharamon's mother caught his arm. "What's going on?"

He murmured, "How often does a wall proofed against flame catch fire? I don't think those were rumors about southerners after all." He dashed out, calling the men to arms and the wall.

Dieharamon's mother pressed clasped hands to her lips and whispered a prayer. Then she gathered her children and fled toward the village center. Dieharamon followed, desperately trying to remember any of this and failing. The rain began with a final peal of thunder, each drop the hard tap of a finger on their heads.

A bell tolled in the distance, calling the villagers to assemble, ushering them through the increasingly muddy streets, and eventually bringing them to a church ringed in a thin iron fence. A man in humble robes occupied the open doorway, his gentle hands ushering villagers inside as he spoke comforting words, "Come inside, *Enecki* will guard us until time destroys the sanctity of his house."

"Hurry up!" Dieharamon's mother urged, pulling his sister and younger self into the courtyard before directing them up the stairs. "Go."

She waited until they disappeared inside, then approached the pastor. "What's going on, Father? Why are they attacking us when we have nothing?"

"I don't know, but you and your children will be safe in this house." He indicated the doors. "Go, my child, there is a fire to warm you inside." Nodding gratefully, she complied, but Dieharamon lingered, his eyes fixed on the distant orange glow and his body frozen to the core even though he could not feel the rain.

The last refugees scurried into the church and the pastor fastened the gate, murmuring scripture that caused the church's cobbles, walls, and fence to quiver with power. Then he returned to the steps, grim about the mouth.

Cries rose soon after, most a whooping exultation, but the rest desperate, terrified pleas. The village guards appeared from the dark, staggering as Avarans pranced around them, butchering and tormenting with gleeful cackles. They harried the survivors to the church's gate and there slaughtered the last one within inches of salvation.

The pastor stepped forward, heedless of the besieging rain, and raised a golden amulet that depicted a burning book and wheel. "This is a house of *Enecki;* sanctuary has been given to those within, and you heathens are forbidden entrance!" Golden light flashed, searing any Avaran within a foot of the fence line.

They shrieked their fury and hurled themselves against the fence twice more, each assault resulting only in burned flesh. After the second, they relented, giving way to a command from the dark. Valeriius, his appearance unchanged by the reverse of sixteen years, emerged from their ranks and planted his cane before the gate. "Come now, Father, is this how you treat guests?" He laid a hand upon the fence, golden light igniting beneath his fingers. "This will go easier if we bargain."

"You cannot enter this sanctuary! Creatures of your ilk do not belong here! Go, before *Enecki* smites you!"

"Your god will not be doing much smiting, Father; in fact, I do not think he will be doing much of anything for you. All I want is one child, and the rest can abide their misery in peace."

"I will not yield one life to you, devil! Even if its costs my own."

Valeriius beckoned, and an Avaran rushed to kneel beside him. "Can a temple of *Enecki* stand on tainted earth, Father? No, of course not, a temple can only stand on hallowed ground. At least, that is the Law of Blood, and unfortunately for you, my blood is purer." Valeriius pulled the kneeling Avaran to his feet and thrust a steel blade into his throat, spraying blood over the fence and church grounds.

The fence's glimmering power died and Valeriius entered the courtyard, his cane tapping with every step. "There was a time, Father, when granting sanctuary would have sufficed to deny almost anyone entrance. But the gods fell with their Age, and their grasp on these Mortal Kingdoms waned." Valeriius delved into his tunic as he walked, retrieving a small, triangular amulet. "New laws took precedence, the Laws of Blood, though few know them."

The pastor flung a hand skyward, light blooming in his palm. "You will not ruin this sanctuary, devi–"

Shadows lanced from the amulet, impaling him without mark or blood and hurling him down the steps as Valeriius ascended to the double doors. There he buried his cane into the floor until it stood autonomously, grasped the twin door handles and heaved them open to expose the terrified villagers within. They cowered back, mothers desperately concealing their children and pleading.

Valeriius retrieved his cane and returned to the Avarans. "Bring the children and ensure no one leaves." They rushed to obey and Dieharamon could only watch as they brought and discarded child after child, knowing all the while that Valeriius sought him.

Inevitably, they threw his sister before Valeriius. She scrambled away, but he snatched the collar of her dress and dragged her back, flipping her so he could inspect her opaque eyes. "I believe it would benefit us to keep track of you." Disregarding her struggles, Valeriius pressed a thumb against her brow and swept it across her skin, causing it to darken and the image of a bird in flight to materialize. "Keep this one safe. I want to revisit her later." He pushed her aside and faced the next child: Dieharamon.

They slammed him onto the cobbles before Valeriius, his hands and feet clenched tight as he snapped at them. Valeriius' eyes instantly flickered with realization and he caught Dieharamon's younger self by the jaw, twisting his face and searching his eyes. "This is the one. Dose him and kill the rest." The Avarans whooped, but his cane whipped out to catch the commanding officer by the shoulder. "No survivors, no witnesses, or I'll feed you to your own soldiers."

A curse drew Valeriius about. One of the two Avarans holding Dieharamon's sister lay on the ground, his eyes ruined, while the other screamed in pursuit. He managed one step before the Raven dove for his eyes.

The dreamscape began to fade, but as it did so, Dieharamon heard an Avaran voice. "Valeriius Kalvonder, we didn't find her…"

22
Lambs For The Slaughter

To all appearances Slade left, hurrying towards whatever disaster required his immediate attention. Appearances, however, were mischievous creatures. In reality Slade shadowed Feylin and Tasha, ensuring they went home as instructed.

When he verified their destination, Slade left for real and signaled his crew, ordering them to their assigned duties. Most went to prepare his unscheduled meeting with the assassins, but two followed Slade at a distance.

Samara was supposed to watch for assassins, instead she found herself watching the newcomer Naric. He moved too well, his sturdy, travel-stained boots landing mutely and his loose, foreign clothing barely rustling. Even the wooden lockets strapped across his chest bounced in complete silence. The only consistent sound he made was two miniature bells. They tinkled sweetly from the ends of side braids he'd tucked behind his ears, both bells strikingly gold when set against the tangled, matt black of his otherwise short hair.

As a member of Slade's entourage, he should have bubbled with speech and laughter, but he rarely spoke and, worse yet, did so in a thick eastern accent that rolled almost as much as the sea.

"So, are you a bodyguard from the Mercenaries' Guild?" Silence. "Why did Slade hire you? He's never commissioned a bodyguard before." Silence. "What is he planning?"

Naric's pace quickened, forcing Samara into a trot.

"Ha! You don't know."

Finally he spoke, voice deeper than any she had ever heard. "Being personally uninformed does not signify ignorance in others. If Slade restricted your knowledge concerning either my origins or his intentions, I shall follow his direction and maintain a similar degree of secrecy."

She glared at his back, scrambling for a rejoinder. Then just as she found a proper retort, Naric hunched, stepped sideways and disappeared, leaving her swearing.

He reappeared a second later, grabbing a pedestrian around the neck, muffling his surprised gasp and then bludgeoning his temple with a knife hilt. In a blink, a nearby alley swallowed both men, leaving nary a whisper to speak of violence.

Samara blundered through the crowd in pursuit, deliberately crushing a few toes so Naric wouldn't guess her true skill. As she ducked into the alleyway, however, a treacherous, umber cobblestone reached up and converted her false stagger to a real one, sending her stumbling past him.

"You cause a remarkable din for a thief." Naric said, his words accompanied by the quiet whimpering of his captive.

"What do you know? You're some mercenary from the East."

"I've had the pleasure to encounter several noteworthy members of your profession as well as some unexceptional specimens. You cause a remarkable din for a thief." Without breaking eye contact, Naric slammed his escaping captive into a wall. "Were I prone to credulity, I'd accept your incompetence." Captive met wall a second time. "But I've a suspicious heart, and I know the competence of your cohorts; it's unlikely Slade Lammerock assessed you so appallingly when he gauged them so accurately." Naric turned to and addressed his sobbing captive, "Now, unless I'm mistaken, you're a spy hired by Syndros Nomarr."

Faster than she thought possible, a knife slashed out.

Naric jerked sideways then punched the man's sternum. As he gasped, Naric caught his wrist and applied a sharp lock, forcing him to his knees. "Perhaps I misjudged your occupation." Naric touched the small cut across his neck. "Respectable technique. Excellent blade. Speed enhancing bracers and"—he licked a bloody finger—"low grade poison."

"Aaawhhhh! Let me go, let me go."

"Do you have a moment to discuss our lord and savior Slade Lammerock? I promise it won't take–" The assassin twisted, broke free and fled toward the exit. Naric slammed him back into place. "Slade Lammerock, the mortal incarnation of light and goodness, wishes to extend a chance for redemption, an opportunity to forsake your blood-soaked past and embrace the divine sanctity that is honest labor." Naric produced two envelopes signed with gold ink. "Deliver–" The assassin spat into his face, then froze as Naric poked him with his own knife. "Be patient a moment longer, please." Calmly Naric wiped away the spittle. "Your first step toward glorious, beautiful spiritual rebirth would be a simple one. Deliver these letters to Carr'Selain and Syndros Nomarr respectively."

"What business does Slade Lammerock have with the Thief Lord and Assassin King?" the man snapped.

"Syndros endeavors to assassinate our glorious savior and Slade Lammerock wishes to express his profound irritation. As for Carr'Selain, do not concern yourself." Naric tucked the letters down his captive's shirt. "Simply deliver these without broaching their privacy and then rejoice in how you've taken your first small step toward eternal peace."

"Like hell I'll do anyth—"

"Please, I implore you, reexamine your self-destructive road, recognize how it leads only to despair and ruin. Take this opportunity, break the cycle, save yourself from the horror of your current choices." Naric gave the man a cautionary knife jab.

After being released, the assassin scrambled to the alley's mouth, where he glanced back at Naric, anger and fear mixing expertly on his face. "Eastern scum," he spat before whirling and promptly tripping over his own feet.

An indistinct figure stepped into view, helped the assassin up, dusted off his clothes, and clapped him on the shoulder; whereupon the assassin shoved him aside and stormed for the street.

"After everything I did for him too." Slade harrumphed, strolling toward Naric and Samara. "So, my two love birds, how are matters progressing?"

Samara made an X with her arms. "Alright now, enough of that. I don't want the others—"

"The affair concluded as predicted; our courier may require further convincing, but I'll provide any necessary encouragement tonight. He should commence his journey in the morning."

"Excellent, now we just need another dozen. Here, see if you can find any starry-eyed volunteers among these." Slade passed over the Ie'Calla supplied portraits.

"Fresh infiltrators, I presume."

"Already? *Jaidar* bless us, we haven't even finished…" Samara fell silent, shooting Naric a mistrustful glance.

"I'm well aware of Tellor's sudden influx of thieves and your difficulties evicting them," Naric said, flipping through the portraits. "That said, these appear to be primarily assassins"—he frowned—"expensive ones. It seems like Carr'Selain sold your whereabouts to the other guilds."

"It was inevitable. Fortunately, he only ever sells a portion of his information, meaning we can exert some control over the situation. By regulating what he discovers, we determine how much the others learn. As for our invasion of murderously minded immigrants and their kleptomaniacal predecessors, we can only do so much right now, so sit tight and avoid the murderous ones; I don't want anyone getting hurt. We'll manage them when we can. In the meantime, let's focus on Syndros Nomarr's assassins. Samara, pop down below and oversee preparations to welcome our unwelcome guests. Naric we'll rendezvous in the sewers; I must issue their invitations."

Even accounting for the heat and crowds their pace dawdled, arising from how Feylin flitted from curiosity to curiosity. Tasha sighed, forcing herself to slow down and quelling impatience yet again. She couldn't really blame the girl. According to Slade, Feylin grew up in careful isolation, surrounded by instructors and their books and not much else apart from Tiberius.

Tasha glanced ahead, then back to where Feylin sorted through beaded jewelry with bright sparkling eyes. Shaking her head, Tasha retraced her steps. *'The assassins aren't hunting us. Might as well let the girl enjoy herself.'* Nevertheless, she checked all her weapons and kept a wary lookout.

Slade waited in a market square, perched atop one of the many fountains and situated between two of its four Northern Wolves. A small audience gathered behind a white line, watching as cards danced through, between, and across his fingers, their curious murmurs gradually rising until he stood. "Welcome friends of old, friends that are, and friends to be." Slade cupped his hands and blew through them, scattering a wave of glittering, multicolored butterflies.

Giggling children pursued the insects while their parents clapped or cheered in their reserved Imperial fashion, attracting a larger audience. As the new arrivals settled in, Slade produced a card from his sleeve: the King of the Divine House. He rotated to show his audience, then began folding and unfolding the card. When he finished, Slade adopted a quizzical expression. "Wherever did the king fellow go?" Apart from a few lonely chuckles, the crowd remained unimpressed until Slade folded the card again and produced the Queen of the Divine House. "Oh my, now I've really lost him." General laughter greeted his words, followed by amazement when he brought the king back.

Amidst the following applause, five people merged with the crowd and used its present activity to ease forward. They offered little besides paper-thin reactions when he produced several colored balls and hurled them skyward before quickly raising himself into a one-armed handstand. Even when he began juggling upside down, they all but ignored his acrobatics and simply blocked any possible escape routes.

Harrumphing at their callous indifference, Slade swapped between hands a few times then popped to his feet and struck a pose, arms aloft.

The crowd cheered, summoning additional spectators while Slade exchanged the balls for two rods with smoking tips. Once again displaying his tools, he began twirling the sticks in a complex pattern, each broad, sweeping stroke trailing a line of shimmering red that persisted. Gradually a shape formed whereupon Slade paused, letting the fiery lines dwindle to mere embers before sipping from a clear vial and spitting its contents over the image. A dragon burst toward the sky, beating its wings and breathing a torrent of flames that had several audience members screaming. Then at the peak of its ascent the dragon exploded.

Embers showered the market, delighting his audience and horrifying the shop keepers. While everyone was thus distracted Slade drew franticly, scarcely finishing before his audience turned around.

Imbibing more liquid, he sprayed in a sweeping arc and sent three couples in flaming dresses and suits to dance among the crowd, their every step kicking up sparks.

The audience recoiled, forming circles in which the dancers tangoed and shrank until they vanished with a final spin.

Hesitant but eager for his next trick, the crowd approached and Slade grinned, beckoning them closer as he paced atop the fountain. Back and forth. Back and forth until he accidentally stepped off the edge, falling forward and smashing against an invisible wall. Frowning and quite obviously perplexed, he slapped at the barrier, discovering its dimensions before shoving off and righting himself. Some more experimentation revealed he now stood within a transparent box. Sitting back atop a Wolf's head, he lapsed into profound thought and then—with a silent 'ah-ah!'—sprang to his feet. Readying himself, Slade kicked at his prison. Except his foot stuck and he was left hauling at it until his temper slipped and he kicked again. This foot stuck as well, leaving him perfectly horizontal.

Slade let his head drop backward, grinning at his stunned audience before wrenching free and walking up the invisible wall to stand upon the ceiling. There he reproduced his six colored balls and tossed them at the ground only to watch as they fell back toward him. Unperturbed, he started juggling upside down.

Murmurs spread through the crowd. Questions about whether his tricks weren't magic after all.

Slade's grin broadened and he dropped down, leaving his boots stuck to the ceiling as he strode to a particular section and pushed. The front wall of his glass prison fell over with a crash.

The audience just stared, too stunned to speak; even the assassins forgot their assigned task.

A heartbeat later, the crowd's approval bellowed and coins rained upon the ground, piling up under his feet as he swept four consecutive bows, once for each direction. Rising, he abruptly tossed his colored balls skyward, eliciting immediate silence. Everyone watched, transfixed to the very moment that the colorful orbs exploded in sparkling pink smoke. When it cleared Slade had disappeared, collecting both his winnings and the assassins' purses.

The audience meandered away, discussing his mysterious disappearance. The assassins, however, sought an answer, searching the fountain and the nearby area for any hint. Soon enough an old sewer entrance suggested itself to them, its grate sitting uncomfortably with one corner resting on the cobblestones.

At first Feylin had enjoyed their indolent pace. Now she wanted to rush home and dispel the mystery shrouding Josi's fortunetelling. True or false, it had spoken of events far beyond her and most people; Tiberius, however, they fit like a glove. "Isn't there a shorter route, a backstreet or perhaps a carriage?"

"Probably," Tasha agreed, grabbing the back of Feylin's dress and hauling her forward when she stopped to look around. "Except, I'd get lost anywhere but the main roads, and a carriage does no one any good; not in these crowds." A memory came unbidden, one of skipping through a market and tripping only to remain down as a thousand people jostled past ignoring her. Tasha shivered. "Stay close to me; it's easy to lose oneself in a crowd."

"Really? Okay." Feylin hurried forward, nearly stepping on Tasha's heels. "Since you don't know your way around, does that mean you're new here?"

"Yep, I'm native to Dol'Cardolani."

"Dol'Cardolani? But your accent originates from the Empire's eastern corner, Sorres or perhaps Temisan."

"Where did you learn to recognize accents? I thought you were a recluse or something."

Feylin blushed. "I am or I was. Apelium has many … visitors and I managed to learn some of their accents. Your speech possesses similarities to Thearcs from the eastern part of the Empire." Her head tilted. "Now that you

mention it, I can hear a broad, mid-Empire dialect and something else...
What is it?"

"Beats me; you're the expert," Tasha snapped, making the girl flinch
back. *My accent is definitely not improving.*

After a moment, Feylin spoke again, her words so quiet they almost
went unheard. "I'm not an expert; I mean I can identify the thicker varieties,
but mostly northern sounds like eastern and eastern sounds like southern."

Tasha stopped mid-stride. "God's above, girl. Are you apologizing?"

"Y-Yes?"

"What in the Abyss for?"

"You sounded so angry when I talked about your accent; as if you
thought I was trying to gloat or mock you. I wasn't. I don't know enough to
gloat and I wouldn't mock. You're a bit … scary."

'Scary? She thinks I'm scary?' Tasha found herself staring for one second
then two, Feylin avoiding her gaze and becoming increasingly restive as the
silence progressed. At last she grabbed the girl's wrist and strode away. "Feylin,
do not repeat what I'm about to say, especially not to Slade." She took a
breath. "Gods help us both, but you might actually benefit from his
acquaintance."

"What's that supposed to mean?"

Before Tasha could answer, a little boy, scarcely ten years old, barreled
into her and almost deposited Tasha on the ground.

"I found her! I found her! I foun–" Retreating a pace, the boy hastily
inspected her face. "You are Mistress Tasha, aren't you?"

"What? Yes. Who are you? What are you–"

A mob of hollering children converged, prompting the boy to wrap
himself around her waist and defend his acquisition. "Back off." Kick. "She's
mine." Kick. "I found her first." Kick. He glanced up at Tasha when she tried,
unsuccessfully, to free herself. "Tell them I found you first, tell them I won.
Tell them!"

"Alright, alright, he found me first. Now will you let me go?"

"No!"

"Feylin, a little help here."

At that very instant, a little girl of inexhaustible dirt sprang onto
Feylin's back, wound skinny arms about her neck and pulled back sharply,
accidentally choking her.

"No no, you're going the wrong way," the boy cried as Tasha waded
through his cohorts to rescue Feylin. "We have to go the other way. No, the
other way. Stop going the wrong way," he wailed, bare feet dragging across the
road as he tried to redirect Tasha with every fiber of his being.

Reaching her destination nonetheless, Tasha unwound the little girl's arms and was rewarded by Feylin's immediate gasp for air. "Stop holding onto a person's neck like that, you'll strangle them."

Chastened, the girl corrected her grip. "I found her," she proclaimed to the other children.

"And I found Mistress Tasha." This brought about many discontented cries, calls of unfair play and demands for a restart given that some of the children had lost their shoes, stubbed their toes, received misinformation, or simply got mugged in a back alley.

"Quiet all of you." The children fell quiet, staring at Tasha expectantly. *'Oh, that actually worked. Maybe I am a little scary.'* "Okay, how did you find me and why did you find me?"

"I found you." The little boy stabbed himself in the chest with a thumb.

"Yes, I know you found me, but why did you find me?"

The girl riding Feylin's back clambered down, latching onto her captive's leg instead. "Master Lammerock told us to. He said find Mistress Tasha and guide her through the alleys; if you got home safe, we'd get a copper crown." This met a chorus of agreements.

Tasha tapped her captor on the shoulder. "Let go." The boy complied neither willingly nor completely. "What does Slade look like?"

He frowned thoughtfully. "A little short for a grown up, and he dresses funny."

"He had strange eyes too." Feylin's captor piped up, dexterously evading any attempt to disengage.

Feylin sighed, relinquishing her freedom. "Well, it sounds like Slade."

"Maybe, but I doubt there's a soul in Tellor who couldn't recognize Slade."

"Tasha, they're children; I hate to believe their planning to mug us."

"Is Slade going to pay you, or I am supposed too?"

"Master Slade said you would."

"Of course he did. Well alright, you two can stay; the rest be about your business." Waiting until the last grumbling child disappeared, Tasha faced their new escorts; the family resemblance between the two was incontestable despite the layers of dirt. "So which way do we go?"

Slade held the ladder's grimy bars and slid down, landing at its base with a quiet splash. He stood on a narrow ledge that ran alongside a river, the turgid current enjoying a robust traffic of discarded toys, ruined clothing, and rotten food, even an old grey rat who sailed by in a fashionable hat.

Giving the little mariner a salute, Slade placed his hand against the wall and stepped deeper into the pungent gloom, his fingers trailing across a series of large murals that staunchly resisted the sewer's corruptive taint.

As the pale light faded, he produced a vial of perfume and sprayed its contents at measured intervals. This left an aroma distinct enough for a deaf bat to follow, perfect for any disoriented guests sneaking along behind him.

"My compliments on your … bold choice of cologne," Naric said from the tunnel ahead of Slade, falling into step. "Such a *lovely* aroma."

"I thought you'd enjoy it; after all I pilfered this particular vial from your vanity." Naric snorted. "I'm curious though, what possessed you to purchase such an extensive supply of women's paraphernalia; doubtless you're the embodiment of grace and beauty, but it's still a peculiar hobby."

"Happenstance secured me employment at a theater, something I intended to gloat over profoundly to Harram … at least until I discovered the current production and my role therein." A smile snuck into his voice. "My employers believed I was the perfect candidate for the titular role of Mad Queen Isabel." Despite the darkness, they grinned at each other. Queen Isabel had, according to legend, murdered eleven successive husbands before meeting her own accidental demise. Few retellings ascribed to her the same motive and all strove to outdo their predecessors in ludicracy.

Abruptly, the wall under Slade's hand fell away. Reaching back, he grabbed Naric's shirt and pulled him down the new passageway, rescuing his friend from an unanticipated bath since the water turned with the wall. He then doused the corner liberally and continued onward.

It was the first of many, each successive turn leading them deeper into the sewers. Strangely, the deeper Slade and Naric went the lighter their surroundings became until vague, inanimate objects crept into sight. At this point they separated, Naric creeping off and Slade rounding the final corner to enter a room lit by firelight.

A giant four-pointed compass dominated the ceiling, designed to resemble a dragon whose northern claw held an ice shard and southern one held an angry sun. As for the western and eastern claws, the first held a sword while the second writhed with shadows.

Along with the compass, various paintings, murals, and tapestries—the later woven from metal wires—decorated the space between the room's many doors. One tapestry on Slade's right depicted a tall, pale-haired necromancer. Opposite that was a mural whose subject crouched in a bloody garden picking wildflowers. To the far left draped another tapestry, this one portraying a battlefield.

Slade smiled; an enormous art gallery resided beneath Tellor, spreading throughout the entire underground maze and offering guidance to those versed in the hidden meanings, yet barely anyone remembered.

Five people rose and drew weapons as Slade entered, toppling three chairs in their excitement. "Samara, Harram, hide the chairs and douse the fire; our guests will arrive shortly."

Naric returned amid the ensuing flurry, his entrance going unnoticed by everyone except Slade, who tossed a roll of wire at Harram and then directed him towards Naric. "String this across the doorway." Except, as it flew, Samara stamped on the fire, submerging the room in darkness and pulling an utterly inoffensive curse from Harram as he dropped the wire.

"Hmm, I guess you'll have to work in the dark. String the wire and hurry to your positions."

After this, the quiet patter of feet took over, interspersed with the occasional curse when people collided or someone splashed into one of the bisecting rivers. Slade alone maneuvered without mishap, collecting an impressive chair and positioning it behind the embers before returning for its ottoman. He then relaxed into his throne. *'There, all set.'*

Seconds trickled by, silence hummed, the coals warmed his damp boots, and a delicious lethargy settled upon his eyelids, the seductive heat whispering *now* was a perfect time to sleep. Slade shook his head, discarding the serpentine whispers.

Muted voices drifted down the sewer's path, doubling the room's tension. People made unintentional sounds, shifting or performing last minute checks of their gear. Slade gave a quiet, "hisst," and the room fell silent.

The muted voices continued their approach, indistinguishable words gradually becoming decipherable. "He went this way."

"How can you tell?"

"Take a deep whiff of the air. Smell that? That's no sewer flower, its rich people perfume."

"It smells like lady's perfume. Are you sure we're following the right trail?"

"What business would a girl, let alone a high-born lady, have down here?"

"Well, you're down here."

"Yeah, but we have no choice. If that *Jaidar* blessed idiot hadn't used these blasted sewers for his disappearing act, I would have gone right back up that ladder. Gods, this place makes my skin crawl. Are you sure there's no magic?"

"Not that I can de—"

"Quiet, both of you."

The mutters stopped, replaced by stealth; few stepped lighter than assassins, and the dead alone breathed softer. This silence lasted until the first assassin stepped through and tripped, almost falling into one of the sewage streams as she stumbled forward with an inadvertent gasp. She never managed to warn her companions, however, because the wire untied itself and wrapped along her entire body, even slithering down her mouth and binding her voice within.

"Lydia what happened? Are you alright? Lydia?"

Slade searched through his satchel, extracting a marble-sized ball of vermillion gel. He tossed this into the embers, and with a burst of acrid scent, the fire erupted into a pillar of green flames that crashed against the ceiling and sprayed outward.

"Hello, gentlemen," Slade purred over the swiftly dying flames.

Assassins were intelligent by necessity, so even as they recognized their predicament, they realized it was a belated revelation. Moving in concert they drew weapons, formed a semi-circle and shuffled backwards, eyes fixed on Slade.

"But my friends, why depart with such unseemly haste?" he asked, rising with arms opened in welcome. "The fireworks are just beginning." Another marble of vermillion gel and another burst of flames.

"This light show doesn't suit us," said one assassin, flinching away then motioning his fellows to collect their indisposed comrade.

"I'm afraid I must insist."

Another flare blinded the assassins, letting Naric and Harram slip up behind, grab two and wrap moist cloths over their faces.

Slade, meanwhile, advanced through the fire, his boots kicking up flared embers and his clothing catching fire for a moment before the flames flickered and died, leaving only one or two patches that he brushed off.

"Mage," growled one assassin, repositioning to face Slade directly.

"I know," the leader snapped, not looking away until his companion crumpled with a gurgle.

"Oh my, it appears your friend drank a little too much. Shall I order beds prepared?"

"*Jaidar* take you, Slade Lammerock." The leader spat, hurling a knife at him and then spinning, his sword whistling through the air to crash off Samara's. But the attack didn't end there, his blade slid down Samara's weapon and hooked it to the side, opening her defenses for a second knife strike.

Naric's intervention alone saved her, the man simply materializing to block the stabbing dagger. Then within the space of a heartbeat, it become a duel between him and the assassin, both men fighting at speeds that rendered them wraiths in the night and their weapons glints in the dark.

It was Harram who eventually ended the struggle, wrapping the assassin in a massive hug from behind and slapping a cloth across his mouth. The man's eyes rolled upward, forewarning a collapse that his captor eased him into.

Slade strolled over, idly tossing the assassin's knife from hand to hand. "Well, that was exciting."

Samara frowned at him. "Did you really use women's perfume?"

"Indeed, I did. I used Clarerye'devacoy; the most expensive fragrance on the market." He delved into his satchel. "Here. Naric purchased some for you as well." Casting a surreptitious glance in either direction, he sidled closer and began whispering loud enough for everyone to hear. "I think he has romantic notions concerning you; few men would go so far to win a fair maid's notice."

Samara stepped away, placing distance between herself and Naric.

Despite being such small children, or maybe because of it, Tasha struggled to keep up. Adding insult to injury they moved constantly, investigating each offshoot before chasing after stray noises and then scurrying ahead to search for danger.

"So what now?" Feylin asked, wincing and grabbing at a stitch in her side. They'd stumbled across an intersection with neither hide nor hair to be seen of their escorts.

"Can't do much more than wait and catch our breath." Tasha said as she circled the area, peering down each damp, shadowed alley without spotting anyone or allaying the hairs prickling on the back of her neck. In the end, she could only follow her own advice, locating an old wooden box and cautiously trusting her weight to its creaking care. "I suspect they're just scouting for trouble. They'll return shortly."

Displaying the first hint of impatience she'd seen from the girl, Feylin sighed and started rooting around for her own crate, the resulting rustle of discarded paper and scrapes of nudged debris masking the approach of boots. "Well, well, what are two beautiful ladies doing in this inhospitable place?" At the man's high, spindly voice, Feylin whirled with a yelp and tripped over her crate, scrambling backward on her hands.

"N-n-nothing."

He followed, stepping smoothly onto the box and then bouncing off, landing with his legs straddling her feet. "Are you lost by any chance? I could help." A grubby, bandaged hand extended, but not with palm turned upward. He offered it as if to shake, only a small twist from grabbing a fist full of her shirt.

Tasha, grabbing Feylin's arm from behind, yanked the girl to her feet and thrust her stumbling back. "We're fine, thank you. Please, be about your business."

"Are you sure? Alleyways can be so disorienting." The man closed to well within arm's reach, his leer displaying rot-blackened teeth and his breath carrying a sickly-sweet odor. "Even the wisest, most knowledgeable wanderer can lose their way."

"We're sure." Her stomach twisting, Tasha grabbed his chest and shoved backward, the brief touch conveying a sense of muscles rather than starved ribs.

Nevertheless, he swayed back agreeably, permitting her the distance even as he followed their retreat. "Well, it seems your mind is made up. Pity. This warren here can be dangerous. I've lost three friends just this month, all new but all dear to my heart." That smile again, only now accompanied by a cudgel and a knife bearing the distinctive blue sheen of Cardolani steel. A sheen her knives lacked.

'Shit.'

"Tasha..."

"Not now. I need space." She knocked Feylin's hand away, then for good measure, knocked the girl herself back. *'Of all the people to get mugged with, the worst is a skirt hugger.'*

"Tasha, there're two men coming from the alleys behind us, one to your left and one to your right." The words sounded high, panicked, but when Feylin's hands gripped her upper arm, they were firm and dragged Tasha into a sharp left turn. A moment later their backs collided with a wall.

'At least the girl's not stupid.' Tasha's somewhat bitter smile faded as all three men drew closer, languidly cordoning them off. *'Shit. No, calm down. There's only three of them. I can deal with this ... maybe. Might be easier to run the blockade, except Feylin would never keep up.'*

The speaker splayed his hands in the universal sign for harmlessness, ragged overcoat barely clinging to his shoulders. "Before we get over-excited ... please, there's no need for violence. We have naught but your pristine health in mind. After all, a damaged product won't sell, and Kalvonders pay handsomely for such untarnished examples of Imperial beauty."

'Jaidar bless me and him and Slade and all our combined relatives.' She straightened to an achingly perfect posture and assumed a tone of old, comfortable authority. "Listen closely, street scum. My lady Feylin"—she nodded toward the girl—"is the illustrious ward to Tiberius Whyte: the Will of the Imperial Emperor. The moment she disappears, Theanne guards will come trawling for the perpetrators and I have no doubt the Imperial Army will come looking as well. You will be punished."

Unconcerned, the speaker pricked his thumb and drew a bloody whorl over one eye. "Even if that were true, by the time soldiers arrive, we'll be long gone. Off to newer and greener pastures.

'Of course they don't believe me. Might as well have said she's ward to the Emperor's Shadow. Jaidar bless me, what do I do? Fight? Leave her behind? No, not yet. They'll back off when I—' Her gaze flicked to Feylin, then she gritted her teeth. *'Whatever. It's better than sailing south.'* "You need to be careful. I am an emissary of Carr'Selain and he does not take kindly to kidnapping." Behind her a gasp, across from her laughter.

"Another obvious lie. Today is just not your day friend. Carr'Selain has no people and no power in Tellor; we can do whatever we want, free of checks, free of balances. But hey, that was at least funny. I'll give you another chance. Make it good."

'Jaidar bless Slade a second time. In any other city! Any City! He doesn't even have the decency to show up and—' Without quite realizing it, a slow, sly smirk crept into place. "Courtesy demands I warn you about my final contact. I have a rather personal acquaintance with the man who rules Tellor's underworld; we might almost be called friends. I even know his name. Imagine his disappointment if I missed our dinner date."

That earned a reaction, shared glances and shuffled feet from everyone except the speaker. "You bluff wonderfully, friend. Sadly you are also misinformed; the renegade thief-lord of Tellor is a butcher, a man who delights in pain and money. Why would he care anything for you, even if you were … acquaintances?"

'Shit.' Her already rapid heartbeat quickened to a murderous tempo, then a tiny gap in the cordon around them opened up. *'Here's my chance. I can make it. Run or fight? Run or Fight?'*

"I can see from those wide, panicked eyes of yours that something very unwise is being considered. I cannot stress enough the danger to be found in running." A lazy, blood dribbled hand lifted and three additional footpads strutted onto the scene, each new arrival taking Tasha's heart and punching a hole through it.

'Shit. I need to run. I need to run. I need to run. I need—' She bared her teeth, crouched and drew her knives. "Alright then, who wants to see their dead relatives first?"

The men, even the speaker, retreated a step, but one retreated sluggishly and Tasha exploded, slashing for his stomach. He proved slow and awkward, stumbling out of range with a frantically swung cudgel. She caught the haft and yanked, pulling herself into place behind him. By the time the others reacted, she had the man prisoner with a knife pressed to his throat. "Back off," she growled, low and guttural.

The speaker did not back off. The speaker exchanged amused glances with his fellows. "He's new. Go ahead and kill him."

So she did. Then as the body spewed warm blood over her hands and arms, as the speaker and his fellows stared in shock, as Feylin's gasping scream burned itself into her memory for that night and several after, Tasha attacked.

Her blades carved the air with swift, harsh strokes that lacked any form of grace, and the slavers stumbled back with more than one bleeding. A second later, however, the men surged forward and Tasha retreated, working her knives in a blurring defense that barely kept their weapons at bay.

Then, just as long bloody cuts began appearing along Tasha's arms and Feylin began awkwardly hurling rocks and other debris, a bone-shaking battle cry brought the conflict to a crashing halt. Two figures slammed into the footpads, scattering them like startled geese and sending more than one flying through sheer force. Each newcomer carried a massive broadsword that they swung in complex, flowing patterns that seemingly rejected the weapons substantial weight and made true opposition impossible.

The slavers fled, some even scrabbling across the ground on all fours.

As the last man disappeared, the taller of their two saviors approached and sheathed his sword, affording Tasha a glimpse at the embossed crossguard: paladins. "My Lady Feylin, are you and your companion well?"

Tasha, her nerves still singing, almost rushed between the powerfully muscled newcomer and the girl, but then Feylin—in her small body, in her barely smudged shoes, in her pristinely shimmering dress and that somehow untarnished sense of cleanness—marched up right under his nose and poked him in the chest. "You followed me."

"Yes," he confirmed, bearing her stabbing finger calmly.

"You. Followed. Me."

"My lady, wandering through the bowels of a foreign city unescorted is foolhardy. Be grateful we did follow, or you might not have escaped unharmed. Please, recognize how fortunate you were today."

False indignation cracked and unwilling eyes traveled to where a footpad lay bleeding. The full weight of recent events broke through her flimsy obstructions, crashing down upon slim shoulders as her breath quickened and she began swaying, eyes losing all focus.

Tasha darted closer ready to catch, but Feylin leaned into the paladin, pressing her brow against his chest and knotting her fists in his shirt, her breath growing increasingly ragged until her entire body was pressed against his, trembling and wholly silent.

Slowly though, the trembling eased and the girl pulled away with a last shuddering breath, unveiling a tear stained face that was a little less clean, a little less new, but still pretty. "I'm sorry, Dreaos. This is unbecoming of me. I'll collect myself in a moment. I also shouldn't have–"

Her wrapped her in an embrace. "There is nothing to forgive. Nor is it unseemly to endure trauma." The man's hard, unforgiving eyes found Tasha. "Where is Slade Lammerock? Lady Feylin was placed in his charge. What drew him elsewhere?"

'Oh nothing too important. Just some blood thirsty assassins.' Tasha bit back her tongue though. "He didn't say, but if Slade thought the matter deserved immediate attention, then I doubt it was innocuous."

The second paladin strode up, sheathing his sword with a slow, wary motion. "Those are inquiries for Lord Tiberius to make, for now, let's return Lady Feylin to safety."

As the paladin moved away, a little boy raced into the alley swinging a makeshift club about his head. "Let her go! I found her! She's mine!" Tasha darted forward, catching their extravagated escort about his midriff before he reached the paladins.

"Careful now, they're friends; they helped us." His struggles ceased, the pitiable club still held at an aggressive angle.

"Are you sure?"

Dreaos lifted a hand as if taking a solemn oath. "May *Jaidar* claim both our souls if we intend mischief."

The boy favored their rescuers with a final distrustful glance then gave a shrug and grinned. "Alright, we go this way." Gesturing down the left road, he spun about and whistled sharply, summoning his sister from hiding before marching off in the indicated direction. The second paladin, however, grabbed his shirt collar.

"We no longer require your services, my Lady Feylin and her companion are now under our protection; you may go."

The little boy shook his head. "I promised master Slade; I promised to take them home."

Tasha approached the pair and attempted to disengage the paladin's hand. When that didn't work, she slapped his wrist. "Let him go." The paladin obeyed. "Now as for you," she said kneeling before the boy. "These are good people, I–"

The boy's arms crossed and his chin stuck out. "I promised."

"I know, but we're safe. You can go play with your friends." Tasha dug into her purse despite its destitution, producing two copper-crowns.

Glancing from the coin to her face, he snatched his reward, collected his sister and disappeared without another word.

"Now that we've dismissed our guides, I hope you brought a map."

"Who needs a map? We have magic." Dreaos closed his eyes, golden light shimmering to life underneath his eyelids. "This way please."

As the paladins led their charges safely into the labyrinth, a man watched from the roof tops, unseen even by the girl's protective thieves who were just now returning from his distraction. Despite the provided opportunity, the slavers below had failed to capitalize, robbing him of an unremarked kill upon a distant ship. Pity.

He drew a thin, hiltless blade that had been stripped of any distinguishing features, but a flutter of dark wings stayed his killing throw and the girl slipped behind a building. He pursued, reclaiming visual even as a voice spoke inside his mind, calling him to dissuade a guest from entering Tellor's sewers. The knife was raised a second time, held for a moment and returned to its sheath as the voice grew insistent. Tonight then.

Crannir held each breath for as long as possible before releasing it as a tightly controlled exhale, practically forgoing oxygen all together in his attempt to avoid notice. Around him, the others did much the same, even Lydia. They'd all just witnessed what happened to their loud-mouthed brethren, the idiots whispering and bickering all the way into a trap. Well, it provided Crannir and his assassins with two bits of information that probably just saved their lives. First, sound carried through the unnaturally thick, grasping air of these sewers, much farther than it should. Second, Slade Lammerock knew they were coming.

Turning as little as possible, he performed a series of sharp hand gestures. *'What now?'*

Lydia made a short, stabbing motion. *'Attack.'*

Tehroc shook his head and performed his own gestures. *'No. Too many. Dark. Confusion. Uncertain. Dangerous.'*

The recently returned Sora said nothing, seeming almost dislocated from the conversation, but Jamus signed the most obvious question. *'Leave then? Plan more? Return later?'*

Crannir hesitated. *'Maybe. Think carefully. Target knew. Trap. Perhaps found on purpose? Maybe not find again?'*

Lydia swore violently with her fingers. Not actually part of the standard curriculum, but she'd invented her own signs. *'What then? Gamble?'*

Tehroc shook his head again. *'Attack better.'*

Lydia reiterated the stabbing motion. *'Attack.'*

Jamus considered, then. *'Gamble.'*

Sora gestured curtly. *'Gamble.'*

And then everyone looked to Crannir, lodging a particularly uncomfortable stone in his throat as he was forced to decide how he'd potentially get them killed. *'Gamble.'* He signed before rising, dusting off his knees and striding around the corner into a room still populated by the bodies of the last assassins who tried killing Slade Lammerock. "Hello, I wonder if I might bend your boss' ear?"

A startled cry, a chemical explosion with a pungent smell, and darkness.

23

Strange Fruit

Crannir woke to a horrid, acrid stench and reflexively cried out, any sound catching and dying on foul, gagging cloth. Worse yet, his inhale coated his tongue with the foul substance which then spread down through his chest, burning vindictively.

In response, a cough scraped free and propelled him into a nauseating swing that revealed two unpleasant facts: first, a tremendous pressure threatened to blow his head inside out; second, he couldn't feel his legs. Their psychotic captors had hung Crannir upside down. *'Well, this is awkward.'*

"It appears our fruit ripens; let's be sure to harvest."

Footsteps forewarned the deft, chilly fingers that rooted through his hair, each digit a point of hyper-focus in his sightless state. Then the blindfold fell away, and light stabbed prongs into his already aching skull.

As the blurriness receded and obscuring tears were blinked away, Crannir couldn't help a low exhale: dangling beside him were four red-faced, slightly bruised companions cocooned in a mixture of corded rope and enveloping blankets.

'Ugly, imprisoned, and hairbrained, but still alive. Thank the gods. Let's see if I can keep them that way.' Not bothering to test his restraints, Crannir flattened the bottom of his tongue to the roof of his mouth, a gentle tingle confirming that Slade and his grunts had overlooked the spell tattooed there. *'Good.'* He maintained the pressure, releasing just enough accumulated magic to loosen and discard his wrist bindings, not activating the spell in full though. *'Not yet. Not until Slade Lammerock reveals himself, sets his head beneath the guillotine. Not until there's no chance of him surviving.'*

Movement on the right drew his attention to a dark-haired woman who sashayed from captive to captive, waving a vial under each nose then proceeding when the owners began thrashing. Under different circumstances, Crannir might have laughed. Instead, he focused on tugging his left hand

289

deeper into its sleeve, thumbing the heavy cuff to confirm Slade's grunts had also missed the needle.

It took everything not to smile savagely. *'Arrogant bastards.'*

Finished, the woman positioned herself by a throne-like chair and leaned behind it, whispering to a shrouded companion.

Crannir squinted, deciphering words from lip movements until a clap jerked his eyes to the throne. He would have sworn it sat empty, but there a young man lounged, his face consumed by a victorious smirk and his left foot resting atop the seat. "Everyone awake? Good. As your host, it is only proper I confirm your suspicions about my identity. Yes, I am indeed Slade Lammerock and you, unless I'm mistaken, were hired to kill me."

Had Crannir not already known they were expected, he would have felt his hair stand on end. It never boded well when a contract introduced themselves. As it was, he hastily began picking at the stiches in his sleeve, gradually freeing the needle.

Slade rose languidly, sauntering around failed and unconscious assassins to squat at eye level. Unnervingly mismatched and sociopathic green eyes then bore into Crannir, curtly halting any work on needles. "Normally"—the young man began—"I'd list all the lovely little ways I intended on torturing you, maybe even practice a few. Today, however, I'm feeling curious." His smirk widened, unwittingly jumpstarting invisible fingers on stitches. "Instead of letting you writhe around begging for clemency, gradually 'persuading' me that you've some modicum of worth, I'll experiment with straightforward honesty. Sounds fun, yes?"

The last thread pulled free and Crannir nodded, concealing a shudder as the deeply grooved needle slid into his bare hand. Somehow, he'd forgotten how it conveyed a phantom impression of cold, slimy film.

"Excellent. The only reason you're still alive is that I have a task to discuss with you; there, wasn't that refreshing?" Slade reached out and, his shirt sleeves brushing against Crannir's face, untied the gag before dancing the filthy, tattered cloth between them. "Be careful now, in Tellor we remove vulgar tongues." And then he remained crouched within touching distance, too close to react.

'Not yet, I need to accommodate for the drop somehow, that or find a way to punch through this bloody blanket.' Crannir coughed and cleared his achingly dry throat, using the moment to measure his response. "I've no doubt that your … past visitors gave ample reason for such practices, but I assure you that neither I nor my fellows would ever engage in vulgar speech." *'Please, let Lydia have heard that and guard her tongue for once. We don't need the bastard killing us before we kill him.'*

Slade laughed. "Oh, what a beautiful response. You really were a diplomate, weren't you?"

Crannir almost dropped his needle. *Morgan bless me, how does he know that? Did he—no! Focus. This is an opportunity, play into your role.'* He pretended to swallow, allowing his eyes to widen for a single instant before wiping away any emotion. "Yes, I was. For most of my life in fact. Made quite a few friends in politics and we're still in contact. They're doing quite well for themselves and might get curious if—"

"Oh hoho, look at the desperate man drawing his last knife. One question though, if I perchance knew about these friends of yours, what would happen if they all died unexpectedly, hmm? Personally, I suspect complications upon complications, barring one certainty: our noble, meticulous, logic-based justice system and its exasperating demands for proof would hang the wrong person. Why would they even suspect me, a perfectly upstanding citizen who's never met the victims or lived in Dol'Cardolani?"

Crannir shifted, pretending discomfort as he began freeing his hand from the blanket's inner layer. "That does seem rather likely, except you don't know who they are. Meaning—"

"What makes you think I couldn't find out? You're here, and I've all manner of magic and alchemy at my disposal."

The bottom dropped from Crannir's stomach and he barely stopped himself from stabbing out with the needle. *'Calm down. The bastard doesn't know yet, and if you kill him, he never will.'* With his hand now extracted from the inner layer, he wormed it toward the blanket's nearest edge. "What did you want to discuss?"

"Perhaps I mislead you with the term discuss. We'll address the exact terms later, for now, simply recognize and accept the reality of your situation." Slade gave Crannir a little push on the chest, sending him swinging into a wide, arching circle that made even nodding a bit harder. "Good. Concerning your assignment, I won't go into details either, but know I've planned an exciting change for you. Not to say our association will be bloodless—I rather expect the opposite—but the amount spilled will depend on you." Slade rose and turned to inspect Lydia, exposing his back, except Crannir was caught in the furthest part of an arc.

He thrust forward, breaking his natural circuit to swing closer, tongue already pressed to the roof of his mouth, the spell's energy building beyond a tingle as ropes slithered loose and the blanket drooped noticeably, a gap opening. The needle pressed into his palm, its engraved runes replicating themselves on his skin. Slade's slim figure grew to an unmissable target, and…

The bastard stepped away, smoothing back Lydia's short, bristling hair. "I will be the musician and your crew my dancers, so long as they can follow and not … improvise?"

'Jaidar bless him.' Crannir released the spell, feeling both the blanket and the ropes reconstricting. "My crew will perform whatever task you assign."

Ignoring the woman's murderous stare, Slade proceeded down the line, scrutinizing each assassin in silent commentary upon their bedraggled state. "Such wonderful confidence you have. And from a man in captivity no less. Confidence is good. Unwarranted confidence, less so. Your present situation hardly inspires my faith."

"I admit our performance leaves something to be desired, but—"

"Shhhh, it's alright. I'm not holding today's events against you." Slade returned and cupped Crannir's cheek, leather gloves cool against his skin. "After all, your colleagues performed significantly worse. Even disregarding your latest failure, though rumor and inconsistency conspire against you. I'm left wondering if I shouldn't wait for your successors."

His grip tightened on the needle. *'Don't get riled up, don't lose control, even if this human butcher's making you justify your continued breathing. Ignore him, find the next opportunity.'* "If you take a moment to reconsider, I'm—"

"Please don't. I thought we'd skipped where you blither and beg."

"Our success rate is purposefully depressed. We serve as one of Syndros Normar's personal hands, trimming the other guilds when deemed necessary. We're portrayed as subpar so as to pass beneath Carr'Selain's concern. Most of our assignments don't even enter the guild ledgers. I have proof, if you just—"

Slade pressed a finger to Crannir's lips. "I believe you. Your honesty though, raises a different question; if a vague threat has you spiling Syndros Nomarr's secrets, how can I expect any dedication to my interests? Most pertinently, an assignment you've undertaken grudgingly."

"We will honor whatever agreement is made."

"Honor is a delightful tale fabricated by the swindlers of yore." Slade strode down the line of assassins, shoving each backward with a firm thrust. "The only way to ensure loyalty is through duly meted out punishment and reward, or in the case of betrayal, the most horrific retribution imaginable."

Most accepted his abuse in stoic silence, all except Lydia. She flung herself toward Slade, head rearing back than snapping forward as she spat a viscous, black globule onto the thigh of his leg. A death spell, courtesy of the tangled, barbed lines tattooed beneath her tongue.

Slade, however, stepped aside, reacting before it even left her mouth then cuffing Lydia as she swung past. "Speaking of reward and punishment, I've prepared a little exhibition for your entertainment. Cut them down."

'Gods dammit.' She'd only had one shot.

The woman from earlier returned, rising on tiptoes and sawing at the rope holding Crannir suspended. When it snapped, his stomach dropped sharply and he braced himself against the fall, but a massive, bespectacled man caught and ferried him to one side.

A short time later, the giant laid a thrashing Lydia beside Crannir, wisely leaving the woman's arms bound. Nevertheless, she sprang to her feet, faceplanting immediately after.

Crannir grabbed the woman's shoulder. "Lydia, enough." When she persisted, he applied pressure and graciously ignored the resulting spew of muttered profanity. "I said enough. Don't tip our hand or force theirs."

Lydia's eyes snapped to him then flicked about his person, locking on his sleeve when he gave it a little shake. Her teeth ground together and a vein pulsed along the side of her brow, but she lay back, adopting a calm that long acquaintance warned Crannir against trusting.

The other captives were gradually freed, and the blond man even returned for Lydia's bindings, leaving her to sulk as Tehroc stretched taught muscles and Jamus meditated. Sora lay predictably still, vacant eyes staring upward.

Like always Jamus felt Crannir's attention, his eyes opening the barest slit.

Hands clenched into fists, Crannir stretched them overhead and snapped his fingers open to simulate an explosion. Jamus glanced toward Slade then shook his head almost imperceptibly.

'Shit, no magic. Probably should have expected it.'

Presumably warned by the same sixth sense, Slade twisted to meet their observation, smirked and then strolled over. "In most dilemmas, people call upon mages for assistance. Especially, if said mage possesses considerable ability." He supplemented this with a kick at Jamus' foot. "I would advise against that." But Crannir barely noticed. The young man had brought himself within killing distance.

Moving at a rate of millimeters, his hand eased back up into its sleeve, recovering the needle. *'Slowly, don't arouse—'* The metal, warm and slick from sweat, slid between his fingers. *'Jaidar bless it. Throwing's too risky. Come closer, you bastard, just a step.'*

Across from him Jamus sat up with a question, but Crannir tapped Lydia, who silenced the poor man with a firm elbow to his ribs.

Crannir winced, he'd wanted that done subtly.

Tut-tutting them, Slade crouched before Jamus. "Ignore those bullies. Go ahead, ask your question; I'm really a very sweet crocodile." Despite his invitation, the man remained silent. "Oh come now, timidity is such a worthless trait. Still no? Very well then, yes, I know about your 'hidden' talents; you well-nigh reek of ashes and charcoal. In fact"—Slade straightened and swung around, nearly making Crannir bite his tongue when the young man's booted foot passed directly in front of him only to continue past, taking his target closer to Tehroc instead—"I know all your secrets, from the grimmest, most twisted memories to those dangerous whispers you thought unheard." Slade gestured sharply and two men seized his cushioned throne, dragging it into place before the assassins. "Let me enlighten you. Do you see this letter? It's an exact copy of the one you 'intercepted' two weeks ago." Displaying it, he then folded the paper into a strange design and sent it gliding toward Crannir. "Admittedly not my best work, but still good enough to fool a couple assassins into thinking it was sent by Carr'Selain."

Hastily stashing the needle, Crannir caught the letter and paled almost instantly. "But this is—"

"The letter I wrote for Carr'Selain to myself, explicitly stating our intention to set differences aside, combine our talents, and actualize an insane scheme. The theft of *Akravast*. Which resulted in you receiving the original version of this." Reaching into his waistcoat, Slade produced another letter which he folded and sent flying as well. "Orders received from Syndros Nomarr demanding that I be killed on sight, authentic for once." Slade snapped his fingers and both letters burst into flames. "The moral of the story? If Carr'Selain's most fanciful estimate of my influence falls short, how incorrect is Syndros Nomarr? The truth is that I could declare dominion over the four guilds, and they would submit without me having to leave Tellor."

Crannir surged to his feet, swayed as his vision swirled and paced anyway. *'What in the gods-dammed Abyss is going on? Is he even working with Carr'Selain? Are we only here because he wanted it?'* Across from him, Slade reclined into the cushions of his throne, smirking and draping a leg across the armrest. *'No, that doesn't matter. Focus. They're letting me move, use that.'* Crannir slowed. On the far side of his thigh, he made a sign. Distract. In his other hand, the needle slid into place.

Tehroc groaned as he rolled to his feet, stretching to his full height with arms reaching overhead. "I think you're lying."

Crannir, the other assassins and even the thieves stilled, all waiting for the response. *'What in the Abyss are you doing? I said distract, not challenge, you idiot. Now he has to respond and—'*

"About anything in particular?" Slade asked, his full attention settling upon Tehroc. "There are so many potential lies. Why should any of it be true?" A smile, thin and malicious, pulled at his lips. "What if I lied about Carr'Selain's letter being my creation, or perhaps you're wondering if Syndros Nomarr sent those crucial orders after all?"

Crannir's tensed muscles relaxed and he continued pacing, leaving Slade's purview without garnering so much as a glance.

"Oh no"—Tehroc shrugged—"I'm fairly certain Syndros Nomarr sent those letters. The rest of your story is what I'm struggling with. The evidence looks nice enough, I'll grant, but I doubt you're so powerful as all that."

"Wisdom and your present captivity would suggest giving me the benefit of the doubt."

'Only, you didn't capture us. We surrendered.' Crannir circled behind the chair and continued past, staring fixedly at the ground and watching for negative reactions, testing his leash by sidling closer. The buffoons didn't even notice.

"Alright," Tehroc said, "then what's stopping you from declaring dominion over all four guilds?"

"The whim hasn't struck."

Crannir twisted and retraced his steps, angling closer to the throne. Closer, closer, and still no reaction.

In that void of interest, Tehroc clicked his tongue and only long hours of practice kept his attention from riveting on the enthralling man, his every word glorious and honest and reasonable.

"You'll understand if I find that hardly conclusive."

"Of course. That's perfectly understandable."

While thieves and assassins stared at Tehroc with glassy eyed expressions, Crannir pressed his needle into the back of Slade's chair, aligning its tip with the young man's heart.

Then the black hatted, ridiculously feathered head tilted back and rested against the woodwork: vibrant, mismatched green eyes smirking up. "Why hello there, you're looking lively."

Fear, bright and staggering, surged, but before the needle could rip through fabric and stuffing, Slade stepped free of the chair. "I'll take that to mean you've all fully recovered." As Crannir locked in place, certain their target was heartbeats from snapping his fingers and ordering their deaths, Slade casually kicked Jamus a second time. "Well come along then, you've malingered enough." Oblivious to the disbelieving, near giggling relief sweeping through Crannir, he turned his back on them and strode away, beckoning imperiously.

"The arrogance of that man." Lydia growled under her breath, grabbing Jamus by the shirt and hauling him to his feet. "If I had my knives, he'd be dead."

"Supposing you had a knife, you really think that'd suffice? Did you see him ignore Tehroc's glamour?" Jamus shook his head. "We just got unbelievably lucky. Face it, we needed to surprise him, but he's had our places set at the dinner table for months."

Sora rose last, following Slade without sparing a glance for his own comrades. The others hurried after him, all except Crannir who lagged behind with a hand pressed to his thundering heart.

"The board's looking a little grim, isn't it?" Jamus asked, smiling his crooked smile from a few steps ahead. "I have a blinding headache and my world spins at the slightest provocation. Lydia is weaponless, Tehroc walks as if they broke his legs, and half our spells are exhausted."

Crannir shook himself and fell into step. "No one's as bad as they seem; an opportunity will present itself or I'll make one. In the meantime, watch Lydia, make sure she doesn't try ripping out the smug bastard's throat. I'll keep an eye on Sora."

Jamus nodded, gaze flitting toward the dead-eyed man. "It's times like these you wish old Vannis hadn't insulted that Marked. At least then we'd know who's working alongside us."

"No sense worrying about it, at least not when we can worry about Slade Lammerock arbitrarily deciding we're incompatible. Focus on remembering the way out or spotting potential exits; even if we don't kill him, we may need to leave fast."

As they and their whispered conversation lagged further behind, Slade's lieutenants materialized to force an increased pace, whereupon Jamus twisted around with an agreeable smile. "So, what are your nam—hang on, Naric?"

Crannir's feet tripped underneath him and he contorted to find charcoal-dark eyes crinkling at them.

"At last. To be frank, I find your belated recognition extremely insulting."

"What are you doing here? Is Slade Lammerock—" Crannir's words stuck in his throat, mind whirling with abrupt, horrifying realizations.

"You two know each other?" the dark-haired woman cut in sharply. Then her eyes narrowed and she leapt back a step, hand falling to the hilt of her knife. "You're a bloody assassin, aren't you?"

Jaidar bless it. A brawl is the last thing we need.' Hastily interposing himself, Crannir extended a hand toward both. "Whatever this is, please solve it later. And you"—he faced Naric, his better judgment losing the argument—"are you the reason he knew we were coming?"

"I never named you fool, Crannir, do not give me cause now."

The calm rebuke cut through Crannir's flaring nerves and paranoia, leaving him flushed. "Yes, yes of course." He quickly swiveled toward the woman. "Look, I'm not privy to whatever conflict this is, but I'd rather you get yourself killed later. If a fight breaks out now, your devil of a boss might punish me and mine. As such–"

Slade, wearing a thinly amiable smile, appeared in their midst and both Crannir and Jamus instantly jerked away, neither reaction affecting the young man. "Since you're lagging behind, I can only suppose you're either lost or discussing something important. Being an optimist, I will assume the latter and ask if there's room for another in this no-doubt scintillating conversation. No? Pity. Ah well, no sense in frittering away the day when there's someplace *I want* to be. Shall we go?" It wasn't really a question; nevertheless, he sat there waiting for their response and Crannir stood stock still, unable to kill him because Naric stood on his direct right.

In the end, Crannir obliged. Soon after, they encountered an old door illuminated by a light without a source, its wood rotten and slimy and hanging from a solitary hinge while an appalling stench wafted out, suffocating the clustered space.

One by one, Slade's smirk settled upon each assassin. Jamus looked away, glancing at Crannir with sick foreboding. Tehroc's jaw clenched and he stared ahead with typical determination. Lydia glowered a promise of enmity. Sora alone met Slade's gaze indifferently.

Their antagonist bowed low, twisted the door handle and pushed inward to reveal dozens of bodies sprawled across the ground or thrown together in tangled heaps. The scent of old murder and fresh death billowed through the breach, managing to subdue even Lydia's colossal obstinacy.

"This is where I house any assassin who seeks fame and fortune at my expense. After all, where better to spend eternity than in the company of those who fought the same impossible enemy." He closed the door with a grating shriek, moving slowly to give each assassin a final grisly memory. Crannir's was a woman whose eyes appeared to have been gouged out. "This door is a crystal ball showing two possible futures. In one, it's open and you've committed the same crime and suffered the same fate. In the other, the door's closed and you're looking into mysterious potential."

Their return to the initial room found it changed. New passageways had opened in the walls, squishing old artworks together while opening space for new ones. Diverse stairwells led to lower levels and the perimeter of the room itself had changed. Gone was the circular design, replaced by room-like protrusions that overlapped and almost resembled puzzle pieces, many creating shadowy alcoves that whispered of surprising depth.

'This place changes? How in the Abyss are we supposed to run away if this bloody place changes?'

Slade approached a featureless table with a sheet of thick yellow paper resting atop it. To the paper's right sat six empty inkwells. To the paper's left lay a red, unadorned quill. At the top brooded a simple, indelicate knife.

Crannir's heart sank and inside his sleeve, he practically crushed the needle with his grip.

Exuding both implacability and inevitability, Slade motioned Crannir into the stiff-backed chair opposite, waiting until he sat before speaking. "Ready? Wonderful. My proposed contract is simple. You will each complete one reasonable assignment for me, after which I'll consider your obligations fulfilled. Provided you pursue no detrimental action during or subsequent to our engagement, I will allow you to leave."

Crannir nodded. *'Think, dammit. I can't let this happen.'*

"To ensure both parties perform as agreed, this contract will be drawn in blood."

The chill already creeping through his veins, worsened to an outright frost.

Across from him, Slade cut into his palm, clenching his fist around the blade and deliberately dragging it free.

Blood seeped from between the fingers, spilling down into the inkwell. As the last scarlet drops fell, Slade set the knife aside and bandaged his hand, tying the knot with his teeth.

'Think, think, think, think.' Fighting against nausea and struggling to control trembling hands, Crannir reached for the bloody knife and wiped it on his sleeve, numbly following procedure. Should any of Slade's blood mix with his, it might have unforeseen repercussions.

'I have no choice. I have to kill him immediately.' He hadn't thought it possible, but his grip tightened around the needle. *'Right now.'* He drew a steadying breath, forcing his trembling hands and rapidly beating heart to subside, but they resisted, and he drew another. There could be no mistakes.

A pen scratching across paper drew Crannir's attention to Slade whose countenance was now disfigured by intense concentration, each achingly slow pen movement creating yet another sharp ugly letter. Crannir's muscles tensed, and then he jerked forward, inspecting what he suddenly realized was an illegible script. Illegible meant dangerous or possibly a spell, or maybe some precaution or trap in case Crannir decided assassination was the wiser bet. "Jamus, get over here."

The mage's head snapped around, then he jogged over. "What is it?"

"Can you read that?"

"Yes, it should just be … no. What is that?" Jamus craned his neck, growled and moved to read from behind Slade's shoulder. To his credit, Slade neither glanced nor flinched at the commotion, never mind that any of them besides Jamus could have broken his neck in a heartbeat. A misspelled word or badly written letter could ruin the whole contract.

Crannir rose, grabbed Jamus' shoulder and dragged him off to the side. "What is it? What's going on?"

But the assassin made a helpless gesture. "I don't know. This is unlike any contract I've seen. It's as if he's using one of the old scripts specifically designed for blood-contracts."

"What does it mean?"

"It means Slade Lammerock learned to write contracts from books rather than a tutor. Really, really old books." Jamus pinched the bridge of his nose. "This means the contract is subject to his intentions more than his exact words, meaning no clever little loopholes."

"*Jaidar* bless it." *'At least it's not an enchantment.'*

"We need to kill him."

"I know."

"Now, Crannir, or we'll find ourselves—"

"I know!"

"Crannir," Slade called, "I think it's time for a decision to be made. Come sit down."

Casting a final, despairing glance at Jamus, Crannir returned but did not resume his seat. He stood behind it, one hand gripping the back while the second hid inside his sleeve. *'Do it now. Breathe in, breathe out. Breathe in, breathe out. Breathe in, breathe out, and—'*

"I'd say take your time because this is a big choice, but frankly my patience has run out. So the hour has come to choose, will you do as I ask and sign the paper, or will you finally use that needle you've been clutching for the past half an hour?"

'Do it! You have no choice. But what if I miss? You won't miss, he's a thief, not a fighter. But he's survived everything else. No, not survived. He's teased you by hovering just within reach. The moment you press him, he'll fall apart. But he dodged Lydia's spell? Of course he's fast, doesn't mean you aren't faster. But he knew about the spells, he's known about everything. What if he expects this? Of course he

expects you, you're a wild animal backed into a corner. But—No, kill him or face slavery. Wouldn't living be better though, with life comes opportunity?'

"Choose, Crannir."

He looked at Slade and found him unmoved except for the outstretched hand, its upturned palm waiting to accept the needle. Gloved, but the needle could pierce the leather easily, unless it wasn't leather. Still, the needle could pierce most things. Unless...

Slowly, Crannir revealed the needle—dark silver except for the bloody red runes—its slim body held horizontally between all five fingers as he lowered it—stopping and starting—into Slade's hand. At the last moment, he changed his grip and stabbed downward. A scratch was all it'd take.

But the needle punched into the wood of the table, only stopping when Crannir's fist slammed atop the surface. Then gut-wrenching horror. *I missed. We're all dead.*'

Steady hands slid the needle from loose fingers. "Good. You have some backbone after all. Sign the contract." Gone was the hint of play. Gone was the arrogance and gloating malice. Gone was the smirk. In its place, cold, unspoken assurances. This was Crannir's last chance.

Strangely, his nerves steadied as he grasped the knife, its handle feeling unremarkable even comfortable in his hand. Now the decision was made, all that remained was a growing acceptance. The affair belonged to **Kis'Maat** and he would manage it as he saw fit.

He cut cleanly, perfectly, but his blood waited as if shy. When it appeared, the liquid slunk into view through a series of slow drops that evolved into a steady flow, filling a second inkwell.

One handed, Slade spun the paper around.

Crannir dipped the pen and wrote his name with a short, inelegant script.

One after the other, his crew signed the contract. Jamus wrote with a long spidery hand, Lydia employed a neat, confined style similar to a scribe's, Tehroc wrote with a simple yet oddly beautiful hand that starkly contrasted its fellows. And Sora ... well Sora scribbled his name.

Finished, their eyes gravitated toward Slade, who gave a cursory nod. "Yes, you may go. I will contact you when your assignments are prepared." He rolled the contract into a scroll, bound it with black lace, and stuffed it into his satchel. "Naric will serve as your guide. Do not search for me, discuss these proceedings, or leave the city. Any infringement will provoke swift punishment." Slade rose, gestured curtly and departed through one of the many doors, his followers trailing along behind.

Seconds and their subsequent minutes ticked by, watching as Crannir and his crew digested the day's events in silence. Naric stood apart, letting them have their time and space.

Eventually, Tehroc voiced their communal question. "What do we do now?"

Jamus collapsed into Slade's vacated throne, head falling to his hands. "Exactly what he told us to."

As soon as a respectable distance separated the two groups, Slade whooped and the soldier-like procession broke apart to cluster around him. "Samara, your acting was superb. I almost believed you were the incomprehensibly loyal subordinate you pretended. Harram, I said act big and mean; you managed cuddly grizzly at best. And you, that guy I'm still pretending I can't remember, I have no idea what you did but you did it fantastically." And so he mingled, complementing or teasing each crew member respectively.

"So what happens now?" Samara asked. "What do you plan for the assassins?"

Slade grinned, wagging a finger at her. "Samara, don't you know that curiosity killed the snoop? What's more, I reincarnated the man's depraved soul and personally oversaw his second execution because the first method dissatisfied me."

"All right, all right; if we snoop, bad things will happen."

"On the contrary if you perform adequately, I will assign errands suited to your predilections." Slade leaned in, kissing her cheek.

Mid-kiss, the scent of decaying bodies wafted down the tunnel, soon followed by a line of shambling skeletons and half-rotted corpses. "Ah, our deceased comrades return," Slade cried cheerfully, throwing his arms wide and capering toward the resurrected dead. "I must say you played your parts to perfection. I would have suspected a dead man before doubting your ruse, even if he moonlighted as a famous thespian."

The two groups mingled, complementing and laughing as they shared respective stories. Some, mostly Slade, elaborated without mitigation while others restrained their imagination and a bare few dealt in base facts.

After tales were exchanged, the restless dead left to wash up while the living hurried home, leaving Slade alone with Samara and Harram.

"Harram, be a dear and organize watches on the assassins. Ensure they neither depart nor wander beyond the third wall." Slade reached into his satchel, produced the blood-contract and handed it to Samara. "Here, take this to Malendor; as it stands, our little forgery won't survive a close inspection. The assassins need to feel the magic taking hold, feel its constraints tightening and burrowing under their skin, preparing to tear and shred should they break confidence. Otherwise, I might as well fry your livers for them."

Samara accepted the scroll and began tapping it against one hand. "That's why I suggested using pig's blood over whatever substitute you concocted, at least for writing the contract. Malendor can only compensate for so much."

"True, but we know precious little about blood magic and nothing about how substituted blood could affect proceedings. We've a contract written in ancient script, drawn with an authentic blood-quill, and signed by people who are swearing an oath they're determined to keep because *to them* they're signing a real blood-contract. Belief alone would muddy the situation, but these are powerful people, willful people. They've more than a dull flickering candle of a soul." Slade shook his head smiling. "The line between perfect deception and reality is thinner than you can imagine, and it's a boundary I don't want to cross."

She smirked. "Well well, self-preservation isn't wholly foreign to Slade Lammerock."

"On the contrary, I've signed an agreement that prevents me from undertaking anything dangerous. What you attribute to self-preservation is actually a fiendish plot dedicated to curtailing my free will." Slade waggled his eyebrows, daring the obvious question.

Harram obliged. "So, who—"

"*Morgan!* The very God of Death himself. Through various clandestine means, he uncovered my deceptively devious scheme to claim dominion over both life and death. Instantly his boots began shaking to such a degree they leapt right off his feet into the nearest lake. *Morgan*, however, was made from sterner leather and took immediate action. Descending from his glass throne and coming to the mortal plane, he offered me a simple proposition: sign the agreement or see my enemies become immortal. I, being a law-abiding individual, had no choice. 'Live and let live' I said, whereupon he smote me with the fury of ten thousand angry hippos."

"Hippos...?"

"Yes, never underestimate an angry hippo."

"Okay..."

"Anyway, this untimely death was the soul of inconvenience. I had countless projects running around and none were capable of finishing themselves; so I conceded momentary defeat and was returned to life."

Samara looked at him skeptically. "How does that keep you from taking over the Underworld?"

Slade scoffed, "I thought that was obvious; only the dead can visit the land thereof. How am I supposed to ravage the Underworld if I can't visit its silver dunes?"

"How were you planning on visiting then?" Samara asked.

Slade threw his hands into the air. "Why do you think I was getting so frisky with danger?"

"Remind me again, what prompted you to conquer the land of the dead?"

"Well, I hoped to sell the place to some fat lazy bum. With an indolent usurper on the throne, there'd be nothing stopping me from escaping death altogether."

Samara sighed and strode away. "Only you would fabricate such an idiotic story."

After she disappeared, Harram turned toward Slade with a slight frown. "Does she know you're planning on leaving yet?"

"Not yet, but she'll learn soon enough, alongside a few secondary secrets."

"Secrets we know about her or secrets she doesn't know about us?"

Slade grinned. "Both." He sidled closer, nudging the other man with an elbow. "On a side note, I noticed you noticing Miss Lydia's great beauty." Harram blushed. "Shall I arrange a meeting, or do you insist on hunting this prize yourself?"

"I would but I can't, not yet. Perhaps in a year or two."

Slade grabbed the man's shoulders. "Harram, you're fifty-six years old; death lurks around the next corner. Lydia's sixteen and only half a block behind. You're perfect for each other."

"Slade, I'm twenty-four, and I doubt she's sixteen."

"Okay, so the age difference poses a larger problem than I expected. You're still perfect for each other and she was eyeing you most appreciatively."

"Really?"

Slade placed one hand on his heart. "*Enecki* strike me down if I lie. She swooned whenever you glanced in her direction." He rose onto his toes, slung an arm over Harram's broad shoulders and dragged the man down to his height. "A little help from me and you'll be kissing in the rain by next month."

"What do you have in mind?"

"I don't know yet."

Harram smiled, then shook his head. "Still no. Maybe next year."

As his subordinate left waving goodbye, Slade shook his head. "Poor guy, Lydia will eat him alive." Grinning to himself, Slade headed home. With a party to attend and negotiations with Carr'Selain's delegates to conduct while at said party, today was far from over.

<hr>

The midnight bells rung distantly by the time Samara knelt outside her bedroom door. All around she could hear the snores of other tenants accompanied by creaking bed springs and the occasional groan as someone tiptoed across the wooden floors. It was a newer house. One of those hastily built as a place marker until the work crews brought the stone and steel for a more permanent building.

The crowded quarters, minimal rent and temporary nature meant it suited her perfectly.

Samara pushed these thoughts aside and concentrated on breaking into her own room. She placed her mouth to the keyhole, muttering a few counter-spells before inserting the lock picks and beginning the delicate process of unlocking her door. An unfortunate necessity ever since she 'accidentally' lost the key.

The lock gave an inaudible click, slight vibrations warning Samara that her door had opened. If she continued fiddling, magical alarms would summon members of the town watch held on secret retainer.

Pushing through, she slipped into a room whose only extravagance was a modest vanity shoved into a back corner. Samara didn't mind. The bed sufficed and downstairs served passable food.

She brought Slade's perfume to her nose, inhaling deeply. Whether from providence or coincidence, it was her favorite scent. Slade couldn't possibly know, of course; she cultivated the deception that she lived from meal to meal and missed her rent as often as she paid it.

Samara smiled. Simple chance then. She set the perfume atop her vanity and froze, remembering something Harram had said during her first days in Tellor. 'This is Tellor, Samara, Slade rules here, and under his dominion, serendipity, chance, dumb luck, and even divine intervention are suspended.'

With a slow, trembling hand, she felt under the vanity and twisted the dial to a combination lock. Ten numbers later, a secret compartment gasped open, revealing a tower of precisely stacked letters. Letters destined for Carr'Selain's libraries.

She'd sent her last pigeon two months earlier, hence the small stack of incriminating evidence. To anyone else the pile would have looked undisturbed, but Samara breathed a quiet curse. A second, identical stack of letters adjoined the first; letters she hadn't written.

A large gold coin sat atop the second pile, beautifully engraved with Slade's head and shoulders. There could be no mistake. The grin was unequivocally his, and the enormous, feathered hat, pulled low to cover his eyes, was undeniable.

Samara picked up the coin slowly, wrapping her fist around the warm metal and knocking it against her forehead. Abruptly she hurled the coin across the room to where it dinged off the wall and landed atop her bed in a pool of moonlight.

She wanted to burn the vanity, letters and all, but a perfect mixture of necessity and curiosity forced her to open the second stack of letters. Each card was a replica of one she had written, except each was written in Slade Lammerock's hand.

He knew she spied for Carr'Selain.

Worse yet, the final card bore her handwriting, except she had never written it.

Samara eased onto the edge of her bed, fighting back tears as Slade's coin smirked at her. "*Kis'Maat*, help me."

24

By Moonlight Witnessed

Every civilization segregates its wealthy and its destitute, and for Sahdaen that distinction manifested in Upper and Lower-Sahdaen, with the impoverished condemned to the Hold's highest levels. There, deprived of rain and caretakers, the dung, filth, dead, dying, addicts, and drunks rot in the sun, swelling into ever-higher heaps and spreading pestilence. Rats and other vermin throng the districts in hoards, assaulting the children, sickly, and unconscious while drug dealers and flesh vendors peddle their wares from every corner. It is governed by famine, devoid of law, forsaken by the Kalvonders, and it was here Dieharamon woke.

He failed to recognize it at first, lulled by the lingering torpor of sleep and the gentle comfort of vague reminiscence. The Hunt constellation gleamed in the sky, merging its pale radiance with *Sarah'Venn's*, currently seated in the sixth-Vigil. Then the realization that he saw the heavens murdered his indolence.

He surged into a crouch, scrutinizing his surroundings for the faintest movement or sound. Nothing betrayed the presence of another living being or his location in the Hold. Still, he darted to a squalid nook between two housing complexes and squeezed in, suppressing the urge to gag at the stench.

The reality that magic had effectuated his relocation was irrefutable and terrified him, but it was also irrelevant; he needed to decide whether to find Dayada Avenar or hide behind Valeriius and deliver the *Pathfinder Shard* to the Dread Lord. He slid to the ground, shivering with clenched fists as memories of the Dread Lord reared in his mind; that fear hadn't been natural, it had destroyed Dieharamon even through Tragnashi apathy, stripped him of everything, debased him. He couldn't face that again, couldn't imagine what it would take to defy him. And yet he had to.

Dieharamon's head fell back with a thud, pricking him with the bone shards in his hair. Sinnitar would do something awful with the *Pathfinder Shard*. Dieharamon had felt his malice in their interaction, glimpsed the horrors he was capable of. Dieharamon couldn't oppose him, but maybe Dayada Avenar could. It just required contracting the Thieves' Guild for information, which in turn necessitated traversing Upper-Sahdaen at night, both of which could kill him. And he had to accomplish this before the Angorat'Wass arrived, where he would slaughter as many other Tragnashi as he physically could before they killed him in turn. Treacherously, that little hope resurfaced: maybe Dayada could save him as well.

He crawled to his feet and vacated the alcove, stretching cautiously to ascertain his body's state, and for the first time in years, felt no pain. He broke into a startled laugh and stared at his limbs, straining them further with no ill-result. Laughing again, he absently checked for the *Pathfinder Shard*, and then tore at his clothing with a muffled cry: it was gone.

Petrified by a vicious amalgamation of shock and terror, Dieharamon stared at the wall. Why would the Dreamer take the *Pathfinder Shard?* Why did the Dread Lord even want it? And what was he going to do when the Dread Lord found him?

Gritting his teeth, Dieharamon forced himself to move. There was no way to retrieve the *Pathfinder Shard* from the *Lake of Dreams,* so his only hope remained unchanged: find Dayada Avenar. He flung a desperate wish to the heavens that he pass undetected and sprinted in search of lights.

Without Kalvonders, Upper-Sahdaen had fallen to the guilds and the Avaran Clergy who spent the millenia warring over it via proxies. Almost every merchant, vendor, gang rat, or common thug owed their allegiance and power to one of the two. Thus territory was marked, street-lords self-crowned, bribes paid, and criminal syndicates baptized in blood and stolen currency. It was these ties Dieharamon feared. For while the guilds and Clergy segregated their various coalitions, they ensured anyone foolish enough to contest one incurred a death mark all would pursue.

Unfortunately, Dieharamon encountered conflicts twice despite his best efforts and tertiary routes. The first instance he managed to avoid entirely as it centered around a solitary drug silo. The second embroiled an entire district: the buildings, streets, and subsidiary bridges all consumed by a storm of shadowy figures slaughtering one another in the near-silent night. He escaped involvement only due to accent, which marked him a resident of Lower-Sahdaen—Kalvonder-owned—and therefore inviolate to the likes of them. He crossed by skirting the district and screaming that he had no association with either party. After that, Dieharamon proceeded through the back alleys, using rooftops and balconies to avoid the streets and search for a tavern's telltale pool of orange light.

Most guilds operated from fortified households, but the Thieves' Guild differed, preferring taverns and public forums, anywhere rumors and secrets abounded because above all else, the Thieves' Guild traded in secrets. Besides, drunks tended to lose their purses.

Being unfamiliar with Upper-Sahdaen, it took Dieharamon a long, tense hour to locate a tavern, but he eventually glimpsed the orange glow of an open door and windows. Exhaling in relief, he swung off his rooftop perch and descended along a stairway of balconies, pillars, clotheslines, and ladders to the street below.

He landed with a soft whoosh of cloth and crouched, scanning the remnants of a third, long-decided, conflict. When no scavenger spooked at his arrival, Dieharamon scurried forward and knelt beside a corpse.

The skirmish appeared to have involved three street-lords, with the smaller two being allies and the instigators. The aggressors had marked themselves with black gloves and faded silver sashes. The third, richer than the first two, defined itself with simple, many-faceted stone earrings.

Dieharamon hurriedly scavenged the bodies, killing any survivors and ultimately acquiring a pair of coarse stone knives and rough bludgeons. When he finished, he whispered a meaningless prayer of gratitude, not because he expected it to ease their passage into the dead realms, but simply because it felt right. His neck started prickling before he ever finished.

Five men prowled from the burnt husk of a tannery, their heavy robes, shaven heads, and clasped hands marking them as acolytes of *Ashshand*, servants of the Clergy. They fanned out behind a full prelate, his jiggling bulk draped in the finery of his station and bone adornments.

Dieharamon stood nervously, the newly acquired knife and bludgeon professing a fabricated composure. He didn't want to kill these men.

"Why did you murder these people?"

"I did not," Dieharamon replied, even though he knew the prelate had only come to retrieve whatever prize instigated the conflict.

"Then why are your weapons bloodied?"

"The blood is dry; they were dead when I arrived. I'm only here to scavenge."

"And why would you need weapons?"

He studied the acolytes instead of answering. They stood with the easy confidence of experienced swordsmen, sickle blades tapping the ground in anticipation and grips light; they had killed before and often enough to forget they lacked proper instruction. No one in the South hired real arms masters when it was cheaper to suffocate your opponent with bodies. The Clergy trained their initiates under failed mercenaries for a week before dispatching them. This, however, still made them more dangerous than the average thug and equally volatile.

He reverted his attention to the prelate, earning a scowl and sharp beckons at his lack of response. Dieharamon retreated, and the prelate's face reddened. He stalked forward, kicking aside a corpse, and snatched Dieharamon's chin. As soon as their skin touched, however, the prelate yanked his hand back, nostrils flaring. "Who's your master, Tragnashi?"

Dieharamon flinched, unable to conceal his master's identity because of ancient laws seared in the Tragnashi pact. "Valeriius Kalvonder."

The prelate snorted. "What does he desire with Upper-Sahdaen?"

Dieharamon re-examined the prelate's apparel; his dark robes hung to mid-calf with the orange flame of *Ashshand* emblazoned on its chest alongside numerous sun lizards, indicating minor authority. "Valeriius Kalvonder is unaware of my current actions."

"I doubt it. I also doubt your allegiance to *Ashshand*, foreigner."

Dieharamon snorted impulsively and spat again. "Damn all gods."

Horrified, the prelate just stared, then slapped him.

Dieharamon endured the blow, not daring a quarrel with the Clergy.

"You would do well to recall I am a servant of *Ashshand*. Moreover, you would do well to remember all *Ashshand* has done for you—"

Dieharamon barked a derisive laugh. "Save it."

The prelate glowered. "This man has forgotten all he owes *Ashshand*. We must remind—"

Dieharamon crushed his head with the bludgeon and lunged; however perilous a quarrel with the Clergy was, it paled before being 'enlightened'.

Compelled by desperation, Dieharamon fumbled for the heat from before, uncertain if it would even answer. It did, rearing in his chest and cascading down his limbs, filling him with fire.

The acolytes recoiled, scrambling for weapons and scattering as he crashed into their midst. One reset his feet and lunged, thrusting a thin, sandstone blade for Dieharamon's side. Dieharamon swept it aside with the bludgeon, stepped in close, drove the knife beneath his assailant's ribs, and then spun, splitting the skull of a second acolyte intent on his back.

The two remaining acolytes charged him; one he fended off with a swipe of the bludgeon, the second danced around his reach and gouged his side before leaping back. Dieharamon made to pursue, pain masked by the fire surging within him. The other acolyte sensed an opportunity and rushed his turned back, sword raised. Dieharamon slammed his foot down, reversed momentum, spun and brought the bludgeon crashing down into his solar plexus. The acolyte collapsed, chest caving as the bludgeon shattered into a spray of bone fragments.

Dieharamon flung the handle aside and turned, searching for the final acolyte. He was already fleeing, discarded sword clattering on the cobbles.

Dieharamon followed, strides propelling him in short bounds that easily breached the distance. The acolyte glanced back, eyes widening in disbelief and terror. He began to scream, but Dieharamon slammed into him, driving the knife through him and into the wall, crushing him.

The instant he died, Dieharamon recoiled, blanching as reason returned. He had killed before, hundreds in the arena, but never in his own pursuits, and never so effortlessly. Even now, the fire pulsed within, a dull, lethargic current eager to erupt at his slightest need and fill him with awful power. It terrified him, the way it swallowed his sanity, its potential for devastation, and most of all because it was magic. *He* had magic.

A giggle shattered his reverie, snatching his gaze up and about to where a boy crouched on the eaves of a verandah. A grin split the dark, bleached unnaturally white by the Sovan drug, and the child vanished, his movement betrayed only by the swish of a falling curtain.

Dieharamon muttered a curse and hastened to scrounge the corpses; the Clergy always compensated informants generously and took pains to advertise it. They would claim him as theirs in minutes and issue a prize to their proxies for his butchering. Valeriius might protect him, but the Clergy valued their prelates and the Immortal Consort would demand restitution in blood.

To worsen matters, he could feel nervous heat starting to fill him, the initial symptom of deprivation from Valeriius' drugs. He'd never experienced full deprivation, but logic dictated he'd deteriorate rapidly, both physically and mentally.

The corpses yielded two daggers and a pewter sword, all of which thrummed at the touch, provoking a shudder at the undeniable presence of enchantments. He stored them on his belt and crossed the street without subterfuge. Word traveled fast in Upper-Sahdaen, and it would forbid anyone unaffiliated with the Clergy from touching him.

Valeriius sat at the edge of a simple fountain, the white tiles glistening, and a sequence of intricate glass lanterns swaying overhead, radiant with sequestered starlight. Eight pillars separated the fountain from the larger chamber, their intervening sections furnished with incense burners, cushioned benches, and sumptuous violet curtains. Valeriius occupied one of these benches, a wine glass in his right hand and his cane resting across a knee. A quartet of guards surrounded his back, and the Aparthii slave kneeled at his feet, head bowed.

Outside the fountain area, the chamber devolved to rough sandstone and torches, the smoke slithering up the walls and across the ceiling to a chimney vent. Seven empty doorways and one stone door offered egress from the chamber, their frames outlined in Isaracc hieroglyphics and the stone door crowned with runes even most Kalvonders could not decipher.

An unassuming book waited beside him, its title worn away by the years but its leather bindings otherwise unblemished.

Taking a sip of golden wine, Valeriius returned the glass to the armrest and retrieved a compass from his coat pocket, its brass case reflecting the starlight. He clicked it open for a brief glance and then deposited it on the book, two of its needles holding firm while the third spun in a ceaseless pattern.

A knock sounded against the barred door, a solicitation for entrance that Valeriius ignored in favor of his wine. The battery persisted, increasingly enraged until he finally gestured at his guards. One strolled to the entrance, hefted the slim iron bar, and heaved it open. "Valeriius Kalvonder offers his welcome and gratitude for having accepted his invitation."

Sharp as a bitter truth, the slap silenced Valeriius' guard and echoed through the chamber. Valeriius sipped again, swirling the wine in its crystal glass to observe a thread of discordant color.

Lyrrh stormed into view, kicking the Aparthii slave from his path. "What idiot put it in your stupid head to threaten me!"

Valeriius glanced at his Aparthii slave. "You will pay for any damage she suffered; rage does not grant leave to impair my property. Now, if you would calm down and take a seat, we may initiate our business. I have a proposal—"

Lyrrh kicked her into the fountain. "I will break anything I wish! You can't summon me like an Avaran! I am a Kalvonder, Valeriius, and I can crush you without spending a single glass piece!" His finger stabbed out, spittle flying from his lip.

"Touch her again and I will feed you to the rabble in Upper-Sahdaen." Valeriius' cane flicked up, catching him by the hand. "Now, take a seat before you make further mockery of yourself." The wine in Valeriius' glass darkened, turning red as he raised it to eye-level, waited for Lyrrh to notice, and then poured it out, soaking his boots and the tiles in sanguine liquid.

Lyrrh sputtered, sweat beading his brow. "You wouldn't dare harm me, not on the palace grounds—"

"The enforced peace does not extend to these clandestine chambers, Lyrrh. They were relinquished so Kalvonders could discuss matters privately and without restraint. By traversing that door, you waived any protection rendered by law, accord, or blood. Take your seat."

Lyrrh shifted, jaw clenched as he glanced between Valeriius and his cane. After delaying long enough to remind Valeriius he could depart if the whim struck him, Lyrrh complied, snapping his fingers to prompt a lone slave of his to scamper inside. She reached into an opulent purse at her side, then withdrew and presented to Lyrrh a burgundy seat-cloth almost entirely decorated with demonic imagery. Lyrrh accepted it before disdainfully facing Valeriius and waiting, the seat-cloth held gently in both hands. Valeriius refrained from moving and rage gradually burgeoned in Lyrrh's visage, converting into a pointed glare at Valeriius' own seat-cloth, which draped the entirety of his bench. Valeriius ignored him and finally Lyrrh snarled, "Your compass is broken; it's not pointing North. Hah, it's not pointing anywhere!" He stalked to the adjacent bench, unfurled his seat-cloth and sat, barking a command for his four guards to enter and for the door to be closed.

The Aparthii slave emerged from the fountain, where she had crouched until Lyrrh relented, and hastened to refill Valeriius' glass before assuming her place.

Valeriius proffered Lyrrh the glass. "Wine? No? Very well, let us proceed. A substantial portion of your wealth is about to evaporate due to this Angorat'Wass."

"As if your prized dog will survive either. He's as doomed as my gladiators, and if I have to sacrifice the three of them to kill him, I will do so gladly. *Ashshand* curse you both, I've lost dozens to that monster you call a Tragnashi. That being said, I am curious, how did you achieve him? Breeding a Tragnashi capable of surviving sixteen years as a gladiator must have been difficult. What did you poison him with that he could keep fighting with a spear in his back, or slaughter half-a-dozen men alone? There are rumors of sorcery or witchcraft, but you know magic is prohibited, except for *brands* to compel unruly Tragnashi. Tell me how you did it, and I'll ensure those rumors disappear. Or don't and face the inquisition."

"You are a serpent without fangs, Lyrrh; you declare Dieharamon doomed in one breath, and threaten to launch an inquisition with the next. No one will care once he's dead. Unless you believe him capable of surviving the Angorat'Wass?"

Lyrrh settled back, throwing an arm along the bench and crossing his knees. "If I am a fangless serpent, why demand my presence?"

"Because I intend to harvest your venom. You will benefit from previously useless assets, and I from our agreement."

"I'll humor you; how am I without fangs when my resources exceed yours, and how do you intend to harvest me?"

"Because, you, Lyrrh Kalvonder, are an addict."

Lyrrh blanched and surged to his feet. "That is a lie! I am no addict, and you would do well to terminate whichever of your operative's confided it!"

Valeriius raised an eyebrow, his mouth curling. "I do not need operatives to inform me of an obvious truth: men are not born with black teeth. Nor does your addiction interest me. I only care that your supply is exhausted, and it is difficult to find demon blood in the vilest markets. You need me, Lyrrh, because you will not find more demon blood otherwise."

"Are you threatening me, again?"

"Obviously. Though to be clear, I will rephrase my statement: accept my alliance or die from deprivation. If you assent, I can satisfy your hunger tonight."

Lyrrh hesitated, the words he had been on the brink of uttering now hollow in his mouth. His tongue flicked out. "Prove you have it."

"Of course." Valeriius stood, cane dipping into the pool as he circumvented it. "But leave your guards." The fountain and the lamp dimmed, casting the chamber into slumber. The Aparthii slave rushed to confiscate a torch and guided both them and Lyrrh's slave from the room, Lyrrh visibly jittering with anticipation.

They emerged onto a descending stair, the torchlight flickering against the shadows of an immense, arching vacuity. Doorways, stairs, and balconies populated the obscurity, vaguely discernible as silhouettes whenever the torch drifted their way, and almost entirely forgotten.

Valeriius advanced to the precipice, gazing down at the cobwebs and the ancient banners of Remanas. Kalvonders had been exploiting these abandoned catacombs for centuries to inter secrets or facilitate machinations, knowing Andeor'Vallen never stirred from his chambers and the palace-keepers rarely ventured beyond the most superficial levels. So much so, that no one could imagine all that transpired within these conduits, some of which persisted despite the progress of decades.

"Come, there are several flights to traverse, and then I will grant a taste of the product."

Two stairways and a bridge brought them to a simple wood door set beneath three spent torches, probably never more than a storage closet until the Kalvonders appropriated it. Its previous owner had converted it into a menagerie for venomous serpents, and routinely imprisoned rivals, treacherous servants, or whatever unfortunate soul stumbled across it.

Oblivious to its history, the slaves pried the door open, prompting a groan of rusted hinges and a waft of rosemary. Lyrrh inhaled, snatching the lingering scents of ashes and charred flesh, before shoving through with a whirl of manic eyes. Valeriius followed, igniting a series of interior lights and indicating the slaves to tarry outside.

The shadows receded from a hallway of burnished prisons, their walls an intricate matrix of carven blooms and dragons. Lyrrh panted at the far end, pressed against the bars of the final cell without heed of the central fire pit or the incarcerated monsters on either side.

Starting to hum, Valeriius crossed the hall, every tap of his cane causing the monsters to flinch. In passing the firepit, he extracted a fine leather purse from his coat and dispersed the crude, black powder onto the ashes. Then, still humming, he returned the purse to its pocket, halted beside Lyrrh, and rested both hands atop his cane.

An emaciated man paced within, his eyes wrought of Chaos and his words reduced to distorted mutters punctuated by bursts of profanity. Lyrrh moaned, nostrils flaring as his lips spread in a foul grin and his teeth clicked.

"If he fails your standards, I have others."

Lyrrh's attention snapped to Valeriius. "And they'll all be mine?"

"Not at once lest your appetite consume you, but yes, all yours if you accede."

Lyrrh grasped the cell bars, fingers paling with the strain, and moistened his lips. "Yesss!"

"I am afraid I need more than that."

"Yes! We have an alliance, Valeriius! Now give me what was promised!" Lyrrh yanked the bars, rattling them in their foundations.

"Just follow me; Chaos and violence agitate the demon; and you for that matter."

Lyrrh dragged him back. "What do you mean? The demon's right there! I want my blood!"

Valeriius pried himself free. "Very well, wait here while I collect the blood already extracted for your pleasure."

He returned to the entrance and claimed two stocky black vials from the Aparthii woman. Storing one in his coat, he returned to Lyrrh who stilled, eyes desperate and tongue flicking between gnashing teeth.

Valeriius tossed him the vial. "I will grant you one now, and the other when the alliance is signed and I control your assets."

"Of course." Lyrrh snapped the vial's neck in a spray of sable ichors and thrust it to his mouth, the broken edges piercing his lips.

Valeriius strolled to the opposite side of the firepit, drawing a match and speaking softly in a dialect Lyrrh would not have understood. The charcoal erupted into life, rising six feet as the monsters and demons hurled themselves against their prisons in a pummeling frenzy.

Oblivious, Lyrrh flung the vial aside and dropped his head back with a desolate shriek of ecstasy and unsatisfied hunger. He dropped, snuffling at the blood stains as his breath wheezed out.

Valeriius pressed his cane into the floor. "Lyrrh…"

The Kalvonder forced himself upright, peering at Valeriius across the flames and completing the bridge. He had a heartbeat to scream before the flames flared deep amethyst and tore his soul free, entrapping it in Valeriius' cane and stripping him of all power. He collapsed, spasming.

"You will tell no one of this, Lyrrh Tragnashi, and you will break your addiction before the year end. I will grant enough blood to wean yourself, but no more. Now, return to the party and proceed as if nothing occurred. To everyone else, you remain Lyrrh Kalvonder."

Valeriius vacated the hall, commanding Lyrrh's slave to assist Lyrrh's return before retracing his steps to the conference room with the Aparthii woman as his shadow. "Dismiss Lyrrh's guards and summon Thanen Kalvonder." She nodded and wordlessly sprinted ahead.

Upon returning to the chamber, Valeriius resumed his seat, restored the compass to his pocket, and drained the wine into the fountain before tossing both glass and pitcher to his guards. "Extinguish the torches." They obeyed and Valeriius reignited the fountain's radiance so he alone inhabited the light. Then he opened the nameless book to a blank page, set an ink bottle on the bench beside him, and drew the second of three quills from his sleeve. Using a sharp but graceful script of his own devising, he began scrawling words on the page, heeding neither rhythm nor logic.

A knock sounded, followed by a rush of air as the Aparthii woman entered, her steps echoing with the light report of Thanen's. Valeriius continued writing, ignoring Thanen as the Kalvonder appeared beside him and the Aparthii woman resumed her place at his feet. Thanen stared at Valeriius pointedly, waiting for him to role aside his seat-cloth.

Valeriius finished a sentence and re-wet the quill. "It is strange and discomforting that a man such as yourself would trust me enough to abandon his guards at the door. What engenders such confidence that you would enter unguarded?" Tapping off the excess ink, he began drawing a square symbol.

Thanen's eyes fastened on the image. "I do not fear you, Valeriius, because I control you. We are all slaves to our secrets, and if I were to die, your secrets would find their way to the light. Therefore, I control you, however much you strive to prove me wrong. It is best to accept this and dispel any remaining illusions of autonomy."

Valeriius completed the symbol's exterior, four walls of curving and interlocking vines crowned at their corners with spears. "If I am to dispel my illusion, you must first resolve my doubts. Prove you know my 'secrets' and can expose them in the eventuality of your demise."

Thanen yawned, but his hands tightened as he continued to wait. "Why should I bother? I did not come to enforce my will. We have an arrangement: how are you progressing with Lyrrh?"

Valeriius completed the second series of walls and interlocked them with the first, joining flames to vines. "Lyrrh Kalvonder is dealt with. You may have seen him on your journey here but give that no credence. The man is dead, and illusions are easily acquired."

"Clever. You replaced Lyrrh with a proxy and now control his resources without yourself appearing any stronger. You really do intend to challenge Ureign."

"Of course; though presently, I am content with amassing power. Which introduces our agreement—you owe me a vow."

Thanen meandered around the fountain, a hand brushing the spray of water. "On the contrary, I've long abandoned adherence to oaths and promises. I am surprised you failed to notice my pledge carried no weight when I tendered it. You've been played, Valeriius. With a few simple words, I contrived for you to murder a Kalvonder; which one never mattered, only that they perished. Now, if you will excuse me."

Valeriius finished the third barrier, a circle of water pressing out against the lines of the fire box. "Before you go, what did you gain from the disappearance of Lyrrh Kalvonder?"

Thanen paused. "It was a wager; a wager that I was unable to control any Kalvonder I chose. I needed to make one of you kill another, and if I succeeded, I would gain all the wealth and influence of the deceased. It was infuriatingly easy, Valeriius. I had hoped for a more significant challenge. Please, try and maintain a higher standard of competence throughout our next discourse." He resumed his departure.

"Why does Trerrock Kalvonder hold any interest for me?"

Thanen froze, face contracting in shock. Valeriius completed the final wall of the symbol: a solid diamond with its four corners drawn out far to pierce the circle.

Thanen controlled his features with a visible effort. "What makes you believe it was Trerrock Kalvonder who wagered against me? What makes him anymore viable than Xexeross, Ureign, or any other Kalvonder?"

Valeriius lifted the page and breathed into it. "It is simple, if one knows how to watch. First, you must acknowledge your opponent needs to be a Kalvonder from the utmost zenith of the pyramid to wager so much for so little gain. Second, the lesser Kalvonders of our pyramid's higher echelons are all too preoccupied with one another and their attempts to supplant one of the Triad. Third, Xexeross is not a man for games, and this is certainly a game. Fourth, Ureign has a slight predilection towards arrogance and refuses to converse with anyone who is not within the general vicinity of being his equal or one of his slaves. This leaves only Trerrock: an enigmatic man known to enjoy games and subterfuge despite avoiding the Angorat'Wass. Also, I know for a fact that he suffers an intense dislike for you." Valeriius stood and ripped the page from his book.

Thanen gestured dismissively and scowled. "If he dislikes me, why would he conduct a wager with me?"

"Because he wanted you to lose." Two of Valeriius guards emerged from the shadows to grasp Thanen's shoulders.

Thanen stared, then threw his head back with laughter. "Don't you remember, Valeriius, you can't kill me! I know all your secrets, and they will find the surface if I die." Expecting the guards to loosen their holds, he attempted to shake free, but their grips tightened.

Valeriius approached him, discarding the nameless book. "Illusions are cheap to procure, but do you know what is cheaper?"

"No."

"Witchcraft." Valeriius lifted the paper holding the symbol—a seal— before Thanen's eyes. With his other hand, Valeriius raised the mirroring amulet and set it against the page.

Thanen squirmed, uncomprehending but fearful nonetheless. The ink began bubbling, and the symbol melted through the paper, leaving a gaping hole before the amulet. Thanen shrieked, two streams of lavender mist flowing from his eyes into the amulet as the paper melted. The transfer concluded promptly, leaving Valeriius with only the amulet.

Thanen slumped, coughing as black tears bled from his eyes. "What did you do to me?"

Valeriius returned to the bench to collect his cane, inspecting the amulet. The once black diamond at its core had changed to glow with a faint white light; the other barriers remained black glass. "Did I take your soul? No, nothing so banal as that. I have no interest in you as an ally, Thanen, but

I would not waste you. So I took everything you knew, including your failsafe." He glanced at the horrified man. "I had hoped you would present more than half-a-night's entertainment, but we cannot have everything given to us. Kill him." Valeriius departed, the Aparthii woman gathering his seat-cloth and falling into his shadow as Thanen Kalvonder died with a gurgle.

25

Borluce Emissaries

Despite having fortified the first breech, the High-Warden's time ran thin. Even now *Malbreyth* labored to expand the *Barrier's* flaws, infusing it with his corrosive presence without thought for his sibling's defeat. Yet the High-Warden waited in an old chair for Caddon to wake.

He slept on a tired mattress beside an open hearth, the floorboards covered with old furs that smelled of cinnamon and the walls ribbed with laden shelves. It was a storage room in Antiark's Citadel, one of the few not repurposed for refugees. The young kelbrok they'd migrated here seemed to enjoy it nonetheless and was currently gnawing on a seasoned rowan log.

The wizard slept feverishly; his mind imprisoned within the disjointed memories of the *Dreamer* that slumbered beneath Antiark. He had exhausted himself achieving the summons, eroding his mental defenses to the point a fragment of the dragon's memories permeated his consciousness, ensnaring him in millennia from its life. The High-Warden could restore him, but that required invading Caddon's mind, so he delayed, hoping the wizard's natural strength could expel the intrusion.

A change occurred in Caddon's breathing, and his eyes flickered open, clouded with nightmares and the claws scraping at his mind.

"How are you?"

"Ill"—Caddon gave a wan smile—"but recovering." His smile crumpled, erased by a sharp inhale of pain and a wave of convulsions as his eyes rolled back.

The High-Warden surged from his seat and caught Caddon's face in both hands, stilling his thrashing instantly, though his muscles remained taught. "Let me in."

Caddon's mental defenses slammed shut, but he could not survive the *Dreamer's* malady alone and after hours of silent vigil the High-Warden could delay no longer. So he enveloped Caddon's mind, clasped his beleaguered thoughts, and crushed his mental defenses, exposing the nightmares. He

319

caught them with a mental hand and then slowly, carefully pried them free like a man disentangling himself from briars. They were hollow recreations, possessing weight and sentience solely because they originated from a *Dreamer*.

Caddon's taut muscles loosened, and he slumped, blinking as consciousness gradually returned. The High-Warden laid a hand upon his brow. "Rest, your strength will return on its own."

Caddon gazed about, speaking with a soft mumble, "Were all the two-bit way-houses taken?"

"Yes, along with every tavern, room, floor, stable, bed, blanket, pillow, chair, and hall. You are alone because we feared the *Dreamer's* memories might spread."

He pulled himself upright with a small grin of triumph. "When do we have to leave?"

"Your labors are complete, and for all you have done, I am in your debt. Unfortunately, time presses me hard."

"Where do you go next?"

The High-Warden stood. "The nightmares will no longer plague your sleep. Rest now before another trial demands your actions. Tumult might preside over The North for now, but it will soon evolve into more controlled violence, and that violence will extend to the Tower of Wizardry; whether I will it or not."

Caddon nodded, eyes closing despite his efforts. The High-Warden started toward the door.

"You never answered my question; where are you going?"

The High-Warden glanced back, eyes flickering with mirth. "To the skies."

Outside the storage room, the High-Warden accosted one of the passing servants in a hushed voice, "Listen please; if you are available, have I a task."

"High-Warden, it is our pleasure to serve; there is no need to ask."

"The man resting in this chamber needs to be awoken when a warm, strengthening repast is prepared. A warm bath will also improve his health; add cedar, hyssop, and melissa to the water. After these, send for his wife at the Tower of Wizardry. Tell her he is cured and rapidly improving. Can you remember all of this?" The servant inclined and hurried for the kitchens nestled far below, his tread soft on the stone floor with indoor shoes.

He resumed his own journey.

The Citadel boasted two complexes that spanned its entire circumference, the first being the entrance floor and the second being the floor reserved for visiting dignitaries. Despite its size, this second floor experienced little use. Even in the most trying political years, only the Borluce and, on occasion, the Paladin Empire, assumed residence. Hence, it principally catered to the mysterious reptilian race, and after representing the floor's sole notable inhabitants for decades, the various Borluce delegations had renovated the floor to their tastes, replacing the ancient artworks with enigmas of every known design and language.

They also needed abundant warmth and compensated for this by installing such an abundance of torches, braziers, and furnaces their quarters assumed a southern disposition. Why they chose such an unwelcoming climate remained unanswered. The Borluce were reticent at the best of times and, more importantly, an Elder Race: their eldest bloodlines anteceded the birth of the gods.

The history of their race had long passed from memory, leaving only their existence in the Deep North, where neither men nor gods could reach them. Only the Weshac shared their territory, and that proximity had engendered an enduring enmity.

As he neared the emissary quarters, the High-Warden began removing his mental defenses and secreting his memories into the further reaches of his consciousness.

A vast, alien presence brushed against him, merging effortlessly into his thoughts. "*Welcome, High-Warden of Winsyria.*" A distant echo reverberated through it, the hundred thousand dispassionate but unique voices of the Borluce.

"Fare thee well on all future roads." A tremor of approbation rewarded his use of the Borluce greeting.

"*Your mind is well ordered, High-Warden; I am Secluath Kellserasven.*"

"It is an honor, emissary, to have earned your respect so swiftly."

"*Respect, High-Warden, is all my people hold for you. We consider ourselves people of Winsyria, regardless of the world's opinion. We are ready to listen.*" The alien mind withdrew, conveying a destination for their discourse.

Traversing several minor chambers, their air laden with foreign scents and their floors cluttered with rodents and birds, the High-Warden arrived at a burgundy door wreathed in delicate strands of cloth and wood. It swung inward at his touch, emitting a wash of burgundy fumes.

Five Borluce reclined on plush cushions within, their immediate surroundings awash in multihued wines and exotic fruit. They dressed similarly except for minor distinctions of personal taste: headdress of interlocked bones and a mask representing animals—the two females a wolf and bear, and the males a serpent, falcon, and catfish. They also wore ebony mantles and skirts of tattered cloth sewn with the achromatized skulls of fox kits and rodents. One of the males examined the High-Warden, the bright feathers of his crest lifting in recognition and darkening to a redder hue in dominance.

"Again I welcome you, High-Warden, please share in our bounty." The central Borluce gestured at a seat, black claws glittering in the obscured firelight. He accepted, kneeling on a cushion distinctly larger than the rest.

The emissaries relaxed, most partaking of food or wine while Secluath collected a rowan pipe. The High-Warden let them proceed unharried, his features impassive. To a people as ancient as the Borluce, one who had straddled the cusp of annihilation, time held little importance.

The pipe's first draft wafted upward, pulling at his consciousness with a powerful odor despite the distance: Borluce adored the dangerous Taytan incense, possibly because they alone could inhale it and remain sober.

A feminine consciousness addressed him, *"High-Warden, you have need of our assistance."*

He returned the gesture and responded aloud. "With *Winsyria's* absence, the New Order has invaded The North, undermining the *Barrier* and forging a conduit between our lands and the external world for their patron deities. *Telacra* attempted to breach the *Barrier,* but the Rhawn opposed her and continue to deny her entrance."

Violet eyes implacable, the Borluce held his stare, uniformly contesting and respectful, countless millennia of history passing through the memories of both. "This threat does not end with her and my time runs short. I must reach Adriat where the *Winter Court* convenes and then to a sanctuary deep in the Rhawn. My intention is to bargain with these other entities and, if need be, force them to uphold the *Barrier* until *Winsyria* returns, to ensure neither *Malbreyth* nor *Jaidar* gain entrance."

"And what of Alkarred, God of Malady?" Secluath inquired.

"*Alkarred* fears his elder brothers too much for open confrontation; he will not stir while they remain active."

"Then what do you need from us?" Secluath exhaled a cloud of black mist, revitalizing the Taytan's sickly-sweet odor.

"By land or sea, the journey exceeds my time, and I dare not allow the gods to gain purchase. I need to fly, and your people have the means." The five Borluce twitched in their seats, becoming guarded as their crests settled. An absence descended over the High-Warden's mind, informing him the

Borluce had segregated their consciousness. They returned after a long silence, their mentality unchanged.

"*This is an unprecedented request. Never have the northern men faced a threat dire enough to solicit aid from our 'abominations'.*"

"The Borluce do not consider their 'creations' perversions of the natural order."

Secluath laughed, his musical voice beautiful despite, or maybe because of, its alienness. "*Those who deride us are fools, either for deceiving themselves or hiding behind hypocrisy.*" He inclined forward. "*Each of them knows they would not hesitate if given the opportunity. They also know, in the secret corners of their hearts, that they would act with far more cruelty.*" The High-Warden disagreed but held his silence. He needed their assistance and contradicting them would not further his ends. "*What of you, High-Warden, are you of those who oppose what we accomplish, or of those that desire in the secrecy of their hearts to imitate our success?*"

"I deem the experiments of your people immoral, Secluath. Yet I admit your skill surpasses the ability of any other to match."

The five Borluce reassessed him, eyes vibrant and calculating through the drifting fumes. "*And what are you willing to sacrifice?*"

The High-Warden responded slowly, a quiet threat warning against inflated demands, "What do you need? I will do what I can after the gods have been defied." His last words echoed, and the eyes of the Borluce flashed, noting their unusual, almost lyrical cadence.

"*Would you draw blood?*"

The High-Warden shifted his attention to the wolf-masked female. "Whose blood?"

Her eyes never shifted, but a shiver of unease infected her low mental voice. "*Renegades.*"

"Borlucian?"

"*Yes,*" Secluath responded through a renewed cloud of fumes, ignoring the true question of how such a thing was possible and appearing unperturbed by the unprecedented rebellion.

The entire Borluce species lived from birth to death interconnected, everyone unique but joined to an immense collective regardless of distance. How could rebellion form when every mind was open to every other?

"Of which city-state are they?"

"*That information is irrelevant. They number a score; only a few are soldiers. None are Shamans or Hunters.*"

"Where are they now?"

"They are between Antiark and Adriat along your intended route. That is fortunate for you and us. If the task is accepted, you will receive every aid we can provide."

He deliberated. The Borluce penchant for secrecy and notorious disdain for sharing motivations made any contract uncomfortable. The fact that they treasured the lives of their own beyond almost any crime magnified his unease. But he had no alternative.

The High-Warden stood with a bow. "Very well, I will eliminate these renegades." A sense of acceptance extended from the Borluce. He did not ask why they pursued their kin, they would only declare the information unnecessary.

Secluath returned the reverence. *"I wish you success, High-Warden of Winsyria; the gods are uneasy. Seated upon his misshapen throne, **Jaidar** besieges his brother, issuing challenges of rightful claim, though he stands alone. The Pantheon is unsettled."*

"I am wary of the gods, but I do not fear them. Tell your people this instead, for this I do fear: the Southern horizon lies bereft of stars, it's every light extinguished as if they were candle flames at the break of dawn."

The Borluce glanced between one another, their crests rippling and darkening to angered scarlet tinged with cobalt fear.

"May the gods never touch you, Secluath Kellserasven."

He moved to depart, but the wolf-masked Borluce spoke anew, *"We will guide you in this pursuit, High-Warden. When the proper time arrives, we will seek your thoughts and you will open them to us, lest those we hunt hide from you, and we gain nothing."*

He stilled and glanced back, recognizing there was another truth seething beneath the surface of her words. "Very well," he said softly, and with that expelled them from his thoughts.

26

Chaos And Winter

The Citadel gradually woke as the High-Warden ascended, filling its arching corridors and sinuous passageways with bleary-eyed servants and shuffling guards. Most hurried past with a perfunctory reverence, eager for the morning repast or struggling to discard the lingering torpor of sleep. To each, he returned a bow and murmured greeting.

His mind quested however, affixed to a trickle of cold air threading up through the Citadel, warning him that the New Order's incursion had eroded some of The North's most dangerous cells, threatening to liberate their inhabitants, and one in particular that could only visit ill upon the world. To worsen matters, the Tower of Wizardry throbbed with *Vydur* and *Kysuir*, two elements of wizardry combined only for the summoning of demons.

The High-Warden growled, his thoughts turning to Falain Durensev. The North did not forbid summoning demons, but this was no minor devil, this was immense, and the whole of the Unseen World shuddered with its advent.

He reached Caddon's chambers and knocked.

The woman from the council of wizards opened the door, her features strained and a white squirrel seated atop her head. "High-Warden? What can we do for you?"

"I would speak with Master Caddon if he has recovered enough."

She hesitated, head half-turning to peer behind her before she stepped aside. "Certainly, High-Warden."

Glancing up from the remnants of breakfast, Caddon smiled as the High-Warden doffed his boots. "Welcome to my humble incarceration. What brought you back?"

"Initially only to see how you fared, but something new has arisen."

The woman returned to a chair at Caddon's side, the white squirrel vaulting from her shoulder to avail itself of his repast. "We'll help any way we can."

"Someone has expended an immense quantity of *Kysuir* and *Vydur* from the Tower of Wizardry; do you know who?"

Caddon paled. "I didn't sense anything. Are you sure?" He looked to his wife, but she frowned as well.

"Yes, The North screams with it. Could a spell have been cast?"

Caddon grimaced and closed his eyes, perspiration beading his brow. "Damn it! I can't sense anything." His head thudded back. "I don't, there might be a spell. There's so many written into the Tower it would require centuries to compile them all. I don't know who it could be, everyone knows not to summon demons over a certain level in The North."

"What of Falain?"

"I don't know. Yes, he hungers for power and often boasts of his intentions to become one of the Methurion, but this feels too radical after years of repairing his image, too impetuous."

"Will the council intervene?"

"If they have not already, then something's impeding them. Maybe that spell's blinding them as well?"

The High-Warden sighed internally, relinquishing any hope that Falain Durensev would not require his personal intervention. "Arch-Wizard Caddon, I will investigate and, if it is required, punish the trespasser. If you are able, please meet me in the courtyard before I depart. Lord Antiark will know when." He paused at the door, a hand resting on the oaken grip. "I apologize in advance for the collateral damage."

The High-Warden slowed as he entered the Tower of Wizardy's grounds, glancing at the demons skulking through its statues in the guises of vagabonds and drunks. He growled low, breathing heavy with fettered wrath as ice crept outward from him.

The demons turned, most cowering but a few jeering in reckless ignorance. One vaulted into flight, flesh warping to crimson iron in the guise of a metallic crane. It landed before him and straightened, body reverting to that of an armored man in a cloud of ash and cinder.

"Falain Durensev stands accused of malignant intent and is summoned to account."

The demon laughed, stained fingernails scratching a disheveled beard. "The arch-wizard ain't seein' anybody right now."

"He doesn't have the authority to refuse."

"And you're not getting in, so sod off before I show you what I really am." It raised a hand, vicious flames bubbling atop its fingertips: Chaos Fire.

"You are a minor demon, belonging to the tenth hell of *Jaidar's* Abyss with six decades left to your sentence."

The demon's morbid grin slipped, replaced by a flash of doubt and then rage. "I could kill you right here and now, erase this city like it never existed!"

"No, you can't, you are just ash on the snow." He reached out and touched the demon's chest, snapping the chains binding it to this Mortal Kingdom. "Enjoy the Abyss." The demon had a single moment of realization, then its body imploded into a cloud of ash.

The remaining demons sobered as one, their guises of poverty and indolence falling away as crimson armor sprouted from their skin.

He scoured them with a scornful glance, and a deep elemental shift swept the courtyard. It all groaned, cracking as ice crept over every statue, river, bench, and path. A demon whined, scratching at the frost enveloping its flanks and the black fissures splitting its iron hide. Then the air screamed, and all warmth fled the court, stripping the demons of life and freezing their crumbling ashes solid.

The High-Warden rolled his shoulders, breaking the crusted ice, and resumed his task. He encountered no further opposition in his ascent to the Tower's entrance where, patience exhausted, he struck the door with such force it shook.

The door opened promptly, emitting something guised as a maid. It allowed a heartbeat for observation and then spoke, its voice human but its words mechanical, annunciated without inflection or accent, "Hello, how may I be of service?"

He constrained his temper. "Arch-Wizard Falain Durensev stands accused by The North and is called to trial." The maid nodded and stepped aside with an obeisance, her body flickering with the emerald light that betrayed a construct of Kysuir. The High-Warden bowed stiffly and entered.

"Where are all of the students?"

"They returned to their homes due to the war; the Tower is mostly unoccupied now."

"Where might I find Falain Durensev."

"He is on the summoning tier. I shall prepare him for your arrival." The maid departed into the wall.

He did not linger for her return for he knew the Tower's composition, and doubted Falain Durensev's hospitality.

She met him a few flights further up the stairs. "I apologize, Master High-Warden, the Arch-Wizard Falain Durensev labors upon an arduous summons, and barriers prevent me from alerting him of your arrival. Disrupting him forcefully would compromise the summons and safety of everyone present."

"Then forewarn any potential casualties; I will not delay."

"Very well, please, follow me." They began their ascent, the maid's figure becoming translucent.

"If it is no insult, what breed of magic are you?"

"I am a design from the Tower of Wizardry's creator, manifested to assist the Tower and her students. Once I kept the Tower through all hours, now only in the night or when the students are absent because the wizards create their own servants."

"Do you know what Falain Durensev hopes to accomplish?"

"I am ignorant of his intention; the magic he harnesses is foreign to *Vydur*, *Kysuir*, or *Asiiu*, though it tastes slightly of *Vydur*. It is wizardry, but a unique, or personal, configuration."

The maid reached an unremarkable door. "This is the summoning floor, reserved for accredited masters. Falain occupies a chamber at the back, reserved for members of the council and visiting arch-wizards. You may experience some discomfort due to the severity of the wards." The lock clicked, and a bar of pale wood slid aside, its enchantments dimming.

"Thank you for your assistance, but I wish to converse with Arch-Wizard Durensev in private." He bowed in farewell and she returned it with a curtsy before retiring through the opposite wall.

Beyond the frail barrier of wood and stone, he encountered an immense antechamber of drifting shadows. Rank upon rank of vast iron walls occupied the floor space, their hollow interiors filled with stacked cell-like rooms, and every wall bedecked with low burning torches that stank of asafetida.

He advanced down the central corridor, searching the abutting rooms for Falain Durensev. Each contained a glowing pentagram and iron gates: the walls, ceilings, and floors a pageantry of lacerated stone, charred surfaces, and cavities large enough to cradle children. Outside the chambers, the black granite of the walls, floor, and ceiling gleamed with the husky wizard lights and enchantments of annihilation against the potential of demons escaping their confinements before the contracts were formed. More runes flared on the cells as he passed, illuminating the lingering ethereal scars of past summonings.

All of this dimmed in his wake, falling dark as his steps echoed off the walls. A glow akin to molten iron blossomed in the distance, mounting with the refrains of a feverish chant that itched at his psyche. A tremor swam through the hall, causing the bars to rattle and unlocked doors to drift open. The pentacles flared in their cages, the latent *rifts* pulsing with momentary life.

He reached the antechamber's opposite extremity and entered a smaller subset of rooms segregated from one another by sheer walls of enchanted stone and silver bars. Falain Durensev occupied the centermost, his form awash in a churning miasma of volcanic light, rampant shadows, and fire-bloated ash. A pentacle fulminated at his feet, its lines spanning the entire alcove, enclosing a burgeoning *rift* of lapping, vine-like flames.

The High-Warden stepped forward and grasped the silver bars, swallowing their molten hue in ice and seizing Falain's attention.

"What are you doing here?" Falain demanded, glancing between the High-Warden and the Raven perched on the chandelier.

He ignored the query, searching the expanding *rift* and the spell revolving around it instead. "How did you muster the power for this?" He knew Falain's capability, and this portal exceeded both it and the ability of any two council members.

Falain laughed, near-delirious from so intimate a contact with the Chaos of the Abyss. "I made a bargain, fool, a bargain you cannot hope to resist! My new allies march upon Antiark and will soon pronounce me lord over The North."

The High-Warden pried the bars open with a snap and stepped through. "If you speak of the New Order, then you have committed an egregious error. No foreign army can survive here; the weather tears their flesh, the rodents despoil their food, and the howling Wolves strip them of courage and respite. They may glimpse the walls of Antiark, but they have already lost. And you"—he shifted his attention to the Raven—"do you intend to introduce yourself this time?"

In response, it cawed and soared from the room, the bars curving from its path. He reverted his attention to Falain. "Who empowered you to open this *rift?*"

"I need no one's help to summon a demon! I am preeminent, unmatched in power or skill! I will conquer every Tower and dance upon the wreckage of this land!"

The *rift* exploded open, hurling Falain into the molten bars and slamming the High-Warden with a wave of heat, drawing his clothing taught as something vast took shape.

Falain peeled himself off the bars, leaving strips of blackened flesh, and knelt before the *rift*, hands raised. He screamed the angelic name of his summons, "Maphael," and slammed his fist into the runes. Then he repeated it, reversed to reflect his subject's descent from grace, "Leahpam!"

The Fallen Nephilim roared in answer, its char-colored face materializing in the *rift*. Again, Falain screamed the two names, and the *rift* strained wider, its edges solidifying around a molten core. The Fallen Nephilim dragged itself free, flames spewing from its corrupted form and its smoldering tread.

The damned monster towered over the High-Warden, its naked form twice his height. Two leathery wings spread from its back, rising past an elongated carapace skull, leering maw, and two crowning goat horns. It had the torso of a man but with sheets of matted fur adorning its back, deepening the air of bestiality it exuded with every infernal breath. Opening its double maw, the demon roared and slammed a cloven hoof, searing the floor black. This was no mere demon. This was a high servant of *Jaidar*: a Nephilim who had forsaken the heavens for violence and fire.

Its voice rupturing with infernal power, Leahpam leaned over the High-Warden. "You are not my supplicant, mortal."

The wizard scrambled to his feet. "I am your master, Leahpam, ignore him!"

Leahpam sneered. "The servants of *Jaidar* owe compliance to no man, idiot. Now, who is this?"

"I am the High-Warden of Winsyria, and you are forbidden."

Leahpam exhaled a mass of boiling air that reeked of burning flesh and flexed, expanding itself in challenge.

Falain scrambled for distance, a golden light flaring on his hand. "Who are you to forbid him? It is time you yield your post to one worthier of *Jaidar*. Kill him!" He stabbed his hand forward, launching a flaming lance from the ring's onyx centerpiece.

The High-Warden deflected the lance with a flick of his hand and stepped after him. Falain backpedaled, energy materializing about the ring in an emerald web and exploding outward. The High-Warden scattered it with his other hand, caught Falain about the head and slammed him into the wall, knocking him unconscious.

The pentacle's brilliance wilted, dimming to low embers as Leahpam grinned and stepped from his prison. The *rift*'s ossified frame cracked, bleeding fire as a new face appeared within its churning core. "They're coming, High-Warden of Winsyria, I hope you're ready." Leahpam charged, long talons sweeping wide.

The High-Warden ducked beneath the swipe and dove past, plunging his hand into the colossal *rift*. Ice flooded outward, freezing the fire solid and sealing the doorway.

Leahpam twisted, spewing flames from its maw and assailing the High-Warden with its tail. The fire billowed harmlessly off him, snuffing to dust as he vaulted the tail and dove past. One of its wings lashed out, striking him a glancing blow, and then recoiled, ice sweeping from the point of contact. Leahpam screamed and drew up, fiery energy gathering along its spine and coursing into the frozen appendage. The wing pulsed once, twice, and shattered, wrenching a shriek from Leahpam as it reeled, blood pumping from its back.

The High-Warden vaulted onto Leahpam's back, fingers enveloping its tawdry fur in ice. Leahpam reared, bashing him against the wall and howling. The High-Warden climbed higher, setting his feet on its shoulders and wrapping an arm about Leahpam's neck.

The Nephilim thrashed, pummeling him with its wing and tail. "Do you really believe yourself strong enough–" The High-Warden grasped its jaw and tore off Leahpam's head. All fell silent, the corpse swaying beneath him until he discarded the gore-doused skull and dismounted, then it collapsed with a thunder, noxious blood fountaining from its throat.

He grabbed Falain and dragged him to the frozen *rift*, shaking him awake. "Who gave you the power to summon a Fallen Nephilim?"

"What…?"

The High-Warden slammed him against the *rift*. "Who gave you the power to summon a Fallen Nephilim?"

Falain whimpered, eyes wheeling and his blood staining the ice. "I … I don't know."

"Who was that Raven? And why are you treating with *Jaidar?*"

"I don't know, I don't know; please, just let me go."

He dropped Falain, recognizing an erased memory. Whoever the Raven was, they possessed enough skill to obliterate the mental defenses of an arch-wizard.

Falain hauled himself up by the *rift*, staring at it in compounding horror. "How…?"

"Falain Durensev, where there was once doubt, now there is none. Twice you have assailed me, once in alliance to a dark god. Your judgement is set."

"You … you can't judge me! I am an arch-wizard on The Northern council, beyond you!"

"Give my greetings to *Jaidar*." He kicked Falain through the frozen *rift*, shattering the ice crust and amputating his agonized shriek.

The flames roared awake, swamping the alcove in heat and swelling to dozens of feet high, liberated of all confining enchantments. He pressed his hand against them, quelling the unchecked flames and dismantling the bridge behind them, vile spell by vile spell. The flames slowly shriveled in upon themselves, subsiding until only an ethereal scar remained.

He departed after that, the warped door rocking on its hinges and the entire hall sweltering from the *rift*. He paused briefly to inform the spectral maid of Falain Durensev's actions, judgement, and fate. She thanked him and vanished to apprise the council. How they did not know already he could not be certain of, but anyone capable of summoning Leahpam was capable of spells to conceal his arrival. Something none of the council were capable of.

Guards met him at the Citadel gates, their crystalline armor glimmering from a brief rain, and their swords murmuring in a troubled wind. He raised a hand in placation and greeting, but they hesitated, disconcerted by the blood covering him.

"Sheath your weapons," he said, and gently clasped one guard's shoulder. "Everything is fine; the threat is resolved." He held the woman's gaze and that of her fellows until they relented. Two white Wolves yawned in roguish irreverence from the gate, and he nodded at them. "Remember, trust the Wolves; they will tell you if something ill is a foot." The guards nodded, returning to their old lax postures with visible effort.

A reptilian cry drew his attention to the courtyard beyond where a Borluce and a Riicann waited. The scaled quadruped resembled a feline with a long neck and four intricately colored wings.

He approached and the Riicann twined its dexterous neck to inspect him. He stopped, arms extended to either side in invitation, permitting the Riicann to press its nostrils against his chest and inhale. It sneezed, stepped back with a shake of its plumed head and submitted, pressing its delicate jaw against the ground.

He knelt and caressed her snout, his callused hand soft against the elaborate scales. She initially shied from the contact, then eagerly pressed her snout into his hand. A smile flickered across his face and he scratched her copper chin, earning a rumbling, catlike purr.

He basked in this moment of uninterrupted peace until the Citadel opened to emit Lord Antiark and a group of derangers. He caught sight of

Caddon leaning on the shoulders of his wife, the irrepressible white squirrel Andrea standing proudly on his shoulder with all the imperiousness of his royal blood.

The High-Warden swung into the Riicann's saddle, situating himself between her four wings, and returned his attention to Lord Antiark and Caddon. "It is heartening to see you afoot again, arch-wizard, but something bothers you?"

"I worry over what occurred in the Tower and my inability to sense it."

He leaned down, beckoning Lord Antiark and Caddon closer. "Falain Durensev was attempting to forge a pact with *Jaidar*, and in the process of summoning the Fallen Nephilim Maphael."

"What? Such a being should transcend any wizard's ability to summon."

"Someone assisted him. Prior to Maphael's entrance, a Raven departed the summoning chamber by *warping* the door from its path."

"What of Maphael?"

"Dead."

"Are you sure? Maphael is—was—a Nephilim. He served the gods millennia before succumbing to *Jaidar*."

"Yes. Send derangers to search the Tower for accomplices in this mad scheme, with the council's consent."

Caddon scowled. "A pact with *Jaidar* exceeds anything the Methurion Conclave would sanction; blood's mercy, they forbid us from summoning demons older than four centuries. They're uncontrollable. Of course the Tower will sanction it; gods, we'll help you."

Lord Antiark nodded appreciation, then asked, "What did you do with Falain?"

"I entrusted him to the company he sought."

A grim satisfaction bloomed on Lord Antiark's features. "That is fitting, though it darkens my heart to consign a soul to the Abyss."

A brush against his consciousness drew his attention inward where, recognizing Secluath Kellserasven, he opened a slit in his defenses.

"Fare thee well on all journeys to come, High-Warden of Winsyria. You have our respect and promised aid. We will contact you again when you near the renegades."

"Very well."

Lord Antiark glanced at the emissary's tier, fully aware of the mental communications, and grimaced. Excluding the Tower—which existed apart from The North—very little occurred in Antiark that eluded his notice. "What did they request of you?"

"I am to eliminate Borluce renegades."

Caddon stared. "Truly? I thought the Borluce refused to kill their own people?"

"They do."

Some past apocalypse had ravaged the Borluce race, pushing them to the brink of extinction. They had yet to recover despite the passage of millennia and, as such, refused to execute any member of their race. The strictest punishment that might befall a Borluce was slavery; a sentence meted out only for a betrayal of their entire race.

Bidding them farewell with a nod, he directed the Riicann southward only to hesitate when Caddon touched his knee. "What is it, arch-wizard? Do you still suffer from the *Dreamer*?"

"No, it's just"—he broke off, trying to find the words—"I was connected with the Rhawn Mountains, I know how this will end, what will be demanded of you"—his breath caught—"the price, it's not worth it, it's too high; she has no right to ask that of you."

The High-Warden gave him a sad smile. "It will never be too high, arch-wizard. You have lived in The North for decades; you should know we Northerners love a good tragedy. I will give whatever The North requires to survive, and I will deem myself blessed for having the chance."

He pressed the Riicann's flanks and it launched heavenward toward a sky black with storm clouds. For a moment, there was nothing, then the wind caught them, dragging them into the storm's furious grasp. Lightning cracked, booming with thunder that shook his world. The Riicann shrieked, its wings beating desperately to climb above the storm, fighting against the raging winds. He pressed close against her, fingers wrapping in the saddle straps and pressing his will out through the deluging rain and hail, calming the tumult just enough. The Riicann twisted itself and lunged, breaching the cloud veil into the brittle sunlight with a triumphant cry.

It shook its plumed head with a huff, dislodging the rain and hail before leveling out. The High-Warden straightened, peering northward where The North's fury ravaged an unseen object. Relaxing, he opened himself to The North's embrace and submerged into its rhythm.

Sometime later, Secluath brushed his mind, speaking with the voices of two others when he gained admittance, *"You near your quarry, High-Warden."*

"Before I act, I would know what they have done to merit death?"

The answer came reluctantly, threaded with sorrow, *"Two are my children, precious to me before avarice and pride corrupted them. Now they have fallen beyond honor. We owe them a debt of life, however, and so will spare them an existence in bondage."*

The High-Warden accepted the evasion without comment and dove, not pretending to comprehend the Borluce. The storm swallowed them, imparting a fulfilled purpose, a destination, and a sense of pity: The North was not kind.

They landed with a burst of snow and ice, and he dismounted into a swath of frozen corpses, most killed before they had a chance to scream. He knelt, scrounging the Outcast and Shorn Borluce for signs of their family medallions. The Outcasts retained their medallions, a symbol of their potential for redemption, but the Shorn carried only its defaced likeness branded on their chest.

He found two renegades with the medallions of a ruling clan: copper stones encircled by brass rings and a fish mask. He pocketed these and continued his search, almost immediately brushing against another medallion. Energy surged at his touch and died, leaving the medallion burning cold through his gloves. He opened its collar and the medallion sparked again, retaliating against his touch with increased vehemence. He snapped its chain and stepped back, a medallion shaped into a gauntleted fist resting in his palm amidst a pool of onyx links: the New Order's sigil.

The amulet was one of a pair enchanted to facilitate conversations across vast distances. Such an alliance should have been impossible, Borluce loathed the gods more than Northern men, yet here it lay, and with it the explanation for their exile.

He grasped the medallion between thumb and forefinger, ice expanding from his touch, cracking the onyx links and draining it of color until it resembled glass. Then he crushed it and threw the dust to the storm.

His obligation accomplished, he returned to the Riicann, but despite his success, something prickled at the back of his thoughts. He scowled, recognizing *Malbreyth's* perversion; the War God accumulated power from all open conflict, including those in The North now that his name had been invoked within its boundaries, and these Borluce had served him via their alliance with the New Order.

Malbreyth struck in that instant, hurling his will against the *Barrier* in an attempt to shatter it before the High-Warden could reinforce it.

The High-Warden staggered, his entire being groaning beneath the War God's assault, and swung into the saddle, pressing the Riicann's flanks to demand all the swiftness its wings could muster. It answered his entreaties with a cry and vaulted heavenward. Unlike earlier, it made no effort to slow its beating wings or release its straining muscles. It pressed harder, seeking the higher heavens and calmer weather.

Secure within the Riicann's beating wings, he closed his eyes, centering his mind and gathering his will. Breathing slowly, he merged his strength to the *Barrier*, fortifying it against the War God's assault. *Malbreyth* hurled himself against the High-Warden and the *Barrier* again, causing the whole North to shudder and him to stoop.

27

The Governor's Mansion

Tiberius leaned against the foyer's back wall, toying with a glass of red wine as he pondered the day's events—namely, Slade's disappearance. *'Where did you go? What was so important that you'd leave Feylin with a practical stranger ... or did you know about her bodyguards? More pressingly, where are you now?'* Both Cain and Senna assured him that Slade disappeared like this frequently, sometimes for an entire day if not longer. Still, Tiberius worried. After all, he had assigned the paladins to protect Slade as much as Feylin.

Motion drew his eyes to his ward and the pattern that began with her inspecting one painting, quickly growing restless and drifting onward, immigrating from piece to piece and from room to room until she encountered the tall mirror. There she fretted over her immaculate appearance, trying to distract herself, but invariably glancing at the door and leaving to repeat the whole pattern yet again.

On her latest circuit, she'd actually refrained from delivering her new withering stare, an expression with odd similarity to Senna's, though the woman denied any hand therein. In Feylin's case, she still needed a little practice, the expression was amusing as much as chastising. *'Regardless, it's deserved. I deceived her and she'd be justified in flinging a book my direction.'* Tiberius looked at the ceiling, staring into a painted blue sky and mocking clouds. *'I let her believe that she had escaped the constant surveillance and could simply be, that Slade's surreal dream was a place even nightmares feared to tread.'*

Thinking of nightmares and surreal dreams, his mind wandered to Senna. She rarely slept nowadays, though one would hardly realize it from watching how she laughed and eagerly participated in the day's activities. Even now she lay off to the side, her bright, attentive eyes absorbing a crime novel and clearly dissecting every possible theory.

The more Tiberius learned about her sickness, the more his initial suspicion gathered credence, slowly dismissing the other possibilities until only one remained: a curse. He had felt the lines of disease spinning through her blood, hints of dark magic tying its threads together while pure malice drove the concoction and twisted her mind. Only a handful in the East possessed the qualities to fabricate such a spell, mostly witches and a few ancient creatures or forgotten terrors, but they all lacked the inclination.

A final, deeply unsettling possibility remained. She may have been exposed to the disease years ago, back when she still lived in the East. It was all too likely that she brushed against a foul, insidious working with no direct relation to her. If so, others were no doubt affected. Countless others.

The front doors burst open and Slade skated across the foyer into a swooping bow, one hand flung back toward the starry night. "I'm afraid that unless you cease and desist your laggardly ways, we shall arrive most informally late. A disaster to be avoided, unless we want an envious crowd ridiculing our audacity."

Senna glanced up from her book, lips twitching. "In that case, we mustn't dawdle." Carefully marking her spot by folding a corner, she swept her legs off the couch and leaned down to collect her shoes.

Feylin, meanwhile, had frozen mid-step, the curiosity gnawing at her since Slade's disappearance reaching a crescendo. His secrecy and her imagination had changed a simple question into an irresistible mystery, and mysteries needed to be solved. From the narrowing of her eyes, Tiberius suspected that she intended to harry Slade until he died.

Amidst these reactions, Cain emerged from his study and gave Slade a quick appraisal followed by a nod. "I am glad you dressed accordingly." Leaving Slade to unconsciously straighten a little, Cain strode to his wife and bowed with an arm extended, earning a smile.

Tiberius set his empty glass on an adjacent table. "Before we leave, there's something Slade and I must discuss in private."

Senna, however, flapped her hand. "Tiberius, I doubt that's necessary. It's obvious Slade knew about Feylin's bodyguards; after all, paladins hardly qualify as masters of stealth."

Tiberius captured Slade's eyes with his own, employing the barest touch of his will to pin the youth in place. "Is this true?"

The young man neither blinked nor looked away, could neither blink nor look away. "I believe their names are Dreaos and Markand, two third level paladins."

"I see; we may now continue." It was quiet, almost inaudible, but the room exhaled in relief.

"Father, about that lady friend you wanted me to bring; I found this lovely little concubine who—" A slipper flew through the door, smacking Slade across the face.

"I don't know what insanity convinced me to do this," Tasha said, storming through the front door towards Slade, "but if you don't behave, I'll make sure you suffer just as much as I do."

"I believe the incentive was a public marriage proposal followed by a pardon for misdeeds entailing debauchery and murder. Really, I can't see why you're complaining. You get to spend an amorous evening with me, at a ball no less. Just imagine it." Slade sprang forward, wrapping an arm about Tasha's waist and spinning her around the room. "The lights, the music, the dancing, the food, the handsome lords, the incorrigibly stuffy ladies and their revealing gowns; oh, this will be an affair to remember."

Tasha stomped on Slade's foot, breaking free as they circled near Tiberius. "Ah, Miss Bloomhale, we meet again." Tiberius placed a hand on his chest and bowed, extending her errant footwear with a smile. "May I commend the ingenious use of this slipper?"

Blushing, Tasha snatched the object and fell into a hasty bow with steepled fingers. Mid-obeisance she remembered she wore a dress and gracefully switched to a curtsey, accidentally giving Tiberius a Thearc's curtsey rather than a commoner's. "My lord, it is a pleasure to make your acquaintance again." When Tasha rose, she flushed a deeper red, clearly recognizing her mistake but also meeting his gaze proudly.

Tiberius looked to Slade. "But wasn't my ward the object of your matrimonial interest?"

"Emotions are flighty creatures; plus, Tasha is my true fiancée, so I've every enticement to fall madly in love with her despite suffering from a horribly broken, desperately bleeding and irrevocably scarred heart." Slade shrugged, dismissing any sign of torment. "Besides, Feylin rejected me."

"So this is the mysterious future Mrs. Lammerock."

Tasha's lips pressed into a thin line. "Please don't encourage him, my lord."

"Hello, dear." Senna interposed, nudging her way in and dragging Cain along behind. "It's wonderful to see you again. But come, Slade grows anxious and not without reason." She laid her free hand upon Tiberius' shoulder. "We can ride together. Let the young conspire and concoct some travesty to enliven our evening."

"Your wish is my command." Tiberius glanced toward Feylin and found his ward stalking Slade, who had opted for flight, resulting in one now chasing the other around the small party.

Hiding a smile, Tiberius changed course and offered his arm to Tasha.

The moment she touched him, Tiberius felt both the anxiety and nervous energy straining to escape her grip. It was a wonder she didn't pace like a caged animal. He smiled and she reciprocated with the most artfully designed smile he'd experienced in years, no inkling of being polite or deceptive. At the same time, he felt old rules waking up and tightening around her thoughts as nearly forgotten habits slowly reestablished themselves. Anything free, impulsive, or simply frivolous quickly submitted to an inflexible propriety. She would not be throwing another slipper this evening.

'Curious. Her grace and diction suggest schooling if not experience, so why the unease?' He renewed his smile, reaching out with a feather-light touch and easing her anxiety through a quiet sense of well-being. He also tried loosening the rigid control settling over her thoughts, but his light touch felt akin to drilling granite with paper. Then Slade jostled past—squeezing between them and the doorframe while proclaiming that Feylin would never catch him alive—and exasperation mixed with amusement flashed across Tasha's thoughts, relaxing them just a little.

Outside they found two grand carriages waiting by the road. As their little procession neared the vehicles, a short man leapt from the second carriage and moved to engage the first pair of bulky, excitedly prancing horses. He stared fixedly into one's eyes, whispering and stroking until the animal calmed. Its companion, conversely, settled after a single word.

Ignoring the other driver's derisive snort, he returned to his own carriage to begin lecturing its horses.

Cain greeted their paladin guards with a nod, then opened the carriage door and politely helped Senna climb the precipitous steps. Tiberius entered next followed by Cain, who gave a firm rap from within. Their driver gave his reins a cursory flick and the horses leapt forward, making the driver bark a short command to suppress their enthusiasm.

The horses from the second carriage proved less agreeable. No sooner would the coachman peer down his great beak of a nose at one horse then its brother would start prancing about until the coachman swapped back over. Of course, whenever that happened the first horse instantly resumed fidgeting and started the whole process over again. "Your brothers listened well enough, yet you two stubborn mules—yes, I called you mules—refuse to behave. You were trained better than this; the Lammerock hostlers aren't near so incompetent as most, and yet you act like foals on your first outing. Here we are going to a grand ol' ball where you can prance all about and impress the pretty mares, but you won't calm down enough to get there. What will Master Tiberius, and don't tell me you haven't heard of Master Tiberius, everybody's heard of Master Tiberius, think when I tell him of your antics? Why he'll be most disappointed, and don't forget about Master Lammerock."

The chastened horse ducked its head, drawing an embarrassed hoof across the ground and stepping up to nudge the coachman. "Well, if you be good, I won't have to tell him anything. Here's what we'll do. If you two comport yourselves, I'll put something sweet in your suppers." Both horses considered his offer. "Or, you can act like the lazy, no-good, stubborn sons of mules you are and get nothing for dinner." Wisely, the horses agreed to his offer.

"Where to, young Master Lammerock? Direct to the party or a detour first?" Delving into his long-tailed coat, the coachman produced a flask and took a prolonged drink.

Coughing slightly, Slade waved at the air. "Straight to the party, Alca."

"As you wish, my lord." And there Alca's formality ended, the man forgetting to so much as to incline his head before heaving his rotund self up the ladder.

"Your carriage awaits, fair ladies." Slade said, opening the door with a flourish.

"Yeah, give us a moment," Tasha called from the walkway, leaning on Feylin's shoulder as she hopped about trying to remove her boots.

"Here, grab my shoulders," Slade said, striding over to kneel down and catch her foot. "Basic wisdom advises wearing the appropriate shoes before going out." Slipping her boot free, Slade tossed the article over his shoulder into the carriage and followed it with a ragged sock.

"I planned to change here so I wouldn't have to walk halfway across the city in slippers. I didn't expect to be rushed out the door on arrival."

"You should have arrived earlier then."

"You promised to pick me up! I expected you to at least reach your own house on time."

"Expecting people to arrive on time is very rude—stop shifting, please—almost as rude as arriving late. We should really polish your social skills." Grumbling, Tasha trusted more weight to his shoulders, and Slade slid the boot's replacement onto her foot. "Alright, next foot and … we're done." Dusting off his knees and returning to the carriage, he caught its door just as a mischievous wind began closing it. "Shall we?"

Practically thrumming, Feylin repeatedly smoothed out her skirts and watched as Slade climbed into the carriage. Watched as he brushed aside one of Tasha's discarded boots. Watched as he plopped down opposite them. Watched as his foot bounced up to land between her and the other woman. Finally, he spoke, "Now, I assume both of you are dying from curiosity, but I must attend to some business first." A heartbeat from surging forward with a question, Feylin fell back with a huff and he patted her knee. "Don't worry, I'll avoid answering your questions soon enough." His attention swiveled toward Tasha, who fidgeted with equal impatience. "My Dear, I've arranged for some acquaintances to meet me at the governor's ball tonight, and I'd like you to join our little engagement; they're practically throttling one another to meet you."

Tasha's countenance darkened into what Feylin was beginning to realize was less her contemplating a brutal thrashing and more a simple frown. "What sort of business? Are they actually interested in me or are you just being facetious?"

"I may have exaggerated their interest a smidgen, but they do know you. As for the subject, we're discussing those thieves who plan on stealing *Akravast*; I thought you might have some insight to offer."

Both women reacted simultaneously, Tasha jerking forward with a half barked, "What?" then for some reason indicating Feylin with a near imperceptible head twitch. As for herself, Feylin grabbed his leg with a little shake. "Slade! Tiberius said not to tell anyone." Immediately after, she blushed to her ears and hastily removed her hand, almost managing it before his lips twitched and his eyebrow quirked.

"He also asked me to poke around, which I can't do unless my friends help me ask some very particular questions. Tasha's incredibly trustworthy; in fact, I think we've just proved that she's less likely to spill the beans than I am." Slade looked to Tasha. "In case you didn't catch that, a group of truly vile, reprehensible hoodlums are planning to steal *Akravast* and Tiberius asked me to look into it for him."

Tasha slumped back into her seat with one hand, rather justifiably, covering her eyes. "If Tiberius Whyte's involved, that means its serious. I guess I should help anyway I can."

"Excellent." Slade swung back toward Feylin. "Now, my dastardly inquisitor, go ahead and fetch your thumbscrews."

'Finally!' "What message did the hawk bring you? And don't say assassins again."

"I wasn't planning to. First some back-story. I and a few young disreputable Thearcs have entered into a little wager, the repercussions for which might entail something as trivial as global annihilation or as horrendous as wearing a pink gown—adorned with all manner of frills and pearls—to the next ball. With such terrors looming over us, the competition to acquire the most wealth by next month is fierce. What's more, my rivals are lowly scoundrels who cheat atrociously, meaning I've no recourse but to cheat as well."

Feylin tried not to frown. *'That story about the assassins, the sudden rushing off, the shooing me home? All because of a wager? I know he's private but still … that situation hardly calls for us rushing home … unless … come to think of it, I don't actually remember him rushing us home, it might have just felt that way.'* She gave a minute shake of the head. *'This is ridiculous. Why would he lie. If he didn't want to tell us, he wouldn't.'* A quick glance confirmed that Tasha, the most dubious person present, seemed fine with the story. "Alright, so what happened?"

"Apparently, one of my less imaginative rivals had an idea—rather uncharacteristically I might add—and hired thugs to disrupt a textile shop I'd invested in, but they accidentally set fire to the place."

She stared at him for a second, unsure if he was exaggerating, then slapped the carriage seat. "Those … those …"

"Bastards?" Tasha offered with a smile.

Feylin flushed. "Umm, yes…" *'I guess that explains the rushing off … and the story about the assassins was probably just him not wanting us to worry.'* "So what did you do?"

"I hurried over and found the beautiful little shop engulfed in flames, the street awash with blue coats as volunteers hurried to evacuate nearby buildings or fight the spreading fire." While speaking, Slade made his usual expansive gestures, detailing the building with his hands, gesturing toward the blue of Tasha's dress, raising an arm as if to ward off a scorching heat. "Luckily for everyone involved, a water-mage wandered by and controlled the situation. At that point, I dashed off to fuss over the shop's owners, a lovely old woman and her thirteen-year-old daughter. While talking to them, I must confess, I got a touch angry."

Feylin's heart gave a short stutter at this, little goosebumps sprouting along her arms. He'd pronounced it so casually, the subtlest of shifts from sounding amused. Tasha perked up as well, shooting a glance that Feylin had to be misinterpreting as a warning.

"How dare he hurt my people? A little old lady and her daughter who adopted cats, loathed tea, and giggled at the slightest provocation. While standing there, I considered how best to take my revenge." He grinned at them. "Eventually I decided to rob a second rival—henceforth dubbed Victim Extraordinaire—and blame our chief villain: the rival who ultimately destroyed my textile shop. With this in mind, I left to find some talented scoundrels. Afterwards, my only dilemma was implicating our fetid and chief villain."

Feylin sucked in a breath. *He can't be serious. That's, that's—*

"So, how do you plan on going about it?" Tasha asked, smiling a rather savage smile.

"Alongside stealing everything of value, I tasked my goons with appropriating a favored cloak from Victim Extraordinaire, intending on giving it to our chief villain." Slade rubbed his hands together, cackling. "In time our chief villain will don this garment—mostly because I confiscated his other cloaks—whereupon Victim Extraordinaire will catch him red handed."

Feylin knew she was staring but couldn't help it. *He seems awfully comfortable with all of … this. Except, not just comfortable. He seems … competent. His mother said he used to steal food, didn't she? But that's nothing like this. It's so much bigger and more complicated.* She bit back several stuttered or confused responses, eventually settling on one she simultaneously did and did not want answered. "What happens to everything else you stole?"

"The goons will earn a quarter of our total profits, and the rest shall fund a new textile shop outfitted with the very best wares. In the meantime, the woman and her daughter can live on a little money I've set aside. Any leftovers I feel no compunction about taking for myself."

Well, that's alright… I guess. Besides, it sounds like the other people employed these underhanded methods first and if they're all acting like 'chief villain' then … well they sort of deserve it. "What stops those goons from taking all the money and simply running away?"

Slade winked. "Now that is a secret worth knowing."

"So you aren't going to tell us?"

"Of course I am. Bragging's impossible unless my audience knows what I'm bragging about."

Which incentivized Tasha to roll her eyes. "Well that's logical."

"My Dear, everything I do has logic behind it. Why I own an army of logic. As we speak, my logical minions and I are planning to conquer the world and rule it with the most insufferable logic." Slade raised his hands overhead and imitated a cheering crowd.

Fighting a smile, Tasha flicked his boot. "Answer the question."

Slade dug into his satchel, produced a sheet of rolled up paper and waved it around, afflicting the atmosphere with a thick, charged texture that caused Feylin's hair to prickle. "I compelled them to sign a fake blood-contract."

Hairline cracks skittered across its surface, the edges were frayed, and a sense of age and power cloaked the document. What made this impression even more unpleasant was the ghost of ugly red handwriting that appeared whenever a passing streetlamp glared inside and shone through the parchment.

Tasha took the blood-contract from Slade, handling it as she would a porcelain doll dropped by a child. "Y-yo-you did what?" Shivering, she quickly handed the document back.

Feylin reached out for it as well, but Slade shook his head and took her hand between his, smoothing out her fingers so he might safely graze the document across their very tips. Icy needles stabbed all the way up her forearm, and Feylin jerked back. "Ow! If that's a fake blood-contract, what does a real one feel like?"

"I'm assuming much worse, then again you're also far more attuned to magic than Tasha is, so you're experiencing the full brunt of it. With a little study, you shouldn't feel anything more than a light sting."

"How do you know I'm—"

"A clever guess."

"Oh, … how did you even get those goons to sign it?"

"I gave them a few necessary hints on looting my rival's estate."

Overhead, Alca tapped the roof as the carriage rolled to a stop. "We've arrived, my lord."

Immediately, Feylin practically leapt across Tasha's lap so she could pull the curtain open. After peering outside, however, and seeing the governor's marble mansion she muttered a quiet, "oh," and scooted back, sinking into the far shadows before peeking through the opposite window. Outside that window was only normal, unassuming Tellor with its tall, square buildings, its flat or shingled roofs, its three enormous walls, and its gradual slant down into the grain fields.

A brush of fingers across her knee drew Feylin's attention back around to Slade. "Is everything alright? Do you want Alca to take you home, or shall I find Tiberius?"

"Finding somebody in a crowd is near impossible," Tasha interjected curtly, looking through the curtains. "Did we agree on a meeting place?"

"No." Slade then winked at Feylin. "But while locating someone is difficult, being found is easy."

"I doubt making a scene will alleviate her social anxiety."

Feylin shook her head. "No, it's not the crowds; I'm just feeling a little overwhelmed." Carefully she leaned across Tasha and peered outside again, feeling her chest constrict as she examined the sweeping stairs pierced by a ramp, the two giant murals carved into either side of the door, the sheer size of the mansion itself, and how it was all illuminated by ambient golden light.

All this without even considering the attendees, an array of the Empire's most intimidatingly rich or powerful or competent Thearchs and Theonaughts.

"You've never attended a ball before?" Tasha asked, giving her a light tap then switching to Slade's side of the carriage, allowing Feylin easier access.

"No, Apelium isn't … Tiberius doesn't throw many parties."

"Well, you're not missing much." The woman sounded darkly amused at first but quickly lost the edge of humor. "I've been to several, and they were dreary affairs that only served to spend money and politic, at least if you were a man. The women generally spent the whole night arranging for the societal murder of their rivals or those they simply didn't like. Vicious people."

"Really? You know, I rather like the solitude. Perhaps we might…"

"Nonsense," Slade declared, rising to his feet. "Nothing you encounter outside will be nearly so terrible as myself; take heart for you walk in the devil's shadow, and all other nightmares cower away. Besides, if necessary, Tasha has a knife thrust down her bosom."

Feylin's head whipped around, but Tasha lifted her hands. "I'm not hiding anything sharp, well not unless you count hairpins."

This roused a slight smile followed by Feylin peering outside yet again, watching for several moments. *As soon as I leave, they'll all stare and then it'll only get worse when I'm introduced. They'll gawk and surround and judge and remember every mistake even while pretending not to notice. The polite will pressure me for information about Tiberius, the desperate will demand an introduction, and the powerful will manipulate.* She laid her forehead against the windowpane, eyes closing. *Enough. Dreading it does no favors and you have to go out eventually. Just take a deep breath and proceed like before. One, two, three and Yaaaah.* Before she chickened out, Feylin straightened and gave a sharp nod. "Alright, let's go."

Outside a small crowd congregated just beyond the road, Thearcs and the occasional Theonaught glided from their carriages to converse with friends or contend with enemies, the gold and silver of their jewelry glittering in the light along with the reserved filigree of their clothes. Interspersed among the ruling class were influential merchants in more richly appointed garb, retinues, and other integral figures, also those who'd earned Governor Warsein's favor. Lastly, a few hollowed cheeked individuals writing notes or making sketches that would fill tomorrow's pamphlets.

Tasha, the picture of elegance, caused a minor stir as observers wondered over her identity and obvious scars. Then Feylin exited and the murmuring doubled, her appearance seeming almost foreign with her slim build and pale skin.

All around her, Tasha could hear the mutters. A Northern princess perhaps? Did The North have princess? Maybe eastern nobility or a little known Theonaught's daughter from the Empire's frozen reaches? Only one thing was for certain, the girl's grace and bearing made her high-born status beyond question.

Feylin, for her part, froze under the scrutiny, a list of questions—that Tasha was all too familiar with—flitting across her face. Did the gown's pale green clash with her eyes or hair? Was the cut too demure? Not enough? Had she worn too much jewelry or– Watching from the corner of her eye, Tasha nearly missed the girl pinch herself sharply. Then, despite the fears no doubt still rattling around inside her head, Feylin donned what she probably hoped was a light, easy smile and descended.

'Good girl.'

Slade appeared last, prompting a third deluge of questions from the observers. He flowed down to and across the ground like water, adopting feigned solemnity as he bent into a slow obeisance with one leg extended and his arms stretched to either side, hands dangling from their wrists.

Gradual, reluctant movement started from deep within the crowd, first as a mere handful then as a growing tide. Grumbling to themselves, the people opened a path for Slade.

Tasha glanced from the path to the imperious-eyed lords and their regal ladies. Regardless of either station or reputation, the Empire's ruling class was bogged down by a wall of people. Disturbingly, several of those lords and ladies stared back with pursed lips, the Thearc equivalent to a deep frown. *'Gods dammit, Slade. Why'd you have to make a scene?'*

"Well, shall we proceed?" Slade asked, tone light as he proffered an arm.

Tasha almost rejected it from simple habit, but the crowd's expectations pressed in from all sides. Old rules asserted themselves and old memories reminded her what happened when she disobeyed.

Tasha took his arm, fighting against restless energy that suggested she pull him into something faster than their current leisurely walk. *'Let's get this Jaidar blessed night over with.'*

"Color me surprised, my Dear; you care about public opinion."

Tasha almost gave a bitter laugh at how true and false that was. "If I cared about public opinion, would I associate with you or strut about in this ridiculous dress? There's so much fabric missing I'm astounded it hasn't fallen off yet."

"You're wearing that most fabulous gown because I requested it. Also, I'm very public in my opinion, as such you care about public opinion. Besides, you look beautiful." Slade, ignoring all proper etiquette, extended his other elbow toward Feylin, who latched onto it as a drowning child might a raft. "Now onward to supreme debauchery and utter depravity." He strode through the gap onto a broad azure carpet, the slightest of un-lordly bounces kicking up his feet.

"So, how'd you do it?" Tasha whispered, looking to distract herself.

"Do what, my Dear, coordinate global salvation? Ruin the livelihood of my enemies? Cause the tides to stop? There are so many possibilities. Why, only yesterday I directed the usurpation of every major guild."

She patted his arm. "I'm sure you did, honey. But no, I'm asking about the crowd's convenient repositioning; I doubt anything besides a visit from Cardolyn Tyier himself would have convinced them to step aside."

"My Dear, are you comparing me to our glorious Emperor? I think I'll blush." He fluttered his lashes at her. "Such things aside, you assume I masterminded this fantastic event; when in truth, the people orchestrated it themselves."

"If that's the case, why are your fellow Thearcs struggling through human quicksand? They can't all be studies in human depravity."

"It's true; a few consider themselves champions of humanity. I, on the other hand, consider myself among those whose depravity is cultivated and distilled to such purity that our subjects pretend we're simply misunderstood rather than admit such villainy exists. That's why the crowd parted: sheer, all-consuming terror."

"Slade, you're no more dangerous than a bunny." Categorically false, but Feylin could use the reinforcement. Tasha had noticed several distinctively weighing expressions during the carriage ride.

"Ah ha, you forgot to mention I was a rabid bunny trained since birth to kill and maim while feeding on nothing but human flesh. Just imagine it, you're meandering through the woods as the sun shines overhead and the birds sing a song meant just for you when a massive bunny springs from the brush and charges, its red eyes spinning insanely while its mouth foams and bleeds around dagger-like teeth. Not the friendliest sight."

This time both Feylin and Tasha eyed him skeptically. "A bunny?" the younger asked.

Slade nodded.

"With blood red eyes?" Tasha followed up.

Slade confirmed it a second time.

"And dagger-like teeth?" Feylin continued.

Slade nodded again.

Tasha, despite struggling mightily, couldn't hold back her smile. "Whatever you say."

"Ignoring the bunny analogy for a moment," Feylin said, struggling against her own laughter, "how did you make the people step aside?"

"A pebble can start a landslide, a single drop can flood the dam, and six people can redirect the river if given proper tools."

Tasha glanced at Slade pensively. "Did your crew push the crowd aside?"

"Yes, and simply because I enjoy the practice, there's also a moral to the story." Slade looked to Tasha, seeming almost serious. "It's always a good idea to arrive early even when you don't do it in person."

Before he could elaborate, a triumphant voice bellowed from up ahead, snapping Tasha's head around and, for some reason, setting her on edge. "Slade Lammerock! I knew you'd make an appearance tonight. The others doubted your spine, but oh no not me. I know you better!" A tall, husky man with dark tousled hair casually forced his way through the oncoming guests.

Slade hastily disengaged from the women and, motioning them back, strode ahead to meet the approaching man alone.

Immediately he grabbed Slade in a rough bear hug, lifting him a foot off the ground. "The lackwits all thought you'd spend the night sniveling in your room, unable to face us after that fire torched your textile shop. But I said no, he's far nastier than you believe and a damn sight cleverer too. He's still in the running, sure as *Jaidar* would damn the innocent. I even bet upon it, and now you've won me a tidy little sum."

'*What in the Abyss?*' Tasha thought. '*The textile story was true?*'

"Amonn. Put. Me. Down." Slade gasped, his face growing steadily red as the man bent him into a severe arch.

Amonn plopped him down. "Oh sorry, I know you hate that, but I couldn't resist." Smirking at Slade, he jingled the new gold in his pockets. "I'm riding a nice buzz is all, what with winning that bet and—ahem—a little drink to be honest. Oh, but shame on me, I meant to commiserate with you. It must be bloody frustrating to suffer at such underhanded methods." Abruptly Amonn threw his head back and laughed. "Ha! If you can believe it, they say that Ab'tucha was the one who planned the whole mess. I'm rather proud of the idiot if it's true. Glad to see he's finally applying himself. Still completely forbidden, of course. Unfortunately, none of us can prove anything, meaning the numbskull's still a contender." He slung a heavy arm across Slade's shoulders, dragging him close. "Just between us, I've heard another rumor saying someone else gave Ab'tucha the idea to destroy your business. Very clever of the *Jaidar* blessed bastard, if it's true anyway. Also makes me curious if the damned fire was as accidental as it seemed. I've been investigating, you see, trying to discover something useful, and the floor's layout was designed to protect against random fires. That shopkeeper and her daughter were very careful; you'd need a long series of coincidences to set the entire building ablaze." Everything Amonn said or did was loud, his voice boomed, his motions rarely qualified as gentle, even his aura seemed to bully those around him.

"I'm grateful for both your faith and your concern, Amonn," Slade said, trying to slip out from under his arm. "But there's no need to investi–"

"Nonsense," Amonn proclaimed, his arm tightening across Slade's shoulders. "I'm simply performing my duty by investigating noteworthy events around my father's city and seeing to the welfare of our fellow Thearcs. I'm just glad you weren't there today, last I heard you'd planned on paying a visit around the time the fire started."

"Yes, there was an abrupt change of plans."

"Something involving your beautiful companions no doubt." Amonn turned Slade around and beckoned for the women, who approached cautiously. "Such beautiful creatures must have names. Or are they fallen stars and therefore nameless?" Amonn's voiced had lost its abrasive boom, instead adopting a low pleasing rumble as he finally released Slade and stepped forward to give Tasha a slight bow with steepled fingers, smiling roguishly. "Amonn Warsein at your service, may *Enecki* and his light shine upon you."

Her eyes narrowed, then a little smile curled Tasha's own mouth. "If we're truly fallen stars, why did *Sammahale* cast us from the heavens? What unspeakable horrors did we commit to deserve such horrendous punishment? Tell me, Amonn Warsein, of what exactly are you accusing us?"

The man laughed. "I should have guessed. Slade would never bring some giggling, simpering, porcelain princess to one of these affairs; he likes someone to contend with. But princess or no, you're still a mystery." Amonn stepped back, rubbing his jaw. "Let's see, a new dress in the fashion of Tellor's seamstresses, a light tan but not dark enough to be native, and a commanding presence. Are you a visiting Thearc perhaps?" He laughed again and, before Tasha could respond, sidestepped in front of Feylin. "What about you? A more delicate flower it seems, but probably fierce in your own way. On second thought, no. I'm guessing you're a curious one, prone to incessant questions and always looking for answers. A reader almost for certain and still malleable. Destined for greatness or he wouldn't bother. Tell me, do you like poetry? I excel at both reading and writing it."

"Not much, my lord," Feylin said, gazing at her feet and then continuing with obvious effort. "I enjoy Chorkerand's writings and I'm warming to Seysil's latest work, but…," she trailed off with an inarticulate shrug.

Amonn frowned, reaching out and tipping her chin up. "What is your name?"

Feylin took a breath and straightened her shoulders, meeting his gaze firmly. "My name is Feylin Sarashell Whyte."

"Ward to Tiberius Whyte?" She nodded and Amonn glanced at Slade, smirking. "Well well, we're certainly walking in high-company now. Who is the other one? Some eastern princess?" He laughed and released Feylin. "No, don't tell me. I've already stolen one secret from you tonight. Let's not spoil the game by giving me another." Reaching inside his coat, Amonn produced a small black book and opened it to a page marked with green silk, quickly jotting something down with a pencil. "There, yet another mystery added to your list of unsolved riddles. Have a lovely night." Tapping the pencil against the book, he strode away.

"Who was that?" Feylin asked Slade as he watched until the other man departed for good.

"The governor's son and a man I'd like you to avoid."

"Why?"

"Have you ever heard the term 'a man is innocent until proven guilty'?"

"Yes?"

"Well here's another one: some men were always killers; society simply didn't realize it until after someone died."

At this Feylin looked confused but Tasha focused on Slade. "Slade, are you calling the governor's son a murderer?"

"No, a murderer is an incompetent killer and Amonn is far from incompetent. Shortly after I first arrived in Tellor, he almost succeeded in getting me executed." Slade finally turned away from the distant man. "Amonn's dangerous, Tellor simply hasn't realized it yet. Avoid him whenever possible, but if impossible then be very careful when you talk to him, he remembers everything." Slade let this sit for a moment, impressing the true gravity of the situation before easing the tension with a grin. "On a side note, the thought that just occurred to me is how a lack of homicidal tendencies doesn't necessarily increase a person's social appeal. At least a murderer can always provide interesting conversation."

"If you're trying to rebrand murder, I wish you'd find a better foundation than the ability to generate engaging discussions. A man shouldn't need to kill someone to enliven the conversation."

"Of course not, but if they're already a murderer then it's better to embrace the topic rather than become a social pariah simply because they exude sheer undiluted tedium." Slade presented his arms. "Shall we find our errant companions?"

The group set off once again, Tasha scanning the notable landmarks while Feylin piped up with, "Just being a terrible conversationalist doesn't mean someone lacks social appeal. People can be simultaneously boring and likeable."

"Yes, but it's rather difficult to uncover their likeability if our hero's staggering tedium prevents anyone from fraternizing."

Spotting their missing companions loitering by one of the pillars that lined either side of the carpet, Tasha tapped his shoulder. "Over there, third pillar from the door."

Slade veered without question. "We need an engaging personality to beguile our violent disinterest in strangers, without it we would simply ignore the poor fellow or avoid him like a card-carrying member of the leper society. At that point, their best option is to lease a shadowy corner and stare broodingly out across the dance floor, letting a mysterious fog descend so we might fantasize and hypothesize about their character. A similar process happens to the preternaturally quiet or secretive members of our society. There is, however, a slight difference between the two. A boring man can't speak lest he dispel the illusion."

Tasha cast him a side-eyed glance. "Why do I get the impression we're about to leap headfirst into one of your cockamamie stories."

Slade climbed atop his dignity and favored Tasha with an expression that would have made a stone quiver. "I never tell cockamamie stories, my Dear; they are all true as day and certain as death."

"You don't say."

"Oh, lots of people say it; I just say it better than most." Grinning, Slade wrapped an arm around Feylin's shoulders. "Returning to our discussion, let's take our companion as an example for the quiet members of society."

"Wait, what?" Feylin squeaked, pushing against Slade's ribs and trying to escape immediate danger.

"She, by way of studious timidity, creates a perception of being innocent and thus trustworthy. As a result, we talk freely, forgetting her and how she's listening with acute interest; not that it matters. We have complete faith in the personality we've assigned her. We know she'll keep our secrets." After a final huffing push, Feylin gave up on escape. "In effect by claiming neither honor nor fidelity, Feylin adopts those very qualities despite standing as our most despicable liar. Her depravity is without end, and her disregard for curiosity boundless!"

Tasha scrutinized Feylin with a discerning eye. "It's possible."

"What!?"

"For all her wickedness though, Feylin is a mere henchman when compared to the true master of deception." Slade whirled upon his other companion. "Tasha, I have finally uncovered your vile plot."

The woman pinched her brow. "I knew I should have stabbed you before this got out of hand."

Feylin, no doubt encouraged by self-preservation, hastily joined Slade's tact shift by leaning forward with an expression of mock innocence. "But I thought you didn't have a knife?"

"I don't," Tasha responded conversationally. "I could have scrounged one up though. A big fork would have done the trick. I could have also stolen—"

"Ahem!"

"Alright alright, Slade, you can do your bit now."

Instantly he dropped to his knees and wrapped arms around her legs. "Please, I beg of you, abandon your deceptions and communicate your dastardly and most assuredly brilliant schemes. I wish to travel beside you and eat beside you and fight beside you and when your mortal aspirations have achieved fruition, I wish to accompany you heavenwards so we might battle the gods and claim *Etherea* together."

In the aftermath, silence and a shocked audience surrounded them. Soon an old, white robed man hobbled out from the spectators, his blue eyes twinkling and gleaming malevolently as he invaded the sanctity of their invisible stage.

Dispelling Tasha's evil through a series of holy signs and gipping *Enecki's* burning wheel and book in a trembling hand, the priest spat at her feet. "Shame on you, and may the Abyss claim your soul for eternity." Denouncement delivered, he stormed away.

Tasha looked down at Slade. "I'm assuming you paid him to screech at me?"

And he, arms still wrapped around her legs, grinned. "Of course."

"If you ever do this again, I'll harvest your brain and sell it to a curiosity shop."

"Ah well. Life's a twisted road and a blind guide; you never know where the old bugger will take you."

"Slade, one could almost call you wise if not for your habit of indulging certain peculiarities," proceeded by the rich, layered tones of his voice, a smiling Tiberius came strolling up behind them, prompting Slade to twist around without releasing Tasha's legs.

"True; but if people considered me wise, they might actually listen and that would spawn all sorts of problems."

"And here I thought you were an agent of chaos."

"I can't be an agent for chaos all the time, that'd be too structured."

"Ah, that makes perfect sense." Tiberius circled around toward Feylin, laying a large hand upon her shoulder and leaning close to ask a few 'well-being' questions.

Tasha, meanwhile, flicked Slade between the eyes and he rose just as Cain's large hand descended onto his shoulder. "Though your mother is amused, please abandon such antics once we enter the governor's mansion. We are guests here, show respect for our hosts." After a moment, his gravity receded before a slight smile. "If it's any consolation, I may host my own party upon returning to our estates, provided your mother's health allows it. That should prove adequate sport for you and excellent entertainment for us."

"Did I hear we're throwing a party?" Senna asked, materializing beside her husband with a mischievous grin. "We'll have to invite everybody, in particular those we don't like."

"I hear the Baron of Northstride has become intolerable of late," Tiberius offered.

Cain raised a hand, forestalling further suggestions. "Perhaps so, but let's delay our planning until after we enjoy the governor's festivities." As he spoke, a bell sounded in the distance, tolling three times and signaling the end of the day. By the final toll, shadows lengthened across the ground and *Sammahale* transitioned to the ninth-Vigil, taking the light and sunsets of the eighth-Vigil with him as he vanished beneath the horizon. Opposite him, the moon assumed her place as warden of the night.

Where *Sammahale* travelled across the sky in short bursts, the moon journeyed with a slow constant grace, and just like *Sammahale* painted the sky whenever he set, *Sarah'Venn* painted the sky whenever she rose. In her case though, she employed all manner of silvers, purples, and blues. Together they guarded the sky, watching the prisons of the Old Gods alongside their children the stars.

With this spray of colors, silver gold lights gradually bloomed across the city, winking to life along streets, over doorways, down alleys, and by shops or across archways. Directly to Slade's left an old, desiccated plant twitched, its drooping branches lifting and its leaves flushing with renewed vigor, displaying a multitude of tiny buds that opened into distinctive swan shaped flowers. From these flowers shone the same light that sparked all across the city.

Slade turned from the Swanlight to his stepfather. "Well, it seems that despite my best efforts, we still arrived on time; the family name will never recover."

Retaking Senna's arm, Cain beckoned to Slade and made for the steps. "Come, I doubt we are missed. Much longer though, and they'll notice our absence." Behind Cain, Slade took Tasha's arm while Tiberius took Feylin's and brought up the rear.

28

The Ball

Outside the mansion's entrance, Slade and his company passed beneath four adari, each cloth swaddled creature marking their arrival in ledgers before continuing to eye them suspiciously. Afterwards, the group encountered a group of servants beautifully uniformed in teal and gold, and lead by a man whose clothing was so starched it bent rather than wrinkled. The butler—so designated by his collar pins—steepled his fingers and bowed to Cain and Senna with exacting correctness before granting Slade and Tasha the barest possible obeisance, due to their lack of personal status. In culmination, he lowered himself far beyond any preceding display to honor Tiberius and, by extension, Feylin.

Cain and Tiberius acknowledged the servants with gracious nods while Senna smiled. In response, the servants bowed a second time, some flushing at being noticed but all returning Senna's smile; except for the butler, who gave a quiet, disdainful sniff.

"My Lord Lammerocks and my Lady Lammerock, my Lord Whyte and my Lady Whyte, it is a pleasure to greet you." The butler intoned, snapping his fingers and commanding his subordinates to collect the cloaks of their guests. "If it pleases your august selves, how may I introduce you tonight?"

Cain, Tiberius, and Senna each chose their preferred title, then proceeded deeper into the mansion as servants rushed ahead. Slade and his company held back, custom dictating their parents or accompanying chaperone appear first. After a suitable period elapsed, the butler warily approached Slade, bitter recognition glinting in his eyes. "If it pleases you, how would my lord like to be introduced?"

Slade grinned and waved his companions ahead before leaning in to whisper something to the butler.

"What do you think he's up to?" Feylin asked, following a servant through the massive, gilded doors.

Tasha's lips pursed. "I haven't the slightest idea and it'll start killing me soon. I wish one of the Emperor's crazy inventors would fabricate something to guard against surprises."

"I doubt anyone could invent anti-Slade armor." Feylin mumbled distractedly, her eyes scanning the absurd wealth displayed all around them. "I don't think a fortune teller would be much use either. Is that real gold on the walls?"

Tasha afforded them a single, cursory glance. "Like I said before, a needless parade of wealth."

Once he finished whispering in the butler's ear, Slade clapped him on the back, slipped a dead mouse into his pocket, and strode for the mansion doors.

Fuming, the butler snatched his nearest underling by the collar, growled something and pointed her after the departing youth. She then rushed past Slade and chased after Feylin and Tasha, dragging their guiding servant into a heated but murmured discussion.

When Slade caught up, he found Tasha leaning back and tapping her head against the wall while Feylin sidled towards the muted argument. Just as she neared, the servants finished negotiating and one fled to her initial posting while the second beckoned them sourly. "My lord and ladies, please follow me."

Slade grinned, extending an arm to either companion. "Come, the guests of this dreary celebration await our most magnanimous arrival with desperate anticipation. Let us brighten their evening as only two beautiful women can. And if saving them from accursed boredom ruins our own enjoyment, then I shall claim the comfort of having made a worthy impression. Public relations aside, let's make the impression a small, forgettable one because allowing it to persist would invite disaster upon my plans."

"What plans?" Feylin asked.

"Oh, you know," Tasha interposed, waving a hand, "simple things like world domination or immortality. The true question is how he intends to accomplish it all: Monetary expenditure? The tramp of steel-shod boots? The rabid manipulation of lesser men?"

Feylin scrutinized Slade, realized what she was doing and flushed. "I can't quite imagine Slade as a general."

"For the record, my plans entail a quiet night spent reading with tea and cookies, but since you asked about my preferred method, I could see myself leading a few dozen men in the future. Heck, I may even lead them to victory; constant defeat can be such a drag. Then again, victory comes with so many hassles." His companions shared perplexed glances that Slade ignored. "After winning the battle, the victor always has to clean up by his lonesome because the other side suffers from the most infuriating indolence. Next he must personally write all the history books so they treat him favorably, thus developing a horrible wrist cramp. Also, at some point he will invariably run out of ink, except it's the middle of winter and he's miles from the nearest city and he's in the middle of a war. Well, he can add a headache to his list of woes. Yes, indeed. This victory business is a terrible pain in the neck."

Tasha gripped his arm tighter, preventing him from making his usual expansive gestures and dragging her around. "So, you'd prefer to lose over clean up?"

"Nah, I'd bribe my adversaries to play dead, paint a couple pictures to serve as proof and then escape, all the while singing songs that celebrate my opponent's absolute annihilation. Much cleaner all around, and they get to write the history books."

Feylin's brow wrinkled. "But if your enemies record the battle or the lack thereof, they might aggrandize their own image while besmirching yours."

"We write history for those living a hundred years in the future. By the time history rolls around, I will have died and won't care what others think of me."

They crossed beneath an arch into the governor's ballroom, the azure carpet underfoot pooling across a dais before giving way to the first of three staircases stacked atop one another, each one varying in width and length. As for the room itself, it resembled a miniature coliseum with three descending balconies that circled the entire room and occasionally broke for additional staircases. The first level provided guests with dinner and a place for idle conversation. The second allowed for aimless pacing but largely served as the strictly delineated battle ground for politics, unspoken rules preventing both the desperate and the powerful from conducting business anywhere else. As for the ground level, it hosted the dance floor along with a central platform that raised the orchestra overhead.

Feylin gawked at the glittering expanse. She had thought Apelium sumptuous, now she realized it barely qualified as rich. Tasha, conversely, stared at the ceiling where an enormous, unsupported stained-glass window opened to the night sky. It depicted the Creation of Soul, a story wherein

Jaidar and *Enecki* took the mindless slaves of their parents, the Fore-gods, and breathed first logic then choice into their empty, obedient minds. The birth of humanity. The beginning of the end for the Fore-gods.

"Impressive, isn't it?" Slade said, breaking Tasha from her awe with a nudge. "Governor Warsein hired a dozen wizards and a legion of glass-smiths to build it over winter, making it for the summer parties. I peeked in when they lifted it. Unsurprisingly, the forging proved far easier than installing three giant pieces of glass."

Following their eyes upward, Feylin gasped. "It's beautiful. Why haven't I heard of it?"

"The governor bought concealment charms from across the Empire and bribed all the laborers, ensuring he could unveil it at the next major event. I only discovered it because I have friends who work here."

"What makes tonight so important?"

"Isn't it obvious?" Tasha asked, then—when Feylin shook her head— she reached over and tapped her lightly on the chest. "You and Tiberius Whyte. Your guardian has reentered the political scene after a decade's absence, with a mysterious ward no less. Described in terms of importance, it's only a feather less earth shattering than the return of a dead prince."

Eyes wide, Feylin sought out and found the now familiar scene of Tiberius surrounded by the wealthy, the powerful, and constant deference. "You're exaggerating, aren't you? I know he's important, Tiberius warned me of as much, but surely he's not … that important?"

"If anything," Slade said, "we're understating. Tiberius Whyte is one of five men with unrestricted access to the Imperial Emperor, more importantly he has the Emperor's ear. At a single word from your guardian, the Emperor would strip the lands from any Theonaught or the city from a Thearc. By the same token, a suggestion from Tiberius Whyte could see a pauper elevated to those recently vacated seats." As he spoke, Feylin underwent the curious sensation of having her vision expand outward, of reordered information and disparate pieces clicking into place. Now, the lords and ladies didn't surround Tiberius so much as flutter about like moths around a light. At the same time, she saw distant Thearcs watching from all across the second floor, passing banalities amongst themselves as they waited for an opportunity to talk with either Tiberius or someone who stood a better chance of reaching him.

"He and Cardolyn Tyier have known each other for decades, as long as anyone can remember. What's more, it's said that members from the Whyte family have advised the Imperial Emperor since he first appeared. Cardolyn Tyier and the Whytes have been working together for centuries."

As the trio discussed Tiberius and gawked at the glass ceiling, their accompanying servant whispered into the announcer's ear. Blinking, he quickly whispered back and started a subdued argument that culminated with the servant giving an unsympathetic shrug before scurrying away.

Seeing their servant flee, Feylin went cold with a sense of impending doom. The premonition only worsened when she glanced toward the announcer and found his countenance glowing a self-conscious red. Beneath her steadily mounting concern, the announcer snapped a glower at Slade before lifting his staff, letting it hang for as long as possible. Finally he tapped the ground once, twice, and thrice, his voice then booming across the golden hall. "Lord Slade Lammerock and his two fiancées: Feylin Whyte, ward to Tiberius Whyte the Will of the Emperor, and Tasha Bloomhale, the most competent spy in the Imperial Emperor's possession. Sadly, his mistress and his third fiancée are absent tonight. My Lord Lammerock, the younger, humbly begs your forgiveness."

Stiff backed lords, ladies with gently parted lips, calculating Thearcs, piercing eyed Theonaughts, and glittering merchants all stared, appetizers, drinks, books, and dancing partners forgotten. Because of Cain's intermittent attendance, most had never encountered Slade—couldn't even remember his name—and thus only heard vague rumors concerning his antics, leading many to reject them as expanded or perhaps tortured versions of the truth.

As for Feylin, it took every ounce of determination to remain, to stand at the railing and endure the sea of upturned faces, to endure even as her frantically beating heart sucked air into barren, gasping lungs.

"Smile and wave politely, Feylin, we want you as unremarkable as possible." Slade, steady, confident and an absolute bastard, eased from her clutching hands, removing Feylin's only support as he contradicted his own words by descending the steps like an exaggerated version of himself. He bounced higher, grinned wider, and oozed more mischief than ever, glorying in the shock and disapproval, somehow towering in his disdain for their gawking.

"Chin up," Tasha murmured, lagging a pace behind the evil man. "We'll kill him later." She then descended in stark contrast to Slade, with blue silk gliding across pale marble and measured progress, her statuesque figure cloaked in cool disregard as her forceful gaze fixated on the horizon. If anyone, lord, lady or merchant, crossed Tasha's gaze and was caught staring, she quirked her lips into the barest hint of a mocking smile.

Which only left her. Slim, half grown, socially intimidated Feylin. *'Oh gods, what do I do? Etiquette doesn't cover this. What would Tiberius do? Tiberius wouldn't care. Tiberius wouldn't get into this awful situation to begin with. What about Slade—oh gods no, he's what started this mess. And Tasha? I've already seen what she'd do, but I'd never pull it off. Oh gods, none of them are any help unless— actually,*

maybe ...' Giving a silent war cry, she simply pretended nothing had happened. She descended quietly, normally, without even a smile as her gaze turned slightly downward, avoiding any potential contact. She acted beneath notice. "Slade," Feylin whispered upon descending the first stair and drawing abreast, "please tell me you had a reason for introducing us like that."

"And won't your father kill you for it?" Tasha asked. "What about Tiberius? Personally, I'd guess he's already measuring the paperwork against your untimely death. Even if he's not, you should still consider skipping town because if neither he nor your parents kill you"—she gave him a confectionary sweet smile—"I will."

"In that case, I know a fantastic undertaker. I'll be sure to leave you his address. Now, in regard to Feylin's enquiry"—Slade nodded across the room, indicating Senna—"I believe an acquaintance of ours is quite breathless with mirth." Feylin, tracking his nod, felt the young man retake her arm and guide her to an unoccupied table. "Strangely, my stepfather seems oblivious to this whole situation. Do not be fooled though."

"Is this really the time for a lecture?" she asked, flushing and lifting her gaze toward the glass roof as, from the corner of her vision, she caught the sight of large, staring eyes or hasty shifts as people looked away. "Both our parents are likely planning your murder."

"There is always time for lectures, and if by chance there's a hired killer behind those flowerpots, I'm sure they'll benefit as well." Slade pulled back a chair, helped Feylin into it and then pulled one out for Tasha, who only accepted because etiquette demanded it. "Listen closely my prodigies and prospective killers: my father is not only aware of the incident he is quite possibly irritated by it; however, being both a decorated general and a politician, he strives to control his emotions while also endeavoring to unravel the mystery. Notice how his brow wrinkles in thought? Does he contemplate some detail from my recent assault on propriety, or maybe he wonders why I would go such lengths to draw attention to myself? That's it! See how his face clears and his posture relaxes. He's guessed my intentions and nods his understanding. Contrary to what Feylin suspects, the idea was not to mock or embarrass but rather the opposite. Think of how we were introduced. I was first, granting me both leadership and, bizarrely, chief importance. Next came

Feylin, burdened by nearly unmatched presence because of her guardian. Lastly there was Tasha, who should have descended with a servant's importance. Instead, she descended with no title, money, or power, and yet was introduced with an obvious lie, bringing her inherent mystery to the fore. When we descended, it was not as Feylin Sarashell Whyte alongside two unimportant companions. Rather, it was as the ward to Tiberius Whyte alongside"—Slade indicated Tasha—"a dangerous, potentially scandalous mystery and the infamous, irreverent, buffoon of a grand general's son who was nevertheless introduced first." Slade tapped himself on the chest then grinned at Feylin. "You are no longer of prime interest to these people. I had other reasons of course—namely, the chance to make my mother laugh."

Tentatively Feylin glanced around and, like before, caught several people quickly looking away, their exchanged mutters coming to an abrupt end. Except, some noticed her more slowly, allowing Feylin to perceive that she wasn't actually the object of their interest.

Tasha, conversely, did not care to look around, she clapped in that small, polite way belonging to high-born women. "Bravo, you've successfully turned a simple explanation into a needless description of your stepfather's reactions."

"I wouldn't say completely needless, I was merely preparing for my unexpected demise. If I turn up missing under peculiar circumstances, you'll instantly know who to blame for my tragic death: Tiberius! Besides, we'll call it a practical lesson on critical thinking and observation."

"Ehhh," Tasha hemmed, fluttering a hand. "The man's your stepfather; not much of a challenge. Try that old geezer over there."

Slade peeked over his shoulder then immediately reeled backwards, arm flung across his eyes. "No, no, no it cannot be. Never have I seen such depravity, such loathsome depths of character, such a putrefying swamp muck of a soul. No, I refuse. I cannot terrorize your psyche by revealing one thought from a mind that is like a weeping sore which bleeds filth and poison into the air."

"In that case"—she rose, one hand smoothing the wrinkles from her dress—"I'm off to find something to eat. Afterwards, I plan to socialize and hopefully hear some interesting rumors."

"A moment, my Dear," Slade said, lifting a hand. "Those are dangerous waters, should you need my help, do not hesitate to call, be it for a kiss on the cheek or a sword in or at your back." He winked, giving her a crooked grin.

"Yeah whatever; I'll return later."

Feylin watched this exchange with head cocked to one side, waiting until Tasha left before touching Slade's arm. "Did her departure strike you as a little abrupt?"

"A little, but I'm sure she has her reasons." Walking around the table, Slade grasped Tasha's chair and slid it back into place. "A friend spotted amid the crowd, an old enemy long since forgotten, perhaps somebody she randomly decided to murder. The possibilities are endless, and people can usually find a reason to lie."

"There's hardly any point in lying if she saw an old friend."

"I wouldn't be so sure; the friend might be a drug addict or a fiancé she hog-tied and threw from a cliff… Actually, that one falls more into the second category which practically explains itself. Why she'd lie about murdering somebody is beyond me though."

"I … guess that's a reasonable excuse."

"Don't forget she could also be telling the truth; one of the more tedious alternatives to be sure but a possibility nevertheless. And we mustn't forge–" He stopped mid-sentence, attention snared on something over her shoulder.

"Slade? Did you see someth–" Sudden bile coated the back of Feylin's mouth, its acrid flavor becoming a point of intense awareness as sights and sounds faded to gray and her own heartbeat filled her ears. Without reason, adrenaline flooded her blood stream and old, long dormant instincts uncoiled within her, demanding that she flee, demanding that she kill whatever crept up behind her, pleading that she find Tiberius.

Twisting about, Feylin's attention caught on the ballroom's entrance just as the latest arrival entered: a physically intimidating man with ugly yellow eyes and entirely black clothing, but not the stark, military style currently favored by the Empire. It was loose, layered garb with an emphasis placed on impact and power rather than utility. Feylin might have laughed at the man's overdone appearance if not for the baleful pressure bearing down upon the room. People flinched just for having his gaze touch them, likely without knowing the reason. Even those near the back shivered when his casual examination passed over, their reactions eliciting a thin pleased smile from him.

Then as the man was being introduced, a woman appeared from behind and glided past without acknowledging him or the amused comment he tried making. Instead, she descended the stairs and waited, sweeping the room with a frigid disdain that included her companion. Following, the man made another smirking comment that she shrugged aside before leaving to attend her own affairs.

"Feylin, do you know that man?" Slade asked, sneaking a hand into his satchel.

"No, but I don't like him."

Slade's eyes narrowed and he began murmuring, for once more preoccupied with himself than those around him. "He seems familiar. Why? *Kis'Maat* help me. Who is he? Why is he here? What does he want?"

Chills running down her spine, Feylin reached across the table and jostled his shoulder, hoping to break the trance. She could feel the strange man approaching; his effect losing its gentle malice in favor of ephemeral hooks. Black hooks; hooks attached to long spiked chains; hooks that burrowed under her skin and pierced her soul; hooks that threatened to drag her soul free with every casual yank.

Again Feylin leaned across the table and shoved Slade. Harder this time. Again he remained unmoved. Springing to her feet, Feylin almost collapsed when her trembling legs simply gave out, but she caught herself on the table and stumbled to the nearest steps.

Tiberius, blessed with an awareness verging on the arcane, was already looking for her. Spotting Feylin from across the room, he gave a lone, meaningful nod. He knew. Striding to meet her, Tiberius placed a large hand on her shoulder and stared into her eyes with all the imperturbability of a mountain. "Feylin, calm down; I barely feel his spirit-presence. He's not powerful enough to harm anyone."

"No, no, no; he lies," Feylin half-moaned, shaking her head with each reiteration. "He's playing, scaring all the little mice."

Tiberius frowned and touched her cheek, keeping her head from swiveling around the room. "Feylin, look at me. It'll be alright. Feylin, look–" He gave up and wrapped his arms around her, consciously pressing her face into his chest so she neither saw nor heard the world. "Breathe. I'm here, right here. Listen for my heartbeat, focus on it. There's nothing to worry about." When she pushed against him, Tiberius held tighter, giving her something physical to fight against as he took a slow, deep breath and delved the room. With this breath, Feylin felt his spirit spread outward: a gentle, near unnoticeable pressure that enfolded her in warmth.

Then Tiberius' eyes snapped open, their iron-gray bleached white. He grabbed her shoulders and pushed Feylin back a pace. "Tell me exactly what you feel."

Her gaze immediately wandered, but Tiberius caught her chin and locked her gaze to his. Even so, she spoke distractedly, "I feel anger and … and hate, and … terror all … all swirling around my head, con … confusing my thoughts while a thousand … in … instincts scream at me all at once:

run, hide, kill, kill, kill." Feylin broke away, clasping both sides of her head. "I can feel them, his hooks digging into me and, and, and–"

Tiberius dragged her back around, pressing a thumb to her brow. Searing heat spilled from the point of contact, burning away the spiked chains and dulling the screaming inside her head. "Feylin, where is Slade?"

Her eyes widened in horrified realization. "Slade!" Grabbing her guardian's wrist, she charged back the way she had come, back toward the malevolent presence. "He's at our table in some kind of trance. He was mumbling about not knowing the man and yet how he seemed familiar. Here, just over here–" Feylin came to an abrupt halt. "Wait, where is he? Where's Slade? He was just here a moment ago."

Tiberius though walked to the balcony's edge and stared at the woman who had entered alongside what he now realized was a Muntalabac. She met and held his gaze from across the room, wearing a smile touched by neither warmth nor pleasure. Tiberius answered with stony regard. "Feylin, go find Cain. Stay by him until I come get you."

———————

'In theory,' Slade thought as Feylin hurried away, *'I might have gotten away with simply asking her to fetch Tiberius, but she'd never leave me behind and he'd never sanction my talking to strangers.'*

Smiling over the last thought, Slade rose and meticulously repositioned their displaced chairs, even adjusted the table's various adornments.

Finally he addressed the writhing terror quarantined in the back of his mind, gripping its throat and squeezing until the dangerous emotion succumbed with a gasp.

Next he tended to his less dangerous but equally undesirable emotions.

The loathing he buried. The bile he swallowed. The instinctive urge to murder this newcomer got locked inside a chest and shoved to the deepest recesses of his mind. Regarding the curious sensation of knowing the man from another place and time, he shuffled that away for later dissection.

In their absence, Slade substituted a thin greasy smile, narrow calculating eyes, and a casual arrogance. With the façade successfully instituted, he meandered off through the guests, intending little more than observation and careful eavesdropping.

Despite this, the newcomer found Slade immediately and repeatedly, forcing him onto a different course. Thus started a strange game. Whenever Slade approached directly, his suppressed anxiety would surge and force a retreat. If he ignored it and pressed forward, his quarry invariably evaded him.

Conversely, when the man approached, Slade was the one who avoided contact.

Abruptly the newcomer's companion intruded upon their game, accosting Slade's opponent for a brief, condescending exchange that ended when she smirked and left to resume her own affairs. The man's features contorted, and he grabbed her arm but instantly recoiled as if burned.

The woman disdained to so much as look at him.

As the newcomer followed her departure with simmering eyes, his attention grazed Slade and their stares met. With a twist, everything fell into place; though neither could say what had been misaligned. Moving in unison, they approached each other, one navigating the intervening space without wrinkle while the other led disorder across the room.

"Are you, perhaps, the remarkable Slade Lammerock?"

Slade bowed, adopting the rigid posture of one unaccustomed to showing deference. "An admirable deduction, one no doubt assisted by those distasteful rumors."

The newcomer's lips curled involuntarily, flashing bared teeth. "I hate rumor. At best it's an excited guess; at worst, it's a tool for deceit, manipulation, and ruin."

Slade donned a shallow smile, disguising calculated words with a casual inflection. "It's always refreshing to discover a shared opinion—it assures one of the other's intelligence—but I wonder how you learned my name without the help of rumor?"

"I heard your name in passing, an unexpected gift while I commissioned the Thieves' Guild. It was accidental, I'm sure, because she initially denied further information, but I managed to extricate a few details."

"Coaxing free information from the Thieves' Guild? You must possess quite the eloquent tongue. Should I be worried?"

Sinnitar chuckled darkly. "Not tonight. Considering your parentage though, perhaps I should exercise caution as well. Adopted or not, immigrant or not, you are Cain Lammerock's son."

The back of Slade's head prickled. "You're remarkably acquainted with my life, and I don't even know your name. Was your acquaintance so well informed?"

"Sinnitar Muntalabac, and no, I simply made a deduction. Lammerock is hardly a Descendant name, and Cain looks as much an immigrant as I look a native." Sinnitar indicated his charcoal-dark skin, which swirled with red dots that formed complex patterns and teased the mind into imagining horrors: here a grinning skull, there a tortured body. "It is curious that Cain took your mother's name though." While subtle, Sinnitar's tone betrayed a predatory enjoyment at holding information about Slade.

"I'm afraid that's a story for another time; if I'm not mistaken, there's a purpose to this conversation." Slade gestured to the side, leading away from Tasha, Feylin, and particularly his mother. "Perhaps you can elaborate on your objective here?"

"Not yet, I think. There's little wisdom in regaling strangers with secrets." Sinnitar commandeered the lead, looming over Slade for the split second of passing.

'So his objective is sensitive but of what sort? The details suggest criminal, but I can't affirmatively link his visiting the Thieves' Guild with his objective here.' Outwardly, Slade adopted subtle annoyance obscured by a perfunctory smile. "I'm hardly a stranger since you stole my story ahead of time. Still, silence is your prerogative, even if I do suspect your purpose concerns me."

"Is that so?"

"Yes. After all, you uncovered my existence while consulting with the Thieves' Guild, implying your project relates to my line of work."

"A random thief mentioning your name does not prove the conversation pertained to you or your occupation. It does beg the question why the Thieves' Guild knows you?"

"Over the years I've developed a modest reputation, in certain circles, for acquiring valuable objects." Slade donned a conceited smirk. "This reached Carr'Selain, who thought to acquire my services. I agreed to negotiate, and you can imagine what followed."

"It seems foolhardy to admit ties with the Thieves' Guild."

"The Thieves' Guild is little short of legalized crime; they provide important services to the Empire, as such Cardolyn Tyier considers them a secondary issue." Slade opened his arms, encompassing the room. "Everyone's either employing their services or attempting to ingratiate themselves with Carr'Selain. Those who don't are morality bound idiots." His amused scorn brought a reflective curl to Sinnitar's lips.

"It's comforting to know I'm surrounded by such open-minded individuals, and it certainly encourages me that my prospects won't arouse your misplaced indignation." Sinnitar casually brushed a preoccupied waiter from his path.

"Does this mean you're prepared to reveal what's tempted you to the Empire?"

"Not yet. I'm still taking your measure."

'Ah, it does concern me. How though? Am I the method to the prize or is he merely paying a courtesy call?' Outwardly, Slade soured his expression. "I see.

Am I a dancing bear then? Destined to prance around in bright silks, balancing atop balls and serving drinks until I earn your confidence?"

Sinnitar's amiable exterior thinned. "Of course not. I'm simply assessing your character. If our dialogue bores you, bear with me; I may extend a proposition at its end."

'Good, he wants whatever it is badly enough to placate me… Something feels off though; this isn't just caution it's … hunger?' "Well, now I'm intrigued. Ask me whatever you like; I promise to answer truthfully."

Triumph flickered in Sinnitar's yellow eyes. "You'll have to forgive me if I abuse your generosity."

"By all means."

"How obedient are the members of your operation?"

"What makes you think I have an operation?"

"Even if you supplied Carr'Selain by yourself, you couldn't control this city alone. So, how many unfortunates have you ensnared? What crimes, what cruelties, are they capable of? How much ink would they pour over their souls for you? What of the other Thearcs? Do they participate?"

"Unless I'm mistaken, you're roundabouts asking what crimes I'm willing to have committed." Without braking pace, Slade lifted a decanter of icy blue wine from a passing servant and then snatched two glasses from the next unoccupied table. Still moving, he filled both glasses and handed the first to Sinnitar before downing his and immediately refilling it.

Sinnitar set his glass aside, watching Slade drink. "Maybe so, but their capacity for evil does interest me."

"Evil seems a strong word."

"But it is appropriate if I'm asking what extremes you're prepared to cross."

"My people are perfectly able to bloody their hands, if that's what you're asking."

"Murder is hardly an extreme; to breathe is to have incentive to kill. The horror develops when unmerited cruelty is employed, or someone discovers a talent for strange and ingenious death."

"A dangerous question to answer; I can't say whether you want honorable thieves or soulless mercenaries." Slade considered for a moment, then presented a smirk. "I've not had occasion to … request my personnel to trespass on moral indignation. And with that said, perhaps we should reconvene elsewhere."

"That's probably wise." Sinnitar redirected Slade toward the back wall. "As for your answer, you won't wriggle free. Tell me, what's your view on the Empire blockading eastern slave nations?"

"I can't say I'm terribly distressed. National policy rarely concerns me, and I've not dabbled in that particular industry—always considered it an inefficient source of labor."

Being circular, the ballroom couldn't claim a back wall. The closest substitute stood just beyond the northern staircase, a line of frosted glass doors that opened to an outside balcony.

"Inefficient, perhaps. But humans also make poor slaves; they're short-lived and they're fragile. In contrast, the Weshac require neither clothing nor shelter and have proven domesticable if caught young enough. The Lynn are tireless and the Ie'Dara immortal."

Slade paused at the foot of the staircase, looking around with amused disbelief. "Are you suggesting we reestablish slavery and invade the Ie'Dara without provocation?"

"Yes. But first I'd resolve the idiotic human wars."

"Enslaving the Ie'Dara would only engender *Enecki's* wroth, risking our abandonment." Slade resumed his ascent as Sinnitar brushed past, replacing disbelieving laughter with faint concern. "In his absence, the other gods would descend. Religious turmoil would ensue, inevitably spawning violence if not outright war."

"And through that crucible people might finally abandon religion and dedicate all that wasted potential to advancing human industry."

"Maybe so, but the inner conflict would expose the Empire to all the wolves lurking and waiting for opportunity, maybe induce them to conspire. Cardolyn Tyier, for all his divine power, cannot guard every border nor influence every battle."

"Do you have so little faith in your soldiers?"

"Generally, no." His neck prickling at the prospect of touching anything Sinnitar touched, Slade exited through a different door and glanced skyward, hoping to see the moon or at least the stars. To his discomfort, clouds shrouded *Sarah'Venn* in a dark dress. "In fact, I've great regard for the Imperial Army, but they can only achieve so much while devastated by inner strife."

"Why so concerned, aren't you indifferent to national policy? I think the ruination of this Empire worries you less than the inconvenience to your operation." His eyes gleamed. "Then again perhaps you simply fear for your peons?"

'Ah, he wants to leverage my ducklings against me.' "I'm sorry to say my associates are all replaceable."

"A practical approach."

"Quite. What's that charming phrase farmers have? Never name a pig destined for the slaughterhouse?"

Sinnitar laughed. "Let's see how far that practicality stretches; if I requested information, what would your response be?"

Slade leaned against the balustrade with carefully tailored interest. "What type of information?"

"Details you might hear on the street: where funds are being allocated, what section of wall is slated for repair, which public official is moving to his summer house."

'He's establishing spies? Interesting.' "I believe I'd react quite practically then. It sounds like perfectly harmless curiosity after all."

"Yes, perfectly harmless curiosity. I'll inform my associates you're open to negotiations."

'If not for himself, then who? A Kalvonder? No, probably one of the Arch-Dukes? Sinnitar doesn't feel like Southern Darkness.' "At risk of coming across like a desperate vendor, is there anything you're curious about? I've uncovered quite a few secrets and, depending on your ambitions, several could prove useful. The location to Cardolyn Tyier's weapon vaults perhaps?"

"Intriguing but I've no army to outfit."

Slade flicked his wrist and a keyring appeared around his finger. "How about a key to the Western Tower of Sorcery?"

"Wizardry offers me nothing."

"Well then, can I rouse your interest for the latest schematics produced by Imperial engineers? Or perhaps who's in line for succession? What about the secret behind the schism of the paladin orders?"

"I've no interest in stolen schematics, Cardolyn Tyier will live for another thousand years, and I already know about the Rock of Kuthyrion."

'Ah, he's with the New Order.' "It seems there's nothing I can offer you. Pity. I suppose we should revisit those prying enquiries of yours."

"That would be unnecessary; you've satisfied my curiosity and the game's starting to irritate me. When I visited the Thieves' Guild, your name emerged because the subject referenced Tellor."

"Ah, of course. Please continue."

"I wanted to acquire something, but my contact indicated that could prove troublesome. When I inquired, she mentioned your name and warned how you dislike competitors. Understandable since that could endanger your arrangement with Carr'Selain."

"I'm guessing you'd like me to acquire this object in their stead?"

"Precisely."

"I'm intrigued to say the least, but tell me what assurances do I have? Unkind as it is, we're ill-acquainted for blind trust."

"I'm willing to provide your compensation upfront. If that's insufficient, we'll have to let matters go because I refuse to sign a blood-contract."

"It seems we'll have to trust one another." Slade leaned toward Sinnitar. "I'll steal whatever you want."

"Excellent. First a secondary note, I'd like to acquire that lovely young woman who shared your table earlier. I am certain you realize her value, especially in the South."

"I'll take it under consideration; she belongs to a powerful family and one I'd not lightly cross."

"If you do undertake my request, I'm prepared to offer appropriate recompense. That aside, I primarily desire several artifacts—seven black disks fashioned from a strange metal—that some idiot hid within this city's damnable sewer system."

"You're lucky Carr'Selain rejected you; I'm perhaps one of a dozen people who can navigate Tellor's sewers. Entire armies have lost themselves below."

"The true difficulty is the vault itself. There's old magic layered over still older magic down there, protections designed to withstand demons and monsters from the time of *Arthramain Roy'al*."

Slade's eyebrows crept upward. "If these defenses are as robust as you claim, how can you expect me to overcome them?"

Sinnitar smirked. "You're practically drowning in *Kis'Maat's* luck; I've no doubt you'll succeed, and if not ... well risk is what makes yours an exclusive profession."

"What do you intend for these artifacts?"

"My intentions do not concern you."

"Alright, let's discuss my price: a week from now I'll send a list of nonnegotiable names—soldiers in the New Order's army—and you will consign them to me under permanent indentured service. These people will be delivered to a specific location with all their belongings, severance pay, three months rations, and fully equipped for battle. If any man has a family, he may bring them according to his own discretion."

"What makes you think I can acquire New Order soldiers for you."

"Because you know about the Rock of Kuthyrion and the only ones privy to that information are its architects: the New Order, Cardolyn Tyier, and the long dead."

"And you, apparently."

"I know a great many things I'm not supposed to."

"A useful characteristic provided you don't inquire about me. I will deliver whatever names you request."

"And I will be reserved in my choices."

"I cannot help but ask why you need an army?"

"Secrets curry only secrets in return."

"Could I motivate you to reconsider? No? Then farewell, Slade Lammerock." He descended into the mansion gardens and departed through its hedgerows.

For a long time afterwards, Slade stared at the night sky, watching as its clouds retreated without apparent reason. Releasing a long pent-up breath, he closed his eyes and bathed in the moonlight streaming from the heavens. But no peace could last forever. He turned, confronting Tiberius as he stepped from concealment.

After sending Feylin to search for Cain, Tiberius quickly ascended to the highest level and walked its inner railing, scanning all three balconies with growing concern. Eventually he espied Slade following Sinnitar out onto the northern balcony and halted.

'What in the Abyss?' Tiberius strode for the doors only to pause while grabbing the handles. As much as his blood burned to explode through the frosted glass doors and shower the Muntalabac with holy fire, that battle would endanger everyone in a thousand yards. He couldn't charge out recklessly. Taking a deep breath, he forced himself to release the handles and step back to watch.

Unnervingly, Slade and the Muntalabac simply conversed with the boy exuding a comfortable familiarity. But whether he was comfortable with the encounter or the subject, the Muntalabac still coated Slade's skin with a bubbling, tar-like substance.

The taint was invisible to most eyes, but some could feel nausea as it seeped into the body and warped thoughts toward violence or poisoned them with imagined enemies. Usually, these persisted until dawn when *Sammahale* incinerated the taint, leaving skin red and blistering. As Tiberius watched, however, moonlight broke through the clouds and enveloped Slade, gently rinsing the black from his slim frame until he listed against the balustrade with a controlled but clearly relieved sigh.

Again Tiberius caught himself before exiting, tripped up by Slade's naked emotion. Giving a shake of his head though, he set aside the boy's vulnerability and marched out across the balcony. Few dealt with a Muntalabac willingly, and those who did often equaled their malice.

Within a few paces, Slade was already glancing over. He displayed no hint of surprise or reaction at all, letting the tension gradually build as his inscrutable gaze met Tiberius' without apology or even acknowledgement of wrongdoing.

"Some might question your choice of company."

"You among them, it seems. I'm guessing you're well acquainted with my former companion?"

"I have history with the family, not this particular scion; they are … evil people."

"I don't suppose you'd accept ignorance as an excuse?"

Tiberius shook his head. Even if Slade knew nothing about Sinnitar Muntalabac, he would have recognized the creature's malice.

"I thought not." Slade hoisted himself onto the balustrade and sat there swinging his legs. "Well, isn't this a bitter situation, or perhaps bleakly amusing. On the one hand, you've already assigned me guilt; on the other, you're hoping I'll provide an excuse so you can avoid condemning me."

At the boy's tone, a little of Tiberius' control snapped and he stepped forward. "Yes, I'm hoping you have an excuse, but don't treat this like some game."

"The only reason it's not a game is because I've enough respect not to make it one. That aside, does it really matter how I comport myself if I'm the one standing trial?"

Behind Tiberius' back, one hand flexed open and closed while the other gripped it by the wrist. "If I felt you treated the situation with the gravity it deserved, I'd be less inclined to condemn you. That accursed family has blighted this world for millennia, driving entire populations insane, putting butchers on thrones, starting plagues. Thousands have died because of them, including some of my best friends."

"And that's exactly why it doesn't matter what I do. Their sins combined with your justifiable prejudice have rendered my actions inconsequential."

"No! Your actions are not inconsequential." Tiberius grabbed him by the shoulders, giving them a light shake. "You can still explain yourself, tell me what happened, show me you're not–"

Slade gave a shiver, and Tiberius found himself gripping empty space as the boy—now standing atop the railing—looked down. "I wish I could. You see I've been declared guilty by a judge who's desperate to find me innocent, meaning I could spout any excuse and he would believe me." Pivoting, he swung one foot out across the garden before delicately setting it down toe first, walking the balustrade with arms thrown out for balance. "The most outlandish lie or the most honest soul bearing truth, it doesn't matter which I present because they'll have the same result: freedom and temporary trust. So what's the point?"

Tiberius walked alongside the boy, prepared to leap forward in case he slipped. "Truth always has a point."

"It certainly does. Truth is complete absolution; not only would I sleep with a clean conscience, but I could also shuck all responsibility, claim that at least I spoke honestly and it's not my fault if you doubted me." Slade bent forward, placed both hands atop a decorative flowerpot and tipped into a careful handstand before transitioning into a slow cartwheel. "Except, I'm not terribly interested in personal absolution and we both know you would believe me, so we return to square one. Do you see it now? How unimportant I am? Worse yet, do you see how little control you have? No matter what excuse I pick, you'll clap my shoulder, sigh with relief and then walk away cocooned in your faith. Later, doubt will creep in. The power of the Muntalabacs will loom large in your mind and certainty will fail. Before long, we'll find ourselves repeating this very scene." The balustrade broke off for the garden steps and Slade leapt across, pausing on the other side to finally look down at Tiberius again. "Seeing as I'm faced by a pointless choice and you're powerless, I think I'll change the rules."

Tiberius Whyte, Imperial councilor, paladin knight, grand general, and Will of the Emperor felt an old familiar weight settle on his shoulders, one he had not experienced since he found a curious bundle and unwrapped a small, blonde child. Who was this boy to summon a *crossroads* seemingly at will? "What do you have in mid?"

"Removing the complications and giving you the decision."

Unconsciously Tiberius brushed the band of white skin adorning his ring finger, then spoke with studied calm, "Which is?"

Slade grinned and dropped from the balustrade. "You can trust me, Tiberius Whyte." He then strode away, whistling an old tune.

———

Feylin was alone. First Slade, then Tiberius had left, and the final departure was announced when Senna began coughing. She had watched the woman's condition worsen with her own breath rapidly constricting, knowing Cain would leave soon but unwilling to accompany them while Slade remained in danger. Feylin had almost begged Cain to stay or at least return, but she knew what was required and so she invented a smile and waved his uncertainty aside.

Now she sat at a table which overlooked the dance floor, twisting a napkin into tortured knots and worried about leaving for fear of not being found. All the while, she searched for Slade. Tasha too, though less assiduously. Something told her the other woman would be fine.

In the end, she only spotted Slade because he met with the terrifying stranger, his choice spawning a storm of profanity that temerity alone prevented her from saying aloud. Of course Slade would indulge his curiosity. Of course he would flaunt caution.

Feylin shoved her chair back and stormed after her friend, barely making a dozen paces before slowing to an uncertain shuffle. *'What am I doing? I can't even fight, gods bless me. I'm just going to make things worse, give Slade yet another thing to worry about.'* Hugging herself, Feylin turned back and slumped into her seat, submitting to an unpleasant stew of chilling anxiety and gnawing curiosity.

Gradually the fever pitch died down and Feylin's attention wandered, catching on the woman who had entered alongside the stranger. At this distance she looked small, so small in fact that Feylin might have enjoyed a few inches on her. Strange. When the woman entered, she had seemed taller.

As Feylin observed her, a handsome older gentleman approached the woman's table and bowed, introducing himself with all the charm instilled in him since birth. Mid-way through his performance, however, the woman shifted her chair and left him addressing her naked back.

Cheeks reddening, the Thearc drew himself up and said something with profound dignity.

She ignored it.

Steam practically boiling out his ears, the gentleman stormed off and made room for a younger man who presented himself only to meet the same disdain. This pattern repeated itself a third, fourth, and fifth time as three more suitors intruded, continuing until Slade slid into the unoccupied seat, braced his elbows atop the table, and introduced himself with a grin. When she spurned this as well, he simply started a conversation with himself. The resulting impasse only broke when Slade delved into his satchel and, still chatting, withdrew something bright.

If Feylin had blinked, she would have missed it. Slade flicked his wrist and the woman spun, caught the projectile and then slammed it down, pinning his hand to the table. Despite this he continued grinning, making her expression gradually warp to one of slight confusion.

Even from this distance, Feylin discerned his next words. "It appears I've finally caught your attention."

The dagger impaling Slade's hand vanished, and the woman's expression cleared, submitting to the slightest of smiles. "So it would seem."

Rising, Slade offered his arm and she accepted, following him to the dance floor, where they made an almost comical couple. She nearly reached his chin and he barely stood above the average woman. The elegance of their movements, however, went unrivaled, and the difference in ability became obvious when they started a completely different waltz midway through, Slade appearing to make it up as he went.

Throughout all of this they engaged incessantly, Slade speaking with his usual energy while she responded impassively, rarely offering extended sentences but never looking away.

When their last dance ended, Feylin expected Slade to sweep forward and plant a kiss on his partner's cheek or indulge another liberty; instead, he merely leaned forward to whisper something. Afterwards, he returned the woman to her chair, bowed, and left.

Feylin immediately sprang to her feet, charging in pursuit only to realize Slade had already disappeared. Frowning, she strode to the railing and scrutinized the area immediately around his former companion, who was pricking her own thumb with a needle. As Feylin watched, the woman dipped the dull end into the blood and drew on her wrist before gliding toward the ballroom's southern side.

Without really deciding to, Feylin mirrored her progress around the room, walking in time, ascending the opposite staircases, even matching the route the woman of her fascination took between tables. When they neared the farthest extremes, a part of Feylin's mind did warn against continuing, but it was a distant unimportant thought. She was curious. So curious, she did not question when they started walking toward each other or when they met at a pair of double doors and each grabbed a handle, stepping through into a room where dusty sheets covered the furniture.

Stopping at the center, they raised their hands and snapped their fingers, waking bright colorless lights in each corner. Then they glanced at each other and the woman spoke, breaking the trance. "If you're not careful, other less benign powers will start noticing you. Where is your Nissassarin?"

Feylin staggered backward then bolted toward the door, woozy vision and a throbbing head making her zigzag around doubling furniture until she crashed over an armrest onto a long couch. She thrashed amidst the pluming dust, rolled off onto the rug and then scrambled to the door, kicking aside the grasping sheet as she went. Grabbing the handle, she wrenched downward only to find it locked. Breathing hard, she looked back at the woman.

"Answer the question, please."

Feylin pressed back against the door. "I don't know what you're talking about."

"Your kind are not fostered in oblivion and Tiberius knows better than to leave you unguarded, unless he's gone senile." The woman's eyes flashed with an indefinable emotion. "Now, I'll ask again. Where is your Nissassarin?"

As Feylin's thoughts reeled from the woman's knowledge, the quiet thump of footsteps sounded from outside the locked door and the handle jiggled then turned smoothly. "Hello, Seren," Tiberius said, sounding tired as he stepped in beside Feylin. "What brings you to the Empire?"

The woman smirked. "Baby-sitting the Muntalabac; wouldn't want him to aggravate that annoying Emperor of yours."

"In that case, I'll thank you to leave my ward alone." Reaching down, Tiberius grabbed Feylin by the arm and lifted her up, eyes fixed on Seren. "Additionally, if you would be so kind, leave Slade Lammerock out of this. He's the son of a very dear friend."

"Ah yes, a delightful young man." Seren's eyes flashed. "Concerning whom I may or may not socialize with, however, you'd be wise to consider making fewer demands and more requests."

"Maybe so, but she is my ward and I will–" Tiberius broke off, running a hand through his hair. "Very well, do as you see fit." He sighed, finally releasing his grip on Feylin's aching arm. "Sinnitar intends to abscond with the Soul-Iron, doesn't he? Why any man would want a single piece of that gods-dammed spear is beyond me, but to want all seven shards means he intends to combine them."

"Slade told you, did he? Strange, I thought his character was more conservative."

"No, the boy kept your secrets; it's the only possible reason for a Muntalabac to burrow this far into the Empire, let alone this close to the DawnHold. I wonder if your companion realizes how dangerous the spear is."

"He knows alright, he simply doesn't care."

"Sinnitar's insane if he presumes himself strong enough to control it."

"Sinnitar's an arrogant fool, but his allies are less afflicted. He knows the spear is beyond him, just as it was for all his ancestors"—another slight smirk—"to their endless chagrin I'm sure."

"Which leaves only one path. You do realize that if Sinnitar succeeds, and *he* realizes what you're planning, it will shatter his remaining sanity and penetrate the fog surrounding his mind. *He* will come to kill you."

An unspeakable sorrow entered her eyes. "Yes, *he* will. It's the last vestige of his former self. *He* is old and crippled and broken in a thousand ways; *he* teeters on the edge of losing a battle *he's* forgotten to even fight. Once *he* falls, *he* shall finally become his nightmare."

"Yes, *he* teeters on the edge, but *he's* not lost yet; and so long as *he* teeters, there is hope. Don't consign him to his own nightmare."

"It has never been, nor will it ever be my place to safeguard him. It is no one's place. It will never be someone's place."

Tiberius lost his faint stoop, embracing his true intimidating height and a fragment of the age and power so rarely shown. "Be warned then, *he* retains some of *his* old power, and *he* is not wholly without allies."

"Azarael, Richard-Cesar, or someone else. It doesn't matter. They are only minor pieces, you included Tiberius. You are not your father and old are the waking powers, some old enough to have seen the fiery birth of this world."

Tiberius shook his head. "I'll ask you one last time, don't give Sinnitar the spear. It will cause more death in a year than you have in the past century. Should all the Archients in the South awake, every shambling corpse in Paranoia crawl from its grave, and Vanner himself rise again, nothing will match the devastation caused by unleashing that horror."

"Run crying to your demi-god king then, or to the last Dragon Lord; let one of them resolve this dilemma."

"Andeor'Vallen is but a shadow of himself; he has not the will to combat this menace."

Seren shrugged. "Then send the Lammerock boy; he certainly seems capable." Walking to the nearest wall, she laid a hand against its surface and turned back. "Rather amusing isn't it? The evil that you—in your depression and dotage and wounded fear—have been content to let sleep for centuries is about to release the monster you couldn't destroy at the height of your powers." Seren glanced at Feylin, and in her gaze Feylin saw none of the sadness she'd witnessed moments earlier. "Get her a guardian, Tiberius; don't waste your only chance. If she matures, a little of *Arthramain* will return, potentially enough to weather this storm … if only for a little while." Feylin shivered as those beautiful sapphire eyes looked at her, so cold and hard. "The girl just had to be silver; a red would've suited your needs better." Seren tapped the wall, opening a window before transforming into a Raven and flying into the night, cawing once.

29

A Demon Bargain

White and serene amidst the black ocean of the New Order's encampment, Salem's tent swayed in the howling winds, teasing Brimares with exhales of seductive heat. Two messengers loitered behind her, one aggravated and nervous, the other morbidly apathetic, neither able to depart until she entered. The hour felt somewhere near midday, but The North's deluge had stripped the days of focus and progression, reducing the world to a perpetual night only the New Order's commanders could differentiate. The rest of them calculated time by the army's encampments and decamps, for they only traveled at night when *Telacra*, and thus her blessings, attained their peak.

She scraped a lock of soaked and ice-crusted hair from her face and stepped through onto a blanket of glistening fox furs. Heat enfolded her, rapturous and seductive after so long in winter's grasp, but she roused a sliver of Chaos and clenched it, igniting pain through her limbs.

Colored head to foot in lurid reds and grays, the tents walls depicted men on strange, fuming machines wading through corpses and blood, slaughtering soldiers and horses with all manner of bizarre weaponry.

Aside from the walls, a long table occupied the center space, its surface cluttered with a dozen books in myriad languages, maps, a decanter of wine, and a plate mutton. Salem's Raven perched on the chair, staring at her with emerald eyes, but Salem himself seemed absent.

She advanced to the table and overturned one of the books, but its glittering red title defied her comprehension. She laid the book aside and turned her attention to the four large maps, each labeled with a corner of the world. Brimares unrolled The Northern map, moving quickly lest her touch burn the vellum.

"I would appreciate it if you restrained yourself from further impairing my cartography." Brimares stepped from the table, relinquishing the map and turning toward the tent's eastern corner, where Salem reclined against a support beam, his white collar and cuffs unbuttoned. "Leave the books, also; some are not just ancient volumes with a propensity for wisdom, but reservoirs of unaligned, malleable power. I'd rather you not mar them."

She retreated further, ignoring the mockery and silent pressure he exuded. When he received no verbal answer, Salem resumed his seat, caressing the Raven in passing and lifting the wine decanter. He gestured to the plate, pouring himself a glass of burgundy wine. "Take some if you wish."

More concerned with what the dish might contain than his potential ire, Brimares refused him.

He just shrugged and drank. Of all who journeyed with the New Order, Salem alone remained unaffected; his skin glowed with vigor, his eyes danced, and his clothing carried no more blemishes than the day she first saw him.

He finished his wine and beckoned her closer. "It is time we discuss the reason for your summons." She complied, matching his gaze despite her crawling skin. Salem pushed the books and maps aside. "You are here to kill the High-Warden; and should you fail, the length of your individual damnations will be increased threefold. Unfortunately, you will fail, regardless of how much Chaos rampages beneath that pretty face.

"Kheldar Ferain and Kale Saragion believe that if sufficient power is levied against him, the High-Warden will fall. While correct to a degree, they forget the High-Warden has already defeated their goddess and currently defies *Malbreyth*. You and your kin are doomed; though I doubt the latter causes you much heartache."

Brimares waited for him to continue, knowing he hadn't called her just to portend her demise. "However, while I will not facilitate the killing of the High-Warden, I can help you survive."

Salem unearthed a tall, thin book from the table, displacing a cascade of scrolls. "This is a unique book of extraordinary rarity. I collected it from a temple just south of Winter's Gate. The priests had no idea it existed, much less its value." He slid the book toward her, inviting her to examine the leather bindings marred with blood and the inverted pentacle seared onto the cover, its edges seeping corruption and malice so dark they suffocated all hope within her. "This is a *Grimoir*, one of thirteen."

She stared at it, entranced though every nerve screamed to distance herself. Dread welled within her, robbing her of will and pulling her spasming hand forward until her fingers twitched inches over its cover. She tried to retreat, to wrench her hand back, but the *Grimoir* held fast.

"It's terrifying, isn't it, the power it holds over you? And it's a mere book. I show you this to demonstrate how far you have traveled, to show you what realm you have entered by presenting you with one of its scions. Through the crime you committed, you took a place in a different world entirely, a world of legends and souls so heavy the earth cracks beneath their tread. You are wholly unprepared." Salem covered the *Grimoir* with another book, severing its hold.

She stumbled back, snapping her hands against her breast in mingled relief and horror, then her Chaos stirred and with it a searing rage. She forced it to heel but kept it alight, fueling her.

"You begin to realize you swim in an ocean, but that knowledge is as insufficient as you are inadequate. Of all the demons summoned by Kale Saragion, only Kell'MachChain has any comprehension of the war you've entered. That understanding comes from being a pawn in it himself and is thus flawed. If any desire to survive endures in the shriveled husk you call a heart, you need me."

Brimares stared at him, gauging, debating, denying. She did not understand him or his motives, but if he desired to elicit supplications or torment, she would refuse. However, he did speak truth, and she had no other real choice. Brimares nodded once.

"I am glad you've seen reason." Shifting his attention to The Northern map, Salem tapped Antiark. "The New Order intends to sack Antiark, destroying the center of the Northerners' power and belief. Without that center, they will collapse, allowing every god, king, and priest mad with desire to invade and conquer this land. Once The North is laid bare, it will fall. You see, every Northern city has a purpose; Adriat is the City of War; Jellark observes and interacts with those of the Deep North, and Antiark is both the library and, more importantly, the graveyard: the dead and all their wisdom are buried in her foundations. There is a truth; all men born to The North find their way back to The North." Salem smiled. "The North has always relied on the Rhawn and the weather, which have long proven insurmountable barriers, but if one is surpassed, an assault is possible.

"In contrast, the New Order endures by virtue of its clerics, whose prayers blunt the storm and warms our legions. But their gifts are finite, and if this host does not find shelter before they exhaust their reservoirs, we will perish within seconds. Therefore we must conquer Antiark so the Dark Pantheon may enter The North, renewing the New Order and sheltering us from the avenging onslaught."

Salem unrolled another map depicting Antiark. "If Antiark is to fall, the High-Warden cannot intervene. But, contrary to the belief held by Kheldar Ferain and Kale Saragion, we cannot just kill him, he is the only thing preserving us from extinction. The North is furious, desiring only to destroy us in retaliation for cheating it of *Winsyria*. However, the High-Warden cannot allow The North to run rampant lest it eradicate all life not born of *Winsyria*: Human, Borluce, and Weshac. Ironically, we survive because he restricts The North's rage, but suffer because he cannot take The North fully in hand without exposing it to our gods. Thus your task is merely to keep him too occupied to affect this war." Salem released the map of Antiark to reroll itself and withdrew a small amulet bearing the New Order's sigil from his pocket. "Until today, the New Order knew little concerning the High-Warden's capabilities, and it cost them dearly. You see, they've been attempting to forge an alliance with Northern outcasts by using whatever spare power their clerics scrape together; mostly outlawed Weshac and iconoclastic Borluce who tire of their forefather's tolerance for lesser races. I assume the High-Warden discovered our negotiations because he sent us a gift. When the clerics activated this amulet to contact the Borluce today, they unleashed a cataclysmic amount of arctic power and died instantly, their blood frozen solid. Another score collapsed containing the fallout."

Salem closed his fist, crushing the amulet to dust while his other hand withdrew a miniature hourglass of black mahogany with an ivory cap and base connected by four marble pillars. He uncapped the top, poured in the amulet's black dust and recapped it. "Use this when you find yourself short on time. Be cautious though, it contains only a few minutes and will serve you ill against the High-Warden. It will also serve you poorly against your 'friend' when he finds you. What? You didn't know he's following you? Well now you do, and he wants his ring back."

She accepted the hourglass, crushing the urge to recoil from his touch.

"Now, I would be a poor host if I presented but one gift." Reaching into another pocket, he tossed a chain and collar of black iron onto the table with a dull crash, its cruel jaws vacillating open and closed. "I find this particularly effective on dogs; you would be surprised how fast any mongrel can learn something if you beat it. This will aid you in controlling your kin and most other feral creatures."

Brimares retreated, hackles rising with a low hiss as her hand involuntarily brushed her own throat, remembering the molten heat snapping taught around her neck, the serrated teeth digging into her flesh. Then she cursed herself for displaying any vulnerability. "Come now, we both know you lack the fortitude to reject this, for all you remember its taste. In fact, it is because you remember it that you will use this. The Abyss has cleansed you of morality, leaving only the fear and the phantom agonies tormenting your dreams and memories. You are little more than a beast, ruled by base passions and fear. So take this and survive a few hours longer." He flung it across the table to her, and she caught it, fingers wrapping between its teeth.

The artifact lashed out, lacerating her fingers and provoking the Chaos within her to retaliate. It spasmed once and settled, allowing her to cinch it around her arm before facing Salem to await his final gift.

He beckoned her closer with a delicate gesture, commanding with naught but her fear of him, of the Abyss, and the feeling of inevitability. When she arrived, he struck with sudden violence, a black shard of glass appearing in his fingers to gash her cheek and shear off a lock of crimson hair.

She recoiled with a snarl, the plates of her armor flaring open and igniting to molten white. Ignoring her, Salem immersed the hair in the bloodied glass shard, and then discarded the glass to hiss and melt on the floor. "Don't be shy, you've seen fouler things than your own blood." She refused, retreating until her back touched the wall. "You have to accept it, it's part of the contract." Brimares remained put. "Can you even conceive the power I'm offering? Yet you balk like a frightened child, distressed by a menial cut even after centuries in the Abyss." He flung the lock of bloodied hair to thud at her feet, transmuted into pewter. "Take it and stop lying to yourself. You are no less the monster than any other in this encampment, and a great deal more than many."

She was not lying to herself, she just did not trust him and continued staring at the piece, blood pounding in her ears. She also had no choice and eventually took it.

"That's better. What you hold there is a life to take or give. If you take, the price shall fall to you; if you give, you shall damn them with the price. Either way, the choice is yours."

Salem returned to his chair and poured himself another glass of wine, the beverage black where before it had been red. "Of course, my gifts and knowledge come at an equal cost. I want a name, but not your name or any other you can spit out, a particular name, one you will owe me at a time of my choosing. Are we agreed?"

She looked at his gifts: the black collar wrapped around her arm, the hourglass, and the petrified lock of hair. Were they worth a name? Was any name more valuable than her life? She didn't know. It depended on the name, and she thought she knew which one he wanted.

Brimares met his gaze and nodded, the bargain already taking hold. Its bindings were fragile however, diminished by the absence of spoken consent and blood; she could break them if the price proved too heavy, consequences be damned.

"You know that's insufficient. If you will not speak, you must bleed." Salem withdrew a stained long knife and laid it on the table. "Your hand will suffice."

Taking the knife, she set his gifts aside, peeled back her right gauntlet, and slit her palm. Blood welled, corroding the dull blade and turning it red as she tossed it back to the table.

Salem cut his own hand, mixing their blood and ossifying the bindings on her soul. In response, the collar stilled and the hourglass warmed, but the hair remained unchanged.

"Now that's concluded, I will enlighten you..." The light flickered, drawing his gaze to the entrance. "They still vie for ingress, despite every attempt earning only failure and pain. It appears Kheldar desires my attendance at some congregation, but do not concern yourself; he cannot enter, and we have all the time required to answer your desperate, corrosive questions. Currently, your sole hope is the paladin, and if you survive the High-Warden with him intact, you may save The North. That, however, is secondary and of no consequence to you. The New Order's going to capture the paladin before dawn; this is inevitable, but his execution is not. You, in particular, can sway his fate. Ask what he has to offer, when he gives something worth your aid, free him and take him deeper North. Your kin will pursue and torment you for your treason, but what's a little pain to the damned? When they arrive, endure for you are not alone. Your friend nears ever closer, and he is more than sufficient to slaughter your kin. He will demand his ring, and you will bargain. He cannot take it by compulsion, so offer to return it for a life; the High-Warden's perhaps. He will agree, and in so doing, save you." Salem rose, returning the wine glass to the table. "But that concludes my advice, and we have a guest."

Brimares moved aside, clamping the pewter hair and hourglass to her breast as the tent flap burst open, admitting a rush of frozen air and a lieutenant.

Salem bowed, gesturing at the decanter. "How may I serve the New Order?"

The lieutenant, whip clasped before him in a taut loop, declined. "Kheldar Ferain requests your presence to discuss the paladin. I am to escort you"—he glanced at Brimares, unconcealed loathing blazing through his eye-slits—"and the demoness to the training grounds."

"Very well, let's not delay; I'm certain a solitary paladin poses immense threat to our endeavor." Salem gathered a pack from beside the table and tossed it to Brimares. "Use this for your gifts; the armor won't damage it."

Thus finished, Salem exited into The North's vindictive cold, unmolested by the plummet in temperature.

Brimares followed, stuffing the hourglass and hair into the pack but leaving the collar on her arm. The instant she stepped outside, the cold tore through her armor, stripping her of warmth and stabbing pain through her limbs. She grimaced, hacking as the frigid air scoured her throat and lungs, and slogged after Salem, forging through the snow while he strolled upon it. The lieutenant followed effortlessly in her path.

A thousand fires burned throughout the camp, spreading light and meager heat to the men trudging around her, their forms distorted beneath heaped ice. Corpses sprawled between the tents, divested of anything valuable and discarded by the convicts the New Order had pressganged. Even the elite soldiers couldn't escape the elements, their numerous privileges powerless before The North's wroth.

A mercenary and convict brawled between two tents to her left, while another man grinned from the shadows behind them, his sable attire marked with a rough skull: a Death Addict. The New Order maintained no compunction about their soldiers' origins, caring only that they killed Northerners. Brimares knew little of Death Addicts, except that acts of killing increasingly empowered and destabilized them, killings that had no relation to *Morgan*. She also knew they had plagued the East for centuries, emerging whenever war brewed or the hours preceding some awful massacre. This incursion marked their first foray into other lands.

Victorious, the convict and Death Addict stripped the mercenary, cementing the truth that whether or not they sacked a city, some would leave this army rich.

Sounds of conflict from ahead redirected her focus and she recognized their destination. The elite gathered here daily to hone skills, soothe boredom, wager, or avenge slurs, but mostly just to maintain heat. The mercenaries and convicts spurned it, contemptuous of the New Order's 'fancy' dueling practices and restrictions. Brimares had watched them often enough, attracted by the training grounds immense fire rather than their skill; she had seen real masters, and in comparison, the best here were brutish, flailing amateurs.

The lieutenant barked a command, clearing their path to reveal two men wrestling in full plate: Kheldar Ferain and the Blond Knight. Salem traversed the spectating soldiers to assume a position at the front while the lieutenant, his task completed, retired on a different obligation. Brimares chose to remain among the ranks, ignoring the hateful glances and sneers.

Kheldar and the Blond Knight crashed together, grappling as the air steamed with their heat. The Blond Knight twisted, attempting to throw

Kheldar, but Kheldar countered, surging in close and driving his knee into the Blond Knight's stomach. The Blond Knight buckled, Kheldar falling on top of him, arm pressed against his throat. The Blond Knight panted for a moment and then surrendered. Kheldar Ferain shoved off and strode toward Salem, hailing someone from the crowd.

The New Order's commanders followed suit, emerging from the spectators to congregate around Salem: Sorran and Eredar together, their strides imperious with fury and lust; Kadrin stalked a few steps behind and Viral scurried anxiously from the opposite side, eyes fixed on Kheldar. The Blond Knight rose, swiped the mud and snow from his armor, and approached with a contemptuous sneer. Kell'MachChain arrived last, Cellar'Veer and the lesser demons lingering just outside the conference.

A group of New Order soldiers approached, leading a stallion bearing a man with two glass arrows protruding from his back.

Kheldar Ferain took the stallion's reins and dragged it into the circle, lips moving in words she could not hear over the deluge. The air surrounding their congregation rippled and the sound faded, leaving Kheldar free to speak. "We are being hunted by two separate forces." He flung the dead man to the ground. "Of the two threats, this is the graver. Our scouts never return to the vanguard alive; they just reappear like this: pierced by two arrows and thrown across their mounts. Viral," Kheldar barked so loud the priest flinched, "I told you to conceal them, why are they still dying?"

Viral stuttered, wringing his hands and staring at the arrows.

Salem crouched beside the corpse, brushing a hand along the shafts, musing, "One arrow to kill, the other to bind." The arrows disintegrated at his touch.

"What do you mean 'bind'?"

"Simple; one arrow kills the man, the other restrains his spirit and thus knowledge. The Ranger-Wardens hunt your scouts and nothing you can concoct, no incantation, armor, or act will stay their hands or betray their location."

"So we are blind and powerless to preserve our scouts? That cannot stand; I will not wander The North ignorant of her legions and movements. You will help Viral resolve this, or I'll put your head on a pike."

"Burn the cadavers and break the arrows, Sir Ferain, and stop dispatching scouts. Also, have your sentries lay down when they watch, otherwise they'll die like your scouts. When you camp, eradicate all shadows and drown the environment in red, anything to reveal their approach. Finally, stop counting the dead, you cannot deter their increase. You have chosen to invade The North; this is the price."

Kheldar Ferain growled and struck the horse's rump, spurring it from the circle. "There's also a paladin tracking us, or so the Dread Lord says, and while I do not trust him implicitly, he has no reason to lie or jeopardize this endeavor. The paladin cannot be ignored, his insignificance aside."

Kadrin spat, eyes igniting with his Shard's resplendence. "We must destroy him!"

"We can't, you fool," Sorran snapped. "If we do, it'll bring Cardolyn Tyier down on our asses. You know he watches his knights."

Kadrin stormed towards Sorran, threads of black fire dancing along his fingers. "We must not fear Cardolyn Tyier! We are the New Order, the rightful paladins; he is a parasite with our name!"

"He's the son of a god! Until the hour of our war against the West rises; we must avoid his notice."

"Let's take the paladin then, extract everything he knows and then make him suffer for his choice of Pantheon!" Eredar licked his lips, eyes alight with imagined agonies.

"Enough," Kheldar interposed, "we cannot risk bringing Cardolyn Tyier into this war. We capture the paladin and restrict his power so he can neither escape nor contact the West. One of us or the demons will have to hunt him; for I will not waste soldiers on this endeavor; we can't spare the fodder."

"Send the demons," Salem advised. "They have a significant reservoir of power and should overcome the paladin with ease."

Kell'MachChain stroked his shaven jaw, unfazed by the bleeding lacerations he opened. "I believe we are the logical choice. We can subjugate the paladin and outpace the derangers with minimal effort. We're also bored and starving from the peace, bickering, and petty criminals of this encampment."

"I am inclined to concur with Salem and Kell'MachChain, any objections?" Kheldar glanced through the company, granting each the opportunity to speak.

Only the Blond Knight accepted.

He stepped forward, stabbing a finger at Kell'MachChain. "Why should we trust demons with this task? You all pounce at the chance for them to die in your stead, but forget they are not beholden to us or our crusade against the abomination that is Cardolyn Tyier! They are a cursed, treacherous race: mortal souls damned to the Abyss for their crimes! Disregard your fear of death, of failure, and ask: Can we trust them?" He dropped his hand and faced Kheldar. "Can you trust them? When rumors abound of paladins forgiving these cursed souls? I do not argue their efficacy or power. I, like all of you, would rather see them die a thousand times over any of us, but I will not stand for folly. I demand caution be measured; these demons need a guide, someone to direct their efforts to our ends and not their own. Give me that responsibility."

Kell'MachChain struck without warning, crushing the Blond Knight's breastplate—despite its prodigious enchantments—and toppling him. The Blond Knight surged back to his feet, lips parting to resume his tirade, but Kell'MachChain spoke, his words shearing through the Blond Knight's, "You don't control us, fool, you didn't summon us. You preach your cause like gospel, but none of you believe it. You 'New Order Lords' are just warmongers, and you will taste the Abyss when you die, branding you what you profess to hate. I intend to enjoy that moment."

Salem interposed, "If I am ever condemned to the Abyss, I'll walk out. Besides, our nameless comrade has just reason for concern and a solution. Let him accompany the demons; I doubt his presence will hinder the endeavor, and even if it does, the demons can resolve the matter."

"Of course we could, but we can't move freely while shackled to a human. Free us of restrictions, let The North burn in our hate!"

"Do not trust them, they were bred in pain. Allow me to kill one, enforce their servility and remind them of their place! Like the she-demon; she serves no purpose in this host."

Salem interposed again, "There is no need for a purge; we are allies and all have parts to play. Furthermore, the she-demon will resist, and how will you guide them while injured, let alone maintain balance between the New Order's lords? You've often warned that Eredar is subservient, his lusts and needs controlling?"

Sorran fixed on Salem with sudden curiosity, but Eredar lunged for the Blond Knight, shoving him. "I won't be insulted! You have no idea what we are, what we are capable of! You should learn to fear us; else, you'll know pain." He shoved off. "I know where you came from, some backwater, rat infested village that's never seen true malignance. You would weep to know of my origin; you and that demon." Eredar flung a hand at Kell'MachChain.

The Blond Knight retaliated, launching Eredar backward before grasping him by the collar and pulling him close.

Salem stepped forward, gesturing mollifyingly. "Come now, there is no need for violence. We are allies! If you fight, you'll disturb Viral and Kadrin."

Kadrin growled. "Do not speak for me, I want no part of these fools."

Kell'MachChain hissed. "You would call me a fool? I, who am centuries old and you scarce decades? Idiot, you will pay in blood for your arrogance."

Brimares scrambled back, half-crouched against the looming fallout and surrounded by her retreating kin. Only Cellar'Veer remained, his maw twitching with excitement and his eyes igniting with Chaos' call. Her own Chaos bayed within her, but she contained it.

Kheldar Ferain finally intervened, striking the embattled men and wrenching them apart. "Enough!"

Kell'MachChain retaliated without thought, scouring furrows in Kheldar Ferain's breastplate with a bestial hand and launching him back. Still snarling, Kell'MachChain stalked after him, Cellar'Veer practically salivating as the fissures in his crimson hide belched steam and molten iron.

Kheldar Ferain surged back to his feet, the night manifesting into a fist over Kell'MachChain's head and slamming down, crushing the demon. Viral, his hands alive with borrowed divinity, advanced to beside Kheldar. Kell'MachChain vaulted to his feet, armor flaring as the Blond Knight half-unsheathed his blade and Sorran and Eredar bared knives.

Salem just laughed, and with it shattered the impending violence.

"What strikes you so funny?" Kell'MachChain demanded, eyes engorged and malefic.

"You bickering children, of course, all striving for dominion without the requisite self-control. I shall resolve this matter; the demons will hunt the paladin, accompanied to preclude deviation, but not by any of you."

"And how do you propose to watch them, Salem?" Kheldar demanded, reluctantly allowing his overwrought presence to subside. The other lords followed suit, with Kell'MachChain and the Blond Knight relenting last.

Salem caressed his Raven. "There is no need to worry, Sir Ferain. If the demons stray from the path you dictate, we will know both their motives and actions. Does this satisfy your concern?"

One by one, the lords accepted.

"Good, I see no further reason for delay. The paladin is still days behind us, and every second precious. Go now, my devils, and collect your prize."

The Raven vaulted from his shoulder and circled the company once. Kell'MachChain glowered at it, trying to pierce its veil without success. After a futile moment, he turned away, an evil mien darkening his features, and sprinted southward. Brimares followed reluctantly, merging with her kin beneath the echo of Salem's laughter. Her Chaos raged within, eager to slaughter the paladin and a part of her shared that desire. Yet she could not. She had to save him.

30

A House Of Thieves

Dieharamon vacated the alley, slippers scraping on the red sand scattered everywhere, and approached the nameless tavern, recognizing it by the profuse smoke, insect lights, and drunken laughter. Its three levels and multiple glass windows conveyed profitability, but its stained walls bespoke unsavory clientele. The corpses tossed outside substantiated the promise of a precarious environment, but he didn't have time to scrounge for safer territory, he had one night to find Dayada Avenar before the Angorat'Wass and the Dread Lord came due. He lengthened his stride, quelling the sensation that he did not belong and clutching his quivering kernel of hope. He needed Dayada Avenar.

Most guilds operated from private abodes throughout Sahdaen, fortified establishments they could defend in case of street wars, but the Thieves' and Assassins' Guilds differed, with the former operating openly from taverns, and the latter generally disturbing only the most auspicious institutions. Still, Dieharamon cringed as he neared the tavern's entrance, gaze darting between the bouncers arrayed to either side of the cloth door. They returned his appraisal, fingers tightening on stone clubs at both the blood splattering his clothes, and the sword he carried, something only the affluent possessed. He slunk to the door, and they admitted him without comment.

Inside the ill-lit common room, seven patrons populated stunted tables of cracked stone encircled by faded mats: two sober and five drunk, three of which were mercenaries by their branded equipment. These mercenaries slumped together atop a central table in a drug-induced coma, their hair absorbing spilled ale and bile while a pickpocket skulked closer, preparing a lure and a glass receptacle to steal the insects from their lamp.

One of the sober patrons occupied the tavern's deepest corner, his surroundings shrouded by uninhabited lamps, and constantly scrutinized by the other patrons. Even the cognizant drunks avoided him, daring only the occasional surreptitious glance to verify his location. The surrounding tables were vacant and unsullied, and a rat that should have died hours ago squirmed before him, skewered on his knife.

Dieharamon instinctively shied from the man, noting the conspicuous twin knives that marked him an assassin of the second tier, though he might belong to the third if the third knife was visible when sheathed.

The other sober patron also fiddled with a knife, twisting it nervously between her hands, as thieves were wont when in the company of assassins. She wore a cloth mask and false auburn hair that further emaciated her lithe build, rendering her anxiety all the more evident and her natural features indistinguishable.

Both inspected him, recognizing a potential client, then resumed their previous activities. He compelled tranquility into his posture and strolled through the clustered tables to kneel opposite the thief, her table's mat retaining a ghost of its previous yellow hue. She continued her inspection throughout, counting his strides, judging the ease of his movements, and ascertaining his temperament until she finally set her knife horizontally between them, just behind a congested lamp. "What is your desire?"

"I'm ... seeking a man named Dayada Avenar. He is a westerner and an influential noble."

She jolted upright. "Why do you seek Dayada Avenar?"

Dieharamon surged forward in response, excitement briefly erasing caution; this woman knew Dayada Avenar well enough to have a vested interest in his safety. He caught her hand, trying to evince as much of his desperation and fear as he could. Before his fingers even tightened, however, the thief whipped a knife from beneath the table and laid it against his throat. He ignored it despite the trickling blood. "Where is he?"

"Why do you need him?"

"I need his help, please."

"And if he does not aid you?" she hissed, almost spitting.

He slumped back, relinquishing her. "I ... will face my damnation alone." Dieharamon forced himself to meet her gaze, knowing his only chance was convincing her he intended Dayada Avenar no harm. If he succeeded in that and rescuing the Avenar, maybe he could devise a means of surviving the Angorat'Wass. Deep within, his hope thrummed a little louder. Maybe he could survive.

After a prolonged interval, the thief clasped his hand with a slow, controlled exhale. "You ask for trust, but are you willing to extend it? Because if you are not, you'll never find Dayada Avenar."

"What do you mean?"

"You must follow me and trust I can help, because I can, just not here, like this. Consider it a test, if you like."

Dieharamon had no choice; he nodded. The thief beckoned him to follow, snatched her insect lantern and strode to a secluded stair. He complied with trepidation, glancing back but failing to ascertain if someone observed them through the haze.

The stairway, stained with drugs and wine, closed around Dieharamon, obliging him to hunch and half-turn to ascend. The thief climbed with ease, her voiceless tread complementing continuous furtive glances both ahead and behind. She trailed one hand along the wall and clutched a knife in the loose apparel of her robes with the other.

She paused at the second-tier landing and peeked around the corners, scanning the floor twice before mounting the final step but never relinquishing the concealed knife. Dieharamon followed, glancing across the secluded room and wealthier patrons. The decorations here were darker, contrasting a clean floor and improved furnishings. Slaves populated the landing, their clothing sheer and bodies unmarked to emphasize their natural beauty.

One approached the thief, indicating a table with a smile of invitation.

"No, thank you; I just need the key to my room."

The slave's smiled degenerated into a lifeless countenance at the thief's decline, but she nodded and tendered the key before departing. The thief spat, "Damn these southerners, they're monsters! Cutting out tongues just so they can't speak, and only the gods know what else."

"Aren't you Avaran? Your skin's dark…"

"Hardly, you have to be raised Avaran; I'm just here because my skin does match the locale." She started up the next flight of stairs. "Speaking of which, how did a Descendant like you end up this far south? Easterners are common enough, but that bastard Cardolyn Tyier keeps his borders, and even if he didn't, there's a war and the Inland Sea to cross."

"I thought we were supposed to remain anonymous for your safety and the guild's?"

A sable rug blanketed the stairs, framed by ceiling-high emerald curtains and infused with incense, subtly forbidding all but the most affluent patrons from ascending. Despite this, the thief advanced with a surer step, emboldened by the seclusion. "Generally, yes, but Dayada Avenar is a special case; there are powerful men invested in his safety. Someone warned the guild to avoid him before he ever arrived, so we keep our distance. Unfortunately, if anything does occur, we will be the first blamed; so we're ensuring nothing does. Now, answer my question."

"I don't know; I was too young to remember." Dieharamon had no intention of revealing his name; it would be best for everyone involved if he and Dayada Avenar could escape Upper-Sahdaen with none the wiser, the Clergy in particular. "Can you tell me who Dayada Avenar is?"

"What? You don't know who you're searching for? That's something of an oversight."

"They told me to find him; the whys and hows were never mentioned."

"Well, I'll just say he's real nobility, blood old as dirt with the heritage to prove it. Unfortunately, I don't know where he is; the Librarians don't always share…"

"Librarians?"

"Librarians of Secrets, middle-line brass."

The stairs concluded at a hallway of cloth doors seated in walls painted to resemble wood. The thief strode to the penultimate door on her left, retrieving a carven whorl of bone—her key—from a pocket. She pressed the key into a purse draped from the doorframe and a ripple arched over the cloth with a rush of moist air and the scent of dye, removing whatever enchantment would have rebuked unsolicited entrance.

They entered, the thief restoring the lock before briefly fumbling the insects into another lantern. After that, she hurriedly suspended one from the ceiling and seated the other on a table mounded with paper. The remains of a dinner, a cracked tea mug, and a thin bone gnawed clean lay on the floor beside the doorway. There was no bed, and travel bags lay heaped in a corner, the upper two thrown open in a cascade of contents: various styles of clothes from one, papers, ink, and books from the other. A box of sand, about four feet in width and length and six inches deep, occupied the room's center.

The thief doffed her cloak and mask, dropping the first carelessly and discarding the second to the table with her false hair. Moving economically, she bound her russet hair with a leather string, snatched a mahogany staff about her height from the wall, and approached the sandbox.

She planted the staff in the sand, its length carved with intricate images: men, dragons, lions, and a dozen other beasts both mythical and ordinary. This done, she returned to her bags and shoved the upper two aside, divulging their contents across the floor and opening one of the secondary bags to reveal basic traveling gear. She discarded it with a mutter and grabbed another, smaller, bag, opening it with caution to a flood of aromas: myrrh, cinnamon, spearmint, lavender, and other fragrances all warring within one another, mixing, suppressing, and supplanting in an increasingly complex conglomeration of scents. Unruffled, the thief rifled through its contents, removing an oval platter, then a pair of incense sticks and a belt of numerous pouches. Fastening the belt to her waist, she returned to the sandbox.

Setting the platter beside the sandbox, she ignited the incense sticks and laid them upon it. The scent of bistort and frankincense quickly dominated the room.

Dieharamon suppressed a visceral shudder. "Divination?"

"Yes, this will confirm your trustworthiness and perhaps grant a gleam of your fate. I am no Oracle, foreigner, but I am no charlatan either. If you wish to find Dayada Avenar, you will accept this before I tell you anything."

Dieharamon inched forward, peering over her shoulder. "I thought divination was with cards or glass spheres?"

Taking the staff, she began to stir. "Divination has many forms; some of us see images in the dark, others on card faces or in tea and water. Some query of the stars—sometimes they answer—and some take the answers we seek and write them on paper or ancient sands."

Dieharamon grit his teeth and stepped beside her. "What do I have to do?"

She spat into the sand pool. "Three drops of blood are required to bind the ritual to you. I will be the conduit, but you are the source. You may experience visions, but they are not truth, merely refractions of infinity. Now, add your blood." She tossed him a knife.

He waivered, mind quailing at the prospect of submitting himself to magic. Then, grimacing, he removed his right glove, scored his palm and squeezed blood onto the sand, the three globules forming a perfect triangle.

The fumes of incense thickened, obscuring Dieharamon's vision and dimming his senses. He rubbed his eyes, attempting to clear blurred vision, and slowly, without realizing it, sank to the floor, staring at the sand as its hue changed to the red of bricks. He slouched forward, entranced by its ebbing flow back and forth across the box. The sand assembled into a tower, prompting him to touch it only for it to collapse, leaving his fingers wrinkled and pale with veins swollen blue. He lurched away, falling back onto unchanged hands.

The sands swelled into seven massive dogs running and baying at the heavens, then morphed into a spinning pillar, and then again into Dieharamon as he fled, stumbling and glancing back. His doppelganger sank, scrabbling for purchase as it submerged.

The sands erupted, matching his height before collapsing into an image of war; men slaughtering one another and trampling the dead beneath desperate feet. He saw himself at the epicenter, awash in the dead and butchering the living.

The scene of war unwove and coalesced into the waist high image of a kneeling man, his arms extended to either side by frail chains. For a moment, other men traversed the periphery, one pausing to address the imprisoned man.

Then the sands turned black.

The sands shrieked and swirled, ascending into a towering pillar, its structure different from before. A shape formed and Dieharamon scrambled backward, staring in mounting horror as Sinnitar Muntalabac stepped from the sand. "I believe you owe me something."

Dieharamon continued retreating, his vision plunging into grainy darkness. "I don't have it!"

The Dread Lord advanced, black lines of corruption bleeding into the stone. "Oh, I disagree. The *Pathfinder Shard* no longer resides in the palace, and it cannot linger in the *Lake of Dreams*. The instant you touched it, you bound yourself; thus, you must have it." The Dread Lord extended his hand, the long, claw-like fingers spread wide.

Dread welled within Dieharamon, clutching his throat and suffocating his mind. "I ... I don't have it."

"Where is it?"

Dieharamon curled against the wall, wrapping shuddering arms about his head. "I don't know."

"I suggest you find it." The Dread Lord hurled him through the door in a whoosh of cloth. "You have until dawn, and I warn you, tomorrow will be the last sun Sahdaen sees for a long time." Then the cloth fluttered down and the darkness subsided.

A long time passed before Dieharamon recovered the physical and emotional strength required to stand and shuffle into the room. The thief lay inside, curled into the fetal position and weeping beside a heap of gray sand. Pain lanced through his midsection as he entered, doubling him over for its duration. He clenched his fist and stumbled over to the thief, ignoring the symptoms of deprivation as best he could.

Dieharamon shook her gently but jerked back, hissing at her icy flesh. His faltering touch sent spasms rocking through her form, eliciting a strangled cry from her lips and driving her into a tighter ball. He rushed to set the two lanterns beside her, hoping their light and warmth would ameliorate her condition, and then draped her with the discarded cloak in the absence of a blanket. Then he settled in to wait.

She stirred after a while and climbed tremulously to her knees, wrapping the cloak tighter. Noticing the leftover wine, Dieharamon offered her the goblet and watched her gulp the dregs before releasing it to clatter across the floor.

"What … what was that?"

"I … don't know what happened, but that was Sinnitar Muntalabac." He grimaced, noting her dangerous pallor, and felt her brow, finding it still frigid. "We … we need to get you downstairs; you're too cold. There will be more wine, and more heat."

"No! Not the corridors; they're dark and, and"—she covered her face—"what if *he's* there? Things like him like the dark. We need to stay here, where there's light. They won't come where there's light; we're safe so long as I don't call the sands. Yes, that's how he got in, the sands; if I don't wake them, he can't get in!" Another onslaught of spasms dragged her back to the floor.

Dieharamon ran a hand over his hair. He needed to warm her, and dull her fear, but short of starting a bonfire, he could only think of alcohol. He stood, intending to retrieve stronger liquor, but her hand snapped to his pant leg.

"Don't leave! What if he comes back? I'll be alone with him and the dark. Please."

He caught her shaking hands. "Shh, shh, it's alright. He … won't be coming back, I promise. He … doesn't want you, he … wants me. This was just a warning."

Dieharamon continued murmuring quiet encouragements, doing what little he could to relieve the terror besieging her mind. Eventually he calmed her enough that the spasms faded and her breathing normalized. She still clutched him, however, so he stayed.

After a long, precious hour, she finally pushed away, rubbing her arms against a chill that refused to abate. "What did … he want?"

"Something I don't have but needed to get."

She dared a glance at the sand pile. "The *Pathfinder Shard* thing?"

He nodded.

"Why don't you have it, or at least try and get it?"

"I did have it, but lost it in the *Lake of Dreams*, and I don't know how to retrieve it."

"So he's going to kill you? Gods! What are you doing still here? You need to run!"

"I can't leave. And if I did find it, I wouldn't survive anyway."

"What do you mean?"

"I'm in the next Angorat'Wass."

"But why? Why do you remain for that atrocity?"

"Because I'm Tragnashi. I have no soul, no will but that which is allowed to me." On the verge of a response, she fell silent, stripped of any possible answer. Dieharamon continued, "If I were you, I would forget the Thieves' Guild and run. You haven't seen the worst Sahdaen can offer, let alone Sinnitar. So, for your own sanity, run."

Unable to respond, she could only sit there.

She slowly crawled to her knees, renewing her cloak's embrace. "Alright, I think I can leave now, or at least make it downstairs."

He helped her rise and then escorted her downstairs, passing the strangely empty second floor with a prickle of fear. Reaching the common room, he stopped. Everyone, from the regular Avarans to the guildsmen, had departed, leaving a mess of overturned chairs, cracked tables, broken lanterns, and spilled alcohol.

The thief leaned over his shoulder. "Where are they?"

"Where you should be."

She grabbed his arm. "What's going on?"

Dieharamon slumped against the wall. "I made enemies tonight, and it seems, my time's run out."

The thief retreated up the stairs, a knife hissing from its sheath. "Who?"

"Where is Dayada Avenar?"

She took another step. "You can't reach him!"

"Why not?"

"The Clergy has him!"

"What? How? I saw nothing of that."

"Because all you did was see. Search with something other than your eyes! Dayada Avenar is imprisoned by the Clergy!"

Dieharamon's hope died. "You ... should leave. They'll be here soon."

The woman spared him a final nod and fled, her footsteps disappearing with the clatter of an opening window.

Dieharamon pushed off the wall with an effort, forcing himself to consider his options. He could allow his own capture, thus infiltrating one of their cathedrals, but there was no guarantee it would house Dayada. Or he could resist, slaughter those dispatched to seize him. This would allow him to preserve his weapons, but also ensure an assault upon a cathedral. It was also the path of the Kalvonder. A path he detested, one he had never selected of his own, where the lives of others meant nothing.

Two prelates and a cluster of acolytes entered the tavern, the foremost prelate scanning the overturned tables until he settled upon Dieharamon with a smirk. He strode forward, kicking aside fallen tankards and splashing the various puddles with obnoxious exuberance. "You are desired by the Clergy of *Ashshand* for the unprovoked slaughter of five sworn to his service. We claim you by law, by right, and by justice for hateful murder!"

"And if I do not consent?" He exhaled a ragged breath and tightened his sagging gloves, unable to explain their split seams and ratty exterior. His power welled within him, and he welcomed its fire to drown his fear even as it inflamed it. He had magic. He didn't know what kind, or how, but he had it. It would torment him later, but for now he couldn't risk being taken to the wrong cathedral.

The prelate faltered, shock distorting his features. "Then you will be taken by for—"

Dieharamon erupted forward, the power searing through his throat and limbs as he vaulted a table and slammed the prelate to the ground.

The second prelate stabbed his hand forward, bellowing a command that died on his tongue, falling impotent on the sterilized air. Dieharamon slowed, one hand drawing the pewter sword while the other grasped an immense clay barrel and hurled it at the prelate, crushing him. The barrel shattered, spilling the hard knuckle-sized seeds of some drug.

The acolytes howled, their voices mingling in rage and feigned despair, and charged, bone swords scraping free as they circumvented the impeding furniture. They moved swiftly, fortified by hours of strength cultivation; but to Dieharamon, they resembled men caught in a morass.

He plowed through their front-most ranks and whirled, scattering them like rag dolls and flailing his assailants with an unrelenting succession of blows. The only way he would survive against so many was if he kept them separated and stayed mobile.

One acolyte managed to parry a strike, but his blade snapped beneath the subsequent blow. He reeled back, waving his truncated sword as Dieharamon advanced and kicked his chest, launching him into the wall with lethal force.

Two swords struck Dieharamon in unison, one scouring his side, the other gouging his shoulder. He pivoted, using the momentum to accelerate his blade, and struck wide, shearing through his two attackers and releasing fonts of blood. The remaining acolytes swarmed him in their wake.

Meanwhile, the surviving prelate retreated to a distant corner, tendrils of molten fire growing between his fingertips and expanding in a web. The prelate—a mage—grinned and flicked his hands, sending the net over his acolytes and onto his quarry.

Dieharamon leapt back, slashing the flaming net and shearing it into particles of molten fire. The prelate flicked again, and the drops veered into

Dieharamon, exploding upon contact. He reversed momentum, lunging and slashing at an acolyte's head. The acolyte attempted a parry, but his sword shattered beneath Dieharamon's. Dieharamon pressed his advantage, crushing the acolyte's throat with a punch, desperate to reach the prelate.

Two acolytes thrust at his back in coordinated unison, the first leading the second by a heartbeat. Dieharamon twisted, battering both thrusts aside as his backward momentum propelled him into a wall. The acolytes pursued with a seamless flurry of blows, opening a dozen thin gashes across Dieharamon's chest.

The further acolytes—making it four in total—closed in, another already prancing at his side, dancing in and out. He lunged, impaling the prancing acolyte before diving away from the renewed flurry of slashes and kicking a table into one of his assailant's legs, toppling him. He hit the ground, rose and lunged again, cleaving the fallen acolyte's skull, and earning himself another barrage of minor injuries while stumbling back through a pair of tables.

The final two acolytes, provoked as much by desperation as his imbalance, leapt atop the tables and hacked down at him with two-handed blows. He wove to the left, blocking one blow and kicking the table out from under the offending acolyte into the other table, upending both into a heap. He reversed his momentum, skewering the closest acolyte while grasping the remaining—one-handed—lifting and smashing him on the edge of an upturned table, snapping his spine.

Without pause, Dieharamon spun, jumped onto a table and dove for the prelate just before a concussive blast of air slammed him into the tavern's front wall. He lay there, panting, for eight heartbeats, fighting to stand through his ringing skull.

A tall, Eastern man strode from the kitchen, his form clad in sleek black-plate armor and his fingers spinning a long-handled mace of pure iron: the man Dieharamon had glimpsed a Turning earlier with Dava. A series of three iron lockets dangled from a chain of steel wood on his throat, each split with a rupture down the center and seething black light.

Dieharamon staggered to his feet, lodged his sword in the floor, grabbed one of the stone tables, and hurled it at the newcomer.

The Easterner waved and the table flew astray, but distracted, he failed to see the subsequent clay barrel, brimming with seeds, until it struck him. He reeled, armor flashing emerald as the clay split upon his chest. He swept the pieces aside, caught them up in a grasp of wind, and threw them back at Dieharamon.

Dieharamon dove, ducking behind a table as the fragments and seeds pulverized themselves on its surface. A second later the table lurched, flipping over him and flying to smash against the wall. He scrambled to his feet and lunged through the dust cloud to hack at the Easterner.

The Easterner caught his slash with the mace's haft, parried his thrust and stabbed for his knee, just barely splitting the floor instead as Dieharamon lurched back. The Easterner pursued, sweeping the mace up and then down. Dieharamon caught its haft in his free hand and stabbed, but the blade scraped harmlessly off the enchanted armor. The Easterner altered his grip and shoved, slamming Dieharamon's stomach with the mace's butt, before flipping his grip again and hammering Dieharamon's chest, flooring him.

The Easterner spun his mace back to his shoulder and strolled away. "I doubt he's still alive but check anyway."

"You should remember who your master is, Renegade!"

The Easterner paused to glance back, his armor unmarred by the blows levied against it. "And you would do well to remember why I bear the title Renegade."

The prelate uttered an incensed squeal and launched his hands forward, flames materializing in his palms. The air between them exploded, hurling him into the southern wall. The Easterner smirked and resumed his departure, the mace once more spinning. Before he took a step, however, flames lanced his back, engulfing and driving him to a knee.

The prelate staggered from the wall's molten ruin. His teeth bared as he intensified the flames roaring from his hands. The Easterner stood slowly, the air visibly consolidating around him as he doffed his coat and draped it over a chair, his armor untouched and gleaming. This contempt further enraged the prelate, who imbued every ounce of strength he possessed into the torrent, feeding the flames until they swelled as wide as his torso. The Easterner waved a hand, and the air crushed the prelate to pulp.

His hand fell, reaching to brush imaginary dust off his coat. "I'm surprised you're alive; hell, you're even standing." He faced Dieharamon, the air whispering off his armor. "Don't try to run, the doors are all closed."

Dieharamon recognized this truth, he could feel the air circling him and the room, almost sentient and entirely unnatural. He started creeping along the wall, raising his sword as a distant hope formed.

"What are you trying?" The air snapped rigid, slamming Dieharamon against the northern wall. "Do you think you have a chance because you've killed a few Avarans? Have you actually seen them? With their dirt and their bones sticking out? It's a wonder they haven't starved into extinction; though

I suppose you get used to even starvation after millennia. The gods should have drowned them upon inception, saved the rest of us the trouble."

Dieharamon desperately fanned the inferno within, fashioning it into strength against the confining wind and restraining it in turn, escalating the pressure.

"Best drop that useless hunk of metal lest I cut off your arm." The sword jostled feebly in Dieharamon's hand, its pommel warming as a muted wind tugged at it. "Not like it's doing you much good with your imbecilic flailing." The wind tightened, constricting ice-cold bonds all across his skin, around his arm in particular.

Dieharamon hissed involuntarily and stoked the power at his core, firing it beyond all previous extents until it felt like he poured the Abyss into his veins. For a moment, it was both elation and agony, then he released the fires and tore free of the wind bonds.

He dropped with a thud and hurled the sword, spinning end over end, at his opponent. The wind instantly amassed before it, and its runes flared in response, but Dieharamon was already running and diving through a cloth-barred window. He hit the ground outside, rolled to his feet and kept sprinting.

The tavern exploded, every orifice screeching with gale-force winds as the Easterner swept out, feet scarcely touching the floor.

Dieharamon bolted down the nearest alley, vaulted, caught the bottom of a ledge and swung onto the balcony, squirreling himself in its shadows. The Easterner appeared a second later, bounding down the alley with a weightless tread, scanning the alcoves and doorways on either side but never looking up, oblivious to Sahdaen's alternate paths. Dieharamon shadowed him from above, stepping lightly from balcony to balcony.

The alley concluded at the bridge's edge in a hundred-foot drop if you were fortunate, or a descent of miles if you were not.

The Easterner halted at the precipice, scanning it with a vexed expression. Dieharamon, meanwhile, dropped down behind him. His landing, however, was not soundless. The Easterner spun, sweeping his right arm out while his left drew a curved knife and thrust.

Dieharamon caught the stabbing arm and rammed close, throwing all his weight against the precariously balanced Easterner. But the Easterner shifted, gliding under his raised arms to step around him and slash his ribs. Dieharamon pivoted instinctively, following as the Easterner slipped around him, but the heel of his foot scraped past the edge as he did so with all of his weight behind it. His arms snapped out, wind-milling, as his weight pulled him back. He barely had time to think as a gauntleted fist clamped onto his collar.

He caught the mailed arm and stabilized, panting over the precipice. The Easterner's face came into focus, reddish hair around a crooked grin. "No easy way out, the Immortal Consort wants you alive."

Dieharamon dragged himself forward, back onto solid footing as the Easterner stepped back, and then immediately slammed his arm sidewise, breaking the Easterner's grip, dropped low and yanked the Easterner's legs out from under him. The man fell hard, crashing against the cobbles as Dieharamon reset his grip and twisted, hurling him off the edge.

The Easterner spun for an instant, arms flailing and fingers spread to marshal the wind. Then he struck some protrusion and ricocheted off into the night.

Dieharamon staggered from the edge and caught himself on a wall, praying to ever-absent Luck that the Easterner died. He knew he could not delay, however, and so compelled his trembling limbs to move, quelling the raging torrent inside with the same breath. Pain seized him in response, grinding down through his muscles and bones until he almost collapsed again. He just grit his teeth and kept moving, diverging only to claim his abandoned possessions.

31

The Winter Court

The Riicann landed in the courtyard of Adriat's Citadel in a spray of fresh snow, jarring the High-Warden from his fatigued half-sleep, and spasming with great, heaving pants. He roused leadenly, cracking the ice layered upon him and retrieving his distant consciousness from his sweeping conflict with *Malbreyth* before dismounting. His feet slid through the snow, descending to the black stone of Adriat and connecting him to the city. She slumbered now, scarred deeply by the New Order's assault, but her rage endured even in sleep. It reflected the wroth that roiled within him: The North's wrath contained lest it spiral beyond control. The city displayed none of this on her exterior. She scaled the Rhawn from the *Annuir'Hyme's* eastern bank, carven purely of the mountains' black stone into a series of slim mesas, each overlooking the previous with a rank of fortified structures. Soldiers patrolled the exterior and unlit citadel walls, but the fields beyond glowed with violet light, illuminated by natural stone furrows, which in turn revealed the sprawling marsh of half-frozen corpses. Much of the city was unlit, for most of Adriat's population consisted of The North's militia soldiers, and the majority of those had pursed the New Order.

The Citadel doors slipped open, painting a sliver of snow and the Riicann gold with light and emitting a lone deranger. The High-Warden bowed a weary greeting and climbed the Citadel stairs with a laborious tread, struggling to remain upright beneath the War God's assault. "I need to converse with Lord Adriat immediately. Please request she bring her key to the Mirror Hall."

"Of course, sir." The deranger returned his bow and then led him inside to an entrance hall ringed in three tiers of looming balconies. Sentries patrolled them, just visible between stone crenellations and suspended casks of oil. Each of the halls various doors, fashioned more of iron and stone than wood, sat in deep embrasures with arrow and spear slits. The tiled floor sounded hollow beneath his strides, promising retaliation on any invader to breach the Citadel. Finally, shadows lingered despite the light, awaiting only Lord Adriat's command to dowse all illumination and cast the Citadel into an obscurity no spell could pierce.

He began his ascent, unfazed by the people slipping silently through the hallways about their obligations with murderous eyes whether they were soldier or servant: there was little difference between the two in Adriat.

He climbed the Citadel's third tower and entered its unassuming door. The guards spared him a glance and a reverential bow before resuming their vigil as he strode to a thin marble stair leading up.

He emerged onto a cracked roof and gazed about it, noting the empty archway at its center and the circle of white stone, all untouched by the ice of millennia. Unbidden, the wind swelled around him, granting images of the New Order, of its tattered sigils on worn lances and debilitated soldiers shuffling past corpses almost lost in the ice as sergeants and lieutenants rode past, whips flaying blood from any exposed skin.

Its warlords rode at the head, and behind them, the demons brought to kill him. He knew Kell'MachChain and Cellar'Veer, but the third greater demon, a woman, escaped his knowledge. Yet none of them concerned him; it was the man dressed in white that concerned him. He appeared human and ungifted but traversed The North without misery, a feat even Northerners could not achieve.

The High-Warden relinquished his grip on the wind, shifting his gaze to the battlefield, which persisted despite their best efforts. A malignant flock of carrion birds presided upon it with jealous hostility, assaulting anyone that approached and preying upon their own kin. Something had corrupted them against their purpose, converting them against *Morgan* so that instead of escorting dead souls to his realm, they stole them.

Descending from the north, a squirrel-like creature alighted on the ramparts beside his hand, its white coat accented by a black streak. It paused, standing on its hind legs to preen and lift its regal head with a flutter of furred wings, making its readiness for worship well known.

He smiled and offered his palm to the annuri queen, marked thus by her crowning streak, who delicately accepted. He raised her to eye level, stroking her breast. "You are a pretty thing, aren't you?" She purred contentedly and returned his affections with a nuzzle. "You shouldn't be here, beautiful. Take your family and climb the mountains where no one can reach you before it all turns foul." He threw her to the wind, earning an affronted squeak before she flew toward the Rhawn.

A muffled profanity attracted his attention to the roof's entrance where Lord Adriat, dressed in thick breeches, a long cotton nightgown, and an unbound oudakc, emerged barefoot onto the ice. He bowed in greeting, but she did not return it, burdened by exhaustion, failure, and a new inflamed scar between her eyes. "What do you want that you must wake me at *this* hour?"

"I apologize, Lord Adriat, but I need to speak with the Winter Queen."

"The Winter Queen? What do you need from her?"

"Aid. The Winter Queen may lack any semblance of human compassion, but she presides over the *Court* which is still beholden to *Winsyria*."

"Alright, but it's your risk; you'll need the other key."

"I have it." He retrieved a pale stone key from beneath his collar, it's flowing chain of water gleaming on his fingers. "I've always had it."

She accepted it, the artifact dwarfing her delicate hands as she turned it over. "Strange that *Winsyria* would entrust this to you and not another lord, though I suppose their movements are restricted." She returned the key, her vexation usurped by simple exhaustion. "Its song compliments mine."

They approached the arch, Lord Adriat extricating a glass key on a string of dark wood from her belt. "I must admit ignorance on how to proceed; neither I nor my predecessor ever found the door."

"Did you ever search beneath moonlight or through a mirror?" He regarded the clouded heavens, a silver sheen illuminating his irises.

"Even if moonlight is the secret, we have none." She fell silent, gaze rising as the storm ebbed, its clouds pulled aside as if by an unseen hand.

"There is always moonlight to be found in The North, Lord Adriat."

An evanescent door thinner than a knife's edge materialized in the arch, first ethereal then hardening to frosted glass. Two keyholes waited at its center, one shadowed and the other brilliant.

He inserted the Stone Key with a click of two locks, one retracting and the other fastening. Spectral lines faded onto the door's visage, assembling into a mural of interwoven vines: Fae script, though no living human could recognize it, let alone decipher its patterns.

Lord Adriat inserted her key and the lines solidified, rising from the surface as she retreated.

He nodded his gratitude and submerged his hands into the glass to grasp and heave the doors open with a grunt, unleashing a cascade of unearthly light and music. He threw his arms wide, forbidding them passage. They quailed in response and receded, loath to heed a mortal's command but unable to defy his will.

He dropped his arms. "Please ensure no one ascends the tower, Lord Adriat, lest the *Court* entrap them."

"I will stand this vigil and hope the *Court* does not exact too severe a price. Go and let the grace bestowed upon you suffice against the *Winter Court*."

"I will not come to harm. Even if they possessed the means to threaten me, they dare not challenge *Winsyria*."

"I know, but the *Winter Court* is still treacherous, lacking the compassion of The North's other scions."

"I have no alternative, Lord Adriat." He paused upon the threshold. "One final word: hunt the crows, they are not of *Morgan*." Then he stepped into the *Winter Court*. For an instant, there was only light, then gradually the Mirror Hall enveloped him.

He appeared beneath the arch of a vast ice mirror as the *Winter Court* expanded into being around him. It started with the floor, its crystalline surface reflecting an altogether different image from the barren hall. Pillars followed, rising in streams of ice and glass to their zenith where lines flared across an unseen roof, giving shape to the white void. Massive ceiling-high mirrors formed between the pillars, colored—as was everything in the hall—a white-cobalt and frosted.

The hall's far end materialized next, assembling a dais, chairs, and glass instruments. Tables, burdened with a feast as long as the hall, ensued. Finally, came a throne of black rock, implanted at the head of a high stair with a secondary throne of glass set below.

He advanced, scanning the floor's reflection: a thousand Fae dancers, their bodies those of porcelain dolls with rosy cheeks and mouths painted in eternal smiles, swirled underfoot, dancing with infinite grace and subtle cruelty. Servants attired in black suits swept through them, bearing laden trays and avoiding him, just as the dancers did, as if he stood in their midst.

In the mirrors to his left he saw more dancers, but they differed from those abiding underfoot, resembling swirling water or agonizingly carved statues of ice. The music was unchanged, but they obeyed a divergent cadence, more ecstatic, though their features expressed no joy. Suddenly he glimpsed someone moving in contrast to the whirling dancers and music, at odds with the *Winter Court's* rhythm. He paused, searching until he understood the discordance: the Jester.

The Jester slipped from the dancers, his tunic checkered black and white and adorned with a dozen tinkling bells of blue glass. He pranced closer and bowed low, his four-tailed cap brushing the floor so its bells chimed, then he straightened—his face garishly painted in the style of his tunic, except for the mouth which bore a grin of blue stretching from ear to ear—and presented him with a harp and painted sphere, his bells tinkling ceaselessly.

The High-Warden declined with a raised hand, the dancers growing frantic to keep pace with music that no human could replicate. Again the Jester presented him with the harp and sphere, pushing them through the mirror. When he refused again, the Jester shrugged, releasing the harp and sphere to crumble into white dust.

Prancing back, the Jester spun, threw his hand high to pirouette and drop in a curtsey, one hand offering a card, the other a coin.

"I advise selecting one, High-Warden; if you persist, he will continue presenting you with your species' inane contrivances."

The High-Warden faced his addresser—an armored Fae thrice the height of a normal man with frosted hair raked back from a colorless, aquiline visage—and bowed. "Lord Knight, I come seeking an audience with the Winter Queen."

"She will receive you when the *Court* enters session. Until then, I'm sure you'll find our company enlightening."

"I shall respect her preferences if I can, but time presses me."

"The Winter Queen heeds not those who worship, love, and revere her. She will arrive in her own time, and you will abide by it, High-Warden." He departed, striding to his place beneath the elevated thrones as the porcelain dancers in the floor's reflection scurried to evade his path. One child failed to escape him and was batted aside by a callous hand, shattering upon the floor without causing so much as a stumble in the ballet.

The High-Warden reverted his attention to the Jester, only to find him likewise departed. He searched for the Jester in the left-hand mirrors and floor without success, then turned his gaze to the right-hand mirrors.

Flesh and blood dancers, their pallid skin glinting with speckled starlight, cavorted in unreserved, frenzied violence, their masks constantly altering between delicate artworks and the visages of horrific beasts. The men wore cloaks, bear hide breeches and metallic bands around their arms, waist, and thighs; and the women wore revealing dresses of black swan feathers. Their faces and bodies carried a thousand swirls of cobalt ink that covered everything but their bare feet.

The Jester reappeared, leaning against the right-hand mirror with a wide grin. Intrigued, the High-Warden followed, only for the Jester to dance back, batting his eyelashes and clapping his hands to his face with an expression of wonder and embarrassment. He indicated the Winter Knight with a long, painted finger and shook his head with an expression of disgust.

"Why do you caution me against the Winter Knight?"

The Jester shrugged and covered his face as if weeping.

"Can you not speak? I remember you singing before."

The Jester dropped his hands, miming laughter before tumbling back and blowing him a kiss.

"The Winter Queen took his voice years ago, punishment for some insult all of us have forgotten. She still remembers, I suppose, and lacks the kindness to return it. Sadly, I too am diminished."

"Then I am grieved, Lady Artist." He bowed in greeting, the gesture warmed by a smile.

She curtseyed in return, her body swirling to the necessary motions. She was ephemeral, her figure crafted of a pale white radiance and snow around a core of silhouettes. Like everything else here, she was beautiful, but unlike many, a gentleness clung to her, bespeaking frailty only a fool would believe.

"How goes your painting and music? I hope the pleasure you find in both is undiminished."

"Both are successful, and I believe we shall be graced with a piece of the latter tonight—oh, no."

He followed her gaze to where shards of the porcelain doll emerged from the floor, assembling into a semblance of the destroyed child and scampering to her side. "He destroyed another. Why cannot he be cautious of them? They are so fragile."

"He has grown stronger, is this due to the Winter Queen's favor or his natural power?"

She knelt, stroking the dolls cheeks with a whisper of music. It collapsed, divested of whatever grace granted it life. "Both. The *Winter Court* grows restless beneath the Winter Queen, and she ever listens to his council more. He no longer stands at her feet but whispers at her ear of conquest and war."

"*Winsyria* would never sanction conflict."

"No, but the Winter Knight's arrogance mounts; he speaks of Lord *Ever-Winter's* debility and challenges the Rhawn openly so all may see them restrain their fury. He claims they fear him, and if they fear him, so must Lord *Ever-Winter*. I do not believe him capable of initiating war with the other courts; the Winter Queen harbors only contempt for them. I fear that he will guide her eye inward to the *Winter Court* itself."

"If she trespasses, she will be cast down, and a new queen crowned."

"How can she be dethroned if Lord *Ever-Winter* does not see her trespass? He has vanished beyond the Keeper's sight, High-Warden, all but abandoning The North. However, I do not believe you came to hear of the *Winter Court*. You bear a purpose in your stride, and though diminished, I offer my aid."

A knocking sound restored their attention to the Jester, who now supported an ancient creature bedecked in roots, moss, leaves, and small animals. Ice-crusted eyes stared from beneath bushy brows and wrinkled green skin as it hunched atop a high staff, its body covered in rich white fur.

The Artist slipped forward. "Here, let me help. Did he get lost again?"

The Jester nodded, motioning at the mass of dancers and easing his companion into her grip before retreating to wrap himself in a shivering embrace and stare wide-eyed.

She frowned, pulling the strange Fae gently through the mirror. "Something frightened him?"

He nodded, indicating the creature and himself, and mimed speech while shaking his head.

"He won't speak to you?"

The Jester nodded again and rejoined the dancers.

She lowered the creature to a seat against the mirror, smiling as its unseeing eyes fastened on her and its quivering hand stroked her cheek. "It gladdens me that you are well, Keeper. But what caused your terror."

Without responding, the Keeper tugged on the High-Warden's pant leg, prompting him to kneel.

"I hope you fare well, Lord Keeper."

The Keeper's hand clutched his hand, feeble despite immortality. "I fare as well as age and my fading memories permit. However, I still recollect much, and more beyond the surface of my consciousness. This past Turning an old memory revisited me, a dark memory of fear and old, long-harbored dread.

"I remembered the Hate-Monger who breached The North through ancient power and corrupted grace, his body stolen from his descendants. He warped those he pretended to serve, granting them immortality, true immortality, and bent their legions to his command. And for this, they paid their gift of redemption."

"You speak of the Andaar Kings. What brought their memory to darken you?"

"Yes, the Mad Kings you call them, and the Hate-Monger. They ruled for twelve generations, a hundred years for each until the treachery of sons usurped them, but all were the Hate-Monger's dogs."

"Do not dwell on these memories, Lord Keeper. Taelan Muntalabac is long past."

The Keeper's hands tightened. "That is a treacherous name, do not utter it aloud. We can never say what dread wraiths might stir when they hear their name spoken. Darkness needs no summons to reenter the Mortal Kingdoms."

"I apologize, Lord Keeper. I am strained; else my tongue would not have slipped. Please, confide what awoke your memories."

"I perceived a darkening, then a moment of absolute dread. It lay there over what it had corrupted, so prevalent it was like a river over the stone. I felt another scream, another corruption and darkening and more dread. I felt the dying of souls, and felt mortal horror stir in my evergreen heart: a new Dread Lord comes."

The High-Warden exhaled slowly, assailed by fear, dread and grim acceptance in equal measure.

The Artist glanced between them, her natural luminescence fading with that name's utterance. "High-Warden, what nightmare has the Keeper remembered? The name ... eludes me?"

He shook his head, denying her both an answer and the ensuing fear. The time to reawaken the *Winter Court* to the Dread Lords would come, but not yet. "I came to the *Winter Court* with a purpose, Lady Artist, and while I hope for your aid, I cannot share it just yet; not until we stand before the entire *Winter Court*. The Queen, in particular, lest she become jealous." He bowed. "I will await the *Court's* convening."

They reciprocated the gesture, but before he could depart, the Keeper touched his knee. "The Star wishes to converse with you, and in light of current events, I believe his wisdom would be invaluable."

The Artist straightened as well, offering a final warning, "Beware the Fae tonight; the *Court's* agitation excites them, and they know not whether to fear or scheme."

"They fear me more than they desire mischief. It is the Winter Queen that concerns me. I need much from her, and she has never been generous."

Though he displayed little sign of it, *Malbreyth's* ceaseless assault taxed him, exhausting his spirit to such extents his mind lagged and his muscles fatigued. He could not restrain the god forever, and *Malbreyth* knew this, expanding the breadth of his assault and stretching him ever thinner. Thus the High-Warden sought respite in solitude and The North. It could not restore him, but it would ease his strain.

Solitude, however, proved hard to find. With the *Winter Court's* assembly nearing, myriad new entities made their appearance. Some resembled beasts, others trees, roots, or flowers. A few wore the faces of men, but all were simultaneously beautiful and terrible, their sundry forms forever surrounded by ephemeral grace. Most arrived and remained in silence, but a few prattled and laughed, delighting in their façades of childlike caprice.

The High-Warden ignored them as best he could and ultimately found his desired respite in a distant corner. He knelt, cloaking himself in forbiddance before laying his palms and brow upon the reflective wall. The image within changed, the *Winter Court* replaced by a vision of The North from the heavens. He released his taut muscles with a sigh and settled against the mirror, releasing his essence to wander The North uninhibited, cherishing it for he knew it could not last. The final price neared.

He submerged into half-sleep, drawing strength from The North just as it borrowed strength from him, and there arrayed his entirety against *Malbreyth*, repelling him a few precious inches. The War God redoubled his assault, seeking to dislodge him with an abrupt surge, but he held fast. *Malbreyth* persisted, pressing ever harder.

Sometime later, a hand broke his slumber, returning him to the present hour and events. He sat on the floor, his skin coated in snow while a frosted pattern of vines and blooms expanded from him in flowing, serpentine motions.

The Artist released her grip. "High-Warden, the Winter Queen calls the *Winter Court* to session."

"Does she wear a fair face tonight?" he asked, discarding all semblance of exhaustion and standing.

"No, she does not. The Winter Crones have arrived, though she dispatched no invitation."

"The Crones awakening is fortunate; they never respected the *Winter Court*, no matter they are part of it. Who else?"

"It is best to list who has not: the *Annuir'Hyme*, obviously, the Rhawn, for they still maintain the *Barrier*, and the North Star, who has disdained us for millennia."

"I believe that will also change, Lady Artist, the Keeper implied that the North Star might attend tonight."

The *Winter Court* high Fae filled the central walkway, their reflections different in each mirror, though their postures remained unchanged. The Winter Queen sat upon the glass throne, a child possessed of stark white hair that fell over albino skin and a frail body to stream down the steps. She wore a dress but scorned slippers and stared at him with calculating eyes, her irises white and extensive. Upon her brow sat a coronet of ice and glass just small enough for her head, and her voice, when she spoke, was mature, sultry even, "Welcome, High-Warden, to the *Winter Court*. Centuries have passed since last you graced us with your presence. What prompts this honor?"

"I seek aid, Majesty." He advanced to the throne, bowed once and knelt, head held aloft. Ire flashed across her features, and she leaned forward, minute silver trinkets glittering in her hair. He continued, "You cannot be blind to the assault upon The North."

"Have you not dealt with the gods? Aligned the Rhawn against them? What further need do you have of the *Winter Court?*"

"This threat is unresolved, Majesty. The *Barrier* is not one wall against every god; no *Barrier* can stand against the joint might of twelve ascended gods. The *Barrier* is layered, twelve layers for twelve gods. Each layer will recognize and react to only one god."

"Very well, your logic is imperfect but valid. And yet this is your *Burden*, your task to uphold! Why should we assume it? Are you inadequate for the task?"

"I was not granted the power to war with a full Pantheon of gods, Majesty. Were *Winsyria* here, I would suffer no need of your aid, but his departure leaves me lessened. Yes, I need your aid, for I cannot accomplish this task alone without paying a price I am unwilling to countenance."

"It is strange to find a mortal who shuns power with one breath and demands more with the next." The Winter Knight interjected. "Mortals are not worthy of our sacrifice; you will receive no power from us."

"I do not request power, Lord Knight, only for aid. The *Winter Court* will assume the same burden as the Rhawn, and I will pay the price demanded for your succor. This is the bargain, and remember, you are beholden to guard The North."

"We are not. You are." The Winter Knight stepped from the dais with a spiteful gesture. "This is your *Burden*, High-Warden. If you cannot hold it, surrender your post to a worthier servant."

"You will not find a man, entity, or Faerie more fit to bear the mantle of High-Warden, Lord Knight. The day another more suited to my station arrives, I will surrender this *Burden* without sorrow. However, that day is not yet come; you lack the wisdom to judge men or recognize their value."

"I am the Winter Knight; I see the hearts of men behind their veils of flesh and lies. No man can disguise his truth, and I deem you unworthy."

The High-Warden laughed, a harsh, bestial laugh. "Do not challenge me, Lord Knight, you will not like the results." Standing, he brushed past the Winter Knight, cloaking himself in arrogance as armor against their unspoken hauteur and a reminder to them of what he was. Ascending the dais, he stopped before the Winter Queen as their brows aligned.

She lounged back, opening a silver box of hard candies and dropping one onto her tongue before offering him the box. When he declined, she shrugged and closed the lid.

"Do you accept, Majesty?"

"I do not know. I am unaccustomed to making rash decisions. You must allow me a moment to consider the alternatives."

He retreated a step, conceding her the moment but leaving one foot upon the dais. As he did so, he glimpsed the left-hand mirrors where an ancient woman sat in the Winter Queen's place. The same crown rested on her brow, and she wore the same dress but faded. She also clutched a ragged doll and addressed the empty space he should have inhabited. Intrigued, he looked right where she became a tall, beautiful woman with harsh features and Fey complexion. Across her knees, she held a scepter, and upon her brow a full crown. As he watched, that Winter Queen returned his gaze and smiled.

The child queen spat the candy into her hand and held it to the light, revealing a glittering pearl. "I believe a test is required to verify your suitability, High-Warden."

"Is *Winsyria*'s selection insufficient? And what happens if I lose? Will you refuse your aid even as the entire Pantheon swallows us?"

"If you fail, I am certain a more fitting High-Warden will assume the *Burden*. Besides, the *Winter Court* will always guard The North; we simply seek to ascertain your continued efficacy. If you wish, consider this your price."

"Why do you insist on playing games, Majesty? The North could burn while you sit here frolicking."

"If you are truly the High-Warden, there is no danger. Now, shall we begin or will you doubt fate?"

"Fate is unreliable, and I distrust its munificence. However"—he stepped from the dais with a slight obeisance—"you leave only one choice; what is your challenge?"

She clapped, giggling childishly. "Wonderful! But a challenge needs competition."

Unprompted, the Winter Knight stepped forward and knelt at her side, earning a stroke of her hand.

"You, my Knight, have long desired to prove yourself the High-Warden's superior. Here is your chance. If successful, you shall bear both the mantle of Winter Knight and High-Warden."

"I will not fail, Majesty." Rising, he assumed his place beside the High-Warden.

The Winter Queen pulled herself to the throne's edge, granting the High-Warden a conciliatory smile. "We do not doubt Lord *Ever-Winter*. No entity, spirit, or creature can see every divergence. We believe Lord *Ever-Winter* selected you under the belief that no war impended; but war is indeed upon us, and we must adapt. Your suitability for conflict on this scale is ambiguous, the Winter Knight's is not."

"I have neither time nor interest in your excuses, Majesty; state your challenge."

"My you are rude, but I shall pardon it on account of your current inconvenience. The three Crones shall each allot a test to you, the rules of which I shall dictate. The *Winter Court* will assume the War God's onslaught, as is our duty. Now, let's commence."

The Winter Queen beckoned, and three Crones emerged from the massed Fae. One crawled, her eyes sharp. One stood tall and unseeing with an arm upon the shoulders of the last. The third walked with a staff, her stride neither swift nor frail, her eyes neither bright nor dull, and possessed no mouth.

Supported by her voiceless sister, the blind Crone shuffled to the fore. "We three offer tests three to achieve failure or success."

The first Crone crawled past her. "Thrice ye will ask, and thrice thy wish granted."

The final Crone raised an azure hand. "Let he who would challenge and usurp, step forward and ask the first question of three."

"I am the Challenger, what is my test."

The first Crone took his arm in a gnarled grip. "From you I take the blessings of the *Winter Court*." He jerked to break loose, but her grip held; and no matter his struggles, he could not shift her an inch. His armor and adornments fell with a clatter, leaving only the blade. The Crone relinquished her grip, and the Winter Knight recoiled with a snarl. "The price is paid, Challenger." Without pause, she turned and beckoned the High-Warden closer. He obeyed and knelt. "You are the Challenged; he who would defend his honor and his people, regardless of those who doubt him."

"Yes, Grandmother. What is the price asked of me?"

She laid her hand on his breast. "From you we will take as we have taken: your blessings." Her hand tightened, dragging him forward and to his hands. He gasped, shuddering with the sudden absence and acclimating to the void. When the shock diminished, he pushed himself upright, not entirely bereft of his abilities, merely those granted the High-Warden. With his blessings, however, they also removed his *Burden*, and the weight of *Malbreyth's* assault.

The first Crone retreated, giving way to the second who stumbled for want of guidance. She beckoned the Winter Knight and grasped his hands when he warily acceded. "Just as something is taken so must it be given. Choose now a gift, Challenger, and know that with your blessings, so were your obligations taken. You are both no more and no less than you are. Choose with forethought–"

"I demand what was taken: restore our blessings!"

"It is not for you to choose the gift of the Challenged. You have chosen power, and the power taken shall be restored." Unbidden, his armor and adornments flew back to him, cladding his form in his former glory. The Crone relinquished her grip and faced the High-Warden, taking his hands in turn. "To you, Challenged, a gift is also due. Choose with forethought and caution for not every gift is blessed and not every loss a tragedy."

"I choose an ally."

"That is permitted but not an ally greater than us, and only if they accept."

"I choose the Artist."

The Crone released his hands and faced the crowd, which parted as the Artist, appearing frail in their towering midst, stepped from their ranks to halt before the Crones.

"Artist, do you consent to ally yourself with Lord *Ever-Winter's* High-Warden? Aiding him without treachery, divergence, or ulterior motivation."

"Yes."

"Then take your place. Grace and Power shall yours remain to aid in this endeavor."

The Artist bowed and moved to the High-Warden's side.

The final Crone stepped forward, her eyes washed of color and enveloped in white haze. Scarce above a whisper, her voice echoed in their thoughts. *"The first test is a test of finding, of seeking, of searching. A riddle fresh, unheard and unsolved must you find before the hour tolls morning. Search in the realms of mortals, seek through the pathways of mirrors and find in the end a riddle. All pathways are open."*

The roots, vines, and insects covering the Crones' tattered dresses scurried in a sudden excitement, almost seeming to echo the Crones as they spoke once in unison, "Begin."

32

The Pieces Of A Riddle

The Winter Knight threw his head back with a peal of artificial laughter and submerged into the floor. Unperturbed, the High-Warden waited for his laughter to subside before addressing the Artist, "Where might we find a riddle?"

"I fear to hazard a guess, High-Warden; riddles are not my forte."

"Then let us ask the Jester from where he contrives his riddles and jests." They strode to the right-hand mirrors and searched the dancers within for signs of the Jester or any the Winter Knight's snares. When he saw neither, the High-Warden stepped through the mirror and entered the vast hall beyond, its floor of earth and rooted vines shifting under his tread. The dancers stilled in their frantic ballet, the world falling dark as the faces on either side turned black, depriving the room of their light. The column-like trees groaned and cracked, spilling vestigial light that elevated the hall into twilight.

The dancers shifted focus to the High-Warden, masks of shadow materializing over their features. "Are these your children, Lady Artist?"

"No, they are lesser Faerie, those unsuited to inhabit the *Winter Court*. If I diminish further, I will join them."

They proceeded through the silent ranks, some translucent and flickering in the light. "Why do they watch us?"

"Because we interest them. They are Fae and adore mischief."

"Can you find the Jester?"

"With luck, perhaps. He is unpredictable and wanders many of the *Court's* forgotten halls." She glanced to the left and chuckled. "But of course, one does not find the Jester..."

The Jester skipped from the crowd, his bells tinkling and his grin widening. Arriving beside them, he batted his eyelashes and pressed his lips coquettishly. He maintained this posture briefly, then faced the Artist with a tinkling invitation to speak.

"Jester, we need your aid. The Winter Queen has ordained a competition between the High-Warden and Winter Knight."

The Jester frowned, the painted grin converting into a leer. With a snap of his wrist and a crack, he opened a paper fan and batted it before his face. An image in green ink churned across its surface, composing first an image describing the Crones then of the Jester.

"He knows and comes to aid us, Lady Artist, but my knowledge concerning the *Winter Court* is incomplete; you will have to translate his meaning into our destination."

The Jester returned their attention to his fan, where the image changed, becoming a forest, a leopard, and then a leaf with a woman formed of veins. The leaf shrunk, revealing more leaves, each with their own inhabitant. The image continued to expand until the leaves merged, becoming the forest from earlier. The image warped again, cycling through leopard, leaf, and tree.

The Jester stroked the fan's ribs, changing the ink to azure, and then exhaled on its surface as the tree attained its peak, casting the leaves into whirling flight. They spun about one another and condensed, assembling into the shape of an ancient, bearded man who separated into three smaller versions of himself.

The three images pirouetted and spun closer, their hands rising and falling in unison as they met and merged into a lake. The water pulsed, its center throbbing with the fan's vibrations as nonsensical words streamed from its edge and off the fan.

The Jester erased those images with a sweep of his hand, leaving behind four crimson streaks. The lines contracted and swirled, forming a braided rope that twisted itself into a noose. Ink poured up from the fan's grip, painting a hanged man who reached up and shook the noose. The rope broke and he fell, holding the rope at a distance but refusing to relinquish it. The rope threads merged further, losing all distinction until they became a serpent that coiled in his grip and struck. The man reeled, clutching his face and throwing the serpent away as it struck again. He fell to his knees and blindly groped for, caught, and yanked the serpent back to him, biting off its head.

The image stilled for a moment, then the man stood, growing in stature and discarding the serpent. Armor and a colossal sword materialized on his body as he threw his arms wide and screamed. The ink faded entirely after that.

"That showed where we must go, who we must find," the Artist said softly, "and a warning concerning the Winter Knight."

"Agreed, but do you know the where and the who we must find?"

"The destination I know, but who they were I do not; though I suspect those three men are the Riddle."

"So we collect the pieces first and bring them to the Crones unheard."

"Yes, unless the Crones intend some trickery, which I doubt: they differ from most Fae. And we should hurry, our journey lengthens and we cannot keep the Winter Knight's pace. Jester, you have our gratitude; I hope your voice is restored." Bowing, she departed for the opposite mirrors to await the High-Warden.

"For all things, there is a price. Since you cannot speak, you cannot tell me yours, and I can only pay what I deem right. Take this but use it with caution lest it be taken again." He pressed his forefinger to the hollow of the Jester's throat, summoning a grace that had existed in his blood since birth.

A grimace contorted the Jester's features and he hacked, the fan tumbling from his fingers with a clatter. The grimace converted into an expression of disbelief as he slowly touched his throat, then his cracked lips, parting them to speak.

"Ask not where or how, Jester, just use the gift as you will."

"Comprehension is beyond my intellect now, High-Warden; I lack all knowledge of precedence for this act. I thank you and deem this a bargain well struck; though I required no payment." The Jester bowed and retreated.

The High-Warden rejoined the Artist before the line of far mirrors, which remained blackened. "Are they closed?"

"Yes, by the Winter Knight's artifice."

"Is there another path, or must we counteract his interference?"

"There are alternatives but none so easy to traverse. Unfortunately, restoring the mirror is arduous."

"I doubt we have the time to spare."

She nodded and started toward the throne. The Winter Queen ignored them, too absorbed with crooning to her doll to notice them as they circumvented the throne and came to an arching frame of unreflective glass. The glass rippled at their approach, issuing a faint melody as the Artist stepped closer and delicately bit her fingertips, spilling violet blood. She began to paint and sing, except her voice lacked any resemblance to human words and sounds, echoing only the music of the Fae with all its attendant beauty, age and sorrow.

Her work gradually took the shape of a door reminiscent of, but ultimately divorced from, the artistry surrounding them. "This leads to the Lynn roads, High-Warden, from before they migrated to your Mortal Kingdoms."

He hesitated. "Are you sure you know these paths, Lady Artist? They derive from the Before Age."

"As much as any living being can."

Nodding but still cautious, he touched the violet door and stepped through into pathways older than mortality.

They entered a hub-chamber of swirling, delicate blue stone, wrought not by hand and implement but by the song of the Lynn. Multiple tunnels branched from the chamber, their circular entrances alight with natural radiance and fashioned of pale, living metal.

"I do not know how to navigate this world."

"And I cannot teach it; the method must be learned alone, else the knowledge evaporates."

"Then let us begin."

The Artist advanced confidently but her memory appeared to fail her, often compelling them to retrace their steps only to find the pathways and their numbers altered. Despite this, she never wavered. It was as if the path dictated itself to her on whim. But a road that rearranged itself at will, even with a fixed destination, was too fickle a prospect for the surety she displayed. She would have had to imagine the path in its entirety in the moment of their departure, designing something that felt right rather than for expedience. Her route's inconsistency bespoke her nature as a Fae more than aught else.

"How many roads did you envision to our destination?"

"Nine, but there may be more as one needs to imagine both the destination and the route."

Refocusing on their surroundings, the High-Warden closed his eyes and brushed the walls. They shifted under his fingers, prickling them with energy as his hands roved over the undulations, curves, niches and imperfections. Every contact with one of the many images imprinted their truth on his mind, reminding him of memories from before his time as High-Warden. "Artist, do you remember what drove the Lynn from this Song-world?"

"No one in the *Winter Court* does, and I, in particular, am ignorant of mortal history. Some do harbor suspicions, however."

"What does the North Star believe? What could drive the Lynn out of a world they fashioned?" Though he asked this, an inkling already stirred in the back of his mind.

"I do not know his thoughts beyond the belief something did uproot them. I know he's explored here personally."

The High-Warden slowed, mind darkening; stars only graced the mortal or godly kingdoms for one reason: a Dread Lord.

They reached their destination shortly thereafter, a circular antechamber with four pathways and a single, gently luminescent pillar. He broached its burgundy light with unvoiced relief and a wary glance at the surrounding dark. The Artist approached the pillar, crouched and stroked it with a low, rhythmic susurration.

"Are you certain these pathways sleep and harbor nothing evil?"

"They cannot wake until a Lynn sings, and I have never encountered any sign of evil in all my centuries walking these halls." She glanced over with a flick of black eyes. "Why?"

The exit manifested behind him and he extended a hand to help her rise. "I advise you to avoid these Song-Worlds in the future, Lady Artist."

"Why? Whatever evil exiled the Lynn should be centuries gone."

"No, merely hiding." He nudged her through the newly formed glass arch and followed, sliding the door closed as he went. In closing, the glass merged with the stone obelisk that housed it, transforming to mimic its texture and hues, but not before an engorged rat scuttled across the pathways within and sat before the door, observing their departure with venomous eyes.

Outside of the Song-World, they found themselves in a jungle, replete with massive vines, trees, leaves that dwarfed even him, prevalent birdsong, and a network of rivers that coursed up through and around the canopy.

"Where are we?"

"One of the *Winter Court's* infrequently used halls; I cannot recall its purpose, and it never had a name." She moved to an immense fallen leaf, the sole one on the ground, and flipped it, revealing an intricate woman shaped by its veins.

The woman blinked repeatedly. "Oh, I fell again, didn't I?"

"I'm afraid so," the Artist replied.

"Oh, it's going to take forever to climb up again. They make me so mad with all their pushing and shoving." The leaf woman shook her fist at the sky, prompting a tinkling laugh.

The Artist set her against a trunk. "If you're unoccupied, could you help us find something?"

"Oh, I do love finding things but not right now, I need a way back up first."

The High-Warden interceded. "We're searching for a riddle, my lady, one unheard. If you help us, we can easily return you."

The leaf woman tittered and blushed. "Oh stop, I am no lady!" She continued giggling. "Besides, there've been no riddles here for an Age. But oh, I remember them, and the Riddle Makers too; they all loved to talk."

"You are certain they're all gone?" the Artist asked.

"Oh, not certain, I just haven't seen any in an awful long time. You can try asking them; they're always scampering about and exploring. Some have been outside! Can you believe it? And oh, the stories they tell!"

"Who are they, my lady?"

"Oh, you must be one of those knights they talk about! So gallant and polite." The leaf woman sighed and swayed side to side. "I do apologize, my mind wanders so often I wonder what's wrong with my head that it doesn't stay put. What I mean is–"

"She means us." Two men and a woman appeared behind them, assembling themselves into the general shape of humans with debris and streams of water.

The woman leaned on her right companion's shoulder, giggling. "He's much smaller outside."

"This is not the time for jests or humor; how may we serve, High-Warden?"

"I need a riddle, unheard and unuttered. It is in three parts and scattered throughout this hall."

"It has been many years since we encountered a riddle, and you desire a new, untouched riddle. Some still wander this hall, those that went lost when the Riddle Makers left. But I cannot say if they've been heard."

"Can you search without exposing yourselves to it?"

"Yes. We shall collect our family and begin our search." They scattered, abandoning the debris that gave them shape.

He addressed the leaf again, "Thank you, my lady."

She tittered and blushed again, covering her face. "You are too gracious. I did nothing; they did everything. Oh, I cannot wait to tell my sisters I met the High-Warden!" Laughing, she spun and sprinted into the leaf, shrinking until she vanished.

"I think it best to await their return, but what should we do concerning our pact with the sprite?"

"She seems to have lost interest, so we won't press the issue."

"A more pressing matter is the approaching storm."

"Then I believe it wise to escape ground level before it arrives."

"Won't the wind dismount you?"

"No, it is otherwise occupied searching for a riddle."

"True, but the rain is a peril, for it will soon drown this hall."

He nodded and moved to an upward flowing stream, immersed his hand then a foot, and rode it upward. The Artist followed suit.

The rain began in large globules, pounding the earth and trees like hammer strikes, so loud each sounded like a crack of lightning. The various sprites danced in their abodes, voices rising in joyful song above the storm yet symphonized with the rain.

The High-Warden, his clothing soaked, dismounted at the top and reclined against the trunk, using it as a shield. He slid to a seat, closing his eyes and marrying his thoughts to the world's rhythm. "Please keep watch, Lady Artist. This is a rare moment of respite and I would like to rest. *Jaidar* fills the skies, impatient for his chance, and I am tired."

"Then rest, but first, may I ask why you selected me? There are others who are older and stronger, who know and remember so much more than I."

"Because for all their power, knowledge, age, and memories they are not my allies."

He woke to the silence of the storm's wake, and found himself staring at the sky's reflection in the water below. This new lake churned with aquatic creatures, many dwarfing him, while the lowest tree branches drooped with the birds stalking them.

"Are you seeking, hunting for your friend?"

His gaze shifted to the tree, scouring its bark until the speaker emerged in the shape of a man.

"No, though I would like to know her whereabouts."

The Bark Man's skin swirled, reforming until he resembled the Artist. "Is this who you look, seek, hunt for?"

"Yes."

"I cannot, will not tell, confide her location, whereabouts. I can, will show, guide you to her location, person." The Bark Man vaulted to the branch on an adjacent tree, his features and bark altering to mimic his new perch. The High-Warden followed, grasping an ancillary branch for stability.

"What called her away?"

"The wind drew, summoned her away, distant, High-Warden. A riddle they, it found, discovered in the forest jungle. And a riddle is what you, search, yearn for?"

"How far did they take her? And what name do you wear?"

The Bark Man spun mid-leap, face changing again. "I wear, use no name because I wear, carry many faces, each with their own name, though many forgotten, memory lost. Call me what you will, desire. In relation to distance, duration between you and her, she is near. The wind called her, carried her away, distant—not long past."

They found her in a clearing, crouched atop a branch just over the water. She spared him a glance as he landed on an adjacent branch and followed her gaze to where the wind ran in circles upon the water, footprints always falling in the same place. An overturned boat sailed beneath the water, its keel breaking the surface and causing ripples as if in motion, but the boat itself never progressed. Its captain propelled the boat with a rod, and whenever he pushed down, its base pierced the surface.

"That is the first piece of our riddle."

"Thank you, Lady Artist." He dove, and there was an instant of obscurity, then pressure and a current downward, then he broke the opposite surface.

Oblivious, the boat slid past, allowing him to grasp its side and haul himself aboard, though not a sound betrayed his actions. The sudden rocking pulled the boatman around, his mouth opening in an unheard cry. The High-Warden scrambled upright, raising his hands in a pacifying gesture. The Riddle calmed, though he still shifted to the boat's stern to continue his vigil.

The Riddle was ancient, with white hair streaked by dark gray and soaked robes that swayed over bare, black-veined feet. Insect swarms filled the air, their evanescent carapaces illuminating the jungle's half-shadow to reveal sable water and a mangrove of crimson trees. The High-Warden glanced over the side, glimpsing both his reflection and the Artist observing him from the other side.

The boat rocked suddenly, restoring his attention to the Riddle who had resumed paddling. He considered briefly, then tore a strip from his shirt, stepped behind the Riddle and bound his mouth. The Riddle dropped his pole and thrashed with wrinkled fists but failed to resist and soon found himself bound. The High-Warden issued a voiceless apology, lifted the Riddle onto his shoulder and dove back into the water.

As before, there was blindness and pressure, which now pulled upward, then he surfaced, oriented himself and swam toward the Artist as the winds giggled. Reaching the tree, he climbed to the Artist and leaned the Riddle against the trunk, discovering in the process that the Riddle had changed; its eyes were vibrant, hair full and dark, and wrinkles erased.

He returned to the water's edge. "Be careful the gag does not slip; I do not know whether he will speak as a man or a riddle, and I must find the second part."

"How? You do not know its location, and what of the third?"

"He is the third, see how his features change? He's becoming younger, and I know where the others are. The third piece, this boatman, resided on the lake's opposite side. So the first piece will be on this side, and the second somewhere in between, each representing a chapter in the story."

She nodded her comprehension, and he dove again. As before, there was blindness and pressure but also the current from below. He caught a submerged root to resist its pull and the whole lake seemed to inhale. A pulse stirred the water, erasing the downward current and giving shape to vague objects: houses crafted of gray lines, dim lights on poles, and spectral men and women mid-motion as they proceeded about various duties, their eyes beaming sharp white light.

The High-Warden released his grip and sank to a path of cobbled stones worn thin from centuries. A girl child, her hair flowing behind her, sprinted past, her movements languorous in the water. He touched her arm and she spun, becoming solid as the light blinked out from her eyes. Her head swung left and right, searching as she fumbled a hand toward him. He guided it to his face, allowing the delicate fingers to trace his eyes, mouth, nose, and stop in his beard.

"Who are you?"

He tried to answer, but his voice issued no sound.

"You're a stranger here! Where are you from?" He shook his head and pulled her fingers to his mouth. "You cannot speak or sing? You must be from above. Or below. That is sad. What do you want? Do you need a voice, a song?" He shook his head. "You've come searching, haven't you?" He nodded. "But for what?" He took her other hand and pressed it to his chest, and then to hers. "You come searching for yourself?" He placed her hand upon his brow and shook his head. "For someone else?" He nodded. "Someone not of here?" He nodded again. She hesitated, looking out across the still expanding city. "I know who you want, the Drowning Man. But it is forbidden."

The High-Warden kissed her hands, pleading.

"... I can lead you, but you must promise not to harm him; he suffers enough." He kissed her brow and released her hands. Her solidness faded, and the light reignited in her eyes.

She guided him through the undulating streets of her submerged city to its outskirts, where she halted upon the last cobble. He stopped beside her, gazing at a struggling man and recognizing the Riddle. It thrashed in the bindings of a thin cord that chained it to the earth, its mouth agape as it drowned, powerless to either see or feel the cord, and thus condemned to forever struggle on blindly.

The High-Warden stepped off the cobbles and his world plunged into darkness followed by an immense pressure. He recoiled into the city and the light returned, bringing with it comprehension of the Riddle's fate. He calmed himself with a breath and stepped into the void. The weight slammed down again, but he ignored it and advanced, hand extended in fumbling search. No contact answered him, nothing but the mud underfoot. The pressure's direction shifted, slamming from his left and staggering him a step. He ground his feet down into the mud and slid one forward and to the left. The pressure shifted again, rising from below and lifting him onto his toes. He grasped the water around his feet with a thought and froze it, anchoring himself. The pressure thrashed again, shoving him forward but the ice held, allowing him to advance again. Another step brought his extended hand into contact with the Riddle's shirt, the threadbare fabric collapsing as the Riddle jerked and clutched for him.

He wrapped one protective arm about the Riddle and uprooted the binding snare with the other. The Riddle instantly thrashed in his grip, desperate for release, but he tightened his hold and trudged back to the light.

He emerged beside the girl, her eyes fixed upon him from the cobbles' edge. Unable to speak, he kissed her brow again, trying to impart all his gratitude in that simple gesture. Then he kicked upward, passing through the darkness and pressure to the surface. The Riddle instantly fell limp, its form already shrinking to a child's.

He swam to the Artist and consigned it into her keeping. "Has the wind found the first yet?"

"Yes, it waits only for you."

"Seal his voice, I believe they will wake when complete." He climbed onto the encircling branches and faced the swirling figures pirouetting through the canopy above him. "I am ready."

They giggled and gusted around him, causing the water to thrash. He spun in accord, attention flicking from one to the next. "Show me," he reiterated, and they surged upward as one. He followed, vaulting through the limbs.

They crashed through the canopy moments later and entered the golden light, only there was no sky. A forest ran across the heavens and across the horizons, its canopy facing downward in a wall of green leaves, chittering birds and dragonflies. Despite the light, there was no sun or source he could see in the space separating the sky forest from that which he currently occupied.

The wind circled him, assuming its various shapes. "Where is it?" he asked.

They spun faster, their laughter gone, and all pointed northward with fluttering hands. He pivoted, searching the open horizon for the Riddle, but it stayed hidden. "I see nothing." Their gesture remained fixed, guiding his attention unwaveringly north.

He closed his eyes, calming himself. The branch beneath him shuddered, forcing him to grasp another for balance as a deep rumbling burgeoned in the north. There upon the horizon, gathered a soaring tumult of water. The rumble cracked, and the tsunami crashed forward, cascading across the two canopies as if they were solid, inundating everything. There, riding upon the ceiling, a wooden ship fought its currents.

"Is that it?"

"Yes."

"I'm going to need your help." Giggling, they merged into one and lifted him above the tsunami as the ship neared. His world went dark, the forest, wind and source-less light replaced by a bleak sea caught in the thrall of a storm. He fell and the ship spun, its final mast snapping as he crashed onto its deck.

Spouts of water burst from the deck, forming frantic sailors and a captain battling with the wheel. Lightning flashed, rupturing the ship with a shower of burning wood and debris, leaving a gaping cavity in its belly. A wave swamped the ship's sides, snatching sailors and almost ousting the High-Warden who caught the truncated remains of the mast.

The water sloshed away, and he lurched for the captain's quarters, slamming against the cabin's waterlogged exterior. He groped for the handle, but it defied his efforts to turn, forcing him to snap the lock and kick the door open as the ship pitched. He staggered inside and glimpsed a child curled in the far corner, trapped behind an oak table.

A voice screamed behind him, "What are you doing?" and a sailor rushed in, brandishing a knife. The High-Warden spun, caught his hand and throat and slammed him against the wall, instantly rendering him unconscious. Another jolt struck the ship, pitching it with an ominous crack.

He dropped the unconscious sailor, flung the oak table aside and scooped up the Riddle as a fissure tore through the wood beneath him. There was an instant of pregnant despair and then the ship split.

He staggered to one side of the rupture, wrapping the child tight. "Hold on and take a deep breath."

The child curled against him, inhaling as the water gushed up and the High-Warden dove. The wind could not assist him for these were scripted events. Time would pass and the vessel would return, still fighting with the storm, forever living the same script.

The water engulfed him, almost unbearably hot against his skin, and he spun, kicking downward toward where the canopy must be.

The water darkened, but as he neared, the canopy grew to an emerald brilliance amid its obscurity. The child began struggling, its breath running short. He caught the first branch and pulled himself through, breaking into the jungle with a torrent of water, and swung to the side as the leaves and branches closed to repel the storm.

The child slumped in his grip, falling unconscious but continuing to cough up water.

He settled the child on a branch and tore another strip of cloth to bind his mouth. Then he hoisted the limp Riddle over his shoulder and began his return to the Artist and the *Winter Court*.

33

Shady Dealings Done In Light And Sound

When Tasha saw a friend from home stroll across the ballroom and wave, her heart soared for an instant then constricted. *'What is he doing here? Did something happen? Is everyone okay? Has Carr'Selain changed my instructions?'* Giving herself a pinch, she smoothed her expression and refocused on the conversation, returning just as Slade concluded his usual spirited protestations. "In that case, I'm going to find something to eat. Afterward, I plan to socialize and hear some interesting rumors." *'Don't question me, don't question me, don't—'*

"A moment, my Dear." She froze, his simple words dragging Tasha's heart up through her chest and spitting it out onto her feet. "Those are dangerous waters, should you need my help, do not hesitate to call, be it for a kiss on the cheek or a sword in or at your back."

She managed a cursory wave, almost laughing at herself for the surge of relief she felt. "Yeah whatever; I'll return later."

Rather than seek out her friend, Tasha meandered across the room, pausing at the occasional display and walking through open spaces where he could spot her easily. At the banquet tables, she grabbed a warm plate from the tall glimmering stack and brushed gentle fingers along the porcelain's gilded edge. Next she found a tray, collected her silverware and proceeded to the wine rack.

While thus occupied, a man circled into her periphery and slumped against the banquet table with a yawn. "Hey there."

Repressing all the energetic butterflies sprouting in her stomach, Tasha matched his casual, almost bored delivery. "Hello yourself, Keliss. Long trip?" She slid down the long table, pointing at several display dishes and prompting the idle chefs to dash around their mobile kitchen. One began carving a selection of meats while his companion's hands blurred across a cutting board, mincing scallions, peppers, and garlic. A third prepared a white sauce, her

428

twin set about arranging a fruit plate, and the attending wizard hastened any dish with a prolonged cooking time.

Keliss responded with an uninformative sound, inspecting her with his head—as usual—canted to one side. "Hmm, happy you're not dead."

"Ehh, give it another week; I predicted a short visit and barely touched the guild coffers. I'll be sleeping on the streets soon."

"Considered pocketing any sparklies?" Keliss moved like summer molasses and slid down after Tasha, his brown, heavy lidded eyes tracking the legion of servants ferrying liquor around the room. "Expect everyone will be half drunk by night's end. Should be fairly easy."

"For you maybe. Me? I'm not so sure, something to do with how my instructors almost gave up on me." Across from her a chef dumped the meat into a sizzling pan.

"Suppose so. Here, give these an eyeing, see if one entices you." The man reached pudgy fingers into the deep, inside pocket of his coat, but Tasha quickly stepped on his foot. "Alright, I'll save presents for later."

"I'm not here for baubles. I'm working. Carr'Selain told me to make-nice with Slade Lammerock."

"Ah, there's one pigeon that's turned out more of a hawk. Anyway I can help?"

"Not likely. You'd engage him with your manicured voice and subtle insinuations, and Slade would laugh himself silly as he misused every word and planned a very public embarrassment."

"Don't say that, I'm rather good at those sorts of things."

Tasha snorted. "What is your business in Tellor anyway?"

"With negotiations opened, Slade Lammerock's lapsing into negligence and"—he broke for a yawn—"and Carr'Selain's infesting Tellor with Mice, yours truly among them."

"If our people are getting in, it's because Slade cracked the gates on purpose." Tasha fell silent as the chefs approached to arrange her chosen entrées atop the display case. Watching them garnish each dish with elegant, slightly overdone gestures, her stomach gave an un-ladylike growl and roused a smile from one as he started indicating various choice portions.

Keliss took advantage and unhurriedly offered his tray up alongside hers. "Makes sense. Still a welcome opportunity to expand the family business and acquire friends and property." He gave the chef a sleepy, thankful smile. "Sadly, Father's only assigned me a few errands then expects me back home."

"Of course he's got you on a short leash. I'd be surprised if you haven't already poked your nose into something that doesn't concern you and really shouldn't involve you."

"Hmm, warning me off Slade Lammerock again?"

"Yes, and before you get all hard eyed about it, I'm not telling, merely strenuously advising."

He blinked at her long and slow. "Didn't think you were. Might be overestimating my tendencies to be inept though."

"Pride cometh before the fall." Food in hand Tasha strode toward a secluded table, walking slower despite herself to accommodate Kelliss' lethargic pace.

"Difficult to distinguish between pride and merited confidence. I just want to help if possible."

"I know, but everything is under control or as controlled as can be expected." Reaching the table, Tasha extended her foot and drew out one of its chairs.

"Everything does seem like it's under control. Not yours, but it is under control."

"Yes, and that's creating a delicate balance wherein he's happy and no one's dying, me in particular. If you get involved, that could endanger the 'balance', so the last thing I need is help."

"Everybody needs help with Slade Lammerock, and I can be circumspect." Keliss slid into the seat opposite her and swept dirty hair from his eyes. "The abundance of gruesome folklore suggests he's more dangerous than we anticipated."

"Slade likes to fabricate those when he's bored. The kid verges on being a pathological storyteller." Tasha began cutting into her dinner, perhaps more aggressively than required as already she felt restless energy building, partially dampened by her grumbling stomach. "If you had ten people ask him about his whereabouts the previous day, each would recount a different story."

Yawning, Keliss made a half-hearted wave in her direction. "Rats excel at breaking into fancy houses and leaving with none the wiser. Mice"—he made an even less enthusiastic gesture towards himself—"excel at talking and bargaining with, or deceiving, people like Slade Lammerock."

"Keliss, you're a child in comparison."

He considered her words, then conceded with an uninvolved shrug. "You know best."

"I do, now tell me about everyone back home."

Keliss leaned to the side, resting chin in hand. "Clayen's no longer chasing women, found himself a bright girl, Maeya, and got married. The two remind me a bit of *The Troll and the Fairy*. They seem happy."

She snorted, her muscles relaxing slightly. "What's the running bet?"

"Month. He's genuinely star struck."

"I give the marriage two months, my usual bet."

"Alright." Keliss took out a notebook and made a few careful marks. "How's Laura?"

"Fine, gave birth a few weeks back: a boy with charcoal hair and eyes like sapphires."

"What did she name him?"

"Julius; said it was a kingly name." Patting his exterior pockets absentmindedly, Keliss produced a nondescript packet and a small paper square then rolled himself a leisurely cigarette. "Laura says her boy'll grow up to be a grand general, that he'll have his father pulled apart by horses."

"It would serve him right, leaving her like that." An unasked question fell between them, one side steeping in desperate curiosity while the other waited, unwilling to offer sensitive information. "How are th–"

"They're fine. They miss you, but they're fine. Clayen and Maeya have moved in. Laura stops by when she can."

"Thank you."

"Ehh, you'd knife us if we didn't."

Tasha stacked her plate atop Keliss', shoved the pile toward the center of the table and then distributed her dirty silverware between the appropriate baskets. "What now? Can you stay or must you see to your errands?" Common sense warned he should leave before he encountered Slade and potentially reveal one of her more dangerous secrets. However, loneliness and homesickness argued Keliss could lie better than most. Surely, he could stay a little longer.

The conflict became mute when a chair was dragged across the floor, spun backwards, and Slade dropped into it, his arms resting on the back and his chin falling onto them. "Hello, you must be Tasha's father. I assure you that we continue to behave most incomprehensibly well, with me entertaining no designs upon your daughter's virtue for tonight. Shamefully, I can't promise the same for tomorrow because the future guards its mysteries even against me." Slade tipped forward, scrutinizing the man. "I must say the resemblance is stunning, though it's obvious her beauty springs from her mother's family. You, I assume, gave Tasha her dark, twisted mind and that strange obsession with daisies."

From the height bestowed by his suddenly rigid posture, Keliss scoured Slade with a glance of scarcely concealed disdain. "I don't believe we've been introduced. Who are you and why have you intruded upon our meal?"

"You are correct, we have never been introduced. Furthermore, I doubt we ever will be, for my name belongs to me alone and I forbid anyone else from holding, using, or carrying it. My name is my one unique possession; should another man steal it I would lose what little novelty I possess and became yet another drudge. I would be nameless, heartless, hopeless, and nameless all over again."

Keliss blinked. "Excuse me?"

"His name is Slade Lammerock."

At this Slade froze in the middle of his distraught seesawing, caught while grasping the sides of his chair and leaning back with both legs thrust out to balance his tilted position. Heaving a comically put-upon sigh, he righted himself and performed a seated bow. "The one and only."

"Slade, what are you doing here?" Tasha asked, crossing her arms.

"I grew concerned by your prolonged absence, so much so I began to perspire and created a miniature swimming pool on the third dais."

"We're sitting in the middle of the Paladin Empire, what could possibly happen?" His eyes came alive and Tasha threw up her hands. "Wait, don't answer. Just tell me why you're really here."

Slade immediately scrutinized Keliss through narrowed eyes and over a scrunched nose. "Can we trust him?" he whispered loudly, holding a hand to the side of his mouth.

"Yes, Slade, we can trust him." She sighed, rubbing her brows.

"Awww, trusting people is so boring. Well alright. My Dear, do you remember when I invited you to a certain business meeting earlier?"

"Yes." Tasha ignored Keliss, who leaned forward with his ears perked like a rabbit's.

"Well, my Dear, the appointed hour has arrived, though I have not."

"I'm a little busy right now. Perhaps you should go without me, and I'll see if I can join you in an hour or so."

"Nonsense." Slade rose, twirled his chair around and meticulously replaced it. "Your friend can join us. I assure you nothing untoward will happen, and he may even acquire some fascinating information."

Tasha glanced at Keliss, noticed him actively considering the offer, and landed a kick under the table. "Ah, yes. While your offer's tempting, I have other engagements to attend. Please, forgive me." Keliss rose, bowed and was grabbed by the shoulders.

"How can you betray me in such a fashion, and not only me but your children, your wife, and your wife's wives?" Slade wore an expression so furious his eyes practically sprung from their sockets. "Tell me, apostate, why can't you join an utter stranger on an obscure, possibly dangerous, certainly murder inducing venture whose details remain a complete mystery?"

"Uhh."

"Shame on you." Slade flung his head from side to side without releasing Keliss, forcing his hapless prisoner to emulate every move he made. "You faithless betrayer! You sodden dishrag of morality! If you refuse my request despite your family, friends, and wives than do it for your country!"

"My country?"

"Yes, your country, my brave inept squire. The world is ending, and only you can stop it! Fire! Death! Pink Frogs! All these shall rain from the heavens, despoiling our fields, rotting our forests, burning our towns, laying waste to our entire civilization. Only you, my hopelessly hapless stranger, can stop it. You must join me in this endeavor because I have chosen you, and I forbid you from denying my wishes. Spit in the eyes of gods if you must, cut off your own foot if you wish, but under no circumstances can you discard my wishes alongside committing these less heinous crimes." Slade abruptly swapped intonations. "Truth be told, the first suggestion does sound rather entertaining."

The two locked gazes for a moment, then Keliss relaxed back into himself, eyes half closing and sleepy timber resurfacing. "Guess we better move along if the world needs saving."

Slade clapped his shoulder. "Well said, my young apprentice."

Tasha gave a short bark of laughter. "With our hierarchy established, would you consider telling us where we are going?"

"I would indeed. For this singular occasion, I will discard my usual reserve to armor you against the forthcoming bedlam lest you emerge bloodied and disillusioned by the disillusionment found within. We're going to a library." Slade strode away. "Now, for the sake of our unexpected guest, a little groundwork. Tonight we're meeting representatives from the Thieves' Guild."

Keliss staggered slightly. "Not sure I should come along; seems rather dangerous."

"Don't worry. The guild is a loose conglomeration of toothless ferrets who've gotten high on too many un-prescribed drugs all in a desperate effort to control their kleptomaniac tendencies and general heliophobia. It's an excellent business racket since I provide both the drugs and the shadows they're so enamored of. Oh, by the way, I know you're a member." Slade threw Keliss a wink. "Regardless, this meeting came about because after accepting Carr'Selain's proposed alliance, I erroneously expected a prompt reply. When delivering a letter proved impossible for the guild's peons, I took matters into my own hands and forwarded one directly to Carr'Selain, entreating he send representatives immediately."

"That seems unlikely," Keliss said, discounting Tasha's cautionary hand waving and then ignoring her exaggerated forehead slap. "Didn't hear anyone mention a letter, so it must have arrived after I departed, yet the resulting delegation reached Tellor the same day as I did."

"Good, I wondered if Carr'Selain could still keep secrets."

"Unable to keep a secret? Secrets are our lifeblood."

"And your propaganda agrees with you, though I've long distrusted that particular source of information." Slade veered toward a door secreted within a shadowy alcove. "I'm simply concerned that our dealings might lack confidentiality. How many personal details will Carr'Selain auction to the highest bidder? Will my true face sell for a thousand gold crowns? My whereabouts for a hundred? My friends and family for a million?" Slade paused at the door, his hand resting on the hidden knob. "The Thieves' Guild is an unmatched purveyor of secrets. Every day I negotiate with Carr'Selain, my anonymity slips away like water pulling sand from the bank. Enemies who have always raged at a shadowy, untouchable menace could now pierce my façade." Slade pushed the door open and held it for his companions. "With this in mind, I hope you'll forgive my distrust."

Keliss' gaze flicked to Tasha. "Her reports suggest you contacted us first, roundaboutly. If true, why make such a dangerous move?"

"Because the guilds have forgotten how much power they possess and they're unwittingly misusing it. I hope to supply a course adjustment, secretly. And speaking of secrets, I've collected some in your name." Slade delved into his satchel, producing a sheaf of paper carpeted with square, unlovely writing. "These contain any material I found significant regarding my lord governor and the other worthies of Tellor's society. The knowledge contained within should fulfill your mission's parameters, but stay a while, enjoy the scenery and the company of friends."

Keliss accepted gingerly, whereupon the donor pivoted and—arms flung toward the ceiling—marched off. "Come, the foretold encounter approaches at the speed of one overly energetic man."

Tearing his gaze from Slade, Keliss looked to Tasha who shrugged. "I have no comment."

Together they followed their disappearing guide, falling into step as he rounded a corner. "How'd you uncover I was a member of the Thieves' Guild?"

"Your travel papers revealed everything for a pittance and I, being a generous entrepreneur, sold it all to Tellor's underworld." Keliss paled. "Never fear, I own the majority of that distinguished company, so your particulars are safe." Slade smirked. "Now, contrary to your obvious impression, self-preservation rather than greed or spite inspired me. Just because I opened the front door doesn't mean I'll let you muck around unsupervised; I don't even know if you're house trained yet. Everybody knows you're in Tellor; everybody knows your friends are in Tellor; everybody knows where you are in Tellor. Everybody is listening and everybody is watching; don't piss on the carpets."

Keliss swallowed, finally understanding a little of what Tasha had tried to convey.

Shortly thereafter they encountered a pair of stone lions that flanked a set of double doors, the pale wood heavily ornamented with carved knights, fae, dragons, and other staples of the fiction genre.

"Won't the governor mind if you appropriate his library to discuss business?" Tasha asked.

"I've routinely raided this hallowed room with nary a word of complaint. I doubt he'll protest." Grinning over his shoulder, Slade grasped the handles. "Prepare your snacks and drinks, the performance is about to begin."

A chill creeping down his spine, Keliss leaned toward Tasha. "Is he planning something?"

"If you read my reports, you'd realize that was a rhetorical question."

"Any idea what?"

"Not the faintest."

"Should I be worried?"

"Oh, undoubtedly," she cackled, rubbing her hands together.

They stepped through the doors, heads swiveling from side to side. The room, however, was empty. This rather stole the wind from Tasha's sails, but Slade smoothly veered toward the library's walls where he clambered up a ladder and began liberating books. Whenever he cleared the desirable tomes from one section, Slade would propel himself along the circular wall by gripping a shelf and pushing. After completing a full circuit, he descended and began examining the lower bookshelves.

Tasha quickly took to pacing while Keliss found a seat. In one of those queer twists of fate, no sooner did he do so then two men entered the library.

The younger shuffled inside, awkwardly concealing a book under his dress-coat while his unkempt, pepper-haired friend followed with an amused smile.

Atop the ladder once again, Slade swung to the outside and smiled, his expression shifting to decidedly wolfish after spotting the first man's predicament. "Don't hide the book, brandish it hither and thither like it belongs to you." Slade slid down, bounced over and draped an arm across the thief's shoulders.

Just as he reached him, a woman entered with a brusque, heavy stride and an identical voice. "We've fallen far if a gutter rat can teach us anything about theft." She swept the room, acknowledging Tasha with a slight nod before noticing Keliss. "What are you doing here?"

"Our host invited me," the man drawled, lounging back.

"Leave," Madame Roshfen barked, jerking a thumb toward the door. "These are delicate proceedings, you've no function here, and I'm certain you have assignments elsewhere." Turning away, she yanked off a dark, rain speckled cloak, gave it a brisk shake and hooked it upon a nearby rack. Turning back, she found an unmoved Keliss. "I said leave." A tabby cat materialized from behind a couch skirt, startling everyone except Slade as it darted past Madame Roshfen to rub against Keliss. "No. He's a potential liability and I don't trust him," she said, peeling off dark leather gloves and slapping them against her palm. The tabby rubbed itself more vigorously, purring loudly. "I said, no. He's … fine, be it on your head." Madame Roshfen stuffed the gloves into the pocket of her stiff, black suit and stomped toward Slade, who was still explaining how to steal a book.

"Okay, so after I set fire to the stables, what do I do?"

"Did you set the horses free first?"

"Of course."

"Good; now you sound the alarm, which is the giant bell sitting to the left of the courtyard. In the ensuing hubbub, you find a suitable enemy, inculpate him, sneak off to the treasuries, steal a couple famous trinkets, plant these on any guards you encounter, then give your love poem to the governor's daughter—"

"Is the poem really necessary?"

"Yes, who else will save you from a life spent wallowing in prison if the guards catch you. Of course you might have to marry the girl afterward, but I hear she's pretty as a rose in winter."

"The lord governor doesn't have a daughter." The pepper-haired man offered around barely controlled laughter.

Slade, however, just flapped a hand. "A minor hitch, nothing more; send the poem to his eminence's wife instead. She's not so pretty, but the darling lady's already married, which saves you from matrimony."

"Ah, good. What's next?"

"Well, my young prodigy, you must catch one of the rampaging horses, find a suitable cape and ride toward the sunset, hopefully departing to trumpeted fanfare or a crowd screaming their adulation."

"Samuel, you're here to take notes, not lessons on horse theft."

"But, Madame Roshfen, I'm not stealing a horse; Slade is teaching me how to steal a book."

"He's not teaching you anything. Stop wasting your time. Master Lammerock, come this way. Master Bohkar, keep watch."

The pepper-haired man placed a hand on Samuel's shoulder, both comforting and restraining his friend. "Yes, Madame Roshfen."

She had already turned away, striding toward center stage with an imperious gesture. "The rest of you sit or stand as you wish but come close. I will not shout and risk being overheard."

Slade picked the largest chair, sat to ascertain its comfort and then dragged it across the room. Samuel seated himself near the back alongside a table and Bohkar sat opposite him, dealing them both a hand of cards, then arranging more atop the table and producing a small hourglass.

Tasha started migrating off to the side where she could pace without distracting anyone, but a sharp glance from Madame Roshfen brought her back and situated her, reluctantly, in a chair.

After everyone found suitable accommodations, Madame Roshfen glanced to where the tabby had just taken up residence in Tasha's lap. She snapped towards the ground at her feet, but this only elicited a wide, tooth-baring yawn followed by a luxuriant stretch. "Now."

Voicing a very human sigh, the tabby rolled off with a feather light landing. Sauntering toward her, its body gave a subtle ripple and shifted, blurring and elongating as the creature slowly evolved into a man. "Really, Beatrice, couldn't you see I was otherwise occupied."

"We are not here to enjoy ourselves, Hacoast."

The wizard shrugged, his various ornaments tinkling. "Just because you've disavowed fun, that doesn't mean Carr'Selain outlawed the practice. Master Lammerock"—he bowed with steepled fingers—"it is a pleasure to make your acquaintance."

Slade returned the bow from his chair. "The sentiment is mutual. I've heard so much about your accomplishments I almost feel outclassed." He grinned. "But not quite."

Madame Roshfen stepped in between the two men. "Master Lammerock, if you're finished with pleasantries, I'd like to begin." She caught Hacoast's eyes then pointedly glanced at a chair. "To begin, I will trust that

Miss Bloomhale's reports didn't exaggerate and you're well acquainted with tonight's project?"

"I'm afraid Tasha doesn't quite have the imagination to exaggerate a report, but don't fret, we're working on that." Slade rose, glanced at his seat, dusted it off and sat back down.

"Please, don't. We need accurate reports. Now if I may–"

"Accurate reports are nice, good reports are better. Can't speculate without an imagination. Can't solve problems either."

"Be that as it may, stop meddling with our personnel. They serve our purposes just fine."

"Yes, but they don't serve my purposes just fine."

Off to the side, Tasha and Keliss shared glances. The former indicating that they needed to discuss this later.

Madame Roshfen's achingly thin fingers tapped out a sharp rhythm atop her armrest. "Miss Bloomhale's reports warned us you might try to derail proceedings; that you would unbalance us for your own peculiar amusement. It won't work. Now, let's attend to the particulars."

"Don't bother. I'm acquainted with the particulars." Slade rose again to frown at his seat.

"How? Miss Bloomhale doesn't know the particulars."

"Well, I'm not Tasha, now am I?" Slade forsook his chair and migrated to a new one, grimacing as he shifted in the seat. "The only way secrets are kept is if the receiver dies soon after. A small population knew what you intended and they're all still running around dribbling secrets. The math seems fairly straight forward."

Hacoast leaned forward, hands clasped. "Are you suggesting we kill anybody who knows anything about our plans? That's a little extreme."

"Another possibility is to sever their hands and remove their tongues, but death is neater."

Madame Roshfen's thick black eyebrows pulled together, her words coming cold and clipped. "Unlike you, Carr'Selain does not advocate the mass slaughter of his employees; wise counsel you might follow if you weren't so convinced of your own brilliance."

"I'm sure he wasn't honestly suggesting we–" Tasha interjected, sitting forward only to fall silent as Slade—having found his way into the adjacent seat—touched her arm.

"Ah, but, Madame Roshfen, I'm not convinced as to my intellectual grandeur. Daily I challenge myself to prove the question one way or the other."

Seeing the subtle interaction between them, Madame Roshfen's already stern countenance iced over. "Enough, you are clearly trying to and succeeding in wasting my time. I won't indulge you any longer. The following are the particulars of our opening offer. When I've finished, we can negotiate and—Master Lammerock, will you sit down!"

"Of course, Madame Roshfen."

"Now, the particulars are as follows." Opening a tarnished brooch clasped to her collar, Madame Roshfen produced a miniscule scroll that expanded as she unrolled it. "The signer of this contract is hereby agreeing to aid Carr'Selain, or his successor, in stealing *Akrahvast* from the Imperial Emperor. Furthermore, the signer will submit to a discretion spell so the Thieves' Guild's secrets remain undisclosed…"

Madame Roshfen droned on, but Slade quickly diverted attention by crawling about with his rear pointed heavenward and his nose pressed to the carpet.

Hacoast looked to Tasha who shrugged despite the malicious excitement starting to fizz within her stomach, for the moment perfectly content to sit and wait. Sharing a perplexed glance with everyone else, he then leaned over his armrest and tapped the brim of Slade's hat. "Master Lammerock, what are you doing?"

"Shush."

Across the room, Samuel's pen stopped scratching, and Bohkar's chair tilted backward for a better view.

"Ha!" Slade pounced, startling Madame Roshfen and landing with hands cupped to the ground, the contents of a nudged table rattling beside him.

"What now, Master—"

"Shush." Moving with agonizing care, Slade stood and cracked two fingers so he could peer inside. Barking a curse, he dropped back to the floor and scrabbled in pursuit of a flicker.

Hacoast shot to his feet, eyes bright and searching. Samuel and Bohkar shoved themselves back from their table and darted closer. Even Madame Roshfen craned her neck.

Keliss also contracted the excitement, half rising before he noticed Tasha's unmoving example and sat back down.

"Quick, after him. He's escaping!" Slade cried, his obvious desperation prompting Bohkar, Hacoast, and Samuel into joining the chase while Madame Roshfen stumbled forward a step then restrained herself.

Tasha watched, barely contained laughter bubbling within her as the hunters collided with a table, then upended a desk before tipping an entire couch onto its back, the rampant excitement and disregard punctuated by Slade shouting things like, "Quick that way, flank him!"—or—"Make sure he doesn't go that way!"—and—"After him!" Until roaring triumphantly, Slade pounced a second time.

"What is it? What did you catch?" Samuel asked breathlessly as they all crowded around.

"A lost soul."

"Be careful. Don't let it escape again," Bohkar said.

"Oh, it's a tricky devil alright, but I got it now." Employing the same caution as before, Slade separated his hands and the other men inched still closer, clogging the space overhead.

"Wait a minute, there's nothing there!"

Slade knocked Samuel with his shoulder. "Of course there's something there. Mortals simply can't see it." Despite this, realization dawned for all his companions.

Hacoast laughed, while Bohkar harrumphed, and Samuel swiveled in bewilderment. "But–"

"It's the soul of a powerful sorcerer," Slade cried, looking around. "He was imprisoned in the Abyss for centuries, but now he's escaped through secret, treacherous roads and hunts the gates of hell, hoping to breach them and free his brethren. They're planning an invasion!" With growing desperation, he darted from person to person, the supposed evil soul forgotten. "You must believe me! They are real, I swear! It's just that only I can see them. You have got to help me, or they'll kill us all!"

Hacoast, still laughing, shook him off and Slade dashed across the room, falling to his knees and sliding forward to wrap his arms around Madame Roshfen's legs. "We're all going to die!"

Tasha watched as Madame Roshfen's countenance descended to raw furry, bursting into outright laughter when the other woman attempted to escape and ended up stumbling over a coffee table, losing her balance, and sitting down atop it. "Let go of me, you gods forsaken … boy!"

Ripping his hat away, Madame Roshfen pressed both hands against his face and shoved, making enough space to fit her shoe against his chest and free herself. Then with sharp vicious tugs, she fixed her rumpled clothing. "Gods damn you, Slade Lammerock. And you!" She whirled on Tasha. "Why didn't you warn me?"

Tasha raised her hands unable to stop chuckling. "I did. I sent Carr'Selain a detailed account of all my dealings with Slade, not least of which were the pranks. Carr'Selain responded with, and I quote, 'How droll'."

Keliss opened his mouth to add his own comment, but Slade, from behind Madame Roshfen, drew a finger across his throat.

"I read those *Jaidar* blessed reports. Why didn't you warn me about this one?" Madame Roshfen's mouth snapped shut on the edge of a scream. "No. I refuse to let him derail us further. Rest assured, Miss Bloomhale, we'll talk later, for now let's–" Madame Roshfen faced about and froze.

Slade stood at the room's center, perusing the contract she'd held only a moment earlier. "Would everyone sit down, please."

And everyone did, except for Madame Roshfen who strode forward with an outstretched hand. "Give that back."

"Sit down, Madame Roshfen. You have directed this engagement long enough."

"If you think I'll permit you–"

"Madame Roshfen, at birth you learned to speak, but in all your forty-eight years, you have not learned to listen. I suggest you learn now. This is not a negotiation. I do not need your help to steal *Akrahvast*. All I lacked was the incentive, but now I'd do it simply to thumb my nose at Carr'Selain."

Her lips pulled into a thin smile. "Really? I wouldn't be sitting quite so comfortably if I were you. In case you haven't noticed, we've flooded Tellor with our people." Madame Roshfen stepped into Slade, nearly smashing her nose against his as she leaned forward. "Even if these negotiations fall apart, your castle is broken and your reign is dead. We've won the war."

"Keliss," Slade said, meeting Madame Roshfen's gaze calmly, "do me a favor and explain why you're at this meeting."

In response the man frowned at his lap, utterly silent even as the tension built and his fellows began shifting in their seats. Finally he touched the sheaf of papers Slade had given him. "Proof."

Madame Roshfen's attention snapped over, words spitting out. "Proof? Proof of what?"

"That I can find your people," Slade said, forceful but measured. "I know where they are. I know who they are. I know what they're after." Stepping back from Madame Roshfen, he moved to stand behind a chair and lightly grasped the sides. "They are not conquerors: they're hostages. And this, this is a petition. We discuss these matters by my sufferance alone, so I'll ask one last time. Please, sit down."

Invisible energy crackled as Madame Roshfen fought for dominion. But in the end, she sat, gripping her armrests so hard the wood all but cracked under the pressure.

Slade inclined his head. "Thank you, Madame Roshfen. It says here you require a demonstration." He tapped the rolled-up contract against his palm.

When Madame Roshfen refused to answer, Hacoast stepped in. "It's a formality, something to assure Carr'Selain your skills are genuine. Almost any display will suffice; you need only indicate a target and how you intend to liberate his possessions."

"Hmm." Slade held the scroll out to Madame Roshfen, who yanked it from his grip. "The governor possesses many fine libraries. I think I shall appropriate them along with the gold from his coffers."

Hacoast touched the side of his head, eyes closing. A long moment passed before they opened again, the bright orange of his magic still fading away. "Carr'Selain accepts your offer."

34

Thrice Purchased

In the aftermath of their meeting with Seren, Feylin pressed Tiberius for answers, but he replied with an infuriating, "It's not time yet, when you're older," followed by distractedly sending her off to Cain yet again. When she informed him of Senna's abrupt exhaustion, Tiberius turned away and gripped the sides of a desk, muscles flexing under his shirt. "Too many fires," he whispered, eyes staring into nothing, "too many directions." His body slumped and he turned back around. "I'm sorry, I have to go. There's something I must … I must track Sinnitar Muntalabac. Go, find someplace inconspicuous and wait until Slade finds you. Tell Cain I'm sorry. I'll return when I can."

Deserted, Feylin trudged back to her table where she sat hoping Tasha would make a sudden appearance. She could almost see it, an exasperated Tasha throwing herself into the opposite chair with some complaint about Slade. Then again, perhaps Slade would arrive first, sneaking up from behind to tickle her ear with that wonderful feather of his before embarking upon an outrageous story. Mostly she hoped for Tiberius. But the minutes crept by and the sense of their absence grew, fed by the crowd fluctuating around her. Still she waited. It was all she could do.

———————

Following his little coup, Slade discarded his usual gregarious mischief for a concise competence that ensured matters proceeded quickly. Within a dozen minutes the participants were already trickling away, Tasha and Keliss leaving in whispered conference and Madam Roshfen departing shortly thereafter. Samuel lingered the longest, delayed by carefully reaching into a vial with a set of pincers and withdrawing a tongue of flame. He then brushed the flame across his notes, causing the ink to flare red and exhale smoke, burning away to reappear in Carr'Selain's libraries.

In Slade's case, he collected a final stack of books before waving a friendly goodbye. After closing the doors, however, he sat there staring at them. "A curious person might wonder why you're still here, and I'm a very curious person."

"Master Lammerock, Carr'Selain wishes to extend a subsidiary proposal." Madame Roshfen said coldly.

"I should be delighted."

"Yes, especially since, despite my warnings, he wants this conducted under the table. The guild ledgers won't even know."

"And my reward?"

"Substantial; Carr'Selain can be generous to those he favors."

"Does he favor me though?"

"No. He hates your guts, but he's willing to forgo this enmity for profit."

"I'm honored by your Master's forbearance."

"Carr'Selain is not my master."

"Ah, the delusions we craft for ourselves; they are such sweet dreams." Madame Roshfen's countenance darkened, but Slade waved aside her forthcoming protests. "Never mind. Tell me what's tickled Carr'Selain's fancy."

"Rumor says you're acquainted with Tiberius Whyte, is this true?"

"Well well, it seems your spies have exceeded my expectations; have your Master send them a bonus for me."

"Carr'Selain is not my master."

"Yes, of course. My apologies. It simply escaped me for a moment."

"I don't care. Answer the question. Are you friends? Acquaintances?"

"Oh, I'm friends with everybody … except your Master. Friends in what sense though, fair weather friends or the type who lets you hide bodies in their backyard?"

"That's what I'm trying to figure out," she growled through gritted teeth. "To what degree are you acquainted with Tiberius Whyte?"

"Hmm, I can't say I appreciate this sifting through my personal life. I suggest your Master molest his own affairs, lest I return the favor."

Madam Roshfen knotted her hands in the fabric of Slade's shirt and slammed him against the wall. "Carr'Selain is not my master! Learn that or by *Kis'Maat* I'll nail it to your forehead."

"My apologies," Slade said, slipping free and bowing with one arm held across his sternum while the other wrapped behind his back and deposited an old, tarnished necklace into his satchel. "I shan't make the mistake again."

Madame Roshfen snarled into his repentant expression, her hands clenching and unclenching at her side. "Are. You. Acquainted. With. Tiberius Whyte. Or not? Or did you spread those rumors purely for our amusement?"

"Ah, Madame Roshfen, there is hope for you yet. This doubt in me, in your spies, is the first step toward becoming a magnificent Thief-Lord. Next is discovering how valid your suspicions are."

"Answer the *Jaidar* blessed question."

"Yes, I am acquainted with Tiberius Whyte; though if I'm not mistaken, you're more concerned with his ward."

"How—"

"Simple logic. Tiberius is strong, far too strong for the guild to challenge idly. His ward, on the other hand, is young and inexperienced; one might call her fragile—like fine porcelain. Add this to a burgeoning magical talent and—"

"She possesses magic?"

"I retract my earlier statement; your spies are useless. Yes, she possesses magic." Slade turned away disgustedly, then paused and made a show of rolling his eyes. "Normally I wouldn't bother but seeing as we are newly minted compatriots… Don't mistake a helpless girl for a defenseless girl; paladins guard her at all times, and she herself could become quite troublesome if incentivized. I should also warn you about the other complications but"—he smiled—"those come with a price tag." Given the choice, Slade would prefer they abstained from any disastrous kidnapping attempts unless he could personally orchestrate the disaster.

"How do you know so much?"

"That's not hardly important, much like this beating around the bush. It's fairly obvious what Carr'Selain wants, so how about you make the official proposal?"

"Carr'Selain requests that you kidnap Feylin Whyte for ransoming. Need I remind you about not damaging her?"

"That won't be necessary."

"I think I will anyway. A broken doll fetches no prize, so don't break her."

"Once again Carr'Selain's weakness rears its head. He fears the sight of blood, little understanding how a little red on white can be useful, or how a child's scream can pull secrets from a stubborn mother."

Madame Roshfen's face contorted in barely concealed loathing at Slade. "Nevertheless, Carr'Selain will be severely displeased if any harm befalls the child. He will also punish you accordingly."

"Carr'Selain is an old, pathetic man who's been wheezing threats ever since I let him spot my shadow. He could no more honor his ultimatum than I could grovel." Again Slade waved aside her protests before they began. "Still, his request has merit. I accept. Let's discuss my reward."

"You will be paid a substantial amount of money—"

"Yes, yes. Yes, shiny metal, yellow, very pretty. What I actually want is the guild's records concerning the Whyte family, the Lammerock family, the Muntalabac family, and *Arthramain Roy'al* or his works, in particular the Dragon Lords."

"Get them yourself if you're so high and mighty."

"I could, but this saves a significant amount of time and trouble." Slade extended his hand. "Do we have a deal?"

She hesitated, the uncertainty continuing even as she clasped his hand. "We do."

———————

Feylin saw him by accident while trying to distract herself with the acrobatic troupe. Slade crossed into the performance space, tapping a man on the shoulder and passing over an official looking envelope alongside a small purse. He then stepped close for a private dialogue before leaving to circle the ballroom, his head panning from left to right.

Feylin leaned forward. *'Who is he looking for? Tasha probably or maybe his mother. After all, he's obviously not look—'* Slade glanced in her direction and his countenance split into a brilliant grin. His feet veered toward the nearest staircase and he bounded upward two at a time, steps gradually slowing as he inspected the empty chairs around her.

"Feylin, where is my mother?" he asked, stopping behind the outermost chair and gripping its back.

"She felt a little under the weather, so Cain took her home. As far as I know, she's fine."

He breathed a quiet exhale and the tension eased from his shoulders, replaced by a touch of guilt. "Is Tiberius nearby?"

Feylin shook her head. "He left an hour or so back. I don't know where to. I don't know where Tasha is either, if that's who you're looking for," she added, trying her best to sound relaxed and comfortable.

"Actually, no; I'm looking for you." Slade pulled out the chair and sat. "Did you happen to see yourself wandering around somewhere? I'm afraid I've quite lost you."

As soon as he sat down, the subtle brew of unease, loneliness, and reeling thoughts within Feylin burst like a bubble. "I can't say I have. It seems I've quite lost myself as well." Finally exhaling the knot in her chest, Feylin's head tipped back to rest against the chair, eyes falling shut. "Any idea where I might have run off to?"

Slade rubbed his chin. "Hmm, where oh where... Ah ha, the dungeon! A pair of thuggish guards undoubtedly caught you stealing something: a dress probably; women are always hunting for more clothes."

"I was not!"

"Yes, I can see it now," Slade said, peering through the picture frame of his fingers. "You approach a beautiful, poised woman who you fear will steal away all your admirers. She offers a friendly smile and you return it, opening your arms as if to embrace her. She—assuming it's a harmless eccentricity— moves to accept, whereupon you grip the shoulders of her dress and rip downwards, leaving her stark naked in a crowd of Thearcs."

Both smiling and shaking her head in futile rejection, Feylin slumped into her chair again, burning countenance hidden behind her hands.

"Come," Slade said, springing to his feet. "Let's check the dungeon. I'm certain we'll find you hunched over in some shadowy corner, hissing at intruders and clutching a tattered ball gown to your avaricious chest."

"Slade, I'm also certain you won't find me in the dungeon."

Heaving a sigh, he sank back down. "Where do we begin then?"

"Well, if I were me, I would have left to find you and Tasha." Feylin winced immediately after. She had meant to play along, not attack him for leaving.

In response, Slade's eyes fell closed and his expression lost the levity so at home there. Opening them again, he leaned forward and laid his hands atop the table, palms up. "Feylin, I'm sorry. I thought you'd have my parents for company or at the very least Tiberius."

Feylin stared at his hands without taking them. "Slade, it's alright; I was fine. I've been alone before. Tiberius routinely departs on secret errands. There is no need to make a big fuss out of this." In truth, even when Tiberius left there was a bevy of familiar servants to keep her company.

"Just because you've survived past experiences doesn't mean I'm entitled to subject you further. Loneliness is an oppressive opponent that bleeds all light and warmth from the world."

His words rang a little too true, so Feylin shrugged the conversation aside. "What were you doing anyway? Something"—she tried waggling her eyebrows like he did—"clandestine I hope."

Slade leveled an appraising glance at her, then allowed the change of subject. "All right, I'll tell you." He motioned Feylin closer and lowered his voice to a whisper, "Tonight representatives from the Thieves' Guild rendezvoused with me in a most clandestine fashion. Frightful characters one and all. They adorned themselves with a jingling cacophony of knives, hooks, charms, beads, and a not few bone ornaments. The first member of the company was a thunderous wizard who dressed in an abundance of violet silks and golden trinkets, none of which compared to his glass eyes. He swore they enabled him to see the unseen or peer into the nether realms. However, his powers extended far beyond that. On a whim, he could change into whatever breed of cat, large or small, he wished. One moment he reared up as a lion, clawing the air and roaring so that I felt it'd tear the very skin from my face. The next he curled in my lap as an orange tabby." Slade leaned to the side, resting his head atop the pillow of his hands before springing back the life. "The second representative, meanwhile, had skin that resembled old papyrus, going so far as to include an ancient script that wound around his arms and disappeared under his shirt only to reappear from his collar and writhe all the way to his jaw line. More mysterious still, he balanced an enormous book on one hand, the pearlescent pages adorned with words going left, right, up, down, opposite directions, in circles, and even atop one another. So many it's a wonder they didn't burst off the page and dribble onto the floor. He also held a swan feather longer than his own arm, every casual gesture leaving trails of sparkling dust hanging on the air." Slade swept the feather from his own hat, swishing the substitute about as if he wielded a rapier. "Also attending our little congregation was a man so painfully deprived of notable features he passed entirely out of the realm of sight, becoming invisible except for when he opened the single starlit, all-seeing eye set upon his brow." Slapping his hands atop the table, Slade vaulted from his chair onto the beautiful silk tablecloth and adopted a heroic pose. "Last was the dragon lady, a woman who towered twelve feet in height, and belched fire and imprecations with every breath. Her most impressive trait though was the shimmering, blue scales covering her body, each one reflecting the light so the room radiated an azure glow."

"What did they want?" Feylin asked, her voice hushed.

"They desire my aid in a grand adventure, the kind suited for story books and destined to shine out from the annals of history." Slade resumed his seat. "What desperate endeavor would require such an awesome gathering you might ask? Well something secreted within the most inhospitable place known to the world: the southern wastes. Something hidden so deftly, armies of treasure hunters have sacrificed their entire lives in its pursuit. Something so powerful it can affect whole nations." He leaned forward, casting a glance over either shoulder. "My compatriots and I plan to steal winter."

"What?" Feylin couldn't help but laugh. "How can you steal winter? Let alone steal it from the South? The South doesn't even have chilly rain."

"True enough but not through the land's design. Millennia ago *Ashshand* seized the frozen winds, the snow, and all the ice in the Avarus Desert and locked them in a white jewel no larger than a river stone. Next he captured sleet, hail, and all manner of frost, and placed them in a second white gem. In conclusion, he took the innocence of freshly fallen snow, the thunder of winter storms, the death found in blizzards, and ensnared them in a third crystal, making the *Akalandari* the three prisons of winter. None know why *Ashshand* made the *Akalandari* only that he locked them away in a box of red stone to be kept safe."

Something in how Slade spoke told Feylin the story was old. She could almost imagine the voices of a thousand storytellers as they wove this story again and again, each version unique yet true.

"So now you and your companions must steal winter back from *Ashshand?*"

"Correct, and we have no idea where they're hidden, at least none beyond a hope that *Ashshand* hid the *Akalandari* in the South. For all we know, *Ashshand* might have tossed our prize into the nearest volcano."

"I can't say I envy your position; if you accepted that is."

"Of course I accepted; two months from now rumors will abound telling how we stole winter right from under *Ashshand's* nose. Imagine all the wealth and fame that shall rain upon me when I return with the *Akalandari* raised overhead to sparkle like stars at night. People will line the streets cheering, waving, and offering themselves up as my eternal slaves, going wild from the sheer excitement of basking in my divine presence."

"So when is this mad throng going to appear?" Tasha asked, sliding into the table's third chair and making Feylin give a start. "And how did they escape from the insane asylum?"

Slade pressed a hand to his chest, fingers splayed. "Well I liberated them, of course. Shame on me if I permit a single person to pass from this life without soaking in my grandeur at least once."

"Slade," Tasha asked, half-exasperated, "did it ever occur to you that we lock the mentally unhinged away for a reason?"

He flapped his hand. "I'm sure it's all political humbug, a scheme to suppress the masses."

And Tasha, who almost felt content, rolled her eyes with a smile. "What started this whole discussion anyway?"

"Slade was telling me how some rather bizarre acquaintances of his want to steal the *Akalandari*."

"Slade, you realize the *Akalandari* has been lost for centuries?"

"Ah, ha." Slade gesticulated toward the ceiling. "That delightful challenge is why I acquiesced so easily to their entreaties."

Tasha shrugged. "If you're going to shoot, aim for the sky."

"I'm glad you agree, though the sky is well within my reach, so I'll reach for the stars."

Slade could almost feel the night taking a breath before it announced the fifth-Vigil and called the dawn laborers to their endless work on improving and industrializing the city. Then as expected, the mighty bells tolled from their tower stations and all across Tellor men slipped outside with conscientious stealth.

Slade, like most people, could ignore the bells, which allowed him to detect the quiet tap of pebbles knocking on his bedroom window. Brow furrowing, he glanced up from his book and listened, gradually recognizing the absence of expected sounds. No servants ghosted along the halls, no mice skittered through the attic, no oversleeping cook snored audibly from below. The house itself seemed to have fallen asleep or perhaps it simply held its breath.

Another pebble knocked against his window and Slade closed the book, setting it aside before extinguishing his stubby, near exhausted candle. Despite the sudden darkness, he crossed to the unwrinkled bed and clambered atop it, crawling across the vast, wine colored expanse to collect his hat from the furthest post. Afterwards, he slid to the ground and strode for the door, where he stepped into his boots and lifted his satchel from a hook.

Outside, the intruder threw a final pebble then sat back to wait.

Notwithstanding his appointment, Slade paused outside his parents' door, listening for sounds of wakefulness. During previous late-night escapades, Cain had invariably appeared to make a few uncomfortable questions, so Slade adapted and began absconding through the window.

On this occasion, however, Cain remained absent.

After peeking inside to check on them, Slade conducted a cursory house inspection. Judging from appearances, everyone suffered from an identical sleep disorder, or maybe he dreamed and everybody else waltzed through a normal day.

Slade snagged an orange from the kitchen counter and passed into the entrance hall, whereupon the front door swung silently open. *'Well, at least the lack of eerie creaking suggests this won't veer into nightmare territory.'* Slade tossed his orange into the air, caught it, and strode for the door, peeling his snack as he went.

Mid-journey he recognized the foreign compulsion urging him onward. While far from annoyed at the manipulation, Slade nevertheless spun around. Instantly the compulsion ceased.

'That's better.' Giving a contented nod, he dropped the last peel into his satchel and stepped outside where, curious, he placed a foot between the closing door and its frame. An unseen force, however, nudged his boot clear.

Slade grinned. *'Yet another interesting development.'*

Tossing an orange slice into his mouth, he settled atop the uppermost step to await future developments. When these proved to be of an indolent character, he searched through his satchel and produced a bone flute densely etched with strange designs.

Fingers falling comfortably over the holes, he began playing a soft, soulful lament whose loudest notes barely sounded above the night's secondary occupants.

After a time, he lowered the flute and said, "Do you know the tale of Shara's flute?" Silence greeted his words. "Well, the legend claims anyone who plays the flute will perform with the skill of a master. There's a catch though."

One of Crannir's fellow assassins stepped out from behind a statue with the answer, "Only a master musician can entice music from the flute."

The corner of Slade's mouth curled. "So who is making the music, the instrument—?"

"Or the musician?"

Slade stored the flute. "Why are you here?"

"I apologize for my intrusion." The man bowed, conveying polite acknowledgement more than remorse. "The present hour seemed the most agreeable to you, and I felt a private meeting was necessary."

"Is this a pressing issue?"

"No, the culmination to a long-term engagement."

"Then, Sora, why are you flaunting my very simple, very strict instructions? You must realize that I'll punish your friends as well you."

His too-azure gaze held Slade's eyes, attempting no intimidation merely offering Slade his full attention. "Please allow me to first correct a minor deception, my name is not Sora, nor am I one of Syndros'Nomarr's assassins."

One of Slade's eyebrows quirked upward. "While I'm grateful for the courtesy, I don't care who you really are, who you really serve or whatever petty secrets you're keeping. You have exactly one excuse before I start killing for your breach of contract."

The man's eyes narrowed, but his tone remained the same: distinct yet gentle, dangerously susceptible to being talked over yet possessed of a subtle quality that heeled the brashest speaker. "I've broken no contract, so do not suggest I have. We both know that contrary to your faultless illusion there is no contract."

Slade leaned back to consider him, elbows resting atop one of the higher steps. "So you no longer wish to play make-believe. Alright. How many layers should we discard? Certainly, not all of them; but perhaps we can risk a few more. Starting with this one." Shifting his weight, Slade drew a finger across his brow then trailed it down his nose. "You wore a different face the first time I saw you. It was the day Miss Bloomhale arrived in Tellor. You loitered in the background, observing while I treated her to supper. Then, a week or so later, I spotted you meandering among the Ie'Calla and observing, unnoticed in a place where neither a field mouse nor distant hawk could go unnoticed. Peculiar to be sure."

"I observed out of curiosity. Despite my best efforts, I can only perceive you through the minds of others. Had I realized you perceived me, I would have introduced myself sooner." The man inclined his head, appearance fading to reveal perfect features, golden brown hair, and the same too-azure eyes. "My name is Bellay Enkarta."

"It is a pleasure to make your acquaintance, Bellay Enkarta. What brings you before my august throne, threats or bargains?"

"I wish to discuss the fate of Feylin Tamara Sarashell Whyte."

"Ah, yes; you wish me to procure her for you."

"No. Despite your recent transactions with Lord Sinnitar and the esteemed Carr'Selain, I suspect your character is more noble than foul. You intend on protecting Lady Feylin with all of your substantial abilities. You see the strands of your two fates weaving together. Maybe you choose to weave a few yourself."

"How does this concern her then?"

"I've been tasked with ending Lady Feylin's life." Slade's idle demeanor shifted, his body becoming a coiled spring as his thoughts abandoned all consideration except for the present. Bellay Enkarta, however, raised a hand. "Please be at ease; I have no designs upon her tonight, and I've come to negotiate. I require your talents. In exchange, I will permit you one month to plan and secure Lady Feylin's continued health."

Marginally, Slade relaxed. "Presuming I'm to be a thief, what am I stealing and from which dragon?"

"The Soul Iron hidden beneath Tellor. I believe Sinnitar requested it earlier tonight."

"Sinnitar Muntalabac is a dangerous enemy."

"One you intended on making."

"It is an intriguing proposal."

"Also not subject to negotiations. If you refuse my offer, I will claim Lady Feylin's life in exactly twenty-four hours."

"Two paladins guard this house–"

"They are without consequence and the famed Tiberius Whyte is far afield."

Slade's skin prickled. In his mind's eye, he watched an executioner's ax gradually rise until he saw little besides blue skies and the tops of buildings. Then it simply hung there waiting. "I accept your offer."

"It is agreed. Oath Holder bear witness." Bellay Enkarta left without mystery, quietly closing the front gate behind him and then diminishing by way of his footsteps.

As for Slade, the prickling gradually ceased, giving way to a ticklish sensation in his gut. This grew and led to him counting off his fingers. "Sinnitar, Carr'Selain, Bellay Enkarta. Sinnitar, Carr'Selain, Bellay Enkarta. Sinnitar, Carr'Selain, Bellay Enkarta." The tickling burgeoned to buzzing that coursed up and down his frame, continuing until his entire body thrummed and he threw back his head and laughed. "OH, WHAT FUN."

35

The Clergy

In the centuries of its existence, the Clergy of *Ashshand* had erected scores of cathedrals throughout Sahdaen, most relegated to its upper tiers and functioning as bastions of power and symbols of fear rather than sites of worship. They trained warriors, hoarded resources, crafted weapons, and converted Avarans to Tragnashi for Kalvonders at exorbitant expense. They all shared a design: sun-blacked, monolithic shards suspended from several tiers of Sahdaen by crooked limbs carven into the imagery of serpents that doubled as entrances.

The one currently before Dieharamon bore the name Dru'Kerack and had once served as the Clergy's preeminent cathedral. Now, draped in the swaddled corpses of wizards long murdered, it imprisoned their most loathed antagonists and had accrued a baleful mythos they delighted in propagating. It was also the only location they would take Dayada Avenar, for Avarans loathed westerners above all other humans.

Dieharamon withdrew from the precipice to the roof's center, gaze rising to the heavens. The stars stared back, countless in their millions and painting all the world into silver clarity. His breath misted before him, visible in the bitterly cold air. Far below in the chasm, its stone walls retained the day's smothering heat long into the night, but here on an edifice that extended above it the Avarus night exerted its authority.

He began pacing, exploring scenario after scenario that all concluded in failure. A frontal assault bordered on suicide and Dru'Kerack's exterior was solid rock, impossible to tunnel through. He couldn't attempt subterfuge with his size and Descendant skin. If he attempted bribery the guards would simply plunder his corpse. This left one inevitable truth: he needed help.

Dieharamon exhaled a resigned sigh, swung onto an attached ladder and slid down to the adjacent living complex's roof. He progressed through the dense clotheslines to the roof's edge, leapt to the balcony below, vaulted that railing and shimmied down the supporting pillar, continuing in this fashion until he reached the main bridge.

He settled in a shrouded alley and, after a glance to verify his solitude, extracted his coin pouch and emptied it into his palm. A meager pile of glass beads greeted him, woefully insufficient for the aid he required. Rumors traveled fast, and the Thieves' Guild was timorous at the best of times. It would balk at aiding him for any price with the Clergy's retribution looming.

Hoping for a shred of luck, he proceeded to the nearest tavern, guided by tattered and stained banners. The bouncers admitted him without complaint, probably because a blue sheen covered their eyes and they swayed on their feet, whispering animatedly to no one.

The common room was sunken beneath a wide balcony that clutched the four walls and stretched across the center. A river of burgundy curtains dangled from its balustrade, their edges trimmed with fine veins of gold, silver, and jade. Entertainers occupied various pedestals scattered throughout and furnaces warmed the bitter southern night. Unlike most taverns, almost every guild maintained a presence here: mercenaries, thieves, merchants, mages, assassins, and others he could not name.

Patrons abounded, spilling into side rooms, upstairs, and out the various entrances to such extents barely a space could be found. Excluding the assassin in his corner. He occupied the sole chair with a black seat-cloth, surrounded in vacant tables and empty lamps. A long knife spun continuously in his hand and bright eyes gazed from beneath a cowl, every motion an act of contempt reinforced by four evident knives.

Across from the assassin, three men huddled around a table with an empty space on the floor mat and untouched tankards. The space surrounding them was smaller than the assassin's but still evident. Only fools sat near thieves.

As Dieharamon squeezed through the packed Avarans toward their table, they noticed him and laid bared knives on the table around their insect lamp. The first was a scarred but still handsome, young man. The second was one-eyed and furtive with hunched shoulders and a disdainful aspect. The third had a gray beard, a stenciled burgundy robe, and a clicking stone hand.

The one-eyed thief greeted Dieharamon with a scowl. "What do you want?"

"Your services."

The young thief snorted and began flipping his knife, earning himself a withering glower before the one-eyed thief repeated his query. "What do you want?"

"I need help accessing a fortress."

The stone-handed thief scratched his beard, speaking in a honeyed voice that made Dieharamon's skin crawl, "Sounds simple enough. Where do you need to get into?"

Dieharamon flinched at the query, then hoping to blind them with avarice, revealed the first of his two pillaged knives. He had barely enough money to finance a guide, let alone entrance into one of the most fortified bastions in Sahdaen; but this knife, with the enchantments scribed into its surface, was worth a month's food, lodging, protection, and water.

The one-eyed thief took the knife with deft fingers, appraising it with calculating ease before restoring it to the table. "So, you wish to enter Jredan'Kor."

"No, Dru'Kerack." Jredan'Kor was Ureign Kalvonder's manor.

The corpulent thief quietly returned Dieharamon's knife. "Such an artifact is worth a fortune, but not our lives; entering Dru'Kerack exceeds our abilities and courage. Take this and depart. We could not aid you even if the Immortal Consort had not taken residence there."

Dieharamon swore; even without the Immortal Consort, the task had verged on the impossible. He forced himself to think. A thought occurred, and returning the knife to his belt, he emptied his purse onto the table. "For Dru'Kerack's cartography, one with the Immortal Consort's chambers marked."

The thieves exchanged glances, and at his corpulent colleague's nod, the one-eyed thief opened a worn satchel and scrounged through various scrolls, vials, and assorted trinkets until he found a roll of worn cloth, which he consigned to Dieharamon. The youngest leaned forward, whispering, "Her chambers are at the base of the cathedral with four guards, two within and two without. Her servants are trained assassins, and she herself is a formidable soul-caster and fire-mage. Dru'Kerack hosts eight score guards, as many acolytes, and forty soul-casters and mages—more than any Kalvonder in the last two millennia."

Dieharamon pocketed the cartography and departed toward the group of mercenaries where they reveled near the common room's center. What he intended reeked of desperation, but if he could enter Dru'Kerack with allies, he might succeed.

The mercenaries quieted, some ignoring him but most facing him with lowered tankards. He withdrew the knife again and offered it to the mercenary captain, who immediately passed it to the man on his left, probably an indentured assessor.

"What do you need?"

"A diversion, nothing more."

The captain snorted. "You're not a poor man, and I doubt there's many people you couldn't butcher on the street, so you've bitten off something nasty. Plus, you feel like somebody who got himself condemned." He reassessed Dieharamon. "Now that I think about it, some idiot initiated a personal war with the Clergy."

"The guilds hold no allegiances, offering their services to anyone capable of paying–"

"We don't throw our lives away either. No contract." He reclaimed Dieharamon's knife and twirled it. "In fact, with the odds arrayed against you, one might suspect ill-intent." He wagged the knife. "We don't like people trying to kill us. Fortunately, I'm feeling generous and will attribute it to alcohol rather than an ill-advised plot to instigate war between the guilds and the Clergy. Forgiveness isn't cheap, however, so we'll be keeping this knife." The mercenaries cackled, slapping one another's shoulders and gulping ale.

Pain lanced Dieharamon's midsection, sharper than before, and doubled him over as bile rose in his throat. It persisted longer as well, squeezing first his stomach then progressing toward his lungs until it became hard to breathe. The pain subsided moments later, but it left him feeling hot and with blurred vision. He needed more of Valeriius' drug, or he wouldn't even make it to the Angorat'Wass. Someone would find him spasming on the street and knife him.

The mercenary captain laughed and slapped Dieharamon's shoulders. "What's wrong, little man?"

Rage suffused Dieharamon, fueled by the beginning thrums of panic over his deprivation and stolen knife, and the burning heat sung into his veins unbeckoned. Almost unaware of himself, he stepped forward, planted the second knife in the captain's heart, removed it and shoved the corpse aside, splashing ale and bowls of red powder.

The mercenaries surged to their feet, grasping for weapons as he leveled his knife on them. "Think carefully; there are only half-a-dozen of you and no mages. I have killed almost a dozen acolytes and three mages, one from the East; what chance do you have?" His rage attenuated, but his fear mutated, warping from panic into horror at himself. Snarling, he throttled his doubts, allowing only the iron purpose necessary to survive. *'Gods. Dayada Avenar, I hope you're someone worth saving. Please, please be someone worth killing for.'*

Dieharamon retrieved his stolen knife and started for the tavern's entrance, a little unsteady on his feet in the press of bodies. As he reached the door there was a hiss followed by a thunk as a bone throwing-knife planted in the door frame inches from his cheek. Every voice and sound died, inevitably pulling Dieharamon about to face the assassin, who lifted a long-fingered hand and beckoned him closer. Dieharamon obeyed.

Assassins advertised their ability by baring knives: a single knife signified a raw operative, two declared a veteran skilled in death, three an artist, four, such as this assassin displayed, a king-killer. Marked bared no weapons because there was no measure of their lethality.

Dieharamon kneeled on the barely-worn mat circling the assassin's table and did his best to ignore the old blood stains.

"Who do you need dead?"

Dieharamon briefly wondered if the assassin could kill Sinnitar Muntalabac, but quickly abandoned the hope. "You can't help me."

The assassin just waited.

"What I need is to enter Dru'Kerack."

"Let me see the knife."

Dieharamon complied.

"What help would you need once inside?"

"None." Armed with the map, he could evade the patrols.

"What's your goal?"

"I need to rescue someone."

"I can get you into Dru'Kerack, but I want both knives."

Dieharamon paid it without hesitation and the assassin rose, slipping toward the entrance through scampering Avarans as the tavern watched, too terrified to so much as whisper. Outside, Dieharamon measured *Sarah'Venn's Vigil* and cursed under his breath; three hours remained until the Angorat'Wass. He hastened his step.

The assassin traversed Sahdaen without subterfuge, conducting Dieharamon to Dru'Kerack's south entrance in minutes. There Dieharamon halted while the assassin continued.

The guards roused, baring weapons and discarding tankards. One, armed with a sword and arrogance, claimed the forefront. "Who are you?"

His companions guffawed, celebrating the inevitable entertainment right until he collapsed, blood spewing from his throat. One rushed to assist him, a shocked cry parting his lips, and died with his first step. The assassin continued, drawing another pair of knives.

Scattered and deeply inebriated, the Avarans fumbled to assemble themselves into some resemblance of cohesion. A barked command stalled their haphazard assault, pulling them back into the gate's recess and about their new commander. He died a second later with a knife in his eye. The Avarans charged, screaming as they threw themselves upon their assailant and died. The assassin proceeded into Dru'Kerack.

Dieharamon stumbled after him, tripping over and staring at the neatly butchered dead. He stopped upon the cathedral's threshold, frozen by the agonized screams within and the blood soaking his slippers, spilt not in some Kalvonder's game but because of him, for him. A spasm shook his hands, but he forced them to still and continued into Dru'Kerack, entering a realm of dense shadows, cavernous rooms and damp, cloying chill.

The assassin crouched just past four twitching corpses, cleaning his blades. Scorch marks fouled the walls, floors, and corpses' scarlet mage coats. A dozen passageways extended from the antechamber, all in either ascent or descent and utter darkness, for torchlight was forbidden in *Ashshand's* temples. Even if light had graced them, Dru'Kerack's floors were a labyrinth of isolated chambers connected by circuitous and illogical routes.

Dieharamon extracted and raised Dru'Kerack's map to the sparse insect light entering via the doorway, scanning it until he found the four rooms marked with the Isaracc hieroglyph for entrance, then memorized the paths leading down.

The door creaked behind him, then boomed shut as the assassin departed, erasing all light. Its echoes reverberated down the halls, making him flinch at every repetition. He hastened to store the map and fumbled his way to, then along the wall to his desired corridor, recognizing it by the raised hieroglyphics and downward trajectory. He needed the bowels of Dru'Kerack, for they would have incarcerated Dayada Avenar in only their foulest dungeon. As for recognizing him, the man would be impossible to mistake with his pale skin and noble heritage.

Dieharamon encountered no one during his descent, but often heard footsteps or the echo of excited voices from abutting passages or thin walls. These encounters grew more prevalent the further he descended, posing little peril but constantly delaying him with the necessity to hide. As time passed, his memory faltered forcing him to attempt less reliable forms of navigation. First he tracked scents, immersing himself in the odors of brine, sulfur, and stale air. Next he touched the pockmarked walls, testing the dampness and chill. Finally he followed the old blood and fingernail scars until he heard the whimpers and mutterings.

He trailed those sounds to a final stair illuminated in sickly viridian light. It spanned the hall's length and spat out a writhing, suffocating conglomeration of scents: rancid blood, urine, rats, fear, and misery. He crouched at its top, breathing through his mouth and shivering at the illumination. This was Dru'Kerack's deepest prison.

Dieharamon rolled his shoulders, attempting to loosen sore muscles in preparation for the inevitable conflict, and pain instantly ripped through him, doubling him over with a gasp. It passed almost as quickly, leaving him with singing nerves and shuddering breath. He compelled his limbs to stand and crept into the icy light. It came from a spectral imitation of fire upon the ceiling, the memory of a fire dragged from an abused soul and implanted in the ceiling by a soul-caster for the Clergy. Dieharamon hurried through it and snuck into an alcove at the stairs' bottom to peek beyond.

He saw a corridor of stone cells with slits for feeding and barred iron flaps. Three hulking men patrolled between the cells with the stumbling tread of drugs, halting only upon collision with walls, whereupon they turned and resumed their shambling march. They blinked often, constantly fidgeted with their stone cudgels, and whenever their patrol brought them toward the stairs, Dieharamon saw a *brand* of violence charred into their skulls.

He scanned the prison block again, sensing something else but seeing nothing. Shadows veiled its extremity, defying the regular soul-lights but occasionally betraying a glimpse of what lurked within. Mangled bones littered the floor and the whole complex reeked of urine and wet animal.

Dieharamon inched further, scouring for what he could sense without success, knowing it sought him in turn. Both lingered for a while, loath to reveal themselves, but time compelled Dieharamon's hand. He stood, igniting the pyre within even as it made him cringe, and emerged, skin hot under the static soul-lights.

Bereft of thought, reduced to pure rage and stripped of all skill, the guards charged instantly, flailing at him with haphazard blows he easily evaded and counterattacked, leaving them sprawled upon the floor spasming in helpless ire. The scuffles conclusion left Dieharamon facing the stairs, the lights extinguished by the conflict. Feet pattered behind him, clicking with claws and a low hiss, roused by the guard's defeat. He tightened his grip on the sword and turned, following it with his ears.

The claws rasped then clicked as the creature drew back and pounced. Dieharamon side-stepped, slashing blindly, and landed a blow, rending flesh with a spray of blood and a howl. Claws scrambled again and he thrust toward them, scoring another injury before retreating and resetting himself.

Largely unfazed, the creature bounded toward him. He lunged aside, slashing again, but the creature compensated. He caught a whiff of foul breath before its massive weight crushed him to the floor, snapping his grip on the sword.

He battered it futilely with his fists and then shoved with his forearms. Claws dug into his chest, locking them together as he thrashed: hammering it with hands and knees, and tasting its dripping blood. Jaws clamped onto his shoulder, eliciting a scream from him. He tore the creature's paws from his chest and flung it aside with a heave from his feet, then scrambled upright and against the wall, listening for it.

Prowling footsteps sounded from the dark, slow and uneven as it paced, and Dieharamon ran a hand along the wall behind him, feeling for a depression in the stone. There! A handle. He spun, digging fingers into the groove, and pulled, but his hand slipped—betrayed by the blood on his fingers—and he fell. The creature rushed forward and Dieharamon flailed, connecting with a kick that drew an agonize yelp and repelled the creature across the hall, stealing the moment he needed.

Wiping his hands clean, Dieharamon clambered back up the wall and fumbled for the handle. He seized it with a sob and dragged it aside, straining against its ancient weight. It gave reluctantly, screeching across the floor and into its pocket, but let him stumble inside.

A soul-light flickered on in the cell and the creature stilled, hissing in the glow. It was a feline beast slightly shorter and wider than a horse, with black fur and an orange crest streaming from brow to tail.

Dieharamon leaned against the wall beside the entrance, muting his breath and listening. The feline crept a few steps and halted, unnerved by the light. Its instincts were to hunt at night, in the dark, but those instincts now warred with the Clergy's commands. It resumed advancing.

The massive creature slunk into the cell, eyes darting left and right. Dieharamon struck, swinging his interlocked hands like a cudgel. The feline lunged forward on instinct, twisting so that his fist only struck its shoulder, and then scrambled to turn as Dieharamon dove out the door. It leapt, yowling just before he slammed it shut.

He slumped forward, shaking as the feline railed against the door. The vibrations gradually attenuated, replaced by the scratch of pacing. He sank to the floor, panting and tentatively probing his injuries. Pain throbbed in his shoulder, chest, and back, and a burning sensation plagued his hand from the feline's smeared blood.

Grimacing, he tore strips from his robes and bound his injuries. The pain burrowed into him as he worked, leaving a dull ache and a curious numbness. He cursed under his breath and flared the pyre at his core, engulfing his limbs in heat and routing the pain. When the surge ended, the pain resumed its slow advance. He was poisoned. He crawled to his feet, collected his sword and shambled to check the guards for keys. No luck. His heart sank. Without knowing who carried the keys he could only gamble, and that meant finding the Immortal Consort. Dieharamon couldn't know for certain whether she possessed the keys or not, but he could leverage her, regardless. Rising again, he stumbled into the cell block's darkened extremity, holding the wall for balance.

The darkness persisted for several steps then ended unnaturally, relinquishing him to a wide chamber of graceful arches lit by warm, orange soul-light. The floors were carpeted, the walls lined with wood desks bearing writing implements and abundant wines. A single wood door waited opposite him: the Immortal Consort's chambers.

Two guards, equipped with ivory weapons and armor crafted from akarhri bones, lounged outside her entrance. They stood at his appearance, blades singing free. He scanned for other guards, wondering at their scarcity. *'She must believe herself safe, secreted so deep in Dru'Kerack,'* he thought.

"Who are you?" the challenge echoed unanswered. The elder guard sank into a blade stance, repeating his challenge, "Who are you?"

Dieharamon wiped the perspiration from his eyes and staggered to a halt before them. The power surged of its own accord, banishing his pain, fatigue, and doubt. The pewter sword flickered darkly as he raised it, contrasting the pale gleam of its ivory foes as the young guard looked on in terror.

The elder guard ghosted forward, gliding from one unrecognizable blade form into another, parrying and fluidly retaliating against Dieharamon's injured shoulder. Dieharamon persevered, throwing himself forward to crush his opponent against the wall, but the elder guard slipped past, slashing his thigh.

The younger guard charged, his thrust wavering and imprecise. Dieharamon slapped it aside with a hand and hammered the youth's head with the flat of his blade, toppling him.

The elder's blade flashed again, slashing upward and driving Dieharamon against the door before pressing his assault, striking first down to pin Dieharamon's sword to the floor, then up. Dieharamon lunged back then forward, ignoring the pain as the elder pricked his injured shoulder.

The elder effortlessly evaded Dieharamon's charge and sweep, which buried his sword in the wall. Still flowing, the elder reversed his momentum and slashed for Dieharamon's hand.

Abandoning his sword, Dieharamon vaulted and kicked the elder with both feet, launching him into the wall half-a-dozen feet away. One of the adorning curtains bounced from its hooks and covered the elder, permitting Dieharamon the moment needed to free the pewter sword and steady himself.

Discarding the curtain with a sweep of his free hand, the elder surged to his feet and into a lunging whirlwind of strikes. Dieharamon responded as best he could, but his sword felt heavy and lethargic, his body battling the poison. The ivory blade slashed and thrust inches ahead of his defense, incessantly weaving around his sword to inflict a dozen minor injuries.

Dieharamon could only retreat, striving to survive while luring the elder into the shadows. With a final step, the unnatural darkness at the entrance enveloped him, both blinding and concealing. The elder hesitated, his onslaught faltering for a heartbeat, then resuming.

There was the swish of a blade probing for its target, then a pause as the elder advanced and adjusted. Dieharamon crept back and aside, easing from the elder's path. The blade swished again, concluding with a rasp as it pierced a wall. The elder grunted and tore his sword free with a patter of fragments.

Discarding his sword as ineffective without vision, Dieharamon rushed close. Hearing the clatter, the elder pivoted to strike, but he was blind in the dark and his thrust missed. They collided, and the elder stumbled, the wall stopping their momentum and serving as the anvil Dieharamon used to crush the elder. The elder screamed, blade clattering to the floor. Dieharamon smashed him against the wall again, pounding until his body turned flaccid and soaked.

He released the corpse and collapsed, gasping through the agony of deprivation and fresh wounds. Gradually the pain receded, along with that of his injuries, the blood clotting as aching muscles soothed and the fire within pulsed. His senses cleared and his body strengthened, the poison's effects diminishing.

When he had the strength to stand, Dieharamon stumbled to the younger guard. The boy scrambled back and Dieharamon caught his collar. "Go home, boy, this isn't where you belong." He punched him, leaving the youth unconscious but alive.

Dieharamon snapped the wooden door with a kick, but there were no answering cries from the incense-filled room. He entered, scanning the fog of burning incense. The chamber's colors and design were opaque, a mixture of cobalt, sable, and emerald with touches of cherry to contrast. Ebony tables, carved with images and inlaid with gems, were draped with velvet and accompanied by padded chairs. A musician played a harp in the corner, her tranquil song and the sensuous languor of her posture belying the fear that should have ruled her.

Four attendants stood in a half-circle about their mistress with bared Arshendi and drugged eyes. Their lady sat behind them, wrapped in a robe of bear fur accented by raven feathers and armed only with an amethyst pendant.

"Did you think I would slumber ignorant of your assault?"

Dieharamon had hoped for this but acknowledged its folly. He advanced, searching for others hidden among the ocean of curtains. They fluttered at his passage, their black and emerald fabric painted with illustrations in gold.

His silence gave her pause, and his actions more so as he began snuffing soul-lights. The attendants hissed at this but remained still. The Immortal Consort surged to her feet with a blow to the armrest of her chair, the amethyst flaring. "Who are you?"

He gave no response, continuing to snuff lights. The attendants screamed their affront and charged. The Immortal Consort remained put and raised the amethyst.

The first attendant came, slashing wildly in unkempt anger, missing Dieharamon completely and exposing herself to a horizontal slash across the midsection. Two others vaulted her body; the first he killed with a reverse sweep, the second with a punch to her throat.

The last attendant came swinging with such force her body lurched. He sidestepped and decapitated her in passing, dropping her head with a dull thud while her body briefly continued past. None of them seemed the trained assassins the thieves promised; the Immortal Consort seemed to trust her own capabilities over the loyalty of hired mercenaries.

The Immortal Consort lowered her amethyst. "You have power, assassin, why not serve a better master than whatever filth hired you? Put yourself in my service, reap true power."

He lunged without answering, sword extended and teeth bared. She recoiled, hissing as the amethyst flashed and a rune of binding materialized. The *brand* landed but fizzled against the fire within his veins.

He swiped at the retreating Immortal Consort, scoring a thin laceration and eliciting a yelp as blood blossomed about the medallion. Amethyst flames erupted, spawning two searing *brands*: *Break and Spirit*. Together they formed a command in the old Arthramainian tongue: a tongue few could remember, let alone possess the spirit to utter.

The *brands* struck him and burst like flash powder. He slashed through their remnants, severing the amulet's chain and dropping it with a ding.

The Immortal Consort reeled and buckled against the bed. Dieharamon's sword anchored her there with a kiss to her throat. She stilled, clutching the bed frame with trembling hands, awash in revulsion and shock at the foreign taste of fear.

"What do you want?"

"I desire a safe departure from Dru'Kerack and a prisoner from your cells."

"You cannot enter the cells; they are guarded by more than stone and locks!"

"Yes, they are. But you have the keys, and I have something you want. This bespeaks a bargain."

"What can you possibly possess that I desire?"

"How highly do you value your life?"

"How am I to trust you?"

"I am not in the mood for rendering proof, so take my word on faith."

She tried to meet his gaze, to deny the validity of his threat, and failed. "Who do you want?"

"The Descendant."

Her breath caught and sudden visceral hate filled her expression. She pushed to rise, but the sword pricked her throat, checking her movements. "What do you want with him? How can you desire aught but to bring the blade down upon his neck with your own hands?"

She pressed closer, heedless of the blade in her hatred of the Descendants and compelling him to turn its flat against her throat. He dared not kill her; if he did, the whole of the Clergy would seek vengeance upon him. Yet he needed to convince her he was both capable and willing.

Dieharamon caught and threw her to lie among her slaughtered servants. She scrambled to rise, but his boot drove her back into the bloody mess and his sword tip bit into her stomach. "I am not Avaran; I reject your beliefs and deities."

Darkness smothered the chamber, sudden and brutal, snuffing the remaining lights and stealing all warmth from his blood. *Ashshand's* wrath constricted about his throat like chain links, and the gods stirred upon their Pantheon, enraged by the insolence of a mortal to reject a divinity.

The Immortal Consort whimpered, "You shouldn't have said that! We have to go!" The entreaty fell on deaf ears and subsided into moans. He ignored her, eyes fixed upon the unseen heavens as all of Sahdaen quaked with *Ashshand's* wroth. Yet Dieharamon still lived.

Realization slowly dawned, and he reverted his attention to the Immortal Consort. "This Hold is not yet *Ashshand's;* other entities exert claim upon it." She shrieked and thrashed, but he crushed her back to the floor. "Where is the Descendant?" She convulsed and slumped, babbling incoherent mumbles.

He nudged her, but the delirium held for she communed with *Ashshand.* Working quickly, he bound and gagged her to the bed, then felt about her throat for the key he needed. His fingers touched the hard cords of two strings. Hope renewing, Dieharamon extracted the cords and found two cumbersome iron keys. Certain these were his goal, his thoughts drifted to his sword; how many lives might he save if he broke his promise? How many would he doom? Would this woman's death alter anything about the Clergy, or would just another tyrant ascend? Would the new monstrosity be any kinder? Dieharamon growled and spared the mumbling woman, refusing to tread their path.

He returned to the cellblock, examining the keys; one was normal, the other carved into the *brand*: *Open*. If inverted, *Open* became *Lock*. Dieharamon discarded the first key and hurried from door to door, trying each without success. Growling in frustration, he spun on a heel, scanning the cell block for a door, a cavity—anything he overlooked—and settled upon the stairway, or more accurately, the paths running to either side of it. He sprinted to the shrouded paths and around the stairway until he came to a solitary door of wrought iron contorted into a grotesque caricature of greed and rage.

Trembling, he inserted the key and turned the lock, changing its rune from *Barred* to *Open*. The door cracked open, easing out of its own accord so he could stumble in.

The Descendant looked up and grinned. He was young, maybe just having seen his twentieth summer, with eyes so crystal blue they seemed to erase the dark. "Hello! I'm Dayada Avenar, son of Tarram Avenar, Lord of the DawnHold. What's your name?"

36

Dayada Avenar

Dieharamon stared at the man, mouth agape, uncomprehending of his radiance, his ... excitement. The man bounded closer, still spouting his lineage though Dieharamon registered none of it. He caught the man's shoulders and shook. "Be quiet, we have to leave, now!"

Dayada Avenar pulled free, straightening his filthy clothing. "Calm down, no need to shake me."

Dieharamon yanked him out of the cell and around the stair, ignoring his continued dialogue. "What are you in here for? I don't know why I'm here; foreign laws are so strange. I had just taken my seat at this lovely, rustic tavern when a pair of burly fellows approached me. Since both had clearly suffered many horrible accidents, I invited them to sit. One took my arm and said something I didn't understand. When I told him so, he switched to terrible Merchant's, saying somebody wanted to see me. I politely declined because, you see, I'm looking for somebody, and I told him as much. That's where everything got awfully jumbled; his Merchant's tongue really was atrocious—"

Dieharamon clamped a hand over Dayada's mouth. Footsteps echoed from above, many and ordered. "Quick," he whispered and scurried toward the stair, trying to gauge their distance.

Dayada followed, humming. "I'm supposed to be finding someone; but I don't know his name or appearance. Father said I would know him, that the ancestors would guide me. Except, I think the ancestors are a little lost! Just think about it, the first level of bridges here alone is larger than Tellor, and there's people everywhere! Plus, the bridges are amazing! I never imagined a city could be built on them!" They rounded the corner. "They're not the largest I've seen, mind you. I saw one of the Annuir Bridges on my way here; it was wider than I could see, longer too, though I guess it has to be to cross the *Annuir'Hyme!* Have you seen the southern bridge? Lord *Arthramain Roy'al* made all of them. They say you can't find a scratch on them! No one knows what they're made of, and I wanted a better look because I've read a lot about them, but Father said I couldn't delay–"

Dieharamon clamped Dayada's mouth again. "Listen, we are not safe. Our lives hang by a thread and every word frays it!" He forced himself to calm. "I need your help, Dayada; a man called Sinnitar Muntalabac is hunting me, and you are an Avenar, correct?"

All mirth died. "That's a *dark* name; you shouldn't say names like that." He shuddered. "You seem sick. There's a light inside you, but it's being strangled and there's so many scars. Don't they hurt?" He touched Dieharamon's chest and jerked back. "You're so cold."

The power within him surged, burgeoning until he felt aflame. He cried out and buckled, unable to stand for the pressure, and knelt there, panting huge gasps as perspiration streamed and the fire slowly diminished. Yet there was no pain: he felt alive, not simply restored but brimming.

Strong hands pulled him back upright. "Of course I'll help, although, they took my money, so I can't help you there. If we get it back, I could, but I only have a few gold crowns."

Dayada adjusted Dieharamon's clothing, naive smile gracefully restored. Dieharamon wanted to cry. How could the Dreamer or the Accumulary ever think this child capable of fighting a Dread Lord?

Unfortunately, what was done was done, and he had neither the cruelty nor the desire to return him to his cell.

"Let's go." The strength was gone from his words; the Avenar couldn't save him, couldn't protect him from the Dread Lord, couldn't even save himself, and no amount of rage or determination could alter that.

Dayada followed with a bouncing step. "Will you help me find him?"

Dieharamon paused atop the stair, peeking for guards. "Who?"

"The man I'm looking for."

"Now?"

"No, later; after we've escaped, whenever you're ready. Oh, have you seen my sword?"

"You have a sword?"

"Yes, er no; they took it."

"Do you really need it?" Dayada nodded. "Can you use it?"

"Yep, Tiberius says he's never seen someone fight like I do; Father agrees. Though he is always smiling when he says it."

Dieharamon raised the map of Dru'Kerack to a soul-light he didn't remember during his descent; they seemed to be multiplying.

If the Avenar truly could vanquish—or at least compete with—the Dread Lord, his weapon likely possessed immense power, augmented by all matter of western magic. The Clergy would preserve such a weapon, hoarding it for a suitable bearer in their most secure vault.

"I know where your sword is; if we hurry, and you actually keep quiet, we might survive."

"Roger that, Captain! Off we go."

"Wait! You don't know where you're going, follow me."

The next chamber contained three stairways, and to reach the armory they needed the center stair, but first he had to ascertain from where the guards approached.

He touched a finger to Dayada's lips, silencing his low hum. "Stay here and stay quiet. That means no humming." Dieharamon kept his finger there until Dayada nodded acquiescence, then felt his way up. If the second stair betrayed no sign of approaching guards they could depart, if it did, they would hide. He barely managed a few steps before a ruddy glow illumined the second stairs' top landing.

Muttering a curse, Dieharamon scrambled back as some twenty acolytes began their descent, guided by soul-lights. Thankfully, they did not see him even as he sprinted across the open floor and down to Dayada, their chatter muting his steps. No doubt more good fortune he would have to repay.

Dayada sprung upright and smiled at his approach, leaving an unfinished dust picture. "Have you seen a dragon? Father says one actually lives here. Can you believe it? A real dragon! My first history instructor said they were myth, but I never believed him, what with Blessed Remanas and all. I told him as much and he acted strangely, face going all red and gasping. So I got him some wine, which he didn't like either. I wonder if he was allergic?"

"Shhh, the guards are almost here!" Dieharamon caught and dragged him along the room's edge, ducking behind the first stair into a nook just as the acolytes reached the floor, voices echoing boisterously and lights swinging. He crouched lower, daring just enough exposure to monitor their progress.

Strangely, the guards moved without haste or excitement; though their dialogue confirmed they knew of his intrusion. They had been dispatched to ensure the Immortal Consort's safety, and thus cared nothing for him. As they crossed the room, a second, frantic, pair of footsteps silenced their boasts. Another guard emerged atop the third of the ascending stairs, almost tumbling in his reckless haste.

Unable to hear their lowered voices, Dieharamon watched them exchange a flurry of words then erupt into frenzied activity. Someone cried, "The Immortal Consort," and together they rushed the descending stair, blades hissing free.

"Let's go." Dieharamon didn't know what had alerted the guards to the Immortal Consort's plight, but he hoped she diverted them long enough to reclaim Dayada's sword. Indicating the second stair, he hissed, "That way," and then slipped through the shadows toward it, ever cautious of the guards. They managed to ascend without alerting anyone and began a stuttering sprint through Dru'Kerack.

They attained the armory after a surprisingly brief journey and found it unguarded, which initially uneased Dieharamon until he realized it was made entirely of stone.

Dayada, a few steps ahead of Dieharamon, paused outside it without guidance, and laid a hand upon its surface, cocking his head as if listening. "We need to open this."

Nodding, Dieharamon grasped the iron handle and heaved, straining until the portal rasped open with a belch of sacrificial ash. "Find your sword; I'll watch the door."

Soul-lights ignited within, providing copious illumination and granting the jumbled heap of weapons unmerited grandeur. Most boasted simple craftsmanship, lacking both the artwork that accompanied skilled artistry and even the basic quality of western swords. Spears, arrows and unstrung bows lined the walls on hooks and in barrels, but the rest comprised the heap, many having slid off to clutter the circumventing path.

Glancing in, Dieharamon noted side exits and swore, realizing it would take hours to search everything. Before the Avenar could advance further, he caught his arm. "We'll never find it in this."

"Of course we will; as if I can't recognize my own sword." Dayada waded deeper, kicking weapons aside without thought for racket or potential harm. Dieharamon cringed and followed, unable to shirk the presentiment that Dayada knew his destination exactly but also unwilling to let the Avenar escape his sight.

They traversed a trio of rooms, each one varying little in size or contents. Dieharamon said nothing, more concerned with chance encounters than where Dayada led. He scanned constantly, jumping at every new sound and smell as his mind paraded through one violent sequence after another. Finally, with his nerves frayed unto breaking, Dayada brought him to the armory's deepest vault.

The cavernous room contained ranks of ceiling-high shelves bulging with spheres of glass, stone, wood, and every conceivable metal. There were masks, bolts of cloth, ornate daggers, opalescent swords, simple staves, and statues both minute and larger than two men could lift. Yet all this paled before the sword planted in the stone floor at its center, glimmering and bound to the walls with chains.

Dayada grinned. "There's Taychran! I wonder how they got it here? Must have used some kind of soulcraft."

"Don't touch anything; it's probably warded."

"Why bother warding Taychran? It's not like anybody could use it."

The sword was exquisite, its worn pommel wrought of gold and inlaid adamants, and its blade an untarnished white metal. Dieharamon cautiously approached and tapped its chains with his sword. Orange light erupted, lashing him with punishing heat as he retreated and swore, waving a hand futilely to shield his face. He began to turn and warn Dayada, but the words died as six acolytes filed into the room.

Dayada followed his gaze. "Oh, hello. Could you give us a moment? We're just trying to get my sword." Dieharamon struck Dayada to the floor and spun, slashing the chain holding Taychran.

The link coiled and snapped, whipping Dieharamon across the face and releasing Taychran. He staggered, but caught the sword and flung it to Dayada, almost screaming as the blade ignited into golden flames in his hand. The acolytes charged with a cry, two engaging Dieharamon and the rest skirting around him with glancing blows to cover their evasion.

He tried to engage them, but the two opposing him doubled their assault. He eluded one strike, parried a second and dove into a straggling acolyte. They crumpled to the ground, Dieharamon on top with his sword caught between them.

Bones cracked as they landed, puncturing the acolyte's almond skin and loose tunic as he screamed. The acolyte flailed as Dieharamon rose, grasped and heaved him onto one of the two Avarans that first engaged him. They tumbled in a heap, and Dieharamon lunged to engage the other one, who spun with a sweep of his axe. Dieharamon blocked with a forearm to its haft and swept in close, hammering the acolyte's chest hard enough to break ribs. The acolyte staggered and collapsed, freeing Dieharamon to reclaim his sword.

Of the two acolytes he entangled, one had managed to stand while the other screamed with his injuries. Shaking off the fog of deprivation, Dieharamon advanced, struck the standing acolyte's defense aside, pursued as he staggered back, and decapitated him. The corpse collapsed and Dieharamon impaled the screaming man.

Freeing his blade, he scanned for Dayada and saw him stumbling between three acolytes, Taychran held crossways across his body at its sheathed tip and pommel. The acolytes assailed him, howling in joint fury as

Dayada lurched between them, awkwardly blocking and parrying. One slashed at his ankles, the other two for his ribs and his neck. Dayada reeled, sweeping Taychran horizontally up to miraculously block the two high strikes while evading the low. His feet betrayed him in that same instant, and he fell with a squeak of surprise.

Dieharamon lunged in response, grasping and hurling one of the fallen blades in a desperate attempt to save the Avenar. The spinning blade impaled an acolyte, separating the others. One immediately confronted Dieharamon.

The acolyte led with an awkward thrust, which Dieharamon batted aside before pivoting into the man, wondering how the acolyte could believe himself the stronger. Then he heard the tinkle of smashing glass as a marble struck his boot. The hoarded flames roared out, engulfing both of them.

He buckled, screaming as the flames lashed his flesh. Before him, Dayada wrestled with the final acolyte as his sight faded. Vying for leverage, the acolyte's groping hand caught Taychran and golden light exploded outward, obliterating the acolyte to a burnt husk: Taychran suffered only the Avenars' touch.

His consciousness fluttered.

Dayada lingered briefly, contemplating the charred corpse, then returned to himself with a start and rushed to Dieharamon, laying Taychran aside.

Cool hands touched Dieharamon's brow, soothing his scattered, fevered thoughts. Words followed, reaching him through the pain, shock, and fear, coaxing him upward, away from the whispering desire to just give up. "Are you all right? Can you move?"

He blinked and shook his head weakly. The pain doubled, effacing all thought from his mind.

Dayada spoke again, finding purchase in Dieharamon's reeling thoughts, "Hey, you need to wake up." The agony flickered, diminishing at the Avenar Prince's words as he pulled him to his feet.

Quivering with effort, Dieharamon pushed Dayada away and breathed long, weighted breaths, shoving the pain into the recesses of his consciousness until it became no more than an itch. Exhaling a final time, he opened his eyes, their natural blue usurped by molten gold. "Why did you not draw Taychran? Retaliate?"

"It was stuck."

Dieharamon groaned. "Well, let's go before more a–" The summons reverberated through his body, echoing again and again as the first etches of day pierced the reluctant night. He was out of time and still needed to bring Dayada to Valeriius' fortress, where he would be comparatively safe. At least until Valeriius deemed otherwise.

He delayed only long enough to don a suit of rare chain mail before absconding through Dru'Kerack, every beat striking like a hammer.

The Dread Lord stood atop Sahdaen's highest bridge, observing the city as it suffocated beneath its own bloated malice. Yet a light blazed within that wallowing morass, almost lost amidst the putrefaction but unaffected: an Avenar princeling had entered Sahdaen.

A cheap prostitute approached him, enraptured by his glory. He returned her inviting smile, drawing a veil about his intent as he extended a hand. Then he tore her fragile soul free and discarded the corpse into the precipice.

The Dread Lord restored his gaze to Sahdaen, admiring his labors. In the hours since he sowed the first seeds of fear, they had bloomed into a garden. Now fully matured, the roots had begun to propagate, swallowing entire buildings and infesting every miserable soul they touched.

Fear made for fertile soil, and soon that fear would begin eroding the Avarans' sanity. When this occurred, the fear would explode beyond even *Ashshand's* ability to control. Such was Sahdaen's fate.

He stepped to the precipice, cupping the prostitute's still shrieking soul in both hands and torturing it into something horrific. He adsorbed this remade soul, fusing it irrevocably into the cacophony of his being and then expelled it again, adding another crow to his flocks.

Restoring his focus to the city, he gorged upon its malice, feeding until shadows seeped from his eyes, the cobbles blackened at his feet, and the very air cowered. When this state manifested, he shifted his attention to two men of the New Order and the brutalized girl they carried. She struggled feebly, an effort born more from instinct than conscious effort.

The men approached, the words of *Telacra* inked onto their hands but faded. They had been intended as a reminder of the Dark Consort's power and a fetter upon him, but they had stepped into his presence and in so doing, erased their individuality. Now they served as extensions of himself, individual and sentient but bereft of autonomous will.

The men staggered and buckled as they neared, crushed by the bared weight of his soul. He took the girl from them and extended her over the precipice, an obsidian knife materializing in his other hand as storm clouds crept into the sky, blinding *Sarah'Venn* and forbidding her from interfering. He marshalled his dread power, chaining it to the beginnings of a *dark labor*, and ended the girl with a slash. In the same instant, he tore her soul out and crushed it from existence, speaking words colder than the heart of winter,

> *"Darkness secreted deep within soul and body,*
> *awaken at my call; come, come quickly.*
> *"Darkness long dormant within your ancient*
> *Hold, come and obscure the heavens once more with*
> *clouds and water.*
> *"Darkness of Cold and Dread at last*
> *awakened by its master's call, rise up and darken the*
> *heavens from the light of sun and moon, and blind*
> *the ancient flame in its fury with ice and cold long*
> *forbidden."*

The *dark labor* flooded out, usurping the heavens and bringing all of Sahdaen to heel with a crushing burden of silence. As one, the Avarans felt the change in their ancestral land, felt its subjugation and the shattering of *Ashshand's* dominion. A drop of searing water landed upon his brow, condemning this land to despair and marking the advent of his night.

He flung the corpse from the bridge, the dread power cresting ever higher within him, and again spoke, uttering words so black they shattered what little sanity remained in the New Order soldiers.

> *"Fly nightmares upon the wings of darkness*
> *spawned by darkness to the minds of those sleeping*
> *deep.*
> *"Fly darkness born of nightmares fair, infest*
> *the dreams of those asleep and those walking with*
> *dread beyond reason.*
> *"Terror born of darkness and fell dreams,*
> *consume and sew hatred, bring to ruin all you touch*
> *until only ruin remains."*

Valeriius watched the storm with indifference; this was not a heavenly tantrum, and he would have known it even blind to the spiritual ether men called magic. Rain never touched the Avarus Desert; the heavens would crack and sunder, flash with lightning and howl, but rain never fell.

He stood alone in a desolate room, illuminated by a dim insect lamp and unknown even to the daemons assembled outside. They knew only their purpose to slaughter anyone who neared within three hundred yards of the structure, regardless of nature or allegiance.

Despite the insect's fluttering wings, the room's shadows refused movement, behaving as if they were old paint and not absent light. He felt their hunger: a young, uncomprehending thirst for blood that only stirred in the night. It was the Dread Lord's doing; his presence that gave them and all things born of or in darkness life.

Superseding them, however, intangible unless sought, was the fear. Sahdaen reeked of it from Tragnashi to Kalvonder, and man to beast. The Dread Lord had arrived, and with him, everything born or subservient to malice would flourish.

The door opened with a soft creak, movement far too quiet for stone. He turned from the window as Bellay Enkarta entered, closing the door with a wave of his hand, unnoticed by the sentries. "Salem sent you to measure current events?"

Bellay Enkarta joined him at the window, too-azure eyes unnaturally bright. "Yes. He wonders how or if you cope with the Dread Lord."

"I do not; the sufferings of this city and her people are of no consequence."

Bellay Enkarta was tall for Avarans but short for the more northern race. He wore a loose tunic and a black vest, high boots, dark trousers, and gloves. Light brown curls adorned his brow while a thick goatee gave color to pale skin. A tattoo obscured the left side of his neck, three black serpents: a cobra, an adder, and a taipan entangled and devouring its predecessor's tail. A scorpion hung at the center, grasping the taipan and the adder and spearing the cobra.

"What of Dieharamon?"

"He is nearly complete."

"When?"

"Soon. Present events strain him, exhausting the limits of his abilities until they expand."

"Will Dieharamon equal Sinnitar Muntalabac?"

"No. However, he is not alone. An Avenar stands with him, along with another."

"Who?"

"I have only supposition, but this land's bane no longer quells Dieharamon. It was broken in the Lake of Dream, during a time neither I nor a **Hound of Karrassain** could see Dieharamon."

"You are certain nonetheless."

"Yes."

"Who is it, and what is his intent?"

"I do not presume to fathom his desires; but when he last walked this mortal realm, war consumed it."

37

Order And Chaos

Lionel crouched before the dying embers of a fire, warming his hands in the outskirts of a forest. The early morning light glistened on the snow and the world bustled with wildlife waking from the night's repose. Arrad waited to the side, already saddled and strapped with Lionel's equipment. He stamped impatiently, anxious after the two days cowering from a storm. Lionel stood, donning his gauntlets and scarf before stamping the fire out and mounting Arrad.

He tapped the destrier's flanks and rode northward, allowing Arrad to navigate the clustered trees and roots with easy, energetic steps. As Arrad advance, Lionel shuffled through his saddlebags to extract a small, golden amulet depicting a hawk.

He ordered his thoughts and activated his Shard of Divinity. The golden hawk pulsed in response, expanding to the size of his hand, where upon it shook its feathered head and disentangled itself from the fine chain. He stroked it, cooing until it settled. "You shall take this message west through Winter's Gate to the court at Dol'Cardolani. It is exclusively for Adjudicator Jaden Attas or the Imperial Emperor: my name is Lionel Iitanen, and this is my report on the New Order's movements.

"The New Order has invaded The North, but its forces suffer heavy attrition. At the beginning, their strength numbered at rough estimation around twenty thousand soldiers. Three-quarters of that were sacrificed at Adriat to gain entrance into The North. The army has bypassed all settlements and foregone any deviation. I believe they seek to enter Winsyria's Cradle and sack Antiark.

"As it stands, the New Order leads Lord Adriat's forces by two days and, to all appearances, seems capable of maintaining that distance. If they are indeed hunting Antiark, they might succeed. Antiark has little in the way of an army; most of The North's soldiers reside at Winter's Gate and along The Northern border to prevent Weshac raids. Because of this, I find *Winsyria's* inaction troubling; he has done nothing to impede the invading host, which has grown lately—possibly from mercenaries smuggled into The North over previous years.

"It may be wise to aid The North; they are currently amicable and possess vast stores of knowledge that might prove useful. I believe the New Order's main intent is to isolate the Paladin Empire from all potential allies. If true, and I have no proof, the New Order will also be seeking allies in the Avarus Desert. Even if I'm wrong, we need to observe the South more diligently, the Avarans and Kalvonders have no love for us."

Finished, Lionel leaned back. The hawk shifted, its large eyes closing for one slow blink as it memorized his message. When they opened again, he tossed it skyward and watched it bank southward to Dol'Cardolani.

He gathered the amulet's fine chain and returned it into his saddlebags alongside roughly eleven other hawk amulets and two emblazoned with the Paladin Empire's maul and circle. He reclaimed the reins and urged Arrad up the gradually rising snow drifts and onto the vast Northern tundra. A quick glance verified the position of the *Annuir'Hyme* to the West, and the New Order to the north. Beyond them the Rhawn formed Winsyria's Cradle, an immense plateau in the center of the human north, accessible via a single pass and only in summer, with the exception of derangers. Even during summer, the roads were treacherous and best taken with a guide.

Lionel restored his attention to the New Order; the scar of their passage ran due north from Winter's Gate toward the pass, a trail of frozen mud, ice, waste, shards of wood, and discarded metal that set his skin on edge. Suppressing the sensation, he nudged Arrad faster.

He reached the trail after a couple hours and reined in at its edge, senses tingling with *Telacra's* residual power. Hoping to ascertain something from the tracks and residue, Lionel dismounted, ignoring the barrage of foul energy this action incurred. He ventured onto the tracks and began his examination, crossing it while judging the distance between himself and the New Order and the condition of their army. He had gained recently, closing to within half-a-day, but their wagons had noticeably lightened, increasing their pace.

"Why does a paladin of Cardolyn Tyier wander The North in the New Order's shadow?"

Lionel froze at the rasping voice. When no arrow pierced his back, he raised his hands. "I am tracking them to gauge their strength and purpose. I intend The North no harm, Ranger-Warden."

"You speak like a western man and a paladin, sir knight; but your accent is a Northerner's."

"I was raised in the Shallow North."

When this earned no response, Lionel peeked over his shoulder. A patch of air twenty yards away rippled, unveiling a deranger in a white oudakc. Lionel sighed in relief and dropped his hands.

The deranger studied him impassively, armed with a black bow, arrows, and a glass sword hanging from a naked loop. Then quivering his arrow, he revealed Lionel's messenger hawk, reverted to an amulet. "What did you report to the Summer-lands, sir knight? And what is your name?"

"I am Lionel Iitanen, that messenger carries only my knowledge of the New Order, advice, and suppositions concerning their intent. If you give me your name, I can open it for you."

The deranger tossed him the amulet. "Tassen, Sir Lionel."

He caught and lifted the amulet to his lips. "Present your message to Ranger-Warden Tassen and then continue to withhold it." The amulet morphed into a hawk, ruffled its feathers and flew to Tassen's shoulder. Its beak opened, issuing Lionel's voice, "This is my report on the New Order's movements, my name is Lionel Iitanen…"

Lionel left the deranger to dissect the message and crossed to Arrad, exhaling as he escaped *Telacra's* incessant burning evil. The destrier snorted and permitted Lionel to touch their brows together. "You could have warned me there was a deranger before I made a fool of myself." Arrad nibbled on Lionel's hair. "I know, you couldn't see him either, but still…" The destriers head jerked up from Lionel's shoulder, nostrils flaring as he stomped the ground. Lionel stepped backed, scanning the panorama.

He saw only the vast white of the northern expanse, but Arrad snorted again and retreated from the trail's edge. Lionel followed his gaze, trying to soothe him with a stroking hand, but again saw nothing. "What do you see, my friend?" The destrier reared, eyes growing large and wild as the wind lashed them with flakes of ice. Lionel shielded his face with a hand and cursed, but the wind pummeled harder, leaving only the deranger unfazed.

An old memory surfaced: 'Lionel, The North is unlike the Summer-lands. It is awake and intelligent, after a fashion. Even when it appears violent, listen to what it's trying to say.'

Lionel exhaled to calm himself and closed his eyes, listening but hearing only the wind's shriek. He felt for what it carried but found only ice and snow. Then he smelled burning, inhaled deeper and gagged, mouth and nose filling with the scent of fire and sulfur: Chaos.

"Damn it!" Lionel lunged into Arrad's saddle, the wind dying, and swung toward the deranger who was already lowering his oudakc's hood and knocking an arrow.

"Sir Lionel—"

"I know. Demons. We need to run, there's more than we can handle."

"You are their target, Sir Lionel. Go, I will delay their advance." He faded into the elements.

"What do you mean, delay their advance?"

"Do not fear for me, this is The North, and The North always keeps its own. You, however, are alone, so I suggest you start running."

Lionel yanked Arrad about and charged for the *Annuir'Hyme*, glimpsing scattered figures in crimson armor as he did so. One jerked—a black arrow protruding from its chest—stumbled and continued, its body warping into a beast.

He leaned into Arrad's neck, awakening the Shard of Divinity, and touched the destrier's flanks. Resplendent energy flooded through his hands into Arrad, strengthening him. Arrad surged, strides pounding the ground like thunder, each step cracking century-old ice.

The *Annuir'Hyme* had no beginning or end, it split the Mortal Kingdoms perfectly, crossing mountains, forests, and oceans. Despite this, it had many derivatives and, while only a few bridges crossed its main body, many smaller bridges traverse its progeny. Despite their size, these smaller rivers were no less the *Annuir'Hyme,* and Lionel could only hope they would forbid the hell-spawn passage.

More demons appeared on his flanks, angling inward to impede his escape. He called more heavily upon his Shard, channeling more power into Arrad. The destrier's soaked flanks heaved forward, spasms wracking his body, destroying his muscles.

The miles melted beneath Arrad's enhanced body, and with every one, the destrier broke further. As his body deteriorated, so did his pace, forcing Lionel to channel more energy and demand more of the already ruined body. Arrad was dead after the third mile, but he kept pushing. The demons inched ever closer, becoming distinct against the white.

Finally the bridge appeared, an arching masterpiece of misted glass forged from the river it crossed. Graceful glass railing framed either edge, every inch of it and the floor fashioned with the frail, beautiful images of vine flowers. Arrad's hooves thundered upon the glass, spraying mud and snow across the surface as blood dripped from his mouth. But they were not alone. A Raven awaited them atop the bridge's arch.

As he and Arrad crested the arch, it cawed and swept its wings back. Arrad shrieked, rearing in a futile attempt to arrest his momentum, and fell thrashing, body breaking beneath Lionel and throwing him before the Raven.

Lionel scrambled upright, but the Raven cawed again and a shapeless force repelled him, sending him tumbling to the floor.

The *Annuir'Hyme* surged with a roar, swelling against the banks as Lionel clambered to his feet and spun. A woman in the blood armor of demons, stood at the bridge's foot, pretty if one ignored her blood-hued curls and vicious, serrated armor. Her eyes roiled with Chaos, contrasting her silence and immobility, while her physique was masculine with wide shoulders and a thick, powerful torso.

Lionel yanked his broadsword from beneath Arrad's corpse and unsheathed it, the sanctified metal singing and flaring golden. The familiar weight settled in his grip and he assessed his foe. She carried no weapon except her armor and a foul collar about her wrist. Strangely, he felt nothing of the Chaos filling her, and saw no sign of it beside her eyes. She could have been human.

She retreated from him, distancing herself from the *Annuir'Hyme* because she knew he had nowhere to go. Lionel sought her fellows, saw them approaching but distant, and refocused upon her. "What is your name, hell-spawn? If I am to die, I will know who killed me."

She did not answer.

Lionel growled, "Justice be done," and charged, reigniting his Shard of Divinity and empowering his broadsword into a mass of golden fire. She evaded his first downward strike, a feint, and Lionel reversed the momentum, sweeping the sword back up and across with barely a pause. She caught it on her bracers, the plates snapping open and latching down. The sword's flames roared and vaulted onto her arms and face, clawing hungrily as he tore free.

He tried to retreat, sweeping the broadsword to ward her off, but she kicked his breastplate, launching herself back and hurling him to crash upon the bridge—a fuming, foot-shaped dent in his breastplate. He rolled to his feet and faced her, broadsword held before him just as the other hell-spawn arrived, some as men and others as grotesque, metallic beasts.

Two eclipsed the rest, one an immense, fulminating bear with a ridged back and barely restrained violence, the other a tall man whose features had been etched solely to evince cruelty. "Hello, sir knight, we welcome your company."

Lionel flared his Shard and thrust his right hand toward the tall demon, hurling a golden lance through his chest and driving him to a knee. Almost instantly, the lance twisted and warped, darkening to a convoluted mimicry of its former glory as the demon stood, tore it free, and crushed it to dust. "That's not how you greet someone. Let me show you: I am Kell'MachChain, and you are?"

Lionel charged, golden flames engulfing his arms and shoulders. The demons—lesser devils for the most part—scattered, but they were too clustered for all to escape. He caught one with a sweep, splitting its skull amidst gouts of golden fire and writhing Chaos. Its kin howled and charged, but he whirled, blasting them aside with golden force. In its wake, Lionel charged the bear demon and impaled its flank.

The demon roared and shook, hurling Lionel to the ground and breaking his grip. Lionel scrambled upright, reeling from the blow, and reached toward the bridge, screaming another word. His arming sword and shield tore from their bindings on Arrad's saddle and soared to him.

He spun, repelling the encroaching demons with a sweep of his sword and a tide of fire. They retreated and he crouched, the words of a psalm rising to his lips as his Shard pulsed with ancient hatred. Light bled from his armor, consolidating at his feet and expanding to form a diamond of incandescent light.

A rat-like demon howled and spat liquid fire at the barrier, but the flames cascaded harmlessly off its surface. Lionel scrutinized their ranks for vulnerability, but only saw Kell'MachChain licking his lips. "Please, kill more of them; I have quite an appetite."

Horrified by the allusion, Lionel charged and smashed the rat demon aside with his shield before cleaving its spine with a hack, the blade's divine enchantments granting it efficacy it would otherwise have lacked. He pivoted, skewering a human-guised demon and engulfing it in fire. He retreated, relinquishing his arming sword and materializing a golden maul in his now empty right hand. Another demon lunged, and he brought the maul crashing down on it.

The demon to his left, shrieking and clawing at the sword, rammed Lionel's shield, hurling him across the ground and tearing his shield free. He rolled to his feet, raising a hand, and called out again. His arming sword wrenched free of the human-guised demon's midsection and flew to him. He turned—still chanting as golden light coalesced in his left hand—and gored a demon charging his flank. It shrieked, the blade perforating its skull. He yanked his sword free, slid his foot wide and swept his left arm in a wide arc before him. A chain of golden links formed in his hand and lashed out with a crack of divine power, scattering half-dozen lesser demons.

Where the golden links struck crimson armor, they exploded, engulfing the demons in flames until it struck the bear demon, whereupon it shattered like glass.

Staggering, Lionel righted himself and lashed out again, the golden chain crackling as it reformed. Before it collided, Kell'MachChain stepped forward and caught it with a savage grin. The links ensnared his arms and ignited, but Kell'MachChain only roared, his body swelling as his eyes erupted. For a moment, Order and Chaos warred, then a crushing force flung Lionel face-first into the ground, dispelling his chain.

Hacking blood, Lionel surged upward, but a boot smashed him back down. He groped for his arming sword and the boot ground harder, ending his struggles.

Kell'MachChain's boots stepped into his vision and the demon dug burning fingers into his hair, lacerating his scalp and drawing blood. "It appears you will be enjoying our company after all."

Lionel's vision flicked and died, leaving him with a final glimpse of the she-demon as she stepped off him and walked past Kell'MachChain.

Kell'MachChain released the unconscious paladin, causing the lesser demons to visibly relax, all except the rat demon, who strove feebly to rise. Kell'MachChain knelt beside it with a grin, and its hisses turned to whimpered entreaties. Kell'MachChain stroked him with a comforting hand. "Don't worry, you will be home soon." Careful to avoid anywhere touched by the paladin, he leaned over the rat, maw unhinging to clamp on and snap its prominent spine.

Kell'MachChain's features warped as he consumed the demon's vital Chaos, reverting to his demonic half and flaring with internal fire. The demon died within seconds; its agonized soul restored to the Abyss. Kell'MachChain straightened, his maw bloody, and flexed with newfound strength. "Come, Kheldar Ferain anxiously awaits our guest."

Lionel woke first to pitch blackness, then recognized the abhorrence of all that surrounded him: living and inanimate, beast and man, the power of his captors, and the wanton death presiding upon all. He curled around his knees, shuddering in a cold that flayed his skin and devoured warmth.

He knew why he lived; they dared not incur Cardolyn Tyier's attention with the death of his paladin. Instead, they incarcerated him, leaving only sufficient warmth to survive and a distant awareness of his surroundings. His mind worked in that darkness, scrounging for potential escape, even if it meant suicide. His purpose had been to scout the New Order, now his sole objective was to impair them, and the greatest detriment he could inflict was summoning the Imperial Emperor's attention; Cardolyn Tyier knew little of forgiveness, and none concerning his knights.

In time, the New Order would question him about the extent of his knowledge and reports, which necessitated opening his prison and granting him an opportunity to strike.

So he waited. Time passed slowly but he gradually acclimated to his reduced senses, recognizing movement and even distinct presences as they traversed his environs. They never fed him and although the darkness muted his hearing, he occasionally caught words from an old Descendant dialect: Alarachi. He recognized the elapse in days by the temperature and the pattern of the army's movements. When it hurt to breathe, he knew night had fallen; when that pain faded and someone arrived to stand vigil, the day had come. At first, he only distinguished it as a demon but eventually recognized her by the feel of her spirit, though she never spoke.

Then on the fourth night of his imprisonment, she came out of time, bringing warmth the clerics had stripped from him as their power failed. She lay against the bars for that whole night, sparing what heat she dared as The North raged so viciously the goddess-blessed New Order could only cower. He slept, bathed in Chaos' writhing fire and hate, warm for the first time in months. When the dawn woke him to the renewed warmth of his prison, she remained present but no longer adjacent, and others crowded the periphery of his perception.

The darkness retracted like a sharp intake, giving way to overwhelming light and sound. Lionel squinted, almost drowning in the deluge of sensations. A key turned the lock and two gauntleted hands pitched him out onto the frozen mud.

Coughing, he climbed to his knees and forced his eyes first open, then up past the black wood of a throne, the armored limbs of its occupier, and into the dark paladin's face. The man reclined, hands clamped on the armrests and brow raised in hatred so absolute it was a physical burden. "I am Kheldar Ferain, a paladin of the New Order. What is your name?"

Lionel examined his captors. He saw Kell'MachChain, Cellar'Veer, and the she-demon along with three dark paladins: Kheldar Ferain, a blond paladin, and a third masked man toying with a dagger. To Lionel's right, there was a tall cleric and a man dressed in white with the Raven from the bridge on his shoulder. Lionel dropped his head.

Kheldar Ferain struck his jaw, knocking him to the ground. "We can do this with minimal pain and a higher degree of civility, or resort to barbarism. I assure you, we prefer the second option, but wisdom advised against it."

Lionel returned to his knees and wiped the blood dripping from his mouth with a tattered sleeve. He reached for his Shard, beginning words of death that would obliterate himself and everyone around him, but Kheldar Ferain reacted first. The dark paladin snapped his fingers, and a thin black chain seething with energy materialized around Lionel's throat, flattening him in gasping agony as the *silence* asserted itself.

"You were *silenced* before we took you from the prison, fool. We are not allowing you to escape and warn your masters. That said, if you deny us your name, you will confide how you survived the night."

Refusing to stay in the mud, Lionel crawled back to his knees as the chain dematerialized. "Your allies are not as loyal as you–" Kheldar Ferain's fist smashed into his jaw again, but Lionel caught himself. "Might as well drop the pleasantries, I will give you nothing."

Kheldar Ferain dragged Lionel closer by the hair. "We will try pain eventually, but first we'll see what the fear of it does to you in the darkness and hate of your cell. How long will you survive when there is only fear, starvation, cold, and insanity to accompany you? Please, enjoy it; the cell was a gift from the friend who told us about you." Kheldar Ferain dropped him. "Put him away and take note that my wager is a week."

Lionel gave no resistance as the she-demon returned him to his cell. At its entrance, she lifted him like a child and whispered in a voice that, though fractured from disuse, was achingly beautiful, "Trust me." Then she shoved him forward and the door slammed shut.

38

A Wizard Of Dreams

In the days trailing the governor's ball, the already abusive weather doubled down and convinced most children to shed their modesty, whereas the adults tugged on their restrictive collars, complained or swore, and stubbornly refused to submit.

Tasha refused right alongside them, glowering silent condemnation at Slade, who pranced about with his usual energy.

"Behold the gutter of the gutters, the slum of the slums; home of thieves who steal rags and footpads who stalk dogs. Rats, the species without crime, exile their most depraved rodents here." He spun a circle, arms thrown wide to indicate the tightly huddled buildings of crumbling clay, rotting thatch, and makeshift supports bolted to awkward repairs. A few exceptions existed here and there, rising from adjacent streets as pristine, warmly colored towers designed to accommodate multiple families. Those were few, however, as this quarter of Tellor rebuffed construction, its ground shirking the dark, loamy soil so prevalent across the Empire for a rippled composite of red metal and granite.

Atop this curiosity squatted what Tasha assumed was their destination. A house with a peculiarly curved roof mounded by dirt and sprouting green, its rear burrowing into a modest knoll while the various apertures hung open, grasping for every stray breeze. An easy mark for theft or espionage, provided passersby could overcome the front yard. A hedge of sparse bushes dressed the building in a tattered skirt while a host of overgrown and browning weeds assailed it from all sides, the tools needed to rout their assault laying strewn over the battlefield. Most peculiarly, several gracefully rusting statues attended the perimeter.

"Your friend seems obsessed with his garden," Tasha quipped, wiping her brow with an already damp sleeve and then—simply because she apparently wasn't hot enough—began restlessly bouncing atop her toes. "However does he find the time?"

"My friend is a wizard," Slade replied, performing an elegantly descriptive shrug. "Indifference toward menial tasks is a requirement for the job. Far more important than housework is a spell that changes the color of his rose bushes."

Feylin, fanning herself with a hat he had foisted upon her claiming it would guard against assassins, glanced over. "Why not simply plant the desired color?"

"Because it's far more entertaining to spend three years creating a spell to avoid that exact task."

Tasha snorted. "I'm astounded by his hardworking dedication to avoiding work."

"Yes, it is quite impressive. A bit problematic too, but luckily for him I undertook all the necessary maintenance so he need not forsake his principles. Hence the new door and its accompanying walkway."

Feylin squinted through the statues and bushes, breaking into an abrupt giggle. "I guess that explains why his door's striped yellow and pink."

"It does, doesn't it." Slade grinned then nodded toward the distant building. "Well, shall we brave the dragon's lair?"

"Not quite yet." Sitting back, Tasha crossed her arms. "We're not braving anything until we know exactly what 'adventure' is lurking inside. This Malendor is a friend of yours, and he's a wizard. You cause enough trouble without supernatural assistance."

"I haven't the faintest idea what you're insinuating. Malendor is a simple shopkeeper, and I'm a poor inoffensive boy who's been framed by circumstance … repeatedly. Hardly the elements of chaos you would suggest."

"Sure you are. What's inside the building?"

"Magic," he intoned impressively, gloved hands giving gentle shakes to either side of his head. "Specifically, magical junk. It is a place where you can find, discover, and encounter any sort of old, discarded, and useless trinkets from some of the greatest, weakest, or most mediocre wizards of our Age. Don't trust the tags, however. They might claim that such—and—such pot has seen five centuries, but an apprentice made and subsequently broke it two weeks ago. A bit of commercial dust, a light scuffing, and bless me, we now hold the royal chamber pot of lord almighty what's-his-name."

"I might have guessed he has a flexible arrangement with morals," Tasha said dryly. "To be fair, I'd be a little disappointed if your friends weren't all a little eccentric.

"He's your friend as well, or he will be unless you act determinably unsociable and continue this completely unnecessary fear mongering." Slade spun atop his heel and thrust a fist overhead. "Onward!"

Meeting Feylin's questioning glance, Tasha held-out for a second then rolled her eyes. "He'll come back and get us if we don't follow."

"It's probably cooler inside too."

Agreed, they set out after Slade, Feylin trotting a step ahead. "What's the shop's name?"

"Artifacts from the Age of Might."

Tasha fell into step on Slade's opposite side, accepting the water skin he dredged from his satchel. "A grand name for this dump of a neighborhood; who are his customers?"

"My friend has earned himself a measure of renown. Colleagues and Thearcs travel hundreds of miles to visit him. If Malendor set-up shop in a more agreeable neighborhood, the surplus customers would steal his every waking moment. Here only the desperate stop by." Slade stepped over a short lip onto Malendor's walkway and followed it through the weed infested yard, occasionally pushing a briar from his path. When Tasha and Feylin crossed into the property, however, a warning thrum sparked and the statues shifted to life, heads grinding through puffs of rust to observe the intruders. Slowly the statues advanced, old, desiccated weeds cracking under foot and the occasional iron hemline dragging furrows through the earth.

Grabbing Feylin's arm, Tasha escaped into the street, whereupon the statues froze and all but two resumed their former postures. One iconoclast was a gnome with a tall, pointed hat, the other a beautiful, armless maiden. She spent several seconds shifting back and forth, endeavoring to make her dress hang appropriately and only settling when it did.

"What's going on?" Tasha demanded, a handhold preventing Feylin from reentering the yard.

Slade, eyeing the armless maiden sympathetically, clucked to himself and dug through his satchel. "There's nothing to worry about, my Dear; it's a spell to ward off thieves."

"But were not thieves," Feylin protested.

"Yes, well these are yet another victim of Malendor's negligence. They'd broken down entirely by my last visit. He promised to do some repair, but they've apparently relapsed and started harassing strangers again." Withdrawing a lily and some lace from his satchel, he approached the maiden to tie the flower around her neck. "There, a beautiful lady deserves a beautiful adornment."

"Forget the adornments for a minute," Tasha said. "Why are you bouncing around so freely? Your shadier than either of us."

A cheeky grin and. "Because I'm not a thief."

"But we're not thieves either," Feylin protested again, stepping around Tasha to lay a cautious toe on the walkway. Instantly the statues roused themselves and Feylin retreated, expecting the figures to freeze like before. Except they didn't. "Slade, why aren't they stopping?" To her credit, the girl sounded more intrigued than frightened.

"Since you returned once, they assume you'll return again; they're preparing."

Tasha stepped between Feylin and the statues. "I'm guessing we're calling this adventure finished then?"

"Nonsense, I'm already formulating a strategy to circumvent these most fiendish defenses." Slade paced through and around the encroaching statues, considering the building and sporadically grabbing a tool off the ground for examination. "Something to do with grappling hooks maybe..."

Feylin stepped closer once again, giving Tasha's stomach a small kink, and waved a hand before the maiden's iron countenance, failing to garner a reaction. She then proceeded to the gnome who, contrasting his companions, shifted from foot to foot, a nervous tick pulling on his right eye.

Feylin knelt before him, and his eyes flicked in either direction followed by a finger raising to his lips. "Shhh." Repeating the whole affair a second time, he beckoned Feylin still closer.

"What are you waiting for, girl? Give these stiffs the password and move on." His voice ground like two stones rubbing together with a pleasant, earthy undertone filling in the cracks.

"I don't know the password."

"What? You don't know the password? How do you expect to get inside without the password?"

"I didn't know I needed a password."

"Humph, well that's becoming painfully obvious. I suggest going home and leaving us to our card game. If you lot stick around, one of those cheaters are bound to peek." He jabbed a thumb at his fellow guardians, one curly toed boot tapping impatiently.

"Umm, …"—Feylin glanced at Slade, who shook his head—"I'm afraid we can't leave yet."

Slade cheered silently.

"Why not, you got some sort of pressing business with our wizard?"

Slade quickly started miming instructions at her from behind the gnome. "Not really…," she began, watching as Slade made a building with two hands and then walked his fingers over to it, "we came here to …"—Slade brought his hands together, placed them underneath one side of his head and tilted his upper body to the right, eyes falling closed—"take a nap?"

Frowning, Feylin switched her attention between Slade and the gnome, clearly hoping one of them would explain.

"Humph, why else does one visit a wizard of dreams. Pure foolishness is what it is, letting some old fart muck around in your head." Feylin's gaze snapped toward Slade, eyes all-a-sparkle, and Tasha felt butterflies sprout within her own stomach, both of which the gnome completely ignored. "Do you even know our wizard, or are you going to let a complete stranger play dolls with your thoughts?"

"I don't know him personally, but I trust somebody who does."

The gnome's head twisted in a circle, imitating an owl. "Who could you possibly trust enough to let a stranger … ah, I should have guessed." He snorted. "I know all about your silver-tongued friend. Rumor says he's a notorious cheat at cards."

Slade gasped, splaying a hand across his chest. "Surely you are mistaken, my good gnome. I would never stoop to such an unforgiveable low."

"It's none of my business one way or the other. What is my business is that we can't return to our game until you people stop slinking around, him in particular."

Tasha knelt beside Feylin. "You could tell us the password, that'd get us out of your hair."

"No can do, lady, telling's against the rules."

"Slade might have some idea what it is," Feylin suggested, casting what she probably thought of as a sly glance toward Tasha, "enough to start us guessing."

"Yeah." Suppressing a smile, Tasha made a pretense at mental calculations. "Phssh, it should only take about half-an-hour or so."

The gnome, firm in his conviction, lasted about twenty seconds before knuckling under to his card game. "Tell you what"—he produced four stone cups from somewhere about his person—"you guess where this bauble is, and I'll tell you the password. Deal?" The gnome displayed a blue pearl between two stubby, large-knuckled fingers.

Tasha swore, bursting to her feet and storming off. "It's a *Jaidar* blessed street scam!"

The gnome grinned, switching to Feylin. "How about you, girl? Willing to test your luck against mine?"

Slade nodded and Feylin mirrored him. "Alright, I accept your challenge."

The gnome beamed. "The rules are simple: I hide the pearl under one of these cups, shuffle them around and then you guess which cup has it."

Tasha, three steps into her grudging return, stopped once again. "Four cups? It's only supposed to be run with three!"

The gnome snorted, slipping the pearl beneath a cup. "That's because human scammers need to bait the hook. You two have already bitten, so I can make this exciting." His hands settled upon the cups with long familiarity, starting slow and ascending to blurred speed.

Feylin leaned forward, brow scrunching tightly, and Tasha knelt beside her, scowling deeply.

All motion stopped abruptly, neither shiver nor wobble moving the cups. "Alright, ladies, pick a cup."

"This one," they chorused, indicating the same cup.

"Wrong," the gnome sang out, deftly tipping their selection to reveal its underside before mixing the cups once more, this time even faster.

Again the cups stopped, and Tasha—still scowling—indicated one of them, checking with and receiving confirmation from Feylin.

The gnome smirked. "Wrong again." He repeated the unveiling process, this time revealing the true hiding place. A second later, the cups were dancing under his skilled manipulation, shifting faster than ever.

Once again Tasha and Feylin settled in to watch, the former leaning in so close her nose almost tipped a spinning cup.

"Alright, make your guess, ladies," the gnome said, smirking at them.

Tasha's finger snapped out impatiently, and he flipped the cup before Feylin could agree. Not that it mattered, empty space greeted them for the third time. Swearing, Tasha shot to her feet and stomped off, muttering words Feylin probably shouldn't repeat and ripping into the 'cheating gnome' under her breath.

The gnome's triumphant expression quickly faded, replaced by furrowed concentration as he immersed himself in mixing the cups.

A soft, "psst," sounded to Feylin's right, stealing the girl's attention towards a tall, handsome statue with generous muscles and less than generous clothing. He gave her a lopsided grin, lifting three fingers before dropping two and holding the final one to his lips. Feylin hesitated then nodded and Tasha, returning for the third time, sighed to herself. *'I suppose it doesn't matter; we've already lost track of the cup.'*

The gnome retracted his hands, holding them out to either side of his body, fingers spread. "Last chance, girl. Choose well."

She tapped the ground in front of the third cup.

"Wrong again," he declared cheerfully, but as the gnome grabbed for the cups, Feylin tipped her selection and revealed a small blue pearl.

Instantly the gnome leapt back with a snarl, hand snapping up in accusation. "You cheated; the deal's off."

Feylin flinched back, curling in a little. "You cheated as well."

"So what? You cheated first." The gnome whirled in place, accusatory finger jabbing at the other statures. "And don't you start frowning down your long noses at me. I know you helped her–"

"While I'm sorry to interject and ruin your eloquent harangue"—Slade glided forward, pinching the gnome's finger to redirect it—"I'm afraid I must insist." Oil described it best, the way he slithered into the conversation and claimed absolute dominion of it. "As I understand, you think this young woman cheated and felt obligated to reciprocate the gesture?"

"Yes, well–"

"Nevertheless, you both cheated, leaving the question of who transgressed first as immaterial." The gnome, in the middle of arming for another harangue, snapped his mouth shut. "The next logical step is to play another round. Unless, of course, someone cheated prior to this latest incident, and let me assure everyone present that you, my good gnome, cheated outrageously."

The gnome spluttered, "Cheat! Cheat! I-I never cheated."

"Cease the theatrics, my good gnome. These wonderful ladies guessed correctly twice, and both times you scooped the pearl up your sleeve." The gnome fumed in truculent silence, prompting Slade to apply a stern expression. "The password, or I will plant poisonous moss atop your head."

"Fine!" the gnome burst out, storming into a patch of weeds, where only the tip of his shiny metal hat peeked into view. "The password is grasswort."

Grinning, Slade stepped forward and helped Feylin to her feet. "Easy enough, yes?" Turning back around, he gave a pompous cough. "Ahem. Grasswort, my hard-hearted friends, is the password."

The statues nodded in perfect synch and Feylin tentatively braved the path, releasing a sigh when nothing happened.

Tasha entered less reservedly, though her wary observation persisted throughout their trek. "If you're this man's friend, shouldn't you know the password?"

"Malendor prefers to trust the statues with such minutia."

"Which, if I remember, are broken."

Slade paused on the low, wooden porch to offer a shameless grin. "Who can fathom the ways of wizards?" With that he took a vine dangling in front of the doorway, hooked it behind a protruding nail, and crossed inside, leaving the women to tramp up the creaking steps and follow him into a dusky, windowless corridor and its thriving spider colony.

This initial poor impression notwithstanding, birds chirped from somewhere inside the building, dust particles floated invitingly through the light streaming in from outside and a summer wind swirled through the open hall, banishing any damp or unpleasant scents.

Slade disdained the various doors spaced along their route, instead following painted arrows to the hall's rear and veering down a stunted offshoot that ended at a tattered sheet. Bending, he grabbed a corner of the fabric and lifted it overhead, ushering his companions through into a descending stair before pulling a cord to ring a small bell.

Tasha, leading down the carved steps, trailed fingers across the metal and granite wall, its vacillating surface smoothed years ago and lined with grooves, some needle thin, others broad enough to accommodate her entire hand, both adorned by decorative offshoots or swirls.

'This seems ... old.'

As they delved further into the earth—two, three, four flights of stairs—the temperature at first cooled dramatically, then gradually warmed again, holding steady well beneath the torturous sunshine up above. Accompanying this mellow heat was the faint tang of iron and the scent of ash, ancient ash long since devoid of heat or life.

Eventually they encountered a stone door, and beyond it a sapphire, predictably-suspicious adari suspended atop its ledger. Past the adari was a wide, high-ceilinged room where every available inch was consumed by a variety of desks, tables, stools, counters, and large dampened forges. All these in turn, suffered under a massive burden of accumulated artifacts. Even the walls struggled for breath, hung with an astonishing selection of hammers and bellows and prongs and other tools belonging to the blacksmith's trade, all distinguished by the same curious blend of red metal and granite, most seeming too large for a normal man.

Altogether, it was the most expansive repository of clutter either woman had ever seen.

"When do you think Slade's friend last organized?" Feylin whispered, rubbing her nose as if to dispel a building sneeze.

"Apparently, indifference toward menial tasks is required for being a wizard," Tasha said, wandering off to investigate.

Behind her, she heard Feylin mutter, "I'm not obsessively clean myself, but this is excessive," before toeing one of the mounds of silvery dust that blanketed the entire room and approaching the nearest table. As Tasha watched, the girl selected one of its innumerable knick-knacks and blew the dust clear, unveiling a beautifully stenciled plate. Curiosity visibly roused, Feylin replaced the item and meandered deeper into the jungle, no doubt seeking further treasures.

As for herself, Tasha shuffled rather than strode across the floor. The precaution failed, however, and she repeatedly kicked objects hidden beneath the silvery dust, each time triggering a minor heart attack followed by an attempt to shelve the unfortunate object.

On one such occasion, she discovered a whole vase, possibly one of the few unbroken specimens left in the room. Bending, she lifted it from squalor and paused to examine the object, gently wiping its surface clear. "Design on its surface … must be at least five hundred years old." Murmuring to herself, she traced the bizarre markings, noticing their similarity to another script she'd seen, "Old style, akin to the writings of scholars who lived before the Paladin Empire…"

"Quite right, young lady." A wrinkled hand stretched past to pluck the vase from her fingers. "Though it's closer to six centuries old, maybe seven depending on which historian you ask. Back then they used a mixture of powdered obsidian, melted silver, and the barest dab of true ink to write. So even dismissing its age, this artifact is quite valuable." If learning, knowledge, and teaching had an accent, this voice spoke with it, going so far as to adopt the hushed tones one hears in libraries.

Tasha turned about and faced a chest, which led her gaze up to an old man's face. Retreating a step, she managed to meet his twinkling eyes without craning her neck.

A disheveled lion's mane, similar in both color and nature, framed the old man's face, its former luster receding from the onslaught of time while a long, braided mustache hung from his upper lip.

"I'm sorry; I shouldn't have picked it up."

The old man ignored Tasha's apologies. "It took me three years to discover what the writing meant. I worked myself, both physically and emotionally, into a frothing state of anticipation. I deluded myself with fantastic imaginings, I bragged to friends, I taunted rivals. Then I puzzled out the key and learned the inscription was quite mundane. Reacting with the expected poise, I threw myself into the soul of depression and the vase across the room." The wizard withdrew some spectacles from his robe and propped them atop his crooked nose. "I believe it says something like … a moment … ah, yes, just as I thought." Attacked by a sudden, harsh cough, he chased it away by muttering several black words and making a note about, "Cleaning this blasted place up."

"Well, what does it says?"

The old man shot her a glance over his cloudy, gold-rimmed spectacles and raised his eyebrows, one of which appeared singed by a recent accident. "Patience is a virtue the young should practice aggressively. Now, where was I? Ah ha, it says here"—a dramatic pause—"with duty bound and by honor led; the Dark to war on disorder, the Light to seek truth."

"What does it mean?"

"It's an old maxim of the Paladin Order. During this era"—he gave the vase a little shake—"few controlled the paladins, primarily kings and the Order itself, so it was a reminder to take personal responsibility for their actions. The second part is more interesting and refers to the split halves of *Enecki*, that of Light and Order. Before Cardolyn Tyier assumed the throne, there were two branches of paladins: the Dark and the Light. The first group fought, preserved order, and enforced the law while their siblings—valuing knowledge and truth—were judges and scholars, many became teachers. Anyway, as I said, this vase is unbelievably old and expensive." He tossed it irreverently over his shoulder.

Tasha gasped, darted around the old man and dove to catch it, but the vase slipped through her fingers. Just before it smashed to pieces, a wave of shimmering dust spiraled up to catch the endangered relic.

"Wonderful spell," he said cheerfully. "A little something I designed to safeguard my merchandise from unwary customers. Now, what might your name be?"

This question snapped Tasha from her astonishment and to her feet. "I'm Tasha Bloomhale, may *Enecki* guard you from chaos." She bowed, steepling her fingers, and he returned the gesture.

"Malendor Atarious Etlin Booklore at your service. It is a pleasure to meet a young woman with such a talented eye. One might suppose you have a scholar in the family, an uncle perhaps?"

"Uh, no. I'm afraid not." Which sparked acute interest in his eyes, prompting her to scrounge for a deflectory question. "I'm assuming you're the friend Slade mentioned?"

"He applies that term somewhat liberally, but yes; despite his propensity for theft, I'm compelled to say." With a gentle cant of his head, Malendor indicated Slade as the young man sifted through ancient scrolls to pocket the odd specimen. "And you? What's your relation to our sticky-fingered subject?"

She opened her mouth—preparing some sort of bland assurance—then paused, struck by his question. '*I … don't actually know.*' Frowning, she glanced back at the wizard and found him staring, far more interested than the question deserved. "Why do you ask?"

"He usually comes alone, so I was curious. There's no need to be suspicious."

"Telling someone not to be suspicious doesn't actually work."

"Ah yes, I suppose not."

Tasha shook her head, smiling a little. "Slade and I are …" Again the appropriate, colorless answer caught in her throat.

"You don't actually know, do you?" Malendor's attention relaxed. "Well, that's unfortunate but scarcely unexpected. Not to worry, I'm sure you'll parse the nuances eventually. In the meantime, how about we…"

The wizards voice faded out as Tasha scowled down at her hands, idly rubbing thumbs over fingers. *I don't know. Not even a little. We're obviously not friends and it'd be too easy … it'd be dangerous to assume we're simply business associates. After the meeting with Madame Roshfen, I've outlived my purpose and Slade clearly needs nothing from me, not even to contact Carr'Selain. My only use is spying for the guild, which he has to realize and yet here I am at a place Slade usually visits alone. Why?'*

"… and you're not listening to me." Malendor concluded, seeming unconcerned by fact.

"I apologize, what did you say?"

"Nothing of import. You, conversely, are giving thought to something deeply engaging and, though its none of my concern, I'd be happy to discuss it with you. I've known Slade longer than most, almost … seven years now?"

Tasha's ears perked up. "You've known him since he was a child?"

"I have indeed. He came skipping down my stairs shortly after he and his mother immigrated. Mind you, I'm in no way claiming to understand him, but I possess certain details that may grant insight."

"What sort of details?"

"What he's working toward, a little of what he wants. Even, perhaps, what he needs."

She couldn't help herself. She stared, wide eyed, for a second. "Well, what are they?"

But the old man merely tapped the side of his nose. "Subjects that are none of your concern. And with that settled, will you allow me to offer my expertise?"

For the third time, Tasha swallowed her instinctive reply. *'Could it really hurt? If I steer clear of secrets and offer as little as possible, especially about myself, could I gain a bit of crucial information? Slade won't care. Hell, he probably expects me to try digging, which means ramifications only happen if I'm the one who slips up.'*

"If it helps, you'll be in complete control of the conversation."

She debated one last time, then said, "Alright."

"Excellent. Let's start with your impression of him."

Tasha's eyes immediately narrowed at the personal question. "Why?"

"Because when charting a relationship, its best to start with what you can verify."

"On second thought, I think this might be a bad idea."

Malendor's eyebrows rose slightly, but otherwise he didn't react. "I understand. Would you like to ask something instead?"

Questions about Slade piled onto her tongue, fighting for this slightest chance at being answered. One by one, she discarded them. Most were subjects for a different person, others crossed the line into secrets that Malendor wouldn't divulge. Growing increasingly frustrated, she realized his initial subject choice had been one of the few they could both discuss without redacting every second word.

Tasha broke from her vetting process to fire a well-deserved but also hypocritical glare in Slade's direction. *'This is all his fault for being so secretive.'* However, as she glowered and he continued plundering, her eyes gradually transitioned from observing to measuring. One second became several, and several became a slow, slightly irritated sentence; she couldn't even say why she spoke, only that it felt … important somehow. "He … distracts me and I … I think he expects something, as if I'm supposed to do a favor for him. Which is bloody concerning because I don't trust him to not sacrifice me. Abyss take it, half the time I'm still worried he's planning on stabbing me later."

"Could those not be true about yourself as well? How safe is he around you?"

'Pretty gods damned safe, I should say. He could kill me in his sleep.' Nevertheless, her frown deepened, preceding gradual words. "If I were the stronger, not very safe at all. If necessary, I would hurt, deceive, and worse. However, I … I find myself hoping it will not be necessary."

"That's a relief, and I might also suggest that Slade has similar thoughts."

"Yes, well you're supposed to say that, aren't you?" The wizard sat back atop a table, ensconcing himself within its mounded articles.

"I suppose it is a rather predictable sentiment. But answer me this. You don't trust him, you suspect he has ulterior motives, you acknowledge your own impotence and yet"—indulging in a short pause, he raised both arms to indicate his shop—"you accompany him on idle adventures. Why?"

"Because it's my job."

"If the situation were so simple, I doubt we'd be having this conversation. You actively wish harm away from him, and despite you lamenting about it, I suspect that his distractions are a nice change of pace, especially with that restless bouncing of yours."

"I'm only restless because there's better things I could be doing."

"Better than making friends with Slade Lammerock?"

"No, better than waiting around until the clock dings and I'm thrust into whatever role or sacrifice I've been curated for."

"You could always ask him. Slade doesn't like to lie."

"No, he simply fabricates blatantly ludicrous stories to pass off as truth. That's hardly enlightening."

"True enough. But just because he has an ulterior motive doesn't mean he intends you harm. The opposite even."

"There's a massive difference between not wishing me harm and pursuing my best interest. There's also a massive difference between pursuing my best interest and risking himself for it. Slade, likeable as he is when not terrorizing me, would risk nothing for my sake. I'm an enemy's pawn." Across the room, Slade moved to inspect a table and began relocating its contents as well.

"Well," Malendor said, swaying gently, "I now understand why you had such difficulty labeling your relationship. It's a concerningly fraught, under explored mess rife with manipulation and distrust. Clearly, the start to a beautiful friendship."

"Oh, really?"

"Yes, because despite it all, you seem to be having a bit of fun. Some of the truest friendships grow from toxic soil, all you need is a little trust to sprout. If it's any help, I'm sure he will heroically risk the lives of his underlings to protect yours."

"Oh, such sacrifice, such altruism; however would he manage without them?" Even as she snorted and shook her head, Tasha felt a smile creep onto her face. "His machinations are probably what landed me in the predicament to begin with."

Malendor smiled back. "More than likely, but at least he has the decency to extricate you afterwards."

"That is close to being the absolute least he could do."

The wizard fell silent, merely looking for a moment. "I can see why he likes you."

"Of course he likes me; I'm a fresh, innocent target for his sadistic humor."

"Not entirely; your sarcasm is likely a fresh wind to him."

"I highly doubt I'm the only sarcastic grouch in his life."

"To my knowledge, you are. His crew prefers knuckling under, his stepfather considers sarcasm to be discourteous, and his mother, well, their humor runs together."

"And what about you?"

"Thankfully, Slade only indulges the occasional prank at my expense; then again, he's also developed the irritating habit of eloping with my merchandise. One time I almost caught him stealing half my collection of eastern lucky frogs."

"Almost?"

"When I turned my back, he stole the other half."

"How can you name him 'friend' if Slade absconds with anything that catches his eye?"

"Slade has certain uses. Uses which I'm sure you've discovered seeing as you're partners in crime." Malendor flicked his fingers at a desk seated opposite his own table. The air rippled, and the nominated desk overturned, throwing its habitants to the floor. "Please sit."

Tasha though, remained where she was. "Are you suggesting Slade and I are criminals?"

"I'm not suggesting anything. Our mutual acquaintance over there"— he nodded toward Slade—"enjoys providing me with merchandise that he acquires in a … mysterious fashion. A few days ago, he dumped five assassins in my back yard prior to which he had requested a fake blood-contract. I'm well aware of both your and his illicit activity."

Tasha lowered herself onto the desk, rubbing her eyes. "Gods above, the bastard's going to get himself killed."

"How are you so certain?"

"Because I am going to kill him."

"Oh, indeed?"

"He's brought bloody assassins into our affairs with nothing more than a fake blood-contract to restrain them. The moment they find out, our lives are forfeit."

"Don't be so sure; according to Slade they're quite charming murderers; though from his story, I found the woman a tad coarse."

"It doesn't matter. They have a real, preexisting contract to kill Slade, a contract with real compensation and real consequences should they fail."

"Slade is adept at complicating the issue, killing him will prove far harder than you suppose."

"It doesn't matter how good he is. Slade dances on a tightrope so thin it's amazing the line hasn't snapped. Worse yet, I think he's managing another dozen projects on the side; it's like he's juggling damned broadswords for no apparent reason.

"You would be correct, unless of course"—Malendor leaned forward with a smile—"our daring adventurer cheats." Sitting back, he grasped a knee and started rocking. "The necklace you're wearing is beautiful. Where did you get it?"

"What? Oh this? Slade bought it for me." Truth be told, she'd forgotten the necklace entirely, couldn't even remember the last time she took it off.

"Curious, Slade bought an identical piece from me early last month."

"It's a tracking device, isn't it?"

"He told you, did he?"

"Yes, and I immediately suspected something far worse."

Malendor caught her gaze. "Allow me to offer you some advice; it is a smart move to befriend the rich or the friendless, one for their wealth, the other for their loyalty. Slade is rich, and you are presently friendless; make use of the opportunity."

Before Tasha could respond, Slade appeared by skidding into place with a finger pointed at Malendor. "Fore-shame, oh decrepit one; never did I guess you'd choose my fiancée as the target for your seductions. My Dear," he said, spinning toward her, "I must take up words and arm you against this man's forked tongue. Malendor is a very old, very talented pessimist capable of striking down all semblances of hope. He is adept at rooting out the smallest, most inconsequential of optimisms and butchering them for his own gruesome amusement." Slade closed his hand into a fist, crushing an imaginary ball of hope. "I have accused and convicted him of these most heinous crimes on multiple occasions, but he always escapes my clutches, running off to continue his reign of ruin while besmirching my name in the process." Slade's eyes bulged with outrage. "He possesses the supreme audacity to claim I walk a dark, treachery-laden path while simultaneously preaching the wisdom of seeking my friendship, mostly because of my inhumanly beautiful face and unbelievable intellect."

"I'm sure she's already aware of your great, though not unbelievable, intellect, so I needn't circulate that particular bit of information. I will, however, admit to feeling a guilty pleasure in spreading my morbid outlook. Apart from that, your allegations are pure fabrication."

Slade's accusatory finger dropped. "Oh, okay then."

Feylin, meanwhile, approached with her usual shyness, stopping a little behind Slade.

Noticing this, Malendor levered himself from the table into a bow and a warm smile. "My lady, I am Malendor Booklore, once a caster of dreams now a humble provider of antiques."

Stepping a little further into view, Feylin performed her own curtsey. "Feylin Whyte, ward to Tiberius Whyte." Her gaze swept his apparel, bright with anticipation only to dim with faint disappointment.

"Ah yes, you expected someone with a more ... fantastic wardrobe. If it's any consolation, during my youth I gallivanted in some of the most ridiculous costumes ever designed. I made quite the entrance."

Feylin smiled, stepping entirely from Slade's shadow. "So, you're a wizard of dreams? When Slade offered to introduce us to his wizard friend, he only mentioned your prodigious skill."

"Did he tell you nothing else?"

Feylin blushed. "He said you enjoy boasting above all other sports."

Malendor chuckled, his green eyes becoming a shimmering violet. "He knows me well." Magic coalescing around his long bony fingers and trailing after them, Malendor began drawing complex designs with swift, articulate gestures. "I walked on air and conversed with creatures both terrible and majestic." A miniature gryphon appeared, soaring around the room. "I've planted a seed with three drops of water and sprouted a tree moments later." He swept a hand through the air, calling forth the image of a forest at whose heart towered a massive oak. "I've won battles and cured sickness, even chased storms out to the sea." Atop a nearby table, a little man's chest expanded and exhaled a mighty gust of wind, blowing a thunder cloud into the distance.

Tasha turned in a circle, watching the gryphon fly. "While impressive, I must say your boasts don't quite equal Slade's sheer disregard for plausibility."

Slade gave a barking cough, concealing a distinct "amateur" under the façade, and Malendor shot him a pointed glance. "At least my claims are supported by actual truth. Yours, well ... they're recognized countrywide as fantastic bluster."

"Of course they are," Slade exclaimed, hands flying into the air. "You can't boast without bluster, and you can't bluster about something accurate. If you do, your recognized everywhere as a truthful braggart."

"That may be so, but–" A coo-coo clock abruptly sounded from amidst the clutter and was swiftly trailed by the gong from a grandfather clock, which, in turn, preceded additional announcements from all across the room. "Ah, it seems time has gotten away from us. As you've probably guessed, Slade brought you here to experience a Dream-Caster's power. So, shall we sail the *Lake of Dreams* together?" His fingers settled upon the air again, painting with sharp, quick movements. Soon runes covered the air around him, his blackboard spanning from the floor to the ceiling.

Feylin stroked one of the violet runes hanging in the air, her finger tickling slightly. "Yes."

Malendor shifted to Tasha. "What about you, Miss Bloomhale?"

Suddenly hesitant, she frowned down at her shoes and their mounded silver dust. "I'm not sure I want you mucking around in my head."

Malendor nodded. "We're journeying to a carefully controlled part of the *Lake of Dreams* rather than your personal psyche. To do otherwise invites disaster: who knows what landscape or nightmares your thoughts might conjure."

"All right. I suppose I'll tag along."

Slade grinned, clapping. "Excellent. Now I suggest we sit down, unless you've mastered the ability to sleep standing up." So saying, he slid to the floor and shimmied back until he leaned against a dresser.

Meanwhile both women frowned at the dusty floor, prompting Malendor to sweep a hand across the room. A wave of shimmering dust rolled forward and coalesced into a silver-gray couch.

The women poked the new furniture before seating themselves cautiously. When neither half of the couch collapsed, they nodded to Malendor, and he—eyes consumed by violet fire—laid a gentle hand upon their brows. Chanting unintelligible words, he eased their minds into the *Lake of Dreams* so smoothly that only Slade noticed the transition.

"Where do you wish to go?" Malendor asked in a whisper that echoed both within and outside their minds.

Feylin's reply carried a childlike glee about it, her request fueled by an evanescent memory of something she'd dreamed years ago: silver wings and a blue sea. "I want go sailing."

Tasha spoke next, a touch self-conscious at baring her soul even this little bit. "Take me to the stars."

———————————

Tasha found herself standing atop a mountain peak thrust so far in the sky she need only extend a hand to touch a passing cloud. Sibling mountains stood on either side of her, humming as air caressed their craggy surfaces and howling when a different gust smashed against their parapets. She felt the noise reverberate under her feet, calling to the valleys below, which answered by singing a song of their own.

Despite feeling unsteady, Tasha crept toward the peak's outer rim and admired the land sweeping away from her: a beautiful tapestry of red and copper split by gigantic ravines. With a flash, Tasha realized she overlooked the trackless waste of the Avarus Desert.

A tail of white fabric snuck into her vision and Tasha twisted around, spotting Malendor as he ascended the lethargic incline winding up the mountain's side. With him came a stilling of the winds.

"Do you like the view?"

"It's wonderful but…"

"But it's not what you requested. Don't worry. All shall be revealed in time." With neither word nor gesture, he strode to the mountain's outermost edge and lifted his arms overhead.

The midday sun began to set in the south, vanishing after a moment and transforming into a giant bird that uttered a single cry before soaring across the heavens, its every wing beat sending rainbows arching outward.

Malendor faced her, smiling as he held out a hand. "Come, let's visit the night sky."

"How?"

Rather than answering, he pointed to the bird still painting the heavens with its colors.

Feylin sailed across an ocean of crystalline water on a sloop sown from silver thread. She sat atop a railing, feeling the wind slide across her face and through her hair as she leaned out over the water, hands clinging to an unnerving figurehead: a woman with a dragon's head.

In the distance, a tidal wave rolled across Feylin's horizon. As it did so, the wave stretched skyward to adopt the shape of an angel, whereupon it crashed down and lost any semblance of form. A second wave rolled in from her right, its brief existence taking the form of a scantily clad man who rode dolphins. No sooner had this one vanished, then a third and fourth wave materialized, charging at each other from opposite directions in the shape of armies. They crashed together and the resulting foam spawned an island decorated by everything from civilians to buildings to vegetation.

Here the performance broke and Feylin pulled herself back into the ship. But the vessel rolled with a degree of violence as the latest attraction sprouted underneath her, a crystalline volcano that erupted with all the kerfuffle one would expect from such things.

Tossed high, so high she abandoned the sky itself, Feylin bent over the ship's railing and peered at the distant world below. She instantly saw Tasha and Malendor petting a colorful bird on a mountain's edge.

Feylin waved and hollered without the slightest hope of being heard, then she sprinted to the opposite side of the ship. There she spotted Slade, who turned cartwheels along the rim of a colossal tower with an utter disregard for both caution and a second Malendor.

At this point, her ship plummeted back to the ocean, the unexpected descent tearing an exhilarated scream from her and the abrupt landing shoving a wave in all directions. As it departed, the wave split into a hundred dancing couples that circled Feylin's ship, lasting until a giant tsunami rolled in and carried her within shouting distance of a land of burnished copper.

Laughing and still riding the tsunami, she located her friends once again. Tasha now sat with her arms thrown wide as if to embrace the myriad constellations swirling all around. What's more, she interacted with the stars, all the fantastical creatures, and near-divine people who spawned the world's core legends. Over the woman's head flew Antisana—the great four-winged lion—while Chorkerand—the first minstrel—danced on Tasha's left with his broken lute. Then Feylin gasped for below them all stood the Three Brothers—also known as the Three Princes, the Three Kings, or for those who studied ancient lore, the King, the Eldest Son, and the Warmonger. Of these three constellations only the King had any lore; and his legend, if written, would have consumed the entire sky. He was *Arthramain Roy'al*: the greatest constellation; though he, along with his brothers, appeared only once a year.

As for Slade, well, he'd fallen asleep.

Slade waited in one of Malendor's back rooms, the secret one with numerous complicated locks and layers of enchantments. The one that served as a threshold to a larger, much deeper complex of sculpted caverns and enveloping silence where only a few dim, lonely hearths resisted the overbearing shadows. The one whose tall, coffered ceiling barely contained the first Sleeping Smiths: looming figures slumped over anvils and dying forges, their chests rising and falling in a slow, endless rhythm.

He was wide awake and, for once, wandering idly as someone else puttered about with dangerous chemicals.

"Tasha's worried that your arrogance is leading you astray," Malendor said, peering intently at a heavily magicked glass vial, dribbling its contents into a measuring spoon. "Are you being careless?"

"I assume this came about because you revealed that I really did ensnare a group of deadly assassins with nothing more than a fake blood contract?" Malendor grunted his confirmation. "Ah well, it doesn't matter. As for my being careless? Only with myself. Naric's here to look after my little ducklings."

Moving slow enough to lose a race with the moon, Malendor tipped the measuring spoon into a beaker of clear liquid, added a dusting of vermillion powder, and then quickly muttered two enchantments. One to start the concoction brewing. The other to seal the resulting explosion. "She is right to worry about your arrogance."

"I know. I even accept that my arrogance condemns me to eventual failure." Grabbing a poker made from the same amalgam of granite and metal as everything else fashioned by the Sleeping Smiths, Slade stabbed the rod into an ancient hearth. "For the moment, however, it is simply merited confidence." Most of the hearth's coals had burned down to charcoal or grey crumbling lumps years ago. Some broke open though, revealing warm, stubbornly glowing centers.

"Pride, arrogance, conceit, all these precede the fall and most begin by whispering truth in your ear. A complement spoken by a reticent master, the awe of the uninitiated, a just reward for heroism served; all can lead to mistaken confidence."

Slade shrugged, set aside the poker and continued wandering. He crossed beneath the raised hammer of a female smith, her vertical horns poking through a blue hood and nearly brushing the ceiling despite her hunching over a centuries cooled sword. "I set foot on that path a long time ago; so long ago it's not worth the effort to retrace my steps." Across from the woman towered a second figure, his hood having fallen back as he pumped the bellows, unveiling a face that might have been described as goatish if not for the squashed muzzle, curving tusks and large braided beard. "On a side note, matters with Carr'Selain are progressing nicely. We've agreed to a contract, and he's demanded that I prove my competence before we proceed."

"All according to plan then. Have the Ie'Calla supplied what I need?"

"Indeed, they have." Slade withdrew a small redwood box from his satchel, set it upon a table and sent it sliding toward the wizard. "I ordered enough to compensate for accidents and to leave some left over. A gift from me to you."

"Ah, wonderful." Malendor navigated the obstacle course of clutter, detouring toward a wall of shelves loaded with boxes, wax sealed jars, and opaque tincture bottles.

Depositing his collection upon the second of the two meticulously clean iron tables, Malendor took the redwood box and cracked its lid. Sniffing the contents, he snapped it shut again. "Perfect." Returning to his ingredients, the wizard dipped two fingers into a mysterious oil and began smearing it over a chunk of quartz.

"You think you could answer a question for me while you work?" Slade asked, starting to produce the usual bevy of fresh merchandise for Malendor to sell.

"Mhhmm."

"Do you know anything about a man called Bellay Enkarta?"

The wizard stilled just before pouring a steaming tincture over the quartz. "There is no concrete information concerning the man, only footnotes in ancient books or stories that old, senile men learned from their grandfathers." Wiping his fingers clean, Malendor turned around and rubbed his face. "These hints rarely agree; and if they do, it's contradicted by other texts. The one consistent piece of information is that he's a Marked. Slade, whatever business you're conducting, you need to get out now."

"Unfortunately, circumstances have contrived against me. Our conflict is now predetermined. The outcome alone remains in flux."

Malendor sighed, turning back to the quartz. "Who among your flock screwed up so royally as to merit Bellay Enkarta's attention?"

Slade considered for a long moment. "I'd rather not say," he admitted finally. Some secrets were best left untold. The fewer people who knew a Marked pursued Feylin, the fewer snared in the potential fallout.

Malendor frowned, drawing a glowing circle and runes above the quartz. "Being nosy, I can't help but wonder if it's not Feylin or Naric?"

"Before you leap to conclusion, might I remind you that Feylin is ward to Tiberius White. The gods wouldn't help whosoever harmed her. As for Naric, the world doesn't know he's intended for greatness and it won't until I reveal it." Slade gave him an almost wolfish grin.

"Gods above you're enjoying this." Malendor shook his head then leaned down until his lips hovered just above the quartz. He hummed softly, a nighttime lullaby occasionally broken by whispered spells. Finally, he placed the quartz in the redwood box and passed both to Slade. "Please remember you're not alone; others are endangered by this crusade."

"I know. I'm not sure there's much I can do about it however."

As Malendor tidied up, Slade made a final circuit of the room, stopping by the third smith. Like both of its predecessors, the figure loomed over him, its broad shoulders mounded with dust and its movement snared in time. For the past two hundred years, the smith had bent over the same table engraving the same pair of tongs, its low thunderous heart patiently marking each passing minute.

Laying a hand over his own heart, Slade found its pace almost frantic in comparison.

Few knew the smiths existed, sleeping away in caverns and ancient forges secreted all across the Empire. None knew when they had succumbed to this enchantment and none knew when they'd wake again. If their last hearth went cold, Slade didn't know if they ever would.

As Alleria called to Skylamaid, a final circuit of the room, looping by the mud spout. The helm of the princess on the figure loomed by a thin

39

Opening Entertainments

His palanquin's burgundy and gold curtains fluttered, spreading the odors of jasmine and lavender while a lantern provided heat and light to the spacious interior, ameliorating the early morning chill. Jeers and muffled voices permeated his surroundings, all celebratory, inebriated, and almost entirely devoted to the Angorat'Wass or the latest Kalvonder murders.

Lacking a pre-heated coat, the Aparthii slave shivered at his feet, rattling the wine tray and capped bowl of roasted salamanders she held. He considered the options, selected a choice morsel and gestured for her to lower the tray, savoring the salamander's bitter mustard and fiery paprika.

He expected someone would accost him soon, though who eluded him. His conversation with Thanen Kalvonder would have aroused suspicions, alerting upper echelon Kalvonders of an unchecked ascent and prompting them to either forewarn his further expansion or coerce his loyalty.

Valeriius had mounted a step higher on the pyramid, entering a new court with subtler laws and different music. All that remained was the acknowledgment of his peers: his unknown guest.

His ascension conferred expectations; he needed a proper retinue to cultivate an illusion of his predilections by selecting, favoring, and impoverishing retainers. Their origins would be replaced to foster the illusion and guide the inquisitive through curated truths and misdirection.

His status was likewise changed; where once he had been tolerated, now he would be expected at galas of the eminent, monthly communions with *Ashshand*, prominent Angorat'Wasses, and the occasional hunt. They would bestow upon him superficial deference and demands, for he had entered their purview and straddled the cusp of the ruling elite.

A voice pierced the hubbub, directing his bearers to depart the main progression. Valeriius motioned the Aparthii woman to remain put, parted the embroidered curtains with his cane and descended sedately onto the red sea of rolling dunes. A disinterested glance revealed a horizon alight with the

508

first tongues of cherry and gold, and a horse near his palanquin's front bearing the accosting Kalvonder.

Both horse and rider were magnificent, with the man huge, armored in bone plate and seated comfortably. A carapace sword favoring the eastern design of substantiality hung from his saddle, warning all viewers of his violent preferences.

The Kalvonder grinned, hand rising in greeting as his retinue shoved through Valeriius' six guards, disdaining ceremony in favor of spectacle.

The dozen guards were richly equipped, and evidently attired and selected for intimidation, with their swords of dark bone fashioned from a single piece rather than many, detailing their master's efficacy at hunting Akhari rather than wealth. The Kalvonder's three retainers halted before Valeriius and clasped their hands in continued demonstration of contempt.

The left-most retainer wore sheer silk tied with ribbons at the waist and just below her breasts. The beautiful artwork adorning her face peaked through the golden veil, verifying the truth her lute alluded to. She blinked long lashes and smiled with a feigned kiss: a courtesan.

The right-most retainer wore only cured leathers, a fanged whip and scars as adornments. A hawk perched on his shoulder, its wings bound but eyes unimpeded. He carried a naked butcher's knife on his belt and a boar pelt across his shoulders: a beast master.

The final retainer led his fellows in lavish attire, featuring a complex design of golden birds catching silver fish across jade cloth. He was muscular, bred for killing, and equipped with a spiked hatchet and loaded crossbow. The bolts were iron and designed for piercing, the wooden shafts properly fletched. He wore a wolf's skull-mask and had tattooed his proudest kills into his forearms: a huntsman.

The Kalvonder affably circumvented his retainers, even deigning to preserve his smile, and reined in before Valeriius, a hand resting truculently on his waist. "Hello, Valeriius."

"I would be more inclined to return your greeting if you introduced yourself, sir."

"You lack humility, especially considering your life balances on my whim." He dismounted with a thud and stepped closer, looming over Valeriius. "I advise increased reverence, lest I snuff you out."

"And I have yet to hear your name..."

The Kalvonder ground a finger into Valeriius' chest. "You tread a thin line, little man—"

Valeriius swept the finger aside with his cane. "Hostilities have been retired for the duration of these negotiations, Kalvonder"—he accessed Thanen's memories from the amethyst atop his cane—"Kyar."

"What?"

"Please, I intend no intimidation. In fact, I admire how you killed Kalvonder Ghevas. It couldn't have been a simple procedure to replace every curtain, rug, and tapestry in his mansion with exact replicates doused in Sheshova oil. They drove him and his entire household cannibalistically mad, I believe, yes? I particularly appreciate how you acquired your entire supply from him a Turning previous; that was an eloquent touch."

Kyar grinned, and in that moment, Valeriius saw Kyar decide to kill him. "Yes, I do take excessive satisfaction in that poetry."

Valeriius gestured toward his palanquin. "Please, accept my hospitality. We journey toward the most prestigious spectacle ever orchestrated in Sahdaen."

"Of course." Kyar dismissed his retainers and entered the palanquin, yanking the curtains open and kicking the kneeling Aparthii woman aside. He flung himself into the seat and propped his sullied boots on the armrest of the opposite side, cautious to avoid the seat-cloth draping it.

Valeriius indicated the journey's resumption and claimed the seat opposite Kyar, examining the bruise growing across the Aparthii woman's cheek. "In the future, refrain from damaging my property."

Kyar laughed. "Who cares about a scarred slave? I promise you prettier in any Kalvonder harem."

Valeriius gestured the Aparthii woman to serve wine. "I care that she's mine, not yours."

"You're too attached. We're already drowning unto starvation with Avarans, I imagine fewer mouths would improve the situation."

"If I am too attached, why did I scar her face? All that matters is she belongs to me."

"It is a matter of inconsequence, Valeriius, being that you are irrelevant and I am indisposed."

"Then what have I done to merit your illustrious presence?"

"Because no one ever bested Thanen." Kyar select a salamander from the plate and split it, consuming half. "This has alerted some Kalvonders of actual relevance as to your existence, engendering interest. Thus I have two purposes: one personal, the other on behest. We will resolve the former immediately: What do you know of me?"

"Your concern is misplaced, Thanen betrayed nothing. I know only hearsay; you are a warmonger by nature and a supplier by profession, preferring akarhri hunts to agriculture. This last Turning you slaughtered three beasts, the smallest a reptile some hundred feet from rump to snout, and the others, mammals: a carnivore with fur and ivory tusks, and an omnivore with carapace. They rendered some thirty-thousand pounds of assorted materials, the prime of which you reserved for yourself.

"For entertainment, your inclined toward beast fights and hunting, with a predilection for the chkaii hives, regardless the cost in lives. You cultivate other lusts, of course. How many courtesans have disappeared from your quarters this last Turning? Three? Four? Tragic. Satisfied?"

"Your attempt to accrue information is admirable but woefully rudimentary. I advise professing more knowledge in the future rather than admitting your lack; you might actually survive." Kyar took a long draught, devoured the salamander's other half and spat the bones onto the Aparthii woman. "How do you view the exchanging of stories? Our legends exceed any man's ability to read, so I exchange the occasional story with fellow Kalvonders. I know one that could be quite educational for you?"

"By all means..."

In their zenith, the Dragon Lords warded three evils. The first they buried in stone, lies, and veils; the second they imprisoned with silver, ice, and twelve keys; the last they broke and scattered. These represented their greatest burden.

Yet these evils constantly stirred, and whether through happenstance or lust, men, children, and beasts always found them. Time and again the Dragon Lords suppressed these evils, but never before they wrought fathomless grief upon the world. The Dragon Lords were mortal, forbidden the omnipresence of gods, and thus lost perception of the evils when they appeared, excluding only the second evil, which never stirred.

Consequently, they sought aid from the Master Artificer, who excelled at the weaving of magics into objects. They embarked for his palace, secluded deep within the ocean, and were greeted as honored guests. There they spoke with him, pleading for a compass to direct their strides when the evils escaped and chains to evermore mute the evils' voices, deafening mortal men to their summons.

He answered with promises of service but also mockery, challenging them as to why they served a dead man's will. He asked why they who descended of dragons, whose blood burned with magic, restricted themselves to the rubble of the Crimson Throne.

They answered that immortality was a curse and power a burden. They maintained their oaths to their Lord—the Crimson Monarch—*Lord*

Arthramain Roy'al. Still laughing, he bade them leave and return with the year's dawn.

They obeyed, trusting in his promise. When that dawn rose, they flew to the shore and echoed his promises. He answered with festivities and music. They entered, stressing they desired his promised item. With many affirmations of his devotion, he unveiled a compass of three tips—one still and the other two in constant shift—explaining how each tip pointed to one evil.

They praised his skill, blessing him for his service. But when they moved to take the compass, he raised an ancient hand and it disappeared. He demanded payment. They asked what he desired, and he responded with brash confidence, proclaiming that as his compass would be as a weapon to them only its equivalent would satisfy him. He demanded *Stolen Wings*: the blade of silver stone gifted into their keeping by their Lord.

They refused, warning that *Stolen Wings* would destroy him. He scattered the feasting table and chairs with a swipe of his hand. Crying out, he demanded whether they thought themselves his superiors. They denied this hubris but affirmed that the Stone Blades had been entrusted to them by the Crimson Monarch, who did surpass the Master Artificer.

He raged, for the Stone Blades far exceeded his capabilities and he yearned to discover their secrets and replicate them. The Master Artificer flung the compass at the Dragon Lords, declaring it theirs, but that he would take his payment whether they willed it or not. They challenged him without fear of his intent. However, they had relinquished their weapons upon entry as the custom for guests dictated. So when the Master Artificer opened his palace to the sea, flooding the ancient halls and expelling them onto the shore before retreating to a vault of stone at the ocean's utmost depths, their blades remained within its confines.

Decrying his treachery, the Dragon Lords rose on wings of fire and tore his palace from its roots, vault of stone and all. Casting it upon the beach, they burned the vault of stone and water to ashes and shattered his palace. In vain the Master Artificer struggled, using all his art and, ultimately, their own weapons, against them. They reclaimed what was theirs and returned him to the ocean amidst the ruins of his palace, banishing him until their Age ended. With the compass in hand, they returned to the South. In their wake, however, he called upon them a curse, swearing that before their stories ended, they would know true betrayal.

"**Of** course, that is only the official version. The truth is Andeor'Vallen had a black skinned whore he was quite fond of. The Master Artificer became infatuated with her, so Andeor'Vallen incinerated his palace." Kyar caressed the Aparthii woman's unsoiled braid. "The Master Artificer later murdered the whore long before his curse ever transpired.

"I find this tale suitable for cautioning a friend against insults, revenge, and getting too attached to one's possessions." He grinned, yanking on the Aparthii woman's braid.

A light knock sounded on the palanquin's frame and Valeriius smiled. "It is unfortunate we lack time for another tale. I, for one, doubt the notion of the three-tipped compass. But the story is entertaining, so thank you."

"Anytime. I have many such tales. I must retire though; my retinue awaits that we might enter in proper order. I depart with a respectful farewell." Kyar vaulted from the palanquin onto his stallion.

Valeriius rummaged beneath his seat and withdrew a basket of chilled atari: a pallid eastern fruit, harmless except during early stages of growth when its skin is sanguine.

"My Lord Kalvonder, I have a parting gift."

"Pray tell?"

Valeriius tossed him the blood-red atari. "A fruit imported from the East; I am told it has a distinct effect. There are legends of them being poisonous, but I have never experienced ill-effect. That said, I have never tried one of this color; I hear they are sweeter."

"I will give this all the consideration it deserves." Kyar slowly— purposefully—bit into the red flesh, chewed and spat it onto the sand.

"Whatever drove you to brawl before the Angorat'Wass is beyond me. Valeriius would whip you dry any other day." Taor cinched another bandage. "And absconding in the middle of the gala? One would think you wanted to die." Reaching blindly toward a cluttered table of medical implements, Taor snatched the dabbing cloth from a bowl of ruddy alcohol. "What did you fight with? A dog? These are tooth marks!"

"Not a dog a cat, one of the big eastern ones." He groaned, gripping his chair as Taor dug the cleaning rag into his shoulder. "That hurts."

"Of course it hurts. Damn it, this needs stitches. I hate doing stitches, there's never clean string. Wait here while I find thread that won't kill you."

Dieharamon slumped forward on his mat, aching, exhausted, and petrified to his very core. He didn't know what to do, if there was anything he could do. The Dread Lord waited out there, delaying his return for a reason Dieharamon could not imagine. But that wasn't what sickened Dieharamon the most. He had killed, murdered, dozens of men to save Dayada Avenar, to save himself, and the Avenar couldn't even wield his sword properly.

A spasm shook Dieharamon, clutching his heart and squeezing his emotions. His despair and horror faded, leaving him hollow but for a burgeoning sense of wrath and a thorn of fear. All those men dead for someone who couldn't even fulfill his function.

Dieharamon forced his thoughts away from that line of reasoning. He shouldn't have expected anything from Dayada. He didn't deserve anything from him. For now he only had one task: survive the Angorat'Wass. The thought restored his nausea.

The occasional tramp of boots or muffled voice intruded through the makeshift infirmary's cracked walls, but no one passed the open doorway. The infirmary's slanted floor might not have invited operating, but it was one of few locations with ample light.

Taor returned, a needle clamped between his teeth while he scraped filth off a string. He spat the needle into the alcohol, then sterilized it with a reed torch before dunking the string in alcohol as well. "What even induced you to brawl? You're only hurting yourself. *Ashshand!* One would think a man of your age would be wiser!"

"It doesn't matter. I'm going to die today regardless. Just finish my shoulder."

"It is the gods' gift to hope, Dieharamon, don't waste it. You stand a better chance of surviving than any other gladiator today. Surviving this past Turning proved it; Vysar's dead, and rumor is Jaur killed him. Not just him either, roughly two dozen gladiators showed up dead, some from hiding, all of them prominent contenders. The Kalvonders are desperate, hundreds of them have invested the majority of their fortune in their Tragnashi; they won't be destitute, but they won't be a Kalvonder.

"And it's not just the Kalvonders. This isn't going to be like anything you've experienced. There was a promise, witnessed by thousands, that the victor will go free. That is something to kill for."

The needle bit into his skin, earning a grimace. "Well, count me overjoyed and hopeful. The gods don't care about us, Taor, we don't have souls to worship them." The anger simmered in Dieharamon, itching under his skin. He clamped down on it, stifling the urge to punch something.

"Well at least try to win for me. I bet three glass pieces on you surviving, and the odds are a hundred thousand to one. You could make us both rich. Valeriius will take it, of course, but it's a long road to Lower-Sahdaen; I'm sure we could find something, maybe some real food, the type they only sell in the Entertainer's Guild. Or perhaps more proper armor to accompany that sword and chainmail you found."

"I thought you didn't bet. Where'd you get the money?"

"Somebody always needs patching-up near Upper-Sahdaen. I go there whenever I can to earn whatever pittance they have to offer. It takes a while, but eventually I scrape enough together for a decent meal. As for the betting, this is my last chance to bet on you, so I decided to play the odds."

The rage surged again, striving against the apathy. "You don't sound much like a Tragnashi."

He snorted. "None of us do; we're not drugged into incoherence, and Valeriius doesn't suppress anywhere near as much as the other Kalvonders. It's one of the reasons you've survived. The other survivors are too suppressed to learn anything; all they have is instinct and whatever their Kalvonders *brand* into them."

"So how did Valeriius pull you out of the Thieves' Guild?"

Taor's low hum died and he stilled briefly. "What do you mean?"

"I don't know if that's it, but I know you came from somewhere. How many Avarans know rudimentary medicine? The Thieves' Guild would have taught you that and information gathering."

He bit off the string. "Yeah, the Thieves' Guild, and nothing interesting about the how. I got sold, like everybody else. Someone wanted me gone, so he paid to make it happen. Valeriius accepted, not often you find someone with my training they'll pay you to take." Taor wiped Dieharamon's shoulder with the last clean rag. "Well, I've done all I can." He stepped back, wiping his hands. "You're lucky, both the bleeding and poison could have killed you. I'm not sure how you survived to be honest."

Dieharamon stood and tested the stitching. The anger surged again, only to immediately recede. "Valeriius is manipulating my emotions."

"Yeah, dampening your conscience as usual for the Angorat'Wass, but also suppressing everything nonessential and funneling it into surges of rage." Taor shrugged. "What can you expect? There are several hundred fortunes owed the victorious Kalvonder. Others are doing far worse. A couple gladiators are so *branded* there's nothing left; they just stare at the wall, hot enough to burn if you touch them."

"Ooh, yes and it smells divine!"

Dieharamon looked over, a snarl tugging his lips at the newly arrived man. "What do you want, Jaur?"

Jaur Tragnashi sauntered inside. "So you're the legendary Dieharamon, Valeriius' big, bad dog. You seem a little ragged, are you sure you're ready?"

"What do you want?"

Jaur toured the room, fondling the various surgical knives. "Nothing, just thought I'd stop in and see you before the killing starts. This is your final bout after all. Did you hear about poor Vysar? I had hoped to kill him on the field, but I guess someone got scared. No matter, there's always you."

"Do you think yourself a wolf, Jaur?"

Jaur lifted one of the bloodied knives. "Is this where you tell me you've seen things that would make my skin crawl? That you've killed bigger dogs than me? I heard it all the night Vysar died. So trust me, there are far more reasons to fear me than the reverse." He licked the blade. "Ach, it tastes burnt!"

"No, because frankly you've done things to make my skin crawl." He took the knife and tossed it back to the table. "Don't worry, I get it, Jaur, you're scary, really scary, but I've met someone worse."

Jaur slid in front of him. "You see those fellows?" He gestured at two Avarans standing outside the doorway. "They're to make sure I reach the Angorat'Wass all nice and healthy. Kyar knows I'm gonna win this for him, so he's got a dozen gladiators bedecked with proper gear all dedicated to protecting me, dying for me. You're alone, and everybody's target." A light flickered in his eyes and he drew a finger-long knife. "I don't think anyone would complain if you showed up dead; the Kalvonders hate you so much, bless their greedy little hearts."

The Avarans shared flashing grins and Taor moved to intervene but Dieharamon forestalled him. "I guess you've been busy. Did you kill all the gladiators or just some? Also, put that away, you're not killing me here."

"Just some here and there when they drank too much. There are other Kalvonders much more desperate than Kyar." Jaur started for the door, flicking a hand in farewell. "See you soon."

____

Valeriius examined the arena from its highest pillar, ruminating on the faltering lights and rousing darkness. He disliked the prominence this position afforded him, but no one ignored a summons from Trerrock Kalvonder. Five other Kalvonders lounged across the pillar in degrees of unease, languor, and anticipation, two of them inconsequential, the others the Triad.

Xexeross towered in a frothing medley of retainers, slaves, and Tragnashi, bellowing drunken laughter and coarse jokes. His retinue contained mostly soldiers and mercenaries, with the rest being a pair of assassins, a huntsman, preening courtesans, and a persecutor.

Ureign sat at the pillar's edge, swimming in food, drink, and courtesans as he swamped his immense throne through sheer fat and golden silk. He carried no weapons, wore an amethyst crown upon his naked brow and suffered none but the courtesans to touch him. Every imaginable retainer accompanied him, garbed in riches.

Trerrock reclined in a chair across from the others, alone but for his wine slave, face masked by weaving strands of scarlet iron. He wore thick black leathers despite the heat, eclipsed Xexeross in height to the point of resembling men from the Winter-lands and carried a crimson-hilted blade at his side. Of the Triad, and their closest competitors, Trerrock alone dispatched no Tragnashi to the arena, preferring to execute them outright rather than submit to the Kalmarads' machination.

Trerrock finally beckoned with a twitch of his hand and Valeriius obeyed, assuming a mien of confidence while arranging his features into a veil of humility. Of all the Kalvonders, Valeriius knew the least of Trerrock, and Thanen's memories supplied only hearsay and rumor. There were only two certainties, and these widely known: the first, Trerrock acted purely at his own discretion, disdaining any oath, agreement, threat, or unspoken law; and second, he was immortal.

"What do you calculate your chances of victory today?"

Valeriius considered his response carefully; conversations between Kalvonders rarely inclined so pedestrian. "A higher chance than many: Dieharamon is an effective instrument."

"Why such faith in Dieharamon?"

Valeriius shrugged, wondering both at Trerrock's use of Dieharamon's name and his question. The answer seemed evident. "Dieharamon has proven himself superior, resilient, and most of all intelligent for over a decade. There is no comparable gladiator."

"No there is not, which makes me wonder what would happen if they learned he was mage-born?"

Valeriius assimilated the revelation and adapted; he could kill Trerrock if the necessity presented itself, but for now, he would allow him to divulge his purpose in exposing his knowledge.

"Don't bother with bribes; I appreciate cheating as much as anyone."

"What is your desire?"

"Declare your stance on the New Order?"

"I have little influence or power."

"When gods stand in opposition, mortals define the balance; do not bore or insult me with lies of insignificance."

"I will favor the alliance."

"When empires collide, kings fall but beggars endure. Not that it matters, I intend a departure and have no interest in Sahdaen's ruin. I'll return when all the murdering's done." His attention flicked to something in Valeriius' periphery. "Our guests have arrived."

The New Order's emissaries emerged from a stairway, headed by their chief priest, a patriarch whose robes merged effortlessly with the shadows and whose eyes burned with feverish power. The patriarch, Daevon Vedren, bowed to Ureign first, Xexeross second, and Trerrock last, who regarded him as he would a wallowing drunk. The patriarch's cordiality splintered like an eggshell, revealing a flash of rage that Trerrock continued to ignore.

Quelling his features, Vedren spun pointedly to Valeriius. "I've not had the pleasure of your acquaintance."

"I am Valeriius, Lord Daevon."

"And I no lord. I serve *Telacra*, though you disdain her here."

"Yes, the far corners of our world do loathe the gods."

The patriarch blatantly measured Valeriius against Trerrock and then marshalled another false grin before leaning close. "I would speak with you privately later, concerning the proposed alliance and your ... leadership."

"Of course," Valeriius bowed submissively, coloring his voice with a hint of glee.

Trerrock finally addressed the patriarch. "Daevon, I do not know if your master intended you as a joke of incompetence, or as an attempt to cultivate underestimation of his abilities, but I tire of your blundering infantility. Go."

"You would dare—"

"Go."

The patriarch snarled, struggling to assert himself as his station and power demanded, and failed. When this failed, he marshalled a visage of disdain, sniffed contemptuously and retired to an empty corner with his retinue.

In their absence, Trerrock readdressed Valeriius, "Your preferred slave has arrived, presumably with a message. Go deal with her, I am done with you."

A glance revealed Valeriius' Aparthii slave at the entrance and he crossed to, then past her. She fell into step.

"What has occurred?"

"Dieharamon has arrived in the catacombs bearing a heavily enchanted sword and a chainmail shirt, both from the Clergy."

"Preserve his acquisitions and inform the lesser Kalvonders allied against Trerrock—for a price—that an opportunity graces them. Confide, anonymously, that he means to depart Sahdaen. Second, ensure that every Kalvonder slave knows that the Kalvonders allying with the New Order will affect them … adversely."

Dieharamon crouched against his pit's earthen walls, listening to the stadium's roaring jubilation. The Kalvonders had constructed a new arena for this Angorat'Wass, expending hundreds of lives and a fortune to accomplish it. As a crowning touch, they had excavated tombs in its floor for the competitors. Dieharamon was uncertain if the irony was intentional. They had also restructured the rule, ordaining that all gladiators serving one Kalvonder would fight as allies. Thus Dieharamon fought alone because Valeriius possessed but 'one' Tragnashi.

Dieharamon absently polished the pewter sword. The Kalmarads should have forbidden its use, just as they should have forbidden the iron chainmail looted from Dru'Kerack that he wore. Both items, the sword with its enchantments and the chainmail with its vast superiority, represented an immense advantage. Valeriius must have intervened, but why expose the influence that would require when he had never displayed any interest in preserving Dieharamon before?

The sword hummed beneath his fingers, magic pulsing within it like blood in veins, and the fire simmering within him echoed the rhythm back. It terrified him but his injuries had healed, leaving only sore muscles, scars, and bandages as testament they ever existed.

He hacked and spat, his gaze wandering to where the specters from the Remanas Palace crowded his pit's far end, wasted and decrepit. He had noticed their reappearance as the storm first manifested, initially just a handful clutching the shoulders of the feeblest Avaran like ashen monkeys—attached via thin bone tubes—but more appeared as the storm waxed and the fire within him seethed higher. Now dozens hovered just outside his reach, hollow eyes full of malice and want.

The drums commenced above, summoning Dieharamon to the ladder as the grate swung open with a spray of sand. He ignited the fire within his core, retreating into the old tracks of battle but failing to shirk one simple question: *'What have we done to deserve this?'*

The audience's elation crescendoed, drawing his gaze up to the blackened sky. Lightning streaked across it, flashing red, black, and soundless. Unbidden, Sinnitar's words echoed in his mind: One way or another, tomorrow's dawn will be the last Sahdaen sees for a long time. Then the drums ceased.

He lunged upward, vaulting from the pit to crouch on the packed sand of an immense arena, surrounded by gladiators emerging from identical pits and dodging a matrix of soaring stone blocks arranged in a revolving pyramid.

A flicker of movement from his periphery sent Dieharamon diving across the treacherous ground, just barely evading the talons of a colossal Roc as they slammed into his earlier position. The creature disdained further pursuit and stalked toward his pit, wings flaring out with a flash of red, violet, and blue in the lightning. It screeched and stabbed its beak into the hole, rifling for prey.

Dieharamon scrambled back to his feet, stumbling as other Rocs slammed to the earth near pits or onto emerging gladiators with ruthless efficiency. Those lingering in the pits soon discovered they were no sanctuary from the massive birds.

A block soared past within reach, revealing handholds. Dieharamon jumped, caught one of the handholds and hauled himself up, beginning his ascent toward the pyramid's zenith in the storm-strangled heavens.

———————————

After allowing an appropriate span for the man to recover his composure, Valeriius approached Daevon Vedren. Surrounded by his adherents, the patriarch sat in a vacant corner, his rigid, high-backed throne garishly at odds with the Avaran half-moon seats.

Valeriius forwent etiquette. "You wished to discuss your purpose here?"

Daevon leaned forward, clasping his hands in benign superiority. "Yes, much can be gained from a union of our cultures. The tyrant in the West—"

"We are not in the East, Patriarch, propaganda is unnecessary."

The patriarch blinked, then grinned. "Very well, what do you desire, Kalvonder?"

Valeriius settled opposite him, resting both hands atop his cane. "It was not I who requested this meeting."

"And I am no simple petitioner; remember that before we continue. The Dark Consort needs soldiers to make war on the Paladin Empire, the South has a plethora."

"You speak one truth but act another. Why does a black storm shadow our Hold and why does a Dread Lord stalk her streets?"

"The storm is not ours, and I do not know who this 'Dread Lord' is."

"Has the East forgotten so much of their history?" Privately he thought, *'Or has it been shrouded?'*

"We remember what is important. That I do not know this 'Dread Lord' signifies he is irrelevant and undeserving of our fear; he cannot compare to The New Order's strongest scions. We are born of *Telacra*, fused with her essence to transcend mortality."

"The Muntalabacs were consuming the blackest nightmares and most holy seraphs centuries before gods sought mortal servants."

"Wait, I know the name Muntalabac, two in fact. One accompanied us here at the Dark Consort's behest, but I assure you he is feeble, eclipsed by even the lowest of *Telacra's* servants."

"Then why is he rampaging through our Hold?"

Daevon's cheeks ticked. "No servant of mine would stray from my will. I am not kind."

"You do not control Sinnitar Muntalabac—"

"Enough of him! You know our desire, Valeriius, and the wealth we offer. Right here, right now, you are laughable and pathetic, a joke propped up by the achievements of a slave. But with our aid, you can ascend beyond what anyone could envision!"

"I see far, and my avarice runs deeper than these canyons."

"Then we share a vista, and the New Order can satisfy it, no matter how vast. Even if it includes dominion over your peers."

"So you desire more than Southern blood to fuel your war, you wish to rule her."

"And such empires need lords acquainted with certain territories."

"The Avarans need many chains. You could but err to liberate them now."

"Like I said, the New Order will need many kings, and of course, a sovereign above them."

"You speak sweet words, but a man once told me a serpent's venom is sweet. I do not trust the sorcerer; men of his nature disregard their promises."

"Hah! A Kalvonder lecturing me on trust! Oh, the irony. Your entire history is betrayal and deceit. Your culture revels in garishly murdering one another! You cannot stand here and posture skepticism."

"Nor can I discard my promises without true need, the retribution would destroy me. A risk you lack. In contrast, I request only proof of your intentions, a small concession considering you could eradicate me on a whim."

"I doubt both your vulnerability and impotence."

"I have no intention of obstructing the New Order or the Army of Purgeance, such a conflict exceeds the South's reach."

"Lives are cheap to Kalvonders; you would not hesitate to initiate such a war."

"Not that cheap; Cardolyn Tyier still presses us from the Inland Sea; and if he decided to march, all our power could not deter him. We cannot fight both the East and West."

"Then logic dictates an alliance, lest Cardolyn Tyier swallow the world whole. We need each other if this world is to survive. But if you refuse..."

"Before you continue that thought, ask yourself this: Why does Cardolyn Tyier delay? I assure you; it is not for concern of Morrehiegann in Paranoia. The South is not something to assail lightly."

"Even The North can and will fall, the South is no different. Your Great-Immortals are debilitated, their ancient power drained away like rain into the sewer. They cannot resist the Pantheon's gods."

"Your avowal might bear more weight were there no other influences in this world, beings we do not know, older than you can conceive, creatures that mayhap would not like this world to change."

"I fear no dead gods; their time ended."

"The wheel turns, Patriarch."

"Leave your ghosts, memories and fears, Kalvonder; this Age calls, and it beckons with power. Heed it."

"Bring proof and you will have all you desire of the South."

"I believe the Dark Consort will find this acceptable."

———————

Dieharamon dropped to a lower block, twisting to evade a sweeping ax and channeling the impact onto his uninjured leg. The assailing gladiator reset his stance and struck again, hacking towards Dieharamon's head. Dieharamon caught the ax just below its head, snapped it in two and eviscerated his foe with a slash of the pewter sword. The man crumpled and Dieharamon migrated toward the block's smooth center, discarding the useless ax head and scanning for threats. When none presented themselves, he knelt gingerly.

His injuries inflicted little pain, but every wound hampered him a little further and the blood loss sapped his strength. He leaned his sword beside himself and stripped cloth from the dead to bind the shallow cuts on his legs, silently thanking whatever entity bestowed him with the chainmail vest. It had saved him continuously, especially in melees, converting many potentially lethal injuries into bruises. The Avaran weapons simply couldn't penetrate the iron. Unfortunately, it only hung to mid-thigh, which had permitted a dying gladiator to gouge his leg.

After binding his wounds, he scavenged for weapons and wine skins, working slowly and feigning debility so his body could heal and his fatigue ameliorate. None of the gladiators on passing blocks assaulted him, too preoccupied with more immediate conflicts or simply disinterested in a nameless opponent. Dieharamon had known he would be hunted from the beginning, and so had disguised his features with the bloodied rags of his first victims.

He accumulated a meager arsenal of hatchets, bludgeons, and arrows over the ensuing minutes, then settled in to observe the arena, lying among the corpses and smearing himself in their blood to appear dead.

A thousand twenty by ten blocks comprised the pyramid, levitated by mages scattered through the bleachers, their vibrant coats pinpricks of color amidst the sea of Avarans. Markings organized the blocks into families, each presided over by a clearly distinguished mage in case Kalvonders desired to influence the match.

Blocks had failed Dieharamon twice, the first simply plummeting while the second upended him. In both instances errant blocks diverged from formation to preserve him. Shortly after the second event, a whole family of blocks fell permanently, their mage murdered and unceremoniously dumped into the arena. Hundreds of gladiators died in the process. The mages ceased interfering with him after that.

Shortly thereafter, the mages had tired of maintaining the pyramid pattern and proceeded to dismantle it, casting the ordered perfection into disarray. Now the blocks collided, spun, and dove at whim, discarding gladiators and crushing dozens more. This of course, only improved the entertainment value.

Having dawdled as long as he dared, Dieharamon reclaimed his sword and vaulted onto a passing block, seeking the pyramid's zenith for both its stability and the protection it afforded against Rocs who hunted the gladiators still embattled on the ground. Another, slightly elevated, block drifted by, embroiled in conflict. One of its gladiators noticed him, hooted gleefully, and launched an arrow. Dieharamon cursed and tried to evade, but the arrow slammed against his chest and splintered on the chainmail. He staggered, a new bruise forming, and scrambled his own bow awkwardly off his shoulders. Before he could aim, however, his block trembled, cracks spiraling from its center. The mage had lost control, either exceeding his abilities, distracted, or murdered.

He cursed again and leapt up off the block, flinging his bow aside as a second arrow whipped past. There was an instant of flight, then he struck the side of his assailant's block, caught a handhold and heaved upward. The gladiator recoiled, scrambling for another arrow, but Dieharamon was already vaulting onto the block.

He landed in their midst and whirled, the pewter sword sweeping from its seat on his belt. It sheared through archer's gambeson, flesh, muscle, and bone like rotten cloth and hurled him into a shrieking descent.

Dieharamon didn't pause, he couldn't if he wished to survive, he ploughed forward, slashing left and right, splitting one gladiator's skull with his sword's spine and hacking two others across the midriff. The crowded block might have obstructed other weapons, tangling them and preventing the windup Avaran weapons relied on, but Dieharamon's strength and the sword's enchanted edge rendered it a lethal advantage.

Slamming to a halt, he grounded his foot amidst the jumbled corpses and spun, butchering the encroaching gladiators. Blood and severed weapons sprayed him, the pewter sword suffering almost no resistance.

The gladiators sharing the block with him reeled and scrambled, some trying to approach and others to flee, all entangling with one another and the dead. Had they known how to fight, or coordinated, they might have killed him. Had they possessed proper weaponry they might have survived. But they did not.

A short gladiator shoved through two of his retreating fellows and thrust a cracked spear at him. Dieharamon slapped it aside with his forearm and impaled him through his bone shield, then swept back around, slashing the pewter sword through the body of another gladiator without pause. The rest, emboldened by desperation, tried to swarm him but stumbled over the dead, reeling from the block's constant shifts. Dieharamon staggered as well, but his size and the chainmail's weight helped to anchor him.

So they flailed toward him in ones and twos and died, slaughtered by artless, sweeping blows. An arshendi-armed gladiator charged his left. He batted the weapon aside and crushed the man's throat with a punch. A spear glanced off his chainmail and he spun, decapitating its master before borrowing the spear and launching it through two others.

More attacked but their efforts proved hopeless; they couldn't muster sufficient numbers or consistency to threaten him. Eventually the survivors fled and he was left swaying on an empty block.

Dieharamon collapsed against a cadaver, sword slipping from his grip. He lay there and panted, letting the fire thrum through his veins, ameliorating his pain and soothing his body. He could rest, these moments of respite paid for in the blood dousing him. It couldn't last, of course. It never lasted.

Atop the Triad's pillar, only Daevon, Xexeross, and Ureign endured the storm without concession, Trerrock having long since departed. Xexeross berated his cowering attendants with a diatribe of inebriated profanity, jokes, and benedictions, vacillating between the three without cause. Daevon paced the column's center, reveling in the cloying malignance, while Ureign sat upon the pillar's precipice laughing.

Wind lashed Valeriius, shearing through his clothing and besieging him with the stench of rotting meat. He grimaced and clutched the railing; this storm served more purpose than to bar *Ashshand* from Sahdaen; it forbid *Sammahale* and *Arawn* as well, stripping the Avarans of all their deities. And more besides.

Even before its manifestation, there had been a sickness on the Hold, a plague of fear spreading through its populous like overgrowth ever since the Dread Lord arrived. Now that plague stirred to life, assaulting not flesh but the mind and the soul. The Dread Lord would reveal his presence soon. But a question remained, why embed himself in the New Order? They possessed nothing Sinnitar could not achieve on his own, and the veil of subservience gained him nothing in the South. Avarans had proven themselves willing vessels for his ancestors on many occasions.

Suddenly, violent as spite, a foreign emotion charged the atmosphere, wrenching Valeriius, Daevon and Xexeross about. Sinnitar stood in the doorway, the darkness cowering at his feet and his visage glistening in the putrid rain. Yet none could shirk the corrosive awe that swallowed them.

Daevon advanced, railing against the fear Sinnitar's presence invoked, compelled by pride that refused any adversary. He marshalled his goddess' benediction, wreathing his form in shadowed armor as he screamed a condemnation, but the words were stolen from his lips by the Dread Lord's storm.

Sinnitar advanced in kind, causing Daevon to stumble beneath his presence then draw himself up. Shadows coalesced before the patriarch, expanding into a barrage of ephemeral hands. They struck Sinnitar and warped, contorting as if in pain to become something entirely other, though their form persisted.

Stripped of his goddess, Daevon recoiled and fell, whimpering as he lifted a hand to shield himself. The Dread Lord wasted neither word nor gesture in destroying his foe, for Daevon's fear alone sufficed, driving him to scramble ever backwards until, with a final horrified shriek, he flung himself over the precipice.

Sinnitar glanced at Ureign. Their eyes locked and Ureign straightened, upending the courtesans and food as his eyes spun. "What must the creature want? Must it want? Yes, it must want. Too great, too great is the creature's power to not lust. Where does it want? Why does it want? Wants the where? It burns, but not with the fires of its origin, but where it has never been."

Sinnitar Muntalabac scanned the remaining Kalvonders with scathing eyes. "I am your new liaison with the New Order, vested with all the incumbent authority."

"Fire! Fire in his tread. Fire obeys law; it cannot burn without wood. Why does his tread burn? Because the fire in his step does not burn. It must burn, it is fire, and I feel its flames! Burning, burning, and I revel in the burning. But it doesn't burn. Why do they burn if they do not burn? All is broken, all is changing, and all is burning. I hear chains in the winds, singing in the heat of flames that do not burn. I hear screams and feel black ashes that are flesh beneath my fingertips! He would command us with this fire, or he would burn us. He wants to bring more of this fire here, no, not here, but there and where. The where he desires is the when from where the fires that do not burn come." Laughing, Ureign resumed his seat, ignoring the Dread Lord even when he came to stand beside him and join his spectating of the Angorat'Wass.

Terrified and cowering, the other Kalvonders hastily called their slaves to erect curtains against the rain, belaboring them with words and blows at every step. Only Valeriius and Xexeross refrained from that practice; one suffered the rain dispassionately, the other drinking through it without qualm.

The Kalvonders gradually relaxed, their focus reverting to the entertainment without ever fully escaping Sinnitar's influence. As general equanimity returned, Xexeross swaggered unsteadily toward Valeriius, a stained decanter dangling from his fingers. He threw a burly arm over

Valeriius' shoulders and squeezed him close, speaking in a slur. "I think you've been keeping secrets, little Valeriius."

"I try my best; it is a wise practice."

Xexeross hiccupped. "Are you saying you try to find secrets to keep?"

"Not at all, though I am curious as to what betrayed me?"

"Because both Daevon and Trerrock Kalvonder seem to find you very interesting." Another hiccup. "Personally, I can't see what they were all fussing about."

"… You think they saw something you do not?"

"No, no. I mean, when was the last time you killed somebody no one else was supposed to know you killed? Never. You're an upright fellow, only kill people straight on, face forward." He swigged heavily. "A shame about you not selling your Anatay crop, I fancied a hit of it every now and then, good for a detox. Killed all your consumers from deprivation, straight on, face forward, no shadows or poison." Another hiccup.

"A flash sand-fire burned the crop, unfortunate but it happens."

"That it does, that it does. So tell you what, I'll buy it from you, fair price, straight up, save you the loss."

"I appreciate the offer, but I'll retain my assets."

The decanter cracked against Valeriius' chest, bruising him to the bone as Xexeross squeezed him close. "You're a gambler! Turning me down. I like gamblers." He ground the decanter harder, cutting through Valeriius' layers of clothing and then skin with a wickedly sharp edge. "I was a gambler once, years ago when I was small and itty-bity, about as big as one of your Anatay plants. But I outgrew it." Xexeross looked at him expectantly, grinning vaguely."

"I'm … sure I'll outgrow it too."

"That's great!" Xexeross ripped the decanter free, its mouth stained with Valeriius' blood. "But not too soon, you gotta have some fun first."

Valeriius stumbled as Xexeross abruptly relinquished him. He leaned into the unsteadiness, flailing for balance so his cane whipped out and smashed Xexeross' decanter. "Oh, my apologies, Xexeross Kalvonder. Here, let me clean you up–"

"No, no, there is no need." Xexeross waved Valeriius off while snapping his fingers for one of his slaves to attend the glass shards. "And don't even think about repaying, it was entirely my action." He clapped Valeriius on the shoulder again. "Well, I expect we'll be seeing more of you. Best of luck!"

Without tarrying for a reply, Xexeross staggered over to a subsequent nameless Kalvonder and clapped an arm over his shoulders, one hand extended back to accept a new decanter.

Valeriius shifted subtly to face away from Xexeross and surreptitiously ran a hand over his shoulders and beneath the lapels of his coat until he found a red and violet chrysalis, tall as a chicken egg but thinner: an avaryat. Avaryat were parasitoid insects that fastened onto the spines of victims and attached themselves to their organs, making them irremovable. They were agonizing and terminal once latched.

He crushed it and clasped his cane in both hands. A light blossomed within its amethyst heart and faded, erasing his injuries and cleaning any potential parasites or diseases. Before the process finished, Sinnitar stepped beside him.

"You harbor an Avenar."

"Yes?"

"Expel him."

"He is impotent—"

"He is an Avenar. Cast him out, or I will destroy you."

"You will fail."

"Do you seriously believe that?"

"Why do you think an Avenar walks my halls?"

"You brought him to challenge me."

"No, he came of his own accord and I saw fit to house him."

"That house can burn with or without the Avenar. Give him to me, and I will spare you from Sahdaen's ravaging."

"Madmen and blind men glimpse what the sane and the seeing cannot. I know the un-burning flames. I know what Kale Saragion intends for the West."

"He will burn like everyone else. I repeat, give me the Avenar princeling."

"You will have the Avenar when I have exhausted his use."

The sword on the Dread Lord's back seethed awake, causing the air about it to palpitate with abrasive, dry heat. Its silver winged crossguard marked it for what it was, naming it for those with the knowledge: *Stolen Wings*.

The blade subsided, leaving Valeriius with naught but the Dread Lord's ravenous presence. "Your Tragnashi has something else I desire."

"What could he possibly possess that you desire?"

"The *Pathfinder Shard*. I sent him to retrieve it, but he no longer has it. Which means you do."

The Dread Lord's presence swallowed Valeriius and he gasped, bending over at the waist, ravaged by starvation, thirst, bloodlust, and wrath. He clamped both hands on his cane and it burned with vicious heat, the rowan wood lacerating his hands with a dangerous chill. It was insufficient, he buckled beneath the Dread Lord's presence. "I have no knowledge of this *Shard!*"

The Dread Lord grabbed Valeriius by the head with a char-colored hand. "Yes, you do. Now, give it over."

"I don't have it! I don't have it!"

"Then find it. Bring me the *Pathfinder Shard* or the Avenar's heart. Bring both and you will survive Sahdaen's ruin." The Dread Lord flung him to the ground, sending his cane clattering across the pillar's roof.

Slowly, the awful weight of Sinnitar Muntalabac abated, diminishing as he departed and allowing Valeriius to stand. He brushed his hair and clothing into some semblance of order and ignored the burn marks on his brow that refused to heal.

41

Demons And Paladins

Brimares stalked through the New Order's inner and outer encampments, ploughing through the deluging sleet past *Telacra's* whispering totems and the fires in their embankments. A few of the officers turned at her passage, their dim lights rising to illuminate her and the steam that seethed off her armor and skin. She snarled at herself, furious at her inability to control her panic. The Chaos within seethed with that panic, escalating until the air rippled with her heat and the snow melted before ever touching her skin. In offering to aid the paladin she had walked the Abyss' precipice and tasted its flames; one false step or utterance that the New Order heard, and she would have toppled over: executed for treason.

She reached the outer encampment's extremity and scaled the frozen wall of mounded snow and ice, traversing between the cowering sentries and startling them into alarmed cries. She continued past, abandoning the encampment for the blizzard beyond and allowing it to swallow her. She forced her armor to flare open, to admit the snow and ice, and bathed in the vengeful cold. Her Chaos roiled in response, but the cold and the ice suppressed it and her rampant emotions, allowing her to begin reasserting control.

Brimares slowly sank to the ground, panting through gritted teeth, and waited. She could neither hear nor see more of the encampment than a haze of light through the storm, but even so she waited, expecting the condemning screams, voices booming through the tempest to demand her execution. They never came.

Brimares forced herself upright and back to her feet, closing her armor and extinguishing the final trickle of panic. She recognized the dregs of a foreign influence on her emotions, and although that alarmed her slightly, she understood it and could combat it. The dregs reeked of the paladin's cage, a foul, tortuous thing even the New Order refused to touch; they coerced mercenaries to guard and transport it instead, usually with abuse and compulsion enchantments. Those who managed the prison daily earned raving dreams for their efforts and became violently suicidal after extensive proximity.

Finally calmed, she returned toward to the encampment, discarding thoughts of the cage to contemplate the paladin and his liberation. The sight of him had engendered a visceral loathing within her that did not entirely originate from her Chaos or the anathema of his Divine Shard to her essence. His kind had damned her to the Abyss, and while she could not logically attribute that action to him, she still did not trust him, or herself around him. Still, he was more likely to keep an oath sworn than break it, which meant she needed to pilfer the key from Kheldar, stockpile supplies, and acquire a suitable mount without arousing suspicion if she wished to save him. Fortunately, she had a mount in mind.

Brimares reentered the encampment's purview and the warmth washed over her, just slightly poisoned by *Telacra's* presence. One of the sentries peeked over the ice barricade to greet her as she began her ascent, and soundlessly crumpled, a black shaft protruding from his throat. She hit the ground with a crack of splintered ice, diving over the barricade and then behind a stack of crates as her armor snapped into place. The dying sentry jerked again, spasming with a second arrow in his stomach as the warning horn shrieked. A second later, black arrows rained from the blizzard, raking the barricade, never missing and always in pairs.

The sentries scattered, hurling themselves behind whatever meager cover they could find and hailing warnings. The arrows pursued relentlessly, piercing tents, sleds, barrels, and even metal armor with implacable ease. The assault lasted all of moments, then ceased as abruptly as it began, leaving Brimares alive with only a flicker of silhouettes retreating into the storm, two-dozen new corpses, and an opportunity.

Distant screams informed her that derangers had struck elsewhere along the encampment's border, but she had already risen and begun striding inward. Soldiers and mercenaries inundated her vicinity moments later, swarming from the inner encampment with fearful cries as they struggled into unavailing armor and prepared weapons. Ravaged by exhaustion, most could barely stand and thus floundered in the snow, stumbling into and shoving one another desperately.

No one in the New Order had slept in days; whenever the encampment began to settle, the Northerners would assault, prompting the sentries to hail warnings, and the battle horns to sound, all to no avail. They never caught more than a glimpse of receding coats. Even worse, their scouts continued to return dead atop unscathed mounts and their supplies to spoil despite the cold. The Northern weather deteriorated constantly, draining the clerics to shambling husks and submerging the entire encampment in snow whenever they dared to rest. Every evening demanded hours of desperate excavation just to unearth themselves from the snowfall.

The milling soldiers began to calm in the assault's wake, their frantic energy subsiding to spent shambles and cursory inspections of the dead until another horn blasted from deeper within the encampment. They lurched aside, squeezing between tents and equipment mounds to clear a path. She shuffled aside but continued pushing through them, head bowed to shirk what attention she could.

Two score fully armored riders—preemptively prepared for this eventuality—charged past, the Blond Knight at their head with an ugly horn pressed to his lips. He blew again, spitting a rasping wail that clawed at her ears. The knights answered with a roar, black energy seething from their armor as they plunged into the storm to hunt the derangers.

The Blond Knight had been accruing power in the New Order recently, disdaining the elite soldiers to instead curry loyalty with the more prestigious mercenaries and convicts. He wooed them with promises of wealth and stature and then fanned their lusts unto the brink of insanity, cultivating and dominating them until their vices mimicked his.

The other lords quickly imitated him, splintering the various mercenary and convict groups into personal factions. As a result, the once infrequent murders were escalating into minor skirmishes and inter-camp scavenging into pillaging. Despite this, Kheldar Ferain maintained a semblance of control through the sergeants and lieutenants who terrified the common soldiers. Still, it was only a matter of time before the army devoured itself.

Brimares veered further from the main thoroughfares, bisecting the rows of tents and rushing soldiers until the inner encampments black palisade materialized from the storm. She vaulted it and retraced her steps from earlier, returning to the paladin's prison compound.

The two jittering guards lurched upright at her approach, unsteady and hollow eyed but vainly hollering against the wind. They relented upon recognizing her and slumped onto soaked seats beneath a woefully inadequate awning. She passed through the compound's tilted palisade into a circle of beaten mud ringed by prison sleds and centered around three of the New Order's totems. The paladin lay across from her, shivering and curled within his black cage, wrapped in the ragged cloak the New Order had deigned to permit him. He faced the entrance, sunken eyes open and staring, though she knew he could not see her through the cell's veil.

Her pace slowed then halted, fists clenched at her sides as her Chaos reared, full of hate, full of fear. He would own her the moment she spoke, empowered by her treason. He would need only to expose her subversion to kill her, and only to threaten it to enslave her, and she had nothing to prevent it.

Rain, melted by the density of *Telacra's* presence here, pattered against her armor, soaking her through and turning the ground to mud. She stepped forward, teeth grinding as she quelled her Chaos. The New Order would kill her anyway, by one means or another.

She crouched outside his cell, raking her soaked hair back, and extended an arm through the bars. Her gauntlet retracted, exposing bare fingers to touch his shoulder and spare a spark of warmth. "Can you hear me, paladin?"

His arm snapped from beneath the cloak and latched onto her wrist, pulling her close heedless of the lacerations this opened. "Who are you and why did you save me?"

"I want your help, and you can't do that if you're dead." Her fingers clamped on his shoulder and bore down hard enough to bruise, but he refused to relinquish her.

"Is that why I am here? You stopped me at the bridge so I would have to help you?"

"I couldn't let you go; your horse was dead. They would have caught you anyway and punished me for allowing it. I was not going to risk death over an impossibility." She twisted her arm free, disregarding the damage it caused him.

He hissed sharply but scrambled after her, fumbling until his fingers touched the prison's bars then recoiling with a stifled profanity. He clutched his hand, the skin infested by a mass of slowly fading venomous tendrils. "What's changed? Why help me now?"

"I can get you out now, and away from them before they notice. Everything's a storm out here, you can't see more than a few feet, let alone hear worth a damn. All you would have to do is trust me, if you could manage it." She returned her hand inside. "I have already saved you once though."

"It could be a ploy."

"What do you have to lose?" She seized his shirt. "What could they possibly gain from you being out that they couldn't gain from you being inside? Think!"

He tensed under the violence of her response, but she saw his mind working and felt his Shard of Divinity subside. "Fine. Who are you and what did you do to earn damnation?"

"That doesn't matter."

"Like hell it doesn't! I'm not setting a mass murderer lose on the world."

"I'm already loose on the world."

"You are on a suicide mission in The North. You are as good as dead."

The Chaos roiled within her, desperate to destroy him. She crushed it and forced words through gritted teeth. "Brimares."

"And what did you do?"

If he knew anything about the East, she couldn't tell him. Not the whole story, not what actually earned her condemnation. "In all my life, I've knowingly killed two people, both in defense. One was a paladin knight, and she earned me the last three hundred years in the Abyss."

"Why did she attack you?"

"It. Does. Not. Matter."

"It does to me. Why? Or I am not leaving this cell with you."

"Because I didn't tell her something she wanted to know, something that would have gotten her killed anyway."

"That can't be all of it. It's not enough to kill, let alone damn someone over."

"Then you don't know your own order that well." She growled softly, armor rippling. "It's also the truth and all you're getting."

He slowly nodded his capitulation. "Okay. I … am Lionel Iitanen, knight errant of the Paladin Order. What do you want from me?"

"*Redemption.* My penance to the Abyss paid."

"I can't. *Redemption* for a greater demon is—"

"You need me! Unless you want to try and find some way to kill yourself in a cage with rotting fabric. They don't want you alive just because of Cardolyn Tyier, you're a paladin in his order. What do you think's going to happen?"

"I can't promise anything. Even if I could, I have nothing to contain your Chaos once it's extracted. And I would have to be stronger than whoever condemned you, a paladin capable of creating a greater demon, and I am not."

"I don't care if I survive, I just don't want to go back. You have to be capable of that much at least. You're a gods-damned paladin."

"It's not that simple…"

"Then what use are you to me? *Morgan's* kiss." She slammed the bars. "I have suffered three hundred years for something that was a crime only because of its consequences, and you can't forgive that?"

"You killed a paladin!"

"She deserved it."

"That's not helping your case."

"Give me something! Anything. Please."

The paladin sagged, strength evaporating, and she realized how pallid he had grown, how many dark veins riddled his exposed skin.

"I did not say it was impossible, just beyond my abilities. I can't promise anything, but if you help me, the Imperial Emperor might bargain for your *Redemption*. That's all I have." His blue eyes somehow found and held hers for a moment, then he lowered himself back to the floor and curled up.

Brimares thrust off his cell, the Chaos within her a storm of pent violence and fury. She needed *Redemption* if she wanted to survive, she needed liberation from the New Order; otherwise her fate led to Antiark where she would be used as battle fodder, butchered so a few more of their soldiers could survive.

Brimares left the compound—eyes aflame with her Chaos' wrath—and began to wander, searching for she knew not what. The New Order continued its unvarying cycle, progressing through assault, bedlam, de-escalation, attempts to sleep, and renewed assault until she barely registered the horn blasts. Hours elapsed in these pursuits and night gradually fell, leaving her where she began, staring at the compounds and its guards.

Alkarred take them, she was not going to stand put while they killed her. Brimares growled to herself and stalked into the compound, disdaining the guard's hailed questions.

Lionel stirred at her approach, but she ignored his murmured greeting and grasped the prison's rear bars in gauntleted hands, waking the Chaos in her blood and calling it to a fevered pitch of violence. Lionel recoiled with a curse, sensing the Chaos but not its intent.

The prison retaliated with icy malice, darkening her gauntlets and freezing her hands. Enraged, the Chaos roared higher, igniting her skin and armor in ugly flames as pain ripped through her. The prison bar began to collapse, hissing and spitting acid fumes between her fingers as it melted.

She tore her hands off and stumbled back, panting as she pacified her Chaos. The pain receded in turn, and the horrid flames subsided.

Lionel tentatively touched the smoking indents her fingers had left, aware of her actions despite the prison's enchantments. "Why?"

"I needed to know if I could break it." She knelt before him. "I'll open your cell at midday tomorrow, but you need to hide that, and I don't know where to go. Once we get out, it'll all be on you." She waited for his confirmation then stood. "I know you want more, but that's all I have."

"Wait." He scooted forward, fumbling with his hands. "Why were you summoned? You and your kin."

"We are meant to kill the High-Warden of Winsyria, but now's not the time; I will answer your questions when we are free. For now, is there anything special you need? Necessities only."

"There is a book in my saddlebags: the *Amarthayiss*. The New Order cannot be allowed to keep, destroy, or, *Enecki* forbid, corrupt it."

"You want a book?"

"Yes."

"The holy scripture of the religion that damned me!"

"Yes."

"I would rather see it burned."

"I will not leave without the *Amarthayiss;* retrieve it or abandon me."

"Fine," she growled. "I'll get the damn book."

"Thank you. I know it doesn't mean anything to you, but we cannot continue to lose the *Amarthayiss* scriptures—"

"I don't care about you, your book, your Order, or anything you have that is not *Redemption*. Keep it to yourself." Brimares left without further comment.

She could acquire armor, sword, and mount easily, but not the book. That would have to come first.

That night and the subsequent half-day concluded in worse failure than Brimares could have feared, leaving her not only without the *Amarthayiss* but unable to even find it. To make matters worse, the New Order had issued orders to decamp hours early, which left her short on time and with precious few options: solicit her kin or Salem, and she already owed Salem.

Grinding to a halt, Brimares scaled atop an adjacent sled, knotting her fingers in its ropes to anchor her against the wind's lashing gusts. The soldiers huddled against its flanks glanced curiously at this, but she ignored them and ignited the Chaos in her eyes. Pain instantly woke in her skull, burning as if she were aflame, but her world slipped into shades of gray, all except a few distant and scattered pyres that blazed through The North's storm: her kin. She rifled through them, dismissing Kell'MachChain, who would use this as an excuse to consume her; and Cellar'Veer, who would know little of the *Amarthayiss*. Unfortunately, most of the lesser demons congregated around the communal fires with the New Order elite, but not all.

She dismounted her perch and directed her steps toward the inner encampment, slogging through the waist-high sludge of partially melted ice and snow. At her approach, the gatekeeper lumbered out from the mismatched sleds serving as an entrance, his jiggling bulk clad in appropriated armor. "What do you want, she-devil?"

Brimares glowered in response, lips curling in the hint of a snarl, but he laughed and scratched his chin with a sullied knife. "I need more than that; my compatriots believe you mute, but I think you just need proper incentive." He sidled closer, grinning and inadvertently drawing her attention to a white cloth wrapped about his neck like a scarf, the Blond Knight's sigil. "So tell me what you want, and we'll see about getting it." He extended a grimy hand and stroked her jaw.

She caught his wrist, the top plates of her gauntlet flaring open.

He chortled. "Come now, a woman like you can't get much attention; you need to welcome those willing to forgive your defects." He grinned and the Chaos within her stirred, causing her teeth to elongate and sharpen. He blanched and snatched the silver knife from his belt. "I don't want to see that, you hear? Keep those things hidden."

Her Chaos mounted, eager for violence, for the pain she would inflict. He ignored the heat rising in her gauntlet and the steam pouring from her to moisten his lips and beckon to the others behind her. "Still won't speak? I'd have expected more fight from a damned-beast." He grasped her chin. "Let's see how much you take before retaliating."

She relinquished her control of the Chaos, and for a moment everything went blank. A memory surfaced, assailing her with a glimpse of white eyes and silver armor. Then she heard the shrieks. Her eyes refocused, and she saw the gatekeeper stumbling from her, clutching the mangled stump of his arm, the bone, muscle, and flesh a knotted mess, not severed but crushed. She glanced to her gauntlet, now splattered with gore, and flicked it clean.

The gatekeeper collapsed, screaming as a pair of soldiers rushed to his side. They dragged him to the side and against a sled. She walked past, wiping her cheek and watching the soldiers scramble for a surgeon's saw and bandages. The gatekeeper saw her and shrieked unintelligibly, but she understood his promises of agony and revenge. She kept walking.

The New Order would not kill him; they would bind his injury, strap him to a horse, and assign him to the vanguard where he could take two arrows in lieu of a healthy soldier.

She found her intended lesser demon crouched within a firepit beneath the eaves of a totem as soldiers stumbled and crawled from their tents. The flames stroked him frantically, incensed by the Chaos in his blood, but dimmed as his voice slithered out from the dark, "What do you want?"

Mounting the surrounding embankment, she offered no reply, recalling all she knew of him; he preferred his human face but had displayed his other half—a reptilian creature with a molten spine, stubbed maw, and four feet of serrated tail—when threatened. He was also a coward, always slinking through the back ranks with hunched shoulders, a breath away from flight. Despite his cowardice, or possibly because of it, he had a mind for quandaries and a desire for power.

His flames swelled, deepening to red in expression of dominance and threat, and she advanced to the embankments edge, knelt atop it, and gazed down at him. "I'm seeking information."

"So you can speak; what so important that you abandon the lie?" His flames subsided, belying his confidence. "Do you perchance wish knowledge about the man called Salem? Or perhaps our kin?"

"No, Athan, just the location of something."

He leaned forward, the flames thickening with his excitement and clinging to him. "You want a bargaining chip?"

"Yes. The paladin carried a copy of the *Amarthayiss* that is now lost."

Athan hissed, rearing as the fire exploded. "You intend to bargain with the Order for *Redemption*! But how will you enter the Paladin Empire without being annihilated on sight?"

"I intend to free the paladin."

"You audacious fool! And a fool twice over! Just imagine what I'll gain for revealing this!" Athan hurled his arms forward, inciting a torrent of flames up from his feet and launching them at her, their tongues warping to reddish-brown with infused Chaos.

Brimares stepped into the fire, rousing her Chaos and hurling Salem's collar to shear through his flames and clamp around his throat. He buckled instantly, clawing at the collar with one hand and scrambling to escape with other. She yanked the collar taught, crossed to him and planted a boot on his back. "Where is the *Amarthayiss*?"

He arched, raking furrows in the coals and wood and gasping a name, "Kadrin!"

Brimares growled. Of course they would entrust the *Amarthayiss* to their leading cleric. Athan kept struggling feebly at her leg. "I am sorry, but better you than me." She crushed his head.

Her Chaos erupted into rabid delight, dragging her to her knees as magma filled her veins. Athan's blood gushed from his ruined skull, soaking the ground and her legs with sizzling, multihued Chaos. She inclined, digging fingers into the fuming blood and rearing fire. His blood latched onto the chinks of her armor, swarming up her body and into her skin. She threw her head back, mouth opening and eyes rolling, and drank his Chaos. Euphoria wracked her, ripping and contorting her muscles, bones, and flesh as her body adapted to and assimilated his Chaos.

She reclaimed herself with a snarl, sick with horror and internally afire with something reminiscent of the Abyss' pain. She heard and felt her bones cracking back into place but refused to look, refused to witness the monster she almost became. And she hated herself for that weakness.

When she knew her body was human, Brimares forced her eyes to open and trembling limbs to stand. She examined her surroundings but saw only black tents and empty sleds, the soldiers occupied with breakfast in a distant section of the encampment.

She departed, dousing the flames so the storm would obscure any lingering signs of Athan's demise.

Brimares directed her steps deeper into the encampment, searching for the clerics and priests' nexus, and found it enshrined in a wall of nebulous, liquid, inky darkness that radiated *Telacra's* essence. She halted outside it to observe the vicinity, which, aside from this darkness, resembled most of the encampment. But it was the darkness that concerned her; it served a similar purpose to the totems in that it rendered this as sacred ground for *Telacra* and her adherents, empowering and rejuvenating them but to exaggerated effect. They converted The North into sacred ground, this converted it into a temple. There would be a device or relic of some sort at its axis, something to contain the darkness while traveling. Like all sacred ground, it would reject her, but she also felt conflict within its depths and knew the *Amarthayiss* lay within.

She tentatively immersed a hand into the liquid night, meeting no resistance and effecting no visible change. Still cautious, she retracted her hand, noticed dark threads clinging to her fingers and yanked it free, muttering a profanity.

The fear dissipated as soon as she broke contact, prompting a slightly exasperated sigh. Suppressing all further disquiet, she explored the liquid night's circumference for potential witnesses or debilities without success.

After completing her circuit, Brimares confiscated one of the bordering torches and thrust it into the liquid night.

The barrier imploded, roiling in a silent tumult of wrath and odium until the torch extinguished. She retreated, the torch re-igniting the instant it escaped. The liquid night subsided, but Brimares heard the clerics stirring within. Taking a last preparatory breath, she fueled the torch with a surge of Chaos and flung it into the priests' nexus. The light faltered, caught the fabric of a tent and exploded in ravenous life. Cries rose, mingled rage and surprise as Brimares sprinted and hurled a half-dozen more Chaos-fed torches into the liquid night. Then she activated her armor entirely, concealing any hint of her identity—excluding her species—and plunged into the inferno.

Even minutes old, the fire swallowed her vision with tides of black smoke, gushing steam, and roaring pandemonium. Many of the clerics knelt in hacking powerlessness, just barley protecting themselves as they crawled toward escape; none of them noticed her arrival, distracted by the flames exploding upon her egress, frenzied by her Chaos.

She scanned for the *Amarthayiss*, caught a glimpse of its radiance through the conflagration, and strode toward it, flames washing over and clinging to her like sand in a southern storm building ever higher.

She reached Kadrin's tent seconds later, its fabric steaming but not aflame, and searched for him. He stood a short distance away, black robes beating his exhaustion-hollowed frame and streaming threads of power. She marshalled her limited control, amassed the Chaos in a hand, and lobbed it at Kadrin. Pain rent through her as reward and the inferno multiplied, engulfing Kadrin utterly.

Turning, she carefully retracted her gauntlets lest the flames clinging to them incinerate the tent, thrust the entrance flap aside, and entered the *Amarthayiss'* light.

Fresh pain ignited across her flesh, searing and devouring her wherever the *Amarthayiss'* light touched. She stumbled, clutching an adjacent table as her Chaos flickered, dimmed by the *Amarthayiss'* mere proximity. Enraged, the *Amarthayiss* flared, magnifying its brilliance and her pain. She continued nonetheless, grasping the holy manuscript in shaking fingers. Her Chaos winked out.

Brimares collapsed and dropped the book, gasping as her strength evaporated. She tried to spark her Chaos, but it refused, leaving her nothing but a trickle of mortal strength. She snarled and crawled to where the *Amarthayiss* had fallen, shoving it irreverently it into Salem's bag. The moment the flap closed, her Chaos re-ignited, sending her reeling back to her feet. She staggered, caught her balance, and bolted westward.

Driven by the ancestral loathing of her Chaos, the flames were hunting Lionel, racing through the encampment in a direct line, consuming everything in their path. She pushed harder, launching herself into huge bounding leaps even as she continued to incite the flames, coercing them to expand universally, anything to distract the New Order further.

The flames began to attenuate as she progressed, eventually stalling at a haggard line of clerics and soldiers. She blasted through without hesitation, disregarding everything to reach the paladin in time, not just before the fire, but before they contained it. A task that would be made multiplicatively easier without her Chaos to incite the conflagration.

She skidded to a halt outside the prison compound, spraying mud and ice, the heat palpable even at this distance. The two guards spun about, half-lowering their spears before recognizing her. "No further, demon. Visiting the paladin is prohibited until the flames are quell—"

Brimares crushed the man's chest with a flat-handed blow, launching him into the second guard who buckled beneath the sudden impact. She crossed to them, projecting the armor from her wrist into a thin spear that punched through the surviving guard's skull and obliterated his attempted screams. He jerked and stilled. She grasped both corpses and dragged them out of sight inside the compound.

Lionel, somehow aware of her, called from his cell, "I smell fire, what's happening?"

"Just a distraction." She crossed to him and gripped the disfigured bars.

"Do you have the *Amarthayiss*? It'll burn like any other book!"

"Yes, now shush." Her Chaos already burned feverishly within, but she needed more; the prison's ice was leeching through her armor, expanding voraciously and feeding off her. She incited her Chaos, blindly funneling all her rage and desperation until it erupted. There was an instant of comprehension, then the Chaos engulfed her.

The prison screamed, echoing her own silent cries as it warped in her hands, liquid iron squeezing through her fingers in huge, freezing globules. Her own armor screeched as well, molding to a new shape, her body starting to break as it changed from human to beast. She screamed again, denying the change, and wrenched her hands free, stumbling to the ground.

She lay thus for a while, waiting for her bones and muscles to snap back into place. Lionel staggered free in the meantime, unsteady after weeks of incarceration and immobility. Brimares groaned softly at his footsteps and rolled to her feet, facing the prison wall where it lay in shambles of freezing liquid.

"What now? Do you have armor for me? A disguise?"

"Give me a second."

She returned to the corpses she discarded earlier and dragged one to Lionel, who reiterated his earlier question and began stripping the guards, "Do you have it?"

"Yes." She flipped the bag open, briefly displaying the *Amarthayiss*.

Lionel paused, examining the corpse's shredded throat with mingled horror and disbelief. "You did this with your bare hand?"

"Yes. Now hurry." She exited the compound to stand vigil, and he joined her there a few minutes later, his new mail still wet with blood.

"What next?"

She started southward, noting he had armed himself with a sword and dagger. "A horse."

"And after that?"

"North. The New Order's not going to allow us to just escape. They'll send one of their knights and my kin after us, and they'll kill us. So we run and hope The North is kind."

Lionel caught her arm. "Wait, there's a better option. I have friends in The North, we should—"

"Whoever your friends are, they are more likely to kill me than anything else." She pulled free and continued south.

42

The Judgement Of Wolves

Lionel followed the she-demon in a crouch, scampering through the ranks of tents beneath heavens that boiled with ash and fumes. The sky had cleared of The Northern storm, depriving the New Order of anything that might quell the flames. Sometimes when he looked up, a face would emerge from the clouds, its features long and distended, insubstantial but for the furnace of its eyes and maw, and visible only for an instant before returning to the ghastly womb of its birth.

The she-demon abruptly dropped flat, sending him to the earth as well. Torchlight appeared several tents ahead, followed by a troop of rushing soldiers. She eased back, her armor retracting soundlessly as the soldiers passed without fuss. The she-demon spared them time to depart, then crept to their current tent row's end and peeked. He followed, the New Order's mail chafing his shoulders. She scurried across the open space as he arrived, watching the departing soldiers all the while. He waited until she reached safety then sprinted after.

When she moved to advance again, he caught her shoulder. "Wait, how much farther to the horses?"

She shook his hand off and her armor inadvertently shredded his gauntlet. He stifled a curse, blood welling from his palm, and yanked off his glove, hastening to tear a strip from his cloak. The she-demon partially straightened to scan the horizon, lips moving in silent count, then glanced at him as he struggled to tie the bandage. She knelt, her gauntlets seamlessly retracting to her elbows, and took the bandage from him, tying it. "Not far. At the end of this last run there's a small pen, meant only for the mercenary horses. It's unguarded."

She continued without another word, and he followed despite years of indoctrination screaming she could not be trusted, demanding he kill her. But—their agreement aside—he doubted he could even kill her, *silenced* or not; he remembered her after she broke his prison, thrashing upon the ground as her armor split and her body twisted, beginning to reveal the demon within. He shuddered.

A light touch and a directing hand focused him on a wide clearing a short distance ahead. Some fifty horses clustered in the pen, evidently distressed at the fire.

The she-demon abandoned their scant cover to examine their surroundings, then nodded toward the horses. "Go."

Lionel hurried over and jumped the penning fence, almost slipping on the icy wood, to begin his appraisal. Despite his best effort, however, both the urgency and his own somewhat lacking knowledge of horses colluded to make an educated decision impossible. Mentally rebuking himself for not paying more attention to his instructors, Lionel drew a knife and severed the closest animal's tether. The mare snorted, resisting him at first before conceding to his gentle coaxing. He glanced about for saddles but found only a pile of riding mats tossed over the fence. Lionel threw one over the mare's back before glancing about for the she-demon.

He spotted her navigating towards him from the corral's opposite end, leading a fully equipped black stallion that, to his eyes, seemed largely equivalent to his mare. She paused before him and swept his horse with a glance. "Put that animal back."

"Why?" The mare shied away from them, whinnying and stamping while it fixed the she-demon with a look.

"It's old, going lame, and already spooked. It wouldn't carry you more than a day, let alone if we have to run like you did before."

Lionel flinched at the mention of Arrad. "And your horse will?"

"This horse would survive it. Now get on."

He complied, even though the stallion snorted at his approach and very pointedly looked away. *'I guess he doesn't realize I'm a paladin.'*

Brimares returned with a final saddle bag and laid it across the stallion's rump. "I don't know where to go from here. My purpose persists, rendering me the enemy of any Northerner we might meet. If you believe you can keep the Northerners from killing me, lead the way. If not, then suggest something."

He signaled confirmation and prodded the stallion into a northward canter, the snow hardening beneath its hooves. The she-demon followed, easily keeping pace despite sinking knee-deep in the icy sludge.

Despite the fire's best havoc-inducing efforts, it took them until dusk to reach the encampment's edge, constantly needing to delay for or circumvent passing patrols and soldiers. Lionel crossed this last barrier with a sigh and tentative optimism. The she-demon lingered at the edge, scanning one final time. The seconds elapsed as she counted once, twice, and a third time, her head beginning to shake and her armor to flare. Lionel pulled about, realizing something had gone terribly amiss. The she-demon's armor opened fully, serrated edges gleaming as it flowed up her throat and over her head. She spun away, sprinting toward him. "We have to go; one's missing."

The stallion whirled with the she-demon, forcing Lionel to clutch the bridle. "The bastard's third mother! What do you mean one is missing?"

"I can't see Kell'MachChain."

Lionel cursed again, ducking low as the stallion bolted into a gallop, and cast his gaze skyward.

A shape soared there amidst the veil of smoke, visible as a silhouette against the conflagration's brilliance. Lionel grasped for his Shard of Divinity, but the *silence* clamped on his throat, choking his *second voice*. He hacked and relinquished his attempts.

A quick glance ahead revealed a forest whose trees thrashed despite the absence of wind and the she-demon sprinting parallel, already far ahead. He yanked the reins toward the forest, and hammered the stallion's flanks, calling after the she-demon, "The forest! Go to the forest!" The she-demon faltered, balking, then veered.

She almost made the forest, Lionel no more than a hundred strides behind, before a shriek split the clouded sky. A winged monster burst from the ash clouds, fire streaming off its hide. It crashed into the she-demon, driving her to ground with a screech of rasping metal, and then flung her from the forest's edge.

The she-demon rolled back to her feet, twisting with the impetus, and crouched, hands splayed on the snow. Her armor flared out, its serrated edges protracting and burning white with heat. Lionel reined in beside her and vaulted to the ground, drawing his sword as the stallion rounded behind him.

Kell'MachChain approached them, surpassing twice the height of an average man with livid metallic flesh drawn taught over a skeleton and overlapping back-plates split by three distended vertebrae and two molten wings.

He halted, shrinking as his wings folded and his features mellowed. Bones snapped and metal flesh peeled away, falling to mound at his feet like a serpent shedding. Armor clicked into place, gliding over his flesh like oil until he wore a man's visage, his long fingers tugging at knots in his white hair as he grinned with desiccated lips. "Where might you be going, sir paladin, and with one of our own no less?"

Lionel leveled his sword. "Away from you."

"After such a short visit? And without bidding farewell." Kell'MachChain leaned back as if mortally struck, laying a hand upon his chest. "And now you bare weapons against us! After we graced you with hospitality!" Tisking loudly, he raised his hand and directed long, cruel fingers at Lionel.

At first nothing happened, then his sword began to smoke. Spitting a profanity, Lionel flung it aside and clutched his burnt hand, the sword melting into a ruined heap. He growled, as much to himself as the demon, drew his knife and charged, only for Kell'MachChain to bat him aside with a flick, his armor shearing through Lionel's as if it were papier-mâché.

"Come on now, we have no need to figh–" The she-demon rammed Kell'MachChain, driving him to the ground with spine-crushing force. She reared atop him, hammering down with blows that sounded like colliding anvils. Kell'MachChain retaliated in kind, exerting such force that Lionel knew to interfere would result in his immediate death.

Suddenly, heat erupted between them, separating the demons and hurling Lionel half-a-dozen feet away. He scrambled upright and saw Kell'MachChain already standing, his armor shredded but his flesh undamaged. The she-demon crouched a short distance away, her armor flared out and grinding against itself, issuing a venomous, rasping sound of warning.

Kell'MachChain directed a crooked finger at her, his features contorted and bestial. "You sicken me; trying even now to maintain yourself as human. You are not human; you are a devil, a monster, a beast. And now I will devour you for rejecting it." The great black wings spread from Kell'MachChain's back, his flesh blackening to cinder and flaking off as the towering monster of before reemerged.

A whistle hissed and Kell'MachChain jerked forward, a black arrow protruding from his shoulder, frost already expanding from it. He roared and spun, more arrows diving from the ash-choked sky. Brimares jerked and buckled as well, two black shafts protruding from her stomach and shoulder and spreading ice.

Kell'MachChain shrieked again, now fully transformed, but two more arrows struck, the first exploding upon contact with his defending hand and the second piercing his stomach. Stumbling, he shattered the twin arrows with a sweep and vaulted heavenwards. Arrows pursued him only to strike a sudden barrier of flame and disintegrate to ash.

Lionel rushed to interpose between the she-demon and the forest, ignoring the stallion as it trotted to her. "Don't kill her! She's an ally." The thrashing trees quieted, prompting Lionel to tentatively lower his arms and doff his helm. "Please, I am a friend."

A figure materialized from the forest with a drawn bow. The deranger approached Lionel, regarding him briefly before loosening his bow and removing his hood. "Welcome back, Sir Lionel. I assume asking us to spare her was appropriately considered."

"It was considered, but I cannot promise it was wise; I know little of her past, Tassen. But she offered me aid when I was imprisoned. While it might be some elaborate deception, I doubt it; she risked herself to retrieve the *Amarthayiss* at my request."

"If it were all a ploy, there would be no risk in retrieving the *Amarthayiss*. Nor would the New Order send someone inexperienced to deceive you."

"I know. But this, whatever it is, feels honest; just give her a chance, please." Lionel touched one of the black shafts and hissed at the bitter cold. The she-demon's features were black now, and she spasmed constantly. One of the arrows collapsed to dust and she curled tighter about the final shaft, wheezing feebly. The stallion lipped her hair.

Tassen carefully bowed his head to the black horse, then knelt beside Lionel and removed the last arrow, causing her to jolt with a ragged breath. "She will live but will need sleep, and you both will be judged. If the Wolves condemn her, she will die; if you are condemned, you will die." Tassen stood. "Come. Bring the damned."

"But how will I carry her? Even if it doesn't cut me, her armor's too heavy."

"She is your burden, Sir Lionel, not ours, and we have no mercy for those who bring war."

The deranger departed, the wind sweeping around to engulf them in the resuming storm. There would be no pursuit. The stallion flicked the back of Lionel's head with its tail and then nudged the she-demon, conveying both expectation and resignation.

Lionel touched the she-demon's side and her armor jittered, reacting to his Shard of Divinity. It briefly continued to protest his touch, then closed seamlessly tight. She curled tighter, the spasms ameliorating now that the arrow had been removed.

He slid his hands beneath her shoulders and knees, and lifted—finding her surprisingly light. Another drop of sleet tapped his armor, raced down his arm and sizzled on her shoulder. He adjusted his grip, heaved her onto the stallion, and then followed Tassen.

A dull roar sounded as they entered the forest, and the skies opened behind them, unleashing all the pending rain, hail, snow, and ice upon the New Order, who had just begun to control the fire.

Lionel hunched his shoulders and shivered. Tassen had spoken truthfully; The North had no mercy for those who brought war.

The black stallion snorted beneath Lionel, prancing slightly with each step and constantly half-threatening to upend him. He tightened his grip on its reins. The fractious beast made him uneasy, though it was smaller than Arrad; too much intelligence glinted in its eyes, and more than a hint of human mischief.

Despite a day's elapse, the she-demon still slumped against him with shallow, whimpered breaths, wracked by persistent, minute spasms of her shoulders and midsection that warned of how closely she straddled death.

He measured her warmth with a hand against her cheek and grimaced; she was like ice, so bereft of heat it sapped his own warmth. He slid his arm back around her waist and pulled the heavy cloak closed again, silently thanking that her armor had not shivered once since she fell unconscious.

Tassen walked a short distance ahead, threading through the landscape with scarcely any effort. Four other derangers accompanied them, fading in and out of sight from the towering forest, the trees magnificent and black with flowing bark. Although a significant distance separated each tree, the branches still entangled one another, their diminutive leaves merging in a fluttering storm of emerald, gold, and sapphire colors. There was no wind, snow, rain, or light this far into the forest; the canopy forbade it, permitting only the glass lanterns the derangers carried and the frail, silver Wisps to grant light.

The stallion halted, drawing Lionel's gaze to where Tassen stood with an upraised hand. A voiceless river bisected the path, consigning everything beyond to shadows and silhouettes. The stallion advanced to drink, tranquil despite the unnatural, recumbent silence.

"Cross the river, Sir Lionel, and continue until you rediscover the lanterns. You will find a glade open to the stars. Once there wait for the Wolves. Leave your weapons here and do not strike or allow her to strike the Wolves; bind her if you must. Return if you survive." The deranger retreated into the forest, leaving him to divest what remained of his plundered armaments.

This done, Lionel tapped the stallion's flanks and rode into the river. The current hastened, rising to his ankles and spraying icy droplets. The she-demon arched and screamed as they struck, her eyes bursting open. He tightened his grip, keeping her from thrashing herself off the horse. Her head rolled back, tears running from her ignited eyes and blue fractures creeping across the demonic maelstroms around her pupils. The river lashed higher, scouring his calves. He pressed harder, grinding his heels into the stallion's flanks, but the creature just snorted and kept its own pace until it finally clambered up the opposite bank.

The she-demon slumped and then gently pressed against his confining arms. He cautiously released her, and she sat thus for a long while, holding herself up with an arm.

"Are you alright?"

She shook her head, her breathing still shallow and forced, and her fingers clamped on the saddle horn. He felt her try to inhale deeper only to erupt into coughs. She tried again with the same result. Lionel pulled her against him. "Don't breathe so deep, your lungs can't handle the cold yet." She resisted his embrace briefly, then surrendered, afflicted with shivers but no spasms.

Lanterns gradually appeared in the distance, expanding the depth of their world. The trees became more numerous, larger and closer, hindering their advance with protruding roots and low branches. Eventually they became too clustered for the stallion, forcing them to halt at the first lantern, which hung over a narrow breech.

Lionel dismounted and helped Brimares down. She managed to keep herself afoot with a hand on the saddle and shuffled to the stallion's head, whispering to it.

The breach broadened at their approach, the roots retreating into the ground and the vines slithering up the trees. A faint pool of light extended from the breach, greeting him with warmth. Brimares, however, recoiled when the light touched her, stifling a snarl. He started to pause, but she prodded him forward, sending them into a glade of starlight and white moss crowned with bluebell flowers.

He stopped at the entrance, mesmerized. A stone pool accented the clearing, the water within swirling with a susurration and a promise of healing in the fine white steam. Lionel advanced onto the moss, half carrying Brimares and setting her on the water's edge before straightening to search for signs of the Winsyrian Wolves, without result.

He knelt beside her and brushed his palm across the water, letting its scalding warmth return life to his fingers. She pulled herself up beside him and slumped forward, pushing her hands into the water as her gauntlets snaked up her forearms. She moaned and leaned forward, immersing her arms to her elbows as heat bloomed in her cheek.

Lionel studied her in that unguarded moment, searching for any truth it might reveal. She felt his eyes and fixed them with her own, the stare unyielding.

"What made you try to bargain with me?"

She looked away, hands swishing through the water, and took a long time to answer in her beautiful, aching voice, "I was told you would help me find *Redemption* as part of a bargain I struck with … someone I should not have."

"Who, and what did you sell?" He rose and dried his hand on his cloak. She refused to answer. "Who was it?"

Removing her arms from the pool, she shook her head. "I don't know…" His eyes fell to her hands, where inflamed scars now crisscrossed the length of her forearms. "He comes from the East and the Dark Consort but belongs to neither. He mocks the New Order yet serves it. He offers to aid me in killing the High-Warden but stipulates I spare him."

"What did you give? What could you even have?"

"He called me before we were dispatched to hunt you, offered me survival. I could not defy him even if I had the strength. He spoke of you, the High-Warden, and others. He told me truths and showed me a book."

"But what did he ask?"

She faced him at last, the maelstrom of her eyes burning low. "He asked for a name. Not my name and not for then. He told me he would ask later."

"Do you know whose name he wanted?"

"Yes."

He inched closer, searching her drawn features. Her armor clicked, the edges opening and closing minutely in quiet disorder. The maelstrom in her eyes subsided.

"Whose name did he ask for and where is its owner?"

"That is a secret you will never learn."

"What can you tell me of the dark paladins?"

"There are six commanders for their army: two paladins, two clerics, and two Death Addicts. Then there is Kell'MachChain, Cellar'Veer, and Salem."

"Kell'MachChain and Cellar'Veer are the demons, correct?" She nodded. "Who are the Death Addicts and this Salem? I know of Death Addicts but have no knowledge of their abilities."

"The Death Addicts are Sorran and, his brother, Eredar. They feed off those they kill, growing stronger and crueler. They are the least of the lords; though they might become the greatest before this war reaches its conclusion. I know little else."

"What of the clerics? How deep is their communion with *Telacra*? What is their influence in the New Order?"

"None of them are prominent within the New Order, and although individually powerful, they are infants compared to the New Order's upper hierarchy. Kadrin, a patriarch, is a blind fanatic. He's driven by hatred for everything not sworn body and soul to *Telacra*. Before the war, he led a monastery near the southwestern border of the East, near the Thousand Pools. Viral is the least of the four, a coward without loyalty or true ambition. His power, however, would be substantial if he ever truly exercised it."

"Who are the dark paladins and how many witnessed the original Order's schism? Which of them is the greatest? What are their strengths and weaknesses?"

"Kheldar Ferain leads the army, and is probably its strongest soldier, powerful even without his goddess. He was a street lord before the New Order recruited him but is self-controlled and forceful enough to direct the wild power of his associates. All that said, he leads only by the Dark Consort's decree." She paused briefly here, considering. "I don't know the fourth man's name; he never gave it. Kheldar Ferain might know, but I doubt it. This man is dark in a way the others aren't, possessed by an evil that ridicules his allies. He is patient, calculating and cruel, and deep in communion with his goddess, but there's more to him I couldn't quite grasp. He never wears a helm, is blond haired, and of that group, the one you should fear."

"What of Salem?"

"He is the bargainer, the one who orchestrated my summoning. I know nothing of him, and I cannot decide if his power is authentic or deception, but he is dangerous regardless. Maybe more so than the Blond Knight but different."

She fell silent, nostrils flaring as a cold wind enfolded them rich with the scents of pine and sap. She shriveled, pressing herself low with a dull growl, her armor running flat. Lionel moved to help her stand, but she shook her head, face pale and strained, refusing to so much as look up.

Before them, the water stilled then undulated outward, turning white as a lotus bloomed from the ripples. A white Wolf entered the glade, its fur weighted with ice and glinting in the starlight. Lionel brushed Brimares' arm, cautioning her against anything to threaten the Wolf, and knelt, touching his brow to the white moss.

The Wolf approached him first, footsteps simultaneously huge and delicate. It captured his eyes with a flash of primeval intellect and raw winter, its irises icy-blue around pale pupils. It exhaled, spilling white steam over his face, and shifted to Brimares who cowered, her eyes locked in shuddering terror.

The Wolf extended its snout and sniffed her, wet nose brushing the crown of her head. It growled and hunched forward, hackles rising. Brimares scrunched lower, trembling as her hands dug into the moss.

A giggle broke the Wolf's spell on Lionel, pulling his attention to where a Fae child lounged across the pool, feet brushing the water. She clapped once and pressed her hands against her wide smile, black eyes unwavering as she observed the Wolf.

Lionel bowed. "How may I serve The North?"

The child laughed again, immersing her feet to the ankles and averting her face. The locks of her white hair wrapped about her features like a scarf, leaving an eye bare to fix mischievously on Lionel. "The North you cannot serve, sir knight of the Lost Order. Never can The North be served because you are nothing to The North. Only Lord *Ever-Winter* cares about those who live two lives. I see two lives hanging upon you, one before and one after. One hangs from your heart and another from the conscious thoughts you conceal. Lord *Ever-Winter* watches you, sir knight of the forgotten Order. The Lord *Ever-Winter* watches her, she who burns within and smells of tears and blood." The child leaned forward, hair falling to brush her shoulders. Her feet slid deeper, up to her knees, and the water glinted with momentary luminescence. "Why do the Wolves judge you?"

Remembering the stories of the Fae, Lionel averted his gaze. "Who are you? What are you?"

She pulled away, pouting as she slipped deeper into a pool that appeared mere inches deep to Lionel, but which she stood up to her waste in. "To the *Court of Winter* do I owe allegiance and birth. I was born of and to The North, in the time before there were those who lived two lives. I watch the rivers and waters and listen when they speak. And speak now to me, to you, to her. They speak in unison three ever-changing words, one each for each of us. Two are to be lost, and the third kept hidden away in dark thoughts and lost secrets. They speak fragile words, like the shells of eggs, to me, telling, commanding I speak to you, confide unto you knowledge and purpose in The North besides the biddings of the West. I must find for you the High-Warden of Lord *Ever-Winter*, you and she who burns within. He is the catalyst of this convergence, the axis upon which this war turns. Even distant, all fear him. They run and they hunt him, but he is lost in The North; and they can never find him unless he chooses to be found. He strives against the Gods of the Dark Pantheon and the men who would challenge him while cowering behind those cursed to pain and fire. Twin swords, sheathed for three five-generation spans, shall at last sing their song of war, and they shall taste their first blood of neither ally nor foe. A life shall be taken, and that life will ally with The North for the promise of a curse returned." The child sank lower, submerging to her chest.

"What are you saying? Speak without the *Court's* riddles!"

She lifted an arm, the sleeve of her dress crusting with frost, giggled and let it submerge again. She spun three times, the water swirling and her hair climbing skyward as if to escape her brow. "There is fear in you, a fear of me. Does this help control the fear plaguing those who live two lives?" Her features changed, waxing fuller and rounder, losing the aspect of the girl and assuming that of a boy. "Do you like me better now?"

Lionel retreated from the pond, shaking his head.

The boy cackled and reclined until the water lapped his face and his hair surrounded him in a halo. "Follow the great river to the mountains high, any mountain, and find a watchtower in the black rock. There the High-Warden will find she who burns within. There is a life to be taken, a life to be spared, and a life to be forgotten." The boy submerged fully, vanishing from sight.

Lionel leaned back and looked to Brimares where she still bowed before the Wolf, shuddering and whimpering.

Another minute passed before the Wolf stepped back. Brimares' eyes snapped open, the Chaos maelstroms within motionless and drained of all color. The Wolf turned, its massive head lifting toward the moon, and howled a lament. Its call sent her cowering back to the earth with clasped ears. Answering howls echoed from the distance: they had been judged. Once more the Wolf lifted its head and howled.

Lionel crawled to Brimares' side, extending a cautious hand to touch her shoulder. Still kneeling with her brow pressed to the snow and her hands locked upon her ears, she gave no reaction, just continued screaming until the Wolves subsided.

The Wolf departed without a glance, its tread soundless in the glade's perfection and the starlit night. She did not rise with the Wolf's departure; she only slid her hands from her ears to clasp her neck. He could feel her shaking, the Chaos writhing within her.

"Let's go, Brimares. We have journeyed long enough, let us find a place to rest. The New Order will continue to hunt us; but for now, The North has accepted our flaws."

———

Thyme

They shadowed him, always just outside his vision, never more than a flit of white clothing between trees. They made their presence known with these constant reminders, a warning without teeth. The derangers feared him, knowing they could not destroy him or challenge any of his intents. They would attempt to, nonetheless, if he struck against The North and those they warded.

The lowest boughs above Thyme's head shifted with a low groan, the leaves quivering in unease. The animals fell silent, even the birds. The hunters fled and the prey cowered at his passing, burrowing into deep earthen holes and pressing against the deepest crannies of their lairs in desperate, futile attempts at survival. Only the Raven remained in his sight, the accompanying flock having faltered at Winter's Gate. She watched him from an arching branch.

He could feel it. His nearness made its presence pulsate beneath all the currents and emotions roiling in The North. It perceived him and called, its desire to return to him burning brightly just beneath his superficial sensations. Still, he advanced with caution. Too many objects and creatures lurked in The North, and one in particular still struggled for release even after millennia. Thyme felt his own hate spark at the other's taint and pressed onward, hastening his pace. He would retrieve his Signet, and all the derangers in The North couldn't deny him, because after all reasoning and compassion ended, everything alive or dead owed him their lives and allegiance.

43

Whispering Silver

Waking gradually, Tasha opened her eyes to the high curved ceiling of Malendor's shop and spent the next several minutes scrutinizing its swirling pattern of metal and granite, dreading the inevitable need for movement. Eventually though, she voiced a groan of distilled misery at comfort lost and bullied herself into sitting upright, wincing and rolling sore shoulders. "That's the last time I ride a phoenix."

From behind her, Slade's voice heralded a pair of hands that kneaded her shoulders with exquisite skill. "Last is such an absolute word. Better to mitigate the promises we make ourselves, that way we can enjoy our failures without breaking trust."

Tasha snorted. "I'd expect nothing less from you."

"Well, I do aim for mediocrity."

"Oh really?"

"Yes. With everyone running around trying to be extraordinary, it befalls the extraordinary to step up and be ordinary."

Tasha barked a laugh, taking Slade's proffered hand and letting him hoist her from the couch. "Where did he send you anyway? Some desert island surrounded by sharks?"

"Not quite. Malendor plunked me atop the Fifth Tower of High-Wizardry, which had me thrumming with excitement until I realized he never provided a key."

"Wasn't the Fifth Tower lost within Paranoia?" Feylin asked indistinctly, arching into a yawning stretch then flopping sideways across Tasha's half of the couch.

"Yes, primarily due to the incalculable foolishness of you mortals. But never fear, I seem to have rediscovered this relic." Shoeing Tasha aside, he struck a heroic pose by raising a fist overhead and wedging a foot between Feylin and a couch arm. "My plans are laid, my pieces in motion, and the time is right; come the apex of summer, I shall embark upon a daring mission to claim Kah'Elecktoral for my own."

"Aren't you supposed to be stealing winter about that time?" Feylin murmured, quickly sliding back to sleep.

"I can multitask."

"Sure you can." Tasha struck Slade across his thigh. "Get off the couch, and you"—she grabbed Feylin underneath the shoulders, lifting her upright—"up you go." When she immediately tried slumping over again, Slade offered his assistance by laying back across the couch, his head landing in the girl's lap.

"Trust me, I've got a plan."

"Alright then, just how many armies do you intend on bringing on this excursion?"

Slade thrust both fists into the air, eyes filling with demented zeal. "As many as required; no sacrifice is too great."

"Pray tell, how will you sneak them past the Silverwood Wall?"

"Subtle creeping, very subtle creeping indeed."

Tasha shook her head. Nothing snuck past the Silverwood Wall. "Does Malendor make dreams often?"

"Not anymore. Dreamcasters are rare, so during his younger years Malendor traveled from household to household, serving as both entertainment and status symbol. He's understandably soured on Dreamcasting but feels the occasional need to show off, and thus calls upon my august self. It is the least I can do for a friend who suffers the most appalling case of inferiority complex I've ever seen." Slade leaned close. "Between us, Malendor likes retreating to a nice dark corner, wrapping himself in a blanket and doling out the wildest compliments to himself, inflating menial achievements to divine status. Peculiar to be sure but also harmless. The true difficulty arises when Malendor doesn't reassure himself and transforms into a puddle of depressed tears." Slade sighed, laying a hand upon his chest. "I cannot help but feel sympathy for such a piteous display of—"

"Slade, be quiet," Malendor cut in amiably, strolling up with his hands thrust into pockets. "Besides, I was only crying because of that horrid book you gave me."

Slade sat up indignantly. "What? It was a masterpiece of modern literature."

"I'd hate to read a less masterful piece then."

"You just don't like tragedies."

"Slade, a tragedy is when something sad happens. Your book was a bloody massacre." Malendor shook his head and turned to the women. "The author, on a whim, decided to kill off every character in the space of two chapters, thereby sentencing his heroine to a lifetime of solitude."

"Bah." Slade threw up his hand. "Half the characters were fools anyway."

"Well obviously, they all died."

Slade huffed, then broke into a sudden grin. "By the way, the author released the sequel two weeks ago." Malendor groaned, trying to ward the youth off as he advanced with a freshly materialized stack of books. "Recognizing your consummate love for the original, I purchased a first edition, along with some secondary titles."

"Please don't, I couldn't possibly–"

"I even included some you might even actually enjoy."

Malendor's hands dropped. "Really? What are they about?"

Slade dropped the stack on a table. "Most are comedies; two, plus the sequel of that one title, are tragedies. The rest cover a variety of subjects you should find interesting."

The wizard grabbed the top book, inspected the title and then passed it to Feylin, who had finally roused with the prospect of books. Opening the second one down, Malendor smiled. "I've been looking for this one; where did you find it?"

"A friend of mine wasn't using it, so in a generous outpouring of generosity, I relieved him of its burdensome weight."

Malendor looked at Slade from over his gold-rimmed spectacles. "I assume he won't notice its absence?"

"I doubt my friend knew he owned a copy."

Overhead and dulled by distance, the shop's front door slammed open to admit a furious bellow that echoed down to them. "Malendor! Where are you?"

The wizard offered Slade a wry smile. "I think you ought to leave; my latest customer sounds notably irritated."

"Right you are, my friend. Feylin, Tasha, let's depart; proprietors who make customers wait seldom endure." Slade shooed his companions out the back door onto a lift, leaving as Malendor's irate customer stormed in with a plucked chicken swinging from one fist.

"Slade? Do you know the story behind the plucked chicken?" Tasha asked, ducking beneath a board trapped between the walls of the alley, one hand braced against it in case the soggy wood collapsed.

"No, but I can invent one if you like." Slade leaned back and shimmied under the board, then extended a hand to Feylin when she crossed underneath it. "I'm sure this whole affair concerns the initiation of that prime specimen into a sect of the dastardliest sort: a cult of carnivores."

"They must have spectacular propaganda," Tasha muttered dryly.

"Don't let the name mislead you; these are notorious cannibals who disdain all meat besides human. I was almost initiated myself but found the cuisine a tad ... reserved."

Feylin's nose wrinkled. "You find cannibalism boring?"

"Remarkably, the flavor of human meat is identical to that of chicken, only without the texture." He brushed a massive cobweb from their path, compressing its silken threads into a pellet before dropping it down his satchel's mouth. "Anyway. There I stood, belongings gathered about my feet, preparing to depart while they implored me to stay. However, I had made my will into stone and refused both their protestations and wailing cries; nothing would dissuade me except for the immediate adjustment of their cuisine to better suit my palate."

"And they, of course, complied without question." Tasha vaulted a garbage pile, splashing down into the middle of a puddle then waiting for her companions.

"On the contrary, they protested mightily," Slade said, tiptoeing his delicate way over the refuse pile. "They called my demands anything from barbaric to heretical while simultaneously offering up entire boats of gold. The sect considered me their patron saint, you see, which is absurd since I'm the patron saint of a different cult."

Feylin, following a brief hesitation, readied herself and then leapt the obstacle like Tasha had, spraying water across Slade when she landed in the same puddle. Both hands immediately flew out. "Oh, I'm so sorry. I–" A giggle interrupted her though, brought on by how Slade bristled his eyebrows.

A moment later, he waved her apology aside. "Regardless, imagine if I were the patron of two sects–"

"They'd murder one another to win your affections, stocking the cannibals' larder for the next decade?" Tasha's suggested, head tilting to the side.

Slade ignored this, flailing his arms overhead with all due excitement. "Panic would descend upon the city, riots would fill the heavens, volcanoes would explode across the world, seas would rage with uncontrolled passion, and monarchs would fall dead upon their golden thrones: in short, total chaos would ensue."

"Is that all?" Tasha asked.

Slade thought for a moment. "Yep, pretty much."

"Well, if you only risked the world, why didn't you accept their offer?"

"Moral principle."

"I thought you mentioned something about bland food."

"Their pedantic cuisine caused my departure, but stout moral principle is why I rejected their attempts to canonize me."

Glancing toward Feylin, Tasha smiled as she found the young woman starring groundward, brow furrowed as she obviously tried to imagine who would nominate Slade as their patron saint. A heartbeat later, the young girl asked, "What was the second cult dedicated to?"

"Moral depravity." He threw a swift grin in their direction before abruptly crouching at a grate from which a swath of lustrous burgundy moss grew. Deftly magicking up a spatula, Slade harvested the wall clean, then scraped his fingers through the mortar lines. Lastly, he bent to collect the large, warty mushrooms poking up from below.

Feylin peered over his shoulder. "What are you doing?"

"Harvesting ingredients, my young protégé."

"For what?" Tasha asked, peering over his other shoulder.

"A love potion," he responded before laughing maniacally and shaking his fist at the sky.

"I see, … is there a particular maiden you intend on beguiling?"

"Ha. As if I require a crutch. No, if a need for wooing ever did arise, I would simply clasp the maiden's soft hands like so, press a chaste kiss to her ivory skin and speak a few inadequate lines of poetry describing my unutterable devotion."

"Slade, you can release my hands now."

"As you wish, my Dear." Tasha's captor rose and brushed off his knees. "It goes without saying that I'd tailor the method according to my subject. If she's already infatuated, this approach could well soften her heart until it puddles right there on the ground."

Feylin crouched in Slade's spot, examining the adolescent mushrooms he had left behind. "If not for wooing a sweetheart, who's it for?"

"Governor Warsein," he tossed back casually while ambling ahead.

"What?" Feylin asked, whipping around. Slade, however, was already gone. "Why does he do that?"

"Because he finds it amusing to spread discord and confusion. Let's go, lingering in alleyways hasn't proven the wisest strategy for us."

Trotting up behind their still chattering host, Tasha tapped him on the shoulder. "Slade, we should proceed quietly; I'd rather not encounter more footpads."

"Worry not my dear, I know all the deplorables stalking these alleys. Shall I enumerate them by name or profession?" Slade began counting off fingers. "Let's see, we have a few common laborers—all inebriated unto death—the occasional urchin, a few depressed courtesans, and those immoral law breakers who're sneaking to the gambling den around here."

Tasha eyed him skeptically. "Any footpads?"

"A couple, but I doubt they'll bother us after how I punished their uppity predecessors." Causing a faint prickle, Slade gave her a smile that was all teeth, savagery, and absent remorse. The sort Tasha would have expected from a lion's mouth.

"Wh-wha-what did you do to them?" Feylin asked, catching a glimpse from behind Tasha.

"I strung them up by their toes and then draped slugs across their bodies, after which I slowly removed their skins by applying paper-thin layers of acid."

Tasha flicked Slade, making him recoil, clutching a supposedly broken arm. "Feylin, this sadist over here had those men placed in the stockade pending a prolonged prison sentence; nothing more and nothing less. The point being, a very poignant message was delivered."

Slade ceased his soft mewling. "Also, since I forgot to mention it earlier, my discerning eye spotted two paladins wandering around as well. Dastardly fellows I'm sure." Sidling close, he wrapped an arm across Feylin's shoulders. "Between us, my spies deduce they're protecting you against further excitement." Slade's voice hiked to a near shout, "They're less obvious than a couple days ago, but I can still smell their flowery soap."

Feylin inhaled deeply then grinned, and Slade, humming cheerfully, led them into the labyrinth of Tellor's alleyways, each slimy turn taking them deeper and deeper until they suddenly reentered the muggy, sunlit world of polite society.

Walking a step ahead of Tasha, Feylin blinked and raised an arm, trying to peer through the glare. "What are we doing here?"

"I promised a tour of the city, so I'd be sorely remiss if I denied you the glory of Echeira'Sollas: foremost and grandest among *Enecki's* temples." Smiling broadly, Slade walked backwards with arms stretched out to either side; and Feylin, almost as if by providence, finally blinked through the glare.

She gasped.

The temple waited at the center of a massive square, and even at this distance, Echeira'Sollas strained easy viewing. Its shimmering, tiered bulk towered above the women like a miniature mountain, making the palaces of ancient kings seem a cowering child in comparison. Unlike most Imperial architecture, it strayed from a simple blockish shape in favor of a more pyramidal design. Additionally, scores of long rectangular structures protruded from the main structure at every possible height, many in different directions and none adhering to any strict specifications.

At the temple's base, ivory sand covered the surrounding prayer-field: a raised dais ringed by onyx stairs. These stairs, like so many structures in the Empire, gleamed with runes; but where other structure's bore enchantments to ward off heat, degradation or intruders, prayer-fields received enchantments to blunt *Sammahale's* noonday glare. Inhabiting this particular prayer-field were thousands of grey obelisks arranged with militaristic precision, each standing about the height of an apple tree and obviously ancient, more so than the temple itself. Among these obelisks people knelt in respectful silence, praying with heads lowered as the final occupants—serene individuals dressed in white—meandered through the neat lines and crouched beside those who were clearly distraught, offering advice or a friendly ear.

One such priest looked up as they approached, pressing a finger to her razor thin lips with a glower that promised instant dismemberment if they caused undue disorder.

Slade mimed sealing his lips then swallowed the key and bent to swap his dirty boots for a pair of the pristine, lightly scented slippers arranged along the stair's edge. At the same time, he motioned for Tasha and Feylin to replicate his swap. As for the priestess, she resumed her duties with obvious suspicion but left his good behavior to the numerous narrow-eyed adari stationed along the dais' edge. Each was perched atop a tall, thin pillar with their ledgers and inks.

Paying no mind to priestess or adari, Slade mischievously beckoned his companions onward.

Progressing down the lanes of worshipers, Slade supplied constant distractions by burrowing into his satchel for an extensive range of gifts. Sometimes he left coins or candy for the worshipers. Other times he bestowed more exotic items, here a dead frog was ensconced in a matriarch's voluminous curls, there a bottle of perfume was placed alongside a rancid beggar. Once he presented an elderly gentleman with an entire violin, and another time he delivered pink heart etched letters to a young man with a snoring problem.

Eventually the women escaped the restrictive rows of attendees and walked across a small, empty space to one of many enormous stairs that protruded from the main bulk of Echeira'Sollas. Slade, the personification of innocence, lounged on the bottom-most step.

"Do you always leave presents?" Feylin asked.

"Once or twice a week, whether rain falls or the sun shines."

Tasha, gauging the warmth of the golden bricks with a touch, sat down and rested her elbows atop a higher step, head falling back to observe the daunting ascent. "Please, tell me we're not supposed to climb all these bloody steps."

"Oh no, only about half of them."

"Are these solid gold or plated stone?" Speaking over Tasha's distraught groan, Feylin meandered further right, inspecting the golden steps with a half bent, side-stepping walk that culminated with her kneeling before them.

An irreverent scoot placed Slade on Feylin's left. "What you're stroking is an estimated five inches of solid gold"—following along behind him, Tasha gave a quiet whistle—"and underneath all that gold, underneath all those impressive expansions and statues and murals and beautiful architecture, lies a honeycombed mountain that existed long before Cardolyn Tyier came along." Slade grinned. "We're going to see its heart."

Feylin nodded distractedly then tapped on the bricks. "And what is this writing?" Etched within each golden brick was a lovely swirling script that formed a series of modest, unique sentences.

Slade's inquisitive look was cursory at best. "Ah, that's a prayer."

Feylin's gaze finally broke away. "Prayers? Why would anyone write their prayers on gold?"

Clapping his thighs, Slade stood and extended a hand to his kneeling companion. "It's a quirk peculiar to those who live in Tellor. We believe that a spoken prayer is one whisper drowned amongst thousands, while a written prayer consigned to fire is forever lost." Slade crouched and sprang over the first couple steps. "Now if someone writes his or her wish in gold, the prayer is shouted and continues shouting until the writing fades. Wood and stonework as well, but gold is *Enecki's* favorite."

Walking around, Tasha saw prayers written upon nearly every brick. "Do people engrave their own prayers, or must they hire a priest's services?"

"Priests perform the task and adari keep their usual, careful records. A person, regardless of their wealth, station, or power can only exercise this particular form of worship once. Furthermore, once written, the prayer will persist until that person's death."

"If anyone can inscribe prayers, does that mean this little quirk is free to partake of?"

"Of course; who'd write a beggar's prayer if the whole business drained one's purse."

"What do they say? Can you read them?" Feylin asked, studying a specimen whose clustered writing nearly burst onto adjacent bricks.

"Many people can actually; it's difficult to recognize through all those swirls, but that's the West's old dialect, the one used before Cardolyn Tyier adopted the Merchant's tongue as our national language. It's still widely taught in academics because much of our literature hasn't been translated yet." Slade led them in a diagonal, searching for an engaging prayer. "Here we are"—he knelt, polishing the golden brick with his sleeve—"this woman asked to live long enough to see her grandchild born." He smiled. "Apparently, *Enecki* felt generous that day; this prayer is almost a decade old." Slade resumed his ascent, reading prayers under his breath until he encountered one which bore repeating. "This man asked *Enecki* to protect his brother, the adjacent prayer begs for increased wealth. Judging from the wording, our foolish supplicant is already rich."

Tasha, a bit self-consciously, touched her own mostly empty purse. "Wealth is hardly foolish."

"Yes, but why spend your single, unrestricted wish on something you already possess?"

"Oh, and I suppose you have some grand, altruistic prayer just waiting to set the world aright?"

Slade brushed the side of his nose with a finger. "My secret." He turned and began climbing, leading them past the multitude of minor entrances to one of the four imposing doors spaced around Echeira'Sollas' midpoint.

After entering through the open doors, they descended a sloping corridor that gradually shirked the humidity so notable outside. At the corridor's center, a line of delicate, curving pillars held the concave ceiling aloft and hosted a series of expansive, semi-circle banners. These bore the shimmering iconography of *Enecki's* burning book and wheel, and helped guide devotees into a giant circular chamber. Therein the ceiling spiraled skyward, building to a socket filled with a ball of molten, ever-churning gold and light. The temple's heart.

Catching herself marveling, Tasha stopped blocking the entrance and claimed a bench by the wall. There she cast an ascertaining glance toward

Feylin and found the young woman standing with her head thrown back, transfixed by the ceiling. Tasha shook her head. *'Look at us. No wonder he reeks of satisfaction.'*

Leaning back, her eye caught on a latticework of silver lines spiraling across the wall; in fact, spiraling across every wall to adopt script-like patterns or simple images like flowered ivy, various birds, and occasionally the beautiful, narrow countenance of a Fae person.

Curious, she brushed one with a finger and felt a chilly metallic bump, jerking back when it twitched away from her. As she watched, the strand jostled against a minute squirrel that reacted as if zapped and fled, pulling its curling vine along behind it and starting a cascade effect that brought the entire wall to life, swiftly followed by the whole room.

Tasha stepped back a pace. "Umm, Slade…" Instantly several people turned vexed expressions her way, but it also brought him.

"You discovered the shifting words, I see."

"This is normal then?"

"Very much so."

"What is it? A spell? A semblance? An illusion?"

"None of the above; its Quicksilver trapped in the walls." Slade, for once, spoke in a perfectly moderate tone; nevertheless, the expressions around them grew positively scandalized at his willingness to hold a conversation during mass.

Feylin, her attention torn from the ceiling by their voices, migrated over and cautiously touched the silver threads as well. Once again the threads retreated; only this time, they returned and played around underneath her fingers. "Quicksilver?"

"A liquid, partially sentient metal. It possesses numerous magical properties, not least of which is the ability to shape itself according to whim; rather intimidating when whole rivers are said to run beneath the northern part of the Empire, particularly Drak'marr." His gaze idly lifted to the glowing heart of Echeira'Sollas. "Once those rivers flowed across the surface of the Empire, stretching from the Rhawn all the way down to the Inland Sea, shifting location from day to day, growing bored and separating into animals or trees, causing very serious problems when they teased the *Annuir'Hyme*. Then Cardolyn Tyier ascended to power and the West lost much of its … strangeness."

Feylin's head cocked to one side. "Why does it flourish within Echeira'Sollas then?"

"Because a long time ago, this temple belonged to *Iothar* and Quicksilver is closely bound to the Western Great-Immortal. When Cardolyn

Tyier occupied the city and repurposed this temple to serve *Enecki*, the Quicksilver was left trapped inside."

"How sad." Feylin placed her other hand against the wall, watching as the silver lines mimicked one another's movements.

"A little, yes. Though I wouldn't indulge too much sympathy; it's spent the last five minutes insulting Tasha's eyebrows."

"My eyebrows? I suppose you speak Quicksilver now?"

"Hardly. Those pretty swirls are characters in the Lynn alphabet."

"Where and how did you learn to read Lynish? It verges on the impossible."

"Two years ago we suffered a month of the most appalling rain. It was as if the Chalice of Tears up and decided to quit its profession, dumping all those accumulated waterworks upon our sorry selves." Slade shrugged. "During that harrowing period, I studied Lynish calligraphy."

"You learned to write Lynish in a month? Yeah, right." This garnered a second shrug, and Tasha shook her head.

"What does it say about her eyebrows?" Feylin asked, nudging him with an elbow.

"That they have a wonderfully masculine appearance."

"They do not," Tasha protested, slapping a hand to her forehead and then biting back a sharp remark when she heard Feylin suppressing laughter.

Slade, however, whirled on the young woman. "And in the same breath they proclaim that you, my young prodigy, resemble nothing so much as a child dunked in a vat of milk." Now Tasha laughed while Feylin protested, but Slade talked over both of them. "And now they say you both look as if— no, I am not going to repeat that!"

"And what do the clever little lines say about you?" Tasha asked, prodding Slade on the shoulder as Feylin nodded eagerly.

"As I understand it, one side thinks I'm the ugliest woman ever born, while the other believes I'm the wimpiest man ever born. It's quite the debate." He sat back and frowned at the wall. "Without a doubt, my apparel's to blame; if I wore a proper dress, my beauty would surpass all others." Slade rubbed his chin. "Blue I think, to accent the color of my eyes, and perhaps a plunging neckline." He proceeded to thrust out his hips and sway with such unnerving skill Tasha forgot his true gender for a second. "Maybe a slit up the leg too; men enjoy a little skin."

Feylin would have liked to say something, but her scattered thoughts offered nothing and so Tasha beat her to it. "I don't know which is more unnerving, how much thought you've given this subject or your salacious wardrobe."

Before he could respond, bells began ringing across the city, calling the end of prayer and indicating the forthcoming Vigil shift. Soon after, *Sammahale* started its inexorable path across the sky, pushing or pulling shadows according to their location. Meanwhile, those genuflecting for prayer also moved, a chorus of groans disturbing the reverent hush.

"Ah," Slade said, digging through his satchel and producing a small redwood box. "Excuse me, it's time I ran a quick errand. Shouldn't take long; it's just a favor for one of my minions."

Tasha glanced around. "They asked you to run an errand up here?"

"Yes, her father's sick and she wanted me to make an offering for her."

"Why not make it herself?" Tasha's mouth quirked upward. "Unless she just wanted to avoid climbing all those steps."

"Before placing an offering at *Enecki's* feet"—Slade gestured to where a gold and sapphire statue of the god towered at the room's center—"one must first sweet-talk the high-priest. My minion gets frightfully nervous around strangers, particularly if she has to talk to them."

"Is that where we're going next? To petition the high-priest?" Feylin asked.

"Nah, the old tub of lard is so corrupt moldy cheese avoids him. I'll just sneak this offering in while everybody's looking away. Now if you'll excuse me." Slade began skulking toward the alter pillar by pillar, peeking around each edge and preparing for his next dash.

Following without feeling the need to skulk, Tasha grabbed the back of his shirt after the third pillar. "Slade, what are you doing?"

"Losing pursuit." He sank even lower, eyes taking on a shifty air. "I can't well deposit this if I'm being watched and there's been two creatures stalking me ever since I woke up this morning."

Meeting Feylin's eyes, Tasha saw her own suspicion mirrored back at her. "What do these pursuers look like?"

"Imagine curving horns, long fangs, forked tails, towering pillars of flame, and the enchanting odor of brimstone."

"Why hasn't anybody else seen these ... creatures?"

"Because, my Dear, both have adorned themselves with signs bearing the simple message that says, and I quote, 'You do not see me'. The words are horribly misspelt, but what can you expect from such creatures."

"Are the signs magical in some way?" Feylin asked.

"No, these creatures are just so horrifying that everybody, with astounding composure, ignores them in the hopes they'll be ignored as well; and the demons, with their glorious intelligence, believe the signs are working." Slade grinned, then slipped free and scurried to an advantageous location that offered easy access to the statue and its heap of offerings.

"So how do you plan on doing this?" Tasha asked. "There are a lot of priests meandering around."

The grin he gave her was pure, untarnished wickedness. But it wasn't until Slade thrust the redwood box at her, lay his plumed hat atop her head and waggled his fingers, that she understood the true disaster awaiting them.

Feylin was already scampering toward safety.

Tasha barely escaped before Slade cast his head back and howled at the sky, spittle flying from his mouth. In one instant, every gaze swiveled toward him: surprise, confusion, and fear sweeping through their ranks as they absorbed the scene.

Slade writhed upon the ground, foam leaking from the corners of his mouth as he screamed one ululating cry after another.

Priests rushed in from every direction, some carrying fresh water while others brought the various necessities for attending injury. The first man to reach the scene hurled himself across Slade's writhing figure, restraining the youth as best he could. The second and third dragged shocked observers away, a fourth grabbed Tasha's shoulder from behind, making her start violently. "What happened? Did you see anything?"

"I don't know," Tasha said, raising the pitch of her voice and nervously gripping the brim of Slade's hat between her hands. "One minute he was fine, the next he's writhing across the floor."

Across from them, Slade squirmed out from underneath the first priest, his flushed countenance standing in stark contrast to the rolling whites of his eyes. Another man threw himself atop of Slade but failed to restrain him as the youth fought to a sit and shrieked his first intelligible words. "They're coming! Doom and Death await! Fear the dusk for it brings darkness not of this world. Thirteen times the bells shall ring, thirteen demons shall arise and thirteen hours shall the slaughter last. Thirteen lives alone shall be spared: the lives of those who killed the rest." Just as another tide of priests arrived, Slade collapsed, eyes rolling backward.

The second priest whirled back to Tasha. "Are you acquainted with him? Has he ever displayed a tendency for divination?"

Tasha pretended to shrink back from his sudden agitation, holding the hat up as she might a shield. "No! I've never seen him before. Surely these are just the ravings of a madman?"

"This is *Enecki's* holiest temple." The priest shook his head. "We can hope these are simple ravings, but in all likelihood, this man has spoken *Enecki's* words."

Temple or not, Tasha doubted Slade spoke for a god. Deranged raving was more his style. Still, she decided against relaying this particular piece of information and let the priest go examine Slade, using the modicum of privacy it afforded her to secret the redwood box at *Enecki's* feet. She then inclined her head, touched two fingers to her brow, and muttered a heartfelt apology before striding off to collect Feylin. "Next time," she grumbled, placing Slade's hat atop her head, "he had better ask before throwing me headlong into one of his demented schemes." *'Somehow, I doubt he will though.'*

She discovered the young woman hiding behind a pillar. "Come," Tasha said, touching her shoulder, "I think we should leave."

Feylin started at the gentle touch, then breathed a sigh of relief. "Tasha, it's you."

"Course it is. Let's get out of here." Tasha jerked her head toward the door, realized a veritable wall of priests was arrayed against them and grabbed her companion's hand.

Looking at the priests, Feylin gave a little shake of her head. "It's amazing what Slade's capable of when you give him an audience."

"Yes, but don't let admiration become emulation; I doubt the world could withstand two of him."

———————

With his distraction having climaxed, Slade addressed the dilemma of how to extricate himself. The perfect opportunity presented itself when somebody knelt beside him, the rustle of his or her robes revealing their priestly occupation and heralding the wet cloth draped across his brow.

As a drop of water trickled down his face, Slade fluttered his eyes lids and moaned softly.

"Quick, Holy One, he's coming around." Though deep and cluttered by a thick accent, it was undeniably feminine.

'She's from the East, how interesting.' Slade allowed his eyes to flutter open and blink repeatedly, bringing a round, concerned face into view.

"Are you all right, prophet?"

"Prophet?" Slade asked groggily, wincing and stiffly trying to sit but failing until she assisted him. "I'm sorry, but you must have me confused with somebody else. I'm no prophet, no way no how." Slade gave her a shy, self-deprecating smile.

Smiling back, she was about to respond when an old man dropped beside her in a billowing of robes. Unceremoniously, he thrust the woman aside and grabbed Slade's face between both hands, filling his vision with damp, calculating eyes hidden behind a veneer of compassion. "Tell me, child, do you remember your fit?"

"My fit, Holy One?" Slade asked, brow crinkled. "What are you talking about?"

"Moments ago you were beset by a violent seizure. We believe *Enecki* may have been speaking through you."

Slade contained his inner amusement with some difficulty. "Why would *Enecki* choose me? There are many worthier than I."

"It is not our place to question *Enecki*. Now, what is your latest memory?" His remonstration was gentle, the kind one expected from an old, fatherly priest. It was a masterful deception.

Slade allowed his eyes to close and his brow to crease as if he struggled with sweeping the fog from his mind, as if he fought to remember anything of value, anything that could help the high-priest. "There was ... a light in my mind, and I floated in it, content, despite a ... a ... burning pain that filled the entirety of my body, consuming me from within." It was the typical fare for one possessed by the gods: a mysterious, benign presence and an unspeakable pain combined with prophecy.

The priests accepted Slade's words like the divine truth they were supposed to be, most forming tight groups to discuss his words while others scurried off on mysterious tasks.

Slade snuck away while they were all thus distracted, humming a hymn to *Jaidar* under his breath.

Tasha and Feylin waited just outside the doorway, sheltering from the sun behind one of Echeira'Sollas' many pillars. Feylin perched atop the uppermost step, idly twisting a lock of hair around one finger as she watched the last remaining people descend from the prayer-field, some stretching achy backs, others prodding at new sunburn. Normally the exodus would have taken longer, but it had been a relatively small crowd today.

Unlike the people, the wind decided to linger and play a little, rushing in to rumple Tasha's clothing or tug at Feylin's hair. Breathing delighted sighs, both women faced it and caught sight of Slade as he jogged over with his usual grin.

"The star performer returns." Tasha called, levering herself from the pillar.

In response, Slade turned a cartwheel and then rolled forward into a bow. "Did you ladies enjoy the performance?"

"Your acting was superb. The material, on the other hand, was overwrought."

Slade clapped a hand to his chest, feigning mortal injury. "You wound me to the quick, my Dear."

"There isn't a tongue flapping that could wound you, and mine doesn't cut all that deep."

He harrumphed. "Here I stand, my intestines spilling out from this gaping hole in my stomach, and you've the gall to declare yourself innocuous." He spun toward Feylin. "Just last night, I visited her room and she cut me to figurative ribbons with that instrument of bloody slaughter."

Blushing at Slade's implications, Feylin glanced to their companion, who threw her hands skyward.

"You can't get into my room, the owner doesn't allow guests and he keeps three guards on duty at all times, plus I've rented an interior room so there's no windows." And this was without mentioning the two black dogs or the cat that yowled whenever a stranger approached. Nobody knew who owned the diabolical creature. According to the landlord, it had simply appeared and declared its dictatorship.

"That might be true if I didn't have forces on the inside—namely, a large white cat with blood-red eyes and a certain partiality for human flesh." His hands formed claws that raked the air. "Don't let his fluffy appearance fool you, he's a mastermind of villainy and devious beyond even my tortured machinations."

"Yeah, yeah; any day now he's going to supplant Cardolyn Tyier and take over the entire Paladin Empire." Tasha gave a brusque wave, unconcerned by Slade's surprisingly accurate description.

"Ah-ha, so you've heard the rumors as well?"

"No, Slade, I stated the most absurd thing I could imagine."

He wagged a finger at her. "Well, you know what they say, in absurdity lies genius."

"No, Slade, they don't say that." Then before he could segue into his next absurdity, she raised a hand. "Anyway, we all done here and ready to terrorize the next venue?"

"Lemme see, we scandalized a roomful of priests, suffered through a history lesson, and served the God of Light some excellent hallucinogens. Yep, I think we're done here."

"Wait, hallucinogens?" Feylin asked.

"Why yes; if you want to be noticed, you can't mindlessly trudge the same road as everyone else. *Enecki* already receives mounds of pretty jewels and expensive incense, so we need to provide more exciting offerings. Now, where shall we visit next? The docks? Or perhaps we'll take a ride beyond city limits and get sequestered by ferocious bandits."

Tasha's eyes flicked toward Feylin. "I suggest the docks; Tiberius might take it amiss if we allowed bandits to sequester his ward."

"Pashaw." He flapped a hand at her. "I'm sure he won't mind. In any case, all such enterprises are undertaken in the name of romance."

"Romance?" If this traveled the road Feylin suspected, Slade had read far too many novels.

"Of course, why do you think bandits exist in the first place? Because women across the Empire need a dashing rogue to elope with. I know this man, ugly enough to attract a warthog, who arranges the sequestering of young ladies and lonely widows by handsome rogues. What follows are a couple months of supposed brutal enslavement at the end of which the lady can be ransomed or remain with her new lover. There's this one duchess whose been kidnapped no fewer than eleven times. All this bad reputation attached to bandits is government propaganda. Our leaders are probably attempting to suppress women and save their Thearcs the odd coin, that or control the economy." He froze. "Gods above, it's a conspiracy against the free-market. What next? Will pickles become a criminal possession? Are carrots the next great murder weapon? Is stone doomed to restriction and seizure? Will thievery be made illegal?" It started calmly enough but ended with Slade hopping around waving his arms.

Feylin squirreled away her amusement behind an expression of mock solemnity. "Slade, I'm sorry to inform you but thievery is already illegal."

He paled. "Gods above, we're all going to die spitted on the ends of carrots." And with that, he collapsed to the ground, moaning softly.

Tasha crouched down beside him, giving his shoulder a few consoling pats. "There, there. I'm sure Cardolyn Tyier would assign you to his propaganda department if you asked nicely. Besides, this all seems a little far-fetched considering there aren't any bandits around Tellor."

Slade heaved a sigh. "I suppose you're right." Rolling backward, he flipped to his feet and extended a hand toward her. "My hat if you please."

"Instead of hats or dresses, next time can you give me a nice ruby?"

In a single fluid motion, he caught and returned his hat to its rightful seat atop his head. "Now if I'm not mistaken, our destination is an hour's walk as the dainty lady shuffles." He flashed his teeth at them. "And we are not dainty ladies."

Tasha's heart sank. "An hour? I don't have enough time; Madame Roshfen expects me before the next Vigil shift."

Slade winced. "Ah, yes."

"Who's Madame Roshfen?" Feylin asked, ears perking.

Slade shook his head. "An unpleasant acquaintance of ours. I hope you'll forgive us if we forgo an introduction; it's best to abstain from certain experiences."

"If I want dinner, I'd best leave now."

"I could arrange for an unexpected mugging or, better yet, a kidnapping. I'm sure Madame Roshfen has a heart chained up somewhere in her chest. Who would consider punishing another person for getting mugged?"

Tasha considered it, then abruptly realized what she was doing. "Nope, no, no; I've been around you too long."

"As you wish, my Dear." Slade's hand dipped into his satchel and reappeared with a slip of paper. "There are things we must discuss, meet me at the time and place specified."

She stuffed the paper into a pocket. "Sure."

Slade watched her go, his lowered brows and crossed arms attracting Feylin's attention. "What's wrong?"

"Betrayal ..."—an instant later his countenance adopted its usual glee—"doom, death, and the eternal destruction of everything we hold dear. In short, the usual shenanigans."

"The usual shenanigans?"

"Of course." Slade threw an arm over Feylin's shoulders, leading her down the steps. "Didn't you know Tasha is *Telacra* in disguise? It was quite the scandal ten thousand years back when she decided to gallivant around with my most illustrious self. *Enecki* suffered from an extreme case of apoplexy that spawned half-a-dozen stories itself. Have you heard of any? No? Well, one goes like this..." And he went on to regale her with his trademarked exaggeration fused to blatant mistruths, ending with an epic so grand it lasted the entire return journey.

Later that same day, a horrid stench wafted in through the library's open door and woke Feylin from an unplanned nap. She jerked forward, mouth clicking shut and head snapping like a whip. The book—hitherto sleeping companionably in her lap—fell to the floor with a muted bang.

Senna, despite sitting closer to the source, unconcernedly flipped a page. "Best pick that up, dear. Slade would throw a fit if someone trod mud across the cover."

"Oh, yes of course, Ms. Senna." Momentarily distracted from the stench, Feylin rescued the book and blindly thrust it toward her end table but knocked against a stack of books that had the poor thing practically trembling under their weight. A cursory inspection revealed that similar pillars of books burdened the other tables as well as the floor and unoccupied couches.

"Don't worry over the books, dear. Slade will neaten up eventually."

"Won't he be angry?" This was the first time Feylin had seen the meticulously ordered Lammerock house in any form of disarray.

"I doubt it; he removed them in the first place."

"Oh," was all Feylin could manage when confronted by yet another of Slade's many contradictions. Adapting to the situation, she returned to where she'd first procured her book; except the library shelves, once packed from side to side, now sat empty. "Err, Ms. Senna…"

"I think Slade transferred *Roy'al* history to the west wall, top shelf."

"But … that's the biology section." Glancing toward the indicated bookcase, Feylin discovered it, too, had been ransacked.

"I know, dear. Slade has … peculiar ideas about organization." Senna turned another page, smiling a little bit. "Three years back a servant absconded with one of his books, and my son demanded that Cain marshal the Theanne Guard to pursue and—ahem—castigate the man; my husband, in his profound wisdom, refused. Ever since, Slade routinely shuffles the books lest someone grow too attached."

"How can you find anything with him doing that?" Feylin asked, stopping at the indicated bookcase and glancing up with a sigh; there was no way she could reach the top shelf. She needed a stool.

"Oh, I rarely search for any book in particular; I choose one at random and carry it around with me until I've finished."

"Doesn't that annoy Slade?" Even as she dragged a stool across the floor, clambered atop it and tipped the book into place, Feylin wishfully contemplated the ease of using the bookshelves as a stepping ladder.

"I suppose, but he understands it's a direct result from his endless shuffling, so he's accustomed himself to my irrationalities."

Hopping from the stool, Feylin found herself waving at the oppressive stench when she accidentally inhaled a noseful. "What is that smell?"

"Slade; he's playing at witch down in the cellar."

"Does he … um, become a witch often?"

"Oh, all the time. On one memorable occasion, he fabricated a potion that changed some poor maid's hair stark white." Senna flipped another page. "More recently he's been infatuated with woodworking, but I assume that's run its course. Such a pity, I've grown to enjoy the scent of saw dust." The woman looked up, her gaze pensive. "I especially liked fresh pine." Giving a shrug, she returned to her book.

Feylin darted across the room, grabbed the woman's couch by its gilded trim and leaned over the back. "Slade changed somebody's hair white?"

"Every hair on the poor girl's body. It was, perhaps, a fortunate accident seeing as he had intended on blue. A strange color, but Slade has funny tastes."

"Blue?"

"Indeed, nor did the matter end with one experiment. Over the succeeding days, we discovered that allowing Slade into the kitchen was an unparalleled disaster. Within the week, everyone except Cain had developed some new fantastic hair color." Senna stroked her own curls, smiling at Feylin. "I had orange."

"Why was Slade experimenting with hair colors?"

"I haven't the faintest idea."

Feeling a touch queasy, Feylin glanced out the library doors. "Shouldn't we see what he's doing then? I'd rather not spend the rest of my life with blue hair."

"I wouldn't worry about it; he perfected those experiments long ago; besides, the effects scarcely lasted a week or two. You can still go visit him though; Slade does enjoy showing off."

'If I visit him, will that nominate me as a test subject? Or might I discover a piece of crucial information?' Covering her eyes, Feylin gave a soft moan. "Where do I find the cellar?"

Reaching the basement required that she descend a series of rickety, bemoaning planks, and while they exemplified every eerie fantasy, it was the cellar itself that exceeded expectations. Cobwebs arched across the ceiling in broad nets or dangled to the floor in a crude semblance of drapes. A chill damp pervaded the room, unaffected by the dim, flickering candles. Muted wind chimes added a perfectly manicured ambience while unseen water dripped and spread across the floor, supplying a variety of lichen whose colors ranged from a bright emerald to a dull yellow to a nice fiery blue. Looking around a second time, she noticed other plants along with a few silhouettes that might belong to miniature trees. It was as much a garden as a cellar.

Contorting past a spider silk curtain, she debarked the final stair and accidentally stepped on something squishy, cringing when she discovered it was a patch of vaguely luminescent moss. As she hastened off it, the plant's delicate bulbs swayed then opened shyly, halting Feylin with the gradual revelation of violet flowers.

Slade materialized beside her, grabbing her waist and lifting her into a short flight that concluded with Feylin stumbling back, blushing ferociously. Otherwise he ignored her, kneeling by the abused plant to hum rhythmically while stroking the flowers, gradually lulling them closed again.

'Oh no, please don't be angry. I didn't mean to step on anything important. I'm sorry. It was an accident.'

But when Slade rose, he wore a crooked smile. "It is not quite time for those to bloom; contact with the premature flowers can result in a rather horrid sickness." Slade lifted his hands, displaying the dark, oiled leather protecting his skin. "After maturing, they're ground into a powder with various medical uses; not least of which is a terrific headache reliever."

For once his smile held more reassurance than scheming intent, so when he offered his hand, Feylin accepted it and let him guide her to where a group of battered yet determined tables convened together. Their scars were plentiful and varied but most notable was the misplaced leg substituted with a stack of bricks, dangerous considering each table carried a clustered forest of colorful bottles, glass beakers, iron pots, blackened pans, and various measuring devices.

Among this visual cacophony was an old pot that simmered without apparent heat source, hissing foul temperedly and spitting the occasional insult at a pretty little scale that crouched beneath a mound of wispy herbs and did its best to ignore the crotchety old pot.

After reaching their destination, Slade scurried around the room trying to clear one space so he might clear another, his endeavors culminating with him setting a stool before her and smacking the seat. "Please, sit." He then rushed to the now bubbling pot.

The herbs on the scale were added to the mixture and soon joined by a vigorously stirred spoon. Slade's free hand then darted across the table snatching up one mystery after the other until, with a plume of violet sparks, he added his final ingredients. A villainous stench quickly subjugated the room, threatening death against anyone who inhaled too deeply.

Feylin reeled back atop her seat, pinching her nose closed. "What is that?"

"This, my young protégé, is a potion to help my mother sleep." He grinned at her, stirring his charge with all the enthusiasm of someone who enjoyed torturing others; then he horrified her delicate sensibilities by leaning forward to inhale deeply. "Hhmm, does this smell flat to you?" he asked, whisking the iron pot up from the table.

"No, no it smells fine," she gasped through a strangled voice, poised on the verge of losing her lunch.

"Are you sure?"

"Gah-yes." Feylin stumbled from the stool, raising a hand to forestall Slade's advance.

"What? It's not like it stinks or anything."

"That? That doesn't stink?" The finger she directed at the offending liquid all but shook from the force of her accusation.

"Truth be told; I find it a little flat. Now if you want something to abuse one's sense of smell …"—returning the pot, he rummaged underneath the table—"try this love potion." Displaying wisdom beyond her age, Feylin fled, leaping the toxic flowers and charging up the rickety stairs.

Whistling, Slade uncorked the flask and poured its contents into the pot, releasing a pleasant scent one might call spring. There was, after all, no reason the governor's guards should suffer while they slept.

After he applied the finishing touches, Slade filled three unremarkable flasks with the smoky liquid, marked them appropriately, and slipped them into his satchel.

The months of planning had reached their conclusion. Tonight he would strike, completing the first step toward both fixing and causing a significant amount of trouble.

44

The Last Gladiator

Sitting on a corpse, drenched in the black rain, Dieharamon wiped blood off his body, clothing, and weapon in unsteady sweeps. The maul he carried was solid iron with a three-foot handle and a square head. Few could have used it at all, let alone with devastating effect. The original wielder had lacked the strength. Dieharamon did not.

It was his third weapon since losing the pewter sword when his block and two others collided; his subsequent two weapons had broken almost immediately, and even the maul already displayed signs of deterioration. Any armor he salvaged proved equally temporary, either shattered or torn beyond use within minutes. Only the battered chainmail endured. Despite all of this, here atop the pyramid's upper-most block, a relatively enormous platform, the Angorat'Wass finally neared its conclusion. The floor around him had almost disappeared beneath corpses and carrion birds, and the surviving gladiators stumbled or crawled about, hacking at one another with slovenly, feeble blows, resembling more caricatures then warriors.

Something scraped behind Dieharamon. He lunged up and spun, reasserting his grip on the maul and swinging wide, his aching muscles drinking in the energy at his core, sustaining him long past natural endurance: a cheat against all the Avarans who had nothing but themselves and their shoddy weapons.

Two of the three gladiators encroaching his back managed to fumble back, mostly because the third absorbed the blow. That gladiator's shattered body tumbled a dozen paces away, flecked with his armor. The remaining two staggered in to counterattack, trusting to the maul's unwieldiness to expose Dieharamon, and in their ignorance, advanced too far. The maul struck the first's unguarded side and continued through to the second, flinging both off the block.

Dieharamon spun in place, reeling from accumulated exhaustion, his vision hazy, and almost tripping in the strewn limbs, but no challenger presented himself. Some gladiators fought in the distance, but none close enough to threaten him. He collapsed, heedless of the corpses mounded three-high beneath him, and breathed an exhausted whimper of relief. He slipped down the mound's front, huddling and concealing himself against it as best he could, stealing another moment of respite.

The minutes trudged by as he fought through the throbbing ache of his body, superficial injuries, and pounding rain to calculate how many gladiators remained. The effort proved futile; he was too fatigued to think properly, and the pyramid's zenith too obscured to glean reliable information.

At some point during the conflict, he had realized why Valeriius orchestrated this genocide: the Kalvonders' true military potency derived from their Tragnashi, but Tragnashi were rare, acquirable solely through breeding or contracts with the Clergy. Furthermore, most Tragnashi were committed to the arena, which meant Valeriius had successfully stripped his rivals of their military core. How he achieved this, Dieharamon could not imagine. While the Kalmarads acted independently from the Kalvonders, and due to ancient affiliations with the Clergy, possessed nominal authority over all Tragnashi committed to the arena, they were still ultimately subservient to the Kalvonders, many with particular loyalties. Achieving this result required more than coercing a few members, it needed the entire stratum, or at least an overwhelming majority.

Ever cognizant of the coward's brand, Dieharamon compelled his body up and shuffled forward, tiptoeing through the bodies and husbanding his strength as best he could. The nearest gladiators responded to his approach. As their predecessors had, some fled; the rest forged hasty alliances, knowing survival depended on unity and cohesion. They succeeded only in the first necessity.

None of them possessed his experience or intellect or the energy refueling his strength, and their native distrust fundamentally sabotaged their endeavor. They faced him, but where there should have been uniform purpose, there was fractured howling and chaos. Some charged, others arrayed defensively, and in the confusion, both faltered.

Realizing their disorder, Dieharamon charged, seeking less to destroy them than to perpetuate their disarray. His first sweeping blow produced little damage, knocking some over and scattering others into a muddled retreat. His reverse sweep crushed two heads and brought him whirling from their clustered mass.

They stumbled and tripped after him, barely capable of raising their weapons, let alone slash or thrust with any convincing momentum. Most missed without any effort from him. He set to massacring them.

Those at the back began eroding within moments, reeling off into the rain with feeble attempts to attack their allies. The remainder died, too exhausted to notice the betrayal, and left Dieharamon to bludgeon his last immediate foe, the maul's head utterly disfigured. He halted unsteadily, swaying on his feet and staring at the ruined maul until he discarded it with a dull thud, the handle warped with finger indentations, sticky with blood and flecked with bone fragments.

In the subsequent comparative silence, a shallow laugh pulled Dieharamon about to peer through the rain.

A man watched him, handsome if not for streaming blood, scars, and sickly gauntness. He leaned against a corpse mound in a growing puddle of water, holding his ribs with ragged gasps.

Dieharamon staggered over and knelt, wondering why the man bothered. "What's so funny?"

"Hello, ... Hooded Man. Always knew ... you would ... kill me."

Dieharamon wiped blood and black water from the man's face, not knowing why he did it. Confusion flickered in the gladiator's eyes but faded, dismissed by its own irrelevance.

"Why does it matter that I killed you?"

"Doesn't. Just knew. Always knew. They ... lied so much. Every time ... said ... you were dead. Going to. But you ... always survived. Defied them ... came back. You ... one of us ... no drugs. Strong. I ... I want a ... truth."

"Why? I don't have any truths, I–"

"They ... lied. All I have ... of you ... their lies. I want ... something real. Something ... of you."

"But I don't have anything." Dieharamon slumped back, sagging. "I don't have anything for you."

"Do you ... enjoy ... killing us?"

"Gods no!"

The dying Avaran smiled. "Thank ... you. I'll ... tell the others. They'll ... be glad." His lolled to the side, eyes growing hazy and unfocused. "I ... wanted to hate you. Listen ... to them. Would ... have made ... it easier. But you ... survived ... survived them. They ... hated you. Couldn't kill you." A wet laugh shook the man. "They tried to ... kill you. One of ... us. Really ... tried ... but couldn't. You ... beat them ... us. Showed us ... we could ... win. Hope. Survive. Our ... Hooded Man."

"What's Hooded Man mean?"

"*Arawn*—The God of Death— ... Kalvonder ... ordered us ... kill you. Entire group. Whatever ... the cost. But ... we hoped ... not to be ... the ones

… that killed … you. Hoped … someone else … or that you … survived. All this … to kill you, I think. No other reason."

Shame without reason filled Dieharamon. Gods. He couldn't tell him that this, all of this, was so that Dieharamon could kill them. He looked away from the man, shuddering.

The gladiator coughed, spewing blood, and dragged Dieharamon close, capturing his eyes for a long stare. The pull lacked strength, but Dieharamon lacked the will to resist. "Glad … it was you … who survived. Hope … you … win … whoever … did this … loses."

He took the dying man and touched their brows together as *Arawn* claimed him. He held the pose for a moment, then released the body, retrieved his mutilated maul, and trudged across the vast zenith block for the survivors.

A dozen remained, segregated into three groups around the bronze capstone. Oblivious to Dieharamon, the gladiators dithered, exchanging screams and posturing for advantage. A thirteenth figure crouched atop the capstone in hiding, small enough that it could only be a child. The gladiators knew the child existed but were terrified others might lurk in the storm's obscurity. Thus they vacillated and refused to commit any definitive action.

It was neither assurance nor courage that finally incited the gladiators to battle but the storm. Startled by a streak of lightning, the child lost his grip, tumbled into their midst, and in so doing, sparked a feeding frenzy. The groups converged in howling desperation, the boy shrieking and scrambling from their lunging grasps. Dieharamon crashed into the conflict seconds later.

Opening with a sweeping blow, he struck for the foremost gladiator, but underestimated his charge and missed. He stumbled, caught himself and straightened, sweeping the maul again to scatter his nearest competitors. Movement flashed in the corner of his eye, and he swung about, bringing the maul up only to recognize the child at the last instant and divert his blow. The maul smashed against the ground and shattered, its haft snapping as Dava ducked and screamed, debris pelting him.

Dieharamon spun, impaled a gladiator through the midsection, and flung him aside, wrenching the maul's haft free to swing it across again, this time as a bludgeon. His opponents continued assailing one another, either ignoring or unable to recognize him. He struck again, hurling a gladiator into a second and gaining himself an instant's respite before more stumbled in close, swinging dully.

He growled, pressed a boot against a mound of bodies and shoved off through them, dropping the maul's haft. He caught one by the throat, crushed his windpipe and broke into the open, dragging a second by the arm.

Twisting, he hefted his captive, skewered him on a protruding sword, and turned just as a javelin pierced his thigh and impaled a corpse.

He snapped it with a profanity and tore his leg free, spinning to halt the javelin-throwing gladiator mid-initiation with a fist to the stomach. The gladiator reeled back, flailing as Dieharamon tore an arshendi from his opponent's belt, the hatchet from his hand and then used the former to slice his throat. Pivoting, he brought the hatchet down on another encroaching gladiator's head.

Gasping from pain, spitting blood, and shaking rain from his eyes, Dieharamon threw the hatchet into a third gladiator and stumbled, almost falling when his foot caught in a dead man's arm. A spear smashed against his shoulder, its momentum driving him back another step, but failed to penetrate the chain mail. Slamming his foot into a corpse, he arrested his backward momentum and lunged, driving his arshendi into his attacker.

Transitioning into a retreat, he yanked a two-headed ax from a corpse and maneuvered around another cadaver mound. His opponents surged forward, too desperate to bother with reason. Swinging the ax up and down, he killed one gladiator and spun, cleaving a second between the ribs. Reversing momentum, he drove the haft into a third's gut before flipping it about and crushing his throat with the head.

Two more blows from undefined weapons glanced off his sides. Both died to the same swipe, one decapitated as the swinging ax attained the peak and the other eviscerated as it descended. A thin arm wrapped about Dieharamon's throat, pulling him back as an arshendi stabbed the back of his chainmail shirt. The arshendi struck twice more, both times scraping ineffectually off. Struggling for air, Dieharamon threw himself back, smashing his attacker into the ground beneath him. Rolling over, he straddled the man and crushed his throat.

Dieharamon surged back to his feet, stumbled as weight strained his injured leg and fell, gasping. He struggled for purchase with a foot, kicking a corpse dully until his slippers caught on the stone. He pushed himself up with his hands, first to his knees then to a swaying stand.

Jaur stood a few feet away, blood trickling from a dozen injuries and prepared bandages, staining what little remained of his clothing and armor. He grinned, the expression stiff with pain and exhaustion, and drew a knife from his belt. "Ah, the mighty Dieharamon... It will be a pleasure to kill you." He advanced, forcing his grin wider and lifting an arm-long kuvash with trembling fingers. The kuvash resembled a sword with two parallel edges that expanded into a hollow circle at the weapon's end.

Jaur threw himself forward, slashing. Dieharamon ducked beneath it, catching Jaur's other hand as it punched forward. He clasped it in both hands and snapped the wrist.

Jaur shrieked and slashed, but Dieharamon slapped the kuvash aside with his forearm and kicked. Jaur recoiled, stumbled, and tripped. Dieharamon charged with a surge of desperation but threw all his weight on his injured thigh. It held for an instant, then buckled.

Teeth gritted against the pain, Dieharamon forced himself back to his feet as Jaur scrambled to stand. Dieharamon led with his good leg and leapt for his opponent's neck. Jaur evaded backwards and responded with a swipe of the kuvash. Dieharamon took the cut on his forearm and pursued, driving his hand into Jaur's throat, fingers burrowing into flesh and tearing out. Jaur stumbled back and buckled, wheezing his finals breaths. Dieharamon followed him to the ground, vision reeling as his leg and all the other injuries screamed.

He knelt there for a moment, his entire existence pulsing with the ebb and flow of agony, then fell to his side. The faces stared at him, their almond skin black from the rain and contorted in the endless visages of death. He could almost hear their voices...

A gentle touch shattered his stupor, snapping his head upright to stare at the boy.

Dava did not run.

"You're not scared of me, are you?"

"You won't hurt me."

Dieharamon shook with a broken, bloody laugh. "I could."

The boy tore a strip of cloth and wiped Dieharamon's face.

His shoulders trembled again with the laugh that was as much at the brutal irony of their situation as it was a sob of despair. "I should kill you here; I have won ... hundreds of Angorat'Wasses, killed thousands, survived for decades and the only thing barring my freedom is you. Why am I too weak to take it?"

"You're not weak."

Dieharamon cursed himself, Dava, and the Kalvonders thrice over. "How would you know that?"

"Because you do not want to kill me."

His body's spasms ground to a stop and Dieharamon shook his head. "That changes nothing." He leaned forward and pressed an arshendi into Dava's hand.

Dava thrust the weapon back with a cry. "No!"

Dieharamon pressed harder. "Take it. One of us has to die, and I will not kill you. Take it, kill me and run. They have to return your soul, that was the prize; you don't need to be there though, so run West or North. Anywhere."

Dava continued to refuse, tears brimming. Dieharamon snatched his hand and wrapped the fingers around the handle, clamping them in place until Dava finally relented.

"It's okay," Dieharamon said, adjusting the boy's hands until the arshendi's tip hovered over his heart.

"No..."

"You're not taking a life; I am giving it."

"I can't; you should win, be free."

"This is not a story of white stallions and heroes." Dieharamon gave him a sad smile. "This is not the world of benign gods. Our world has no place for such things, and I am tired of this life."

Dava continued to shake his head and, with a trembling step, retreated. Dieharamon closed his eyes, leaned back and racked his mind for a solution. Dava could not win the Angorat'Wass unless he killed Dieharamon.

Opening his eyes, he saw Dava again and wondered if the boy's freedom was worth the lifetime of nightmares it would cause. It was a moot point, Dieharamon would not kill Dava, and neither of them could kill themselves. Dieharamon could only wait. But if he waited too long, Valeriius would act.

He knew how lost Dava was, could see his pain but refused to look away, even though his heart was breaking. He could not show less courage than he demanded. "There is no shame or betrayal; take my life and be free of them."

Slow as a rousing dawn, determination filled Dava's eyes. He raised the arshendi with a gentle but firm grip and Dieharamon lifted his head, feebly raising the chainmail to bare his chest.

Lightning flashed—white where before it had been dark—outlining a silhouette behind Dava. The sell-sword struck before Dieharamon could even cry out, steel blade flashing down once, the action concealed from the spectators by the storm.

Dieharamon lurched up, a scream strangled on his lips as the small body fell, head lolling and blood gushing. The eyes were white with shock.

The sell-sword stepped back, sheathing his knife with a sharp, professional motion, unhurried because he knew the storm concealed his presence and actions. That was his error; his skill far surpassed Dieharamon's, but with the fire in his blood, Dieharamon was stronger by far. Rage catalyzed his power, and he charged, traversing the separating distance in a heartbeat. The sell-sword reacted quickly, far more so than any Avaran, but it was insufficient. They fell, Dieharamon on top.

The sell-sword hammered and thrust Dieharamon aside, flowing to his feet with a horizontal slash from the sheath. Dieharamon pursued, accepting the new laceration across his chest where the blade found a gap in his chainmail.

They collided again, but this time Dieharamon held them upright, wrapping the sell-sword in a death-embrace. The sell-sword struggled, pummeling Dieharamon's sides and kicking his shins. But Dieharamon kept squeezing until, with a grotesque snapping of bones, he broke the sell-sword's spine.

The sell-sword slumped and Dieharamon dropped him, turning back to Dava for a final look; he knew the boy was dead. Dazedly, he began to stumble away, realizing with cruel irony and bitter relief that he was free.

Despite his injuries, Dieharamon started toward Sahdaen, not intending to return to Valeriius, but to seek his own death in Upper-Sahdaen for only death seemed to offer any mercy now.

In the storm of his despair, a thought took hold, that of finding the *Pathfinder Shard*. He would not find it for the damned Dread Lord. No, never for him. No, he would destroy that horror and cast its ashes across the city. He would cause the whole of Sahdaen to burn until only ashes blacker than night remained. He would cleanse the city of its every sin until nothing remained. Then he would leave it for the crows and whatever horrors desired its ruins.

Within him dread gathered about his heart. He feared to fail in the distribution of justice and vengeance. A black, unnatural strength arose from this fear, pulling him unconsciously deeper into its fold.

45

The Night Court

The *Winter Court's* doors opened at their approach, shimmering as their core dimmed with a thousand spiraling threads. He entered, the Artist a step behind with the Riddle clasped protectively in her delicate hands.

They had fashioned a vessel for it, a wooden doll with gnarled limbs and an ill-carven face that bespoke the Artist's absolute distaste for prisons. Nevertheless, it served its purpose, containing the Riddle to a unified mute form.

They strode down the hall, the colors of dusk painting everything before them until the oncoming night usurped all that was of glass. Outside, the day was breaking, but the *Winter Court* was an inversion of that world; here stars bloomed one after another, forming constellations that stretched and yawned as the *Night Court* convened. The eldest and largest woke first, shaking immense forms and voicing complex, ethereal songs; the younger followed, their music simpler and subdued. All of them were the legends of The North, told best during the night and to music. Not all were heroes, but each belonged to The North.

Spanning the Hall's entire ceiling, Vysera lifted her serpentine neck and snarled, quieting the lesser constellations with her ancient song. She was among the oldest, one of the first to appear during the Before-Age, but her legend was contradictory, sometimes painting her as the hero and other times the monster.

It began with her slumber of millennia during the Before-Age, buried deep in the Rhawn as they grew about her. Vysera's sleep cast an incantation of dreams and illusion over The North, drawing all who submitted into her web. For eons, she entangled minds, harvesting their passions and memories to supplement her own dreams. But on the brink of a new century, *Malbreyth* and *Enecki*, still children fettered to their parents, bickered and fell to the earth amidst flames. Oblivious in their struggles, they woke Vysera. Enraged, she rose, shattering the mountains under which she slept.

Malbreyth and *Enecki* fled to *Etherea* and the aid of their siblings. Vysera pursued, assailing the twelve infant gods in *Etherea* and devouring all their people. The gods retaliated, striking at her and the world she came from. It was futile; Vysera devoured them in turn and then settled to rule the night for a millennium, weaving her dream spell over any who slept, ensnaring all but a few.

In time her spell expanded through the heavens, transcending the Mortal Kingdoms into the subsequent realms. Others who transcended the Mortal Kingdoms began suffering the effects of her dreams. Her draconic kin perceived her incantations and became wary of her intent. The Fore-gods remained unaffected by the spells of a dragon and only watched the brewing storm coalesce. In the end, both lesser and elder dragons converged upon their sister.

Vysera cast herself against them, devouring the lesser and ravaging the greater. However, she was one against thousands, and the conclusion was inevitable: she fell.

She crashed into the northern tundra, her body a fuming husk still alive with boundless rage. The dragons descended upon her and opened Vysera's massive girth, shredding her form and burying what remained of her in the Rhawn.

In the wake of this battle, the devoured gods escaped her wreckage and set about rebuilding the Mortal Kingdoms. Vysera, however, was immortal, thus she received a seat in the heavens and a body of starlight.

Lowering his gaze, the High-Warden continued to the Mirror Hall's extremity and yielded a slight obeisance to the Winter Queen. She replied with a smile, her form no longer resembling a child but that of a young woman. She held a spear in her left hand and had grown beautiful with age, but that beauty failed to mask her cruelty.

The Artist bowed as well, shifting uneasily; she was small now, out of place in the *Night Court* for she belonged to the day.

The Winter Queen noted the wooden doll and scowled. "So you succeeded."

The High-Warden nodded, the mirrors beneath his feet vacant of constellations for a dozen paces. This was not disfavor or respect; this was fear, for the *Winter Court* remembered and saw much that was hidden.

The Winter Knight emerged from a mirror and advanced to the room's center, the constellations swirling about his passage, some hissing and others humming. He bowed to the Winter Queen. "I will begin this demonstration and prove my superiority."

The Crones did not answer. All three huddled over twisted canes, weighted with robes and amulets. They owed their birth to neither day nor night and served both with equanimity.

The central Crone straightened, her gray hair parting to reveal a youthful face. "We are ready."

The Winter Knight advanced eagerly, but the High-Warden's attention strayed, distracted by a flutter of black wings sliding into one of the many alcoves. He trailed it, ignoring the Winter Knight's recount.

He paused between two pillars, searching the shadows beyond as a foreign heat settled on his skin. A small Raven sat perched on an extinguished torch in a corner, listening beneath a motionless constellation: The Crown. It was a circle of twelve stars with the twelfth resting just above the foremost two. It represented the lost crown of the *Roy'al* dynasty.

"Who are you?" He advanced to the Raven's perch and it shifted, emerald eyes defying his attempt to pierce its façade. "This is not your place, sorceress; I request that you depart."

The Artist stepped beside him, examining their surroundings. "What is it, High-Warden?"

"This Raven does not belong here, in The North or the *Winter Court*."

"I see no Raven; are you certain this isn't just one of the *Night Court's* tricks?"

"Yes, the *Night Court* cannot deceive me. Whoever this is, shields their true self in the Raven."

"But how? I cannot sense it, nor can the *Winter Court;* maybe it does belong, or perhaps is insignificant?"

"It is foreign; it smells of warmth, sunlight, and forests, plus I have already encountered it in the company of hell-sworn."

"Who in all The North would swear to *Jaidar?*"

"Someone not born to The North would be corruptible."

"Did you know this 'someone'?"

"Yes."

"What happened to him?"

"I dealt with him." He returned his attention to the Raven and found it gone. He scanned the Hall but saw only the night, constellations, and solitary stars. "It is gone now, let us return."

They resumed their places, arriving just as the third Crone silenced the Winter Knight with a raised hand. "You weave us a tale, Knight of Winter, but that was not the ordeal. Give us your riddle or admit failure."

The Winter Knight's cheek ticked, but he forced a smile. "Of course, I have my riddle. What walks on four legs in its youth, on three in its twilight years, and two in its prime? That is my riddle, drawn from the oldest courts of winter!"

"It is an old riddle, yes, Knight of Winter. But it is not a riddle unheard, unsolved, and unspoken. Your submission fails to satisfy the requirements of the ordeal. You have failed through arrogance; learn this lesson for it did not come free."

A void of sound and pressure descended upon the Hall, freezing all into stasis. The Winter Knight advanced, cold billowing off him in frozen mist, threads of frost cracking and expanding from his feet, sprawling to encircle the Crones. "I am the Winter Knight; you cannot declare my efforts a failure. You and your sisters are insignificant, lesser members of an innumerable court."

"We are small in the *Winter Court*, Knight of Winter, but we are the Crones. While this trial persists, our word is absolute. Your failure stands, though it is incomplete. There remain two challenges."

The Winter Queen seethed, glowering at the Crones but unable to dispute their verdict. The Winter Knight snarled and strode from the center, dispelling the ice with a wave. The chill of his wrath lingered, palpable and brooding.

The unveiled Crone lowered her brow and retreated, covering her face as her sister advanced. Her face was gray with withered skin, sunken eyes, and hollowed cheeks, but her movements and hair were youthful. She beckoned the High-Warden with a thin hand adorned by intricately painted fingernails and lithe rings.

He reclaimed the wooden doll from the Artist and approached the Crone, bowing. She touched his brow. "There is no lie about you, High-Warden; you have operated within the confines of the ordeal. Have you managed to retrieve a riddle?"

"Yes."

She took the doll and explored it. "There is a riddle here; it is unspoken, unheard, and unsolved, even by you. However, it is incomplete, ridden with strife."

"The Riddle is three separate entities, but I dared not reconstruct them lest they speak. The doll holds them silent and bound but disjointed. When they are joined, the Riddle will be complete."

The Crone lifted the doll to her ear and listened. "Yes, it is a riddle full, High-Warden. You have accomplished your task and are considered victorious. Take this as a reward." The Crone returned the doll and rejoined her sisters. He hesitated, uncertain of what to do with the doll, then bowed and returned to the Artist.

The Winter Queen rose and stamped her spear. "The second test will not be so kind, High-Warden; you succeeded only due to the Winter Knight's unjust failure. I will declare the next and final challenge!"

"I know the *Winter Court's* laws; you may ordain the next test because your champion was bested, but you will not dictate the third. Either I am defeated and gain the privilege of selection, or am I am victorious and invalidate the third trial."

Smiling, The Winter Queen sat anew and leaned toward him. "I am sure we can come to some agreement. Anything can be purchased, if you possess the correct currency."

"Leave off your temptations, you have nothing I desire; I linger only because this was the price demanded."

"You are still a mortal, despite your power. How can you not be a man? No burden needs to be carried alone."

"I am hardly mortal, as well you know. Name your ordeal."

"What if I offered something of more personal value. We know what fate awaits you, what price will be demanded. It is unjust, it is cruel, and we could see it undone. You could be liberated of it and still fulfill your onus."

His heart wavered, qualms silenced by what she offered. He knew his fate just as well as they, and he dreaded it for reasons he could not share. There was a history there, complex and conflicted, full of consequence he did not wish to embark upon yet.

He pushed the temptation aside. "I will not surrender The North's fate over to chance, and I will not cheat my *Burden*, Majesty. Name your ordeal."

"Very well, High-Warden; though I warn you, there is more mortal within you than you would care to admit. Your last ordeal was of searching and intellect, and you have proven yourself adept in these, but there is more to guardianship; a guardian is a warrior, willing and capable of taking lives. Thus the subsequent ordeal shall be mired in violence. You and the Winter Knight shall race to destroy one of the evils beleaguering The North. There shall be no restrictions, barring aid in the definitive conflict. You have a day. If the evil persists or you arrive late, you will have proven yourself inadequate."

The Winter Knight grinned, his eyes flicking toward the High-Warden for a reaction.

The High-Warden bowed. "As you wish."

The Winter Queen crossed her legs and tapped her lips. "I see no reason to tarry, so let the Crones declare your prey." Reclining back on her throne, she extracted a small, circular hand mirror of silverwork from her throne's side. "I shall observe you both."

The final Crone lifted her head, her features obscured by a taut, white mask without mouth or eyes. Her shoulders, once the straightest of the three, slumped, growing thin and fragile. "In these days, there are a fortune of evils besetting The North. Some are born of hell, others of fear or malice. Winter Knight, your prey is one of these vultures. She is an old, eastern creature who spent centuries feasting on the wild animals in the High Maze's foundation. With time, she tasted human suffering and became addicted. She now feeds on humans alone, devouring and supplementing their pain over months. Destroy her and bring her scythe as proof. Beware, she may not be alone."

The Crone, now shriveled and bent, extended a hand toward the High-Warden, her knuckles swollen and arthritic. "To you we give an older evil, one who has plagued The North for millennia. You know of *It* for you have hunted *It*. *It* is one from a number of shards from a parent evil and the last. *It* hides in the city of Adriat, concealing itself high upon the Rhawn's foundations where footing is treacherous and the sole visitors are children. *It* survives through abstinence and blood-craft, feeding only when necessary and using the excess to convert every truth of *Its* presence into a lie that deceives even Lord *Ever-Winter*."

She slid to the floor, the white mask stretching across her features, conforming to a toothless skull.

The High-Warden crossed the distance separating them and caught her mid-collapse. She slipped through his hands as if she were silk and draped to the floor, the mask flowing down her throat and over her bosom. He knelt, querying her sisters, "What is this sickness?"

"We age with the day, High-Warden. At dawn we are children, young and innocent with a vision unclouded by age, memories, and travails. As the hours pass, we grow older and acquire biases through the events that occur. At dusk we become old, as you see us now, with all the wisdom learned through life and much of the bias forgotten. One by one we die as the night progresses and are reborn with the dawn. Those deaths are not always ... mortal."

"So when I return you will all wear a different face ... and a different personality, one that is, perhaps, less kind to me?"

"Yes, we will change. All of us will be crueler, for that is the way of the *Winter Court*. We will become capricious, eager to speak and loath to listen. We will abandon interest in these events lest they prove themselves more energetic. We will become children, and prey to all of the child's hindrances. The laws of this challenge will remain within us and grow stronger as we age. If we stray as our interest wanes, the *Winter Court* will correct us."

The High-Warden spared the dying Crone a final glance and retreated.

The Winter Queen reclined, eyes flicking between the High-Warden and Winter Knight as the constellations' music quickened to match her drumming fingers. Her second hand rose to shoulder height and snapped open. "Let us begin." Her fingers ceased drumming and the music died. The Winter Knight spun, each stride resounding as he departed.

The High-Warden bowed to the Artist. "Thank you. I do not believe there is anything I can do for you, but please ask if so."

Her black eyes closed for an instant of consideration. "To serve was honor enough; call upon me in Antiark if ever you need my aid."

"I wish you well." He strode for the door, steps long but inaudible, grasped the crystalline handles and heaved them open, welcoming dawn into the *Night Court*. He exited and the doors vanished, their music fading.

He found Lord Adriat staring northward with hands clasped behind her. The wind rustled, encircling her with murmured sounds and fragrances and flecking her close-cropped hair with glittering frost. She turned, blinking away distant sights and older memories. "I am glad you survived; I owe you an apology. My behavior earlier was not as it should have been. I owed you greater respect but was ill-tempered from exhaustion, though that is a poor reason. To explain myself, my husband and son were injured in the recent conflict. When you first arrived, I feared for them. Thankfully, they have been improving ever since we started hunting those birds."

"There is no fault, we are both mortal—after a fashion—and the ability to love is a shared gift." He moved to the western edge and peered at Adriat. The city sprawled proudly against the *Annuir'Hyme* and up both the Rhawn's northern and southern flanks. The structures were short, never more than two stories and always disconnected. Waist-high walls fortified every roof, overlooking the matrix of narrow roads and alleys. The roads themselves were crafted of thin cobbles, easily broken in the event of siege or breach. The windows and doors all boasted stone embrasures and bundles of dried myrrh or fresh mints to ward off evil and enliven the dour stonework. The wealthier houses displayed silver chains at their thresholds, and wards inked at every corner.

Beyond the city, Adriat's walls merged with the Rhawn, their turrets carved in the resemblance of past northern lords or heroes, weapons held aloft as warning to any who would challenge the City of War. Despite their grandeur, the walls paled in the shadows of the Guardians: two immense statues towering before Winter's Gate.

Every Northern city served a purpose. Antiark—the twelfth city— housed The Northern dead and secrets. Jellark—the tenth city—served as the City of Forges and Labor, creating all the implements necessary for daily life, including armor and weapons. Dellak—the third city—was the City of Cloth, but its lords were also known for clairvoyance. Khensect—the eleventh city—was the deepest in The North and the City of Rangers. Adriat—the first city—was the City of War.

Lord Adriat shifted to stare southeast, watching the last of the carrion birds. She wore a thick fur oudakc and wrapped it tighter, shivering despite the warming day. Her high, prim cheekbones and large, soft eyes belied the truth told by the cut of her hair and the scars on her hands. "At least it's over; the *Winter Court* plays too many games, even if it's their nature." She sighed, the anger abandoning her as suddenly as it came. "The books say they were once kinder."

"They were, centuries before men inhabited The North. The *Winter Court* is a balancing influence; when The North grows warmer, more forgiving and kinder, the *Winter Court* hardens, taking on aspects of the wild. In elder days, only beasts, elementals, and immortals inhabited The North; it did not need to support the frailties of men. Our world was inhospitable, defiant of the Summer-lands, and so the *Winter Court* was kind to balance that cruelty."

"Sometimes, I wonder if The North is truly an improvement on the East. There is savagery here; it's just quieter, more lurking or brooding in nature. When I step on the Rhawn, I feel a trace of it, something primordial that loathes my touch. I feel anger well up within me, wild and foreign; I fear it, that wildness, despite embracing it with my *Burdening*."

"The North does not suffer the whims of change, Lord Adriat. It changes only at its own pace, at *Winsyria*'s pace. What you feel is not evil; it is the memory of a land that will not surrender, of elder days when the world gave no heed to mortal masters. It is the essence of wild things, of the Before-Age, when there was no time, only the continuous ebb and flow of an unfettered existence. If you openly embrace it, it will welcome you."

"Just how old are you?"

"I am the High-Warden of Winsyria; I was born of winter and erased by it. I have no name and no past, no age and no laws; I surrendered such things when I accepted this *Burden*. I know them, but they are no longer mine and will not be until my *Burden* is lifted."

"I suppose it doesn't really matter; I'm glad the *Winter Court's* concluded. You'd best come along though, I had the kitchens prepare something hot for us."

"I apologize for misleading you, but the matter of the *Winter Court* remains unresolved."

"What do you mean?" she asked, halting on the stair.

"I find myself participating in one of their games. But come, I will tell you while we eat."

"I should have known they would not release you without spinning webs." She pounded the stair's edge and descended.

"Do not fret, it was not in your power to avert what transpired."

"That does not matter; I was entrusted with keeping of the Glass Door and surveying the *Winter Court*."

"Do not presume to believe yourself in control of the *Winter Court*."

"I know, but all the same, I am held to higher standards than the other lords, both by myself and The North by virtue of being a foreigner."

"Accepting the *Burden* is enough for The North. Any extra weight is your own artifice."

She shook her head, dismissing the topic as inconsequential. "We are at war, and you have a task to accomplish. Tell me of the *Winter Court*, and I will aid however I can."

"The Winter Queen challenged my suitability for the *Burden* of High-Warden."

"She did what? Damn, her arrogance! To challenge your station is to challenge *Winsyria*!"

"Yes, but she validates it by declaring my selection an act of convenience. She holds that *Winsyria* would have selected another had he known this war loomed. Her reasoning was not intended for belief, merely as an excuse. It is the *Winter Court's* nature to play games, and I prove no exception. They arranged three tasks to test my and my opponent's strength and skill. The first was an ordeal of finding; I am currently engaged in the second, which entails hunting an evil hidden within Adriat upon the Rhawn's slopes."

"That ... that is impossible; I would have sensed it."

"This evil has lurked here for centuries, since before your time; there would never have been any disturbance to sense."

"I do not know... But then again, I cannot fathom the Rhawn or much of The North."

Removing their shoes in the prepared alcove, they entered a modest stone chamber nestled between two massive furnaces and blanketed in furs that smelled of apples. A round table occupied the center, surrounded by cushioned chairs and outfitted with a repast. Other chairs lounged before the kelbroks chuffing in their hearths, which shared the walls with shelves of well-loved books. A boy slept in the largest of the furnace chairs, clutching a stuffed Wolf and a throw blanket. He shifted, revealing a dark head of curls and high cheekbones.

Lord Adriat quietly approached her youngest son, and an older girl—perhaps thirteen—stood from the opposite chair with a look of anxious fatigue. She favored her father with a Northerners' brow and pronounced jaw. Her daughter began to speak, but Lord Adriat lifted a finger and whispered, "Your father and Drannen will survive." The girl sagged in relief and slipped an embrace around her mother, shoulders shaking with muffled tears.

After a moment of shared relief, Lord Adriat separated. "Lina, they both should be strong enough for visitors, take your brother and see them; it will do you all good." Lina nodded, woke her brother with a shake and escorted him from the room, whispering the news.

Lord Adriat sat at the table and pulled an empty plate toward her, piling it high with steaming fish, dark bread, and venison with one hand while the other poured coffee. After amassing her desired repast, she briefly cupped the clay mug in both hands and inhaled, savoring its warmth and aroma before returning it to the table and tearing into the bread. "Tell me what you can of this evil."

He sat opposite her but declined to eat. "The Crones said *It* hides on the Rhawn's foundations where children play. Is there a tract of the Rhawn known for infrequent deaths?"

She began carving into a roasted fish. "Yes, the northeastern corner of Adriat; we abandoned it years ago due to avalanches. Since then it has deteriorated into a ghost town. The precinct sits higher on the Rhawn than most and, while mostly solid, there are cavities in the surface that lead to a natural subterranean maze. My predecessors blocked what entrances they could, but many reopen in the storms. There have been deaths, one every three or four years."

"I suspect this evil conceals itself within those catacombs. *It* probably survives by luring children to eat."

"We search the catacombs every time a child goes missing, we would surely have sensed a lingering malice."

"These catacombs run deep, Lord Adriat; this evil can probably hide far beyond what your searchers would explore. There might be natural barriers *It* can surpass with negligible difficulty. Any rivers or chasms?"

"Yes, but they're relatively minor. The sheer number of routes pose a greater hinderance. Thankfully, we have guides familiar with them."

"I do not need their assistance; those catacombs are of the Rhawn."

"Those catacombs extend for miles; you cannot search them in less than two full Turnings. I know the *Winter Court* forbade you any assistance, but these are just men and they will carry no weight in the *Court's* decision."

"I doubt this evil will flee when a solitary man enters its abode, but rather see them, me, as prey. I doubt I will need to hunt for long."

"I doubt this evil will consider you helpless."

"How many years since the last child disappeared?"

"A girl, some two winters ago. Her father refused to give up and spent months searching until he bordered on madness. We tried to deter him, but he gave no heed and entered the catacombs with torches and a sword. We never saw him again. I wonder if he knew or suspected."

"Probably, if he carried a sword. I assume there is a Ranger-Warden who can show me where he entered?"

Lord Adriat laid her knife aside. "Please, let me accompany you. I know the *Winter Court* will doubt you further, but I need to help."

"... You doubt yourself, Lord Adriat, even after all these years." He shook his head. "This must cease; you cannot rule with doubt. You must find balance."

"It is better to think less of myself for my failures than to grow fat on my successes and allow my arrogance to grow untamed." She gave a wry smile.

"That is a matter of choice. It is the habit of men to forever deem themselves less or more than they are, when they should simply strive for honesty. Both unfounded arrogance and excess modesty are perilous." He stood with an obeisance. "You have my gratitude for your aid. I will return shortly. In the meantime, I suggest you spend time with your family; this war is not yet won, and Antiark will need you."

46

Winter's Wrath

The city around him was barren, like a slate scraped clean, haunted by an emptiness that lingered in the broken windows and crumbling doorways. The buildings loomed desolately, riddled with scaling fractures, careworn vines, and branches from the scattered trees. Rubble and snow obstructed most of the roads, sometimes rendering entire streets impassable, but it was the lack of sound that was most daunting. There was no creak of rusted hinges, no bird calls or skittering rodents, not even a breeze as the High-Warden and his deranger guide traversed the forsaken precinct.

They moved cautiously through the streets, her with an arrow already nocked and him with a constant vigil on their surroundings. A regular black wolf trotted beside them, whining with its ears pinned back and tail down. It had initially balked at the abandoned district but capitulated when his mistress pressed forward.

A creaking window shattered the silence, yanking the deranger about with bow fully drawn. The High-Warden glanced up as well, a sliver of the previously absent wind rustling his clothing and slithering toward an edifice. He caught a glimpse of tattered gray cloth disappearing from a window, then the wind eased the shutters closed.

"Just a ghost, nothing to fear," he said softly and resumed the journey.

The roads inclined sharply as they ascended the Rhawns' roots, converting to unscathed black stone while the houses first diminished in size then disappeared entirely until the only sign of human construction before them was the distant, northern edge of Adriat's outer wall. The earth ached with death, leeched dry by whatever evil lurked below, the stones and pebbles crumbling underfoot like poorly baked clay and all the flora eradicated. In all the expanse of rolling stone dells before them only one desiccated tree rose from the black rock. The desolation concluded at Adriat's wall, where the Rhawn's need to diminish themselves for mortals ended and the monster dared not venture.

The High-Warden growled quietly, as much from the earth's pain as goaded wrath. Of all The North only the Rhawn Mountains were disconnected from him, their essence too vast to perpetually contain in his consciousness. In sleeping, they would draw him into slumber; in wakefulness they would affect his reckoning, expanding it to transpire over eons rather than hours. This creature had exploited that debility and shrouded itself from him and his predecessors for centuries, even from the Lords Adriat.

He slowed where the city surrendered to the expanse of unamended foothills, extending a hand to delay his companion. "You have aided me sufficiently, Ereal, return to Adriat before whatever sickness afflicts this land infects you."

She nodded and wordlessly departed, strides lengthening and shoulders straightening as she escaped the tormented earth, her wolf close upon her heels. He watched her throughout her departure, ensuring she reached Adriat's inhabited precincts safely, before facing the lone tree.

It stood straight with a ring of splintered limbs and one crooked bough stretching northward, swathed in thin yellow veins of corruption. The Raven perched at the bough's center, keen eyes fastened upon him. He nodded a greeting and continued, prompting her to caw and follow.

The infection deepened the further he ascended, riddling the stone with gray veins and causing it to depress beneath his strides. Cavities appeared, most boarded up and fenced in, but some gaped wide and spilled a subtle malice, the kind one misses until they physically entered it. Derangers had no cause to visit this area, and normal men would not have recognized the evil beyond a vague illness or disquiet. No wonder the Lords Adriat never discovered it.

The High-Warden bypassed these initial pits, knowing the source lurked deeper in.

He found what he sought around midday; a cavity surrounded by land so broken it verged on impassable. He advanced to the edge and peered into the ravenous darkness, smelling the stench of old carcasses. There far below the surface, the land screamed, pleading for an end, any end. He felt hate also, insidious and festering.

He crouched and dipped his hand into the cavity, but the shadows slithered away from his touch. He withdrew his hand and the obscurity returned. "If you are involved with this," he said to the Raven, "there will be no mercy and no salvation. Remember this if you desire to linger: when wronged, The North cares nothing for justice or honor. You will scream with the vengeance wrought for your sins, and you will do so until the mountains break and the sea burns." The Raven cawed and dove into the cavity.

"Thus is your choice made, sorceress."

Kneeling down, he dug his fingers into the crumbling stone and sang a song older than the race of man. Tendrils of frost crept from him, striking out in all directions. The earth whimpered beneath him and sighed, falling into slumber as new life bloomed. Then he stepped to the precipice and plummeted down.

The force of his impact drove him to a hand and knee, but he suffered no ill effect. He spent a moment in preparation, allowing his eyes to adjust to the dark and exploring his surroundings, disturbing dust and littered bones. The intangible malice roiled all about him, enraged at his invasion and absolute. He inhaled, extending his dominion and dragging the malice toward him. It clawed at the walls and his skin, digging furrows in the first and blunting against the second. He spoke, words like thunder, "You've hidden from us a long time, Del'Vacion. But you are not really him, are you? You are just a shard, a watered-down facsimile eroded by time. You have survived enough to surpass the other pieces he splintered, to develop ambitions, but you remain an infant trying to survive on borrowed power, and your time's depleted."

"It is never up. I am eternal and I will rule this world or watch it and every heaven burn!"

The High-Warden faced the voice and the shadows scattered from a decrepit man with broken teeth and a broken mind. He held a tall staff in his left hand, the wood convoluted and blackened beneath its obsidian crown.

Sneering, the man spoke again, gesturing with a crooked finger, "You will submit to me one day, High-Warden; all this land will succumb, for I am the rightful lord of all nations, all mortal worlds!"

"You are but the shadow of the man you resemble, and he did not rule these lands." The High-Warden advanced, kicking aside skeleton fragments.

Del'Vacion scuttled back, hissing and brandishing his staff. "It was to be mine, the crown and the kingdom. I was the heir, and he took it from me. If you will not accept my rule, I will kill you!" Del'Vacion slammed his staff against the ground, shattering a skeletal hand. The native shadows coalesced about the staff's obsidian centerpiece and charged the High-Warden, only to sputter and disintegrate upon his chest.

"You made an error when you poisoned this land, Del'Vacion. It would have been wiser to flee; you could have feasted for centuries in the East without notice, perhaps growing strong enough to develop into an original being. Instead, you chose to remain, to poison my land."

Del'Vacion fled, merging into the gloom with a low hiss.

The High-Warden let him run; The North had found him now, and no sanctuary would protect him.

A cold wind swept from the cavern entrance, screaming as it hunted, blanketing the walls in ice and coating the floor in frost. The earth groaned, belching tenebrous fumes, exorcised. The temperature continued to plunge, strangling the malice and stalking its purveyor. The wind—gentler now—returned, gliding from the catacombs to enfold him with knowledge. Images rose before his eyes, lasting split-seconds with teasing sounds: the drip of water, the crack of ice, and the skittering of insects. Beneath those, there were words, Del'Vacion muttering to himself and cursing the High-Warden. His strides landed with inaudible force, betraying the truth of his existence; he was merely a hollow replica, an amalgamation of memories and desires sustained by stolen energy.

The High-Warden set off in pursuit, choosing an alternate route than his quarry and summoning the winds again. In answer they swept through the catacombs to their extremities, baring their secrets to his questing eye. He proceeded patiently, unleashing winter with every step, eradicating the lurking malice, healing the land, and forbidding his quarry's escape. Every step tightened the noose, forcing Del'Vacion closer.

The passageway began shrinking, forcing him to first bend, then crawl as its edges turned jagged. A distant, chittering cacophony reached him from ahead, increasing as he advanced until the very stone reverberated and a dim light colored the dark. The walls receded again, delivering him to the edge of a pit where insects crawled over one another in a roiling ocean of swollen carapaces and forked pinchers, devouring one another regardless of size or species.

A few insects were elevated above the rest on small daises, each bloated a dozen times their natural size and pearly white: the queens. There was only one for each species, but they still numbered scores: cockroaches, scorpions, beetles, centipedes and locusts of every variety, all rabid and black.

Ignoring the grotesque sea, he scanned for an alternate path without success, denied even so much as a crack along the wall. A breeze touched his cheek, revealing images of Del'Vacion in flight. He dispelled it with a thought and inhaled, causing the insects to still. The foul air grew dense, weighted with more than malice now. The queens released a universal screech and the masses convulsed, swallowing them into the hive as the strongest burrowed down. He crouched, exhaling a breath much longer than that which he inhaled. The cavern's ceiling cracked, a forest of icy veins erupting across the stone to coat the walls.

The insects panicked, scrambling for the warmth of the cluster. The ice reached them, and the foremost creatures grew sluggish, white threads creeping across their forms. The cold eradicated the malice as it expanded, freezing the sea insect by insect, queen by queen. The High-Warden exhaled through all of it, ceasing only as the last queen expired, her retainers unable to warm her through the winter he brought.

Seeing the exit across the chamber, he vaulted from the edge, sunk to his waist in the frozen carapaces and waded through. At the far ledge, he brushed off the skeletons and proceeded from the chamber, the wind murmuring in his ears once again. Del'Vacion continued to flee, seeking refuge in the centuries of accumulated malice.

That malice thickened as the High-Warden explored further into the catacombs, becoming a physical impediment and dulling his senses. The passageway slowly expanded enough for him to walk, then beyond the scope of his arms. Its jagged edges smoothed, replaced by a sheet of condensation, a skirt of lichen, and the odor of death.

He discovered the first skeleton in a disrupted pile, most of its small, fragile limbs broken or shattered. He crouched, sifting through the bones until he uncovered a forlorn skull. It was a child's, ravaged with fractures, perforations, and claw marks, and possessed by an unnatural chill; something lingered inside, imprisoned or unwilling to depart, and he doubted the second.

Setting the skull aside, he refocused on the mound, ruffling through half-rotted bones and cloth shreds until he found a piece of obsidian clutched in a skeletal fist. He liberated it and stepped back, pressing it against his ear. A voice answered him, too muffled to distinguish but sufficient to condemn the obsidian as a cage. But for what?

A murmur tickled at his mental defenses, drawing his gaze to where a spectral creature waited in silence, formless beneath a tattered cloak and barely as tall as the High-Warden's thigh. He inclined his head in greeting, but the specter just watched. "What is this?" he asked, lifting the stone. "And what are you?"

It gave no answer but cowered from the obsidian, cloth-bound hands rising to shield its face as it shrunk to the ground and prostrated itself in supplication.

Listening carefully for any sound it might make, the High-Warden stepped over the bone mound and crouched before the sorry creature. It inched forward, bleeding a thin black trail from its hands and feet. He reached behind himself, grasped a cloth shred from the bone pile and measured it against the creature. At this, it froze and whimpered. "Come here, child, I mean you no harm."

It crawled toward him, the blood from its hands growing thicker, and its whimpers louder until he lifted its cowl. The shadows within recoiled, swirling around a pair of shockingly blue, pleading eyes. Tears filled those eyes, giving testament to the pain and fear of centuries. The small mouth opened, the lips quivering to speak but issuing only the long whimper. He glanced from the child to the obsidian piece, knowing instinctively that breaking it would not free the child. "How am I to free you? Or is this not you, but the force that feeds off you?" Behind it, more specters accumulated, hundreds now, filling the passageway with a low susurration and an overpowering fear. He moved the obsidian piece closer and it shied away, scrambling back as its bandages turned red.

He relented and stood, the obsidian piece splitting perfectly down the center with a hairline fracture from his protracted contact. He muttered a curse and relinquished it, fearing to inflict further damage. The specter visibly calmed, straightening as he faced it again. "I cannot help you without knowing more."

The specters quietly addressed one another, their susurrations gradually increased until, with a final murmur, they fled down the tunnel, urging him to follow.

They led him downward, passing bone mound after bone mound, each adorned with a skull and an obsidian piece. A specter would halt beside every mound—unable to proceed—but there was never a break in the ghastly procession; whenever one fell—cowering—a dozen more materialized. Gradually, they became a river of gray cloth and ephemeral voices around him, never drawing close enough to touch.

The passageway continued to expand, swelling enough to pass for a chamber and acquiring images along the ceiling and floor, a line of hieroglyphics and runes obscured by dirt. He briefly attempted to decipher them without success, for they derived from the previous Age and exceeded his knowledge. Every so often, however, he noticed one he recognized: the *Roy'al* sigil.

The sound of running water summoned his attention ahead, causing the specters to halt and him to lengthen his stride. The gloom deepened further as he advanced, clutching at the specters as if to deny them. A breeze glided past, offering him visions of tunnels and caverns, of bone mounds and more writhing insect hives. Near the end of the flood, came one of a river, surrounding a blade-like islet illuminated by a thin beam of captured moonlight where the malice and the natural darkness of buried earth warred, and the Raven watched.

The flood of images ceased, returning him to the crowding specters. "Where are we going?" he asked. "And what lies on that island?" They gave no answer, simply watching and waiting. He obeyed their voiceless pressure and proceeded.

Time passed, delivering him to the foreseen river's bank. The specters streamed past, floating over the water to gather upon the islet. They faced the High-Warden in a crowd, calling him across from between a ring of pale braziers. His skin prickled at the sight and his mind itched; the islet concealed something ancient. The weight of centuries draped heavily here, taxing his mind. Whatever the islet held, it wasn't mortal.

He crouched, calming the turbulent river with a murmured word, and submerged his hand. Ice spread from his palm, expanding into a bridge that provided him passage.

The braziers faltered at his approach, shrinking until they died as he set foot on the islet. Something metallic gleamed in the pale moonlight, drawing him forward to gaze upon an abandoned ring. He refrained from touching it, but a premonition itched at the back of his neck. It was a Signet piece, though not that of any living king, and crafted into the likeness of a hundred accreting vines wrapped about one another. There was no sigil to mark its dynasty or architect, but its presence was profound, worrying at his mind with a quiet, blanketing power.

He finally took it, ignoring how his skin prickled, and spun the item between his fingers, searching for an inscription. "What are you?" It yielded no answer, and the pressure it exuded remained constant, unbroken by his touch. The amassed specters cringed, their murmurs a muted, harmonious whine, distressed by the displayed ring.

He returned his gaze to the Signet, recalling a description that might apply to it. The book had been ancient, almost rotting with years, written at this Age's commencement to preserve its predecessor's knowledge. If this ring was what the book described, then an era of upheaval approached.

"Do not touch that! It's mine!"

"This is not yours, for you are not truly Del'Vacion."

"It will always be mine! It can only be taken when it is given, and it always returns in blood!"

The High-Warden closed his fist upon the ring, and the stolen moonlight winked out, never to return.

Laughter reverberated the walls. "You dared to challenge me, High-Warden, and incurred the price of arrogance! You cannot defeat me; I am your rightful Lord and Master!

"I think not." All sound died at his words, deafening in its sudden absence.

Del'Vacion hissed, casting about, then smiled and thrust his hand forward, shadows coalescing into his palm. The High-Warden waited, impassive as the darkness swelled first into a roiling mass of threads larger than the High-Warden and then became a scorpion. The insect dropped and scuttled forward, rearing to tower over him. Del'Vacion screamed and thrust his staff forward. The scorpion responded by vaulting off a protruding boulder and slashing its pincers.

The High-Warden ducked beneath the strike and stepped into its reach, catching its left pincher in one hand and crushing its skull with the other. The corpse thundered to the ground and he stepped beyond it.

Del'Vacion lunged back, hurling a torrent of inky black threads that washed off the High-Warden and disintegrated.

The High-Warden advanced, calling the river to rise and swirl about his quarry on the far bank. Del'Vacion hissed and struck the surging water with his staff, converting it to black dust. But the water surged higher and his form diminished with every blow he struck until he stumbled backward, braced on his staff.

The High-Warden strode through the waist-high torrent, ice forming upon contact with his skin. Del'Vacion stumbled again and lurched to strike him. The High-Warden shattered the staff with a sweep of his hand, scattering its fragments across the rapidly freezing water.

Del'Vacion collapsed, scrambling over the razor ice until his hands bled inky malice. The High-Warden followed and grasped his collar, hefting the man aloft.

Del'Vacion began battering the High-Warden's arms, his breath growing labored and his form flaking black ash until he finally sagged. A moment passed and he spoke in a shuddering hiss, expending his last strength in a final curse, "I will kill this land, High-Warden, and you will see it die."

"That is not a curse you have the power to fulfill." He hurled Del'Vacion into the river, where he crashed through the ice and was consumed with a roar.

Leaving the river to its vengeance, he deposited the Signet into a pouch of red silk. Its presence vanished instantly, but he could not ignore what it signified; objects like the ring were often lost and never found without consequences.

For centuries, the Imperial Emperor Cardolyn Tyier had expanded his empire, swallowing all western lands unto the Rhawn in the North, the *Annuir'Hyme* to the East and the Inland Sea to the South. If the New Order deemed itself ready to confront Cardolyn Tyier, as their incursion implied, they had surpassed what anyone deemed possible. And now, compounding this impending conflict, one of the *Roy'al* Signets had resurfaced, and that was terrifying.

Winter crept into the cavern as he stood there, spreading pale luminescence and healing the earth. At first, the tattered creatures flinched from it, then they stood and immersed themselves in it, their clothes disintegrating. One by one, they fled heavenward while he and the Raven watched, waiting until every tortured soul had departed and everything surrounding him was ice before leaving.

Questions plagued him however: Who had buried the Signet here, how had they done so without alerting any of the Northern Lords or his predecessors, and why?

The Raven flew above him, silent and unfazed by the Signet's appearance.

47

Iconoclastic Beliefs

Waiting as his final alchemical potion simmered quietly, Slade wandered through the corridors of his mind, barely realizing it as he selected various knick-knacks and started juggling them.

If he succeeded tonight, it would ensure a journey across half the Paladin Empire. Neither the distance nor the dangers concerned him, however. Slade had crossed greater divides in the past. No, it was the nagging fear that if he left Senna would die. He'd never see her again. Worse was that he might have prevented it.

Slade scoffed at himself. What could he accomplish that Tiberius Whyte found impossible? Still, the thought lingered, and so fear and logic chased each other round and round.

At some point, descending footfalls interrupted his ruminations, waking him to the now violent grumbling of his potion. Hastily sweeping it from the warming stone, Slade snatched up a sieve and strained the pot into five cryptically annotated bottles with strange pendants floating inside them. At the same time, he listened for the distinguishing features of his guest.

Their stride possessed neither the measured thunder of Cain's boots nor the efficient stealth of a servant's, eliminating everyone except his mother or Feylin. This last mystery was solved by the notable lack of hesitance.

Pushing various items aside, he seated himself atop the table and patted the open space to his left. "So, Mother, what grim purpose brings you down into my tenebrous lair?"

"Why does anyone venture into a cold, mysterious place that's home to an eccentric man? I'm looking for answers to questions." Rather than immediately accepting his offered seat, Senna tiptoed through his moss and set about examining the new plants, poking around the cupboards and pressing her face to his long running experiments. "I'm curious about my son. He's been acting suspiciously of late and while that's common for him, it generally means he's getting himself into trouble."

"It sounds like he's usually in trouble. I wouldn't worry about it."

"Sage advice were it not for him planning an especially dangerous adventure this go around."

"Is he now?"

"Yes, he's leaving town." Senna scooted onto the table beside him. "Mostly, I wondered if he needed something for his journey."

"His journey? Are you sure he's actu–"

She gave him a level stare.

"Ah yes, that journey. Ahem, how did you know?"

"The signs are evident. Cain knows you're up to something and even Tiberius smells mischief. It would be downright embarrassing if me and my searing intellect didn't at least guess what you planned."

Slade rubbed his chin, scratching at the bristles. "I left the maps lying around, didn't I?"

"You've also been stock piling quite aggressively"—she gestured around the room—"leading me to suspect that you're preparing our poor helpless selves for your absence." She smiled at him, a gentle, understanding smile that flickered once or twice as it died. "Will you be gone long?"

"A couple months no more, about the time winter starts moseying on down south." He grinned, knocking his shoulder against hers. "I'll return once everybody's grown accustomed to life without me, riding atop a storm of hellfire and brimstone with all *Jaidar's* lackeys following in my wake."

She grinned back. "I'll hire a prophet to foretell the coming doom. In the meantime, do you need anything? Money? Food?"

"No, I've already collected the essentials."

"Your father wants to send a detachment of guards; foreign breeds of Weshac are creeping into the Empire and though most are disappearing to the Grain Sea, some aren't."

Slade kissed her cheek. "Tell him not to worry; I've recruited a fine company of rogues for companionship." Levering himself off the table, he cleared his throat, adjusted his shirt, and struck a pose. "First, he who brings trouble and who's vision doubles"—grinning he tapped one eye—"second, he who slays woes and bears witness to souls; last, she who serves three: the Lord of Lies, the King of Knives, and the Worst of Wives."

Senna clapped politely. "Very mysterious and an excellent beginning to your quest. Tell me, do you hunt treasure or dragons?"

"Treasure, dragons pose too slight a challenge."

Senna returned his kiss from earlier, feather light. "Wherever did my humble little boy go? Come, let's head upstairs, dinner left the oven fifteen minutes ago."

It didn't matter if she'd visited because she knew about his turmoil or not. Senna had settled his mind by smiling and sending him off without even knowing why he needed to go. Perhaps she thought it important that he leave, or perhaps she knew she'd survive the separation. It didn't matter.

'I wonder what she'd say if she knew I'm being contracted to help Carr'Selain steal Akravast?' Slade chuckled. *'Good luck, no doubt.'*

Dinner passed without incident, Feylin hesitantly regaling them with the afternoon's adventure, Cain responding dryly and then listening to Senna's chatter while a freshly returned Tiberius quizzed Slade on his concoctions; and Slade, delighted, responded comprehensively. At one point, Tiberius and Cain discussed recent troop movements, but that topic closed when Slade developed too keen an interest.

The difficulties arose when Slade excused himself for an evening stroll and his fellow diners lauded the idea. When polite efforts failed to dissuade them, Slade confessed his intentions to carouse through the night, drink himself insensible, marry half-a-dozen women, and institute a new world order. Senna patted his hand, saying they'd stroll in the other direction.

In truth, he needed to instruct his little ducklings on their assignments for tonight. So after turning a corner, he discarded his strolling pace for one better suited to a schedule. Already *Sammahale* rested at the eleventh-Vigil, threatening to drop below the horizon in less than an hour.

As he trotted toward his destination, Slade inspected the statues stationed on each corner. Most resembled either humans or animals and fell into one of three categories: beautiful, serviceable, or expedient. A doe exemplified the first type, while dogs and cats occupied the second. Birds monopolized the final category for obvious reasons. Of these, Slade sought a bird.

While his minions possessed a general idea of tonight's agenda, other parties were less apprized. Madame Roshfen didn't realize Slade planned to rob the governor tonight, and Crannir was uninformed as to the whole affair. A courtesy letter would ensure both meetings proceeded swiftly.

Slade crossed under an archway into one of Tellor's lesser markets, the encroaching night leaving it barren and melancholy.

'Such is always the case,' he mused, striding to a plinth squashed between a bakery and a painter's shop. *'Not that I'd change anything, the desolation provides an excellent opportunity for a smattering of alternative religion.'*

The plinth, despite its beautiful engravings, was insignificant compared to its charge: an ivory wren whose subtle yet elegant markings teased an impossible degree of life from the stone.

Digging into his satchel, Slade withdrew a fragile sheet of paper, the contact dusting his gloved fingers with a green powder. He rolled it into a thin tube and bound the paper with indigo silk, laying it alongside the ivory wren. One sharp, efficient movement later and a match hissed to life, leaving yet another scrape among the countless that already marred the plinth.

At the match's insistence, the paper kindled to a bright, multi-colored flame, releasing a hint of rosemary followed by vanilla then sandalwood. It was an expensive blend and one of the few that could awaken a bird, though its true expense resided in Slade's inability to reproduce the substance, meaning he had to actually pay for it.

Before his eyes, the bird transitioned from inanimate stone to a breathing creature. It began with a partial softening of feathers, then the sparking of intelligence and finally idle movements that culminated with it stepping onto Slade's proffered hand.

It weighed less than one might expect, something he attributed to its subsistence on the ephemeral. Pushing such ruminations aside, he cleared his throat and spoke with slow articulation, "A private message to Madame Roshfen from Slade Lammerock. Madame Roshfen, I have some business to discuss with you. Please expect my visit later tonight." Slade clicked his tongue, signaling the end of the message. "Second message to Crannir Quen from Slade Lammerock. We've business to discuss; start a fire and expect my arrival soon." After clicking his tongue a second time, Slade tossed the wren skyward where it gave a single chirp before darting off.

That task finished, he strode for the market's center to prepare as his protective detail skulked out from their respective alleyways. The first man carried a wooden crate, his face pink from exertion, while the second, Naric, transported a pair of jewel encrusted candelabras.

Upon nearing, both faltered, espying what dangled from his hand and Slade, grinning, waved them closer. "Don't be shy, set the box down here."

The first man, a pasty fellow of admirable girth, edged forward and deposited his burden, eyes flicking in every possible direction. "Uh, boss, what are you doing?"

"Oh, nothing much, just enacting a simple ritual." Producing a stick of chalk and crouching alongside the box, Slade marked the cobblestones with a succession of long, sweeping, vivid red lines. "You worry too much; relax, learn to sail down river. Trust me, Annaise, it really is the wisest strategy: trusting me that is."

"But Slade"—Naric leaned over his shoulder—"you're drawing a pentacle in the middle of an Imperial market."

"Bah"—Slade flicked the chalk away—"rumors and spiteful tales; don't trust everything you hear, particularly when it concerns me."

"Bu-bu-but this isn't a rumor," Annaise spluttered, clutching at his pendant of *Eneki's* burning wheel and book. "This-this is sacrilege. How dare you—"

Slade gave a polite cough. "What's immoral about the expression of new ideas, or the desire to parade one's art before an adoring crowd? Are you a misoneist? Do you abhor free speech? Is art a foreign concept to you?" With each question, Slade gestured, one hand holding something bright and reflective while the other held something that flopped about wetly. "It's not as if I'm conducting a profane ritual or anything exciting."

"But—"

"Now now, don't you realize it's unprofessional to argue with your employer? Here, hold this for a moment." Slade thrust a rabbit carcass toward Annaise, its intestines flopping about in a grotesque imitation of dance while its vacant staring eyes swung from the ends of long cords. Annaise, a man of unquestionable bravery, decided wisdom was indeed the better part of valor and fainted; sanity, after all, must be preserved.

Without losing stride, Slade flipped the rabbit toward Naric who, to his credit, caught the poor animal. Immediately the man's brows scrunched, followed by him repeatedly squeezing the rabbit carcass, each renewed application causing a loud squelch. "It's false."

"Of course it's false." Slade pulled a robe from his satchel, the demonically inscribed fabric swirling ominously. "Do you have the slightest notion of how difficult it is to preserve fresh meat at this time of year? So difficult the gods tried issuing it as a divine labor before all the heroes failed catastrophically." Slade slipped the robe over his head, directed his arms through the sleeves and donned the hood. "Well, how do I look?"

"Exceedingly sinister." Naric bent to collect the strange broad knife Slade had discarded. "But what, if I may inquire, is the purpose behind these preparations?"

"We, my Slayer of Woes, are summoning a demon of the most spectacular damnation." Naric raised one eyebrow first, then raised its sibling when Slade took the knife and started detaching pieces to give it a serrated edge.

"We're committing this heinous sacrilege armed with nothing more than a false carcass and a knife I'm certain would find its nemesis in warmed butter?"

"Of course we are. Modern practitioners of the nefarious arts haven't the vaguest idea what they're doing—hand me those candles, please—according to them, it's all pomp and ceremony and strict rules. You need this many torches, this many sacrifices, this type of incense, this type of accent, in this location at this time of night during this time of the month; it's quite mind-numbing." In a twinkling, both candelabras sat atop the crate, blazing away with all the cheerful sacrilege they could muster. As a final act, Slade arranged his sacrifice between the two candelabras and impaled it with the knife. "There, all done."

"Hmm, looks a smidgen off-center to me," a newcomer pronounced, prompting both men to lean in for a closer look.

"He may be correct," Naric murmured.

"You think you so?"

"Slade arranged it fine," Samara interrupted from just behind the approaching Haram. "Let's finish our business here and move on; I don't want to explain this to the Town-Watch."

"Has everyone arrived?" Slade asked.

Harram shrugged. "More or less. Your profane temple has our brave soldiers cowering in their alleyways."

Slade whirled about, dropping into a wide legged stance and chest expanding to unleash a hurricane. "Cowards! Wretches!" he bellowed. "Here my words and tremble, for I damn you to the blackest pits of my service. Pray, I command you, pray for *Jaidar's* aid because his damnation is infinitely preferable to mine." Slade swiveled back toward his lieutenants, the very soul of good humor. "Alright, we have several tasks to complete tonight, so I hope you all slept well. If everything goes according to plan, we'll catch that much lauded disease known as sickening wealth." Slade grinned, rubbing his hands with as much glee as any money-grubbing merchant.

"Before we get too excited," Harram interrupted, raising a hand though his impressive stature made that unnecessary. "I snooped around the mansion earlier. The governor's doubled his guards, changed their patrols, and removed the usual soldiers from rotation. All our intel's useless."

"Finally." Slade threw his hands into the air. "I informed him of our impending visit ages ago."

Naric crossed his arms. "That seems a bit fool—"

"Yes, yes, I know," Slade said, flapping the budding reprimand away. "It's irrational, it's insane, and what creepy crawler ate my brain while I was sleeping? Tediously, I'm not insane, merely unconventional. Your efforts tonight have a single, specific purpose. My efforts are less restrained and the guards are a result thereof, though not entirely unrelated to your purpose.

Normally, a child in phosphorescent clothes could steal from the governor and escape by riding atop molasses. These additional measures will ensure we impress upon Carr'Selain our abilities."

"We don't need to impress the bloody Thieves' Guild," Samara snapped, still playing the part of his devoted follower. She was bound to the charade until he unmasked her before the entire crew or allowed an escape attempt to succeed. "We're doing fine without them, and I don't care if it's less productive, it's safer than robbing the gods-damned Imperial Emperor."

"O ye of little faith."

"Slade, Cardolyn Tyier is god-spawn and the Imperial Emperor to an entire nation. What could you possibly do when he decides to kill us?"

It was a pertinent question that deserved an answer. The future, however, was an expensive luxury and the truth even more so; therefore he grinned his most assured grin. "Leave such trivialities to me."

"I'd be a lot happier knowing you actually have a plan."

"I do have a plan. I'm simply not revealing it. The poor thing has stage fright. In the meantime, follow my present and less consternating schemes to significant wealth and slight infamy." Samara's shoulders caved in silent resignation, and Slade clasped his hands behind him, pacing in front of them. "Tonight our tasks are simple. We must divert or distract the guards and nullify the servants, after which we raid the vault, ferry our spoils to the wharf, and abscond with unseemly haste."

"Are you planning one spectacular distraction or various smaller ones?" Harram asked, pensively scratching at his beard.

"Various smaller ones. Samara, the servants require your subtle talents. Harram, be an absolute sweetheart and organize the transportation of our prize; Crannir's assassins and I shall administer to the guards."

"The governor poses a challenge to our aspirations as well," Naric warned, his slow, articulate speech contrasting the brisk efficiency of his fellows. "According to my acquaintances, he suffers from mild insomnia and thus frequently ventures down to the kitchens for the remains of supper."

"The governor's out of town for the week; we needn't worry about him. Your task, my friend, is subduing any nobles who sleep near the treasury or the governor's rooms." Reaching into his satchel, Slade extracted a vial of shimmering pink liquid. "Take this and avoid all contact. If even a drop spills, take one of these immediately." Three gray tablets swapped hands, lending an air of danger to their shimmering predecessor.

Naric, accepting a handkerchief from Harram, wrapped the vial before tucking it down his breast pocket. "What are its effects?"

"Fifteen minutes after contact the victim will begin experiencing very … amorous thoughts. Place three drops on their pillow and repeat the process with his or her partner. Bind and gag any lonely hearts."

Harram shuffled surreptitiously away from Naric. "Is pink its natural color or did you alter it?"

"I altered it, naturally." Slade grinned then faced Samara who, despite herself, began exuding the same excited greed as her fellows. "These are for you." He proffered three bottles, each stoppered with pale wax. "They're sleeping potions, administer some to the servants' food."

"Why aren't we knocking out the entire mansion?"

"Because the nobility and the guards eat before the servants, making it exceedingly difficult to sedate all parties. Harram, take the remaining crew with you. Safety is your primary concern, so post watchers and prepare diversions."

"How are we supposed to extract the gold?"

"I recently cultivated a disturbance in the mansion. It damaged several choice sections and there's now a pulley system erected outside the eastern balcony; it just so happens to excel at lowering treasure chests onto specially prepared carts. Transport the gold to the governor's private dock and assemble the waterproof crates."

A corner of Naric's mouth curled up. "I take it you're raiding the governor's library again."

Slade grinned, throwing his arms wide. "On this historic occasion, we rescue every book he's cruelly imprisoned." Grin fading to a mere quirk of the lips, he stepped forward and gripped each of Samara and Harram's shoulders. "May *Kis'Maat's* benign eye rest upon you and if it does not, remember to cheat. Now off you go." He shooed them away, offering another silent blessing before removing the robe and kneeling to arrange it like someone had cast it aside after being discovered.

Naric lingered, watching Slade from across the altar. "Are you prepared for the ramifications of tonight's caper? We're stealing an entire quarter of revenue from Tellor, one of the richest cities in the Empire. Cardolyn himself will take notice. Are you prepared to forsake your obscurity and step forward onto a grander stage?"

"Yes, though mine will be a brief tour as the audience will soon forget, turning shocked gazes toward Carr'Selain and the sheer audacity of his attempt on *Akravast*. I'll recede into the shadows, allowed to tinker and fiddle and maneuver my pieces into a new, more advantageous position: the interior of the Thieves' Guild."

Naric nodded, eyes traveling the city's gradual ascent to where it crested with the governor's mansion. Still he lingered, letting a hesitant silence grow between them. "I know you safeguard your intentions jealously, and I've attempted to respect that, but I'm … concerned. What of your parents? This adventure could prove harmful to Cain if scrutiny fell upon your family."

Slade crossed his legs beneath him and then leaned back onto his hands, eyes gazing up at the waking stars. "Out of all possible outcomes, that is the one to be avoided. Cain would ruin himself trying to atone for my crimes and he'd never accept my help, not then or ever again, not even if I proved the money was honest. I'd be unclean and forever doubted."

"Tomorrow when this report reaches Cardolyn Tyier, he will automatically question the Thieves' Guild and they'll inevitably redirect his suspicions here."

"Luckily a bare handful know and that"—Slade raised a bottle, the pendant floating within clinking softly against the glass—"is a manageable number."

"Deceit is a fragile web easily broken by complication. Be careful."

Slade grinned. "Whenever am I reckless?"

"Reckless? Never. Unnecessarily complicated? Frequently." Naric nudged the unconscious Annaise with a toe. "Regarding complications, what would you suggest for this particular one?"

"Nothing. He'll awake, find himself abandoned by a profane altar, and rush home to hide under his covers. We'll collect him in the morning."

With another shrug Naric glided toward the nearest alley, lifting a hand in farewell.

Slade also lifted a hand, the act mattering more than if Naric saw it. Farewells completed, he departed for the next order of business. Soon enough he lurked across from his destination, spying through the windows as his assassins puttered around their temporary home.

48
The Art Of Socializing

Excepting Sora, the assassins were all home. Crannir idled in a chair with a book, Lydia paced, Jamus juggled a dozen tiny fireballs, and Tehroc slept on the couch alongside some half-eaten snacks.

Players waiting for a game they neither wanted nor controlled.

Dropping to his butt, Slade pulled off his boots and, in the dark, produced six nails, a hammer, and two metal plates. Hastened along by a chilly damp seeping into his socks, he affixed the metal plates to his boots, returned them to his feet and then delved back into his satchel for a decanter. This, upon being uncorked, exhaled a sharp, tangy aroma that he briefly smothered with a soluble nut powder.

Finished, he collected his belongings and crossed to a side alley, tiptoeing around the usual collection of fastidiously ordered refuse crates until he found a suitable window. After searching for observers, Slade stretched up and grabbed a mortar joint. Seconds later, he slipped inside the second-floor window.

Purposefully landing with a muted thump, Slade paused and then tut-tutted when the idle chatter continued below. During the succeeding and final preparations, clothing was adjusted, stolen uniforms were laid atop beds, and four beautiful glasses escaped from his satchel's bottomless stomach. As a final touch, the decanter was hung from a finger and allowed to swing as he crossed the room.

———

Crannir had fallen out of the conversation, distracted by a million thoughts and dragged ever deeper into lethargy by his dangerously comfortable chair, never mind the unseasonable fire grumbling on his right. Why Slade Lammerock wanted a fire was beyond him, but Crannir had shelved that mystery for the one behind Slade's impending visit. Somehow, he doubted it was to throw a party.

They all gnawed the same mystery, at least until an ominous footstep sounded overhead. Conversation and movement ceased. Then a measured distance after the first, another thump landed.

Nobody glanced to Crannir for instructions. Lydia snuck to a cabinet stationed near the back, opening its bottom doors and removing a brace of knives before freeing the short sword strapped to its roof.

The intruder's footsteps turned down the upstairs hall, still moving with the same measured pace.

Tehroc donned his boots and knelt beside an awkward carpet, flipping one corner to reveal the trapdoor underneath. Lifting it by way of an empty knothole, he revealed another cache of weapons.

Jamus grabbed an iron-bound staff from the front door and Crannir caught the short-sword Lydia tossed him, laying its naked blade across his knees.

Overhead the stairway door creaked open, and the assassins dispersed to their predetermined corners, leaving Crannir at center stage. He would distract their uninvited guest, be it a thief or something worse, so they could strike, killing if necessary.

The intruder's boots pounded down the staircase, no longer muffled by the ceiling. Greedily, they also claimed first introduction, but Crannir paid little attention as a creeping suspicion eased into his mind. What sort of intruder attached metal plates to his boots? The kind who wanted to announce their presence.

A green sash lined with silver runes lowered into view.

Crannir glanced at his companions and saw his own suspicion mirrored back at him.

A hand appeared, crystal decanter swinging idly from one finger. Its sibling followed, holding a cluster of glasses between its fingers. Then the intruder's face dropped into view, its owner bending forward so he could inspect his audience. "Hello, Crannir." Slade smirked at them one by one, exuding such arrogant superiority even Jamus' hackles rose. "It's nice to see I haven't caught you off guard." Lydia uttered an indignant sound, provoking Slade into crouching down and leaning out over the room, his arm braced against the ceiling. "Don't hiss, Lydia, it's unfeminine."

Descending with suddenly silent steps, he reached the floor and observed everything with a cursory inspection. His hosts, conversely, stared solely at him. Jamus flinched every time Slade's boots should have clomped, Tehroc broke eye contact whenever their gazes met, and Lydia stared as if she might burn holes through his skin. Regardless of their reaction, each assassin stored their weapons when Slade treated them to a pointed glance. Except Lydia, who gripped hers tighter.

Finishing his silent inspection, Slade ghosted to a quaint table set behind the couch and arranged the glasses atop it. "I suppose you're curious as to what Sora is doing?"

Around him the assassins' eyes flicked toward each other, this simple gesture no doubt confirming his supposition. "I assume you know where he is?" Crannir asked, signing for the others to remain silent.

"Yes. He had pressing business elsewhere, so we struck a deal between ourselves." Uncorking the decanter, Slade filled each glass with careful, controlled movements. "However, this is no honorable agreement between gentlemen; this is the staying of an execution and the beginning to a long uncomfortable relationship." Slade smirked at them. "Sora didn't just step further than you; he ran, leapt, sprouted wings, and flew."

Crannir offered up a silent prayer to *Morgan* that Sora never regretted his decision. "What type of pressing business?"

Slade selected a glass, holding its rim between his fingers as he navigated the various obstacles between him and Tehroc. "The type I'll leave shrouded in mystery, but let your imaginations run wild. Perhaps he had an important rendezvous, or perhaps his mother suffered from financial troubles. Believe whatever you like so long as it is not the truth."

Haltingly, Tehroc took the glass' delicate stem between his fingers, later changing his grip so he could brush a thumb across the glass' frolicking otter. "Thank you."

Slade's lips quirked into a slight smile. "You're welcome." He retraced his steps and chose another cup, this one adorned by a bird wreathed in icy flames. "Now to address what I assume is your other, more pertinent question, I'm calling in that favor you promised me." Slade presented Jamus with his glass of wine then motioned to an unoccupied chair. "Sit. As for the task, you shall infiltrate the governor's mansion tonight and distract the guards. You may formulate your own strategy, or I can suggest one; it doesn't matter so long as I'm aware of what you intend, and it diverts any pesky soldiers from the eastern side of the mansion."

Crannir swallowed, mouth suddenly feeling very dry. It was ludicrous, the type of mission he would have dismissed instantly if not for that bloody contract. "How are we supposed to distract a veritable army?"

"From my perspective, you have three immediate options: the first of which is devising a harebrained scheme amongst yourselves." Slade began a scenic journey around the room. Crannir, however, refused to swivel as the man left his sight, ignoring the prickles crawling down his spine and staring straight ahead when Slade reached over his shoulder to dangle the third glass before him. "Your second and third options are to enlist mercenaries or request my aid. Be careful though, two of the three options are … ill-advised."

Crannir set the glass atop his arm rest—its ornamenting albatross becoming saturated in the fire's cherry-orange light—and opened his mouth only to close it. Should he capitulate to Slade's wishes, indebting himself, or formulate his own plan despite knowing nothing about tonight's events or the governor's mansion.

"Miss Lydia," Slade said calmly, rousing Crannir from his inner debate, "I would advise against that."

Lydia paused, the final glass raised to her lips. "Why in the gods-damned Abyss not?"

"Because this, wayward child, is meant for another." Slade caught her arm, deftly liberating the wine when she tried drinking it anyway. "I don't begrudge you a taste, of course, but insider knowledge warns me that you would find it exceedingly disagreeable."

Lydia's eyes narrowed. "How so?"

"I'm afraid you'll simply have to accept my word, call it an experiment."

Jaw clenching, she stalked away and Slade, giving a little shrug, readdressed Crannir. "Shall we proceed?" Snagging an unoccupied chair, he strode toward the fire and, after pausing to kick the displaced rug back over its trapdoor, set the chair down across from Crannir. "Well, have you decided yet?"

"Alright," Crannir sighed, rubbing his face. "How would you prefer we handle this?"

Slade's answering smile startled Crannir. He'd expected arrogance or perhaps smirking triumph; instead, he was met with a pleasant, albeit mischievous, grin.

"Because of certain activities of mine, the governor's hired many new faces. You'll be able to masquerade as guards, feign inebriation, intoxicate a few bystanders, and start a full-scale brawl."

Crannir's brow creased. "Do the guards sleep in the mansion or in barracks?"

"Barracks on the property."

"Imperial Army or Theanne?"

"Theanne. I'm not so cruel as to pit you against the Imperial Army."

"How long before the Imperial Army arrives from the city?"

"Not sure. They'll be taking a detour along the way."

"They will?"

"Yes."

"Brief or extended?"

"Extended."

"Do I need to be concerned about this detour?"

"No."

"It's … possible. What about–" Before Crannir's next question, something fragile expressed a violent distaste for being dropped. He whirled and found Lydia standing above the shattered remains of the decanter, clutching her throat as an ugly purple slowly colored her face.

All thoughts of Slade Lammerock vanished and Crannir sprinted across the room, catching Lydia just as her supporting hand slipped from the table. Shutting out her horrid gasping wheezes, he lowered Lydia to the ground and flung an arm in the door's general direction. "Tehroc, fetch a doctor; Jamus, see if you can force air into her lungs. Lydia, gods damn it, what did you do?" She thrashed in his grip, freeing herself until Jamus fell to his knees and pressed down on her chest. A moment later, she arched upward with the slightest of gasps. Jamus' magic wouldn't be enough though. "Come on, Lydia, speak to me. Tell me what the hell happened."

Wrenching an arm free, she thrust it at Slade.

"Him? What did he do?" Then Crannir saw his wine glass, forgotten and precariously balanced on the armrest of his chair. "You poisoned her!"

"Now that's a baseless accusation. If anything, Lydia poisoned herself. I did warn her against tasting this particular wine. Walnuts are its preeminent flavor, which you might have realized if you took a sip as courtesy demands." Slade strolled over with hands tucked into his pockets, the steel-bound thump of his boots adopting an ominous tone.

"Walnuts? How do you–"

"Because I do." Slade's voice rose to a half shout, "Tehroc, the situation's well in hand. There is no need for a doctor."

Crannir burst to his feet, storming across the few steps separating them. "There's no need for a doctor?" He shoved Slade in the chest, forgetting all sense of caution. "Is this some cruel joke? Were you choking back laughter as you poured the wine? She's dying, you bleeding idiot, or didn't you realize her allergy's fatal."

"I know exactly how deadly it is, a degree of knowledge that extends to all of you and your weaknesses."

Tehroc thrust back through the door, slamming it against the opposite wall. "What happened? Did somebody have medicine?" His frantic eyes settled on Lydia's now swelling face, confusion sweeping in to replace agitation before surrendering to outright horror and the whispered, "May you face judgement at *Morgan's Glass Throne*, Slade Lammerock."

The sentiment was met with a dismissive wave. "Jamus, for example, has a wife and two children, one of which is developing into a powerful fire mage like his father. Tehroc"—Slade favored the second assassin with a curt glance—"also had a wife, but she died in childbirth, leaving him a wealthy estate and many, many dependents. As for Lydia, well, we all know her secret. In culmination, there's you, Crannir. I'm pleased to inform you that I'm intimately acquainted with every gory detail, every shady secret, every grievous decision of your past. Between us, it's enough to give children nightmares." Slade stepped around the appalled Crannir. "Shoo," he ordered, kicking Jamus aside and kneeling in his place.

"What are you doing?" Jamus cried, shoving back at Slade. "She needs my help."

"Yes, but she need's mine more." Slade caught the man's wrist in a lock, twisting to the edge of discomfort and forcing Jamus back. "If I'm allowed to work, I can resolve this issue promptly. If I fail, I will have broken the terms of our contract and you three may brutally murder me. If, that is, the contract doesn't exact its retribution first."

Everyone looked to where Crannir stood trembling with clenched fists, but he didn't answer the unspoken question; not until Lydia's gasping wheezes broke through the roar building in his mind. "Fine, just do something."

Returning to Lydia, Slade withdrew a sprig of fresh leaves and a vial of liquid from his satchel. "Please understand, this was not without purpose. There are two truths I'd prefer if you recognized: the amount of control I can exert over your lives, and … well, something that's harder to believe, and belief starts with acknowledging that my warnings are not frivolous. This"— he tapped Lydia's throat—"should serve as an adequate demonstration. The second step is accepting that I feel no animosity toward you."

"You picked a funny way of showing it," Tehroc snapped, pacing and blatantly struggling with the inspired notion of strangling him.

"How so? I am saving Lydia's life—" One of her arms slipped free, flailing at him in an only partially controlled attack, but Slade trapped it under a knee. "I also spared your lives during our first encounter and supplied a strategy for tonight despite being equally well-served by abandoning you to an ill-conceived plan." Slade plucked the leaves free, rubbing each between his fingers until they became a moist, crumpled green. "Considering our acquaintanceship could have begun with my grizzly murder, I should think my goodwill has been established." Forcing Lydia's jaw open, he placed the leaves under her tongue. "The final step is realizing that everything I do has a specific purpose. You may not understand my instructions, but that hardly means you should ignore them. Lydia, once again, is a glaring testament of this." He poured a single drop from the vial onto his finger and, holding the woman's head steady, rubbed it across her swollen purple lips. Tapping out a second, larger dose, he treated her nose, applied some beneath the eyes and then massaged her windpipe. "So in the future, it'd be wonderful if you'd recognize that you can and probably should trust me."

All of a sudden, Lydia inhaled a massive gasp of air, hacking and coughing until she recovered enough to react violently toward Slade. Her fist carried more anger than actual power though, merely tickling a grin from him. "Rest for now," he said, laying a hand upon her forehead. "You can punish me later." He stepped away, letting her friends swarm in.

"Crannir," she gasped, "go kill him."

Crannir delayed as long as possible before joining Slade by the fire, hoping he would simply depart. When that became a clear fantasy, he marshalled himself and approached the young, slim, foreboding man.

Slade gave him a cursory inspection then nudged Crannir's former seat with a toe.

Sighing, the assassin obeyed. "The excitement isn't over yet, is it?"

"One's travails never truly end. Take heart though, this next surprise shouldn't require audience participation." Slade brought out a sheaf of papers and offered them to Crannir. "These are your contracts to me, the Assassins' Guild, and Syndros Nomarr, as well as that unfortunate document wherein you promised to kill me." A measure of his arrogance resurfaced. "They all belong to me now."

"Impossible." Crannir tore the papers from Slade's hands. "Syndros Nomarr would never sell our contracts. Our records are perfect. Our loyalty is unquestionable. Our"—his breath caught as the tips of his fingers began prickling, reacting to a powerful magic—"... not unless he knew we'd signed a blood-contract."

Upon induction to the Assassins' Guild, every man would sign two contracts, one promising their loyalty to the guild and the other to Syndros Nomarr. Neither compared to a blood-contract.

"Don't worry"—Slade reached out and gave the contracts a light tug— "I ensured he wouldn't ... tie up loose ends."

'By Morgan's grace, I hope he's telling the truth.' Taking a deep, steadying breath, Crannir released the contracts. "So, we belong to you now." Silence stilled everyone and everything except the fire. Even Slade adhered to it. Then a strange expression crept onto the young man's countenance, confusing Crannir until he recognized it as barely controlled glee.

"Nonsense." Abruptly forsaking any attempt to conceal his delight, Slade tossed the contracts into the fire and sat back, grinning as Crannir's heart simply stopped.

A moment later, Crannir was diving toward the fire, repeatedly snatching into the flames but failing to stop the inevitable blaze. "What have you done, you gods-damned fool?"

"I think that's fairly evident. You're now free men, excluding Lydia, who's a woman."

"You burned the gods-damned blood-contract. Do you have the tiniest inkling of what could happen as a result of that sheer unmitigated idiocy?" Crannir kicked the fireplace bricks, then whirled to look for his short sword. It stood beside Slade, sheathed and idly turning as he twirled the pommel.

"Seeing as our exteriors remain our exteriors, and our minds continue puttering along with their modicum of sanity, I assume nothing will happen. I foresee no giant explosion, no century-long curse, not even a paper cut. By destroying the contract, I've simply terminated it as was my prerogative from the start."

Crannir massaged his temples and collapsed into his seat, waiting until the vertigo retreated and his heart stopped pounding to ask the obvious question. "Now you've burned our contracts, what's stopping us from cutting your throat?"

"Stupidity isn't something I ascribed to you, don't make me start. Barely ten minutes ago I demonstrated my appalling control over your lives. If self-preservation doesn't suffice, consider the lack of profit. Without your contract, who'll pay for my head?"

"There's always personal satisfaction," Crannir muttered under his breath, before forcefully shunting aside his resentment. It served no purpose. "Why purchase our contracts if you intended to burn them?"

"Because there's still a job for you to complete, and it's simpler for me if I needn't worry about a man who's chained between two masters."

Crannir gave a short bark of laughter. "What makes you think we'd consider helping you?"

"There are worse friends to make."

"Not many."

"Agree to disagree. I'd make a convenient associate, either as a shadow looming behind your shoulder or as a secret ally."

"And I suppose you want our services free of charge? In retribution for planning to assassinate you."

Slade flapped this suggestion aside. "On the contrary. If I arranged a date between you and death yet failed to offer suitable compensation, how could I expect your loyalty to remain loyal?"

"The thing about guild contracts is they protect our interests as much as the guild's; it's one of their few benefits. Once this caper's finished, what's guaranteeing your good faith? Forgive me, but I don't trust you enough to walk on the same side of the street."

"If I intended to murder you from the beginning, why did I hire the piper and make you dance?"

"You're a sociopath who enjoys manipulating those around you."

"In that case, who would I play puppets with after killing you?"

"You're not reassuring me."

Slade grinned. "I know. How about this, peruse all the rumors you've heard of me. Do any of them suggest I'm dishonorable?"

Crannir quizzed his fellow assassins with a glance, receiving their shaken heads before responding. "No, they don't. Rumor suggests everything else but not that."

"Excellent. Now if the rumor mill hasn't heard it, can it be true?"

'Believable but not exactly empirical evidence.' Crannir conducted a second conference, but his friends only shrugged, so he crossed his arms and sat back with a sigh, one finger tapping against his bicep. *'Would this be beneficial? Yes. Do I think he'll kill us after? No. Would he abandon us? Best to assume he would. Could we survive that? Probably. Will he pay us? I don't know, but Naric seems to trust him.'* Crannir sighed again. "Alright, I accept your offer. We shall start a brawl in the governor's barracks, *Morgan* help us."

"You won't need his help anymore, you've got me. Also, if you're amenable, I'd like to extend your service beyond sparking a minor war; this second task will entail the sequestering and subsequent protection of my crew as they ferry valuables through pirate-infested waters. The voyage commences at sunrise."

"We're assassins, Slade; we don't protect people; we kill them."

"Well then, this should be a nice change of pace." Slade rose, flipped the sword—pommel over tip—and caught its sheathed blade, offering Crannir the hilt. "Your compensation will fall under the generous category, and I'll add some choice spoils from tonight."

"Sounds fair."

"Don't be absurd, I am both overpaying and cheating you quite horrendously." Sword relinquished, Slade stretched up onto his toes then strode for the door. "You have one hour to infiltrate the guard. I left your uniforms on the beds upstairs. Start the brawl when Echeira'Sollas' bells toll. I assume you'll recognize the sound as it's accompanied by the usual fanfare, a call to arms, screaming mobs, mad cows dancing the Kae'kae."

Crannir and the other assassins trailed Slade while only half listening as he doled out their final instructions, distracted by a parade of immodest cows dancing salaciously through their minds.

"Jamus, be miserly with your magic. If the governor hired a mage, the guards would have taken note. All of you avoid killing, it's rude and tends to inspire more zealous pursuit." Slade faced Lydia from over his shoulder, grinning as she immediately stepped back a pace. "Sweet, Lydia. I'd like to apologize for any inconvenience I may have caused."

"You don't sound sorry."

"I'm not, but there's a friend of mine who's desperate for your amorous attentions."

"What?"

"I swore on the grave of my three-headed sibling to champion his cause, resorting to whatever means necessary: be it horrid mistruths, outrageous bragging, or desperate pleading."

"Is that supposed to intrigue me? Your friend sounds like a lily-livered wimp."

Slade shrugged. "It's not my fault he chose a bad representative. Anyway, I hereby champion his cause." Pausing for a dainty cough, he adjusted his collar and then adopted a soulful expression. "Ah-hem, my friend is dreadfully taken with you. Day in, day out, he dreams of your face to the ruin of everything he does and the total shame of his family. Fear not, however. Being an exceptional sociopath, he will butcher any relatives for your amusement. I'm afraid he has a strangle hold on the idea of marriage though. If I were you, I would take precautions against getting kidnapped." Slade clapped her shoulder then exited into the silver-gold luminance of the porch Swanlight.

As Crannir stepped after him, Lydia yanked on his arm. "How am I supposed to know who this lunatic is?"

"Why?"

"I want to know in which direction to run."

"I'm not sure it matters. According to our employer, you'll be sharing a boat with him." Pulling his arm free, he left an increasingly distraught Lydia in his wake.

Slade met him just beyond the door's threshold, his countenance lacking the grin that felt so appropriate. "I have no instructions for you; listen to your head and stay safe. I hate replacing tools."

Crannir nodded. "So which poor soul are you tormenting next?"

"Nobody you're fond of." Grinning, he disappeared with the grace expected of his profession.

Slade's next destination revealed itself as a tall, apparently vacant housing complex, whose primary decorations were a low stone wall, barren flower beds, and a few curious smudges. There wasn't even a respectably crutched rocking chair on the front porch. Confronted by this egregious lack of piled riches waiting for some clever individual with clever fingers, Slade could only huff, shake his head and drop from his seat atop the wall.

Striding up to the house, he knocked twice, employing a firm, measured rap. During the following delay, he uncorked a vial and emptied its cryptic smelling contents into a flowerpot before pocketing the newly freed pendant. A moment later, the sound of nimble fingers pulled aside innumerable locks and preceded Keliss peering out through a cracked door. "Hiring a messenger hawk to herald your visit seems expensive."

"I considered sending a dog so he could piddle on all your plants but"—Slade glanced over his shoulder—"you don't have any."

Keliss stepped aside with a slow, unenthused shrug. "Don't see much point bothering with decorations, we'll be leaving when you've finished with the governor." He nodded down the hall. "Madame Roshfen's waiting in the library, first door on the right."

As Slade slipped by, he paused to stomp on the doormat, but soon realized this wouldn't dislodge his generous allotment of mud. Promptly divesting his boots, he positioned them on the shoe rack and then spent a moment ordering its utter disarray. About half-way through, he noticed the other man's quizzical look and cleared his throat, quickly leaving off the project to slink down the hall in his socks. Apart from briefly dropping into a crouch, he behaved himself.

Shaking his head, Keliss gave Slade's boots a thorough examination before treating the others to a cursory review: Slade hadn't touched any long enough for mischief. His own he gave more attention but still missed the slim pendant pinned under a flap.

The library, Slade realized upon entering, would have embarrassed its brethren the world over. Fewer than a dozen books lined its shelves, and each

lacked those clustered white creases that usually adorned a novel's spine—
badges of honor detailing the many adventures someone had taken within it.
These poor tomes looked as if Madame Roshfen bought them as an
afterthought.

'Well, we can't have this, now can we?'

Its severe depression aside, the library presented a respectable display
with ivory bookcases set into the walls and the occasional fantastic, wooden
creature standing at proud attention along the shelves. Most agreeable were
the portly armchairs that dominated the space, each welcoming him forward
with an open, generously padded embrace.

Madame Roshfen brooded by an imposing marble fireplace, seated
with her back to Slade and wrapped in her dressing gown, the taught lines of
fabric detailing the rigid, knife's edge of her frame. "What do you want?"

"Oh, nothing significant; some mayhem followed by a little profit and
maybe world domination. Here, I found this out in the hall." He set an
unadorned locket with a broken chain atop her armrest then crossed to the
desolate bookshelves, slithering up a ladder and plucking a dapperly attired
frog from the top shelf. "Mostly, I came to discuss affairs of state, starting
with a piece of information that'll probably send you scurrying home sooner
than anticipated." Dropping the frog down his satchel, Slade continued along
the shelves, examining every book or bookend before storing it alongside his
earlier procurement.

Eying the locket for a moment, she picked it up and checked the seal.
Satisfied, she pocketed the locket without noticing the slight added weight of
the pendant within. "What is so pressing as to require my attention at this
ungodly hour? Did one of your crew stub a toe?"

"Yes, but I'm saving that morbid tale for tomorrow's gossip markets."
Slade flipped open a hefty book, checking for the author. "Though far less
scintillating, what I'm about to relate deserves your attention regardless of the
hour."

"Get on with it."

"My apologies." One hand grabbing a ladder rung, Slade bowed.
"Conveyed succinctly, a right scallywag is planning to rob the governor
tonight. Judging from the rumors, it'll be a sensational event."

"What?" she asked quietly, tone practically shredding the bookcase
behind him.

While the room's furniture quaked in their collective boots, Slade
appropriated a porcelain terrier in a reed-hat. "Don't worry; I'm well
acquainted with these immoral goons, and I fully intend on delivering a
grueling sermon regarding the evils of theft." Frowning, Slade crossed his

arms and leaned back against the ladder. "It's actually rather aggravating because no matter how often I tell them thievery doesn't pay, they insist on proving me wrong."

Madame Roshfen rose slowly, forcing her next words out through grinding teeth. "These 'goons', by any chance do they belong to your crew?"

"They do, which explains why I'm compelled to sermonize them. If their crime were less heinous, I might excuse it with a partial beheading; but sadly any punishment that doesn't cause unbearable suffering would only display weakness. Rebellion could ensue, foreshadowing the total collapse of my autocratic government." Slade knelt, fixing a drunkenly slanted shelf before continuing down the line of bookcases and pausing by a plinth with an upside-down vase.

"We thought you needed a month to prepare." She growled, stalking him down the lines of bookshelves. "I sent a letter to Carr'Selain appraising him of that. Why in *Kis'Maat's* name did you lie to us?"

"When I suggested I needed a month to prepare, I failed to convey that I'd already taken said month. This was a simple yet horrendous oversight, and I apologize with all the snot-soaked tissues in my guilt-ridden soul. Rest assured I shall punish myself with chain whips and many sugared delicacies." Slade lifted the vase, inspecting the pearl-colored object for any chinks or cracks before tucking it under his arm and striding for the kitchen.

"I'm going to explain something you desperately need clarified," Madame Roshfen hissed from behind, one hand slithering into place around his throat and squeezing to the edge of strangulation. "We are prepared to overlook some lies, we accept your need for privacy, and we've resigned ourselves to the inevitability of machinations." The tip of a stiletto poked into Slade's side. "Withholding pertinent information does not enjoy the benefit of our tolerance, and before you show me that arrogant, disgusting grin, remember that we can be as treacherous, as deceitful, as you. Maybe the report mentioning the dragon in Cardolyn Tyier's vault will land on the wrong desk, or you'll be issued an outdated map, or our best locksmith will have to rush your order because of a sudden demand."

"Yes, those would all be exceedingly unfortunate." Slade spun the knob on the kitchen faucet, causing the pipes to gurgle and spew steaming water so he could rinse Madame Roshfen's vase. "Let me assure you that moving forward I will adhere to the strictest lack of confidentiality and would already barring a slight snag."

"Snag? You actually had a reason?"

"People always have a reason, even if it only amounts to whim. The question is whether my reason can satisfy your indignation." Turning off the faucet, he tapped Madame Roshfen's hand and returned the sloshing vase to its plinth in the library.

"Get on with it."

"Before our partnership can flourish, there's a final lesson that needs to be taught. During our last encounter, we determined who truly needed who and agreed upon suitable recompense, which may have generated the misapprehension that I was now a contracted laborer, likely one serving beneath you and another dozen superiors." Slade delved into his satchel, pulling out a bouquet of blue and violet roses for the vase. "I felt obliged to disabuse this misconception. Carr'Selain and I are equals." He stopped arranging the flowers to raise a finger, forestalling her instinctive contradiction. "How does my deceit prove this? Well, if you can neither predict nor compel my actions, it grants me autonomy which, combined with my indispensability, means I decide when, how, and why we strike; much like Carr'Selain." Giving the vase one final polish, he stepped back to admire his work. "There, aren't they beautiful?"

"They're perfect." She pushed the vase and sent it smashing to the floor, pottery shards skittering in all directions as flower petals and water washed over Slade's socks. "Now, was there more to this stunt than a declaration of independence, because you are not equal to Carr'Selain."

"Nothing more, but I'd like to continue my litany of those decisions that remain solely under my jurisdiction." Slade dropped into a chair, the plummet kicking his feet onto an adjacent footstool. "I decide our objectives, I decide our allies, and I, Madame Roshfen, decide when to inform a prospective target of our impending visit."

She stilled. "What?"

Slade gave her a hard smile. "What's the point of misleading one another; we've already established your distaste of falsehoods."

"I have no idea what you're babbling about."

"Very well, force me to use a hammer. Shortly after our first encounter, the lord governor began doubling his guards, replacing the old ones and making my life difficult. Suspicious, yes?"

Madame Roshfen strode across the room and grabbed a decanter roughly, splashing a generous dose of its amber liquor into a glass. "If you're suggesting that I informed the governor of your intentions, you can take *Jaidar's* blessing and be done here. I would never act so unconscionably as to damage my guild's interests."

"We're thieves, Madame Roshfen, our consciences are all a bit ragged." He shrugged then grinned at her. "Well at least your amendments will make tonight entertaining. If it's any consolation, I can't blame you. I might have conceived something worse in your position." The grin widened. "Murder perhaps; it's warranted considering I swaggered onto the scene and disregarded all those pretty little, absolutely integral rules between guilds. Warranted or not, however, I'm curious what Carr'Selain's response will be."

"To gut you for lying." She smirked, taking the seat opposite him and resting her glass atop a knee.

"Ah, but who else would sabotage this operation? One of my crew? Laughable; tonight threatens them with untold wealth. An interloper? Unlikely, past retaliations have made spying an unpopular occupation. In comparison to these, you've shown an evident disdain for me and forcefully warned against seeking an alliance. Most importantly, I've repeatedly seen Samara entering the governor's mansion."

"Ah, so you do know she's our mole. Regardless, if you can prove she spoke with the governor, you may punish her. The guild will not retaliate."

"Despite my best efforts, Samara's a worker bee. She's not big on initiative."

Her eyes narrowed, fingers tightening around her glass. "You two are colluding then, to arrange this exact—thrice-damned—scenario."

"You're remarkably quick to accuse your own."

"Samara's loyalty has been suspect ever since Tasha arrived in Tellor and began delivering accurate reports."

"So cold, so quick to disown her when you personally assigned Samara here." Slade leaned forward onto his elbows. "Why would I endanger this opportunity to ransack the Imperial palace?"

"*Jaidar* bless you, Slade Lammerock, if you believe for an instant that I'll submit to blackmail."

"Ahh blackmail. What a charming idea. Do you even possess something I want? Gold is scarcely a commodity and certainly not in the amount you could offer. Aside from that, you're barely in a position of power and Carr'Selain's house already reeks of my spies; spit once and you'll probably hit two."

"Then what's the point of your accusations."

"Oh, didn't I tell you? I'm making idle conversation to pass the time."

"And *Jaidar* masquerades as a school girl. What do you want?"

"I thought you intended on disregarding my blackmail threats?"

"Tell me already!" She exploded from her chair, hands slamming down on Slade's armrests.

"Are you willing to give it to me?"

"If it'll get you out of my house, I'll consider anything."

Slade leaned forward, grinning at her with such wolf-like intensity Madame Roshfen's skin prickled for the first time in years. "I want Tasha Bloomhale's debt contracts: the original ones, the buried ones. The ones explaining what was purchased, from whom, and why."

"Don't be a fool; Carr'Selain doesn't have those."

"No, but the Merchants' Guild ledger does and you've the importance necessary to access it."

"What makes you think I'd be so stupid as to steal a page from that guild's ledger."

"I'm not asking you to steal it, merely position my pretty friend here to steal it." Slade displayed a thin, silver vial, its surface layered with clustered runes that shifted chaotically, forever indenting themselves or exchanging places when they bothered to persist at all. "Don't worry, it's just Quicksilver. I helped the poor thing escape from behind a wall and now it owes me a favor. It might almost be grateful enough to still remember in a couple hours."

"This doesn't make any sense," Madame Roshfen snapped, starting to pace. "Why Miss Bloomhale? She barely exceeds the average, she possesses no secret information, and she has no powerful friends. Her one redeeming quality is an aptitude for administration and learning. It's a wonder she was sent on this mission at all."

"My secrets are my own."

She stopped to glare at him, eyes calculating between acquiescing and refusing while simultaneously trying to account for the most dangerous factor: what she didn't know, but he did. "If I acquire your information, you will renounce these accusations?"

"Yes, but the transaction comes with a slight catch."

"What is it?"

"I need the contracts by tomorrow."

"And how am I supposed to do that? The Merchants' ledger is kept in Dol'Cardolani, half an empire away should you have forgotten."

"Perhaps your eavesdropping wizard could offer assistance." Slade nodded toward the tabby cat sprawled in the doorway and stood, fingers interlacing as his arms lifted into a back-bending stretch. "Truth be told, I don't care. If you can't deliver by tomorrow, I'll be submitting a detailed report to Carr'Selain."

Madame Roshfen's incredulous gaze locked with his, an explosion building in her eyes. Then just as she stepped forward, a warning bell tolled out across Tellor, the precursor to a swelling wave of screams.

Slade sprang from the chair, dashing past her to the library's window and flinging it open.

"What's going on?" Madame Roshfen barked, following a step behind and shoving him aside. His broad, excited grin stopped her from taking his place though. "What have you done?"

"An excellent question, Madame Roshfen. So excellent, in fact, it has multiple answers; the first of which is that I've brought a taste of chaos to this land of order." He motioned out the window, inviting her to gaze past the harsh silhouettes of buildings to where Echeira'Sollas burned.

Madame Roshfen stepped forward, grabbing the windowsill until her knuckles turned white. "How dare you. To attack Echeira'Sollas is to attack *Enecki* himself. You insult the gods with this travesty."

"Hardly. Any number of them would find this wonderfully amusing." Slade chuckled, provoking a murderous glance from her. "Another answer is that I have caused a distraction that will tempt a garrison away from their other duties. In a curious way, all this"—he gestured out the window—"is a byproduct of your actions, making the blame yours as much as mine."

"I had nothing to do with this! I would never condone such rampant disrespect, such outright disgust for *Enecki*."

"You may not have intended this, but our actions frequently have unforeseen consequences. Now, to give a final answer–"

"I don't want to hear it," Madame Roshfen snarled. "Leave or I'll throw you out." She then stormed from the room, each step landing with a dull boom.

In the following silence, he reapproached the window, setting his elbows upon its sill as he leaned out into the night. "Your final answer is that I have told an elaborate lie." A slow grin crawled onto his face.

Bringing dreams into the waking world verged on the impossible; one needed an appropriate container, a rare herb, and a dream wizard of exceptional power. "Do stick around, Madame Roshfen; tonight's entertainments have just begun."

After closing the window, he turned and found the tabby cat watching him from atop the back of a chair, its tail swishing expectantly. "Ah, just the cat I wanted to see." He reached out a hand and Hacoast extended his paw, allowing the shake. "You can probably smell these, can't you?" Slade produced the third pendant, letting it swing before Hacoast's nose. "I suppose you've also told Carr'Selain what they are. More importantly, I would hope you've told him they're harmless. With Carr'Selain's permission, I'd like the pendants to remain undisturbed. His delegates shouldn't forget anything more than my face and recent events here in Tellor. You'll be able to lie to Cardolyn Tyer without endangering the guild or me."

The cat's eyes closed for a long time. When they finally opened, it leaned forward and presented its chest to Slade, permitting him to pin the final pendant to its collar.

49

Secrets And Revelations

A commotion at the door brought the revelries to a halt and the few remaining Kalvonders about on their lavish thrones. Valeriius converted his attention more leisurely, feigning disinterest until a slap split the air, pulling him—still disinterested—to gaze upon a quartet of fresh guards opposing an indistinct figure.

At a second slap, he exerted himself further, cultivating a display of exasperation, and peered between the guards. His Aparthii slave straightened from the blow, defenseless against their abuse. The guard lifted his hand again, anger mounting at her tenacity. But before he could strike, Valeriius caught his arm with his cane. The guards blanched and retreated, bowing and pleading. They could strike any free woman they pleased, but the Aparthii slave belonged to Valeriius, and to damage her was to indebt themselves to him.

She knelt before Valeriius, and he leaned close so they could conversely privately. He straightened, beckoned her and the rest of his attendants to follow before departing the arena. Outside the storm hadn't yet evolved into a deluge, but it still sufficed to douse his skin in oily filth despite his precautions. A pair of horses waited for them, accompanied by two masked servants in a secluded alcove. He mounted one, the Aparthii woman another with grace, and departed along the solitary cobbled road. His attendants would follow on foot.

They found Sahdaen's bridges empty and reeking as decades of accumulated grime eroded, with every window shuttered and barred, every light extinguished, and thousands of carrion birds perched on every spare precipice, from clotheslines and windowsills to rooftops and bridges. They jeered as he descended Sahdaen's lifts, their wings sopping in the storm's filth and imprisoned souls tethered to their backs.

At his mansion, Valeriius consigned his horse to a waiting Tragnashi and immediately directed his steps downward, accompanied only by the

633

Aparthii slave. His ancestors had harbored and amassed many things better left alone over the centuries, a practice Valeriius perpetuated, and to contain these objects they excavated catacombs, which included prisons for their more volatile captives.

Valeriius halted alongside a bare wall far below the surface and laid his hand upon it. Radiant white lines dashed from beneath his palm, painting a door and surrounding it in curses. He withdrew his hand, replacing it with his cane, whose amethyst head flared.

Fetid air burst free in response, followed by a crack as the door opened. An old, malignant darkness poured out, clawing at them with ravenous hands: dry and hot. The Aparthii slave withdrew with a whimper, her fearful hands clutching Valeriius' arm. Scowling, he struck the floor with his cane. Its head again burst with amethyst light and the darkness scattered, routing as the wind disperses autumn leaves.

Five seconds passed and a man emerged from the gloom, sniffing to compensate for his vacant eye sockets. His face carried the fingernail scars and tooth marks bestowed upon those who cared for the insane, some still a livid red. The guard knelt before his master and pressed his pallid brow to the cold stone. Valeriius strode past without a word, and the Aparthii woman followed, clutching to his left arm. The guards might endure this darkness and she survive it, but he ruled it.

Drawn by the light they could not see, other guards appeared from the shadows like adherents to their god. Their obligation was to preserve the darkness and study those Valeriius sent to experience it. The screams and pleadings of those incarcerated gnawed from every direction, for they saw the light and knew instinctively that their horror would end if they could but touch it. Thus they begged, promising everything for but a moment in the light.

When all the guards had gathered, Valeriius addressed the eldest, "Take me to them." In unison, the two dozen keepers slipped away, guiding him to his destination.

Valeriius heard the communion before he saw them—twelve men and women indifferent to his light—and halted a short distance away, lest he interrupt their ritual.

They knelt in the configuration of a twelve-point sigil, the lines etched from their own blood. Normally a different material would have sufficed, but the Dread Lord's madness festered in their minds even as they prostrated themselves with cries of supplication, ensorcelled in the Chaos ritual.

Valeriius had concealed these twelve individuals for years, harboring them for the day they proved useful. Whether through lies, mistake, or lust they had surrendered to the God of Chaos and become his acolytes—soldiers in his mortal host. Through them Valeriius gained insight into the god's intent, all for just a minor fortune.

Each day of a Turning belonged to one of the Pantheon's gods; a day devoted to their worship when they eclipsed all their siblings. These twelve votaries were no different; without fail or divergence, they enacted a ritual on their deity's sacred day. Now, after years, these men and women had initiated a second ritual not on *Jaidar's* day but the Lost God's, which could only mean that *Jaidar's* influence expanded and he had begun marshalling followers.

Valeriius indicated the paramount worshiper, a young man sworn to *Jaidar* since infancy. "Take him, kill the rest."

The worshipers persisted with their devotions, mounting toward a distant, overwhelming crescendo as Valeriius' custodians intruded and silenced them with efficient brutality. They perished without turmoil, and even the survivor protested only when they extricated him from the sigil and pitched him before Valeriius, bound and gagged.

Alight with the ritual's glory and his deity's magnificence, the adherent cast himself upon Valeriius, flailing his head for want of a better weapon. Valeriius sidestepped, cane flaring amethyst and flicking to the acolyte's chest, siphoning the ritual's power and reducing him to a heap. There ensued a moment of stillness, then the imploring from the adjacent cells—previously suppressed by the ritual—resumed.

Valeriius circumvented the body, readjusting his grip on the cane, and addressed his custodians, "Bind him to the Door-Unto-Light and ensure that last spark of Chaos survives." Beckoning sharply, he continued further into the catacombs. The murmurs from the other incarcerated diminished, growing distant before fading entirely as he reached the prison's nexus, where his choicest prizes languished: three cells excavated from the rock, bound with worn silver and white runes, and an effigy so dark its surroundings resembled twilight.

He approached the second cell, relinquished its enchantments with a rap of his cane, and peered in. A woman crouched far below, hissing and mumbling in forgotten tongues as she dug at the floor with crooked, bleeding fingers lacerated so deep it exposed bone.

Valeriius crouched, speaking almost in singsong, "Belladona, you're digging the wrong way."

She halted, fixing large milky eyes on Valeriius as a dry tongue flicked out, tasting the air. "I thought this prison was growing heavier." He felt her senses extending, tasting the darkness against his light, and allowed her to believe she escaped his notice, to suckle on the chamber's malice. When she acquired sufficient strength to accomplish his desire, he disrupted her connection with a cane tap, launching her into a howling frenzy of rage and pain.

In seasons past, she had been powerful: the matriarch of an eastern coven until Valeriius enticed her south, first deceiving then incarcerating her far from her sisters, entombed so deep no beast, curse, or incantation could locate her.

Her mewling attenuated, usurped by guffawing laughter. "I can feel it, a storm shrouding all; and he at its heart, breeding evil, a tumor in the city. They—we—cannot resist for he is our sovereign by blood and power. We were born to serve, and he to rule. Fear rots my heart and I cower, wallowing in dreaded water … an ocean of souls corrupted and bound; all of us are his wretches now. How do you know my name, mortal? Maybe you will confide yours?"

"My name is inconsequential, Belladona, and I needed yours to bind you, thus I found it written in black blood."

"What do you desire of us? We have much."

"I need courage, and for you to read blood."

"Yes, courage we can do; it is easy, so few use it and all have it. But the reading of blood strays too close, too close for us, forbidden magics: his magic."

"It does not cross into blood-magic; it breaks no laws, and it is a skill you possess."

"It will cost us much, yes, everything we have. You must give us something in return, a trinket, something you treasure."

"You will have your trinket, after the courage and blood reading."

"Yesss, it is done." She crawled forward, greasy hair dragging through years of vomit and waste, masking a feral grin. Her pallid face appeared black in the wilting light, almost hollow; she was old and it showed in the thousand wrinkles, a testament to the longevity of witches and their craft.

The shriveled hag scaled the wall, sinking long fingers into the stone as if it were putty until she crouched before Valeriius, dressed in little more than rags, and they, like her hair, reeked.

Valeriius had used Belladona twice before; on each occasion she demanded a gift of him. The first time, Valeriius gave her an old dagger from the East, valuable to her with its memories and the bridge they formed to the original possessor. The second time, he presented her with an assortment of colorful trinkets on strings, ripe for the imbuement of witchcraft.

A prodigious weight lifted from Balladona's shoulders as she emerged and straightened, the years sliding off her visage one after another. She drew in a long dry breath and with it a storm of witchcraft. Valeriius felt her summon the prison's malevolence but did not hinder her. This malignance was not hers, and eventually it would betray her like all others who sought to wield it.

Still, prudence dictated caution. Thus while she drowned in the euphoria of power, Valeriius unveiled a silver collar and latched it about her throat. The witch recoiled, snarling and clawing at her neck to no avail, skin boiling wherever it contacted the silver. He departed, knowing she would follow him even to the Door-Unto-Light.

Vibrant with suppressed but evident relief, the Aparthii woman hastened to the verge of Valeriius' light, pressing its boundary until a distant, agonized screaming silenced the cavern's incessant whispered begging. She faltered and returned to his side, less for terror than recalling her station and what waited at the door. The scream persisted, accompanying them through the dark to the open door, revealing *Jaidar's* servant as its progenitor.

The custodians kowtowed at Valeriius and the Aparthii's advent into the natural light, but Belladona recoiled at its boundary, skin charring further under *Sammahale's* light; Valeriius' illumination was manmade and thus generally innocuous, but *Sammahale's* brilliance, conveyed to these depths via mirrors, scorned all things of malice. Irrevocably, however, the witch could not defy Valeriius, and so obeyed his advance, writhing as smoke billowed from her.

"Read him."

Belladona slunk forward, murmuring in the tongue of witches as her skin seared and smoked, regenerating constantly. A dagger of black bone slithered from her tattered sleeve, its tip crusted with blood from her eyes, tongue, fingers, ears, and nose. Extending a quivering hand, she caressed the acolyte from throat to stomach, drawing black lines of filth upon his flesh. The acolyte screamed twice, once in terror of failing his god and again in rage at death, then the dagger struck, rending him from throat to groin.

Blood sprayed Belladona, inciting her voice to song, though only Valeriius comprehended it. "Rising waters, drowning the cries of prisoners, the oceans of Chaos swell. He unleashes his summons, calling his mortal servants to the rites of blood and suffering beyond the hells. Within his domain of charred iron and raging Chaos, the god calls for his legions; he summons his fallen Seraphim and Nephilim, his devils and nightmares, his fiends and imps, all the hordes and might of the hells. And he marshals his sons: the Princes of the Hells, the Lords of Chaos, his lieutenants and the masters of his legions. Through every hell and in every stone, the fires echo his words: the True King shall rise. All hear his secrets and know terror; all hear his words and begin to realize a truth. These are memories in the blood. These are the visions of those mortals taken by Chaos."

The witch collapsed, sobbing in the emptiness left by the reading. Valeriius grasped the back of her soiled neck. "Give me the courage."

Wordless and shuddering, she restored to him one of his previous gifts, an amulet carved in the semblance of arachnids. He deposited it into his breast pocket, the courage within warming his palm. "Return her to her cell with this"—he presented the elder keeper with an ancient wooden bracelet— "and permit her a sliver of power."

"And the corpse?"

"Add it to the rest."

Dieharamon slammed into the wall, clutching his skull and raving, eyes wide with golden flames turned black. Something festered within him, rearing high on Sahdaen's ancient malice and infecting his veins, subjugating him. He roared again, battering his head against the wall until the stone cracked.

He needed the *Pathfinder Shard*. With it, he could preserve himself from the Dread Lord, dominate Sahdaen, rule like the tyrants of old. He could enact due retribution on the Kalvonders, Tragnashi, and Avarans, liberate himself of fear and inspire it instead.

His screams brought three guild Rats scurrying down the alleyway, hoping to pillage his corpse. He tried to scare them off, but his only utterance was a terrified wail.

Rage and loathing surged within him again; why should he fear power? He was no corrupt monster and could accomplish so much, save so many with the *Pathfinder Shard*, restore hope and sanity to the Avarus Desert.

A thrust launched him from the wall, intent on recovering the *Pathfinder Shard*, but his feet betrayed him. He fell, hands splashing in blood, and a face appearing before him, wide eyed and mired in the sludge. He recoiled, wailing and kicking the dead girl aside, cowering against the wall as he clutched his face, fingers leaving a bloody reminder of those he had sworn to never kill.

No more children needed to die; the *Pathfinder Shard* could avert their deaths, prevent a thousand lifetimes of agony, end this madness. The needs of the few could not outweigh the needs of the many; they could not. A few must sacrifice themselves–

"No!" Dieharamon shoved himself upright, eyes flaring molten gold. He spun desperately, searching for something, anything to help him but saw nothing. He slammed himself into the wall again, pummeling it until his knuckles bled. Shadows crept inward from the edges of his vision and he shrieked defiance, scattering them. He must not find the *Shard*; he could not permit whatever malignance his body harbored to obtain it. The poison reared again...

How dare they oppose him? The fools—the traitors—would pay. They resisted righteous justice for the whims of a false god! They would learn Dieharamon deserved worship. He possessed the power of gods and refused to allow his new life to die; he would smite this evil into ruin!

He convulsed, reeling back, his throat raw from ceaseless cries. Corpses surrounded him; acts of violence he could not recall. A young woman retreated from him, the bloody marks of his hands blemishing her throat. She scrambled to her feet and stumbled into sobbing flight.

Dieharamon collapsed, weeping for all the lives he had taken, and all those he had watched taken. His nightmare subsided, rejecting vacillating madness and sanity for perpetual suffocating horror. Dieharamon could only curl against the wall, barely capable of autonomous thought.

Thundering hooves roused him, affixing his eyes involuntarily upon the alleyway's mouth where riders with steel swords cantered past. He shrunk against the wall instinctively; the riders were foreigners and hunting someone. One of the horses neighed and returned to the entrance, its rider grinning at Dieharamon from within a halo of torchlight.

The horseman spoke, in an eastern dialect that Dieharamon could not understand, and his subordinates rushed into the alley. He retreated but knew it was futile; the easterners caught him in half-a-dozen strides and pinned him against the wall. He snarled, trying to summon his fire, but it rebelled, suffusing him with an aching sense of loss. They pummeled him in retaliation, but it was the void within him more than his injuries that conquered Dieharamon. He buckled, the blows increasing as riders encircled him. His conscious receded to a vestige, just sufficient to perceive a sense of motion and to drown in the floods of his nightmare: horror, fear, hatred, despair. Time elapsed and he shriveled further in on himself, dissolving further into the madness, lost and drowning.

Something minute appeared in the obscurity enshrouding him, distant and burning hot to the touch: a spark of light, a candle flame.

Emotions, thoughts, and sensations returned to him, the world seeping into focus.

Dayada stood before him, grinning up, and for that heartbeat he seemed ablaze with inner light, warming Dieharamon to his core. The Avenar Prince pulled himself up to Dieharamon and wrapped him in an embrace, earning a snort from the horse he straddled and a fragile reciprocation from Dieharamon.

They dismounted gingerly, Dieharamon supporting himself on Dayada's shoulder as the Avenar Prince pierced the haze. "Are you alright? They said you were competing in some grand event, that you wouldn't return. I said of course you would; I'm still here. They laughed and said you were fighting hundreds of people! Can you believe that? I mean what kind of competition has those odds."

Rough hands thrust Dieharamon off the Avenar. "Valeriius Kalvonder demands your immediate presence, Tragnashi. You and your friend."

Stumbling, Dieharamon fell. "I am no longer Tragnashi—"

"You are whatever Valeriius dictates, now move!"

The lead horseman moved to strike again, but Dayada interceded. "Leave him be! Can't you see he's hurt?"

The horseman's eyes narrowed, features distorting with contempt. He advanced a deliberate, heavy step, flexing wide shoulders over Dayada, but the Avenar maintained his gaze with silent reprimand, persevering even as the man thumbed a knife handle. "Fine! Just make sure he moves."

Dayada knelt instantly, wrapping arms about Dieharamon's shoulders. "Here, let me help." Warmth enveloped him, lifting the nightmares again settling upon him and restoring life to inert limbs. "I think we should cooperate; they don't seem very nice."

"No, they are not." They shuffled after the horseman, migrating through the lower mansion's labyrinth of dusty passageways, locked doors, and forgotten rooms. The atmosphere of abandonment regressed as they ascended, capitulating to immaculate floors, vibrant illumination, and ornate furnishings. They passed an open hall brimming with light and sound, aglow with golden murals, gilded floors, and bustling slaves. Mahogany tables lined the walls, abounding with wine vessels, platters, and displays.

The horseman shoved Dieharamon, stimulating his slackened pace and encouraging him to ignore the upper mansion's new splendor.

Their procession concluded at a wooden door, which the horseman opened without ceremony and ushered them in. "He's waiting."

Dieharamon stumbled forward, froze mid-stride, and stared in awe. A forest bloomed around him, replete with rowans, oaks, ashes, birches, sumac, and dozens unknown to him. The ground hid beneath a blanket of ferns and moss interrupted only by the rare, cobbled path and streams overflowing with lilies and cattails. Most of all, Dieharamon stared at the birds on their perches, soaring amidst the branches, or crouched in the shrubbery: falcons, peacocks, macaws, lorikeets, cranes, and scores of other species he could not name.

At the center of it all, Valeriius occupied a simple bench draped with his seat-cloth beside one of the streams, his cane in one hand and a falcon on the other. His favorite Aparthii slave accompanied him, presenting a variety of delicacies. The door closed behind them with a soft click, prompting Valeriius' attention.

He examined them, absently feeding the falcon, then beckoned. Dieharamon warily complied, listening with half-an-ear as Dayada, wowed, at the aviary and lingered by the entrance.

Valeriius indicated a space opposite the Aparthii slave and offered the falcon another morsel. "You are to be commended, Dieharamon, the recount of your exploits sweeps Sahdaen, propelling you into the realm of legends." He shifted focus toward the approaching Dayada and Dieharamon's heart fluttered. "I apologize for delaying my welcome, Lord Dayada, urgent matters demanded my attention. I hope it caused no inconvenience?"

Retrieving his meandering attention, Dayada bowed. "It is a pleasure to make your acquaintance, Valeriius Kalvonder. And don't trouble yourself on my account, everything's been delightful, if a bit strange. The food in particular's proving an adventure, though I guess that's to be expected, and it's so dark on the lower floors. Please don't take that the wrong way, your house is beautiful, it's just so big I get lost. Do you have a map I could use? Nobody's interested in talking, and when I try the Merchant's Tongue, they just stare at me so I can't ask for directions."

"There's no recourse against the lamentable obscurity I'm afraid. I cannot light every hall. I can, however, provide you with an insect lamp and a map, or a guide if you prefer? I can also arrange for western cuisine."

"Oh no, strange food is part of the fun, and I'll decline the guide; I don't want to be a burden. I'll take the lamp and map though, and one of Sahdaen as well."

"You are no burden; I will assign you an interpreter and guide promptly. Should I expect a visit from your father or Tiberius Whyte?"

"No, they're busy; that's why I'm here. I'm supposed to be finding somebody?"

"It will be ... difficult locating anyone in Sahdaen, Lord Dayada, but I will assist you if I can. Now, if you would please leave us, I must converse with Dieharamon privately."

"Okay, bye. Dieharamon, I'll see you later." Dayada trotted off, oohing and aahing, every other stride, and with his absence the crushing despair of what Dieharamon had done returned to him.

Valeriius waited for the aviary's door to close before reverting his attention to Dieharamon. "This is a rare breed of falcon called Palvarus. It inhabits the eastern forests, hunting rodents and small birds, and is renowned for three things: its speed, love of flight, and impossibility to tame. Either they die in captivity, or the prospective trainer kills them for their violent temperaments. I had this Palvarus brought to me from the wilds, fully grown, but still young so I could break its wings." Valeriius stroked it. "Then I made it try to fly by dropping it from various, non-fatal heights. It took some time; but eventually the falcon accepted it could not fly. At this point, I repaired its wings and taught it to fly again. Again this took a while, but it learned." Valeriius fed the falcon another morsel. "Soon it was able to fly again, and the period where it was incapable of flight was nothing more than a memory; so I broke its wings again and again and again. After a few months, it learned I was the god giving it the gift of flight, and it has never shown me anything but love ever since."

Valeriius tossed it into flight and faced Dieharamon. "What does the Dread Lord desire from you?"

Dieharamon swallowed, trying to muster his thoughts, to remember he no longer served Valeriius even as fear swamped him, dense with a baleful premonition. "He ... he wanted something called the *Pathfinder Shard*."

"Why?"

Dieharamon kept answering, unable to prevent the words tumbling from his lips. "I do not know. I found it in the Remanas Palace but lost it in the *Lake of Dreams*."

"This *Pathfinder Shard* is an object of immense physical potency, yet you lost it in a realm without substance? That incompatibility aside, whatever provoked you to abandon it?" Valeriius tapped the Aparthii slave with his cane and she rushed to fill a goblet with river water. He sipped and directed her to resume her earlier position.

"The Dread Lord wanted it! Isn't that enough? And I do not know how I lost it, only that I did, and I hope it stays lost!" Dieharamon bellowed the last words, surging upright with a slash of his hand.

Valeriius presented neither opposition nor reprimand. "What does the *Pathfinder Shard* do?" Dieharamon refused to answer, to surrender anything else to him. Dava had died to secure Dieharamon's freedom, he would not waste it aiding someone like Valeriius. The boy deserved that and more, even if Dieharamon didn't.

Valeriius permitted his moment of rebellion, then inclined. "What does it do?"

"I no longer serve you." He tried to utter Valeriius' name without quiver or subservience but couldn't even muster the courage to speak it. Desperate, he roused the memory of Dayada's light and clutched it, wrapping himself about it and the vestiges of its warmth. "I do not serve you, Valeriius."

"When predators surround you, do you heed the runt? Who would imagine the lion can kill a hundred hyenas set upon him by greedy masters? The lion itself did not believe in survival. Yet, here it is, alive and demanding freedom. Lies, Dieharamon, are an easily spent and acquired currency. I swore no oaths, for none required me to."

Horror burgeoned within Dieharamon. "N—no. That's not possible. You have to free me. I survived! You have to free me, please."

"I do not." Valeriius never swore to uphold the Kalmarad's reward. "Now, what does it do?"

Dieharamon shook his head, but the truth clutched his heart, prying the answer free, "The *Pathfinder Shard* creates a portal mortal men can traverse without ill-effect at the cost of a soul."

"Interesting... Dieharamon, current events near their culmination; simple negotiations have evolved into a lethal ballet. The Kalvonders, Dread Lord, and New Order all pursue distinct, potential conflicting interests, and now the Clergy and Guilds have dispatched representatives. A multitude of labors are unfolding, laying the course we are intended to tread. The Kalvonders will believe you are free; to portray else would be a death sentence. Therefore you will play my game. Your days in the Angorat'Wass are concluded; you now enter a more treacherous arena orchestrated by chaotic tides." Valeriius sipped. "You will serve as assassin, thug, and commander, and convey yourself as a prominent figure in my hierarchy with extensive liberties and resources. Learn to dance quickly, for they will not allow a grace period. They will attempt to discern truth from lies, and to purchase or coerce your loyalties. Henceforth, consider yourself an extension of me with all the incumbent perils."

"But why? I know nothing of this game!"

Valeriius ignored him. "Publicly, I remain undecided and potentially ambivalent to the negotiations. Two Kalvonders share my indecision, and together we dictate the outcome. At present, Kalvonder Vaydrun favors the New Order; he is weak, possessing scant more than I profess to, and knows an alliance would debilitate wealthier Kalvonders while enrichening the lesser. This is obviously one of the New Order's intentions: sowing discord makes Sahdaen easier to control. Vaydrun desires this turmoil and expresses his ambition openly. His counterpart is Kalvonder Nearus, who declines either party's courtship.

"Nearus sees too much for caprice or blind avarice, thus he supports maintaining Southern isolation. His affluence exceeds Vaydrun's, but he has secluded himself for decades, unassailable by inferior Kalvonders and irrelevant to the pyramid's higher seats. Only the New Order's arrival, which agitated Sahdaen to its foundations, and tonight's festivities, prompted his resurgence. He, and every other Kalvonder with a shred of influence, intends to exploit my gala as a stage to berate and extort their rivals."

"Here? Why?"

"Because I alone remain an absolute mystery concerning the alliance, and this gala provides the opportunity to court me. Thus everyone of importance will answer the invitation and drag in their wake everyone else. The wealth I shall receive tonight will beggar the mind in its immensity; I shall receive slaves, Tragnashi, Artisan Silk, precious gems, steel weapons, and magical trinkets of past eras beyond counting."

Valeriius stood, prodding Dieharamon's hand with his cane. "I see you wasted another pair of gloves." His cane flicked up, raising Dieharamon's chin. "I see you've also rediscovered your power." He released Dieharamon's head and poured the almost untouched water back into the river. "You are mage born, as you have obviously discovered, what you fail to realize is you are also cursed."

He set the glass on the bench, motioning for the Aparthii to hand him something. She lifted a wine pitcher from behind the bench and gave it to Valeriius, who uncorked it. "All mages derive their gift from within; most describe it something as a well of fire. They use this gift to manipulate their bound element. Through use, they exhaust their energy; though it replenishes itself. Each mage operates with an innate cap on their reserves, which they can expand via mastery." Valeriius began pouring the wine. "You, Dieharamon, have no cap"—the glass overfilled—"but a mortal body can contain only so much power; eventually it cracks under the strain. You are no different; you can hold only so much power, but unlike the rest of us, you merely overflow instead of breaking." Valeriius dumped all of the wine into the glass, knocking it over with a splash. "Whenever you … 'overflowed', it tended to unleash a sequence of devastation. At first, when you were young, it was outbursts of wild anger and other emotions. As you aged, your power matured, and with it, the outbursts exacerbated. You started killing servants, speaking in lost tongues and foreign voices. Over a couple months, the outbursts increased in number, their destruction augmenting further, obliging me to control it through your gloves and intoxicants. The first dulled your connection to the power; the second restricted your ability to regenerate it."

Valeriius nudged Dieharamon's head up again. "You were like a rabid animal, killing everything whenever the dam burst." He gazed down without malice. "That is why you are drugged.

"Now, when you leave here, you will take a double dose of your drugs. Do not mourn the loss, the drugs dull your memory, and this is not the first instance of recollection." With a final tap on his chin, Valeriius released him and rifled through a pocket. "On a different matter, I have two gifts. The first is this amulet to protect you from the Dread Lord; courage is also both cheap and easy to acquire. Beware though; it burns quickly." He dropped the amulet into Dieharamon's dully-open hand, causing him to inhale sharply at its energy. He stared, feeling the imprisoned courage stir, then grit his teeth and slid the amulet about his neck, a single word echoing in his mind: witchcraft.

"I have one more gift, keep it safe until the time comes to use it." The *Pathfinder Shard* landed on the floor with a dull note and glinted up at him. "Don't lose it again." Valeriius left then, leaving Dieharamon to shrink away in unthinking revulsion.

He remained there for a long time, caught in an infinite cycle of memories. His mind besieged him with all the horrors he had committed, all the promises he had broken, and all his failures. And after all of that, he was still in chains.

50

The Last Bargain

The High-Warden found Lord Adriat seated outside the *Winter Court*, meditating before its crystalline doors with a sword across her knees. She roused at his advent, sheathing the blade and dispelling the images that populated its visage. "How did it go?"

He replied slowly, thoughts preoccupied, "It is done, but there was ... something in those catacombs, and I fear what it bodes."

"What did you find?"

"I discovered one of the *Roy'al* Signets—no, discover is not the correct word." He joined her at the edge. "I think, perhaps, it intended to be found, or that maybe some design unearthed it from obscurity."

"What's that doing here? They were all lost when the Crimson Empire collapsed! Even if one survived, they have no reason to surface; their bearers are all dead and the third never had a bearer to begin with, unless...?"

"No, it's the second Signet, belonging to *Lord Arthramain Roy'al's* brother." He rubbed tired eyes. "As for the first ring, it was never lost. I know who carries it."

"Who and how have they retained their sanity?"

"Who doesn't matter; what does matter is that it has recently entered The North, meaning we now host two *Roy'al* Signets. You must contact the Winter Lords and assemble them in Antiark; there is more afoot than a simple incursion."

"What could they possibly desire if not conquest?"

"I do not know, but two of *Arthramain Roy'al's* Signets are on the verge of meeting after millennia of absence, and I cannot help but wonder if the third is about."

She frowned, thoughts turning dark. "I know this is less than an opportune time, but three paladins are demanding entrance into The North and refuse to abandon their armaments. They inquire after their kinsman who entered previously but has disappeared. I admitted him without restrictions because The North welcomed him, but these others concern me; they intend violence, though not upon The North."

"Tell them their brother lives and that The North will preserve him if she can, but we cannot guarantee his safety. Inform them also of the New Order."

"Should I admit them?"

"We have sufficient god-sworn in The North; they can wait beyond Winter's Gate. Ensure they are cared for." Nodding farewell, he moved toward the glass doors, opened them with a touch, and stepped through.

The instant he set foot inside, a ripple shook the *Winter Court* to its foundations and every constellation whirled to stare at him, their starlit eyes hunting the Signet. He defied them, allowing them to search without impediment until their eyes reached his throat where he stole their true vision and replaced it with absence. Their music grew discordant with ire and unease.

He strode down the hall, the Signet scalding his skin through the pouch; he was not its master, and it had not been given to him, thus it reviled his touch, but suffered it because he had merely found it, and its proper master was lost.

The Winter Knight waited at the foot of the Winter Queen's throne, grinning at him with a decapitated head hanging from his fingers on knotted hair and the shattered remnants of a pale scythe in his other hand. He brandished the head. "I found success, but it appears you failed. Where is your trophy? Certainly, you have more than words for proof?"

"I did not fail; I chose a less macabre trophy."

The Winter Knight's grin shriveled to a sneer. "Your success means nothing; that creature's mere existence proves your inadequacy."

Ignoring his diatribe, the High-Warden scanned for the Artist without success; she was a creature of the *Day Court* and had no place in its counterpart once his need of her concluded. He restored his attention to the fuming Winter Knight. "When you keep silent, you resemble a collared dog far less, Lord Knight."

"Is that a challenge?"

"No. I just tire of you and your inane mumblings. These challenges squander my energy, and when I depart, I still have to resolve *Jaidar*. Thus I would prefer if you maintain a semblance of voluntary action and keep quiet." Dismissing the knight, he advanced to the Winter Queen's throne and presented her with the pouch from his neck. "Do not open it."

She scolded him with a look before raising the pouch to her ear. The seconds passed, and she returned it, lips tight. "You have succeeded, High-

Warden. Congratulations are in order, to both of our champions. There is time for rest before we commence the last challenge."

"There is no time. *Jaidar* marshals himself in the Abyss, wreathed in flames and awash in black iron. I must be prepared to confront him; initiate the last task without delay."

Her eyes flashed violence, but her features softened as she inclined to the side and cupped her cheek. "Such haste for a Northern man is unbecoming. I thought your people were patient. Has this changed?"

He deliberately ascended the stairs and clamped his hands on the armrests of her throne. "I am done with your games. This next ordeal will begin without delay, or the Winter Knight will forfeit. If you decline both alternatives, I will break your crown and sunder this throne."

Her lips parted in a visceral grin, and her black eyes turned white, brimming with winter. "You would set yourself against the *Winter Court?* Such a position can only be treason against The North. Are you certain of its wisdom? You cannot hope to vanquish us while alone and debilitated. Even if you succeeded, *Jaidar* remains, as does the war besetting The North, the land you swore to protect. You would assail us while your people die?"

"Her people are not my burden, Winter Queen, I am the keeper of the land, and the land is beyond your laws."

A massive hand clamped his shoulder, dragging him back. The High-Warden relinquished the chair and turned on the Winter Knight, grasping his outstretched arm. The Winter Knight hissed, a white vapor boiling from between the High-Warden's fingers. He struggled, pummeling the High-Warden's arm, but failed to escape and weakened with every passing second, diminishing in size and grandeur.

"I warned you, Saleas: you are not my equal." The *Winter Court's* doors burst open with shrieking wind that engulfed the hall, building until it was a storm in the fullness of Northern wrath.

He shoved the Winter Knight away and faced the Winter Queen again, amassing the gale about him. The constellations abandoned their poses of leisure, some roaring in open opposition and others fleeing. Vysera yawned and shifted for a better view. Their music grew dissonant with anger, fear, aggression, composing a screaming, staccato melody.

The High-Warden returned to the Winter Queen's throne, assuming his earlier posture. "Are we agreed, or must I disrupt this *Court?*"

"The *Winter Court* will not suffer your tampering! It will defy you as you exert the entirety of your mortal power in a futile battery! You have declared war upon us, and we will destroy you in restitution!" She slapped him, then yanked her hand back with a hiss, skin inflamed and blistered.

"I believe the *Winter Court* will tolerate my tampering. Besides, it is not in your authority to declare war"—he stared heavenwards, past Vysera and deeper into The North—"that is the *Burden* of another."

He refocused upon her and tore the glass throne from its dais with her upon it, shattering its foundation and hurling it to the floor. She landed with a cry and scrambled to her feet, clutching the spear before her. He stepped from the dais, a swirl of water rising behind him and freezing into a new throne. "You are no longer the Winter Queen, Lytia." The spear in her hands melted, cascading through her fingers to splash on the ground and reform as the crown tumbled from her brow with a piercing crash.

He lifted the crown with gentle fingers and straightened, exploring every facet for blemish or scar. Turning his back on Lytia, he laid the crown upon the newly reformed seat, bowed to it and retreated with lowered eyes. He faced the assembled *Winter Court*, still suffering from the upheaval of usurpation. "My business here is concluded. I will depart so that you might discover for yourselves the subsequent Winter Queen. I will offer you no advice; it is not my place to decide this."

Strangely, as he spoke, all the discord within the *Winter Court* subsided, its members ceasing their erratic movements or dispassionate ease to peer behind the High-Warden. Even Vysera descended and affixed her attention to the throne. "No, High-Warden, it is not your place to decide who wears the *Winter Court's* crown, that is my geas. The sentence, however, is within your rights and will be sustained."

The High-Warden turned and, with every other being in the room, knelt. "My lord."

The entity stood upon the throne's dais, one hand upon the throne's back and the other delicately holding the crown. He was an entity of burning, empyreal starlight forged into a body of molten armor with wings of light that were not of eagles, bats, or insects, but an amalgamation of all.

"Stand, High-Warden, it is neither your place nor your nature to kneel, and I am no god or Great-Immortal."

The High-Warden acquiesced. "I do not bow for fear, my lord."

"I know, but it was my brothers' sacrifice not mine. They surrendered their essence to combat the darkness; I am merely the guide, for power is at best useless when uncontrolled and destructive at worst."

"It is equally hard to lose and to be lost."

"I have wasted millennia pondering their sacrifice, you can say nothing I have not already discovered and weighed. Thus this discussion is without purpose. I will decide a new Winter Queen in time, but for now, I would speak with you. This court is dismissed, return with the next day; yes, even you Vysera."

When the last of them faded, the entity waved a hand and the night disappeared, parts of it fading in echo of the constellations and others becoming liquid and flowing through the doors and mirrors into distant halls.

"You would speak to me of the Dread Lords, warn of their advent and confide how to destroy them?"

"No, High-Warden, you already recognized their resurgence, and destroying them exceeds your abilities. In all likelihood, they will achieve their desire in The North, for only the annihilation of everything behind Winter's Gate could deter them."

"Then why have you come?"

"For five hundred years, the Mortal Kingdoms have believed the Dread Lords extinct, that Sedition Muntalabac was the last. A scattering have maintained the truth, and a few discovered it through my efforts; including your predecessor. Others who once believed, lost their memory through misfortune or the machinations of others. As it stands, I know of only seven who know of the Dread Lords; Tarram Avenar, his children, you, a man in white who rides with the New Order, a Kalvonder of the South, and Tiberius Whyte. Of these, two are not our ally. This leaves us five, two of whom are still children. As for Tarram, his spirit is exhausted. The long war has sapped his strength as it did his forefathers'. This leaves you and Tiberius Whyte. High-Warden, the Dread Lords are ready to conclude the Long War, and the Avenar are not. When this conflict ends, you must go west to the DawnHold and Dol'Cardolani."

"I hold no love for the West or its Imperial Emperor. If Cardolyn Tyier understood The North, he would unleash his legions upon us in a heartbeat; even now his mind works at the puzzle of how to break us, to consume our land as he did the West."

"Cardolyn Tyier's ambitions are not your concern; he is a wrinkle in the tapestry." The entity waved again, and a thousand colors streamed across the floor, ceiling, and mirrors, painting an image of war. "He rules the current centuries, but he will pass, just as the gods' reign passed with the coming of *Lord Arthramain Roy'al*. The Dread Lords do not heed the laws of time, death, or any mortal governance, and the Avenar are exhausted; they need your help.

"More than just the Dread Lords' reappearance, catalysts are emerging from the masses, appearing from dead and hollow bloodlines to shred the tapestry of Fate; a convergence is upon us. The New Order believes itself the instigator, but I doubt that assertion: Dread Lords have never served another outside their own. So go west and join Tiberius Whyte, the Avenar Princes, and the Last Lord of the First Great House."

The images faded and the High-Warden sighed. "My place is in The North; it is the blood in my veins, the words in my voice, the colors of my soul."

"It was, but the hour changes and you are still mortal, beholden to the rigors of time. There is greater need for you outside Winter's Gate than there has ever been within. It is beyond your strength to resist the rising storm; find allies now before the Dread Lords destroy The North."

The entity directed the High-Warden's attention to the southern wall where the mirrors rippled, their glass blackening in warning of a god's advent.

"*Jaidar* gathers himself, my lord, I am out of time. I will do what I can for the West when this war is done."

"While to aid you in the war is forbidden, I can give you the time you need to finish it. The night will endure, hampering the day and the passing hours. So long as the price need only be paid on the next dawn, she will suffer you to remain in The North. The day cannot be withheld forever though, so do all you can to shorten this conflict. Rest assured the *Winter Court* will keep its bargain; you no longer need concern yourself with *Malbreyth* and that your gifts shall be restored upon your return to the mortal world. I must now speak with my mother and help prepare her for the long vigil awaiting us." The entity lifted a hand in farewell. The brilliance of his form grew, swallowing all defining lines and colors in white heat. The entity submerged into the floor, his brilliance cascading across every mirror until he disappeared into the *Winter Court's* depths.

Bowing his head one last time, the High-Warden departed with a gentle murmur that called the winter he had summed to depart as well. He stepped through the arching doors and onto Adriat's tower, his gaze rising to the constellations where they pierced the dense clouds, their radiance spilling across the land in a blanket of soothing light. He looked north; there upon the horizon's peak, was a space devoid of starlight. Despite being the brightest star in the heavens, the North Star remained unseen, its position in the sky vacant.

Lord Adriat straightened at his arrival; a hand raised against the winter his advent brought. "Will they aid us?"

"Do not fear, I spoke with the North Star, and though he gave grim tidings, he also assured me the *Winter Court* will restrain *Malbreyth*."

"*Jaidar* is ready, High-Warden. I feel him, a burning presence in the back of my thoughts, searing and corruptive. I feel an unnatural heat along my skin, a warmth that brings my hair to stand. I sense his power, stretched out across the whole of The North in oppressive dominion. And when the wind dies, I can hear a ghost of rattling chains and screams."

"Yes, he is prepared and will soon descend upon us." He walked past her, descending the stairs to a side corridor and beckoning her to follow. "Lord Adriat, I need you to dispatch messenger birds to the Twelve Cities. Again, if you have already sent some; it is vital the Northern Lords bring their counselors on old magic and the rules of blood to Antiark, and that must be stressed." He reached the corridor's last door and entered, the torches and candles within igniting.

Lord Adriat followed, scanning the book-stacked shelves. "How does the Old Blood of the Great Houses concern the New Order's invasion? They died out centuries ago."

"Not entirely. They built many things, many wonders and horrors regardless of allegiance. Moreover, some thin bloodlines—bastard bloodlines—survived, as well as some that are not so thin. I do not know these survivors, but the House of Shadows has a new lord."

"*Kis'Maat* does keep his own, but how do you know this?"

He continued around the small chamber, running his fingers along hundreds of books. "The North Star instructed me to bind my actions to the Lord of the First Great House: the House of Shadows that was born of Light and in the Dark." He completed his loop. "That is not my focus now, however. Where are the dangerous manuscripts?"

"Far below us, buried in the earth and bound with silver. Why do you need them?"

"Show me."

She hurried passed. "What book are you seeking?"

"The *Grimoir*."

She stopped mid-stride, but he continued past. "Why do you want that book? It drove its author, his entire family and every descendent mad."

"I am aware, Lord Adriat, but I need to read the new pages."

"Are you sure? The *Grimoir* is a compendium of evil from centuries, compiled by a man with no inkling of what he attempted!"

"Yes, but there will also be a name I need."

"I know names have power, but what if you lose control, or the evil bleeds out?"

"I will not lose control; yes, to open the *Grimoir* is dangerous, but it is the least of what I must attempt."

"... All right, follow me." She conducted him down through Adriat's citadel, passing droves of servants lighting torches against the sudden onset of night. Even with the army's absence, soldiers seethed through Adriat in the guise of merchants, maids, fishermen, hunters and more, for everyone carried a weapon here and knew war.

The torches grew rarer as they ventured deeper in the Citadel, and through it into the Rhawn; the walls became gray with dust, the floors uncarved stone, and the sounds of life faded. They paused briefly at the final intersection for Lord Adriat to light a candle, then continued down the corridor as it led them beneath the Rhawn.

A half-hour's journey brought them to Adriat's northernmost corner and a massive iron door spanning the corridor's width. A dozen locks clamped its seam, and an equal number of iron bars rested in hooks, each heavier than one man could lift. Lord Adriat raised her candle, revealing a mass of carved vines crisscrossing the iron portal. The vines stirred in the light with a soft hiss. "I do not like this place, there is evil here I would rather see destroyed."

"The North has always preferred to bury something foul so deep it can never see the light of day again, rather than to eradicate it for fear of backlash or future need. To preserve it here means the past Lords Adriat must have known someone would need it."

"If you permit me, High-Warden, if you bury something it almost always find its way to the surface eventually. The East knows that lesson well. The North might benefit from some change."

"No, it would not. The moment it changes is the moment the Summer-lands crash in upon us." He ran a hand along the tangled vines and the locks snarled among them. The vines initially tightened, then loosened as they recognized his spirit. One by one, the locks clicked open and fell with a clatter. The last to withdraw were the bars, shuddering in their handles until a brush of his hand compelled their release.

The last bar slid into the wall, and grasping the long parallel handles, he pulled the reluctant doors open just enough to permit passage into the stale air beyond. Taking the candle from her, he entered first, cautiously keeping the flame close. Its light flickered but illuminated dilapidated books in silver cages of frosted glass, their words glinting gold and crimson from spines and loose pages. The floor shone in the torchlight due to the countless silver rivulets spanning its surface. "Was this chamber built on a plate of molten silver, or entirely encased?"

"I don't know, it was built long before my time and my predecessor never mentioned it either way." She crossed the chamber, touching each case as she passed it, prompting them to issue a soft melody. "They are keyed to The Northern Lords and the High-Warden; only those *Burdened* may open them. The previous Lord Adriat brought me here on the eve of my *Burdening*, and taught me everything he knew of this place, but also to warn me away.

He said it was not my purpose to seek knowledge in the ancient tomes of the Mortal Kingdoms, but to preserve them until I, the High-Warden, or another Lord had need of them. He confided that he had entered here only twice, once at his *Burdening*, and then at mine."

"I remember him. He was cold, like the Rhawn and The North. Two centuries he upheld his *Burden*, unmarried and unaided. He began life as a tall man and ended it as a husk, a thing of fragile bones and yellowing skin."

"How do you know that? I never saw you until after my *Burdening*."

"I visit every new Lord and Ranger-Warden chief in the days succeeding their *Burdening*, to make myself known and to take my measure. Thus I knew him before you were born." Sliding his hand into one of the cases, he retrieved a book and laid it upon a wax-splattered table beside an old lantern. "Bar the way, nothing must leave until the *Grimoir* is returned."

She complied, almost stumbling when the door yielded silently and without effort, far more willing to close than to open. "I thought you could control it?"

"I can, and you as well, but there's no reason to test fortune's grace." He began to unravel the book's worn string, but the thread frayed and snapped. The *Grimoir* burst open, the torchlight flickering across the sallow, bare parchment of its first page and diminishing: leeched into the book. The page darkened, ink stains bleeding to the surface as two feathered wings spread from the page's center, their tips brushing the book's corners. A crow's head followed, emerging from the ink spattered between the wings, its eyes red in an otherwise black image. The ink ceased its expansion, calming into a state of restless immobility. From obscure corners and cracks in the floor and walls, there came a skittering of rodents and insects, and the High-Warden looked to the floor where Lord Adriat lingered near the entrance. He raised the candle higher and its light fell over a mass of spiders, cockroaches, rats, and mice hurling themselves against the iron or scratching at the seams in a desperate bid to escape.

"High-Warden, the book ... it's bleeding!"

He continued to watch the panicking animals, and the blood beginning to appear on the iron from their paws. "Yes, Lord Adriat, the *Grimoir* bleeds. There is too much agony within its pages; some must bleed out." He reverted his attention to the *Grimoir*. The crow twisted to look at them and he stabbed his hand forward in sudden haste, grasping for any page. The crow screamed, its inky head rising off the parchment, feathers defined but spraying ink. Then the pages crashed down, sealing it inside.

He exhaled slowly and pressed on the open page, kneading the thrashing bulge until it disappeared. When it finally subsided, he glimpsed the words beneath his fingers and scowled. "Of course it would open to you."

Lord Adriat approached, a long knife flashing silver in her right hand. "Taelan Muntalabac, the Hate-Monger." She looked at him. "What does this book detail exactly? My predecessor spoke of it particularly but left its origin and nature ambiguous."

"It details the history and members of the Muntalabac family. Taelan Muntalabac was the last man to invade The North. He was a parasite of sorts, feeding and growing stronger off hate in all of its forms. It did not matter for whom or why; all that mattered was you hated. Thus he is the Hate-Monger. If you do not know of the *Grimoir*, why does it terrify you?"

"You do not need to know something to hate or fear it. My predecessor brought me here, taught me of what this room contained. One by one, he pulled out all these books: good, evil, and unaligned. He never let me read any but told me what they contained and asked that I lay a hand upon their covers. When I touched this book, I felt my thoughts turn cruel. I lusted for my *Burdening*, for the power it brought; the need to destroy him and gain power all the sooner arose within me. Logic held that I would be *Burdened* in a matter of days, but my thoughts revolted against that logic. The *Grimoir* controlled me, only when the previous Lord Adriat broke my contact with it was I freed. So, I hate it and fear it because of what it can do to me. Why does it show Taelan's name?"

"Because Taelan Muntalabac brought suffering to The North, and the *Grimoir* rejoices in reminding us." He removed his hand and flipped further into the book. Name after name, written with ink-like dried blood, in a dozen differing dialects and languages, appeared for an instant before fading as he turned pages until he reached the final page. That blank page stared up at him, and he tapped it. "None of that, you know his name." The page turned black. In a thin spidery hand and crimson ink, words appeared on the page as if being written.

Sinnitar Muntalabac: first born of the Sedition Brood, the SoulReaver.

Ignoring the words that continued to expand down the page, a list of atrocities he had no desire to learn, he grasped the book's back cover and sought to close it. The *Grimoir* resisted, hemorrhaging to coat the table. On the open page, the crimson writing also hastened, scribbling out line after line of horror. The High-Warden grasped both ends of the book and slammed it shut. Binding it closed, he spun on a heel and thrust the *Grimoir* back into its glass case. The room immediately brightened.

"Why did you need that name?"

"Its master, this Sinnitar Muntalabac, is coming North, Lord Adriat. I do not know when."

"What can we do to prepare?"

"There is nothing you can do. We can hope, of course."

"What will you do, High-Warden?"

"There is one last god that requires my attention before I can return to Antiark."

"*Jaidar?*"

"Yes. He waxes even now. I can feel him marshalling himself. The time nears. I must go."

The High-Warden emerged from Adriat's citadel, his senses screaming with *Jaidar's* mounting influence. He had mere moments before the god attained his peak and the assault began. The land sensed it as well and crouched silently about him, like an animal amidst predators, reduced to feral instinct by the vastness of the descending god. A foreigner might consider it conquered; a wise man would barricade himself inside with food, water, and wood to weather the coming storm.

He lengthened his stride, approaching the Riicann where it waited a few feet shy of the stairs, swaddled in riding blankets within a patch of cleared snow. It shifted nervously beneath the preternatural night, huffing and whining. He extended a hand to it as he arrived, soothing it with murmured praise and a gentle touch before swinging into the saddle. Its protests diminished, capitulating to resignation and a roll of flexing muscles. He leaned close, wrapping the reins about his hands and pressing its flanks. The Riicann bent and launched skyward, veering to the northeast on a breath of kind wind.

In that moment, as he started toward the final pact, *Jaidar* reached his culmination and manifested upon The Northern heavens, submerging them unto to their extremities in volcanic clouds, ashen chains, and livid cores. His being suffused the High-Warden's mind, overriding his senses and thoughts and plunging him into an incomprehensible deluge of existence. Then *Jaidar* struck from *Etherea*, the entirety of his essence crashing upon the High-Warden in that instant's breadth, bending him double.

The Riicann shrieked and buckled beneath the god's authority, plummeting. The High-Warden retaliated, answering insane fire with unchanging winter and fusing himself with the *Barrier*. The Riicann managed another shriek as it flailed, almost pitching him from the saddle when the burden of *Jaidar's* consciousness lifted. He grasped the reins in both hands and heaved, forcing the Riicann straight. Its wings caught and flared open, violently arresting their descent and slamming him forward in the saddle. He caught himself and slowly pushed upright, panting beneath the Chaos god's wroth as his senses and thoughts reeled. A storm of ice rose about, wrenching itself free of his slipping grip to assail the sky. He struggled and expanded his beset consciousness further, corralling the storm from the land below, protecting the humans and wilds from its insensate fury.

For several long minutes he could do nothing more than exist in that conflict, then his mind gradually achieved equilibrium, acclimating to the strain and allowing him to achingly direct the Riicann northward toward Winsyria's Cradle.

Hours passed, conducting them over frozen lakes, forests that waved gently despite the fearsome winds and miles of trackless tundra. The further they flew, the faster the temperature dropped until ice began collecting on the Riicann's wings, slowing their pace and compelling them to fly lower. They passed over Winsyria's Cradle, an enormous plateau nestled high within the Rhawn. Beyond it the land became more forested, broken only by lakes, rivers, and the rare village. Finally, through the haze of war, he caught the whisper from a friendly wind and knew he had arrived. Exhausted, he urged the Riicann downward.

It landed with a crash, stumbled a couple steps and slumped in the snow, steam pouring off its hide. The High-Warden dismounted and buckled beside its head, submerging to his knees beneath Jaidar's onslaught. He staggered upright and began coaxing it to toward a small cave in the mountain face, crooning words of encouragement. It rose tremulously and shuffled forward, limping until they reached the cave, where it collapsed. He knelt wearily to stroke it, offering a final word of praise and eliciting a low thrum of pleasure. Then he stood and faced deeper into the cave toward wall of azure honeycomb from where a calm buzzing originated. Northern bees crawled over it, buzzing contentedly and mending a man-sized cavity in the center, their bodies covered in downy white and blue fur and as large as his hand. He crossed to them and slipped through the cavity into the hive.

Within, the buzzing became deafening and the air filled with the scents of honey and propolis. Comb covered the ceiling and walls, much of it capped with honey or brood and all of it aswarm with nurse and worker bees.

More extended from the ceiling in wide sheets, bisecting the tunnel into corridors and filling the space with budding life.

He ventured into the warm depths, stepping sidewise to navigate the hallways as bees crawled over and alighted upon him, unperturbed by his presence. He moved carefully to avoid crushing any of them and felt his way through the dark, fingers sliding over the wax cells to either side. Occasionally he felt punctured cells, vestiges from when a Northern man came to extract honey, but these disappeared as he explored further into the hive and the brood cells became more prevalent and the air warmer.

He followed the hive to its end and there emerged into an empty corridor of stone and natural glass. The sound of waves reached from ahead, urging him toward a wavering light that glistened off damp rock. He obeyed its call and stepped from the passage onto a soaked cliff high above the roaring ocean. A tidal wave smashed the mountain face to welcome him, hurling water heavenward, soaking the passage's outcropping. A shrieking wind rushed into his face, berating him with flecks of ice and water, compelling him to shield his eyes as he advanced to the precipice.

The Ocean stretched before him in unconstrained violence, the waves tumbling over one another in a tumult of black water, ice, and half-seen leviathans. It swelled, crashing against the Rhawn with such force they quaked.

There was no peace here; the Ocean was at storm and its rage at the gods' invasion boundless.

Old as the world, the Ocean was *Winsyria*'s first daughter, though daughter is an inapt description. The Ocean was not a creature of intelligent thought; it is wild and bestial, a creature of instinct alone, much like The North, only there is no High-Warden to temper it.

Closing his hand into a fist, he flung the rage-maddened wind and the ice aside, ejecting them from the cove to lay the furious water bare. Then he braced himself against the Ocean's rage and spoke, "I call you, daughter of *Winsyria*, to answer this need. You are bound to your father and will answer this summons!" The Ocean roared, the waves withdrawing from him and rising to form a mountain of their own.

Up and up it rose, emptying its cove and leaving the floor parched, revealing the crabs that scuttled along its fissures. The Ocean slammed forward, hammering the Rhawn and hurling the High-Warden against the mountain face. He recovered his balance and returned to the edge; his strides labored but steady beneath *Jaidar's* assault. His hand snapped forward, closed into a fist, and then drew back, pivoting his whole body with its force. A hundred threads of water erupted from the turbulent Ocean, winding about one another as they writhed to escape his grip. He lowered his hand, and the stream of water latched onto the outcropping's edge. He stepped forward, planting a boot firmly on the current. The sound of cracking ice rose from beneath his step and frost exploded from his heel, converting the roiling stream inch by inch into a staircase of ice.

The Ocean roared and hurled herself against him, but froze upon contact, thickening the stair. Heedless of this, the High-Warden advanced onto the stair, extended a warding hand and closed it, pulling the Ocean irresistibly into his authority. It recoiled, desperate to escape, but failed to liberate itself. He stumbled, dragged by the sheer power she exerted, and then drew back with a grimace, hauling her up the stair. The water around him froze in a sweeping arc, encompassing the entire cove. He inhaled and exhaled again, thrusting the ice deeper, forcing the Ocean to solidify down to its dregs within the cove.

Jaidar beleaguered him all the while, hammering his thoughts to whittle him away. The High-Warden shoved back, jaw taught from the strain, then grasped the stairs' railing and descended to where they became the hallway of a palace delving into the frozen water.

A thin layer of powdered frost billowed up from stairs and walls as he passed, coloring his hands and clothing white in the seconds before they melted. The stair concluded at a pair of double doors which opened to an empty hall filled with empty chairs and empty tables. Pillars devoid of torches and decorations ran along the walls and the hall's center while candelabras adorned the ceiling, bearing hundreds of frosted candles. Tall furnaces occupied the spaces between pillars and doors but contained neither flame nor wood, while an abandoned dais for musicians and performers waited at chamber's far extremity. The power that forged this palace was his, but the design was the Ocean's.

He crossed the chamber, each step exposing a tiled floor from beneath the powdered ice, and exited through a door thrown open on the far wall. Beyond, he discovered a kitchen—with a feast made of ice spread upon every surface—and a plethora of doors, only one pair of which were open.

He could feel the Ocean surrounding him, her movements sluggish within the ice but still wrathful. Even now, the palace's edges were beginning to crack and split as she resisted her confinement. He touched the door frame in passing, sending a burst of energy cascading through the ice to repair the widening fractures.

Past the kitchen, he found a library with high walls and shattered bookcases, and faltered at the devastation. Truncated chairs cluttered the room with the bottom halves relegated to the left side of the room and the upper halves to the right; the shattered bookcases' skeletal frames remained upright against the walls, but their splintered shelves were strewn across the floor, abandoned atop the sea of frozen pages and book covers; in fact, the only thing not broken was a solitary table at the center and the few open books on it.

The High-Warden approached the table, shuffling the frozen pages aside with his feet. Once there, he leaned over the open books and blew away the ice powder. The words were legible despite being written in an old dialect. He traced a finger over the page, murmuring to himself as he read. He did not recognize the manuscript, but he knew the event it detailed. The words described a conflict, and though other men were mentioned, only one name was ever written: his name.

He retreated from the table, scanning the walls, broken shelves, and ravaged books. Kicking aside the fragments of ice, he circumvented the table for the open door and exited onto a balcony suspended in a soaring circular hollow. A forest of suspended roads crossed the space both above and below him, connecting doors on the exterior wall with mirroring entrances on the face of a reflective central column. Ice animals swam through the hollow spaces between and around those walkways, moving with the grace of living creatures despite their frozen skin and absent water, many far larger than their natural size and others a hundredfold smaller.

An emerald road extended from his balcony to an unwelcoming door of the same hue. He crossed and touched the portal's center, searching for a handle or crevice in the smooth perfection. The door melted at his touch and swirled once around his feet before vanishing, admitting him. He entered, feeling the Ocean more acutely here than anywhere else.

On the inside, the column's walls flowed ever upwards, a river of moving ice filled with incorporeal faces that would surface for a heartbeat before resubmerging. He recognized some of the faces, but the majority were unfamiliar.

There was little else besides the door and the faces, just a floor, ceiling, and a chandelier of flowing water. He advanced to the chamber's center, waving a hand to form a chair of ice. He scanned the chamber once for any sign of the Ocean before taking his seat to wait.

Abruptly the walls ceased their flow and pulled the faces into their depths. The Ocean spoke to him, and though she used no words, her meaning cascaded through him: "How dare he summon her?"

Her meaning ricocheted through him, leaving his bones vibrating and his hearing dulled. "I am the High-Warden of Winsyria: Lord *Ever-Winter*.

When I call, you must answer. That is the law, and I can suffer no harm for enacting it."

She lashed out again, her rage mounting. Her meaning drowned him again: "She served only *Winsyria*, never a mortal."

"I do not seek to master you. I seek your aid; the aid you are bound to give. Gods beset The North, and though you rage at their transgression, you have not punished them. I call you to battle, to avenge this violation. You will answer this need."

Jaidar, sensing his defeat, screamed in *Etherea* and hurled his might against the High-Warden with such force the chair shattered beneath him, scattering splinters of ice across the floor. On his hands and knees, the High-Warden rasped and coughed, spitting a mouthful of violet blood.

He retaliated, hurling his strength against the god and breaking his assault for an instant before it renewed. He pushed himself to stand, fighting against the god's assault and his own fatigue to reiterate his earlier avowal, "You will answer this need."

The walls erupted, their water turning first black than the green of oceans. Again the Ocean impressed her meaning upon and through him, wracking his form with the weight of her consciousness: "She was beholden to none, the master of sailors, beloved and hated by all. She was kind on a caprice and cruel on a whim. She would never suffer the laws of gods or men."

He straightened his caving shoulders and held his hands out to the sides, palms up and fingers spread as if welcoming the Ocean into an embrace. "You will answer this need of your own volition, or the laws of your father will force your hand." His hands closed into fists, and the water raging within the walls ceased its struggles. He could feel her against his grip, thrashing in his hands, striving to hurl her might against him, to break him as she would any ship that sailed her waters. She could not, for with his words he had laid a geas upon her. She was bound to *Winsyria* as his daughter, and therefore to The North. Though she was a thousand-fold greater than him, the High-Warden of Winsyria was the keeper of The North, and all the powers of The North are given to him to aid in that keeping. She could not defy him.

A shriek erupted into life around him, echoing through the walls and his body. The chamber split, a massive rupture sundering the floor from one edge to the other. In that scream, he heard her meaning, her will, and her defiance: "She would not submit, no matter what." In her scream, he heard the wild animal terrified of the man and his collar.

He closed his eyes and rotated. He continued to spin, arms pulling close and pushing away, gathering the Ocean to him. He ceased his spinning, standing astride a fissure in the ice with his arms pressed to his chest and wrists crossed. He exhaled, turning his fists outward and pushed. The cracks and the rupture spread further, scaling the walls, breaking off into more and more cracks. When his arms reached their full extension, the whole of the chamber was a vista of cracked ice. He opened his fists and the walls melted, unleashing a torrent of water.

The raging liquid spiraled up his form to engulf him. Even as it touched him, however, it recoiled. The water rose into a pillar and froze from the bottom up, hairline threads of ice racing along the outer edges and worming inward, forcing the Ocean into a new shape: a statue of a woman, water swirling up about her as she held it to her bosom like a dress.

Jaidar roared and unleashed all his might in a final, desperate assault against the High-Warden. The Ocean, however, could no longer sit idly by; she had been called to battle and now she answered that summons. Water and fire clashed in a deafening roar as *Jaidar* battled against the Ocean's power. The High-Warden slumped forward, tension flowing from his form like a spring melt. When his breathing calmed, he clambered to his feet, ready to hear the final price, his irrefutable sentence for using the Ocean's power. "What is to be my price?"

It did not matter that his actions served The North, even if the Ocean had conceded, it would not have mattered; he must pay for the power he used. The Ocean sold the power, but the power would demand its own price. She would speak it and her anger would fuel it, but the price had been determined long ago. Even if she desired to, she could no more rescind the price than he could ignore it.

Cold fury surrounded him, but its violence was gone, spent on her continued war with *Jaidar*. The soft ripple of her meaning found him, sliding into his mind with the grace of a lily on the pond: "You will leave The North with the dawn, relinquishing your *Burden* to another. You will never return to or touch any ocean again. This is my condemnation, High-Warden; rejoice, for you alone forced the Ocean to your will." She left him alone in the frozen palace with his price.

He permitted himself a second to mourn, then straightened his shoulders and departed; a war still ravaged The North, and the dawn would not tarry long if the North Star spoke true. He left the ice palace, heedless of the halls and corridors that melted around him. Only the statue remained, its brow visible just beneath the surface.

51

A Stroll Through Starlight

Slade dodged through the people running to or from Echeira'Sollas, fiddling with his collar and committing the minor evil of removing his pin. After the little gold disk was safely tucked inside his satchel, he extracted its two substitutes: the first was an unadorned bronze that denoted his status as a lower-class citizen while the second—a silver, slightly larger disk—bore the sword and shield of military service. Slade considered adding a third pin to promote himself but decided rank would make him too memorable. He removed his hat for the same reason and stuffed the distraught article down his satchel. Next he wandered the temple's outskirts for several minutes before a priest finally dragged him about. "Help us, oh gods, please help us; Echeira'Sollas is under attack!"

"What?" Slade roared, reeling backward. "Who possesses the gull to attack *Enecki's* own temple?".

"*Jaidar, Jaidar* attacks us. The Abyss' gates opened before our very eyes. Blood came from everywhere, dripping from the ceiling, bubbling up through the cracks, dribbling down the walls, pooling at my feet until with every step I kicked splatters across my fellows. Then a demon emerged and he darkened the temple's own light, his fire boiling the blood and blackening the walls. Oh gods we're all going to die!" The priest stumbled away, falling to his knees and clutching at his head. "Butchered, we're all going to get butchered and eaten and burned and staked and–" His head snapped up, preceding his frantic scramble across the ground to paw at Slade's legs. "Help us, I beg you, take word to the governor and tell him Echeira'Sollas is being attacked and–" A temple window exploded behind the priest, and he shrieked into the ground, spewing prayers at an alarming rate.

Donning a resolute expression, Slade touched the man's quivering shoulder. "Fear no longer, you brave, brave soul; I shall requisition a mount and ride to the governor's mansion without delay."

663

"Hurry, oh gods please hurry." Behind the priest another window shattered, an enormous, mottled arm thrusting itself through the gap.

Without even looking, the priest squealed and fled toward the nearest war-shelter. Witnessing this, Slade chuckled then spun in a slow circle, searching for a suitable mount. Fortunately, more than a dozen horses fidgeted nearby, small knots of priests fluttering around them while trying to either saddle or mount them.

One particularly frazzled priest suggested himself to Slade, the man's arms flailing, desperately grasping for either the saddle horn or reigns as he slid around atop his mount. What fiction of control he had vanished when the horse reared, casting him to the earth in a billow of white fabric.

Lured by the clear inexperience, Slade straightened his back, broadened his shoulders and marched across the square. "Perhaps, I can assist you, Holy One," he said, extending a hand to the priest who stared up, eyes filling with relief upon noticing the military pin.

"Yes, yes you may." Taking Slade's hand with a firm unwavering grip, he scrambled to his feet. "Take this horse and ride to the city's southern barracks, tell them one of *Jaidar's* demons is attacking Echeira'Sollas."

Wordlessly, Slade swung up into the saddle, his years of practice granting an unshakable confidence that his mount noticed. "What about the governor, shall I inform him of your plight?"

"No. Two men were already dispatched to the governor's mansion; you alone ride to the southern barracks. Go swiftly, go safely, and may *Enecki's* light shine upon you."

Slade nodded and kicked his mount into a canter, travelling the expected road until he escaped observation; whereupon he tugged the reins and set course for the governor's mansion.

He traversed the extinguished city with the clatter of hooves both leading and trailing behind, warning any who slept of something irregular. Windows came to flickering life, some thrusting open as their owners leaned out to observe. Soon curious eyes were redirected to the reddish glow filling the sky above Echeira'Sollas, alarmed gasps swiftly following along with the men arming themselves and rushing for the temple. Their wives meanwhile dropped heavy beams into place behind doors.

At last, Slade sighted the mansion, its bulk glaring with the light of a thousand torches that reflected off the armor of an extremely prepared, extremely restless army of Theanne. Immediately he dropped from his horse and rolled behind a partially unloaded cart, letting the animal continue on alone.

One industrious soldier caught its reigns only to blanch as his fingers came away bloody. A superior officer was called for, and she concluded the messenger had been killed while riding to the mansion. With a signal to her horn blower, the officer's troops formed up and marched to Echeira'Sollas' aid, parading right past the source of all their troubles.

After that, Slade easily infiltrated the mansion's grounds, rendezvousing with Harram's group along the east wall. As universal nods were exchanged, a man to Slade's left muttered a quiet prayer before hefting his crossbow. A harsh snap split the air, followed by the dull clatter of a grappling hook latching onto a windowsill. The archer then tested its grip with a sharp tug and stepped back, rubbing sweaty hands against his thighs. "It's ready, but we need to ascend one at a time."

Slade nodded. "I'll climb first and check for inconveniences; but remember I've personal errands to attend, so I won't be waiting at the top." Some of his crew shuffled in place or traded glances at this, prompting Slade to clap the nearest man on his shoulder. "Don't look so worried; I'm out chasing trouble, so if you encounter any, just remember I'm riding on its tail." With a final, wave Slade scrambled up the rope and rolled through the window, sliding to the luxuriously carpeted hall floor.

He lay perfectly still, listening for the potential hum of magic or the sound of approaching footsteps, eyeing the walls for moving shadows or the muffled glow of concealed runes. He even sniffed, checking for more mundane traps. Nothing. They all remained disarmed from his earlier visit.

A moment later, Harram half slid through the window, stopping to stare down at his employer. "Shouldn't you have swept off in a storm of mystery and chaos by now?"

"Ideally yes, but I'm resting after the ascent of a thoroughly disagreeable wall that bedecked itself with all manner of boiling oil, flaming tar pits, and serrated spikes."

"I can assure you it possesses none of those. It's a regular sweetheart of a wall." Harram walked forward on his hands to fully enter the building, cautiously positioning them around Slade.

"Of course it doesn't; I removed the undesirable elements. Pulling the stakes out by hand, mopping the oil up with my shirt, etcetera." Slade kicked his legs up, rolled onto his shoulders and flipped onto his feet.

"What about the flaming tar pits?"

"I spat vitriol upon them until they recognized the error of their ways. Why else would the ascent have taken so long?"

A set of hands appeared at the window and Harram leaned outside, helping the next thief into the mansion. As the newcomer collapsed, he twisted back around to discover Slade had disappeared.

His companion, meanwhile, gasped his way through a sentence. "Tell me again ... why couldn't we ... knock on the front ... door?"

Grabbing the man under his shoulders, Harram hoisted him up. "Because Slade says that's unspeakably rude, at least after midnight, and he's woken me up enough times that I agree with him."

Slade's first errand took him to the kitchen where Samara probably loitered. Ever since her true loyalties came to light and her subsequent departure had its hiccup, she'd avoided him. Tonight was the perfect opportunity to rectify that.

Locating the nearest staircase, he descended to the ground level. From there he traced the scent of smoke, spices, and a myriad of secondary aromas to where they escaped from a wide open door. Stepping through, he found clutter so pervasive it almost scaled the walls, consuming every inch of available space and making its fellow inhabitants—everything from the kitchen equipment to the walls themselves—grapple for the mere chance to breathe.

This general lack of space stemmed from several enormous ovens squatting along the back wall, their bulk encroaching on the room's center where a giant, multiple tiered, many-legged table consumed the remaining space. Samara's smoky silhouette could be seen dashing down the few, sliver like walkways these behemoths tolerated. She struggled against a budding apocalypse, pots hissing and spitting all across the room while cooking sheets bellowed smoke and some frying pans hosted budding fires.

His gallant nature roused by the smell of burning delicacies, Slade leapt into action, dodging through the slumbering staff, tiptoeing across a floor begrimed with flour, eggs, and old sauces, and finally reaching a series of broad skylights.

Seconds later the smoke began gliding past him, escaping through the newly opened skylights as Slade popped a rescued delicacy into his mouth. He then joined Samara in rushing about the room, endeavoring to stay the wholesale slaughter.

At long last, Samara collapsed into a seat with a deep, exhausted sigh. Slade, meanwhile, began picking through their salvaged foods. "In the future, warn me against allowing you anywhere near a kitchen. We might lose the whole castle next time."

"I'm well aware I'm a walking disaster in the kitchen. That doesn't make it funny."

"Only because you're the subject; trust me, the others will find this hysterical. That aside, I assume everything progressed swimmingly?"

"One or two momentary hitches arose."

"All suitably dealt with I presume?"

"Some of the staff ate earlier, so I prepared a tea with … creative ingredients."

"Nicely done. Without those distractions, we can discuss something of vital importance to us both."

Samara stiffened, her fingers tightening around her armrests. "Our present situation doesn't exactly lend itself to a heart to heart."

"Nonsense," he said, flapping a hand. "The only time better than now is yesterday, and since yesterday will invariably elude us, we must settle for the present."

"Slade, we should really discuss this another time. Distracting ourselves will only invite disaster."

"Disaster is the spice of life, or one of them anyway."

"Some spices don't agree with everybody. I, for one, am allergic to disaster."

"I admit, it is an acquired taste." Slade offered Samara a plate with various morsels. "Sweetmeat? No? Alright." Sitting back, he popped one into his mouth. "In all honesty, I can't imagine what you're fussing about. I let other people dupe me and none of them are expecting imminent death. There was an existential crisis or two, but you're the only one who's avoiding my poor benign self."

"Others?"

"Not all from Carr'Selain obviously; I'm hosting spies from each of the major guilds and one from Cardolyn Tyier's secret police. They're the primary reason I remain such an enthralling mystery." He smirked at her, his self-satisfaction rolling off in tangible waves. "Anyway, to make a long, exciting story short and boring, I've known your true loyalties from the start. In fact, I'm responsible for making you slink down here to snoop through all my terribly secret business."

She stared at him, mouth all but hanging open. "You wanted a spy in your midst?"

"Oh yes, it became incredibly tedious to uncover and deport every new spy that strolled through my gates. I thought it best to open my door and let the wolf wander around; that way, in a moment of inattention, I could paint his toenails pink. Besides, I had an ulterior motive, a notion to mold you for a grand design. But, to my everlasting despair, you proved inflexible."

"Oh, … what did you intend for me?"

"World domination of course, or at least domination of the West."

"Oh." Samara stared down at her lap, eventually voicing a short, bitter laugh. "So that's why Tasha had such an appalling time dealing with you: false information. I'd chalked it up to her being incompetent, but no, I was the incompetent one." She shook her head, suppressing another burst of laughter. "Since I botched the exams, I'm assuming Tasha's my replacement?"

"Yes."

"Were there other candidates?"

"Yes, a handsome, agreeable character with one major flaw; a certain murderous inclination toward myself. Apart from him, you and Tasha were my only hopefuls."

Samara frowned, shifted in place then picked at a scab, never once looking up. "Did"—she swallowed—"did you kill him, this … third candidate?"

Slade scoffed. "Except for sociopaths, we only kill because of weakness or mistakes. Have you ever known me to make a mistake?" Samara shook her head a tad sheepishly. "Excellent, but if that's not convincing enough, perhaps this'll help. What nobody seems to understand is that killing makes for a terrible hassle. First you have to kill the poor fellow and then you're obligated to bury or cremate him; because if you don't, the government will fine you for littering. Except you can neither bury nor cremate someone without a license, and we all know what bureaucracy's like. After that you must convince the victim's family of his general mediocrity if not outright ineptitude, and hopefully they'll compensate you for his elimination."

"If I'm useless, disgraced, and reprieved, why can't I leave? With Tasha writing accurate reports and your own meeting with Madame Roshfren, I can't believe keeping me here provides any benefit. Unless"—she took a deep, shuddering breath—"unless you want to punish me."

"I have no interest in causing unnecessary pain; I simply enjoy being mysterious. You're a treasure trove of my secrets, and I can't very well be mysterious without secrets, now can I."

Samara rubbed her brows, only vaguely aware of Slade puttering around the kitchen. "So, I'm to be a prisoner?"

"I'm afraid I can't supply a gilded cage, but yes."

"What happens when Carr'Selain recalls me?"

"Unfortunately, here's where you uncover a black mark in my record. He won't recall you, not after Madame Roshfen verifies you snuck into the mansion and divulged our plans to Governor Warsein."

Samara burst to her feet, arms flying open. "But you told me to inform the governor!"

"Something of which neither Madame Roshfen nor Carr'Selain are aware and will remain ignorant to. This, combined with fears of you having gone native, will prompt Carr'Selain to liquidate your contract."

"But that will force an immediate settling of debts; I don't have enough savings. I could lose everything." The blood drained from her face. "And the frank dismissal will blacklist my name; I'll never work for a guild again."

"An unfortunate repercussion."

Samara snatched a glass from the table and flung it across the room with a scream. "So much for not punishing me. Why, why would you do this?"

"Is there a reason I shouldn't have?" Slade asked calmly. "Do I owe you something? You, the woman who's been pedaling secrets without regard for how it might harm, even kill, my family or her own friends?" He shook his head. "You are so possessed by the idea of serving your guild that you would sacrifice us for the mere chance at returning, even in disgrace."

Samara looked away, unable to meet his eyes. "That's my job; it's what I was supposed to do."

"Just like I'm supposed to protect all my little ducklings from whatever threats arise."

"Alright fine, I'm the villain. I'm—" She fell back into her seat, hands tangling in her hair. "Oh gods, what am I going to do?"

"You'll work for me, unless of course, you're beguiled by the notion of becoming an honest citizen."

"What?"

"I don't trust you and probably won't for several years, but it's an opportunity to build upon the fortune you earned tonight."

"You're actually letting me keep it?"

"Yes, you embraced the danger and did your part right alongside everyone else."

Cupping her mouth and nose, Samara began rocking in her chair, struggling to process the unlooked-for miracle. "What would I be doing?"

"Working here under careful supervision, managing my organization so it doesn't go up in flames while I'm gone."

Her gaze snapped toward him. "What?"

"I need Harram elsewhere, which means you're my only experienced alternative. Besides, you never did any damage, so there's no point in holding a grudge."

Samara stared at him, the seconds strolling by until, finally, she acceded; whereupon Slade swooped in to place a loud, smacking kiss atop her head. "Marvelous. Sadly, I must fly, disasters won't cause themselves." A heartbeat after vanishing, his head poked back into the kitchen, nodding toward the freshly prepared sandwich that had materialized beside her. "Do eat something; you're looking a bit peckish."

As he disappeared a second time, Samara tentatively peeked under the top slice. *What's this, chicken, celery, and ... are those apples?*

Slade ascended to the upper levels, dodging around shrouded Swanlights and passing through as many vaulted chambers as he did the long shadowy hallways that forever riddled powerful homes. Thrice, nobles or wandering servants forced him into a nearby alcove, and once, an attentive guard chased him into a broom cupboard. There, to his amusement, Slade found the man's drunken compatriot humming and talking to himself, cheerfully oblivious to the world.

Capitalizing upon the opportunity, Slade stripped the man to his undergarments and, after the first guard left to be competent elsewhere, resumed his journey with one liquor-stained uniform tucked under his arm. A short ascent through a claustrophobic stairwell brought him to where one of Harram's scouts peeked out from behind a corner.

"Did you observe anyone coming this way?" she asked, striding out to meet him then shifting sideways to maintain a clear view of the hallway.

"Happily, I can report no imminent invasion." Slade extended his hand toward the woman, pilfered boots swinging from two fingers. "Happier still, I can report the presence of gifts." He dropped the boots at her feet, wrapped the coat around her shoulders and presented the trousers. "Wear these and goose step around as if you're patrolling. Keep the pins when you're done; such objects have innumerable uses."

She nodded once, easily slipping into the uniform before pulling her hair into a severe ponytail and buckling the weapon around her waist. "How do I look?"

"Like a girl wearing her father's clothing. Luckily, passersby will assume you're a new recruit who the quartermaster couldn't equip properly. Now return to your post with all the militaristic ardor of a child who learned about death and glory on her grandfather's knee."

Slade left the woman to her assigned task and hurried through the intervening corridors until he smelled the singed odor of accidentally triggered defenses and heard the low mutterings of conversation happening over the soft clink of coins. Interlaced with these was the occasional curse; a muted exclamation always following on the heels of an inadvertent noise.

Harram stood amidst the bustle, tucking various unconscious Theanne guards in for the night by carefully moving each to safety before draping a blanket across them and lifting their heads onto a pillow. All the while, a glittering room waited patiently behind him, its entrance rising an impressive twenty feet skyward, though its massive double doors stood open a mere crack, just enough to permit a steady stream of bag-toting thieves.

Each thief paused alongside Harram to deliver a brief record of their spoils, the process continuing even as Slade approached.

"How generous and varied have Governor Warsein's gifts been?" he asked, returning Harram's cursory nod.

"Gold-crowns and -scepters mostly, though we've also encountered a fair amount of bejeweled goblets and impractical swords. An occasional trinket will crop up as well."

"Place those in a separate bag. We'll have Malendor peruse them when we're done, they may possess interesting characteristics."

"As you say." Harram scribbled a quick note on a clipboard lying to his right. "Not to rush you, but the bags are forming a rather ostentatious pile beneath the eastern balcony. Have you secured Governor Warsein's ship yet?"

"Due to problematic circumstances involving three pixies, a wine barrel, and numerous irascible dragons, I was avoidably detained. I'll look into the ship as soon as I'm through here."

In the distance, a man roared bloody vengeance, spurring a cascade of similar shouts and signaling the start to a nighttime disturbance that, here in the Paladin Empire, was a little short of heinous.

In response, Slade doffed his hat. "Farewell, Harram, it appears I'm needed elsewhere."

"What did you do, start a riot?"

He grinned over his shoulder. "Among other things."

Upon locating a suitable window, Slade flipped its meticulously oiled latch and leaned out into the night, looking for and finding eight squat, rectangular buildings with red shingles. Unassuming architecture aside, a couple of the barracks made for interesting observation, flourishing with movement and noise as the aforementioned riot took place within.

Overlaying this excitement was the occasional grumble from a disgruntled sky, briefly stealing Slade's attention before he slipped out the window and dropped to the earth below. There a quick glance checked for potential witnesses and then he was dashing forward, steps carrying him low while the verdant pasture muted any suggestion of sound.

This first barracks he encountered stewed in shadows and silence, suggesting the occupants were off assisting Echeira'Sollas. Ignoring it, Slade advanced to the next structure, which practically ballooned outward from the violence ensuing within.

A sliding halt brought him beneath its nearest window, after which he slithered up the bricks to peek over the sill.

Inside verged on total bedlam and, despite standing as a lone bulwark against law and order, Crannir thrived in the violence, spinning through it elegantly as he dealt indiscriminate injustice to his attackers.

One of Slade's eyebrows quirked. *'He may surpass my already grand expectations, how delightful.'*

Crannir's opponents, on the other hand, suffered from the battlefield chaos. What had started as a united army determined to apprehend him was devolving into a mess of enraged, drunken or desperate bellows with even the staunchest peacekeeper beginning to retaliate against any accidental blows.

Assured that Crannir had the situation well in hand, Slade slunk further down the line, bypassing two unlit barracks before reaching Tehroc's domain. The assassin had acquired two makeshift clubs and was cheerfully belaboring his opponents with them. As a result, most lay in sundry forms of awkward, uncomfortable repose.

The next barracks sounded livelier than either of its predecessors, suggesting far more of its inhabitants remained conscious. Providing another contrast was Jamus, who sat outside the building, leaning against its front wall, smoking contentedly and utterly uninvolved with the conflict.

Slade offered a little wave then stopped a centimeter or two from a temporary, shining path that streamed through the busted doorway, leery of crossing lest a guard spot him.

Jamus smiled. "You treat light as a cat treats water, with infinite disdain."

Slade flashed the assassin a grin and, moving with exaggerated care, placed a lone toe on the path. A moment later, he had crossed the divide, using a single fluid motion that was both half-leap and half-step. "I've always appreciated cats; they have this magnificent air of superiority and an unequaled talent for dismissing other creatures. Cats truly are excellent role models."

"I know a few dogs who'd disagree." Jamus drew deeply upon his cigarette, head falling back against the barrack's wall as he exhaled a respectable cloud of smoke. In so doing, he revealed the colorful bruise swelling his left eye.

Instantly Slade knelt and took Jamus' head between his hands. "I'm assuming this was collected so you could brag when exchanging stories with your friends?" Slade maneuvered Jamus' head toward the light. "If so, I must condemn your efforts. It's too unsightly to display proudly, and yet so minor that you can't proclaim your imminent demise."

Jamus watched Slade closely but submitted to the administrations, voicing a muted hiss when his impromptu doctor touched the swollen purple skin around his eye. "I doubt either would have impressed them anyway; as assassins, we value escaping unscathed and unremarked more than winning lopsided fights. Believe it or not, this"—he tapped his eye with a slight, amused smile—"was intentional; a reason to excuse myself early. However, I never clarified that I wanted a light tap and so voila, I'm seeing stars. New constellations aside, I think I succeeded quite nicely. The plan was obviously genius."

"A plan working doesn't make it genius," Slade snorted, digging into his satchel. "Look at generals across history. Most survived, thrived, and or died according to luck's whim."

"I'm not sure I believe—"

"Pashaw"—Slade flapped a hand—"you just haven't realized that I've already convinced you. If those men were true geniuses, their empires wouldn't have crumbled the moment they died. All that said, I will acknowledge one benefit of your condemned scheme, it enables that glorious all-consuming depravity known as indolence."

"Oh, I wouldn't call myself lazy, more of … bookish."

"What a shame; I heartily advocate wallowing in indolence. It's one of our more sublime predilections and we should cultivate it to excess, though reading's good too." Slade placed a small clay jar atop the assassin's head. "Spread this over the bruise, it'll decrease the swelling."

Jamus froze for a second then—somewhat uncertainly—tilted forward so that the jar could slide free, dropping into his waiting hands. "You know, I've always wondered how people like you choose their personality for the day?"

"What do you mean?"

"You wear a different personality every time we meet. First, you're a sneering, vindictive thief lord. Then, coldly indifferent as you weave threads, twist minds, and modify the world. And tonight, you're a man who tends to someone he's only met twice."

"I'm impressed, you've guessed my true chaotic nature."

"Don't be. Naric dropped in after you left, and we told him of our harrowing experience, expecting surprise or at least sympathy. To our irritation and growing horror, he laughed as he recounted several far more harrowing stories."

"Ah yes, we've enjoyed quite a few adventures together; happily, he's endured them marvelously."

"So how do you choose your personality for the day?"

"Whichever tickles my fancy."

"And how does a sweet, innocent child become such a complicated man?"

"Well, many years ago—when I was but a wee lad—my well-intentioned mother filled my head with all sorts of perverted concepts. Foremost among which was the belief I could be anybody I wished. This innocuous statement proved to be an invasive one and soon its roots burrowed into every facet of my psyche."

Jamus chuckled. "Ah, I see. Thank you for sharing."

"My pleasure."

Strangely, the last barracks sat in well-mannered silence despite the light shining from within. Creeping up to the door and easing it open a bare sliver, Slade grinned at the scene beyond. Lydia sat in a precariously balanced chair, feet propped atop a mound of bodies as she dined on various sweets scavenged from the soldiers' dinner, periodically sipping a glass of their captain's wine.

Slade rapped his knuckles against the doorframe and entered, causing Lydia to almost capsize her chair before he strode across the room and steadied her. "Although I appreciate the sentiment, there's no need; I'm not a king, nor do I aspire to become one." Leaning past her, he collected the half-finished decanter for a sniff of its contents. "Either the captain's embezzling, or he's got rich friends."

"Give that back, it's mine." Lydia snatched the wine from his hand, pressing the cherished liquid to her chest as if that might protect it from his villainy. "I took forever to find it, so go get your own."

"My, my, my, hear the dragon roar." Slade crossed to where the last serviceable chair waited, tipped its occupant to the floor and dragged the seat back. "However did you know to look?"

"Fool left it uncorked; I smelled wine as soon as I stepped through the door." She shifted her feet atop the mounded bodies, making room for Slade.

"Sounds like the start to a grand adventure. Where did you find it? Sitting on his desk or in a pit guarded by slavering dogs?"

"Credit where credit's due, our friend knew how to hide things. He's stashed one of those new combination safes behind a false wall in his desk. Problem was, whoever made the safe is completely inept. A sneeze could've broken it open." Grabbing the well-endowed purse from the floor beside her chair, Lydia bounced it atop her palm. "Also, he's definitely embezzling."

"Consider me impressed," Slade said clapping softly, prompting her to level a glower. "Don't worry, I meant it honestly. When I mock, I mock through comedic hyperbole, anything else annoys people."

"I think you annoy people whatever you do."

"Seeing as I engender that pesky emotion involuntarily, I renounce all blame in the matter." Slade grinned, then a thought striking him, dug into his satchel. "Speaking of wine, there's something I forgot to give you earlier." He revealed a frosted cup like those her friends had received, complete with Lydia's own decorative animal. "The hawk is delightfully appropriate, yes?"

Setting the decanter aside, Lydia tipped forward and warily took the gift from Slade. "So you chose animals that reflected our personalities. Have you really been studying us that long?"

"Yes, though I didn't match the animals to your personalities; I simply requested whichever ones I found pleasing. The hawk suited your character, so I gifted it to you, enjoying the correlation as much as the creature itself."

"Meanwhile, our resident fire-mage received a phoenix and Crannir an albatross, no doubt referring to his luck and his role as our leader."

"A happy accident."

"Sure. The only animal I can't understand is Tehroc's. What possessed you to give him an otter?"

Slade shrugged. "The artisan suffered a brief spat of artistic license; claiming that, and I quote, 'Mindless boredom infected me'."

"Well, with your artistic genius now in doubt, what's your animal?"

Slade considered her for a short time, then with a shrug, reached into his satchel. "I could not say why I picked these particular animals, only that they seemed suited to the task." Where the other glasses boasted one animal, Slade's glass had four.

"Raven, magpie, rook, and crow," she said, turning the glass in her hands. "All birds with a taste for shiny trinkets."

"Indeed." The cup traded hands again, and Slade returned it to his satchel. "Seeing as we've dealt with the pleasantries; I have a task for you."

"I'm busy so send Jamus. Last I checked, he lazed around like a dog at noon."

"I had intended on both of you going."

"Two of us? Must be important."

"Desperately so. You see, the governor's personal ship needs commandeering."

Lydia smiled. "That's a cheeky way to steal from the governor."

"Yes, I rather thought so."

52

In Search Of A Key

The storm's first raindrops plipped atop his hat as Slade abandoned Lydia to her barracks. A quick glance gauged its approach and sent him sprinting to the mansion, where thunder boomed much louder and much closer than earlier; but Slade was too busy sneaking back through the window to notice.

A brief delay saw the window latched so its soon-to-be violent banging wouldn't disturb anyone, after which he skulked his way across the mansion, hurrying through barren halls until encountering his desired staircase and its spiraling ascent.

Outside the storm arrived in full, rumbling and proclaiming its ascendency to all those beneath it. Sheets of rain rattling upon the roof as lightning struck out across the sky and saturated the world in white pigment. Thunder trailed closely behind, roaring at the lightning for its audacity in striking first.

As Slade neared the top of the staircase, a silver gold luminance appeared ahead of him, spurring a crouch and a slow ease forward until he could peer around the stair's curving edge.

Up atop the landing, a crescent-shaped room was illuminated by a hanging Swanlight, its glow pooling on the armored shoulders of two tense, sharp-eyed guards in the official gear of the Imperial Army. Theanne were competent enough; but for protecting his son, Governor Warsein demanded Cardolyn's best, especially when Echeira'Sollas was under siege.

Slade leaned back, sighing as he raised a mental glass. *'Here's to you, fat, sleepy, overpaid guards; you'll forever be in our hearts.'* No defense was seamless though. He simply needed to find the crack. A slow pivot and search of the unassuming stairway yielded nothing until he lifted his eyes to the arched ceiling. Then it yielded a grin.

Quickly he touched his palms to either wall, grin broadening as his elbows were left slightly bent. Bracing himself, Slade pressed his feet to the walls and repositioned his arms higher, working toward an elevation from which he could leap, grab a rafter, and swing up atop it. There, submerged in shadows and dust, he listened for the guard's response. Nothing.

Without precursor, he catapulted himself from one rafter to the next, landing with perfect balance as dust puffed up all around his feet. Nary a whisper had marked his passage.

Slade leapt three more rafters in quick succession, each bound taking him further down the steps.

When safe skullduggery was reinstated, he crossed his legs, sat, and pulled his satchel around into his lap. Some quick rummaging materialized a long-necked vase, a creaky board, and a dozen marbles: many of which housed unconventional objects. In one there was a bug's wing, while another held a miniature dog, even Slade's own figure could be seen waving from a larger specimen.

A few moments elapsed as he arranged the marbles into a smiling face, then a few more as he arranged a frown. Finally lightning struck and Slade scooped up his marbles, jumping from the rafter to land just as thunder issued its belated report.

The marbles were redistributed across two steps with Slade occasionally breaking off to fetch one after it rolled off in search of adventure. Errant subjects notwithstanding, he finished quickly and resumed his place among the rafters, there reclaiming his discarded board.

Waiting until the last rumbles of thunder died, Slade braced the wood across a rafter and pressed downward, creating a long moaning creak. He let silence reign for a few seconds then created another tortured groan, this time accompanying it with a muttered curse.

Further up, both guards shifted in place, their armor clicking and their boots scuffing the stone underfoot. The younger man glanced to his companion for advice but received nothing more than a shrug. Any doubts vanished when something porcelain crashed to the floor below.

As one the guards leveled their polearms, but long seconds ticked by without excitement, funding a mounting tension that began to feel like a screeching violin until, as all things must, it peaked, marking the start of its decline.

Relaxing slightly, the older guard tapped his companion's pauldron and nodded at the steps, concealing a smile as his dragooned subordinate turned a little green but tip-toed forward. In all likelihood, the disturbance was someone who'd lost their way in the dark. Assassins usually possessed more stealth, and Amonn Warsein wasn't as important as he liked to believe.

The younger guard shot a final glance over his shoulder before inching out of sight, eyes wider than ever and no doubt entertaining a hundred terrible fantasies as to what caused the sound: a vengeful ghost or a flame-wreathed demon or a horrifying animal hybrid with ten arms and three heads. These fanciful imaginings with all their vibrant colors would fade over the coming years, buried beneath the weight of compounded tedium. But for now, he descended the curving stair with sweat slicking his grip and his heart beating louder than the world itself.

Shortly after he turned the corner, the younger guard gave a sharp, startled cry followed by the crash and clatter of metal.

Instantly, the older guard slung the shield from his shoulder and set his polearm aside, exchanging it for the shorter, more maneuverable sword strapped across his back. Then with golden magic sparking in his eyes, he descended, enhanced vision easily piercing the gloom.

He found the younger guard sprawled across the stairs but continued past. After confirming their relative safety, he knelt alongside the groaning man and slipped gentle fingers under his head, feeling for blood.

The youth hissed in response, eyes focusing somewhat as pain bore through his daze. It was only a bruise though, and the older guard breathed a quiet sigh. "What happened? Did you see anything?"

"I slipped on a stone or a … a … don't know what." He blinked repeatedly, trying to clear muddled vision. "What about … about the governor's son?"

"He's alright; I didn't see anyone as I came down."

The younger guard's head dropped to the ground, tension fleeing his body until his eyes snapped back open, staring wide-eyed at something above the older guard, who, stomach clenching, whirled around and looked up.

Rafters. Just rafters.

Then realization struck and the older guard swore. Snatching his weapon from the ground, he dashed back up to the steel bound door. There he grabbed its handle and twisted the bare centimeter allowed by the locking mechanism.

Still locked.

Much of his fear released with a quiet pop, leaving him to slouch against the adjacent wall; few assassins locked a door after passing through. Nevertheless, he reached for the key and, after a short fumble, stepped into Amonn's room.

Beautiful, vibrant Artesian Silk draped every available surface: the silverwood furniture, the golden coat hooks, the oil lamps, even the luxurious carpets sweeping across the floor. It was frivolous and to excess, and amidst it Amonn slept undisturbed, snoring loud enough to rival the storm.

Taking advantage of Amonn's legendarily sound sleep, the guard conducted a cursory inspection; first searching any alcoves hidden beneath the draped silk, then peeking and feeling inside the room's closets, before dropping the window's latch and checking its protective runes. These efforts revealed nothing more than Amonn's bed companion and her robust perfume.

As soon as the guard departed, Slade flung the covers aside, silently hacking on the cloying scent as he rolled from the bed and staggered to a safe distance. There he turned to glare at the perfume-soaked pillow. *'Out of all the possible accidents, little ones are the worst. Large ones at least have the decency to make things interesting.'*

Still grumbling to himself, Slade collected his freshly emptied perfume bottle then strode to the linen cupboard. Two Artesian Silk pillowcases were produced, one leaving for adventure with his satchel, while the second dressed a new pillow for Amonn's bed. The overly scented predecessor got tossed from the window.

Noxious fumes cleared, he gave the room a quick rifling, opening all the dressers, feeling inside the drawers, and disturbing any potential hiding spots; but his efforts only uncovered a variety of cheap merchandise fashioned to look expensive. Whoever crafted the false wealth was an absolute artist though, and Slade appropriated most of it.

Afterwards, he switched to a more concentrated frisking of Amonn's desk. The ugly, hulking affair was lousy with secret compartments—all empty—so with a quiet huff, Slade scanned the room again. Unfortunately, nothing whispered of secrets.

Then his eyes passed over the bed and he grinned. *'Where better to hide something important than one's own person?'*

Crossing the room, he knelt alongside the governor's son, feeling around Amonn's throat until his fingers touched the warm, sweaty metal of a necklace. With a gentle tug, he drew a strange key out from underneath Amonn's shirt, its smooth featureless metal briefly exposed by a flash of lightning.

Pocketing the key, Slade shook his head at the man. Most would awake when another fiddled with their throat but not Amonn; Amonn would sleep through his own murder.

He swapped sides and clambered atop the bed only to have it accept him like quicksand. Luckily, the mattress stopped short of full consumption, meaning he could still dig through his satchel and produce a medium sized lockbox. Inside were keys. Keys belonging to every class, every shape, and every size. Keys in need of sifting.

After discarding those cursed with obvious differences, he placed any moderately similar ones to his left where he could observe them in case the bed grew peckish. The second sorting took longer and culminated in a choice between two imperfect candidates, one weighing a hair too much while the other only passed for a close relative.

Sighing, Slade tossed the first key up into the air, snatched it mid-plummet, and returned the poor thing to its lock box. *'People ignore the familiar; better a passing resemblance than the wrong weight.'*

In a twinkling, he leaned over Amonn and chained the replacement key around his neck, starting a sullen grumble among its rejected compatriots, warning of their imminent revolt. He ignored the threat and shoveled the keys back into their lockbox as well.

With business attended to, Slade stood atop the bed, digging through his satchel for a length of expensive silk—Amonn deserved the best—and an old knife whose blade was smeared with a viscous green dinner sauce, the edge dulled to the point of incompetence.

He bound the silk to the knife and then pinned both to the bed's canopy, letting the contraption dangle so as to position the menacing yet harmless weapon directly above Amonn's face.

Far from done, however, Slade returned to his satchel and produced fresh tools: tins of rouge, various lipsticks, a panoply of eyeshadow, white powder, and a selection of thin, specialized brushes.

Of these the white powder came first, a series of careful dabs generating puffy clouds and gradually transforming Amonn's ruddy complexion into one of seamless ivory. This was accented by a touch of rouge, just a hint to warm the man's cheeks.

For the mouth, Slade wanted a lively, brazen color to fully exploit his broad canvas. As such, he chose a sparkling lavender and augmented it with a gold lining.

'Perfect.'

Now was not the time for admiration, however, so he proceeded to Amonn's eyebrows, selecting a pair of delicate pincers and remorselessly attacking the miniature hedges until Amonn's brows adopted a more feminine disposition. All the while he hummed a popular, rather promiscuous song from the East about a king's courtesan who applied her makeup.

After plucking the eyebrows, Slade deftly attended to Amonn's eyelashes then found himself enmeshed in the difficulty of which eyeshadow to use: a bright vermillion, a sparkling sapphire, or a reflective yellow. In the end he couldn't decide and applied a strip of each.

As a final touch, Slade rustled up a pot of ink, dipped a slim brush, scraped the brush across the inkwell's rim and, employing a slow, graceful motion, painted swirling lines across Amonn's forehead.

Grinning, he sat back to admire the perfect copy of an eastern fertility rune.

The older guard flinched and his companion near jumped from his boots when the door creaked opened behind them. Instead of an assassin, they saw Slade with the top buttons of his shirt undone, his waistcoat slung over one shoulder, his boots dangling from two fingers, and his long midnight hair falling in messy curls.

"Good evening, gentlemen," he purred, oozing sleepy contentment and using their shock to slip in between.

"Pardon me—" The younger guard started only to stop when Slade trailed fingers across his cheek.

"Shhh, let's just keep this between us, yes?" Waving goodbye, he sauntered off, swaying with every step and murmuring the words to a half-remembered song.

It was a colorful introduction; one they'd mostly forget by morning, remembering his presence more than any features or details. By tomorrow night, they'd have forgotten him entirely.

"Their loss," Slade murmured, slipping back into his waistcoat as he stole across the mansion, "would have made an excellent story."

At the foot of the eastern tower, he paused to listen as a sixth sense tickled the back of his neck. Nothing presented itself, so he continued, eyes delving every shadowed nook while he climbed. Only upon reaching the summit did insight strike.

Grinning, he looked toward the rafters and the man crouched above him. "Salutations, oh great lord; please pardon my delayed greeting."

"Rest easy, lowly peasant, no insult was taken." Naric slipped from the rafters, landing beside Slade with a muted thud then immediately leaning back, nostrils flaring. "Everlord's prince! When and where did you engage a perfume store in mortal combat?"

"Accusing me of both vandalism and poor odor in the same breath? I'm deeply insulted." Skirting past Naric, Slade knelt to examine the door's lock. "Anyway, my story is a terrifying one. Are you determined to accompany me on the retelling? It likes to eject those pale, colorless souls who quiver when mice roar."

"My soul travels in the wake of your storm; I doubt mice, even such fearsome ones, will cause it undue distress."

"Alright then; would you believe that mere heartbeats after your departure earlier, some dastardly hooligan swaggered up all bedecked with a sacrilegious outfit identical to mine?"

Naric quirked an eyebrow, lips twitching. "That seems remarkably ... coincidental."

"Downright disconcerting is what it was." Slade withdrew a set of lockpicks from his sleeve and began sorting through them. "We noticed each other simultaneously, and I exhorted him to leave, but the scoundrel refused. Refused! The unmitigated cheek of the man. Didn't he realize I was a high-prelate and he a lowly acolyte?" Slade thumped his knee with a fist, eyes bulging from their sockets. "His audacity was of such cataclysmic proportion that my opponent had the gall to demand that I leave lest he summon the Theanne Guard. Of course, I had to refuse on moral principle, politely suggesting that I dissect his various interiors and sell them to a butcher's shop."

"A reasonable suggestion considering the circumstances." Naric managed to say around his grin.

"Or so one might think," Slade grumbled, inserting the lockpicks only for a hand to glide past his face, twist the knob, and push the door open. "... I see. Anyway, my opponent proceeded to discard all reason, let alone protocol, and fetched out an evil-looking knife, waving it about in the most competent display of incompetence I've ever seen."

"Oh, the horror."

"Worse yet, while I desperately rummaged for a bigger, eviler knife, this paragon of indecency took advantage and charged me, his heart set upon murder." Slade pulled an imaginary knife from his waistcoat and lunged forward, hacking and slicing and stabbing at the air. "Robbed of ulterior options, I could only snatch up a nearby ladle—"

"A ladle?"

"Don't ask questions, I have no idea how it got there."

"Alright, so you snatch up a ladle and...?"

"Proceeded to engage in a battle of comedic legend. To your misfortune, I'm linguistically ill-equipped to denounce my opponent's incompetence, so let's skip to the conclusion wherein I strip the fool naked, bind him with leather straps, and leave him in a thoroughly embarrassing establishment."

"It's heartening to realize that some vestige of justice lingers in our world. That said, I'm still curious about how this explains your debacle with a perfume shop?"

Slade crossed the luxurious, tightly ordered room to the governor's bed. "That particular mystery gets resolved in act two."

"Ahh, I look forward with breathless anticipation then." Naric closed the door behind them, idly gazing around. "In the meantime, could you elaborate on what we're looking for?"

"A lever, button, or trigger of some sort. Anything that might open that secret passageway for us." Slade waved ambiguously from underneath the bed, his voice coming slightly muffled. "Be sure to replace everything as you found it; if we can escape without tipping someone off about this visit, our lives become significantly less complicated."

Naric stepped over Slade's legs to a bedside table and selected the top volume from a stack of adventure novels, letting it fall open so he could check the pink bookmark for any scribbled reminders. "Not to prattle on about my ignorance, but I don't believe you've told me what our grand prize is either."

"That's because I'm not entirely sure; it's a material called soul-iron, but neither the Imperial records nor Tellor's libraries were terribly versed on the subject."

Naric twisted toward Slade with a frown. "The absence of records suggests it was hidden before the Paladin Empire, or that Cardolyn Tyier wanted it forgotten. Neither bodes well for a happy discovery. Some relics are best left to their obscurity."

"Unfortunately, leaving things to their obscurity only works if you're the last to remember them." Slade's boots followed him under the bed, removing any trace of the man until his head popped up on the other side. "While the moral forget and pray, the immoral remember. Now two shadowy actors have materialized upon the stage, one bargaining, one threatening, and both seeking something so dangerous it was buried under a labyrinth. Meanwhile, our noble predecessors have successfully forgotten, their prayers have failed, and I've been blinded, deprived of the tools I need, and forced to measure a life against an ancient, possibly destructive relic."

His frown deepening, Naric migrated to the left and gave an ancient wardrobe a few inquisitive raps on its side, then crouched to sift through the lower drawers. "As I recall from your somewhat exaggerated recounting, both men made offers concerning Feylin and even Carr'Selain mentioned an interest. Why?"

Laying his face upon a rug, Slade felt around beneath the governor's bedside table. "That's another mystery, this one not so much forgotten as hidden; I've tasked a few moles with unearthing any secrets they can from Carr'Selain's libraries."

Naric closed the wardrobe, had a thought, and fetched a chair to help search its top. "Any chance they could uncover more information on the soul-iron?"

"Not in a timely manner; there's an entire wing of Imperial records dedicated to our mysterious sewers, and Carr'Selain's undoubtedly collected far more over the years: rumors, passing mentions, potential allusions, insane theories, gibberish spoken by the prophetic; I'd call him obsessed if not for him showing an identical thoroughness toward other subjects."

"Well then, as I'm understanding the situation, our best avenue to learn anything is through examining the soul-iron itself."

"Precisely. Now stop procrastinating and help; it'd be straight up criminal if I slaved away all by my lonesome on top of planning and securing our fortunes." Slade's hands slid across a wall, his slim fingers probing any peculiar divots or lumps.

"Plan may be an overly generous term, because any plan that includes poisoning a volatile assassin in preparation for ending her contract hardly qualifies as one." Naric started walking a circuit around the room, lifting the various paintings to examine the spaces underneath. "And this without mentioning your intention to falsely accuse and coerce Carr'Selain's foremost delegate, or such unimportant events like sparking a riot in the governor's backyard. At this point, need I even mention your masterful notion of assaulting Echeira'Sollas?"

"The quality of a plan does not alter its nature."

"Maybe not, but your methodology still seems a touch … extreme."

"I prefer to call it thinking outside the box. It's less alarming to the uninitiated."

Naric shook his head. "The wise thrive and so, apparently, does inspired madness."

"The first man to ride a horse was ridiculed, declared insane, and hospitalized for treatment and scientific experimentation. Years later, after people recognized his true genius, our hero was released, given a medal and put right back as he was now masterfully insane." Slade worked his way down a bookshelf, sliding a finger into each spine and tipping it forward.

"What a charming story."

"The scientists, when brought to account for their failures, claimed that if they could make lunatics out of geniuses, they could make geniuses out of lunatics."

"A bold claim to be sure. How did the judge respond?"

"He declared them insane and jailed the poor frauds right alongside our genius horse-rider, who promptly ate their liver, escaped from the asylum tower with their entrails, encountered Ahlacia Luckless, staged a successful rebellion and went on to live a long, happy life as a beloved king who only occasionally ate his prisoners." Slade approached an arrangement of miniature statues. He tipped each without result then bent and dragged a finger along the mortar separating the wall from the floor, seeking any seam or texture shift.

Naric, meanwhile, wandered around and fiddled with the room's various fixtures, eventually hooking a finger through an extinguished oil-lamp and tugging absentmindedly. Without so much as a scrape or whine, it pulled straight down, mechanism clicking at its lowest depression then whirring as the lamp slid back up, muffled gears clacking behind the wall.

Both men whirled toward the northern wall, listening as the gears slowly dwindled to silence without causing a visible effect. They shared frowns, then Slade snapped his fingers. "Ah." He strode to the bookcase, grabbed a large volume and tossed it across the room. "Here, drape this across the supporting hook."

Once again the lamp sank, clicked into place, and started whirring. This time it persisted as the hidden gears resumed their labor, both sounds continuing for several moments without offering any hint of stopping.

"I believe we're missing a step." Naric grabbed the adventure novels from the nightstand. "Let's try anchoring all the lamps simultaneously."

The room held six in total—two flanked the solitary door, one graced the northern and southern walls respectively, with two more loitering above the bed as reading lights—and each accepted their burdening gracefully, gliding downward to click in place and increase the muted, unseen clamor.

When Slade anchored the final lamp, the rapid clacking compelled a deep groan from somewhere and an unseen weight went clunk, compressed air whooshing free as a section of the northern wall pushed out into the room.

Sharing triumphant expressions, each man conscripted a marble bust and wedged it behind the door, only then squeezing through. Immediately beyond, they encountered a sharp turn onto new flooring and a narrow hall that led to a descending staircase.

Motioning Naric back, Slade toed one of the hall's beige tiles. When flames neither burst from the wall nor darts spat from the ceiling, he trusted his actual weight to the floor and tiptoed across, Naric trailing in his exact footsteps.

Abruptly Slade tossed a mischievous look over his shoulder and leapt the remaining distance, landing upon the lip where he feigned a teeter before winking and disappearing below.

Swearing under his breath, Naric duplicated the leap, but rushed his launch and landed incorrectly, part of his foot crossing onto an adjacent tile. Immediately he dove down the staircase, hearing a slight gasp from above then feeling something brush across the top of his head. Out snapped his arms and legs, slamming into the tight walls of the staircase and stalling his tumbling descent. Now precariously ensconced, he sat perfectly still, holding his breath, waiting to see if he had triggered any other traps.

After several tense moments, Naric breathed a quiet exhale and stood. Below him, an unseen, idly chattering Slade continued his descent without complications; so Naric followed, traversing the pitch blackness cautiously but steadily. His predecessor would shout out any traps.

Over time the mutterings dissipated and Naric's pace slowed, the man listening for terrified shouts or pained gasps, and sniffing at the air for anything beyond the slight damp. Upon hearing nothing, he shrugged and proceeded another dozen steps.

"Be careful with your feet, I'm right here."

"Ah, I was wondering where you'd run off to. Why the delay?" Feeling out into the darkness, Naric found the smooth waxy texture of Slade's waistcoat and edged around him, reaching out to see if anything blocked their path.

"Oh, nothing in particular. Just figured I'd delay the door breaching ceremony until you caught up."

"How thoughtful of you." Naric's fingers brushed over the chilly, raised head of a steel bolt, further exploration uncovering the smooth metal of the door pinned beneath it. *Why the bolts if the door is metal? Multiple slabs stacked behind one another?*

"Also, there might be lions on the other side."

"You should have brought Harram then, animals are invariably pleasantly disposed toward him. More advantageously, he runs slower than either of us." Naric's hand slid across the door, traveling across the increasingly impressive expanse to where smooth metal met the rough texture of stone. Except there were neither seams nor hinges. The door simply disappeared behind the stone. "Is this a door or wall?"

"Bit of both." Slade grabbed Naric's wrist, lifted it from his shoulder and upturned the palm, allowing him to deposit Amonn's key. "Momma Door wanted it to study as a load-bearing wall, but Daddy Door wanted Junior to follow in his footsteps, so our door"—Slade slapped the metal portal—"became both, albeit with a slight inclination toward swinging; there's a keyhole in the bottom left."

Naric crouched, stuffed one end of the key into his mouth and began searching the door's surface. Sooner than he anticipated, one of his fingers passed over a small hole; however, as he explored its dimensions, his thumb brushed over a second directly underneath the first. "Slade, … there appears to be multiple keyholes."

"Well now, that's an interesting turn of events."

"Which do I pick?"

"Not a clue, though I am convinced one has a murderous predilection or, if we're lucky, a simple paralyzing habit."

"Which leaves us to decide between returning later or taking a gamble."

"The gamble I think; our benefactor wants his prize within the week, and I don't have time to arrange for such beneficial circumstances again." Slade brushed past Naric, fingers gliding down his arm to find and pluck the key. "Me first."

Naric's fingers tightened around the key. "Why?"

"Because if it's poison, I'll be able to analyze the symptoms, internal or otherwise, and promptly deduce which type. I will also know if I have the antidote in my satchel."

"I think it's more important that you remain unimpaired to administer the antidote. As for prompt deductions, I've received a comprehensive education on the subject of poisons and antidotes; I even have first-hand experience in many."

"Really?"

"My master thought it an excellent prank."

"Now that you mention it, maybe I should–"

"Please don't. It's remarkably unpleasant."

"In that case, there's also the lions to think about."

"They can eat me just as well when I'm paralyzed."

"You historically have worse luck and, it seems, a penchant for getting poisoned."

"… Fair enough."

Key in hand Slade knelt, acutely conscious of his heartbeat, of its sudden volume and newfound obsession with speed. At the same time, his mind dashed between every bloody or crippling possibility, lingering upon their consequences and then following those consequences down their spiraling descents into futures he could neither foresee nor safeguard. Biting back a laugh, he discarded those distractions and chose the bottom keyhole.

About halfway in the key snagged on something. With a jiggle and a light pressure, Slade shoved past. Instantly the key warmed, scorching his gloved fingers and then thrumming violently, discharging a tearing sensation up through his arm. Its severity diminished somewhat after encountering the silver lining on his gloves, but soon faded entirely as a needling numbness began spreading from the tips of his fingers.

"What's wrong? Did something happen?" Naric asked, pressing forward to accidentally knock against Slade in the dark, and Slade—caught in the middle of flexing fingers that were rapidly turning uncommunicative—blinked. He hadn't thought he'd made a sound.

"Of course not; I haven't even decided which I'm betting on yet." Sneaking the key free, Slade slotted it into the second lock and then paused when it encountered a similar snag to earlier. "I wonder ..." Removing the key, he measured its teeth against the depth of the blockage and grinned. "You clever devil." Flipping the key vertically, he slipped one tooth into either hole, swapped hands when his fingers stopped responding altogether, and pulled the handle in a slow, grating circle. "And voila." He pivoted, arm flung wide as the door spun horizontally, light slicing into the darkened staircase.

With the entrance came a view of circular dirt walls, their surfaces bathed in fractals of pale blue light that rippled and glistened and shared the space with broad swathes of moss or lichen.

"Happily," Naric said, peering into the chamber without crossing its threshold, "I can report a complete absence of lions. Unhappily, I must report that something's happened to your arm."

Slade glanced at the dangling appendage. "It's gone on strike, spouting some nonsense about me forcing it to undergo paralyzing magic. The big baby." Slade poked his shoulder, assessing how much he felt if anything at all. "Luckily, my arm seems to be the only disaffected party."

"That's good to hear." Naric grabbed the bowl of Slade's hat and lifted, spurring Slade to throw a protective hand over his head just before Naric smacked the top of it. "Stop taking every risk for yourself; generous as it is, your luck will fail eventually."

Slade scoffed. "What risk? I'd already discovered the dangerous keyhole, so any risk was minimal at worst."

"Obviously not, or you wouldn't have lied." Naric returned Slade's hat and started toward the entrance, pausing when the other man caught his arm. "While our lions may have ended up in a different vault, I still think I should enter first." He nodded at Slade's arm.

"Maybe so, but for the sake of anonymity, you need to stay outside."

"I agree that anonymity is a lovely thing, but how does it warrant subjecting you to danger while impaired?"

"Because in the event of a disaster, it's easier for the whole man to rescue the cripple. More importantly, if I go, we stand a lesser chance of subjecting others to danger."

The two locked gazes, both keeping a grip on the other's arm until Naric finally sighed. "Alright."

Before the other man could reconsider, Slade eased forward onto a short ledge, the climate changing dramatically as he crossed between rooms. Gone was the musty chill, replaced by a steamy warmth and the scent of sulfur, both stemming from the miniature lake shimmering just beneath the ledge. It swirled gently, stirred by schools of elegant turquois fish that swam the same path over and over again, all the while emitting a soft glow that left phosphorescent particles trailing in the water behind them. Living, breathing runes.

Giving a low whistle, Slade scanned the ledge for complications, crossed to its edge, and hopped a slight gap, landing atop a circular steppingstone. This sunk under his weight, barely supporting him enough for a second jump with similar results, the pattern continuing until he graced the room's centerpiece with soggy boots.

Even the island bobbed under Slade's gentle landing, though it steadied as he ascended a short stair and found three waist-high pedestals. Each stood at one corner of a golden triangle, the first baring a grey plate crisscrossed by healed fractures and heaped with live coals. From these sprouted four golden stems holding a miniature wolf mask aloft, its onyx features scrubbed by untold centuries yet still possessing the markings of incredible skill.

Slade dug through his satchel for a suitable replacement, found none, and swiped the statue from its throne, immediately ducking behind the pedestal lest a thunderbolt scorch his vicinity. When nothing enlivened the scene, Slade quickly pillaged the other pedestals, acquiring a bear carved from amethyst and a red ceramic feather.

At the final one, he paused. Two faded engravings—two family crests—hid beneath the supporting plate, and abruptly he understood why the defenses had so exceeded his expectations.

Whatever secrets the wolf, bear, and feather hid, whatever doors they unlocked, whatever dangers the soul-iron posed, they were serious enough to merit the attention of both Cain Lammerock and Tiberius Whyte. And if either Cain or Tiberius had their eye on the soul-iron, then so did the Imperial Emperor.

Slade spoke little during their return, consumed by his need to reassess the game board, assign new positions, reevaluate his pieces, and consider different strategies, primarily the novel idea of involving both Cain and Tiberius.

By the time he surfaced from his reverie, Naric had gone ahead to oversee the docks with Harram and Slade was trudging across the vast green of the governor's backyard, lagging a few paces behind the final treasure cart. It—unlike him—rattled along the path, sensibly avoiding the impromptu bog that had sprouted during the storm.

Boots squelching with every step, he began ascending a subtle incline, soon mounting a small hill where he paused and stole a brief respite. Here, unlike down amidst the bustle and barrage of the city, the sea dominated everything. It filled his nose, dressed his tongue, shouted over all other sounds, and consumed the entire horizon, its waves glimmering with the first hints of sunrise.

As he watched the sea's unrelenting struggle to dominate the land, his stolen second became a stolen minute and then several minutes, each wave pushing the necessity for movement back another slow breath. Time pressed however, and the need for escape was at its most dire. So, at last, Slade shook his head and descended the hill, striding across the lawn to where it met a low stone wall.

Unable to boost himself with both hands, he sat atop it first then swung up his legs and—without his left arm to help balance himself—nearly fell over the side, but a quick grab for the lip saved his dignity.

With a bounce he was strolling along the wall, never mind that a short sway to his right had the grass dropping into a soul sucking void that made the bravest queasy. It wasn't the largest drop Tellor offered as the land continued slanting upward for another hundred meters before ending in one of the city's famous spear tips, but it was close to the highest elevation people were allowed to climb.

Encountering a wide gap bridged by a metal gate, Slade dropped outside the wall and walked a short path to where his treasure cart waited atop a stone lift. Ducking under the steel, zinc-coated framework, he nodded to a crew member and they pulled the lever, starting their trundling descent to the first landing. There were six in total, enormous structures of steel and stone that were bolted to the cliff face and supported by titanic pillars that disappeared into the sea below. The landings served primarily as the waypoints for goods traveling to and from the docks, the towering stacks of boxes carried upward by the efforts of the immense wharf cranes and the intricate lift system. The landings also supported vast swaths of warehouses filled with nonperishable goods, keeping them safe until buyers appeared or holding them in reserve for when a disaster struck the Empire.

Debarking from the final lift just as the morning bells began tolling out across the city, Slade grinned at his newly acquired ship: a three-masted beauty built for speed and luxury, and now escape.

Oblivious to his arrival, Slade's three lieutenants continued shouting orders, directing the ship's final loading process as a strange three-headed king with neither head supplanting the others, though Crannir—having the most travel experience—shouted more than his fellows. Naric and Harram took full advantage of this by occasionally breaking off to continue a whispered argument.

"Friends," Slade called, waving and grinning his way across the bobbing docks, "there's been a change of plans."

All three men twisted around, Harram's eyes immediately searching for Slade's arm and sending Naric a reproachful glance, while Naric raised his hands in a helpless gesture before signaling a hesitant Crannir to accompany them as they strode out to meet Slade.

"How dramatic is this change of plans?" Naric asked.

"Very. I intend to sell one of you into unwilling labor and drag a second into a stormy sea, leading him so far out that green becomes a distant memory."

Crannir checked his companions' reaction to this and found them equally unperturbed. "Well, that's a faintly alarming proclamation in serious need of explaining. Also, about your arm; is that going to cause us problems?"

A crewmember strolling past with a crate, laughed. "Oh ye of little faith; he's probably done that intentionally just to make things interesting."

Crannir looked to Slade. "That so?"

"Not in this specific instance, but his sentiment is suitable enough."

Harram leaned back against a wooden railing, making it creak under his weight. "So which of us is going where?"

"Harram, sadly this is where we part ways; I'm sure your new master will be of entirely humane character. As for the swimming out to sea, Naric, I require your finely-honed skills."

"What a coincidence, I was just struck by the fancy to go for a swim. Feel like sharing any details?"

"Something seated so far beyond the borders of crazy it delves into those nightmarish lands known as insanity." Slade grinned. "We, my friend, shall oppose none other than a Marked." Crannir swore, Haram muttered a prayer, and Naric paled.

53

The Avenar Song

Dieharamon straightened from the small table, jostling the ivory washing bowl with its murky contents and sullied rags. His reflection peered back, the scars of years almost unseen in the lamp-cast shadows. They had cut his hair and unraveled the Tragnashi braid. Now it hung to his shoulders, constrained only by a string of fine ornaments dictating Valeriius' high favor; a favor echoed in his rich apparel and many useless embellishments. He wore a cuirass of dark reeds laced tight over his golden robes with a secondary layer of molded bone on his chest and shoulders for extra protection. The most significant change, however, was he felt cold inside. The drugs Valeriius fed him had suppressed the fire of his power, of his curse. He still sensed it, but the heat was gone, leaving him vulnerable.

Moving stiffly from the fresh bandages and stitching, he returned to his sleeping room, the last in a series of chambers comprising his new quarters. An iron broadsword lay on the bed, simple in design and of flawed make but iron nonetheless, another of Valeriius' gifts.

When he touched the sword, a spark of energy lanced up his arm, revealing its crafting had involved wizardry's first facet: *Vydur*. Or it simply had been enchanted with it earlier; regardless, the blade would shear through armor like paper and shatter what it could not cut. Its weight defied expectation, scarce half of what it should have weighed.

Unbidden, memories gnawed at his consciousness, harrowing him with images of every atrocity he had committed on the night of the Angorat'Wass. No matter how many times he washed his hands, he could still see the blood on them, and he couldn't sleep for the condemning nightmares. Not that he'd had much time to sleep.

Knowing that to linger in solitude was to invite madness, Dieharamon strapped the sword across his back, preformed a hasty inspection to ensure he had everything, and exited his sleeping quarters. An untouched repast occupied the sandstone table in the southern corner, its enticing odors still present. He considered the sliver of charred meat and wine pitcher, then shook his head; he no longer had time to eat. Dieharamon crossed his chambers, surrounded by all the trappings of wealth and splendor that he did not deserve and had slaughtered to attain, and exited.

Three guards and Dayada languished outside, two reclining against the wall while the other two knelt, throwing their Bidding Knuckles. They glanced at him as he emerged, lips curling in contempt. Dayada stopped inquiring about the rules and results to beam a welcome. "Oh, hey Dieharamon, we've been waiting!"

Dieharamon forced himself to smile in response, sick to his stomach. He had hunted this man down, determined to be saved by him without reason or justification, and through his effort had only delivered Dayada into Valeriius' enslavement. That he had rescued him from the Clergy was small solace against what his future held. But Dayada kept smiling up at him—vibrant, full of confidence and trust, ignorant of his position, yet almost unbearably warm. Dieharamon did not deserve this man, but maybe he could save him from Sahdean's wretchedness and, above all else, Valeriius. "How are you, Dayada?"

"I'm fine." Dayada brushed the question aside with a wave. "Did you know somebody snuck into a really old fortress a couple nights ago? Dru'Kerack or something; it's supposed to be an ancient stronghold of your Clergy. Are they the resident religion? I know the South doesn't worship the Pantheon. I can see why, *Enecki* being so stern all the time; you would think he could loosen up. I mean he is a god; he should enjoy it! Anyway, this intruder fought to the very heart of Dru'Kerack, massacring hundreds before finally confronting his quarry. There he struck her to the stone and pressed a knife against her throat, declaring in a black voice, 'This is the sole warning you shall receive.' Then he left, leaving not a scar on her. I wonder who he is; he's becoming something of a legend."

"Come on, maybe you'll meet him tonight."

Dayada followed happily; the Avarans, however, scowled, balking at his command. Dieharamon ignored them; he had been hated ever since he became a gladiator and, honestly, found their abhorrence trivial, not just because of his preoccupation with Dayada but because the Dread Lord had yet to call him due.

It was a long trek to the gala chamber through vacant corridors drowning in torchlight. Dieharamon found himself hunching against that light, the unfamiliar brilliance rasping at his senses like sandpaper. The silence acerbated it, rendering the corridors—vibrant with color and the memory of bustling life—eerily hollow now that they were bereft even of the slaves.

Eventually the silence relented to distant murmurs and enticing scents. These distant signs of festivity far exceeded the designated gala area, which made the wandering man all the more out of place.

Dieharamon called out, heralding his approach to ensnare the wanderer, "What brings you so far from your master?"

The man spun, hunting for an escape route. "I got lost searching for the … the …"

"You have no need to search for anything; Valeriius Kalvonder has provided for every eventuality. Come, we will escort your return." One of Dieharamon's guards clamped the man's arm, and knowing his life depended on Dieharamon's mercy, the Tragnashi uttered no complaint. Spies usually fared far worse.

They attained the gala soon after, its festivities and guests presenting a drastic change from the mansion's customary stillness. Dieharamon stepped into the festivities with a casual perusal of his surroundings, skin crawling at the gross excess. The displays alone must have cost a fortune and, however generous, the Kalvonders' gifts would not balance that cost. Even excluding the deficit he accrued tonight, Valeriius discarded a potent advantage by exposing his wealth. Why?

Fools would label Valeriius an idiot. Everyone else would recognize purpose.

The flicker of something in a corner caught his attention. Shock and fear stirred as he recognized the Clergy's Easterner casually draped against the wall alongside one of the many entrances.

The Easterner beckoned him with a wave and a poisonous little smile. Dieharamon suppressed his shock and gestured for his guards to continue escorting the lost Tragnashi. Dayada hurried forward as well, eager to join in the festivities. He let them pass the Easterner before approaching.

"How swift fortune changes, Tragnashi. I had marked you as more principled than this; mere hours after attaining freedom you renewed your servitude."

"Influence and wealth are potent encouragements," Dieharamon replied disinterestedly, "and much was offered to perpetuate my service; all I desired, in fact. What mortal man could resist?"

The Easterner stepped into the doorway, hindering him. "Yes, power is a commanding incentive, yet I wonder if you stunted yourself. I have to imagine better masters than Valeriius would eagerly present themselves if you auctioned your loyalty."

"Doubtful, everyone's hated me a long time."

The Easterner laughed. "The might of one man is another's bane, but power has a way of soothing old grievances. Every Kalvonder, Guild Lord, and Clergyman in Sahdaen would humiliate themselves to acquire you; there's no one in this Hold with half the legend you've amassed. Oh, the heights you could have achieved!"

"I have no interest in conversing with you." Dieharamon moved to circumvent the Easterner, struggling to restrict his anger.

The Easterner interposed smoothly. "I and my mistress have witnessed your abilities firsthand; to infiltrate and traverse Dru'Kerack alone is in itself a feat worthy of tales, but to do so and escape with a prisoner after confronting the Immortal Consort herself? That borders on the inconceivable for a mortal man. You have promised yourself to Valeriius; the Immortal Consort invites you to forget these promises."

"And if they were made in blood?"

"Valeriius is a weak Kalvonder and a trifling man. Treachery can drive knives into his back like any other. All you need to do is wait; and when the time comes, bind yourself to us in blood."

"It is an ill-time for such offers. Evil creatures are gaining interest in Sahdaen, and I don't mean the New Order."

The Easterner snorted. "Fool, all the true evils of old are dead or buried, reduced to myth. There is no terrible darkness haunting this earth; except Morrehiegann, who is confined and inconsequential."

"And what of Cardolyn Tyier?"

"... Well, he's not a threat to Sahdaen just yet."

"Yes, that's why half of the word is allying against him."

The Easterner laughed and stepped aside. "It will be a joy to renew our interrupted discussion from the tavern. I assure you the results of our next discussion will be more permanent."

"I have yet to decline your offer; does the Immortal Consort permit so little time to decide?"

"Oh, no, she's given you all the time in the world to decide; I just happen to want you dead, and no one on this waste of a continent will stop it."

"I just survived thousands of people trying to kill me, what chance do you have?"

The Easterner leaned close, grinning. "I'm not an Avaran." Then he straightened and disappeared into the gala. In his departure, Dieharamon glimpsed his armor's back plate, which shone with a web of hairline fractures: damaged.

The sudden urge to assail him, exploiting his vulnerability, reared within Dieharamon. He suppressed it instantly; even if he could kill the Easterner, now was neither the time nor the stage for it, and it would cause less inconvenience to remove him later by some uninspired, anonymous means. Dieharamon hated himself for knowing this.

When he finally entered the gala chamber, its transformation shocked him. In a day's span, Valeriius had expanded the once modest chamber twentyfold, gilded it in gold and silver, burnished it to a reflective sheen, and illuminated everything with suffocating brilliance. Such was its luster, the multitudes within looked doused in gold regardless of their apparel, skin tone, or dyes. And, speaking of the multitudes, almost every Kalvonder in Sahdaen was in attendance, accompanied by a throng of retainers.

Thankfully, most of the guests inhabited the designated surrounding corridors, reserving the central chamber for Sahdaen's most prominent magnates. In other cultures, this would have manifested as crowds of soft-handed noblemen and merchants; here, everyone killed personally: the whole gala could devolve into a blood bath at the slightest provocation.

The New Order congregated at the center of it all, arrayed in black finery like a bruise amidst the regalia. The festivities swirled around them in a constant deluge of narcotics and alcohol, beleaguering and besieging until they finally consented as an act of exhausted desperation and tasted the infinite bounty of Sahdaen's debauchery. The Kalvonders and retainers soon followed, smelling of heady scents, plying them with gifts and contracts they could barely grasp.

Sahdaen's other influencers had presented themselves as well, attracted by the New Order's inevitable presence. The Clergy occupied the alcove furthest from the New Order, surrounding their Immortal Consort as lavish adornments for her austere person, and a trio of mercenary-lords caroused in a secluded corner with their already inebriated soldiers.

Valeriius presided over all of it from a wooden throne on a dais of ivory, jade, and onyx, segregated by a girdle of slaves.

A ringing laughter pierced the cacophony of music and words, attracting Dieharamon's attention to where Dayada stood near the New Order. Confusion expanded from his echoing mirth, ensued by silence: it had been decades since any here heard sincere laughter. Dieharamon shoved forward, suddenly terrified someone would harm Dayada.

He arrived just as the prelate Dayada conversed with recoiled furiously, hand delving into his robes for the handle of a black knife. Dieharamon caught the prelate's arm before it could emerge.

The prelate replied with a venomous scowl but relinquished his grip, knowing Dieharamon would snap his neck before he could utter the first syllable of a spell. He yanked free, railed Dayada with a scathing look, and departed.

Oblivious, Dayada smiled at Dieharamon. "Hey, you, where've you been? That man just asked how much I wanted for my soul! Can you believe it? As if anyone would sell their soul!" Dayada shifted focus to the chamber's other occupants. "So who do you know? I obviously only know Valeriius, and he seems busy. Is Valeriius a lord? I would have sworn he wasn't, but some people like to go unnoticed, like Tiberius. He hates attention."

"Just Valeriius, and no he's not a lord. You're better off meeting no one here, Dayada."

"Oh, ... okay."

Dieharamon flushed, pained at ruining Dayada's ebullience, even it if was necessary. He could not let more Kalvonders develop an interest in Dayada. "Forgive me; I just really don't like parties."

"How can you not like parties? There's lights, color, music, food, and people!"

Dieharamon leaned back, barely avoiding Dayada's gesticulations. "I don't know, I just…," he trailed off, unable to express his aversion without dejecting Dayada. "Listen, Dayada, you should leave Sahdaen; the Kalvonders, Avarans in general, don't like westerners. They—"

"Not until I find who I'm looking for; Father said he's important."

"Do you know who he is; his name, appearance, station, anything?"

"Nope," Dayada replied, regarding the arrayed feast predatorily.

Not bothering to inquire how he intended to find this individual, Dieharamon towed Dayada toward the nearest wall, ignoring his pointed fixation on the tables. "Dayada, I cannot stress how important it is to find this person and get out of here. Sahdaen's not safe."

Suddenly a bitter cold slithered into the hall, snuffing every light in its wake and swallowing what remained in a hush. The Dread Lord followed, striding through the widest entrance as the crowd parted, the floor blackening beneath every step. He had grown in height and bulk to the point he barely resembled human; even the second largest man in the room—a simpleton purchased from a freak show—reached only his shoulders.

A shiver swept the assembly. Inferior men cowered into corners or against another while the mighty shriveled, neither able to avert their gazes, fascinated by his dark majesty. For that one eternal moment, almost everyone present devolved into his insensate pawns, quelled by his mere presence.

Dieharamon was no different until a hand touched his shoulder, and Sinnitar Muntalabac's hold shattered. He jerked and there was Dayada, standing beneath the solitary torch.

"Can we leave? That man feels ... wrong."

Voiceless and quivering, Dieharamon could only concede. He pulled Dayada low and wove through the transfixed masses, praying to escape notice all the while. They had almost reached a door when Sinnitar's eyes fixed on them, black with malevolence. He dismissed Dieharamon instantly and settled on Dayada.

Hatred deeper than anything Dieharamon could have envisioned flared in the Dread Lord's eyes. An ancient hate that was unrelenting at birth, and now, after festering for millennia, bordered on insanity. It had been cultivated with the sole purpose of fulfillment and distribution. Dayada stilled, his eyes finding the Dread Lord's. Avenar Prince and Dread Lord, nemeses by birth and inarguable fate, locked stares.

Grabbing Dayada more forcefully than intended, he rushed out the doorway.

As they broke eye contact with the Dread Lord, Dayada returned to himself. "Where are we going?"

"I don't know."

———————

Valeriius watched the masters of Sahdaen cower at the Dread Lord's advent, awash in the unveiled reality of his being. A shiver of unease glided across the floor, imperceptible to any other except Valeriius: Sinnitar Muntalabac disconcerted the *mansion*, and it feared for Valeriius.

The flicker of dying flames drew Valeriius' eyes to the servants gathering outside, clutching bowls of embers. He touched his cane and the slaves rushed in, light blooming across the room and corridors with their advance to check the shroud wrought by the Dread Lord's presence. Now only direct incantation would dispel the light.

Sinnitar approached Valeriius' dais and genuflected, pressing a hand to his breast before rising and extending the gesture to all present with a sweep of his arm.

Valeriius replied with an indifferent nod; outside these halls, Sinnitar Muntalabac might transcend him, but this was his mansion; within its walls, he was strengthened, and strengthened the *mansion* in turn.

The Dread Lord grinned, hand falling to the pommel of that terrible sword: *Stolen Wings*. Valeriius readied himself, though his hand upon the cane displayed no change.

The Dread Lord spoke, his words a languid smoothness, terrible in their utterance, "I greet you, Valeriius Kalvonder, like an equal in your long-hallowed halls and extend congratulations for your triumph. I come seeking an alliance to the benefit of both. Know this, I harbor no treachery, so do not allow fear to tarnish your words or trust, for I merit both."

Valeriius felt the Dread Lord's enchantment enfold him and saw it ensnare the other Kalvonders. The *mansion* stirred in response, affronted at the poisoned words. He calmed it with a thought, assuring it of his absolute safety. It quieted but remained invigorated, ready to intercede if the Dread Lord angered.

"Let us converse as equals and display our trust for all to witness with the utterances of our names and let us brook no violence between us tonight. I am Valeriius, a Kalvonder of Sahdaen, the son of a house forgotten."

"I am Sinnitar Muntalabac, Lord of the House Muntalabac, born of the Old Blood and crowned for perpetuity by the *Roy'als*." Again the Dread Lord bowed, and his words echoed, soundless but corporeal, for such was the impact of a true naming.

He straightened, having revealed himself for all those with the knowledge to see. "Let all who doubt, be appeased. A courtship demands the exchange of gifts, thus I request the honor of first gift." He stepped aside, extending an arm toward the doors through which he entered and again parting the assembly.

Valeriius reclined, knowing one must occasionally dance as the music dictated. "Granted."

The Dread Lord grinned, a savage light erupting in his eyes, and gestured toward the doors from which came the clank of chains. A line of shuffling, grotesque children entered, their limbs broken and scarred and their clothes thin and reeking. They approached Valeriius, blood dripping from their shackles, beneath the Kalvonders' gleeful scrutiny.

"These are my gift, Kalvonder. Decide their fate."

Valeriius regarded them impassively as his body slaves averted their focus, knowing the temperament of Kalvonders all too well. The Aparthii did not turn, for her people had long memories and no love for Avarans.

"Rip out their throats with your hands and scatter their blood, consecrate this chamber with it."

A shiver of anticipation swept the chamber and all eyes fastened on the first child as she, scarce knee high, began to scream.

Sinnitar advanced languorously, the girl scrambling to escape but failing to eek more than a foot before he caught her. She screamed, adorable little feet dangling as he hefted her and caressed one supple cheek, savoring the moment. Then he plucked out her small, unformed soul and tore her throat, spilling blood.

Eighteen children followed, each pleading and sobbing amidst futile attempts to flee. One after another, they died, nurturing the ground and the Dread Lord's lust with every spent soul. But even as he gorged upon their misery, the *mansion* drank their innocence, for innocent blood consecrates any ground it touches against malice: even a Dread Lord's.

The last child differed; he did not scream at the Dread Lord's touch, nor cry at his soul's theft. He fixed his unseeing gaze upon Valeriius, wide with knowledge, and shed one tear, blessing him. Then his blood ruptured from a second, unnatural grin, and the Dread Lord cast his corpse to the stone with a snarl of rage, shattering the body.

Valeriius sighed in resignation. Had he realized the last child's gifts beforehand, he would have spared him. Alas, he could not revert death without revealing more than he desired.

Contentment spread through the assembly, segueing into murmured discussions regarding the gift's value. In that silence, Ureign Kalvonder knelt in the blood, immersing his fingers then pressing them into his face, drawing incoherent symbols.

Valeriius rose quietly and stepped from his dais, summoning every Kalvonders' attention as he crossed to the blood and planted his cane into it, clasping its head in both hands. Its crown glowed, imperceptible unless one searched for it, but no one looked, for all eyes obeyed Valeriius. "I know many a glorious gift will be given this night and many gestures of esteem presented. However, I would be a meager host if I did not provide entertainment."

The blood at his feet swirled gently, empowering his cane as he slowly woke the old magics, rousing a font of energy long in its slumber.

An Avaran brought a quartet of slaves from a side chamber, two men and two women. Valeriius had demonstrated mercy without good council once this night, now he must show malice so that the Kalvonders learned to fear but never understand him.

"This will be your entertainment. There are two pairs, each lovers with children. The males are friends and the women sisters. Two will be allowed to leave this night into a life of leisure. Two will not." The four slaves reached the center of the chamber, the men shielding their lovers. The Avaran warrior separated them, pairing one woman with each man and presenting each man with a knife. "The woman standing before each man is the lover of the other man. Thus each man faces his lover's sister. Each man has a knife with which to torture his lover's sister and his friend's lover. The man who causes the woman in front of him the most pain over the longer span will have his lover cared for and be allowed to depart. Each pair has two children. The children whose father and mother are the victors will be killed without pain. Those whose parents perish this night will be given over to the victors to be cared for in their life of leisure. Let it be known to the contestants that if they attempt to do aught but what is expected of them, the punishments their children suffer will make these games seem like a festival."

Valeriius returned to his seat, and the Dread Lord followed, discarding all pretense of respect. "I set two obligations on your life, are they fulfilled?"

"With only partial success, I'm afraid; the Avenar is gone, but the *Shard* eludes me."

The Dread Lord pressed his fist beside Valeriius' face. "Strange, I glimpsed the Avenar consorting with your new captain only minutes ago, and this room resounds with the *Pathfinder Shard*."

"I assure you I know nothing of this; if I had either, prudence would demand I surrender them. Any other course is lunacy."

"So you understand my confusion. What lust compels you to harbor the *Shard*."

A burden levered onto Valeriius' mind, suffocating his conscious thoughts, but he disentangled himself from it as one shirks a coat. "I am armored against your compulsions both within and outside my house, Sinnitar, and you will not strike me in ire before all those with whom you would ally. So I will retain the *Shard* until my purpose for it is satisfied. The Avenar is antithetical to you, medicine against what you have wrought on this city; he will vacate these halls only on my sufferance; halls now sanctified in innocent blood."

"You exaggerate your reach, Kalvonder, I am Old Blood, not by conquest or election but true lineage."

"No, I cannot expel you, that was never my intent, but your teeth are blunted, your mind shackled, and your reach stunted. Here, now, we are equal."

At this proclamation, the Stone Sword woke, its presence dense as stone on Valeriius' mind and skin, though it extended but a foot from the Dread Lord. "Do not presume divinity, Valeriius, even now I could reduce this mansion and all those present to untethered creation. Nor will the Dragon Lord rouse from his sorrow-sleep to challenge me, for your ancestors enchanted it upon him and to release him would destroy all of you. Now, what do you desire with the *Pathfinder Shard?*"

Valeriius contemplated, then submitted. "I intend to keep it until my machinations attain their culmination and whatever you intend poses no threat. Then I will sell it for power."

"You will surrender the Avenar Prince and the *Pathfinder Shard.*"

"No, I will not. I know what transpires in *Etherea*. I know *Jaidar* is assembling his legions and I see what you intend with the *Shard*, what you hope to achieve from our alliance. You will have opportunity to receive the *Shard* in due course."

Sinnitar relinquished the sword's presence and withdrew, his fingerprints a bloody stain on the throne. "You have your reprieve, Kalvonder, but it is my final kindness. Deny me again, and *Stolen Wings* will sing."

The Dread Lord departed, strides carrying him to the left-hand wall, where Dieharamon and the Avenar princeling left.

Resigned, Valeriius focused his mind inward and rose. The Aparthii slave moved to follow, but he gestured for her to remain, prompting a flash of emotions and wordless compliance. Then he vacated the gala, unnoted by all.

Dieharamon pressed his ear to the door, listening with one hand over Dayada's mouth. When no sound spoke, he sighed and ushered Dayada inward, preforming a final inspection on the corridor before following inside and barring the door.

"Can we get some light?"

"Give me a moment." After a second's fumbling, he found and kindled the room's enchanted lantern, introducing a frigid scent to the heavy air, which already smelt bitterly of Bhakra: Valeriius' preferred incense. The scarcity of wood made light and heat commodities in the South, compelling Avarans to rely on insects for illumination, or for the wealthy, soulcraft. Valeriius employed wizardry in his mansion's more secluded quarters, flaunting the Clergy's prohibition.

The lamp bloomed lethargically, gradually dispelling the shadows to expose the room's treasures: four walls and a hundred shelves of books, silk scrolls and *Acculm* in the guise of glass tablets; just one of over a dozen libraries Valeriius maintained, another facet of the wealth he and his ancestors accumulated.

The libraries occupied specific chambers throughout the mansion, dictated by their contents' value; this particular library harbored the Avarus

Desert's expunged histories. Dieharamon hoped its wards would conceal them from the Dread Lord. Safer places certainly existed in Valeriius' mansion, but none Dieharamon could access or with a means to pass time.

Dayada made a sound, pulling Dieharamon's attention to where he stood, a hand pressed against the cracked walls. "What is it?"

The Avenar glanced over, flashing a bittersweet smile. "These walls are old, rich with memories. Different from the rest of the mansion somehow."

"How can you know that?"

"Because they live, full of emotion, of impressions."

Dieharamon set the lamp on the table amidst a sprawl of books and scrolls. He flipped over one of the open books, preserving the page with a finger and examining its spine. He could read the Merchant's Tongue and the Avaran Shi (low) tongue passably, but other tongues eluded him. Even so, he recognized its gilded lettering and shuddered: the *Amarthayiss.*

Dieharamon reopened the book, wondering why Valeriius studied the Pantheon's scripture and if he possessed others. Twelve books existed for the Pantheon, each pertaining to and defined in purpose by a particular deity. Raised in the South, Dieharamon knew of only the *Amarthayiss,* the book of Cardolyn Tyier's father, and the *Book of Souls: Arawn's* book.

The wide, yellowed pages scratched as he perused what had interested Valeriius, only for their contents to elicit a shiver of horror. The left page displayed a black pentacle diagram etched with foul runes, while an accompanying incantation in archaic two-columned calligraphy occupied the right page. They detailed the summoning and condemnation of demons.

Dieharamon returned the book and covered it with another volume, skin crawling. What could Valeriius possibly desire from demons?

"Dieharamon, what do you do with your dead?"

"Why do you ask?"

Dayada raised a thin, worn book: *Death Rites of Blessed Remanas.* "It's just, I haven't seen any graves. Do you burn them?"

"No," Dieharamon replied, settling into one of the richly cushioned chairs.

"You don't throw them in the *Annuir'Hyme* do you?" Dayada asked aghast. "The *Annuir'Hyme's* sacred everywhere, even here! I know it is, my guide spent hours every day praying to it!"

"No, Dayada, we don't foist our dead on the *Annuir'Hyme,* even the Kalvonders couldn't institute that."

"Then what do you do with them?"

"We have the Reaping. It's a summons that only sounds at night, an enchantment of some kind from Paranoia that wakens the dead. The West doesn't hear it because of Cardolyn Tyier, and The North has always kept its own dead. Only the East, where there's no sovereign immortal or entity, and the South, so long ruptured, hear it. We think it's Morrehiegann's call to restless souls, those who suffered or failed in life. Those buried in sacred earth are safe, but there's none in the South, and no one here dies happy. The strongest souls have thoughts and vestigial wills, but most are simply husks. When the Reaping calls, they go north to Paranoia." Dieharamon fell silent, remembering the Reapings he had witnessed, the dead of months shuffling past in voiceless procession. The Reaping represented a day of festivity in the South, a relief, however brief, from the carrion.

"Paranoia must be so dreary with all those dead people walking around. I mean sure you can see your uncle occasionally whenever he shambles by, but wouldn't it get gross after a while?"

"I think they're probably used to it after a couple hundred years, and there's maybe some ghosts that are worth it." Even after the *Lake of Dreams*, he barely remembered his family more than muffled voices and silhouettes.

"I wish I could speak with my uncle."

"I thought Tiberius Whyte was still alive?"

"No, I mean yes, Tiberius is alive, but he's my foster uncle, goes way back with my father. He was there when we buried Uncle, when I was seven or so. We buried them together: him, Grandfather, and Mother; like they died. A piece of Father died that day I think, all our family gone in a blink, and him alone with only my sister and I. Tiberius was there for it all, spent months helping my sister and I adjust." He quieted for a long while, then began again, "Dieharamon, who was that at the ball? I think I know him, but ... I don't."

"Sinnitar Muntalabac."

"That's an ugly name: Muntalabac. I remember others ... a man named Sedition. Father spoke of him ... years ago, and he had two brothers, Jezran and Marriss, but he was the eldest. Krahvan was a second born, not the Brood Lord, but stronger than the first born. His sire was Vanner Muntalabac. Vanner was the first, the Dread King, Andrea's Bane, Avenar Bane. There are so many names. I feel them in my thoughts, screaming, demanding, but I don't want to look at them. They are shades; shades of the past even death could not destroy. When I recall them, I hurt."

Dieharamon rested a hand on Dayada's quivering shoulder, striving to provide comfort he himself could not take. The names Dayada had uttered scraped at his mind, leaving him feeling hollow and fragile. He rubbed Dayada's shoulders again and the Avenar looked back, smiling gratefully. A little of the unease plaguing him eased and, almost involuntarily, a small smile rose to answer Dayada's.

Scarce loud enough to hear, a groan intruded on their silence, at first dismissed before the realization that it sounded of wood fastened Dieharamon's eyes on the door. It groaned again, warping inward as wards manifested upon its surface in blackened, decayed runes. He crept forward, hand extending only to recoil as it touched the ice-cold wood. Dieharamon buckled, whimpering as his palm blackened. Within his mind, a shade rose before him, guised at its extremities as a man, but vast and consuming. It stooped low, reaching for his head with a skeletal hand of shadows, and he cowered, heart failing. Fingers wrapped in his hair and from his lips tore a shriek, not of pain but of terror. He had failed, and now the Dread Lord would destroy him, would destroy all of them.

A gentle brilliance woke behind Dieharamon, spilling through the chamber on a bloom of warmth, enfolding him, protecting him, reminding him he was not alone. The shade within his thoughts recoiled from the light, shriveling to nothing, but he was no longer looking at it, his gaze drawn involuntarily up and back. The Avenar Prince stood behind him, *Taychran* drawn and radiant, his eyes ablaze with inner light. There was something else as well, soft as a mother's caress, a song more in his heart and mind than his ears. It hummed through and around him, gentle as *Taychran's* light was fierce, usurping the despair that seeped into his spirit and kindling in its place an ember of hope: the Avenar Song. They could survive this.

Beneath the brilliance, the pressure upon the door relented. There was a moment of respite, then it redoubled, melting the wood, peeling its fibers away in blackened strips and depositing them on the floor where they boiled in a tumult of fumes and reeking fire. Ashen clouds billowed from the entrance, heralding a baleful figure and clawing with spectral hands only to shrivel as they neared Dayada. "Did you really trust a door to defy me?"

Dieharamon drew his blade, quivering as the Dread Lord's malice enfolded him, almost buckling beneath its burden, almost unable to fashion coherent thought, but the Song whispered through him, full of warmth, full of strength. He stepped back and leveled his blade, calling his fire to ignite, to fill his veins with strength and remove hesitation. It answered with a sputter, failing to sear through the drugged suppression.

The Dread Lord advanced, malice swirling about him like fetid water but failing to consume the chamber, defied by the Avenar's Light. "Let's test this Avenar princeling."

Dieharamon stepped to meet him and slashed, his blade crashing with enough impetus to shatter a lesser man's body. Yet darkness billowed into life about the Dread Lord and cast the blade from his hand. He staggered and Sinnitar flung him aside, launching Dieharamon into the library shelves amidst a cascade of books.

Still advancing, the Dread Lord extended his hand to extinguish the Avenar princeling, the world darkening about them. The light flared brighter and the darkness clutching Sinnitar rent, exposing his flesh. Dayada slashed, *Taychran* flashing gold and the Avenar Song swelling.

Sinnitar recoiled, a golden scar rending him from shoulder to hip and the ravenous dark faltering further. He slammed his foot back, stabilizing, and the darkness roused higher about him, mountainous and engulfing, swallowing the room entirely except for an orb about Dayada. He advanced anew, and even though the light stripped him of his darkness, he seemed immense, towering over the Avenar as a bleak monolith. Dayada slashed, but the Dread Lord's hand struck downward and caught the blade bare. It scoured his palm, searing into muscle and bone in a livid scar. His other hand snapped forward, grasping Dayada's shirt and thrusting him into the wall. The darkness surged, invading the light with burrowing tendrils and cascading cracks, dimming the Avenar Song as Dayada struggled vainly within his grip.

Dieharamon stumbled to his feet from beneath the books and toward his sword, gasping for air beneath the Dread Lord's oppression. His fingers wrapped about the hilt and he spun into a racing thrust, sobbing as he struck with both hands. For an instant, the tip stalled on the Dread Lord's back and he despaired. Then it plunged through with a grating rasp and impaled the wall, missing Dayada by an inch.

He recoiled and fell, sending a fine wooden chair sprawling with a clatter as he gazed upon the impaled Dread Lord from the confines of a darkness that did not relent.

Sinnitar stepped back, the sword scraping free of the wall, and faced him, the tip protruding from his chest unstained by blood and rusting to dust. He stepped close and pressed a boot against Dieharamon's sternum, grinding him to the ground while Dayada struggled, light failing. "You owe me the *Pathfinder Shard*." The boot pressed harder, denying him speech. "Surrender it and you will be spared torment."

"I would rather you ignore that request, Dieharamon." The pressure besieging Dieharamon vanished, redirected with the Dread Lord's gaze as the darkness stilled and the light steadied.

Valeriius stood in the doorway, hands resting on the amethyst head of his cane, awash in the malice yet indifferent, the corridor behind him alight with mundane, human light, but alight all the same.

Sinnitar inhaled slowly, extending neither hand nor consciousness to assail the Kalvonder. Instead, he spat and tormented specters rose from his bile to form twisted men.

Valeriius remained impassive, simply raising his chin and setting his stance, his cane glimmering.

The twisted creatures lunged with alien shrieks and the Avenar Song swelled again. Valeriius whirled, cane thrusting into the lead creature and flaring violet, dissolving it. He wove away from the second without pause, sweeping his cane wide, but its body split and flowed around it. Valeriius flowed further back, barely avoiding a lash of black talons. The creature pursued, cackling triumphantly as the cane flicked up, its crown blazing amethyst, and evaporated the creature.

In the same moment, Dayada yanked Taychran free of the Dread Lord's grasp and stuck the hand holding him aloft. The blow struck shallowly, opening a mere gash, but it seared with the Avenar's radiance and pried from the Dread Lord's lips a hiss. His fingers spasmed open and Dayada dropped, his brilliance reigniting.

Sinnitar spun towards him, hand rising to strike, but the floor swam up the Dread Lord's calves, shackling him in place. The light and the Avenar Song brightened. He yanked, rupturing the stone with his efforts, but the bindings held. He twisted back to Valeriius, hand stabbing out and darkness lancing from his palm faster than eyes could track. The spear struck Valeriius and he shattered in a flash of amethyst light.

He reappeared a second later not as one but as twin reflections of himself, standing at the shoulders of his earlier position. Sinnitar raised his hands to strike, yet the two Valeriius' spoke and the Dread Lord's darkness stilled once more. "Your deceit betrays you, harbinger. Through action and intent you have desecrated the halls of my fathers and your own blood. You swore oaths of harmony, yet now have wrought violence upon me, my servants and possessions, spilt innocent blood, and sought cruelty upon a guest under my sanctuary." As the words fell from Valeriius' lips, the darkness about the Dread Lord thinned and the tyranny of his will lessened. He had named himself a scion of the Old Blood and in so doing subjected himself to their laws, laws he had now transgressed upon, diminishing himself.

Sinnitar unleashed a howl and whirled back toward Dayada, the darkness that wreathed his form tightening into armor. His hand stabbed toward the Avenar princeling, shadows manifesting into bared talons on his fingers. Dayada slashed *Taychran* again, the blade and his environs engulfed in blinding radiance, and where his blow fell on the Dread Lord's stomach, darkness poured out.

Still howling, the Dread Lord ripped free of his stone fetters and hurled the massed shadows outward, striking a final ineffective blow. In the ensuing moment, a rent split the air before him, no thicker than a child's finger, made of a liquid darker than any night or evil Dieharamon had ever felt. Frothing shadows, the Dread Lord slipped into the *rift*, and it closed behind him, leaving the room cold with only hollow light.

Valeriius materialized slowly, clutching his right arm with a drawn face. He eased himself to the floor, releasing his cane.

There came a pattering of feet, and his Aparthii rushed into the library, face beaded with perspiration. She knelt beside Valeriius, already retrieving bandages from her clothing. "I told you to stay," his voice rang out harsh with pain, shocking Dieharamon with its honest fury.

She commenced bandaging. "Yes, Master."

Valeriius indicated the quivering Dayada. "Take him to your chambers until he recovers. The Dread Lord won't return tonight, though his strength is unabated. The Avenar Song has temporarily diminished him, and I've blunted any direct efforts he could levy against us. When you are done, I have a task you will not like. A gift of immense value and import approaches and you must prepare yourself for your role." Dieharamon did not respond, only obeyed as the Avenar Song's final notes faded like a lingering kiss, leaving only a sweet memory.

54

Inquisition

The fortieth day of the New Order's incursion.

Seated upon the furs of a sparse room, Brimares listened to the world bustle outside her cell with closed eyes. The furnishings amounted to little more than an ash-stained furnace—with a strange reptilian creature inside it—table, chairs, and a tousled bed pillaged of blankets. A repast cluttered the table along with a clay pitcher, presumably of water, but both remained untouched. Despite having propped herself against the furnace, a bone-deep chill persisted on her skin and in her veins, plaguing her with relentless shivers and slackening her Chaos to sludge. They had stripped her of her armor while she lay unconscious, supplying instead three layers of northern clothing: soft, colorless tunic and trousers, a blue inner coat of fur that fell to her knees, and a significantly heavier white outer coat that swept the floor.

Despite the cold and her imprisonment, Brimares felt quiescent here, almost safe with the vehemence of her Chaos slumbering. Shrouded in this tranquility, she absently reached beneath her tunic and clasped her ring. It issued a pulse, a throb of energy that stilled her blood and caused her heart to stutter. He was closer. Fear and old anger stirred within her, and her memories itched to surface, to relive history but unwilling to confront what they contained. She suppressed them.

Although no one visited her silver-lined cell, Brimares occasionally caught scraps of conversation. They rarely provided anything of merit, but she recognized the parlance of a military company. In all the fractured conversations, however, she never heard Lionel's voice, anything concerning him or aught to explain her absent armor.

Brimares restored the ring to her tunic; worrying what the pulsing signified afforded no benefit. Instead, she wrapped the blankets tighter, crossed to the door and peeked out the small window. The dawn, or what passed for it, was her third in confinement if she reckoned correctly. Keeping

711

time had grown difficult due to the permanent night that descended two days prior. Although it disturbed her, the Northerners appeared unconcerned. The soldiers discussed it with interest and the derangers addressed it only once to inquire of its purpose.

Out of habit more than desire to escape, Brimares tried the handle. It resisted her perfunctory efforts and retaliated with the familiar cold bite of silver, prompting a shrug and a return to the table. Sitting, she inspected the clay pitcher and smelled its contents: wine not water, still warm from when they heated it. This was her fifth repast since arriving and the first to include alcohol. She wondered if it would combust if she drank it.

Brimares returned the pitcher and crossed her arms, resting her head atop them and once more listening to the world. She heard the wind hiss between trees and structures, the crunch of boots on snow, and the murmurs of a conversation. Unlike previously, these voices stopped outside her door, one intensifying in annoyance, "I know the Wolves judged her, and I trust the Wolves, but we can't know if or what infection she might carry."

Another spoke, abandoning the pretense of whispers, "The Wolves would know if she was tainted. Besides, she traveled in the company of a paladin, Cathas, you cannot disregard that. Any evil she carried would have latched onto him."

"Not necessarily. The New Order might have bound it to a particular race or man, such as a Northerner."

"Then it would have triggered when I brought her food. I have visited her five times, Cathas."

"Then it is doubly certain you should not speak with her; we mustn't tempt luck."

A third voice spoke, his words graceful and measured, "I trust the Wolves, Cathas. If they deem her no danger to us or an asset, I will accept their judgement. Now open the door, unless deaf, she's been listening to our conversation." After a brief silence and the clink of keys, the lock clicked and the door opened.

Her interrogator sat opposite her, examining the untouched bread and wine. "Let me first apologize for the last three days. We only intended to detain you for a couple hours, just long enough for you to rest and answer a few questions, but events intervened. I also apologize for the food and admit ignorance to your cuisine. What can we bring you?"

She withheld her response, unsettled by his amicable tone. Judged by their Wolves or not, all of her actions thus far meant nothing because of her nature. She irrevocably remained their enemy, and they knew it. Thus she sat in silence and scrutinized her captor. He wore his numerous scars without thought and held himself still despite the room's sweltering heat and her scrutiny.

One of his eyebrows lifted. "You are deciding whether or not to trust me. You are cautious, which I understand. I promise I intend you no harm."

Still, she denied him her voice, judging his response, waiting for his anger.

"If now is uncomfortable, I can return later?"

"We don't eat or sleep; the Chaos in our blood strengthens us, effacing all physical weakness."

"So you have been sitting here sleepless for the last three days?"

"Yes."

"Then I must apologize again; Thale often wondered why you were always awake when he brought you food."

"Just give me your name and ask what you want to know."

"Very well, we'll begin. I am Maern. Why did you run from the New Order? Why did you help a paladin? Why did you come to us? Why did you not bolt alone long before now? Why were you damned to the Abyss, and what is hanging around your neck? It burned us when we tried to remove it. After all of those questions are answered, what can you tell us of the New Order?"

"Not all of those answers belong to you."

"Which don't?"

"Those concerning my damnation, and what's around my neck."

"Do they concern us?"

"They do not. They are mine alone."

"Very well. You may keep your secrets on the promise that if they become relevant, you will tell us." She agreed wordlessly, and he continued, "Is there anything else you wish to know?"

"What of the paladin, Lionel?"

Maern smiled. "Yes, your paladin knight is accounted for. He has improved from his incarceration, and we have removed the *silence* they inflicted on him. The effects of his ordeal are not entirely ameliorated, however. There is a sickness we cannot cure. It is no danger to his life to our knowledge, but it exhausts him and saps his strength. We aim to bring him to Antiark where more proficient healers abide." His sharp eyes focused on her, boring through her flesh like a knife. "Why do you care for his health? He is a paladin."

"He owes me, and I intend to collect."

"What was it he promised you?" He paused, realization dawning in his eyes. "Oh, I see; a chance at *Redemption*, the purging of the Chaos. Why did you run from the New Order? Are you not bound to them?"

"I am not bound to the New Order, only to the man who summoned me and his assignment. Within the incursion force, only Kheldar Ferain received authority to control me, and I need to hear him speak."

"Who is Kheldar Ferain? Is he the Dark Consort?"

"No. Kheldar Ferain is the dark paladin assigned command of the incursion force, more enforcer than a general."

Maern ruminated briefly, fingers drumming a rapid beat on the table. "You say he is a brute, and yet he leads? Why?"

"Because he is competent and strong enough to coerce the rest. What he is not, is perceptive or conniving."

"So he's a linchpin? And without him the chain of command would likely collapse?"

"Yes. He stands on tremulous ground, but I don't think his position is threatened, at least not yet. I implied he was an enforcer, but that means he was merely intended to preserve the incursion's integrity. To be a placeholder."

Maern's fingers briefly stopped. "For whom?"

"I don't know who, the Dark Consort perhaps, but I doubt it. There was someone else, a visitor awhile back…" She drifted off, her mind revisiting the Dread Lord's appearance. She remembered him deriding the army's lords, and Salem mentioning something about a Dread Lord come to declare his ownership.

"Who was it and what did he look like?"

"He was not there in truth. He appeared from a black fire, taking possession of a lieutenant. His visit seemed to serve no purpose other than to disparage the lords and demons, as if he was flaunting his superiority, demanding we submit, and maybe something else; though I do not know what."

"You believe Kheldar Ferain unknowingly was intended to hold the New Order together until this visitor arrives?" She nodded and shivered. Maern leaned back, his fingers resuming their drumming. "What can you tell me of the New Order's lords? What are their weaknesses and strengths, were factions forming among them?"

"There are six lords directing the army; Kheldar Ferain, the Death-Addicts—Sorran and his brother Eredar—Viral, Kadrin, and the Blond Knight, I don't know his name for he never gave it to us. Besides them, there is Kell'MachChain, who assumed command over all demons, and then there is Salem…" She continued speaking, paraphrasing how Salem described the

New Order's lords and recounting her own interactions. Maern listened without interruption except for an occasional clarification. While she spoke, Brimares watched his fingers tap increasingly complex patterns on the table.

As the inquisition proceeded, they delivered a new plate of food for Maern, who ate while she talked. When she finished, Brimares sat back and watched him. Maern continued to dine, using the time to contemplate all she had said and give her the opportunity to share anything else she remembered. "Only a few more questions," he said, placing his wine glass on the table, "so I beg your tolerance a little longer. It is well known that priests sworn to the service of any god refrain from the use of the damned. This is in part because many of them have damned souls to the Abyss, and in part, because your allegiance is ultimately with *Jaidar*: a rival entity. Of course the servants of the Dark Pantheons tend to be more lenient on the subject and occasionally welcome the company of bound demons. So why did the Dark Consort summon a score of damned, you included, and dispatch them with his host?"

She regarded him, striving to see past the self-control and discern his reasons behind the query. She assumed Lionel had confided her purpose to the derangers, which might have led to both her detention and the removal of her armor in the wake of her judgement. Maern was either ignorant of her purpose, or Lionel had spoken and the deranger now tested her. "I am to kill the High-Warden of Winsyria."

Maern resumed tapping his fingers on the table; the rhythm slow and measured, the pattern long. She knew he resolved upon a decision when the tapping ceased. "You seem to work under the duress of equal portions courage, genius, and imprudence. You do realize the Northern people view the High-Warden as something akin to a prophet, an emblem of our somewhat ramshackle religion. Still, you admitted you are bound to murder him when surrounded by dozens of individuals intent on his survival. This signifies you are either suicidal, or you just wagered we already knew your purpose. You can stop fidgeting with your hands, your wager paid off. We know your objective, the paladin insisted on disclosing it, Madam Brimares."

"I am no lady."

Maern smiled. "Would you rather be called 'Miss' like a girl, or 'Ms.' like a mother? I hesitate to use your surname due to our lack of familiarity, but if that is your preference…?"

"Just use my name."

"Very well, Madam Brimares." She caught him concealing a smile behind the wine goblet. He returned the goblet to the table; his features composed. "I have no more questions for you. Use this night to rest and prepare yourself. Tomorrow you will be permitted to wander the encampment. I advise you to stay within the perimeters unless accompanied by a Ranger-Warden or Sir Lionel."

She shrugged, feeling no actual desire to vacate her room. She preferred its warmth to the expansive, frozen tundra now offered her.

Maern stood. "I know this is not what you hoped for, but with our help, you should survive this war. If you trust me in nothing else, trust me when I say you cannot survive against the High-Warden."

"You know they'll come for me, right? My kin. The New Order will want revenge."

"We don't much care what they want; we are at war after all." He collected the platter of food and the pitcher of wine onto a tray and moved to depart. He gave the door a light kick, and it opened.

"Wait."

Maern turned, propping the door with a foot, his clothing fluttering in a wind that failed to invade the room. "Yes?"

"Did you destroy my armor?"

"No. It is somewhere in the encampment being examined for its attributes. It will be returned."

"One last thing, I would like to see Lionel."

"Sir Lionel should be fully recovered tomorrow and will mostly like desire to see you as well." He bestowed a final nod and departed.

Brimares returned to the furnace and sat, pressing her shoulders against its face and reaching inside to stroke the creature without incurring reaction. It felt hot against her fingers and tempted her to crawl inside with it. She suppressed the urge. They had just measured and judged her again, though she could not decide whether the verdict was good or ill, or what the deranger had hoped to learn of her.

She leaned back and stared at the candlelit ceiling, ruminating on Maern, deliberating on whether or not to trust him or any of them.

The morning, if those sunless hours deserved that name, arrived slowly. It was announced by the faint click of a lock and the clear rasp of a bolt being drawn. She heard the door creak, then the steps of boots on ice.

Maern stood in the doorway, a hand still resting on the handle. "Did you sleep well?"

Brimares crawled to her feet, clutching the furs and blankets about her shuddering form. "Well enough."

"Come, it's colder outside, but it is also beautiful and we have a fire prepared."

The cold slammed Brimares the instant she emerged, assailing her with ice shards and wind. She shuddered and wrapped herself tighter, gaze rising to the cloudy yet star-laden skies and stilled. She had always loved the stars, learned from a thousand nights staring at them in the wilds with their horses while her grandmother told stories of the constellations. Brimares no longer remembered any of them; they, and so much else, abandoned in the Abyss. "How can they pierce the clouds?"

"Because they are the heroes this land chose to remember and the evils it birthed and suffered, forever obligated to survey and guard us in reconciliation."

Brimares shivered again and retrieved her focus. Noting this, Maern confiscated a cloak, one of the few she had seen among Northerners, from a bundle a nearby soldier transported. "Here, put this on." She accepted and snuggled into its dense warmth, though the cold never fully abated. He nudged her shoulder, directing her leftward. "Let's go, we have a fire ready for you and Sir Lionel. He is anxious about your health, almost desperate to verify we haven't made a glass cross and stuck you on it at some crossroad."

"You crucified people?"

"Not for many thousands of years and the dawning of this new Age." He met her stare. "The North is not kind, Brimares. It has a long memory, and it does not forgive; do not make the mistake of believing different."

"If The North is cruel, why do you love her?"

"We are bound to this land in our hearts and souls. We love it because of its imperfections, not in spite of them. You cannot love something that is perfect. You can adore, even worship perfection but never love it."

The scents of roasting meat and fresh embers in concert with sounds of gaiety gradually teased Brimares, encouraging her through the sparse structures of what seemed an abandoned village. The font of these scents appeared soon after, a prodigious bonfire situated amidst several rings of low, rectangular stones supporting an animated congregation of Northerners. Brimares kept moving, disregarding the stares fastening on her and the attenuating conversations.

Lionel appeared amidst the derangers, cautiously weaving through them toward her with an expression of relief. "Hey, Brimares. Are you alright? Do you ... need anything? Another cloak?"

"No."

Her response stymied further dialogue, but he still regarded her, thoughts mounting behind his eyes until the words on his tongue finally pried themselves free. "Brimares, I know what I said earlier, that I couldn't *Redeem* you, but this doesn't sit well with me. I promised to take you to Dol'Cardolani and petition for your *Redemption* from those higher in *Enecki's* graces, but I would be lying to say that was anything short of a long shot.

They don't like your kind, they don't trust, and my word matters little. I'll take you there, but I can't advise it; I can't even say you'd come out alive, let alone *Redeemed*."

She shifted toward him more directly, the Chaos stirring and heat swelling off her in visible distortions. "Then what are you saying? That I freed you for nothing?"

"No, I will keep my word, but I ... I want to offer something else as well. I can attempt a *Redemption* ritual on you, but it probably won't work, and in the event of a failure it'll hurt a lot, but there is a chance it will work and unlike taking you to Dol'Cardolani, the endeavor won't probably kill you. It's your choice, and, again, I don't think it will work, but I'm willing to try and still take you to Dol'Cardolani if it fails."

Brimares silently considered him, measuring his avowal and offer before slowly nodding. "If there is little to no chance of the attempt killing me, then yes. I am used to pain."

"Okay." His jaw tightened into an expression of grim acceptance. "Not here though, it's not safe for anyone. I discussed this with Maern earlier, and he says we'll find ourselves somewhere a bit safer soon. I couldn't get any more out of him, but we'll do it there if it's appropriate. And if not there, Antiark."

She considered him a while longer, contemplating his personality and whether or not to speak. Her focus eventually incurred a question. "What is it? Did I ... say something?"

"I do not know you that well, but if you are concerned about what might happen if my kind find me after I am *Redeemed* and left ... helpless, don't be. If I die *Redeemed*, then I will pass on happily and you should accept no guilt."

He chuckled awkwardly. "Your concern for my concern is heartwarming."

She shrugged and resumed walking. They continued into the circle and she sat with her back inches from the fire, the warmth easing an involuntary purr from her lips. Lionel settled on a stone facing her, having acquired a plate of mutton and dark bread from somewhere. He offered her some, but she declined. Conversation, having attenuated after her arrival, gradually resumed its earlier volume, punctuated with laughter and exclamations. Brimares leaned her head back into the flames, cautious to avoid igniting the cloak, and basked.

"So you're who's supposed to kill the High-Warden?" A tall woman with blond hair cut ragged and short stepped before Brimares. "I'm not usually one to inflict advice on people but trying to kill the High-Warden is not a good idea. Just saying."

"So I've been told...," she replied cautiously, disconcerted by the combination of friendly tone and warning.

"Either way, welcome to the company. I am Kaea of Dellak, third city of The North."

"My name is Brimares, and you know where I come from."

"Bah, no one's from the Abyss. Where did you live before that? And I suppose 'when' would also be appropriate."

"The East, near the Thousand Pools about three hundred years ago. I can't remember who ruled."

Kaea examined her again, noting the large eastern eyes. "Yes, I can see it; they're kind of disguised by the burning eyes. I think I would hate to see you angered."

"Haven't you seen damned before? My eyes can't be much different."

"Oh, we've seen them before, just none with eyes quite as bright as yours." She hesitated. "If it's alright, and don't answer if you don't want to, have you seen your other face?"

"No. I have not." She let a scowl bare a sliver of her razor teeth; it was not a subject she enjoyed.

"I'm sorry; I wouldn't have asked if I realized it was a source of torment; please forgive me."

Brimares waved her off and Kaea replied with a grin. Before she could speak again, a young, flustered man entered the circle, muttering to himself and tapping the fingers of his right hand against his thumb. He glanced about, saw Kaea and rushed over, waving a crimson gauntlet overhead. "Kaea, it's amazing. See how the ridges move? Opening and closing? It's like they're alive! Do you have any idea what they're doing? Look, they're accelerating!"

Kaea's grin turned into a gentler smile. "I have no idea, love, but you might ask her. It is her gauntlet."

He spun toward Brimares, running a hand through disheveled hair. "You're the demon? Yes, I can see the eyes. It is a pleasure to meet you." He performed a hasty reverence. "Can you tell me why your armor's started moving? It's been growing livelier all morning. How do you make it? What sort of iron is it?"

"Love, give her a chance to answer and maybe your name."

"I suppose that would be appropriate. Hello, my name Daelus, what's yours?"

"Uh ... Brimares. As for the armor, it's symbiotic and bound to the Chaos in my blood. It's moving like that because it's near me. How did you get it off?"

Daelus laughed and clapped his hands. "Really? That's wonderful! So it doesn't actually consume the Chaos inside you? And it protects you? We pulled it off without any trouble, regular metal armor. Where does it come from and what iron is it?"

"I think the Abyss, but I just woke up here with it on. I think it's to mark us as demons."

"Are you one of the powerful demons?"

"No, I am not. I believe the warning is more for Cellar'Veer and Kell'MachChain."

Daelus' smiled faded. "I know that name. Oh, ... yes. Kell'MachChain, a member of the Mad Kings' inner circles for years. He died during the invasion."

"Kell'MachChain fought other wars against The North? Died in one?"

Kaea grimaced. "Yeah, he attacked The North, killed hundreds and tortured dozens. There's whole chapters on him in our histories."

Daelus refocused on her, his demeanor muted. "Will they come for you?"

"Yes. I must, will, be punished."

Maern emerged from the crowd. "Don't worry, we have made preparations to escape deeper into the forest." He addressed a deranger at his side, "When you are finished here, speak with the regulars. Tell them they are free to depart and ensure those who remain understand the risks." The addressed deranger nodded and departed.

Brimares stood, wrapping herself in the cloak once more. "If you can conceal Lionel and I, we can avoid them entirely, and perhaps hide long enough to reach Antiark where Lionel can attempt my *Redemption*. If he succeeds, I would be liberated of my charge."

Kaea shook her head. "No, there's no guarantee of that working, and more importantly, this is an opportunity. Your treason has baited the demons—one of the New Order's strongest asset—and one of their commanders into isolation. They have erred and we intend to capitalize. You are not required to fight, of course." She stood. "Don't molest her too long, love, she's been through hell, literally. Now I am going to go pay those bastards a visit." She exited the firelight, drawing her cowl down over her features, and disappeared. The other derangers followed suit in ones and twos, with Daelus bidding an excited farewell before disappearing into the white.

"Well, that went pretty well," Lionel said, "considering you're doomed to attack the High-Warden." He graced her with an uncertain smile that faded quickly when she failed to react. "Look," he began again, "just bear with us a little longer, time enough for us to kill your kin and attempt your *Redemption*. After that they'll let you walk free."

"They won't. If your *Redemption* fails, my bondage will sooner or later compel me to attack the High-Warden. Then he will kill me, or the Northerners will first."

"What if you run? Escape The North after your kin are dead?"

"My purpose would inevitably recall me. Escape is futile while my mandate remains. So I will help The Northerners kill my kin, because I have no other option; though you might dislike what happens after. All the Chaos that infects their blood will merge with mine; I will grow stronger, but also become more like them. Whenever I kill one of them, the human part of me will die a little more." She slipped a hand into the fire, exaggerating it for the moment required to grasp a handful of flames and withdraw. The captured fire danced across her undamaged skin, morphing first gray then into the guise of a hare that sprinted around her wrist, marking her flesh with ephemeral, gray footprints. Brimares closed her fist, crushing the hare mid-leap.

"If you plan on killing demons, you'll need your armor." He stood and tentatively beckoned her to follow.

"Do you have the authority for that?"

"So long as you agreed to help us, then yes."

She regarded him for a long while before accepting.

Lionel guided her through the roughshod encampment, indicating the various stone structures and elucidating their purposes. The massive open stables initially prompted confusion, until he explained, "You'll never see a lost Ranger-Warden's horse, they stick close to their riders."

After the stables, they passed her quarters and arrived at the armory, which hummed with lively conversation and radiated candlelight from a series of glass windows. Inside, barrels of swords, arrows, spears, and bows cluttered the floor while shields hung from the walls alongside dusty pennants depicting The North's running Wolf on a black field. The spear heads, arrow tips, sword blades, and shields were crafted of either crystalline glass or misted ice. "How can glass swords serve their purpose," she asked, "won't they shatter?"

Lionel chuckled. "Very little in The North heeds the rules that govern the Summer-lands. Come, I believe your armor is on the upper floor." He directed his steps to a flight of stairs on the right wall and ascended. Brimares followed, grasping the delicate handrail and doing her best to ignore stares from soldiers loitering throughout the armory.

The upper floor was an attic so cluttered with overburdened tables she could barely see the floor. Black iron helms and broken swords blanketed those tables, each one branded with the New Order's clenched fist. Shields and other pieces of armor littered the tables also but in far fewer quantity. "Why are they keeping these?"

"The derangers are examining everything they can of the New Order before fighting them in earnest. You can learn much about an enemy from their armor. If it is well made, they are wealthy and willing to sacrifice much for success; if it's well kept, the army is disciplined, etc." They progressed along a thin pathway to the room's back, where her armor decorated a pair of tables. "Furthermore, you can learn how many enchantments your opponents worked into their iron…" He fell silent and stared at the undulating mass of crimson metal. The larger pieces shuddered, while the smaller fragments practically danced.

Brimares continued passed and, undoing the cloak and two coats, pressed her hands on the table. Her armor flowed toward her, scaling up her wrists, arms, across her shoulders, down her back and front, around her legs and finally about her feet. She rolled her shoulders to adjust the fit, and the metal tightened on her figure like a second skin, warming to shield her against the cold.

Lionel scratched his jaw, humming a brief lyric, then grinned. "I need armor like that."

55

Forbidden Power

After ensconcing Dayada in his chambers and requisitioning a new sword from Valeriius' abundant armories, Dieharamon wearily returned to the gala. He found it abuzz with residual excitement and plastered with a new swath of dried blood. He grit his teeth against the spectacle and navigated the crowd to where Valeriius occupied his throne in satisfied languor, displaying no indication of his recent skirmish.

Mounting the dais, Dieharamon knelt and waited for the Kalvonder to acknowledge him before assuming his position on Valeriius' left. The Aparthii slave occupied Valeriius' right, her jaw set against unseen pain.

"Vaydrun Kalvonder has determined his position concerning the New Order, ensure it remains unvoiced."

Surprise wormed through Dieharamon's exhaustion, rousing to a whispered, "You wish him killed?" Even as the words escaped him, Dieharamon recognized his error and cursed his buzzing thoughts.

"Of course not, we operate under armistice while these negotiations transpire. The Kalvonders must comport peacefully if we are to outmaneuver the New Order; we cannot sabotage ourselves with personal turmoil." Despite his rebuke, Valeriius' eyes belied the truth; if all else failed, Vaydrun died.

Dieharamon vacated the dais and merged with the crowd, scanning for and locating his quarry beside the enormous liquor table and its resplendent bounty, validation of his notorious appreciation for fine wine. Dieharamon maintained distance, exploiting his obligations as guard captain to surreptitiously assess Vaydrun and scheme.

Dieharamon could lure him from the festivities on pretense of negotiating an alliance and imprison him somewhere remote, provoking Vaydrun's servants to investigate his absence. They would easily locate him via the Tragnashi bond, and citing concern, Dieharamon could follow them and kill Vaydrun while implicating his slaves.

Vaydrun lacked the wealth to possess many Tragnashi, and would have brought two at most, only one of which he dared expose. Tragnashi, due to the devastation inflicted by the Angorat'Wass, had multiplied in importance recently, converting them from high-value—if ultimately expendable resources—into vital blood lines that needed to be preserved. Most Kalvonders bred their Tragnashi abusively to maintain numbers, expelling the inferior products in the Angorat'Wass while husbanding the more desirable members of their flock for further breeding and guaranteed victories in the arena. This latest Angorat'Wass annihilated that cycle and ecosystem, reducing most of the Kalvonders' carefully engineered bloodlines to infants and their non-combat members. To expose one his few surviving adult Tragnashi, would be for Vaydrun to invite their assassination and the possible extinction of their bloodline.

By separating him, Dieharamon could compel Vaydrun to either reveal his Tragnashi or risk being attended merely by a slave who would be untrained in combat.

It was far from perfect, but the best Dieharamon could conceive in his current state; this allowed for non-violent negotiations and, if murder became inevitable, no one would question spoilt slaves, reducing the chance of inquiries.

His course decided, Dieharamon altered his trajectory and started toward Vaydrun's body servants—five in all, each beautiful with exquisite physique. Vaydrun reflected and accentuated this description, having meticulously arrayed himself in adornments, apparel, and makeup to amplify his allure.

Upon arriving, Dieharamon performed a full bow, expressing gratuitous respect and obligatory subservience; not all Kalvonders disdained flattery.

Vaydrun replied with an immaculately painted smile, his slaves rearranging with flawless elegance; the females to press lasciviously against him and the males to interpose. One, an ursine Avaran armored in bone, advanced further, close enough that Dieharamon felt the scarred hollow of his soul.

Dieharamon presented a vacant smile. "Valeriius has learned you intend to support unification but he himself is unsure and unfortunately occupied. He dispatched me to seek your thoughts and relay his concerns." This being Valeriius' gala, Vaydrun could neither refuse a request for counsel nor conduct negotiations publicly.

Vaydrun's smile devolved smoothly into irritation; Valeriius had rendered insult by sending Dieharamon, stating, in essence, that Dieharamon equaled Vaydrun. Only the fouling smile advised Dieharamon of his error.

"By all means; I'm sure you have a private room prepared, Dieharamon Trag-Varnashi?" The smile returned, slim and condescending but perfectly arranged.

Ignoring Vaydrun's barbs, Dieharamon bowed again and gestured for the Kalvonder to follow. When Vaydrun began assembling his slaves, Dieharamon raised a hand and spoke in a supplicant but firm tone, "Please, bring only Tragnashi." This request was elective etiquette: slaves gossiped, Tragnashi did not. Regardless, it compelled Vaydrun to choose between revealing his Tragnashi or relying on a slave. Vaydrun motioned for his retinue, minus one slave, to remain. That slave scrambled to collect Vaydrun's fine teal seat-cloth of Artisan Silk, its surface woven with the intricate image of ships in black and gold.

Outside of the main gala hall, the floors were dressed in new, lush burgundy carpets and the walls in dense tapestries. Most would discard these as decorations, intelligent Kalvonders would recognize the implicit threat the resulting silence conveyed. Screams would not echo, and footsteps would not sound.

They proceeded unmolested except for hasty obeisances from the staff and wary greetings from lesser Kalvonders regulated to the carpeted halls. Occasionally they glimpsed where the carpets ended, always attended by loitering, if unarmed, sentries to enforce the gala's boundaries.

After several turns deeper into Valeriius' mansion, Dieharamon slowed and raised a borrowed insect-light to illuminate a wooden door. Halting, Vaydrun scowled almost imperceptibly; he had not credited Valeriius with such affluence, and it conflicted with the lantern Dieharamon held. Feigning ignorance of Vaydrun's lapsing control, Dieharamon tested the door for warmth, which would signify vacancy, and entered.

The chamber within boasted richly furnished chairs, tables, and carpets, with a floor of polished black marble, glinting with jade veins. The high walls depicted radiant scenes of conflict and glory, featuring dragons, devils, seraphim, and even more esoteric species. A side cabinet, fashioned of wood and glass with enchantments, displayed a plethora of wines and exotic delicacies, all sealed to prove their innocence.

Vaydrun sat, the slave racing to drape it with his seat-cloth before retiring to kneel in the corner, head meekly bowed. "I must condemn the treatment your gross ignorance has inflicted upon me thus far; insults from a station of advanced social prominence are to be expected, suffered, and ignored, as is right. His recent fortune aside, Valeriius does not possess advanced social prominence. Not yet, nor likely ever if he persists in such ill-conceived decisions as electing you his representative. Fortunately, I understand ignorance and idiocy are inevitable, if aggravatingly rampant, irritants. Particularly in the impoverished, but they at least understand the value of compliance." Vaydrun doffed a black, soft-furred glove and extended the naked hand, nails glinting vermillion, lethally venomous. "Take my hand."

Dieharamon's skin crawled. He knew the rumors, heard the verifications from Valeriius, of merchants, slaves, even Kalvonders who shook Vaydrun's hand. They died minutes later screaming, the flesh of their hands red and blistering, and no sign of incision. He'd heard other stories as well, one from just days before the New Order's arrival about the absence of Vaydrun's chief rival. She had spent the previous year boasting about the impregnability of her abode only for her and her entire household to disappear. Sahdaen learned what transpired a few days before the New Order; someone had inverted every lock, exit, and window from her mansion, barred them and laid enchantments of silence to strangle all sound. The household had spent a year incarcerated in the impregnable fortress, surviving on cannibalism. Well, the handful that survived at least. She did not.

Dieharamon retreated a step as submissively as possible. "I ... appreciate your understanding, but I can't accept."

Vaydrun snorted softly and donned his glove again. "At least you're not entirely benighted. Pour wine."

Dieharamon complied, selecting a sapphire brew and an ivory glass. He needed an excuse to leave without arousing suspicion, otherwise Vaydrun would easily recognize he intended subterfuge and dismantle it. "I ... assure you every insult's come only from my ignorance; Valeriius' interest in your opinion is honest. He's indecisive right now, wary of the New Order but concerned by the Imperial Emperor. There are rumors that the Blood-Soul is failing. Cardolyn Tyier presses harder, and his forces amass along the Inland Sea, swelling as summer dies. If the god-spawn breaks through, we cannot restrain him again.

"The New Order is powerful," he continued, "an army of enchanters, clerics, mages, and sorcerers but also volatile and pugnacious. Can we trust such people? When they loathe our culture and are our theological opposites? Valeriius begs your council and promises compensation."

Vaydrun accepted the glass, smoothing a lock of glossy hair, and stifled the twitch of a smile. He could feel Dieharamon's anxiety. "Of course not; it's foolish to presume otherwise. If they survive the contract, they might even prove inconvenient. If they survive, superior minds have already orchestrated their calamity. Valeriius just needs to recline and amass the spoils."

"Forgive me, but...," Dieharamon faltered, a shift in color attracting his attention to where Vaydrun's slave now knelt by the door, "would Valeriius actually receive any spoils? You've already expressed his impotence in Sahdaen, and the powerful always exploit the weak. Without guarantee of fair distribution, isn't an alliance with the New Order just him taking a risk without reward?"

"Don't worry about my slave, he's just making sure you don't run off to spread rumors. As for Valeriius, even he's not so incompetent as to permit that. He'll have insurances to ensure he receives a bounty, so would you like to revise your concerns? Except ... I wonder ... what insurances does he have for you?"

Dieharamon's blood ran cold. "What do you mean?"

Vaydrun lowered his glass, swirling its contents as his slave roused. "Acquiring your services after decades of abusive servitude, granting significant influence in his organization and even electing you as representative, you must represent significant value to him." Vaydrun drank, the blue staining white-painted lips. "I believe I require another servant to convey a message to Valeriius. Let's see how much he values your survival."

Dieharamon recoiled from the seated Kalvonder. "You want to ransom me?" He scrambled for something to dissuade him. "That ... that would not be wise. Valeriius will..." Inspiration struck. "Nearus opposes the alliance! It'll fall apart if you spite Valeriius."

Vaydrun's eyes remained fixed on Dieharamon, blithely contemplating malice. "I suppose that's possible, but desperation makes liars of men."

"Look, I can kill your slave—"

"But you can't touch me, especially with the armistice. You leave so much as a bruise on me and I tell everyone Valeriius broke his oath of harmony. Kill me, and Valeriius executes you as a rogue agent. Run, I kill you and pay Valeriius remuneration plus a little extra to ensure he votes my preference. Or, you comply, summon another of my slaves without leaving this room and I send a message to Valeriius to ransom your life. Valeriius will carve the price from your flesh, but you'll live and learn. Everyone profits."

Dieharamon quelled his racing thoughts, forcing his exhausted mind to work, then spoke in a furious quiver, "I can't hurt Valeriius, not so much as a glass piece. I just physically ... can't. There's a spell."

"I suppose that follows, considering how you must hate him. Very well, you may resume. You were revising Valeriius' concerns..."

Dieharamon permitted himself an internal sigh. "One does not survive Sahdaen by being capricious or hasty, Valeriius simply desires a little insurance."

"Extortion? Is that the entirety of what this debacle amounts to?" Vaydrun extracted a silk pouch and tossed it to the table with a thud. "That is my gift for tonight, and a pittance of what we'll receive from the New Order. The imbeciles have offered us too much to deny them, and anyone who opposes the unification will ultimately pay from their own blood."

Dieharamon snatched the purse and upended its contents: a petite statue carved in the exquisite semblance of a kneeling man. He touched it cautiously and jerked when it retaliated, something sparking in his core. "Wizardry is forbidden."

"As is murder, but you threatened to kill my slave a few minutes ago. This statue has cluttered my family vaults for three millennia; its use casts either an incantation of binding or release, though I don't know their strength. It stores sufficient energy for three successive uses and accumulates naturally."

An idea formed in Dieharamon's mind. "Do you have another?"

"Of course, it's a pair."

"Let me see it, I wish to verify your claim."

Vaydrun delved into his clothing and extended the statue of a kneeling woman, lips quirking as he tapped it with his nails. Dieharamon took the statue, ignoring the jolt of painful energy it expelled. The jolt conveyed the statue's purpose: binding and release. Moreover, it sparked his core, causing his drugged power to flare briefly.

He set the statue beside its companion; they were opposites but linked, one a lock and the other a key. Their invested wizardry was significant, else they would not have conveyed their purpose. If one was destroyed, its power would transfer to the counterpart, maintaining balance.

"How easily destroyed are they?"

"We're not negotiating; either take them or get out of my sight."

Before Vaydrun could deter him, Dieharamon drew his sword and split the female statue. An invisible force imploded, rupturing the table and hurling everything near it into the walls.

Dieharamon shoved upright, sloughing debris and ignoring Vaydrun's muffled cry. He staggered to the table, thrust its upright half aside, and knelt in the wreckage. Sifting through it, he excavated a piece of the female statue glowing white with heat, though it chilled his fingers. He discarded the useless fragment and continued searching for the male figure. Upon finding it, he faltered, unsure of what to expect, and then grasped it. The familiar jolt of energy surged up his arm, confirming the statue remained functional. His power sparked again, burning in his gut like coals as nausea twisted his stomach. This time, it stayed alight.

He straightened, turning as Vaydrun extricated himself from his ruined chair, clothing torn and oiled-skin befouled. The Kalvonder stalked forward, kicking his slave to rise in passing. "I should flay your skin into rope and hang you by it. That was worth a fortune!"

Dieharamon shoved past, unearthed his sword from beneath the sundered table and decapitated the slowly rising slave.

Vaydrun recoiled instantly, jade runes waking upon his white and golden silks. His hand stabbed forward, the glove burning away from a seething ring as fire leapt from the imbedded jewels. Dieharamon pursued him, catching the torrent of flames on the flat of his blade. The iron warmed, turning cherry, but within him, his power slowly churned faster, replacing nausea with a grinding headache.

Without relinquishing the torrent of flames, Vaydrun reached into his robes and hurled something at Dieharamon's feet. The artifact struck the ground and rent with an ear-splitting crack, emerald fumes boiling out. Dieharamon leapt aside, swiping at the fumes and covering his mouth.

Vaydrun's flames dissipated, introducing a breath of silence. Then a shape swelled in the emerald fog: a *daemon*.

Dieharamon shifted into a defensive posture, desperately inciting his power without response. The kindled flame remained, but it was as if cloud choked it, denying him access.

The *daemon* slipped from the fog, vaguely serpentine with mist pulling at its limbs and pouring from its eyes and maw. Bright sapphire skin split by incandescent white veins gleamed in the insect-lantern. Its twin tails thrashed as it crouched, the seven digits of its hands digging furrows in the carpets and crushing an upturned seat. Its long head twined, observing Dieharamon from every angle with distended, azure pupils.

"Kill him."

The *daemon* voiced an unearthly shriek and charged. Dieharamon dove aside, swinging wildly and connecting with the *daemon's* flank. The foreign magics flared—the *daemon's* sapphire and the sword's orange—launching them apart. Dieharamon tumbled and scrambled back to his feet, swiping his sword to forestall pursuit. The *daemon* staggered and reoriented toward him, pacing warily.

Dieharamon snarled and charged, slashing two reversing strokes. The *daemon* leapt back, and he followed, ploughing it into the wall with his shoulder. It snapped at him with its beak but missed as Dieharamon rammed an arm into its throat, pinning it against the wall. The *daemon* bucked, hurling Dieharamon across the room and crashing over a table half. He rolled to his feet and swung as the *daemon* slithered over one of the table's halves in pursuit. His blow landed and magic, stronger than before, flared with the collision again, the resulting discharge propelling him into the wall and flipping the table half onto the *daemon*.

The *daemon* writhed free, sapphire energy coalescing between the fingers of its forehands. Dieharamon stood and hurled his sword spinning end over end. It impaled the creature, orange flames erupting down its length.

The *daemon* howled, thrashing and clawing at the blade. Dieharamon retreated from its reach, fumbling for Valeriius' last gift: a stunted silver knife. He waited for its convulsions to present an opportunity, then darted in and stabbed its flank. The entity spasmed, curling unnaturally about the silver weapon, and disintegrated into cobalt ash.

Sagging, Dieharamon turned for the Kalvonder, but Vaydrun was gone, the door swinging on its hinges. He groaned, snatched fragments from the shattered statue on the chance they proved necessary and sprinted in pursuit.

———————

Careful to avoid physical contact, Valeriius navigated a pair of Tragnashi standing in opposition, mimicking their respective Kalvonders. His passing incurred no more than a flicker of attention and summary dismissal without recognition. He continued, perusing the gathering en route to his destination, accumulating every bawdy laughter, conceited murmur, veiled threat, and outlandish promise his guests ventured in the crowd's security. The drivel information he purged, the rest he hoarded against future potential. He slowed only near Xexeross, tarrying until his approach brooked no reaction before skirting the man's ravenous vision.

Valeriius had received most of tonight's gifts, excluding only Ureign's, the absent Trerrock's, and Vaydrun's, though he expected none from the last. The Immortal Consort also withheld her tribute, and it was to her he traveled.

She occupied a reserved corner, swaddled in dull-eyed Tragnashi, cowering slaves, and swirling Artisan Silk strung from ivory poles in aesthetically domineering fashion. He relinquished his manifested will, reemerging fully into the world, and she fastened instantly upon him, eyes narrowing.

He assembled a smile and offered a bow of veneration, affecting arrogance muted by trepidation.

Anger flashed in response, spited by how such an inferior individual dare approach her, but also doubt. "What desire prompts this insolence, Valeriius?"

"Not desire but disquiet; my fellows contemplate inviting a foreign theocracy onto our soil, and I cannot imagine *Ashshand* tolerating their incursion. I seek the Clergy's insight, and perhaps ... more. I cannot be the first to contact you, currying favor." His words wavered, eloquence excised for uncertainty.

"Typical Kalvonder rat, eating the fruit from either tree. You are not selling this city into sin and then painting your brow with our blood, hiding under my hand as *Ashshand* eradicates the faithless. You've set your fate, live it..."

"I haven't signed my name yet."

"You think I don't realize this charade is a scam? As if you would capitulate to whatever pittance the Kalvonder dregs bribed you to vote against the alliance. Still, I suppose words are hollow."

"Not entirely ... hollow. I have a design for tonight, one that requires your benediction and a significant, if temporary, concession. If leveraged appropriately it would debilitate my colleagues severely."

"Impelling them further toward the New Order..."

"Supplying your excuse for their genocide."

"Continue."

"The Plutocracy shares one, certain stimuli: Cardolyn Tyier. Apply it via the right messenger, portending the border's collapse and the Kalvonder's will concede to whatever devastating insurance he requires."

"... You believe we possess part of the Blood-Soul's key."

"The Clergy is the only organization that's persisted since their creation, it's hard to believe one hasn't found its way home."

"You would still need the other two."

"What would I do with one piece?"

"So, all you require from us is our piece for the night, its return guaranteed by your aggregate holdings of course, and my protection when the faithless pay their due for inviting a foreign god into our city?"

"Provided you can motivate *Ashshand* as required."

"Then it is done; we enter accord. Expect your device within the hour."

Valeriius bowed, wordlessly expressing his gratitude, and withdrew to his approaching Aparthii slave. Her eyes darted aside, guiding his focus to where Nearus Kalvonder waited before his throne. Valeriius reassembled his will, enshrouding his presence, and departed.

Those who observed him during this veiling felt their attention diverted, their thoughts straying to new ruminations. A few recognized this and refocused their attention, rediscovering him easily, only for their minds to drift anew.

Nearus Kalvonder was short even for Avarans, and physically soft—his shoulders, arms, legs, and middle all slightly too round—but his eyes were razors, devoid of addiction, and his bearing indifferent, tempered by caution. He wore rich, flowing orange and gold silks. His shoes were cushioned, and his hands bedecked with jewelry that glowed with the internal illumination of enchantments. Yet, beneath all of this, the shroud of something inhuman polluted him.

Valeriius donned a nondescript ring of belabored gold from his pocket.

The Kalvonder shifted minutely, eyes slashing to fasten on Valeriius who slowed, then relinquished his concealment and hastened forward, extending one hand while the other slipped into his ivory sash. It was a quick movement, a sleight of hand to avoid notice.

Valeriius greeted Nearus with a grin, left hand clasping the Kalvonder's shoulder. "It is humbling for such an auspicious and reclusive man to grace my gala."

Nearus grinned wide in reflection, something baleful flickering through his eyes as he grasped Valeriius' arm. "Yes, and a pleasure to attend after so many years detached from society." The gold ring on Valeriius' finger flared violently cold, burning his skin.

He woke the archaic device taken from his sash with a thought, sending the metallic spider crawling under his shirt, up his arm, and across his shoulder. Nearus began to retreat, but Valeriius maintained his grip. Again, the foreign malice glimmered in Nearus' eyes, and this time, Valeriius caught it. It was a different set of eyes, with a darker iris and an ominous soul hidden within. The spider device slid down his left arm and onto Nearus' hand.

Nearus recoiled instantly, but Valeriius held fast, giving the device time to bite Nearus' shoulder. Hissing at the sharp pain, Nearus pulled free, displaying inhuman strength.

Valeriius caught the device as it tumbled free and restored it to his waist. "Hello, Belladona, are you enjoying your pretties?"

"Yes. Such a vast price for a wee bit of courage; we wondered if Valeriius tricked us. Now we feel cheated; we asked for a gift, and we received a poisoned flower." This was not Belladona liberated from her cell, but rather her soul infesting Nearus' body, a curse facilitated by the gifts he'd given her.

"Do you wish for a different gift?"

"No! We like our pretties. The poison tastes so foul and sweet we hope for more gifts. Gifts from Valeriius' own hand, mayhap? We could kiss you then, and you would like our kisses. We will be pretty soon, and then, maybe, we will give you a lovely ring. You will taste so sweet. You will like our kisses and you won't pull out that horrid, horrid, horrid silver when we are pretty again."

"I won't share any kisses with you, Belladona."

"We would not hurt you! We would never hurt you!"

"Perhaps. Your ... rebirth intrigues me, maybe I should visit?"

"Yes, visit us, we have a gift, a ring for you, a ring for me, for all of us. But first we must finish it. Them."

"Could you fashion a ring from the storm overhead?"

"No! We dare not! It belongs to Dread-Born, nightmares of past eras always returning to haunt. They cannot be killed, for Death itself fears them. The Abyss will not restrain them. All of darkness and dread is their birthright, and always three in a brood named after the father; the Lord, the Deceiver, the Firstborn."

"If Death fears them, why are we not all their thralls?"

"Because the Princes, Shadows, and Crowned. They break dread and darkness, cheat them. Kill them."

"And Death fears neither the cheated nor the broken." Valeriius pondered: he knew 'the Princes' represented the Avenar and who the Crowned were, but the Shadows stirred no memory. He needed to research this later; if one of the Old Families survived, they merited addressing.

"Who are the Shadows?"

"We do not know, we could never find them. But perhaps we could with a Kiss?" Valeriius began to rebuff her but paused. A witch's Kiss ensorcelled men, rendering them permanent thralls to her whim. It required more than just physical contact, however, including sanity, else she would never remember what a Kiss was.

Valeriius quieted his thoughts and directed them to the witch. He threaded a spectral hand along the connection Belladona used to hold Nearus captive and severed it. Nearus flinched, hissing as Belladona's façade of madness receded. The witch retaliated instantly, striking through the connection Valeriius' act had created. Putrefaction filled his mouth and his heart seized, aching within his chest. He snapped their connection and retreated, ignoring her internal shriek of fury and pain.

"Fool, I almost had you! You fell for those pitiable words of madness. The mighty Valeriius Kalvonder caught in a snare! How your pride stings!

And your heart beat with remembered terror! I will be young again soon, and you will not escape! I know what you are!"

"I cannot prevent your resurgence, Belladona, but you will not claim me. You are bound in silver and imprisoned beneath the tomb of an evil that transcends you. If you are wise, you will subside less you awaken it." His cane flicked out as he spoke, tapping her leg and transferring a memory.

She quailed. "Fool! Are you ignorant of him, what he has done, what he can do?"

"As I said, do not awaken him; he's most likely hungry after six thousand years." He brushed past her, leaving the witch to retreat into her vessel and hide behind whatever shadow of Nearus Kalvonder persisted.

Valeriius resettled into his throne, absently watching his slaves flock through the gala, replacing old platters and wines with coastal variants, replenishing braziers, and ushering the various poets, jugglers, musicians, and dancers to their stands.

Like a shadow the Aparthii appeared beside him, her head bowed. She first extended a glass of wine and next a warm platter. On it lay a coiled serpent roasted and seasoned to perfection with ancillary potatoes and mushrooms. Valeriius tore the crisp tail off, contemplating what he knew of *Stolen Wings*.

There were twelve Stone Blades, one each for Blessed Remanas' Dragon Lords, and all forged of alien stone. No one knew its origin only that *Lord Arthramain Roy'al* forged the blades from it: the most powerful weapons produced by man.

Stolen Wings had belonged to Leeana, the silver Dragon Lord. Histories asserted that Leeana was the kindest of the twelve: a skilled healer, and the Dragon Lord most inclined toward personal intervention.

Stolen Wings before its corruption had imitated its mistress. It wielded magnificent healing magic, capable of bringing men from the brink of death or ceasing a rampaging plague. Despite its inclination, it was still a weapon. Its chief purpose was war, and it was manifold stronger at annihilation than healing. Only a few records detailed *Stolen Wings*' destructive abilities, and those few were vague at best. The most Valeriius had learned was that the Stone Blades amplified their wielders' power.

Like the other Stone Blades—excepting Andeor'Vallen's—*Stolen Wings* had been corrupted with Leeana's death, and whatever healing abilities it possessed eradicated by its madness.

Rumors referencing the Stone Blades existed of course. They were lost or hidden initially, but men or other entities unearthed them as the centuries transpired, always resulting in firestorms, craters, fear, other such calamites, and screams. Valeriius found the last tidbit intriguing; when recounting tales of devastation, one rarely lingered on the screams, yet no recounting lapsed in that detail.

A cry erupted from the gathered slaves alongside voices of outrage from the Kalvonders, arresting his musings. Vaydrun tumbled from the assembly, Dieharamon, huge and armored, stomping in his wake. The Kalvonder spun, a thin, needle-thin bone whipping from his sleeve and thrusting toward Dieharamon, who snapped it with a swat. The Kalvonder continued to retreat, light burgeoning upon his finger, but Dieharamon caught him by the collar and slammed him to the floor, snuffing the light.

Valeriius allowed an eyebrow to arch in question, a smile tugging his lips, and settled in for a spectacle.

Reaching the chamber's now vacant center, Dieharamon pitched Vaydrun forward to center stage, whereupon the Kalvonder immediately scrambled upright, perfectly manicured features snarling and ugly. "He lies!" His words lashed out like an assault, yet all eyes regarded Dieharamon for he was magnificent.

"This man"—Dieharamon's finger thrust toward Vaydrun—"has tampered with wizardry! The curse that held our people, your ancestors, enslaved for millennia to the burning tyranny of demons and *Jaidar*, a magic forbidden by *Ashshand!* This man crafted an item with it, one that would bind foes and release allies from any restraint!"

"That artifact was inherited! An heirloom of my family for generations! Ignore him!"

Dieharamon spun toward him, strident with righteous fury. "How could it be? Your family has been sacked, raped, and slaughtered incessantly! Are we to believe this item went miraculously undiscovered through all of that?"

"You have no proof I made it–"

"I need no proof! You tried to use it! To bribe Valeriius. After trying to hold me ransom!" The last comment snarled with the bite of truth. Not that it mattered, Kalvonders rarely required more than an excuse to execute a rival.

"As if your intentions were–"

"Dieharamon, if you present evidence of his crime, we can conclude this discussion," Valeriius' words silenced Vaydrun's enraged retort.

Dieharamon accessed a pouch on his belt, extracting two perfect halves of a statue and flinging them to the floor beside Vaydrun. They struck with a resounding echo, and all heard the faint, unnatural tone of wizardry. "That is my proof."

Sensing his end, Vaydrun turned and fled, screaming as if succumbed to madness, but Dieharamon caught and hurled him to the stairs of Valeriius' dais with a crack. He tried to rise again and crumbled, legs failing him.

Valeriius stood, handing his plate to the Aparthii and regarding Vaydrun with fabricated contempt. "Let us decide his fate. A man with no feud has accused Vaydrun of treachery and presented evidence he could not dispute. For summary execution, raise your hand." Excitement swelled through the room, carried by a sea of hands.

Vaydrun shrieked a wordless command.

An answering scream echoed through the chamber, heralding a tall Avaran who burst from the crowd, charging Dieharamon with an arshendi. Dieharamon spun, iron singing free of an unseen scabbard, and the Tragnashi's headless corpse toppled past. Dieharamon flicked the sword, wiped the blood on his sleeve, and strode after the crawling Vaydrun.

A transitory hush fell, dense with anticipation, then voices rose in a low, guttural harmony taught since birth. It suffused the chamber, resounding and amplifying to drown all else in the advent of death.

Valeriius strode to the edge of his dais as the lights dimmed and the humming swelled, a reflection of the impending condemnation. It pitched, carnal with desire, and Valeriius spoke, "Let him die as his Tragnashi before the hour concludes."

The humming music diminished, changing tone from verdict to execution. Dieharamon reached Vaydrun and grasped him by the collar; to delay even a moment past the hour would result in his own death, but the execution could not be rushed, it must worship *Arawn* as he deserved.

Dieharamon reset his grip and hoisted Vaydrun, bringing him about as the death hymn intensified. From somewhere in the crowd, a child's voice pierced the dirge, singing in ancient, haunting Remanasi.

Dieharamon hurled Vaydrun back to the center and pursued, features dispassionate and steps measured. There were those who wept as they executed men, those who laughed, and those who looked dead themselves. The best engendered delicious anxiety in the spectators, and Dieharamon resembled these in his indifference, as if death meant nothing.

The humming built and the child's voice rose in kind, seeming to swirl about Dieharamon as he advanced. Vaydrun clambered to his knees, lips moving and hands splayed in supplication, but his words lost in the song. Dieharamon laid a booted foot on his back and ground him to the tiles.

He readied his sword, the death hymn nearing its final crescendo and the child's voice breaking. He swung high and brought the weapon crashing down, sending Vaydrun's head thudding across the ground, though none heard it.

His task complete, Dieharamon departed without a glance, cleaning his blade as the guests before him parted.

Valeriius returned to his throne, reclaiming his food platter from the Aparthii and waving to summon a messenger slave. The boy hastened forward, listened intently and then scrambled to retrieve the artifact halves before disappearing behind the throne anew.

Examining the fragments, Valeriius explored the vestiges of their magic, divining an echo of their purpose and former state. He smiled—silently applauding his Tragnashi—and reclined, tapping the fragments together. The *mansion* stirred, energized by the death chant's lingering energy.

down, sending writhing heat shuddering across the ground, though more
listless.

His task complete, the champion departed with one's glance, leaving his
bloodless prisoners behind him parted.

Valerius edged up to the body, reclaiming his steel pilfered from the
...and waving to someone in the snow's drave. The boy listened,
toward... lineage threatened, his path harried... thinner the unnameable...
become than a thing behind the silhouette.

Examining the fragments, Valerius noticed a blood mark... of the corpse...
the meager edge of their prompts and forms that the... halt and awaited
...

The Blond Knight dismounted beside the two corpses with a thud, his
posse of mounted soldiers and demons congregated beneath the meager
protection afforded by a copse of trees. The wind ripped through them,
lashing with hail and ice shards, thrashing the trees. He grinned and kicked
one of the corpses over, dislodging it from the ice and revealing two glass
shafts. "We're closing and, if the priests haven't lied, too far from any
settlement for them to entrench in."

Kell'MachChain eased beside him, radiating heat and seething steam as
he whispered, "If you need help tracking her, I can assist; this blizzard would
foil the best trackers..."

The Blond Knight whirled, ripping a silver knife from his belt and
gouging it into the demon's eye. "If I want your help, I'll ask for it. As for our
quarry, they'll veer towards the mountains. Typical Northerners." He yanked
the knife free, spraying blood and Chaos.

Kell'MachChain snarled, features convulsing across crooked bones, but
did not retaliate.

"Good, you're learning, maybe next time I'll allow you to tag along
without the oath of subservience." He sheathed the knife and began
humming. His heart spasmed, its beats slower and heavy. The Blond Knight
grinned. "I think I like The North, it respects the natural order of dominion.
But"—he slapped Kell'MachChain's shoulder—"this's no time for soliloquy, I
have a she-demon to butcher."

Enormous spruce trees surrounded Lionel and his companions,
affording scant protection from the wind and shrouding the forest from the
starlight above. But they did not travel in complete darkness, streams of light
played beneath the ice underfoot, shifting hues through azure, silver, and

emerald as they swayed, illuminating the path and the riders from beneath within the unnatural night.

A column of thirty-odd Northerners rode behind him, the majority regular soldiers equipped in delicate crystalline armor with naked blades dangling from their sides, infused with reflected light. Scattered derangers, including a returned Kaea, patrolled the flanks, culminating with Maern a few paces ahead of Lionel, unarmored despite the impending conflict and apparently unconcerned.

As if sensing Lionel's attention, the deranger slowed to ride beside him. "Another Ranger-Warden told me you were once a Northern foundling, is this true?"

"Yes," Lionel replied, his voice muffled by the ice-crusted scarf over his face."

"I imagine that's why they dispatched you to trail the New Order, but I am also curious why you left us?"

"Is there a purpose behind this question?"

"Just curiosity; you were raised a Northerner, and we habitually prefer to stay here. So why did you leave?"

"My adoptive family was murdered by monsters, horrible things from beyond Winter's Gate. Someone else killed them a few days later but I had still lost everything, again. I had nowhere to go and no path to take, so I made a choice to try and protect as many people as I could from that fate. I couldn't do that here in The North, it's safe and Ranger-Wardens don't leave its borders. I knew of the paladins from the stories, that they didn't just protect people, they hunted monsters and could teach me how while giving me the autonomy to do it." He chuckled softly. "Now here I am, escorting a demon. Funny how life works."

"Do you harbor enmity towards her, Sir Lionel? Not specifically for your tragedy but in general? You assumed your current mantle to eradicate creatures like her, to hunt them, and she is an avatar of chaos, your antithesis."

"I ... don't want to. I look at her and I can see that she's human, then she looks at me and I see her eyes and her armor and I'm reminded that she's a demon; that she's probably committed atrocities I can't imagine."

"And yet you intend to *Redeem* her?"

"She saved me, without guarantee, despite having just as much reason to hate me. It might just have been desperation, but I don't think that matters. She saved me and I gave my word."

A caw, raucous and vile, tore through the forest, snapping their focus to the canopy and the black stallion beneath him to a rearing halt. The Raven screeched again, the trees all around her sagging beneath the burden of her kin, tinted rust red in the ghastly radiance of their eyes. Her second cry brought his New Order blade singing free of its sheath and the procession to a cringing halt, the soldiers and derangers gazing up with foul looks.

Maern reined in, features contorted in a scowl. "What ails those birds?"

The black stallion bucked and stamped beneath Lionel, almost unseating him. "I do not know, but they're not allies!"

Brimares' voice rang out from behind, taught with strain, "Shoot that Raven, it belongs to Salem!"

Maern strung his bow without hesitation, knocked an arrow, and released it. The Raven evaded it with a laughing caw and its kin followed in a roaring cacophony. Lionel slashed at the swarming birds and felt his blade connect. Others followed suit, hacking with swords or launching arrows until the final crows swarmed beyond the canopy.

Lionel lowered his arm, searching the forest for any lingering signs of the flock without success. The black stallion continued to buck beneath him, neighing loudly as it moved to the side. "What is it with you?" Lionel demanded, attention snapping down only to freeze. A swath of matted black feathers surrounded them, ugly and coated with fetid bile. Erratic lines sectioned the feathers, each perfectly defined, forming a pentacle.

He recoiled, nausea clutching his gut as his throat tightened. "Look down. It's an inverse pentacle."

Maern commenced unstringing his bow. "That is a Summer-land evil, what do you know of them?"

"Very little; normally a pentacle restrains devils throughout a summons, if inverted it becomes more of a welcome sign."

"So, someone's summoning something."

Brimares reined in beside them, pale and sickly. "This ... isn't a summons."

"Then what is it?" Maern asked, restoring the dismantled bow to his quiver.

She licked her lips. "It's a mark of possession, and a ... harbinger. Someone's claimed us, and those aren't Salem's crows. It's his Raven, for sure, but those others..."

Maern tapped his saddle thoughtfully. "They're expending extraordinary effort to retrieve a single demon; is there anything special about you?"

"No, nothing. I was entirely human before my damnation, not even gifted...," she trailed off, thoughts turning inevitably to the ring.

"I know you have secrets, but you promised if they endangered us, you would share them. I am sorry, but there are more lives at stake than yours."

"Later, not here, not in the open."

"Tonight when ancient walls guard us."

"I will not tell you everything, but I will give you the reason and nothing more."

"I hope that will suffice."

The trees, which had been tightening as they advanced, parted abruptly, revealing a black tower behind a stout wall of seamless glass crusted with ice. Despite its ominous aesthetic and the strange twilight, Lionel found it a welcome sight.

Brimares emerged to his left and reined to a halt, gaze widening in awe. The streams of light continued beyond the forest and into the clearing, refracting off the crystalline wall and filling the space with a haze of swirling colors.

Lionel couldn't help but grin, though he immediately regretted it when her eyes tightened. "Why build this here? So far north?"

"I don't know if Northerners actually built it, or if the derangers just followed the wind."

She considered the tower. "Perhaps it was a refuge?"

Lionel prodded the stallion forward. "Against what? War? Military disputes, in general, are rare in The North."

She followed. "It doesn't matter, a fortress like this will last centuries, more than long enough for a war to occur."

"Well, if it's a refuge, we owe its architect our gratitude." He absently examined the short wall as they neared with the column's tail, noticing its interior swirled. "I hope it serves us well."

He ducked beneath the low door and Brimares imitated him, shivering as they crossed an unseen threshold. A deranger stepped into their wake, brushing the wall's interior with a murmured phrase. She turned, endeavoring to catch his words, only to see the door fade from view and her reflection staring back.

Lionel glanced over at her pause. "All Northern gates do that, prevents enemies from finding the entrance."

"How will we find it?"

"The gatekeepers and derangers can see it." He dismounted the black stallion, which permitted him to guide it toward the stables sprawling on the courtyard's northern side. Strangely absent of mounded snow, the tower came alive as they advanced, with Northerners bustling about gathering wood to waken the hibernating kelbroks, unfurling banners, unloading packhorses, exploring the various structures, and disappearing into the tower to prepare it for habitation. A gentle harmony gradually filled the castle, half-heard chimes and flutes that no one played and never faded.

Brimares entered the stables, traipsing through hay and following her stallion to an unoccupied stall where she unsaddled him. Lionel did the same further down, fingers moving deftly from long practice while he absently observed her.

"I thought horses were rare in the East, reserved for the lords. How did you learn to tend them, or judge them?"

"They are, but my father was a breeder and trader; his bloodlines were among the most sought in the Thousand Pools."

"So you traveled a lot, selling your horses to whichever lord paid more? That must have been hard. Were you part of a caravan?"

"No, we were alone. No mother nor siblings either."

"What happened?"

"Father was an ugly drunk, and she was beautiful; so she fled with the next caravan after my birth. At least, that's what Father said."

"Why would she marry him?"

"Even though we were poor, Father's bloodlines were worth a fortune. We could date them back centuries, some of them had blood more noble than our nobles. Almost as noble as that stallion you're torturing."

Lionel's hand froze and he stared at the black horse, which seemed to bestow an imperious look upon him." When you say 'noble' you mean..."

"Old Blood, High Men, the Crimson Monarch's Court, whatever you call them. And you've been riding him like he was a common, lunkhead warhorse."

"Oh, ... I bet you have some neat stories to tell?"

Her hand tightened on the brush, and her armor clicked, vacillating by fractions. She gave no answer and forced her hand to resume brushing.

Rebuffed, Lionel quelled his curiosity and focused on the stallion. After finishing, he exited the stall and waited for Brimares. She ignored him and continued brushing the stallion long after all the Northerners finished. Occasionally, her armor would click and her head would tilt back, checking if he still lingered. By the time she resigned herself to his company, Lionel was shivering.

"You should have left."

"Undoubtedly, but my prying seemed to anger you and I wanted to offer an apology." He extended his hand in a gesture of peace, as much for her as for himself. The Shard of Divinity continuously seethed within his chest, always incensed by her presence, and her eyes stared at him, unreadable and brimming with crashing flames and colors. He could feel the violence beneath her skin, the searing pressure of her Chaos to attack him, to be unleased. "This will be easier for both of us—for everyone—if we're not at odds."

"Do you plan on spending long in my company? I imagine I'll be free, dead, or imprisoned after tonight. None of those require additional interaction from you." She started across the courtyard and he fell into step.

"You don't plan on helping the Northerners after this?"

"Do you?"

"Yes. I was raised here, but even if I wasn't, they will kill thousands if they succeed and claim an entire country for the Dark Pantheon. I have the power to help prevent that; I can't standby without intervening."

They ascended the tower's stairs and entered. Inside, the rooms remained sparse and unlit besides a few scattered candles. Two soldiers crouched in the doorway with steaming soup bowls. They nodded at Lionel and Brimares and indicated a set of stairs. "Kitchens are down those stairs; it's just soup and old bread for tonight, but they're warm and there's a fat kelbrok."

Lionel paused for a half-step. "Do you know where Ranger-Warden Maern is?"

"Sorry, I don't; ask someone in the kitchen."

Lionel signaled his gratitude and descended, laughter beckoning them onward, supplemented by the scent of potato rosemary soup, bread, and relaxed conversation.

"I don't know what you want from me, Lionel. To kill myself in a war for people I don't know? You have no right to ask that of me."

"I don't know what I want. Maybe just confirmation that what I'm about to do isn't a mistake."

"Confirmation you're not going to get; when this is done and my dues paid, I'm gone, and you had better keep your end of the bargain. I've already been cheated once." She broke away, entering the kitchen and crossing to sit at the least frequented furnace.

He moved to follow, but Kaea called from the stairs above, forestalling him. "Sir Lionel, Maern has dinner prepared for you and Madam Brimares, he needs answers as soon as possible."

"Would you mind informing her as well? I'm afraid I've angered her."

"All right." Kaea spoke briefly with Brimares, incurring a nod, then conducted them up two flights of stairs and through a series of obscured corridors to a brightly illuminated doorway. She motioned them in and closed the door behind them.

A rectangle table dominated the room, amplifying the sense of confinement. The table itself was intricately worked rowan with a pageantry of wolves, bears, caribou, and falcons carved into its surface and limbs. A sheet of glass covered it to preserve the artwork and provide a smooth surface. The smell of wine, coffee, dark bread, and potato soup ignited Lionel's hunger.

Maern ruminated before a kelbrok in a hearth, flanked by two other derangers in tall-backed chairs, Daelus and an unknown man. This deranger's unkempt hair, pallid skin, and sunken cheeks gave the impression of malady, further augmented by his posture. He sat with his arms draped on the armrests, bony fingers loosely gripping the tired wood, their knuckles swollen and chafed. He blinked slowly, as if the movement was a conscious action and a chore.

Maern stirred at their appearance and moved barefoot across the fur-covered floor to the table, his outer coat, an oudakc, draped over one of the chairs. "Good, you're here. Please help yourselves."

Lionel removed his boots in the alcove then joined him at the table and began to ladle soup into a bowl. "Thank you."

Maern indicated the stranger. "That's Ranger-Warden Hrann, Sir Lionel; you'll have to forgive his silence, he is mute. I solicited his and Daelus' help because they are versed with Summer-land's magic and items. Please sit, Brimares."

Lionel turned to see Brimares hovering near the door, fixated on Hrann. She advanced hesitantly, talons vacillating open and closed and the armor flowing off her feet in emulation of their removed boots.

"What is it?"

She stilled, hands on the back of a chair, then retracted it and sat. "He's a witch."

Neglecting his food, Lionel extended a thread of consciousness toward Hrann, prompting a faded pulse of power, long abandoned, reduced to memory, but unmistakable and prompting an involuntary spark of loathing.

"Yes, Hrann was a practitioner of malignant witchcraft. He found redemption in The North at the cost of his voice; though he remains capable of minor witchcraft. He will stay, regardless of your sensibilities, Sir Lionel."

"I understand; he poses no issue."

The four derangers assumed their seats, each with a mixture of anticipation and curiosity. Hrann settled opposite Brimares, scrupulously inspecting every detail about her but provoking no comment.

Maern began without preamble, "Recently, a group of Ranger-Wardens has been shadowing a new foreigner in The North. He's acted peacefully thus far but has displayed a stalking a pattern with us. I can surmise only one target. Brimares, do you know anything about this?"

"Does he look ancient, decrepit, with only silver pools for eyes?"

"Yes, but he's armored in silver as well and bears two long swords, one on his back and one on the hip...," Kaea began, but Maern shook his head slightly and she subsided.

Moving slowly, Brimares retracted her gauntlets, the armor from her throat, and then removed the ring, dangling it from her fingers by the necklace. "This is why he follows us; it erases all other drives that compel him." She released it and the ring thudded to the table with a piercing note. Hrann flinched and a shiver coursed through the other derangers, leaving only Lionel unaffected.

Lionel grasped the ring, exploring its infinitesimal silver threadwork briefly, then returned it to the table and shrugged. "It is exquisite, but I can ascertain nothing unique about it. I hear no echo of power."

"And yet we were affected." Maern lifted it by the delicate chain, watching it sway. "I have never seen it before, but it feels familiar, teasing my oldest memories. There is magic here, even if we cannot grasp it." He tapped the twisting sinews with a bare finger and grimaced. "It guards itself, but there is no active sentience." He restored it to the table, redonned his glove, and reclined.

Daelus snatched the ring next, eager despite Maern's reaction. His form jerked, but he maintained his grip, a circle of coruscating silver fire blooming around his iris. "This is ancient. It has experienced sufficient agony and joy to imprint the metal. There is a purpose as well, a geas that consumes its existence, one of fear but also love. Its purpose is to guard, blind, and deafen, but against what?" Daelus' face gradually tightened as he spoke, hollowing against his bones. "It is either imperfect or incomplete, but there is no evil within."

"Daelus, you need to let it go! It is not bonded to you." Kaea jostled him.

"There is so much here! Real history, I cannot fathom! I am frightened and elated, exhausted and exhilarated!" He convulsed and pitched from his chair, the ring clattering across the table. Kaea cursed and rushed to her husband, holding him as he vomited, waiting for the ring's infection to fade.

Maern readdressed himself to Brimares, "What are we dealing with, Brimares?"

"I don't understand it myself. It's his ring, though it is bonded to me. It was given to him long before we crossed paths, and he gave it to me. I don't know its purpose."

"How did it survive the Abyss?"

"It can never be taken, only given. He said it was a safeguard, and that it would always return to me. It shredded any demon that tried to take it."

Hrann finally moved to evaluate the ring, long fingers dancing along the chain, reading a story in the links. He blinked in rapid bursts, lips forming words that never found utterance. Maern circumvented the table, steadily regarding Brimares.

Hrann relented, preforming sharp gestures that Maern translated, "We cannot discern what the ring is. Hrann confirms it is ancient, but he also says it is unaligned, straddles not only good and evil, but several elements he can neither discern nor quantify. Why did he give this to you?"

"That is a secret you will never learn, but if I give him the ring, he will leave you alone."

"Then if it's not evil and you assure us we will incur no peril, there is no reason to break alliance. But I dislike the mystery, and you have no answers."

"I have answers, just none you can hear. One thing I can say is that inverted pentacle we encountered comes from someone else, maybe someone else trying to claim this ring. I don't know." As she moved to don the necklace, the ring pulsed twice in her hand and a third against her breast. She curled into her chair and stared at the kelbrok as the discussion resumed.

Thyme

Thyme stood alone and wrathful at the brand's perfect center. He felt his Signet writhing as someone vastly distant tried to dominate it with half-forgotten spells and ignorant words. How dare another claim what belonged to him by right! The feathers of the inverted pentacle swayed once. He thrust a warning hand toward the masses of perched carrion birds staring down at him like a jury of the damned. "It is mine, it will always be mine! You cannot deny me; no one can deny me!" The birds shifted, feathers rustling and claws clicking, but remained stationary. The accusatory hand fell. "Power over Blood, Blood over Power. Power over Blood, Blood over Power! Blood is power!" Thyme spun in place, swinging his hand out to encompass the entire realm. "And you will learn I still rule here! I am firstborn, and you are the third of a lesser bloodline; you will submit! They are mine; mine by blood, by right, by conquest, by power, and by blood again! You will submit!"

Thyme stalked from the circle of feathers, footprints white in the black stain. Cracks grew, shattering the brand's integrity. The carrion birds erupted into a storm of pounding wings and inky feathers, but not one spoke.

57

A False Fire And A True Purpose

The longer Tasha knew Slade, the more she suspected that three factors controlled his decisions: the shock value, how amusing he found the potential scenario, and how well it served whatever grand design was lurking behind his cheery exterior.

When Slade handed her a note outside Echeira'Sollas, Tasha expected instructions to a dingy, grime slathered location from where they would depart on his next business venture. What she did not expect was a blind alley defined by its singular lack of privacy. To the left sat a disreputable, though still meticulously clean, tavern that heaved with shouts, excited brawling, and surprisingly bawdy songs. To the right crouched what was undoubtably an illegal gambling den, every windowpane, metal fixture, and piece of decorative paneling polished to the same extremes as respectable society while a tastefully decorated sign proudly listed its various legitimate practices. Mostly, she did not expect the alley to sit within easy sight of Echeira'Sollas.

'Well it's certainly shocking and ironic that whatever he's got planned will take place right under Enecki's nose.' Tasha's smile faded, a faint queasiness unfurling in her stomach as she remembered the package Slade had deposited earlier. *'Oh no, … please tell me he's not sacking Echeira'Sollas. Slade's not that insane, right? Right.'* Nausea increasing, she leaned forward, hands braced upon her knees. *'Oh gods, I helped him, didn't I? And now I'm involved and—'* Abruptly nausea changed to bubbling giggles and she straightened, pushing hands through her auburn locks. *'Oh, this must have been a really long day if I'm taking this seriously. Not even Slade would provoke an actual god.'* She thrust off the wall and strode down the alley, abandoning its relative chill for the night's sticky heat.

Out on the street, she checked on Echeira'Sollas, then tried settling down to resume vigil. Her patience lasted a single night-time traveler. By the time the man and his horse clopped off to explore some distant forest or forgotten castle, Tasha was pacing.

748

Hoping for distraction, she looked skyward and found her favorite constellation: Chockerand, the first bard to garner world renown, not necessarily for his music. Smiling, she sifted through her mother's old stories and found their accompanying constellations, lingering longest upon the ancient heroes.

Standing there watching *Sammahale's* children glimmer and shine across the sweeping sky, her tension eased somewhat, enough to glance around, not find Slade and simply shrug. *'I'll give him another five minutes. Whatever needs discussing can wait until morning, and if not, Slade should have arrived on time.'*

Upon finishing the allotted period, coincidence struck with its usual peculiar timing.

Alarm bells shattered the night's tranquility, their volume increasing as a dull, red luminance expanded over the tops of buildings. All along the street windows flew open, people leaning out to peer around, exchange shouts, and eventually point toward Echeira'Sollas. Seeing this, Tasha lowered her head and charged off, joining a growing stream of half-dressed men belting on swords.

Her feet skidded to a halt the moment she rounded the last corner. Echeira'Sollas burned, exhaling huge gouts of unnaturally green fire and ringing with a clamor of voices, some cursing others screaming but thankfully none dying. Not yet at least.

Shunting aside her paralysis, she charged deeper into the chaos, closer to the burning temple and its awful blistering heat. She found a place in the bucket lines as close to the fire as she could tolerate then began the somehow frantic task of passing one bucket after the next. All the while, a bitter, twisted foreboding grew in the back of her mind, constantly pulling her eyes from the blazing temple to scan the frightened priests.

Just as she began to breathe easier, Tasha saw him; a slim, dark figure slicing through a sea of billowing white robes, unaffected by the terror or the orange glow enveloping their world.

In the glimpses of him she caught between buckets, Slade approached a group of priests who struggled with a terrified horse. Evading its violent kicking and rearing, he caught the saddle horn, jammed a foot into the stirrup, and swung up. Instantly the horse stilled to examine its rider, but Slade didn't allow much delay. He kneed its side and cantered off through the giant obelisks, gaze fixated on the road ahead.

'What's your game?' Tasha stepped from the line, watching Slade until he disappeared, struggling to direct flailing thoughts and control the burgeoning urge to lash out. *'Was this you? Are you capable of burning people*

alive just to … to … what? Distract someone? I hope not; but if you are and if you did, may someone save your soul from **Enecki**, *because you and I need to have an uncomfortable conversation.'* Turning back, she dragged her twelve-year-old replacement from the line and booted him toward a cooler, safer section. *'If Slade orchestrated this whole affair, why am I here? Was I supposed to see this or do something? What purpose does my presence serve?'*

These questions continued throughout the night, offering little besides the occasional fumbled bucket.

An hour or so after she first arrived, a detachment of Theanne guards marched onto the temple's pale sand with the hand-pumps and hoses, the various commanders shouting orders at anything that moved. Those who disobeyed were summarily ejected along with any observers. Within minutes, the square settled into a clean, ordered landscape inhabited by determined people and copious amounts of water. The flames, however, resisted their best efforts as well as those of a helpful storm.

Later, sometime after the midnight bells, an exceedingly irritated Cain Lammerock rode into the square. Eyes glowing a fierce silver despite the firelight, he approached to within a hundred feet of Echeira'Sollas. Rising in his stirrups, he grabbed the air as if it were a fluttering curtain and wrenched downward. In a blink, the flames were gone, having flowed sideways like paint-streaked water swirling into a drain.

Gradually word spread. The whole affair was nothing more than a clever illusion, which implanted the near pervasive question of who and why? Among the chattering crowd, Tasha alone knew the answers; though she still pondered the same question as before. *'Why am I here? Did he want to gloat, to parade his talent for chaos? No, when Slade gloats, he does so in person.'*

Other possibilities flitted through her mind, oscillating between absurd theories and machiavellian schemes, none of which could be discarded since Slade was the perpetrator. So she paced and brooded her way around Echeira'Sollas until early dawn. When her revelation finally arrived, it was no sunshine filled epiphany but rather a moody sky. *'He wants me someplace where he or someone else can find me. Or maybe he wants me to be found here.'*

A prickle ran down Tasha's spine and she headed for the nearest alley, in the process spotting a squad of hitherto unseen guards. *'Were they left behind to guard Echeira'Sollas? No, they're not wearing any armor and their uniforms are dry. Did they arrive after?'* Watching the guards from the corner of her eye, Tasha forcibly slowed to a more leisurely stroll, almost piercing her palms with her fingernails as she made fists.

Unlike her, the Theanne wandered around directionless, questioning any stragglers and changing her prickle into a rapid pulse.

A wispy guard noticed her leaving and tapped his squad leader on the shoulder, jerking a thumb in Tasha's direction. The second man pulled a piece of paper from his inside pocket and tilted it toward the gray morning, face creasing as he compared it to her. Abruptly he gave a nod, destroying any chance of an unremarked escape.

Swearing under her breath, Tasha continued toward the alley as if she hadn't just seen them assign her a cell for the night, all the while preparing for the inevitable shout. When it came, Tasha found herself tempted by the alley, despite everything: the fact she was in a foreign city, the fact that even if she escaped she'd have to leave Tellor entirely, the fact that leaving meant she was abandoning Carr'Selain's interests here, the fact that her only possible destination was Dol'Cardolani and whatever ramifications waited there, the fact that in so doing she was sacrificing everything that brought her here in the first place.

Closing her eyes, Tasha drew a slow breath to calm her frantic heart and twisted about, affecting a searching glance. *'Why are these men searching for me in particular and does it have anything to do with why I'm here? Hopefully, they're unrelated but somehow I doubt that.'*

Seeing her glance around, the squad leader beckoned her closer and then nodded when Tasha tapped herself on the chest. They met halfway, the red-haired man stepping forward and dipping into a normal, relaxed bow. "Pardon the interruption, ma'am, but I need a second of your time." His eyes flicked to the bronze pins on her collar, no doubt checking her supposed profession and class status against whatever record he possessed. "Are you Tasha Bloomhale?"

"Yes, that's me." *'Well, that's just perfect; they know my name.'*

The man's shoulders squared, his hand fell to his sword hilt, and he spoke with deep, clear toned formality, "I, Kayja Retryn, squad leader in Tellor's Theanne guard, with powers granted by Governor Warsein, hereby place you under arrest for the desecration of, but not limited to, public property, temple grounds, and Echeira'Sollas itself."

"What?" Tasha stumbled back a pace. "I didn't do that, not any of it!"

"Please, ma'am—"

"And you're just arresting me without asking any questions?"

The red-haired man quirked an eyebrow. "Were you expecting questions?"

"I should bloody well hope there'd be questions if I'm getting arrested."

"Several eyewitnesses reported seeing you enact a profane ritual. One … industrious citizen provided us with this." Digging inside his coat, Kayja extracted the sheet of paper. "It would seem that you've caught *Kis'Maat's* Grim Eye."

"*Enecki*, save me," she whispered after unfolding it. Calling the portrait a fair description was akin to likening a three sentence explanation to a book. Tasha held a resemblance so perfect, so detailed, she could almost confuse the paper with a mirror. Eventually she tried smoothing out the wrinkles, failed and handed the portrait back, fighting to control the snarl building in her throat. "Out of curiosity, how many guards did you bring to arrest me?"

"Enough." Something in his voice warned Tasha, sending her eyes in a sweeping arc. All around her, uniformed soldiers strode toward her from across the damp sand, many appearing from between buildings on the street and even the alley directly behind her, one by one sealing off her escape routes.

'Jaidar bless it all, Slade. Why?'

About midway through the journey, Tasha's long day began asserting itself, making her little more than a damp, shambling husk with a splitting headache. Her mind actually relinquished the constant wheel of questions and profanity directed at Slade. She couldn't even muster a faint queasiness at her future prospects, but that resulted more from how Dol'Cardolani's guards dragged Rats in for interrogation once a week. With time the most-timid Rat considered it just another unpleasant facet of their job.

At the guard house, Tasha blinked through blurry eyes for a more than vague impression of colorless rooms lined with sharp-cornered desks, the latter learned from an unfortunate collision. After the immediate and thorough frisking that followed this collision, they guided her under an interior portcullis into a long, curving hall with steel doors.

Tasha's clearest memory was of her cell, though it amounted to little more than an impression of sterile odors, dry surfaces, and white-washed walls, all collected in the few seconds before she dropped onto her mattress and instantly slipped into dreams.

While she lived, Tasha's mother had documented every dream in the household, from servant to family member, believing any one of the beautiful, macabre, or bizarre images could hold a secret meaning. Tasha's father—in his few diplomatic moods—called such beliefs childish, otherwise he preferred the terms idiotic or sacrilegious. Her mother would always nod, smile agreeably and then wink at Tasha behind his back.

Later, when her father and brother slept, they'd sneak onto the balcony together, Tasha crawling up onto the railing and leaning back against her mother to learn about the stars. Tasha vaguely remembered her brother joining them at first, but he quickly grew out of his childhood and turned to money ledgers and equations, leaving Tasha to her mother's stories of *Sarah'Venn* and *Sammahale*.

"Many, many years ago, the sun and moon walked the sky together, but one day the Fore-gods looked up from ruling the mortal world. They saw the stars in the night sky and they grew hungry. One by one, they devoured *Sammahale's* children until the night was left cold and dark and empty. Come morning, when *Sammahale* found that emptiness, the sky blazed with his fury and he descended to the mortal plane. The old gods met him with laughter only to find him beyond words and his charcoal skin burning white, too hot to touch. They fled across the world and he chased, round and round until the land itself bubbled under his step and all living things cried out in torment. Their cries reached *Sarah'Venn*, lifting her cloud of misery and waking her to the destruction of the world. She followed her husband down, braved his heat until her own skin blackened beneath his fury. She calmed him, returned him to the sky so that the world might heal. In the centuries since, neither has forgotten their loss. To this day *Sarah'Venn* stands vigil over the night, guarding our dreams and guarding the heavens until dawn when her husband rises to safeguard the day. Only in those brief moments between night and day, are they together. Yet we, blinded by *Enecki's* scripture, never honor their sacrifice."

Out of everyone Tasha knew, her mother alone observed the ritual of burning cinnamon at dawn and vanilla at night, worshiping the gods most had all but forgotten.

Forgotten or not, Tasha wished *Sarah'Venn* would clarify her message because it felt akin to a drug addled hallucination. First she was a white rabbit, bounding through the forest, chasing a carrot that dangled just before her nose. Then the dream changed with a violent ripple and Tasha fled from grasping hands with crooked, spindly fingers and ragged nails that clawed bloody furrows into her skin.

Another ripple and the dream changed from forest to grassy landscape. Still the hands reached for her, chasing Tasha around a corner into view of a thicket, its thorny embrace promising safety. Doomed or fated, Tasha never found sanctuary for a stone giant appeared, one enormous stride carrying it over the horizon into view, where it bent down and pinched her scruff between cruel fingers. She was lifted high above its mouth and lowered into yawning darkness; whereupon she opened her eyes to a golden ballroom that stretched away endlessly, its walls lined with stained glass windows pulled unnaturally thin by the distant ceiling.

On the step below her, a fox stood frozen in time, his familiar dark eyes staring up possessively as he extended a paw. No, not a fox. A man in a mask and russet suit, his paw a clever affectation of his gloves.

Looking down, Tasha found herself wearing similarly fanciful garb, complete with a full mask and long white ears.

Her stomach suddenly roiling, she turned from the man only to find him in whatever direction she faced. At last she accepted the proffered hand, causing time to resume as a sharp, triumphant smile split his features.

Taking license not afforded to him, the fox kissed her palm before leading her down the steps; but Tasha wrenched free in a flutter of white silk and found their wrists bound by a delicate silver chain. Unable to escape, she was dragged to the dance floor, where a black-feathered bird unexpectedly stole her away.

Laughing, he spun her round and round until the world transformed into swirling colors, and dizziness made her laugh even as it pulled her into a dreamless sleep.

Clang ... Clang ... Clang. The sound of a guard tapping cell doors with his bludgeon, each strike measuring the distance between cells. Clang ... Clang ... Clang.

Tasha rolled over, burying her face within the pillow's doughy embrace as if that might delay the morning. All around her, inmates groaned mournfully or cursed hangovers, some of the more bright-eyed leaning against their cell doors to exchange news with the older inmates, others waiting in patient silence for their release, and a bare few causing a ruckus. These the guards ignored, bypassing them to continue methodically releasing one prisoner at a time.

From the sound of things, Tasha was in the overnight cells. Unlike her fellow inmates, however, she doubted anyone had orders to release her within the next decade let alone by tomorrow. At this thought, Tasha's stomach began knotting and she pressed against her pillow harder, breath quickening. *'No, stop that. This is not the way to react, you've been in prison before and nothing's decided yet. Besides, you've somehow lucked into simple calamity rather than wholesale catastrophe. You should be able to escape this place given enough time; if not, Carr'Selain might still come for you.'* Breath slowing, Tasha rolled onto her back. *'So long as I'm kept in Tellor, anyway.'*

In old mines picked exclusively for their isolation, Cardolyn Tyier built stronger, deeper prisons where the maze-like corridors and perpetual night kept the prisoners secure if their cramped iron boxes did not.

Tasha shivered, wrapped her arms around herself, then whirled sharply and kicked the wall. *'Gods damn it, Slade. Just how badly have you skinned me?'* Rather than bruise her other foot, she sprang up and stomped around her cell's perimeter, passing the door several times before a low whistle drew her to its barred window.

Across the stone, featureless hall stood an identical door with its own number, pristine lock, and oiled hinges, also its own restless inmate staring back at her. "Good morning, miss."

Tasha snorted. "I'm not entirely sure how, but alright."

"It doesn't take much if you're not dead."

"You're remarkably cheerful for a prisoner."

"It's been a few days since I had a neighbor to talk to."

"Ah."

"Speaking of which, what news of the outside world?"

"Nothing you haven't already heard."

"In that case, may I ask what landed a respectable lady like yourself in this here establishment?"

"Respectable is it? No one's called me that in years." Tasha smiled, feeling a little of the knotted sensation ease. "Nothing too exciting, just burned down Echeira'Sollas."

"That was you? No wonder you're feeling grumpy. Why aren't they trundling you up north, all wrapped up in blankets and chains?"

"Hopefully, because they're verifying their evidence and discovering I was framed."

"Were you now? My sympathies, though it'll make for a grand story if they absolve you."

"Could be grander if they condemn me and I escape."

"True."

"What are you in for?"

He grinned through the bars. "Take a look at my pretty face and guess."

"A brawl?"

"Ah, not just any brawl. I went drinking a couple days back and got into a fight with Amonn Warsein."

"That explains the bruising. Did his goons jump in?"

"Aye, but some other patrons took issue with that and followed, so it was a fair fight. Now we're all here, excepting his lordship."

Off beyond the hall's gentle curve, a winch creaked and gears clanked, the unseen portcullis rattling upward to admit multiple sets of boots. Tasha and her new friend shared raised eyebrows then pressed against their window bars. Usually, only one guard was sent to release prisoners.

Lead by Kayja four grim faced Imperial soldiers stomped into view, each gazing around warily as they escorted Amonn Warsein toward her cell, his normally long forceful strides curtailed by their protective ring.

Muttering a curse, Tasha stole back to her mattress, flung away the crumpled blanket and lay down facing the wall. Behind her the sound of boots stopped, and her already dim cell darkened further as someone peered through the window. Under their observation, the knots in her stomach tightened until it felt a struggle to breath.

"So you're our … what? Our anarchist? Terrorist? Militant atheist? If I'm being honest, you seem a bit small. I expected someone tall, half-starved with a malevolent glint to their eye; the sort to make one shiver and be thankful they're on the opposite side of the door. But you? You've gone and hidden yourself in a corner." As Amonn spoke, his voice adopted the low pleasing rumble that appeared whenever he abandoned his normal booming tones.

Tasha gritted her teeth, biting back a sharp retort. "If I seem ill suited, perhaps it's because I am."

At her voice, Amonn's head cocked to the side. "Though much of the evidence appears to have gone missing, they assure me it was nearly conclusive."

"If I'm practically swinging already, what are you doing here?"

"Echeira'Sollas was just vandalized; I believe the bastard responsible deserves my personal attention, don't you? Besides, I'm curious about a few things and this interrogation seems the obvious starting point."

"If you're looking for answers, I'm afraid you're talking to the wrong person," Tasha's neighbor drawled through his bars. "Rumor has it that she was framed for that."

Amonn barked a laugh. "Is that so? One should always listen to rumors; they tend to reveal questions that need asking. Also"— he strode to the opposite cell, his guards quickly stepping aside—"I believe we've met before." He reached through the bars, grabbed the man's jaw, and turned it to the side. "In that popular tavern down among the Ie'Calla, yes? We tried to beat the shit out of each other if I recall. Well, I'm willing to let bygones be bygones; and since we need privacy to interrogate our potential anarchist, I believe we can end your sentence early. As for you"—he returned to Tasha's cell—"your voice sounds familiar, but I can't place it. Have we met before?"

"Yes. You made a pass at me; it was uncomfortable and you overstayed your welcome." If possible, her stomach muscles tightened even further, cramping until all she wanted was for him to leave so she could just lay there and breathe.

"That's less illuminating than I'd like. Turn around."

"Let me consider it … mmm no." Tasha waved a hand. "Something about being in a cell just saps my energy."

"Could I convince you to reconsider?"

"Not while that door's there."

"I see. Lieutenant Kayja, find me the key."

'Oh for the love of– Can't I catch a single, gods-damned break? Think. I can't cover up, there's no dirt and–' Behind her, Amonn thumped away down the hall, returning just as her cell door swung open and setting something down with a clatter of wood.

Instinctively she tensed, but Amonn simply grabbed the back of her shirt with one hand, the fabric pulling tight across her throat as he lifted and thrust her into the chair he'd just brought in. Immediately his eyes narrowed, preceding a slow, broad smile. "Why hello again, my nameless star."

"I have no idea what you're talking about." Despite herself, Tasha looked away, letting a curl of hair fall across her face.

"Miss Bloomhale, I've only forgotten one face in my life, so believe me when I say that I remember yours vividly." He took a lock of auburn hair and looped it behind her ear. "You accompanied Slade Lammerock to my father's ball and caused quite the commotion. If the bootlickers weren't bribing or begging or threatening someone to present their name before Tiberius Whyte, they were all a titter with questions about you." He threw back his head and laughed. "Hell, I asked around myself, but nobody knew anything; and the Thieves' Guild deflected my questions with some story about needing time to 'reevaluate' the information. Which is the same response I got after inquiring about Slade Lammerock two years ago. Obviously they know as much as I do, perhaps less."

Her gaze snapped back to him. "You asked about Slade?"

"Of course I asked about Slade Lammerock, half the city would be asking about him if Cain let him attend more events. Slade's a black, grinning fox with a penchant for trouble making and not much concern for how it affects others." Amonn paused, good humor vanishing and eyes narrowing; rather than voicing his thought, he waited until her neighbor hobbled off on a crutch. "Is Slade Lammerock the one who framed you?"

Tasha forced a short barking laugh. "If you're serious, that's a dangerous insinuation to make."

"Why? I doubt you'll be telling him anything given the current situation, and Imperial soldiers don't gossip."

"No, Slade is not the reason I am here." *'Why am I bothering? Slade sure as hell doesn't deserve the courtesy. Except … if I squeal on him, that could complicate Carr'Selain's bid for Akravast… Do I really care though?'*

Amonn didn't break his stare, making Tasha contend with a growing urge to fidget or look away. "Very well. It's odd though for the condemned not to leap upon salvation, but let's see where the evidence leads. Lieutenant Kayja and his men have just returned from searching your lodgings."

Tasha lounged back in her chair. "I don't suppose Lieutenant Kayja found something to absolve me?"

"Not as such," Kayja said, rubbing his chin, beard rasping quietly. "Though if you have an imagination, it does lend credence to the theory of you being framed." He joined Amonn Warsein in Tasha's cell, producing a slip of paper from his coat pocket. "We found several bags stuffed with duplicates of this note and nearly a dozen crates with alchemical substances that we're trying to identify."

Amonn took the paper between two fingers and flipped it over, eyebrows rising. "I did it. It was me. I claim all credit. Well, that certainly seems damning." He flipped the paper toward her. "Is this your handwriting?"

Tasha squinted and then swore; whereupon Kayja took the opportunity to answer for her. "Yes, my lord, it matches the bits of writing we found scattered about her room. Additionally, we pulled a couple travel bags from her closet and checked all gate ledgers; the one at Trader's Gate mentioned her passing through a little under a month ago and the description seems to match. The writing on these confessions is identical to her entrance signature."

"I didn't write it!" Tasha slammed both hands against her arm rests, half rising from the chair before Kayja caught her shoulder and pressed her back down. "Why would I even write that once, let alone a hundred times?"

Amonn shrugged and stepped away to examine her cell's bare amenities, making Kayja answer, "A guilty conscience perhaps, or maybe a scheme to parade how you successfully desecrated one of the Empire's holiest places."

Tasha flung up her hands. "Or this could be a ham-fisted attempt to frame me. Didn't a miraculous witness provide you with an astoundingly accurate sketch of me?"

This failed to attract Amonn's attention beyond an idle rebuttal. "Perhaps, though I'm struggling with the notion that whoever desecrated Echeira'Sollas would be so heavy handed. Powerful magic was used in the attack as well as extensive planning. That aside, the sketch is among the evidence that appears to have disappeared, so it won't be serving either of our cases."

"Miss Bloomhale, do you have any enemies in the city?" Kayja asked.

"No, because in case it's escaped your notice, I'm not from here."

Wordlessly Kayja produced a cloth bundle and offered it to Tasha, who blinked when it unraveled into a shirt. "I don't understand; why do you have one of my shirts?"

Grabbing the shirt's collar, he folded it down to reveal an embroidered symbol. "Do you know what this means?"

Tasha choked back a stark, humorless laugh. "Let's not ask rhetorical questions. Every child above the age of five knows what that means."

"Humor me."

Fine yellow threads depicted a pentagon with a rat holding a keyring while standing atop an open book. "It's the official marker of the Thieves' Guild." Abruptly, her bitter humor vanished and, blood roaring in her ears, she reached up to feel inside her own collar, any lingering hope dying with a strangled whimper as her finger brushed across the damning lump of threads. Rolling off her chair before Kayja could stop her, Tasha grabbed two of its wooden slats and spun, hurling it against the back wall with a scream.

Unconcernedly, Kayja righted the chair and set it alongside the simple toilet. "Miss Bloomhale, do you have ties to the Thieves' Guild?"

"I've spent years fending for myself, of course I have ties to the bloody Thieves' Guild. I've talked to dozens of members and I know I'm friends with at least one and I've probably worked for several unknowingly. None of that means I'm a member and neither does this." She kicked the shirt across the floor.

"What a pity." Amonn stooped, hooking a finger through the collar. "We haven't had a delegate pass through in years. I've resorted to conducting all my business through mail, which is distinctly insecure." He turned from Kayja to wink at her. "If you had been a member, I'd have had several uses for you. Hell, I might have had enough to call in a few favors and see this whole messy business cleared up. But you're not—"

"My lord!"

Amonn sighed, pinching the bridge of his nose. "Lieutenant, don't tell me you're actually unaware of how common dealing with the Thieves' Guild is?"

"No, my lord, I am well aware of such transactions. However, I must protest your willingness to exchange clemency for personal–" Running feet interrupted him.

"My Lord Warsein, my Lord Warsein!" A young woman burst onto the scene, coming to a sliding halt and nearly colliding with Amonn as he exited from Tasha's cell.

"What's the–" But she grabbed Amonn's shoulder and pulled herself up to his ear, whispering furiously.

His eyes widened briefly before giving way to studied calm. "Thank you for telling me. Run outside and inform my advisors that I'll be along shortly, there are still a few details that need my attention in here. Lieutenant"—he swiveled toward Kayja—"I'll be discussing a sensitive subject with Miss Bloomhale, please leave."

"My lord, I feel I should remind you that it is forbidden to collude with or abus–"

"Yes, yes, I'm aware. Leave."

Still frowning, Kayja inclined his head. "As you wish, my lord."

"You four as well." Amonn nodded at his guards, sending them tromping after Kayja and watching until the portcullis rattled closed. Instantly his façade dropped, lips pulling into a snarl. "Well, this just became a royal shit fest. What in *Enecki's* name am I supposed to do now? Why didn't the little bastard tell me? How in the gods-damned Abyss am I supposed to complete his 'favor' if I don't have all the information? Why would he even ask me if that was his ulterior motive to this whole *Jaidar* blessed disaster? Hell, he probably didn't tell me because he knew I'd refuse."

Tasha edged back warily, watching Amonn pace outside her cell. "Refuse what? Who are you talking about?"

Amonn waved dismissively. "Slade. He sent me to extract you–"

"He did what?" Surprise took her an unconscious step forward, the knots in her stomach loosening ever so slightly.

"He asked me to get you out. We trade favors on occasion, and he said this was just another one of his stupid pranks. Of course that was a lie like every other thrice-damned word spilling from his mouth. I don't know how I'm supposed to free you if he steals my father's entire gods-damn treasury the same night as 'you' torch Echeira'Sollas. That's just too much bloody coincidence to sweep under the rug."

"What, how can–" Tasha bit down on her tongue, barely stopping herself.

"How can I know about Slade stealing my father's treasury–"

"No! How can you be certain it was him?"

"Oh come now, I've been helping him for years. Do you really think he's kept Carr'Selain out all by himself? He'd need at least a little help from the Theanne Guard."

"What are you talking about? Slade's not some thief; he's not waging a shadow-war against Carr'Selain."

Amonn stopped pacing and stared at her fixedly. "Are you saying he hasn't told you any of this?"

"Any of what? That he's a secret thief lord who's powerful enough to challenge Carr'Selain and yet has somehow evaded the notice of an entire empire? Give me a break, his crew only has ten people."

The corner of Ammon's mouth curled upward, anger falling away like a performer's mask. "A crew is it? You know, I think I'd like to contact them. I don't suppose you remember any of their names?"

'Gods dammit.' "Why would I? They're all thieves and murderers; aren't they? Real low-lifes. Hell, they're all probably demons in disguise."

"You're not taking this very seriously are you?"

"Of course I'm not; it's completely ludicrous."

"I guess it was a bit fanciful." Amonn shrugged. "Him chasing out the entire Thieves' Guild is quite absurd."

"I'm not entirely sure I buy him desecrating Echeira'Sollas either, let alone stealing your father's treasury."

Amonn reentered her cell, ignored Tasha as she scrambled away and dragged the chair back out the doorway. "Cain Lammerock is a paladin lord, so Slade has access to everything his insidious heart could want, including the tools and knowledge for desecrating Echeira'Sollas. It's a moot point though as you're committed to his innocence, and you would know best since it's your head on the chopping block. Then again, you could be deliberately misleading us, which would be stupid if he's actually guilty. After all, that would mean he's utterly unconcerned by betraying you."

"You can't honestly believe Slade's guilty?"

"It doesn't matter what I believe so much as what you tell."

"Are you suggesting that I—"

"Wrongfully accuse Slade? Yes. Or that you stop protecting him and rightfully accuse Slade? Yes. I don't care and you shouldn't either."

Tasha opened her mouth to reject this, but the words caught in her throat. *'Why does it matter, really? I wouldn't be sacrificing an innocent and looking after guild interests doesn't gain me anything; I'll land in prison whatever path I choose. Whatever path except this one.'*

That slight curl began teasing Amonn's mouth again. "You're just an innocent caught in the webbing of someone else's scheme. Break free or embrace your role as a simple piece on the board, a pawn already walking toward the sacrificial alter."

"How would my falsely condemning Slade make me any less of a pawn?"

"A living pawn can still evolve into a greater piece, maybe flip the game altogether."

Even as she debated, another question wormed its way to the forefront of her thoughts. "Why do you want me to frame him?"

"Because he introduces himself as having three fiancées and the whole world forgets him two days later. Because I write notes in a book and the ink bleeds off the page. Because I hire people to follow him and come an hour later they can't even remember walking into my office. Because I scry him and he doesn't exist. Because I don't understand." Amonn turned and strode from her cell. "I'll give you a day to weigh the deep prisons against freedom and a moral blemish. Think carefully." The lock scraped into place and the governor's son marched off, his eventual knock on the portcullis bouncing back to her. "We're finished in here."

"Right away, my lord."

"Order a twenty four hour watch on her. She makes a strong argument for being set up, but it could be a ruse and I don't want her escaping."

"As you command, my lord."

Tasha laid her forehead against the door's cool metal, pressing both fists against it until her knuckles hurt as she breathed through a building scream. *'You know. You know I'm innocent. Bastard. I'll rot in jail before telling you anything.'* As the scream slowly released her throat, Tasha forced herself to reach overhead, stretching muscles that were rapidly growing sore from last night's exertions. *'Nothing for it at the moment, might as well try getting some sleep.'*

Before she even knelt atop her mattress, Kayja reappeared outside the door and rapped his knuckles against the frame. "Miss Bloomhale, one of the governor's personal aides has just arrived and wishes to speak with you."

"Tell them I'm busy." She flopped onto her back, draping an arm across her eyes and taking a series of long, slow breaths to try and loosen her stomach muscles. "Have them call again tomorrow; perhaps I'll have perfected my plans for demolishing the Imperial Emperor's statue by then."

"He wishes to negotiate your possible release."

"Har, har. Amonn Warsein just left, but not without making it clear that he wanted me kept right here in this cell. Your 'personal aide' must not have heard."

A key ring jingled, the lock clicked, and her cell door swung open. "Dellyune Grey is permitted significant autonomy. Apparently, he suspects you have something the governor might want."

Tasha raised her arm slightly, searching Kayja's calm, guileless face for any hint of deception. At the same time, she fought to curtail her own fluttering heart. "Alright."

A few minutes later, Kayja ushered her through an unremarkable door into an interrogation room and Tasha froze just beyond the threshold.

Mirrors surrounded her in numerous shapes and sizes. They were nailed to every inch of the room from the ceiling to floor, several had even been given carefully cultivated fractures or raised facets. They displayed Tasha's dirty face, her frizzled hair, her blood-shot eyes, her rumpled clothing, and her slouching posture, every possible detail from a thousand different angles.

'Well, this isn't disconcerting at all and it does wonders for my concentration.' She growled, took a step forward, and instantly regretted it as a cascade of fractured images spilled across the room, duplicating themselves again and again until her head swirled and her stomach rebelled. *'I think I might be sick.'* She snapped her eyes closed, swallowing back a surge of bile.

Keeping them closed, she felt her way toward the room's center where she encountered a glass table and two chairs. Within seconds of getting comfortable, the door that she felt certain was in front of her opened behind her.

Tasha began listing every profanity, curse and obscenity she knew while silently damming the person to each and every known hell simultaneously, none of which made it onto her face.

By the time she reopened her eyes, the man had ghosted half-way around the room, moving with a controlled, wooden bearing that accentuated his slight stature but did nothing to suppress his cavalcade of reflections. All the while, his unblinking eye stared at Tasha or perhaps one of her reflections. She couldn't tell. As for Tasha, she thought she stared at the man himself until the opposite chair was pulled to the wrong side, and he sat down across from her, his iron gray suit pulling into thin, restrictive creases across his slim frame.

Gray hair—with a tenuous grip on its former black—framed pale but smooth features, making his age elusive while a battered eyepatch and an impressive mustache lent him the aspect of an old soldier.

"Miss Bloomhale, I am here to negotiate the possibility of your release." He spoke with faultless pronunciation, clipping the end of each word so it ended with a slight abruptness. "You may call me Mister Grey." One eyebrow quirked upward, awaiting the usual response, but Tasha had spent the last weeks with Slade and merely snorted. "You will answer my questions simply and honestly or this meeting will end." Mr. Grey laid a smoky quartz on the table. "This truth stone will glow red if you lie."

Tasha jerked forward. "Where in the Abyss did you find that?"

"I feel that's largely unimportant, Miss Bloomhale." His single dark-jade eye speared Tasha to her chair. "Shall we begin?"

She swallowed, glancing over her shoulder toward the door. *'Why do I get the impression I just walked into something I really shouldn't have?'* She turned back to the man, pressing down on her leg to keep it from bouncing. "Might as well."

Mr. Grey produced a slender beige folder with one hand, his other one resting in a basic sling. As the silence continued, he perused the folder's contents, barely moving except to glance from one page to the next. On one such occasion, Tasha managed to glimpse his collar pins. There were three in total, all aligned on the right side of his collar. The furthest back offered nothing besides the glint of silver, maybe detailing his station as a minor noble or wealthy merchant. The second—silver as well—bore the sheathed sword of a retired soldier. His last was bronze and displayed the ornate crown of Imperial service.

Mr. Grey glanced up from his folder. "Is your birth name Tasha Bloomhale?"

"Of course it is, why would–" To her left, the crystal exploded with a sickening red light.

"Hmm...," the man said without referring to his truth stone. "Imperial records claim your family has existed for decades, but you yourself only appeared six years ago. Either you changed your name, or you immigrated from the East."

"I've lived here my entire life, so the records are either wrong or misplaced."

Mr. Grey's eyes flicked to the quartz, looking for any reaction. "This is the Paladin Empire, my Dear. Clerical errors don't happen. That said, it seems you were indeed born in the Paladin Empire, leaving a name change as the likeliest answer. Miss Bloomhale, did you change your name approximately six years ago?"

"No."

"Did you pay someone to change it for you?"

Beneath the table, Tasha's hands clenched into fists. "Yes."

"Who?"

"Yinn'Sarr of the Merchants' Guild."

"Considering how much the Merchants' Guild charges for those services as opposed to legal channels, it's obvious you altered your records to escape a grievous error. Either a serious misdemeanor, or you ran afoul of an underworld power."

Tasha's nausea returned, this time completely independent from the room.

"It says here that you are potentially a member of the Thieves' Guild. Is that true?"

"Yes."

"Since Carr'Selain arguably rules the underworld, his guild is the perfect place to disappear ... provided he's willing to offer shelter. I can't see him harboring you—a stranger—against another underworld power, even a minor one. There's no profit in it. Acting on a hunch, I researched the crimes committed six years ago. In particular, those near or inside Dol'Cardolani. After all, the best place to hide is at the center of a nationwide man hunt. Men committed most of the viable transgressions, leaving a bare handful to women. Of these, all but one was caught or killed." Mr. Grey leaned forward, fixing her with a penetrating stare. "I think you committed that final, unresolved crime, Miss Bloomhale; the murder of Duke Racheaos Sivarra who was also"—Tasha glared at the hateful man—"your husband."

58

The Aparthii

Dieharamon emerged into the outside world—nauseas to his core from the Kalvonders festivities—and his skull already pounding from the Dread Storm's malice. He could barely see beyond the entrance, for no light penetrated the night and neither mage nor soulcraft could incite them. Only the oldest Kalvonder mansions and the Remanas Palace harbored light now, and even those in the mansions guttered.

He ducked, shielding himself as the agonized wind flung needles of freezing water. The droplets bit like thorns and seeped along his skin, thick and cloying as honey but black with filth. He swiped at them and only succeeded in smearing the muck. He sighed forcefully, besieged with seeping frustration he could neither shirk nor explain and which festered in his thoughts like a parasite, rejoicing in the storm's renewed dominance. It had briefly diminished after the Dread Lord's foiling, but whatever reprieve had blessed Sahdaen seemed concluded.

There, concealed from the Kalvonders and all others, Dieharamon dropped his head and wept.

He had hoped Vaydrun's execution would not haunt him, had tried to convince himself Vaydrun deserved death, even if it were purchased by deceit. Reality disillusioned him of his fantasy; Dieharamon had degraded himself in orchestrating Vaydrun's demise, and again by achieving it duplicitously, painting himself ever more into the Kalvonders' reflection.

He slumped onto the deceptively delicate railing, fingers finding nooks in the raised, draconic iconography, and reopened his eyes to watch the storm batter Sahdaen. The rain fell in toxic sheets, drowning any half-starved animal or drunk unable to find shelter and swallowing the structures in mire. Thunder roared, preempting a bolt of black lightning that rent a lone tower into blackened rubble and scattered its debris across the rotting beds of Quosh reeds: the Dread Lord's power increased.

Dieharamon rubbed his face, plagued by questions without answers. He needed to smuggle Dayada from Sahdaen before the Dread Lord completed his conquest. But how? Dayada would never leave without the man he sought. He kneaded his brow harder, his headache deteriorating to splitting pain beneath the storm's influence. He needed a solution else Dayada would die, but there was no epiphany to be found in the suffering surrounding him, so he roused from the railing and returned inside, the storm's effects receding within the corridors. Valeriius would have more errands; Kalvonder Nearus still posed a threat and other Kalvonders certainly expressed opinions divergent from Valeriius' will.

The Aparthii slave awaited him outside the gala chamber with a demure posture and clasped hands. He initially circumvented her, assuming she expected another, but she interposed, quietly requesting permission to speak.

"Do you bring word from Valeriius?"

"Yes. 'Ware of Nearus Kalvonder.' He also bids you assemble four guards."

"As he commands."

As Dieharamon redirected his steps away from the gala's carpeted halls toward the nearest barracks, a murmur crested above the festivities, setting his teeth to grinding with apprehension; he could practically feel Valeriius' hooks boring into his flesh, into every attendee's flesh, arranging them into whatever shape he designed: an impending catastrophe Dieharamon could no more envision than he could elude.

Retracing familiar passageways to the sections of the mansion he formerly inhabited, Dieharamon arrived at a simple doorway and parted the bead curtains. The shadows within parted grudgingly, revealing a dozen robust Avarans curled on mats or hunched around tables.

An aging Avaran advanced, marked with diminutive command braids and scars from years of instruction. "I thought he freed you?" His approach knotted the familiar chill of another Tragnashi in Dieharamon's stomach; and the man's voice, bitter and exhausted, layered another burden of failure upon him.

He averted his gaze. "I'm to requisition a quartet of guards, preferably Tragnashi, to accompany me in the gala. My true status is to remain a secret."

"For what service, Varnashi?"

"I don't know."

The commander nodded comprehension and barked a series of names. Four Tragnashi marshalled, equipped with shields and armor of bone, and iron swords, all emblazoned with a dragon-mask helmet as the legions of old wore.

Dieharamon shook his head, indicating stacks of tattered reed gambesons. "No, clay or reed armor only, and stone weapons."

Although inferior materials, the inedible Quosh reeds growing along the *Annuir'Hyme*, and the clay sustaining them, were abundant and easily harvested. Bone was harder to procure, as it necessitated hunting the enormous akarhri and often cost a Kalvonder dozens of warriors. Iron was unheard of except for mercenaries and sell-swords.

Valeriius' guards attending the gala with iron and bone equipment would dismantle his carefully tended illusion of frailty.

The guards re-equipped themselves and trudged to the gala, finding it barred by spectators and draped in a mien of ritual. Scanning for an easier route, Dieharamon spotted a pathway cutting to where Ureign addressed Valeriius.

Even standing at the foot of another man's throne, Ureign strove to overshadow his host. A dozen statuesque slaves attended him, and as many warriors furnished with iron blades and bone-armor. For himself, the ursine Kalvonder appeared pleased, dressed in gilt clothing and weighted down in several fortunes. As always, madness glinted in his eyes.

No one knew what form Ureign's madness took, but all recognized it when he devolved into violence and smelled it when in close proximity. Rumors abounded of his inclinations and abilities, some fanciful and others terrible, but copious evidence existed of his martial and intellectual dominance.

Mounting the dais, Dieharamon motioned his Tragnashi to tarry, and greeted Ureign with a low bow, demonstrating reverence devoid of submission.

"Rise, Dieharamon. Ureign Kalvonder implies his gift is perilous."

Dieharamon repositioned before Valeriius and his Tragnashi knelt at their feet. In some Kalvonder households, impeding their Kalvonder's vision would have incurred execution, in others, a physical reprimand. Valeriius preferred the insurance.

Ureign barked a command in Isaracci and his body slaves scurried off, replaced by half-a-dozen male Tragnashi shuffling forward with Ureign's gold throne, unusual since he usually preferred his silver throne. They set it beside Valeriius then draped it with the radiant white canvas that was his seat-cloth—swathed in black imagery of stunning beauty and intricacy, predominant among them being an immense sun lizard in the midst of consuming a serpent by its tail in a loop along the cloth's edge. Ureign sat, punctuating this insult with additional barked commands. In response, four of his warriors entered via the primary entrance and assumed guard positions to either side. A procession followed, heralded by flutes and drums, and burdened unto collapse with every form of wealth imaginable. They sprawled it about Valeriius with abandon, mounding it as the dais filled until it swaddled Valeriius like the cushions of a boudoir.

However, despite its immensity, this wealth was only an appetizer. Escorted by six guards, an Aparthii man shuffled before Valeriius, wreathed in four iron chains—one on each ankle and wrist—and his mask torn to expose almond eyes. His clothing reeked of sewage and mold, his step limping from heaped abuse, and his unshod feet soundless except for the clink of manacles. The scant clothing accentuated corded muscles and faded battle scars. His appearance provoked an excited murmur, for Aparthii were rare in Avaran Holds, hated for their failure to worship *Ashshand* and coveted for their knowledge in traversing the desert.

Dieharamon met the procession at the dais' edge, forestalling their advance with a raised hand. They glowered but conceded the chains so he might drag the feebly struggling Aparthii before Valeriius, heralded by the man's gasped profanity. Dieharamon could not understand the words, but he understood the cant.

Valeriius grasped the ranting Aparthii by the jaw, maneuvering his face for examination and purring. "You will breed well."

The Aparthii recoiled. "I not serve you, not give sons. Soul my own."

"Oh, but you will. I shall take your soul, your children, and your children's children, and everything your bloodline accomplishes will be in my service." The Aparthii's defiance warped to horror, eliciting a pleased grin. "Take him away."

Dieharamon bowed affirmation and dragged the Aparthii from the gala chamber, his guards rushing to secure the loose chains. The congregation resumed festivities as they progressed, deterring and embroiling his guards. It swallowed members of his troop twice during departure, reducing their progress to a knotted shamble, but ultimately relinquished them without incident. Dieharamon escaped first, fighting from the crowd to stumble through a minor secondary entrance into a mostly unpopulated hallway. He sighed in relief at the leavened pressure, then again as his guards trickled through the wooden doorway, staggering and fighting off guests that strained after the Aparthii.

He noted their precarious holds, weakened by the guests tugging on them, with a spike of alarm and tightened his own grip, wrapping the chain twice. The movement seemed to jar the Aparthii awake. His eyes darted to either side, muscles tensing. "Don't even try–" Then the Aparthii's eyes met his and Dieharamon recognized the look: better to die than live the life awaiting him.

The Aparthii exploded into motion, snapping the embattled guards' tenuous holds in a whirlwind of chains. The crowd recoiled with elated screams, dragging the guards' further back, and the links whipped out, knocking one guard unconscious and a second to the floor. Their prisoner whirled away, slipping his emaciated hand, slick with spilled wine from the revelers, free of Dieharamon's chain while his other hand lashed out, shattering the final guard's clay breastplate and toppling him.

Dieharamon surged forward, discarding his useless chain.

The Aparthii sneered, his rich eyes bright with dangerous fever, charged, spun with his first step to gather momentum and vaulted up, whipping his remaining wrist chain down. Dieharamon twisted aside and stomped on the chain as it landed. The Aparthii landed and leapt back, wrenching on the chain but failing to free it. He jerked violently and crashed onto his back a couple feet from Dieharamon.

He rolled instantly to his feet, thrashing the chain futilely. Dieharamon caught the links near where his foot anchored them and dragged the Aparthii closer. His captive wasted a final second in resistance and flung himself at Dieharamon, who smashed him to the floor.

The Aparthii attempted to rise again but shuddered and collapsed, deprivation, fever, and injuries finally exerting themselves. Dieharamon loosened his hold and knelt. The Aparthii did not struggle as Dieharamon wrapped him in the chains, and when Dieharamon glanced into his eyes he saw only despair. Whether from fever, pain, or defeat, the Aparthii no longer believed he deserved freedom.

Dieharamon finished binding him and hoisted the Aparthii to his shoulders. His four guards inched closer; one of them braced by two others. He nodded at the incapacitated guard. "Two of you return him to the barracks and ensure he's treated. When done, rendezvous at the cells. Bring a sleeping draft and a thick, medium length piece of cloth." They bowed and departed.

Dieharamon adjusted the Aparthii on his shoulder and headed for the cells.

An old door barred the upper cells' solitary entrance, its stonework gray in the feeble torchlight, and its handle eroded. The obscurity beyond belched a gust of stagnant air as Dieharamon's remaining guard heaved it open. Dieharamon kicked the wedge into place and entered, stifling his urge to retch.

The paltry lighting flared at the onset of fresh air, illuminating two rows of stacked cells. The prison's three guards stood from a dilapidated reed table, squinting in the renewed brilliance. They had joined Valeriius years ago, brought from Upper-Sahdaen for their reputation and had promptly verified the rumors, raping wantonly and murdering when they deemed it safe from Valeriius' wrath. Valeriius had promoted them to his chief prison guards, for what fool would attempt escape when these monsters lurked outside?

Eager to glimpse the new arrival, the inmates pressed against their cells' stone rungs. Most were Avarans who had angered Valeriius. One was an eastern sell-sword Valeriius had purchased from the Border War to serve as a pseudo arms master training the Avarans in actual warfare.

Advancing to the furthest cell, Dieharamon alternated between kicking the nastier rats and warning the prisoners off when they clutched at the Aparthii. He signaled the cell guards to open the door, and the larger two hastily volunteered their one-eyed companion. The man snarled and spat incomprehensibly, terrified of Dieharamon, but ultimately capitulated when his associates emphasized their position with a mild battering.

Dieharamon entered in the cell guards wake, surveying the interior for anything that could facilitate the Aparthii's escape or suicide. When only putrid reeds, contaminated by the previous inhabitant's waste, and maggots presented themselves, he deposited the Aparthii down and began liberating his bindings, cautious of renewed violence, but the Aparthii attempted no escape. Finished, he retreated to the door and the Aparthii crawled to where the Quosh straw had been compiled into a makeshift bed.

Dieharamon's other guards arrived moments later, their eyes watering at the stench, and hurried toward him, one bearing a steaming mug and the other a strip of green cloth. Dieharamon took both, waving for them to depart. They shot him looks of gratitude and joined their fellows at the primary entrance.

He reentered the cell and set the steaming mug beside the Aparthii, who warily inspected him before accepting it. Dieharamon proffered the cloth. "For your face." The Aparthii froze instantly, staring at Dieharamon. Recognition dawned and he seized the cloth, spilling the cup in his haste. He covered his face and brow, leaving only his eyes visible. "I'm sorry, but I have nothing for your eyes."

The Aparthii reclaimed his cup. "You are not a Lost Avaran, for all you speak this awful tongue like one born to it. You have something this city has long tried to excise; what permitted you to retain shreds of compassion through the monstrosities of this place?"

"You know this tongue?"

"I deemed it better to appear ignorant and a fool to the Lost Avarans than a potentially dangerous hostage."

"What do you mean Lost Avarans?"

"They are a lost race, and thus we name them such. They were deceived and broken as the river flowed unceasingly, and false prophets prevailed in the wake of this deception. They filled the void of stolen wisdom with cunning lies. Now they rule over the Lost Avarans and are those you know as Kalvonders; though some are of true descent. Why does a man with your bright soul serve one such as Valeriius Kalvonder?"

"I am Tragnashi, my spirit—my essence—is held by another."

"You are of the Shorn? That is impossible; your soul alights with power and your eyes brim with fire. Yours is a soul that cannot be bound short of destruction or an eternal-creature's interference. You are what the Lost Avarans call mage born."

"How do you know I am mage born?"

"Your eyes burn like the guide-fire during a night's journey. Your step warms the earth, and your breath gives life to the air. When you ignite your gift, the calluses of the Deceived Fallen should have loosened. You cannot be of the Shorn; the chains would not bind your soul."

"I have the power but no training; I cannot free myself. Even if I did, I would injure this existence."

"It is chains of fear wrought from lies that bind you, not the lack of knowledge or weakness. The light in your soul and the fire in your eyes are enough to break the chains the False Prophets placed upon your essence."

"Then why am I still chained?" Dieharamon faltered, breath catching.

"You strangle yourself and your power. The fear must be discarded if your soul is to ignite. Please, help me. I can bring you to my people. We can teach you to control what they have taught you to fear, and you will be freed."

"I cannot help you." Dieharamon closed his eyes, restoring control. Hope was a treacherous emotion, and he couldn't afford it. "I cannot leave when another man holds my soul. I cannot aid you, I—" He caught himself again, strangling the words before he devolved into useless reiteration. There was nothing in that cell for him but the Aparthii's frail hope.

"It is not your captor's dominion preserving your enslavement, but your acceptance of it."

Dieharamon had no answer and so left, trying to crush the dreams sparked by the Aparthii's words. He failed.

59

Path Of Redemption

Brimares stepped from the chamber of her inquisition and closed the door, hand splayed heavily across its surface as her jaw involuntarily turned rigid from clamped teeth. Her fingers bored into the wood, blackening it from the Chaos strident within her, and she forced them straight, recognizing her sense of violation as irrational and loathing it. Brimares shoved off the door, crushing the shudders of her treacherous vulnerability. She understood the purpose of their inquiry and the necessity of her responses, but the ring was a vestige of her previous life, and she hated showing it to anyone; it exposed her both physically and emotionally, and represented more than even the Ranger-Wardens realized.

The corridor guided her upward, flanked on either side by a continuous mural of stained glass in various shades of blue, gray, and white: depicting winged people in flight, fleeing some grand denizen of the heavens while carrying two paper eyes fashioned of real paper attached to the mural. The narrative soothed her frayed emotions and she followed it absently despite the deteriorating cold and receding candlelight, bypassing several sealed doors and the occasional alternate path where the story diverged.

Her ascent and the story ended at a secluded doorway in the tower's zenith, the walls—illuminated by a solitary candle stand—recounting a scene of devastation in reds and blacks around the sole surviving thief. She tugged the handle, expecting it to deny her, but the ancient ice crunched encouragingly on the other side, so she exerted greater effort. The door relented with a sharp crack and wind invaded through the gap, greeting her with a chilling kiss and ushering her out with the aroma of pines.

She crossed to the tower's western edge, ice and snow melting beneath her steps, and leaned on the ramparts, regarding the stars on their high thrones and relinquishing the remnants of her tension. Brimares' gauntlet retracted unbidden from her hand, dropping the ring onto her bare skin. She stroked its surface with her thumb, humming a snatch of song as old memories stirred in her mind's recesses. A part of her hoped he had not reverted to the monster, that her damnation was unmerited. The honest part knew he had long since returned to his customary state of violence and rampant pride.

Brimares clenched her fist, suffocating the memories before they ensnared her, and transferred her attention to the western horizon, hunting for signs of the New Order. Initially only trees and the eternal Northern whiteness answered her search, then she noticed the thousands of birds perched at the forest's edge, silent in their ravenous expectance. She straightened, teeth baring and armor flaring, the razor edges steaming with ignited flame. She began to depart, but wingbeats disrupted the volatile silence, dragging her attention left to where Salem's Raven had alighted just within reach. Brimares let her lips part into a full snarl. "What are you doing here?"

The Raven just preened, evincing no threat or desire.

Brimares growled softly but relented and resumed leaning on the ramparts. "You're probably just as much a slave as I am." She raked it with another glance. "Don't suppose you can tell me anything about Salem?"

"Who are you talking to?"

Brimares whirled about, gauntlets clamping shut and serrated armor flaring.

Half through the doorway Lionel recoiled, one hand snapping up in mollification. "Wait! Just me, it's just me."

She exhaled and relaxed, smoothing her armor. "Hello, Lionel." She gestured at the Raven. "That's Salem's bird, probably sent to watch me."

He eased through the door and joined her on the ramparts. "Should we be worried?"

"The Raven's no danger; they probably already know everything they need to. At least Salem does." She slid away from him, reaffixing her attention on the tree line. "What do you want, Lionel?"

He shifted toward her, leaning one arm on the wall's crenel. "I wanted to discuss your *Redemption*."

"Why? Are you backing out?"

"No! Just ... wondering if you need time to prepare. If this fails—goes cataclysmically poorly because of The North or Enecki's distance—it might kill you."

"You aren't strong enough to kill me, Lionel. If you fail, nothing changes. Even if I succeed in killing the High-Warden without the Northerners butchering me, Cardolyn Tyier won't sanction my *Redemption*." That, however, didn't mean she wouldn't try.

"Okay." He extended a hand to her. "Let's go, then."

Her Chaos stirred in response to the proximity, incensed by the gesture, and she could feel his Shard reacting in kind. "You go on ahead," she answered, quelling her Chaos, "get everything ready. I'll follow."

The hand dropped with a nod of his head, soothing her still fractious Chaos. "Don't tarry, I don't know how long we have, or what this will do to you." He departed, tension evident in his shoulders.

Once more alone atop the ramparts, Brimares opened her hand and scrutinized the ring nestled atop its ivory links. It glinted in the starlight, superficially insignificant. She studied it, her eyes exploring the countless wrinkles of its surface before slipping it back over her head and beneath the collar of her breastplate.

She restored her attention to the Raven, where it still perched on a rampart, and seized her Chaos. Pain seared through her veins and twining streams of fire lashed from her fingertips at the Raven.

The Raven reared back with a caw, raising ebony wings to shield itself, and vaulted into the air. It screamed at her and dove away, flying westward.

Brimares clenched her fist, extinguishing the flames, and strode back toward the door, teeth gritting as a wind scoured her unguarded face in pursuit of the Raven. She shoved the door open and entered, ice cracking across her footprints in the snow as a dense fog washed down from the mountains, enshrouding the tower. She shut the portal against the creeping tendrils, muttering about how The North would have more allies if it were friendlier to outsiders.

A soft, lyrical voice answered her statement from the vacant corridor behind her, "The North chooses to be alone, Brimares hell-born."

Brimares turned, skin crawling, to observer a speaker no taller than her knee with a form of autumn leaves bound into a humanoid shape by delicate vines. A dozen legends stirred her memories, cautioning against what she faced and provoking her Chaos to an uncertain hum. She sank to a crouch with deliberately inoffensive motions, retracting and smoothing her armor. "You're a Fae of the *Court*."

"No, I am of The North, Brimares hell-born. I dwell in the world of men, in the forests and the rivers and the flowers that only bloom beneath the freshly fallen snow. I leave the glass halls to the greater of my kind and their dances."

Brimares leaned closer, exploring the Fae's beautiful form. "Who are you?"

The long fingers of its hands splayed wide. "I have no name, for I am absolute—unique—and there is no variation in what I am or can be. I have no need of a name because I cannot be categorized with words."

"Why are you here?"

"Because boots trample soft ground, crushing the burrows. Because the screams of men disturb the birds in their trees and the slumber of those who cannot wake in winter and survive. I am here because in a forest old as the world we now hear the thunder of ancients falling to the steel and hunger of men. I am here because we ask why."

"I think you know that answer, otherwise you wouldn't be here talking to me." Her Chaos kindled, incensed by the accusation the Fae's questions implied, almost drawing her fingers taught with prepared violence, but she forced them limp.

"We ask not why they come or why ours suffer; we ask why one who burns is welcome in a castle of winter. We ask why the men of dark iron hunt one of their own. We ask what is the song and music that play within you; what is the truth you have spent so long drowning?"

"I am damned; there is no music in me." Brimares released a sliver of her Chaos' mounting aggression, causing her armor to flare minutely and the air to ripple with heat. Her hands flipped over and splayed, mimicking the Fae's prior gesture.

"All life is music and song. The music within you is distant and coarse. It is the sound of iron and screams, of fire and pain wrapped tight, suffocating a softer vein hidden so deep it goes unseen not unheard. I can hear love, mortality, and sacrifice. It is a song that is far from complete, and yet it is no answer to the questions we asked."

"Just tell me what you want."

"We take an interest because the High-Warden of Lord *Ever-Winter* has developed an interest in you extending beyond your purpose in The North; and when the High-Warden takes an interest, The North takes an interest."

"Why's he interested? It's been made clear I am no threat."

"The High-Warden takes an interest because despite burning within, you were welcomed by Lord *Ever-Winter's* Wolves."

"And what does that have to do with me?"

"There is more I would ask you and of you, and much I would tell in turn of your foes and your allies."

"Spare me." Brimares rose. "I have nothing to offer you and have no intention of fighting for you any longer than I need to survive. Find someone else, someone who will actually help you." Brimares marched past the creature, but it followed, teasing her with the scent of autumn.

"If you do not answer, that is your choice, but you must listen. A geas is upon me to confide what I know, and I can no more ignore it than you can break the bonds which make you our enemy."

Brimares lengthened her strides. "I don't intend on being your enemy much longer, and this is not my war."

The Fae creature's form shifted abruptly and thickened, its vines blossoming into radiant white and sapphire blooms, manifesting its unseen soul. "The paladin cannot free you, Brimares hell-born. It is beyond his energy and far beyond his station among the gods. If you insist on this futile attempt, your only reward will be pain. Aid The North and you will be freed."

"And what would you have me do? Fight blindly for you until someone deems my service sufficient? For how long? On faith? Faith is what got me into this nightmare!" Brimares' words ground from her teeth as a taut snarl.

The Fae creature diminished anew, regarding her with cold, inhuman eyes. "We cannot lie, from the greatest of the four queens to the smallest changeling child. Although this night offers many possible results, and your destination stretches furthest into shadow, if you aid The North, you will be freed."

Brimares stifled a retort before it could pass her lips, unable to refute the Fae for she knew the legends. "Why are you telling me this?"

"Because it will define your choice and compel you down a road beneficial to The North." The Fae stepped closer, hand rising toward her brow as the scent of autumn filled the air, burdened with memories and slumber. "You might think me cruel for this, but all creatures are, and you have been alone long enough." The Fae's hand fell without making contact and in the same motion she began to fade, vanishing entirely before Brimares could voice an utterance.

In her wake, she left a snare of confusion and frustration that held Brimares fast, struggling to comprehend the interaction. She understood the Fae's response, but the logic failed her; she had no choice but to assist The North in killing her kin, otherwise the New Order would kill her. So how had this dialogue altered her intentions?

A hail from below roused Brimares from her ruminations, directing her attention toward Kaea—dressed in the soft medium-length coats and slippers Northerners wore inside—as she ascended toward her. "Brimares!"

Brimares faced her warily. "Why are you here? Weren't you discussing my ring with Maern?"

"That concluded shortly after you left, so I went looking for Lionel, thinking you might like some company for the *Redemption* ritual, and he sent me to fetch you. He's ready."

"You know the destination, lead the way. And there's no reason to stay after, I doubt it's a pleasant experience."

"I'm not staying because it's a pleasant experience. I'm staying because you could use the support; *Redemptions* are supposed to be a rough ordeal."

"I've experienced worse."

The deranger bestowed a sobered look on her. "I imagine you have. It's not far now, just the next floor down. Out of the way in case things go sour."

True to her word, they rounded a final corner and attained their destination: one of the previously ignored doors with Lionel stationed outside. He greeted them with a terse nod and led them inside onto a floor blanketed in silver pentacles, their lines stacked atop one another and offset to ensure no energy escaped.

Brimares hesitated upon the threshold, then advanced, crossing the first silver line. Her Chaos stilled, turning icy in her veins before lethargically resuming its burning flow. Lionel closed the door after Kaea, tracing its confines with a murmured phrase.

Kaea slipped to the side. "Maern suggested this place; it was used in acts of high-magic to contain superfluous energy. It will serve us the same way."

Brimares nodded, a dull ache growing in her breast as the chill returned and expanded. The North was powerful here, condensed into a mantle that suppressed her and her Chaos. She continued inward, crossing each pentacle with a flare of pain and cold. After the fourth pentacle, neither the pain nor the cold abated. It persisted, throbbing within her blood and augmenting the ache within her breast. She advanced to the chamber's heart, a small dais of wrought stone, black as a starless night. She mounted it and all heat fled her body, leaving only the pain, the cold, and the festering agony of the Chaos within. She staggered and braced herself on one of the dais' four pillars.

Lionel hurried toward her. "Are you alright?"

"I'm fine." She compelled her body straight and faced him. "Just get this over with."

He froze, bewilderment swallowing his features as his eyes squinted at her. His hand rose to graze the space between her eyes with a thumb, accompanied by a distracted question, "Where did you get this?"

"What?" Brimares brushed his hand aside, her gauntlets receding so she could touch her brow.

"There's a white Fae mark between your eyes. At least, I think it's Fae?"

"I met a Fae creature when I left the roof, but it never touched me. I imagine that's its origin."

Kaea approached to inspect Brimares. "Don't worry, the Fae are of The North, they won't harm you with the Wolves acceptance still fresh on the air."

"What does it mean?"

Kaea shrugged apologetically. "I do not know; I have no dealings with the Fae or the *Winter Court*. You'd be better served asking one of the ambassador Ranger-Wardens who treat with them regularly. Maern's one."

"Will this mark interfere with us?" Lionel asked.

"It should not, it's currently dormant, but I have no real idea."

"Brimares, do you want to continue?"

"Yes." The thought of the Fae's mark made her Chaos writhe with paranoia, but she did not believe the creature had intended her malice, so Brimares repositioned to the dais' center and knelt.

Kaea retired to the door, reclining against it with a final gesture of confidence. Lionel stepped opposite Brimares, armored but unarmed, and bowed his head in prayer. Brimares shivered, the layers of her armor vacillating in response.

Lionel raised his brow, golden light blooming in his eyes as his voice resounded, "Let a Light be now lit against the Darkness of god and man. Lord of *Etherea* and Light, *Enecki*, this soul was cast into flames to burn and suffer for crimes judged by a remote viewer. She has suffered this damnation, and all crimes she birthed have been paid for."

The strength fled her, crushed as the ache within her breast multiplied. She felt a presence, an intellect, focus upon her, incomprehensibly vast and solid as iron crypts, and yet merely a fragment of its true shape.

Then she heard someone screaming in her mind and it took a moment to recognize her own voice. Scrambling against the stone, she clutched her ears, trying to deafen herself to the god's presence while it crushed her piece by piece. And above this, his voice inhuman, Lionel continued his prayer, "Father of deities and guardian of men, *Enecki*, I plead for your mercy to right a wrong done in your service. I beg that you revoke the excessive judgement of damnation and allow me to cleanse her." His eyes unwavering and wholly dominated by the golden light within them, Lionel withdrew the *Amarthayiss* from a satchel at his side, its cover blooming with the same golden light in his gaze. Hefting the book level to his breast, he extended his arms as if to grant the *Amarthayiss* to another. Then as if there was indeed another standing opposite to him, the book rose from his hands and opened. Now, Brimares screamed aloud, her consciousness inundated with a thousand words, each burning and solitary, spoken in the voices of souls that transcended her. They were the voices of god-spawn, of Seraphim and Nephilim speaking the words of a god, the words that detailed his laws to those who worshiped him across the Mortal Kingdoms. They were also the words of Light and Order, the anathema to Chaos. She felt no pain, but still she suffered. Lionel's voice boomed across the chamber, no longer recognizable as his, "*Enecki,* Lord of the Immortal Pantheon, upholder of justice and guardian against the Dark. I implore and beseech you, grant me your blessing and your forgiveness for the pride that drives me to contend against your sentence. I stand here as your servant—a paladin knight errant—and will accept your judgement if I am to be judged. Let this Chaos, this curse and this damnation's hold be broken. This corruption shall no longer have right or privilege to remain a parasite upon this beloved soul that wants to reenter the Light of justice and order." The vacillating pages of the *Amarthayiss* ceased their movement and settled at last. Lionel looked down, his hand falling to rest on the book.

Brimares felt the blood streaming from her ears and tasted it on her tongue. The war continued within her; words of abolition and *Redemption* struggling with Chaos. The Chaos within her lashed back, burning all the brighter for the conflict, incinerating her from within. Now, there was pain.

Lionel spoke and his words fell dead on laden air. His invocation remained simmering on the air, reaching higher of its own accord and searching with an inevitable energy. The pulsing blood, the strident heartbeats, and all magic, burning, frozen or ordered fell into rhythm with Lionel's prayer. Those words dragged Brimares from the floor, first to her knees, then to stand in helpless thrall. She saw Kaea crouched in a corner, another victim of the storm.

Brimares could only clutch at her head, bleeding from her nose, ears, and mouth. She heard each drop of her blood hiss as it hit the ground. The Chaos roiled, retaliating against the exorcism and threatening to sunder her from within rather than be parted. She could feel its burning fingers digging into her like a thousand needles, binding them together with iron thread. She tried to scream, to free herself of the taint. But she was powerless to escape the war within her. Lionel's words were spoken in silence now, each like the crack of a whip against her skin, searing at the Chaos within. Every word bellowed and sparked, building on itself toward an inevitable climax. Each word was a brand on her mind and on her skin; a summons, a challenge for the Chaos to answer. Brimares felt herself breaking from the strain and the climax of Lionel's prayer as he spoke the concluding word, the final condemnation. The crescendo ascended, and every heartbeat spent a moment in tune. And then the world crashed back down upon Brimares. The last sensation she had was of her body tearing open and her skin shredding as the Chaos shattered its fetters.

Lionel started from his doze as Brimares erupted to a crouch atop her bed, shredding the blankets as her armor clamped around her face and flared open with a searing rasp, igniting. He lurched to his feet, arms swinging wide as he scrambled away from her. "Brimares, wait! You're fine!"

His words snapped her rigid but the sear of her Chaos on his mind and Shard swelled, immersing the room in a dry, sweltering heat and the smell of ash. She faced him, fingers boring deeper in the mangled mattress before registering him and the room and relaxing. She sagged back, armor retracting and smoothing with a ragged exhaled. "It didn't work, I assume."

Lionel miserably righted his upended chair and sat. "I'm sorry, there was too much Chaos for me to purge. I couldn't control it and ... it got out of hand."

Her armor rippled subtly, and her voice dropped. "What do you mean—out of hand?"

"Kaea..." Lionel fell silent as the door opened to admit the woman in question, a new scar and numerous burns marring her features.

"Hello, Brimares, thought I heard you talking."

"I'm sorry."

"I do not blame you for this. What you were in that chamber is not who you are. That was a creature wrought of pain and suffering, driven mad by the language of warring gods. I chose to be there, and my being there helped contain you to that room away from the people who couldn't handle it."

Brimares snorted. "And yet that is who I am, the monster they made me, and it seems no *Redemption* can cure me." She shifted her gaze to Lionel and for once her eyes were human, a vibrant swirling blue. Lionel flinched internally at the sight, remembering her shriek as his prayer failed, and all the Chaos within her escaped. Her eyes had changed from maelstrom to human as her face changed to the devil within.

"Not quite, there's still a chance a stronger paladin could *Redeem* you; Cardolyn Tyier for certain." That her eyes remained human instead of their customary maelstroms signified the madness of Chaos persisted in her mind to some extent, but she appeared unaffected. Even now, her eyes bored into him.

"Do you ... remember what happened?"

"No."

"Hey"—Kaea moved to sit beside Brimares—"do you want us to describe if for you? Your other face?"

"No." Brimares stood, flames slowly reigniting in her pupils. "I want nothing to do with that monster. What happened while I was asleep?"

Kaea exhaled softly and stood as well, her amicability disappearing. "The New Order arrived; they will demand to see you, and we will not lie about your presence."

"What do you want me to do?"

"Nothing for now, but you'll have to be present if they demand an audience."

"Then there's no value in lingering here. I'll wait with Maern; where is he?"

"In the courtyard below, I'll show you."

Kaea led from the room, spilling moonlight onto its furs from a window past the open door as she emerged and commenced her descent. Brimares followed, armor encasing her bare feet again as she stepped onto the icy stone beyond, but Lionel remained in the vacant bedchamber long after them, staring at the rumpled bed before slowly sinking onto it. The Shard of Divinity fumed in his breast, frigid in its wrath and righteous in its hatred of her, demanding her annihilation. Images of the pentacles shattering one after another besieged him, always culminating with the memory of Brimares' human face ripping into something hellish. He'd always known her nature, yet seeing it exposed with such violence and brutality had impressed upon him the reality of her; she was not human and, deserving or not, she had murdered. It was a reality he had learned to ignore, but being forcefully reawakened to it had left him unravelling and his Shard pulsing louder than it ever had since entering The North. He stifled the memories with an effort and stood once more; now was not the time for this. He donned his boots at the door and followed the women.

Lionel exited the tower into the courtyard and the unnatural atmosphere presiding over it. Derangers crouched upon the slender, rampart-less, wall while soldiers congregated in small clusters throughout, occupied in various entertainments or endeavors.

Maern knelt at the courtyard's epicenter beneath the tails of a long Northern banner, amidst a circle of blue flame candles and four bowls: one of pewter, one of glass, one of hawthorn, and one of white marble. Lionel joined Brimares and Kaea where they observed the ritual from several feet's distance, near enough to hear the low murmurs Maern uttered and guess at the phantom images he sketched on the air.

The twelve candle flames flared, turning white at their peak as milk swirled up out of the marble bowl into a sphere a foot from the ground. It continued swirling, in and out of itself, never breaking its perfect sphere. The undefined blood in the hawthorn bowl followed suit, spiraling upward in a red cone opposite the white. Ashes followed suit from the pewter bowl, only instead of spinning elegantly, they churned, their shape constantly in flux, sometimes a symbol and sometimes an animal. The last to rise was a stream of white lily petals, from the glass bowl, to form a pillar.

Lionel felt Brimares stiffen beside him, an act compounded by the snick of her armor opening further. He first glanced at the walls, fearing the New Order had commenced its assault, then at her when he saw nothing. "What do you see?" She gave him no response other than to indicate the hawthorn bowl. He followed her direction, at first still seeing nothing. Then he noticed the blood sphere's diminished size. He unfocused his gaze. A figure constructed of twigs connected by red veins sat perched on the hawthorn bowl imbibing the levitating blood.

Peering at the other three bowls, he glimpsed Fae creatures clustered around Maern. One, a creature with long, delicate fingers and a brow crowned with antlers, drank the milk, its blue forked tongue piercing the white sphere over and over. A second with skin of starlight and the liquid black eyes of the Fae laughed softly to himself, weaving the flower petals into a dress about his frail body. The final eldritch creature danced with the ashes, twirling to and fro, her laughter tinkling and her glass limbs reflecting the light. Then they evaporated, leaving the candles snuffed and the bowls empty.

Lionel couldn't find words in the ensuing moments, and it took Maern beginning to collect the bowls for him to find his voice again. "What was that for?"

"It was a ritual of appeasement and apology. The eldritch keepers of this forest are frightened and angry at the New Order's transgression; they came seeking answers for why their burrows are crushed underfoot, for why their foxes are slaughtered, and their trees hewed. I answered as I could, offering blood, milk, ash, and bloom to appease their wrath."

Brimares shook her head. "But they know of the New Order? One came to me yesterday, and it knew why."

"The Fae are unlike us, Brimares. They are quick to tease and slow to anger; but when angered they lose all sense of reason, turning insane with violence and forgetting much of their conscious thought. They are aware of the New Order on some level of their consciousness, but it is buried beneath their rage. The lesser Fae can be appeased with offerings; the greater often demand the harm undone and the culprit surrendered to their judgement.

The lesser are quick to release their anger, the greater often hold onto their anger for generations, causing the land to wither. I am a Ranger-Warden and an ambassador, a peacekeeper between the mortals and the Fae."

Before Lionel continued his inquiry, a call rose from the battlements, "A rider approaches beneath a white flag!" Maern stood and stepped over the circle of extinguished candles, beckoning them to follow.

They watched the rider approach, the horse thrashing in his grip and struggling against the depths of freshly fallen snow. He approached the wall, yanked his beast about so his left side faced them. He raised the spear and white flag. "My master bids you come forth and speak before blades are drawn. This is war, yes, but not all lives need to be lost! You all have families, and my master bids you think upon them, on your wives and children. The New Order is kind and knows much of mercy, for we all have found salvation in the arms of truth and honest justice. That hope is now being offered to you; think with care before you discard it for the lies and evil that reign unchecked across this beautiful land!"

The messenger lowered his spear and searched the ranks of Northern men atop the wall. Maern leaned forward onto the ramparts. "Tell your master we will hear his words, but he is to come unarmed and with only two companions, also unarmed. We will not tolerate treachery."

The messenger scowled. "Let there be three who accompany both commanders, and you will bring the hell-spawned traitor."

"Very well," Maern conceded, "but the hell-spawn that accompany your master will come bound at the wrists and wearing their human faces. They will come armored to display them for what they are, but their armor will be retracted; its edges sheathed."

"Do not think we trust you implicitly, Northerner! You will obey every restriction you place upon us! You will come unarmed, and that traitor will come human and bound!"

Maern glanced at Brimares for confirmation, and she agreed. "Very well, may the violence of this day be averted. Now return to your master and convey our words truthfully."

The messenger guided his horse about and looked back at the walls. "Yes, let this bloodshed be averted and lives spared."

"Why did you agree to this parlay?" Lionel asked. "They can offer us nothing, even if we cared to negotiate."

"This is The North, Sir Lionel, and time is our ally. Every hour that passes, their strength will wane and their courage weaken. More than that, their commander is a man of violence given to rage, and rage is easily manipulated. When angered, he will hurl his forces futilely against this wall, wasting many lives for no gain. Also, look behind you on the mountain side. We will not stand alone for long."

Lionel cast his eyes on the Rhawn. At first he saw nothing, then he saw a blur of white on the black rock. He focused in on it, seeing a White Wolf standing in absolute stillness watching them. Someone, or something, was coming.

The designated envoys waited for the appointed hour beneath the tower's wall with their horses, bathed in moonlight that draped the world unopposed, painting all of them in silver clarity. Seated atop the black stallion, still nameless, Lionel readjusted his grip on the reins, feeling exposed without a sword despite the sleek, crystalline Northern armor he'd borrowed. Maern waited a short distance from him, watching the gentle snowfall while his fingers traced the edge of a long blade, causing the glass to sing softly and glisten. Hrann crouched beside him, cowled and fully armed with quiver, bow, and sword, scarcely more than a specter even within the walls safety. He would stalk the negotiations unseen, insurance against treachery and whatever dark magic the New Order might attempt to employ. Brimares stared at the wall, features expressionless and armor smooth but eyes churning and her hands bound in azure chains.

"The hour's come," Maern stated as his attention fell to the wall. He flicked the blade and it collapsed in a spray of water droplets, all but the handle which he attached to his saddle. "Let us proceed." His stallion snorted and trotted forward, the door receding before them. Hrann slipped out in advance, vanishing entirely despite the moon's brilliance. Brimares came last, the air distorting around her and snowflakes melting in proximity.

Four riders emerged from the forest, mounts laboring through the snow, two in crimson armor and a third in black with his blond hair brushed suavely to the side and a Raven perched on his shoulder. The last wore sable robes and pulsed with vestiges of divinity.

The parties converged at the brink of the forest's shroud, far from the tower and well within the purview of the New Order's concealed troops. Kell'MachChain spared Brimares and Lionel a grin as they arrived, but ceded authority to the Blond Knight, who performed a perfunctory reverence to Maern. "I assume you're in command? Pray tell, what's your name?"

"No. I know you, and you will not have my name without giving yours."

786

The Blond Knight sneered. "That's not a wise attitude, northman. Those short walls cannot protect you or your scant soldiers. This parlay is to save me lives and give you a chance at redemption. If you can't respect that, return to die."

"I have no need of redemption."

The Blond Knight's jaw and cheek ticked and his brow lowered as he scanned the ground, granting Lionel a revelation. *'He has no name.'*

Eventually a grin split the Blond Knight's lips and he said, "Fine, I have a name for you. I am Mallicinth."

A false name, the name of a monster from a child's story, and yet it made Lionel's skin crawl all the same.

"That's not your name." Brimares snarled quietly, her armor writhing across her skin.

"No, but it's the only one I have." His grin widened. "The rest were taken from me and replaced with the vessel you see before you. A wise man would see the calamity I represent, but you are not wise and so you will fight, you will die, and then, at the end of it all, you will lose."

"The name will suffice for now. I am Ranger-Warden Maern, and yes, I am in command. What do you want?"

"What we stated at the onset! I want the she-demon; she belongs to us and only the inconvenience of distance has prevented her master from reminding her of it. She betrayed us and ultimately will betray you because she cannot help it. She is our demon; one word from the right man and she will kill all of you. Give her to us, she's only a liability to you and will only get you all killed tonight. We also want the paladin. No one knows he's here, there'd be no repercussions for giving him up and you could all save yourselves for a battle that actually matters. I assure you, he doesn't. He's also a foreign agent in your country, spying on us and probably you. He belongs to us as well, to do with as we see fit. Even if you do win, he'll betray you to Cardolyn Tyier. These people are not worth dying over."

"You are ill-prepared for a siege; I think it would cost you more to take them, than us to die defending them. You don't have demon's enough to spare or squander and your soldiers are dead on their feet, starved and exhausted."

"Soldiers die, that is their purpose, and I doubt your country could tolerate the loss of so many Ranger-Wardens without grief. But I am not intractable, name a price for their return, something your king or whoever rules you could countenance." His hand extended in invitation, the baleful magnificence of *Telacra* manifesting palpably within him and expanding into coiling shadows.

Maern snorted. "There is no king in The North."

The Blond Knight laughed, his hand falling with a dull clatter, but *Telacra's* presence and her shadows persisted. "Is no one strong enough in this frozen hell to rule it? You really are pathetic. But why haven't your vaunted Fae claimed the throne?" The Blond Knight raised his hand again, and this time a miniature woman struggled in his fingers. "I found this thing wandering the woods not two hours ago. A little spy of yours perhaps? Surely not one of the elder Fae?"

Maern stiffened. "Do not harm her, Mallicinth."

"Why? Is it truly a member of the *Winter Court*? And to think Kheldar Ferain feared their intervention! If this is all they are, I believe that fear lacked justification."

"Do not harm her! She is neither a part of the *Winter Court* nor this war!"

"Well, then give me what I want: the she-demon and the paladin. Or is this immortal being worth less to you than a pair of foreigners and enemies?"

Maern's hands tightened on the reigns, drawing them taught until they groaned. His teeth ground together visibly and audibly, clamped on words that eventually pried themselves free. "Don't. You don't know what you could bring down on all of us. The Great Fae—"

"Are not so terrible if they can't even claim the throne over the lot of you."

"They are forbidden to wear the Midnight Crown," Maern ground out.

"The fact they can't defy your second-rate deity attests their frailty. They're just hollow specters, and since this little thing is not part of their renowned *Court*, there should be no repercussion for her death." The Blond Knight crushed the Fae.

Maern roared, his hand grasping the handle of his dismantled blade and slashing at the Blond Knight in a lethal, seamless motion, ice spilling from the handle into the edge of a crystalline sword. The Blond Knight reacted as he began however, snapping his other hand up and into a fist, materializing a gleaming, metallic barrier of black energy. Maern's sword struck and sheared through it, singing a bitter refrain unlike anything Lionel had heard. It stilled inches shy of the Blond Knight's throat, visibly quivering from Maern's strain and its own vibration.

The Blond Knight leaned away, raising a finger to tap its point. "Now that wouldn't have been appropriate for a flag of truce." The tap pierced the steel guarding his fingers, drawing a thimble of blood and his gaze down while the color drained from his features. Even an enchanted blade should not have sheared through his prayercraft so effortlessly, and his armor would boast enchantments of its own to defy weapon and magic alike, yet his blood stained the glass of the Northern sword.

The forest stirred behind them, its branches waving as the wind died and the temperature plummeted. The Blond Knight flicked the Fae woman to the ground and Maern slipped from the saddle, dispelling his blade to cradle her crumbling form of delicate bloom and vine.

The Blond Knight relinquished his barrier and chuckled. "This is why The North is doomed. Look at him crying over a creature he didn't even know. These men are weak and godless, you'd be better served joining us, paladin. At least then this land would be opened to the Pantheon."

Lionel matched his glare. "This land does not belong to the gods, Mallicinth, yours or mine, and I will not surrender it to you or them if I can help it."

"You're in no position to prevent it. You're alone and subject to the will of your host. Though, seeing as he's otherwise occupied, if you want to give the she-demon to us I'll let you go free."

"There will be no agreement," Maern snarled, his voice rising from his kneeling form like an omen. "There will be no treaty. And there will be no mercy." He rose, his irises gone dark. "There will be judgement and there will be retribution. I promise you, Mallicinth of the New Order, you will not survive the dawn."

"Now, now, there's no need to be hasty. It was only a—"

"Run!" Hrann appeared from nothing with a ripple of hues, his blade slashing in a spray of blood. "They're surrounding us!" A corpse tumbled from the conjured shadows beside him, clutching at a severed throat.

The Blond Knight wrenched his horse back, the shroud he'd manifested dispelling with a gasp to reveal dozens of encroaching New Order mercenaries and demons. "Take them!"

The lesser demon erupted forward, shattering its bonds like they were nothing and roaring laughter. Lionel recoiled, scrambling for his weapon only to remember he had none and cursing as the demon dove for him. Brimares crashed into it, driving it to the ground as the links of her bonds melted. He struck at her, digging four massive, bone-deep furrows across her face, but unaffected, she reared her head back, her mouth opening far wider than humanly possible, and dove forward, her distended jaws clamping about her foe's throat. The demon jerked once, thrusting its body against her before expiring with a whimper.

Lionel kicked the black stallion's flanks, screaming, "Go, go, get back to the tower!"

Hrann vanished then reappeared seconds later beside the mounting Maern, his crystalline blade slashing effortlessly through a pair of soldiers. Maern reached a hand down to help him mount as well, but a black bolt of divine energy blasted through his horse's head, obliterating it. They tumbled free, Maern rolling back to his feet as his blade sang free and the New Order troops swarmed to within a few steps.

Hrann retreated with a grimace, yanking Maern with him as black lines spread across his face like fractures in a vase. The pulse of witchcraft scraped across Lionel's skin then Hrann leaned forward and shrieked, his cry all the more terrible for want of a tongue. The New Order's charge faltered and broke, the men staggering as a wild, reasonless scream rose.

The scars on his face bleeding from his broken vows, Hrann wrapped an arm about Maern, who limped, and aided by some fell power, sprinted for the tower, his footprints leaving bloodstained tracks in the snow. Lionel steered the black stallion around and raced back toward them. "Take him." He leapt from the saddle activating his Shard with a hasty prayer.

Someone screamed a command and a hail of black shafts flew from the forest, diving toward them. Lionel flung his hands skyward, his left wrist clasped in his right palm, and a wall of golden lights materialized between them and the New Order. The arrows struck the wall and shattered.

Lionel snapped the energy flow to his wall with a ragged command, staggered and fell. The Shard of Divinity pulsed within his breast and he shuddered as waves of pain throbbed in sync with his heartbeat. He had the energy to conjure the wall, but the sudden expenditure of energy and the lack of proper incantation had shocked his body and left him reeling. A second hail of arrows barraged his wall, followed by the massive force of soldiers hurling their weight against it. He felt the wall flicker but hold, stalling the charge.

Hands grabbed his shoulders from behind, dragging him upright. He smelled Chaos-tainted blood and heard Brimares screaming in his ear, though her words sounded distant, "Get up, that wall won't hold forever!" He tried to stand, to support himself, but even with her hands under his shoulder he could not, his Shard rebelling at him as much as her touch. She growled and threw him over her shoulder as she would a child, then sprinted toward the tower.

The Shard of Divinity pulsed again in his breast, bringing some measure of rage-born clarity to his vision. Peering through the golden concave of his wall, he watched the Blond Knight fling his hand toward it. A hammer of inky energy materialized over the barrier and crashed down. Hairline cracks of black exploded outward from the hammer and the wall imploded, hurling golden shards of divine energy in all directions. The obliteration of his wall, something that held such a vast amount of his energy, slammed into Lionel seconds later, hurling him further into shock.

Brimares skidded to a halt at the base of the wall beside Hrann and Maern. "What's wrong? Where's the door?"

Maern hissed beside them, struggling to stand in Hrann's grasp. "The door won't open with the New Order so close; not even if I told it to." Brimares hurled a torrent of flames at the ground between them and the New Order. The fire sizzled on the snow and caught, surging to an impassable height of ten feet.

"Can we get in anywhere else? Maybe a rope?" She stepped back, scanning the wall.

Maern shook his head. "There's no other way for you or Lionel to get in."

She shifted Lionel higher on her shoulder. "Is there another way for you to get?" He nodded. "Then go."

"What about the horse?"

"He'll be fine, just let him go!"

"And you?"

She shoved him toward the wall. "Don't worry about us; we can get inside." He matched her stare for a moment, then nodded and slipped to the ground. Staggering toward the wall, he laid a hand on the smooth ice, inhaled once, and merged into it. Hrann followed promptly, the ice offering no resistance to their passage as the black tore off toward the forest.

Brimares readjusted Lionel on her shoulder with a soft warning, "Hold on tight." She back-pedaled from the wall, gathered herself and sprinted forward. Then at the last possible second, Brimares vaulted, hurling herself and Lionel three-quarters of the way up the wall. Lionel heard the rasp of metal scraping on ice as the edges of her bracers snapped open and latched onto the wall. The New Order soldiers crashed against the wall's base, shaking it with their impetus but failing to unseat them. Brimares pulled her legs up and grasped the wall with the serrated armor of her boots before detaching one arm and embedding it further up. Thus, inch by inch, she scaled the wall, carrying Lionel to safety through a hail of arrows and javelins, until her hand finally clamped on its peak.

Ranger-Wardens perched atop it pulled Lionel over the palisade and then slid down the other side, their fingers submerging in its surface for purchase. Brimares lurched as she hauled herself over the wall, her back arching from some external force as her grip broke, then tumbled forward.

Brimares crashed to the inner courtyard on her hands and knees, two black shafts protruding from her back, one between her shoulders and one at the base of her spine. She pushed herself up, armor clamping on the shafts and yanking to remove them with no effect. "Will someone please pull these arrows out?"

The nearest Ranger-Warden hesitated, then grabbed the upper arrow in her right hand, ice spreading from the touch. Bracing against the wall with a foot, she yanked the arrow free, causing it to shatter and Brimares to lurch but otherwise issue no sound. She repeated the procedure with the other arrow.

Brimares reclined against the ramparts and searched for Lionel. "You alright?"

"I didn't just have two arrows pulled from my back. I think I should be asking you that and saying thanks for saving my life … again."

"Arrows are nothing; most of the pain came from the enchantments on them. That's how they got through the armor. My guess is one of their clerics cast a prayer on them to target me."

Outside the wall, horns sounded the retreat over the incessant thrum of bowstrings from the Ranger-Warden's perched atop it. "Seems like we're to have a moment's respite."

She stood. "Stay where you are until you have recovered, Lionel. The wall won't survive the next assault."

He snorted. "This is a Northern wall, it will self-repair any damage they dealt to it. This wall is not falling anytime soon."

"Lionel, they have paladins and clerics of *Telacra* and over a dozen demons; this wall is going to fail."

60

The Rise Of Valeriius Kalvonder

Valeriius waited for a long-anticipated guest beneath the eaves of a gray archway. The stone stooped from age, its foundation riddled with fissures and split with resilient gold ivy. The passage behind him climbed at a sharp gradient, the dust at the entrance strangely absent from the passage's smooth floor and walls. The passage led to the maze-like catacombs beneath his mansion and provided him a secret conduit from Sahdaen. Even if someone found this entrance, they would never survive the catacombs.

His various absences from the gala had gone unnoticed, even when they exceeded an hour. A simulacrum, an echo of his soul given form and colored by deceptions of magic, occupied his place. It spoke the required pleasantries and greeted his guests with the appropriate gifts or veiled insults, but never touched them because it was incapable of physical contact. Every now and then he would peer from its eyes to ensure all proceeded accordingly but had yet to discover an event that warranted intervention.

Satisfied all proceeded as projected, Valeriius withdrew his awareness from the simulacrum and inhaled the oppressive malice besieging Sahdaen. Poisonous energy swamped him, scouring his throat and lungs. He caught the pollution in his mouth, rolling it over his tongue and tasting its intricacies before expelling it.

He inhaled again, refreshing the taste. Although diluted, the storm's essence still lurked in that breath, foul with the Dread Lord's touch and purpose. The Dread Storm was a curse, a plague of misfortune upon all who bided within its shade, for misfortune bred malice, and malice fed the Dread Lords.

The rain poured in black sheets, pummeling the ground before parting at the entrance. In spite of this, his defenses failed; black veins infested the entrance walls, cracking and corrupting the brittle stone, and the air hung thick with moisture. The passage would collapse soon.

A grunt of anger pulled at his lips, and Valeriius lifted the rowan cane and struck the floor. The shrieking winds died and the rain faltered; a vast pressure lifted from the stone to descend on his shoulders instead. The veins of corruption receded, leaving mutilated stone in their wake.

A lone rider materialized from the anomalous night, galloping toward Valeriius. Not the guest he expected but a herald. The sell-sword's charger pitched forward grotesquely and threw its rider. The man hit the ground, rolled, and sprinted toward Valeriius, who stepped aside as he entered.

The sell-sword flung his helmet to the floor with a profanity and a spray of putrid water, the article black with rot. "That's the third horse I've had die on me! The third in as far as this bloody tempest reaches! The wretched horse should have lasted another hour at least! Your land is cursed, Kalvonder."

"Yes. It is wilder than the East or West, untamed by the hands of men. Does he approach?"

"Yes, our scouts saw your man, everyone saw him; he's only minutes behind."

"Describe him."

The sell-sword snarled. "A year ago, you approached us, promising wealth and violence. The first you've supplied, but the second's still absent. Where's the war?"

"Are the rewards insufficient? Is your payment late? Are you bullied, assaulted or given spoiled food? Are the whores I send thieves, hideous, or murderers? What more can you desire of me? Your existence is one of leisure with nothing asked of you in return. Yet you complain. How have I wronged you?"

"We're bored, and whatever's happening here is starting to kill us. Two days ago, my lieutenant randomly butchered two of your whores and then drowned himself in the blood. Yesterday, my brother started raving and carving signs in his chest! By morning he was dead and the first sigil rotted black! I have a dozen other incidents from just this last Turning, and they're not witchcraft. At least, not the sort witnessed since we entombed the Mad Kings. This is something else. So give us protection and start whatever it is you're planning, or we leave tonight."

Valeriius did not reply, his concentration arrested by something far more significant than dying sell-swords. His guest, Avanhier—the Kalvonders' Blood-Soul—neared, blazing through the storm on enormous gouts of amethyst flame, launching himself in soaring bounds, visible even from miles.

"Bring your brothers and kin," Valeriius addressed the sell-sword, "it's almost time, but not quite yet. Until then, these bulwarks will protect you." The sell-sword wordlessly obeyed.

Avanhier arrived minutes later, crashing to the fragmented earth and rupturing it further, flames gushing from the point of impact. He stomped forward, garbed in sickly yellow robes stained with blood and filth, his body rippling with distended muscles beneath stitched skin—a mismatched creation of Kalvonders from centuries before, born of soulcraft and sustained on the essence of mages.

A scarlet, many-faceted eye fixed on Valeriius while the other, human, orb rolled ceaselessly in its socket with a black iris and violet pupil.

"Hello, Avanhier."

"Hello, fool." Avanhier stepped into the tunnel, black rain sloshing off his figure and spreading from his steps. He was tall, engulfing Valeriius in his shadow even when stooped, and still his robes sprawled across the floor, dragging behind him and scraping with sand. He leaned close, sniffing. "You smell ... strange." Hunger woke in the scarlet eye and the black eye stilled.

"Do you believe I summoned you here to feed, Avanhier? I have a purpose for you."

"They all do at the beginning and I always end up feeding."

"You're not the worst horror I've confronted."

"Yes, I smell him, and he senses me, but I am not him." His gaze, briefly directed heavenwards, refocused on Valeriius. "I do not think you have the pieces of Command or Keeping, Kalvonder." Avanhier glided closer, his hand reaching for Valeriius.

Unperturbed, Valeriius pressed the butt of his cane against the Blood-Soul's chest. "Fortunately, I do possess the full piece." He reached into his robes and retrieved a circular talisman, designed as five interconnected iron circles clutching a glowing ruby.

In the hour of Avanhier's creation, the Kalvonders had crafted an amulet to curtail and control their monstrosity, fashioning it of sanctified metal so he could never touch it. Then they divided it into three fragments to ensure equality amongst themselves, one to command, one to summon, and one to protect the user. The era's wealthiest Kalvonders claimed these shards as sigils of supremacy and thus initiating the Triad. The amulets, however, proved more curse than boon, for all Kalvonders desired them and preyed upon their possessors. The original triumvirate died within a decade and their prizes slipped into obscurity. A fragment resurfaced every so often, immediately instigating months of rigorous bloodshed and inevitably concluding with the possessing Kalvonder's death and the fragment's disappearance.

Avanhier halted, but scarred lips retracted from inch-long incisors and his hand remained outstretched, boasting ill-fitting claws and talons alike. "I think"—his black eye resumed it frantic revolutions—"I should test it anyway." His maw ripped open inhumanly wide and he struck forward, one hand batting aside Valeriius' cane while the other sought his throat. The striking hand imploded, the bone shattering and rupturing through flesh that peeled and blistered, spraying acidic blood and noxious vapors up to his shoulder. Yelping, Avanhier recoiled with a whimper and clutched his mauled appendage.

"Are you satisfied?"

"Yes." The sniveling Blood-Soul sank to a knee and rested his flaccid arm atop the other leg. He began prying the protruding bones free, causing more noxious blood to gush, then retrieving dark string from his robes, began sewing the lacerations closed. "You know? I'm actually somewhat excited. This is the first time I'll get to do something else. All the others forgot a piece, or had fake pieces, and I got to eat them. But you, I am yours to command."

"First, keep this talisman and your allegiance a secret."

"Of course." Avanhier rose, his black eye resuming its frantic revolutions, and all vestige of its distress eradicated. "I am yours until dawn, Kalvonder, then I return to the Border War for my next summons, probably from someone else. I wonder what they'll taste like." His lips parted again, grinning.

"Inconvenient but acceptable. I assume the protection against you will persist so long as I possess the amulet?"

"Yes, but only against direct assault. I maybe could bring this tunnel down by accident, then eat you." He reached up to the ceiling, scraping it with his claws and talons. "It could collapse at any minute; we should find someplace sturdier."

"It will hold. I've heard baleful rumors from the front lines, are they true?"

"If you mean the rumors concerning our defenses failing, then they're true." Avanhier's attention remained fixed upon the ceiling as he scratched pictograms on its surface. "I can't hold Cardolyn Tyier any longer than a decade. He'll kill me and conquer all of you within a century, founding the largest empire since Arthramain Royal. Then he'll take the East and rule everything outside of The North. And, in time, even that may change. You're all doomed. Shame I have to die first."

Valeriius smiled. "That is ideal."

Valeriius felt a rare spark of impatience in his stride; a culmination engineered by decades of preparation neared, an evolution of necessity for all its violence and horror. He schooled his limbs into a controlled saunter, reprimanding himself for his impatience. Even now, he could not afford to err.

Footsteps echoed from the corner ahead, preceding his simulacra and a quintet of guards. It resembled him perfectly in every physical aspect one could assess because it had been fabricated of him, of his blood, his hair, and his skin. Upon seeing Valeriius, the simulacra froze and stiffened, the warmth fading from its visage to assume a doll-like appearance. Valeriius gestured for his guards to return the simulacra to its cupboard and resumed his trek.

The animate had spent the previous hour espousing Valeriius' abhorrence of the New Order, ensuring all of Sahdaen would recognize he detested the potential union. This was a lie. Valeriius intended to coerce his rivals into the alliance even as he strove against it.

He reentered the gala without grandeur, discarding spectacle for a far defter appearance. He disdained a veil to conceal his arrival for the remaining Kalvonders were potent individuals and, in their reduced number, wary of the slightest inconsistency or disturbance.

Those who remained, numbering two and a score, were the elite of Sahdaen's self-crowned oligarchy. Many had disencumbered themselves of their outer clothing, revealing the plainer and more practical garments they wore underneath. The potentates dressed more for the benefit of lesser Kalvonders and the oppressed Avarans than from whim. Only Ureign remained unchanged, dressed in gaudy colors and ornate feathers from some rare avian.

Xexeross noticed Valeriius first and silenced his companions with a gesture, ending their discourse and transferring their attention to Valeriius.

Valeriius positioned himself at the gala's axis, assembling a smirk, and began, "It has been my unadulterated joy to confer upon you, my friends, my gratitude and what meager luxuries I can. You have made me exponentially wealthier, and for that, I can only dare an obeisance alongside sublime gratitude. Still, all things must end. Our wanton revelries have reached their conclusion and we must again turn our attention back to the New Order. We have all made our decisions concerning their proposed alliance, so I call for the final vote." Every sound in the chamber died.

As host, Valeriius wielded unmitigated political authority, including—but not limited to—the license to initiate a vote. For any other in the room to initiate a vote would require a monumental amount of support and resources. Even then an opposing faction could suppress their attempts if they amassed a comparable influence. However, after five thousand years of political maneuvering, the original laws and amendments had multiplied exponentially. It was not a question if one knew the law, but how much one knew.

Valeriius left them their calculations, enjoying each spark of revelation that struck his rivals. For a decade, he had labored to achieve variations to the law through annulments and resurrections of new and old laws, one of these being numerous host privileges. No matter how they struggled, the Kalvonders could not deter him. The impossibility did not dissuade them, however.

Xexeross spoke first, chuckling boisterously, "I am disinclined to conclude these festivities, Valeriius; I have found tremendous pleasure in them. I know you want to conserve the power the New Order's arrival has afforded you, but this is a little far. You have to let go, my friend, let things take their own course. I will not sanction this."

Valeriius smiled. "Three years back we passed a motion returning power to hosts: greater majority to abstinence. Among, but not restricted to, these powers was the privilege to judge and execute crimes, and the license to initiate a ballot even if said ballot concerns the governance of Sahdaen. You cannot deter this."

"We repressed that idiocy a month later. Or do you not recall: extreme majority versus minority?"

"I recall very well. We eliminated useless privileges or those defunct. I recall and can verify the cited concessions that remained. If it pleases you, I can designate the detached rights? Among them I believe was the privilege of tribute this night employed. It was reinstated roughly seventeen Turnings ago from this day when the illustrious, but deceased, Barrun Kalvonder's wealth was devastated by every Kalvonder attending his gala with their entire household."

Xexeross fell silent, his ebullience faltering to a flicker of venom swiftly suppressed, but in his silence Ureign rose and commanded every eye to him like flies to a lamp. One would not notice it, for Ureign rarely stood, but the Kalvonder towered over every man present. "I evoke the amendment of denial and call for a judgement concerning the wisdom of such deliberations at this time." A murmur followed Ureign's words, amplifying the two and score hands being raised.

Valeriius shook his head. "The amendment requires all who are affected by the outcome be present. We are missing several hundred members."

"The Fifteenth Article in the Second Declaration, Concerning the Modifications to Current Restrictions and Privileges, declares a denial can be enforced by the lords of Sahdaen if the raised matter is construed to be fabricated. We are two and twenty, the lords."

"No, you are not. You are two and twenty, but it requires all the lords of Sahdaen to be present. One is absent, unless some merciless accident has befallen Trerrock Kalvonder?"

"Due to his departure, Trerrock Kalvonder cannot be present, but as the chief among us, it is my right to declare a substitute. That substitute brings us to a full score, Valeriius."

Valeriius grinned, taking pleasure in how far they delved the annals of Sahdaen's laws. The privilege of substitution, a privilege reserved for members of the Triad, had been invoked only twice before; first three thousand years ago and then four hundred years after.

"It is your prerogative to demand a substitute in hours of travail, but the host designates who. The limitations are, the selected cannot be a Kalvonder, one of the Clergy, or the progeny of either." Valeriius gestured toward one of the many slaves bearing wine. The woman blinked, cowering beneath the attention coalescing upon her. Furious, but soft, growls escaped the Kalvonders as they recognized their defeat.

Ureign resumed his seat, burning madness and reasonless hate raging in his eyes. A perilous air collected about his shoulders, revealing the writhing alien shadow encased in his bulk.

No man knew the tracts of Ureign's insanity, only that he was and some of its effects. They varied from eating the hearts of the opponents he vanquished, to shrieking laughter when he bathed in blood. Transcending his madness, however, was the man's genius. Despite his psychosis, Ureign Kalvonder's intellect was consummate. Valeriius did not know the extent of Ureign's intelligence, whether it equaled, surpassed, or fell short of his own.

"Let us begin, Valeriius."

The Kalvonders stepped forward, forming an expansive oval, crowned at the peak by Ureign and at the base by the Immortal Consort, the twenty-third member of the assembly. Valeriius, as the initiator, entered the circle, counting the passing seconds and readying himself. He needed to be perfect. He could not construct ill-formed prevaricating features as he had done before; his emotions and their demonstration must be flawless, lest others see his farce. When he reached the center, Valeriius lifted his brow towards the ceiling.

Valeriius opened his mouth to speak, but the gala's doors—which were shut after his return—burst open. The Kalvonders turned as one, breaking the circle to stare at the intruder. A pulsing throb of energy swept across the chamber to meet them, causing the air to waver and grow cold. The Blood-Soul loomed in the doorway, towering and monstrous. Valeriius smiled inwardly *perfect* and slowly twisted his cane, decreasing the temperature and the light further.

Avanhier advanced while grinning, his right leg swinging wide beneath his robes as if it were a stump or immobile to propel him forward with a thud and scrape.

Xexeross strolled from the congregation, his voice booming cheerily, "What are you doing here, you foul creature? You're supposed to be on the border? Did you get lost?"

Avanhier shriveled beneath the Kalvonder's denunciation, but his grin resurfaced almost as quickly and he swept forward and around Xexeross. "No... No, I was summoned." He flung his arms high with such force his putrid robes billowed, then lowered his hands to stroke the air over Xexeross' shoulders, his black eye stilling. "Because you are all fools playing at your ancestors' games, comprehending little and controlling less. You can't command me here, you don't have the talisman, nothing to protect you either." He leaned closer, biting his lower lip until it bled bile. "But first a message, tidings from the West: Cardolyn Tyier presses and vast ships marshal upon the far coast, transporting legions to swell his war efforts. Soon the Imperial Emperor will have marshalled his host, then I and all my hordes will die and you will lose."

Xexeross whirled, striking the creature's arms aside with one hand and driving a steel knife into the Blood-Soul's flank with the other. "You shouldn't touch your betters, creature."

Avanhier squealed and retreated, but unlike when he assaulted Valeriius or dealt injury to himself, no blood poured from his side and the doughy flesh pressed back together like soft clay. None remarked upon this, however, silence had assumed dominion over the room.

The Avaran Army, amassed by the Kalvonders a century ago, was not the equivalent of Cardolyn's. The original Kalvonders had known this; the Avarus Desert, however, was vast and the Avaran race innumerable. The Kalvonders had kept the Imperial Emperor at bay through sheer weight of numbers. One day every year for a century, each of the Avaran Holds sent five to ten thousand warriors to supply the Blood-Soul's defense. This was an insignificant burden; children and men abounded in the Holds. There was never sufficient work for the hands, never enough food to feed the mouths, and so the Blood-Soul never ran short on warriors to engage the Imperial Emperor's lines.

Avanhier's whimpers faded and he surged close to Xexeross again, the spread fingers of both hands prodding the Kalvonder's chest, only this time his claws snagged on the rich apparel and held. "If you want to survive, I need more men." No Kalvonder responded. Most recalculated their machinations and the cascading changes to the power balance; the rest measured the exponential growth in Avanhier's strength such a concession would cause. He already feasted on hundreds yearly, growing stronger on every banquet and further straining the spells that enslaved him to them. The price in lives the Kalvonders could pay; the cost in power they would not dare.

"How many lives would you require, Avanhier?" Ureign asked, and the Kalvonder's parted before his seat.

"I need fifteen-thousand from every Hold, twenty from the largest, mages also, at least a thousand every year. Beyond those immediate necessities, I want capital sufficient to contract thirty thousand sell-swords from the East, which I will use to reclaim the Inland Sea. With the Inland Sea in our control, all your fat purses will benefit."

"And we're supposed to believe these lies?" Valeriius claimed the stage, painting violence in his gait and voice. He circled and halted a dozen strides from Avanhier like a man striving to master his fury. Responding to his bellowed words, the Kalvonders' guards swarmed in from an adjacent room, weapons and shields readied, over a hundred in all. Valeriius sneered at the Avaran guards, gesturing to allay their unease and aggression. "For a hundred years, you have fortified the beaches against every incursion! We have given the blood price for this service without fail; we have paid to the utmost extent of mortal tolerance. Now, ahead of all word but for your own, you demand more of us! Have we not provided you enough? Will you bleed this land dry? Will you take the life of all who live to satiate your hunger? For over a hundred years, two mortal lifetimes, you have held that defense. I think it is time you stop holding ground and start taking it. It is time for us to receive something in return for your inflated extortions."

Murmurs of agreement rose from the Kalvonders, prompting some to advance as well, lending their support.

Others, however, condemned Ureign and his followers, demanding they heed caution and supply the warriors. At the forefront of these, a laughing Xexeross opposed Ureign. "You are a senile old fool. You fail to see this creature speaks the truth. We know Cardolyn Tyier has a host larger than any he has yet sent against us. He has finally decided to end this war."

Valeriius knew Xexeross was intelligent in his own way, but this maneuver was more spite for Ureign than actual belief in the Blood-Soul. Xexeross feared Ureign and would blindly oppose everything he endeavored.

The de facto master of Sahdaen thrust the full might of his contempt on Xexeross with a glare and lumbered past. Ureign spat a command at the Blood-Soul and the creature recoiled anew. Foam spewing from his mouth, Ureign withdrew a talisman from his clothing that mirrored Valeriius' own and hurled it to the floor at Avanhier's feet, believing it the authentic fragment intended to control the Blood-Soul.

Avanhier flinched, his hands shielding his face as the talisman flared a blinding white. A crack split the air, severing the cries of those blinded. The illumination flickered once and perished as Avanhier ground the talisman to dust and grinned.

Ureign stared at the lie of his talisman then stabbed his hand at the creature. "Kill it!" His warriors lunged forward, hurling their spears.

Javelins drove into the Blood-Soul, but he dove forward, cackling, and crashed among them. Avanhier whirled and flailed, biting the head off one Avaran and eviscerating another, his head and hands moving disjointedly from one another, bending at sickening angles and toward opposite directions. Screams of horror and agony rang at his assault, then warped as amethyst flames erupted from his person, incinerating the soldiers and suffocating their wails. He came to a stop, crouched amidst the carnage, chewing on a hunk of flesh, panting contently and dripping gore. He swallowed. "You're next, it's only what you deserve really, sending me to die and hurt for you."

The other Kalvonders of Sahdaen scrambled to distance themselves from Ureign, calling for their own guards to raise no weapon against Avanhier. Valeriius pretended to aid Ureign, but his aid proved of little consequence. He stepped forward, reaching for an amulet imbued with flames. The Blood-Soul noted his advance and flicked his hand, discharging an unseen force to hurl him across the chamber.

Ureign screeched, the sound half laughter and half vindictive cry. All eyes swarmed to him and where he stood unguarded for the first time in decades. The obese Kalvonder threw his weight forward, his screech convoluting into a keen.

Bent almost double, Avanhier charged Ureign, casting his clawed hands forward and hurling flames. The torrent enveloped Ureign, but he only laughed harder as the inferno caught on his flesh and erupted into true fire. The Blood-Soul lowered his hands, letting the flame soaring from his fingers attenuate until they extinguished. Ureign's screams dwindled, leaving only ashes and brittle bone.

Feigning weakness, Valeriius stood. He swayed, placing a hand on the wall and the other on his cane. The Avarans and Kalvonders tentatively reassembled near the straightening Avanhier, their eyes and postures ripe with fear, utterly cowed. Valeriius had needed more than Ureign Kalvonder's death to force the more obstinate Kalvonders into aligning with the New Order. The demise of a single Kalvonder, however prominent, would only have increased their resistance. They would have dithered over inconsequential quarrels until the shock dissipated and then killed the alliance under a counterfeit principle.

Avanhier's warnings, however, added an immediate threat they needed to resolve and they were too scared of Avanhier to rebuff his demands; demands Valeriius had made purposefully onerous even for the wealthiest Kalvonders. The increased burden on their finances, particularly for poorer Kalvonders, combined with the fear engendered by Avanhier's predictions and Ureign's death would drive the Kalvonders to accept the New Order's alliance. They could spare the cost in lives, but not the funds for the equipment, food, transport, and all the myriad expenditures an army demanded. The New Order would alleviate that financial burden and the ensuing drain to the Kalvonder's authority.

"I anticipate this incident has not distorted your opinions, but I believe an interval to recuperate ourselves is necessary." The Kalvonders murmured among themselves, acknowledging that a reprieve was prudent. They moved to partake of the cool wines and sorbets while Avanhier prowled their company.

Valeriius retired from the primary gala hall and beckoned to one of his slaves. The youth hurried forward and knelt. "Bring Ureign's heir from the cells, it is time he assumes his father's place. Then contact the Immortal Consort. Tell her, I acknowledge a crime was committed against her by one of my assets. I would redress this grievance now as we stand on the brink of chaos. In the approaching years, I and those akin to us who would deny the New Order their foothold will need allies. These allies are few. Thus I propose a last duel between champions. Dieharamon will combat a champion of the Immortal Consort, with her consent, unto death. If he is defeated, she will receive restitution for my lapse. If he is victorious, I will return to her the foreigner known as Dayada Avenar to do with what she wills, and in return, I will be granted influence in the selection of the next Immortal Consort."

61

Truths Revealed

Silence reigned following Mr. Grey's accusation, its authority uncontested by entreaties, declarations of innocence, or bursts of anger. It clotted the air with its growing expectation, pressing in to try and squeeze a response from Tasha, but every second it reigned was an opportunity to marshal some defense or deception. And so she stared into Mr. Grey's relentless accusation, refusing to concede, praying the silence would continue for she had nothing.

"My Lady Sivarra—"

"Don't call me that."

Mr. Grey gave a curt nod. "Miss Bloomhale, time likes to smudge certain memories while outlining others in bold ink. Thanks to the diligence of those assigned to Duke Sivarra's murder, the evidence collected against you has been impeccably preserved. It remains quite damning."

"I'm already bound for the Empire's northern-most cell, so you'll have to forgive me if I don't muster up any waterworks."

"I'm not looking for theatrics, Miss Bloomhale."

"Oh? Then why did you bother dredging up my murderous history? Someone's already supplied the bludgeon you need to coerce me."

"That bludgeon, as you've so accurately described it, has a slippery handle. I've read the reports, and if you're as clever as I suspect, you're already spinning the harrowing story of your false imprisonment. If evidence continues disappearing or they assign a gullible judge, you could wriggle free."

"You needn't have worried; Amonn Warsein's made it clear that my innocence or guilt is completely irrelevant."

Mr. Grey stilled mid-page flip. "Amonn Warsein was here?"

"Oh yes, he made my heart all a flutter when he marched under that portcullis to attend my interrogation with Lieutenant Kayja." Tasha patted her chest a few times before recognizing it as one of Slade's mannerisms and grimacing.

Ignoring this display, Mr. Grey flipped to the first page with a frown. "Amonn Warsein expressed these sentiments while in the presence of Lieutenant Kayja?"

"No, he arranged for a private conversation."

In a spiral of reflected images, Mr. Grey slid from his chair, glided around the table and hooked a finger on her collar, tugging down to reveal the skin of her neck and collar bone.

"Hey, keep your hand to yourself." Tasha snapped, batting him away only for Mr. Grey to catch her wrist and shake gently, causing her sleeve to bunch around her elbow. "I said don't touch me." She yanked her arm free.

"Forgive my presumption, but Amonn Warsein rarely has as much concern for his strength as he should." Mr. Grey circled to her other side. "I am merely checking to—"

Tasha gave his chest a one-handed shove. "Spare me your concern, I'm fine."

"As you wish." Mr. Grey retreated and flipped to a blank page within his folder, then—somewhat awkwardly on account of his sling—withdrew an ink well and quill pen. "Answer with a simple yes or no. Does Amonn Warsein suspect you're innocent?"

"Yes."

Mr. Grey's eyes flicked to the truth stone, checking for any flare of red. "Is he intentionally withholding this information in order to pressure you?"

"Yes."

"I see." He wrote several small, square notes in his folder. "I'll bring this to the governor's attention when he returns."

Tasha lounged back, picking a piece of flint from her sleeve and flicking it away. "You do that, I'll go find some shmuck who believes it'll come to anything."

"If possible, I'd like to conclude our business here first. Shall we proceed?"

"By all means, lets proceed from one coercion straight into the next."

"This is no coercion with trumped up charges; it is a rope thrown to a drowning woman, an offer to exchange decades in prison for information and comfortable service."

"Well that's a noble spin on the situation, almost makes it sparkle enough to ignore the squalid—if I don't—part. Go on, toss your rope. Let's hear the governor's offer."

"In due time, Miss Bloomhale. There are some questions I still need to ask. Were you the one responsible for raiding Tellor's treasury?"

"No."

"Were you involved with the planning or execution thereof?"

"No; and while we're verifying what crimes I did and did not commit, I had nothing to do with the desecration of Echeira'Sollas."

"Mhm," Mr. Grey said without looking up from his notes to gauge the truth stone's response. "In what capacity do you serve Carr'Selain?"

Tasha's eyes narrowed. "Why?"

"I must confirm that you possess the information Governor Warsein wants."

"Ahh, I see. And if I don't, the governor will imprison me for the rest of my life, yes?"

"Your lack of illusions is commendable, Miss Bloomhale."

"A life spent navigating Imperial politics will strip away the most tenacious illusions."

"I suppose it would. Now, in what capacity do you serve Carr'Selain?"

Tasha crossed her arms, meeting Mr. Grey's stare for several minutes before finally sighing. "As a Rat."

"Hmm, the governor was hoping for a Mouse. How important is your position?"

Again they locked eyes, the apparent confrontation giving Tasha a moment to pick her words. "Not so important as to inconvenience the guild through my death."

"I see. How expansive is your guild's roster of members?"

Tasha laughed. "I have no idea. There are thousands, perhaps hundreds of thousands of people in the Thieves' Guild. We are everywhere and we are there all the time."

"And how many could you provide an accurate description of?"

"To a useful degree? Hardly any." The crystal flashed red and Tasha swore. She'd forgotten about it. "What I mean is that most have a talent for disguising themselves."

Mr. Grey's mouth thinned and he leaned forward. "Miss Bloomhale, shall we review how many times you've successfully deceived me?"

"I'm not trying to deceive you, that's what I honestly—" The crystal flashed red, causing Mr. Grey to quirk an eyebrow. "Fine, let's pretend we did and that I, when faced by your scathing rebuke, promised to mind my manners."

"Whether you mind your manners or not is immaterial. What you need to realize is that truth is like oil and water—"

Tasha snorted. "It doesn't mix with lies?"

"On the contrary, my Dear, a lie interwoven with truth endures far better than any fabrication. What you need to realize is that a truth will always rise to the surface. You cannot deceive me, Miss Bloomhale. Please stop trying."

At the endearment, Tasha's eyes narrowed and Mr. Grey, noting her interest, gave his mustache a villainous twirl.

Deep within her mind—beyond the first corridors of logical thought, past the lockbox with her irrational paranoia, and through the wall imprisoning all her twisted imaginings—a part insane, part furious, part hopeful disbelief formed. Tasha leaned forward, mentally stripping away the mustache, dying the hair black, and flipping up the eyepatch.

Slade, *Jaidar* blessed, Lammerock.

A variety of emotions swelled within Tasha, most demanding she vault the table and strangle the deranged creature opposite her. *'How dare you embroil me in your machinations? How dare you lock me in a cell? How dare you pull hidden strings, play an invisible pipe and make me dance with cursed slippers? Why? Why? WHY! Must I be your puppet?'* For the first time in six years, Tasha felt her true, very dangerous anger stir.

"Mr. Grey, I think it's time that you reveal what exactly the governor wants from me."

"Yes, I think it is. Unlike the majority in Cardolyn Tyier's court who view the Thieves' Guild as a way to humiliate and defeat their enemies, Governor Warsein finds it morally reprehensible if not outright harmful to the Empire."

"Is that so?" She leaned forward, staring at Tellor's thief lord fixedly. "Well, he might want to reconsider that notion. If Governor Warsein partook of their services, he might realize all the snakes lurking in his employ."

"You needn't fear on the governor's behalf; I personally vet and purge any undesirable elements. His fellow lords and state officials though, are another matter and he cannot ensure they adhere to the conduct expected of their station. Governor Warsein is prepared to exchange your freedom for aide in curtailing the guild's access."

Tasha barked a laugh. "The governor would let a murderer walk free so that he could fight his righteous war?" She shook her head. "Seems more like a thinly veiled power play, not that it matters. What he wants is impossible."

"Miss Bloomhale, what the governor requires is simplicity itself: names and accompanying descriptions."

Except this whole affair was anything but simple, neither its convoluted beginning nor the inquisition bearing down upon her, and ethics— omnipresent meddlers without shame—delighted in muddying the water. "I told you it's impossible. I can arrange for information on anything else the governor or you want, but I cannot, I will not, sell information about the guild itself."

Slade leaned forward, bracing his arms atop the table and spearing Tasha to her chair with a single eye. "Allow me to illustrate a fictional situation. You're swinging from a noose and gasping for breath when the rope slips from your wrists. Instantly you grab for the noose but scrabbling at the knot does nothing. Worse yet, each renewed effort steals more oxygen. Running out of time, you resort to pulling yourself up with the very rope that's killing you. Soon enough blood leaks from between your fingers, staining the cord as you tighten your grip and try to forestall the inevitable slide downward. Even so your grip slips, leaving behind a bloody trail. The noose constricts. Mere inches remain. As your vision fades, an indistinct figure approaches with the handle of a knife raised to you. What do you do?"

'Screw this. I'm done playing his game.' Tasha leaned forward, bracing her elbows on the table. "Very well. If the governor want's information on the Thieves' Guild, how about this? Amonn Warsein is an avid customer of ours."

"The governor is well aware of his son's activities; furthermore, I'm not entirely sure I see the relevance."

"The relevance is that Amonn has also expressed an interest in my services. Imagine how tempting a prospect I'll make after he learns I'm a member of the Thieves' Guild. Up to now all he wanted was for me to verify one of his theories about who desecrated Echeira'Sollas—apparently he suspects that I'm personally acquainted with the man responsible—but I'll be able to offer so much more now."

"These theories, I suppose he wanted them verified regardless of their accuracy?"

"Yes."

"And you would prefer this over an honest transaction with Governor Warsein?"

"At least Amonn's not asking me to sell information about the guild. If I did that, Carr'Selain would excommunicate me within days and my creditors would come sniffing, most likely accompanied by a harmless, inoffensive man tasked with solving the problem permanently."

Slade tilted his chair back, head swiveling idly as he watched the reflections scatter across the room. "Ignorance, Miss Bloomhale, is bliss. Unfortunately, you can enjoy neither ignorance nor bliss."

"What?"

Slade's chair tipped forward, its legs clattering upon the floor. "Your creditors already hunt you. Six years will exhaust the most tolerant man's patience, and you borrowed from the Black Lenders who, even among their own guild, are considered blackguards. Do you really think Amonn Warsein would be willing to speak on your behalf, especially after you've already given him what he wanted?"

Tasha swallowed, feeling dizzy all of sudden. "They can't be coming already. It's not time yet."

"Perhaps, but assuming that you're here on special assignment from Carr'Selain, you likely disappeared several months ago."

"It doesn't matter. I'm a member of the Thieves' Guild, to attack me is to assault the guild itself."

"True enough for minor lords or petty criminals, but you made a bargain with Yin'sarr and the Merchants' Guild. You borrowed money from someone with the power of an entire country behind them, more importantly the power to ruin entire countries. There are new rules, new consequences. Carr'Selain will not intervene. Even if he did, Yin'sarr need only inform the authorities that she found an escaped murderess and produce the documents proving it." Slade shook his head. "I can't say I approve of how you managed this whole affair. It seems very—"

"You think I don't know that?" Tasha slammed her fists on the table. "I had maybe twelve hours before they found my so-called husband, twelve miserable hours to decide if I should hide or flee. I chose to buy time and a future disaster. Was it a terrible choice? Yes. But no more so than grabbing a horse and charging past the gate guards."

Slade held up a hand, meeting and holding her gaze. "The correct alternative was turning yourself in, but that obviously never crossed your mind. As things stand, either you produce the money or the Merchants' Guild recoups their losses however they can. Carr'Selain may purchase your debts, but he's not known for gambling. You need a new benefactor."

His last sentence stole Tasha's thoughts, replacing them with a gradually unfurling understanding and the sensation of the floor dropping away beneath her.

Truth: Slade needed to protect the city during his forthcoming absence. Truth: he knew about Tasha's past and he could use it as leverage. Truth: he chose her specifically as the guild's delegate; he intended to use her knowledge to catch any Rat or Mouse Carr'Selain sent sniffing around Tellor.

Tasha slumped forward, gripping the back of her neck. "I can't give the governor what he wants." In the end, it was simple. Either she fled Yin'sarr's collectors or she found temporary shelter and made a new enemy in Carr'Selain. An enemy she could not buy off.

Tap … Tap … Tap.

Looking up slightly, she found Slade tapping a finger pensively.

Tap … Tap … Tap. Then all his fingers drummed down in quick succession and he leaned in, his breath tickling her ear. "Walls are such nosy creatures, my Dear. They hear everything and even enable the spying of others. An entire squad of guards lurks behind them, straining at the cracks to hear every word and see every subtlety, writing in their ledgers so nothing will be forgotten or misrepresented. You have an audience, smile for the crowd." Straightening, he gestured in a sweeping arch, directing her attention to the mirrors and down their endless corridors with her countless reflections.

When she saw it—the lie—her world came to a grinding halt. Mouth agape she watched her mirror-self move without direction; she watched herself smile with smirking self-satisfaction; she watched herself raise a rebellious hand; she watched herself wave that hand; she watched as one by one her errant selves blew a raspberry. Then, all across the room, Tasha watched herself hesitate and nod her assent.

She rose with a shout, but Slade—unseen by the mirrors—materialized behind her and pricked Tasha's neck with a needle, causing a buzzing sensation to spread up her throat to her tongue. All the while he somehow remained seated across from her, even offered a pleased smile. "I'm glad you've seen fit to accept the governor's offer."

She tried shouting for help, tried yelling her refusal only to realize she couldn't control her tongue. Finally, she tried making any sound at all.

'What did he do to me? What the hell did he do to me?' She grabbed for her throat, feeling for enchantments or blood or swelling. At the same time, she glanced around desperately. Surely the guards had seen, surly they were coming. But in the mirrors, her and Slade's reflections remained seated. *'What is going on here?'*

As she stared at the disobedient reflections, insight struck for the second time. Truth: Slade new more about the Thieves' Guild than she did. Truth: he planned to use Tellor's forces as his proxy. Truth: the governor would never believe him if Slade, an eccentric, produced the list of names himself.

Tasha broke for the wall, intent on shattering the lying mirrors but Slade wrapped his free arm around her shoulders and dragged her back into his chest. "Relax, my Dear, nobody will suffer for this transaction, least of all you."

Ignoring the whispered words, she punched his ribs with an elbow and grabbed his arm, shrugging free. Immediately she spun in place, applying a vicious wrist lock before rearing back with a fist.

"Have you ever inspected the inside of a clock?" Slade gasped, his upper body contorting to alleviate some of the pressure. "No? Well, imagine a hundred gears locked in perpetual motion, forever pushing at their adjacent companions."

Tasha frowned at him, barely restraining the blow. *'What is he going on about? Why isn't he breaking free?'*

"Because of this, clocks are delicate machines; if one part falls out, the whole contraption stops working. My plan is a clock, and you are a piece therein, a large piece but no less important than any other. Should you or any one of a dozen parts 'break', the clock will stop working. Can you envision how many lives I need to safeguard? Now imagine if one of those lives fought against me as a sinner does salvation."

She swept an arm around the room then slapped her chest roughly. *'All this for me?'*

"Not at all, this was very much for my benefit. However, that does not change the fact that I need to protect you, never mind that you're fighting against my attempt to do so. I'm not simply referring to this business with Echeira'Sollas, you're also keeping me from cutting those leaden shackles you've worn for the past six years. Short of vandalizing every record vault across the Empire, an official pardon is the best way I know to loosen that spiked knot of your past. So please stop fighting me."

Slowly, Tasha released the pressure on his wrist, letting him straighten and begin rolling it around. Then before that annoying triumphant grin of his could appear, she slugged him across the jaw and stomped around the table, stealing his chair.

Slade, wincing and rubbing at the red blotch spreading across his face, sat across from her, completely inverting what the mirrors displayed. "Provided you're amendable, the last step is you accompanying me to Dol'Cardolani, where you shall run a couple errands for me"—she scoffed—"and I will settle your debts."

Tasha's heart stopped and all she could do was stare at him, mouthing a single word.

"Why? Because I am your friend, Tasha." No sparkle lit his eyes and no grin tugged at his mouth. The expression contrasted his usual levity so starkly that Tasha breathed a quiet sigh when the grin swept into place. "Besides, I need your help to conquer the world."

For the umpteenth time, she turned to look at the lying mirrors, watching as a thousand Slades laid a thousand sheets of paper upon a thousand tables. Then she watched as a thousand Tashas signed a thousand, thousand names.

62

Blade Dance

The New Order spent an hour preparing their assault: enchanting its weapons, assessing the fortress, and calculating their strategy. Those not involved in these preparations loitered on the camp's borders, sharpening weapons, tightening armor, or making wagers and boasts, anything to calm their nerves. Wiser soldiers stood apart, surveilling the forest and thanking their goddess they had erected their camps outside its border. They knew the rumors, remembered the legends and the myths; none of them trusted the tranquility.

Behind the wall, the Northerners waited in somber clusters—a fair distance from said wall for fear of the demon's vaulting the barrier and devastating them—murmuring to one another, sharing final promises and confessions. The derangers moved among them, warning the soldiers to keep their distance from the demons, and patrolling for subterfuge from the New Order. That all changed when a horn—deep, rolling, and gleeful—blared from the woods.

The Northerners assembled in the courtyard, unsheathing blades and donning helms. They made no attempt to defend the wall; it had only ever been intended as a barrier by the architects, not to endure a dedicated assault, and there was no purchase atop it for the common man.

The lesser demons surmounted the wall first, vaulting over the battlements in soaring bounds. The ground splintered beneath them, livid cracks of hellfire melting the accumulated ice and snow. They charged with a howl, some setting themselves alight with hellfire while others turned bestial and metallic, but all exhaling a tide of ashes and embers before them to obscure their advance.

Black shafts flew from the Northerners, rending the ash cloud and staggering the demons when they struck. The derangers released another volley, but the demons twisted and vaulted, evading or incinerating the shafts while those struck in the first volley buckled in a tumult of shrieks, tugging at the arrows as their blood froze in their veins and frost sprawled across their armor. Their skin blackened and then shattered like porcelain, restoring them to the Abyss.

The surviving lesser demons, still a majority, dashed the remaining distance, and unperturbed, the derangers met them, unsheathing their glass blades with notes of eldritch song. The demons flailed with talons and fire, but the derangers ghosted through and about them, extinguishing their flames with a touch of their blades and spreading ice with every step, depriving the demons of solid footing.

A second horn sounded and ladders clattered against and over the ramparts, spewing New Order mercenaries into the courtyard. They landed and spread, exploiting the conflict between derangers and demons for cover. Without need of command, the Northerner soldiers drew their blades and split to either side of the central conflict. The mercenaries scrambled to form ranks and engage them, locking shields and raising their axes or hatchets. The forces collided, Northern glass blades shearing through armor and piercing shields, but the New Order maintained formation.

Brimares smashed to the ground between three Northern soldiers and their foes on the outskirts of the melee. The Northerners recoiled with a choir of muffled curses, two-handed blades sweeping into defensive stances while the two lesser demons assailing them instantly redirected their assaults toward her, hurling flames from their fingertips and maws. The inferno drove her back a step, worming at the perfect sheet of her armor, hunting for puncture or seam. She snapped her left arm forward, the ugly chain given to her by Salem uncoiling to clamp around the leftmost demon's throat. Its flames extinguished with a gasp and it fell, screaming and clawing at the collar until she decapitated it with a jerk.

The second demon, some grotesque combination of an ape and dog, lunged at her. She caught its charge bodily, her gauntleted fingertips piercing the fuming, crimson metal of its shoulder and spilling streams of molten ichor. Its jaws clamped on her shoulder, gnawing futilely at her armor. Brimares slammed the demon to the ground, crushing its body and shattering its spine. The familiar urge to consume its chaos burgeoned within her, tugging at her sanity and inflaming the suppressed bloodlust. She thrust her hand into the demon's chest, her gauntlets extending into a blade. The demon spasmed beneath her and died.

She stood, ashes swirling around her as the corpses disintegrated and her gauntlets clicked back into place. One of the Northern soldiers spared her a nod before rejoining the fray, leaving her to resume her hunt. More New Order had swarmed into the courtyard over the last few minutes, deepening their ranks as they vaulted off the palisade and stretching the Northerners thin as the battle lines expanded to fill the space dying demons left. Already three score thronged the courtyard, and dozens more lay dead. Most engaged the Northern soldiers, the rest swarmed the derangers, surrounding and mobbing them while avoiding their wicked glass blades, having learned very quickly that their armor, whether mail or gambeson, afforded scant protection. A few more perched awkwardly atop the ladders, spraying arrows. Of the demons, only Cellar'Veer seemed to remain, immense and seething flames as a knot of derangers wove about him with glass spears.

Brimares growled, corralling her raging, jubilant Chaos, and charged, dodging through the embattled soldiers and then vaulting over the derangers battling Cellar'Veer to land between them. She bent low, snarling and flaring her armor in threat, challenging him.

Cellar'Veer retaliated with a massive swipe, hammering her side and hurling her crashing across the ground. She snarled and twisted with the momentum, warping her armor to latch onto the ground, snapping her body to a halt and scarring livid furrows in the stone. She surged to her feet, hurling Salem's collar to snare Cellar'Veer's arm. He reared back, roaring and wrenching on the chain, but she spun, grabbing the links in both hands, and yanked him to his knees.

Slamming to all fours, Cellar'Veer roared again, his maw wider than a man's torso, and charged. She bent low and leapt, flipping over him and pulling the chain taught. He followed her up, rearing and slashing wildly. Brimares landed and immediately dove, barely escaping his gore-stained claws. The four derangers capitalized on his distraction and darted in, spears flashing.

Brimares rolled to her feet behind Cellar'Veer as he retaliated against the derangers, and yanked the collar taught, burying its fangs into his metal hide. He roared again but continued pursuing the retreating derangers, dragging her staggering along. She answered in kind and stabbed the armor of her calves and feet into the ground, anchoring her and stalling his advance. The derangers again capitalized on his immobility, dancing in and out of his reach with their spears, but ultimately inflicting only glancing blows. Brimares wrapped the chain about one arm and heaved herself into a soaring leap at Cellar'Veer, armor flowing past her hands to form blades.

She slammed into him, staggering him to his knees, blades driving through his flank with an eruption of volcanic ichor and noxious fumes. He snapped at her, twisting her blades deeper into his hide. She tried to wrench free, but her blades refused to relinquish their grip. In the second she wasted struggling with them, his jaws clamped on her torso, shearing through her armor. She howled furiously and kicked at him, sawing her blades.

He ground his teeth, snapping her ribs, and tore her from his side, whipping her back and forth. Brimares snarled and drove her fist into his eye, eliciting an enraged bellow before he spat her onto the ground and reared back. She rolled to the side, hauling awkwardly on the chain to no effect. He yanked back, dragging her towards him, and caught the chain in his mouth. She snarled and scrambled to her feet, again heaving on the chain, but his jaw slammed shut, severing it in an explosion of energy that shredded his mouth and slammed her to the ground, dislocating her shoulder.

The derangers struck again, one—sprinting past Brimares as she slammed her shoulder back into place—driving his spear into Cellar'Veer's foreleg. Before the others could land their blows, however, the plates of Cellar'Veer's skin flared open, revealing the molten core within, and exploded with heat, scattering the derangers across the courtyard.

Brimares scrambled to her feet as he settled onto his forelegs and scraped the cobbles with one burning paw. She retreated from him and sank into a crouch, breathing slowly as her ribs snapped back into place and muscles knit together.

She ignited the Chaos in her blood and pressed her palms into the ground, fingers warping into claws as he charged. Inhaling deeply, she drove the fire within her out from her hands, sending a tract of blood-hued Chaos rending through the ground at Cellar'Veer. The ground beneath his feet split with a crack and a blood-colored stalactite pulsing with black veins erupted into his path. He plowed through it undeterred, spraying molten ichor from where the stalactite gouged him, and trampled over her.

Cellar'Veer continued past, scraping to a halt before turning back to her as she stood. His neck arched back, then shot forward, his mouth opening to spit a stream of thick, oil-like fire. Brimares slammed her arms together, drawing the armor off her back and shoulders to her front. The crimson metal coalesced and expanded, forming a shield just before the flames rolled over her. She thrust back against the torrent, hurling the Chaos from her own blood up through her arms and into the fire.

Lionel ducked beneath the mercenary's wild swing and thrust his borrowed Northern sword up, piercing his adversary's gambeson. The man shuddered and collapsed, his mace and shield clattering against the stained ice as he futilely tried to stem the flowing blood.

Lionel slid the sword free, his hand aching from the blade's constant, whispering vibration, and retreated through a pair of Northerners for a moment's reprieve. Almost all of the New Order's forces had entered the courtyard, and in truth, it was only the derangers keeping them in check. They danced through the conflict, their blades a shimmering blur as they reaped one life after another. But even they had not escaped the conflict unscathed; their battles with the demons had left barely a half-dozen alive.

A cheer broke across the New Order, drawing Lionel's attention. Three riders in full plate descended to the courtyard from above the wall in the conclusion of an enormous leap, their forms wreathed in sable energy and the clenched fist of the New Order emblazoned upon their breastplates: paladins. Behind them levitated two clerics, suspended on colossal hands of black energy, and Kell'MachChain.

The demon was already changing, his body splitting at the seams as it swelled and sprouted wings. Those wings slammed downward, hurling him heavenwards as fire bloomed in his palms and the clerics woke their Shards.

Lionel cursed and flung his shield aside, activating his own Shard and molding its divinity into a golden lance he launched at Kell'MachChain. It struck the demon's midsection and shattered, blowing him from his ascent and sending him plummeting to the ground.

Lionel sprinted forward, chanting to invoke a shield of light about his person. He passed Maern battling a pair of New Order mercenaries, and screamed, "Maern! Clerics at the back!" The deranger whirled through his opponents, eviscerating both with a stroke, and then nodded a fatigued acknowledgement toward him. Lionel returned his attention to the demon, forcing his legs faster.

He arrived as Kell'MachChain crawled from the fiery crater of his landing, wings merging into his back and clawed hands fuming as they touched the courtyard's stone. Lionel stilled, raising his blade toward the demon, who regarded him with a smirk across the dozen feet separating them. "So you would test yourself against me?"

Lionel roused his Shard higher, sheathing his blade in molten flames, and thrust at the demon. The golden flames roared free, expanding into a torrent, bridging the gap and engulfing Kell'MachChain, but the demon hurled them aside with a sweep of his arm. "You are not my equa–"

Lionel slammed to a halt before the demon, his advanced concealed by the flames, and slashed upwards, twisting with the strike and both hands clamped on the long handle.

Kell'MachChain recoiled from the first slash, caught the second on the bracer of his right arm and stabbed with his left hand. Flames erupted from his fingers, blasting and cascading across Lionel's barrier of light with such force he reeled back.

Lionel staggered, caught his balance, reversed momentum, and drove forward again, blade striking forward to renew his torrent of flames, but Kell'MachChain was already in his reach, grinning as his hand stabbed forward. Lionel pivoted aside, Kell'MachChain's hand scouring furrows in his pauldrons, and threw himself stumbling backward. Kell'MachChain turned with him, his free hand swinging wide as the crimson armor of his gauntlets swelled then stabbed forward into a barrage of blades. They struck Lionel's barrier and buckled. Lionel capitalized, setting his feet and driving into a lunging thrust as the blades retracted. He crashed into Kell'MachChain and drove his sword through the demon's stomach. The demon lurched and then hammered Lionel's barrier over his chest, shattering the light and throwing him a dozen feet away.

"You'll have to try harder." Kell'MachChain tore the sword free and melted it in a surge of fire.

Lionel staggered to his feet, summoning power from his Shard, and spoke, "Heavens of the Earth and Sea in the Sky, the Widow cries and the Cripple walks. The Old Night bows and the Young Day rises. Give luster to the knight's armor and fire to his soul." One after another, plates of golden, spectral light clamped into place over his body, swelling around and lifting him higher until he towered over Kell'MachChain, armored in an *Avatar* of divine light.

Lionel charged, his golden heel fracturing the cobbles and his body moving faster than the human eye could follow. Kell'MachChain's face contorted as his body grew to match Lionel's size, vast wings spreading from his back. The two collided with a thunder of anathematic magic.

Links of golden chain materialized in Lionel's hands and whipped outward, ensnaring Kell'MachChain, but the demon flared his wings outward, breaking the chains with a surge of hellfire. He slashed with the black claws of his hands, digging furrows in the *Avatar* that immediately mended. Lionel struck Kell'MachChain on the chest with joined palms, drew back and lifted his hands as the demon stumbled. A maul materialized in his fingers, and he brought it crashing down onto the demon's skull. Kell'MachChain fell to a knee, a cascade of golden cracks spreading out across his crimson hide. The hammer faded from Lionel's hand, replaced by an incandescent great sword. He slashed twice through Kell'MachChain, reversed his grip and drove the now serrated blade down, impaling Kell'MachChain from his throat through to his pelvis.

Gagging as ichor spewed from his mouth, Kell'MachChain clamped burning hands on the *Avatar's* arms, his armor melting as the golden light fractured. Lionel began to reverse the twist of his sword, but Kell'MachChain tore Lionel's grip from the hilt and bit the blade in half, dispelling it.

Lionel leapt back, breaking the demon's grasp, then surged close anew, a spear materializing in his hands.

Kell'MachChain slapped the spear aside and two burning chains erupted from his other palm, coiling then striking to lash around Lionel's *Avatar*, close taught and stab into the ground to anchor him.

Grinning through the ichor of his injuries, Kell'MachChain flicked his hand, disconnecting himself from the chains, and vaulted skyward. Lionel spun to keep track of him, but the chains binding him tightened and multiplied, dragging him to the ground. He strained and, hearing the creek of his fetters beginning to give way, screamed his challenge. One restraint broke and he surged up, hurling another golden lance at the almost completely healed Kell'MachChain, who simply evaded the missile and redoubled his bindings.

Dozens of chains enveloped Lionel, but he thrashed again, snapping them like strings of glass. Yet for each he broke another three encircled him, dragging him inevitably back to the ground until he knelt in the courtyard, ensnared. Kell'MachChain descended to hover just overhead, chuckling gleefully. "Let this exorcism commence."

Lionel thrashed to no avail, watching a storm of fire, crimson lightning, and black mist grow between the demon's hands. Then screaming his triumph, Kell'MachChain hurled the sphere of Chaos energy.

Lionel rocked back, the chain's holding him stable. Twice more Kell'MachChain hurled a sphere of Chaos at him, each riddling the *Avatar* with fractures until it imploded, hurling Lionel across the courtyard before the chains could cinch on his physical body.

He tumbled to a stop against the tower's stairs, his whole body screaming in pain. He heard the beat of wings and the scratch of boots as Kell'MachChain landed next to him. He looked up as Kell'MachChain crouched and wrapped fingers in his hair.

"If I could, I would damn you. But since that is not one of the gifts bestowed upon us by the Chaos, your suffering will have to suffice." Then he crushed Lionel's hand.

Brimares twisted to stare at the tower, her ears ringing with the agonized shriek. She saw Kell'MachChain standing over Lionel, grinding his boot down onto the ruins of Lionel's left hand. She hurled herself into a roll, evading yet another of Cellar'Veer's charges.

Despite everything she had attempted, Cellar'Veer remained uninjured. This was a war of attrition; neither of them could inflict enough damage to kill the other outright, and whatever damage they did inflict was simply healed by the Chaos in their veins.

Cellar'Veer glanced toward Kell'MachChain and grinned, saliva dripping between his incisors. He spoke, his words a deep, rumbling bellow distorted by Chaos, "What will you do when the paladin is dead? Where will you discover your salvation?" He lunged forward, flames gushing from the cracks in his hide.

She dove, but his flames still engulfed her, biting down as if they were a living beast, shearing the armor of her right shoulder and side. She landed with enough force to shatter the ice and rolled to her feet, one hand braced on the ground, and threw herself toward the stairs, leading with a bolt of Chaos. The Chaos flames struck Kell'MachChain across the shoulders, dismounting him from Lionel and bringing him whipping about. She slammed into him, hands impaling his chest as her impetus drove him onto the stairs. He bucked and retaliated, his armor erupting into a churning wall of blades that sawed through her armor and tore into her flesh, spraying her ichor. She tore her hands free as violently as she could, extracting his throbbing steel heart in one hand and a clutch of ribs with the other, and leapt off. He shrieked through gushing ichor, thrashing up the stairs in his spasms and clutching at his gaping injury, but the flesh was already mending.

She landed beside Lionel and caught him about the shoulders, lifting him to his feet. "How many times am I going to save your sorry hide?"

"Don't rub it in; I'm already feeling more like a damsel in distress than a resplendent knight."

Kell'MachChain pushed himself up from the stairs, ichor still seeping from his chest cavity. Cellar'Veer shuddered to a halt opposite him, flanking them. Lionel glanced between them. "Well, at least there are only two of them. Any suggestions?"

"Stay back and do what you can."

Kell'MachChain sneered unsteadily, lips parting for some proclamation or other, but Brimares was already charging, spinning as she hurled flames from her right hand and cast the newly regenerated collar from her left.

Cellar'Veer charged through the flames without heed while Kell'MachChain spun, catching the collar mid-flight. But the collar coiled and snapped around Kell'MachChain's hand, shearing through his armor. Brimares twisted, evading Cellar'Veer and yanking Kell'MachChain into his path.

Clutching his crushed hand as his Shard screamed its nearing exhaustion, Lionel flung his uninjured hand toward Cellar'Veer as he trampled over Kell'MachChain and clenched it into a fist. A golden wall blazed into existence and the demon crashed into it, arching upward and hide screeching. Lionel rolled weakly, conjuring and hurling another lance at the rising Kell'MachChain, causing him to stumble but inflicting no damage. All the while, his Shard ached deeper.

Brimares rammed into the stumbling Kell'MachChain's back and drove the blade of her right gauntlet into his still regenerating heart. The metal of their armor screeched on contact, his parting and her blade piercing. She tore the blade out and thrust again, wrenching it in a circle. Heart, lungs, brain, these were nucleases of living creatures, but demons lacked the same necessity; their Chaos healed any damage losing their vital functions inflicted and restored the damaged organ or muscle. Even destroying the brain would simply render them catatonic until healed rather than dead; their nuclease was their soul, which physical weapons could not damage. Silver, which annihilated their Chaos and impeded healing, and the exhaustion of their Chaos through repeated injury were the only means of banishing demons. Standard weapons could deal them injury, but most commonly failed to pierce even the lowliest of demons' armor, rendering magical enhancement or spells a necessity.

Kell'MachChain spun, heedless of her gauntlets shearing through his body, and grabbed her shoulders, maw opening and eyes igniting. She slammed her head forward, hammering her helm into his chin. Kell'MachChain's head jerked back, but his grip remained. She formed a second blade on her right hand and stabbed him again, joining the right blade with her left. Kell'MachChain snarled and bit for her throat. She pivoted in his grip, feeding him her shoulder instead, and stoked the Chaos, igniting every inch of her body in putrid flames.

The flames vaulted to Kell'MachChain, and he screamed in rage, refusing to release her. She felt the flames birthed of her Chaos latch onto the ichor pouring from Kell'MachChain then erupt beyond her control.

The fire exploded across both of them, feeding off them in unison and showing allegiance to neither. Brimares tore herself free, searing with the agony of being incinerated, and stumbled backward, snarling.

Lionel reeled as the heat slammed his flank, dragging his gaze toward Brimares and Kell'MachChain for an instant before Cellar'Veer's roaring impact against his flickering barrier of light restored it to him. Lionel wiped the perspiration from his eyes with a bloodstained glove and pressed his hand against the barrier, wheezing as he scraped more power from his Shard of Divinity, prompting a weak pulse of compliance and rasping pain through his chest. The scent of nutmeg filled his nostrils and throat, overpowering his other senses and expelling the air from his lungs with a cough.

Cellar'Veer paced before him, scoring the courtyard beneath the slush with seething footprints. "I can't feel your god anymore, paladin. You're hollow."

Lionel dragged a simple iron knife from his belt and settled into a crouch.

The two clerics of the New Order never noticed his approach, too focused on the battle. He gave them no reason to turn, not when he dropped from the wall nor when he drew blades: one from his shoulder and one from his hip. Obsidian and silver flashed, and the two clerics crumpled with severed throats. He continued forward. A few soldiers in black registered their gurgled cries and spun toward him, initiating a sequence of revelations and decisions that culminated in a muddled charge.

Thyme batted his first opponent's sword aside and continued past, thrusting his silver blade past the man's shield and into his heart. He spun on a heel, his silver blade parrying a wild strike while his obsidian sword flicked, piercing the second man's Adam's apple. Another man charged, and Thyme killed him with a thrust from the silver blade.

821

He continued through the New Order's ranks, but let the Northern men live; they were not his foes nor was he theirs. If they struck at him, either in accident or by intent, he slaughtered them and continued onward. He kept allegiance to none.

His massacre drew the attention of the Blond Knight. Thyme advanced on him, dispassionately reaping lives as he went, caring no more for those he slaughtered than he would for a paper wall. The Blond Knight disengaged from the deranger he battled with a burst of black force and spun to present his blade's tip to Thyme, instinctively recognizing a transcendent threat.

Thyme just continued his advanced at the same measured pace until the tip of the Blond Knight's sword touched his faded breastplate. His silver blade flashed, batting aside his opponent's blade as his obsidian sword struck upward like a serpent. The Blond Knight retreated, pushing the thrust aside with a hand. Thyme continued his assault, spinning as he slashed his silver blade and reversing his grip on the obsidian blade. The Blond Knight continued backpedaling, slashing at empty air in a pathetic attempt to keep pace with his foe. At the peak of his spin, Thyme stomped the ground and reversed momentum, stabbing the obsidian blade into the Blond Knight's side. His opponent fell to the ground, blade clattering away, and screamed a command summoning darkness to armor him. Thyme swept forward and slashed his silver blade. The sword sheared the barrier easily, devouring even divine magic. The Blond Knight tried to scramble back, but the obsidian blade drove forward.

Thyme kept walking.

He saw her battling two demons near the steps—recklessly charging to the aid of a paladin—and hastened his approach for the first time, slaughtering another pair of New Order soldiers: one with a slash to the throat and the other with an impaled heart.

Kell'MachChain moved to pursue Brimares but froze in the act, recognizing—even more than the Blond Knight had—the presence of something dangerous. He faced Thyme and flared his wings even as his heart quailed. He spat flames at Thyme, but Thyme cut them asunder with two flicks of his silver blade. The demon manifested burning chains as he had against Lionel and cast them forward only for Thyme to sever them with another casual slash. Kell'MachChain snarled and advanced, summoning mountainous flames to crush his opponent, but Thyme traversed them, swords whispering before him.

Past the barrier of flames, Thyme quickened his pace. Kell'MachChain, having no other option, reacted by slashing with his hands. The silver blade flashed, and Kell'MachChain recoiled with a hiss, clutching a stump that did not heal. Thyme's obsidian blade flashed, taking the other hand as the silver blade severed his legs. Thyme continued past as Kell'MachChain crawled backward, Chaos-tormented ichor boiling from his limbs as those severed by obsidian regenerated. The silver blade rose and fell, decapitating him.

Thyme kept walking, a wall of ash rising behind him with Kell'MachChain's demise.

The bear demon smashed a paw down, just missing Brimares as she dodged to the side. It reared back, maw opening to spew fire. Dashing forward, Thyme vaulted onto its back, both blades impaling it. The demon shrieked and flailed at him as he tore the silver blade free and impaled it again, this time higher-up. One after the other, he planted his blades, scaling its spine until he stood on its shoulders. The demon spun and thrashed, striking wildly in a madness of agony. Thyme impaled the demon's skull with the obsidian blade and hacked at its neck with the silver until the head ripped free with a spasm.

The demon crashed to the ground, and Thyme stepped off it, advancing until he stood before Brimares. Stabbing the obsidian blade effortlessly into the ground, he extended his hand and spoke, his words grasping her like chains, "I will have my ring back."

She shook her head, her eyes losing focus beneath the weight of his eldritch will. He frowned. "Give it to me or every life you see is forfeit."

Again she shook her head, in defiance as much as denial. "No." She took a breath, trying to calm her ragged nerves. "If you kill them, I won't give it to you, so don't threaten me with them."

He laid the silver blade upon her shoulder, the edge kissing her throat with a promise. "Give … it … back."

She shook her head again, fighting the urge to prostrate herself. Desperate, she reiterated the law he had told her all those centuries ago. "The ring will not suffer you to take it by force. If you kill me, you will have to wait until the Abyss releases me again."

His inhuman, unblinking eyes—devoid of iris, pupil, and whites— glowered. "I am immortal, centuries are insignificant to me, mere moments in my existence, while yours will be agony. You shall suffer far more than I."

Brimares flinched. She was under no illusions that he would kill her if she refused. "You cannot take it, Thyme; nor will I ever return it if you kill me or any Northerner here." All logic and morality screamed for her surrender it, yet she could not. She had no use for whatever power it held, but it was the last thing she had left, and she hated herself for that weakness.

"You would return to damnation and cause the deaths of others to keep possession of a ring you cannot use and is not yours to keep?" The silver blade lifted from her shoulder, and she gasped in relief. Thyme held the blade still, pointed at where Lionel was trying to stand. "Give me my ring, Brimares." His hand remained lifted, palm toward her. She felt the old power of his words wash over her, silencing her doubts, calming the tension. His words called to every part of her—mind, body, and soul—to surrender the ring. Her hand started creeping upward.

Before she could grab the chain, a stillness descended upon the courtyard, a physical weight upon their minds and bodies.

Everyone, powerless to defy the reasonless urge, peered west, seeking the origin of the unnatural silence. Thyme also looked, his open hand falling. As one the Northern soldiers, derangers, and Lionel all fell to a knee.

Taller than any man Brimares had ever known and flanked by the White Wolves of Winsyria, the newcomer stood beside a massive, winged reptile, his eyes focused on her. She inched away, blood running cold as he moved closer.

Thyme pivoted, directing the silver blade toward him and casting his silken voice like a veil to dissuade the newcomer, "There is nothing here to involve yourself in, nothing at all that warrants your intervention. I intend this woman no harm. I only desire the return of what is rightfully mine."

The newcomer continued walking, unaffected by Thyme's voice. He stopped before Thyme, his words a soft rumble discordant with his size, "The grace and majesty of your blood has abandoned you, Wanderer; it is no longer your privilege to command men."

All pretense abandoned, Thyme snarled, "It is not for you to name me! I am born of kings, and you are beholden!"

"Your birth name no longer belongs to you, and you can never wear a mortal's name. Thus I name you Wanderer, for you have wandered lost through the centuries."

Thyme struggled against this open denial, combating rage and the ancient prerogative of his blood. Finally he spoke, forcing his words through gritted teeth, "Yield!"

"I am not your foe, Wanderer, do not make yourself mine or The North's."

She saw a flicker of hesitation in Thyme, then the raised sword steadied. "I will have what is mine." He stared at Brimares. "Give me my ring now, or I start taking lives."

She tried to speak, to bargain with him, but the newcomer spoke first, "These are not your lives to take, Wanderer, and I will not suffer their deaths."

"I will kill as I desire; it is still my right to execute traitors." Brimares saw Thyme move only as a blur, completing the perfect, lethal pattern before anyone realized he moved. At that moment, Brimares recognized the newcomer's death. Then she heard the ring of clashing blades and the song of drawn swords. Somehow, the newcomer parried Thyme's assault.

The duelists' individual movements defied every spectator's attempt to follow, all heard only the ceaseless ring of their song. She remembered all those who had previously challenged Thyme. She remembered the blade masters with their beautiful intricate dances promising swift, perfect deaths. She remembered Thyme scarring them with a series of cuts, one beneath each eye and a third between to mark their failure. He never inflicted more than that, just as they never lasted longer than a minute.

The two warriors separated. The newcomer standing at ease with lowered blades, and Thyme half crouched with his blades raised before him, both recognizing the outcome before Thyme reignited the conflict.

The spectators watched in fascination and awe. She stood apart, hands pressed to her mouth, desperate to turn away but incapable of that simple act.

It all ended in a screech and a shattering of obsidian.

Brimares flinched, lifting a hand to shield her eyes from the countless black needles whistling through the air and clattering across the slush. Looking, she saw the newcomer standing with a shard of Thyme's obsidian blade driven into his side but no blood from the fatal injury.

She saw Thyme reeling back, silver blade lifted before him and only the stump of his obsidian left. The newcomer advanced, and Thyme lunged forward, silver blade a whirl of death surrounding him. The silver of his sword rang out twice upon contact before it was struck from his hands. Reeling back again, Thyme faced his opponent with a snarl, and the newcomer's blade flashed again, decapitating him.

Brimares fell to her knees with a strangled gasp and tore her eyes away, a storm of emotions mounting within her. Maern broke from the ranks of Northern men. "High-Warden, she is not ..." But fell silent at the High-Warden's raised hand.

He advanced to her, searching her face with unfathomable eyes. She braced herself and met his gaze. "The Abyss has broken you beyond my skill to heal; I am sorry for this." Her heart stopped, and though he continued speaking, she never heard his words.

The moments passed in agonized horror. All she could think was that she was being returned to the Abyss despite everything. She tried to find the courage to flee, even as she readied herself for the pain. He crouched, pressing his right hand upon her chest, his lips moving, though she still heard nothing.

A searing cold swept through her at his touch, silencing the Chaos and robbing her of warmth. There was an instant of agony, and she felt something shatter inside, the absolute cold of his touch settling over her.

She collapsed to the ground, hacking and vomiting fetid, writhing bile.

The High-Warden continued to kneel beside her but did not touch her. "I broke your bindings; whoever summoned you, can no longer command your actions. You are free to go, to leave The North or to stay in search of peace or vengeance. So long as you do not harm her, The North will accept you. I regret that I cannot lift your damnation, if that is your goal, you must continue to aid Sir Lionel Iitanen." He straightened, addressing Maern, "Clear away the dead, burn those not of The North and bring the rest into the citadel; except for him." The High-Warden gestured to the Blond Knight's corpse. "Bind him to the earth and set a vigil. As for the Wanderer, take his body and weapons into the forest." He walked toward the citadel, and in that instant, Brimares felt a shift in her world. It was not a physical shift, but more of a massive, coercive premonition and she knew, in that instant, that something inevitable was grinding into motion.

63

Mage-Born

Dieharamon sat with his arms on his knees and his face in his hands, isolating himself from the world as Dayada chattered. He knew he needed to return to Valeriius, but his resolve failed him at every attempt. More than that, he needed to rescue Dayada from Sahdaen; if he succeeded in that then maybe, just maybe, Dava's death and all those he murdered would be worth it.

Dayada wandered around the chamber, reciting memories with gesticulations for emphasis and laughing. "... My father's not a big man, but you wouldn't know it with how others act around him. Well, everyone except Tiberius, who doesn't make way for anybody. Ha, I mean what's there to be afraid of? Sure, he's kind of reclusive, but–"

"What's your home like?"

Dayada paused, lips pursing comically as he rubbed at a vestigial beard. "It's like a lot of things, did you have anything in mind?"

"Can you describe it?"

"I can try." He settled back, still stroking his chin and humming. "It sits on a plateau of stone, like on a fist or a palm, surrounded by wheat as far as you can see. In summer, everything smells like the wheat, even the houses and the furniture. There's never a cloud except when it rains, and it's always a refreshing rain; the kind you like to watch or listen to. A river flows eastward along the north wall carrying all sorts of passersby and merchants inland. There's always something new and exciting going on at the port, some new wonder and a hundred people with stories to tell. I've actually become good friends with many of them.

"The city itself is all white marble that shines at night for leagues. Father calls it an offering of sanctuary to everyone. He says it's the light of dawn, and we hold it so the night will never set foot in our home."

Dayada fell silent, gently kicking his heels against the bed. "What's your home like?"

"I think I had one once, but I can't remember it now."

"What about your family?"

Dieharamon avoided Dayada's gaze. "I don't remember my family." He did remember his family, or rather the feeling of them, of warmth and laughter, of being safe. He also possessed his memories from the *Lake of Dreams*, but those weren't really his.

"But you must have a family; everyone has a family."

"The South isn't like other lands; there are no true families here."

Dayada grew silent, and Dieharamon made no effort at conversation. Dayada's query, however, lingered in his mind.

"Why don't you leave?"

"I am bound to Valeriius, I can only walk the path he dictates."

"But you have to leave. How am I supposed to bring you back to Father if you can't come?"

Something plummeted in Dieharamon's chest. "What?"

"I didn't tell you?"

"No."

"Oh, okay. You know the person I was supposed to find?"

"Yes?" Dieharamon tried to mask his horror but failed, the single word crawling from his lips more as a plea than affirmation. Dayada failed to notice.

"He's you! It took a while to realize it because of everything, but *Taychran* helped!"

The horror in his stomach became a twisting knife. "Me?"

Dayada grinned. "Yep."

Dieharamon lurched off his seat and dropped to his knees before the Avenar. "Dayada, I can't be the man you're looking for. I just can't! I am Tragnashi, a monster almost. I have nothing to offer the likes of your father and Tiberius Whyte. Damn it, I can't even help myself!" He barely even recognized the words he spoke; he couldn't leave Sahdaen, he couldn't, and Sahdaen would destroy Dayada. Everything Dieharamon had done, every futile sin he had committed to save himself, and it was Dayada who would suffer.

"You're no monster, Dieharamon; actually, you're kind of sweet, and you'll like Father. He's like you, in some ways."

"Dayada, I am not the one you want! I am nobody, nothing!"

"Bah, everybody's somebody."

"That doesn't matter. What matters is you've got it wrong—"

"Nope."

"You're wrong, you have to—"

"No, I am not."

Dieharamon faltered at the confidence in Dayada's words, momentarily shocked, then he slowly relinquished his grip on the Avenar's hands and slumped. "I can't be; I just can't be." After all he had done, all he had survived, this was the price; he was going to kill Dayada. Dieharamon sank forward, pressing his head to his knees and clasping the back of his neck.

A thunderous knock sounded from the doorframe, rousing Dieharamon's head and heralding a man's voice through the door curtain, "Dieharamon, you and the foreigner Dayada Avenar are summoned to partake in the closing festivities." The fist, silent throughout the summons, resumed pounding.

Dayada leapt to his feet. "Hey, maybe Valeriius will release you. I have some money I can get from the Merchant's Guild, and it wouldn't have to be long, just enough to meet Father and Tiberius."

Dieharamon caught Dayada arm's, scrambling for words that failed him, "Dayada, I … I don't think you should go. Stay up here away from the festivities. Avarans don't care for westerners."

"I've been invited, it would be rude to decline."

"Dayada, you have to leave here, not just here, but Sahdaen entirely. Return home as soon as possible, tonight, before the party's over if you can."

"Will you come with me? Because I can't leave without you; Father trusted me to find you, and I won't fail."

"Fine! I'll meet you along the way, or at the DawnHold, just somewhere else, anywhere else. But don't wait for me though, just leave now."

"Okay, I'll leave right after the gala. A party sounds fun and I haven't eaten anything all night."

Dieharamon wanted to weep. But he could only release Dayada. The Avenar immediately sprang forward and out the cloth door, right into the unprepared messenger with a squeak. They crashed to the floor in a heap, the Avaran spitting profanity and Dayada apologizing profusely.

Dieharamon crawled to his feet and shuffled to the door frame, fists clenched at his sides as he prayed to every god and entity he knew; he didn't care that prayers died in his thoughts, he just prayed for them to work and prayed again.

Dayada finally extricated himself and vaulted to his feet, slapping dirt from his clothing.

Dieharamon asked, "Ready?"

"Yes, I do believe I am." Dayada blushed, and continued slapping his clothing and blushing deeply. "I really am sorry, oh and umm, … Dieharamon, I lost *Taychran* again. Do you happen to know where it is?"

"I think it's in the library; we can pick it up on our way."

"Oh, that's a relief; Tiberius is always saying I should keep a better handle on it."

For once in his life, Dieharamon found others waiting for him. Dozens of Kalvonders inhabited the gala chamber alongside their most prominent retainers despite the late hour, many attired in traveling gear. Valeriius stood at the forefront conversing with the Immortal Consort, her features emanating savage glee.

Dieharamon slowed, extending a hand to keep Dayada back, unable to reject the awful premonition rising within him. He tried to find the source of his unease, to understand it, but failed. He saw only Valeriius beckoning him onward.

Powerless to resist, Dieharamon obeyed, motioning Dayada to remain outside. The Avenar grumbled but complied, squirming as if feeding on the room's palpable excitement. Reaching Valeriius, Dieharamon laid his brow upon the floor. "You summoned me?"

Valeriius knelt, his rich clothing flashing gold and auburn in the light, and stroked the back of Dieharamon's head. "We come full circle. The first time we truly met, you knelt without command, face marked with blood. That was the eve of your first kill, of your new allegiance, of becoming Tragnashi. You do not remember it, of course. I needed a gladiator for the arena, one who could defy all plausibility and survive. You were one of two. The other was your sister.

"I had to destroy your minds with drugs so you would kill each other, after that you crushed her skull without complaint, maybe even enjoyed it.

"Just as that was your first kill in my service, this next bout will be your last. I confide this because I have a final jest at your fate. There is more at stake here than your life. I have bound the Avenar Prince's future to the conclusion of this conflict. If you survive, you will live with more wealth and prestige than your grandest aspirations, and in the process, condemn Dayada to the Immortal Consort. If you die, I will restore the Avenar to his father unharmed. The choice is yours."

Valeriius called Dieharamon to his feet with a touch and withdrew to the Immortal Consort, his smile challenging his peers to present a more perfect specimen of war. His unseen will grasped Dieharamon when he failed to rise, compelling him to stand, muscles flexing as they unsheathed the iron broadsword and drove it into the stone tiles.

With his introduction complete, attention shifted to the Immortal Consort, who summoned her champion with a gleeful call. The Easterner emerged from the chittering spectators and halted beside Dieharamon, offering his mistress a cursory bow that she ignored. Thus disregarded, the Easterner addressed Dieharamon, "You should have been here earlier; your Blood-Soul thing arrived with tidings of a dire war to frighten them."

"The Kalvonders are already at war with the world; one more won't frighten them."

"It's the foe not the war; Cardolyn Tyier prepares his legions, and I hear he intends to march in person."

"I imagine they took that news well."

"Not to the result you would expect. Ureign Kalvonder and a score of his elite protested the warnings and will now feed Morrehiegann's lust when the Reaping comes." The Easterner finally looked at Dieharamon. "I promised you we would fight again, and this time you'll die."

The Immortal Consort concluded her introduction with the flourish of a hand, ceding attention back to Valeriius, who said, "There will be no abilities or strengths disregarded in this contest. The champions must use everything they possess until one dies, raising the other to unprecedented heights. We begin at my mark. *Ashshand* favor the worthy."

Valeriius beckoned Dieharamon with a lethargic hand and took him by the shoulder, pulling him aside. "You will have a few moments to prepare yourself, Dieharamon, but first there is someone awaiting you." Valeriius motioned to where the Aparthii slave waited outside one of the numerous side doors.

Dieharamon gave Valeriius a dull nod and crossed to the Aparthii slave, ignoring her reverence.

She followed him through the cloth door into a secluded corridor and assumed a servile position with her back to the entrance. Dieharamon slumped against the wall, struggling with a mixture of guilt and relief; he could not defeat the Easterner, even if he strove with all his abilities, which meant Dayada would survive. It also meant Dava had died for nothing. The reality of his own impending demise barely registered.

The Aparthii woman chided him softly, "Continue please, Master Dieharamon, the Immortal Consort is not a patient woman."

He nodded and started down the corridor, following it to a room of sterile white stone, devoid of embellishments and presided over by a prevalent, source-less white illumination. It was a soft light, but nevertheless irritated his eyes like the sun's reflection off a book page. Besides the light, only a simple chair occupied the room. A man sat in the chair, dressed in loose silks and a leather vest. He wore no visible armaments to contrast the brown curls adorning his brow or languid posture. He sat with elegant hands clasped in his lap while his too-azure eyes stared at Dieharamon from the room's exact center. He tapped the floor once with a boot. "Hello, Dieharamon, I am Bellay Enkarta. We have already met, though you will not remember it. I locked away your memories along with your gifts. Alone, each was unsettling to Valeriius' agenda, together they proved explosive. You were rather vindictive about the murder of your village, which made enforcing your obedience difficult. After I suppressed the violence-inducing memories, it was a simple matter to make you Tragnashi. Even a mage-born's soul can be transferred if it submits, and you had no resistance left."

"Why are you here?"

"To undo what I wrought fourteen years ago."

"No! You can't, I won't be able to control it! I'll kill everybody around me!" He stumbled back, fumbling for the door.

"You already kill men, Dieharamon; this will just make you less precise—"

"No! Valeriius will punish me if I damage anything that belongs to him." That was a lie, he was dying anyway; uncontrolled his abilities would hurt Dayada.

"You have no choice in the matter, I am afraid," Bellay Enkarta's voice boomed in his mind. *"It will not be easy; coping with all your restrained power and memories, but you will survive. They won't come all at once, but they will come."* Dieharamon felt something shift inside him, a subtle change that sent tremors through his consciousness. It took him a moment to realize they were emotions: a sea of hate, anger, desire, hope and, most of all ... fear for Dayada. *"One way or another, your life here is ended for better or worse. There is one last battle for you to fight, one you will lose and when it is over, you will be free."* Then Bellay Enkarta was gone, leaving only the white room, the vacant chair, and a mounting inferno in his breast.

Dieharamon stumbled out, grasping the wall for support and struggling just to breathe through the onslaught of emotions. He caught flashes of memories. He saw his sister's face, truly recognized it for himself, and then was swallowed by all the decades of suppressed hate. The Aparthii slave hurried to part the curtains.

He staggered into the gala chamber, one hand extended and waving. The Easterner awaited him in an arena of spectators, spinning his mace and grinning. The Kalvonders closed around them and a spasm racked through his body, bringing a ravenous heat in its wake. He forced his twitching hands to still and drew the iron sword, turning his right shoulder to the Easterner.

Valeriius occupied his throne at the chamber's back, the Aparthii slave at his feet, and Dayada to his right. The Avenar Prince squirmed in his chair, practically bouncing with every shift, obviously oblivious to the stakes.

Valeriius lifted a delicate hand and let it fall. "Begin."

The Easterner rushed Dieharamon, mace spinning up and then sweeping down. Dieharamon retreated, blearily, the iron sword feeling leaden in his hands as he lifted it to intercept. The mace fell with crushing force, driving him to a knee and splintering the tiles beneath him. Dieharamon pushed the mace aside and lunged upward into a slash. Before he even managed a step, however, a wall of solidified air slammed him to the ground. The Easterner laughed and circled, spinning his mace.

The compressed air receded, allowing Dieharamon to stand. He faced the prowling Easterner and unsteadily pivoted with him as the man circled him, smashing the floor tiles with his mace every other step. The fragments quivered and swirled about him in a serrated cloud. Dieharamon tried to concentrate, to extricate his thoughts from the morass of emotions roiling within him, to stabilize his mind's reeling trajectory, but he couldn't; he was drowning in himself.

Dieharamon growled and lurched toward the Easterner, one arm raised to protect against the cloud and the other tensing to slash. The Easterner's mace shot from his hand, smashing into Dieharamon's solar plexus, and driving him back to the ground with a crack as his bone armor fractured.

The Easterner recalled his weapon and strolled forward, the air visibly coalescing around him as Dieharamon scrambled to his feet and charged again. The whirlwind lashed out, tearing the sword from his grasp and staggering him. He lurched after the blade, fighting to keep his balance beneath the wind's force.

Unrelenting, the Easterner swept his free hand up, clenching it into a fist. The wind clamped around Dieharamon, lifting him up and hurling him after his sword. There was a moment of weightlessness, then he slammed into the wall on the other side of the room, colliding with and scattering spectators as he did so. His sword lay a few feet away. He clambered to his feet and grimly reached for it.

<hr>

Valeriius reclined in his throne, watching the Easterner pummel Dieharamon. Tension washed off the Aparthii slave at his side, and she flinched whenever Dieharamon took a particularly violent blow. The Avenar princeling watched in horror, unable to speak or protest. Valeriius could feel the excitement building throughout the chamber. No Kalvonder or clergymen present had ever seen Dieharamon lose, or even the hint of it in a fair conflict, and now the prospect teased them into a frenzy.

The *mansion* susurrated through him, a ghost of sorrow tainting Valeriius' implacability. It had grown fond of Dieharamon after sixteen years, as it would anything it housed and protected for so long. Only his command kept it from interceding, not that it could do much. A light footstep stole Valeriius' attention.

The Immortal Consort approached him, unattended by her retinue. Valeriius nodded in greeting and tapped his Aparthii slave with a foot, sending her to his other side. "I hope the spectacle pleases you."

"Yes, most entertaining. However, I am here to discuss the terms of our arrangement. You desire a voice for the subsequent Immortal Consort; this is an unusual request. The Clergy alone decides who will wed themselves to *Ashshand*, for we alone comprehend his intricacies and desires."

"I understand, Consort, and I am willing to sacrifice whatever I must to achieve my desire. I will become a disciple of the Clergy if I must."

"You would be placing yourself under my command, all your resources, influence, and power; your every secret."

"You would command me, yes; but in return, I would gain power over thousands throughout Sahdaen, including this Easterner of yours should he achieve victory, which I anticipate. He is quite impressive, and a skilled mage." Valeriius caressed the Aparthii slave's cheek. "His children will make fine soldiers."

"I have tried to breed him, but he kills the little bastards at birth. He refuses to have his bloodlines tarnished by Avarans; he was a lord back in the East before his family exiled him for brutality and oath breaking."

"I am sure he feels right at home in Sahdaen."

The scent of burning leather reached them. "Valeriius, is Dieharamon … smoking?"

"It appears your Easterner is more than the common mage, Consort. Now are we agreed?"

"I believe we are."

Dieharamon collapsed, bleeding from a dozen injuries and gasping. An inferno raged within him, searing everything it touched, fighting for release. He could smell his clothes burning and saw the smoke, but still he groped toward his fallen sword.

The Easterner caught the back collar of his shirt. "Well aren't you the little fire mage. Too bad you can't control it."

Dieharamon struck at him, trying to channel all the power burning within his body into the iron sword. There was an instant of relief as the heat flooded out of him, then the sword melted—its grip crumbling to ash—and the tempest renewed.

"Now stop that, we can't have you burning everything." The Easterner slammed Dieharamon into the floor and ground him into it.

Dieharamon shoved back, his fingers melting furrows into the cracked floor, but failed to even shake the Easterner's grip. The inferno within surged higher, filling his head with their roar and obscuring his vision. He vomited, eschewing a mix of blood and bile as a Raven's caw pierced the fire within him. He looked up, barely conscious of the Easterner anymore, and saw it.

He knew that bird, remembered it from the dream and his own slowly awakening memories. He remembered it flying away, and he remembered his sister running beneath it. And suddenly he remembered something else, something that rewrote every pathway of his soul. His sister had not died that night. A part of his mind riled at the thought; it defied logic. Why would Valeriius lie to him if he planned on returning Dieharamon's memories? It did not matter; the sudden revelation was a catalyst shattering his restraints.

Flames exploded from his skin as the maelstrom roiling within him swelled, obliterating his finite control. A terrible flame kindled into life around Dieharamon and surged outward, devouring everything, scattering everyone.

He slowly stood as the flames expanded, marveling in their brilliance, marveling at the sheer power that enveloped him. He lifted his burning hand, his mind drowning in a sea of emotions, and pressed outward, willing the fire to swell until it stroked the rafters. He heard nothing but the crack of snapping tiles and the roar of the fire; not the terrified screams of Kalvonders, nor Dayada's startled cry. A single thought entered Dieharamon's mind: *So this is what it is to be a god.'* Then in the clarity of release he remembered Dayada and swept about, causing the flames to whirl. *'Gods, please no. Not him.'* He staggered toward where he had last seen the Avenar, extending a hand before him. *'Not Dayada, not Dayada,'* the words echoed in his thoughts as a mantra, ringing louder as he shuffled through charred corpses and Kalvonders burning alive. He reached the steps of Valeriius' dais, weeping without even realizing it for the flames consumed his tears. The mantra died within him, silenced by a glimmer of gold. No one could have survived him, and yet there through the flames a shape materialized, radiant blade in hand.

Dieharamon crumbled to his knees, clutching himself and sobbing openly as Dayada reached him, untouched by the flames and bearing Taychran aloft.

"Are you okay, Dieharamon?"

Dieharamon could only nod. *'Thank you, thank you, thank you.'*

Dayada's hand touched his shoulder. "You need to turn it off, or you'll destroy everything."

Dieharamon shook his head; he couldn't, but Dayada seemed to understand.

"That's okay, you don't need to do it alone. I'll help." And again, that strange, heavenly warmth filled Dieharamon. It swaddled all the pain, fear, rage, and shame within him, all the violence, and soothed them. "It's okay, I understand now, it's okay." The inferno receded, and Dayada knelt before him. "We can go now, Dieharamon, I understand, but I don't know where to go. You have to show me."

Dieharamon nodded fitfully, answering the only solution he possessed. "Aparthii, dungeons."

"Show me." As he spoke, the Avenar slipped an arm beneath Dieharamon, raised him to his feet and began walking through the still diminishing conflagration.

Unharmed by the inferno, the Raven descended into the flames, searching until it found Valeriius Kalvonder standing with his amethyst cane held aloft. Violet energy engulfed the Kalvonder, shielding him and the Aparthii while the Immortal Consort burned beside them. The Raven cawed once, veered and flew through the crumbling walls.

Twin circles of blood, the second inside the first, glowing with malignant light. Thirteen lances of blood pierced the circles, completing the mark of Chaos. A thousand runes, their lines horrific and convoluted, decorated the edges, giving definition to the blood.

Chains bound a woman within the two circles, her arms outstretched almost to the point of dismemberment while the corpses of thirteen unblemished daughters fashioned a third circle around the first two. Wordless chanting climbed from the mouths of shrouded men where they knelt in a huddle mass, rising and descending in veneration.

Unarmored, Sinnitar Muntalabac stood at the heart of it all, straddling the kneeling woman, her hair tangled in his fingers. He towered a head above the tallest man there, his bloated body gorged on Sahdaen. Crows and vultures saturated the air, each as distended as he was, each carried a tormented soul stolen from some distant realm of the world; a wealth of power for him to harvest, and this was but the southern flock.

He pulled the woman's head back, baring her face to the blinded heavens, and the woman sobbed, her mind utterly gone.

A Raven alighted upon Sinnitar's shoulder and he grinned. "Lady Seren, you finally arrive. I have grown impatient for this beginning. Are we to unfetter *Jaidar* and permit his sundering of the Mortal Kingdoms?"

"It is not your place to succumb to impatience. Salem deems the unleashing of **Jaidar** suitable for his intentions."

"Ah, at last you reveal who holds your leash." Bleeding darkness from his eyes, Sinnitar Muntalabac tore out the woman's throat, bathing the mark of Chaos in her blood. The gory lines flared, blinding all but the Raven, and consuming the shrouded men. A pillar of flames erupted from the prostrated sacrifices, merging above the Dread Lord's head into a *rift*.

The crimson fire throbbed, spewing molten iron as an infernal shape formed. The first of *Jaidar's* devils stepped from the portal and sniffed the air with a shudder of anticipation, its flames burgeoning.

The Dread Lord grinned. "Hello there, why don't you go have some fun?"

Epilogue

There was a stillness to the world, a quiet only The North seemed capable of, like the tranquility of cherry blossoms dropping onto a garden pond. The snow fell around her, but it felt distant, almost as if she were looking at the world from a glass box. The flakes swirled and danced, each movement achingly clear and defined, but they never touched her, even if she tried to grasp one.

She walked through the forest, searching for him without knowing where he was but never doubting her steps. She ached from the day's battle, a cold that afflicted every muscle. She did not know how much longer she had, how much more Chaos she carried, how many more battles she could fight without burning out and returning to the hell that awaited her. She knew her return was inevitable, but that just made her desperate need to delay it stronger. It was this desperation that had driven her from the warming fires into the night.

Shortly thereafter, she found him laying at rest in a circle of rowans. He lay with his hands crossed upon his breast, and his swords at his side. The obsidian one lay shattered with all its glittering fragments arranged into a semblance of its former glory. She knelt beside him, observing his worn features, exhausted armor, and graying hair. Somehow, even in death, Thyme maintained an aura of power, a presence that weighed upon her mind and oppressed the mortal pieces of her soul.

She continued her inspection for another moment, taking in how they had laid his decapitated head above his shoulders, before she grasped him by the shoulders and stood. Ignoring his wayward head for the moment, she trudged across the partial clearing, dragging his corpse to one of the twelve rowan trees and propping him against it. There was no blood from his injuries or stiffness to his corpse, though he had died hours ago.

Brimares took her eyes from his throat and laid her right hand upon his breast, retracting her gauntlet. It clicked open softly and streamed down her fingers, first contracting and then smoothing out into a rope. The armor up to her shoulder soon followed, and Thyme's headless corpse was bound to the tree seconds later. This finished, she collected his head and set it atop his shoulders. There was no need to balance it, to hold or prop it up; the head sat there as certainly as if it had still been attached.

Her preparations complete, Brimares stepped back and crouched down to wait. It wouldn't be long with his ring in such close proximity.

Thyme woke from death with the ease of someone who had done it a thousand times: first with a slight shift as he drew himself up and then with an opening of his silver eyes. He glanced around, his eyes moving like slashing knives to assess his surroundings before focusing upon her without so much as a glance at his bindings. "Give me back my ring, Brimares."

The old power of his words struck her, clawing at her mind and emotions, demanding her servitude, but she shook her head. "No." It was a simple word, a basic refusal uttered without eloquence or power, but it shattered his hold as surely as a hammer can shatter frozen iron. "You owe me, Thyme."

"I owe you nothing. Death breaks all promises, all oaths, all vows whether they are written in blood or bound in souls, and I have died a thousand times since we last met."

She leaned in close, unable to stop her lips from pulling up in a snarl, unable to still the simmering rise of her anger. "You owe me a soul, Thyme, and I don't care if it's mine or yours."

His too-wide eyes flashed perilously, and he leaned forward with a savage look to answer the challenge her rage unconsciously presented. "I owe you nothing."

"If you ever want to have your ring back, you will free me of this hell, Thyme."

"So be it." He snapped his fetters and stood. "My ring for your soul." His hand reached out, palm up to accept what she offered.

Brimares shook her head. "No, Thyme, you forgot me once; I will not return your ring until I am freed."

He shrugged and stepped past her to where his swords lay. He knelt, sheathing the silver blade and grasping the obsidian blade's hilt. Ignoring the black shard at his feet, he plunged the broken sword up to its onyx hilt into the snow and earth. He maintained that posture for a heartbeat and then stood, unsheathing the newly remade blade. He strode northward without another glance at her, knowing she would follow; and she did, shadowing his steps with a mixture of fear and hope until they reached The Northern tower.

Glossary

Accumulary is an autonomous device crafted in the Age of Gods that accumulates knowledge, materials, objects, magic, and spells that it comes in contact with. *Acculm* is an inferior replication of the Accumulary, serving only to preserve knowledge acquired in the near vicinity.

Adari are mystical grain spirits that paladin citizens form contracts with to take notes and watch over their wares.

"Through the course of the war {The Fae War, 6465-6467AOM} most of the Fae of the Laughing Court (Western Fae) met extinction and much of the land itself burned, withered or rotted, all except for the grains, for there were spirts hiding in the wheat."

Archients are naturally occurring, magic rich denizens of the Avarus Desert.

Artisan Silk is a very particular illustrious silk from specific weaving methods that are only found in the South and closely guarded secrets of certain Kalvonders.

Daemons are lesser incorporeal beings who inhabit the ether between primary realms (Abyss, Mortal, Death and Etherea.) Lesser daemons are mortal, after a fashion. Upon their death, they are reincarnated into new forms and personalities. A lesser *daemon* can on occasion recover its old memories, though how remains unknown to mortals. This recovery of memories elevates them to higher states of existence, though the number of recoveries they can experience in any given lifetime is limited. If they successfully recover memories over sequential lives, they eventually ascend to a Greater Daemon and retain new memories even upon death. Daemons often frequent the *Lake of Dreams*, which is adjacent to their realms and comprised of related material.

Fore-gods are the gods who preceded the present gods. Those who created the world with the Great-Immortals.

Great-Immortals are equitable to gods, except gods are incorporeal: beings of spirit apart from the word; Great-Immortals are physical beings in the world.

The Hunt is a constellation.

Imperial Army is beholden to the Emperor. They are better trained and better equipped. They are currently involved in a skirmish with the South.

Indakc is a Northern coat intended for indoor use, and an **Oudakc** is a Northern coat intended for outdoor use. Both coats follow clothing trends and styles.

Kelbrok are native northern fauna that consume wood to produce heat. More efficient than simply burning wood and are often consider family pets.

Lake of Dreams is an incorporeal realm that often attracts the unconscious minds of those attuned to magic and a variety of incorporeal beings.

Marked is the highest rank of an assassin.

The **Gods** are vast, incorporeal beings that ruled the world through the millennia of the Age of Gods until Arthramain Roy'al rebelled and ousted them in the Immortals War. They were forbidden access to the world unless invoked, and so chose aspects that might appeal to humans so as to incur their prayers.

Rat and **Mouse** are designations for a Thief Guild member. A rat has perfected all forms of theft from pick-pocketing, to mugging, to burglary, and grander heists. A mouse is skilled at insinuating themselves unremarked into positions near people of power or households of influence to gather useful intel for Carr'Selain.

Shards of Divinity are slivers of one of the Pantheon's twelve ruling gods that are ritualistically bestowed into mortal servants.

Theanne Guards are beholden to nobles and serve as the defense force for cities and towns, similar to a militia.

Theonaughts are hereditary caretakers for lands and cities, similar to governors.

Thearcs are individuals that Cardolyn Tyer assigned to positions of power.